KU-121-072

THE TWELVE

ALSO BY JUSTIN CRONIN

The Summer Guest
Mary and O'Neil

IN *THE PASSAGE* TRILOGY

The Passage

THE
TWELVE

JUSTIN CRONIN

First published in Great Britain in 2012 by Orion Books,
an imprint of The Orion Publishing Group Ltd
Orion House, 5 Upper Saint Martin's Lane
London WC2H 9EA

An Hachette UK Company

1 3 5 7 9 10 8 6 4 2

Copyright © Justin Cronin 2012

The moral right of Justin Cronin to be identified as the author
of this work has been asserted in accordance with
the Copyright, Designs and Patents Act of 1988.

All rights reserved. No part of this publication may be
reproduced, stored in a retrieval system, or transmitted
in any form or by any means, electronic, mechanical,
photocopying, recording, or otherwise, without the
prior permission of both the copyright owner and the
above publisher of this book.

All the characters in this book are fictitious, and any resemblance to
actual persons living or dead is purely coincidental.

A CIP catalogue record for this book is
available from the British Library.

ISBN (Hardback) 978 0 7528 9786 8
ISBN (Export Trade Paperback) 978 0 7528 9788 2
ISBN (Ebook) 978 1 4091 1213 6

Printed in Great Britain by Clays Ltd, St Ives plc

Excerpt from 'In the Afterlife' by Mark Strand, extracted from
ALMOST INVISIBLE. Copyright © 2012, Mark Strand, used by
permission of The Wylie Agency (UK) Limited.

The Orion Publishing Group's policy is to use papers that are natural,
renewable and recyclable products and made from wood grown in sustainable
forests. The logging and manufacturing processes are expected to
conform to the environmental regulations of the country of origin.

www.orionbooks.co.uk

CAVAN COUNTY LIBRARY
ACC No. C/264344
CLASS NO. F
INVOICE NO 9356 O'H
PRICE £14.38

For Leslie, foot-to-foot

She stood beside me for years, or was it a moment? I cannot remember. Maybe I loved her, maybe I didn't. There was a house, and then no house. There were trees, but none remain. When no one remembers, what is there? You, whose moments are gone, who drift like smoke in the afterlife, tell me something, tell me anything.

—MARK STRAND, "IN THE AFTERLIFE"

CONTENTS

PROLOGUE

From the Writings of the First Recorder ("The Book of Twelves")
Presented at the Third Global Conference on the
   North American Quarantine Period
Center for the Study of Human Cultures and Conflicts
University of New South Wales, Indo-Australian Republic
April 16–21, 1003 A.V.

[*Excerpt begins.*]

CHAPTER ONE

1. For it came to pass that the world had grown wicked, and men had taken war into their hearts, and committed great defilements upon every living thing, so that the world was as a dream of death;

2. And God looked upon his creation with a great sadness, for his spirit no longer abided with mankind.

3. And the LORD said: As in the days of Noah, a great deluge shall sweep over the earth; and this shall be a deluge of blood. The monsters of men's hearts shall be made flesh, devouring all in their path. And they shall be called Virals.

4. The first shall walk among you disguised as a virtuous man, concealing the evil within him; and it shall come to pass that a sickness will befall him, such that he is made into the likeness of a demon, terrible to gaze upon. And he shall be the father of destruction, called the Zero.

5. And men shall say: Would not such a being make the mightiest of soldiers? Would not the armies of our enemies lay down their weapons to cover their eyes at the very sight of him?

6. And a decree shall go forth from the highest offices that twelve criminals shall be chosen to share of the Zero's blood, becoming demons

also; and their names shall be as one name, Babcock-Morrison-Chávez-Baffes-Turrell-Winston-Sosa-Echols-Lambright-Martínez-Reinhardt-Carter, called the Twelve.

7. But also I will choose one among you who is pure of heart and mind, a child to stand against them; and I will send a sign so that all may know, and this sign shall be a great commotion of animals.

8. And this was Amy, whose name is Love: Amy of Souls, the Girl from Nowhere.

9. And the sign went forth in the place of Memphis, the beasts howling and screeching and trumpeting; and one who saw was Lacey, a sister in the eyes of God. And the LORD said to Lacey:

10. You too are chosen, to be as a helpmate to Amy, to show her the way. Wither she goes you shall go also; and your journey shall be a hardship, lasting many generations.

11. You shall be as a mother to the child, whom I have brought forth to heal the broken world; for within her I shall build an ark to carry the spirits of the righteous.

12. And thus did Lacey according to all that God commanded her, so did she.

CHAPTER TWO

1. And it came to pass that Amy was taken to the place of Colorado to be the captive of evil men; for in that place the Zero and the Twelve abided in chains, and Amy's captors intended that she should become one of them, joining to them in mind.

2. And there she was given the blood of the Zero, and fell into a swoon as unto death; but neither did she die, nor acquire monstrous form. For it was not the design of God that such a thing should come to pass.

3. And in this state Amy lingered through a period of days, until a great calamity occurred, such that there should be a Time Before and a Time After; for the Twelve escaped and the Zero also, unleashing death upon the earth.

4. But one man befriended Amy, and took pity upon her, and stole her away from that place. And this was Wolgast, a man righteous in his generation, beloved of God.

5. And together Amy and Wolgast made their way to the place of Oregon, deep in the mountains; and there they abided in the time known as the Year of Zero.

6. For in that time the Twelve beset the face of the world with their great hunger, killing every kind; and those they did not feed upon were taken up, joining to them in mind. And in this manner the Twelve were multiplied one million–fold to form the Twelve Viral Tribes, each with his Many, who roamed the earth without name or memory, laying waste to every living thing.

7. Thus did the seasons pass; and Wolgast became as a father to Amy, who had none, nor he a child of his own; and likewise did he love her, and she him.

8. And also did he see that Amy was not as he was, nor like any living person upon the earth; for neither did she age, nor suffer pain, nor seek nourishment or rest. And he feared what would become of her, when he himself was gone.

9. And it came to pass that a man came to them from the place of Seattle; and Wolgast did slay him, lest the man should become a demon in their midst. For the world had become a place of monsters, none living but they.

10. And in this manner they remained as father and daughter, each attending to the other, until a night when a blinding light filled the sky, too bright to gaze upon; and in the morning the air was foul with a rank odor, and ashes descended upon every surface.

11. For the light was the light of death, causing Wolgast to fall ill with a lethal sickness. And Amy was left to wander the ravaged earth alone, with none but the Virals for company.

12. And in this manner time passed, four score and twelve years in sum.

CHAPTER THREE

1. So it was that in the ninety-eighth year of her life in the place of California Amy came upon a city; and this was The First Colony, four score and ten souls abiding within its walls, the descendants of children who had made their way from the place of Philadelphia in the Time Before.

2. But at the sight of Amy the people became frightened, for they knew nothing of the world, and many words were spoken against her, and she was imprisoned; and much confusion occurred, such that she was forced to flee in the company of others.

3. And these were Peter, Alicia, Sara, Michael, Hollis, Theo, Mausami, and Hightop, eight in sum; and each had a cause of righteousness in

his heart, and desired that they should see the world outside the city where they dwelled.

4. And among them Peter was first in name, and Alicia second, and Sara third, and Michael fourth; and likewise were the others blessed in the eyes of God.

5. And together they left that place under cover of dark to find the secret of the world's undoing, in the place of Colorado, a journey of one-half year in the wilderness, enduring many tribulations; and the greatest of these was The Haven.

6. For in the place of Las Vegas they were taken as captives to stand before Babcock, First of Twelve; for the dwellers of that city were as slaves to Babcock and his Many, and would sacrifice two of their number for each new moon, so that they might live.

7. And Amy and the others were cast into the place of sacrifice, and did battle with Babcock, who was terrible to behold; and many lives were lost. And together they fled from that place, lest they too should die.

8. And one among them fell, who was the boy, Hightop; and Amy and her fellows buried him, marking it as a place of remembrance.

9. And a great grief was upon them, for Hightop was the most beloved of their number; but tarry could they not, for Babcock and his Many did pursue them.

10. And after more time had passed Amy and her fellows came upon a house, untouched by time; for God had blessed it, making it hallowed ground. And this was known as the Farmstead. And there they rested in safety, seven days in sum.

11. But two among them chose to stay in that place, for the woman was with child. And that child was to be born Caleb, who was beloved of God.

12. Thus the others continued while two remained behind.

CHAPTER FOUR

1. And it came to pass that Amy and her fellows made their way through the days and nights to the place of Colorado, where they came into the company of soldiers, five score in sum. And these were known as the Expeditionary, from the place of Texas.

2. For Texas was in that time a place of refuge upon the earth; and the soldiers had traveled abroad to fight the Virals, each taking a pledge to die for his fellows.

3. And one among them chose to join their ranks, becoming a soldier of the Expeditionary; and this was Alicia, who was to be called Alicia of Blades. And one of the soldiers elected to join with them in turn; and this was Lucius the Faithful.

4. And there they would have tarried, but winter was upon them; and though four of their number desired to travel with the soldiers to the place of Texas, Amy and Peter chose to press on alone.

5. And it came to pass that the pair arrived at the place of Amy's making, and there atop the highest peak they beheld an angel of the LORD. And the angel said to Amy:

6. Fear not, for I am the same Lacey whom you remember. Here have I waited through the generations to show you the way, and to show Peter also; for he is the Man of Days, chosen to stand with you.

7. For as in the time of Noah, God in his design has provided a great ship to cross the waters of destruction; and Amy is that ship. And Peter shall be the one to lead his fellows to a place of dry land.

8. Therefore will the LORD make whole what is broken, and bring comfort to the spirits of the righteous. And this shall be known as The Passage.

9. And the angel Lacey summoned Babcock, First of Twelve, from out of the darkness; and a great battle was joined. And with a burst of light did Lacey slay him, casting her spirit to the LORD.

10. And thus were Babcock's Many set free of him; and likewise did they remember the people they had been in the Time Before: man and woman, husband and wife, parent and child.

11. And Amy moved among them, blessing each in turn; for it was the design of God that she should be the vessel to carry their souls through the long night of their forgetting. And thereupon their spirits departed the earth, and they died.

12. And in this manner, Amy and her fellows learned what lay before them; though the way of their journey was steep, and only just beginning.

I

THE GHOST

SUMMER, 97 A.V.
FIVE YEARS AFTER THE FALL OF FIRST COLONY

Remember me when I am gone away,
Gone far away into the silent land.

—Christina Rossetti,
"Remember"

I

ORPHANAGE OF THE ORDER OF THE SISTERS, KERRVILLE, TEXAS

Later, after supper and evening prayer, and bath if it was bath night, and then the final negotiations to conclude the day (*Please, Sister, can't we stay up a little longer? Please, one more story?*), when the children had fallen asleep at last and everything was very still, Amy watched them. There was no rule against this; the sisters had all grown accustomed to her nighttime wanderings. Like an apparition she moved from quiet room to quiet room, sidling up and down the rows of beds where the children lay, their sleeping faces and bodies in trusting repose. The oldest were thirteen, poised at the edge of adulthood, the youngest just babies. Each came with a story, always sad. Many were thirdlings left at the orphanage by parents unable to pay the tax, others the victim of even crueler circumstances: mothers dead in childbirth, or else unwed and unable to bear the shame; fathers disappeared into the dark undercurrents of the city or taken outside the wall. The children's origins varied, yet their fates would be the same. The girls would enter the Order, giving their days to prayer and contemplation and caring for the children they themselves had been, while the boys would become soldiers, members of the Expeditionary, taking an oath of a different but no less binding nature.

Yet in their dreams they were children—still children, Amy thought. Her own childhood was the most distant of memories, an abstraction of history, and yet as she watched the sleeping children, dreams playfully flicking across their slumbering eyes, she felt closer to it—a time when she herself was just a small being in the world, innocent of what lay ahead, the too-long journey of her life. Time was a vastness inside her, too many years to know one from the other. So perhaps that was why she wandered among them: she did it to remember.

It was Caleb whose bed she saved for last, because he would be waiting for her. Baby Caleb, though he was not a baby anymore but a boy of five, taut and energetic as all children were, full of surprise and humor and startling truth. From his mother he had taken the high, sculpted cheekbones and olive-hued complexion of her clan; from his father the unyielding gaze and dark wonderings and coarse black cap, shorn close,

CAVAN COUNTY LIBRARY

that in the familial parlance of the Colony had been known as "Jaxon hair." A physical amalgamation, like a puzzle assembled from the pieces of his tribe. In his eyes Amy saw them. He was Mausami; he was Theo; he was only himself.

"Tell me about them."

Always, each night, the same ritual. It was as if the boy could not sleep without revisiting a past he had no memory of. Amy took her customary position on the edge of his cot. Beneath the blankets the shape of his lean, little-boy's body was barely a presence; around them, twenty sleeping children, a chorus of silence.

"Well," she began. "Let's see. Your mother was very beautiful."

"A warrior."

"Yes," Amy replied with a smile, "a beautiful warrior. With long black hair worn in a warrior's braid."

"So she could use her bow."

"Correct. But most of all she was headstrong. Do you know what that means, to be headstrong? I've told you before."

"Stubborn?"

"Yes. But in a good way. If I tell you to wash your hands before dinner, and you refuse to do it, that is not so good. That is the wrong kind of stubborn. What I'm saying is that your mother always did what she believed was right."

"Which is why she had me." He focused on the words. "Because it was . . . the right thing to bring a light into the world."

"Good. You remember. Always remember you are a bright light, Caleb."

A warm happiness had come into the boy's face. "Tell me about Theo now. My father."

"Your father?"

"Pleeease."

She laughed. "All right, then. Your father. First of all, he was very brave. A brave man. He loved your mother very much."

"But sad."

"True, he was sad. But that was what made him so brave, you see. Because he did the bravest thing of all. You know what that is?"

"To have hope."

"Yes. To have hope when there seems to be none. You must always remember that, too." She leaned down and kissed his forehead, moist with childlike heat. "Now, it's late. Time for sleep. Tomorrow is another day."

"Did they . . . love me?"

Amy was taken aback. Not by the question itself—he had asked this on numerous occasions, seeking assurance—but by his uncertain tone.

"Of course, Caleb. I have told you many times. They loved you very much. They love you still."

"Because they're in heaven."

"That's right."

"Where all of us are together, forever. The place the soul goes." He glanced away. Then: "They say you're very old."

"Who says so, Caleb?"

"I don't know." Wrapped in his cocoon of blankets, he gave a tiny shrug. "Everyone. The other sisters. I heard them talking."

It was not a matter that had come up before. As far as Amy was aware, only Sister Peg knew the story.

"Well," she said, gathering herself, "I'm older than you, I know that much. Old enough to tell you it's time for sleep."

"I see them sometimes."

The remark caught her short. "Caleb? How do you see them?"

But the boy wasn't looking at her; his gaze had turned inward. "At night. When I'm sleeping."

"When you're dreaming, you mean."

The boy had no answer for this. She touched his arm through the blankets. "It's all right, Caleb. You can tell me when you're ready."

"It's not the same. It's not like a dream." He returned his eyes to hers. "I see you too, Amy."

"Me?"

"You're different, though. Not how you are now."

She waited for him to say more but there was nothing. Different how?

"I miss them," the boy said.

She nodded, content for the moment to let the matter pass. "I know you do. And you will see them again. But for now you have me. You have your uncle Peter. He'll be coming home soon, you know."

"With the . . . Expe-dishunary." A look of determination glowed in the boy's face. "When I grow up, I want to be a soldier like Uncle Peter."

Amy kissed his brow again, rising to go. "If that's what you want to be, then that is what you'll be. Now, sleep."

"Amy?"

"Yes, Caleb?"

"Did anyone love you like that?"

Standing at the boy's bedside, she felt the memories wash over her. Of a spring night, and a wheeling carousel, and a taste of powdered sugar; of a lake and a cabin in the woods and the feel of a big hand holding her own. Tears rose to her throat.

"I believe that they did. I hope they did."

"Does Uncle Peter?"

She frowned, startled. "What makes you ask that, Caleb?"

"I don't know." Another shrug, faintly embarrassed. "The way he looks at you. He's always smiling."

"Well." She did her best to show nothing. Was it nothing? "I think he is smiling because he's happy to see you. Now, sleep. Do you promise?"

He groaned with his eyes. "I promise."

Outside, the lights were pouring down: not a brightness as total as the Colony's—Kerrville was much too big for that—but, rather, a kind of lingering dusk, lit at the edges with a crown of stars above. Amy crept from the courtyard, keeping to the shadows. At the base of the wall she located the ladder. She made no effort to conceal her ascent; at the top she was met by the sentry, a broad-chested man of middle years with a rifle held across his chest.

"What do you think you're doing?"

But that was all he said. As sleep took him, Amy eased his body to the catwalk, propping him against the rampart with his rifle across his lap. When he awoke he would possess only a fragmented, hallucinatory memory of her. A girl? One of the sisters, wearing the rough gray tunic of the Order? Perhaps he would not awaken on his own but would be found by one of his fellows and hauled away for sleeping at his post. A few days in the stockade but nothing serious, and in any event, no one would believe him.

She made her way down the catwalk to the empty observation platform. The patrols moved through every ten minutes; that was all she had. The lights spilled their beams onto the ground below like a shining liquid. Closing her eyes, Amy cleared her mind and directed her thoughts outward, sending them soaring over the field.

—Come to me.

—Come to me come to me come to me.

They came, gliding from the blackness. First one and then another and another, forming a glowing phalanx where they crouched at the edge of the shadows. And in her mind she heard the voices, always the voices, the voices and the question:

Who am I?

She waited.

Who am I who am I who am I?

How Amy missed him. Wolgast, the one who had loved her. Where are you? she thought, her heart aching with loneliness, for night after night, as this new thing had begun happening inside her, she had felt his absence keenly. Why have you left me alone? But Wolgast was nowhere, not in the wind or the sky or the sound of the earth's slow turning. The man he was, was gone.

Who am I who am I who am I who am I who am I who am I?

She waited as long as she dared. The minutes ticked away. Then, footsteps on the catwalk, coming closer: the sentry.

—You are me, she told them. You are me. Now go.

They scattered into the darkness.

2

SEVENTY-SIX MILES SOUTH OF ROSWELL, NEW MEXICO

On a warm September evening, many miles and weeks from home, Lieutenant Alicia Donadio—Alicia of Blades, the New Thing, adopted daughter of the great Niles Coffee and scout sniper of the Second Expeditionary Forces of the Army of the Republic of Texas, baptized and sworn—awakened to the taste of blood on the wind.

She was twenty-seven years old, five foot seven, solidly built in the shoulders and hips, red hair shorn close to her scalp. Her eyes, which had once been only blue, glowed with an orange hue, like twin coals. She traveled lightly, nothing wasted. Feet shod in sandals of cut canvas with treads of vulcanized rubber; denim trousers worn thin at the knees and seat; a cotton jersey with the sleeves cut away for speed. Crisscrossing her upper body she wore a pair of leather bandoliers with six steel blades ensheathed, her trademark; at her back, slung on a lanyard of sturdy hemp, her crossbow. A Browning .45 semiautomatic with a nine-shot magazine, her weapon of last resort, was holstered to her thigh.

Eight and one, was the saying. Eight for the virals, one for yourself. Eight and one and done.

The town was called Carlsbad. The years had done their work, sweeping it clean like a giant broom. But still some structures remained: empty husks of houses, rusted sheds, the becalmed and ruined evidence of time's passage. She had spent the day resting in the shade of a filling station whose metal awning somehow still stood, awakening at dusk to hunt. She took the jack on her cross, one shot through the throat, then skinned it and roasted it over a fire of mesquite, picking the stringy flesh from its haunches as the fire crackled beneath it.

She was in no hurry.

She was a woman of rules, rituals. She would not kill the virals while they slept. She would not use a gun if she could help it; guns were loud and sloppy and unworthy of the task. She took them on the blade, swiftly, or on the cross, cleanly and without regret, and always with a blessing of mercy in her heart. She said: "I send you home, my brothers and sisters, I release you from the prison of your existence." And when the killing was done, and she had withdrawn her weapon from its lethal home, she touched the handle of her blade first to her brow and then her chest, the head and heart, consecrating the creatures' deliverance with the hope that, when that day should come, her courage would not fail her and she herself would be delivered.

She waited for night to fall, doused the flames of her fire, and set out.

For days she had been following a broad plain of lowland scrub. To the south and west rose the shadowed shape of mountains, shoulders shrugging from the valley floor. If Alicia had ever seen the sea, she might have thought: That's what this place is, the sea. The floor of a great, inland ocean, and the mountains, cave-pocked, time-stilled, the remains of a giant reef from a time when monsters unimaginable had roamed the earth and waves.

Where are you tonight? she thought. *Where are you hiding, my brothers and sisters of blood?*

She was a woman of three lives, two befores and one after. In the first before, she had been just a little girl. The world was all lurching figures and flashing lights, it moved through her like a breeze in her hair, telling her nothing. She was eight years old the night the Colonel had taken her outside the walls of the Colony and left her with nothing, not even a blade. She'd sat under a tree and cried all night, and when the morning sun found her, she was different, changed; the girl she'd been was no more. Do you see? the Colonel asked her, kneeling before her where she sat in the dust. He would not hold her for comfort but faced her squarely, like a soldier. Do you understand now? And she did; she understood. Her life, the meager accident of her existence, meant nothing; she had given it up. She had taken the oath that day.

But that was long ago. She had been a child, then a woman, then: what? The third Alicia, the New Thing, neither viral nor human but somehow both. An amalgamation, a composite, a being apart. She traveled among the virals like an unseen spirit, part of them but also not, a ghost to their ghosts. In her veins was the virus, but balanced by a second, taken from Amy, the Girl from Nowhere; from one of twelve vials from the lab in Colorado, the others destroyed by Amy herself, cast into the flames. Amy's blood had saved her life, yet in a way it hadn't. Making her, Lieutenant Alicia Donadio, scout sniper of the Expeditionary, the only being like herself in all the living world.

There were times, many times, all the time, when Alicia herself could not have said precisely what she was.

She came upon a shed. A pockmarked and pitted thing, half-buried in the sand, with a sloping metal roof.

She . . . *felt* something.

Which was strange, nothing that had happened before. The virus had not given her that power, which was Amy's alone. Alicia was yang to Amy's yin, endowed with the physical strength and speed of the virals but disconnected from the invisible web that bound them together, thought to thought.

And yet, did she not? Feel something? Feel *them*? A tingling at the base of her skull, and in her mind a quiet rustling, faintly audible as words:

Who am I? Who am I who am I who am I who am I . . . ?

There were three. They had all been women, once. And even more: Alicia sensed—how was it possible?—that in each one lay a single kernel of memory. A hand shutting a window and the sound of rain. A brightly colored bird singing in a cage. A view from a doorway of a darkened room and two small children, a boy and a girl, asleep in their beds. Alicia received each of these visions as if it were her own, its sights and sounds and smells and emotions, a mélange of pure existence like three tiny fires flaring inside her. For a moment she was held captive to them, in mute awe of them, these memories of a lost world. The world of the Time Before.

But something else. Wrapping each of these memories was a shroud of darkness, vast and pitiless. It made Alicia shudder to the very core. Alicia wondered what this was, but then she knew: the dream of the one called Martínez. Julio Martínez of El Paso, Texas, Tenth of Twelve, sentenced to death for the murder of a peace officer. The one Alicia had come to find.

In Martínez's dream, he was forever raping a woman named Louise—the name was written in a curling script on the pocket of the woman's blouse—while simultaneously strangling her with an electric cord.

The door of the shed was hanging kitty-corner on its rusted hinges. Tight quarters: Alicia would have preferred more room, especially with three. She crept forward, following the point of her cross, and eased into the shed.

Two of the virals were suspended upside down from the rafters, the third crouched in a corner, gnawing on a hunk of meat with a sucking sound. They had just fed on an antelope; the desiccated remains lay sundered on the floor, clumps of hair and bone and skin. In the dazed aftermath of feeding, the virals took no notice of her entry.

"Good evening, ladies."

She took the first one in the rafters with her cross. A thud and then a squeal, abruptly squelched, and its body crashed to the floor. The other two were rousing now; the second released its hold on the rafter, tucked its knees to its chest, and rolled in the midst of its decent to land on its clawed feet, facing away. Dropping the cross, Alicia drew a blade and in a single liquid motion sent it spinning into the third, which had risen to face her.

Two down, one to go.

It should have been easy. Suddenly it wasn't. As Alicia drew a second blade, the remaining viral turned and swatted her hand with a force that sent the weapon spiraling into the dark. Before the creature could deliver another blow, Alicia dropped to the floor and rolled away; when she rose, fresh blade in hand, the viral was gone.

Shit.

She snatched her cross from the floor, loaded a fresh bolt, and dashed outside. Where the hell was it? Two quick steps and Alicia launched herself to the roof of the shed, landing with a clang. Quickly she surveyed the landscape. Nothing, no sign.

Then the viral was behind her. A trap, Alicia realized; it must have been hiding, lying flush to the far side of the roof. Two things happened simultaneously. Alicia spun on her heels, aiming the cross instinctively; and with a sound of splintering wood and tearing metal, the roof gave way beneath her.

She landed face-up on the floor of the shed, the viral crashing on top of her. Her cross was gone. Alicia would have drawn a blade, but both of her hands were now occupied in the stalemated project of holding the viral at arm's length. Left and right and left again the creature darted its face, jaws snapping, toward the curve of Alicia's throat. An irresistible force meeting an immovable object: how long could this go on? The children in their beds, Alicia thought. That's who this one was. She was the woman looking through the doorway at her sleeping children. Think about the children, Alicia thought, and then she said it:

"Think about the children."

The viral froze. A wistful expression came into its face. For the thinnest instant—not more than half a second—their eyes met and held in the darkness. Mary, Alicia thought. Your name was Mary. Her hand was reaching for her blade. *I send you home, my sister Mary,* thought Alicia. *I release you from the prison of your existence.* And with an upward thrust she sank her blade, tip to hilt, into the sweet spot.

Alicia rolled the corpse away. The others lay where they had fallen. She collected her blade and bolt from the first two, wiped them clean, then knelt by the body of the last. In the aftermath Alicia usually felt nothing beyond a vague hollowness; it surprised her now to discover that her hands were shaking. How had she known? Because she had; with absolute clarity, she had known that the woman's name was Mary.

She pulled the blade free, touched it to her head and heart. *Thank you, Mary, for not killing me before my work is complete. I hope you are with your little ones now.*

Mary's eyes were open, gazing at nothing; Alicia closed them with her fingertips. It wouldn't do to leave her where she was. Alicia hoisted the body into her arms and carried it outside. A rind of moon had risen, washing the landscape in its glow, a darkness visible. But moonlight wasn't what Mary needed. A hundred years of nighttime sky were enough, Alicia thought, and laid the woman on a patch of open ground where, come morning, the sun would find her and cast her ashes to the wind.

Alicia had begun to climb.

A night and a day had passed. She was in the mountains now, ascending a dry creekbed through a slim defile. The feeling of the virals was stronger here: she was headed toward something. Mary, she thought, what were you trying to tell me?

It was nearly dawn by the time she reached the top of the ridge, the horizon jumping away. Below her, in the wind-scraped blackness, the valley floor unfurled, none but the stars for company. Alicia knew it was possible to parse discrete figures from their arbitrary-seeming arrangement, the shapes of people and animals, but she had never learned to do this. They appeared to her only as a random scattering, as if each night the stars were flung anew against the sky.

Then she saw it: a gaping maw of blackness, set in a bowl-like depression. The opening was a hundred feet tall or more. Curved benches, like an amphitheater, carved from the rocky face of the mountain, were situated at the cave's mouth. Bats were flicking through the sky.

It was a door to hell.

You're down there, aren't you? Alicia thought, and smiled. *You son of a bitch, I've found you.*

II

THE FAMILIAR

SPRING
YEAR ZERO

'Tis now the very witching time of night,
When churchyards yawn and hell itself breathes out
Contagion to this world.

—Shakespeare,
Hamlet

Denver Police Dept.
Case File 193874
District 6
Transcript of Interview with Lila Beatrice Kyle
VIA: Det. Rita Chernow
3 May 4:17 A.M.

RC: Let the record show that the subject has been fully apprised of her rights and has declined to have an attorney present at this interview. Questioning conducted by Detective Rita Chernow, Denver PD, District Six. The time is four-seventeen A.M. Dr. Kyle, would you please state your full name?

LK: Lila Beatrice Kyle.

RC: And you're an orthopedic surgeon at Denver General Hospital, is that correct?

LK: Yes.

RC: And do you know why you're here?

LK: Something happened at the hospital. You wanted to ask me some questions. What is this room? I don't know it.

RC: We're in the police station, Dr. Kyle.

LK: Am I in trouble?

RC: We talked about this, remember? We're just trying to figure out what happened in the ER tonight. I know you're upset. I have just a few questions for you.

LK: There's blood on me. Why is there blood on me?

RC: Do you recall what happened in the ER, Dr. Kyle?

LK: I'm so tired. Why am I so tired?

RC: Can we get you something? Coffee maybe?

LK: I can't drink coffee. I'm pregnant.

RC: Water, then? How about some water?

LK: Okay.

(*Break.*)

RC: So let's start at the beginning. You were working in the emergency room tonight, is that correct?

LK: No, I was upstairs.

RC: But you came down to the ER?

LK: Yes.

RC: At what time?

LK: I'm not sure. Sometime around one A.M. They paged me.

RC: Why did they page you?

LK: I was the orthopedist on call. They had a patient with a broken wrist.

RC: And was that patient Mr. Letourneau?

LK: I think so, yes.

RC: What else did they tell you about him?

LK: Before I went downstairs, you mean?

RC: Yes.

LK: He had some kind of animal bite.

RC: Like a dog bite?

LK: I suppose so. They didn't say.

RC: Anything else?

LK: He had a high fever. He'd vomited.

RC: And that's all they told you?

LK: Yes.

RC: And what did you see when you got to the ER?

LK: He was in the third bed. There were only a couple of other patients. Sunday's usually quiet.

RC: What time would this be?

LK: One-fifteen, one-thirty.

RC: And did you examine Mr. Letourneau?

LK: No.

RC: Let me rephrase. Did you see the patient?

(*Pause.*)

RC: Dr. Kyle?

LK: I'm sorry, what was the question?

RC: Did you see Mr. Letourneau tonight in the ER?

LK: Yes. Mark was there, too.

RC: Are you referring to Dr. Mark Shin?

LK: He was the attending. Have you talked to him?

RC: Dr. Shin is dead, Dr. Kyle. He was one of the victims.

LK: (inaudible)

RC: Could you speak up, please?

LK: I just . . . I don't know. I'm sorry, what did you want to know?

RC: What can you tell me about Mr. Letourneau? How did he seem?

LK: Seem?

RC: Yes. Was he awake?

LK: He was awake.

RC: What else did you observe?

LK: He was disoriented. Agitated. His color was strange.

RC: How do you mean?

(*Pause.*)

LK: I have to go to the bathroom.

RC: Let's just get through some questions first. I know you're tired. I promise I'll get you out of here as quickly as I can.

LK: Do you have children, Detective Chernow?

RC: I'm sorry?

LK: Do you have any children? I was just curious.

RC: Yes, I have two boys.

LK: How old? If you don't mind my asking.

RC: Five and seven. I have just a few more things to ask you. Do you think you're up to that?

LK: But I bet you're trying for the girl, aren't you? Believe me, there's nothing like having a baby girl of your own.

RC: Let's focus on Mr. Letourneau for now, would that be okay? You said he was agitated. Can you elaborate on that?

LK: Elaborate?

RC: Yes. What did he do?

LK: He was making a funny noise.

RC: Can you describe it?

LK: A clicking sound, in his throat. He was moaning. He seemed to be in a great deal of pain.

RC: Had they given him anything for the pain?

LK: They'd given him Tramadol. I think it was Tramadol.

RC: Who else was there besides Dr. Shin?

(*Pause.*)

RC: Dr. Kyle? Who else was there when you examined Mr. Letourneau?

LK: One of the nurses. She was trying to calm him down. He was very upset.

RC: Anyone else?

LK: I don't remember. An orderly? No, two.

RC: What happened then?

LK: He started to seize.

RC: The patient had a seizure, you mean?

LK: Yes.

RC: What did you do then?

LK: Where's my husband?

RC: He's right outside. He came with you. Don't you remember?

LK: Brad is here?

RC: I'm sorry. Who's Brad?

LK: My husband. Brad Wolgast. He's with the FBI. Maybe you know him?

RC: Dr. Kyle, I'm confused. The man who came with you is named David Centre. He's not your husband?

(*Pause.*)

RC: Dr. Kyle? Do you understand what I'm asking you?

LK: Of course David is my husband. What a strange thing for you to say. Where did all this blood come from? Was I in an accident?

RC: No, Dr. Kyle. You were at the hospital. That's what we're talking about. Three hours ago, nine people were killed in the ER. We're trying to figure out how that happened.

(*Pause.*)

LK: It looked at me. Why did it just look at me?

RC: What looked at you, Dr. Kyle?

LK: It was horrible.

RC: What was?

LK: It killed the nurse first. There was so much blood. Like an ocean.

RC: Are you speaking of Mr. Letourneau? He killed the nurse? I need you to be clear.

LK: I'm thirsty. Can I have some more water?

RC: In a minute. How did Mr. Letourneau kill the nurse?

LK: It happened so fast. How could anybody move that fast?

RC: I need you to focus, Dr. Kyle. What did Mr. Letourneau use to kill the nurse? Was there a weapon?

LK: A weapon? I don't remember a weapon.

RC: How did he do it then?

(*Pause.*)

RC: Dr. Kyle?

LK: I couldn't move. It just . . . looked at me.

RC: Something looked at you? Was there somebody else in the room?

LK: He used his mouth. That was how he did it.

RC: Are you saying that Mr. Letourneau bit the nurse?

(*Pause.*)

LK: I'm expecting, you know. I'm going to have a baby.

RC: I can see that, Dr. Kyle. I know this is very stressful.

LK: I need to rest. I want to go home.

RC: We'll try to get you out of here as quickly as we can. Just to clarify, is it your statement that Mr. Letourneau bit the nurse?

LK: Is she all right?

RC: She was decapitated, Dr. Kyle. You were holding the body when we found you. Don't you remember?

LK: (inaudible)

RC: Can you speak up, please?

LK: I don't understand what you want. Why are you asking me these questions?

RC: Because you were there. You're our only witness. You saw nine people die tonight. They were ripped apart, Dr. Kyle.

LK: (inaudible)

RC: Dr. Kyle?

LK: Those eyes. It was like looking into hell. Like falling forever into darkness. Do you believe in hell, Detective?

RC: Whose eyes?

LK: It wasn't human. It couldn't have been human.

RC: Are you still speaking of Mr. Letourneau?

LK: I can't think about this. I have to think about the baby.

RC: What did you see? Tell me what you saw.

LK: I want to go home. I don't want to talk about this anymore. Don't make me.

RC: What killed those people, Dr. Kyle?

(*Pause.*)

RC: Dr. Kyle, are you all right?

(*Pause.*)

RC: Dr. Kyle?

(*Pause.*)

RC: Dr. Kyle?

4

Bernard Kittridge, known to the world as "Last Stand in Denver," realized it was time to leave the morning the power went out.

He wondered what had taken so long. You couldn't keep a municipal electrical grid running without people to man it, and as far as Kittridge could tell from the nineteenth floor, not a single human soul was left alive in the city of Denver.

Which was not to say he was alone.

He had passed the early hours of the morning—a bright, clear morning in the first week of June, temperatures in the mid-seventies with a chance of bloodsucking monsters moving in toward dusk—sunning on the balcony of the penthouse he had occupied since the second week of the crisis. It was a gigantic place, like an airborne palace; the kitchen alone was the size of Kittridge's whole apartment. The owner's taste ran in an austere direction: sleek leather seating groups that were better to look at than sit on, gleaming floors of twinkling travertine, small furry rugs, glass tables that appeared to float in space. Breaking in had been surprisingly simple. By the time Kittridge had made his decision, half the city was dead, or fled, or missing. The cops were long gone. He'd thought about barricading himself into one of the big houses up in Cherry Creek, but based on the things he'd seen, he wanted someplace high.

The owner of the penthouse was a man he knew slightly, a regular customer at the store. His name was Warren Filo. As luck would have it, Warren had come into the store the day before the whole thing had broken to gear up for a hunting trip to Alaska. He was a young guy, too young for how much money he had—Wall Street money, probably, or one of those high-tech IPOs. On that day, the world still cheerily humming along as usual, Kittridge had helped Warren carry his purchases to the car. A Ferrari, of course. Standing beside it, Kittridge thought: Why not just go ahead and get a vanity plate that says, DOUCHE BAG? A question that must have been plainly written on his face, because no sooner had it crossed Kittridge's mind than Warren went red with embarrassment. He wasn't wearing his usual suit, just jeans and a T-shirt with SLOAN SCHOOL OF MANAGEMENT printed on the front. He'd wanted Kittridge to see his car, that was obvious, but now that he'd allowed this to happen, he'd realized how dumb it was, showing off a vehicle like that to a floor manager at Outdoor World who probably made less than fifty grand a year. (The number was actually forty-six.) Kittridge allowed himself a silent laugh at that—the things this kid didn't know would fill a book—and he let the moment hang to make the point. *I know, I know,* Warren confessed. *It's a little much. I told myself I'd never be one of those assholes who drive a Ferrari. But honest to God, you should feel the way she handles.*

Kittridge had gotten Warren's address off his invoice. By the time he moved in—Warren presumably snug and safe in Alaska—it was simply a matter of finding the right key in the manager's office, putting it into the slot in the elevator panel, and riding eighteen floors to the penthouse. He unloaded his gear. A rolling suitcase of clothes, three lockers of weaponry, a hand-crank radio, night-vision binoculars, flares, a first-aid kit, bottles of bleach, an arc welder to seal the doors of the elevator, his trusty laptop with its portable satellite dish, a box of books, and enough food and water to last a month. The view from the balcony, which ran the length of the west side of the building, was a sweeping 180 degrees, looking toward Interstate 25 and Mile High field. He'd positioned cameras equipped with motion detectors at each end of the balcony, one to cover the street, a second facing the building on the opposite side of the avenue. He figured he'd get a lot of good footage this way, but the money shots would be actual kills. The weapon he'd selected for this task was a Remington bolt-action 700P, .338 caliber—a nice balance of accuracy and stopping power, zeroing out at three hundred yards. To this he'd affixed a digital video scope with infrared. Using the binoculars, he would isolate his target; the rifle, mounted on a bipod at the edge of the balcony, would do the rest.

On the first night, windless and lit by a waning quarter moon, Kittridge had shot seven: five on the avenue, one on the opposite roof, and one more through the window of a bank at street level. It was the last one that made him famous. The creature, or vampire, or whatever it was—the official term was "Infected Person"—had looked straight into the lens just before Kittridge put one through the sweet spot. Uploaded to YouTube, the image had traveled around the globe within hours; by morning all the major networks had picked it up. Who is this man? everyone wanted to know. Who is this fearless-crazy-suicidal man, barricaded in a Denver high-rise, making his last stand?

And so was born the sobriquet, Last Stand in Denver.

From the start he'd assumed it was just a matter of time before somebody shut him down, CIA or NSA or Homeland. He was making quite a stir. Working in his favor was the fact that this same somebody would have to come to Denver to pull the plug. Kittridge's IP address was functionally untraceable, backstopped by a daisy chain of anonymizer servers, their order scrambled every night. Most were overseas: Russia, China, Indonesia, Israel, Sudan. Places beyond easy reach for any federal agency that might want to pull the plug. His video blog—two million hits the first day—had more than three hundred mirror sites, with more added all the time. It didn't take a week before he was a bona fide worldwide phenomenon. Twitter, Facebook, Headshot, Sphere: the images found their way into the ether without his lifting a finger. One of his fan sites alone had more than two million subscribers; on eBay, T-shirts that read, I AM LAST STAND IN DENVER were selling like hotcakes.

His father had always said, *Son, the most important thing in life is to make a contribution.* Who would have thought Kittridge's contribution would be video-blogging from the front lines of the apocalypse?

And yet the world went on. The sun still shone. To the west, the mountains shrugged their indifferent rocky bulk at man's departure. For a while, there had been a lot of smoke—whole blocks had burned to the ground—but now this had dissipated, revealing the desolation with eerie clarity. At night, regions of blackness blotted the city, but elsewhere, lights still glittered in the gloom—flickering streetlamps, filling stations and convenience stores with their distinctive fluorescent glow, porch lights left burning for their owners' return. While Kittridge maintained his vigil on the balcony, a traffic signal eighteen floors below still dutifully turned from green to yellow to red and then to green again.

He wasn't lonely. Loneliness had left him, long ago. He was thirty-four years old. A little heavier than he would have liked—with his leg, it was hard to keep the weight off—but still strong. He'd been married once, years before. He remembered that period of his life as twenty months of oversexed, connubial bliss, followed by an equal number of months of yelling and screaming, accusations and counteraccusations, until the whole thing sank like a rock, and he was content, on the whole, that this union had produced no children. His connection to Denver was neither sentimental nor personal; after he'd gotten out of the VA, it was simply where he'd landed. Everyone said that a decorated veteran should have little trouble finding work. And maybe this was true. But Kittridge had been in no hurry. He'd spent the better part of a year just reading—the usual stuff at first, cop novels and thrillers, but eventually had found his way to more substantial books: *As I Lay Dying, For Whom the Bell Tolls, Huckleberry Finn, The Great Gatsby.* He'd spent a whole month on Melville, drilling his way through *Moby-Dick.* Most were books he felt he ought to read, the ones he'd somehow missed in school, but he genuinely liked most of them. Sitting in the quiet of his studio apartment, his mind lost in tales of other lives and times, felt like taking a long drink after years of thirst. He'd even enrolled in a few classes at the community college, working at Outdoor World during the day, reading and writing his papers at nights and on his lunch hour. There was something in the pages of these books that had the power to make him feel better about things, a life raft to cling to before the dark currents of memory washed him downstream again, and on brighter days, he could even see himself going on this way for some time. A small but passable life.

And then, of course, the end of the world had happened.

*   *   *

The morning the electricity failed, Kittridge had finished uploading the previous night's footage and was sitting on the patio, reading Dickens's *A Tale of Two Cities*—the English barrister Sydney Carton had just declared his everlasting love for Lucie Manette, the fiancée of the haplessly idealistic Charles Darnay—when the thought touched him that the morning could only be improved by a dish of ice cream. Warren's enormous kitchen—you could run a five-star restaurant out of the thing—had been, unsurprisingly, almost completely bereft of food, and Kittridge had long since thrown away the moldy take-out containers that had constituted the meager contents of the fridge. But the guy obviously had a weakness for Ben and Jerry's Chocolate Fudge Brownie, because the freezer was crammed with the stuff. Not Chunky Monkey or Cherry Garcia or Phish Food or even plain old vanilla. Just Chocolate Fudge Brownie. Kittridge would have liked some variety, considering there was going to be no more ice cream for a while, but with little else to eat besides canned soup and crackers, he was hardly going to complain. Balancing his book on the arm of his chair, he rose and stepped through the sliding glass door into the penthouse.

By the time he reached the kitchen, he had begun to sense that something was off-kilter, although this impression had yet to coalesce around anything specific. It wasn't until he opened the carton and sank his spoon into a soft mush of melted Chocolate Fudge Brownie that he fully understood.

He tried a light switch. Nothing. He moved through the apartment, testing lamps and switches. All were the same.

In the middle of the living room, Kittridge paused and took a deep breath. Okay, he thought, okay. This was to be expected. If anything, this was long overdue. He checked his watch: 9:32 A.M. Sunset was a little after eight. Ten and a half hours to get his ass gone.

He threw together a rucksack of supplies: protein bars, bottles of water, clean socks and underwear, his first-aid kit, a warm jacket, a bottle of Zyrtec (his allergies had been playing hell with him all spring), a toothbrush, and a razor. For a moment he considered bringing *A Tale of Two Cities* along, but this seemed impractical, and with a twinge of regret he put it aside. In the bedroom he dressed himself in a wicking T-shirt and cargo pants, topping this off with a hunting vest and a pair of light hikers. For a few minutes he considered which weapons to take before settling on a Bowie knife, a pair of Glock 19s, and the retrofitted

Polish AK with the folding stock: useless at any kind of range but reliable close in, where he expected to be. The Glocks fit snugly in a cross-draw holster. He filled the pockets of his vest with loaded magazines, clipped the AK to its sling, hoisted the backpack over his shoulders, and returned to the patio.

That was when he noticed the traffic signal on the avenue. Green, yellow, red. Green, yellow, red. It could have been a fluke, but he doubted it.

They'd found him.

The rope was anchored to a drainage stack on the roof. He stepped into his rappelling harness, clipped in, and swung first his good leg and then his bad one over the railing. Heights were no problem for him, and yet he did not look down. He was perched on the edge of the balcony, facing the windows of the penthouse. From the distance he heard the sound of an approaching helicopter.

Last Stand in Denver, signing off.

With a push he was aloft, his body lobbing down and away. One story, two stories, three, the rope smoothly sliding through his hands: he landed on the balcony of the apartment four floors below. A familiar twang of pain shot upward from his left knee; he gritted his teeth to force it away. The helicopter was closing in now, the thrum of its blades volleying off the buildings. He peeled off his harness, drew one of the Glocks, and fired a single shot to shatter the glass of the balcony door.

The air of the apartment was stale, like the inside of a cabin sealed for winter. Heavy furniture, gilt mirrors, an oil painting of a horse over the fireplace; from somewhere wafted the stench of decay. He moved through the becalmed space with barely a glance. At the door he paused to attach a spotlight to the rail of the AK and stepped out into the hall, headed for the stairs.

In his pocket were the keys to the Ferrari, parked in the building's underground garage, sixteen floors below. Kittridge shouldered open the door of the stairwell, quickly sweeping the space with the beam from the AK, up and down. Clear. He withdrew a flare from his vest and used his teeth to unscrew the plastic top, exposing the igniter button. With a combustive pop, the flare commenced its rain of sparks. Kittridge held it over the side, taking aim, and let go; if there was anything down there, he'd know it soon. His eyes followed the flare as it made its descent, dragging a contrail of smoke. Somewhere below it nicked the rail and bounced out of sight. Kittridge counted to ten. Nothing, no movement at all.

Three flares later he reached the bottom; a heavy steel door with a push bar and a small square of reinforced glass led to the garage. The floor was littered with trash: pop cans, candy bar wrappers, tins of food.

A rumpled bedroll and a pile of musty clothing showed where someone had been sleeping—hiding, as he had.

Kittridge had scouted out the parking garage the day of his arrival. The Ferrari was parked near the southwest corner, a distance of approximately two hundred feet. He probably should have moved it closer to the door, but it had taken him three days to locate Warren's keys—who kept his car keys in a bathroom drawer?—by which time he'd already barricaded himself inside the penthouse.

The fob had four buttons: two for the doors, one for the alarm, and one that, he hoped, was a remote starter. He pressed this one first.

From deep within the garage came a tart, single-noted bleep, followed by the throaty roar of the Ferrari's engine. Another mistake: the Ferrari was parked nose to the wall. He should have thought of that. Not only would this slow his escape; if the car had been facing the opposite way, its headlights would have given him a better look at the garage's interior. All he could make out through the stairwell door's tiny window was a distant, glowing region where the car awaited, a cat purring in the dark. The rest of the garage was veiled in blackness. The infected liked to hang from things: ceiling struts, pipes, anything with a tactile surface. The tiniest fissure would suffice. When they came, they came from above.

The moment of decision was upon him. Toss more flares and see what happens? Move stealthily through the darkness, seeking cover? Throw open the door and run like hell?

Then, from high overhead, Kittridge heard the creak of an opening stairwell door. He held his breath and listened. There were two of them. He stepped back from the door and craned his neck upward. Ten stories above, a pair of red dots were dancing off the walls.

He shoved the door open and ran like hell.

He had made it halfway to the Ferrari when the first viral dropped behind him. There was no time to turn and fire; Kittridge kept on going. The pain in his knee felt like a wick of flame, an ice pick buried to the bone. From the periphery of his senses came a tingling awareness of beings awakening, the garage coming to life. He threw open the door of the Ferrari, tossed the AK and rucksack onto the passenger seat, got in, and slammed the door. The vehicle was so low-slung he felt like he was sitting on the ground. The dashboard, full of mysterious gauges and switches, glowed like a spacecraft's. Something was missing. Where was the gearshift?

A *wang* of metal, and Kittridge's vision filled with the sight of it. The viral had bounded onto the hood, folding its body into a reptilian crouch. For a frozen moment it regarded him coolly, a predator contemplating its prey. It was naked except for a wristwatch, a gleaming Rolex thick as an ice cube. *Warren?* Kittridge thought, for the man had been wearing one like it the day Kittridge had walked him to the car. *Warren, old buddy, is that you? Because if it is, I wouldn't mind a word of advice on how to get this thing in gear.*

He discovered, then, with the tips of his fingers, a pair of levers positioned on the undersides of the steering wheel. Paddle shifters. He should have thought of that, too. Up on the right, down on the left, like a motorcycle. Reverse would be a button somewhere on the dash.

The one with the R, genius. That one.

He pushed the button and hit the gas. Too fast: with a squeal of smoking rubber, the Ferrari jolted backward and slammed into a concrete post. Kittridge was hurled back into his seat, then tossed forward again, his head smacking the heavy glass of the side window with an audible thud. His brain chimed like a tuning fork; particles of silver light danced in his eyes. There was something interesting about them, interesting and beautiful, but another voice inside him said that to contemplate this vision, even for a moment, was to die. The viral, having tumbled off the hood, was rising from the floor now. No doubt it would try to take him straight through the windshield.

Two red dots appeared on the viral's chest.

With a birdlike quickness, the creature broke its gaze from Kittridge and launched toward the soldiers coming through the stairwell door. Kittridge swung the steering wheel and gripped the right paddle, engaging the transmission as he pressed the accelerator. A lurch and then a leap of speed: he was thrust back into his seat as he heard a blast of automatic weapon fire. Just when he thought he'd lose control of the car again he found the straightaway, the walls of the garage streaming past. The soldiers had bought him only a moment; a quick glimpse in the rearview and Kittridge beheld, in the glow of his taillights, what appeared to be the detonation of a human body, an explosive strewing of parts. The second soldier was nowhere visible, though if Kittridge had to bet, he'd say the man was surely dead already, torn to bloody hunks.

He didn't look back again.

The ramp to the street was located two floors above, at the far end of the garage. As Kittridge downshifted into the first corner, engine roaring, tires shrieking, two more virals dropped from the ceiling, into his path. One fell under his wheels with a damp crunch, but the second leapt over the roof of the barreling Ferrari, striding it like a hurdler. Kittridge felt a stab of wonder, even of admiration. In school, he had learned that you couldn't catch a fly with your hand because time was different to a fly: in a fly's brain, a second was an hour, and an hour was a year. That's what the infected were like. Like beings outside of time.

They were everywhere now, emerging from all the hidden places. They flung themselves at the car like suicides, driven by the madness of their hunger. He tore through them, bodies flying, their monstrous, distorted faces colliding with the windshield before being hurled up and over, away. Two more turns and he'd be free, but one was clinging to the roof now. Kittridge braked around the corner, fishtailing on the slick cement, the force of his deceleration sending the viral rolling onto the hood. A woman: she appeared to be wearing, of all things, a wedding gown. Gouging her fingers into the gap at the base of the windshield, she drew herself onto all fours. Her mouth, a bear trap of blood-lined teeth, was open very wide, a tiny golden crucifix dangled at the base of her throat. *I'm sorry about your wedding,* Kittridge thought as he drew one of the pistols, steadied it over the steering wheel, and fired through the windshield.

He blasted around the final corner; ahead, a shaft of golden daylight showed the way. Kittridge hit the ramp doing seventy miles an hour, still accelerating. The exit was sealed by a metal grate, but this fact seemed meager, no obstacle at all. Kittridge took aim, plunged the pedal to the floor, and ducked.

A furious crash; for two full seconds, an eternity in miniature, the Ferrari went airborne. It rocketed into the sunshine, concussing the pavement with a bone-jarring bang, sparks flying from the undercarriage. Freedom at last, but now he had another problem: there was nothing to stop him. He was going to careen into the lobby of the bank across the street. As Kittridge bounced across the median, he stamped the brake and swerved to the left, bracing for the impact. But there was no need; with a screech of smoking rubber, the tires bit and held, and the next thing Kittridge knew he was flying down the avenue, into the spring morning.

He had to admit it. What had Warren's exact words been? *You should feel the way she handles.*

It was true. Kittridge had never driven anything like it in his life.

5

For a time, a long time, which was no time at all, the man known as Law-rence Grey—former inmate of Beeville Men's Correctional Facility and registered sex offender of the Texas Department of Public Safety; civilian employee of Project NOAH and the Division of Special Weapons; Grey the Source, the Unleasher of Night, Familiar of the One Called Zero—was nowhere at all. He was nothing and no place, a being annihilated, possessing neither memory nor history, his consciousness dispersed across a shoreless sea of no dimension. A wide, dark sea of voices, murmuring his name. *Grey, Grey.* They were there and not there, calling to him as he floated alone, one with the darkness, adrift in an ocean of forever; and all above, the stars.

But not just the stars. For now had come a light—a soft, golden light that swelled above his face. Blades of shadow moved across it, gyring like a pinwheel, and with this light a sound: aortal, heartlike, a *thrum-thrum-thrum* that pulsed to the rhythm of its turning. Grey watched it, this wonderful, gyring light; and the thought crept into his consciousness that what he beheld was God. The light was God in his heaven above, moving over the waters, brushing the face of the world like the hem of a curtain, touching and blessing his creation. The knowledge blossomed inside Grey in a burst of sweetness. Such joy! Such understanding and forgiveness! The light was God and God was love; Grey had only to enter it, to go into the light, to feel that love forever. And a voice said:

It's time, Grey.

Come to me.

He felt himself rising, lifted up. He rose and as he rose the sky spread its wings, receiving him, carrying him into the light, which was almost too much to bear and then was: a brightness blinding and obliterating, like the sound of a scream that was his own.

Grey, ascending. Grey, reborn.

Open your eyes, Grey.

He did; he opened his eyes. His vision crawled into focus. A dark form was whirling unpleasantly above his face.

It was a ceiling fan.

He blinked the grime away. A bitter taste, like wet ashes, painted the walls of his mouth. The room where he lay possessed the unmistakable sense of a chain motel—the scratchy coverlet and cheap foam pillow, the cratered mattress below and popcorn ceiling above, the smell of recycled, overused air in his nostrils. His brain felt as empty as a leaky pail, his body a shapeless mass, vague as gelatin. Even to move his head seemed to require a feat of strength beyond his power. The room was lit with a sticky yellow daylight filtered through the drapes. Above his face, the fan spun and spun, rocking on its bracket, its worn-out bearings rhythmically creaking. The sight was as abrasive to his senses as smelling salts, and yet he could not look away. (And wasn't there something about a thrumming sound, something in a dream? A brilliant light, lifting him up? But he no longer recalled.)

"Good, you're awake."

Sitting on the edge of the second bed, eyes downcast, was a man. A small, soft man, filling out his jumpsuit like a sausage in its casing. One of the civilian employees of Project NOAH, known as sweeps: men like Grey whose job it was to clean up the piss and shit and back up the drives and watch the sticks for hours and hours, slowly going loony; sex offenders to a one, despised and forgotten, men without histories anyone cared to remember, their bodies softened by hormones, their minds and spirits as neutered as a spayed dog.

"I thought the fan would do it. Tell you the truth, I can't even look at the thing."

Grey tried to respond but couldn't. His tongue felt toasted, as if he'd smoked a billion cigarettes. His vision had gone all watery again; his goddamned head was splitting. It had been years since he'd drunk more than a couple of beers at a time—with the drugs, you were too sleepy and pretty much lost interest in everything—but Grey remembered what a hangover was. That's how this felt. Like the worst hangover in the world.

"What's the matter, Grey? Cat got your tongue?" The man chuckled at some private joke. "That's funny, you know. Under the circumstances. I could go for a little cat tartare right now." He turned toward Grey, his eyebrows arcing. "Don't look so shocked. You'll see what I mean. Takes a few days but then it kicks in, real hard."

Grey remembered the man's name: Ignacio. Though the Ignacio that Grey remembered was older, more worn-down, with a heavy, creased brow and pores you could park a car in and jowls that sagged like a bassett hound's. This Ignacio was in the pink of health—literally *pink,* his cheeks rouged with color, skin baby smooth, eyes twinkling like zircs.

Even his hair looked younger. But there was no mistaking who it was, on account of the tat—prison ink, blurred and bluish, a hooded snake rising up his neck from the open collar of his jumpsuit.

"Where am I?"

"You're a regular riot, you know that? We're at the Red Roof."

"The what?"

He made a little snort. "The fucking Red Roof, Grey. What did you think, they'd send us to the Ritz?"

They? Grey thought. Who were *they*? And what did Ignacio mean by "send"? Send for what purpose? Which was the moment Grey noticed that Ignacio was clutching something in his hand. A pistol?

"Iggy? What are you doing with that thing?"

Ignacio lazily raised the gun, a long-barreled .45, frowning at it. "Not much, apparently." He angled his head toward the door. "Those other guys were here for a while, too. But they're all gone now."

"What guys?"

"Come on, Grey. You know those guys. The skinny one, George. Eddie whatzisname. Jude, with the ponytail." He looked past Grey toward the curtains. "Tell you the truth, I never did like him. I heard about the stuff he did, not that I'm anyone to talk. But that man, he was flat-out disgusting."

Ignacio was talking about the other sweeps. What were they all doing here? What was *he* doing here? The gun wasn't a good sign, but Grey couldn't call up a single memory of how he'd come to be where he was. The last thing he recalled was eating dinner in the compound cafeteria: beef bourguignon in a rich gravy, with a side of scalloped potatoes and green beans and a Cherry Coke to wash it all down. It was his favorite meal; he always looked forward to beef bourguignon. Though as he thought about it, its greasy taste, his stomach clamped with nausea. A squirt of bile shot up his throat. He had to take a moment just to breathe.

Ignacio gave his pistol a halfhearted wave toward the door. "Look yourself if you want. But I'm pretty sure they're gone."

Grey swallowed. "Gone where?"

"That depends. Wherever they're supposed to go."

Grey felt totally at sea. He couldn't even figure out what questions to ask. He was pretty sure he wouldn't like the answers, though. Maybe the best thing was to lie quietly. He hoped he hadn't done something terrible, like in the old days. The days of the Old Grey.

"Well," Ignacio said, and cleared his throat, "as long as you're awake, I guess I better be moving on. I've got a long walk ahead of me." He rose and held out the gun. "Here."

Grey hesitated. "What do I want a gun for?"

"In case you feel like, you know, shooting yourself."

Grey was too stunned to reply. The last thing he wanted was a gun. Somebody found a gun on him, they'd send him back to prison for sure. When he made no move to accept the weapon, Ignacio placed it on the bedside table.

"Give it some thought, anyway. Just don't drag your feet like I did. It gets harder the longer you wait. Now look at the fix I'm in."

Ignacio moved to the door, where he turned to cast his gaze a final time around the room.

"We really did it. In case you were, you know, wondering." He took a long breath, blowing out the air with puffed cheeks, and angled his face toward the ceiling. "Funny thing is, I really don't see what I did to deserve this. I wasn't so bad, not really. I didn't mean to do half those things. It was just the way I was built." He looked at Grey again; his eyes were filmed with tears. "That's what the shrink always said. Ignacio, it's just the way you're built."

Grey had no idea what to say. Sometimes there was nothing, and he guessed this was one of those times. The look on Ignacio's face reminded him of some of the cons he'd known in Beeville, men who'd been inside so long they were like zombies in some old movie. Men with nothing but the past to dwell on and, ahead, an endless stretch of nothing.

"Well, fuck it." Ignacio sniffled and rubbed his nose with the back of his wrist. "No use complaining about it now. You make your bed you have to lie in it. Think about what I said, okay? Be seeing you, Grey." And with a wash of light from the open door, he was gone.

What to make of that? For a long time Grey lay still, his mind spinning like a bald tire on ice. Part of him wasn't sure if he was awake or still sleeping. He reviewed the facts to give his mind a point to fix on. He was on a bed. The bed was in a motel, a Red Roof. The motel was somewhere in Colorado, probably, assuming he hadn't gone far. The light in the windows said morning. He didn't appear to be injured. Sometime in the last twenty-four hours, maybe more and maybe less, but probably not more than a day, he'd blacked out.

He'd have to go from there.

He drew himself up on his elbows. The room reeked of sweat and smoke. His jumpsuit was stained and torn at the knees; his feet were bare. He gave his toes a wiggle, the joints cracking and popping. Everything seemed to be working.

And come to think of it, wasn't it true that he was feeling better? And not just better—a lot better. The headache and dizziness were gone. His vision had cleared. His limbs felt firm and strong, full of fresh, coiled energy. His mouth still tasted foul—finding a toothbrush or a pack of gum was job one—but other than that, Grey felt right as rain.

He swiveled his feet to the floor. The room was small, just space enough for the beds, with their brown-and-orange coverlets, and a little table with a television. But when he picked up the remote to turn it on, all he got was a blue screen with a sound like a dial tone. He flipped through the channels; the network affiliates, CNN, the War Channel, GOVTV—all were blued out. Well, didn't that just figure. He'd have to tell the manager about that. Though as far as he recalled he hadn't paid for the room, and his wallet had been confiscated months ago, when he'd first arrived at the compound.

The compound, Grey thought, the word dropping to his gut like a rock. Whatever else was true, he was in a heap of trouble. You didn't just up and leave. He remembered Jack and Sam, the two sweeps who'd gone AWOL, and how pissed off Richards had been. Who was not somebody you wanted to piss off, to put it mildly. Just a glance from the man made Grey's bowels twist.

Maybe that's why the sweeps had all run off. Maybe it was Richards they were afraid of.

His thirst hit him then—a mad, crazy thirst, like he hadn't had a drink in days. In the bathroom he jammed his face under the tap, gulping fiercely, letting the water stream over his face. Slow down, Grey, he thought, you're going to make yourself sick if you drink like this.

Too late; the water hit his stomach like a crashing wave, and the next thing he knew he was on his knees, clutching the sides of the toilet bowl, all the water coming up.

Well, that was dumb. He had no one to blame but himself. He stayed on his knees a moment, waiting for the cramping to pass, breathing in the stink of his own vomit—mostly water, but in the final instance a gooey, yolk-like glob, no doubt the undigested remnants of the beef bourguignon. He must have strained something, too, because his ears were ringing: a faint, nearly subaural whine, like the sound of a tiny motor whirring deep inside his skull.

He struggled to his feet and flushed the puke away. On the vanity he saw a little bottle of mouthwash in a tray with soaps and lotions, none of it touched, and he took a swig to clear the taste in his mouth, gargling long and hard and spitting into the sink. Then he looked at his face in the mirror.

Grey's first thought was that somebody was playing a joke on him: an elaborate, unfunny, improbable joke, in which the mirror had somehow been replaced by a window, and on the far side stood a man—a much younger, better-looking man. The urge to reach out and touch this image was so strong he actually did it, the man in the mirror perfectly mimicking his movements. What the fuck? Grey thought, and then he said it: "What the fuck?" The face he beheld was slim, clear-skinned, attractive. His hair brushed over his ears in a lush mane, its tone a rich chestnut. His eyes were clear and bright; they actually sparkled. Never in his life had Grey looked so good.

Something else drew his eye. Some sort of mark on his neck. He leaned forward, tilting his head upward. Two lines of symmetrical bead-like depressions, roughly circular in their arrangement, the top of the circle reaching to his jawline, the bottom skimming the curve of his collarbone. The wound had a pinkish color, as if only lately healed. When the hell had this happened? As a kid he'd been bitten by a dog once; that was what this looked like. A surly old mutt-dog from the pound, but still he'd loved it, it was something that was his, until the day he'd bitten Grey on the hand—no good reason for it; Grey had only meant to give him a biscuit—and his father had dragged him to the yard. Two shots, Grey recalled that clearly, the first followed by a yelping squeal, the second dimming the dog forever into silence. The dog's name was Buster. Grey hadn't given him a thought in years.

But this thing on his neck. Where had it come from? There was something familiar about it—a feeling of déjà vu, as if the recollection had been stored in the wrong drawer in his mind.

Grey, don't you know?

Grey spun from the mirror.

"Iggy?"

Silence. He returned to the bedroom. He opened the closet, knelt to look beneath the beds. No one.

Grey. Grey.

"Iggy, where are you? Quit fucking with me."

Don't you remember, Grey?

Something was wrong with him, really wrong. It wasn't Iggy's voice he was hearing; the voice was in his *head*. Every surface that met his eyes seemed to throb with vividness. He rubbed his eyes, but it only got worse. It was as if he weren't just seeing things, but touching and smelling and tasting them too, as if the wires in his brain had crossed.

Don't you remember . . . dying?

And all at once he did; the memory pierced him like an arrow to the chest. The aquatic blue of the containment chamber, and the slowly opening door; Subject Zero rising above him, assuming his full and terrible dimensions; the feel of Zero's jaws on the curve of his neck and the clamp of boring teeth, picketed row upon row; Zero gone, leaving him alone, and the blare of the alarm and the sound of gunfire and the screams of dying men; his stumble into the hall, a vision of hell, blood everywhere, painting the walls and floor, and the grisly remains, a slaughterhouse of legs and arms and torsos with their roping entrails; the sticky, arterial spurt through his fingers where he held them to his throat; the air whooshing out of him, and his long slide to the floor, blackness enveloping him, his vision swimming; and then the letting go.

Oh God.

Come to me, Grey. Come to me.

He tore from the room, daylight blasting his eyes. It was crazy; he was crazy. Across the parking lot he ran like a great, lumbering animal, sightless and without direction, his hands clamped to his ears. A few cars dotted the lot, parked at haphazard angles, many with their doors standing open. But in its white-hot state, Grey's mind failed to register this fact, just as it failed to note other troubling details: the smashed front windows of the hotel; the highway on which not a single vehicle could be seen to move; the vacant filling station across the access road, its windows smeared with red, and the body of a man slumped against the pump in the manner of an impromptu siesta; the wrecked McDonald's, its chairs and tables and ketchup packets and Happy Meal toys and patrons of various ages and races hurled through the windows in violent disgorgement; the plume of chemical smoke from the still-burning wreckage of a tractor-trailer two miles away; the birds. Great wheeling clouds of large, black birds, crows and ravens and buzzards, the scavengers, idly spinning overhead. All of it suspended like the aftermath of a terrible battle, bathed with pitiless summer sunshine.

Do you see, Grey?

"Stop it! Shut up!"

He stumbled on something soft. Organically damp and squishy, under his feet. It sent him crashing to his hands and knees, skidding on the blacktop.

See the world that we have made.

He squeezed his eyes shut. He was heaving for breath. He knew without looking that the squishy thing was a body. *Please,* he thought, not sure whom or even what he was addressing. Himself. The voice in his head. God, whom he'd never quite believed in but was willing to believe in now. *I'm sorry for whatever I did. I'm sorry, I'm sorry, I'm sorry.*

By the time he finally looked, all hope had left him. The body was a woman. The flesh of her face was sucked so tightly to the bones it was hard to tell how old she was. She was dressed in sweatpants and a scoop-necked T-shirt with a little frill of pink lace at the neckline; Grey supposed she'd been in bed and had come out to see what was happening. She was splayed on the pavement, her back and shoulders twisted. Flies were buzzing over her, dipping in and out of her mouth and eyes. One arm lay outstretched on the pavement, palm up; the other was bent across her chest, the tips of her fingers touching the wound at her throat. Not a cut or gash, nothing as tidy as that. Her throat had been chomped away, down to the bone.

She was not the only one. Grey's vision widened, like a camera lifting over the scene. To his left, twenty feet away, a Chevy half-ton was parked with the driver's door open. A heavyset man in suit pants with suspenders had been pulled from his seat and now hung half in and half out of the truck, dangling head-down over the running board, though his head wasn't there; his head was somewhere else.

More bodies lay near the hotel entrance. Not bodies, strictly speaking—more like a zone of human parts. A woman police officer had been eviscerated as she'd stepped from her cruiser. She rested with her back propped against the fender, pistol still clutched in her hand, her chest opened like the flaps of a trench coat. A man in a shiny purple tracksuit, wearing enough gold around his neck to fill a pirate chest, had been hurled upward, his torso lodging like a kite in the limbs of a maple tree; his bottom half had come to rest on the hood of a jewel-black Mercedes. The man's legs were crossed at the ankles, as if the lower half of his body hadn't heard it was missing the rest.

By this time, Grey knew himself to be in something close to a trance. You couldn't look at something like this and allow yourself to feel anything.

The one that finally did it was the one that wasn't there. Two vehicles, a Honda Accord and a Chrysler Countryside, had collided head-on near the exit, their front ends crumpled into each other like the bellows of an accordion. The driver of the sedan had been shot through the windshield. The sedan was otherwise untouched, but the minivan looked ransacked. Its sliding door had been ripped away and hurled across the parking lot like a Frisbee. On the pavement by the open door, in a plume of debris—suitcases, toys, a jumbo pack of diapers—lay the prostrate body of a woman; just beyond the reach of her outstretched hand, tipped on its side, was an empty baby carrier. *What happened to the baby?* Grey thought.

And then: *Oh.*

*　　*　　*

Grey chose the pickup. He wouldn't have minded driving the Mercedes, but he guessed a truck would be more sensible. He'd owned a Chevy half-ton, back in a life that didn't seem to matter now, so the pickup was something familiar to cling to. He eased the decapitated driver free and laid him on the pavement. It was troubling, not having the head to give back to the poor guy. It didn't seem right to leave him there without it. But the head was nowhere obvious, and Grey had seen enough. He looked around for a pair of shoes his size—13EEE; whatever Zero had done to him, it hadn't shrunk his feet any—and finally chose a pair of loafers from the feet of the man on the Mercedes. They were Italian lambskin, soft as butter, and a little narrow in the toe box, but leather like that would stretch. He got in the truck and started the engine. There was a little more than three-quarters of a tank of gas; Grey figured that would get him most of the way to Denver.

He was about to pull away when a last thought occurred to him. He put the vehicle in park and returned to the room. Holding the pistol a little distance from his body, he walked back to the truck and deposited it in the glove compartment. Then, with only the gun for company, he put the truck in gear and drove away.

6

Momma was in the bedroom. Momma was in the bedroom, not moving. Momma was in the bedroom, which was forbidden. Momma was dead, precisely.

After I'm gone, remember to eat, because you sometimes forget. Bathe every other day. Milk in the fridge, Lucky Charms in the cupboard, and hamburger casseroles to reheat in the freezer. Put them in at 350 for an hour, and remember to turn off the oven when you're done. Be my big boy, Danny. I love you always. I just can't be afraid anymore. Love, Momma.

She'd left the note tucked beneath the salt and pepper shakers on the kitchen table. Danny liked salt, but not pepper, which made him sneeze. Ten days had gone by—Danny knew this from the marks he put on the calendar every morning—and the note was still there. He didn't know what to do with it. The whole place smelled something awful, the way a raccoon or possum did when it had been run over again and again for days.

The milk was no good, too. With the electricity off, it had gone sour, warm and unpleasant in his mouth. He tried the Lucky Charms with water from the tap, but it wasn't the same, nothing was the same, everything was different because Momma was in the bedroom. At night he sat in the dark in his room with the door closed. He knew where Momma kept the candles, they were in the cupboard over the sink where she kept her bottle of Popov for when her nerves got to her, but matches were nothing for him. They were on the list. It wasn't an actual list, it was just the things he couldn't do or touch. The toaster, because he kept pushing the button back down and burning the toast. The pistol in Momma's nightstand, because it wasn't a toy, it could shoot you. The girls on his bus, because they wouldn't like it, and he wouldn't get to drive the No. 12 anymore, which would be bad. That would be the worst thing in the world to Danny Chayes.

No electricity meant no TV, so he couldn't watch Thomas, either. Thomas was for little boys, Momma had told him so a million times, but the therapist, Dr. Francis, said it was okay to watch it as long as Danny tried other things, too. His favorite was James. Danny liked his red color and matching tender, and the sound of his voice the way the narrator did it, so soothing it made his throat tickle at the top. Faces were hard for Danny, but the expressions on the Thomas trains were always precise and easy to follow, and it was funny, the things they did to each other, the pranks they liked to play. Switching the tracks so Percy would run into a coal loader. Pouring chocolate all over Gordon, who pulled the express, because he was such a haughty engine. The kids on his bus sometimes made fun of Danny, calling him Topham Hatt, singing the song with not-nice words in place of the real ones, but for the most part Danny tuned this out. There was one kid, though. His name was Billy Nice, and nice was not what he was. He was a sixth grader, but Danny thought he'd probably been held back a few times, on account of he had a body like a full-grown man's. He boarded each morning without so much as a book in his hands, sneering at Danny as he mounted the steps, high-fiving and what-upping the other boys as he sauntered down the alley between the seats, dragging a smell of cigarettes.

Hey, Topham Hatt, how are things going on the Island of Sodor today? Is it true that Lady Hatt likes to take it in the caboose?

Har-har-har, Billy laughed. Har-har-har. Danny never said anything back, because it would only make things worse; he'd never told Mr. Purvis anything, because he knew what the man would say. *Goddamnit, Danny, whatcha let the little shit treat you like that for? Lord knows you're one weird duck, but you've got to stand up for yourself. You're the captain of that ship. You allow a mutiny and the next thing you know everything goes in the dumper.*

Danny liked Mr. Purvis, the dispatcher. Mr. Purvis had always been a friend to Danny, and Momma, too. Momma was one of the cafeteria ladies, so that was how they knew each other, and Mr. Purvis was always coming around the house, fixing things, like the disposal or a loose board on the porch, even though he had a wife of his own, Mrs. Purvis. He was a big bald man who liked to whistle through his teeth and was always hitching up his pants. Sometimes he visited at night, after Danny was in bed; Danny would hear the TV going in the living room, and the pair of them laughing and talking. Danny liked those nights. They gave him a good feeling in his mind, like the happy-click. When anybody asked, Momma always said that Danny's father "wasn't in the picture," which was precisely true. There were pictures of Momma in the house, and pictures of Danny, and pictures of the two of them together. But he'd never seen one with his father in it. Danny didn't even know the man's name.

The bus had been Mr. Purvis's idea. He'd taught Danny to drive in the parking lot at the depot, and went with him to get his Class B license, and helped him fill out the application. Momma hadn't been so sure at first, on account of her needing Danny to help around the house, being a useful engine, and the Social Security, which was money from the government. But Danny knew the real reason, which was the different and special way he was. The thing with a job, Momma had explained, using her careful voice, was that a person needed to be "adaptable." Things would happen, different things. Take the cafeteria. Some days they would serve hot dogs, and some days lasagna, and other days chicken cutlets. The menu might say one thing, but it turned out to be another; you couldn't always know. Wouldn't that upset him?

But a bus wasn't a cafeteria. A bus was a bus, and it ran on a schedule, precisely. When Danny got behind the wheel, he felt the happy-click bigger and deeper than he'd ever felt in his life. Driving a bus! A big yellow one, all the seats in their orderly rows, the gearshift with its six speeds and reverse, everything laid out nice and neat before him. It wasn't a train but it was close, and each morning as he pulled away from the depot, he always imagined he was Gordon or Henry or Percy or even Thomas himself.

He was always on time. Forty-two minutes from depot to drop-off, 8.2 miles, nineteen stops, twenty-nine passengers, precisely. *Robert-Shelly-Brittany-Maybeth-Joey-Darla/Denise (the twins)-Pedro-Damien-Jordan-Charlie-Oliver (O-Man)-Sasha-Billy-Molly-Lyle-Dick (Dickhead)-*

Richard-Lisa-Mckenna-Anna-Lily-Matthew-Charlie-Emily-JohnJohn-Kayla-Sean-Timothy. Sometimes a parent would wait with them on the corner, a mother in a housecoat or a father in a jacket and tie, holding a mug of coffee. *How's it going today, Danny,* they might say, wearing a good-morning smile on their faces. *You know, a person could set their watch by you.*

Be my useful engine, Momma always said, and that's what Danny was.

But now the children were gone. Not just the children: everyone. Momma and Mr. Purvis and maybe all the people in the world. The nights were dark and still, no lights burning anywhere. For a while there had been a lot of noise—people yelling, sirens wailing, Army trucks roaring down the street. He'd heard the pop of guns. *Pop!* went the guns. *Pop-pop-pop-pop!* What are they shooting at, Danny wanted to know, but Momma wouldn't say. She told him to stay inside, using her strong voice, and not to watch TV, and to keep away from the windows. What about the bus, Danny asked, and Momma only said, Damnit, Danny, don't worry about the bus now. School's out today. What about tomorrow, Danny asked. And Momma said, It's out tomorrow, too.

Without the bus, he didn't know what to do with himself. His brain felt as jumpy as corn in a hot pan. He wished Mr. Purvis could come over and watch TV with Momma, it always made her feel better about things, but the man never did. The world went quiet, the way it was now. There were monsters out there. Danny had figured that out. As a for instance, there was the woman across the street, Mrs. Kim. Mrs. Kim taught the violin, kids coming over to her house for their lessons, and on summer days when the windows were open Danny could hear them playing, twinkle-twinkle and Mary-had-a-little-lamb and other things he didn't know the names of. Now there was no violin and Mrs. Kim was hanging over the porch railing.

And then one night Danny heard Momma crying in the bedroom. Once in a while she cried like this, all alone, it was normal and natural and nothing for Danny to worry about, but this felt different. For a long time he lay in his bed listening, wondering what that must be like, to feel something so sad it made you cry, but the idea was like something on a shelf he couldn't reach. Sometime later he awoke in the dark to the feel of someone touching his hair and he opened his eyes to see her sitting there. Danny didn't like to be touched, it gave him the jangly feeling something awful, but it was okay when Momma did it, mostly, on account of he was used to it. What is it, Momma? Danny said. What's wrong? But all she said was Hush now, hush now, Danny. Something was resting in her lap, folded in a towel. I love you, Danny. Do you know how much I love you? I love you, too, Momma, he said, because that was the right answer when someone said I-love-you, and to the feel of her hand caressing him he fell asleep, and in the morning her bedroom door was closed and never opened and Danny knew. He didn't even have to look.

He decided to drive the bus after all.

Because maybe he wasn't the only person still living. Because it gave him the happy-click, driving the bus. Because he didn't know what else to do with himself, with Momma in the bedroom and the milk spoiled and all the days gone by.

He'd laid out his clothes the night before the way Momma always did, a pair of khakis and a white collared shirt and brown tie shoes, and packed a lunch. There wasn't much left to eat except for peanut butter and some graham crackers and a bag of stale marshmallows, but he'd saved a bottle of Mountain Dew, and he put it all in his backpack with his pocket knife and his lucky penny, then went to his closet to get his hat, the blue-striped engineer's cap that Momma had bought him at Traintown. Traintown was a park where kids could ride the trains, just like Thomas. Danny had gone there since he was little, it was his favorite place in the world, but the cars were too tight for Danny to fit in with his big legs and long arms, so he liked to watch the trains go round and round with their little puffs of smoke chuffing from their stacks. Except for trips to Traintown, Momma didn't let him wear the hat outside the house, on account of she said people would make fun of him, but Danny figured it would be okay to wear it now.

He set out at dawn. The bus's keys were in his pocket, flat against his thigh. The depot was 3.2 miles away, precisely. He hadn't walked a block before he saw the first bodies. Some were in their cars, others were lying on their lawns or draped over garbage cans or even hanging in the trees. Their skin had turned the same blue-gray color as Mrs. Kim's, their clothing stretched tight over limbs that had swollen in the summer heat. It was bad to look at, bad but strange and also interesting; if he'd had more time, Danny would have stopped to get a closer look. There was a lot of litter, bits of paper and plastic cups and fluttering grocery sacks, which Danny didn't like. People shouldn't litter.

By the time he got to the depot, the sun was warm on his shoulders. Most of the buses were there but not all. They were parked in rows with empty spaces, like a mouth with missing teeth. But Danny's bus, the No. 12, was waiting in its usual spot. There were many different kinds of buses in the world, shuttle buses and charter buses and city buses and coaches, and Danny knew about them all. That was something he liked to do—to learn everything there was to know about one thing. His bus was a Redbird 450, the Foresight model. Built to the most exacting engineering standards, with all-permanent frame fixtures, Easy Hood Assist™, an advanced driver's information display providing a wealth of system knowledge to both the operator and service technicians, and the purpose-built, single-scope Redbird Comfortride™ chassis, the 450 was the number one choice for safety, quality, and extended life-cycle value in the industry today.

Danny climbed aboard and wedged the key into the ignition; as the big Caterpillar diesel roared to life, a warm surge filled his belly. He checked his watch: 6:52. When the big hand hit the twelve, he put the bus in gear and pulled away.

It seemed odd at first, driving through empty streets with no one around, but by the time Danny was approaching his first stop—the Mayfields', Robert and Shelly—he'd settled into the rhythms of the morning. It was easy to imagine that today was just an ordinary day. He brought the bus to a halt. Well, Robert and Shelly were sometimes late. He'd honk the horn and they'd come dashing out the door, their mother calling after them to be good, have fun, and sending them off with a wave. The house was a bungalow not much bigger than the one Danny lived in with Momma but nicer, painted the color of a pumpkin and sitting behind a wide front porch with a swing. In spring there were always baskets of flowers hanging off the rails. The baskets were still there, but the flowers had all wilted. The lawn needed mowing, too. Danny craned his neck to look up through the windshield. A window on the second floor looked like it had been ripped from its frame. The blind was still hanging in the space where the window used to be, lolling out of it like a tongue. He honked the horn and waited a minute. But still nobody came.

Seven-oh-eight. He had other stops to make. He pulled away from the corner and guided the bus around a Prius lying on its side. He came to other things in the road. An overturned police car, smashed flat. An ambulance. A dead cat. A lot of the houses had X's spray-painted on their doors, with numbers and letters in the spaces. By the time he arrived at his second stop, a townhouse complex called Castle Oaks, he was already running twelve minutes late. *Brittany-Maybeth-Joey-Darla/Denise.* He gave the horn a long honk, then another. But there wasn't any point. Danny was just going through the motions now. Castle Oaks was a smoking ruin. The entire complex had burned to the ground.

More stops: all were the same. He guided the bus west into Cherry Creek. The houses were bigger here, set back from the road behind wide, sloped lawns. Big leafy trees draped curtains of dappled shade over the street. There was a quiet feeling here, more peaceful. The houses looked like they always did, and there were no bodies that Danny could see. But still there were no children.

By now his bus would have had twenty-five kids in it. The silence was unnerving. The noise in the bus always built along the route, each stop adding a little more with every kid who got on, the way music rose in a movie, approaching the final scene. The final scene was the bump. A speed bump on Lindler Avenue. *Do the bump, Danny!* they'd all cry out. *Do the bump!* And though he wasn't supposed to, he'd give the bus a little extra gas, jolting them from their seats, and for that one moment he'd feel himself to be a part of them. He'd never been a kid like they were, just a kid going to school. But when the bus went over the bump, he was.

Danny was thinking about this, missing the children, even Billy Nice and his stupid jokes and har-har-har, when up ahead he saw a boy. It was Timothy. He was waiting with his older sister at the end of their drive-way. Danny would have known the boy anywhere, on account of the cowlick—two spikes of hair that stuck up from the back of his head like antennae on a bug. Timothy was one of the youngest kids, second grade or maybe third, and small; sometimes the housekeeper waited with him, a plump brown woman in a smock, but usually it was the boy's older sister, who Danny guessed was in high school. She was a funny girl to look at, not funny ha-ha but funny strange, with hair streaked the color of the Pepto that Momma gave him when his stomach got nervous from eating too fast and heavy black eyeliner that made her look like one of those paintings in a scary movie, the kind with eyes that moved. She had about ten studs in each ear; most days she was wearing a dog collar. A dog collar! Like she was a dog! The odd thing was that Danny thought she was sort of pretty, if not for all the weird stuff. He didn't know any girls her age, or any age, really, and he liked the way she waited with her brother, holding his hand but letting it go as the bus approached so the other kids wouldn't see.

He drew up to the end of the driveway and pulled the lever to open the door. "Hey," he said, because that was all he could think of. "Hey, good morning."

It seemed like their turn to talk, but they didn't say anything. Danny let his eyes quickly graze their faces; their expressions were nothing he could read. None of the trains on Thomas ever looked like these two did. The Thomas trains were happy or sad or cross, but this was something else, like the blank screen on the TV when the cable wasn't working. The girl's eyes were puffy and red, her hair kind of smooshed-looking. Timothy had a runny nose he kept rubbing with the back of his wrist. Their clothing was all wrinkled and stained.

"We heard you honking," the girl said. Her voice was hoarse and shaky, like she hadn't used it in a while. "We were hiding in the cellar. We ran out of food two days ago."

Danny shrugged. "I had Lucky Charms. But just with water. They're no good that way."

"Is there anybody else left?" the girl asked.

"Left where?"

"Left alive."

Danny didn't know how to answer that. The question seemed too big. Maybe there wasn't; he'd seen a lot of bodies. But he didn't want to say so, not with Timothy there.

He glanced at the boy, who so far had said nothing, just kept nervously rubbing his nose with his wrist. "Hey, Timbo. You got allergies? I have those sometimes."

"Our parents are in Telluride," the boy stated. He was looking at his sneakers. "Consuela was with us. But she left."

Danny didn't know who Consuela was. It was hard when people didn't answer your question but instead answered some other question you hadn't even thought of.

"Okay," said Danny.

"She's in the backyard."

"How can she be in the backyard if she left?"

The boy's eyes widened. "Because she's *dead.*"

For a couple of seconds, nobody said anything. Danny wondered why they hadn't gotten on the bus yet, if maybe he'd have to ask them.

"Everybody's supposed to go to Mile High," the girl said. "We heard it on the radio."

"What's at Mile High?"

"The Army. They said it's safe there."

From what Danny had seen, the Army was pretty much dead, too. But Mile High would give them someplace to go. He hadn't really thought of that before. Where was he going?

"I'm April," the girl said.

She looked like an April. It was funny how some names were like that. They just seemed to fit.

"I'm Danny," he said.

"I know," said April. "Just please, Danny? Get us the hell out of here."

7

The color wasn't right, Lila decided. No, it wasn't right at all.

The shade was called "buttercream." On the sample from the store it was a soft, faded yellow, like old linen. But now, as Lila stood back to inspect her work, dripping roller in hand—honestly, she was making such a mess; why couldn't David do these things?—it looked more like: well, what? A lemon. An *electrified* lemon. Maybe in a kitchen it would have been all right, a bright, sunny kitchen with windows looking out to a garden. But not in a nursery. My God, she thought, a color like that, the baby wouldn't sleep a wink.

How depressing. All her hard work wasted. Hauling the ladder up the stairs from the basement, laying the drop cloths, lowering herself onto her hands and knees to tape off the baseboards, only to find she'd have to go back to the store and start over. She'd planned to have the room done by lunch, leaving enough time for the paint to dry before she hung the wallpaper border, a repeating pattern of scenes from Beatrix Potter. David thought the border was silly—"sentimental" was the word he'd used—but Lila didn't care. She'd loved the stories of Peter Rabbit when she was a girl, crawling onto her father's lap or snuggling down in bed to hear, for the hundredth time, the tale of Peter's escape from Mr. McGregor's garden. The yard of their house in Wellesley had been bordered by a hedgerow, and for years—long after she should have stopped believing in such things—she'd patiently searched it for a rabbit in a little blue jacket.

But now Peter Rabbit would have to wait. A wave of exhaustion enfolded her; she needed to get off her feet. The fumes were making her dizzy, too. Something seemed to be wrong with the AC, although with the baby, she always felt a little overheated. She hoped David would get home soon. Things were crazy at the hospital. He'd called her once to let her know he'd be late, but she hadn't heard from him since.

She made her way downstairs to the kitchen. The place was an awful mess. Dishes piled in the sink, counters stained, the floor beneath her bare feet tacky with grime. Lila stopped in the doorway, feeling puzzled. She hadn't realized how badly she'd let things go, and what had happened to Yolanda? How long since she'd been here? Tuesdays and Fridays were the housekeeper's regular days. What was today? To look at this kitchen, thought Lila, you'd think Yolanda hadn't been to the house in weeks. Okay, the woman's English was not the best, and sometimes she did strange things, like confusing the teaspoons with the tablespoons—how David grumbled about that—or depositing the bills, unread, straight into the recycling bin. Annoying things like that. But Yolanda wasn't one to miss even a day of work. One winter morning she'd shown up with a cough so bad that Lila could hear it from upstairs; she'd practically had to pry the mop from the woman's hands, saying, *Por favor, Yolanda, let me help you, I'm a doctor. Soy médico.* (Of course it was bronchitis; Lila had listened to the woman's chest right there in the kitchen and written the prescription for amoxicillin herself, knowing full well that Yolanda probably didn't even *have a doctor,* let alone insurance.) So, okay, she sometimes threw the mail away and mixed up the silverware and put the socks in the underwear drawer, but she was a hard worker, tireless really, a cheerful and punctual presence they depended on, what with their crazy schedules. And now not even a call.

Which was another thing. The phone didn't seem to be working, on top of which there was no mail. Or newspaper. But David had told her not to go outside under any circumstances, so Lila hadn't checked. Maybe the newspaper was sitting in the driveway.

She fetched a glass from the cabinet and turned on the faucet. A groan from below, a burp of air, and . . . nothing. The water, too! Then she remembered; the water had been out a while. Now she'd have to call a plumber on top of everything else. Or would have, if the phones were working. Wasn't it just like David to be away when everything went to hell in a handbasket. That had been one of Lila's father's favorite expressions, hell in a handbasket. A curious turn of phrase, now that Lila thought about it. What exactly was a handbasket, and how was it different from a regular basket? There were lots of phrases like that, even just simple words that could suddenly look strange, as if you'd never seen them before. Diaper. Misled. Plumber. Married.

Had that really been her idea, to marry David? Because she didn't remember thinking, *I will marry David.* Which a person *should* think, probably, before they went ahead and did it. Strange how one minute life was a certain way and then it was another, and you couldn't remember what you'd done to make it all happen. She wouldn't have said that she loved David, exactly. She *liked* him. She *admired* him. (And who could fail to admire David Centre? Chief of cardiology at Denver General, founder of the Colorado Institute of Electrophysiology, a man who ran marathons, sat on boards, held season tickets to both the Nuggets and the opera, who daily hauled his patients from the very brink of death?)

But did these feelings add up to love? And if not, should you actually marry such a man because you were carrying his child—nothing planned, it had simply happened—and because, in a moment of characteristically David nobility, he had announced that he intended to "do the right thing"? What *was* the right thing? And why did David sometimes seem not like David but someone *resembling* David, *based on* David, a man-sized, David-like object? When Lila had told her father the news of their engagement, she'd seen it in his face: he knew. He was sitting at his desk in his study, surrounded by the books he loved, stroking glue onto the bowsprit of a model ship. In just the tiniest lift of his generous eyebrows, the truth was written. "Well," he said, and cleared his throat, pausing to screw the top onto the little jar of glue. "I can see how, under the circumstances, you might want to. He's a good man. You can do it here if you like."

Which he was, and which they had, flying off to Boston on the front edge of a spring blizzard, everything rushed and jammed into place, just a handful of relatives and friends able to make it at the last second to stand awkwardly in the living room while vows were exchanged (it had taken all of about two minutes) before making their excuses. Even the caterer had left early. It wasn't the fact that Lila was pregnant that made it all so awkward. It was, she knew, that someone was missing.

Someone would always be missing.

But never mind. Never mind David, and their awful wedding (really, it had felt more like a wake), with its piles of leftover salmon and the snow and all the rest. The important thing was the baby, and taking care of herself. The world could go to hell in a handbasket if it wanted to. The baby was what mattered. She would be a girl; Lila had seen her on the ultrasound. A baby girl. Tiny hands and tiny feet and a tiny heart and lungs, floating in the warm broth of her body. The baby liked to hiccup. *Hiccup!* went the tiny baby. *Hiccup! Hiccup!* Which was a funny word as well. The baby breathed the amniotic fluid in and out, contracting the diaphragm, causing the epiglottis to close. A synchronous diaphragmatic flutter, or singultus, from the Latin *singult,* "the act of catching one's breath while sobbing." When Lila had learned this in medical school, she'd thought: Wow. Just, wow. And of course she had immediately started to hiccup herself; half the students had. There was a man in Australia, Lila knew, who had been hiccupping continuously for seventeen years. She'd seen him on *Today.*

Today. What was today? She had made her way to the front hall, becoming gradually aware, as if her mind were lifting on tiptoes to peer above a ledge, that she had drawn the curtain aside to take a look outside. Nope, no newspaper. No *Denver Post* or *New York Times* or that trashy little neighborhood thing that went straight into the bin. Through the glass she could hear the high, tree-borne buzz of summer insects. Usually you'd see a car or two gliding by, the postman whistling his way down the block, a nanny pushing a stroller, but not today. *I'll be back when I know more. Stay inside, lock the doors. Don't go out under any circumstances.* Lila remembered David saying these things to her; she remembered standing at the window to watch his car, one of those new hydrogen-powered Toyotas, zip silently down the drive. Good God, even his car was virtuous. The pope probably drove one just like it.

But wasn't that a dog? Lila pressed her face closer to the glass. The Johnsons' dog was toddling down the middle of the street. The Johnsons lived two doors away, a pair of empty nesters, the daughter off married somewhere, the son away at college. MIT? Caltech? One of those. Mrs. Johnson ("Call me Sandy!") had been the first neighbor to show up at their door the day they'd moved in, all bundt cake and big hellos, and Lila saw her nearly every evening when she wasn't on call, sometimes in the company of her husband, Geoff, out walking Roscoe, a big grinning golden retriever so submissive he'd hurl himself tummy-up on the pavement when anyone approached. ("Excuse my fucking fairy of a dog," Geoff said.) That was Roscoe out there, but something wasn't right. He didn't look the same. His ribs were sticking out like the keys on a xylophone (Lila was touched, fleetingly, by a memory of playing the glockenspiel in grammar school, and the tinkling melody of "Frère Jacques"), and he was walking in a disconcertingly aimless manner, gripping something in his mouth. Some sort of a . . . floppy thing. Did the Johnsons know he'd gotten loose? Should she telephone them? But the phones weren't working, and she'd promised David she'd stay indoors. Surely someone else would notice him and say, Why, that's Roscoe; he must have gotten out.

Goddamn David, she thought. He could be so stuck on himself, so inconsiderate, out doing God knows what when here she was, no water and no phone and no electricity and the color in the nursery all wrong. It wasn't even close! She was only twenty-four weeks along, but she knew how the time raced by. One minute you were months away and the next thing you knew you were hustling out the door in the dead of night with your little suitcase, driving pell-mell to the hospital, and then you were on your back beneath the lights, huffing and puffing, the contractions roaring down upon you, taking you over, and nothing else would happen until you had the baby. And through the fog of pain you would feel a hand in your own and open your eyes to see Brad beside you, wearing a look on his face you had no name for, a beautiful terrified helpless look, and hear his voice saying, *Push, Lila, you're almost there, one more push and you'll be done,* and so you would: you would reach inside yourself and find the strength to do this one last thing and push the baby out. And in the stillness that came after, as Brad handed you the magical swaddled present of your baby, rivers of happiness running down his cheeks, you would feel the deep and permanent rightness of your life, knowing that you had chosen this man above all others because you were simply meant to, and that your baby, Eva, this warm new creature you had made together, was just that: the two of you, made one.

Brad? Why was she thinking about Brad? *David.* David was her husband, not Brad. Pope David and his popemobile. Had there been a Pope David? Probably. Lila herself was a Methodist. She wasn't the person to ask.

Well, she thought, Roscoe having wandered out of sight, enough was enough. She'd had it with being trapped in a filthy house. David could do as David liked; she saw no reason to sit out this perfectly beautiful June day, not with so much to do. Her trusty old Volvo awaited her in the driveway. Where was her purse? Her wallet? Her keys? But here they were, sitting on the little table by the front door. Just where she had left them some period of time ago.

Upstairs, she went to the bathroom—my God, the toilet was in such a state, she didn't even want to *think* about that—and examined her face in the mirror. Well, that was not so good. You'd think she'd been in a shipwreck—her hair a rat's nest, her eyes sunken and bleary-looking. Her skin was all washed out, like it hadn't seen the sun in weeks. She wasn't one of those women who needed an hour to primp before leaving the house, but even so. She would have liked a shower, but of course that was impossible; she settled for washing her face with water from one of the jugs on the sink, using a washcloth to scrub her skin pink. She ran a brush through her hair, applied blush to her cheeks, stroked mascara onto her lashes, and put on a bit of lipstick. She was wearing only a T-shirt and panties in the heat; she retreated to the bedroom, with its guttered candles and heaps of dirty laundry and the musty smell of un-washed sheets, and pulled one of David's long-tailed shirts from the closet. What to wear below this was a problem—nothing really fit anymore. She settled on a pair of loose jeans she could wriggle into if she didn't do the top button, and a pair of sandals.

Once more to the mirror. Not bad, Lila concluded. A definite improvement. It wasn't like she was going anyplace special, after all. Although it might be nice to stop for lunch, once her errands were done.

She certainly had earned it after all this time indoors. Someplace nice, where she could eat outside. Few things were nicer than a glass of tea and a salad, sitting outdoors on a spring afternoon. Café des Amis— that was just the ticket. They had a marvelous patio draped with vines of fragrant flowers, and the most wonderful chef—he had visited their table once—who had trained at Cordon Bleu. Pierre? François? The man could do the most amazing thing with sauces, teasing the deepest flavors from even the simplest dishes; his coq au vin was to die for. But the desserts were what Des Amis was known for, especially the chocolate mousse. Lila had never tasted anything so heavenly in her life. She and Brad always shared one after dinner, spooning it into each other's mouths like a couple of teenagers so besotted that the world barely existed beyond the two of them. Such blissful days—courtship days, all the promises of life opening before them like the pages of a book. How they'd laughed when she'd damn near swallowed the engagement ring he'd tucked within its airy cocoa folds, and again on the night when Lila had sent Brad out into the pouring rain—anything would do, she told him, a Kit Kat or Almond Joy or a plain old Hershey's—and awakened an hour later to see him standing in the doorway of the bedroom, soaked to the bone, wearing the most hilarious smile on his face and bearing a giant Tupperware container of François's—Pierre's?—famous chocolate mousse, enough to feed an army. Which was just the kind of man Brad was. He'd gone around to the back, where a light was still burning, and pounded on the door until somebody came to receive his rain-drenched fifty-dollar bill. Which was the sweetest thing of all. *My God, Lila,* Brad said as she spooned a mouthful to her lips, *the way you're going, this baby is going to be born half chocolate.*

But there she went again. *David.* David Centre was her husband now. Lila really had to get a handle on that. Not that she and David had ever shared a chocolate mousse or been to Café des Amis or done anything remotely of the kind. The man didn't have one romantic bone in his body. How had she let a man like that talk her into marriage? As if she were merely one more item on a glorified to-do list? Become a famous doctor, check. Get Lila Kyle pregnant, check. Do the honorable thing, check. He hardly seemed to know who she was.

Down the stairs she went. Outside the sun was pouring down, filling the hall like a golden gas. By the time she reached the door, a pure excitement was coursing through her. What sweet release! After so much time cooped up, to venture out at last! She could only imagine what David would say when he found out. *For God's sake, Lila, I told you it's not safe. You have to think of the baby.* But it was the baby she was thinking of; the baby was the reason. That's what David didn't understand. David, who was too busy off saving the world to help with the nursery, who drove a car powered by asparagus, or pixie dust, or wholesome thoughts, or whatever it was, and who had left her here alone. Alone! And what was worse, really the worst thing of all, was that he didn't even *like* Peter Rabbit. How was it possible she was going to have a baby with a man who didn't like Peter Rabbit? What did that say about him? What kind of father would he be? No, it was none of David's business what she did, Lila concluded, lifting her purse and keys from the hallway table and unbolting the door. It was none of his business if she went outside, or if she painted the nursery chartreuse, or vermilion, or puce. David could go screw himself. That's what David could do.

Lila Kyle would buy the paint herself.

8

It was not a good day in the office of the deputy director. Today, May 31—Memorial Day, not that it mattered—was an end-of-the-world kind of day.

Colorado was gone, basically. Colorado was kaput. Denver, Greeley, Fort Collins, Boulder, Grand Junction, Durango, the thousand little towns in between. The latest aerial intel looked like a war zone: cars crashed on the highways, buildings burning, bodies everywhere. During daylight hours, nothing seemed to be moving except the birds, huge spiraling swarms of them, like the word had gone out from Vulture Central Command.

Would somebody please tell him whose idea it had been to kill the entire state of Colorado?

And the virus was moving. Spreading in every direction, a twelve-fingered hand. By the time Homeland had sealed off the major interstate corridors—those dithering assholes couldn't get themselves out of a burning house—the horse was already galloping from the barn. As of this morning, the CDC had confirmed cases in Kearney, Nebraska; Farmington, New Mexico; Sturgis, South Dakota; and Laramie, Wyoming. And those were just the ones they knew about. Nothing yet in Utah or Kansas, though that was a matter of time, maybe just hours. It was five-thirty in northern Virginia, three hours till sundown, five in the west.

They always moved at night.

The briefing with the Joint Chiefs had not gone well, though Guilder hadn't expected it to. To begin with, there was the whole "problem" of Special Weapons. The military brass had never been particularly comfortable with, or especially clear on, what DSW did, or why it existed outside any military chain of command, drawing its budget from, of all things, the Department of Agriculture. (Answer: Because nobody gave a shit about agriculture.) The military was all about hierarchies, who urinated highest on the hydrant, and as far as the brass could see, Special Weapons answered to no one, its pieces cobbled together from a dozen other agencies and private contractors. It resembled nothing so much as a game of sidewalk three-card monte, the queen always moving, not quite where you thought it would be. As for what DSW actually did, well, Guilder had heard the nicknames. "Distraction from Serious Warfare." "Department of Silly Wingnuts." "Deep-Shit Weirdness." And his personal favorite: "Discount Shoe Warehouse." (Even he had started calling it the Warehouse.)

So it was that Deputy Director Horace Guilder (were there any actual directors anymore?) had found himself sitting before the Joint Chiefs (enough stars and bars around the table to start a Girl Scout troop) to offer his official assessment of the situation in Colorado. (Sorry, we made vampires; it seemed like a good idea at the time.) A full thirty seconds of dumbfounded silence ensued, everyone waiting to see who would speak next.

Let me see if I have you right, the chairman intoned. He leaned his folded hands over the table. Guilder felt a bead of sweat drop from his armpit to slither the length of his torso. *You decided to reengineer an ancient virus that would transform a dozen death row inmates into indestructible monsters who live on blood, and you didn't think to tell anybody about this?*

Well, not exactly "decided." Guilder hadn't been with DSW at the outset. He'd come in at the change of administration, so much money and so many man-hours already down the rat hole that he couldn't have put the brakes on if he tried. Project NOAH was under a chain of command so obscure, even Guilder didn't know where it had originated— probably NSA, though he'd gotten the sense it might have gone even higher than that, even to the White House itself. But sitting before the Joint Chiefs, he understood that this distinction was pointless. Guilder had spent three decades working in agencies where so much was a secret that nobody was actually responsible for anything. Ideas seemed to flower of their own accord. *We did what? No, we didn't.* And so, off into the shredder it went. Which was exactly what was about to happen to Special Weapons; probably even to Guilder himself.

But in the meantime, there was blame to be doled out. The meeting had quickly devolved into a shouting match, Guilder taking verbal punch after verbal punch. He felt relieved when he was banished from the room, knowing that the situation was out of his hands. Henceforth, the military would deal with this the way they dealt with all problems: by shooting everything in sight.

In hindsight, Guilder might have put the situation more diplomatically. But the CDC's projections spoke for themselves. Three weeks, four at the outside, and the virus would take out Chicago, St. Louis, Salt Lake. Six weeks and they were looking at the coasts.

Vampires, for Christ's sake. What had he been thinking?

What had *everyone* been thinking?

And yet there was no doubt that Lear had been on to something. The great Jonas Lear—even Guilder was intimated by the man, a Harvard biochemist with an IQ of a zillion who had, for all intents and purposes, invented the field of paleovirology, retrieving and resuscitating ancient organisms for modern use. Within his professional circle it was generally assumed that Lear was a shoo-in, someday, for a Nobel Prize. Okay, maybe using death row inmates hadn't been the smartest move. They'd gotten ahead of themselves there. And certainly Lear wasn't rowing with his oars entirely in the water. But you had to admit the idea had possibilities. Such as, for instance, not dying. Ever. A matter in which Guilder had lately found himself holding a not-inconsiderable personal stake.

His only hope was the girl.

Amy NLN. The thirteenth test subject, snatched from a convent in Memphis, Tennessee, where her mother had abandoned her. Guilder hadn't felt exactly comfortable signing off on that. A kid, for the love of God. Somebody was bound to notice, and they had; by the time Wolgast had brought her in, everybody from the Oklahoma Highway Patrol to the U.S. Marshals was scouring the country for her, and Richards, that lunatic, had left a trail of bodies a mile wide. The nuns at the convent, shot in their sleep. A pair of small-town cops. Six people at a coffee shop whose only mistake was coming in for breakfast at the same time as Wolgast and the girl.

But the request for the girl, which had come from Lear himself, was nothing Guilder could make himself refuse. Each of the cons had been infected with a slightly altered variant of the virus, though the effects had been the same. Illness, coma, transformation, and the next thing you knew they were hanging upside down from the ceiling, gutting a rabbit. But the Amy variant was different. It hadn't come from Fanning, the Columbia biochemist who'd been infected on Lear's misbegotten excursion to Bolivia; it had come from the group of tourists who'd started the whole thing—terminal cancer patients on a lark in the jungle with an ecotour group called Last Wish. They'd all died within a month: stroke, heart attack, aneurysm, their bodies blowing apart. But in the meantime, they'd shown remarkable improvements in their condition—one man had even grown back a full head of hair—and they'd all died cancer-free. Reading Lear's mind was a fool's errand, but he'd come to believe this variant was the answer. The trick was keeping the first test subject alive. For this he'd chosen Amy, a young, healthy girl.

And it had worked. Guilder knew it had worked. Because Amy was still alive.

Guilder's office, on the third floor of an otherwise nondescript low-rise federal office building in Fairfax County—DSW shared space with, among other entities, the Office of Technology Assessment, the Department of Homeland Security Special Energy Task Force, the National Oceanic and Atmospheric Administration, and a day care—looked out on Interstate 66. Monday of Memorial Day weekend, yet there was almost no traffic. A lot of people had left the city already. Guilder imagined a lot of chits were being called in. A mother-in-law in upstate New York. A friend with a cabin in the mountains. But with all air transportation grounded, people could get only so far, and it wouldn't make much difference in the end. You couldn't hide from nature forever. Or so Horace Guilder had been told.

The girl had made it out of Colorado somehow. They'd caught her signature in southern Wyoming in the first few hours. Which meant she was in a vehicle, and not alone—somebody had to be driving. After that, she'd disappeared. The transmitter in her biomonitor was short-range, too weak for the satellites; she had to be within a few miles of a cell tower, and not some rural co-op but one connected to the federal tracking network. Which, in southern Wyoming, as long as you stayed off major highways, would be easy to avoid. She could be anywhere now. Whoever was with her was smart.

A knock at the door broke his train of thought; Guilder swiveled from the window to see Nelson, the department's chief technical officer, standing in the doorway. Christ, what now?

"I have good news and bad news," Nelson announced.

Nelson was dressed, as always, in a black T-shirt and jeans, his dirty feet shoved into a pair of flip-flops. A fast-talking Rhodes scholar with not one but two PhDs from MIT—biochemistry and advanced information systems—Nelson was the smartest guy in the building by a mile, a fact that he knew only too well. He still had the young person's predisposition to regard the world as a series of vaguely irritating problems created by people less cool and smart than he was. Though their relationship was cordial, Nelson had a habit of treating Guilder like a doddering elderly parent, a figure of respect but no longer quite worthy—which was exasperating, coming from a guy who seemed to comb his hair every fourth day, though not, Guilder had to admit, entirely unwarranted. He was twenty-eight to Guilder's fifty-seven, and everything about Nelson conspired to make him feel old.

"Any sign of her?"

"Nada." Nelson scratched his scraggly beard. "We're not getting any of them."

Guilder rubbed his eyes, which stung of sleeplessness. He needed to go home for a shower and a clean suit. He hadn't left the office in two days, grabbing only a few winks on the couch and living on junk from the vending machines. He was having trouble with his fingers, too. Numbness, tingling.

"You said something about good news?"

"Depends on how you look at it. From a free-speech point of view, probably it's not the best, but it looks like somebody finally shut down that lunatic in Denver. My guess would be NSA, or else one of Lear's little pets finally got to him. Either way, the dude's off-line in a permanent way."

Last Stand in Denver: Guilder had watched his videos, like everybody else. You had to hand it to the guy for balls. Theories abounded about his identity, the general consensus being that he was ex-military, Special Forces or SEALs.

"So what's the bad?"

"New numbers just came in from the CDC. It seems the original algorithm failed to take into proper account just how much these things like to eat. Which I could have told them if they'd asked. Either that or some summer intern moved a decimal place when he was daydreaming about the last time he boned his girlfriend."

Sometimes talking with Nelson felt like trying to corral a five-year-old. A genius five-year-old, but still. "Please, just spit it out."

Nelson shrugged. "As it now stands, based on the most recent projections, it appears we're looking at a more succinct timeline. Something on the order of thirty-nine days."

"For the coasts you mean?"

"Um, not exactly."

"What then?"

"The entire North American continent."

A gray shadow swooped over Guilder's vision; he had to sit down.

"A response is already in the works at Central," Nelson continued. "My guess is they'll try to burn it out. Major population centers first, then anyone else who gets left behind."

"Christ almighty."

Nelson frowned. "Small price to pay, on the whole. I know what I'd do if I were, say, the president of Russia. No way I'd let this jump the pond."

The man was right, and Guilder knew it. He realized his right hand had begun to tremble. He reached for it with his left, trying to bring the spasms under control while also making the gesticulation seem natural.

"You okay there, boss?"

His right foot had begun to shake as well. He felt the incomprehensible urge to laugh. Probably it was the stress. He swallowed effortfully, a taste of bile in his throat.

"Find that girl."

Once Nelson was gone, Guilder sat in his office for a few minutes, trying to collect himself. The trembling had passed, but not the impulse to laugh—a symptom euphemistically known as "emotional incontinence." Finally he just gave in, ejecting a single, cleansing bark. Jesus, he sounded possessed. He hoped nobody outside had heard.

He departed the building, got his car from the garage—a beige Toyota Camry—and drove to his townhouse in Arlington. He wanted to clean himself up, but this suddenly seemed like work; he poured himself a Scotch and flipped on the TV. It hadn't taken long for each of the networks, right down to the Weather Channel, to brand the emergency with a catchy slogan ("Nation in Crisis," etc.), and all the broadcasters looked harried and sleep-deprived, especially the ones reporting from beside a highway somewhere—a cornfield in the background, long lines of vehicles creeping past, everybody pointlessly honking. The whole country was seizing up like a bad transmission. He checked his watch: 8:05. In less than an hour, the middle of the country would go dark.

He heaved his disobedient body from the couch and climbed the stairs. Stairs—that had been a concern for the future. What would he do when he could no longer climb the stairs? But it hardly mattered now. In the master bath he turned on the shower and stripped to his shorts, standing before the mirror while the water heated. The funny thing was, he didn't look especially sick. A little thinner, perhaps. There was a time when he'd thought of himself as athletic—he'd run cross-country at Bowdoin— though those days were long past. His line of work, with its attendant demands for secrecy, had made marriage impossible, but well into his forties Guilder had managed—well, if not to turn heads exactly, then at least to keep himself occupied. A series of discreet affairs, everyone apprised of the facts. He had prided himself on the well-managed quality of these encounters, but then one day it had all simply stopped. Glances that might have been returned slid past him, conversations that before had merely served as elaborate preambles went no place. Inevitable, Guilder supposed, but nothing to cheer about. He surveyed his reflection, taking stock. A square-jawed face that had once looked rugged but had long since sagged at the jowls. A scrim of thinning hair swept back over his scalp, trying not quite successfully to conceal the ghostly white presence of his scalp. Bags of skin beneath his eyes, a rubbery paunch at the waist, legs skinny and insubstantial looking. Not a pretty sight, but nothing he hadn't accepted as the inescapable degradations of late middle age.

To look at him, you'd never know he was dying.

He showered and changed into a clean suit. His closet contained almost nothing else; an understated two-button—dark navy usually but sometimes gray with a subtle pinstripe, occasionally khaki poplin in summer—paired with a shirt of powder blue or starched white and a tie as neutral as Switzerland was so closely aligned with his sense of himself that he felt naked without one. Minding his balance, he descended the stairs to the living room, where the television was dutifully barking out its parade of bad news. Though he possessed no appetite, he heated up a frozen lasagna in the microwave, standing before it as the seconds ticked away. He sat at the table and did his best to eat, but the diazepam made everything taste bland and vaguely metallic, and the tightness in his throat had not abated, as if he were wearing a collar two sizes too small. His doctor had suggested he try milk shakes, or something soft like macaroni, but resorting to kiddie food was nothing he could face. From there, everything would go downhill.

He dumped the unfinished lasagna down the disposal and checked his watch again. A little after nine. Well, whatever was happening in the middle of the country was happening. Nelson would call if he needed him.

He left the townhouse and drove to McLean. What lay ahead was a grim duty, but Guilder was the only one to do it. The facility was set back from the road behind a sweeping green lawn; by the driveway a sign read, SHADOWDALE CONVALESCENT CENTER. At the check-in desk, Guilder presented his driver's license to the nurse, then proceeded down the medicinal-smelling hallway, past its mass-produced paintings of green fields and summer sunsets. The place was quiet, even for the hour; usually there were orderlies around, and patients in the common room, those who still got some benefit from human company. Tonight the place was a tomb.

He came to his father's room and gently knocked, opening the door without waiting for an answer.

"Pop, it's me."

His father was propped in his wheelchair by the window. His jaw drooped open, the muscles of his face as slack as pancake batter. A pendulum of spittle dangled from his mouth to the paper bib around his neck. Somebody had dressed him in a stained sweat suit and orthopedic shoes with Velcro tabs. He gave no sign of recognition as Guilder stepped into the room.

"How you doing, Pop?"

The air around his father tanged of urine. The Alzheimer's had progressed to a point where he recognized no one, but still one had to go through the motions. How terrifying it was, Guilder thought, the solitude of the mind. Yet his father's silence, the feeling of absence, was nothing new. In life—as now, in death—he had been a man of almost reptilian coldness. Guilder knew that this was just the way his father had been raised—the son of small-town dairy farmers who'd attended church three times weekly and slaughtered their own hogs—yet still he couldn't bring himself to put aside his resentments for a boyhood spent hoping to win the attention of a man who was simply incapable. It had been a small thing, a natural thing, what he'd asked of his father, simply by being born: to treat him like a son. A game of catch on a fall afternoon, a word of praise from the sidelines, an expression of interest in his life. Guilder had done everything right. The good grades, the dutiful performances in auditoriums and on athletic fields, the full ride to college and swift ascent into a useful adulthood. Yet his father had had virtually nothing to say about any of this. Guilder could not, in fact, recall a single instance when his father had told him he loved him, or touched him with affection. The man just didn't care.

Hardest of all had been the toll it had taken on Guilder's mother, a naturally sociable woman whose loneliness had driven her to the alcoholism that eventually killed her. In later life, Guilder came to believe that his mother had sought comfort elsewhere, that she had had affairs, probably more than one. After his father had been moved to Shadowdale, Guilder had cleaned out the house in Albany—an absolute mess, every drawer and cabinet crammed with stuff—and discovered, in his mother's dressing table, a velvet Tiffany box. When he'd looked inside he'd found a bracelet—a *diamond* bracelet. Probably it had cost as much as his father, a civil engineer, had made in a year. It was nothing he could have afforded, and the box's location—concealed in the back of a drawer beneath a pile of moldering gloves and scarves—had told Guilder what he was looking at: a lover's gift. Who had it been? His mother had been a legal secretary. One of the lawyers at her firm? Somebody she had met in passing? A rekindled romance of her youth? It had gladdened him to know that his mother had found some happiness to brighten her lonely existence, yet at the same time this discovery had sank him into a depression that had continued unabated for weeks. His mother was the one warm memory of his childhood. But her life, her real life, had been a secret from him.

Always these visits to his father brought these memories to the surface; by the time he left, he was often so dispirited, or else seething with unexpressed rage, that he could barely think straight. Fifty-seven years old, yet still he craved some flicker of acknowledgment.

He positioned the room's only chair in front of his father. The old man's head, bald as a baby's, was tipped at an awkward angle against his shoulder. Guilder retrieved a rag from the bedside table and wiped the spit from his chin. An open container of vanilla pudding sat on a tray with a flimsy metal spoon.

"So how you feeling, Pop? They treating you okay?"

Silence. And yet Guilder could hear his father's voice in his head, filling in the spaces.

Are you kidding me? Look at me, for Christ's sake. I can't even take a proper shit. Everyone talking to me like I'm a child. How do you think I am, sonny boy?

"I see you didn't eat your dessert. You want some pudding? How would that be?"

Fucking pudding! That's all they give me around this place. Pudding for breakfast, pudding for lunch, pudding for dinner. The stuff's like snot.

Guilder tucked a spoonful between his father's teeth. Through some autonomic reflex, the old man smacked his lips and swallowed.

*Look at me. You think this is a picnic? Drooling on myself, sitting in my
own piss?*

"Don't know if you've been following the news lately," Guilder said,
delivering a second spoonful into his father's mouth. "There's something
I thought you should know about."

So? Say your piece and leave me alone.

But what did Guilder want to say? I'm dying? That everyone was
dying, even if they didn't know it yet? What purpose could this information possibly serve? A chilling thought occurred to him. What would
become of his father when everyone was gone, the doctors and nurses
and orderlies? With everything that had happened in the last few weeks,
Guilder had been too preoccupied to consider this eventuality. Because
the city was emptying out; soon, in weeks or even days, everyone would
be running for their lives. Guilder remembered what had happened in
New Orleans in the aftermath of the hurricanes, first Katrina and then
Vanessa, the stories of elderly patients left to wallow in their own waste,
to perish slowly of hunger and dehydration.

*Are you listening to me, sonny boy? Sitting there with that big dumb
look on your face. What's so all-fired important that you came here to tell
me?*

Guilder shook his head. "It's nothing, Pop. Nothing important." He
spooned the last of the pudding into his father's mouth and wiped his
lips with the rag. "You get some rest, okay?" he said. "I'll see you in a few
days."

Your mother was a whore, you know. A whore a whore a whore . . .

Guilder stepped from the room. In the vacant hallway, he paused to
breathe. The voice wasn't real; he understood that. But still there were
times when it felt as if his father's mind, departed from his bodily person,
had taken up residence inside his own.

He returned to the front desk. The nurse, a young Hispanic woman,
was penciling in a crossword puzzle.

"My father needs his diaper changed."

She didn't look up. "They all need their diaper changed." When Guilder didn't move, her eyes darted upward from the page. They were very
dark, and heavily lined. "I'll tell someone."

"Please do."

At the door he stopped. The nurse had already resumed working on
her puzzle.

"So *tell* someone, goddamnit."

"I said I'd get to it."

A fierce protective urge came over him. Guilder wanted to shove her pencil down her throat. "Pick up the fucking phone if you're not going to do it yourself."

With a huff she lifted the phone and dialed. "It's Mona at the front. Guilder in 126 needs changing. Yes, his son is here. Okay, I'll tell him." She hung up. "Happy?"

The question was so absurd he didn't know where to begin.

Guilder wouldn't die like his father—just the opposite. ALS: amyotrophic lateral sclerosis, more commonly known as Lou Gehrig's disease. Major motor function would be the first to go, the muscles spasming and dimming into uselessness, followed by speech and the ability to swallow. The spontaneous laughing and crying were a mystery—nobody knew quite why this happened. Ultimately he would die on a respirator, his body utterly stilled, unable to move or speak. But worst of all was the fact that he would experience no diminishment of his ability to think or reason. Unlike his father, whose mind had failed first, Guilder would live every moment of his decline with full awareness. A living death, no one but some sulky nurse for company.

It was clear to him that in the aftermath of his diagnosis, he had gone through a period of profound shock. That was the explanation he gave himself for the foolish thing he'd done with Shawna—though, of course, that wasn't even her real name. For two years Guilder had been visiting her on the second Tuesday of each month, always at the apartment provided by her employers. She was dark-skinned and slim, with subtly Asiatic eyes, and young enough to be his daughter, though this was not the attraction—if anything, he would have preferred that she were older. He had originally found her through a service, but after a probationary period he had been permitted to call her directly. The first time, he had been as nervous as a college boy. It had been a while since he'd been with a woman, and he'd found himself worrying that he wouldn't measure up—in hindsight, a preposterous concern. But the girl had quickly put him at his ease, taking command of the occasion. Always the ritual was the same. Guilder would ring the bell outside; the buzzer would sound; he would mount the stairs to the apartment, where she would be waiting in the open door, wearing a welcoming smile and dressed in a black cocktail dress beneath which lay an erotic treasure of lace and silk. A few pleasantries, as might be exchanged by any two lovers meeting in the afternoon, followed by the unremarked-on placement of the envelope of cash on the dresser; then on to the thing itself. Always Guilder undressed first, then watched as she did so herself, allowing the cocktail dress to fall to the floor like a curtain before stepping regally away from it. She made love to him with an enthusiasm that seemed neither manufactured nor overly professional, and for those slender minutes, Guilder's mind found a serenity that nothing else in his life came close to matching. At the moment of his release, Shawna would say his name over and over, her voice losing itself in a wholly persuasive facsimile of womanly satisfaction, and Guilder would find himself floating on these sounds and sensations, riding them like a surfer onto a tranquil shore.

Why don't I see you more often? she would ask him after. Are you happy with the things I do? There isn't anybody else, is there? I want to be your only one, Guilder. Very happy, he would say, stroking her velvety hair. I couldn't be happier than I am with you.

He knew nothing about her at all—at least, nothing real. Yet in the weeks that followed his diagnosis, the only refuge his mind could take was in the absurd idea that he was in love with her. The memory embarrassed him now, and the psychological subtext was obvious—he didn't want to die alone—but at the time, he'd been utterly convinced. He was madly, hopelessly in love, and wasn't it possible, likely even, that Shawna shared his feelings? Was that what she meant when she said she wanted to be his only one? Because what they did and said to each other *couldn't* be false; those things occurred on a plane that only two people who were truly connected could share.

On and on like this, until he had worked himself into such a state that Shawna was all he thought about. He decided he would give her something—a symbol of his love. Something expensive and worthy of his feelings. Jewelry. It had to be jewelry. And not something new from a store, but something more personal: his mother's diamond bracelet. Energized by this decision, he wrapped the Tiffany box in silver paper and drove to Shawna's apartment. It wasn't Tuesday, but that didn't matter. What he felt wasn't anything a person could schedule. He rang the bell and waited. Minutes passed, which was strange; Shawna was always very prompt about the bell. He rang again. This time the speaker made a little burst of static and he heard her voice. "Hello?"

"It's Horace."

A pause. "I don't have you in the book. Do I? Maybe this is my fault. Did you call?"

"I have something for you."

The speaker seemed to go dead. Then: "Hang on a second."

A few minutes passed. Guilder heard footsteps descending the stairs. Perhaps the buzzer wasn't working; Shawna was coming down to open the door. But the figure that turned the corner wasn't Shawna. It was a man. He looked about sixty, bald and heavyset, with the piggish face of a Russian gangster, wearing a rumpled pin-striped suit, his necktie loosened. The implications were obvious, yet in its agitated state, Guilder's mind refused them. The man stepped through the door, giving Guilder a cursory glance as he passed.

"Lucky you," he said, and winked.

Guilder hurried up the stairs. He knocked three times, waiting with buoyant anxiety; at last the door swung open. Shawna wasn't wearing the dress, just a silk robe cinched at the waist. Her hair was disheveled, her makeup smeary. Perhaps he'd caught her taking a nap.

"Horace, what are you doing here?"

"I'm sorry," he said, suddenly breathless. "I know I should have called."

"To tell you the truth, it's not really the best time."

"I'll only be a minute. Please, can I come in?"

She eyed him skeptically, then seemed to soften. "Well, all right. It'll have to be quick, though."

She stood aside to let him enter. Something felt different about the apartment, though Guilder couldn't say exactly what. It seemed dirty, the air unpleasantly dense.

"Now, what's this I see?" She was eyeing the silver-papered box. "Horace, you shouldn't have."

Guilder held it out to her. "This is for you."

With a warm light dancing in her eyes, she undid the wrapping and removed the bracelet.

"Isn't that thoughtful. What a pretty thing."

"It's an heirloom. It belonged to my mother."

"That makes it even more special." She kissed him quickly on the cheek. "You give me a minute to clean up and I'll be right with you, baby."

A titanic wave of love broke over him. It was all he could do not to throw his arms around her and press his mouth to hers. "I want to make love to you. Real love."

She glanced at her watch. "Well, sure. If that's what you want. I don't have the full hour, though."

Guilder had begun to undress, madly unbuckling his belt, yanking off his wingtips. But something was wrong. He sensed her hesitation.

"Isn't there something you're forgetting?" she asked.

The money. That's what she was asking for. How could she think about money at a time like this? He wanted to tell her that what they shared couldn't be counted in dollars and cents, words along those lines, but all he managed to say was "I don't have it with me."

She frowned. "Honey, that's not how this works. You know that."

But by this time Guilder was so frantic he was barely processing any of it. He was also standing in front of her wearing only his boxers and undershirt, his pants bunched around his ankles.

"Are you all right? You don't look so good."

"I love you," he said.

She gave an airy smile. "That's sweet."

"I said, I love you."

"Okay, I can do that. That's no problem. Put the money on the dresser and I'll say anything you want."

"I don't have any money. I gave you the bracelet."

Suddenly there was no sign of warmth or even friendship in her eyes. "Horace, this is a cash business, you know that. I don't like the way you're talking."

"Please, let me make love to you." Guilder's pulse was throbbing in his ears. "You can sell the bracelet if you want. It's worth a lot of money."

"Baby, I don't think so." She held it out to him with unconcealed contempt. "I hate to break it to you, but this is glass. I don't know who sold it to you, but you should get your money back. Now go on, be sweet. You know the drill."

He had to make her understand how he felt. In desperation he reached for her, but his feet were still tangled up in his trouser legs. Shawna released a yelp; the next thing Guilder knew, he was sprawled on the floor. He raised his face to discover a pistol aimed at his head.

"Get the fuck out."

"Please," he moaned. His voice was thick with tears. "You said you wanted to be my only one."

"I say a lot of things. Now get out of here with your crappy goddamned bracelet."

He rose heavily to his feet. Never had he experienced such humiliation. And yet what he mostly felt was love. A helpless, melancholy love that would devour him whole.

"I'm dying."

"We're all dying, baby." She waved the pistol at the door. "Do like I say before I shoot your balls off."

He knew he could never face her again. How could he have been so stupid? He drove to his townhouse, pulled into the garage, shut off the engine, and sealed the door with the remote. He sat in his car for a full thirty minutes, unable to muster the energy to move. He was dying. He had made a fool of himself. He would never see Shawna again, because he meant nothing to her.

Which was when he realized why he was still sitting in the Camry. All he had to do was turn the engine back on. It would be like falling asleep. He'd never have to think about Shawna again, or Project NOAH, or live in the prison of his own failing body, or visit his father at the convalescent center—none of it. All his cares lifted, just like that. Following an impulse he could not explain, he removed his watch and took his wallet from his back pocket, placing them on the dashboard—as if he were getting ready for bed. Probably it was customary to write a note, but what would he say? Who would the note be for?

Three times he tried to make himself turn the key. Three times his resolve failed him. By then he had begun to feel silly, sitting in his car—one more humiliation. There was nothing left to do but put his watch back on and return his wallet to his pocket and go into the house.

As Guilder was driving home from McLean, his handheld buzzed. Nelson.

"They're on the move."

"Where?"

"Everywhere. Utah, Wyoming, Nebraska. A large group massing in western Kansas." He paused. "That's not why I called."

Guilder drove straight to the office. Nelson met him in the hallway. "We picked up the signal a little before sunset. Grabbed it off a tower west of Denver, a town called Silver Plume. It took some doing, but I was able to call in some favors at Homeland and reroute one of the drones to see if we could get a picture."

At his terminal he showed Guilder the photograph, a grainy black and white. Not the girl; it was a man. He was standing beside a pickup truck parked on the side of the highway. It looked like he was taking a leak.

"Who the hell is this? One of the docs?"

"It's one of Richards's guys."

Guilder was perplexed. "What are you talking about?"

For a moment, Nelson appeared faintly embarrassed. "Sorry, I thought you were in the loop on this. They're paroled sex offenders. One of Richards's little projects. For security reasons, all sixth-tier civilian personnel were harvested from the national registry."

"You're shitting me."

"I shit you not." Nelson tapped the image on the screen. "This guy? Our lone survivor of Project NOAH? He's a fucking pedophile."

9

The pickup gave out late on the morning of Grey's second day on the road.

The hour was just shy of noon, the sun high in the sky. After a restless night in a Motel 6 near Leadville, Grey had picked up I-70 near Vail, then made his descent toward Denver. As far east as the town of Golden, the interstate corridor had been mostly clear, but as he moved into the city's outer suburban ring, with its huge shopping centers and sprawling subdivisions, things began to change. Portions of the highway were choked with abandoned cars, forcing him onto the access road; the vast parking lots lining the highway were scenes of frozen disorder, store windows smashed, merchandise strewn over the pavement. The stillness was different here, too—not a simple absence of sound but something deeper, more ominous. A lot of the bodies he saw were headless, like the suspendered man at the Red Roof. Grey guessed maybe Zero and the others liked to take the heads.

He did his best to keep his eyes on the road, forcing the carnage to the fringes of his vision. The weird, buzzing energy he'd felt at the Red Roof had not abated; his brain was humming like a plucked string. He hadn't slept in a day and a half, but he wasn't tired. Or hungry, which wasn't like him at all. Grey used to slam it down, but for some reason the thought of food wasn't remotely appealing. In Leadville he'd gotten a Baby Ruth from a vending machine in the lobby of the Motel 6, thinking he should try to put something in his stomach, but he couldn't get the damn thing past his nose. Just the odor of it made his insides clench. He could practically smell the preservatives in the thing, a nasty chemical stink, like industrial floor cleaner.

By the time the city's core rose into view, Grey knew he would have to abandon the interstate. There was simply no way around the cars, and the situation was only going to get worse the closer he got. He drew the truck into the parking lot of a 7-Eleven and checked his map. The best route would be circling downtown to the south, he decided, though this was just a guess; he didn't know Denver at all.

He veered south, then east again, picking his way through the suburbs. Everywhere was the same, not a living soul about. He wished he could at least have had the radio for company, but when he scanned up and down the dial, all he could get was the same empty wash of static he'd heard for a day and a half. For a while he honked the truck's horn, thinking this might alert anyone left alive to his presence, but eventually he gave up. There was no one left to hear it. Denver was a crypt.

By the time the engine died, Grey had entered a state of such complete despair that for several seconds he actually failed to notice. So disturbing was the silence that it had begun to seem possible that he would never see a living soul again—that the whole world, not just Denver, had been swept clean of humanity. But then he realized what was happening, that the engine had lost power. For a few seconds the truck coasted on its own momentum, but the steering had locked up, too; all Grey could do was sit and wait for it to glide to a halt.

Christ, he thought, this is all I need. Sliding Iggy's gun into the pocket of his jumpsuit, he climbed out and lifted the hood. Grey had owned enough junky cars in his day to know a broken fan belt. The logical step would have been to abandon the truck and find another vehicle with the keys in it. He was on a wide boulevard of big-box retail outlets: Best Buy, Target, Home Depot. The sun was glaring down. Each lot had a scattering of cars in it. But he had no heart to look inside them, knowing what he would find. He'd swapped out a fan belt lots of times. All he needed was the belt and a few basic tools, a screwdriver and a couple of wrenches to adjust the tensioner. Maybe the Home Depot had auto parts. It couldn't hurt to look.

He crossed the highway and headed for the door, which stood open. The cage of propane tanks by the entrance had been pried open, all the canisters taken, but otherwise the front of the store appeared undamaged. A phalanx of lawn mowers, chained together, rested undisturbed by the doorway, as did a display of patio furniture dusted with yellow pollen. The only other sign that anything was amiss was a large square of plywood propped against the wall, spray-painted with the words NO GENERATORS LEFT.

Grey drew the pistol from his pocket, wedged the door open, and stepped inside. The power was out, but a semblance of order had been maintained; a lot of the shelves had been stripped bare, though the floor was mostly clear of debris. Holding the gun out before him, he advanced cautiously along the front of the store, his eyes scanning the signs over the aisles for one that said AUTO PARTS.

He had made it halfway down the rows when Grey stopped in his tracks. From ahead and to his left he heard a quiet rustling, followed by a barely audible murmuring. Grey took two steps forward and peered around the corner.

It was a woman. She was standing in front of a display of paint samples. She was dressed in jeans and a man's dress shirt; her hair, a soft brown, was swept behind her ears, fixed in place by a pair of sunglasses perched on top of her head. She was also pregnant—not have-the-baby-right-this-second pregnant, but pregnant enough. While Grey watched, she pulled a little square of color from one of the slots and angled it first this way and then the other, frowning pensively. Then she returned it to its slot.

So unexpected was this vision that Grey could only gaze at her in mute astonishment. What was she doing here? A full thirty seconds passed, the woman taking no notice of his presence, wholly engaged by her mysterious business. Not wanting to frighten her, Grey gently placed the gun on an open shelf and took a cautious step forward. What should he say? He'd never been good at icebreakers. Or even talking to people, really. He settled for clearing his throat.

The woman glanced at him over her shoulder. "Well, it's about time," she said. "I've been standing here for twenty minutes."

"Lady, what are you doing?"

She turned from the display. "Is this or is this not the paint department?" She was holding out a group of sample chips, fanned like a deck of playing cards. "Now, I'm thinking maybe Garden Gate, but I'm worried it will be too dark."

Grey was utterly dumbfounded. She wanted him to help her pick paint?

"Probably nobody ever asks your opinion, I know," she continued briskly—a little too briskly, Grey thought. "Just put it in a can and take my money, I'm sure that's what everybody says. But I value the judgment of someone who knows his business. So, what do you think? In your professional opinion."

Grey was standing within just a few feet of her now. Her face was fine-boned and pale, with a subtle fan of crow's-feet at the corners of her eyes. "I think you're confused. I don't work here."

She narrowed her eyes at him. "You don't?"

"Lady, no one works here."

Confusion swept over her face. But just as quickly it disappeared, her features reorganizing into a look of irritation. "Oh, you hardly need to tell me that," she said, tossing his words away. "Trying to get a little help around this place is like pulling teeth. Now," she went on, "as I was saying, I need to know which of these would go best in a nursery." She gave a bashful smile. "I guess it's no secret, but I'm expecting."

Grey had known some crazy people in his days, but this woman took the cake. "Lady, I don't think you should be here. It's not safe."

Another little hitch of time passed before she answered; it was as if she was processing his words and then, in the next instant, rewriting their meaning.

"Honestly, you sound just like David. To tell you the truth, I've had just about enough of this kind of talk." She sighed heavily. "So, Garden Gate it is then. I'll take two gallons in an eggshell finish, please. If you don't mind, I'm in kind of a hurry."

Grey felt completely flustered. "You want me to sell you paint?"

"Well, are you or aren't you the manager?"

The manager? When had that happened? The fact was dawning on him that the woman wasn't just pretending.

"Lady, don't you know what's going on around here?"

She pulled two cans from the shelves and held them out. "I'll tell you what's going on. I'm buying some paint, and you're going to mix it for me, Mr.— Now, I don't believe I got your name."

Grey swallowed. Something about the woman seemed to make him absolutely powerless, as if he were being dragged by a runaway horse. "It's Grey," he said. "Lawrence Grey."

She pushed the cans toward him, forcing him to take them. Christ, she practically had him filling out an employment application. If this went on much longer, he'd never get a fan belt. "Well, Mr. Grey. I'd like two gallons of Garden Gate, please."

"Um, I don't know how."

"Of course you do." She gestured toward the counter. "Just put it in the whatchamacallit."

"Lady, I can't."

"What do you mean, you can't?"

"Well, just for starters, the power's out."

This remark seemed to have some beneficial effect. The woman tilted her face toward the ceiling.

"Now, I think I did notice that," she said airily. "It does seem a little dim in here."

"That's what I was trying to tell you."

"Well, why didn't you just say so?" she huffed. "So, no Garden Gate. No color at all, from what you're saying. I have to tell you this comes as a disappointment. I was really hoping to get the nursery done today."

"Lady, I don't think—"

"The truth is, David should really be the one doing this, but oh no, he has to go off and save the world and leave me stuck in the house like a prisoner. And where the hell is Yolanda? Pardon my French. You know, after everything I've done for her, I'd expect a little consideration. Even just a call."

David. Yolanda. Who were these people? It was all completely baffling, and not a little weird, but one thing was obvious: this poor woman was completely alone. Unless Grey found a way to get her out of here, she wouldn't last long.

"Maybe you could just paint it white," he offered. "I'm sure they got lots of that."

She looked at him skeptically. "Why would I want to paint it white?"

"They say white goes with anything, right?" For the love of God, listen to him; he sounded like one of those fags on TV. "You can do anything with white. Maybe add something else with color in the room. The curtains and stuff."

She hesitated. "I don't know. White does seem a little plain. On the other hand, I did want to get the painting done today."

"Exactly," Grey said, and did his best to smile. "That's just what I'm saying. You can paint it white, then figure out the rest when you see how it looks. That's what I'd recommend."

"And white does go with anything. You're correct about that."

"You said it was a nursery, right? So maybe later you could add a border, to jazz it up a little. You know, like bunnies or something."

"Bunnies, you say?"

Grey swallowed. Where had that come from? Bunnies were the glow-sticks' all-time favorite food. He'd watched Zero gobble them down by the cartload.

"Sure," he managed. "Everybody likes bunnies."

He could see the idea taking hold of her. Which raised another question. Assuming the woman agreed to leave, what then? He could hardly let her go off on her own. He also wondered just how pregnant she was. Five months? Six? He wasn't a good judge of these things.

"Well, I think you really may have something there," the woman said with a nod from her fine-boned chin. "We really seem to be on the same wavelength, Mr. Grey."

"It's Lawrence," he said.

Smiling, she held out her hand. "Call me Lila."

* * *

It wasn't until he was sitting in the woman's Volvo—Lila had actually left a wad of cash at one of the registers, with a note promising to return—that Grey realized that somewhere between his carrying the cans to the car and loading them into the cargo area, she had successfully maneuvered him into agreeing to paint the nursery. He didn't recall actually doing this; it just kind of happened, and the next thing he knew they were driving away, the woman steering the Volvo through the abandoned city, past wrecked cars and bloated bodies, overturned Army trucks and the still-smoking rubble of gutted apartment complexes. "Really," she remarked, guiding the station wagon around the burned-out hulk of a FedEx delivery truck with barely a glance, "you'd think people would have the sense to call a wrecker and not just leave their cars sitting in the road." She also chattered on about the nursery (he'd hit pay dirt with the bunnies), tucking in more snide asides about David, who Grey figured was her husband. Grey guessed the man had gone off somewhere, leaving her alone in her house. Based on the things he'd seen, it seemed likely he'd gotten himself killed. Maybe the woman had been crazy before, but Grey didn't think so. Something bad had happened to her, really bad. There was a name for this, he knew. Post-traumatic something. Basically the woman knew but didn't know, and her mind, in its terrified state, was protecting her from the truth—a truth that, sooner or later, Grey would have to tell her.

They arrived at the house, a big brick Tudor that seemed to soar above the street. He'd already guessed the woman was well-off from the way she'd spoken to him, but this was something else. Grey retrieved the supplies from the Volvo's cargo area—in addition to the paint, she'd selected a package of rollers, a tray, and an assortment of brushes—and mounted the steps. At the front door, Lila fumbled with her keys.

"Now, this always sticks a little."

She shouldered the door open to a wash of stale air. Grey followed her into the foyer. He had expected the interior of the house to be like something in a castle, all heavy drapes and overstuffed furniture and dripping chandeliers, but it was the opposite, more like some kind of office than a place people actually lived. To his left, a wide arch led to the dining room, which was occupied by a long glass table and some uncomfortable-looking chairs; to the right was the living room, a barren expanse interrupted only by a low-slung couch and a large black piano. For a moment Grey just stood there, dumbly holding the cans of paint, trying to put his thoughts together. He smelled something, too—a pungent whiff of old garbage coming from deep within the house.

As the silence deepened, Grey scrambled for something to say. "Do you play?" he asked.

Lila was depositing her purse and keys on the little table by the door. "Play what?"

Grey gestured at the piano. She swiveled her head to look at the instrument, seeming vaguely startled.

"No," she answered with a frown. "That was David's idea. A little pretentious, if you ask me."

She led him up the stairs, the air thickening as they made their ascent. Grey followed her to the end of the carpeted hall.

"Here we are," she announced.

The room felt disproportionately snug, considering the dimensions of the house. A ladder stood in one corner, and the floor was covered by a plastic drop cloth taped to the baseboards; a roller sat in a tray of paint, hardening in the heat. Grey moved farther in. The room's original tone had been a neutral cream, but someone—Lila, he guessed—had rolled broad, haphazard stripes of yellow up and down the walls, following no organized pattern. It would take him three coats just to cover it.

Lila was standing in the doorway with her hands on her hips. "It's probably pretty obvious," she said with a wince, "I'm not much of a painter. Certainly not a professional such as yourself."

This again, Grey thought. But as long as he'd decided to play along, he saw no reason to disabuse her of the notion that he knew what he was doing.

"Do you need anything else before you get started?"

"I guess not," Grey managed.

She yawned into her hand. A sudden weariness seemed to have overcome her, as if she were a slowly deflating balloon. "Then I suppose I'll leave you to it. I'm going to get off my feet for a bit."

With these words, she left him alone. Grey heard the snap of a door closing down the hall. Well, wasn't this the damnedest thing, he thought. Painting a baby's room in some rich lady's house certainly wasn't anything he'd imagined himself doing when he'd woken up at the Red Roof. He listened for more sounds from her but heard nothing. Maybe the funniest thing of all was that Grey didn't mind, not really. The woman was as nutty as they came, and not a little bossy. But it wasn't as if he'd deceived her about who he was, since she'd never even asked. It felt good to be trusted by someone, even if he didn't deserve it.

He retrieved his supplies from the foyer and got to work. Painting wasn't anything he'd ever done much of, but it was hardly rocket science, and he quickly settled into its rhythms, his mind a pleasant blank. He could almost forget about waking up at the Red Roof, and Zero and Richards and the Chalet and all the rest. An hour passed, and then another; he was cutting in the edges along the ceiling when Lila appeared in the doorway, bearing a tray with a sandwich and a glass of water. She had changed into a high-waisted denim maternity dress that, despite its roominess, made her appear even more pregnant.

"I hope you like tuna."

He climbed off the ladder to receive the tray. The bread was covered with furry green mold; there was a smell of rancid mayonnaise. Grey's stomach flipped.

"Maybe later," he stammered. "I want to do a second coat first."

Lila said nothing more about this, instead stepping back to look around the room. "I have to say, this really looks better. *So* much better. I don't know why I didn't think of white before." She pointed her eyes at Grey again. "I hope you don't think me too forward, Lawrence, and I don't want to assume anything, but you don't by chance need a place to stay the night?"

Grey was caught short; he hadn't thought that far ahead. He hadn't thought ahead at all, as if the woman's delusional state were contagious. But of course she'd want him to stay. After so many days alone, there was no way she was letting him get loose now—keeping him here was the point. And besides, where would he go?

"Good. It's settled then." She gave a nervous laugh. "I have to say, I'm very relieved. I feel so guilty, dragging you into this, never even asking if you have someplace else to be. And after you've been so helpful."

"It's okay," Grey said. "I mean, I'm glad to stay."

"Don't mention it." The conversation seemed over, but at the doorway Lila turned, wrinkling her nose with distaste. "Sorry about the sandwich. I know it probably isn't very appetizing. I keep meaning to get out to the market. But I'll make you a nice dinner."

Grey worked through the afternoon, completing the third coat as the sun was setting in the windows. He had to say, the room didn't look half bad. He deposited his brushes and rollers in the tray, descended the stairs, and followed the central hallway back to the kitchen. Like the rest of the house, the room had a spare, modern appearance, with white cabinets, black granite countertops, and appliances of gleaming chrome, the effect marred only by the garbage bags that were piled everywhere, reeking of old food. Lila was standing at the stove—the gas appeared to be working—and stirring a saucepan by candlelight. The table was set with china, napkins, and silverware, even a tablecloth.

"I hope you like tomato," said Lila, smiling at him.

Lila directed him to a small room behind the kitchen with a utility sink. There was no water to wash the brushes, so Grey left them in the basin and used a rag to clean his hands as best he could. The idea of tomato soup repelled him, but he would have to do a convincing job of trying to eat—there was simply no way to avoid it. By the time he returned, Lila was ladling the steaming soup into a pair of bowls. These she carried to the table with a plate of Ritz crackers.

"Bon appétit."

The first spoonful nearly made him gag. It didn't even seem like food. Against every instinct, he managed to swallow. Lila appeared to take no notice of his distress, breaking the crackers into her soup and spooning it into her mouth. By sheer force of will, Grey took another spoonful, then a third. He could feel the soup lodging at the base of his gut, an inert mass. As he attempted a fourth, something viselike clamped inside him.

"Excuse me a second."

Trying not to run, he retreated to the utility room, arriving at the sink in the nick of time. Usually he made a racket when he puked, but not now: the soup seemed to fly effortlessly out of his body. Christ, what was the matter with him? He wiped his mouth, took a moment to steady himself, and returned to the table. Lila was looking at him with concern.

"Is the soup all right?" she asked gingerly.

He couldn't even look at the stuff. He wondered if she could smell the puke on his breath. "It's fine," he managed. "I'm just . . . not very hungry, I guess."

The answer appeared to satisfy her. She regarded him for a long moment before speaking again. "I hope you don't mind my asking, Lawrence. But are you looking for work?"

"More painting, you mean?"

"Well, certainly there's that. But other things, too. Because I have the impression, and forgive me if I'm leaping to conclusions, that you may be a little bit . . . at loose ends. Which is fine. Don't get me wrong. Things happen to people." She squinted across the table. "But you don't really work at Home Depot, do you?"

Grey shook his head.

"I thought so! Really, you had me going for a while there. And regardless, you've done a beautiful job. A *beautiful* job. Which only proves my point. If you see what I'm saying. Because I'd like to help you get back on your feet. You've been so helpful, I'd like to return the favor. God knows there's plenty that needs doing around here. There's putting up the border, and of course the problems with the AC, and the yard, well you've seen the yard . . ."

If he didn't stop her now, Grey knew, he'd never get her out of here. "Lady—"

"Please." Holding up a hand, she gave him a warm smile. "It's Lila."

"Lila, okay." Grey drew a breath. "Have you noticed anything . . . strange?"

A puzzled frown. "I don't know what you mean."

Best to back in slowly, Grey thought. "Like, take the electricity, for instance."

"Oh that," she said, and waved a hand dismissively. "You already mentioned that, at the store."

"But doesn't it seem odd that it's still out? Don't you think they would have fixed it by now?"

A vague disturbance moved across her face. "I haven't the foggiest. Honestly, I don't see where you're going with this."

"And David, you said he hasn't called. How long has it been?"

"Well, he's a busy man. A very busy man."

"I don't think that's the reason he hasn't called."

Her voice was absolutely flat. "You don't."

"No."

Lila's eyes narrowed suspiciously. "Lawrence, do you know something you're not telling me? Because if you're a friend of David's, I hope you would have the decency to tell me."

Grey might just as well have tried to snatch a fly out of the air. "No, he's not a friend of mine. I'm just saying . . ." There was nothing to do but just come out with it. "Have you noticed there aren't any people?"

Lila was staring at him intently, arms crossed above her pregnant belly. Her eyes held a look of barely contained rage. She rose abruptly, snatched her bowl from the table, and carried it to the sink.

"Lila—"

She shook her head emphatically, not looking at him. "I won't have you talk this way."

"We have to get out of here."

With a clatter she tossed the bowl into the sink and turned on the tap, violently pumping the lever back and forth, to no avail. "Goddamnit, there's no water. *Why is there no fucking water?*"

Grey got to his feet. She spun to face him, her fists balled with anger.

"Don't you understand? I can't lose her again! I can't!"

Did she mean the baby? And what did she mean by "again"?

"We can't stay." He took another cautious step, as if approaching a wary animal. "It's not safe here."

Furious tears began to spill down her cheeks. "Why do you have to do this? Why?"

She lurched toward him, fists raised like hammers. Grey was thrust back on his heels. She began to pummel his chest as if she were trying to break down a door. But her attack wasn't organized; it was an expression of pure panic, of the storm of emotion breaking inside her. As she reared back again, Grey regained his balance and pulled her into him like a boxer into a clinch, encircling her upper body and pinning her arms to her sides. The gesture was reflexive; he didn't know what else to do. "Don't say that," Lila pleaded, thrashing inside his grip. "It isn't true, it isn't true. . . ." Then, with a rush of breath and a whimper of surrender, the air let out of her and she collapsed against him.

For a period that might have been a full minute they stayed that way, locked in an awkward embrace. Grey couldn't have been more astonished—not by her violent reaction, which he could have foreseen, but by the mere presence of a woman's body in his arms. How slight she was! How different from himself! How long had it been since Grey had hugged a woman, hugged anyone? Or even been touched by another person? He could feel the hard roundness of Lila's belly pressed against him, an insistent presence. A baby, Grey thought, and for the first time, the full implications of this fact dawned in his mind. In the midst of the chaos and carnage of a world gone mad, this poor woman was going to have a baby.

Grey relaxed his grip and backed away. Lila was looking at the floor. The brisk, officious woman he'd met in the paint aisle was gone; in her place stood a frail, diminished creature, almost childlike.

"Can I ask you something, Lawrence?" Her voice was very small.

Grey nodded.

"What did you do before?"

For a moment he didn't understand what she was asking; then he realized she meant what job. "I cleaned," he said, and shrugged. "I mean, I was a janitor."

Lila considered his statement without expression. "Well, I guess you've got me there," she said miserably. She rubbed her nose with the back of her wrist. "To tell you the truth, I don't think I was anything at all."

Another silence descended, Lila staring at the floor, Grey wondering what she would next say. Whatever it was, he sensed their survival depended on it.

"I lost one before, you see," Lila said. "A baby girl."

Grey waited.

"Her heart, you understand," she said, and placed a hand against her chest. "It was a problem with her heart."

It was strange; standing in the quiet, Grey felt as if he'd known this about her all along. Or, if not the thing itself, then the kind of thing. It was as if he were looking at one of those pictures that made no sense when you saw it up close, but then you backed away and suddenly it did.

"What was her name?" Grey asked.

Lila raised her tear-streaked face. For a moment she just looked at him, her eyes pulled into an appraising squint. He wondered if he'd made a mistake, asking this. The question had just popped out.

"Thank you, Lawrence. Nobody ever asks me that. I can't tell you how long it's been."

"Why wouldn't they?"

"I don't know." Her shoulders lifted with a tiny shrug. "I guess they think it's bad luck or something."

"Not to me."

A brief silence passed. Grey didn't think he'd ever felt so awful for anybody in his life.

"Eva," Lila said. "My daughter was Eva."

They stood together in the presence of this name. Outside, beyond the windows of Lila's house, the night was pressing down. Grey realized it had begun to rain—a quiet, soaking, summer rain, pattering the windows.

"I'm not really who you think I am," Grey confessed.

"No?"

What did he want to tell her? The truth, surely, or some version of it, but in the last day and a half, the idea of truth seemed to have slipped its moorings completely. He didn't even know where to begin.

"It's all right," Lila said. "You don't have to say anything. Whoever you were before, it doesn't make much difference now."

"It might. I've had . . . some troubles."

"So that would make you just like the rest of us, wouldn't it? One more person with a secret." She looked away. "That's the worst part, really, when you think about it. Try as you might, nobody will ever truly know who you are. You're just somebody alone in a house with your thoughts and nothing else."

Grey nodded. What was there to say?

"Promise me you won't leave," Lila said. "Whatever happens, don't do that."

"Okay."

"You'll look after me. We'll look after each other."

"I promise."

The conversation seemed to end there. Lila, exhaling a weary breath, pushed her shoulders back. "Well. I guess I'd better turn in. I expect you'll want to be leaving first thing in the morning. If I'm reading you correctly."

"I think that's best."

Her eyes wistfully traveled the room with its shiny appliances and overflowing trash bags and dirty dishes in piles. "It's too bad, really. I did want to finish the nursery. But I guess that will have to wait." She found his face again. "Just one thing. You can't make me think about it."

Grey understood what she was asking. *Don't make me think about the world.* "If that's what you want."

"We're just . . ." She looked for the words. "Taking a drive in the country. How does that sound? Do you think you can do that for me?"

Grey nodded. The request struck him as strange, even a little silly, but he would have put on a clown suit if that's what it took to get her out of there.

"Good. Just so long as that's settled."

He waited for her to say something more, or else leave the room, but neither thing happened. A change came into Lila's face—a look of intense concentration, as if she were reading tiny print that only she could see. Then, abruptly, her eyes grew very wide; she seemed about to laugh.

"Oh my goodness, what a scene I made! I can't believe I did that!" Her hands darted to her cheeks, her hair. "I must look terrible. Do I look terrible?"

"I think you look fine," Grey managed.

"Here you are, a guest in my home, and off go the waterworks. It drives Brad absolutely crazy."

The name wasn't one he'd heard from her before. "Who's Brad?"

Lila frowned. "My husband, of course."

"I thought David was your husband."

She gave him a blank stare. "Well, he is. David, I mean."

"But you said—"

Lila waved this away. "I say a lot of things, Lawrence. That's one thing you'll have to learn about me. Probably you think I'm just some crazy woman, and you wouldn't be wrong."

"I don't think that at all," Grey lied.

An ironic smile creased her fine-boned face. "Well. We both know you're only saying that because you're being nice. But I appreciate the gesture." She surveyed the room again, nodding vaguely. "So, it's been quite a day, don't you think? I'm afraid we don't really have a proper guest room, but I made up the couch for you. If you don't mind, I think I'll just leave the dishes for the morning and say good night."

Grey had no idea what to make of any of this. It was as if Lila had broken her trance of denial, only to slip back into it again. Not slip, he thought; she had done this to herself, forcing her thoughts back into place with an act of will. He watched in dumb wonder as she made her way to the doorway, where she turned to face him.

"I'm so very glad you're here, Lawrence," she said, and smiled emptily. "We're going to be good friends, you and I. I just know it."

Then she was gone. Grey listened to her slow trudge down the hallway and up the stairs. He cleared the rest of the dishes from the table. He would have liked to wash them, so she could come down to a clean kitchen in the morning, but there was nothing he could do but deposit them in the sink with the others.

He carried one of the candles from the table to the living room. But the minute he lay down on the sofa, he knew sleep was out of the question. His brain was bouncing with alertness; he still felt a little nauseated from the soup. His mind returned to the scene in the kitchen, and the moment when he'd put his arms around her. Not a hug, exactly; he'd just been trying to get Lila to stop hitting him. But at some point it had become something hug*like*. It had felt good—more than good, actually. The feeling wasn't anything sexual, not as Grey recalled it. Years had gone by since Grey had experienced anything that even approximated a sexual thought—the anti-androgens saw to that—on top of which, the woman was pregnant, for God's sake. Which, come to think of it, was maybe what was so nice about the whole thing. Pregnant women didn't just go hugging people for no reason. Holding Lila, Grey had felt as if he'd stepped into a circle, and within this circle there were not just two people but three—because the baby was there, too. Maybe Lila was crazy and maybe she wasn't. He was hardly the person to judge. But he couldn't see that this made a difference one way or the other. She'd chosen him to help her, and that was exactly what he'd do.

Grey had almost talked his way into sleep when the silence was cut by an animal yelp. He lurched upright on the couch, shaking off his disorientation; the sound had come from outside. He hurried to the window.

That was when he remembered Iggy's gun. He'd been so distracted, he'd left it at the Home Depot. How could he have been so dumb?

He pressed his face to the glass. A dog-sized hump was lying in the middle of the street. It didn't seem to be moving. Grey waited a moment, his breath suspended. A pale shape bounded through the treetops, the image fading, then gone.

Grey knew he wouldn't shut his eyes all night. But it didn't matter. Upstairs Lila slept, dreaming of a world that was no more, while outside the walls of the house, a monstrous evil lurked—an evil Grey was part of. His mind returned to the scene in the kitchen, and the image of Lila, standing at the sink, desperate tears flowing down her cheeks, her fists clenched with rage. *I can't lose her again. I can't.*

He would stand guard at the window till morning, and then, come sunrise, get them the hell out of here.

Lila Kyle was brooding in the dark.

She'd heard the yelp from outside. A dog, she thought; something had happened to a dog. Some thoughtless motorist, speeding down the street? Surely that was what had happened. People should be more careful with their pets.

Don't think, she told herself. Don't think don't think don't think.

Lila wondered what it would be like, being a dog. She could see how there might be some advantages. A purely thoughtless existence, nothing on one's mind but the next pat on the head, a walk around the block, the sensation of food in one's belly. Probably Roscoe (because it *was* Roscoe she had heard; poor Roscoe) hadn't even known what was happening to him. Maybe a little bit, at the end. One minute he was snuffling down the street, searching for something to eat—Lila recalled the floppy thing she'd seen in his mouth that morning, instantly pushing this unpleasant memory aside—and the next: well, there was no next. Roscoe was sailing into oblivion.

And now there was this man. This Lawrence Grey. About whom, Lila realized, she knew exactly nothing. He was a janitor. He cleaned. What did he clean? Probably David would have a conniption if he knew she'd let a total stranger into the house. She would have liked to see the look on David's face. Lila supposed it was possible she'd misjudged the man, this Lawrence Grey, but she didn't think so. She'd always been a good judge of character. Granted, Lawrence had said some disturbing things in the kitchen—*very* disturbing. About the lights being out and people missing and all the rest. (Dead, dead, everyone was dead.) He'd certainly gotten her upset. But to be fair, he'd done a wonderful job with the nursery, and she could tell just by looking at him that his heart was in the right place. Which was another of her father's favorite expressions. What did it mean, exactly? Could the heart be anywhere else? Daddy, I'm a doctor, she'd told him once, laughing; I can tell you for a fact, the heart is where it is.

Lila heard herself sigh. Such an effort, just to keep everything straight in her mind. Because that was what you had to do; you had to look at things in a certain light and no other, and no matter what happened, you couldn't break your gaze away. The world could overwhelm you otherwise, it could drown you like a wave, and then where would you be? The house itself was nothing she would miss; she had secretly hated it from the moment she'd stepped inside, its show-offy dimensions and too-many rooms and gaseous yellow light. It wasn't at all like the one that she and Brad had lived in on Maribel Street—snug, homey, full of the things they'd loved—but how could it be? What was a house but the life it contained? This pompous monstrosity, this museum of nothing. It had been David's idea, of course. The House of David: wasn't that something from the Bible? The Bible was full of houses, the house of so-and-so and the house of such-and-such. Lila remembered being a little girl, snuggled up on the sofa to watch *A Charlie Brown Christmas*—she'd loved Snoopy almost as much as Peter Rabbit—and the moment when Linus, the smart one, the one who was really just a man pretending to be a boy with his blanket, stepped downstage to tell Charlie Brown what Christmas was all about. *And there were in that same country shepherds abiding in the field, keeping watch over their flocks by night. And lo, the angel of the Lord came upon them, and the glory of the Lord shone round about them, and they were sore afraid. And the angel said unto them, Fear not, for behold, I bring you good tidings of great joy, which shall be to all people. For unto you is born this day in the city of David a Savior, which is Christ the Lord.*

City of David, House of David.

But the baby, Lila thought. The baby was where her thoughts belonged. Not with the house, or noises from outside (there were monsters), or David not coming home (dead David), or any of the rest. All the literature had clearly shown, indisputably shown, that negative emotions affected the fetus. It thought as you thought, it felt as you felt, and if you were frightened all the time, what then? Those upsetting things Lawrence had said in the kitchen: the man meant well, he was only trying to do what he thought was best for her and Eva (Eva?), but did these things have to be true, simply because he'd said them? They were *theories*. They were just his *opinions*. Which wasn't to say she disagreed. Probably it was time to go. It had gotten awfully quiet around this place. (Poor Roscoe.) If Brad were here, that's what he would have said to her. Lila, it's time to go.

Because sometimes, lots of times, all the time, it felt to Lila Kyle as if the baby growing inside her wasn't somebody new, a whole new person. Since the morning she'd squatted on the toilet with the plastic wand between her thighs, watching in mute wonderment as the little blue cross appeared, the idea had taken root. The baby wasn't a new Eva, or a different Eva, or a replacement Eva: she *was* Eva, their own little girl, come home. It was as if the world had righted itself, the cosmic mistake of Eva's death undone.

She wanted to tell Brad about it. More than wanted: his name produced a longing so powerful it brought tears to her eyes. She hadn't meant to marry David! Why had Lila married David—sanctimonious, overbearing, eternally do-gooding David—when she was already married to Brad? Especially now, with Eva on the way, coming to make them a family again?

Lila still loved him; that was the thing. That was the sad and sorrowful mystery of it all. She'd never stopped loving Brad, nor he her, not for a second, even when their love was too much pain for either to carry, because their little girl was gone. They had parted as a way to forget, neither being able to accomplish this in the company of the other—a sad, inevitable sundering, like the primordial separation of continents. Until the very end they'd fought it. The night before he'd moved out, his suitcases in the hall of the house on Maribel Street, the lawyers properly apprised, so many tears having been shed that no one even knew what they were crying about anymore—a condition as general as the weather, a world of everlasting tears—he'd come to her in the bedroom he had long since vacated, slid beneath the covers, and for a single hour they'd been a couple again, silently moving together, their bodies still wanting what their hearts could no longer bear. Not a word had passed between them; in the morning Lila awoke alone.

But now all of that had changed. Eva was coming! Eva was practically here! She would write Brad a letter; that's what Lila would do. Surely he was going to come look for her, it was just the kind of man he was, you could always count on Brad when things went to hell in a handbasket, and how would it be for him to find she wasn't there? Her spirits restored by this decision, Lila crept to the little desk under the windows, fumbling in the drawer for a pencil and a sheet of notebook paper. Now, what words to choose? *I am going away. I don't know quite where. Wait for me, my darling. I love you. Eva will be here soon.* Simple and clear, elegantly capturing the essence of the thing. Satisfied, she folded the paper into thirds, slid it into an envelope, wrote "Brad" on the outside, and propped it on the desk so she would see it in the morning.

She lay back down. From across the room, the letter watched her, a rectangle of glowing whiteness. Closing her eyes, Lila let her hands drift down to the hard curve of her belly. A feeling of fullness, and then, from within, a gaseous twitch, then another and another. The baby was hiccupping. *Hiccup!* went the tiny baby. Lila closed her eyes, allowing the sensation to wash over her. Inside her, in the space beneath her heart, a small life was waiting to be born, but even more: she, Eva, was coming home. The day was catching up to her, Lila knew; her mind was riding the currents of sleep like a surfer paddling on the curve of a wave; in another moment the wave would wash over her, taking her under. Eva had quieted under her fingertips. I love you, Eva, thought Lila Kyle, and with that she fell asleep.

10

It was nearly ten A.M. by the time they got to Mile High. Driving into downtown, Danny found himself caught in a maze of barricades: abandoned Humvees, machine-gun positions with their piles of sandbags, even a few tanks. A dozen times he was forced to backtrack in search of an alternate route, only to find his passage blocked. Finally, as the last of the morning haze was burning off, he found a clear path under the freeway and ascended the ramp to the stadium.

The parking area was a grid of olive-green tents, eerily becalmed under the morning sun. Surrounding this was a ring of vehicles, passenger cars and ambulances and police cruisers, many of them looking half-crushed: windows smashed, fenders torn from the frames, doors ripped off their hinges. Danny brought the bus to a halt.

They disembarked into a stench of decay so thick that Danny nearly gagged. Worse than Momma, worse than all the bodies he'd seen that morning, walking to the depot. It was the kind of smell that could snake inside you, into your nose and mouth, and linger there for days.

"Hello!" April called. Her voice echoed across the lot. "Is anybody here? Hello!"

Danny had a bad feeling in the pit of his stomach. Some of this was the smell, but some wasn't. He had the jangly feeling all over.

"Hello!" April called again, her hands cupped around her mouth. "Can anyone hear me?"

"Maybe we should go," Danny suggested.

"The Army's supposed to be here."

"Maybe they left already."

April removed her backpack, unzipped the top, and withdrew a hammer. She gave it a swing, as if to test its weight.

"Tim, you stay by me. Understand? No wandering off."

The boy was standing at the base of the bus's steps, pinching his nose. "But it smells gross," he said in a nasal voice.

April slid her arms into the straps. "The whole *city* smells gross. You'll just have to deal with it. Now come on."

Danny didn't want to go either, but the girl was determined. He followed the two of them as they made their way into the maze of vehicles. Step by step, Danny began to comprehend what he was seeing. The cars had been positioned around the tents as a defense. Like in pioneer times, the way settlers would circle the covered wagons when the Indians attacked. But these weren't Indians, Danny knew, and whatever had happened here, it looked to be long over. There were corpses, somewhere—the smell seemed to intensify the farther they went—but so far they'd seen no trace of them. It was as if everyone had vanished.

They came to the first of the tents. April entered first, holding the hammer up before her, ready to swing. The space was a mess of overturned gurneys and IV poles, debris strewn everywhere—bandages, basins, syringes. But still there were no bodies.

They looked in another tent, then a third. Each was the same. "So where did everybody go?" April said.

The only place left to look was the stadium. Danny didn't want to, but April wouldn't take no for an answer. If the Army said to come here, she insisted, there had to be a reason. They moved up the ramp toward the entrance. April was leading the way, clutching Tim with one hand, the hammer with the other. For the first time, Danny noticed the birds. A huge black cloud wheeling over the stadium, their hoarse calls seeming to break the silence and to deepen it at the same time.

Then, from behind them, a man's voice:

"I wouldn't go in there if I were you."

*   *   *

The Ferrari had died as Kittridge was pulling into the parking area. By this time the car was bucking like a half-broke horse, plumes of oily smoke pouring from the hood and undercarriage. There was no mistaking what had happened: Kittridge's rocket ride out of the parking ramp—that leap into space and then the hard bang on the pavement—had cracked the oil pan. As the oil had drained away, the motor had gradually overheated, metal expanding until the pistons had seized in their cylinders.

Sorry about your car, Warren. It sure was good while it lasted.

After what he'd seen in the stadium, Kittridge needed some time to collect himself. Jesus, what a scene. It wasn't anything he couldn't have predicted, but staring it in the face was something else. It sickened him to the core. His hands were actually shaking; he thought he might be ill. Kittridge had seen some things in his life, horrible things. Bodies in pits lined up like cordwood; whole villages gassed, families lying where they'd fallen, their hands reaching out in vain for the last touch of a loved one; the indecipherable remains of men and women and children, blasted to bits in a marketplace by some lunatic with a bomb strapped to his chest. But never anything even remotely on this scale.

He'd been sitting on the hood of the Ferrari, considering his options, when in the distance he'd heard a vehicle approaching. Kittridge's nerves snapped to attention. A large diesel engine by the sound of it: an APC? But then, lumbering up the ramp, came the surreal vision of a big yellow school bus.

How about that, Kittridge thought. Holy son of a bitch. A goddamned school bus, like a class trip to the end of the world.

Kittridge watched as the bus came to a stop. Three people emerged: a girl with a streak of pink in her hair, a knobby-kneed boy in a T-shirt and shorts, and a man in a funny-looking hat, whom Kittridge guessed was the driver. Hello! the girl called out. Is anybody here? A moment of conferral, then they advanced into the tangle of vehicles, the girl leading the way.

Probably it was time to say something, Kittridge thought. But alerting them to his presence could incur a host of obligations he'd vowed to avoid from the start. Other people weren't part of the plan; the plan was to get gone. Travel light, stay alive as long as possible, take as many virals with him as he could when the end came. Last Stand in Denver making his bright, meteoric descent into the void.

But then Kittridge realized what was about to happen. The three of them were headed straight for the stadium. Of course that's where they'd go; Kittridge had done the same. These were *kids,* for God's sake; plan or no plan, no way could he let them go in there.

Kittridge grabbed his rifle and hustled to head them off.

At the sound of Kittridge's voice, the driver reacted so violently that Kittridge was momentarily frozen into inaction. Erupting with a yelp, the man lurched forward, stumbling over his feet while simultaneously burying his face in the crook of his elbow. The other two scurried away, the girl yanking the little boy protectively to her waist, swiveling toward Kittridge with a hammer held before her.

"Whoa, steady there," Kittridge said. Pointing the rifle skyward, he raised his hands. "I'm one of the good guys."

Kittridge saw that the girl was older than he'd first guessed, seventeen or so. The pink hair was ridiculous, and both her ears had so many studs in them they looked like they'd been riveted to her head, but the way she regarded him, coolly and without a hint of panic, told him she was more than she appeared. There was no doubt in his mind that she'd use the hammer on him, or try to, if he went another step. She had on a tight black T-shirt, jeans worn to threads at the knees, a pair of Chuck Taylors, and bracelets of leather and silver up and down both arms; a backpack, crime-scene yellow, hung from her shoulders. The boy was obviously her brother, their familial connection evident not only in the unmistakable arrangement of their features—the slightly too-small nose with its buttony tip, the high, sudden planes of the cheekbones, eyes of the same aquatic blue—but also in the way she had reacted, shielding him with a fierce protectiveness that struck Kittridge as distinctly parental.

The third member of their group, the driver, was harder to quantify. Something was definitely off about the guy. He was dressed in khakis and a white oxford shirt buttoned to the collar; his hair, a reddish-blond mop peeking from the sides of his peculiar cap, looked like it had been cut by pinking shears. But the real difference wasn't any of these things. It was the way he held himself.

The boy was the first to speak. He had just about the worst cowlick Kittridge had ever laid eyes on. "Is that a real AK?" he said, pointing.

"Quiet, Tim." Drawing him closer, the girl lifted the hammer, ready to swing. "Who the hell are you?"

Kittridge's hands were still raised. For the moment, the notion that the hammer presented an actual threat was something he was willing to indulge. "My name's Kittridge. And yes," he said, speaking to the boy, "it's a real AK. Just don't go thinking I'll let you touch it, young man."

The boy's face lit with excitement. "That's *cool*."

Kittridge lifted his chin toward the driver, who was now gazing intently at his shoes. "Is he okay?"

"He doesn't like to be touched is all." The girl was still studying Kittridge warily. "The Army said to come here. We heard it on the radio."

"I expect they did. But it looks like they've flown the coop on us. Now, I don't believe I caught your names."

The girl hesitated. "I'm April. This is my brother, Tim. The other one is Danny."

"Pleased to meet you, April." He offered his most reassuring smile. "So do you think it would be all right with you if I put my hands down now? Seeing as we've all been properly introduced."

"Where'd you get that rifle?"

"Outdoor World. I'm a salesman."

"You sell guns?"

"Camping and fishing gear, mostly." Kittridge replied. "But they give a nice discount. So what do you say? We're all on the same team here, April."

"What team's that?"

He shrugged. "The human one, I'd say."

The girl was weighing him with her eyes. A cautious one, this April. Kittridge reminded himself that she wasn't just a girl; she was a survivor. Whatever else was true, she deserved to be taken seriously. A few seconds passed, then she lowered the hammer.

"What's in the stadium?" Tim asked.

"Nothing you want to see." Kittridge looked at the girl again. She seemed like an April, he decided. Funny how it sometimes worked that way. "How'd you all get by?"

"We were hiding in the wine cellar."

"What about your folks?"

"We don't know. They were in Telluride."

Jesus, Kittridge thought. Telluride was ground zero, the place where everything had started.

"Well, that was smart. Good thinking." He gestured toward Danny again. He was standing ten feet off to the side with his hands in his pockets, looking at the ground. "What about your friend?"

"Danny was the one who found us. We heard him honking."

"Well, good for you, Danny. I'd say that makes you the hero of the day."

The man gave Kittridge a darting, sidelong glance. His face bore no expression at all. "Okay."

"Why can't I see what's in the stadium?" Tim cut in again.

A look passed between April and Kittridge: *Not a good idea.*

"Never mind about the stadium," April said. She returned her attention to Kittridge. "Have you seen anybody else?"

"Not for a while. That doesn't mean there aren't any."

"But you don't think so."

"Probably it's wisest if we assume we're alone."

Kittridge could see where this was all headed. An hour ago he'd been riding down the side of a building, fleeing for his life. Now he was facing the prospect of looking after two kids and a man who couldn't even meet his eye. But the situation was what it was.

"That your bus, Danny?" he said.

The man nodded. "I drive the blue route. Number twelve."

A smaller vehicle would have made more sense, but Kittridge had the feeling the man wouldn't be leaving without it. "Feel like maybe driving us out of here?"

The girl's expression hardened. "What makes you think you're coming with us?"

Kittridge was taken aback; he hadn't considered the possibility that the three of them wouldn't want his help.

"Actually, nothing, you put it that way. I guess you'd have to invite me."

"Why can't I *see*?" Tim whined.

April rolled her eyes. "For fuck's sake, Tim, just shut up about the stadium, will you?"

"You said the F word! I'm telling!"

"And who are you going to tell?"

The boy was suddenly on the verge of tears. "Don't say that!"

"Listen," Kittridge cut in, "this really isn't the time. By my count we've got eight hours of daylight left. I don't think we want to be anywhere near here after dark."

Which was when the boy, sensing his opening, spun on his heels and bolted up the ramp.

"Shit," Kittridge said. "Both of you stay here."

He took off at a hobbling run, but with his leg, he was in no condition to close the gap; by the time Kittridge caught up to the boy, he was standing in the open mouth of one of the gates, staring dumbly at the field. Just a few seconds, but it was enough. Kittridge snatched him from behind and hoisted him to his chest. The boy went limp, collapsing against him. He made no sound at all. Jesus, Kittridge thought. Why had he let the kid get the jump on him like that?

By the time he reached the base of the ramp, Tim had begun making a sound that was half hiccup, half whimper. Kittridge lowered him to the ground in front of April.

"What do you think you were doing?" Her voice was thick with angry tears.

"I'm . . . s-sorry," the boy stammered.

"You can't go running off like that, you *can't.*" She shook him by the arms, then pulled him into a desperate hug. "I've told you a thousand times, you stay with me."

Kittridge had moved to where Danny was standing, gazing at the ground with his hands in his pockets.

"They were really all alone?" he asked quietly.

"Consuela was with them," Danny stated. "But she left."

"Who's Consuela?"

He gave a loose-limbed shrug. "She waits with Tim at the bus sometimes."

There wasn't much else to say on the subject. Maybe Danny wasn't all there, but he'd rescued two helpless kids whose parents were almost certainly dead. It was more than Kittridge had done.

"So how about it, my friend," Kittridge said. "Feel like firing up that bus of yours?"

"Where are we going?"

"I was thinking Nebraska."

11

They left an hour after dawn. Grey took whatever he could find in the kitchen that still looked edible—a few remaining cans of soup, some stale crackers, a box of Wheaties, and bottles of water—and loaded it into the Volvo. He didn't have so much as a toothbrush of his own, but then Lila appeared in the hall with two wheeled suitcases.

"I took the liberty of packing you some clothes."

Lila was dressed as if leaving on vacation, in dark leggings paired with a crisply-starched, long-tailed shirt. A brightly colored silk scarf lay over her shoulders. She'd washed her face and brushed her hair, and was even wearing earrings and a bit of makeup. The sight of her made Grey realize how dirty he was. He hadn't washed in days; probably he didn't smell the best.

"Maybe I should clean up a bit."

Lila directed him to the bathroom at the head of the stairs, where she'd already laid out a change of clothes for him, neatly folded on the toilet seat. A brand-new toothbrush, still in its wrapper, and a tube of Colgate rested on the vanity beside a jug of water. Grey peeled off his jumpsuit and washed his face and splashed his armpits, then brushed his teeth, facing the broad mirror. He hadn't looked at his reflection since the Red Roof, and it still came as a shock, how young he looked—skin clear and taut, hair growing lushly over his scalp, eyes radiating a jewel-like glitter. He looked like he'd lost a lot of weight, too—not surprising, since he'd eaten nothing in two days, but the degree to which this had occurred, both in quantity and kind, was startling. He wasn't just thinner; it was as if his body had rearranged itself. Turning to the side, holding his gaze on his reflection, he ran a hand experimentally over his belly. He'd always run on the chubby side; now he could discern the taut outline of muscles. From there it was a small step to flexing his arms, like a kid admiring himself. Well, look at that, he thought. Actual biceps. God damn.

He put on the clothing Lila had left for him—white boxers, a pair of jeans, and a checked sport shirt—discovering, to his continued amazement, that it all fit rather well. He took one last look at himself in the mirror and descended the stairs to the living room, where he found Lila sitting on the sofa, paging through a *People* magazine.

"Well, there you are." She regarded him up and down, smiling in her airy way. "Don't you look nice."

He wheeled the suitcases to the Volvo. The morning air was weighted with dew; birds were singing in the trees. As if the two of them were just taking a drive in the country, Grey thought, shaking his head. Yet as he stood in the driveway wearing another man's clothes, this almost seemed true. It was as if he had stepped into a different life—the life, perhaps, of the man whose jeans and sport shirt now graced his newly slender, muscled body. He took a deep sniff, expanding his chest. The air felt fresh and clean in his lungs, full of scent. Grass, and new green leaves, and damp earth. It seemed to contain no trace of the terrors of the night before, as if the light of day had cleansed the world.

He sealed the hatch and looked up to see Lila standing at the front door. She turned the lock, then removed something from her purse: an envelope. She withdrew a roll of masking tape from her purse and taped the envelope to the door, standing back to look at it. A letter? Grey thought. Who would it be for? David? Brad? One of these, probably, but Grey still had no idea who was who. The two seemed virtually inter-changeable in Lila's mind.

"There," she announced. "All set." At the Volvo, she handed him the keys. "Would it be all right if you drove?"

And Grey liked that, too.

Grey decided it would be best to stay off the main roads, at least until they were out of the city. Though this fact was unstated, it also seemed part of his agreement with Lila that he should avoid passing the sorts of things that might upset her. This turned out not to matter: the woman barely looked up from her magazine. He picked his way through the sub-urbs; by midmorning, they were in a parched, rolling land of empty fields the color of burnt toast, moving east on a rural blacktop. The city faded away behind them, followed by the blue bulk of the Rockies, va-porizing in the haze. The scene around them possessed a barren, forgot-ten quality—just a scrim of feathery clouds high overhead, and the dry fields, and the highway unspooling under the Volvo's wheels. Eventually Lila gave up her reading and fell asleep.

The oddness of the situation was inarguable, yet as the miles and hours passed, Grey felt a swelling rightness in his chest. Never in his life had he really mattered to anyone. He searched his mind for something, anything to compare the feeling to. The only thing he could come up with was the story of Joseph and Mary and the flight into Egypt—a boy-hood memory, because Grey hadn't been to church in years. Joseph had always seemed like an odd duck, taking care of a woman who was carry-ing somebody else's baby. But Grey was beginning to see the sense in it, how a person could become attached just by being wanted.

And the thing was, Grey liked women; he always had. The other thing, with the boys, was different. It wasn't about what he liked or didn't like but what he *had* to do, because of his past and the things that had been done to him. That was how Wilder, the prison shrink, had explained it. The boys were a compulsion, Wilder told him, Grey's way of returning to the moment of his own abuse, to reenact it and, in so doing, seek to understand it. Grey no more decided to touch the boys than he decided to scratch an itch. A lot of what Wilder said sounded like bullshit to Grey, but not that part, and it made him feel a little better, knowing he wasn't entirely at fault. Not that it let him off the hook any; Grey had beaten himself up plenty. He'd actually felt relieved when they sent him away. The Old Grey—the one who'd found himself lingering on the edges of playgrounds and cruising slowly past the junior high at three o'clock and dragging his feet in the locker room at the community swimming pool on summer afternoons—*that* Grey was nobody he ever wanted to know again.

His mind returned to the hug in the kitchen. It wasn't a boy-girl thing, Grey knew that, but it wasn't nothing either. It made Grey think of Nora Chung, the one girl he'd dated in high school. She hadn't been a girlfriend, exactly; they'd never actually done anything. The two of them were in the band together—for a brief period, Grey had gotten it in his head to play the trumpet—and sometimes after practice Grey would walk her home, the two of them not even touching, though something about those walks made him feel for the first time that he wasn't alone on the earth. He wanted to kiss her, but he'd never summoned the courage; eventually she'd drifted away. Curious that Grey should remember her now. He hadn't so much as thought her name in twenty years.

By noon, they were approaching the Kansas border. Lila was still sleeping. Grey himself had lapsed into a half-dream state, barely paying attention to the road. He'd managed to avoid towns of any considerable size, but this couldn't last; they'd need gas soon. Ahead he saw a water tower poking from the plain.

The town was named Kingwood—just a short, dusty main street, half the store windows papered over, and a few blocks of dismal houses on either side. It looked harmlessly abandoned; the only evidence that anything had happened was an ambulance parked in front of the fire station with its rear doors hanging open. And yet Grey sensed something, a tingling at his extremities, as if their progress was being observed from the shadows. He cruised the length of the town, finally coming to a filling station on its eastern edge, an off-brand place called Frankie's.

Lila stirred when Grey shut the engine off. "Where are we?"

"Kansas."

She yawned, squinting through the windshield at the desolate town. "Why are we stopping?"

"We need gas. I'll just be a sec."

Grey tried the pump, but no dice: the power was off. He'd have to siphon some off somehow, but for that he'd need a length of hose and a can. He stepped into the office. A battered metal desk, covered with stacks of paper, stood by the front window; an old office chair rested behind it, rocked back on its hinges, giving the ghostly impression of having only recently been vacated. He moved through the door that led to the service bays, a cool, dark space that smelled of oil. A Cadillac

Seville, late-'90s vintage, was perched on one of the lifts; the second bay was occupied by a Chevy 4x4 with a jacked-up suspension and fat, mud-choked tires. Resting on the floor was a five-gallon gas can; on one of the workbenches, Grey located a length of hose. He severed off a six-foot section, slid one end into the 4x4's fuel port, drew in a sip that he spat away, and began to siphon gas into the can.

The can was nearly full when he heard a scuffling above his head. Every nerve in his body fired simultaneously, clenching him in place.

Slowly he lifted his face.

The creature was suspended from one of the ceiling beams, hanging upside down with its knees folded over the strut like a kid on monkey bars. It was smaller than Zero, more human-seeming. As their eyes locked, Grey's heart froze between beats. From deep inside the creature's throat came a trilling sound.

You don't have to be afraid, Grey.

What the fuck?

His feet tangled under him as he lurched backward, sending him pitching to the hard concrete. He snatched the gas can off the floor, fuel still gushing from the siphon, and charged from the service bay into the office and out the door. Lila was standing with her back braced against the car.

"Get in," he said breathlessly.

"You didn't notice if they had a vending machine inside? I'd really like to get a candy bar or something."

"Damn it, Lila, get in the car." Grey threw open the Volvo's hatch, tossed the can inside, and slammed it closed. "We have to go *right now.*"

The woman sighed. "Fine, whatever you say. I don't see why you have to be so rude about it."

They raced away. Only when they were a mile from town did Grey's pulse begin to slow. He let the Volvo coast to a stop, threw the door open, and stumbled from the car. Standing at the side of the road, he placed his hands on his knees, breathing in huge gulps of air. Jesus, it was like the thing had *spoken* to him. Like those clicks were a foreign language he could understand. It even knew his name. How did it know his name?

He felt Lila's hand on his shoulder. "Lawrence, you're bleeding."

He was. His elbow looked ripped open, a flap of skin dangling. He must have done it in the fall, although he'd felt nothing.

"Let me look."

Wearing an expression of intense concentration, Lila gently probed the edges with her fingertips. "How did it happen?"

"I guess I tripped."

"You should have said something. Can you move it?"

"I think so, yeah."

"Wait here," Lila commanded. "Don't touch it."

She opened the hatch of the Volvo and began to rummage through her suitcase. She removed a metal box and a bottle of water and dropped the tailgate.

"Let's sit you down."

Grey positioned himself on the tailgate. Lila opened the box: a medical kit. She rubbed a dab of Purell into her hands, removed a pair of latex gloves, snapped them onto her hands, and took his arm again.

"Do you have any history of excessive bleeding?" she asked.

"I don't think so."

"Hepatitis, HIV, anything like that?"

Grey shook his head.

"How about your last tetanus shot? Can you remember when that was?"

What Lila was this? Who was Grey seeing? Not the lost woman of the Home Depot, or the defeated soul in the kitchen; this was someone new. A third Lila, full of efficiency and competence.

"Not since I was a kid."

Lila took another moment to examine the wound. "Well, it's a nasty gash. I'm going to have to suture it."

"You mean like . . . stitches?"

"Trust me, I've done it a million times."

She swabbed the wound with alcohol, removed a disposable syringe from the box, filled it from a tiny vial, and tapped the needle with her forefinger.

"Just a little something to numb you up. You won't feel a thing, I promise."

The prick of the needle and in just a few seconds, Grey's pain melted away. Lila unfolded a cloth onto the tailgate, laying out a pair of forceps, a spool of dark thread, and a tiny scissors.

"You can watch if you want, but most people prefer to look away."

He felt a series of tiny tugs but that was all. Moments later, he looked down to see the gash and its flap of skin replaced by a tight black line. Lila spread ointment over it, then dressed it with a bandage.

"The stitches should dissolve in a couple of days," she said as she was snapping off her gloves. "It may be a little itchy, but you can't scratch it. Just leave it alone."

"How did you know how to do that?" Grey asked. "Are you a nurse or something?"

The question appeared to catch her short. Her mouth opened like she was about to say something; then she closed it again.

"Lila? Are you okay?"

She was sealing up the kit. She returned her supplies to the Volvo and closed the hatch.

"We better be going, don't you think?"

Just like that, the woman who'd stitched his arm was gone, the moment of her emergence erased. Grey wanted to ask her more but knew what would happen if he did. The pact between them was clear: only certain things could be said.

"Do you want me to drive?" Lila asked. "It's probably my turn."

The question wasn't really a question, Grey understood. It was the natural thing to ask, just as it was his job to decline the offer. "No, I can do it."

They got back in the Volvo. As Grey put the car in gear, Lila took up her magazine from the floor.

"If it's all right with you, I think I'm going to read a bit."

A hundred and twelve miles to the north, traveling east on Interstate 76, Kittridge had also begun to worry about fuel. The bus had been full when they'd started; now they were down to a quarter tank.

With a few minor detours, they'd managed to stay on the highway since Fort Morgan. Lulled by the motion of the bus, April and her brother had fallen asleep. Danny whistled through his teeth while he drove—the tune was nothing Kittridge recognized—gamely spinning the wheel and working the brakes and gas, hat tipped to his brow, his face and posture as erect as that of a sea captain facing down a gale.

For the love of God, Kittridge thought. How in the hell had he ended up in a school bus?

"Uh-oh," said Danny.

Kittridge sat up straight. A long line of abandoned vehicles, stretching to the horizon, stood in their path. Some of the cars were lying upside down or on their sides. Bodies were scattered everywhere.

Danny stopped the bus. April and Tim were awake now as well, gazing out the windshield.

"April, get him out of here," Kittridge directed. "Both of you to the back, now."

"What do you want me to do?" Danny asked.

"Wait here."

Kittridge stepped down from the bus. Flies were buzzing in vast black swarms; there was an overwhelming odor of rotten flesh. The air was absolutely still, as if it couldn't bring itself to move. The only signs of life were the birds, vultures and crows, circling overhead. Kittridge moved up the line of cars. Virals had done this, there was no mistaking it; there must have been hundreds of them, thousands even. What did it mean? And why were the cars all together like this, as if they'd been forced to stop?

Suddenly Danny was beside him.

"I thought I told you to wait with the others."

The man was squinting into the sunlight. "Wait." He held up a hand, then said, "I hear something."

Kittridge listened. Nothing at all, just the creak of the crickets in the empty fields. Then it came: a muffled pounding, like fists on metal.

Danny pointed. "It's coming from over there."

The sound became more distinct with each step. Somebody was alive out there, trapped inside the wreckage. Gradually its components began to separate, the pounding underscored by a strangled echo of human voices. *Let us out! Is somebody out there? Please!*

"Hello!" Kittridge called. "Can you hear me?"

Who's out there? Help us, please! Hurry, we're cooking to death!

The sound was coming from a semitrailer with the bright yellow FEMA insignia printed on its sides. The pounding was frantic now, the voices a shrill chorus of indistinguishable words.

"Hang on!" Kittridge yelled. "We'll get you out!"

The door had been knocked kitty-corner in its frame. Kittridge looked around for something to use as a lever, found a tire iron, and wedged the blade under the door.

"Danny, help me."

The door refused them at first; then it began, almost imperceptibly, to move. As the gap increased, a line of fingers appeared beneath the lip, attempting to draw it upward.

"Everybody, on three," Kittridge commanded.

With a screech of metal, the door ascended.

They were from Fort Collins: a couple in their thirties, Joe and Linda Robinson, the two of them still dressed for a day at the office, with a young baby they called Boy Jr.; a heavyset black man in a security guard's uniform, named Wood, and his girlfriend, Delores, a pediatric nurse who spoke with a thick West Indian accent; an elderly woman, Mrs. Bellamy—Kittridge was never to learn her first name—with a nimbus of blue-rinsed hair and an enormous white purse that she kept clutched to her side; a young man, maybe twenty-five, named Jamal, with a tight fade haircut and brightly colored tattoos winding up and down his bare arms. The last was a man in his fifties with the coarse gray hair and barrel-shaped torso of an aging athlete; he introduced himself as Pastor Don. Not an actual pastor, he explained; by trade, a CPA. The nickname was a leftover from his days coaching Pop Warner football.

"I always told them to pray we didn't get our asses kicked," he told Kittridge.

Though Kittridge had initially assumed they'd traveled together, they had wound up with one another by accident. All told versions of the same story. They'd fled the city only to be stopped by a long line of traffic at the Nebraska border. Word passed down from car to car that there was an Army roadblock ahead, that nobody was being let through. The Army was waiting for word to let people pass. For a whole day they'd sat there. As the light had ebbed, people had begun to panic. Everyone was saying the virals were coming; they were being left to die.

Which was, more or less, what happened.

They arrived just after sunset, Pastor Don said. Somewhere ahead in the line, screaming, gunshots, and the sound of crunching metal; people began to tear past him. But there was nowhere to run. Within seconds, the virals were upon them, hundreds blasting out of the fields, tearing into the crowd.

"I ran like hell, just like everybody else," Pastor Don said.

He and Kittridge had stepped away to confer; the others were sitting on the ground by the bus. April was passing out bottles of water they'd collected at the stadium. Pastor Don removed a box of Marlboro Reds from his shirt pocket and shook two loose. Kittridge hadn't smoked since his early twenties, but what could it hurt now? He accepted a light and took a cautious drag, the nicotine hitting his system instantly.

"I can't even describe it," Don said, ejecting a plume of smoke. "Those goddamn things were everywhere. I saw the truck and decided it was better than nothing. The others were already inside. How the door got jammed I don't know."

"Why wouldn't the Army let you through?"

Don shrugged philosophically. "You know how these things work. Probably somebody forgot to file the right form." He squinted at Kittridge through a trail of smoke. "So what about you, you got anybody?"

He meant did Kittridge have a family, somebody he had lost or was looking for. Kittridge shook his head.

"My son's in Seattle, a plastic surgeon. The whole package. Married his college sweetheart, two kids, a boy and a girl. Big house on the water. They just redid the kitchen." He shook his head wistfully. "The last time we spoke, that's what we talked about. A fucking kitchen."

Pastor Don was carrying a rifle, a .30-.06 with three rounds remaining. Wood was carrying an empty .38. Joe Robinson had a .22 pistol with four cartridges—good for killing a squirrel, maybe, but that was about all.

Don glanced toward the bus. "And the driver? What's his story?"

"A little off, maybe. I wouldn't try to touch him—he'll just about have a seizure. Otherwise he's okay. He treats that bus like it's the *Queen Mary.*"

"And the other two?"

"They were hiding in their parents' basement. I found them wandering around the parking lot at Mile High."

Don took a last, hungry drag and crushed the butt underfoot. "Mile High," he repeated. "I'm guessing that was nothing nice."

There was no way around the wreckage; they would have to backtrack and find another route. They scavenged what supplies they could find— more bottles of water, a couple of working flashlights and a propane lantern, an assortment of tools, and a length of rope that had no obvious use but might find some purpose later on—and boarded the bus.

As Kittridge mounted the bottom step, Pastor Don touched him on the elbow. "Maybe you should say something."

Kittridge looked at him. "Me?"

"Somebody has to be in charge. And it's your bus."

"Not really. Technically, it's Danny's."

Pastor Don met Kittridge's eye. "That's not what I mean. These people are worn out and frightened. They need somebody like you."

"You don't even know me."

He gave a cagey smile. "Oh, I know you better than you think I do. I was in the reserves myself, way back when. Just doing the quartermaster's books, but you learn to read the signs. I'm guessing ex–Special Forces. Rangers, maybe?" When Kittridge said nothing, Pastor Don shrugged. "Well, that's your business. But you obviously know what the hell you're doing better than anyone else around here. This is your show, my friend, like it or not. My guess is, they're waiting to hear from you."

It was true, and Kittridge knew it. Standing in the aisle, he surveyed the group. The Robinsons were seated up front, Linda holding Boy Jr. on her lap; directly behind them was Jamal, sitting alone; then Wood and Delores. Don took the bench across the aisle. Mrs. Bellamy sat at the rear, clutching her big white purse with both hands, like a retiree on a casino junket. April was sitting with her brother on the driver's side, behind Danny. Her eyes widened as their glances met. *What now?* they said.

Kittridge cleared his throat. "Okay, everybody. I know you're scared. I'm scared, too. But we're going to get you out of here. I don't know just where we're going, but if we keep heading east, sooner or later we're going to find safety."

"What about the Army?" Jamal said. "Those assholes left us here."

"We don't really know what happened. But to be on the safe side, we're going to keep on back roads as far as we can."

"My mother lives in Kearney." This was Linda Robinson. "That's where we were headed."

"Jesus, lady." Jamal scoffed. "I told you, Kearney's just like Fort Collins. They said so on the radio."

In every group, Kittridge thought, there was always one. This was all he needed.

Linda's husband, Joe, twisted in his seat. "Close your mouth for once, why don't you?"

"I hate to break it to you, but her mother's probably hanging from the ceiling right now, eating the dog."

Suddenly everybody was speaking at once. Two days in the truck, Kittridge thought. Of course they'd be at one another's throats.

"Please, everybody—"

"And just who put you in charge?" Jamal jabbed a finger at Kittridge. "Just because you're all, like, strapped and shit."

"I agree," said Wood. It was the first time Kittridge had heard the man's voice. "I think we should take a vote."

"Vote on what?" Jamal said.

Wood gave him a hard look. "For starters, whether or not we should throw you off this bus."

"Fuck you, Rent-a-Cop."

In a flash, Wood was up. Before Kittridge could react, the man gripped Jamal in a headlock; in a flurry of arms and legs, they went tumbling over the bench. Everyone was shouting. Linda, clutching the baby, was trying to scamper away. Joe Robinson had joined in the fray, attempting to grip Jamal around the legs.

A gunshot slapped the air; everyone froze. All eyes swiveled to the rear of the bus, where Mrs. Bellamy was pointing an enormous pistol at the ceiling.

"Lady," Jamal spat, "what the *fuck*."

"Young man, I think I speak for everyone when I say I'm tired of your crap. You're just as afraid as the rest of us. You owe an apology to these people."

It was completely surreal, Kittridge thought. Part of him was horrified; another part wanted to laugh.

"Okay, okay," Jamal sputtered. "Just put that cannon away."

"I think you can do better than that."

"I'm sorry, okay? Quit waving that thing around."

She thought a moment, then lowered the pistol. "I suppose that will have to do. Now, I do like the idea of a vote. This nice man in the front— I'm sorry, my hearing isn't what it used to be—what did you say your name was?"

"Kittridge."

"Mr. Kittridge. He seems perfectly capable to me. I say all in favor of his running things, let's see a show of hands."

Every hand went up except Jamal's.

"It would be nice if it could be unanimous, young man."

His face was burning with humiliation. "Christ, you old bag. What else do you want from me?"

"Forty years of teaching public school, believe me, I've dealt with more than my share of boys like you. Now, go on. You'll see how much better you feel."

With a look of defeat, Jamal raised his hand.

"That's better." She directed her attention at Kittridge again. "We can go now, Mr. Kittridge."

Kittridge glanced at Pastor Don, who was trying not to laugh.

"Okay, Danny," Kittridge said. "Let's turn this thing around and find a way out of here."

12

They'd lost him. How the good Christ had they lost him?

Last they knew, Grey had been driving into Denver. He'd dropped off the screen at that point—the Denver network was a mess—but a day later they'd picked up his signature from a Verizon tower in Aurora. Guilder had asked for another drone to sweep the area, but they'd found nothing; and if Grey had gotten off the interstates, as now seemed likely, and headed into the sparsely populated eastern half of the state, he could travel for miles without leaving a mark.

And no sign at all of the girl. For all intents and purposes, she'd been swallowed by the continent.

With little to do but wait for news from Nelson, Guilder had plenty of time to ponder Grey's file, including the psychiatric workup from the Texas Department of Criminal Justice. He wondered what Richards had been thinking, hiring men like this. Human disposables—although that was, Guilder supposed, the point; like the original twelve test subjects, Babcock and Sosa and Morrison and all the creepy rest, the sweeps were no one anybody was ever going to miss.

To wit: Lawrence Alden Grey, born 1970, McAllen, Texas. Mother a homemaker, father a mechanic, both deceased. The father had served three tours in Vietnam as an Army medic, honorably discharged with a bronze star and a purple heart, but it had done the guy in anyway. He'd shot himself in the cab of his truck, leaving Grey, just six years old, to find him. A series of common-law stepfathers followed, one drunk after another by the looks of it, a history of abuse, etc.; by the time Grey was eighteen, he was on his own, working as a roughneck in the oil fields near Odessa, then on rigs in the Gulf. He'd never married, though that was no big shocker; his psychiatric profile was a bag of problems, everything from OCD to depression to traumatic disassociation. In the shrink's opinion, the guy was basically heterosexual, but with so many hang-ups it didn't even figure; the boys had been Grey's way of reliving his own childhood abuse, which his conscious mind had repressed. He'd been arrested twice, the first time for exposure, which he'd pled down to a misdemeanor, the second for aggravated sexual assault. Basically, he'd touched the kid—not exactly a hanging offense, but nothing nice, either. With the first conviction on his sheet the judge had sentenced him to the max, eighteen to twenty-four years, but nobody did the full bid anymore, and he'd been paroled after ninety-seven months.

After that, there wasn't much of a story. He'd moved back to Dallas, done little bits of work but nothing steady, met with his PO every two weeks to pee in a cup and swear eight ways to Sunday he hadn't set foot within a hundred yards of a playground or school. His court-ordered regimen of anti-androgens was standard, as was a fresh psychiatric evaluation every six months. By all accounts, Lawrence Grey was a model citizen, at least as far as a chemically neutered child molester could be.

None of which did anything to tell Guilder how the man had survived. Somehow he'd escaped the Chalet; somehow he'd managed to avoid getting himself killed since then. It simply made no sense.

Nelson's new plan was to retraffic all the cell towers in Kansas and Nebraska, shutting down both states for a period of two hours and trying to isolate the signal from Grey's chip. Under usual circumstances, this would have required a federal court order, a pile of paperwork ten miles high, and a month's lead time, but Nelson had used a back channel at Homeland, which had agreed to issue a special executive order under Article 67 of the Domestic Security Act—more commonly known in the intelligence community as the "Do Whatever the Fuck You Want" Act. The chip in Grey's neck was a low-wattage transmitter at 1432 megahertz; once everything else was cleared out, and assuming Grey passed within a few miles of a tower, they could triangulate his position and retarget a satellite to get a picture.

The shutdown was scheduled for eight A.M. Guilder had come in at six to find Nelson typing away at his terminal. A buzz of music was leaking from the earbuds stuffed in the sides of his head.

"Let Mozart work," he said, shooing Guilder away.

Guilder was running on coffee and adrenaline; he went down to the break room to get something to eat. All they had were vending machines; he'd already paid his three dollars for a Snickers when he realized it would take too much effort to swallow. He tossed it in the trash and got a Reese's, but even that, with the sticky peanut butter, was difficult. He snapped on the TV, tuned it to CNN. New cases were suddenly popping up all over: Amarillo, Baton Rouge, Phoenix. The U.N. was vacating its New York headquarters, relocating to The Hague; once martial law was declared, the military would be recalled from overseas. What a fiasco that would be. It would make Pandora's box look like a picnic basket.

Nelson appeared in the door. "Bow down," he declared with a grin. "Houston, we have a sex offender."

Nelson had already targeted the satellite. By the time they reached the terminal, the image was coming in.

"Where the hell is this?"

Nelson worked the keyboard, bringing the picture into focus. "Western Kansas."

A grid of cornfields came into aerial view and, at the center, a long, low-slung building with a grid of parking spaces in front. A single vehicle, some kind of station wagon, was in the lot. A figure stepped from the building, pulling a suitcase.

"Is that the same guy?" Nelson asked.

"I'm not sure. Bring it in closer."

The image faded, then resolved again, assuming an approximate aerial distance of eighty feet. Now Guilder felt certain he was looking at

Lawrence Grey. He'd changed out of his jumpsuit, but it was him. Grey returned to the building; a minute later he reemerged with a second suitcase, which he deposited in the car's cargo compartment. He stood a moment, as if lost in thought. Then a second figure emerged from the building, a woman. A little heavy, with dark hair; she was wearing slacks and a light-colored blouse.

What the hell?

They had less than thirty seconds left. Already the picture had begun to lose its crispness. Grey opened the passenger door; the woman lowered herself into the car. Grey glanced around the parking lot one more time—as if, thought Guilder, he knew he was being watched. He got into the vehicle and drove away, just as the image dissolved into sparkles of static.

Nelson looked up from his terminal. "Looks like our target made a friend. From the psych workup, I have to say I'm a little surprised."

"Call back the last shot with the woman in it. See if we can enhance it."

Nelson tried, but the results were only a modest improvement.

"Can we figure out what that building is?"

Nelson had slid his chair to an adjacent terminal. "Thirty-eight-twelve Main Street, Ledeau, Kansas. A place called Angie's Resort."

Who was she? What was Lawrence Grey doing with a woman? Was she from the Chalet?

"Which direction was he going?"

"Looks like straight east. He's headed right into the thick of it. If you want to grab him, we'd better move."

"Locate our nearest asset. Something outside the quarantine line."

More taps of the keys; then Nelson said, "The closest for something like this would be the old NBC lab in Fort Powell. The Army shut it down three years ago, when they moved everything to White Sands, but it should be an easy matter to get the lights turned on."

"What else is around there?"

"Not a lot except for Midwest State, which is about three miles east. It's your basic football factory with a few classrooms attached. Otherwise you've got a National Guard armory, some hog and cattle processing, a little light manufacturing. There's a small IAC hydroelectric facility, but it was mothballed when they built a larger one downstream. Pretty much the only reason the place exists is the college."

Guilder took a moment to think. They were the only ones who knew about Grey, at least so far. Probably it was time to bring in the CDC and USAMRIID.

Yet he hesitated. Partly because of the bad taste in his mouth from his meeting with the Joint Chiefs. How would it go down when Central Command learned that they'd put Lear's monstrosities under the surveillance of a bunch of paroled sex offenders? He'd never hear the end of it.

But that wasn't the real reason.

A cure for everything. Weren't those Lear's exact words? Wasn't that where the whole misbegotten thing had begun? And if Grey was infected but for some reason hadn't flipped, was it possible that the virus in his blood had changed somehow, achieving the very result Lear had hoped for? That he was in every way a prize as valuable as the girl? And wasn't it also true that, although death was everyone's problem, especially now, it was for Guilder just as pressing and personal even more so, because the fate that awaited him left nothing to chance? Didn't he have some right to muster whatever resources he could on behalf of his own survival? Wouldn't anybody do the same?

We're all dying, baby. Fair enough. But some of us more than others.

Maybe Grey was his answer, and maybe he wasn't. Maybe he was just some lucky schmuck who'd managed to claw his way out of a burning building and avoid the glowsticks long enough to make his way to Kansas. But the more Guilder ruminated over it, the more he didn't think so. The odds were simply too long. And once he turned the man over to the military, he doubted they'd hear anything from Grey, or this mystery woman, again.

Which wasn't going to happen. Horace Guilder, deputy director of the Division of Special Weapons, would keep Lawrence Grey for himself.

"So? What do you want me to do?"

Nelson was staring at him. Guilder calculated the mechanics. Who else did he need? Nelson wasn't somebody Guilder would have described as loyal, but for the time being he could appeal to the man's naked self-interest, and he was the best person for the job, a one-man band of biochemical know-how. Sooner or later he'd catch wind of what Guilder was up to, and decisions would have to be made, but that was a bridge Guilder would cross when he came to it. As for making the pickup: there was always somebody off the books for tasks like that. One phone call and everything would be set in motion.

"Pack your things," he said. "We're going to Iowa."

13

Sunrise of the second day: they were deep into Nebraska now. Danny, hunched over the wheel, his eyes stinging with sleeplessness, had driven through the night. Everyone except for Kittridge had fallen asleep, even the obnoxious one, Jamal.

It felt good to have people on his bus again. To be useful, a useful engine.

They'd found more diesel at a small airport in McCook. The few towns they'd passed through were empty and abandoned, like something from a movie about the Old West. Okay, so maybe they were lost, kind of. But Kittridge and the other man, Pastor Don, said it didn't matter, as long as they kept heading east. That's all you got to do, Danny, Kittridge said. Just keep us headed east.

He thought of what he'd seen on the highway. That was really something. He'd seen a lot of bodies in the last couple of days, but nothing as bad as that. He liked Kittridge, who sort of reminded him of Mr. Purvis. Not that he *looked* like Mr. Purvis, because he didn't at all. It was the way the man spoke to Danny—as if he mattered.

While he drove, he thought about Momma, and Mr. Purvis, and Thomas and Percy and James and how useful he was being. How proud of him Momma and Mr. Purvis would be now.

The sun was peeking over the horizon, making Danny squint into its brightness. Before long, everyone would be awake. Kittridge leaned over his shoulder.

"How we doing on gas?"

Danny checked. They were down to a quarter tank.

"Let's pull over and refill from the cans," Kittridge said. "Let folks stretch their legs a bit."

They pulled off the road, into a state park. Kittridge and Pastor Don checked the bathrooms and gave the all clear.

"Thirty minutes, everyone," Kittridge said.

They had more supplies now, boxes of crackers and peanut butter and apples and energy bars and bottles of pop and juice and diapers and formula for Boy Jr. Kittridge had even gotten Danny a box of Lucky Charms, though all the milk in the grocery store's cooler had spoiled; he'd have to eat it dry. Danny, Kittridge, and Pastor Don unloaded the jugs of diesel from the back of the bus and began to pour it into the tank. Danny had told them that the bus had a fifty-gallon capacity, precisely; each full tank would get them about three hundred miles.

"You're a very precise guy," Kittridge had said.

When they'd finished refueling, Danny took the box of Lucky Charms and a can of lukewarm Dr Pepper and sat under a tree. The rest were seated around a picnic table, including Jamal. He wasn't saying much, but Danny had the feeling that everyone had decided to let bygones be bygones. Linda Robinson was diapering Boy Jr., cooing to him, making him wiggle his arms and legs. Danny had never been around babies much. He'd been led to understand that they cried a lot, but so far Boy Jr. had kept quiet as a mouse. There were good babies and there were bad babies, Momma had said, so Boy Jr. must be one of the good ones. Danny tried to remember being a baby himself, just to see if he could do it, but his mind wouldn't go back that far, not in any orderly way. It was strange how there was this whole part of your life you couldn't recall, except in little pictures: sunshine flaring on a windowpane, or a dead frog squashed in the driveway by a tire tread, or a slice of apple on a plate. He wondered if he'd been a good baby, like Boy Jr.

Danny was watching the group, feeding fistfuls of Lucky Charms into his mouth and swilling them down with the Dr Pepper, when Tim rose from the table and walked over to him.

"Hey, Timbo. How you doing?"

The boy's hair was standing all whichaway from his sleeping on the bus. "Okay, I guess." He gave a loose-boned shrug. "Mind if I sit with you?"

Danny scooched over to make room.

"I'm sorry the other kids tease you sometimes," Tim said after a minute.

"That's okay," said Danny. "I don't mind."

"Billy Nice is a real dickhead."

"He picks on you, too?"

"Sometimes." The boy frowned vaguely. "He picks on everybody."

"Just ignore him," Danny said. "That's what I do."

After a minute, Tim said, "You really like Thomas, huh?"

"Sure."

"I used to watch him. I had, like, this huge layout of Thomas trains in my basement. The coal loader, the engine wash, I had all that stuff."

"I'd like to see that," said Danny. "I bet that was great."

A brief silence followed. The sun was warm on Danny's face.

"You want to know what I saw in the stadium?" Tim asked.

"If you want."

"Like, a thousand million dead people."

Danny wasn't sure what to say. He guessed Tim had needed to tell someone; it wasn't the kind of thing you should keep bottled up inside.

"It was pretty gross."

"Did you tell April?"

Tim shook his head.

"You want to keep it a secret?"

"Would that be okay?"

"Sure," said Danny. "I can keep a secret."

Tim had scooped up a little bit of dirt from the base of the tree and was watching it sift through his fingers. "You don't get scared much, do you, Danny?"

"Sometimes I do."

"But not now," the boy stated.

Danny had to think about that. He supposed he should be, but he just wasn't. What he felt was more like *interested*. What would happen next? Where would they go? It surprised him, how adaptable he was being. Dr. Francis would be proud of him.

"No, I guess I'm not."

In the shade of the picnic area, everyone was packing up. Danny wished he could find the words to make the boy feel better, to wipe the memory of what he'd seen in the stadium from his mind. They were walking back to the bus when the idea came to him.

"Hey, I've got something for you." He reached into his pack and removed his lucky penny and showed the boy. "You hold on to that, I promise, nothing bad can happen to you."

Tim took the coin in his palm. "What happened to it? It's all squished."

"It got run over by a train. That's what makes it lucky."

"Where'd you get it?"

"I don't know, I've just always had it." Danny dipped his head toward the boy's open hand. "Go ahead, you can keep it."

A moment's hesitation, then Tim slipped the flattened penny into the pocket of his shorts. It wasn't much, Danny knew, but it was something, and there were times like these when just a little thing could help. As a for-instance: Momma's Popov, which she visited when her nerves got bad, and the visits from Mr. Purvis on the nights when Danny could hear them laughing. The roar of the Redbird's big caterpillar diesel coming to life when he turned the key each morning. Driving over the bump on Lindler Avenue, and all the kids hooting as they shot from the benches. Little things like that. Danny felt pleased with himself for thinking of this, like he'd passed along something he knew that maybe not everybody did, and as the two of them stood together in the morning sunshine, he detected, from the corner of his eye, a change in the boy's face, a kind of lightening; he might have even smiled.

"Thanks, Danny," he said.

Omaha was burning.

They saw it first as a throbbing glow over the horizon. It was the hour when the light had flattened. They were approaching the city from the southwest, on Interstate 80. Not a single car was on the highway; all the buildings were dark. A deeper, more profound abandonment than anything they'd seen so far—this was, or should have been, a city of nearly half a million. A strong odor of smoke began to flow through the bus's ventilation. Kittridge told Danny to stop.

"We have to get over the river somehow," Pastor Don said. "Go south or north, look for a way across."

Kittridge looked up from the map. "Danny, how are we doing for gas?"

They were down to an eighth of a tank; the jugs were empty. Fifty more miles at the most. They'd hoped to find more fuel in Omaha.

"One thing's for sure," said Kittridge, "we can't stay here."

They turned north. The next crossing was at the town of Adair. But the bridge was gone, blasted away, no part left standing. Only the river, wide and dark, ceaselessly flowing. The next opportunity would be Decatur, another thirty miles to the north.

"We passed an elementary school a mile back," said Pastor Don. "It's better than nothing. We can look for fuel in the morning."

A silence descended over the bus, everyone waiting for Kittridge's answer.

"Okay, let's do it."

They backtracked into the heart of the little town. All the lights were out, the streets empty. They came to the school, a modern-looking structure set back from the road at the edge of the fields. A marquee-style sign at the edge of the parking area read, in bold letters: GO LIONS! HAVE A GREAT SUMMER!

"Everybody wait here," Kittridge said.

He moved inside. A few minutes passed; then he emerged. He exchanged a quick look with Pastor Don, the two men nodding.

"We're going to shelter here for the night," Kittridge announced. "Stay together, no wandering off. The power's out, but there's running water, and food in the cafeteria. If you need to use the facilities, go in pairs.".

In the front foyer they were met by the telltale scents of an elementary school, of sweat and dirty socks, art supplies and waxed linoleum. A trophy case stood by a door that led, presumably, to the main office; a display of collages was hung on the painted cinder-block walls, images of people and animals fashioned from newspaper and magazine clippings. Beside each of them was a printed label bearing the age and grade of its creator. Wendy Mueller, Grade 2. Gavin Jackson, Grade 5. Florence Ratcliffe, Pre-K 4.

"April, go with Wood and Don to find some mats to sleep on. The kindergarten rooms should have some."

In the pantry behind the cafeteria they found cans of beans and fruit cocktail, as well as bread and jam to make sandwiches. There was no gas to cook with, so they served the beans cold, dishing everything out on metal cafeteria trays. By now it was dark outside; Kittridge distributed flashlights. They spoke only in whispers, the consensus being that the virals might hear them.

By nine o'clock, everyone was bedded down. Kittridge left Don to keep watch on the first floor and climbed the stairs, carrying a lantern. Many of the doors were locked but not all; he selected the science lab, a large, open space with counters and glass cabinets full of beakers and other supplies. The air smelled faintly of butane. On the whiteboard at the front of the room were written the words "Final review, chaps. 8–12. Labs due Wednesday."

Kittridge stripped off his shirt and wiped himself down at the washbasin in the corner, then took a chair and removed his boots. The prosthesis, which began just below his left knee, was constructed of a titanium alloy frame covered in silicone; a microprocessor-controlled hydraulic cylinder, powered by a tiny hydrogen cell, adjusted fifty times per second to calculate the correct angular velocity of the ankle joint, imitating a natural gait. It was the very latest in prosthetic limb replacements; Kittridge didn't doubt it had cost the Army a bundle. He rolled up his trousers, peeled off the mounting sock, and washed his stump with soap from the dispenser by the basin. Though heavily callused, the skin at the contact point felt raw and tender after two days without care. He dried the stump thoroughly, allowed it a few minutes of fresh air, then fixed the prosthesis back in place and drew down his pant leg.

He was startled by a sound of movement behind him. He turned to find April standing in the open doorway.

"Sorry, I didn't mean—"

He quickly drew on his shirt and rose to his feet. How much had she seen? But the light was dim, and he'd been partially concealed by one of the counters.

"It's no problem. I was just getting cleaned up a little."

"I couldn't sleep."

"That's okay," he said. "You can come in if you want."

She advanced uncertainly into the room. Kittridge moved to the window with the AK. He took a moment to quickly scan the street below.

"How's everything outside?" She was standing beside him.

"Quiet so far. How's Tim doing?"

"Out like a light. He's tougher than he looks. Tougher than I am, anyway."

"I doubt that. You seem pretty cool to me, considering."

April frowned. "You shouldn't. This calm exterior is what you'd call an act. To tell you the truth, I'm so scared I don't really feel anything anymore."

A wide shelf ran the length of the room beneath the windows. April hoisted herself onto it, bracing her back against the frame and pulling her knees to her chest. Kittridge did the same. They were face-to-face now. A stillness, expectant but not uncomfortable, hovered between them. She was young, yet he sensed a core of resilience in her. It was the kind of thing you either had or you didn't.

"So, do you have a boyfriend?"

"Are you auditioning?"

Kittridge laughed, felt his face grow warm. "Just making talk, I guess. Are you like this with everybody?"

"Only the people I like."

Another moment passed.

"So how'd you get the name April?" It was all he could think to say. "Is that your birthday?"

"It's from 'The Waste Land.'" When Kittridge said nothing, she raised her eyebrows dubiously. "It's a poem? T. S. Eliot?"

Kittridge had heard the name, but that was all. "Can't say I got to that one. How's it go?"

She let her gaze flow past him. When she began to speak, her voice was full of a rich feeling Kittridge couldn't identify, happy and sad and full of memory. "'April is the cruellest month, breeding/Lilacs out of the dead land, mixing/Memory and desire, stirring/Dull roots with spring rain . . .

"Winter kept us warm, covering
Earth in forgetful snow, feeding
A little life with dried tubers.
Summer surprised us, coming over the Starnbergersee
With a shower of rain . . ."

"Wow," said Kittridge. She was looking at him again. Her eyes, he noted, were the color of moss, with what looked like flecks of shaved gold floating atop the surface of her irises. "That's really something."

April shrugged. "It goes on from there. Basically, the guy was totally depressed." She was tugging a frayed spot on one knee of her jeans. "The name was my mother's idea. She was an English professor before she met my stepdad and we got all, like, rich and everything."

"Your parents are divorced?"

"My father died when I was six."

"I'm sorry, I shouldn't have—"

But she didn't let him finish. "Don't be. He wasn't what you would call an admirable sort. A leftover from my mother's bad-boy period. He was totally loaded, drove his car into a bridge abutment. And that, said Pooh, was that."

She stated these facts without inflection; she might have been telling him what the weather was. Outside, the summer night was veiled in blackness. Kittridge had obviously misjudged her, but he had learned that was the way with most people. The story was never the story, and it surprised you, how much another person could carry.

"I saw you, you know," April said. "Your leg. The scars on your back. You were in the war, weren't you?"

"What makes you think that?"

She made a face of disbelief. "Gosh, I don't know, just everything? Because you're the only one who seems to know what to do? Because you're all, like, super-competent with guns and shit?"

"I told you. I'm a salesman. Camping gear."

"I don't believe that for a second."

Her directness was so disarming that for a moment Kitteridge said nothing. But she had him dead to rights. "You're sure you want to hear it? It isn't very nice."

"If you want to tell me."

He instinctively turned his face to the window. "Well, you're right, I was. Enlisted straight out of high school. Not Army, Marines. I ended up as a staff sergeant in the MPs. You know what that is?"

"You were a cop?"

"Sort of. Mostly we provided security at American installations, air-bases, sensitive infrastructure, that kind of thing. They moved us around a lot. Iran, Iraq, Saudi. Chechnya for a little while. My last duty was at Bagram Airfield, in Afghanistan. Usually it was pretty routine, verifying equipment manifests and checking foreign workers in and out. But once in a while something would happen. The coup hadn't happened yet, so it was still American-controlled territory, but there were Taliban all over the place, plus Al Qaeda and about twenty different local warlords duking it out."

He paused, collecting himself. The next part was always the hardest. "So one day we see this car, the usual beat-up piece of junk, coming down the road. The checkpoints are all well marked, everybody knows to stop, but the guy doesn't. He's barreling straight for us. Two people in the car that we can see, a man and a woman. Everybody opens fire. The car swerves away, rolls a couple of times, comes to rest on its wheels. We're thinking it's going to blow for sure, but it doesn't. I'm the senior NCO, so I'm the one who goes to look. The woman's dead, but the man is still alive. He's slumped over the steering wheel, blood all over. In the backseat is a kid, a boy. He couldn't have been older than four. They've got him strapped into a seat packed with explosives. I see the wires running to the front of the vehicle, where the dad is holding the detonator. He's muttering to himself. *Anta al-mas'ul,* he's saying. *Anta al-mas'ul.* The kid's wailing, reaching out for me. This little hand. I'll never forget it. He's only four, but it's like he knows what's about to happen."

"Jesus." April's face was horrified. "What did you do?"

"The only thing I could think of. I got the hell out of there. I don't really remember the blast. I woke up in the hospital in Saudi. Two men in my unit were killed, another took a piece of shrapnel in the spine." April was staring at him. "I told you it wasn't very nice."

"He blew up his own *kid*?"

"That's about the size of it, yeah."

"But what kind of people would do that?"

"You've got me there. I never could figure that out."

April said nothing more; Kittridge wondered, as he always did, if he'd told too much. But it felt good to unburden himself, and if April had gotten more than she'd bargained for, she had a way of hiding it. In the abstract, Kittridge knew, the story was inconsequential, one of hundreds, even thousands like it. Such pointless cruelty was simply the way of the world. But understanding this fact was a far cry from accepting it, when you'd lived it yourself.

"So what happened then?" April asked.

Kittridge shrugged. "Nothing. End of story. Off to dance with the virgins in eternity."

"I was talking about you." Her eyes did not move from his face. "I think I'd be pretty screwed up by something like that."

Here was something new, he thought—the part of the tale that no one ever asked about. Typically, once the basic facts were laid bare, the listener couldn't get away fast enough. But not this girl, this April.

"Well, I wasn't. At least I didn't think I was. I spent about half a year in the VA, learning to walk and dress and feed myself, and then they kicked me loose. War's over, my friend, at least for you. I wasn't all bitter, like a lot of guys get. I didn't dive under the bed when a car backfired or anything like that. What's done is done, I figured. Then about six months after I got settled, I took a trip back home to Wyoming. My parents were gone, my sister had moved up to British Columbia with her husband and basically dropped off the map, but I still knew some people, kids I'd gone to school with, though nobody was a kid anymore. One of them wants to throw a party for me, the big welcome-home thing. They all had families of their own by now, kids and wives and jobs, but this was a pretty hard-drinking crowd back in the day. The whole thing was just an excuse to get lit, but I didn't see the harm. Sure, I said, knock yourself out, and he actually did. There were at least a hundred people there, a big banner with my name on it hung over the porch, even a band. The whole thing knocked me flat. I'm in the backyard listening to the music and the friend says to me, Come on, there are some women who want to meet you. Don't be standing there like a big idiot. So he takes me inside and there are three of them, all nice enough. I knew one of them a little from way back when. They're talking away, some show on TV, gossip, the usual things. Normal, everyday things. I'm nursing a beer and listening to them when all of a sudden I realize I have no idea what they're saying. Not the words themselves. What any of it *meant*. None of it seemed connected to anything else, like there were two worlds, an inside world and an outside world, and neither had anything to do with the other. I'm sure a shrink would have a name for it. All I know is, I woke up on the floor, everybody standing over me. After that, it took me about four months in the woods just to be around people again." He paused, a little surprised at himself. "To tell you the truth, I've never told anybody that part. You would be the first."

"Sounds like a day in high school."

Kittridge had to laugh. "Touché."

Their gazes met and held. How strange it was, he thought. One minute you were all alone with your thoughts, the next somebody came along who seemed to know the deepest part of you, who could open you like a book. He couldn't have said how long they'd been looking at each other. It seemed to go on and on and on, neither possessing the will, or the courage, or even the desire, to look away. How old was she? Seventeen? And yet she didn't seem seventeen. She didn't seem like any age at all. An old soul: Kittridge had heard the term but never quite understood what it meant. That's what April had. An old soul.

To seal the deal between them, Kittridge removed one of the Glocks from his shoulder holster and held it out to her. "Know how to use one of these?"

April looked at it uncertainly. "Let me guess. It's not like it is on TV."

Kittridge dropped the magazine and racked the slide to eject the cartridge from the pipe. He placed the gun it in her hand, wrapping her fingers with his own.

"Don't pull the trigger with your knuckle, the shot will go low. Just use the pad of your fingertip and squeeze, like so." He released her hand and tapped his breastbone. "One shot, through here. That's all it takes, but you can't miss. Don't rush—aim and fire." He reloaded the gun and handed it back. "Go on, you can have it. Keep a round chambered, like I showed you."

She smiled wryly. "Gee, thanks. And here I don't have anything for you."

Kitteridge returned the smile. "Maybe next time."

A moment passed. April was turning the weapon around in her hand, examining it as if it were some unaccountable artifact. "What the father said. *Anta*-something."

"*Anta al-mas'ul.*"

"Did you ever figure out what it meant?"

Kittridge nodded. "'You did this.'"

Another silence fell, though different from the others. Not a barrier between them but a shared awareness of their lives, like the walls of a room in which only the two of them existed. How strange, thought Kittridge, to say those words. *Anta al-mas'ul. Anta al-mas'ul.*

"It was the right thing, you know," April said. "You would have been killed, too."

"There's always a choice," Kittridge said.

"What else could you have done?"

The question was rhetorical, he understood; she expected no reply. *What else could you have done?* But Kittridge knew his answer. He'd always known.

"I could have held his hand."

*　　*　　*

He kept his vigil at the window through the night. Sleeplessness was not a problem for him; he had learned to get by on just a few winks. April lay curled on the floor beneath the window. Kittridge had removed his jacket and placed it over her. There were no lights anywhere. The view from the window was of a world at peace, the sky pinpricked with stars. As the first glow of daylight gathered on the horizon, he let himself close his eyes.

He startled awake to the sound of approaching engines. An Army convoy was coming down the street, twenty vehicles long. He unsnapped his second pistol and passed it to April, who was sitting up now as well, rubbing her eyes.

"Hold this."

Kittridge quickly made his way down the stairs. By the time he burst through the door, the convoy was less than a hundred feet away. He jogged into the street, waving his arms.

"Stop!"

The lead Humvee jerked to a halt just a few yards in front of him, the soldier on the roof tracking his movements with the fifty-cal. The lower half of his face was hidden by a white surgical mask. "Hold it right there."

Kittridge's arms were raised. "I'm unarmed."

The soldier pulled the bolt on his weapon. "I said, keep your distance."

A tense five seconds followed; it seemed possible that he was about to be shot. Then the passenger door of the Humvee swung open. A sturdy-looking woman emerged and walked toward him. Up close her face appeared worn and lined, crackled with dust. An officer, but not one who rode a desk.

"Major Porcheki, Ninth Combat Support Battalion, Iowa National Guard. Who the hell are you?"

He had only one card to play. "Staff Sergeant Bernard Kittridge. Charlie Company, First MP Battalion, USMC."

Her eyes narrowed on his face. "You're a Marine?"

"Medically discharged, ma'am."

The major glanced past him, toward the schoolhouse. Kittridge knew without looking that the others were watching from the windows.

"How many civilians do you have inside?"

"Eleven. The bus is almost out of gas."

"Any sick or wounded?"

"Everybody's worn out and scared, but that's it."

She considered this with a neutral expression. Then: "Caldwell! Valdez!"

A pair of E-4s trotted forward. They, too, were wearing surgical masks. Everyone was except Porcheki.

"Let's get the refueler to see about filling up that bus."

"We're taking civilians? Can we do that now?"

"Did I ask your opinion, Specialist? And get a corpsman up here."

"Yes, ma'am. Sorry, ma'am."

They jogged away.

"Thank you, Major. It was going to be a long walk out of here."

Porcheki had removed a canteen from her belt and paused to drink. "You're just lucky you found us when you did. Fuel's getting pretty scarce. We're headed back to the guard armory at Fort Powell, so that's as far as we can take you. FEMA's set up a refugee-processing center there. From there you'll probably be evaced to Chicago or St. Louis."

"If you don't mind my asking, do you have any news?"

"I don't mind, but I'm not sure what to tell you. One minute these goddamned things are everywhere, the next nobody can find them. They like the trees, but any sort of cover will do. The word from CENTCOM is that a large pod's massing along the Kansas-Nebraska border."

"What's a pod?"

She took another gulp from the canteen. "That's what they're calling groups of them, pods."

The corpsman appeared; everyone was filing out of the school. Kittridge told them what was happening while the soldiers established a perimeter. The corpsman examined the civilians, taking their temperatures, peering inside their mouths. When everyone was ready to go, Porcheki met Kittridge at the steps of the bus.

"Just one thing. You might want to keep the fact that you're from Denver under your hat. Say you're from Iowa, if anyone asks."

He thought of the highway, the lines of torn-up cars. "I'll pass that along."

Kittridge climbed aboard. Balancing his rifle between his knees, he took a place directly behind Danny.

"God *damn*," Jamal said, grinning ear to ear. "An Army convoy. I take back everything I said about you, Kittridge." He poked a thumb toward Mrs. Bellamy, who was dabbing her brow with a tissue taken from her sleeve. "Hell, I don't even mind that old broad taking a shot at me."

"Sticks and stones, young man," she responded. "Sticks and stones."

He turned to face her across the aisle. "I've been meaning to ask you.

What is it with old ladies and the snot-rag-in-the-sleeve thing? Doesn't that strike you as just a little unsanitary?"

"This from a young man with enough ink in his arms to fill a ditto machine."

"A ditto machine. What century are you from?"

"When I look at you, I think of one word. The word is 'hepatitis.'"

"Christ, the two of you," Wood moaned. "You really need to get a room."

The convoy began to move.

14

The plan was in motion. His team was assembled, the jet would meet them at dawn. Guilder had been in touch with his contact at Blackbird; everything had been arranged. The server and the hard drives at the warehouse had all been wiped. Go home, he'd told the staff. Go home and be with your families.

It was after midnight when he drove to his townhouse through quiet, rain-slickened streets. On the radio, a continuous stream of bad news: chaos on the highways, the Army regrouping, rumblings abroad. From the White House, words of calm assurance, the crisis was in hand, the best minds were at work, but nobody was fooling anybody. A nationwide declaration of martial law was sure to come within hours. CNN was reporting that NATO warships were churning toward the coasts. The door would slam on the North American continent. The world might despise us, Guilder thought; what will it do when we're gone?

As he drove, he kept a watchful eye on the rearview. He wasn't being paranoid; it was just how things tended to unfold. A roar of tires, a van pulling in front of him, men in dark suits emerging. *Horace Guilder? Come with us.* Amazing, he thought, that it hadn't happened already.

He pulled into the garage and sealed the door behind him. In his bedroom, he packed a small bag of essentials—a couple of days' worth of clothes, toiletries, his meds—and carried it downstairs. He fetched his laptop from the study and placed it in the microwave, sizzling its circuitry in a cloud of sparks. His handheld was already gone, tossed from the window of the Camry.

In the living room he doused the lights and peeled back the drapes. Across the street, a neighbor was loading suitcases into the open hatch of his SUV. The man's wife was standing in the doorway of their townhouse, clutching a sleeping toddler. What were their names? Guilder either had never known or couldn't remember. He'd seen the woman from time to time, pushing the little girl in a brightly colored plastic car up and down the driveway. Watching the three of them, Guilder was touched by a memory of Shawna—not that last, terrible encounter but the two of them lying together in the aftermath of lovemaking, and her quiet, whispering voice, tickling his chest. *Are you happy with the things I do? I want to be your only one.* Words that weren't anything more than playacting, a bit of cheap theatrics to crown a dutiful hour. How stupid he'd been.

The man accepted the child from his wife's arms and gently lowered her into the backseat. The two of them got in the car. Guilder imagined the things they'd be saying to each other. *We'll be all right. They have people working on it right now. We'll just stay at your mother's a week or two, until this all blows over.* He heard the engine turn over; they backed from the drive. Guilder watched their taillights vanish down the block. Good luck, he thought.

He waited five more minutes. The streets were silent, all the houses dark. When he was satisfied he wasn't being watched, he carried his bag to the Camry.

It was after two A.M. when he got to Shadowdale. The parking area was empty; only a single light burned by the entrance. He stepped through the door to find the front desk unmanned. An empty wheelchair sat beside it, a second in the hall. There were no sounds anywhere. Probably there were security cameras watching him, but who would examine the tapes?

His father was lying on his bed in darkness. The room smelled awful; nobody had been in for hours, perhaps as long as a day. On the tray by his father's bed, somebody had left a dozen jars of Gerber's baby food and a pitcher of water. A spilled cup told him his father had attempted the water, but the food was untouched; his father couldn't have opened the jars if he'd tried.

Guilder didn't have long, but it was not an occasion to rush. His father's eyes were closed, the voice—that hectoring voice—silenced. Better that way, he thought. The time for talk was over. He searched his memory for something nice about his father, however meager. The best he could come up with was a time when his father had taken him to a park when Guilder was small. The recollection was vague and impressionistic—it was possible it had never happened at all—but that was all he had. A winter day, Guilder's breath clouding before his face, and a view of bare trees bobbing up and down as his father had pushed him on a swing, the man's big hand at the center of his back, catching him and launching him into space. Guilder recalled nothing else about that day. He might have been as young as five.

When he slid the pillow from beneath his father's head, the man's eyes fluttered but didn't open. Here was the precipice, Guilder thought, the mortal moment; the deed, that, once done, could never be undone. He thought of the word *patricide.* From the Latin *pater,* father, and *caedere,* to cut down. He had lacked the courage to kill himself, yet as he placed the pillow over his father's face, he experienced no hesitation. Gripping the pillow by the edges, he increased the pressure until he was certain no air could reach his father's nose or mouth. A minute crept by, Guilder counting out the seconds under his breath. His father's hand, lying on the blanket, gave a restive twitch. How long would it take? How would he know when it was over? If the pillow didn't work, what then? He watched his father's hand for additional movement, but there was none. Gradually it came to him that the stillness of the body beneath his hands meant only one thing. His father wasn't breathing anymore.

He drew the pillow away. His father's face was just the same; it was as if his passage into death represented only the subtlest alteration in his condition. Guilder gently placed his palm beneath his father's head and moved the pillow back into place. He wasn't trying to hide his crime—he doubted anybody would be around to examine the situation—but he wanted his father to have a pillow to lie on, especially since, as now seemed likely, he would be lying there for a very long time. Guilder had expected a rush of emotion to overcome him at this moment, all the pain and regret unloosed inside him. His awful childhood. His mother's lonely life. His own barren and loveless existence, with only a hired woman for company. But all he felt was relieved. The truest test of his life, and he had passed it.

Outside, the hallway was quiet, unchanged. Who could say what degradations lay behind the other doors, how many families would be facing the same cruel decision? Guilder glanced at his watch: ten minutes had passed since he'd entered the building. Just ten minutes, but everything was different now. He was different, the world was different. His father was nowhere in it. And with that, tears came to his eyes.

He strode briskly down the hallway, moving past the empty common room and the vacant nurse's station and farther still, into the early morning.

15

It was late on the second day, approaching the Missouri border, that Grey saw an obstruction ahead. They were in the middle of nowhere, miles from any town. He brought the car to a halt.

Lila looked up from the magazine she was reading: *Today's Parenting*. Grey had gotten it for her at a mini-mart in Ledeau, with a pile of others. *Family Life, Baby and Child, Modern Toddler*. In the last day, her attitude toward him had shifted somewhat. Perhaps it was the mental effort of maintaining the fiction that their journey was nothing out of the ordinary, but she was becoming increasingly impatient with him, speaking to him as if he were an uncooperative husband.

"Will you look at that." She dropped the magazine to her lap. On the cover was the image of a ruddy-cheeked girl in a pink jumper. WHEN PLAY DATES GO BAD, the caption read. "What *is* that?"

"I think it's a tank."

"What's it doing there?"

"Maybe it's lost or something."

"I don't think they just *lose* tanks, Lawrence. Like, excuse me, have you seen my tank anyplace? I know it was around here somewhere." She sighed heavily. "Who just parks a tank in the road like that? They'll have to move it."

"So you're saying you want me to ask them," Grey stated.

"Yes, Lawrence. That's exactly what I'm saying."

He didn't want to, but to say no seemed impossible. He exited the car into the falling dusk. "Hello?" he called. He glanced back at Lila, who was watching him with her head angled through the open passenger window. "I think it's empty."

"Maybe they just can't hear you."

"Let's just turn around. We can find another road."

"It's the principle of the thing. They can't just block the road like that. Try the hatch. I'm sure there has to be somebody inside."

Grey doubted this, but he didn't want to argue. He clambered up on the exposed treads and hoisted himself to the top of the turret. He positioned his face above the hatch, but it was too dark to see anything down there. Lila had exited the Volvo and was standing at the base of the tank, holding a flashlight.

"I'm not sure this is such a good idea," Grey said.

"It's just a tank, Lawrence. Honestly. Sometimes you men are all the same, you know that?"

She passed him the flashlight. There was nothing to do now but look inside. Grey pointed the beam through the hatch.

Jesus fuck.

"So? What's down there?"

Grey guessed there had probably been two of them. It wasn't the easiest thing to sort out, visually. It looked like somebody had dropped a grenade, that's how torn up the soldiers were. But it wasn't a grenade.

Do you see, Grey?

He startled, as if hit by a jolt of current. The voice. Not like the one in the garage; the voice was in his head. The voice of Zero. Lila was staring at him from the base of the tank. He tried to say something, to warn her, but no words would leave his mouth.

Are you . . . hungry, Grey?

He was. Not just hungry: famished. The sensation seemed to take hold of every part of him, each cell and molecule, the tiniest atoms whirring inside him. Never in his life had he felt a hunger so profound.

It is my gift to you. The gift of blood.

"Lawrence, what's the matter?"

He swallowed. "I'll be . . . just a sec."

Down the hole he went. He had dropped his flashlight, but that didn't matter; the tank's dark interior was bright to his eyes, each surface glowing with its beautiful coating of blood. A titanic need seized him, and he pushed his face against the cold metal to drag his tongue along it.

"Lawrence! What are you doing in there?"

He was on his hands and knees now, licking the floor, burying his face in the syrupy remains. So wonderful! As if he hadn't eaten for a year, a decade, a century, only to be presented with the richest banquet in the history of the world! All the joys of the body rolled into one, a trance of purest pleasure!

The spell was broken by a violent boom. His fingers were in his mouth; his face was covered in blood. What the hell was he doing? And what was that sound, like thunder?

"Lawrence! Come quick!"

Another boom, louder than the first. He scrambled up the ladder. Something was wrong with the sky; everything seemed lit by a fiery glow.

Lila took one look at his bloody face and began to scream.

A pair of jets roared low overhead, splitting the air with their velocity; a violent white sheen lit the sky, and Grey was slapped by a wall of heated air that knocked him off the roof of the tank. He landed hard, the wind sailing out of him. More planes shot past, the sky to the east flashing with light.

Lila was backing away from him, her hands held protectively before her face. "Get away from me!"

There was no time to explain, and what would he have said? It was clear what was happening now, they had wandered into the war. Grey grabbed her by the arm and began to drag her to the car. She was kicking, screaming, thrashing in his grip. Somehow he managed to open the passenger door and shove her in, but then he realized his mistake: the instant he closed the door, Lila hit the locks.

He pounded on the glass. "Lila, let me in!"

"Get away, get away!"

He needed something heavy. He scanned the ground near the car but found nothing. In another moment Lila would realize what she had to do; she would take the wheel and drive away.

He couldn't let that happen.

Grey reared back, squeezing his hand into a fist, and sent it plunging into the driver's window. He expected to be met by a wall of pain, all the bones of his hand shattering, but that didn't happen; his hand passed through the glass as if it was made of tissue, detonating the window in a cascade of glinting shards. Before Lila could react, he opened the door and wedged himself into the driver's seat and jammed the car into reverse. He spun into a 180, shifted into drive, and hit the gas. But the moment of escape had passed; suddenly they were in the midst of everything. As more planes rocketed past, a wall of fire rose before them; Grey swung the wheel to the right, and in the next instant they were barreling through the corn rows, the tires spinning wildly in the soft earth, heavy green leaves slapping the windshield. They burst from the field and, too late, Grey saw the culvert. The Volvo rocketed down, then up, the car going aloft before crashing onto its wheels again. Lila was screaming, screaming-screaming-screaming, and that was when Grey found it: a road. He yanked the wheel and shoved the accelerator to the floor. They were racing parallel with the culvert; the sun had dipped below the horizon, sinking the fields into an inky blackness while the sky exploded with fire.

But not just fire: suddenly the car was washed with a brilliant light.

"Stop your vehicle."

The windshield filled with an immense dark shape, like a great black bird alighting. Grey jammed his foot on the brake, pitching both of them forward. As the helicopter touched down on the roadway, Grey heard a tinkle of breaking glass and something dropped into his lap: a canister the size and weight of a soup can, making a hissing sound.

"Lila, run!"

He threw the door open, but the gas was already inside him, in his head and heart and lungs; he made it all of ten feet before he succumbed, the ground rising like a gathering wave to meet him. Time seemed undone; the world had gone all watery and far away. A great wind was pushing over his face. At the edge of his vision he saw the space-suited men lumbering toward him. Two more were dragging Lila toward the helicopter. She was suspended face-down, her body limp, her feet skimming the ground. "Don't hurt her!" Grey said. "Please don't hurt the baby!" But these words seemed not to matter. The figures were above him now, their faces obscured, floating bodiless over the earth, like ghosts. The stars were coming out.

Ghosts, Grey thought. *I really must be dead this time.* And he felt their hands upon him.

16

They drove through the day; by the time the convoy halted, it was late afternoon. Porcheki emerged from the lead Humvee and strode back to the bus.

"This is where we leave you. The sentries at the gate will tell you what to do."

They were in some kind of staging area: trucks of supplies, military portables, refuelers, even artillery. Kittridge guessed he was looking at a force at least the size of two battalions. Adjacent to this was a gated compound of canvas tents, ringed by portable fencing topped with concertina wire.

"Where are you off to?" Kittridge asked. He wondered where the fight was now.

Porcheki shrugged. *Wherever they tell me to go.* "Best of luck to you, Sergeant. Just remember what I said."

The convoy drew away. "Pull ahead, Danny," Kittridge said. "Slowly."

Two masked soldiers with M16s were positioned at the gate. A large sign affixed to the wire read: FEDERAL EMERGENCY MANAGEMENT AGENCY REFUGEE PROCESSING CENTER. NO REENTRY. NO FIREARMS PAST THIS POINT.

Twenty feet from the entrance, the soldiers motioned for them to halt. One of the sentries stepped to the driver's window. A kid, not a day over twenty, with a spray of acne on his cheeks.

"How many?"

"Twelve," Kittridge answered.

"City of origin?"

The tags had long since been stripped from the bus. "Des Moines."

The soldier stepped back, mumbling into the radio clipped to his shoulder. The second was still standing at the sealed gate with his weapon pointing skyward.

"Okay, kill the engine and stay where you are."

Moments later the soldier returned with a canvas duffel bag, which he held up to the window. "Put any weapons and cell phones in here and pass it to the front."

The ban on weapons Kittridge understood, but cell phones? None of them had gotten a signal in days.

"This many people, the local network would crash if people tried to use them. Sorry, those are the rules."

This explanation struck Kittridge as thin, but there was nothing to be done. He received the bag and moved up and down the center aisle. When he came to Mrs. Bellamy, the woman yanked her purse protectively to her waist.

"Young man, I don't even go to the beauty parlor without it."

Kittridge did his best to smile. "And right you are. But we're safe here. You have my word."

With visible reluctance she withdrew the enormous revolver from her purse and deposited it with the rest. Kittridge toted the bag to the front of the bus and left it at the base of the stairs; the first soldier reached inside and whisked it away. They were ordered to disembark with the rest of their gear and stand clear of the bus while one of the soldiers searched their luggage. Beyond the gate Kittridge could see a large, open shed where people had gathered. More soldiers were moving up and down the fence line.

"Okay," the sentry said, "you're good to go. Report to the processing area, they'll billet you."

"What about the bus?" Kittridge asked.

"All fuel and vehicles are being commandeered by the United States military. Once you're in, you're in."

Kittridge saw the stricken look on Danny's face. One of the soldiers was boarding the bus to drive it away.

"What's with him?" the sentry asked.

Kittridge turned to Danny. "It's okay, they'll take good care of it."

He could see the struggle in the man's eyes. Then Danny nodded.

"They better," he said.

The space was packed with people waiting in lines before a long table. Families with children, old people, couples, even a blind man with a dog. A young woman in a Red Cross T-shirt, her auburn hair pulled back from her face, was moving up and down the lines with a handheld.

"Any unaccompanied minors?" Like Porcheki, she'd given up on the mask. Her eyes were harried, drained by sleeplessness. She looked at April and Tim. "What about you two?"

"He's my brother," April said. "I'm eighteen."

The woman looked doubtful but said nothing.

"We'd like to all stay together," said Kittridge.

The woman was jotting on her handheld. "I'm not supposed to do this."

"What's your name?" Always good, Kittridge thought, to get a name.

"Vera."

"The patrol that brought us in said we'd be evacuated to Chicago or St. Louis."

A strip of paper slid from the handheld's port. Vera tore it off and passed it to Kittridge. "We're still waiting on buses. It shouldn't be long now. Show this to the worker at the desk."

They were assigned a tent and given plastic disks that would serve as ration coupons, then moved into the noise and smells of the camp: wood smoke, chemical toilets, the human odors of a crowd. The ground was muddy and littered with trash; people were cooking on camp stoves, hanging their laundry on tent lines, waiting at a pump to fill buckets with water, stretched out in lawn chairs like spectators at a tailgate party, a look of dazed exhaustion on their faces. All the garbage cans were overflowing, clouds of flies hovering. A cruel sun was beating down. Apart from the Army trucks, Kittridge saw no vehicles; all the refugees appeared to have come in on foot, their gasless cars abandoned.

Two people had already been billeted in their tent, an older couple, Fred and Lucy Wilkes. They were from California but had family in Iowa and had been visiting for a wedding when the epidemic hit. They'd been in the camp six days.

"Any word on the buses?" Kittridge asked. Joe Robinson had gone off to find out about rations, Wood and Delores to see about water. April had let her brother run off with some children from the adjacent tent, warning him not to wander far. Danny had accompanied him. "What are people saying?"

"Always it's tomorrow." Fred Wilkes was a trim man of at least seventy, with bright blue eyes; in the heat he'd removed his shirt, displaying a fan of downy white chest hair. He and his wife, as generously proportioned as he was undersized—Jack Sprat and the missus—were playing gin rummy, sitting across from each other on a pair of cots and using a cardboard box as a table. "If it doesn't happen soon, people are going to lose patience. And what then?"

Kittridge stepped back outside. They were surrounded by soldiers, safe for the time being. Yet the whole thing felt stopped, everyone waiting for something to happen. Infantrymen were stationed along the fence line at one hundred meter intervals. All of them were wearing surgical masks. The only way in or out seemed to be the front gate. Abutting the camp to the north he saw a low-slung, windowless building without visible markings or signage, its entrance flanked by concrete barricades. While Kittridge watched, a pair of sleek black heliocpters approached from the east, turned in a wide circle, and touched down on the rooftop. Four figures emerged from the first helicopter, men in dark glasses and baseball caps and Kevlar vests, carrying automatic rifles. Not military, Kittridge thought. Blackbird, maybe, or Riverstone. One of those outfits. The four men proceeded to take up positions at the corners of the roof.

The doors of the second helicopter opened. Kittridge placed a hand to his brow to get a better look. For a moment, nothing happened; then a figure emerged, wearing an orange biosuit. Five more followed. The rotors of the helicopters were still turning. A brief negotiation ensued, then the biosuited figures removed a pair of long steel boxes from the helicopter's cargo section, each the approximate dimensions of a coffin, with wheeled frames that dropped from their undercarriages. They guided the two boxes to a small, hutlike structure on the roof—a service elevator, Kittridge guessed. A few minutes passed; the six reappeared and boarded the second helicopter. First one and then the other lifted off, thudding away.

April came up behind him. "I noticed that, too," she said. "Any idea what it is?"

"Maybe nothing." Kittridge dropped his hand. "Where's Tim?"

"Already making friends. He's off playing soccer with some kids."

They watched the helicopters fade from sight. Whatever it was, Kittridge thought, it wasn't nothing.

"You think we'll be okay here?" April asked.

"Why wouldn't we be?"

"I don't know." Though her face said she did; she was thinking the same thing he was. "Last night, in the lab . . . What I mean is, I can be like that sometimes. I didn't mean to pry."

"I wouldn't have told you if I didn't want to."

She was somehow looking both toward him and away. At such moments she had a way of seeming older than she was. Not seeming, Kittridge thought: being.

"Are you really eighteen?"

She seemed amused. "Why? Don't I look it?"

Kittridge shrugged to hide his embarrassment; the question had just popped out. "No. I mean yes, you do. I was just . . . I don't know."

April was plainly enjoying herself. "A girl's not supposed to tell. But to put your mind at ease, yes, I'm eighteen. Eighteen years, two months, and seventeen days. Not that I'm, you know, counting."

Their eyes met and held in the way they seemed to want to. What was it about this girl, Kittridge wondered, this April?

"I still owe you for the gun," she said, "even if they took it. I think it might be the nicest present anybody ever gave me, actually."

"I liked the poem. Call it even. What was that guy's name again?"

"T. S. Eliot."

"He got any other stuff?"

"Not much that makes sense. You ask me, he was kind of a one-hit wonder."

They had no weapons, no way to get a message to the outside world. Not for the first time, Kittridge wondered if they shouldn't have just kept driving.

"Well, when we get out of here, I'll have to check him out."

17

Grey.

Whiteness, and the sensation of floating. Grey became aware that he was in a car. This was strange, because the car was also a motel room, with beds and dressers and a television; when had they started making cars like this? He was sitting on the foot of one of the beds, driving the room—the steering column came up at an angle from the floor; the television was the windshield—and seated on the adjacent bed was Lila, clutching a pink bundle to her chest. "Are we there yet, Lawrence?" Lila asked him. "The baby needs changing." The baby? thought Grey. When had that happened? Wasn't she months away? "She's so beautiful," said Lila, softly cooing. "We have such a beautiful baby. It's too bad we have to shoot her." "Why do we have to shoot her?" Grey asked. "Don't be silly," said Lila. "We shoot all the babies now. That way they won't be eaten."

Lawrence Grey.

The dream changed—one part of him knew he was dreaming, while another part did not—and Grey was in the tank now. Something was coming to get him, but he couldn't make himself move. He was on his hands and knees, slurping the blood. His job was to drink it, drink it all, which was impossible: the blood had begun to gush through the hatch, filling the compartment. An ocean of blood. The blood was rising above his chin, his mouth and nose were filling, he was choking, drowning—

Lawrence Grey. Wake up.

He opened his eyes to a harsh light. Something felt caught in his throat; he began to cough. Something about drowning? But the dream was already breaking apart, its images atomizing, leaving only a residue of fear.

Where was he?

Some kind of hospital. He was wearing a gown, but that was all; he felt the chill of nakedness beneath it. Thick straps bound his wrists and ankles to the rails of the bed, holding him in place like a mummy in a sarcophagus. Wires snaked from beneath his gown to a cart of medical equipment; an IV was threaded into his right arm.

Somebody was in the room.

Two somebodies in fact, the pair hovering at the foot of the bed in their bulky biosuits, their faces shielded by plastic masks. Behind them was a heavy steel door and, positioned high on the wall in the corner, watching the scene with its unblinking gaze, a security camera.

"Mr. Grey, I'm Horace Guilder," the one on the left said. His tone of voice struck Grey as oddly cheerful. "This is my colleague Dr. Nelson. How are you feeling?"

Grey did his best to focus on their faces. The one who'd spoken looked anonymously middle-aged, with a heavy, square-jawed head and pasty skin; the second man was considerably younger, with tight dark eyes and a scraggly little Vandyke. He didn't look like any doctor Grey had ever met.

He licked his lips and swallowed. "What is this place? Why am I tied up?"

Guilder answered with a calming tone. "That's for your own protection, Mr. Grey. Until we figure out what's wrong with you. As for where you are," he said, "I'm afraid I can't tell you that just yet. Suffice it to say that you're among friends here."

Grey realized they must have sedated him; he could barely move a muscle, and it wasn't just the straps. His limbs felt like iron, his thoughts moving through his brain with a lazy aimlessness, like guppies in a tank. Guilder was holding a cup of water to his lips.

"Go on, drink."

Grey's stomach turned—just the smell of it was revolting, like some hideously overchlorinated pool. Thoughts came back to him, dark thoughts: the blood in the tank, and Grey's face buried greedily in it. Had that actually happened? Had he dreamed it? But no sooner had these questions formed in his mind than a kind of roaring seemed to fill his head, a vast hunger lurching to life inside him, so overwhelming that his entire body clenched against the straps.

"Whoa now," Guilder said, backing away suddenly. "Steady there."

More images were coming back to him, rising through the fog. The tank in the road, the dead soldiers, and explosions all around; the feel of his hand crashing through the Volvo's window, and the fields detonating with fire, and the car sailing through the corn, and the bright lights of the helicopter, and the space-suited men, dragging Lila away.

"Where is she? What have you done with her?"

Guilder glanced toward Nelson, who frowned. *Interesting,* his face seemed to say.

"You needn't worry, Mr. Grey, we're taking good care of her. She's right across the hall, in fact."

"Don't you hurt her." His fists were clenched; he was straining against the straps. "You touch her and I'll—"

"And you'll what, Mr. Grey?"

But there was nothing; the straps held firm. Whatever they had given him, it had taken his strength away.

"Try not to excite yourself, Mr. Grey. Your friend is perfectly fine. The baby, too. What we're a little unclear on is just how the two of you came to be together. I was hoping you might help us with that."

"Why do you want to know?"

One eyebrow lifted incredulously behind the faceplate. "For starters, it seems that the two of you are the last people to come out of Colorado alive. Believe me when I tell you, this is a matter of some interest to us. Was she at the Chalet? Is that where you met her?"

Just the word made Grey's mind clench with panic. "The Chalet?"

"Yes, Mr. Grey. The Chalet."

He shook his head. "No."

"Then where?"

He swallowed. "At the Home Depot."

For just a moment, Guilder said nothing. "Where was this?"

Grey tried to put his thoughts together, but his brain had gone all fuzzy again. "Denver someplace. I don't know exactly. She wanted me to paint the nursery."

Guilder quickly turned toward the second man, who shrugged. "Could be the fentanyl," Nelson said. "It may take him a little while to sort things out."

But Guilder was undeterred. There was something more forceful about the man's gaze now. It seemed to bore right into him. "We need to know what happened at the Chalet. How did you get away?"

"I don't remember."

"Was there a girl there? Did you see her?"

There was a girl? What were they talking about?

"I didn't see anyone. I just . . . I don't know. It was all so confusing. I woke up at the Red Roof."

"The Red Roof? What's that?"

"A motel, on the highway."

A puzzled frown. "When was this?"

Grey tried to count. "Three days ago? No, four." He nodded his head against the pillow. "Four days."

The two men looked at each other. "It doesn't make sense," Nelson said. "The Chalet was destroyed twenty-two days ago. He's not Rip Van Winkle."

"Where were you for those three weeks?" Guilder pressed.

The question made no sense. Three weeks?

"I don't know," Grey said.

"I'll ask you again, Mr. Grey. Was Lila at the Chalet? Is that where you met her?"

"I told you," he said. He was pleading now, his resistance gone. "She was at the Home Depot."

His thoughts were swirling like water going down a drain. Whatever they'd given him, it had screwed him up good. With a thump in his gut, Grey realized what the straps were all about. They were going to study him. Like the sticks. Like Zero. And when they were done with him, Richards, or somebody like him, would put the red light on Grey, and that would be the end of him.

"Please, it's me you want. I'm sorry I ran away. Just don't hurt Lila."

For a moment the two men said nothing, just stared at him from behind their faceplates. Then Guilder turned toward Nelson, nodding.

"Put him back under."

Nelson took a syringe and a vial of clear liquid from the cart. While Grey looked on helplessly, he inserted the needle into the IV tube and pushed the plunger.

"I just clean," Grey said feebly. "I'm just a janitor."

"Oh, I think you're much more than that, Mr. Grey."

And with these words in his ears, Grey slipped away again.

Guilder and Nelson stepped through the air lock into the decontamination chamber. First a shower in their biosuits; then they stripped and scrubbed themselves head to foot with a harsh, chemical-smelling soap. They cleared their throats and spat into the sink, gargling for a minute with a strong disinfectant. A cumbersome ritual but, until they knew more about Grey's condition, one they were wise to observe.

Just a skeletal staff was present in the building: three lab technicians—Guilder thought of them as Wynken, Blynken, and Nod—plus an MD and a four-man Blackbird security team. The building had been constructed in the late eighties to treat soldiers exposed to nuclear, biological, or chemical agents, and the systems were buggy as hell—the aboveground HVAC was on the fritz, as was video surveillance for the entire facility—and the place had a disconcertingly deserted feel to it. But it was the last place anybody would look for them.

Nelson and Guilder stepped into the lab, a wide room of desks and equipment, including the powerful microscopes and blood spinners they'd need to isolate and culture the virus. While Grey and Lila were still unconscious, they'd each had a CT scan and blood drawn; their blood tests had been inconclusive, but Grey's scan had revealed a radically enlarged thymus, typical of those infected. And yet as far as Nelson and Guilder could discern, he'd experienced no other symptoms. In every other way he appeared to be in the pink of health. Better than that: the man looked like he could run a marathon.

"Let me show you something," Nelson said.

He escorted Guilder to the terminal in an adjacent office where he'd set up shop. Nelson opened a file and clicked on a JPEG. A photo appeared on the screen of Lawrence Grey. Or, rather, a man who *resembled* Grey; the face in the photograph looked considerably older. Sagging skin, hair a thin flap over his scalp, sunken eyes that gazed into the camera with a dull, almost bovine look.

"When was this taken?" Guilder asked.

"Seventeen months ago. These are Richards's files."

God damn, Guilder thought. It was just like Lear had said.

"If he's got the virus," Nelson said, "the question is why it's acting differently in his body. It could be a variant we haven't seen, one that activates the thymus like the others and then goes dormant somehow. Or it could be something else, particular to him."

Guilder frowned. "Such as?"

"Your guess is as good as mine. Some sort of natural immunity seems the likely culprit, but there's no way of really knowing. It might have something to do with the anti-androgens he was taking. All the sweeps were taking pretty big doses. Depo-Provera, spironolactone, prednisone."

"You think the steroids did this?"

Nelson shrugged halfheartedly. "It could be a factor. We know the virus interacts with the endocrine system, same as the anti-androgens." He closed the file and turned in his chair. "But here's something else. I did a little digging on the woman. Not much to find, but what there is is mighty interesting. I printed it up for you."

Nelson presented him with a fat file of papers. Guilder opened to the first page.

"She's an MD?"

"Orthopedic surgeon. Keep going."

Guilder read. Lila Beatrice Kyle, born September 29, 1974, Boston, Massachusetts. Parents both academics, the father an English professor at BU, the mother a historian at Simmons. Andover then Wellesley, followed by four years at Dartmouth-Hitchcock for her medical degree. Residency and then a fellowship in orthopedics at Denver General. All impressive, but telling him nothing. Guilder turned to the next page.

What was he looking at? The first page of an IRS form 1040, dated four years ago.

Lila Kyle was married to Brad Wolgast.

"You're kidding me."

Nelson was wearing one of his victorious grins. "I told you that you were going to like it. *The* Agent Wolgast. They had one child, a daughter, deceased. Some kind of congenital heart defect. Divorced three years later. She got remarried four months ago to a doctor who works at the same hospital, some big cardiologist. There's a few pages on him, too, though it doesn't really add anything."

"Okay, so she's an MD. Is there any record of her at the Chalet? Was it possible she was on the staff?"

Nelson shook his head. "Nothing. And I seriously doubt Richards would have missed this. As far as I can see, there's no reason not to think Grey found her just like he said."

"She could have been in the truck in that first aerial we got. We wouldn't have seen her."

"True. But I don't think Grey's lying about where he met her. The story's just too weird to make up. And I checked: her Denver address puts her within just a couple of miles of a Home Depot. The way Grey was headed, he would have gone right through there. You've talked to her. She seems to think Grey is some kind of handyman. I don't think she has a clue what's going on. The woman's crazy as a bedbug."

"Is that your *official* diagnosis?"

Nelson shrugged. "There's no history of psychiatric illness in the paperwork, but consider her situation. She's pregnant, hiding, on the run. People are getting ripped to shreds. Somehow she manages to stay alive, but she gets left behind. How would you feel? The brain's a pretty nimble organ. Right now it's rewriting reality for her, and doing a hell of a good job. Based on Grey's file, I'd say she's got plenty in common with the guy, actually."

Guilder thought a moment and returned the file to the desk. "Well, I'm not buying it. What are the chances that these two would simply bump into each other? It's too big a coincidence."

"Maybe," Nelson said. "Either way, it doesn't tell us much. And the woman might be infected, but we're just not seeing it. Maybe her pregnancy masks it somehow."

"How far along is she?"

"I'm no expert, but from fetal size, I'd say about thirty weeks. You can check with Suresh."

Suresh was the MD Guilder had brought in from USAMRIID. An

infectious diseases doc, he'd been tasked to Special Weapons only six months ago. Guilder had told him little, only that Grey and the woman were "persons of interest."

"How long before we can get a decent culture from him?"

"That depends. Assuming we can isolate the virus at all, somewhere between forty-eight and seventy-two hours. If you're really asking my opinion, the wisest course would be to pack him off to Atlanta. They're the ones who are best equipped to handle something like this. And if Grey's immune, I can't see why they wouldn't just let bygones be bygones. Not with so much at stake."

Guilder shook his head. "Let's wait until we have something solid."

"I wouldn't wait long. Not with the way things are going."

"We won't. But you heard the guy. He thinks he's been sleeping in a motel. I doubt anybody's going to take us seriously if that's all we've got. They'll lock us both up and throw away the key if we're *lucky*."

Nelson frowned, touching his beard with a thoughtful gesture. "I see your point."

"I'm not saying we won't tell them," Guilder offered. "But let's move cautiously. Seventy-two hours, then I'll make the call, all right?"

A frozen moment followed. Had Nelson bought it? Then the man nodded.

"Just keep digging." Guilder clapped a hand on Nelson's shoulder. "And tell Suresh to keep the two of them sedated for the time being. If either of them flips, I don't want to take any chances."

"You think those straps will hold?"

The question was rhetorical; both men knew the answer.

Guilder left Nelson in the lab and rode the elevator to the roof. His left leg was dragging again, a hitch in his step like a hiccup. Outside, the Blackbird officer in charge, named Masterson, nodded a terse greeting but otherwise left him alone. Vintage Blackbird, this guy: built like a dump truck with arms as thick as hydrants and a face petrified into the self-satisfied sneer of an overgrown frat boy. In his wraparound sunglasses and baseball cap and body armor, Masterson seemed less a person than an action figure. Where did they get these characters? Were they grown on some kind of farm? Cultured in a petri dish? They were thugs, pure and simple, and Guilder had never liked dealing with them— Richards being Exhibit A—though it was also true that their almost robotic obedience made them ideally suited for certain jobs; if they didn't exist, you'd have to invent them.

He moved to the edge of the roof. It was just past noon, the air breathless under a shapeless white sun, the land as flat and featureless as a pool table. The only interruptions to the perfectly linear horizon were a gleaming domed building, probably something to do with the college, and, just to the south, the bowl-like shape of a football stadium. One of those kinds of schools, Guilder thought—a sports franchise masquerading as a college where criminals drifted through phony courses and filled the coffers of the alumni fund by pounding their opposite numbers to pieces on autumn afternoons.

He let his eyes peruse the FEMA camp below. The presence of refugees was a wrinkle he hadn't anticipated, and initially it had concerned him. But when he'd considered the situation more closely, he couldn't see how this made any difference. The word from the Army was that in a day or two they'd all be gone anyway. A group of boys were playing near the wire, kicking a half-deflated ball around in the dirt. For a few minutes Guilder watched them. The world could be falling apart, and yet children were children; at a moment's notice they could put all their cares aside and lose themselves in a game. Perhaps that was what Guilder had felt with Shawna: a few minutes in which he got to be the boy he never was. Maybe that was all he'd ever wanted—what anybody ever wanted.

But Lawrence Grey: something about the man nagged at him, and it wasn't just his incredible story or the improbable coincidence of the woman in question being Agent Wolgast's wife. It was the way Grey had spoken of her. *Please, it's me you want. Just don't hurt Lila.* Guilder never would have guessed Grey was capable of caring about another person like that, let alone a woman. Everything in his file had led Guilder to expect a man who was at best a loner, at worst a sociopath. But Grey's pleas on Lila's behalf had obviously been heartfelt. Something had happened between them; a bond had been forged.

His gaze widened, then taking in the entirety of the camp. All these people: they were trapped. And not merely by the wires that surrounded them. Physical barricades were nothing compared to the wires of the mind. What had truly imprisoned them was one another. Husbands and wives, parents and children, friends and companions: what they believed had given them strength in their lives had actually done the opposite. Guilder recalled the couple who lived across the street from his townhouse, trading off their sleeping daughter on the way to the car. How heavy that burden must have felt in their arms. And when the end swept down upon them all, they would exit the world on a wave of suffering, their agonies magnified a million times over by the loss of her. Would they have to watch her die? Would they perish first, knowing what would become of her in their absence? Which was preferable? But the answer was neither. Love had sealed their doom. Which was what love did. Guilder's father had taught that lesson well enough.

Guilder was dying. That was inarguable, a fact of nature. So, too, was the fact that Lawrence Grey—this disposable nobody, this goddamn janitor, a man who had in his pathetic life brought nothing but misery to the world—was not. Somewhere in the body of Lawrence Grey lay the secret to the ultimate freedom, and Horace Guilder would find it, and take it for his own.

18

The days crawled past. And still no word on the buses.

Everyone was restless. Outside the wire, the Army came and went, its numbers thinning. Each morning, Kittridge went to the shed to inquire about the situation; each morning, he came away with the same answer: the buses are on the way, be patient.

For a whole day it rained, turning the camp into a giant mud bath. Now the sun had returned, cooking every surface with a crust of dried earth. Each afternoon more MREs appeared, tossed from the back of an Army five-ton, but never any news. The chemical toilets were foul, the waste cans overflowing with trash. Kittridge spent hours watching the front gate; no more refugees were coming in. With each passing day, the place had begun to feel like an island surrounded by a hostile sea.

He'd made an ally of Vera, the Red Cross volunteer who had first approached them in the check-in line. She was younger than Kittridge had first thought, a nursing student at Midwest State. Like all the civilian workers, she seemed utterly drained, the days of strain weighing in her face. She understood his frustration, she said, everyone did. She had hoped to take the buses, too; she was stranded like the rest of them. One day they were coming from Chicago, then next from Kansas City, then from Joliet. Some FEMA screwup. They were supposed to get a bank of satellite phones, too, so people could call their relatives and let them know they were okay. What had happened to that, Vera didn't know. Even the local cell network was down.

Kittridge had begun to see the same faces: an elegantly dressed woman who kept a cat on a leash, a group of young black men all dressed in the white shirts and black neckties of Jehovah's Witnesses, a girl in a cheer-leading outfit. A listlessness had settled over the camp; the deflected drama of nondeparture had left everyone in a passive state. There were rumors that the water supply had become contaminated, and now the medical tent was full of people complaining of stomach cramps, muscle aches, fever. A number of people had radios that were still operating, but all they heard was a ringing sound, followed by the now-familiar statement from the Emergency Broadcast System. *Do not leave your homes. Shelter in place. Obey all orders of military and law enforcement personnel.* Another minute of ringing, and the words would be repeated.

Kittridge had begun to wonder if they were ever getting out of there. And all night long, he watched the fences.

Late afternoon of the fourth day: Kittridge was playing yet another hand of cards with April, Pastor Don, and Mrs. Bellamy. They'd switched from bridge to five-card poker, betting ludicrous sums of money that were purely hypothetical. April, who claimed never to have played before, had already taken Kittridge for close to five thousand dollars. The Wilkeses had disappeared; nobody had seen them since Wednesday. Wherever they'd gone, they'd taken their luggage with them.

"Jesus, it's roasting in here," Joe Robinson said. He'd barely been off his cot all day.

"Sit in a hand," Kittridge suggested. "It'll take your mind off the heat."

"Christ," the man moaned. The sweat was pouring off him. "I can barely move."

Kittridge, with only a pair of sixes, folded his cards. April, wearing a perfect poker face, raked in another pot.

"I'm bored," Tim announced.

April was sorting the slips of paper they used for chips into piles. "You can play with me. I'll show you how to bet."

"I want to play crazy eights."

"Trust me," she told her brother, "this is a lot better."

Pastor Don was dealing a fresh hand when Vera appeared at the flap of the tent. She quickly met Kittridge's eye. "Can we talk outside?"

He rose from the cot and stepped into the late-day heat.

"Something's going on," Vera said. "FEMA just got word that all civilian transportation east of the Mississippi has been suspended."

"Are you certain?"

"I overheard them talking about it in the site director's office. Half the FEMA staff has bugged out already."

"Who else knows about this?"

"Are you kidding? I'm not even telling you."

So there it was; they were being abandoned. "Who's the officer in charge?"

"Major something. I think her name is Porcheki."

A stroke of luck. "Where is she now?"

"She should be in the shed. There was some colonel, but he's gone. A *lot* of them are gone."

"I'll talk to her."

Vera frowned doubtfully. "What can you do?"

"Maybe nothing. But at least it's worth a try."

She hurried away; Kittridge returned to the tent. "Where's Delores?"

Wood lifted his eyes from his cards. "I think she's working in one of the medical tents. The Red Cross put out a call for volunteers."

"Somebody go get her."

When everyone was present, Kittridge explained the situation. Assuming Porcheki would provide fuel for the bus—a big if—they would have to wait to leave until morning, at the earliest.

"Do you really think she'll help us?" Pastor Don asked.

"I admit it's a long shot."

"I say we just steal it and get the hell out of here," Jamal said. "Let's not wait."

"It may come to that, and I'd agree, except for two things. One, we're talking about the Army. Stealing it sounds like a good way to get shot. And two, we've got at most a couple of hours of light left. It's a long way to Chicago, and I don't want to try this in the dark. Make sense?"

Jamal nodded.

"The important thing is to keep this quiet and stick together. Once this thing gets out, all hell's going to break loose. Everybody stay close to the tent. You, too, Tim. No wandering off."

Kittridge had stepped from the tent when Delores caught up with him. "I'm concerned about this fever," she said quickly. "The med tents are being completely overrun. All the supplies are used up, no antibiotics, nothing. This thing is getting out of hand."

"What do you think it is?"

"The obvious culprit would be typhus. The same thing happened in New Orleans after Hurricane Vanessa. This many people crammed in, it was just a matter of time. If you ask me, we can't leave fast enough."

Another worry, Kittridge thought. Quickening his stride, he made his way to the shed, past overflowing dumpsters where crows were picking at the garbage. The birds had showed up the prior evening, attracted, no doubt, by the reek of accumulating trash. Now the place seemed full of them, so brazen they would practically snatch food from your hand. Never a good sign, he thought, when the crows showed up.

At the command tent, Kittridge chose the most direct approach, doing nothing to announce his presence before stepping inside. Porcheki was seated at a long table, speaking into a satellite phone. Three non-coms occupied the room, a densely packed jumble of electronic equipment. One of the soldiers yanked off his headset and shot to his feet.

"What are you doing in here? This area is restricted, no civilians."

But as the soldier stepped toward Kittridge, Porcheki stopped him.

"It's all right, Corporal." Her face a mask of weariness, she put down the phone. "Sergeant Kittridge. What can I do for you?"

"You're pulling out, aren't you?" The idea had formed in his mind even as he'd spoken the words.

Porcheki weighed him with her eyes. Then, to the soldiers: "Would you excuse us, please?"

"Major—"

"That's all, Corporal."

With visible reluctance, the three exited the tent.

"Yes," Porcheki said. "We've been ordered back to the Illinois line. The entire state goes under quarantine at eighteen hundred hours tomorrow."

"You can't just leave these people. They're totally defenseless."

"I know that, too." She was looking at him closely. She seemed on the verge of some announcement. Then: "You were at Bagram, weren't you?"

"Ma'am?"

"I thought I recognized you. I was there, with the Seventy-second Medical Expeditionary Group. You wouldn't remember me, I don't think." Her eyes darted downward. "How's the leg?"

Kittridge was almost too stunned to reply. "I get around okay."

A faint nod and, on her troubled face, what might have passed for a smile. "I'm glad to see you made it, Sergeant. I heard about what happened. That was a terrible thing, with the boy." Her officious manner returned. "As for the other, I've got two dozen coaches en route from the arsenal at Rock Island and a pair of refuelers. Plus your bus, that makes twenty-five. Not enough, obviously, but it's what I could put together. This is not for general consumption, mind you. We don't want to start a panic. I'd be lying to you if I didn't say I'm going way off the reservation here. Are we clear?"

Kittridge nodded.

"When those buses pull in, you'll want to be ready. You know what these things are like. You keep control as long as you can, but sooner or later it gets ragged around the edges. People will do the math, and you can bet nobody's going to want to be left behind. We should have time to make four trips before the border closes. That should do it, but we'll have very little margin. You have a driver for your bus?"

Kittridge nodded again. "Danny."

"The one with the hat? Forgive me, Sergeant, I mean no disrespect to the man. But I need to be sure he can handle this."

"You won't do better than him. You have my word."

A quick hesitation, then she agreed. "Have him report here at oh-three-hundred. The first load departs at oh-four-thirty. Just remember what I said. You want to get your people out of here, get them on those buses."

The next thing surprised Kittridge most of all. Porcheki leaned down, opened the bottom drawer of her desk, and removed a pair of pistols. Kittridge's own Glocks, still in their holsters. She handed him a blue windbreaker with FEMA stenciled on the back.

"Just keep them under wraps. Report to Corporal Danes outside and he'll escort you to the armory. Take all the rounds you need."

Kittridge slid his arms through the straps and put on the jacket. The woman's meaning was plain. They were behind the lines; the front had passed them by.

"How close are they?" Kittridge asked.

The major's expression darkened. "They're already here."

Lawrence Grey had never known such hunger.

How long had he been here? Three days? Four? Time had lost all meaning, the passage of hours broken only by the visits of the space-suited men. They came without warning, apparitions emerging from a narcotic haze. The hiss of the air lock and there they were; then the prick of the needle and the slow filling of the plastic bag with its crimson prize. Something was in his blood, something they wanted. Yet they never seemed satisfied; they would drain him like a slaughtered steer. What do you want? he pleaded. Why are you doing this to me? Where's Lila?

He was famished. He was a being of pure need, a man-sized hole in space needing only to be filled. A person could go mad with it. Assuming he *was* a person, still, which hardly seemed likely. Zero had changed him, altered the very essence of his existence. He was being brought into the fold. In his mind were voices, murmurings, like the buzz of a distant crowd. Hour by hour the sound grew stronger; the crowd was closing in. Against the straps he wriggled like a fish in a net. With every stolen bag of blood his strength drained away. He felt himself aging from within, a precipitous decline, deep in the cells. The universe had abandoned him to his fate. Soon he would vanish; he would be dispersed into the void.

They were watching him, the one named Guilder and the one named Nelson; Grey sensed their presence lurking behind the lens of the security camera, the probing beams of their eyes. They needed him; they were afraid of him. He was like a present that, when opened, might burst forth as snakes. He had no answers for them; they'd given up asking. Silence was the last power he had.

He thought of Lila. Were the same things happening to her? Was the baby all right? He had wanted only to protect her, to do this one good thing in his wretched little life. It was a kind of love. Like Nora Chung, only a thousand times deeper, an energy that desired nothing, that took nothing; it wanted only to give itself away. It was true: Lila had come into his life for a purpose, to give him one last chance. And yet he had failed her.

He heard the hiss of the air lock; a figure stepped through. One of the suited men, lumbering toward him like a great orange snowman.

"Mr. Grey, I'm Dr. Suresh."

Grey closed his eyes and waited for the prick of the needle. Go ahead, he thought, take it all. But that didn't happen. Grey looked up to see the doctor withdrawing a needle from the IV port. With careful movements he capped the needle and deposited it in the waste can with a clang. At once Grey felt the fog lift from his mind.

"Now we can talk. How are you feeling?"

He wanted to say: How do you think I'm feeling? Or maybe just: Fuck you. "Where's Lila?"

The doctor withdrew a small penlight from a pouch on his biosuit and leaned over Grey's face. Through the faceplate of his helmet his features swam into view: a heavy brow, skin dark with a yellowish cast, small white teeth. He waved the beam over Grey's eyes.

"Does it trouble you? The light."

Grey shook his head. He was becoming aware of a new sound— a rhythmic throbbing. He was hearing the man's heartbeat, the pulsing swish of blood through his veins. A blast of saliva washed the walls of his mouth.

"You have not had a bowel movement, yes?"

Grey swallowed and shook his head again. The doctor moved to the foot of the bed and withdrew a small silver probe. He scraped it quickly along the soles of Grey's bare feet.

"Very good."

The examination continued. Each bit of data was jotted onto a hand-held. Suresh pulled Grey's gown up over his legs and cupped his testicles in his hand.

"Cough, please."

Grey managed a small one. The doctor's face behind his faceplate revealed nothing. The throbbing sound filled Grey's entire brain, annihilating any other thought.

"I am going to check your glands."

The doctor reached his gloved hands toward Grey's neck. As the tips of his fingers made contact, Grey darted his head forward. The action was automatic; Grey couldn't have stopped it if he'd tried. His teeth bore into the soft flesh of Suresh's palm, clamping like a vise. The chemical taste of latex, profoundly revolting, then a burst of sweetness filled his mouth. Suresh was shrieking, struggling to break free. His free hand pushed on Grey's forehead, fighting for leverage; he reared back and struck Grey across the face with his fist. Not painful but startling; Grey broke his hold. Suresh stumbled backward, clutching his bloody hand at the wrist, thumb and forefinger wrapping it like a tourniquet. Grey expected something large to happen, the sound of an alarm, men rushing in, but nothing of the kind occurred; the moment felt frozen and, somehow, unobserved. Suresh backed away, staring at Grey with a look of wide-eyed panic. He stripped off his bloody glove and moved briskly to the sink. He turned on the tap and began to scrub his hand fiercely, muttering under his breath:

"Oh God, oh God, oh God."

Then he was gone. Grey lay still. In the struggle, his IV had torn loose. There was blood on his face, his lips. With slow pleasure he licked them clean. The merest taste, but it was enough. Strength flowed into him like a tide upon the shore. He tensed against the straps, feeling the rivets start to give. The air lock was another matter, but sooner or later it would open, and when it did, Grey would be waiting. He would alight like an angel of death.

Lila, I am coming.

19

0330 hours: The group was gathered at the tent, gear packed, awaiting the dawn. Kittridge had told them they should sleep, to prepare for the journey ahead. Shortly after midnight, the promised buses had appeared outside the fence, a long gray line. From the Army, no announcement, but their arrival hadn't escaped attention. All through the camp the talk was of leaving. Who would get to go first? Were more buses coming? What about the ill? Would they be evacuated separately?

Kittridge had gone with Danny to the command tent for Porcheki's briefing. What was left of the civilian staff, FEMA and Red Cross, would directly supervise the loading, while the last of Porcheki's men, three platoons, would manage the crowds. A dozen Humvees and a pair of APCs would wait on the far side of the fence to escort the convoy. The trip to Rock Island would take a little under two hours. Assuming everything went as planned, the last of the four loads would reach Rock Island by 1730, just under the deadline.

When the meeting broke up, Kittridge took Danny aside. "If anything happens, don't wait. Just take what you can carry and go. Stay off the main roads. If the bridge at Rock Island is closed, head north, like we did the last time. Follow the river until you find an open bridge. Got that?"

"I shouldn't wait. Stay off the main roads. Go north."

"Exactly."

The other drivers were already headed for the buses. Kittridge had only a moment to say the rest.

"Whatever happens, Danny, we wouldn't have gotten this far without you. I'm sure you know it, but I wanted to say so."

The man nodded tightly, his gaze slanted away. "Okay."

"I'd like to shake on it. Do you think that would be all right?"

Danny's brow furrowed with an expression, almost, of pain. Kittridge was worried he'd overstepped when Danny extended his hand with furtive quickness, the two men's palms colliding. His grip, though hesitant, was not without strength. A vigorous pump; for a second Danny met his eye; then it was over.

"Good luck," said Kittridge.

He returned to the tent. Nothing to do now but wait. He sat on the ground with his back against a wooden crate. A few minutes passed; the flaps of the tent parted. April lowered herself beside him, drawing her knees to her chest.

"You mind?"

Kittridge shook his head. They were looking toward the compound's entrance, a hundred yards distant. Under a blaze of spotlights, the area around it glowed like a brightly lit stage.

"I just wanted to thank you," April said. "For everything you've done."

"Anybody would have."

"No, they wouldn't. I mean, you'd like to think so. But no."

Kittridge wondered if this was true. He supposed it didn't matter. Fate had pushed them together, and here they were. Then he remembered the pistols.

"I've got something of yours."

He reached under his jacket and pulled one of the Glocks free. He racked the slide to chamber a round, turned it around in his hand, and held it out to her.

"Remember what I told you. One shot in the center of the chest. They go down like a house of cards if you do it right."

"How did you get it back?"

He smiled. "Won it in a poker game." He nudged it toward her. "Go on, take it."

It had become important to him that she have it. April took it in her hand, leaned forward, and slid the barrel into the waistband of her jeans, resting against her spine.

"Thanks," she said with a smile. "I'll use it in good health."

For a full minute, neither spoke.

"It's pretty obvious how all this is going to end, isn't it?" April said. "Sooner or later, I mean."

Kittridge turned his face to look at her; her eyes were averted, the lights of the spots glazing her features. "There's always a chance."

"That's nice of you to say. But it doesn't change a thing. Maybe the others need to hear it, but I don't."

A chill had fallen; April leaned her weight against him. The gesture was instinctive, but it meant something. Kittridge draped his arm around her, drawing her in for warmth.

"You think about him, don't you?" Her head lay against his chest; her voice was very soft. "The boy in the car."

"Yes."

"Tell me."

Kittridge took a long breath, exhaling into the darkness. "I think about him all the time."

A deeper silence fell. Around them the camp had fallen quiet, like the rooms of a house after everyone had gone to bed.

"I'd like to ask a favor," April said.

"Name it."

Kittridge felt her body tense just slightly. "Did I mention I was a virgin?"

Despite himself, he laughed; and yet this did not seem wrong. "Now, I think I'd remember something like that."

"Yeah, well. There haven't been what you'd call a lot of men in my life." She paused, then said, "I wasn't lying about being eighteen, you know. Not that it matters. I don't think this is a world where stuff like that means much anymore."

Kittridge nodded. "I guess maybe it doesn't."

"So what I'm saying is, it doesn't have to be any big thing."

"It's always a big thing."

April wrapped his hand with her fingers, slowly brushing her thumb over the tops of his knuckles. The sensation was as light and warm as a kiss. "It's funny. Even before I saw your scars, I knew what you were. Not just the Army—that was obvious to everyone. That something had happened to you, in the war." A pause, then: "I don't think I even know your first name."

"It's Bernard."

She pulled away to look at him. Her eyes were moist and shining. "Please, Bernard. Just please, okay?"

It was not a request that could be refused; nor did he want to. They used one of the adjacent tents—who knew where its occupants had gone? Kittridge was out of practice but did his best to be kind, to go slow, watching April's face carefully in the dim light. She made a few sounds, but not many, and when it was done she kissed him, long and tenderly, nestled against him, and soon was fast asleep.

Kittridge lay in the dark, listening to her breathe, feeling her warmth where their bodies touched. He'd thought it might be strange but it wasn't strange at all; it seemed a natural part of all that had occurred. His thoughts drifted, touching down here and there. The better memories; the memories of love. He didn't have many. Now he had another. How foolish he'd been, wanting to give away this life.

He had just closed his eyes when from beyond the gate came a roar of engines and a flare of headlights. April was stirring beside him. He dressed quickly and parted the flaps as he heard, coming from the west, a roll of thunder. Wouldn't you know they'd be leaving in the rain.

"Are they here?" Rubbing his eyes, Pastor Don was emerging from the tent. Wood was behind him.

Kittridge nodded. "Get your gear, everybody. It's time."

Where the hell was Suresh?

Nobody had seen the man for hours. One minute he was supposed to be examining Grey; the next he'd vanished into thin air. Guilder had sent Masterson to search for him. Twenty minutes later, he'd come back empty-handed. Suresh was nowhere in the building, he said.

Their first defection, Guilder thought. A crack like that would widen. Where could the man hope to get to? They were in the middle of a corn-field, night was pressing down. The days had passed in futility. Still they had failed to isolate the virus, to draw it forth from the cells. There was no doubt that Grey was infected; the man's enlarged thymus told them so. But the virus itself seemed to be hiding. Hiding! Those were Nelson's words. How could a virus be hiding? Just fucking find it, Guilder said. We're running out of time.

Guilder was spending more of his time on the roof, drawn to its sense of space. Past midnight once again, and here he was. Sleep was only a memory. No sooner would he drift off than he would jolt awake, the walls of his throat closing in. The seventy-two-hour deadline had come and gone, Nelson only raising his eyebrows: *Well?* Guilder's windpipe was so tight he could barely swallow; his left hand fluttered like a bird. One whole side of his body was dragging as if a ten-pound dumbbell were tied to his ankle. There was no way he could hide the situation from Nelson much longer.

From the rooftop, Guilder had watched the Army's ranks diminishing over the days. How far away were the virals? How much time did they have?

His handheld buzzed at his waist. Nelson.

"You better come see this."

Nelson met him at the door of the elevator. He was wearing a dirty lab coat, his hair askew. He handed Guilder a sheaf of paper.

"What am I looking at?"

Nelson's face was grim. "Just read."

DEPARTMENT OF THE ARMY
U.S. CENTRAL COMMAND
7115 SOUTH BOUNDARY BOULEVARD
MACDILL AFB, FL 33621-5101

010500JUN16

USCENTCOM OPERATION ORDER—IMMACULATA

REFERENCES: EXECUTIVE ORDER 929621, 1st HL Recon BDE OPORD 18–26, Map Sheet V107

TASK ORGANIZATION: Joint Task Force (JTF) SCORCH, including elements of: 388th Fighter Wing (388 FW), 23rd Fighter Group (23 FG), 62nd Homeland Aerial Defense Group (62 HADG), Colorado Army National Guard (CO ANG), Kansas Army National Guard (KS ANG), Nebraska Army National Guard (NE ANG), and Iowa Army National Guard (IA ANG)

1. SITUATION
   a. Enemy Strength: Unknown, +/- 200K
   b. Terrain: Mixture of high plains/grasslands/urban
   c. Weather: Variable conditions, moderate day visibility, limited night visibility, low to no moonlight
   d. Enemy Situation: As of 010500JUN16, 763 infected person groups ("pods") observed massed in Designated Areas 1–26. Enemy movement expected immediately following sunset (2116).

2. MISSION
JTF SCORCH conducts combat operations from 012100JUN16 through 052400JUN17 within designated Quarantine Zone in order to destroy all infected persons.

3. EXECUTION
Intent: JTF will conduct air and ground combat operations within Quarantine Zone. Priority task for JTF SCORCH is elimination of all infected personnel within Quarantine Zone. *All personnel, including civilians, within Quarantine Zone are assumed to be infected and are authorized for elimination in accordance with Executive Order 929621. End state is elimination of all infected personnel within Quarantine Zone.*

Concept of the Operation: This will be a two-phase operation:

PHASE 1: JTF deploys tactical air units of the 388 FW, 23 FG, and 62 HADG 012100JUN16 to conduct massed bombing of Designated Areas 1–26. PHASE 1 complete with 100% bombing saturation of Quarantine Zone. PHASE 2 will commence immediately following PHASE 1 complete.

PHASE 2: JTF will deploy 3 Mechanized Infantry Divisions from tactical ground units of the CO ANG, KS ANG, NE ANG, IA ANG to conduct free-fire assaults on remaining enemy forces within Designated Areas 1–26. PHASE 2 complete with 100% infected personnel destroyed within Quarantine Zone.

It went on from there: logistics, tactical, command, and signal. The bureaucratese of war. The upshot was clear: anyone behind the quarantine line was now forfeit.

"Jesus."

"I told you," Nelson said. "Sooner or later, this was bound to happen. It's less than two hours till dawn. We're probably okay for the night, but I don't think we should wait."

Just like that, the clock had run down to zero. After all he'd done, to accept defeat now!

"So what do you want me to do?"

Guilder took a breath to steady himself. "Evacuate the techs in the vehicles, but keep Masterson here. We can box up Grey and the woman ourselves and call for pickup."

"Should I notify Atlanta? You know, so they're at least aware of the situation."

It was, he thought, to Nelson's credit that he didn't indulge himself with a second I-told-you-so. "No, I'll do it."

There was a secure landline in the station chief's office. Guilder made his way upstairs and down the empty hallway, his left leg dragging pitifully. All the offices had been stripped bare; the only things in the room were a chair, a cheap metal desk, and a telephone. He lowered himself into the chair and sat there, staring at the phone. After some time he realized his cheeks were wet; he had begun to weep. The strange, emotionless weeping that had come to seem like a harbinger of his fate, and the body's unbidden confession of his wretched little life. As if his body were saying to him: Just you wait. Just you wait and see what I've got in store for you. A living death, sonny boy.

But this would never happen; once he picked up the phone, it would all be over. A small comfort, to know that at least he wouldn't live long enough to suffer the full brunt of his decline. What he had failed to accomplish that day in the garage would now be done for him.

Mr. Guilder? Come with us. A hand on his shoulder, the march down the hall.

No.

20

By the time they reached the buses, the soldiers had established a perimeter. A crowd was forming in the predawn darkness. Danny's bus was in the third slot; Kittridge glimpsed him through the windshield, hat wedged onto his head, hands clamping the wheel. Vera stood at the base of the steps, holding a clipboard.

God bless you, Danny Chayes, Kittridge thought. This is going to be the ride of your life.

"Please, everyone, keep calm!" Porcheki, moving up and down the line of buses behind the barrier of soldiers, was yelling through a megaphone. "Form an orderly line and load from the rear! If you don't get a seat, wait for the second load!"

The soldiers had erected barriers to serve as a kind of gate. The mob was pressing behind them, funneling toward the gap. Where were they going? people were asking. Was the destination still Chicago, or somewhere else? Just ahead of Kittridge's group was a family with two children, a boy and girl, wearing filthy pajamas. Dirty feet, matted hair—they couldn't have been older than five. The girl was clutching a naked Barbie. More thunder rolled in from the west, accompanied by flashes of light at the horizon. Kittridge and April were both keeping a hand on Tim, afraid the mob would swallow him.

Once through the gap, the group moved quickly to Danny's bus. The Robinsons and Boy Jr. were the first to board; at the bottom of the steps were Wood and Delores, Jamal and Mrs. Bellamy. Pastor Don brought up the rear, behind Kittridge, Tim, and April.

A burst of lightning, ghostly white, ignited the air, freezing the scene in Kittridge's mind. Half a second later, a long peal of thunder rolled. Kittridge felt the impact through the soles of his feet.

Not thunder. Ordnance.

A trio of jets shot overhead, then two more. Suddenly everyone was screaming—a high, shrill sound of undammed panic that built from the rear, engulfing the crowd like a wave. Kittridge turned his face toward the west.

He had never seen the virals in a large group before. Sometimes, from his perch on the tower, he had seen three of them together—never less or more—and of course there'd been the ones in the underground garage, which might have numbered as many as twenty. That was nothing compared to this. The sight suggested a flock of earthbound birds: a coordinated mass of hundreds, thousands even, rushing toward the wire. *A pod,* Kittridge remembered. *That's what they're calling them, pods.* For a second he felt a kind of awe, a pure breathtaken wonder at its organic majesty.

They'd sweep over the camp like a tsunami.

Humvees were racing toward the western wire, rooster-tails of dust boiling from their wheels. Suddenly the buses were unguarded; the crowd surged toward them. A great human weight crashed into Kittridge from behind. As the crowd enveloped him, he heard April scream.

"Tim!"

He dove toward her voice, fighting his way through the mob like a swimmer against the current, tossing bodies aside. A clot of people were trying to jam themselves into Danny's bus, pushing, shoving. Kittridge saw the man who had been ahead of them in line holding his daughter over his head. He was yelling, "Please, somebody take her! Somebody take my daughter!"

Then Kittridge saw April, caught in the crush. He waved his hands in the air. "Get on the bus!"

"I can't find him! I can't find Tim!"

A roar of engines; at the back of the line, one of the buses drew clear, then another and another. In a burst of fury, Kittridge rammed his way toward April, grabbed her by the waist and plunged toward the door. But the girl would have none of it; she was fighting him, trying to break his grip.

"I can't leave without him! Let me go!"

Ahead he saw Pastor Don at the base of the steps. Kittridge shoved April forward. "Don, help me! Get her on the bus!"

"I can't leave, I can't leave!"

"I'll find him, April! Don, take her!"

A final thrust through the melee, Don reaching forward, finding April's hand, pulling her toward the door; then she was gone. The bus was only half full, but there was no time to wait. Kittridge's last glimpse of April was her face pressed to the window, calling his name.

"Danny, get them out of here!"

The doors closed. The bus pulled away.

In her basement chamber of the NBC facility, Lila Kyle, who had spent the last four days in a state of narcotic suspension—a semiconscious twilight in which she experienced the room around her as if it were but one of several movie screens she was viewing simultaneously—was asleep, and dreaming: a simple, happy dream in which she was in a car at night, being driven to the hospital to have her baby. Whoever was driving the car, Lila couldn't see; the fringes of her vision were draped in blackness. Brad, she said, are you there? And then the blackness lifted, like the curtain over a stage, and Lila saw that it *was* Brad. A shimmering golden joy, weightless as June sunlight, thrummed through her entire being. We'll be there soon, my darling, Brad said. We'll be there any second. This isn't all going to hell in a handbasket. You just hold on. The baby is coming. The baby is practically here.

And those were the words Lila was saying to herself—the baby is coming, the baby is coming—when the room was buffeted by a violent explosion—glass shattering, things falling, the floor beneath her lurching like a tiny boat at sea—and she began to scream.

21

The viral pod that swarmed the eastern Iowa refugee-processing center in the early morning hours of June 9 was part of a larger mass gathering out of Nebraska. Estimates made later by the joint task force, code-named JTF Scorch differed on its size; some believed it was fifty thousand, others many more. In the days that followed, it would convene with a second, larger pod, coming north out of Missouri, and a third, larger still, moving south from Minnesota. Always their numbers increased. By the time they reached Chicago, they were half a million strong, penetrating the defensive perimeter on July 17 and overwhelming the city within twenty-four hours.

The first virals to breach the wires of the refugee-processing center arrived at 4:58 CTD. By this time, extensive aerial operations in the central and eastern portions of the state had been under way for eight hours, and, in fact, all but one of the bridges over the Mississippi—Dubuque— had already been destroyed; the timing of the quarantine had been deliberately misreported by the task force. It was generally believed by the leaders of the task force—a conclusion supported by the combined wisdom of the American military and intelligence communities—that a concentrated human presence within the quarantine zone acted as a lure to the infected, causing them to coalesce in certain areas and thus make aerial bombardment more effective. The closest analogue, in the words of one task force member, was using a salt lick to hunt deer. Leaving behind a population of refugees was simply the price that needed to be paid in a war that lacked all precedent. And in any event, those people were surely dead anyway.

Major Frances Porcheki of the Iowa National Guard—in her civilian life, a district manager for a manufacturer of women's sporting apparel— was unaware of the mission of JTF Scorch, but she was no fool, either. Though a highly trained military officer, Major Porcheki was also a devout Catholic who took comfort in, and guidance from, her faith. Her decision not to abandon the refugees under her protection, as she had been ordered to do, followed directly from this deeper conviction, as did her choice to devote the final energies of her life, and those of the soldiers still under her command—165 men and women, who, nearly to a one, took up positions at the western wire—to provide cover for the escaping buses. By this time, the civilians who had been left behind were racing after the vehicles, screaming for them to stop, but there was nothing to be done. Well, that's it, Porcheki thought. I would have saved more if I could. A pale green light had gathered to the west, a wall of quivering radiance, like a glowing hedgerow. Jets were streaking overhead, unleashing the fury of their payloads into the heart of the pod: gleaming tracers, spouts of flame. The air was split with thunder. Through a gauntlet of destruction the pod emerged, still coming. Porcheki leapt from her Humvee before it had stopped moving, yelling, "Hold your fire, everyone! Wait till they're at the wire!," then dropped to a firing position— having no more orders to give, she would face the enemy on the same terms as her men—and began to pray.

*   *   *

Time itself acquired a disordered feel. Amid the chaos, lives were over-lapping in unforeseen ways. In the basement of the NBC facility, a bitter struggle was ensuing. At the very moment that the Blackbird helicopter was alighting on the rooftop, Horace Guilder, who had been hiding from Nelson in the office when the assault commenced, his decision not to telephone his counterparts at the CDC having lifted one burden from his mind only to create another (he had no idea what to do next), had descended the stairs to the basement with considerable difficulty to find Masterson and Nelson frantically cramming blood samples into a cooler packed with dry ice, yelling words to the effect of "Where the hell have you been?" and "We have to get out of here!" and "The place is coming down around our ears!" But these sentiments, reasonable as they were, touched Guilder only vaguely. The thing that mattered now was Lawrence Grey. And all at once, as if he'd been slapped in the face, Guilder knew what he had to do.

There was only one way. Why hadn't he seen it all along?

His whole body was poised on the verge of paralyzing spasms; he could barely draw a breath through the narrowing tube of his throat. And yet he mustered the will—the will of the dying—to reach out and seize Masterson's sidearm and yank it free of its holster.

Then, amazing himself, Guilder shot him.

Kittridge was being trampled.

As the buses pulled away, Kittridge was knocked to the ground. As he attempted to rise, somebody's foot caught him in the side of his face, its owner tumbling over him with a grunt. More pummeling feet and bodies; it was all he could do to assume a posture of defense, pressing himself to the ground with his hands over his head.

"Tim! Where are you?"

Then he saw him. The crowd had left the boy behind. He was sitting in the dirt not ten yards away. Kittridge hobbled to his side, skidding in the dust.

"Are you okay? Can you run?"

The boy was holding the side of his head. His eyes were vague, unfocused. He was crying in gulps, snot running from his nose.

Kittridge pulled him to his feet. "Come on."

He had no plan; the only plan was to escape. The buses were gone, ghosts of dust and diesel smoke. Kittridge hoisted Tim at the waist and swung him around to his back and told him to hold on. Three steps and the pain arrived, his knee shuddering. He stumbled, caught himself, somehow stayed upright. One thing was certain: with his leg, and with the boy's added weight, he wouldn't make it far on foot.

Then he remembered the armory. He'd seen an open-backed Humvee parked inside. Its hood had been standing open; one of the soldiers had been working on it. Would it still be there? Would it function?

As the soldiers at the western wire opened fire, Kittridge gritted his teeth and ran.

By the time he reached the armory, his leg was on the verge of collapse. How he'd made it those two hundred yards, he had no idea. But luck was with him. The vehicle was parked where he'd seen it, among the now-empty shelves. The hood was down—a good sign—but would the vehicle run? He lowered Tim to the passenger seat, got behind the wheel, and pressed the starter.

Nothing. He took a breath to steady himself. Think, Kittridge, think. Hanging beneath the dash was a nest of disconnected wires. Somebody had been working on the ignition. He pulled the wires free, picked two, and touched the ends together. No response. He had no idea what he was doing—why had he thought this would work? He arbitrarily selected two more wires, red and green.

A spark leapt; the engine roared to life. He jammed the Humvee into gear, aimed for the doors, and shoved the accelerator to the floor.

They barreled toward the gate. But a new problem lay before them: how to make it through. Several thousand people were trying to do the same thing, a roiling human mass attempting to wedge itself through the narrow exit. Without taking his foot off the gas, Kittridge leaned on the horn, realizing too late what a bad idea this was—that the mob had nothing to lose.

It turned. It saw. It charged.

Kittridge braked and swung the wheel, but too late: the hordes swallowed the Humvee like a breaking wave. His door flew open, hands pulling at him, trying to break his grip on the wheel. He heard Tim scream as he fought to keep control. People were lunging at the vehicle from all directions, boxing him in. A face collided with the windshield, then was gone. Hands were reaching over his face from behind, clawing at him, more pulling at his arms. "Get off me!" he yelled, trying to bat them away, but it was no use. There were simply too many, and as more bodies rolled over the windshield and under the vehicle's tires and the Humvee began to tip, he reached for Tim, bracing for the crash; and that was the end of that.

*　　*　　*

Meanwhile, at a distance of three miles, the line of buses—carrying a total of 2,043 civilian refugees, 36 FEMA and Red Cross workers, and 27 military personnel—was roaring eastward. Many of the people on board were sobbing; others were locked in prayer. Those with children were clutching them fiercely. A few, despite the earnest pleas of their fellows to shut the hell up, were still screaming. While a handful were already undergoing the wrenching self-reproach of having left so many behind, the vast majority possessed no such misgivings. They were the lucky ones, the ones who'd gotten away.

At the wheel of the Redbird, Danny Chayes was experiencing, for the first time in his life, an emotion that could only be described as a magnificent wholeness of self. It was as if he had lived all of his twenty-six years within an artificially narrow bandwidth of his potential personhood, only to have the scales fall abruptly from his eyes. Like the bus whose course he guided, Danny had been shot forward, propelled into a new state of being in which a range of contrary feelings, in all their distinctive contours, existed simultaneously in his mind. He was afraid, genuinely and soulfully afraid, and yet this fear was a source of not paralysis but power, a rich well of courage that seemed to rise and overflow within him. *You're the captain of that ship,* Mr. Purvis said, and that's what Danny was. Over his left shoulder, Pastor Don and Vera were talking away, speaking in urgent tones about this and that and the other; behind them, on the benches, the others were huddled together in pairs. The Robinsons with their baby, who was making a kind of mewing sound; Wood and Delores, who were holding hands as they prayed; Jamal and Mrs. Bellamy, the two of them actually hugging; April, sitting woefully alone, her face too stunned for tears. Their deliverance had become the sole purpose of Danny's life, the fixed point in his personal cosmos around which everything else revolved, yet in the excitement of the moment and Danny's discovery of the amazing fact of his aliveness, their presence was a pure abstraction. At the wheel of his Redbird 450, Danny Chayes was in union with himself and with the universe, and when he saw, as no doubt the drivers of the other buses did as well, the second mass of virals rising from the predawn darkness to the south, and then the third, coming from the north, and discerned in his mind's eye with swift three-dimensional calculation that these two bodies would subsequently unite to form a single encircling mass that would swarm over the buses like hornets loosed from a nest, he knew what he had to do. Swinging the wheel to the left, he broke free from the convoy and jammed the accelerator to the floor, soaring past the other buses in the line. Seventy, seventy-five, eighty miles an hour: with every ounce of his being, he willed the bus to go faster. What are you doing? Pastor Don yelled. For the love of God, Danny, what are you doing? But Danny knew just what he was doing. His goal was not evasion, for there could be none; his goal was to be the first. To hit the pod at such barreling velocity that he would sail right through it, carving a corridor of destruction. The space behind him had erupted in a chorus of screams; beyond his windshield the pods were merging, a swelling legion of light. His knuckles were white on the wheel.

"Get down, everyone!" he yelled. "Get down!"

"What the fuck!"

Nelson was backing away, holding his hands protectively before his face. Guilder realized the man pretty much expected him to shoot him, too. Which was nothing he was particularly averse to, though in the near term he had other requirements.

"Get the woman," he said, gesturing with the pistol.

"There's no time! Christ, you didn't have to kill him!"

There were more concussions from above. The air was swirling with dust. "I'll be the judge. Move."

Later, Guilder would have cause to wonder how he'd known to get the woman first, one of the more fateful decisions of his life. He might have chosen to leave her, bringing about an altogether different outcome. Intuition, perhaps? Sentimentality for the bond he'd discerned between her and Grey—a bond that had eluded him all his life? Pushing Nelson forward at the end of his pistol, he crossed the lab to the door of Lila's chamber.

"Open it."

Lila Kyle, aroused by the explosions, had given herself over to incoherent and terrified screaming; she had no idea where she was or what was happening. She was strapped to a bed. The bed was in a room. The room and everything in it were moving. It was as if she'd awakened from one dream to find herself lost in another, each equally unreal, and she experienced only a partial awareness of Nelson and Guilder as they entered the room. The two men were arguing. She heard the word "helicopter." She heard the word "escape." The smaller of the two was plunging a needle into her arm. Lila could offer no resistance, yet the instant the needle pierced her skin a jolt of energy hit her heart, as if she'd been connected to a giant battery. Adrenalin, she thought. I have been sedated, and now they are injecting me with adrenalin, to wake me up. The smaller man was hauling her to her feet. Beneath her gown, a cold nakedness prickled her skin. Could she stand? Could she walk? Just get her out of here, the second man said.

With a tremendous urgency she could not make herself share, he half-dragged, half-carried her across the wide room, some kind of laboratory. The lights were out; only emergency beams shone from the corners. In the distance, a series of roars, and after each a moment of prolonged shuddering, like an earthquake. Glass was jostling, making a pinging sound. They came to a heavy door with a metal ring, like something on a submarine. The smaller man swung it open and stepped inside. She was being held by the larger man now; he was brandishing a pistol. He gripped her from behind, one hand wrapping her waist, the other pressing the barrel to her midsection. Her thoughts were coming clearer now. Her heart was clicking like a metronome. What would emerge from the door? She could smell the man's breath close to her face, a warm rottenness. She felt his fear in his grip; his hands, his whole body were trembling. "I'm pregnant," Lila said, or started to say, thinking this might alter the situation. But her voice was cut short as, from the far side of the door, came a womanly sound of shrieking.

The aerial operations over western and central Iowa on the night of June 9 were not without risks. Chief among them was that the pilots might fail to carry out their orders, and, in fact, some did not: seven flight crews refused to deploy their payloads over civilian targets, while three more claimed to have suffered mechanical malfunctions that prevented them from doing so, an operational failure rate of six percent. (Of these ten flight crews, three were court-martialed, five were reprimanded and returned to duty, and two dropped to the deck and were never seen again.) In the coming weeks, as the mission of JTF Scorch expanded to include centers of population throughout the nation's middle section and the Intermountain West, members of the task force would recall this statistic with something like nostalgia—the good old days. By the first of August, so many aviators were either sitting in the stockade as prisoners of conscience or had vanished with their aircraft into the skies above the dying continent that it became increasingly difficult to mount a coherent aerial offensive, casting the very mission of JTF Scorch into doubt. These difficulties were compounded by secessionist movements in California and Texas, both of which proceeded to declare themselves sovereign and appropriate all federal military resources within their borders, effectively daring Washington to stop them by force—a remarkably shrewd gambit, both militarily and politically, as by this time the situation was in pure free fall. Much bluster ensued on both sides, culminating in the Battle of Wichita Falls and the Battle of Fresno, in which vast numbers of American military, both on the ground and in the air, threw in the towel, laid down their arms, and asked for sanctuary. Thus, by mid-October of the year that came to be known by subsequent generations as the year zero, the nation known as the United States could be said to exist no more.

But in the early morning hours of June 9, beneath a moonless Iowa sky, JTF Scorch was still on-line, enjoying the full, or nearly full, cooperation of its assets. In confirmation of the task force's projections, great masses of Infected Persons had collected in four distinct hot spots across the state: Mason City, Des Moines, Marshalltown, and the FEMA refugee-processing facility in Fort Powell. By 0200, the first three had been dispensed with; Fort Powell was the final prize. A combination of A-10 Warthogs and F-18 fighter-bombers began the assault; concurrently a C-130 transport was inbound from MacDill. Within its bay lay an explosive device called a GBU-43/B Massive Ordnance Air Blast Bomb, or MOAB. Containing 18,700 pounds of H6 high explosive, the MOAB was the largest non-nuclear bomb in the United States military arsenal, capable of producing an impact crater five hundred feet in diameter and a blast wave sufficient to level an area the size of nine city blocks; its fires would burn for days.

When Nelson bent to undo Grey's straps—straps no longer attached to anything—Grey lurched forward, seizing him by the biceps and burying his teeth in the man's neck. A deep bite: he felt Nelson's windpipe being crushed beneath his jaws. As the two tumbled backward over the bed, Grey shook him like a wolf with a rabbit in its teeth; a jet of hot blood filled Grey's mouth. They were on the floor now, Nelson face-up, Grey above him. An agonal twitch of Nelson's hands and feet, and that was all. Grey burrowed his jaws deeper, into the soft meat.

He drank.

Had it been this easy for Zero, Grey wondered, this pleasurable? A rich vitality poured through him, a glorious immensity of pure sensation. With a final, soul-satisfying inhalation of blood, Grey pulled his face away. He allowed himself a couple of seconds to regard the corpse on the floor. The flesh of Nelson's face looked as if it had been shrink-wrapped to its underlying structure; his eyes, like the eyes of the woman in the parking lot of the Red Roof, bulged reptilianly from their bony orbits, staring into the heart of eternity. Grey searched his mind for some emotion that corresponded to his actions—guilt, perhaps, or pity, or even disgust. He was a murderer, a man who had killed. He had stolen the life of another. But he felt none of these things. He'd done what he had to do.

The door to his chamber stood open. Lila, he thought, I am coming to save you—all that has happened has ordained it.

He stepped through.

What emerged from the door was a man. The figure was backlit, sunk in shadow. As he advanced, beams from the emergency lights slanted across his face. His gown was bathed in blood.

Lawrence?

"Don't." The man with the gun was dragging Lila backward, jabbing its barrel deep into her ribs. His steps were uncertain, fluttering. His whole body was shaking like a leaf. It seemed that any second he might fall. "Keep your distance."

Grey reached his bloody hands plaintively forward. "Lila, it's me."

Horror, revulsion, a protective mental numbness at the violent swiftness of events—all combined in Lila's mind to grip her in a frozen, focusless terror in which her body and her brain seemed like only tangentially associated phenomena. Through the fog she realized what the screams from the chamber meant. If the state of his gown was any indication, Lawrence had not merely killed the small man but torn him to pieces. Which made a kind of sense; Lila should have seen this coming. She remembered the tank. She remembered Lawrence's face, a mask of gore like some Halloween horror, as it popped from the hatch, and the glass of the Volvo's window splintering under his fist. Lawrence had become a monster. He had become one of those . . . things. (Poor Roscoe.) And yet there was something about his eyes, which she could not look away from, that told her not to be afraid. They seemed to bore straight into her, shining with an almost holy light.

"Don't you know what's happening?" the man barked. "We have to get out of here."

"Let her go."

Another blast from above and a lurching wave passed through the floor. Glass was falling; everything was caving in. The gun's barrel was pressed against her ribs like a cold finger pointing at her heart. The man angled his head toward a corner of the room.

"Up the stairs. There's a helicopter waiting."

"Put the gun down and I'll go with you."

"Goddamnit, there's no time for this!"

Something was happening to her. A kind of awakening, and it wasn't just the gun. It was as if she were returning to consciousness after years of sleep. How foolish she'd been! Painting the nursery, of all things! Pretending they were taking a drive in the country, as if that could change anything! Because David was dead, and Eva was dead, and Brad, whose heart she had broken; she had convinced herself the world wasn't ending, because it already had. And here was this man, this Lawrence Grey, who had come upon her like a redeemer, an angel to lead her to safety, as if the baby she carried were his own, and she knew what she had to say.

"Please, Lawrence. Do what he asks. Think about our baby."

A fraught moment followed, so suspended as to seem outside the flow of time. Lila could read the question on Lawrence's face. Could he get to the pistol before the man fired? And if he could, what then?

"Show us the way out of here."

By the time they reached the roof, the helicopter's blades were turning, casting a whirling wind across the rooftop. The sky was glowing with an eerie, emerald-tinged light, like the insides of a greenhouse. It seemed the helicopter would leave without them, a final irony, but then Lila saw the pilot urgently waving to them from the cockpit. They climbed aboard; Guilder slammed the door behind them.

Upward.

Kittridge became aware that he was face-down in the dirt. A taste of blood was in his mouth. He tried to get to his feet but realized he had only one; his prosthesis was gone. He lifted his face to see the Humvee tipped on its side a hundred yards away, like a beached sea creature. Its windshield was smashed; steam was pouring from its hood and undercarriage. The mob had fallen on it like a pack of animals; some were attempting to rock it back onto its wheels, but the effort was disorganized, coming from all sides. Others were standing on the top, shoving and kicking competitors away, defending their positions as if the mere possession of such a thing might offer some protection.

Kittridge crawled to where Tim lay. The boy was breathing but unconscious—a small mercy. His body was splayed at a tortured angle; his hair was matted with blood. More was running from his mouth and nose. Kittridge realized the shooting had stopped. Soldiers were tearing past, but there was nowhere to run. A mass of virals lay at the wire, felled by the soldiers' bullets, but as his eyes scanned the scene, Kittridge understood that the attack had been a test, an advance force sent to exhaust the soldiers' defenses. A second, vastly larger pod was now amassing. As it roared toward them, the image stretched, flowing like a shimmering green liquid as it surrounded the encampment. The final assault would come from all directions.

He lifted Tim's body by the shoulders and held his chest against his own. They were in the midst of chaos, people running, voices shouting, bombs falling; yet as they crouched in the dust, a bubble of silent inactivity seemed to encase them, protecting them from the destruction. Kittridge turned his face toward the east. For a brief moment he imagined he could see Danny's bus streaming away in the darkness, though this was an illusion, he knew. By now they were gone, far beyond the reach of his vision. *Godspeed to you, Danny Chayes.* A deep stillness wrapped his being and, with it, a feeling of the past, an experience like déjà vu: he was where he was but also not, he was here and also there, he was a boy at play and a man at war and the third thing he'd become. Images flashed through his consciousness: the viral in her wedding dress clinging to the hood of the Ferrari; a view of sparkling sunlight on a river he had fished for years; April, on the night when they had sat together in the window of the school, watching the stars, and the look of quiet peace on her face as the two of them made love; the boy in the car, his eyes full of a terrible knowledge, and his hand—his little boy's hand—desperately reaching, then gone. All of these and more. He recalled his mother, singing to him. The warmth of her breath on his face, and the feeling of being very small, a new being in the world. *The world is not my home,* she sang in her silky voice, *for I'm just passing through. The treasures are laid up somewhere, high beyond the blue. The angels beckon me from heaven's open door, and I can't feel at home in this world anymore.*

Tim had begun to make a choking sound; his eyes flickered, fought to open, then stilled. The virals, having completed their encirclement, were surging toward the wire. Kittridge became aware of an absence of sound around them. The battle was over; the planes had broken away. Then, in the quiet, he detected, high above, the drone of a heavy aircraft. Kittridge angled his face to the sky. A C-130 transport, coming from the south. As it passed overhead an object released from its belly, its dive abruptly stalled by the puff of a parachute. The plane climbed away.

Kittridge closed his eyes. So, the end. It would happen instantaneously, a painless departure, quicker than thought. He felt the presence of his body one last time: the taste of air in his lungs, the blood surging in his veins, the drumlike beating of his heart. The bomb was dropping toward them.

"I've got you," he said, hugging Tim fiercely; and again, over and over, so that the boy would be hearing these words. "I've got you, I've got you, I've got you, I've got you."

The blast wave from the MOAB struck the helicopter carrying Grey and Lila broadside: a blinding sheen of light, followed by an earsplitting slap of heat and sound. As if lifted on the crest of a wave, the helicopter lurched forward, its nose pointed earthward at a forty-five-degree angle, rocketed up again and began to spin, its angular momentum accelerating like a line of skaters wheeling on an ice rink. It spun and as it spun the pilot pitched to the side, his neck broken by the force of impact with the windshield; but by this time, between the sound of the alarm—a harsh blaring—and the centrifugal force of their velocity, nobody inside the helicopter was thinking very much at all. The forces that had held them aloft were gone, and nothing else would happen until they reached the ground.

Lawrence Grey experienced the crash itself as a severing in time: one moment he was pressed against the wall of the helicopter in its death spiral, the next he was lying in the wreckage. He felt but did not specifically recall the moment of impact; it had lodged in his body as a ringing sensation, as if he were a bell that had been struck. There was a smell of fuel, and hot insulation, and an electrical crackling sound. Something heavy and inertly soft was lying on top of him. It was Guilder. He was breathing but unconscious. The helicopter, what was left of it, lay on its side; where the roof should have been was now the door.

"Lawrence, help me!"

The voice came from behind him. He shoved Guilder's body off his chest and felt his way to the rear of the helicopter. One of the benches had twisted loose, pinning Lila to the floor, crushing her at the waist. Her bare legs, the flimsy fabric of her gown—all glistened with a heavy, dark blood.

"Help me," she choked. Her eyes were closed, tears squeezing from the corners. "Please, God, help me. I'm bleeding, I'm bleeding."

He tried to pull her free by her feet, but she began to shriek in agony. There was no other way; he'd have to move the bench. Gripping it by its frame, Grey began to twist. A groan and then a pop and it broke away from the decking.

Lila was sobbing, moaning in pain. Grey knew he shouldn't move her, but he had no choice. Positioning the bench beneath the open door, he hoisted her to his shoulder, stepped up, and laid her gently on the roof.

He followed, climbing up the opposite side. He slid down the fuselage, circled back, and reached up to receive her, easing her body down the side of the helicopter.

"Oh, God. Please, don't let me lose her. Don't let me lose the baby."

He lowered Lila to the ground, which was strewn with rubble from the destroyed laboratory—twisted girders, concrete blasted into chunks, shards of glass. He was weeping, too. It was too late, he knew; the baby was gone. Gouts of blood, clotted with black, were spilling from between Lila's legs, an unstoppable flow. In another moment she would follow her baby into darkness. A childhood prayer found Grey's lips and he began to murmur, again and again, "Holy Mary, Mother of God, pray for us sinners, now and at the hour of our death, amen. Holy Mary, Mother of God, pray for us sinners, now and at the hour of our death, amen. . . ."

Save her, Grey.

You know what to do.

He did; he knew. The answer had been inside him all along. Since the Red Roof and Ignacio and the Home Depot and Project NOAH and long before.

Do you see, Grey?

He lifted his face to behold them. The virals. They were everywhere and all around, emerging from the darkness and flames: flesh of his flesh, unholy and blood-driven, encircling him like a demonic chorus. He was kneeling before them, his face streaked with tears. He felt no fear, only astonishment.

They are yours, Grey. The ones I give to you.

—Yes. They are mine.

Save her. Do it.

He needed something sharp. His hands searched the ground, lighting upon a sliver of metal, some broken shard from a world of broken, piecemeal things. Eight inches long, the edges ragged as a saw. Positioning it lengthwise across his wrist, he closed his eyes and slashed a deep gash into his flesh. The blood spurted forth, a wide, dark river, filling his palm. The blood of Grey, the Unleasher of Night, Familiar of the One Called Zero. Lila was moaning, dying. Any breath might be her last. A moment's hesitation—some last, extinguishing human light inside him—and Grey placed his wrist against her lips, tenderly, like a mother easing her breast to the mouth of a newborn babe.

"Drink," he said.

Grey never even saw it: the chunk of concrete, thirty-four pounds of solid rock, that Guilder, with all the strength he could muster, hoisted into the air above Grey's head and then brought down upon him.

22

They made their way into Chicago as the sun was setting, filling the sky with a golden light. First the outer ring of suburbs, empty and still; then, rising before them like a promise, the shape of the city. The lone survivors, their lives joined by the mysterious bond of their survival: they traveled in silence, dreamers in a forgotten land, their progress marked only by the grumble of the bus's engine, the hypnotic whoosh of asphalt beneath their wheels. Ghosts sat beside them, the people they had lost.

As the city came into focus, Pastor Don bent forward from his seat behind Danny. Helicopters were floating over the city, buzzing among the skyscrapers like bees around a hive; high above, the contrails of aircraft cast ribbons of color against the deepening blue. A zone of safety, it seemed, but this couldn't last. In their hearts they knew there was none.

"Let's pull off a minute."

Danny drew the bus to the side of the roadway. Pastor Don rose to address the group. The decision was upon them. Should they stop or continue? They had the bus, water, food, fuel. No one knew what lay ahead. Take a minute, Pastor Don said.

A murmur of agreement, then a show of hands. The verdict was unanimous.

"Okay, Danny."

They circled the city to the south and continued east on a rural blacktop. Night fell like a dome snapping down on the earth. By daybreak they were somewhere in Ohio. A landscape of pure anonymity; they could have been anywhere. Time had slowed to a crawl. Fields, trees, houses, mailboxes streaming by, the horizon always unreachable, rolling away. In the small towns, a semblance of life continued; people had no idea where to go, what to do. The highways, it was said, were jammed. At a mini-mart where they stopped for supplies, the cashier, glancing out the window at the bus, asked, Can I go with you? On the wall behind her head, a television screen showed a city in flames. She spoke in a hushed tone so as not to be overheard. She didn't ask where they were going;

their destination was simply away. A quick phone call and minutes later her husband and two teenage sons were standing by the bus, holding suitcases.

Others joined them. A man in overalls walking alone on the highway with a rifle over his shoulder. An elderly couple, dressed as if for church, their car expired on the side of the road with its hood standing open, steam exhaling from its cracked radiator. A pair of cyclists, Frenchmen, who had been riding across the country when the crisis began. Whole families squeezed aboard. Many were overcome, weeping with gratitude as they took their places. Like fish joining a school, they were absorbed into the whole. Cities were bypassed, one after the other: Columbus, Akron, Youngstown, Pittsburgh. Even the names had begun to feel historical, like cities of a lost empire. Giza. Carthage. Pompeii. Customs evolved among them, as if they were a kind of rolling town. Some questions were asked but not others. Have you heard about Salt Lake, Tulsa, St. Louis? Do they know what it is yet, have they discovered the answer? Only in motion was there safety; every stop felt fraught with peril. For a time they sang. "The Ants Go Marching," "On Top of Spaghetti," "A Hundred Bottles of Beer on the Wall."

The landscape rose and fell, enfolding them in a green embrace: Pennsylvania, the Endless Mountains. Signs of human habitation were few and far between, the leavings of an era long passed. The battered coal towns, the forgotten hamlets with a single factory shuttered for years, red-brick smokestacks forlornly poking a blue summer sky. The air smelled strongly of pine. By now they numbered over seventy, bodies crammed into the aisles, children on laps, faces pressed to the windows. Fuel was a constant worry, yet somehow they always found more in the nick of time, their passage protected by an unseen hand.

By the afternoon of the third day, they were approaching Philadelphia. They had traveled half the width of a continent; ahead lay the eastern seaboard, with its barricade of cities, a wall of humanity pressed to the sea. A feeling of finality had taken over. There was no place else to run. They homed in on the city along the Schuylkill River, its surface as dark and impenetrable as granite. The outer towns felt to be in hiding, houses boarded, roads empty of cars. The river widened to a broad basin; heavy trees, dappled with sunlight, draped like a curtain over the road. A sign read: CHECKPOINT 2 MILES. A brief conferral and all were agreed: they had come to the end. Their fates would find them here.

The soldiers gave them directions. Curfew was two hours away, but already the streets were quiet, virtually without movement except for

Army vehicles and a few police cars. Narrow, sun-drenched lanes, ramshackle brownstones, the infamous corners where packs of young men had once lingered; then suddenly the park appeared, an oasis of green in the heart of the city.

They followed the signs past the barricades, masked soldiers waving them through. The park was teeming with people, as if for a concert. Tents, RVs, figures curled on the ground by their suitcases as if lodged there by a tide. When the crowds grew too thick they were forced to abandon the bus by the side of the road and continue on foot. A terminal act: to leave it behind felt disloyal, like putting down a beloved dog who could no longer walk. They moved as one, unable to let go of one another yet, to fade into a faceless collective. A long line had formed; the air was as heavy as milk. Above them, unseen, armies of insects buzzed in the darkening trees.

"I can't do this," said Pastor Don. He had halted on the path, a look of sudden horror on his face.

Wood had stopped, too. Twenty yards ahead lay a series of chutes, harshly lit by spotlights on poles; people were being patted down, giving their names. "I know what you mean."

"I mean, Jesus. It's like we only just came from here."

The mob was streaming past. The two Frenchmen moved by with barely a glance, their meager belongings bundled under their arms. They could all feel it: something was being lost. They stepped to the side.

"Do you think we can find gas?" Jamal asked.

"I just know I'm not going in there," Pastor Don said.

They returned to the bus. Already a man was trying to jimmy the ignition. He was skinny, his face blackened with grime, his eyes roving in their sockets like he was on something. Wood seized him by the scruff of the neck and hurled him down the steps. Get the fuck out of here, he said.

They boarded. Danny turned the key; the engine roared under them. Slowly they backed away, the crowd parting around them like waves around a ship. The air was drinking up the last of the light. They turned in a wide circle on the grass and pulled away.

"Where to?" Danny asked.

No one had an answer. "I don't think it matters," Pastor Don said.

It didn't. They spent the night in Valley Forge park, sleeping on the ground by the bus, then headed south, staying off the highways. Maryland, Virginia, North Carolina: they kept on going. The journey had acquired its own meaning, independent of any destination. The goal was to move, to keep moving. They were together; that was all that mattered. The bus jostled beneath them on its tired springs. One by one the cities fell, the lights went out. The world was dissolving, taking its stories with it. Soon it would be gone.

Her name was April Donadio. The child that even now had taken root inside her would be a boy, Bernard. April would give him the last name Donadio, so that he might carry a piece of each of them in name; and across the years she spoke to the boy often of his father, the kind of man he was—how brave and kind and a little sad, too, and how, though their time together was brief, he had imparted to her the greatest gift, which was the courage to go on. That's what love is, she told the boy, what love does. I hope someday you love somebody the way that I loved him.

But that came later. This bus of survivors, twelve in sum: they could have continued that way forever. And in a sense, they did. The green fields of summer, the abandoned, time-stilled towns, the forests thick with shadow, the bus endlessly rolling. They were like a vision, they had slipped into eternity, a zone beyond time. There and not there, a presence unseen but felt, like stars in the daytime sky.

III

THE FIELD

NORTH AGRICULTURAL COMPLEX
ORANGE ZONE, EX-MURUS
KERRVILLE, TEXAS
JULY 79 A.V.

For he today that sheds his blood with me shall be my brother.

—SHAKESPEARE,
Henry V

*** WARNING ***

YOU ARE ENTERING THE <u>ORANGE ZONE</u>.

WATCH THE CLOCK.
KNOW THE LOCATION OF THE NEAREST HARDBOX.

DO NOT ENTER UNSWEPT AREAS.

IF YOU MISS THE LAST TRANSPORT,
DO NOT EXPECT TO BE RESCUED.
SHELTER IN PLACE.

OBEY ALL COMMANDS OF THE DOMESTIC AUTHORITY.

VIOLATORS SUBJECT TO FINE AND/OR IMPRISONMENT
UNDER ARTICLE 694, SECTION 12 OF THE
TEXAS REPUBLIC CODE OF MODIFIED MARTIAL LAW.

WHEN IN DOUBT, RUN.

23

It was Dee Vorhees who said she wanted to bring the children.

Though she was not the only one. All the women, as her husband, Curtis, was soon to discover, were in on the plan. Dee's cousin Sally, and Mace Francis, and Shar Withers and Cece Cauley and Ali Dodd and even Matty Wright—the permanently nervous, twittering Matty Wright—told their husbands the same thing. A veritable ambush, the women flanking their men from left and right with a wifely insistence that could not be refused: *A few hours in the sunshine,* they all said, lying in bed or washing the dishes or readying the children for school. *What's the harm? Let's bring the children this time.*

And it wasn't as if they hadn't taken the girls ex-murus before, Dee reminded him, the two of them sharing a quiet moment in the kitchen after putting the girls to sleep. There was that time, she said—how long ago?—when they'd gone to Green Field for Nitia's birthday. Little Siri just a toddler, Nitia still dragging that filthy blanket wherever she went. Those peaceful hours under the spillway, and the butterflies—did he remember? The way they seemed to float along an airborne river, their bright wings falling and pumping to rise again, and the one that, surprising them all, had alighted on Nitia's nose. Dee said: Could you not feel God's presence in a thing like that? The sweet, free feeling of it, the little girls laughing and laughing, the warning siren hours off, some distant future time, and the blue sky suspended like heaven itself above their heads and the four of them being ex-murus together. The Green Zone, it was true, she didn't say it wasn't, but they could *see* the perimeter from there, the watchtowers and the sentries and the fences with their curling razor wire, and who decided these things, anyway? Who decided where one zone ended and the next began? How was an outing to North Ag any different, any more dangerous, really? Cruk would be there, and Tifty as well (the name had popped out before she could stop herself, but what could you do?); there were the hardboxes if anything happened, but why would it? In the middle of a summer day? The traps had gone empty for months, not even any dopeys around. Everyone was saying so. A few hours in the sunshine, away from the gray and grime of the city. A summer picnic in the field. That was all she was asking.

Would he do it, this one thing? For the girls? But why not just come out and say it. Would he do it for her, the wife who loved him?

Which was how, two days later, on a sultry July morning, the temperature already rising through the eighties and headed for a hundred, Curtis Vorhees, age thirty-two, foreman of the North Agricultural Complex, his father's old .38 tucked into his waistband with three rounds in the cylinder (his father had shot the other three), found himself on a transport full of whole families, and not just families: children. Nitia and Siri and their cousin Carson, just turned twelve but still so slight his feet dangled three inches above the floor; Bab and Dunk Withers, the twins; the Francis girls, Rena and Jules, seated at the rear so they wouldn't have to pay attention to the boys; little Jenny Apgar, riding on her older brother Gunnar's lap; Dean and Amelia Wright, the two of them old enough to act bored and put out; Merry Dodd and her baby brother, Satch, and little Louis Cauley, still in a basket; Reese Cuomo and Dash Martinez and Cindy-Sue Bodine. Seventeen in all, a concentrated mass of childlike heat and noise as distinct to Vorhees's senses as a buzzing swarm of bees. It was common for the wives to join their husbands for planting, and of course at harvesttime, when every pair of hands found work to do; but this was something new. Even as the bus cleared the gate, its old diesel engine roaring and sputtering, its tired chassis swaying under them, Curtis Vorhees felt it. A hot, dull job had suddenly become an occasion; the day possessed the hopeful spirit of a tradition being born. Why hadn't they thought of this before, that bringing the children would remake the day into something special?

Past the dam and fuel depot and fence line, with its sentries waving them through and down, down into the valley they went, into the golden light of a July morning. The women, seated at the rear with the hampers and supplies, were gossiping and laughing among themselves; the children, after a fruitless attempt by one of the mothers—of course it would be Ali Dodd—to organize them into a rousing chorus of the Texas anthem, the only song everyone knew (*Texas, our Texas! All hail the mighty State! Texas, our Texas! So wonderful, so great!*), had sorted themselves into various warring factions, the older girls whispering and giggling and elaborately ignoring the boys, the boys elaborately pretending not to care, the little ones bouncing on the benches and darting through the aisle to launch their various assaults; the men up front were sitting in their customary guarded silence, communicating only through the occasional exchange of a wry look or a single raised eyebrow: *What have we gotten ourselves into?* They were men of the fields, their hands thickened from work; hair shorn close, crescents of dirt under their nails, no beards. Vorhees withdrew his timepiece from his pocket and checked the hour: 7:05. Eleven hours until the siren, twelve for the last transport, thirteen until dark. *Watch the clock. Know the location of the nearest hardbox. When in doubt, run.* Words imprinted on his consciousness as indelibly as a childhood rhyme, or one of the sisters' prayers. Vorhees twisted in his seat to catch Dee's eye. She was balancing Siri on her lap, the little girl's nose pressed to the window to watch the passing world. Dee gave him a weary smile, made of words: *Thank you.* Siri had begun to bounce, pumping her knees with pleasure. The little girl pointed a chubby finger out the window, squealing with delight. *Thank you for this.*

And then, before they knew it, they'd arrived. Through the windshield of the transport, the fields of North Ag Complex leapt into view, its vast patchwork laid out below them like the squares of a motley quilt: corn and wheat, cotton and beans, rice and barley and oats. Fifteen thousand acres stitched together by a fretwork of dusty roads, and, at their edges, windbreaks of cottonwood and oak; the watchtowers and pump houses with their catch basins and nests of pipe and, dispersed at regular inter- vals, the hardboxes, marked by tall orange banners, hanging limply in the breathless air. Vorhees knew their locations cold, but when the corn was tall, you couldn't always find them quickly without the flags.

He rose and moved to the front, where Dee's brother, Nathan— everybody called him Cruk—was standing behind the driver. Vorhees was foreman, but it was Cruk, as the senior Domestic Security officer, who was really in charge.

"Looks like we've got a good day for this," Vorhees said.

Cruk shrugged but said nothing. Like the field hands, he was dressed in whatever he had: patched jeans and a khaki shirt frayed at the collar and wrists. Atop this he wore a plastic vest, bright orange, with the words TEXAS DEPARTMENT OF TRANSPORATION printed on the back. He was hold- ing his rifle, a long-barreled .30-06 with a sniper scope, across his chest; a reconditioned .45 was holstered to his thigh. The rifle was standard issue, but the .45 was something special, old military or maybe police, with an oiled black finish and a polished wood grip. He even had a name for it; he called it Abigail. You had to know somebody to get a weapon like that, and Vorhees didn't have to think too hard to figure out who this person might be; it was pretty much common knowledge that Tifty was on the trade. Vorhees's .38, with its paltry three rounds, felt meager in comparison, but there was no way he could have afforded a weapon like that.

"You can always say it was Dee's idea," Cruk said.

"So you don't think this is smart."

His brother-in-law gave a stifled laugh. It was at such moments that Cruk's resemblance to his sister was the most striking, though it was also true that this was more suggestion than actual physical similarity, and something only Vorhees would have noticed. Most people, in fact, remarked on how different the two of them looked.

"Doesn't matter what I think. You know that as well as I do. Dee sets her mind to something, you might as well just hang up your balls and call it a day."

The bus gave a bone-jarring bang; Vorhees fought to stay upright. Behind them, the children shrieked with happiness.

"Hey, Dar," Cruk said, "you think maybe you can miss some of those?"

The old woman at the wheel responded with a wet *harrumph;* telling Dar what to do with her bus was tantamount to an act of war. All the transport drivers were older women, usually widows; there was no rule about this—it was just how things were done. With a face ossified into a permanent scowl, Dar was a figure of legendary cantankerousness, as no-nonsense a woman as ever walked the earth. She kept time with a stopwatch hung around her neck and would leave you standing in a cloud of dust if you were so much as one minute late for the last transport. More than one field hand had spent a night in a hardbox scared out of his wits, counting the minutes till dawn.

"A busload of kids, for Christ's sake. I can barely think with all this noise." Dar shot her eyes to the pitted mirror above the windshield. "For the love of it, pipe down back there! Duncan Withers, you get down off that bench this instant! And don't think I can't see you, Jules Francis! That's right," she warned with an icy glare, "I'm talking to you, young lady. You can wipe that smirk off your face right now."

Everyone fell abruptly silent, even the wives. But when Dar returned her eyes to the road, Vorhees realized her anger was false; it was all the woman could do not to break out laughing.

Cruk clapped a big hand on his shoulder. "Relax, Vor. Just let everyone enjoy the day."

"Did I say I was worried?"

Cruk's expression sobered. "Look, I know you'd rather Tifty wasn't coming along. Okay? I get it. But he's the best shot I've got. Say what you like, the guy can punch out a hanger at three hundred yards."

Vorhees wasn't aware that he'd been thinking about Tifty at all. But now that Cruk had brought the subject up, he wondered if maybe he was.

"So you think we'll need him."

Cruk shrugged. "Summer day like this, we'll have no problems. I'm just being careful is all. They're my girls too, you know." He broke the mood with a grin. "Just so long as Dee doesn't make a habit of this. I had to call in about fifty favors to put this little party together, and you can tell her I said so."

The bus drew into the staging area. The last of the sweepers were emerging from the corn, dressed in their bulky pads and heavy gloves and helmets with cages obscuring their faces. An assortment of weapons hung off their persons: shotguns, rifles, pistols, even a few machetes. Cruk instructed the children to remain where they were; only when the all clear was given would they be permitted to exit the bus. As the adults began carting out the supplies, Tifty descended from the platform on the bus's roof, rendezvousing with Cruk at the rear to confer with the DS officer in charge of the sweeping squad, a man named Dillon. The rest of Dillon's team, eight men and four women, had gone to take water from the trough by the pump house.

Cruk strode back to where Vorhees was waiting with the rest of the men. Already the sun was blazing; the morning's humidity had burned away.

"Clean as a whistle—the windbreaks, too." He shot Vorhees a wink. "That'll cost Dee extra."

Before Cruk could even finish making the announcement, the children were bolting from their seats and streaming off the bus, clearing space for the sweepers, who would return to the city. Watching the children as they fanned over the grounds, their bodies and faces lit with excitement, Vorhees was momentarily transfixed, his mind caught in a tide of memory. For many, the youngest especially, the day's excursion represented their first trip beyond the walls; he'd known this from the start. Yet to witness the moment was something else. Did the air feel different in their lungs, he wondered, the sun on their faces, the ground beneath their feet? Had these things felt different to him, stepping from the transport the first time, all those years ago? And of course they had: to go ex-murus was to discover a world of limitless dimensions—a world you knew existed but had never believed yourself to be a part of. He recalled the sensation as a kind of weightless physical joy, but frightening too, like a dream in which he had been given the gift of flight but found himself unable to land.

By the watchtower, Fort and Chess were sinking poles to erect a sunshade; the women were toting out the tables and chairs and hampers of food. Ali Dodd, her face shaded beneath the brim of her wide straw hat, was already trying to organize some of the children into a game of takeaway. All just as Dee had foreseen when she'd broached the subject of bringing the children along.

"It's something, isn't it?"

Vorhees's cousin, Ty, was standing beside him, holding a hamper to his chest. Over six feet, with a narrow, mournful face, he always reminded Vorhees of a particularly sad-looking dog. Behind them, Dar gave three beeps of the horn; with a belch of oily smoke, the bus pulled away.

"I ever tell you about my first time out?"

"I don't think so."

"Trust me," Ty said, shaking his head in a way that told Vorhees the man had no intention of elaborating. "That's a story."

When everything had been unloaded, Cruk called the children under the tarp to review the rules, which everybody already knew. The first thing, Cruk began, was that everyone needed a buddy. Your buddy could be anyone, a brother or sister or friend, but you had to have one, and you had to stay with your buddy at all times. That was the most important thing. The open ground at the base of the watchtower was safe, within those boundaries they could go wherever they liked, but they were not to venture into the corn under any circumstances; the stand of trees at the south end was also off-limits.

Now, do you see those flags? Cruk asked, gesturing over the field. The orange ones, hanging down like that? Who can tell me what those are?

Half a dozen hands went up; Cruk's eyes roamed the group before landing on Dash Martinez. Seven years old, all knees and elbows, with a mop of dark hair; under the beam of Cruk's attention, he froze. He was seated between Merry Dodd and Reese Cuomo, who were covering their mouths, trying not to laugh. The hardboxes? the boy ventured. That's right, Cruk replied, nodding. Those are the hardboxes. Now tell me, he continued, addressing all of them, if the siren goes off, what should you do?

Run! someone said, then another and another. *Run!*

"Run where?" Cruk asked.

A chorus of voices this time: *Run to the hardboxes!*

He relaxed into a smile. "Good. Now go have fun."

They darted away, all except the teenagers, who lingered an extra moment by the awning, seeking to separate themselves from the younger children. But even they, Vorhees knew, would find their way into the sunshine. The playing cards came out, and skeins of yarn for knitting; before long, the women were all occupying themselves, watching the children from the shade, fanning their faces in the heat. Vorhees called the men around to hand out salt tablets; even drinking constantly, a man working in this heat could become dangerously dehydrated. They filled their bottles at the pump. There was no need to explain the task before them; detassling was a grueling if simple job they had all done many times. For every three rows of corn, a fourth row had been planted of a second strain. That row would be stripped of its tassles to prevent self-pollination; come harvesttime, it would produce a new, crossbred strain, more vigorous, to be used as seed corn for the following year. When Vorhees's father had first explained this process to him, years ago, it had seemed exciting, even vaguely erotic. What they were doing was, after all, part of the reproductive process, even if it was only corn. But the physical discomforts of the job—the hours in the grueling sun, the ceaseless rain of pollen on his hands and face, the insects that buzzed around his head, seeking any opportunity to bore into his ears and nose and mouth—had quickly disabused him of this notion. His first week in the field, one man had collapsed from heat stroke. Vorhees couldn't recall who that was or what had become of him; they'd put him on the next transport and gotten back to work. It was entirely possible the man had died.

Heavy canvas gloves and wide-brimmed hats and long-sleeved shirts buttoned to the wrists: by the time the men were ready to go, they were sweating profusely. Vorhees cast his gaze to the top of the watchtower, where Tifty had taken his position, scanning the tree line with his scope. Cruk was right; Tifty was the man to have up there. Whatever else was true about Tifty Lamont, his skills as a marksman were inarguable. Yet even to hear the man's name spoken, so many years later, aroused in Vorhees a fresh turning of anger. If anything, the passage of time had only magnified this feeling; each year that slipped past was one more year of Boz's unlived life. Why should Tifty grow to be a man when Boz had not? In more circumspect moments, Vorhees understood his emotions to be irrational; Tifty might have been the instigator on that fateful night, but any one of them could have said no, and Boz would be alive. Yet no matter what Dee said, or Cruk, or Tifty himself—who even now, sweeping the tree line with his rifle, was offering a silent promise to protect Vorhees's children—nothing could dissuade Vorhees from the belief that Tifty bore a singular blame. In the end, he was forced to accept his feelings as a failure of his own character and keep them to himself.

He divided the workers into three teams, each responsible for four rows. Then they made their way to the shelter to say their goodbyes. A game of kickball was under way in the field; from the far side of the watchtower came the ring of horseshoes in the pit. Dee was resting in the shade with Sally and Lucy Martinez, playing a round of hearts. Their games were epic, sometimes lasting for days.

"Looks like we're ready to go."

She lay down her cards, lifting her face toward him. "Come here."

He removed his hat and bent at the waist to receive her kiss.

"God, you stink already," she laughed, wrinkling her nose. "That's your last one for the day, I'm afraid." Then: "So, should I tell you to be careful?"

It was what they always said. "If you want."

"Well, then. Be careful."

Nit and Siri had wandered into the tent. Bits of grass were caught in their hair and the weave of their jumpers. Like puppies who'd been rolling around in the dirt.

"Hug your father, girls."

Vorhees knelt and took them into his arms as a warm bundle. "Be good for Mommy, all right? I'll be back for lunch."

"We're each other's buddies," Siri proclaimed.

He brushed the grass from their sweat-dampened hair. Sometimes just the sight of them moved him to a rush of love that actually brought tears to his eyes. "Of course you are. Just remember what your uncle Cruk told you. Stay where Mommy can see you."

"Carson says there are monsters in the field," Siri said. "Monsters who drink blood."

Vorhees darted his eyes to Dee, who shrugged. It wasn't the first time the subject had come up.

"Well, he's wrong," he told them. "He's trying to scare you, playing a joke."

"Then why do we have to stay out of the field?"

"Because those are the rules."

"Do you promise?"

He did his best to smile. Vorhees and Dee had agreed to keep this matter vague as long as they could; and yet they both understood that they could not keep the girls in the dark forever.

"I promise."

He hugged them again, each in turn and then together, and went to join his crew at the edge of the field. A wall of green six feet tall: the corn rows, a series of long hallways, receded to the windbreak. The sun had crossed an invisible border toward midday; nobody was talking. Vorhees checked his watch one last time. *Watch the clock. Know the location of the nearest hardbox. When in doubt, run.*

"All right, everybody," he said, drawing on his gloves. "Let's get this done."

And with these words, together, they stepped into the field.

In a sense, they had all become who they were because of a single night—the last night of their childhood. Cruk, Vorhees, Boz, Dee: they ran together in a pack, their daily orbits circumscribed only by the walls of the city and the watchful eyes of the sisters, who ran the school, and the DS, who ran everything else. A time of gossip, of rumor, of stories traded in the dust. Dirty faces, dirty hands, the four of them lingering in the alley behind their quarters on the way home from school. What was the world? *Where* was the world, and when would they see it? Where did their fathers go, and sometimes their mothers as well, returning to them smelling of work and duty and mysterious concerns? The outside, yes, but how was it different from the city? What did it feel like, taste like, sound like? Why, from time to time, did someone, a mother or a father, leave, never to return, as if the unseen realm beyond the walls had the power to swallow them whole? Dopeys, dracs, vampires, jumps: they knew the names but did not feel the full weight of their meanings. There were dracs, which were the meanest, which were the same thing as jumps or vampires (a word only old people used); and there were dopeys, which were similar but not the same. Dangerous, yes, but not as much, more like a nuisance on the order of scorpions or snakes. Some said that dopeys were dracs that had lived too long, others that they were a different sort of creature altogether. That they had never been human at all.

Which was another thing. If the virals had once been people like them, how had they become what they were?

But the greatest story of all was the great Niles Coffee: Colonel Coffee, founder of the Expeditionary, fearless men who crossed the world to fight and die. Coffee's origins, like everything about him, were cloaked in myth. He was a thirdling, raised by the sisters; he was an orphan of the Easter Incursion of 38 who had watched his parents die; he was a straggler who had appeared at the gate one day, a boy warrior dressed in skins, carrying a severed viral head on a pike. He had killed a hundred virals singlehandedly, a thousand, ten thousand; the number always grew. He never set foot inside the city; he walked among them dressed as an ordinary man, a field hand, concealing his identity; he didn't exist at all. It was said that his men took an oath—a blood oath—not to God but to one another, and that they shaved their heads as a mark of this promise, which was a promise to die. Far beyond the walls they traveled, and not just in Texas. Oklahoma City. Wichita, Kansas. Roswell, New Mexico. On the wall above his bunk, Boz kept a map of the old United States, blocks of faded color fitted together like the pieces of a puzzle; to mark each new place, he inserted one of their mother's pins, connecting these pins with string to indicate the routes Coffee had traveled. At school, they asked Sister Peg, whose brother worked the Oil Road: What had she heard, what did she know? Was it true that the Expeditionary had found other survivors out there, whole towns and even cities full of people? To this the sister gave no answer, but in the flash of her eyes when they spoke his name, they saw the light of hope. That's what Coffee was: wherever he came from, however he did it, Coffee was a reason to hope.

There would come a time, many years later, long after Boz was gone, and their mother as well, that Vorhees would wonder: why had he and his brother never spoken of these things with their parents? It would have been the natural thing to do; yet as he searched his memory he could not recall a single instance, just as he could not recall his mother or father saying one word about Boz's map. Why should this be so? And what had become of the map itself that in Vorhees's memory it should be there one day and gone the next? It was as if the stories of Coffee and the Expeditionary had been part of a secret world—a boyhood world, which, once passed, stayed passed. For a period of weeks these questions had so consumed him that one morning over breakfast he finally worked up the nerve to ask his father, who laughed. *Are you kidding?* Thad Vorhees was not an old man yet, but he seemed so: his hair and half his teeth gone, skin glazed with a permanent sour dampness, hands like nests of bone where they rested on the kitchen table. *Are you serious? Now, you, you weren't so bad, but Boz—the boy could not shut up about it. Coffee, Coffee, Coffee, all day long. Don't you remember?* His eyes clouded with sudden grief. *That stupid map. To tell you the truth, I didn't have the heart to tear it down, but it surprised me that you did. Never seen you cry like that in your life. I guessed you'd figured out it was all bullshit. Coffee and the rest of them. That it would come to nothing.*

But it wasn't nothing; it had never been, could never be, nothing. How could it be nothing, when they'd loved Boz like they did?

It was Tifty, of course—Tifty the liar, Tifty the teller of tales, Tifty who wanted so desperately to be needed by someone that any fool thing would leave his mouth—who professed to have seen Coffee with his own two eyes. *Tifty,* they all laughed, *you are so full of shit. Tifty, you never saw Coffee or anybody else.* Yet even in the midst of their mockery, the idea was staking its claim; from the start, the boy possessed that talent, to make you believe one thing while simultaneously knowing another. So stealthily had he inserted himself into their circle that none could say just how this had occurred; one day there was no Tifty, and the next there was. A day that began like any other: with chapel, and school, and three o'clock's agonizingly slow approach; the sound of the bell and their sudden release, three hundred bodies streaming through the halls and down the stairs, into the afternoon; the walk from school to their quarters, faces winnowing as their classmates' paths diverged, until it was just the four of them.

Though not exactly. As they made their way into the alley, its jumble of old shopping carts and sodden mattresses and broken chairs—people were always tossing their junk back there, no matter what the quartermaster said—they realized they were being followed. A boy, stick thin, with a gaunt face topped by a cap of red-blond hair that looked as if it had fallen from a great height onto his head. Though it was January, the air raw with dampness, he wore no coat, only a jersey and jeans and plastic flip-flops on his feet. The distance at which he trailed them, his hands buried in his pockets, was just close enough to encourage their curiosity without seeming to intrude. A probationary distance, as if he were saying: I might be someone interesting. You might want to give me a chance.

"So what do you think *he* wants?" Cruk said.

They had reached the end of the alleyway, where they had erected a small shelter from scraps of wood. A musty mattress, springs popping out, served as the floor. The boy had halted at a distance of thirty feet, shuffling his feet in the dust. Something about the way he held himself made it seem as if the parts of his body were only vaguely connected, as if he'd been pieced together from about four different boys.

"You following us?" Cruk called.

The boy gave no reply. He was looking down and away, like a dog trying not to make eye contact. From this angle, they could all see the mark on the left side of his face.

"You deaf? I asked you a question."

"I ain't following you."

Cruk turned to the others. The oldest by a year, he was the unofficial leader. "Anybody know this kid?"

No one did. Cruk looked back at the boy again. "You. What's your go-by?"

"Tifty."

"Tifty? What kind of name is Tifty?"

His eyes were inspecting the tips of his sandals. "Just a name."

"Your mother call you that?" Cruk said.

"Don't got one."

"She's dead or she left you?"

The boy was fidgeting with something in his pocket. "Both, I guess. You ask it like that." He squinted at them. "Are you like a club?"

"What makes you say that?"

The boy lifted his bony shoulders. "I've seen you is all."

Cruk glanced at the others, then looked back at the boy. He huffed a weary sigh.

"Well, no point in you standing there like a dumbass. Come over so we can have a look at you."

The boy made his way toward them. Vorhees thought there was something familiar about him, his hangdog look. Though maybe it was just the fact that any one of them could have been alone like he was. The mark on his face, they saw, was a large purple shiner.

"Hey, I know this kid," Dee said. "You live in Assisted, don't you? I saw you moving in with your daddy."

Hill Country Assisted Living: a warren of apartments, families all crammed in. Everybody just called it Assisted.

"That right?" Cruk said. "You just move in?"

The boy nodded. "From over in H-town."

"That's who you're with?" Cruk said. "Your daddy?"

"I got an aunt, too. Rose. She looks after me mostly."

"What you got in your pocket there? I see you fooling with it."

The boy withdrew his hand to show them: a foldaway knife, fat with gizmos. Cruk took it, the other three pressing their faces around. The usual blades, plus a saw, a screwdriver, a pair of scissors, and a corkscrew, even a magnifying glass, the lens clouded with age.

"Where'd you get this?" Cruk asked.

"My daddy gave it to me."

Cruk frowned. "He on the trade?"

The boy shook his head. "Nuh-uh. He's a hydro. Works on the dam." He gestured at the knife. "You can have it if you want."

"What I want your knife for?"

"Hell, he doesn't want it, I'll keep it," Boz said. "Give it here."

"Shut up, Boz." Cruk eyed the boy slowly. "What you do to your face?"

"I just fell is all."

His tone was not defensive. And yet all of them felt the hollowness of the lie.

"Fell into a fist is more like it. Your daddy do that or somebody else?"

The boy said nothing. Vorhees saw his jaw give a little twitch.

"Cruk, leave him be," Dee said.

But Cruk's eyes remained fixed on the boy. "I asked you a question."

"Sometimes he does. When he's on the lick. Rose says he doesn't mean to. It's on account of my mama."

"Because she left you?"

"On account of she died having me."

The boy's words seemed to hang in the air. It was true, or it wasn't true; either way, now his plea was nothing they could refuse.

Cruk held out the knife. "Go on, take it. I don't want your daddy's knife."

The boy returned it to his pocket.

"I'm Cruk. Dee's my sister. The other two are Boz and Vor."

"I know who you are." He squinted uncertainly at them. "So am I in the club now?"

"How many times I have to tell you," Cruk said. "We're not a club."

Just like that, it was determined: Tifty was one of them. In due course they all came to know Bray Lamont, a fierce, even terrifying man, his eyes permanently lit with the illegal whiskey everyone called lick, his drink-thickened voice roaring Tifty's name from the window every night at siren. *Tifty, goddamnit! Tifty, you get in here before I have to come looking for you!* On more than one occasion the boy appeared in the alley with a fresh shiner, bruises, once with his arm in a sling. In a sodden rage, his father had hurled him across the room, dislocating his shoulder. Should they tell the DS? Their parents? What about Aunt Rose, could she help? But Tifty always shook his head. He seemed to possess no anger over his injuries, only a tight-lipped fatalism that they could not help but admire. It seemed a kind of strength. Don't tell anyone, the boy said. It's just how he is. No changing a thing like that.

There were other stories. Tifty's great-grandfather, or so he claimed, had been one of the original signatories of the Texas Declaration and had supervised the clearing of the Oil Road; his grandfather was a hero of the Easter Incursion of 38 who, mortally bitten in the first wave, had led the charge from the spillway and sacrificed himself on the battlefield in front of his men, taking his own life on the point of his blade; a cousin, whose name Tifty refused to give ("everybody just calls him Cousin"), was a wanted gangster, the operator of the biggest still in H-town; his mother, a great beauty, had received nine separate proposals of marriage before she was sixteen, including one from a man who would later become a member of the president's staff. Heroes, dignitaries, criminals, a vast and colorful pageant of assorted higher-ups, both in the world they knew and in the one that lurked below it, the world of the trade; Tifty knew people who knew people. Doors would fly open for Tifty Lamont. Never mind that he was the son of a drunken hydro from H-town, another skinny kid with bruises on his face and ill-fitting clothing he never washed, who was looked after by a maiden aunt and lived in Assisted, just like they did; Tifty's stories were too good, too interesting, *not* to believe.

But seeing Coffee—that was simply too much. Such a claim flew in the face of the facts. Coffee was unknowable; Coffee was, like the virals, a creature of the shadows. And yet Tifty's story possessed the tincture of reality. He had gone with his father to H-town, its lawless, shantied streets, to meet Cousin, the gangster. There, in the back room of the machine shed where the still was located—a colossus of a thing, like a living dragon of wires and pipes and huffing cauldrons—among men with dangerous eyes and greasy smiles of blackened teeth and pistols tucked into their belts, the money changed hands, the jug of lick was procured. These excursions were routine, Tifty had described them many times before, yet on this occasion something was different. This time there was a man. He was distinct from the others, not on the trade—Tifty could tell that right away. Tall, with the erect bearing of a soldier. He stood to the side, his face obscured, wearing a dark overcoat belted at the waist. Tifty saw that his head was shorn. Evidently this man, whoever he was, was there on urgent business; usually Tifty's father lingered, drinking and trading stories of H-town days with the other men, but not tonight. Cousin, his great round form wedged behind his desk like an egg in its nest, accepted his father's bills without comment; no sooner had they arrived, it seemed, than they were hustling out the door. It wasn't until they were well clear of the shed that his father said, *Don't you know who it was you saw in there, boy? Huh? Don't you? I'll tell you who that was. That was Niles Coffee himself.*

"I'll tell you something else." The five of them were crowded into the shelter in the alleyway. Tifty was carving in the dust with the pocketknife, which had, after all, stayed his. "My old man says he keeps a camp below the dam. Right out in the open, like being outside was nothing. They let the dracs come to them, then crisp 'em in the traps."

"I knew it!" Boz burst out. The younger boy's face practically glowed with excitement. He swiveled on his knees toward Vorhees. "What did I tell you?"

"No fucking way," Cruk scoffed. Of all of them, his role was the skeptic's; he wore this mantle like a duty.

"I'm telling you, it was him. You could just *feel* it. The way everybody was."

"And what would Coffee want with a bunch of traders? You tell me that."

"How should I know? Maybe he buys lick for his men." A new idea came into Tifty's face. He leaned forward, lowering his voice. "Or guns."

Cruk gave a sarcastic laugh. "Listen to this kid."

"Joke all you want, I've seen them. I'm talking real Army weapons, from before. M16s, automatic pistols, even grenade launchers."

"Whoa," Boz said

"Where would Cousin get guns like that?" Vorhees asked.

Tifty eased up on his knees to look around, as if making sure no one could hear them. "I'm not sure I should be telling you this," he continued. "There's a bunker, an old Army base near San Antone. Cousin runs patrols up there."

"I can't listen to this another second," said Cruk. "You didn't see Coffee or anybody else."

"You saying you don't believe he exists?"

The idea was sacrilege. "I'm not saying that. You just didn't see him is all."

"What about you, Vor?"

Vorhees felt caught. Half of what Tifty said was pure bullshit—maybe more than half. On the other hand, the urge to believe was strong.

"I don't know," he managed. "I guess . . . I don't know."

"Well *I* believe him," Dee proclaimed.

Tifty's eyes widened. "See?"

Cruk waved this away. "She's a girl. She'll believe anything."

"Hey!"

"Well, it's true."

Tifty leveled his eyes at the older boy. "What if I said you could see Coffee for yourself?"

"Just how would I do that?"

"Easy. We can go through one of the spillway tubes. I've been down there lots of times. This time of year, they don't release until dawn. The vents go right to the base of the dam—we should be able to see the camp from there."

The challenge had been laid down; there was no way to say no.

"There's no goddamn camp, Tifty."

*   *   *

It took them three days to work up the nerve, and even then Cruk forbade his sister from coming. The plan was to sneak out after their parents were asleep and rendezvous at the shelter; Tifty had plotted a route to the dam that would keep them out of site of the DS patrols.

It was after midnight by the time Tifty arrived. The others were already waiting. He appeared at the end of the alleyway and made his way toward them quickly, the hood of his jacket drawn up over his head, hands stuffed in his pockets. As he ducked into the shelter, he withdrew a plastic bottle.

"Liquid courage." He unscrewed the cap and passed it to Vorhees.

It was lick. Vorhees and Boz's parents, prayerful people who went to church at the sisters' every Sunday, wouldn't have it in the house. Vorhees held the open bottle under his nose. A clear liquid with a harsh chemical odor, like lye soap.

"Give it here," Cruk commanded. He snatched the bottle and sipped, then handed it back to Vorhees.

"You ain't never drunk lick before?" Tifty asked Vorhees.

Vorhees did his best to look offended. "Sure I have. Lots of times."

"When did you ever drink lick?" Boz scoffed.

"There's plenty you don't know, brother." Wishing he could hold his nose, Vorhees took a cautious sip, swallowing fast to avoid the taste. A blast of stinging heat filled his sinuses; a river of fire tumbled down his throat. God, it was awful! He finished with a wheezing cough, tears swarming his eyes, everybody laughing.

Boz drank next. To Vorhees's embarrassment, his little brother managed to take a respectable sip without much more than a wince. Three more times the bottle traveled around the circle. By the fourth pass, even Vorhees had gotten the hang of it and managed a solid swallow without coughing. He wondered why he wasn't feeling anything, but the moment he stood he realized he was; the ground lurched beneath his feet, and he had to put out a hand to steady himself.

"Let's go," Tifty said.

By the time they reached the dam, they were all giggling like maniacs. The passage of minutes had altered somehow; it seemed as if they had spent a long time getting there, and no time at all. Vorhees had a fragmented memory of hiding from a DS patrol under a truck but couldn't remember the exact circumstances, nor how they had avoided capture. He knew he was drunk, but this fact was nothing his mind could focus on. They paused in the shadows while somebody—Boz, Vorhees realized, who was the drunkest of them all—vomited into a stand of weeds.

And Dee, what was she doing here? Had she followed them? Cruk was barking at her to go home, but Dee was Dee: once she'd fixed her mind to something, you might just as well try to pull a bone from a dog's mouth. The fact was, Vorhees loved Dee. He always had. It was suddenly overwhelming, this love, like an expanding balloon of emotion inside his chest, and he was working up the nerve to confess his feelings when Tifty stepped toward them from wherever he'd gone and told them to follow.

He led them to a small concrete building with a flight of metal stairs descending belowground. At the bottom was a maintenance shaft, dank and gloomy, the walls dripping with moisture. They were inside the dam, somewhere above the spillway vents. Bulbs in metal cages cast elongated shadows on the walls. A building rush of adrenaline had started to bring Vorhees's senses back into focus. They came to a hatch in the wall, sealed with a rusted metal ring. Cruk and Tifty positioned themselves on opposite sides and heaved with all their might, but the wheel wouldn't budge.

"We need a lever," said Tifty.

He disappeared down the tunnel and returned with a length of pipe. He threaded it through the spokes of the ring and leaned in. With a squeal, the wheel began to turn; the door swung open.

Inside was a vertical shaft and a ladder leading down. Tifty produced a cap flare, scraped the striker, and dropped it into the hole. Tifty descended first, then Vor, Dee, and Boz, with Cruk bringing up the rear.

They found themselves in a wide tube. A spillway vent, one of six. Through these vents, water was released from the impoundment once a day and funneled down the spillway to the fields. Behind them lay a million gallons of water held in place by the dam. The air was cold and smelled of stone. A trickle of water ran the length of the floor toward the outlet, a pale disk of moonlit sky. They crept toward it, away from the light of Tifty's flare. Vorhees's heart was thudding in his chest. The world of night, outside the walls: it was beyond imagining. Ten feet from the outlet, Tifty dropped to a crouch; the others followed suit. Bars of heavy steel guarded the opening.

"I'll go first," Tifty whispered.

He moved on his hands and knees toward the end of the tunnel. Everyone else held absolutely still. In Vorhees's drunken mind, seeing Coffee's camp had become an ancillary purpose; the evening was a pure test of courage, its object irrelevant. The bars were sturdy enough to keep out a viral, but that wasn't the danger; Vorhees half-expected a clawed hand to reach through and grab their friend and tear him to pieces.

Through the lingering haze of the lick, the thought came to him that Dee must be afraid too, and that he might offer her some reassurance, but he couldn't think of what to say, and the idea died in his mind.

At the tunnel's mouth, Tifty eased up onto his knees, gripping the bars, and peered out.

"What do you see?" Cruk whispered.

A pause. Then, from their friend, two words: "Holy . . . shit."

The tone hit Vorhees as wrong. Not an exclamation of discovery but of sudden fear.

"What is it?" Cruk whispered, more harshly. "Is Coffee there?"

"I want to look!" Boz cried out.

"Quiet!" Cruk barked. "Tifty, goddamnit, what is it?"

Vorhees felt it through his knees. A rumbling, like thunder, followed by a shrieking groan of metal gears engaging. The sound was coming from behind them.

Tifty jumped to his feet. "Get out of here!"

It was water. The sound Vorhees was hearing was water being released from the impoundment. One vent and then the next and then the next, moving in a line. That's what Tifty had seen.

They would be smashed to pieces.

Vorhees rose and grabbed Boz by the arm to yank him away, but the boy wriggled free.

"I want to see him!"

"There's nothing there!"

The boy's voice cracked with tears. "There is, there is!"

Boz made a dash for the outlet. Tifty and the others were already racing toward the ladder. The sound of thunder was closer now. The adjacent tube had released; theirs would be next. In another few seconds, a wall of water would slam into them. At the tunnel's mouth Vorhees gripped his brother around the waist, but the boy held fast to the bars.

"I see him! It's Coffee!"

With all his might, Vorhees pulled; the two of them crashed to the floor. The others were calling: *Come on, come on!* Vorhees gripped his brother by the hand and began to run. Cruk was waving at them from the base of the ladder. Vorhees felt a pop of pressure in his ears; an ice-cold wind was pushing in his face. As Cruk disappeared up the ladder, Vorhees began to ascend, his brother right behind him.

Then the water arrived.

It slammed him like a fist, a hundred fists, a thousand. Below him, Boz cried out in terror. Vorhees managed to keep his grasp on the ladder, but could do nothing more; to release even one hand was to be swept away. Water swarmed his nose and mouth. He tried to call his brother's name, but no sound came. This was how it ends, he thought. One mistake and everything was over. It was so simple. Why didn't people die like this more often? But they did, he realized, as his grip on the ladder began to fail. They died like this all the time.

It was Cruk who pulled him free. Cruk, who would forever be his friend; who would one day stand with him while he married Dee; who would watch over his children on the day when everyone had brought the children for a summer picnic in the field; who would join him in the final battles of their lives, many miles and years away. As Vorhees's hands tore away, Cruk reached down and seized him by the wrist and yanked him upward, and the next thing Vorhees knew they were climbing, they were ascending the shaft to safety.

But not Boz. The boy's body wouldn't be recovered until the next morning, crushed against the bars. Maybe he'd seen Coffee and maybe he hadn't. Tifty never gave them an answer. Over time, Vorhees came to think it didn't matter. Even if he had, there'd be no comfort in it.

By midday, the detassling crew had covered sixteen acres. The sun was blazing, not a cloud in the sky; even the children, after a morning of games and laughter, had retreated to the shelter. At the pump, Vorhees removed his hat, filled a cup and drank, then filled it again to pour the water over his face. He removed his sweat-sodden shirt and wiped himself down with it. God almighty, it was hot.

The women and children had already eaten. Beneath the shelter, the work crew gathered for lunch. Bread and butter, hard-boiled eggs, cured meat, blocks of cheese, pitchers of water and lemonade. Cruk came down from the tower to fill a plate; Tifty was nowhere to be seen. Well, so what? Tifty could do as he liked. They ate heartily, without speaking. Soon all of them would be dozing in the shade.

"One hour," Vorhees said after a while, rising from the table. "Don't get too comfortable."

He ascended the stairs to the top of the tower, where he found Cruk scanning the field with the binoculars. His rifle was resting against the rail.

"Anything interesting out there?"

For a second, Cruk didn't answer. He passed Vorhees the binoculars. "Six o'clock, through the tree line. Tell me what that is."

Vorhees looked. Nothing at all, just trees and the dry brown hills beyond. "What do you think you saw?"

"I don't know. Something shiny."

"Like metal?"

"Yeah."

After a moment, Vorhees drew the binoculars away. "Well, it's not there now. Maybe it was just the sun flaring in the lenses."

"Probably that's it." Cruk took a sip of water from his bottle. "How's it going down there?"

"They'll all be asleep soon enough. A lot of the kids are down already. I don't think anybody expected it to be this hot."

"July in Texas, brother."

"Gunnar wanted to know if he could help. That boy is all heart and no sense."

Cruk took up his rifle. "What did you tell him?"

"Just you wait. Someday you'll realize how crazy you sound."

Cruk laughed. "And yet we were the same. Couldn't wait to get out into the world."

"Maybe you couldn't."

Cruk fell silent, gazing out over the rail. Vorhees sensed that something was troubling his friend.

"Listen," Cruk began, "I made a decision, and I wanted you to hear it from me. You know there's talk about the Expeditionary getting back together."

Vorhees had heard these rumors, too. It was nothing new; rumors circulated all the time. Since Coffee and his men had disappeared—how many years ago?—the subject had never really died completely.

"People are always saying that."

"This time it's not just talk. The military's taking volunteers from the DS, looking to build a unit of two hundred men."

Vorhees searched his friend's face. What was he telling him? "Cruk, you can't be seriously thinking about it. That was all kid stuff."

Cruk shrugged. "Maybe it was, back then. And I know how you feel about it, after what happened to Boz. But look at my life, Vor. I never married. I don't have a family of my own. What was I waiting for?"

The meaning sank in all at once. "Jesus. You already signed on, didn't you?"

Cruk nodded. "I turned in my resignation from the DS yesterday. It won't be official until I take the oath, though."

Vorhees felt stunned.

"Look, don't tell Dee," Cruk pressed. "I want to do it."

"She'll take it hard."

"I know. That's why I'm telling you first."

The conversation was broken by the sound of a pickup coming down the service road. It drew into the staging area and pulled up to the shelter; Tifty climbed out. He stepped to the rear of the truck and drew down the tailgate.

"Now, what's he got?"

They were watermelons. Everyone crowded around; Tifty began to carve them up, passing fat, dripping wedges to the children. Watermelons! What a treat, on a day like this!

"For Christ's sake," Vorhees groaned, watching the performance. "Where the hell would he get those?"

"Where does Tifty get anything? You got to hand it to the guy, though. He's not going to die friendless."

"Did I say that?"

Cruk looked at him. "You don't have to like him, Vor. That's not for me to say. But he's trying. You've got to give him that."

The door to the stairs opened. Dee stepped out, carrying two plates, each bearing a pink wedge of melon.

"Tifty brought—"

"Thanks. We saw."

Her face fell with an expression Vorhees knew too well. *Let it go. Please, just for today. They're only watermelons.*

Cruk took the plates from her. "Thanks, Dee. That'll really hit the spot. Tell Tifty thanks."

She glanced at Vorhees, then returned her eyes to her brother. "I'll do that."

Vorhees knew he looked like a resentful fool, just as he knew that if he didn't say something, change the subject, he'd carry this sour feeling inside him for the rest of the day.

"How are the kids?"

Dee shrugged. "Siri's out like a light. Nit's gone off with Ali and some of the others. They're picking wildflowers." She paused to wipe her brow with the back of her wrist. "Are you really going back out there? I don't know how you stand it. Maybe you should wait until the sun's a little lower."

"There's too much to do. You don't have to worry about me."

She regarded him for another moment. "Well, like I said. Anything else I can bring you, Cruk?"

"Not a thing, thanks."

"I'll leave you to it then."

When Dee was gone, Cruk held out one of the plates. But Vorhees shook his head.

"I'll pass, thanks."

The big man shrugged. He was already wolfing down his slice, rivers of juice running down his chin. When all that remained was the rind, he gestured toward the second plate, resting on the parapet. "You mind?"

Vorhees shrugged in reply. Cruk finished off the second slice, wiped his face on his sleeve, and tossed the rinds over the side.

"You should tell Dee soon," Vorhees said.

Three o'clock, the day draining away. A faint breeze had picked up late in the morning, but now the air had stilled again. Under the tarp, Dee was playing a halfhearted game of roundabout with Cece Cauley, little Louis resting at their feet in his basket. A plump, good-natured baby, fat fingers and fat toes and a soft, pursed mouth: despite the heat, he had barely fussed all day and now was sound asleep.

Dee remembered those days, baby days. Their distinctive sensations, the sounds and smells, and the feeling of profound physical attachment, as if you and the baby were a single being. Many women complained about it—*I can't get a moment to myself, I can't wait until she's walking!*—but Dee never had; just thirty, she would have gladly had another, maybe even two. It would be nice, she thought, to have a son. But the rules were clear. Two and done, was the saying. The governor's office was discussing an extension of the walls, and maybe then the ban would be lifted. But probably that would come too late, and until then, there was only so much food and fuel and space to go around.

And Vor—well, what could she do? Boz's death was an intractable barrier in the man's mind, the truth distorted and enlarged over the years until it was the singular injury of his life. Tifty was Tifty, he always would be. One day he was being tossed into the stockade for putting a man's head through a window in a barroom brawl, the next he was producing, through a kind of Tifty magic, a truck of black-market watermelons on a scorching summer afternoon. Probably it was just a matter of time before he ended up in the stockade for good. Yet there was no denying it: Tifty would always be a part of them, and Dee most of all. There were times when Dee looked at her older daughter and honestly didn't know what the truth was. It could be one thing, or it could be the other. In a certain light Nitia was all Vor, but then the little girl would smile in a particular way or do that squinty thing with her eyes and there was Tifty Lamont.

A single night, not even. The whole thing, the entirety of their affair, had been more like ninety minutes, start to finish. How was it possible for ninety minutes to make so much difference in a life? Dee and Tifty had agreed in the aftermath that it had been a terrible mistake—inevitable, perhaps, a force of years that neither could refuse, but nothing to repeat. They both loved Vor, did they not? They'd made a big joke of it, even shaking hands to seal the deal like the two old friends they were, though of course it wasn't a joke at all: not at the time and not nine months later; it wasn't a joke now.

I will never let any harm come to you, Tifty had told her, not just that night but many times, many nights. *Not you or the girls or Vor. Whatever else is true, that's my solemn promise, my vow before God. I'll be the ground beneath your feet. Always know I'm there.* And Dee did; she knew. If she allowed herself to admit it, it was only because Tifty had agreed to accompany them that the idea of today, of a summer picnic in the field, had come about at all.

Did Dee love him? And if she did, what kind of love was it? Her feelings for Tifty were different from her feelings for Vor. Vor was steady, reliable. A creature of duty and endurance, and a good father to the girls. Solid where Tifty was vaporous, a man composed of rumor as much as actual fact. And there was no question that she and Vor belonged together; that had never been an issue. Alone in the dark, in private moments together, he spoke her name with such longing it was almost like pain; that's how much Vor loved her. He made her feel . . . what? More real. As if she, Dee Vorhees—wife and mother; daughter of Sis and Jedediah Crukshank, gone to God; citizen of Kerrville, Texas, last oasis of light and safety in a world that knew none—actually existed.

So why should she find herself, once again, thinking of Tifty Lamont?

But the cards, and this hot-hot-hot afternoon in July, when they had brought the children to the field. Dee's mind had wandered so badly, she hadn't realized what Cece was doing. Before she knew it, the woman, grinning with victory, had successfully maneuvered her into taking the queen. Two tricks, three, and it was over. Cece gleefully jotted the tally on a pad.

"Another?"

Ordinarily Dee would have said yes, if only to occupy the hours, but in the heat the game had begun to feel like work.

"Maybe Ali wants to play."

The woman, who had come back into the tent for water, waved the offer away, the ladle poised at her lips. "Not a chance."

"C'mon, just a couple of hands," Cece said. "I'm on a hot streak."

Dee rose from the table. "I better go see what the girls are up to."

She stepped away from the shelter. In the distance, she could see the

tops of the cornstalks quivering where the men were working. She angled her face toward the tower's apex, positioning a hand over her eyes
against the glare. A ghostly moon, daytime white, was hovering near the
sun. Well, that was strange. She hadn't noticed that before. Cruk and
Tifty were both on station, Cruk with his binoculars, Tifty sweeping the
field with his rifle. He caught sight of her and gave a little wave, which
flustered her; it was almost as if he knew she'd been thinking about him.
She waved guiltily in reply.

A group of a dozen children were playing kickball, Dash Martinez
waiting at the plate. Acting as pitcher was Gunnar, who had become an
unofficial babysitter over the course of the afternoon.

"Hey, Gunnar."

The boy—a man, really, at sixteen—looked toward her. "Hey, Dee.
Want to play?"

"Too hot for me, thanks. Have you seen the girls anywhere?"

Gunnar glanced around. "They were here just a second ago. Want me
to look?"

Dee's weariness deepened. Where could they have gone? She supposed
she could climb the tower and ask Cruk to track them down with the
binoculars. But the hike up the stairs, once she imagined it, seemed too
effortful. Easier, on the whole, to find the girls herself.

"No, thanks. If they come back, tell them I want them out of the sun
for a while."

"Gunnar, pitch the ball!" Dash cried.

"Hang on a second." Gunnar met Dee's eye. "I'm sure they're nearby.
They were here, like, two seconds ago."

"That's fine. I'll find them myself."

The wildflower field, she thought; probably that's where they had
gone. She felt more irritated than concerned. They weren't supposed to
wander off without telling anyone. Probably it had been Nit's idea. The
girl was always into something.

They had five minutes left.

From the observation deck, Tifty watched Dee walk away.

"Cruk, pass me the binoculars."

Cruk handed them over. The wildflower field was located on the north
side of the tower, adjacent to the corn. That's where she appeared to be
headed. Probably she just wanted to get away for a few minutes, Tifty
thought, away from the children and the other wives.

He passed the binoculars back to Cruk. He scanned the field with his rifle, then lifted the scope toward the tree line.

"The shiny thing is back."

"Where?"

"Dead ahead, ten degrees right."

Tifty peered hard into the scope: a distant rectangular shape, brilliantly reflective, through the trees.

"What the hell is that?" Cruk said. "Is it a vehicle?"

"Could be. There's a service road on the far side."

"Nothing should be out there now." Cruk drew down the binoculars. He paused a moment. "Listen."

Tifty willed his mind to clear. The creak of crickets, the breeze moving through his ears, the trickle of water through the irrigation system. Then he heard it.

"An engine?"

"That's what I hear, too," Cruk said. "Stay put."

He descended the stairs. Tifty pressed his eye to the rifle's scope. Now the image was clear: a big semi, the cargo compartment covered with some kind of galvanized metal.

He took out his walkie-talkie. "Cruk, it's a truck. Far side of the trees. Doesn't look like DS."

The line crackled. "I know. Double up."

He saw Cruk emerge from the base of the tower and stride toward the shelter, waving to Gunnar to bring the children over. Tifty dragged his scope across the field: the men working, the rows of corn, the marker flags for the hardboxes drooping in the afternoon stillness. All just as it should be.

But not exactly. Something was different. Was it his vision? He lifted his face. A blade of shadow was moving over the field.

Then he heard the siren.

He turned toward the sun; instantly he knew. It had been many years since he'd felt afraid, not since that night in the dam. But Tifty felt fear now.

One minute.

Vorhees first experienced the altering illumination as a diminishment of visual detail, a sudden dimming like premature twilight. But because he was wearing dark glasses, a defense against the rain of pollen and the afternoon brightness, his mind did not initially compute this change as anything noteworthy. It was only when he heard the shouts that he re-moved his glasses.

A great round shape, wrapped with a glowing penumbra, was sliding over the sun.

An eclipse.

As the sirens went off, he tore down the row. Everyone else was run-ning, too, yelling, *Eclipse! Eclipse! The hardboxes, get to the hardboxes!* He burst from the corn, practically running straight into Cruk and Dee.

"Where are the girls?"

Dee was frantic. "I can't find them!"

The darkness was spreading like ink. Soon the whole field would be enveloped.

"Cruk, get these people in the boxes. Dee, go with him."

"I can't! Where are they?"

"I'll find them." He drew his pistol from his waistband. "Cruk, get her out of here!"

Vorhees raced back into the field.

Tifty, his heart pounding with adrenaline, was sweeping the field from the tower. No sign yet, but it was only a matter of time. And the truck: what was it? Still it idled on the far edge of the windbreak. He tried to get Cruk on the walkie but couldn't raise him. In all the chaos, probably the man couldn't hear him.

He tightened the stock against his shoulder. Where would they come from? The trees? An adjacent field? Everything had been swept by Dil-lon's team. Which didn't mean the virals weren't there, only that he couldn't see them.

Then: at the periphery of his vision, a faint movement of the corn-stalks, no more than a rustling, near one of the flags at the edge of the field. He swung the scope in close and pressed his eye to the lens. The hatch of the hardbox stood open.

It was the one place they hadn't looked. They'd never checked the hardboxes.

Everyone was running, grabbing their children, dashing into the field toward the flags. Tifty emerged from the base of the tower at a dead sprint.

"No!"

Cruk was carrying two children, Presh Martinez and Reese Cuomo, under his arms. Dee was running beside him, Cece and Ali just steps behind—Cece hugging little Louis to her chest, Ali with Merry and Satch.

"The hardboxes!" Cruk was yelling. "Get to the hardboxes!"

"They're *in* the hardboxes!"

A burst of gunfire exploded in the field. Dee saw Tifty drop to a knee and fire off three quick rounds. She turned as the first of the virals burst from the corn.

It landed right on top of Ali Dodd.

Dee felt an urge to vomit. Suddenly she couldn't make her feet move. The viral, which had finished with Ali, was now burying its jaws in Cece's neck. The woman was twitching, shrieking, arms and legs flailing like an overturned insect's. The image seared Dee's vision like a burst of light; all she could do was watch in helpless horror.

Cruk stepped forward, shoved the barrel of his rifle against the side of the creature's head, and fired.

Where was Satch? The boy was suddenly nowhere. Merry was standing in the dust, screaming. Dee hoisted the little girl to her waist and began to run.

The virals were everywhere now. In blind panic, people were dashing for the tent, a pointless gesture; it could offer no safety at all. The virals swarmed over it, tearing it to pieces, the air filling with screams. "The tower!" Tifty was yelling. "Head for the tower!" But it was too late; nobody was listening. Dee thought of her daughters, saying goodbye. How stark everything became, at the end, all the wishes for one's children distilled by the world's swift cruelty into the desperate hope that death would take them fast. She prayed they would not suffer. Or, worse, be taken up. That was the worst thing: to be taken up.

An immense force careened into her from behind. Dee tumbled to the ground, little Merry rocketing from her arms. Face-down in the dirt, she lifted her eyes to see her brother, twenty feet away, pointing his rifle at her. Shoot me, Dee thought. Whatever's about to happen, I don't want it. A prayer of childhood found her lips and she closed her eyes and muttered it quickly, into the dust.

A shot. Behind her, something fell with an animal grunt. Before her mind could process this, Cruk was yanking her to her feet, his mouth moving incomprehensibly, saying words she couldn't quite make out. His rifle was gone; all he had was the pistol, Abigail. Why would a man name a gun Abigail? Why would he name it at all? Something must have happened to her head, she realized, because here she was, worrying over Cruk's gun, when everyone was dying. Other thoughts came to her, strange things, awful things. How it would feel to be ripped in two, like Ali Dodd. Her daughters, in the field, and what was happening to them now. How terrible, Dee thought, to live one second longer than one's own babies. In a world of terrible things, surely that was the most terrible of all. Cruk was dragging her toward the door. He was doing what he thought she wanted, but she didn't, not at all—she couldn't die fast enough, in fact—and with a burst of strength Dee tore away from him, racing into the field, calling to her children.

Vorhees could hear his daughters, laughing in the corn. They were, he knew, too young to be afraid. They had snuck away to do exactly what they'd been told not to, and it was all a kind of game to them, this funny thing with the light. Vorhees raced down the rows, shouting their names, his breath heaving with panic, trying to home in on their voices. The sound was behind him, it was ahead, it was on either side. It seemed to be coming from everywhere, even inside his head.

"Nit! Siri! Where are you?"

Then there was a woman. She was standing in the middle of the row. She was draped in a dark cloak, like a woman in a fairy tale, some dweller of the forest; her head was covered by a hood, her eyes by dark glasses that concealed the upper half of her face. So total was Vorhees's surprise that for a moment he thought he might be imagining her.

"Are they your daughters?"

Who was she, this woman of the corn? "Where are they?" he panted. "Do you know where they are?"

With a languid gesture she removed her glasses, revealing a face sensuously smooth and youthfully beautiful, with eyes that glinted in their sockets like diamonds. He felt a surge of nausea.

"You're tired," she said.

Suddenly, he was. Curtis Vorhees had never been so tired in his life. His head felt like an anvil; it weighed a thousand pounds. It took every ounce of will for him to remain standing.

"I have a daughter. Such a beautiful daughter."

Behind him he heard the final, random pops of panicked gunfire. The field and sky had sunk into an unearthly darkness. He felt the urge to weep, but even this seemed beyond his command. He had dropped to his knees; soon he would fall.

"Please," he choked.

"Come to me, beautiful children. Come to me in the dark."

Somebody yanked him to his feet: Tifty. His face was very close. Vorhees could barely focus on it. The man was pulling him by the arm.

"Vor, come on!"

His tongue was thick in his mouth. "The woman . . ." But there was no one; the place where she had stood was empty. "Did you see her?"

"There's no time! We have to get to the tower!"

Vorhees would have none of it; with the last of his strength he jerked away.

"I have to find them!"

It was the butt of Tifty's rifle that brought everything to a halt. A single, crisp blow to the head, expertly aimed; Vorhees's vision swarmed with stars. Then the world turned upside down as Tifty grabbed him by the waist and hurled him to his shoulder and began to run. Fat leaves streamed past, slapping his face. Vorhees was calling, "Nit! Siri! Come back!" But he had no strength to resist. His family was dead, he knew that; Tifty would not have come for him if they were still alive. More gunfire, the shouts of the dying all around. The hardboxes, a voice said. They came from the hardboxes. Who would survive this day? And Vorhees knew, to his infinite sorrow, that once again he would be one of the lucky ones.

They burst from the corn onto open ground. The shelter was wrecked, the tarp torn away, everything scattered. Bodies strewn everywhere, but he saw no children; the little ones were gone. *Come to me, beautiful children. Come to me in the dark.* And as the door of the tower slammed behind him and he tumbled to the floor, slipping at last into a merciful unconsciousness, his final thought was this:

Why did it have to be Tifty?

IV

THE CAVE

AUTUMN, 97 A.V.

No light, but rather darkness visible
Served only to discover sights of woe.

—MILTON,
Paradise Lost

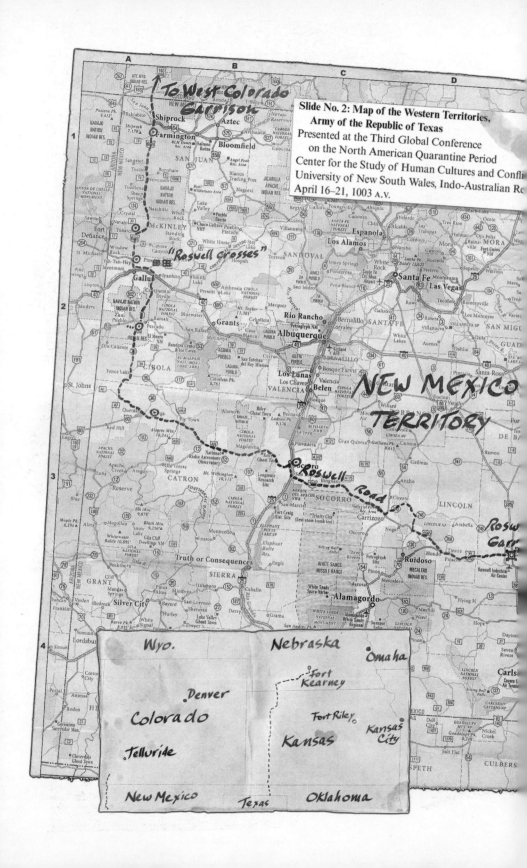

**Slide No. 2: Map of the Western Territories,
Army of the Republic of Texas**
Presented at the Third Global Conference
on the North American Quarantine Period
Center for the Study of Human Cultures and Confli...
University of New South Wales, Indo-Australian Re...
April 16–21, 1003 A.V.

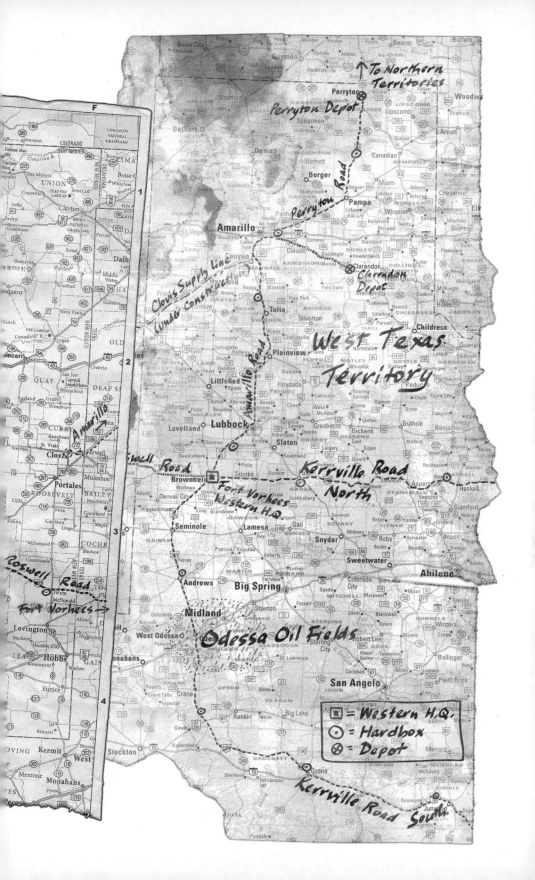

To Northern Territories

Perryton Depot

Perryton Road

Clovis Supply Line
(Under Construction)

Amarillo Road

West Texas Territory

Clarendon Depot

Roswell Road

Fort Vorhees
Western H.Q.

Kerrville Road North

Roswell Road

Fort Vorhees

Odessa Oil Fields

Kerrville Road South

☐ = Western H.Q.
⊙ = Hardbox
⊗ = Depot

24

Wolgast had come to Amy at last. He had come to her in dreams.

They were sometimes in one place and sometimes another. They were stories of things that had happened, events and feelings from the past replayed; they were a jumble, a pastiche, an overlap of images that in their reconfiguration felt entirely new. They were her life, her past and present commingling, and they occupied her consciousness with such completeness that upon awakening she would startle to discover herself existing in a simple reality of firm objects and ordered time. It was as if the waking world and the sleeping world had exchanged positions, the latter possessing a superseding vividness that did not abate as she moved into the traces of her day. She would be pouring water from a pot, or reading to the children in circle, or sweeping leaves in the courtyard and without warning her mind would drown with sensation, as if she had slipped beneath the surface of the visible world into the currents of an underground river.

A carousel, its gyring lights and ringing, bell-like music falling. A taste of cold milk and the dust of powdered sugar on her lips. A room of blue light, her mind floating with fever, and the sound of a voice—Wolgast's voice—gently leading her out of the darkness.

Come back to me, Amy, come back.

Most powerful of all was the dream of the room: dirty, stale-smelling, clothing scattered in piles, containers of old food atop every surface, a television blaring with meaningless cruelty in the corner, and the woman Amy understood to be her mother—she experienced this awareness with a gush of hopeless longing—moving through the cramped space with panicked energy, scooping things from the floor, tossing them into sacks. *Come on, honey, wake up now. Amy, we got to go.* They were leaving, her mother was leaving, the world had cleaved in two with Amy on one side of the gap and her mother on the opposite, the moment and its sentiments of parting unnaturally prolonged, as if she were watching her mother from the stern of a boat as it sailed away from the pier. She understood that it was here, in this room, that her life had actually begun. That she was witnessing a kind of birth.

But it wasn't just the two of them. Wolgast was there as well. This made no sense; Wolgast had entered her life later. Yet the logic of the dream was such that his presence was intrinsically unremarkable; Wolgast was there because he was. At first Amy experienced his presence not as a bodily reality but a vaporous glow of emotion hovering over the scene. The more she felt her mother moving away from her, into a private urgency Amy neither shared nor comprehended—something terrible had happened—the more vivid became her sense of him. A deep calm infused her; she watched with a feeling of detachment, knowing that these events, which seemed to be occurring in a vivid present, had actually happened long ago. She was simultaneously experiencing them for the first time while also remembering them—she was both actor and observer—with the anomaly of Wolgast, whom she now discovered was sitting on the edge of the bed, her mother nowhere to be seen. He was wearing a dark suit and tie; his feet were bare. He was gazing absorbedly at his hands, which he held before him with the tips of his fingers touching. *Here is the church,* he intoned, weaving all but his index fingers together, *and here is the steeple. Open the door*—his thumbs separated to reveal his wriggling digits—*and see all the people. Amy, hello.*

—Hello, she said.

I am sorry I have been away. I've missed you.

—I've missed you, too.

The space around them had altered; the room had dispersed into a darkness in which only the two of them existed, like a pair of actors on a spotlit stage.

Something is changing.

—Yes. I think that it is.

You will need to go to him, Amy.

—Who? Who should I go to?

He's different from the others. I could see it the first time I laid eyes on him. A glass of iced tea. That was all he wanted, to cool himself off in the heat. He loved that woman with his whole heart. But you know that, too, don't you, Amy?

—Yes.

An ocean of time, that's what I told him. That's what I can give you, Anthony, an ocean of time. A sudden bitterness came into his face. *I always did hate Texas, you know.*

He had yet to look at her; Amy sensed that the conversation neither required nor even allowed this. Then:

I was thinking just now about the camp. The two of us, reading together, playing Monopoly. Park Place, Boardwalk, Marvin Gardens. You always beat me.

—I think you let me.

Wolgast chuckled to himself. *No, it was always you, fair and square. And Jacob Marley.* A Christmas Carol, *that was your favorite. I think you had the whole book memorized. Do you remember?*

—I remember all of it. The day it snowed. Making the snow angels.

He wore the chains he forged in life. Wolgast frowned in sudden puzzlement. *It was such a sad story.*

Here was the river, Amy thought. The great, coursing river of the past.

I could have gone on that way forever. Wolgast angled his eyes upward, addressing the darkness. *Lila, don't you see? This was what I wanted. It was all I ever wanted.* Then: *Do you . . . know this place, Amy?*

I don't think it's anywhere, I think that I'm asleep.

He considered these words with a faint nod. *Well. That does sound right to me. Now that you say it, that makes a lot of sense.* He took a long breath and let the air out slowly. *It's strange. There's so much I can't remember. That's what it's like, you know. Like there's only this little bit of yourself you get to keep. But things are coming clearer now.*

—I miss you, Daddy.

I know you do. I miss you, too, sweetheart, more than you'll ever know. I don't think I've ever been happier than I was with you. I wish I could have saved you, Amy.

—But you did. You saved me.

You were just a little girl, alone in the world. I never should have let them take you. I tried, but not hard enough. That's the real test, you know. That's the true measure of a man's life. I was always too afraid. I hope you can forgive me.

A wave of sorrow broke inside her. How she longed to comfort him, to take him in her arms. Yet she knew that if she attempted this, were she to move even one step closer, the dream would dissolve, and she would be alone again.

—I do. Of course I do. There's nothing to forgive.

There's so much I never told you. He was staring intently at his hands. *About Lila, and Eva. Our own little girl. You were so much like her.*

—You didn't have to, Daddy. I knew, I knew. I always knew.

You filled my heart, Amy. That's what you did for me. You filled the place where Eva had been. But I couldn't save you any more than I could save her.

As if these words had willed it, the image of the room had begun to recede, the space between the two of them elongating like a hallway. A sudden desperation took her in its grip.

It's good to remember these things with you, Amy. If it's all right, I think I'll stay here for a while.

He was leaving her, he was telescoping away.

—Daddy, please. Don't go.

My brave girl. My brave Amy. He's waiting for you. He's been waiting all this time, in the ship. The answers are there. You need to go to him when the time comes.

—What ship? I don't know any ship.

But her pleas were no use; the dream was fading, Wolgast was almost gone. He was poised at the very edge of the enveloping darkness.

—Please, Daddy, she cried. Don't leave me. I don't know what to do.

At last he turned his face toward her and found her with his eyes. Bright, shining, piercing her heart.

Oh, I don't think I will ever leave you, Amy.

25

CAMP VORHEES, WEST TEXAS
Western Headquarters of the Expeditionary

Though Lieutenant Peter Jaxon was a decorated military officer, a veteran of three separate campaigns and a man about whom stories were told, he sometimes felt as if his life had stopped.

He waited for orders; he waited for chow; he waited for the latrine. He waited for the weather to break, and when it didn't, he waited some more. Orders, weapons, supplies, news—all were things he waited for. For days and weeks and sometimes even months he waited, as if his time on earth had been consecrated to the very act of waiting, as if he were a man-sized waiting machine.

He was waiting now.

Something important was happening in the command tent; he had no doubt in his mind. All morning Apgar and the others had been sealed away. Peter had begun to fear the worst. For months they'd all heard the rumors: if the task force didn't kill one soon, the hunt would be abandoned.

Five years since his ride up the mountain with Amy. Five years hunting the Twelve. Five years with nothing to show for it.

Houston, home of Anthony Carter, subject Number Twelve, would have been the logical place to start, if the place hadn't been an impenetrable swamp. So, too, New Orleans, home of Number Five, Thaddeus Turrell. Tulsa, Oklahoma, seat of Rupert Sosa, had yielded nothing but disaster; the city was a vast ruin, dracs everywhere, and they'd lost sixteen men before making their escape.

There were others. Jefferson City, Missouri. Oglala, South Dakota. Everett, Washington. Bloomington, Minnesota. Orlando, Florida. Black Creek, Kentucky. Niagara Falls, New York. All distant and unreachable, many miles and years away. Tacked to the inside of the lid of his locker Peter kept a map, each of these cities circled in ink. The seats of the Twelve. To kill one of the Twelve was to kill his descendants, to free their minds for the journey into death. Or so Peter believed. That was what Lacey had taught him when she'd exploded the bomb that killed Babcock, subject Number One; what Amy had showed him, stepping from Lacey's cabin into the snowy field, where the Many had lain in the sun to die.

You are Smith, you are Tate, you are Dupree, you are Erie Ramos Ward Cho Singh Atkinson Johnson Montefusco Cohen Murrey Nguyen Elberson Lazaro Torres . . .

They had been a group of ten then. Now they were six. Peter's brother was gone, and Maus, and Sara, too. Of the five that had made the trip to Roswell Garrison, only Hollis and Caleb had escaped—"Baby Caleb," though he was hardly a baby anymore, now in the orphanage in Kerrville, being raised by the sisters. When the virals had broken through the Roswell Garrison's perimeter, Hollis had run with Caleb to one of the hardboxes. Theo and Maus were already dead. No one knew what became of Sara; she had vanished into the melee. Hollis had looked for her body in the aftermath but found nothing. The only explanation was that she'd been taken up.

The years had scattered the others like the wind. Michael was at the refinery in Freeport, an oiler first class. Greer, who had joined them in Colorado, was in the stockade, sentenced to six years for deserting his command. And who knew where Hollis was. The man they'd known and loved like a brother had broken under the weight of Sara's death, his grief casting him into the dark underbelly of the city, the world of the trade. Peter had heard he'd risen through the ranks to become one of Tifty's top lieutenants. Of the original group, only Peter and Alicia had joined the hunt.

And Amy. What of Amy?

Peter thought of her often. She looked very much as she always had— like a girl of fourteen, not the 103 she actually was—but much had changed since their first meeting. The Girl from Nowhere, who spoke only in riddles when she spoke at all, was no more. In her place was a person much more present, more *human*. She spoke often of her past, not just her lonely years of wandering but her earliest memories of the Time Before: of her mother, and Lacey, and a camp in the mountains and the man who had saved her. Brad Wolgast. Not her real father, Amy said, she had never known who that was, but a father nonetheless. Whenever she spoke of him, a weight of grief entered her eyes. Peter knew without asking that he had died to protect her, and that this was a debt she could never repay, though she might spend her life—that infinite, unknowable span—trying to do just that.

She was with Caleb now, among the sisters, having taken up the gray frock of the Order. Peter didn't think Amy shared their beliefs—the sisters were a dour lot, professing a philosophical and physical chastity to reflect their conviction that these were the last days of humanity—but it was a more than adequate disguise, one Amy could easily pass off. Based on what had happened at the Colony, they'd all agreed that Amy's true identity, and the power she carried, was nothing anybody outside the leadership should know.

Peter walked to the mess, where he passed an empty hour. His platoon, twenty-four men, had just returned from a reconnaissance sweep to Lubbock to scout up salvageables; luck had been on their side, and they'd completed their mission without incident. The biggest prize had been a junkyard of old tires. In a day or two they'd return with a truck to take as many as they could carry for transport back to the vulcanizing plant in Kerrville.

The senior officers had been in the tent for hours. What could they be talking about?

His mind drifted back to the Colony. Odd that he wouldn't think about it for weeks or even months at a time, and then, without warning, the memories would sail into his mind. The events that had precipitated his departure now seemed as if they had happened to somebody else— not Lieutenant Peter Jaxon of the Expeditionary or even Peter Jaxon, Full Watch, but a kind of boy-man, his imagination circumscribed by the tiny patch of ground that defined his entire life. How much energy had he devoted to nurturing his own feelings of inadequacy, manifested in his petty rivalry with his brother, Theo? He thought with wistful pride of what his father, the great Demitrius Jaxon, Head of the Household, Captain of the Long Rides, would have said to him now. *You've done well. You've taken the fight to them. I'm proud to call you son.* Yet Peter would have given it all back for just one more hour in Theo's company.

And whenever he looked at Caleb, it was his brother he saw.

He was joined at the table by Satch Dodd. A junior officer like Peter, Satch had been a toddler when his family had been killed in the Massacre of the Field. As far as Peter was aware, Satch never said anything about this, though the story was well known.

"Any idea what it's all about?" Satch asked. He had a round, boyish face that made him appear completely earnest at all times.

Peter shook his head.

"Good haul up in Lubbock."

"Just tires."

Both their minds were elsewhere; they were simply filling time. "Tires are tires. We can't do much without them."

Satch's squad would be departing in the morning to do a hundred-mile sweep toward Midland. It was bad duty: the area was a cesspool of oil, bubbling up from old wells that had never been capped.

"I'll tell you something I heard," Satch said. "The Civilian Authority is looking into whether or not some of those old wells can still be operated, for when the tanks go dry. We may find ourselves garrisoning down there before too long."

Peter was startled; he'd never considered this possibility. "I thought there was enough oil in Freeport to last forever."

"There's forever and forever. In theory, yeah, there's plenty of slick down there. But sooner or later everything runs out." Satch squinted at him. "Don't you have a friend who's an oiler? One of your crew from California, wasn't it?"

"Michael."

Satch shook his head. "Walking all the way from California. That's still the craziest story I ever heard." He placed his palms on the table and rose. "If you hear anything from upstairs, let me know. If I had to bet, they'll be sending all of us down to Midland to wade in the slick before too long."

He left Peter alone. Satch's words had done nothing to cheer him; far from it. A half dozen enlisted clomped into the mess, talking among themselves with the rough-edged, profanity-laced familiarity of men looking for chow. Peter wouldn't have minded a little company to take his mind off his worries, but as they moved from the line in search of a table, none glanced in his direction; the tarnished silver bar on his collar and the poor spirits he was radiating were evidently enough to ward them away.

What could the senior officers be talking about?

To abandon the hunt: Peter couldn't imagine it. For five years he had thought of little else. He'd signed on with the Expeditionary right after

Roswell; a lot of men had. For every person who'd perished that night, there was a friend, or brother, or son who had taken his place. The ones motivated solely by a need for revenge tended to wash out early or get themselves killed—you had to have a better reason—and Peter had no illusions about himself. Payback was a factor. But the roots of his desire went deeper. All his life, since the days of the Long Rides, he'd longed to be part of something, a cause larger than himself. He'd felt it the moment he'd taken the oath that bound him to his fellows; his purpose, his fate, his person—all were now wedded to theirs. He'd wondered if he'd be somehow less himself, his identity subsumed into the collective, but the opposite had proved true. It was nothing he could speak of, not with Theo and the others gone, but joining the Expeditionary had made him feel alive in a way he never had before. Watching the soldiers eat— laughing and joking and shoveling beans into their mouths as if it were the last meal of their lives—he recalled those early days with envy.

Because somewhere along the way, the feeling had left him. As campaigns were waged and men died and territory was taken and lost, none of it seeming to amount to anything, it had slowly slipped away. His bond to his men remained, a force as abiding as gravity, and he would have sacrificed himself for any one of them without a flicker of hesitation, as, he believed, they would have done for him. But something was missing; he didn't quite know what it was. He knew what Alicia would have told him. *You're just tired. This is a long slog. It happens to everyone, be patient.* Not wrong, but not the whole story, either.

Finally Peter could stand it no longer. He exited the tent and marched across the compound. All he needed was some pretext for knocking; with any luck, they'd let him inside, and he could glean some sense of what they were up to.

He needn't have bothered. As he made his approach, the door swung open: Major Henneman, the colonel's adjutant. Trim, a bristle of blond hair, slightly crooked teeth he showed only when he smiled, which was never.

"Jaxon. I was just going to look for you. Come inside."

Peter stepped into the shade of the tent, pausing in the doorway to let his eyes adjust. Seated around the broad table were all the senior staff— Majors Lewis and Hooper, Captains Rich, Perez, and Childs, and Colonel Apgar, the officer in charge of the task force—plus one more.

"Hi, Peter."

Alicia.

* * *

"There are two entrances I could find, here and here."

Alicia was directing everyone's attention to a map spread over the table: U.S. GEOLOGICAL SURVEY, SOUTHERN NEW MEXICO. Beside it was displayed a second map, smaller and faded with age: NATIONAL PARK SERVICE, CARLSBAD CAVERNS.

"The main opening to the cave is about three hundred yards wide. There's no way we can seal it even with our largest ED, and the terrain is too rugged to haul a flusher up there anyway."

"So what are you proposing?" Apgar asked.

"We box him in," She pointed to the map again. "I scouted another entrance, about a quarter mile away. It's an old elevator shaft. Martínez has to be somewhere between these two entrances. We set off a package of H2 at the base of the main entrance, inside the tunnel that leads toward the shaft. This should drive him toward the bottom of the elevator, where we position a single man to meet him on the way out."

"A single man," Apgar repeated. "Meaning you."

Alicia nodded.

The colonel leaned back in his chair. Everyone waited.

"Don't get me wrong, Lieutenant. I know what you're capable of. We all do. But if this thing is anything like the one you saw in Nevada, it sounds to me like a one-way trip."

"Anybody else will just slow me down."

He frowned skeptically. "And you're positive Martínez is down there."

"It all makes sense, sir. Babcock used a cave, too. And El Paso is just a hundred miles from Carlsbad. It's his home turf."

Apgar thought a moment. "I agree, the pattern fits, but how can you be so sure?"

Alicia hesitated. "I can't really explain it, Colonel. I just know."

Peter was seated at the far end of the table. "Permission to speak, sir."

Apgar rolled his eyes. "Fine, Jaxon, go ahead and say what we all know you're going to say."

"I'm the only other person here who's seen one of the Twelve. I trust Lieutenant Donadio. If she says Martínez is down there, he's down there."

"We're all aware of your history, Lieutenant. That doesn't change the fact that we're just playing a hunch here. I don't see risking anyone unless we know for sure."

"So maybe there's another way. All of the original test subjects were chipped, like Amy. We can use the signal to locate him."

"I already thought of that. Just one problem. Radio waves can't pass through rock. How do you propose to get a signal from a thousand feet underground?"

"We don't get it from the surface. We get it from the cave."

Peter drew their attention to the diagram again. "We do like Alicia says, positioning an H2 pack inside the tunnel that leads from the base of the main entrance into the other chambers. The Twelve are big, but in tight quarters that ought to be enough to get Martínez's attention. The package is wired back to the base of the main entrance, where it's connected to the surface by a radio detonator, so we can blow it at a safe distance. Call that Blue Squad."

Apgar nodded. "I'm with you so far."

"Okay, but we don't send a single man down the elevator shaft to meet Martínez on the way out. We send two, with a radio direction finder. Call that Red Squad. The first thing Red Squad does is plant a second pack of H2 near the base of the shaft. We put it on a short timer, say fifteen seconds. Man one proceeds into the cave, using the RDF to locate Martínez, but man two holds his position at the elevator. The trick will be keeping lines of sight to maintain radio contact with the surface, so that's man two's job. He's the go-between. Basically we use a daisy-chain system. Man one is connected by radio to man two, who's connected to whoever's positioned at the top of the shaft, call him man three, who's connected to Blue Squad. That way we can coordinate all the elements of the operation. No guesswork."

Apgar nodded. "Fair enough, but I'm already seeing the problems, Lieutenant. It's a maze down there. What if men one and two lose contact? The whole thing collapses."

"It's a risk, but there's no reason they should, so long as the first man doesn't go any farther than these three junctures." Peter showed them on the map. "It won't give us a whole view of the cave, but we should be able to survey most of it."

"Go on."

"So. We set the two packages, man one goes looking for Martínez, man two waits to hear. After that it's just a question of the timing. Once man one locates Martínez, he radios back to man two, who contacts the surface. Blue Squad blows the hole. Martínez is pissed. Man one beats it back to the shaft, drawing him toward the elevator. Man two sets the timer. Up they go, the second package blows, Martínez is history." He clapped his hands. "Simple."

Apgar considered this. "Not a lot of margin for error there. I know Donadio's fast, but fifteen seconds won't be much to get clear of the blast. I don't know if we can winch anybody up that quickly."

"We won't have to. The shaft itself will offer enough protection. Fifty feet should do it."

"Just to be clear, you're talking about using man one as a decoy."

"Correct, sir."

"Sounds like you've done this before."

"Not me. Sister Lacey."

"Your mystic nun."

"Lacey was a lot more than that, Colonel."

Apgar placed the tips of his fingers together, glanced at the map, then raised his eyes to Peter's face. "Man one is Donadio, obviously. Any idea who this other suicidal character might be?"

"Yes, sir. I'd like to volunteer."

"And why am I not surprised?" Apgar turned to the others. "Anybody else want to chime in here? Hooper? Lewis?"

Both men were agreed.

"Donadio?"

She glanced at Peter—*Are you sure about this?*—and then gave a tight nod. "I'm good with it, Colonel."

A brief pause, followed by a sigh of surrender. "All right, Lieutenants, this is your show. Henneman, you think two squads should do it?"

"I believe so, Colonel."

"Brief Lieutenant Dodd and put a detail together to outfit the portables. And let's see about that RDF. I'd like to move on this within forty-eight hours." Apgar looked at Peter again. "Last chance to change your mind, Lieutenant."

"No, sir."

"I didn't think so." He lifted his eyes to the room. "All right, everybody. Let's show Command what we're made of and kill this bastard."

Two nights later, they made camp at the base of the mountain. A pair of portables, twenty-four men sleeping on racks; they awoke at dawn to prepare their ascent. The ground around the portables was littered with tracks in the dust, the nighttime visitors, drawn by the scent of two dozen dozing men, a grand feast denied by walls of steel. The mountain was too steep for vehicles, the path winding. Anything they brought they would have to hump on their backs. Without the portables to protect them on the mountaintop, there would be no second chance. In the bright light of morning, the terms of their mission were starkly defined. Find Martínez and kill him, or die in the dark.

Henneman was the senior officer—an irregularity. Rarely did he go outside the walls of the garrison. But he had made his way, over the years, to this position of relative safety by doing just the opposite. Tulsa,

New Orleans, Kearney, Roswell—Henneman had ascended through the ranks on a ladder of battle and blood. No one doubted his capabilities, and his presence meant something. Peter would lead one squad, Dodd the other. Alicia was Alicia: the scout sniper, the odd man, the one who didn't quite fit and seemed, by and large, to answer to no one. Everyone knew what she could do, yet her status was a source of unease among the men. No one ever said anything that Peter was aware of—if they spoke of their concerns, it wasn't to him—yet their discomfort was evident in the way they kept their distance, the cautious glances they gave her, as if they could not quite bring themselves to meet her eye. She was a bridge between the human and the viral, situated somewhere between: where did she fall?

They set out just after dawn. Now it was a race against the hours. They would need to set the charges and have everybody in position before sunset. The cool desert night had yielded to a scorching sun, its thrumming rays hitting their backs, then their shoulders, then the tops of their heads. There was no time to rest; rations were passed down the lines as they climbed, Alicia leading the way, occasionally doubling back to confer with Henneman. By the time they reached the mouth of the cave, it was late afternoon.

"Jesus, you weren't kidding," Henneman said.

They were standing at the cave's mouth. The western sun lit the interior, though its rays traveled only so deeply; beyond lay a maw of blackness. The amphitheater with its curved stone benches, the spaces between them littered with dry leaves and other debris, was inexplicable; if an audience sat here, what did they watch? Metal banisters framed a curving trail that switchbacked down into the cave. They had three usable hours of daylight left.

They reviewed the plan a final time. Dodd's squad would set the charges at the base of the cave. According to Alicia's map, the switchbacks ended two hundred feet belowground, where a narrow tunnel descended another three hundred feet to the first of several large chambers. The charges would be laid inside this tunnel, wired to a radio detonator with a clear line of sight to the cave's mouth. The explosion would shoot a compression wave through the tunnel, its destructive force magnified exponentially by its trip through the narrow space—in theory, sending whatever was down there running toward the elevator shaft. Once the charges were in place and Dodd's men had returned to the surface, Peter and Alicia would commence their descent. The elevator car was resting at the bottom, seven hundred feet below the surface, held in place by its counterweights, which were lodged at the top. A winch would lower

Peter and Alicia by rope to the base of the shaft and pull them back up when they made their escape.

Dodd and his team set out. Fifteen minutes later, he radioed from the bottom. They'd made it to the mouth of the tunnel.

"Creepy as hell down here," Dodd said. "You've got to see this for yourself."

They would, soon enough. Dodd's squad had three hundred feet of cable to connect the detonator to the package. A five-minute silence ensued; then Dodd's voice returned. The bomb and the cable were laid; his team had begun their ascent. Peter and Alicia were waiting at the top of the elevator shaft, which was located a quarter mile away, in a structure that once had housed the park's offices. The winch was in place. The time was 1700 hours; they were cutting it close.

Dodd's voice on the radio: "Blue Squad, good to go."

Alicia and Peter clipped into their harnesses; Henneman wished them good luck. They balanced at the edge of the shaft and pushed off, dropping into the blackness like coins into a well. Portable fluorescents clipped to their vests bathed the walls in a yellowish glow. Peter's mind was clear, his senses acute. There was a kind of fear that deepened awareness, bringing focus to the mind; his was that kind. The temperature dropped swiftly, prickling the hair on his arms. A hundred feet, two hundred, three, their downward passage swift, their weight suspended by the harnesses, as if they were descending in two cupped hands. The elevator's cables—a thick trunk of twined steel and two smaller lines wrapped in plastic—flowed past. A dark shape emerged below: the top of the elevator. The cables were bolted to a plate on the roof. They landed with a soft thunk.

"Red Squad down."

Alicia pried loose the hatch, and they dropped inside. The doors of the car stood open. A feeling of immeasurable space beyond, as if they were standing at the entrance to a cathedral. The air was damp and cold with a strong earthen smell, vaguely ureic. They scanned the space with the lights of their rifles, their beams volleying into the immense blackness. All around were strange, organic-looking forms, as if the walls were made of crumpled flesh.

"Flyers, get a load of this place," Alicia said.

Alicia had removed her glasses; she was in her element now, a zone of permanent night. By the glow of the fluorescents, she knelt and removed two objects from her rucksack. The first was the explosives pack—eight sticks of HEP wired to a mechanical timer. She gingerly placed this on the floor of the cave. The second was the radio direction finder, a small, boxy object with a directional antenna and a meter to register the strength of an incoming signal at 1432 megahertz. She flicked the power switch and stepped from the car, holding the RDF before her to sweep the space beyond. It began to issue a faint but regular beeping. The needle nudged to life.

"Gotcha."

Peter radioed the surface: the target was present. He'd had no cause to doubt Alicia's claim, yet suddenly the situation had acquired a more potent reality. Somewhere in these caverns, Julio Martínez, Tenth of Twelve, lay in wait.

"Tell Dodd to stand ready and wait for my signal," Peter told Henneman.

"Acknowledged. All eyes, Lieutenants."

The moment had come. A final look passed between Peter and Alicia, freighted with meaning. Once again, here they were, the two of them poised at the precipice. There was no need to acknowledge this with words; all had been said. Neither could exist without the other, yet the distance between them could never be crossed. They were who they were, which was soldiers at war. The bond transcended all others but one, the one thing they could not have. Alicia was wearing, as ever, her trademark bandoliers, but she'd given up the cross for an M4 rifle with the fat tube of a grenade launcher fixed under the barrel. Martínez would receive no mercy from her, no final benediction.

"See you soon."

She faded into the darkness.

At the mouth of the cave, Satch Dodd's squad had formed a firing line along the lowest tier of the amphitheater. The sky had begun a discernible darkening, an enrichment of its colors as day spilled toward night. Dodd was clutching the detonator. Its signal, transmitted to the receiver at the base of the cave, would close a simple electric circuit, sending a jolt of current down the wire to the bomb.

Even at this distance, it would make a hell of a boom.

Though it was nothing he could let his men see, the journey to the bottom of the cave had rattled him. Dodd had never experienced any place like it in his life—an unearthly world of alien shapes, strange colors, and distorted dimensions, pockets of darkness everywhere he looked, spiraling down into nothingness. The trip down the tunnel had felt like crawling into his own grave. In the orphanage, Dodd had learned about hell, a realm of everlasting gloom where the souls of the wicked writhed forever in agony. Although the idea had initially terrified him, something about it had struck him, even then, as faintly unbelievable. Though only a boy, he'd sensed that hell was just a story the sisters had concocted to keep the children in line, not unlike the fables they read the children to teach simple moral lessons. Dodd's status as the youngest survivor of the Massacre of the Field had always afforded him a slightly elevated rank among the children, as if this experience had somehow made him wise. This, of course, was completely misplaced—having never really known his parents, he did not feel the loss of them, and he remembered nothing of that day—but under the spell of his playmates' admiration for the imaginary mantle of his grief, Dodd came to see himself as a boy with special powers of perception, especially where the sisters' mystical proclamations were concerned. God, okay, Dodd was good with that, it made a kind of sense. Heaven was a pleasant idea he was happy to go along with, since believing in it cost him nothing. But that was as far as he was willing to go. Hell: it was pure nonsense.

Now, standing at the mouth of the cave, detonator in hand, Dodd wasn't so sure.

The waiting was never easy. Once the shooting started a feeling of clarity always took over. You'd die or you wouldn't, you'd kill or be killed—it was one or the other and nothing in between. You knew where you stood, and for those violent, heart-pumping minutes, Dodd felt himself lifted on a wave of adrenaline that eradicated virtually everything about him that was even vaguely personal. It could be said that in the chaos of combat, the man known as Satch Dodd ceased to exist, even to himself; and when the dust cleared, and he found himself still standing, he experienced a rush of raw existence, as if he'd been shot from a cannon back into the world.

It was in the waiting that a person experienced too much of himself. Memories, doubts, regrets, anxieties, the whole range of possibilities the future contained—they all swirled together in the mind like a soup. While half of Dodd's attention was intently focused on the situation at hand—the detonator in his grip and the presence of his men around him and the walkie clipped to his shoulder, through which Henneman's command to blow the hole would come—the other half was ricocheting through the chambers of his private self. Only when Henneman gave the signal to explode the bomb would this feeling, a kind of whole-body psychological nausea, abate, igniting his power to act.

The major's voice crackled through the radio: "Blue Squad, all eyes. Donadio's going in."

Something tensed inside him; he felt himself returning to the moment. "Acknowledged."

It couldn't happen soon enough.

Seven hundred feet below, in the lightless caverns left behind when sulfide-rich waters had leached upward into the fissured limestone deposits of an ancient reef, Alicia Donadio was advancing on the signal. That this signal emanated from the chip implanted in the neck of Julio Martínez, one of twelve death row inmates infected with the CV virus created by Project NOAH at the dawn of the present age, she had no doubt.

Louise, she thought, *Louise.*

The moment they'd touched down in the cave, this name had taken ahold of her mind. Which was strange: according to the records they had salvaged from the NOAH compound, Martínez had been sentenced to death for killing a policeman, not the rape and murder of a woman. Perhaps her death had gone unrecorded, or else had never been connected to him. The shooting of the policeman was present also, a flash of violence like a white-hot spark, but within each of the Twelve lay a singular story—the one story that was the true essence, the core of who they were. For Martínez, that story was Louise.

According to her map, two tunnels led from the elevator to individual caves, marked with names suggesting their grandeur. King's Palace. Hall of Giants. Queen's Chamber. And, simply, the Big Room. To maintain a line of sight with Peter, and thus stay in communication with the surface, Alicia could go no farther than the junctures at the far end of each passageway. Beyond that, she would be on her own.

King's Palace, she thought. Somehow, that sounded like him.

"Going left."

As she proceeded down the passageway, the meter of the RDF leapt, the beeping accelerating in kind. She'd guessed right. The walls pressed around her, shards of some bright substance embedded in their surface glinting under the raking beam of her rifle. There were virals here, a great horde, like buried treasure, Martínez presiding. Alicia could see it all plainly now; the images deepened with every step, taking hold of her mind. Louise, the tightening cord encircling her neck; the precise demarcation of color above and below, her neck milky white, the skin of her face rosy and swollen with blood; the look of astonished terror in her eyes, and the cold finality of death's approach. It was all as clear as if Alicia had lived it herself, but then something shifted. Now Alicia was experiencing this event in two directions simultaneously. She was look-ing at Louise while also looking *from* her. How was this possible? When had she acquired this attunement to the unseen world? Through Louise's eyes she saw Martínez's face. A well-groomed man of precise features, silver hair swept back from his forehead to form a delicate widow's peak. A human face, though not precisely: there was nothing you could call a person behind his eyes, only a soulless vacancy. The pleasure he was tak-ing was an animal's. Louise was nothing to him. She was an organization of warm surfaces created only for his desire and dispatch. Her name was written plainly on her blouse, and yet his mind could not connect this name to the human person he was strangling in the midst of raping, be-cause the only thing real to him was himself. She felt Louise's terror, and her pain, and then the dark moment when the woman understood that death was imminent, her life at its end; that she would die without any acknowledgment from the universe that she had existed in the first place, and the last thing she would feel as she departed the world would be Martínez, raping her.

Alicia had reached the juncture, a place called the Boneyard. A strong smell of urine tanged in her nostrils, coating the membranes of her mouth and throat. In the moist air, her breath puffed before her in an icy cloud. The beep of the RDF, steadily accelerating, had become a con-tinuous stream of sound.

She knew then what she intended to do. She had intended it all along. The plan was a cover, an elaborate ruse to conceal her purpose.

She wanted to kill Martínez herself. She wanted to feel him die.

At the elevator, Peter became aware that something wasn't as it should be just a few seconds before Alicia stepped from his line of sight. There was no rational explanation for this knowledge; it simply came to him out of the stillness, a feeling deep in his bones.

"Lish, come in."

No answer.

"Lish, can you read me?"

A hiss of static, then: "Stay there."

There was something unsettling in her voice. A feeling of resignation, as if she were severing a rope that held her over an abyss. Before he could respond, her voice returned: "I mean it, Peter."

Then she was gone.

He radioed the surface. "Something's wrong, I've lost her."

"Hold your position, Jaxon."

Had she said the left tunnel? Yes, the left.

"I'm going after her," he told Henneman.

"Negative. Stand pat—"

But Peter failed to hear the rest of Henneman's message. He was already moving away.

At the same time, Lieutenant Dodd had commenced a mad dash down the switchback into the cave. He was unaware that the chain of radio transmission had been broken and that neither Peter nor, by extension, Alicia knew that the bomb at the base of the main entrance had disarmed itself—the first mishap in a cascade of events that would never be fully reassembled to the satisfaction of Command. Somehow—a short in the line, a mechanical defect, a whim of fate—the receiver at the base of the cave had lost contact with the surface. A first-class, A1 screwup if ever there was one, and now Dodd was racing into the mouth of hell.

His first descent had taken fifteen minutes; moving at what counted as a dead sprint down the treacherous, hairpinning pathway, he made it to the bottom in fewer than five. At the edge of his vision he perceived a scuttle overhead, accompanied by a high-pitched squeaking, but in his haste he failed to process this; if Hennemen's order to blow the package came before he'd made it back out, his team would fire it anyway, killing him in the blast. The only thing on his mind was reaching the bottom, repairing the detonator, and getting back out.

There it was. The receiver. Dodd had left it on a smooth, tablelike boulder situated at the tunnel's mouth; now it lay on the ground, tipped onto its side. What force had knocked it away? Dodd dropped to his knees, his breath heaving in his chest. Rivers of perspiration spilled down his face. A ghastly stink was in the air. He gently took the device in his hand. The receiver had two switches, one to arm the detonator, another to close the circuit and fire the bomb. Why wasn't it working? But then he understood that the antenna had come loose, knocked askew in the fall. He withdrew a screwdriver from his pack.

The ceiling began to move.

Alicia noticed the bones first. The bones and the smell, an overpowering stench—rank, biological, like the bottled gas of a grave. She took a step forward. As her boot touched down she felt, then heard, a crunch of bone. The skeleton of something small. The tininess of the skull, its mocking grin of teeth: a kind of rodent? Her field of view widened. The floor was carpeted with the brittle remains, in many places piled knee- or even waist-high, like drifts of snow.

Where are you? she thought. *Show yourself, you bastard. I've got a message from Louise.*

Martínez was close, very close. She was practically on top of him. For the first time in many years Alicia knew the taste of fear, but more than that: she knew hatred. A pure force, binding and suffusing every part of her. All her life seemed called to this moment. Martínez was the great misery of the world. It was not glory she sought or even justice. It was vengeance; not killing but the act of killing. To say, *This is from Louise.* To feel his life leaving him under her hand.

Come to me. Come to me.

From out of the gloom a shape appeared, a flash of white skin in the beam of her rifle. Alicia froze. What the hell . . . ? She took a step forward, then another.

It was a man.

Ruined and sagging, old beyond old, his figure emaciated, a sketch of bones; his skin was bleached of all color, almost translucent. He was huddled in nakedness on the floor of the cave. As the light of her rifle passed over his face, he did not flinch; his eyes were like stones, inert with blindness. A bat was writhing in his hands. Its long, kitelike wings, the sheerest membranes stretched over the attenuated fans of fingered bone, fluttered helplessly. The man brought the bat to his face and, with a shocking energy, enveloped its dainty head in his mouth. A final, muffled squeal and a tremor of the creature's wings and then a snapping sound; the man twisted the body away and spat its head to the floor. He pressed the body to his lips and began vigorously to suck, his body rocking with the rhythm of his inhalations, a faint coo, almost childlike, pulsing from his throat.

Alicia's voice sounded clumsily huge in the cavernous space. "Who the hell are you?"

The man pointed his blind, rigid face toward the source of the sound. Blood slicked his lips and chin. Alicia noticed for the first time a bluish image crawling up the side of his neck: the figure of a snake.

"Answer me."

A faint puff, more air than speech: "Ig . . . Ig . . ."

"Ig? Is that your name? Ig?"

". . . nacio." His brow crumpled. "Ignacio?"

From behind her came a sound of footsteps; as Alicia spun around, the beam of Peter's rifle swept her face.

"I told you to wait."

Peter's face was a blank, transfixed by the image of the man huddled on the floor.

Alicia pointed her rifle to the man's forehead. "Where is he? Where's Martínez?"

Tears swelled from his sightless eyes. "He left us." His voice was like a moan of pain. "Why did he leave us?"

"What do you mean, he left you?"

With a searching gesture, the man raised one hand to the barrel of Alicia's rifle, wrapped it in his fist, and pulled the muzzle hard against his forehead.

"Please," he said. "Kill me."

They were bats. Bats by the hundreds, the thousands, the millions. They exploded from the roof of the tunnel, a solid airborne mass, swarming Dodd's senses with the heat and weight and sound and smell of them. They blasted into him like a wave, sealing him inside a vortex of pure animal frenzy. He waved his arms madly, trying to deflect them from his face and eyes; he felt but did not yet wholly experience the sting of their teeth, drilling into his flesh, like a series of distant pinpricks. They are going to tear you to pieces, his mind was telling him; that's how this is going to end; your awful fate is that you're going to die in this cave, torn to shreds by bats. Dodd screamed, and as he screamed his awareness of the pain became the thing itself, attaining its full dimensions, his mind and body instantly achieving a unity of pure annihilating agony, and as he pitched forward toward the detonator, with its glowing lights and switches, his physical person assuming in that elongated instant the properties of a hammer, falling, his one thought—*oh, shit*—was also his last.

The blast wave from the prematurely detonated first package, rocketing from the tunnel into the cave's complex of halls and cavities with the energy of a runaway locomotive, reached the King's Palace as a terrific bang, overlapped by a pop of pressure and a deep subterranean trembling. This was followed by a second lurch underfoot, like the deck of a boat tossed by a giant wave. It was an event in equal measures atmospheric, auditory, caloric, and seismic; it had the power to rouse the very core of the earth.

They were known as hangers: sleeping virals who, their metabolic processes suppressed, existed in a state of extended hibernation. In this condition they could endure for years or even decades, and preferred, for reasons unknown—perhaps an expression of their biological kinship to bats, a buried memory of their race—to dangle upside down, arms folded over their chests with a curious tidiness, like mummies in their sarcophagi. In the various chambers of Carlsbad Caverns (though not the King's Palace; this was Ignacio's alone) they awaited, a dozing storehouse of biological stalactites, a somnolent army of glowing icicles excited to consciousness by the bomb's detonation. Like any species, they perceived this adjustment to their surroundings as a mortal threat; like virals, they instantly snapped to the scent of human blood in their midst.

Peter and Alicia began to run.

Alicia, had she been alone, might have stood her ground. Though she would have been swallowed by the horde, it was so embedded in her nature to turn and fight that this impossible task would have felt oddly satisfying: a thing of fate, and an honorable exit from the world. But Peter was with her; it was his blood, not hers, that the virals wanted. The creatures were funneling toward them, filling the underground channels of the cavern like the undammed waters of a flood. The distance to the elevator, roughly a hundred yards, possessed a feeling of miles. The virals roared behind them. Peter and Alicia hit the elevator at a sprint. There was no time to set the charge; their initial strategy was now moot. Alicia scooped the package from the floor of the elevator, seized Peter by the wrist, kneed him through the hatch, and launched herself behind him, touching down with a clang.

"Grab a cable!" she yelled.

A moment of incomprehension.

"Do it and hold on!"

Did he understand what she had in mind? It didn't matter; Peter obeyed. Alicia dropped the package to the roof of the elevator, pointed her rifle downward at the cable plate, and pulled the trigger.

Freed from the mass of the elevator car, the counterbalancing weights plunged downward. A hard yank and then a massively accelerating force rocketed them skyward: Peter experienced their ascent in a blur, a sense of pure motion that focused on his hands, his only link to life. He would have lost his grip entirely if not for Alicia, who, below him, her grasp unassailable, acted as backstop, preventing him from slithering down the cable and plunging into the maw. In a confusion of arms and legs, they spun wildly, overwhelmed by a bombardment of physical data beyond Peter's ability to compute; he did not see the virals leaping up the shaft behind them, ricocheting from wall to wall, each jolt of movement propelling them upward, narrowing the gap.

But Alicia did. Unlike Peter, whose senses were merely human, she possessed the same internal gyroscopes as their pursuers; her awareness of time and space and motion was capable of constant recalculation, enabling her not only to maintain her grip but also to point her rifle downward. It was the grenade launcher she intended; her target was the package on the elevator's roof.

She fired.

26

FEDERAL STOCKADE, KERRVILLE, TEXAS

Major Lucius Greer, late of the Second Expeditionary, now known only as prisoner no. 62 of the Federal Stockade of the Texas Republic—Lucius the Faithful, the One Who Believed—was waiting for someone to come.

The cell where he lived was twelve feet square, just a cot and a toilet and sink and a small table with a chair. The room's only illumination came from a small window of reinforced glass set high on the wall. This was the room where Lucius Greer had spent the last four years, nine months, and eleven days of his life. The charge was desertion—not completely fair, in Lucius's estimation. It could be said that by abandoning his command to follow Amy up the mountain to face Babcock, he had simply followed orders of a deeper, different kind. But Lucius was a soldier, with a soldier's sense of duty; he had accepted his sentence without question.

He passed his days in contemplation—a necessity, though Lucius knew there were men who never managed it, the ones whose howls of loneliness he could hear at night. The prison had a small courtyard; once a week the inmates were allowed outside, but only one at a time, and only for an hour. Lucius himself had spent the first six months of his incarceration convinced he would go mad. There were only so many push-ups a man could do, only so much sleep to be had, and barely a month of his imprisonment had passed before Lucius had begun to talk to himself: rambling monologues about everything and nothing, the weather and the meals, his thoughts and memories, the world beyond the walls of the stockade and what was happening out there now. Was it summer? Had it rained? Would there be biscuits with dinner tonight? As the months had passed, these conversations had focused increasingly on his jailers: he was convinced that they were spying on him, and then, as his paranoia deepened, that they intended to kill him. He stopped sleeping, then eating; he refused to exercise, even to leave his cell at all. All night long he crouched on the edge of his cot, staring at the door, the portal of his murderers.

After some period of time in this tortured condition, Lucius decided he could endure it no longer. Only the thinnest vestige of his rational self remained; soon it would be lost to him completely. To die without a mind, its patterns of experience, memory, personality—the prospect was unendurable. Killing yourself in the cell wasn't easy, but it could be accomplished. Standing on the table, a determined suicide could tuck his head to his chest, tip forward, and break his neck in the fall.

Three times in a row Lucius attempted this; three times he failed. He began to pray—a simple, one-sentence prayer seeking God's cooperation. *Help me die.* His head was chiming from its multiple impacts on the cement floor; he had cracked a tooth. Once more he stood on the table, calibrated the angle of his fall, and cast himself into the arms of gravity.

He returned to consciousness after some unknown interval. He was lying on his back on the cold cement. Again the universe had refused him. Death was a door he could not open. Despair gripped him utterly, tears rising to his eyes.

Lucius, why have you forsaken me?

They were not words he heard. Nothing so simple, so commonplace, as that. It was the *feeling* of a voice—a gentle, guiding presence that lived beneath the surface of the world.

Don't you know that only I can take this from you? That death is mine alone to make?

It was as if his mind had opened like the covers of a book, revealing a hidden reality. He was lying on the floor, his body occupying a fixed point in space and time, and yet he felt his consciousness expanding, joining with a vastness he could not express. It was everywhere and nowhere; it existed on an invisible plane the mind could see but the eyes could not, distracted as they were by ordinary things—this cot, that toilet, these walls. He plunged into a peacefulness that flowed through his being on waves of light.

The work of your life is not done, Lucius.

And, just like that, his incarceration was over. The walls of his cell were the thinnest tissue, a ruse of matter. Day by day his contemplations deepened, his mind fusing with the force of peace and forgiveness and wisdom he had discovered. This was God, of course, or could be called God. But even that term seemed too small, a word made by men for that which had no name. The world was not the world; it was an expression of a deeper reality, as the paint on the canvas was an expression of the artist's thoughts. And with this awareness came the knowledge that the journey of his life was not complete, that his true purpose had yet to be unveiled.

Another thing: God seemed to be a woman.

He had been raised in the orphanage, among the sisters; he had no memories of his parents, of any other life. At sixteen he had enlisted in the DS, as nearly all the boys in the orphanage did in those days; when the call had gone out for volunteers to join the Second Expeditionary, Lucius had been among the first. This was right after the event known as the Massacre of the Field—eleven families ambushed on a picnic, twenty-eight people killed or taken—and many of the men who had survived that day had joined up as well. But Lucius's motives were less decisive. Even as a boy he had never been swayed by the stories of the great Niles Coffee, whose heroics seemed transparently impossible. Who in his right mind would actually *hunt* the dracs? But Lucius was young, restless as are all young men, and he had wearied of his duties: standing watch on the city walls, sweeping the fields, chasing down kids who broke curfew. Of course there were always dopeys around (picking them off from the observation platforms, though frowned upon as a waste of ammunition, was generally allowed if you didn't overdo it) and the diversion of the occasional bar brawl in H-town to break up. But these things, distracting though they were, could not compensate for the weight of boredom. If signing on with a bunch of death-loving lunatics was the only other option for Lucius Greer, then so be it.

Yet it was in the Expeditionary that Lucius found the very thing he needed, that had been absent from his life: a family. On his first detail he'd been assigned to the Roswell Road, escorting convoys of men and supplies to the garrison—at the time, just a threadbare outpost. In his unit were two new recruits, Nathan Crukshank and Curtis Vorhees. Like Lucius, Cruk had enlisted straight out of the DS, but Vorhees was, or had been, a farmer; as far as Lucius knew, the man had never even fired a gun. But he'd lost a wife and two young girls in the field, and under the circumstances, nobody was going to say no. The trucks always drove straight through the night, and on the return trip to Kerrville, their convoy was ambushed. The attack came just an hour before dawn. Lucius was riding with Cruk and Vor in a Humvee behind the first tanker. When the virals rushed them, Lucius thought: That's it, we're done. There's no way I'm getting out of this alive. But Crukshank, at the wheel, either didn't agree or didn't care. He gunned the engine, while Vorhees, on the fifty-cal, began to pick them off. They didn't know that the driver of the tanker, taken through the windshield, was already dead. As they ran alongside, the tanker swerved to the left, clipping the front of the Humvee. Lucius must have been knocked cold, because the next thing he knew, Cruk was dragging him from the wreckage. The tanker was in flames. The rest of the convoy was gone, vanished down the Roswell Road.

They'd been left behind.

The hour that followed was both the shortest and the longest of Lucius's life. Time and time again, the virals came. Time and time again, the three men managed to repel them, saving their bullets until the last instant, often when the creatures were just steps away. They might have tried to make a run for it, but the overturned Humvee was the best protection they had, and Lucius, whose ankle was broken, couldn't move.

By the time the patrol found them, sitting in the roadway, they were laughing till the tears streamed down their faces. He knew that he'd never feel closer to anyone than the two men who'd walked with him down the dark hallway of that night.

Roswell, Laredo, Texarkana; Lubbock, Shreveport, Kearney, Colorado. Whole years passed without Lucius's coming in sight of Kerrville, its haven of walls and lights. His home was elsewhere now. His home was the Expeditionary.

Until he met Amy, the Girl from Nowhere, and everything changed.

He was to receive three visitors.

The first came early on a morning in September. Greer had already finished his breakfast of watery porridge and completed his morning calisthenics: five hundred push-ups and sit-ups, followed by an equivalent number of squats and thrusts. Suspended from the pipe that ran along the ceiling of his cell, he did a hundred chin-ups in sets of twenty, front and back, as God ordained. When this was done, he sat on the edge of his cot, stilling his mind to commence his invisible journey.

He always began with a rote prayer, learned from the sisters. It was not the words that mattered, rather their rhythm; they were the equivalent of stretching before exercise, preparing the mind for the leap to come.

He had just begun when his thoughts were halted by a thunk of tumblers; the door to his cell swung open.

"Somebody to see you, Sixty-two."

Lucius rose as a woman stepped through—slight of build, with black hair threaded with gray and small dark eyes that radiated an undeniable authority. A woman you could not help but reveal yourself to, to whom all your secrets were an open book. She was carrying a small portfolio under her arm.

"Major Greer."

"Madam President."

She turned to the guard, a heavyset man in his fifties. "Thank you, Sergeant. You may leave us."

The guard was named Coolidge. One got to know one's jailors, and he and Lucius were well acquainted, even as Coolidge seemed to possess no idea of what to make of Lucius's devotions. A practical, ordinary man, his mind earnest but slow, with two grown sons, both DS, as he was.

"You're sure?"

"Yes, thank you. That will be all."

The man departed, sealing the door behind him. Stepping farther inside, the president glanced around the boxy room.

"Extraordinary." She directed her eyes at Lucius. "They say you never leave."

"I don't see a reason to."

"But what can you possibly do all day?"

Lucius offered a smile. "What I was doing when you arrived. Thinking."

"Thinking," the president repeated. "About what?"

"Just thinking. Having my thoughts."

The president lowered herself into the chair. Lucius followed her lead, sitting on the edge of the cot, so that the two were face-to-face.

"The first thing to say is that I'm not here. That's *official*. Unofficially, I will tell you that I am here to seek your help on a matter of crucial importance. You have been the subject of much discussion, and I am relying on your discretion. No one is to know about our conversation. Is that clear?"

"All right."

She opened the portfolio, withdrew a yellowed sheet of paper, and handed it to Lucius.

"Do you recognize this?"

A map, drawn in charcoal: the line of a river, and a hastily sketched road, and dotted lines marking the fringes of a compound. Not just a compound: an entire city.

"Where did you find it?" asked Lucius.

"That's not important. Do you know it?"

"I should."

"Why?"

"Because I drew it."

His answer had been expected; Lucius discerned it in the woman's face.

"To answer your question, it was in General Vorhees's personal files at Command. It took a little digging to figure out who else had been with him. You, Crukshank, and a young recruit named Tifty Lamont."

Tifty. How many years since Lucius had heard the name spoken? Though, of course, everybody in Kerrville knew of Tifty Lamont. And Crukshank: Lucius felt a twinge of sadness for his lost friend, killed when the Roswell Garrison had been overrun, five years ago.

"This place on the map, do you think you could find it again?"

"I don't know. It was a long time ago."

"Have you ever told anyone about this?"

"When we reported it to Command, we were told in no uncertain terms not to speak about it."

"Do you remember where the order originated?"

Lucius shook his head. "I never knew. Crukshank was the officer in charge of the detail, and Vorhees was second. Tifty was the S2."

"Why Tifty?"

"In my experience, nobody could track like Tifty Lamont."

The president frowned again at the mention of this name: the great gangster Tifty Lamont, head of the trade, the most wanted criminal in the city.

"How many people do you think were there?"

"Hard to say. A lot. The place was at least twice the size of Kerrville. From what we could see, they were well armed, too."

"Did they have power?"

"Yes, but I don't think they were running on oil. More likely hydro-electric and biodiesel for the vehicles. The agricultural and manufacturing complexes were immense. Barracks housing. Three large structures, one at the center, a kind of dome, and a second to the south that looked like an old football stadium. The third was on the west side of the river—we weren't sure what it was. It looked like it was under construction. They were working on the thing day and night."

"And you made no contact?"

"No."

The president directed Lucius's attention to the perimeter. "This here . . ."

"Fortifications. A fence line. Nothing insubstantial, but not enough to keep the dracs out."

"Then what do you think it was for?"

"I couldn't say. But Crukshank had a theory."

"And what was that?"

"To keep people in."

The president glanced at the map, then back at Lucius. "And you've never spoken about this? Not to anyone."

"No, ma'am. Not until now."

A silence fell. Lucius had the impression that no more questions were forthcoming; the president had gotten what she'd come for. She returned the map to her portfolio. As she rose from the chair, Lucius said:

"If I may, Madam President, why are you asking me about this now? After all these years."

The president stepped to the door and knocked twice. As the tumblers turned, she turned back to Lucius.

"They say you've become a prayerful man."

Lucius nodded.

"Then you might want to pray that I'm wrong."

27

Peter was in the medical bay for ten days. Three cracked ribs, a dislocated shoulder, burns on his legs and feet, his hands scraped raw like slabs of meat; bruises and gashes and cuts all over, too many to count. He'd been knocked cold but had apparently failed, despite his best efforts, to crack his skull. Every movement hurt, even breathing.

"From what I hear, you're goddamn lucky to be alive," the doctor said—a man of about sixty with a bulbous nose veined from years on the lick and a voice so coarse it sounded dragged. His bedside manner involved using the same tone, more or less, that a person might take with a hopelessly disobedient dog. "Stay on your back, Lieutenant. You're mine until I say otherwise."

Henneman had debriefed Peter the day the team had returned to the garrison. He was still a little out of it, doped up on painkillers; the major's questions glided over his brain with the disassociated contours of a conversation occurring in another room among people he only vaguely knew. A man, a very old man, with a tattoo of a snake on his neck. Yes, Peter confirmed, nodding his head heavily against the pillow, that was what they saw. Did he tell them who he was? Ignacio, Peter replied. He told us his name was Ignacio. The major obviously had no idea what to make of these answers; neither did Peter. Henneman seemed to be asking the same questions again and again, in only slightly altered forms; at some point, Peter drifted off. When he opened his eyes again— as he would soon discover, a day and a night having passed—he was alone.

He saw no one else except the doctor until the afternoon of the fourth day, when Alicia appeared at his bedside. By this time Peter was sitting up, his left arm dressed in a sling to hold his shoulder in place. That afternoon he'd taken his first walk to the latrine, a milestone, though the voyage of just a few shuffling steps had left him enervated, and now he was faced with the problem of trying to feed himself with hands encased in mittenlike bandages.

"Flyers, you look like hell, Lieutenant."

The light in the tent was dim enough that she'd removed her glasses. The orange color of her eyes was something Peter was accustomed to, though she rarely let others see them. She slid into a chair at his bedside and gestured toward the bowl of cornmeal mush that Peter, without much success, was attempting to spoon in his mouth.

"Want a little help with that?"

"Don't you wish."

She flashed a smile. "Well, it's good to see you've still got your pride. Henneman grill you?"

"I barely remember it. I don't think he liked the answers very much." The spoon slipped from his grip, dragging a glob of the gluey paste onto his shirt. "Shit."

"Here, let me."

He was now endeavoring to clamp the spoon between his thumb and the edge of the bowl to wedge it into his palm. "I told you, I've got this."

"Will you? Just stop."

Peter sighed and let the spoon drop to the tray. Alicia dipped it into the bowl and aimed for his mouth. "Open up for mama."

"You know, you never struck me as the maternal type."

"In your case, I'm willing to make an exception. Just eat."

Bite by bite, the bowl was emptied. Alicia took a rag and wiped his chin.

"I can do that myself, you know."

"Nuh-uh. Comes with the service." She leaned back. "There, good as new." She put the rag aside. "We had the service for Satch this morning. It was nice. Henneman and Apgar both spoke."

Though Satch was presumed killed in the explosion, Henneman had led a squad back up the mountain to look for him. The gesture was symbolic; still, it had to be made. In any case, they'd found nothing. What had happened at the base of the cave would never be known.

"So that's that, I guess."

"Satch was a good guy. Everybody liked him."

"We always say that."

Alicia shrugged. "Doesn't make it any less true."

Peter knew they were thinking the same thing: the plan had been theirs, and now Satch was dead.

"Seeing as you're fed, I should be heading off. Apgar's sending me south to recon some of those oil fields."

"Lish, how did you know something was down there?"

The question seemed to catch her short. "I don't really have an answer, Peter. It was just . . . a feeling."

"A feeling."

She was staring past him. "I don't really know how to put it into words."

"I thought only Amy could do that."

Alicia shrugged, pushing the subject aside: *Don't press.* "I guess I owe you for going out on a limb for me like that. Nice to have a little company in the doghouse at least."

"This whole thing has had it, hasn't it?" he said glumly.

"Apgar's going to do what he's going to do. I'm not a mind reader."

"Do you think he believes us?"

Alicia said nothing. Her eyes had gone away again. Then, with a quizzical expression:

"Peter, do you remember that movie *Dracula*?"

The memory called him back five years. Peter had been watching it with Vorhees's men in the Colorado garrison on the night Alicia had returned from the mission that had found the nest of virals in an old copper mine.

"I didn't know you saw it."

"Saw it? Hell, I *studied* it. The thing is like a viral owner's manual. Never mind the cape and castle and all that nonsense. It's the rest that fits. A human being whose life has been 'unnaturally prolonged.' Using the stake in the heart to kill him. The way he has to sleep in his native soil. The whole business with the mirrors—"

"Like the pan in Las Vegas," Peter cut in. "I thought the same thing."

"It's as if their reflection, I don't know, screws them up somehow. The whole movie is like that."

"Lish, where are you going with this?"

She hesitated. "Something always nagged at me, a piece I couldn't place. Dracula has a sort of adjutant. Somebody who still looks human."

Peter remembered. "The crazy one who eats the spiders."

"That's the guy. Renfield. Dracula infects him, but he doesn't flip, at least not completely. He's more like somebody caught in the early stages of infection. It got me wondering, what if they all have somebody like that?" She was looking at him keenly now. "Do you remember what Olson said about Jude?"

Olson was the leader of the community they'd found in Nevada, the Haven—a whole town of people who would sacrifice their own to Babcock, First of Twelve. Olson had been nominally in charge, but the fact had emerged that it was Jude who really ran the place. He had some kind of special relationship to Babcock, though its nature had gone unexplained.

"'He was . . . familiar,'" Peter quoted. "I never understood what Olson meant. It didn't really make sense. And you *were* pointing a gun at his head."

"So I was. And believe me, there are days when I wish I'd gone ahead and pulled the trigger. But I don't think it was gibberish. I looked up the word at the library back in Kerrville. The dictionary said the definition was archaic, so I had to look that up too, which basically just means old. It said that a familiar is a kind of helper demon, like a witch's cat. A sort of assistant. Maybe that's what Olson was talking about."

Peter allowed himself several seconds to process this. "So what you're saying is that Ignacio was Martínez's . . . familiar."

Alicia shrugged. "Okay, it's a stretch. I'm sort of cobbling things together here. But the other thing to consider is the signal. Ignacio had a chip in him, just like Amy and the Twelve. That means he's connected to Project NOAH."

"Did you tell Apgar any of this?"

"Are you serious? I'm in enough trouble as it is."

Peter didn't doubt that. Nor did he doubt that whatever blame she had incurred for the botched raid on the cave was his as well.

Alicia rose to go. "Either way, we should know more about where we stand by the time I get back from Odessa. No point in worrying for now. I know you think you're indispensible, but we can get along without you for a few days."

"You're not making me feel any better."

She smiled. "Just don't expect me to come back to feed you again, Lieutenant. You only get that once."

As she moved toward the door, Peter said, "Lish, hold up a second."

She spun to look at him.

"What Ignacio said. 'He left us.' What do you think it means?"

"I don't have an answer for that. All I know is he should have been there."

"Where do you think he went?"

She didn't answer right away. A shadow moved over her face, a darkening from within. It wasn't anything Peter had seen before. Even in the most perilous circumstances, her composure was total. She was a woman of absolute focus, always giving her attention to the task at hand. This was similar, but the energy wasn't the same. It seemed to come from a deeper place.

"I wish I knew," she said, and slipped her glasses on. "Believe me."

Then she was gone, the flaps of the tent shifting with her departure. Peter felt her absence immediately, as he always did. It was true: they were always leaving each other.

Peter did not see her again. Six days later, he was released. His ribs would need longer to heal, and he would have to take it easy for a couple of weeks, but at least he was out of bed. Making his way across the garrison to report for duty, a surge lifted his steps. The sensation reminded him of a time many years ago when, just a boy, he'd been sick with a high fever, and after the fever had broken how just being up and about made even ordinary things seem charged with a fresh vitality.

Yet something else was different; Peter could feel it. Everything appeared normal—the soldiers on the catwalks, the roar of generators, the ordered movements of military activity all around—yet he sensed a shift, a discernible lessening of intensity.

He entered the command tent to find Apgar standing behind his desk of battered metal, scowling at a stack of papers.

"Jaxon. I didn't expect to see you for a couple more days. How are you feeling?"

The question struck Peter as uncharacteristically personal. "Fine, sir. Thank you for asking."

"Take a seat, won't you?"

For a while Apgar continued to shift his papers. Though not a large man—Peter stood at least two hands taller—the colonel exuded a strong, physical presence, his movements precise, nothing wasted. After a period of time that might have been two full minutes, he appeared to achieve a satisfactory ordering to the documents and lowered himself into his chair to face Peter across the desk.

"I have new orders for you. They came this morning in the pouch from Kerrville. Before you say anything, I want you to know this has nothing to do with what happened in Carlsbad. I've been expecting this for some time, actually."

The last of Peter's hopes sank beneath the waves. Going, going, gone. "We're abandoning the hunt, aren't we?"

"'Abandoning' would be too strong a word. Putting under review. There's a feeling at Command that some of our resources have to shift. For the time being, you're being transferred to the Oil Road."

It was worse than Peter had expected. "That's a job for Domestic Security."

"Generally, yes. But this isn't without precedent, and it comes from the president's office. Apparently she's of the opinion that security for oil shipments has been too lax, and she wants the Army to take a role. A transport leaves at the end of the week for Kerrville, and I want you on it. From there you'll report to the DS in Freeport."

Despite what Apgar said, Peter knew the decision had everything to do with Carlsbad. He was being demoted—if not in rank, then in responsibility.

"You can't do that, sir."

A lift of his eyebrows, no more. "Perhaps I misheard you, Lieutenant. I could swear you just told me what I could and could not do."

Peter felt his face grow warm. "Sorry, Colonel. That's not what I meant."

Apgar studied Peter a moment. "Look, I get it, Jaxon. Tell me something. How long have you been out here?"

Of course the colonel knew the answer; he was asking only to make a point. "Sixteen months."

"A long time in the sticks. You should have been rotated out a while ago. The only reason you haven't is that you always put in a request to stay. I've let it go because I know what the hunt means to you. In a way, you're the reason all of us are here."

"There's no place else I want to be, sir."

"And you've made that abundantly clear. But you're only human, Lieutenant. Frankly, you need the break. I'm headed back to Kerrville after we button things up, and as soon as I can, I'll put in a request at Division to move you back out to the territories. I'm not in the habit of making deals, so I suggest you take this one."

There was nothing to do but agree. "If I may ask, Colonel, what about Lieutenant Donadio?"

"She's got new orders, too. This isn't just you. As soon as she returns from the slicks, she's going north to Kearney."

Fort Kearney was the northernmost outpost of the Expeditionary. With a supply line stretching all the way from Amarillo, it was typically shut down before the first snowfall.

"Why there? Winter's only a couple of months away."

"Command doesn't tell me everything, but from what I hear it's gotten pretty thick up there. Given her talents, I'm guessing they want a new S2 to help clear out the hostiles before they evac."

The explanation felt thin, but Peter knew better than to press.

"I'm sorry about Satch," Apgar continued. "He was a good officer. I know you were friends."

"Thank you, sir."

"Dismissed, Lieutenant."

Peter spent the rest of the week in a state of suspension. With nothing else to occupy his time, he mostly stayed in his quarters. The map on the inside lid of the locker, once a badge of purpose, now felt like a bad joke. Maybe there was something to Alicia's theory, and maybe there wasn't. It seemed likely they would never find out. He thought of the time before he'd joined the Expeditionary, wondering if he'd made a mistake by enlisting. Back then, the fight had been his alone. Now it belonged to a larger enterprise, one with rules and protocols and chains of command in which he had little, if any, say. He had surrendered his freedom to become just another junior officer about whom people would someday remark, "He was a good guy."

The morning of his departure arrived. Peter carted his locker to the staging area where the transport awaited, a semitrailer loaded with the tires Peter's men had brought down from Lubbock. He hoisted his baggage into the cargo compartment of the escort vehicle and climbed into the passenger seat.

"Good to be going home, sir?"

Peter merely nodded. Anything he might have said would have sounded peevish, and the driver, a corporal from Satch's squad, didn't deserve to bear the brunt of his bad mood.

"I'll tell you the first thing I do after I collect my scrip," the corporal said, his exuberance barely contained. "I'm going straight to H-town to spend half of it on lick and the other half in a whorehouse." Suddenly embarrassed, he glanced at Peter with a flustered look. "Um, sorry, sir."

"That's all right, Corporal."

"Anybody at home for you, Lieutenant? If you don't mind my asking."

The answer was too complicated to even begin. "In a way."

The corporal gave a knowing smile. "Well, whoever she is, I'm sure she'll be happy to see you."

The order was given; with a belch of diesel fumes, the convoy began to pull away. Peter was already settling into the trancelike state he hoped to maintain for the next three days when he heard someone yelling over the racket of engines.

"Hold at the gate!"

Alicia was jogging toward the Humvee. Peter drew down the window.

"I just got back an hour ago," she said. "Who do you think you are, leaving without saying goodbye?"

Her face was a mask of oily grime; she smelled faintly of petroleum. But the thing that caught his eye was a glint of metal on her collar: a pair of captain's bars.

"Well, look at that," he said, managing a wry grin that he hoped masked his envy. "I guess I'll have to start calling you 'sir.'"

"I like the ring of that. About time, if you ask me."

"Apgar's cycling me out."

"I know. The Oil Road." There was no reason to elaborate. "It's easy duty, Peter. You've earned it."

"That's what they tell me."

"Say hi to the Circuit for me. And Greer, if you see him."

Peter nodded. There was only so much that could be said with the driver present. "When do you leave for Kearney?"

"Two days."

"All eyes up there. Apgar says it's gotten pretty thick."

"You, too." She glanced at the driver, who was studying the wheel with his eyes, then back at Peter. "Don't worry. What we were talking about before. It's not over, okay?"

He felt, inside her words, the pressure of something unstated. From behind them rose an impatient roar of engines. Everyone was waiting.

"Sir, we really have to be going," the driver said.

"That's okay, we're done here." Alicia regarded Peter one last time. "I mean it, Peter. It'll be all right. Just go see your boy."

28

The first pain arrived, like a late train roaring into the station, on an afternoon in late September of warm Texas sunshine and a high blue sky. Amy was in the courtyard, watching the children play; in another few minutes the bell would sound, summoning them inside to finish their lessons, and Amy would return to the kitchen to help make dinner. An island of rest in the midst of the day's never-ending rhythm of tasks done and, just as swiftly, undone; always, when lunch was concluded and the dishes put away and the children set loose to burn off the morning's accumulated antsiness, Amy followed them outside and took up a position at the edge of the playground that was near enough for her to enjoy the bright energy of their activity while not so close as to allow the children to draw her in. These were her favorite thirty minutes of the day, and Amy had just closed her eyes and tilted her face to receive the warm rays of the early autumn sun when the pain hit: a powerful clenching in her midriff that caused her to bend sharply at the waist, stagger forward, and exhale a soft cry of shock that even in the busy hubbub of the courtyard could not fail to go unnoticed.

"Amy? Are you all right?"

The image of Sister Catherine—pale, long-faced, irises as blue as cornflowers—came into Amy's focus. The sweat was pouring off her; her hands and feet had turned to cold jelly. Everything below her waist seemed to have lost some essential density; in another moment Amy would, literally, melt to the ground. Part of her wanted to vomit while another part refused, creating an internal stalemate that rendered her unable to speak.

"Maybe you better sit down. You're white as a ghost."

Sister Catherine steered her to a bench against the wall of the orphanage—a distance of twenty feet that could have been a mile. By the time they reached it, Amy couldn't have taken another step without collapsing. With a bustle of concern, Sister Catherine left her, then returned with a cup of water, which she pressed into Amy's hand. Activity on the playground seemed to have proceeded without interruption, but Amy could sense that some of the children were watching her. The pain had dissipated into a more general nausea but not the feeling of weakness. She felt both hot and cold. More sisters had crowded around, all speaking in hushed, earnest voices, questioning Sister Catherine. Amy didn't want the water but everyone was insistent. She took a small sip.

"I'm sorry," she managed to say. "One minute I was perfectly fine . . ."

"Over here, Sister," Catherine said, waving toward the doors to the orphanage. "Come quickly."

The small crowd parted as Sister Peg strode forward. The old woman studied Amy with a pinched expression that managed to seem both worried and irritated at the same time.

"Well? Will somebody tell me what happened here or will I have to guess?"

"I don't know," said Sister Catherine. "She just collapsed."

The playground had been brought to a standstill. All the children were staring at her now. Amy looked for Caleb, but her view was blocked by Sister Peg. She couldn't recall a time when she'd ever felt ill; she understood the principle but had never experienced the reality. Almost worse than the pain was the embarrassment. It made her want to say something, say anything, to get everyone to stop looking at her.

"Amy? Is that what happened?"

"I just felt dizzy. My stomach hurt. I don't know what it was."

The old woman pressed her palm to Amy's forehead. "Well, I don't think you have a fever."

"It was probably something I ate. I'm sure if I sit here another minute I'll be okay."

"She doesn't look good," Sister Catherine chimed in, and the others nodded. "Honestly, Amy, I thought you were going to pass out."

A general murmuring ensued. No, she didn't look good, not good at all. Could it be the flu? Something worse? If it was something the girl had eaten, would they all become sick, too?

Sister Peg allowed the group its moment of conjecture, then brought them to silence with a raised hand. "I don't see a reason to take chances. Off to bed with you, Amy."

"But I'm really feeling much better. I'm sure I'll be all right."

"I'll be the judge of that, thank you. Sister Catherine, will you assist her to the dormitory?"

Catherine helped her to her feet. She felt a little unsteady, and her stomach wasn't quite what it should be. But the worst of it had passed. Catherine led her into the building and up the stairs to the room where all the sisters slept, except for Sister Peg, who, being in charge, had quarters of her own. Amy undressed and got into bed.

"Can I do anything else?" Sister Catherine was drawing the shades.

"I'm fine." Amy did her best to smile. "I think I just need to rest a bit."

Standing at the foot of the cot, Catherine regarded her for a moment. "You know what this could be, don't you? A girl your age."

Your age. If Sister Catherine only knew, thought Amy. Yet Amy also understood what the woman was suggesting. The idea took her by surprise.

Sister Catherine smiled with sympathy. "Well, if it is, you'll know soon enough. Believe me, we've all been through it."

Making Amy promise to call her if she needed anything, Catherine made her departure. Amy leaned back on her cot and closed her eyes. The afternoon bell had rung; downstairs, the children would be filing in for their lessons, smelling of sun and sweat and fresh afternoon air, some of them, perhaps, wondering what all the fuss on the playground had been about. Surely Caleb would be worried about her; Amy should have told Sister Catherine to say something to the boy. *She's just tired. She was feeling out of sorts. She'll be right as rain in a jiff, you'll see.*

And yet: *A girl your age.* Was it possible? All the sisters complained about the "ordeal," as they called it; it was a common joke of the orphanage that living in such tight quarters, everybody menstruated at the same time, making one week of every four a nightmare of bloody rags and quick tempers. For a hundred years Amy had lived in complete innocence of these basic facts; even now she could not have said she understood the phenomenon completely, but she grasped the gist. You bled, not a lot but some, and this would be uncomfortable, extending over a period of days. For a while Amy had regarded the prospect with horror, but over time this feeling had yielded to a fierce, almost biological yearning, and the fear that none of this would ever happen to her, that this door of human belonging would always stay closed and she would live in a child's body forever.

She checked: no, she wasn't bleeding. If Sister Catherine was correct, how long before it started? She wished she'd taken the opportunity to ask Catherine more. How much blood would there be, how much pain, how would she feel different? Though in her case, Amy reasoned, nothing would quite be the same. Maybe it would be worse; maybe it would be better; maybe it would never happen at all.

She would have liked to be a woman. To see it reflected in another's eyes. For her body to know what her heart already did.

A scratchy mewing interrupted her train of thought. Of course Mouser would come to check on her. The old gray cat ambled to her bedside. A pitiful sight he was—eyes fogged with cataracts, fur matted and tacky, his tail dragging with age. "Did you come to look in on me? Did you, boy? Well, come here." Amy lifted him from the floor, leaned back on her cot, and balanced him on her chest. She ran her hands through his coat; he replied in kind, butting his head against her neck. *The sun is out, why are you in bed?* He circled three times before settling down on her chest, loudly purring. *It's fine. You sleep. I'll be right here.*

Amy closed her eyes.

Then it was night, and Amy was outside.

How had she gotten outside?

She was still wearing her nightgown; her feet were bare and damp with dew. The hour was impossible to know but felt late. Was she dreaming? But if she was still asleep, why did everything feel so real? She took measure of her surroundings. She was near the dam on the upstream side. The air was cool and moist. She felt a lingering urgency, as if she'd awoken from a dream of being chased. Why was she here? Had she been sleepwalking?

Something brushed her leg, making her startle. She looked down to see Mouser, staring at her with his clouded eyes. He began, loudly, to meow, then trotted toward the dam, stopping a few feet away to look at her again.

His meaning was clear; Amy followed. The old cat led her toward a small concrete structure at the base of the dam. Something mechanical? Mouser was standing at the door, meowing.

She opened the door and stepped inside. The darkness was total; how would she find her way? She felt along the wall, searching for a switch. There. A bank of lights flickered to life. At the center of the small room was a metal rail guarding a circular staircase. Mouser was standing on the top step. He turned to look at her, issued one more insistent meow, and descended.

The stairs spiraled down. At the bottom she found herself once again in blackness. Another fumbling search for a light switch; then she saw where she was. A wide tube, leading in only one direction, forward. Mouser was well ahead of her, dragging elongated shadows over the walls. His urgency was contagious, drawing her deeper into this underground world. They came to a second hatch, sealed with a ring. A length of pipe lay on the floor beside it. Amy threaded it between the spokes and turned; the door swung open, revealing a ladder. She turned to consult Mouser, who met her gaze with a skeptical look.

Not for me, I'm afraid. You're on your own now.

She descended. Something awaited her at the bottom; she felt its presence, deep in her bones. Something terrible and sad and full of longing.

Her feet touched down. Another shaft, wider than the first. Water trick-led along the floor. At the far end, she saw a circle of light. Now she knew where she was: one of the spillway tubes. It was moonlight she was seeing. She moved toward its penumbral glow just as a shadow moved across it. Not a shadow: a figure.

She knew.

Amy, Amy, daughter of my heart.

He reached toward her through the bars: a long, crooked claw, the digits distended, tipped with curving talons. As their palms touched, his fingers curled first through and then around her own. She felt no fear, only a spreading lightness. Her vision blurred with tears.

Amy, I remember. I remember everything.

Their hands held fast. The feel of his touch had dispersed to every part of her, bathing her in its warmth—a warmth of love, of home. It said: *Always I will be here. I will be the one to keep you safe.*

My brave girl. My brave Amy. Don't cry now.

A great sob shook her, a flood of pure emotion. She was happy, she was sad, she felt the weight of her life.

—What's happening to me? Why do I feel like I do? Please, tell me.

His face made no expression, for there could be none; all that he was, was in his eyes.

All your questions will be answered. He is waiting for you, in the ship. I will show you the way when the time comes.

—When? When will it come?

But Amy knew the answer even as she spoke the words.

Soon, said Wolgast. *Very, very soon.*

V

THE OIL ROAD

Can I see another's woe,
And not be in sorrow too?
Can I see another's grief,
And not seek for kind relief?

—WILLIAM BLAKE,
"On Another's Sorrow"

Guadalupe River bridge #1

San Marcos River bridge

Guadalupe River bridge #2

Slide No. 3: Map of the Oil Road, Texas Republic
Presented at the Third Global Conference
   on the North American Quarantine Period
Center for the Study of Human Cultures and Conflicts
University of New South Wales, Indo-Australian Republic
April 16–21, 1003 A.V.

29

REFINERY COMPLEX
Freeport, Texas

Michael Fisher, oiler first class—Michael the Clever, Bridger of Worlds—aroused from a deep and dreamless sleep to the sensation, unmistakable, that somebody was fucking him.

He opened his eyes. Lore was straddling him, her spine bowed forward, her brow glazed with a glinting, sex-fired sweat. Flyers, he thought, hadn't they just done this? Most of the night, in fact? Hugely, hilariously, in every position allowable to human physiology in a sleeping berth the approximate dimensions of a coffin?

"Good morning," she announced with a grin. "I hope you don't mind I got started without you."

Well, so be it, Michael thought. There were certainly worse ways to face the day. From the flush of her cheeks, he could tell that Lore was well on the way, and, come to think of it, he wasn't far behind. She had begun to rock her hips, the weight of her sex lapping against him like waves on a beach. In and out went the waves.

"Not so fast, mister."

"For Christ's sake, keep it down!" a voice barked from above.

"Shut up, Ceps," Lore replied, "I'm working in here."

"You're making me hard! It's disgusting!"

This conversation seemed to Michael to be occurring in some distant orbit. With everyone bunked together, nothing but thin curtains for privacy, you learned to tune things out. But the feeling was more than that. Even as his senses sailed away into pure physicality, something about sex, its hypnotic rhythms, prompted in him a kind of disassociation. It was as if his mind were lagging three steps behind his body, sightseeing its way through a landscape of various concerns and sadnesses and emotionally neutral images that rose before him like bubbles of expanding gas in the boiler. A decaying gasket that needed replacing. The delivery schedule of fresh crude down from the depot. Memories of the Colony, which he never otherwise thought about. Above him, Lore continued on her journey, while Michael drifted in this current of mental disloyalty, trying to will his attentions into alignment with hers. It seemed the least he could do.

And in the end, he did. Lore's accelerating passion won the day. By the time they pulled the curtain back, Ceps was gone. The clock above the hatch read 0630.

"Shit."

Michael swung his feet to the floor and yanked on his jumpsuit. Lore, behind him, wrapped her arms around his chest.

"Stay. I'll make it worth your while."

"I'm first shift. If I'm late again, Karlovic will chew my ass for breakfast." He stuffed his feet into his boots and swiveled his face to kiss her: a taste of salt, and sex, and something all her own. Michael wouldn't have said it was love between them, exactly. Sex was a way to pass the time, but over the months their relationship had evolved, little by little, into something more than habit.

"You were thinking again, weren't you?"

"Who, me?"

"Don't lie." Her tone wasn't bitter, merely correcting. "You know, someday I'm going to fuck all the worries out of you." She sighed and relaxed her grip. "It's all right. Go."

He rose from the berth and took his hard hat and gloves from the post. "I'll see you later?"

She had already lain back down on the cot. "That you will."

As Michael exited the barracks, the sun was just lifting over the Gulf, making its surface shimmer like a sheet of hammered metal. It might have been the first week of October, but the heat was already building, the ocean air tart as ever with salt and the sulfurous stench of burning butane. With his stomach growling—food would have to wait—he strode at a brisk clip across the compound, past the commissary and weight cages and DS barracks to the Quonset hut, where the workers on the morning shift had gathered. Karlovic, the chief engineer, was calling out assignments from the roster. He shot Michael a cold glance.

"Are we interrupting your beauty sleep, Fisher? Our mistake."

"Right." Michael was zipping his jumpsuit. "Sorry."

"You'll be even sorrier. You'll be firing up the Bomb. Ceps will be your second. Try not to blow up your crew."

Distillation Tower No. 1, known as the Bomb, was the oldest of the lot, its rusty bulk held together by a combination of patch welds, baling wire, and prayer. Everybody said it was a matter of time before she was either decommissioned or launched a cooking crew halfway to Mars.

"Thanks, boss. That's swell of you."

"Don't mention it." Karlovic swept his gaze over the group. "All right, everyone. Seven days until we ship. I want those tankers full, people. And Fisher, hang back a minute. I want a word with you."

The crews dispersed to their towers. Michael followed Karlovic into the hut. Christ, what now? He hadn't been late by more than a couple of minutes, hardly worth a dressing down.

"Listen, Dan, I'm sorry about this morning—"

Karlovic didn't let him finish. "Forget it, that's not what I want to talk to you about." Hitching up his pants, he lowered his bulk into the chair behind his desk. Karlovic was heavy in the true sense, not fat but large in every aspect, a man of weight and heft. Tacked on the wall over his head were dozens of sheets of paper—duty rosters, work flows, delivery schedules. "I had you on the Bomb anyway. You and Ceps are the best I've got for hotwork. Take it as a compliment I'm putting the pair of you on that cranky old bitch. If I had my druthers, that thing would be in the scrap pile."

Michael didn't doubt that this was so; on the other hand, he knew strategically timed praise when he heard it. "So?"

"So this."

Karlovic slid a sheet of paper across his desk. Michael's eyes fell quickly to the signature at the bottom: Victoria Sanchez, President, Texas Republic. He quickly scanned the letter's three short paragraphs. *Well, I'll be,* he thought.

"Any idea what this is about?"

"What makes you think I would?"

"You were the last crew chief on the offload. Maybe you caught wind of something while you were up there. Talk around the depot, extra military hanging around."

"Nothing that rings a bell." Michael shrugged. "Have you spoken to Stark? Maybe he knows."

Stark was the refinery's chief security officer. He was something of a loudmouth and liked the lick too much, but he generally commanded respect among both the oilers and DS, if for no other reason than his prowess at the poker table. His caginess with the cards had cost Michael a bundle, not that the scrip was any big loss—within the fences of the refinery, there was nothing to spend it on.

"Not yet. This won't sit well with him, though." Karlovic studied Michael. "Aren't you guys friends? That whole California thing."

"I know him, yeah."

"So maybe you can grease the gears a bit. Act as a sort of, I don't know, unofficial liaison between DS and the military."

Michael allowed himself a few seconds to probe his feelings. He'd be glad to see someone from the old days, but at the same time he was aware of an inner disturbance, a sense of exposure. The self-contained life of an oiler had, in many ways, rescued him from the grief of losing his sister, occupying the mental space she had left behind. Part of him knew he was hiding, but the rest of him didn't care.

"It should be no problem."

"I'll count it as a favor. Handle it how you like." Karlovic angled his head toward the door. "Now get out of here, you've got oil to cook. And I meant what I said. Watch your ass with that thing."

Michael arrived at the distillation tower to find his crew, a dozen roughnecks, standing around wearing expressions of puzzlement. The tanker with its cargo of fresh slick sat idle. Ceps was nowhere to be seen.

"Okay, I'll bite. Why aren't you people filling this thing?"

Ceps crawled from beneath the heating element at the base of the tower. His hands and bare arms were caked with black goo. "We'll have to flush her first. We've got at least two meters of residuum in the base."

"Fuck sake, that will take all morning. Who was the last crew chief?"

"This thing hasn't been fired in months. You'd have to ask Karlovic."

"How much crude will we have to drain off?"

"A couple of hundred barrels anyway."

Eight thousand gallons of partially refined petroleum that had been sitting for who knew how long: they would need a large waste tanker, then a pumper truck and high-pressure steam hoses to flush the tower. They were looking at twelve hours minimum, sixteen to refill it and light the heating element, twenty-four before the first drop came out of the pipe. Karlovic would pop an aneurysm.

"Well, we better get started. I'll call in the order, you get the hoses ready." Michael shook his head. "I find who did this, I will kick his sorry ass."

The draining took the rest of the morning. Michael declared the leftover oil unusable and sent the truck to the waste pools for burning. Bleeding off the junk was the easy part; flushing the tank was the job everyone dreaded. Water injected into the top of the tower would clean out most of the residuum—the sticky, toxic residue of the refining process—but not all; three men would have to suit up and go inside to brush down the base and flush out the asphalt drain. The only way in was a blind port, a meter wide, through which they'd have to crawl on their hands and knees. The term for this was "going up the anus"—not an inaccurate description, in Michael's opinion. Michael would be one of the three. There was no rule about this; it was simply his habit, a gesture toward morale. For the other two, the custom was to draw straws.

The first to pull a short straw was Ed Pope, the oldest man on the crew. Ed had been Michael's trainer, the one to show him the ropes. Three decades on the cookers had taken their toll; the man's body read like a logbook of catastrophes. Three fingers sheered off by the thrown blade of a rebar cutter. One side of his head and neck seared to a hairless pink slab by a propane explosion that had killed nine men. He was deaf in that ear, and his knees were so shot that watching him bend made Michael wince. Michael thought about giving him a pass, but he knew Ed was too proud to accept, and he watched as the man made his way to the hut to suit up.

The second short straw was Ceps. "Forget it, I need you out here on the pumps," said Michael.

Ceps shook his head. The day had left them all impatient. "The hell with it. Let's just get this done."

They wriggled into their hazard suits and oxygen packs and gathered their gear together: heavy brushes on poles, buckets of solvent, high-pressure wands that would feed back to a compressor. Michael pulled his mask down over his face, taped the seals on his gloves, and checked his O_2. Though they'd vented the tower, the air inside it was still as lethal as it got—an airborne soup of petroleum vapors and sulfides that could sear your lungs into jerky. Michael felt a positive pop of pressure in the mask, switched on his headlamp, and knelt to unbolt the port.

"Let's go, hombres."

He slithered through, dropping down to find himself in three inches of standing muck. Ed and Ceps crawled in behind him.

"What a mess."

Michael reached down into the sludge and opened the asphalt drain; the three of them began to sweep the residuum toward it. The temperature inside the tower was at least a hundred degrees; the sweat was raining off them, the trapped moisture of their breath fogging their faceplates. Once they'd cleared the worst of it, they dumped the solvent, hooked up their wands, and commenced spraying down the walls and floor.

Inside their suits, with the roar of the compressor, conversation was just about impossible. The only thing to think about was finishing the job and getting out. They'd been at it for only a couple of minutes when

Michael felt a tap on his shoulder. He turned to see Ceps pointing at Ed. The man was just standing there, facing the wall like a statue, his wand held loosely at his side. While Michael watched, it slipped from his hand, though Ed seemed not to notice.

"Something's wrong with him!" Ceps yelled over the racket.

Michael stepped forward and turned Ed by the shoulders. All he got was a blank stare.

"Ed, you okay?"

The man's face startled to life. "Oh, hey, Michael," he said, too brightly. "Hey-hey, hey-hey. Woo-woo."

"What's he saying?" Ceps called out.

Michael drew a finger over his throat to tell Ceps to cut the compressor. He looked at Ed squarely. "Talk to me, buddy."

A girlish giggle escaped the man's lips. He was heaving for breath, one hand lifting toward his faceplate. "Ashblass. Minfuth. Minfuth!"

Michael saw what was about to happen. As Ed reached for his mask, Michael seized him by the arms. The man was no kid, but he was no weakling either. He wriggled fiercely in Michael's grasp, trying to break free, his face blue with panic. Not panic, Michael realized: hypoxia. His body convulsed with a massive twitch, his knees melting under him, his full weight crashing into Michael's arms.

"Ceps, help me get him out of here!"

Ceps grabbed the man by his feet. His body had gone limp. Together they carried him to the port.

"Somebody take him!" Michael yelled.

Hands appeared to pull from the far side; Michael and Ceps shoved his body through. Michael scrambled into the port, tearing off his faceplate and gloves the moment he hit fresh air. Ed was lying face-up on the hardpan; someone had stripped off his mask and backpack. Michael dropped to his knees beside the body. An ominous stillness: the man wasn't breathing. Michael placed the heel of his right hand at the center of Ed's chest, positioned the left on top, laced his fingers together, and pushed. Nothing. Again and again he pushed, counting to thirty, as he had learned to do, then slipped one hand behind Ed's neck to tip his airway open, pinched his nose, and pressed his mouth over the man's blue lips. One breath, two breaths, three. Michael's mind was clear as ice, his thoughts held in the grip of a singular purpose. Just as all seemed lost, he felt a sharp contraction of the diaphragm; Ed's chest inflated, taking in a voluminous breath of air. He turned his face to the side, gasping and coughing.

Michael rocked back on his heels, landing ass-down in the dust, his pulse pounding with adrenaline. Somebody handed him a canteen: Ceps.

"You okay, pal?"

The question didn't even make sense to him. He took a long drink, swishing the water inside his mouth, and spat it away. "Yeah."

Eventually somebody helped Ed to his feet. Michael and Ceps escorted him into the hut and sat him down on one of the benches.

"How you feeling?" Michael asked.

A bit of color had flowed back into Ed's cheeks, though his skin was damp and clammy-looking. He shook his head miserably. "I don't know what happened. I could have sworn I checked my oxygen."

Michael had already looked; the bottles were empty. "Maybe it's time, Ed."

"Jesus, Michael. Are you firing me?"

"No. It's your choice. I'm just saying there's no disgrace in calling it a day." When Ed made no reply, Michael rose to his feet. "Give it some thought. I'll back you, whatever you want to do. You want a ride to the barracks?"

Ed was staring disconsolately into space. Michael could read the truth in his face: the man had nothing else.

"I think I'll sit here a while. Get my strength back."

Michael stepped from the hut to find the rest of the crew hovering by the door. "What the hell are you all standing around for?"

"The shift's over, Chief."

Michael checked his watch: so it was.

"Not for us it isn't. Show's over, everybody. Get your lazy asses back to work."

It was past midnight when Lore said to him, "Lucky thing, about Ed."

The two of them were curled in Michael's berth. Despite Lore's best efforts, his mind had been unable to move on from the day's events. All he kept seeing when he closed his eyes was the look on Ed's face in the hut, like someone being marched to the gallows.

"What do you mean, lucky?"

"That you were there, I mean. That thing you did."

"It wasn't anything."

"Yes, it was. The man could have died. How did you know how to do that?"

The past loomed up inside him, a wave of pain.

"My sister taught me," said Michael. "She was a nurse."

30

THE CITY
Kerrville, Texas

They arrived behind the rain. First the fields, sodden with moisture, the air rich with the smell of dirt, then, as they ascended out of the valley, the walls of the city, looming eight stories tall against the brown Texas hills. At the gate they found themselves in a line of traffic—transports, heavy mechanicals, DS pickups crowded with men in their thick pads. Peter climbed out, asked the driver to deposit his locker at the barracks, and showed his orders to the guard at the pedestrian tunnel, who waved him through.

"Welcome home, sir."

After sixteen months in the territories, Peter's senses were instantly assaulted by the vast, overwhelming humanness of the place. He'd spent little time in the city, not enough to adjust to its claustrophobic density of sounds and smells and overflowing faces. The Colony had never numbered more than a hundred souls; here there were over forty thousand.

Peter made his way to the quartermaster to collect his pay. He'd never really gotten used to the idea of money, either. "Equal share," the governing economic unit of the Colony, had made sense to him. You had your share, and you used it how you liked, but it was the same as everybody else's, never less or more. How could these slips of inked paper—Austins they were called, after the man whose image, with its high, domed forehead and beaked nose and perplexing arrangement of clothing, adorned each bill—actually correspond to the value of a person's labor?

The clerk, a civilian, doled out the scrip from the lockbox, snapping the bills onto the counter, and shoved a clipboard toward him through the grate, all without once meeting his eye.

"Sign here."

The money, a fat wad, felt odd in Peter's pocket. As he stepped back into the brightening afternoon, he was already scheming how to be rid of it. Six hours remained until curfew—barely enough time to visit both the orphanage and the stockade before reporting to the barracks. The afternoon was all he had; the transport to the refinery was leaving at 0600.

Greer would come first; that way Peter wouldn't have to disappoint Caleb by leaving before the horn. The stockade was located in the old jailhouse on the west edge of downtown. He signed in at the desk—in Kerrville you were always signing things, another oddity—and stripped off his blade and sidearm. He was about to proceed when the guard stopped him.

"Have to pat you down, Lieutenant."

As a member of the Expeditionary, Peter was accustomed to a certain automatic deference—certainly from a junior domestic, not a day over twenty. "Is that really necessary?"

"I don't make the rules, sir."

Irritating, but Peter didn't have time for an argument. "Just be quick about it."

The guard ran his hands up and down Peter's arms and legs, then produced a heavy ring of keys and led him back into the holding area, a long hall of heavy steel doors. The air was dense and smelled of men. They came to the cell marked with the number 62.

"Funny," the guard remarked, "Greer doesn't see anyone in close to three years, and now he's had two visitors in just a month."

"Who else was here?"

"I wasn't on duty. You'd have to ask him."

The guard located the correct key, inserted it into the tumbler, and swung the door open to a sound of groaning hinges. Greer, shoeless, clothed only in a pair of rough canvas trousers cinched at his waist, was seated on the edge of his bunk. His broad chest gleamed with perspiration; his hands were serenely folded in his lap. His hair, what remained of it, a silvering white, fanned to his massive shoulders, while a great tangle of beard—the beard of a prophet, a wanderer in the wilderness—straggled halfway up his cheeks. A deep stillness radiated off him; the impression he communicated was one of composure, as if he had reduced his mind and body to their essences. For an unsettling moment, he gave no indication that he was aware of the two figures standing in the doorway, causing Peter to wonder if the isolation had done something to his mind. But then he lifted his eyes, his face brightening.

"Peter. There you are."

"Major Greer. It's good to see you."

Greer laughed ironically, his voice thick with disuse. "Nobody's called me that in some time. It's just Lucius now. Or Sixty-two, if you prefer. Most people seem to." Greer addressed the guard. "Give us a few minutes, will you, Sanders?"

"I'm not supposed to leave anyone alone with a prisoner."

Peter shot him a cold glare. "I think I can take care of myself, son."

A moment's hesitancy; then the guard relented. "Well, seeing as it's you, sir, I guess ten minutes would be okay. After that my shift ends, though. I don't want to get in trouble."

Peter frowned. "Do we know each other?"

"I saw your signature. Everybody knows who you are. You're the guy from California. It's, like, a legend." All pretense of his authority was gone; suddenly he was just a starstruck kid, his face beaming with admiration. "What was it like? Coming all that way, I mean."

Peter wasn't quite sure how to respond. "It was a long walk."

"I don't know how you did it. I would have been scared shitless."

"Take my word for it," Peter assured him, "that was a big part of it."

Sanders left them alone. Peter took the room's only chair, straddling it backward across from Greer.

"Looks like you made quite an impression on our boy there. I told you it would be a hard story to keep quiet."

"It's still strange to hear it," Peter said. "How are you doing?"

Greer shrugged. "Oh, I get by. And you? You look well, Peter. The uniform suits you."

"Lish says hello. She just got bumped to captain."

Greer nodded equably. "A remarkable girl, our Lish. Destined for big things, I'd say. So how goes the fight? Or do I have to ask?"

"Not so good. We're oh-for-three. The whole Martínez thing was a catastrophe. Now it looks like Command is having second thoughts."

"That's always what they've been best at. Not to worry, the winds will turn. One thing you learn in here is patience."

"It's not the same without you. I can't help thinking it would be different if you were there."

"Oh, I very much doubt that. This has always been your show. I knew it the moment I met you. Caught upside down in a spinning net, wasn't it?"

Peter laughed at the memory. "Michael puked all over us."

"That's right, I remember now. How is he? I imagine he's not the same kid I knew back then. Always had an answer to everything."

"I doubt he's changed much. Either way, I'll find out tomorrow. They're posting me down to the refinery."

Greer frowned. "Why there?"

"Some new initiative to secure the Oil Road."

"DS will love that. I'd say you've got your hands full with that lot." He gave his knees a slap to change the subject. "And Hollis, what do you hear of him?"

"Nothing good. He took Sara's death hard. The story is he's on the trade."

Greer considered this news for a moment. "On the whole, I can't say I blame him. That may seem strange to say, knowing Hollis, but more than one man has gone that way under those circumstances. I imagine he'll come around sooner or later. He's got a good head on his shoulders."

"And what about you? You're getting out soon. If you want, I can put a word in with Command. Maybe they'd let you reenlist."

But Greer shook his head. "I'm afraid those days are over for me, Peter. Don't forget, I'm a deserter. Once you cross that line, there's no going back."

"What will you do?"

Greer smiled mysteriously. "I imagine something will come along. It always does."

For a while they talked of the others, bits of news, stories from the past. Being with Greer, Peter felt a warm contentment, but accompanying that, a sense of loss. The major had entered his life just when Peter needed him; it was Greer's steadfast presence that had given him the will to move forward in the days when his resolve had wavered. It was a debt that Peter could never fully repay: the debt of borrowed courage. Peter sensed that Greer's incarceration had changed him. He was still the same man, although something inside him ran deeper, a river of inner calm. He seemed to have drawn strength from his isolation.

As the end of the ten minutes approached, Peter told the major about the cave, and the strange man, Ignacio, and Alicia's theory about what he was. Even as he spoke the words, he realized how far-fetched the idea sounded; and yet he felt its rightness. If anything, his feeling that the information was important had grown over the days.

"There may be something to that," Greer agreed. "He said, 'He left us'?"

"Those were his words."

Greer fell silent, stroking his long beard. "The question, of course, is where did Martínez go. Did Alicia have any ideas about that?"

"Not that she told me."

"And what do you think?"

"I think finding the Twelve is going to be more complicated than we planned on."

He waited, watching Greer's face. When the major made no reply, he said, "My offer still stands. We could really use you."

"You overestimate me, Peter. I was always just along for the ride."

"Not to me. Alicia would say the same thing. All of us would."

"And I accept the compliment. But it doesn't change a thing. What's done is done."

"It still doesn't seem right that you're in here."

Greer shrugged carelessly. "Maybe it is, maybe it isn't. Believe me, I've brooded plenty on the subject. The Expeditionary was my whole life, and I miss it. But I did what I thought was right in the moment. In the end, that's all a man has to measure his life, and it's plenty." His eyes narrowed on Peter. "Which isn't something I need to tell you, is it?"

The major had him dead to rights. "I suppose not."

"You're a good soldier, Peter. You always have been, and I wasn't lying about that uniform. It does suit you. The question is, do you suit it?"

The question wasn't accusing—if anything, the opposite. "Some days I wonder," Peter confessed.

"Everybody does. The military is what it is. You can hardly take a trip to the latrine without filling out a form in triplicate. But in your case, I'd say the question runs deeper. The man I met hanging upside down in that spinner—he wasn't following anybody's orders but his own. I don't think he would have even known how. Now here you are, five years later, informing me that Command wants to give up the hunt. Tell me, are they right?"

"Of course not."

"And can you make them understand that? Make them change their minds?"

"I'm just a junior officer. They're not going to listen to me."

Greer nodded. "And I agree. So there we are."

A silence followed. Then Greer said, "Maybe this will help. Do you remember what I said to you that night in Arizona?"

"There were lots of nights, Lucius. A lot of things got said."

"So there were. But this one in particular—I'm not sure where we were exactly. A couple of days out from the Farmstead, anyway. We were sheltering underneath a bridge. Crazy-looking rocks everywhere. I remember that part because of the way the light hit them at sunset, like they were lit from the inside. The two of us got to talking. It was the night I asked you what you intended to do with the vials Lacey gave you."

It was all coming back. The red rocks, the deep silence of the landscape, the easy flow of conversation as the two of them sat by the fire. It was as if the memory had been floating in Peter's mind for five years, never quite touching the surface until now. "I remember."

Greer nodded. "I thought you might. And let me just say, when you volunteered to be injected with the virus, that was, hands down, the ballsiest thing I'd ever seen, and I've seen some ballsy things. It was nothing I ever could have done myself. I had a lot of respect for you before that, but after . . ." He paused. "That night, I said something to you. 'Everything that's happened, it feels like more than chance.' I was really just talking to myself at the time, trying to put something into words I couldn't quite figure out, but I've given the matter a lot of thought. You finding Amy, me finding you, Lacey, Babcock, everything that happened on that mountain. Events can seem random while you're living them, but when you look back, what do you see? A chain of coincidences? Plain old luck? Or something more? I'll tell you what I see, Peter. A clear path. More than that. A *true* path. What are the chances these things would have just happened on their own? Each piece falling into place exactly when we needed it? There's a power at work here, something beyond our understanding. You can call it what you like. It doesn't need a name, because it knows yours, my friend. So you wonder what it is I do all day in here, and the answer is very simple. I'm waiting to see what happens next. Trusting in God's plan." He gave Peter an enigmatic smile; the film of sweat that dampened his face and his bare, muscled chest sharpened the air of the room. "Does it seem strange to hear me say that?" His manner lightened. "Probably you're thinking, *That poor guy, all alone in this little box, he must have lost his mind.* You wouldn't be the first."

It took Peter a moment to answer. "Actually, no. I was thinking how much you reminded me of someone."

"Who was that?"

"Her name was Auntie."

Now it was Greer's turn to remember. "Of course. The woman we buried when we got back to the Colony. You never told me anything about her, and I wondered. But I didn't want to pry."

"You could have. You could say we were close, though with Auntie it was hard to tell. Half the time I think she thought I was somebody else. I used to go around to check up on her. She liked to talk about God, too."

"Is that right?" Greer seemed pleased. "And what did she have to say?"

How strange, thought Peter, to find himself thinking of Auntie now. Like Greer's story of their night in Arizona, his memory of the old woman, and the time they'd spent together, emerged in his mind as if it were yesterday. Her overheated kitchen, and the awful cups of tea; the precise, even reverential arrangement of objects in her cramped house, furniture and books and pictures and mementos; her gnarled old feet, always shoeless, and her puckered, toothless mouth and the vaporous tangle of white hair that seemed to hover in the air around her head, not even really attached to anything. As Auntie herself was unattached; alone in her shack at the edge of the glade, the woman seemed to exist in a wholly different realm, a pocket of accumulated human memory, outside of time. Now that Peter considered it, probably that was what had drawn him to her. In Auntie's presence, the daily struggles of his life always felt lighter.

"More or less the same. She wasn't the easiest woman to make sense of." A specific recollection bubbled to the surface. "There is one thing. It was the same night Amy appeared outside the gate."

"Oh?"

"She said, 'The God I know about wouldn't give us no chance.'"

Greer was watching him with studious intensity. "She said that to you."

He was still a little surprised by the clarity of the memory. "At the time I just thought it was, you know, Auntie."

Greer broke the mood with a sudden, flashing smile. "Well," he said, "it sounds to me like the woman knew a thing or two. I'm sorry I never met her. I bet the two of us would have gotten on just fine."

Peter laughed. "You know, I think you would have."

"So maybe it's time for you to trust a little more, Peter. That's really all I'm saying. Let things come to you."

"Like Martínez, you mean."

"Maybe, maybe not. There's no way to know until you know. I've never asked you what you believe, Peter, and I'm not going to. Every man gets to decide that for himself. And don't get me wrong—I'm a soldier, too, or at least I was. The world needs its warriors, and the day will come when very little else is going to matter. You'll be there for the fight, my friend, I have no doubt. But there's more to this world than meets the eye. I don't have all the answers, but I know that much."

"I wish I had your confidence."

The major shrugged this away. "Oh, you're just trying to work things out, same as the rest of us. When I was growing up in the orphanage, the sisters always taught us that a person of faith is someone who believes something he can't prove. I don't disagree, but that's only half the story. It's the end, not the means. A hundred years ago, humanity just about destroyed itself. It'd be easy to think that God doesn't like us very much. Or that there *is* no God, there's no rhyme or reason to anything and we might just as well hang it up and call it a day. Thanks, planet Earth, it was nice knowing you. But that's not you, Peter. For you, hunting the Twelve isn't an answer. It's a question. Does anybody out there care? Are we worth saving? What would God want from me, if there is a God? The greatest faith is the willingness to ask in the first place, all evidence to the contrary. Faith not just in God, but in all of us. It's a hard place you're in, and my guess is you'll be in it for a while. But it's the right one, and it's yours."

It was then that Peter understood what he was seeing. Greer was free, a free man. The walls of his cage held no meaning for him at all; his life was entirely elsewhere, unbounded by physical things. How surprising, to envy a man whose whole life was conducted in a prison cell not much larger than a good-sized latrine.

The sound of turning tumblers; their time was at an end. As Sanders entered the cell, the two men rose.

"So," Greer said, and clapped his hands conclusively. "A little downtime in Freeport, courtesy of Command. Not the best-smelling town, but the view is nice. A good place to get a little thinking done. You've certainly earned it."

"That's what Colonel Apgar said."

"Smart fellow, Apgar." Greer extended his hand. "It was good to see you, my friend."

They shook. "Take care of yourself, all right?"

Greer grinned through the pocket of his beard. "You know what they say. Three hots and a cot. It's not such a bad life when you get down to it. And as for the rest, I know you, Peter. You'll figure things out when the time is right. That's a lesson you taught me, actually."

Sanders escorted him into the hall. Only then did it occur to Peter that he'd forgotten to ask Greer about his other visitor. And something else: the major had never asked about Amy.

"Listen," Sanders said as they were passing through the second door, "I hope you don't mind my asking, but could you sign this?"

He was holding out a scrap of paper and a stub of pencil.

"It's for my wife," he explained. "To prove I met you."

Peter accepted the paper, scrawled his name, and handed it back. For a moment Sanders just looked at it.

"Wow," he said.

"Uncle Peter!"

Breaking away from the other children, Caleb flew toward him across the playground. At the last instant he took three bounding steps and catapulted into Peter's arms, nearly knocking him over.

"Whoa now, easy."

The boy's face was lit with joy. "Amy said you were coming! You're here! You're here!"

Peter wondered how she had known. But he quickly corrected himself; Amy simply seemed to know things, as if her mind were linked to the world's hidden rhythms. Holding Caleb in his arms, Peter was washed with his distinctive physical presence: his boyish weight and heat; the warmth of his breath; the milky smell of his hair and skin, moist with exertion, mixed with the lingering scent of the harsh lye soap the sisters used. Across the playground, the other children were watching. Peter caught a glimpse of Sister Peg eyeing him coolly from the monkey bars, his unannounced presence a disruption to her beloved routine.

"Let me have a look at you."

He lowered Caleb to the ground. As always, Peter was struck by the boy's uncanny resemblance to Theo. He felt a stab of regret at the time he'd carelessly allowed to pass.

"You're getting so big. I can hardly believe it."

The little boy's chest puffed with pride. "Where have you been, what did you see?"

"Lots of stuff. I was in New Mexico."

"New Mexico!" The look of wonder on his face was total; Peter might just as well have told him he'd visited the moon. Although the prevailing custom in Kerrville was not to shelter the children from knowledge of the virals, as had been done in the Colony, his child's mind had yet to absorb the ramifications. To Caleb, the Expeditionary was a grand adventure, like pirates crossing the seas or tales of the knights of old that the sisters read to them from storybooks. "How long can you stay?" the boy pleaded.

"Not long, I'm afraid. But we have the rest of the afternoon. And I'll be back soon, probably just a week or so. What would you like to do?"

Caleb's answer was instantaneous: "Go to the dam."

"Why there?"

"You can see everything!"

Peter smiled. At such moments he felt something of himself in his nephew, the same undeniable force of curiosity that had governed his life. "The dam it is."

Sister Peg came up behind the boy. Possessing a birdlike slightness, Sister Peg was nonetheless an intimidating figure, her dark eyes capable of shrinking your insides with a single censorious glance. Peter's comrades who had been raised in the orphanage—men who weathered horrible conditions and constant peril—spoke of her with an awe verging on terror. *My God,* they all said, *that woman scared the living shit out of us.*

"Hello, Sister."

Her face, a weathered topography of deep crevices and arid planes, possessed the immobility of judgment withheld. She had taken a position just beyond a normal conversational distance, a small but significant alteration that magnified her commanding presence. Her teeth were stained a yellowish brown from puffing on corn silk—an incomprehensible habit, widespread in Kerrville, that Peter regarded with a combination of wonder and revulsion.

"Lieutenant Jaxon, I didn't expect you."

"Sorry, it was all pretty sudden. Do you mind if I take him for the rest of the day?"

"It would have been better if you could have sent word. Things here run a certain way."

Caleb's body was jangling with energy. "Please, Sister!"

Her imperious gaze flicked down toward the boy, taking accounts. Delta-like fans of wrinkles deepened at the corners of her mouth as she sucked in her cheeks. "I suppose under the circumstances it would be all right. An exception, you understand, and keep an ear to the horn, Lieutenant. I know you Expeditionary feel yourselves to be above the rules, but I can't allow it."

Peter let the barb pass; it did, after all, possess an element of truth. "I'll have him back by six." Under her withering gaze, he found himself, with the next question, attempting to sound curiously offhanded. "Is Amy around? I'd like to visit with her before we go."

"She's gone to the market. You've just missed her." This declaration was followed by a tart sigh. "I suppose you'll want to stay for dinner."

"Thank you, Sister. That's kind of you."

Caleb, bored by these formalities, was tugging at his hand. "Please, Uncle Peter, I want to *go.*"

For a breadth of time no longer than half a second, the woman's stern countenance appeared to crack. A look of almost maternal tenderness flickered in her eyes. But it just as quickly vanished, leaving Peter to wonder if he'd imagined it.

"Mind the clock, Lieutenant. I'll be watching."

The dam was, in many ways, the heart of the city and its mechanisms. Along with the oil that powered the generators, Kerrville's mastery of the Guadalupe River, which provided both water for irrigation and a barrier to the north and west—nobody had ever seen a viral even attempt to swim; it was widely believed that they either had a phobia of water or simply could not stay afloat—accounted for its longevity. The river itself had been a feature of scant dimension in the early days, thin and inconsequential, falling to barely a trickle in summer. But a devastating flood in the spring of 22, a harbinger of a meteorological shift that would raise the river permanently by as much as ten feet, had necessitated its taming. It had been, by all accounts, a massive project, requiring the temporary diversion of the river's currents and the movement of huge quantities of earth and limestone to dig the bowl-like depression that would form the impoundment, followed by the erection of the dam itself, a feat of engineering on a scale Peter had always associated with the Time Before, not the world he knew. The day of the water's first release was regarded as a foundational occurrence in the history of the Republic; more than anything else in Kerrville, the dam's corralling of natural forces had impressed upon him how flimsy the Colony had been in comparison. They were lucky to have made it as long as they had.

Grated steel stairs ascended to the top. Caleb took them at a dash over Peter's shouted protests to slow down. By the time Peter made the final turn, Caleb was already gazing over the water, toward the undulating ridge of hills at the horizon. Thirty feet below, the face of the impoundment possessed a stunning transparency. Peter could even see fish down there, white shapes piloting lazily in the glassy waters.

"What's out there?" the boy asked.

"Well, more Texas mostly. That ridge you're looking at is only a few miles away."

"Where's New Mexico?"

Peter pointed due west. "But it's really, really far. Three days on a transport, and that's without stopping."

The boy chewed on his lower lip. "I want to see it."

"Maybe someday you will."

They walked along the dam's curving top to the spillway. A series of vents released water at regular intervals into a wide pool, from which gravity pumps piped it down to the agricultural complex. Looming in the distance, regularly spaced towers marked the Orange Zone. They paused again, absorbing the view. Peter was once again struck by the elaborateness of it all. It was as if in this one place, human history still flowed in an uninterrupted continuum, undisturbed by the stark separation of eras that the virals had brought down upon the world.

"You look like him."

Peter turned to see Caleb squinting at him. "Who do you mean?"

"Theo. My father."

The statement caught him short; how could the boy possibly know what Theo had looked like? Of course he couldn't, but that wasn't the point. Caleb's assertion was a kind of wish, a way to keep his father alive.

"That's what everyone said. I can see a lot of him in you, you know."

"Do you miss him?"

"Every day." A somber silence passed; then Peter said, "I'll tell you something, though. As long as we remember a person, they're not really gone. Their thoughts, their feelings, their memories, they become a part of us. And even if you think you don't remember your parents, you do. They're inside you, the same way they're inside me."

"But I was just a baby."

"Babies most of all." A thought occurred to him. "Do you know about the Farmstead?"

"Where I was born?"

Peter nodded. "That's right. There was something special about it. It was like we would always be safe there, like something was looking after us." He regarded the boy for a moment. "Your father thought it was a ghost, you know."

The boy's eyes widened. "Do you?"

"I don't know. I've thought a lot about it over the years. Maybe it was. Or at least a kind of ghost. Maybe places have memories, too." He rested a hand on the boy's shoulder. "All I know is that the world wanted you to be born, Caleb."

The boy fell silent. Then, his face blooming with the mischievous grin of a plan unveiled: "You know what I want to do next?"

"Name it."

"I want to go swimming."

It was a little after four by the time they reached the base of the spillway. Standing by the edge of the pool, they stripped to their shorts. As Peter stepped out onto the rocks, he turned to find Caleb frozen at the edge.

"What's the matter?"

"I don't know how."

Somehow Peter had failed to foresee this. He offered the boy his hand. "Come on, I'll teach you."

The water was startlingly cold, with a distinct mineral taste. Caleb was fearful at first, but after thirty minutes of splashing around, his confidence grew. Another ten and he was moving freely on his own, dog-paddling across the surface.

"Look at me! Look at me!"

Peter had never seen the boy so happy. "Hold on to my back," he said.

The boy climbed aboard, gripping Peter by the shoulders. "What are we going to do?"

"Just take a deep breath and hold it."

Together they descended. Peter blew the air from his lungs, stretched out his arms, and with a whip kick sent them gliding along the stony bottom, the boy clutching him tightly, his body pulled like a cape. The water was as clear as glass. Memories of splashing in the grotto as a boy filled Peter's mind. He had done the same thing with his father.

Three more kicks and they ascended, bursting into the light. "How was that?" Peter asked.

"I saw fish!"

"I told you."

Again and again they dove this way, the boy's pleasure inexhaustible. It was past five-thirty, the shadows lengthening, when Peter declared an end. They stepped gingerly onto the rocks and dressed.

"I can't wait to tell Sister Peg we went outside," Caleb said, beaming.

"It's probably best if you don't. Let's keep that between us, okay?"

"A secret?" The boy spoke the word with illicit pleasure; they were part of a conspiracy now.

"Exactly."

The boy slid his small, moist hand into Peter's as they made their way to the hydro gate. In another few minutes, the horn would sound. The feeling came upon him in a rush of love: *This is why I'm here.*

He found her in the kitchen, standing before a massive stove covered with boiling pots. The room roared with heat and noise—the clatter of dishes, sisters racing to and fro, the accumulating racket of excited voices as the children gathered in the dining hall. Amy's back was to him. Her hair, iridescent and dark, descended in a thick braid to her waist. He hesitated in the doorway, observing her. She appeared totally absorbed in her work, stirring the contents of the nearest pot with a long wooden spoon, tasting and correcting with salt, then nimbly stepping to one of the room's several red-brick ovens to withdraw, on a long paddle, half a dozen loaves of freshly risen bread.

"Amy."

She turned, breaking into a smile. They met in the middle of the busy room. A moment of uncertainty, then they embraced.

"Sister Peg told me you were here."

He stepped back. He had sensed it in her touch: there was something new about her. Long departed was the voiceless, traumatized waif with the matted hair and scavenged clothes. The progress of her aging seemed to occur in fits and starts, not so much a matter of physical growth as a deepening self-possession, as if she were coming into ownership of her life. And always the paradox: the person standing before him, though to all appearances a young teenager, was in reality the oldest human being on earth. Peter's long absence, an era to Caleb, was for Amy the blink of an eye.

"How long can you stay?" Her eyes did not move from his face.

"Just tonight. I ship out tomorrow."

"Amy," one of the sisters called from the stove, "is this soup ready? They're getting loud out there."

Amy spoke briskly over her shoulder: "Just a second." Then, to Peter, her smile widening: "It turns out I'm not such a bad cook. Save me a place." She quickly squeezed his hand. "It really is so good to see you."

Peter made his way to the dining hall, where all the children had gathered at long tables, sorting themselves by age. The noise in the room was intense, a free-flowing energy of bodies and voices like the din of some immense engine. He took a place on the end of a bench beside Caleb just as Sister Peg appeared at the front of the room and clapped her hands.

The effect was like a lightning bolt: silence tensed the room. The children joined hands and bowed their heads. Peter found himself joined in the circle, Caleb on one side, on the other a little girl with brown hair who was seated across from him.

"Heavenly Father," the woman intoned, her eyes closed, "we thank you for this meal and our togetherness and the blessing of your love and care, which you bestow upon us in your mercy. We thank you for the richness of the earth and the heavens above and your protection until we meet in the life to come. And lastly we thank you for the company of our special guest, one of your brave soldiers, who has traveled a perilous distance to be with us tonight. We pray that you will keep him, and his fellows, safe on their journeys. Amen."

A chorus of voices: "Amen."

Peter felt genuinely touched. So, perhaps Sister Peg didn't mind his presence so much after all. The food appeared: vats of soup, bread cut into thick, steaming slices, pitchers of water and milk. At the head of each table, one of the sisters ladled the soup into bowls and passed them down the line as the pitchers made their way around. Amy slid onto the bench beside Peter.

"Let me know what you think of the soup," she said.

It was delicious—the best thing he'd eaten in months. The bread, pillowy and warm in his mouth, nearly made him moan. He silenced the urge to ask for seconds, thinking it would be rude, but the moment his bowl was empty one of the sisters appeared with another, placing it before him.

"It's not often we have company," she explained, her face rosy with embarrassment, and scurried away.

They talked of the orphanage and Amy's duties—the kitchen, but also teaching the youngest children to read and, in her words, "whatever else needs to be done"—and Peter's news of the others, though they phrased this information in a general way; it wouldn't be until after the children had gone to bed that the two of them would be able to talk in earnest. Beside him, Caleb was engaged with another boy in a vigorous conversation that Peter was only passingly able to follow, something about knights and queens and pawns. When his companion left the table, Peter asked Caleb what it was all about.

"It's chess."

"Chest?"

Caleb rolled his eyes. "No, *chess.* It's a game. I can teach you if you want."

Peter glanced at Amy, who laughed. "You'll lose," she said.

After dinner and dishes, the three of them went to the common room, where Caleb set up the board and explained the names of the various pieces and the moves they could make. By the time he got to the knights, Peter's head was spinning.

"You really can keep all this straight in your mind? How long did it take you to learn to play?"

He shrugged innocently. "Not long. It's pretty simple."

"It doesn't sound simple." He turned to Amy, who was wearing a cagey smile.

"Don't look at me," she protested. "You're on your own."

Caleb waved over the board. "You can go first."

The battle commenced. Peter had considered taking it easy on the boy—it was, after all, a children's game, and no doubt he would quickly get the hang of it—but he instantly discovered how badly he had underestimated his young opponent. Caleb seemed to anticipate his every tactic, responding without hesitation, his moves crisp and assured. In growing desperation Peter decided to attack, using his knight to take one of Caleb's bishops.

"Are you sure you want to do that?" the boy asked.

"Um, no?"

Caleb was studying the board with his chin resting on his hands. Peter could sense the complex movements of his thoughts: he was assembling a strategy, imagining a series of moves and countermoves projected forward in time. Five years old, Peter thought. Amazing.

Caleb advanced a rook three spaces, taking Peter's other knight, which he had inadvertently left open. "Watch," he said.

A quick exchange of pieces and Peter's king was boxed in. "Checkmate," the boy declared.

Peter stared hopelessly at the board. "How did you do that so fast?"

Beside him, Amy laughed—a warm, infectious sound. "I told you."

Caleb's grin stretched a mile wide. Peter understood what had happened; first the swimming, now this. His nephew had effortlessly turned the tables on him, showing Peter what he was capable of.

"You just have to think ahead," Caleb said. "Try to see it like a story."

"Tell me the truth. How good are you at this?"

Caleb gave a modest shrug. "A few of the older kids used to beat me. But not anymore."

"Is that so? Well, set it up again, youngster. I want my revenge."

Caleb had racked up his third straight victory, each more mercilessly decisive than the last, when the bell sounded, summoning him to the dormitory. The time had passed too quickly. Amy departed for the girls' quarters, leaving Peter to escort the boy to bed. In the large room of cots, Caleb exchanged his clothing for a nightshirt, then knelt on the stone floor at the side of his bed, hands pressed together, to say his prayers, a long series of "God bless"es that began with "my parents in heaven" and concluded with Peter himself.

"I always save you for last," the boy said, "to keep you safe."

"Who's Mouser?"

Mouser was their cat. Peter had seen the poor creature lounging on a windowsill in the common room—a pitiful rag of a thing, flesh drooping over his brittle old bones like laundry on a line. Peter drew the blanket up to Caleb's chin and bent to kiss him on the forehead. Sisters were moving up and down the lines of cots, shushing the other children. The room's lights had already been extinguished.

"When are you coming back, Uncle Peter?"

"I'm not sure. Soon, I hope."

"Can we go swimming again?"

A warm feeling spread through his entire body. "Only if you promise we can play more chess. I don't think I have the hang of it yet. I could use a few pointers."

The boy beamed. "I promise."

Amy was waiting for him in the empty common room, the cat nosing around her feet. He had to report to the barracks at 2100; he and Amy would have only a few minutes together.

"That poor thing," Peter said. "Why doesn't anybody put him down? It seems cruel."

Amy ran a hand along the animal's spine. A faint purr trembled from him as he arched his back to receive her touch. "It's past time, I suppose. But the children adore him, and the sisters don't believe in it. Only God can take a life."

"They've obviously never been to New Mexico."

A joke, but not entirely. Amy regarded him with concern. "You look troubled, Peter."

"Things aren't going very well. Do you want to know about it?"

She considered the question. She seemed a little pale; Peter wondered if she was feeling all right.

"Maybe some other time." Her eyes searched his face. "He loves you, you know. He talks about you all the time."

"You're making me feel guilty. Probably I deserve it."

She lifted Mouser to settle him on her lap. "He understands. I'm only telling you so you know how important you are to him."

"What about you? Are you doing okay here?"

She nodded. "On the whole, it suits me. I like the company, the children, the sisters. And of course there's Caleb. Maybe for the first time in my life I actually feel . . . I don't know. Useful. It's nice to be just an ordinary person."

Peter was struck by the frank, easy flow of the conversation. Some barrier between them had dropped. "Do the other sisters know? Besides Sister Peg, I mean."

"A few do, or maybe just suspect. I've been here for five years, and they'd have to notice I'm not aging. I think I'm a bit of a wrinkle to Sister Peg, something that doesn't really fit her view of things. But she doesn't say anything about it to me." Amy smiled. "After all, I make a mean barley soup."

Too quickly, the moment of his departure was at hand. Amy walked him to the entrance, where Peter pulled the wad of bills from his pocket and held it out to her.

"Give this to Sister Peg, all right?"

Amy nodded without comment and slid the scrip into the pocket of her skirt. Once again she pulled him into a hug, more forcefully this time. "I really have missed you." Her voice was soft against his chest. "Be safe, all right? Promise you'll do that."

There was something fraught in her insistence, a feeling, almost, of finality, a graver parting. What wasn't she saying? And something else: her body was giving off a feverish heat. He could actually feel it pulsing through the heavy fabric of his uniform.

"You don't have to worry about me. I'll be fine."

"I mean it, Peter. If anything happened, I couldn't . . ." Her voice trailed away, as if pulled to the currents of a hidden wind. "I just couldn't is all."

Now he was certain: there was something Amy wasn't telling him. Peter searched her face for what it was. A faint glaze of perspiration shone on her brow.

"Are you okay?"

Taking his hand in her own, she lifted them in concert, pressing her palm against his so that the pads of their fingers were just touching. It seemed a gesture with equal measures of togetherness and parting, connection and separation.

"Do you remember when I kissed you?"

They had never spoken of this—her quick, birdlike peck at the mall, the virals streaming toward them. Much had happened, but Peter had not forgotten. How could he?

"I always wondered about that," he confessed.

Their raised hands seemed to hover in the darkened space between them. Amy studied them with her eyes. It was as if she were attempting to divine a meaning she herself had made. "I'd been alone so long. It's nothing I can even describe. But all of a sudden, there you were. I couldn't believe it." Then, as if jarred from a trance, she withdrew her hand, her face suddenly flustered. "That's all. You better go—you'll be late."

He didn't want to. Like the kiss, the feeling of her hand seemed to possess a unique power to linger in his senses, as if it had taken up a permanent residence in his fingertips. He wanted to say more but couldn't find the words, and the moment slipped away.

"You're sure you're all right?"

Her face assembled a smile. "Never better."

She really did look ill, he thought. "Well, I'll be back in ten days."

Amy said nothing.

"I'll see you then, right?" He wondered why he was asking this.

"Of course, Peter. Where would I go?"

After Peter had left, Amy made her way to the sisters' residence, a smaller version of the dormitories where the children slept. The other sisters were all asleep, a few of the older ones softly snoring. She stripped off her tunic and lowered herself onto her cot.

Sometime later she awoke with a start. A cold sweat glazed her body, drenching her nightshirt. The turbulence of uneasy dreams still roiled through her.

Amy, help him.

She froze.

He is waiting for you, Amy. In the ship.

—Father?

Go to him go to him go to him go to him . . .

She rose, seized with a sudden purposefulness. The moment had come.

Yet one duty remained, one final task to be performed in these last days of a life she had loved, if briefly. Through the silent hallways she padded her way to the common room. She found Mouser just where she had left him, resting on the couch. Exhaustion radiated from his eyes; his limbs were limp, he could barely raise his head.

Please, his eyes said. *I'm in pain. It's all gone on too long.*

Gently she lifted him to her chest. Running a hand along his back, she turned so he could face the window, with its view of the starry night.

"See the pretty world, Mouser?" she murmured, close to his ear. "See the pretty stars?"

It's . . . beautiful.

His neck broke with a snap, the body going limp in her arms. Amy stayed that way for a few minutes while his presence faded, stroking his fur, kissing his head and face. *Goodbye, Mouser. Godspeed to you. The children love you; you will be with them again.* Then she carried him outside to the garden shed to see about a shovel.

31

"Will you look what the wind blew in."

A grease-stained man had directed Peter to the commissary, where he'd found Michael sitting with a group of a dozen men and women, using forks grasped in filthy hands to shovel plates of beans into their mouths. Michael leapt off the bench and clapped him on the shoulder.

"Peter Jaxon, as I live and breathe."

"Flyers, Michael. You're enormous."

His friend's chest seemed to have doubled in size, straining the fabric of his jumpsuit; his arms were roped with muscle. A robust growth of blond stubble roughened his cheeks.

"Tell you the truth, there's not much else to do around here besides cook oil and lift weights. And word to the wise, nobody uses that word around here. It's all 'fuck this' and 'fuck that.'" He gestured toward the table. "This here's my crew. Say hello to Peter, hombres."

Introductions all around. Peter did his best to record the names but knew they'd be gone within minutes.

"Hungry?" Michael asked. "The chow's not bad if you breathe through your mouth."

"I should report to the head of DS first."

"He can keep. Since it's past twelve hundred, odds are good Stark is pie-eyed anyway. It's Karlovic you really need to see, but he's gone up to the reserve. Let me get you a plate."

They shared their news over lunch, returned their trays to the kitchen, and stepped outside.

"Does it always smell this bad?" Peter inquired.

"Oh, this is a good day. When the wind switches around you'll be crying. Blows all the crap down from the channel. Come on, I'll give you the grand tour."

Their first stop was the barracks, a cinder-block box with a rusty tin roof. Curtained sleeping berths lined the walls. A huge, long-faced man was sitting at the table in the middle of the room, shuffling and reshuffling a deck of cards.

"This here is Juan Sweeting, my second," Michael said. "Goes by Ceps."

They shook, the man greeting him with a grunt.

"How'd you get the name Ceps?" Peter asked. "I haven't heard that before."

The man curled his arms, popping a pair of biceps like two large grapefruits.

"Ah," said Peter. "I see."

"Not to worry," Michael said, "his manners aren't the best and his lips move when he reads, but he pretty much behaves himself as long as you don't forget to feed him."

A woman had emerged from one of the berths, wearing only her underclothes. She yawned into her fist. "Jesus, Michael, I was trying to get some rack." To Peter's astonishment, she draped her arms around Michael's neck, her face lighting with a greedy smile. "Unless, of course . . ."

"Not the time, *mi amiga.*" Michael gently freed himself. "In case you didn't notice, we've got company. Lore, Peter. Peter, Lore."

Her body was lean and strong, her hair, bleached by the sun, cut short. Attractive but in an unconventional, slightly masculine way, radiating a frank, even carnivorous sensuality.

"You're the guy?"

"That's right."

She gave a knowing laugh. "Well, good luck to you, friend."

"Lore's fourth-generation oiler," Michael said. "She practically drinks the stuff."

"It's a living," Lore said. Then, to Peter: "So you guys go way back, I guess. Let a girl in on the secret. What was he like?"

"Pretty much the smartest guy around. Everybody called him the Circuit. It was sort of his nickname."

"And a stupid one, too. Thanks a bunch, Peter."

"The Circuit," Lore repeated, seeming to taste the word in her mouth. "You know, I think I kind of like that."

At the table, Ceps, who had said nothing, gave a feminine moan. *"Oh Circuit, oh Circuit, make me feel like a woman . . ."*

"Shut up, the both of you." Michael was blushing to a degree at odds with his newfound muscularity, though Peter could also tell that part of him enjoyed the attention. "What are you, thirteen? Come on, Peter," he said, steering him toward the door, "let's leave these children."

"See you later, Lieutenant," Lore called merrily as they made their exit. "I'll want to hear *stories.*"

In the intensifying heat of the afternoon, Michael gave Peter the lay of the land, taking him to one of the towers and explaining the refining process.

"It sounds pretty dangerous," Peter said.

"Things happen, it's true."

"Where's the reserve?" The oil, Peter knew, came from a holding tank deep underground.

"About five miles to the north of here. It's actually a natural salt dome, part of the old Strategic Petroleum Reserve. Oil floats, so we pump in seawater and out it comes."

His friend had acquired a bit of Texas in his voice, Peter noted. Not "oil" but "awhl."

"How much is left down there?"

"Well, a shitload, basically. By our estimates, enough to fill the cookers for another fifty years."

"And once it's gone?"

"We go looking for more. There are plenty of tanks spread along the Houston ship channel. It's a real toxic swamp up there, and the place is crawling with dopeys, but it could tide us over awhile. The next closest dome is Port Arthur. It wouldn't be easy to move the operation up there, but with enough time we could do it." He gave a fatalistic shrug. "Either way, I doubt I'll be around to worry about it."

Michael announced that he had a surprise to show Peter. They walked to the armory, where Michael retrieved a shotgun, then to the motor pool for a pickup. Michael clipped the shotgun into a stand on the floor of the cab and told Peter to get in.

"Where are we going?"

"You'll see."

They drove out of the compound, then turned south on a cracked blacktop that ran parallel with the water. A salty wind gusted through the truck's open windows, taking the edge off the heat. Peter had seen the Gulf only a couple of times; its ancient span, too huge to hold in his mind, unfailingly took his breath away. Most entrancing were the waves, long tubes gathering size and momentum as they approached, falling in a curl of brown foam at the water's edge. He couldn't take his eyes off them. Peter knew he could sit on the sand for hours, just watching the waves.

Stretches of the beach were swept clean, while others still bore the evidence of catastrophe on a grand scale: mountains of rusting metal twisted into incomprehensible shapes; beached ships of every size, their hulls bleached and pitted or else stripped to the struts, tilted on the sand like exposed rib cages; ridges of undifferentiated debris, pushed inshore on the tide.

"You'd be surprised how much stuff still washes in," Michael said, gesturing out the window. "A lot of it comes down the Mississippi, then curves along the coast. The heavy stuff's mostly gone, but anything plastic seems to last."

Michael had veered off the road and was now driving close to the water's edge. Peter stared out the window. "Do you ever see anything bigger?"

"Once in a while. Last year, a barge still loaded with big containers washed in. The damn thing had been drifting for a century. We were all pretty excited."

"What was in them?"

"Human skeletons."

They came to an inlet and turned west, following the edge of a tranquil bay. Ahead was a small concrete structure perched on the water's edge. As Michael brought the truck to a halt, Peter saw that the building was just a shell, although a sign in the window still read, in faded letters, "Art's Crab Shack."

"Okay, I'll bite," Peter said. "What's the surprise?"

His friend smiled mischievously. "Leave that smoke poker here," he said, gesturing to the Browning strapped to Peter's thigh. "You're not going to need it."

Wondering what his friend had in mind, Peter deposited the gun in the glove compartment, then followed Michael to the rear of the building. A small dock on concrete piers, perhaps thirty feet long, jutted out over the water.

"What am I seeing?"

"A boat, obviously."

A small sailboat was tied up at the end of the pier, gently bobbing in the swells.

"Where did you get it?"

Michael's face shone with pride. "A lot of places, actually. The hull we found in a garage about ten miles inland. The rest we cobbled together or made ourselves."

"We?"

"Lore and me." He cleared his throat, his face suddenly flustered. "I guess it's pretty obvious—"

"You don't owe me an explanation, Michael."

"I'm just saying it's not quite what it looks like. Well, maybe it is. But I wouldn't say we're together, exactly. Lore's just . . . well, she's just like that."

Peter found himself taking perverse pleasure in his friend's embarrassment. "She seems nice enough. And she obviously likes *you*."

"Yeah, well." Michael shrugged. "'Nice' wouldn't necessarily be the first word I'd choose, if you know what I mean. To tell you the truth, I can barely keep up with her."

As Michael stepped aboard, Peter suddenly became aware how meager the boat looked.

"What's the problem?" Michael asked.

"We're actually going to sail that thing?"

Michael had started busily coiling lines and setting them in the bottom of the hull. "Why'd you think I brought you out here? Quit your worrying and get in."

Peter cautiously lowered himself into the cockpit. The hull moved strangely under him, responding to his weight with a sluggish shift. He gripped the rail, willing the boat to stay still. "And you actually know how to do this."

His friend laughed under his breath. "Don't be such a baby. Help me raise the sail."

Michael quickly ran through the basics: sail, rudder, tiller, mainsheet. He cast off the line, scrambled aft to the tiller, did something to make the sail abruptly fill with air, and suddenly they were off and running, streaming away from the dock with astonishing speed.

"So what do you think?"

Peter nervously eyed the receding shoreline. "I'm getting used to it."

"Here's a thought," Michael offered. "For the first time in your life, you're in a place where a viral can't kill you."

"I hadn't considered that."

"For the next couple of hours, you, my friend, are out of a job."

They tacked across the bay. As they moved into deeper water, the color changed from a mossy green to a rich blue-black, the sunlight ricocheting off the irregularities of its surface. Under the tightness of the sail, the boat possessed a more solid feel, and Peter began to relax, though not completely. Michael seemed to know what he was doing, but the ocean was still the ocean.

"How far out have you taken this thing?"

Michael looked ahead, squinting into the light. "Hard to say. Five miles anyway."

"What about the barrier?"

It was generally held that in the early days of the epidemic, the nations of the world had banded together to enforce a quarantine of the North American continent, laying mines all along the coastlines and bombing any vessels that attempted to leave shore.

"If it's out there, I haven't found it yet." Michael shrugged. "Part of me thinks it's all bullshit, you want to know the truth."

Peter eyed his friend cautiously. "You're not looking for it, are you?"

Michael didn't answer, his face telling Peter that he had hit the mark. "That's insane."

"So is doing what you do. And even if the barrier exists, how many mines could still be floating around out there? A hundred years in the ocean would eat just about anything. And all the debris would have set them off by now, anyway."

"It's still reckless. You could blow yourself to bits."

"Maybe. And maybe tomorrow one of those cooking towers will launch me into outer space. The standards for personal safety around these parts are pretty low." He shrugged. "But that's beside the point. I don't think the damn thing was ever there to begin with. The whole coast? If you include Mexico and Canada, that's almost two hundred and fifty thousand miles. Impossible."

"What if you're wrong?"

"Then someday I may, as you say, blow myself to bits."

Peter let the matter drop. A lot had changed, but Michael was still Michael, a man of insatiable curiosity. They were moving through the inlet into open water; the breeze had picked up, casting jeweled waves over the bow. Something in his stomach dropped. It wasn't just the lurching of the boat. So much water, everywhere.

"Maybe just this once you could keep us close to land."

Michael adjusted the sail, stiffening his grip on the tiller. "I'm telling you, it's a whole other deal out there, Peter. I can't even explain it. It's like all the bad stuff just drops away. You really should see it for yourself."

"I should be getting back. Let's save it for another time."

Michael glanced at him and laughed. "Sure," he said. "Another time."

32

Alicia made her way northward, into the wide-open countryside. The Texas Panhandle: a landscape of limitless flatness like a great becalmed sea, wind drifting over the tips of the prairie grasses, the sky immense above her in its autumnal blueness, the encircling horizon broken only by the occasional creekside stand of cottonwoods or pecans or long-armed willows, their melancholy fronds bowing in submission as she passed. The days were warm but at night the temperature plunged, weighing the grass with dew. Using fuel from caches spread along her route, she'd complete the journey in four days.

She arrived at the Kearney garrison on the morning of November 6. It was as Command had feared when the resupply convoy had failed to return: not a living soul remained to greet her. The garrison was an open grave. The echoes of the soldiers' dying cries seemed to hover on the air, locked into the windswept stillness. Alicia spent two days loading the desiccated remains of her fellows into the bed of a truck and carrying them to the place she had selected, a clearing on the banks of the Platte. There she lay them in a long row, so they could be together, doused them with fuel, and set them alight.

It was the following morning that she saw the horse.

He was standing just beyond the barricades. A blue-roan stallion, his long, masculine neck bent to graze upon the heavy grasses at the edge of the parade ground—his presence unaccountable, like a single house left untouched by a tornado. He stood eighteen hands at least. Cautiously Alicia approached him, palms upturned. The animal seemed prepared to spook, nostrils flaring, ears pinned back, one great eye roving toward her. Who is this strange being, it was saying, what does she intend? Alicia advanced another step; still he did not move. She could feel the wildness that coursed in his blood, his explosive animal power.

"Good boy," she murmured. "See? I'm not so bad. Let's be friends, the two of us, what do you say?"

When an arm's length separated them, she eased her open palm beneath his nose. His lips pulled back, revealing the yellow wall of his teeth. His eye was like a great black marble taking in the sight of her. A moment of decision, his body tense and alert; then he lowered his head, filling her open hand with the warm moistness of his breath.

"Well, I think I just found my ride." The animal was nuzzling her hand now, bobbing his head. Flecks of foam stood at the edges of his mouth. She stroked his neck, his glossy, sweat-dampened coat. His body was like something chiseled, hard and pure, yet it was his eyes that radiated the full measure of his strength. "You need a name," Alicia said. "What shall I call you?"

She named him Soldier. From the moment she swung up onto his back, they belonged to each other. It was as if they were old friends, long separated, who had found each other again; lifelong companions who could tell each other the truest stories of themselves but who could also, if they chose, say nothing at all. In the empty garrison she lingered three more days, taking stock, planning the journey ahead. She sharpened her blades to their finest point. Her orders were in her pouch. To: Alicia

Donadio, Captain of the Expeditionary. Signed: Victoria Sanchez, President, Texas Republic.

On the morning of November 12 they rode out, headed east.

One bridge over the Missouri still stood, fifty miles north of Omaha, at the town of Decatur. They reached it on the sixth day. The mornings were glazed with frost, winter in the air. The trees had given up their bashfulness, showing their bare limbs. As they made their approach Alicia sensed in Soldier's gait a notch of hesitation: *The river, really?* They came to the bluffs; below them, the water churned in its broad course. Eddies swirled upon its face, dark as stone. A quarter mile north, the bridge traversed its width on massive concrete pilings, as if bestriding the river on giant legs. *Yes,* Alicia said. *Really.*

There were moments when it seemed that this decision had been hasty. In places the concrete surface had fallen away, revealing the churning waters below. She dismounted and took Soldier by the reins. Painstakingly, every step fraught with the possibility that the bridge would collapse under them, they threaded their way across. Whose stupid idea was this? Soldier seemed to ask. Oh, yours.

On the far side they halted. It was just evening; the sun had begun its descent behind the bluffs. Alicia's rhythms had reversed: on foot, she would have been free to sleep during the day and travel at night, her habit. But not on horseback. Alicia lit a fire on the bank of the river, filled her pan, and set it to boil. She took the last of her stores from her saddlebag: a fistful of dried beans, paste in a can, a wedge of hardtack dense as a rock. She was in the mood to hunt but did not want to leave Soldier alone. She ate her meager supper, washed her pot in the river, and lay down on her bedroll to watch the sky. She had discovered that if she looked long enough, she would see a shooting star. As if responding to her thoughts, a bright streak blazed across the heavens, then two more in quick succession. Michael had told her once, many years ago, that some were leftover creations of mankind from the Time Before, called satellites. He had attempted to explain their function—something to do with the weather—but Alicia had either forgotten what he'd said or else tuned it out as yet another instance of know-it-all Michael lording his intelligence over other people. What had stuck in her mind was an abstract sense of them, their marriage of light and force: unaccountable objects of unknowable purpose that swung around the earth like stones in a sling, locked in their trajectories by counterbalancing influences of will and gravity until they gave up their trials and plunged to earth in a blaze of glory. More stars fell; Alicia began to count. The more she looked, the more she saw. Ten, fifteen, twenty. She was still counting when she fell asleep.

The day broke fresh and clear. Alicia slipped on her glasses and stretched, the pleasurable energy of a night's rest flowing through her limbs. The sound of the river seemed louder in the morning air. She had saved some hardtack for breakfast. She polished off half and fed the rest to Soldier and rode on.

They were in Iowa now; their journey was halfway done. The landscape changed, rising and falling in loamy hills with a slumped appearance and, between them, flat-bottomed valleys of rich black soil. Low clouds had moved in from the west, tamping the light. It was late afternoon when Alicia detected movement from the ridgeline. On the wind, a scent of animals; Soldier could sense it, too. Willing herself into stillness, Alicia waited for the source to reveal itself.

There. A herd of deer appeared in silhouette at the top of the ridge, twenty head in all, and, among them, a single large buck. His rack was massive, like a tree stripped for winter. She would have to make her approach from the downwind side; it was a wonder they hadn't detected her already. She placed her rifle in its holder, took up her crossbow and a sling of bolts, and dismounted. Soldier eyed her warily.

"Now, don't give me that look. A girl's got to eat." She patted his neck in assurance. "No wandering off, all right?"

She circled the ridge to the south. The deer still appeared oblivious to her presence. On knees and elbows she inched her way up the incline. She was fast, but they were faster; one shot of the cross, maybe two, would be all she had. After long minutes of patient climbing, she reached the top. The deer had fanned out into a V shape along the ridge. The buck stood forty feet away. Alicia, still pressed to the ground, pulled a bolt into her cross.

A puff of wind, perhaps. A moment of deep animal perception. The deer exploded into movement. By the time Alicia had risen to her feet, they were bounding down the ridge, away.

"Shit."

She flung the cross to the ground, drew a blade, and took off after them. Her mind was firmly locked onto the task now; nothing would deny her. Fifty feet down the ridge the ground abruptly fell away, and Alicia saw her chance: a convergence of lines that her mind beheld with absolute precision. As the buck darted below the drop-off, she raised her blade and launched herself into the air.

She fell upon him like a hawk, swinging the blade forward in a long-armed arc to drive it upward into the base of his throat. A spurt of blood and his front legs folded under him. Too late Alicia realized what was about to happen. As she pitched over his neck, her body was snatched by gravity, and the next thing Alicia knew she was tumbling head over heels down the hillside.

She came to rest at the base of the ridge. Her glasses had been stripped away. She rolled quickly onto her stomach, burying her face in her arms. Fuck! Would she be forced to lie here, utterly helpless, until dark? She eased one arm free and began to pat the ground around her. Nothing.

The only thing to do was open her eyes and look. Her face still nestled in the crook of her arm, Alicia rose to her knees. Her heart was hammering against her ribs. Well, she thought, here goes nothing.

At first she perceived only whiteness—an obliterating whiteness, as if she were staring into the heart of the sun. The shock was like a needle in her skull. But then, with unexpected swiftness, something began to change. Her vision was resolving. Colors and shapes emerged like figures from a fog. She was peering through the barest slits; she allowed her eyes to open just a little more. Bit by bit, the brightness receded to unveil more of her surroundings.

After five long years in shadow, Alicia Donadio, captain of the Expeditionary, beheld the daylit world.

Only then did she realize where she was.

She called it the Field of Bones. Though neither was it a field, in the strictest sense, nor were they bones, exactly. Rather, the crumbling, sun-blasted remains of a viral multitude, covering the tableland to a far horizon. How many was she seeing? A hundred thousand? A million? More? Alicia stepped forward, taking her place among them. From each footfall rose a cloud of ash. The taste was in her nose and throat, painting the walls of her mouth like a paste. Tears rose to her eyes. Of sadness? Of relief? Or simple amazement at this unaccountable event? It was not their fault what they were. It had never been their fault. Dropping to one knee, she drew a blade from her bandolier and touched it to herself, head and heart. Eyes closed, she bowed her head and cast her mind outward in prayer. *I send you home, my brothers and sisters, I release you from the prison of your existence. You have departed the earth to unlock the truth of what lies beyond this life. May your strength pass into me that I may face the days ahead. Godspeed to you.*

Soldier was just where she'd left him. His eyes flashed with irritation at her approach. I thought we had a deal, they said. Where the hell have you been? But as she neared, his gaze deepened knowingly. Alicia stroked his withers, kissed his long, wise face. His muscular tongue licked the tears from her bare eyes. You are my good boy, she said. My good, good boy.

She would have liked to press on, but her prize wouldn't wait. She pitched her tarp between the trees, sat on the ground, and removed her pack. Inside, wrapped in oilcloth, lay the quivering, bloody lump of the buck's liver. She pressed it to her nose and inhaled deeply, drawing in its delicious, earthen, blood-tinged smell. There would be no cooking fire tonight; it was perfect as it was.

Something was changing; the world was changing. Alicia could feel it, deep in the bone. A profound shift—seismic, seasonal—like the earth tipping on its axis. But there would be time to worry over this later.

Now, on this night, she would eat.

33

Peter saw little of Michael for the next three days. The deadline of departure loomed; all the cooking crews were running double shifts. With no scrip to spend at the card table, Peter passed his time sleeping, taking restless walks around the compound, and milling about the commissary. Karlovic he liked, but Stark was a different matter. Peter's arrival had elicited all the resentment Greer had predicted. The man would barely speak to him. Fine, Peter thought, let him stew. It's not like I wanted this duty, anyway.

His most interesting time was spent with Lore. Her appetite for information about the Colony, and Michael in particular, was as robust as everything else about her. Between shifts she would seek him out in the commissary, taking him to an empty table where they could speak out of earshot. No matter what Michael had said, it was plain that beneath her bawdy exterior her attachment to him was serious. Her inquiries possessed a probing quality, as if Michael were a lock she couldn't quite open. What had he been like back in those days? Smart, yes—that was obvious to anyone who knew him—but what else? What could Peter tell her about Sara? And their parents, what was the story? Of their journey from California, the woman knew only the public account: with the Colony's power source failing, they had made their way east in search of others, stumbling by sheer chance on the Colorado garrison. Of Amy, and what had occurred on the mountain in Telluride, she knew nothing at all, and Peter left it that way.

The most surprising turn in the conversation was Lore's interest in Alicia. Evidently Michael had spoken of her a good deal. Beneath the surface of Lore's questions, Peter detected an undercurrent of rivalry, even jealousy, and in hindsight he suspected that much of the discussion had been circling toward this subject. Peter even went so far as to assure Lore that she had nothing to worry about. Michael and Alicia were like oil and water, he said. Two more different people you'd never meet in your life. Lore responded with a confident laugh. What gave you the idea I was worried? Some crazy woman in the Exped, way the hell and gone? Believe me, she said, waving the notion away, that's the last thing on my mind.

Peter spent his last day conferring with Karlovic and Stark, going over the details of the trip. Ten tankers full of fuel, evenly mixed between diesel and high-octane, were parked by the gate. Before morning there would be two more. The convoy would travel with an escort of six security vehicles, Humvees and 4x4s with fifty-cals mounted in the beds. The distance was three hundred miles: north from Freeport on Route 36, west on Highway 10 at Sealy, a straight shot to the outskirts of San Antonio, where they would circumnavigate the city on a mix of rural highways, then back on I-10 for the final fifty miles. Hardboxes were dispersed at regular intervals along the route, but the practice was to drive without stopping. Traveling at an average speed of twenty miles an hour, they would pull into Kerrville a little after midnight.

Peter's attention was drawn to five major chokepoints on the route: a bridge over the San Bernard River west of Sealy; another at Columbus, where they would cross the Colorado; the San Marcos bridge at Luling; and a pair spanning the Guadalupe, the first just west of Seguin, the second at the town of Comfort. The first three were a small concern—the convoy would be crossing in daylight—but they wouldn't reach Seguin until after sunset. Virals had been seen moving up and down the rivers as they hunted, and the sound of idling diesel engines was a known attractor. To make matters worse, the San Marcos bridge was in such poor repair that only one tanker would be permitted to cross it at a time. Flaring the area would provide a measure of protection, but the convoy would be broken up for nearly an hour.

Everyone gathered at the tankers in the predawn darkness. The air was damp and cold. For nearly all of them, the trip was old hat. They had become inured to it, even a little bored. Cups of chicory coffee were passed. As ranking oiler, Michael would ride in the lead Humvee, with Peter. Ceps would drive the first tanker, Lore the second. Peter had planned for Stark to ride up front, as a gesture of goodwill, but to Peter's relief the man had declined, choosing instead to remain at the refinery with the remaining DS detachment.

With the first rays of light, the gates were opened. A dozen big diesels roared to life, clouds of dense black exhaust chuffing from their smoke-stacks. Michael moved up the line from the rear, distributing the walkies and conferring with each of the drivers a final time. He took his place at the wheel of the Humvee and radioed each of the drivers in turn.

"Tanker One."

"Good to go."

"Tanker Two."

"Good to go."

"Tanker Three . . ." And so on. Michael handed Peter the radio and put the Humvee in gear.

"You'll see," he said. "The whole thing is a big yawn. One time, I slept most of the way."

They moved out, into the breaking day.

By late morning they had moved through the Rosenberg bypass and were angling west toward I-10. The state highways were a series of pot-holes, forcing the tankers to move at a creep, but once they picked up the interstate their speed would improve.

Ceps's voice came over the radio: "Michael, I've got a problem back here."

Peter swiveled in his seat. The convoy had come to a halt behind them. Michael braked the Humvee and backed up. Ceps had exited the cab of the truck and was standing on the front bumper, jimmying the hood.

"What's the problem?" Michael called.

Ceps slapped at the engine with a rag, pushing the steam away. "I think it's the coolant pump. It could take a while to fix. A couple of hours, anyway."

Two options: wait for the repair to be completed or leave the tanker behind. To complicate matters, the land on either side was an impenetra-ble thicket. The closest turnout was six miles back. They would have to back the convoy up all the way to Wallis.

"Can he do it?" Peter asked.

"We've got the parts. I don't see why not."

Peter gave the go-ahead. Michael took up the walkie again. "Okay, everybody, let's power down."

"Are you serious?" Lore came back. "Tell Ceps to move that hunk of junk out of the way."

"Yes, I'm serious. Kill your engines, people."

Peter positioned the security teams on either side of the convoy, their guns trained on the walls of trees and scrub. It was highly unlikely anything would happen in the middle of the day, but a tangle like that was perfect viral cover. Ceps and Lore got to work on the engine. Most of the drivers had climbed from their cabs. The cards came out as the minutes ticked away.

By the time Ceps declared the cooling system fixed, it was past three o'clock. The repair had taken nearly four hours. Kerrville was still twelve hours away—more, since they'd be doing more of the trip in the dark.

"It's not too late to go back," Michael said. "We can use the Columbus exit on the interstate to turn around. The ramps are in good shape."

"What's your call?"

They were standing by the Humvee, away from the others. "If you ask me, I think we should go. A few more hours in the dark, what's the difference? It's not like this hasn't happened before. These old junkers break down all the time. And we've got wide lanes all the way to Seguin." Michael shrugged. "It's really your decision."

Peter took a moment to think. It was a risk, but what wasn't? And Michael's logic seemed sound.

He nodded. "We go."

"That's the spirit. All eyes, brother."

The exit markers, pitted and rusting, leaning like drunks; the ancient highway with its tipping guardrails, calling them forward; the cratered roadside restaurants and filling stations and motels, some with their signs still standing against the wind, declaring incomprehensible names. McDonald's. Exxon. Whataburger. Holiday Inn Express. Peter watched the scenery flow past. They were making better time, but that wouldn't last. Darkness was coming on.

The light gave out at Flatonia. They were thirty miles east of the third bridge, moving at a steady twenty-five. The radio, which had crackled all day with banter between the vehicles, fell silent. As they approached the town of Luling there appeared, in the cones of light from the Humvee's headlamps, an exit sign marked with a red X. A hardbox. Peter glanced at Michael, looking for any change in his face, but detected none. They were moving on.

They were approaching the bridge when Michael suddenly leaned forward in his seat, peering intently over the wheel.

"What in the hell . . . ?"

Peter braced himself against the dash as Michael slammed on the brakes. The cab filled with light as the second Humvee nearly careened into them from behind, braking just in time. They skidded to a halt.

Michael was staring out the windshield. "Am I seeing things?"

Lore's voice crackled on the radio. "What's going on? Why did we stop?"

Peter snatched the radio off the dash. "DS three and four, up front on the double. One and two, hold position. Everybody else stay in your cabs."

A figure was standing in the road. Not viral: human. It appeared to be a woman, head bowed, wearing a kind of cloak.

"What's she doing?" said Michael. "She's just standing there."

"Wait here."

Peter climbed from the cab. The woman had yet to move or otherwise acknowledge their existence. The two floater DS vehicles, 4x4s, had pulled into position alongside the Humvees. Drawing his sidearm, Peter stepped cautiously forward.

"Identify yourself."

The woman was standing at the front edge of the bridge. Its iron struts carved lines of darkness against the sky. Peter raised his weapon, inching closer. She was clutching something in her hand. "Hey," he said, "I'm talking to you."

The woman raised her head. Her face filled with the light of the trucks' headlamps. Peter couldn't tell what he was seeing. Woman? Girl? Crone? The image of her face seemed to flutter in his mind, forming and reforming like something seen through fast-moving water. He felt a jostle of nausea.

"We know where you are." Her voice was as ethereal as tissue. "It's just a matter of time."

Peter cocked his weapon, aiming at her head. "Answer me."

Her eyes shone an intense, twinkling blue. As they locked onto his own, Peter realized that what he was seeing was a beautiful woman, maybe the most beautiful of his life. The plump, pillowy lips. The delicately upswept nose. The proportionate arrangement of the facial bones and the glowing skin of her cheeks. To look at her was to be swept into a current of almost unbearable sensuality. His mouth was suddenly dry.

"You're tired," she said.

The statement, utterly baffling, jarred him from his stupor. He was what?

"I said," the woman repeated, "you're tired."

"I don't know what you're talking about."

Her face fell with puzzlement; it appeared he had disappointed her. Peter's eyes fell to the object clutched in her hand. A metal box. With her free hand she withdrew a long, metal rod from its side.

Peter knew what it was.

He leapt toward her as her finger found the switch. A sheen of light and a crack of sound like the slamming of an enormous door: a wall of scalding heat blew him backward, off his feet. The bridge, Peter thought. Whoever she is, this woman has blown the bridge. Peter was on his back, blinking at the sky. Time had briefly slipped its moorings. Something large, on fire, was descending toward him from the heavens in a languid arc.

The burning road tie crashed to the ground a few feet from his head. As Peter rolled away he felt someone's hands upon him, and suddenly he was on his feet again; Michael was pulling him toward the Humvee.

"Back up!" One arm wrapping Peter's waist, Michael was yelling into the walkie. "Everybody back up now!"

Lights were blazing at them from all directions. Before Peter could fully process the information, a pickup barreled out of the brush, its great mud-choked tires bounding over the ditch. It swerved to a halt before them, angled sideways. Four figures rose like dark apparitions from the truck's bed, simultaneously raising long, cylindrical objects to their shoulders.

"Oh, shit," said Michael.

They flung themselves to the ground as the rockets, in a white burst, jetted from their tubes. Behind them, the sound of gunfire was instantly swallowed by the DS vehicles' detonation. Flaming debris whizzed over their heads.

"Ceps," Michael barked into the walkie, "get out of there!"

The figures in the truck had paused to reload. Ceps's tanker would be next. Peter reached for his sidearm, but it was gone; he'd lost it in the first explosion. From the rear of the convoy came another tremendous bang. The oilers were leaping from their trucks, running, shouting. The attack was coming from both ends of the convoy now. They were trapped between the river and whatever was approaching from the rear, presumably more pickups with RPGs. Their fuel was forfeit, the only thing to do was run. Peter and Michael broke for the first tanker just as Ceps leapt down from the cab, tossing Peter a rifle. He snatched it from the air, swung around, took aim at the pickup, and released a barrage of strafing fire, sending the figures diving for cover. He'd bought them a moment, but that was all. Michael grabbed Lore by the wrist as she emerged from her cab and swung her to the ground. He was shouting, waving toward the rear of the convoy. "Get away from the trucks!"

The apparitional figures rose again. One clean shot at the first tanker and it would all be over. Three thousand gallons per truck, thirty-six thousand gallons in all. The entire convoy would go up, detonating like sticks of dynamite in a line. Peter realized that one of the figures was the cloaked woman. He lifted his rifle again and squeezed the trigger, only to hear the click of an empty chamber.

The woman raised her arms and spread them wide.

At the tail end of the convoy, an altogether different sort of vehicle had appeared. It swooped upon them at high speed, engine roaring, banks of sodium vapor lights blazing from the roof of its cab. A six-wheeled semi-tractor: daisy-chained behind it were two large cargo boxes constructed of galvanized metal buffed to a highly reflective finish. In the weeks to come, this curious aspect—it resembled nothing so much as two mirrored boxes rolling down the highway—would emerge as a matter of significance, a clue in a sequence of clues; but at the moment of the truck's air-braking descent upon the scene, no one paid that much attention. Some of the fleeing oilers, their panicked brains washed clean of logic, and failing to notice that the smaller vehicles that had taken out the rear guard had conveniently vanished into the undergrowth, even permitted themselves the hope of rescue. They were under attack. The attack, mercilessly discombobulating, had come from nowhere. The containers, in their fortified appearance and shining bulk, resembled portables.

Which they were. Though toting a cargo of an altogether different kind.

One to see this was OFC Juan Sweeting. Despite his off-putting manner and intimidating muscularity, Ceps was a man with the soul of a poet. Alone in his rack at the end of each day, he privately put pen to paper, rendering his deepest thoughts in lines of uncommon sensitivity and verbal music. Despite the trials of his life, he steadfastly believed the world to be a beautiful, God-touched place worthy of human hopefulness; he wrote a great deal about the sea, whose companionship he treasured. Though he had never shown anyone these poems, they formed the heart of his life, like a secret lover. Sometimes, scraping oily gunk from a cooker or hurling a bulk of iron above his head in the weight cages, Ceps was so inflamed by the desire to write a poem that it was all he could do not to abandon his task and race back to his rack to celebrate the magnificence of creation.

The arrival of the gleamingly reflective semitruck coincided with his blossoming suspicion, like Peter's, that not all was as it appeared. Indeed, nothing about the attack made sense. Why would human beings prey upon one another in this manner? Did they not possess a common foe? Why destroy an energy source that maintained the very existence of their species? The idea taking shape in his mind was the correct one, that their attackers were not in league with their own kind, and as the first of the two shining compartments released its cargo, his suspicions became certainty. But by then it was too late; it had always been too late.

The virals swarmed over the convoy. There were hundreds. But in the moment that followed, Ceps realized that the virals were not, in fact, killing everyone. Some were set upon with merciless, blood-splashing swiftness, but others were snatched bodily, flailing and screaming as the virals seized them around their waists and leapt away.

A far worse fate, to be taken. To be taken up.

He made a quick decision.

The semi had come to a halt less than twenty yards from the last tanker in the line. Ceps had seen a tanker blow before. The destruction was instant and total, a great fiery wallop, but in the preceding tenth of a second something interesting occurred. Seeking the weakest point in the structure, the expanding fuel sent the tanker's end plates shooting horizontally like corks from a bottle. In essence, an exploding tanker truck was a gun before it was a bomb. Ceps had reached the last tanker now. The silver truck was parked twenty yards straight behind him, well within range. With his massive arms, Ceps unscrewed the cap of the offload port and opened the valve. Gasoline spouted from the pipe in a glistening gush. He stood in this current, soaking his clothes. He filled his hands and splashed his hair. This ravishing world, he thought, his senses filling with the smell of fuel, like bottled fire. This achingly bittersweet, ravishing world. Perhaps someone would find his sheaf of poems tucked beneath his mattress and read in its pages the hidden truths of his heart. The words of a poem he loved came back to him. Emily Dickinson: a boy of eight, he had found a book of her poems in the Kerrville Library, in a room nobody ever went to. Because it seemed no one had any use for it, and in a state of anthropomorphic sympathy for its loneliness on the shelf, Ceps had tucked it into his coat and stolen off to an alleyway, where, sitting on an ash can, he'd discovered a voice long gone from the earth, that seemed to strike straight to his most secret self. Now, standing in the path of the gushing port, he closed his eyes to let its words, etched in memory, pass through him one last time:

> *Beauty crowds me till I die*
> *Beauty, mercy have on me*
> *But if I expire today*
> *Let it be in sight of thee—*

He removed his lighter from his pocket and flicked it open to balance his thumb upon its flinted wheel.

A hundred yards away, in the cab of the third tanker, Peter was attempting to put the thing in gear. The knob, its markings long since worn off, told him nothing. Each attempt was met with a grinding sound.

"Move over."

The door swung open and Lore scrambled in, Michael following. Peter slid across the bench to let him take the wheel.

"Our plan is?" Michael asked.

"We don't have one."

Michael glanced into the side-view. His eyes widened. "Now we do."

He jammed the gearshift into first, swung the wheel all the way to the left, and hit the gas, clipping the second tanker. Instead of reversing, Michael pressed the accelerator again. A screech of metal and suddenly they were free, a fifteen-ton wheeled missile bounding into the undergrowth.

Behind them, the world exploded.

The truck shot forward like a rocket; Peter was thrust back in his seat. The rear of the truck lifted, swerved, then somehow found traction again. The cab was bouncing so fiercely it seemed certain they would shake apart. Michael worked through the gearbox, still accelerating. Brush swept over the windshield; they were flying blind as bats. He turned the wheel left again, guiding them in a long arc across the tangled field, and then with a second toss they were on the highway again, racing east.

Their flight had not escaped attention. In the side-view, Peter saw a bank of pale green light gathering behind them.

"We can't outrun them in this thing," Michael said. "The only chance is the hardbox."

Peter jammed a magazine into his rifle. "What have you got?" he asked Lore, and she showed him a pistol.

"That's not the only problem," Michael said. "We've lost our brake coupler."

"Meaning what?"

"I can't slow down or she'll jackknife. We'll have to jump."

The virals were closing. Peter guessed two hundred yards, maybe less.

"Can you get us up the exit ramp?"

"At this speed, there's no way I'll make the turn at the overpass. It's ninety degrees."

"How far's the box from the top of the ramp?"

"A hundred yards straight south."

There was no way they would make it if they jumped at the base of the ramp. A hundred yards would be cutting it close as it was, and that was assuming they escaped the fall uninjured.

The hardbox marker appeared in Michael's headlights. Lore climbed over the bench and took a place by the door as Michael downshifted, cutting their speed to thirty, and veered to the right, guiding them up the ramp. They flung the doors wide, filling the cab with swirling wind.

"Here we go."

As they hit the top of the ramp, Michael and Lore leapt from the cab, Peter just behind them. He hit the ground on his feet, knees flexed to absorb the impact, then rolled end over end on the pavement. The air poured from his chest. He came to a stop just in time to see the taillights of the tanker barreling through the guardrail. For the thinnest instant, the vehicle, all thirty thousand pounds of it, seemed on the verge of taking flight. But then it sank from sight, its disappearance followed by one more titanic explosion on a night of them, a roiling cloud with a white-hot center that blazed like an enormous flare.

From his left, the sound of Lore's voice: "Peter, help me!"

Michael was unconscious. His hair was slick with blood, his arm twisted in a way that seemed broken. The first virals were at the foot of the ramp now. The light of the burning truck had bought them a moment, but that was all. Peter hoisted Michael over his shoulder. Christ, he thought, his knees buckling under the weight, this would have been easier a few years ago. The hardbox flag stood in dark silhouette against the stars.

They ran.

34

She appeared in the doorway as Lucius was concluding his evening devotions. From her hand dangled a chiming ring of keys. Her plain gray tunic and tranquil demeanor did nothing to communicate the impression of someone in the midst of a jailbreak, though Lucius noted a glaze of perspiration on her face, despite the evening chill.

"Major. It's good to see you."

His heart was full of a feeling of events set in motion, circles closing, a destiny unveiled. All his life, it seemed, he had been anticipating this moment.

"Something's happening, isn't it?"

Amy nodded evenly. "I believe it is."

"I've prayed on it. I've prayed on *you*."

Amy nodded. "We will have to move quickly."

They stepped from the cell and continued down the dark hallway. Sanders was asleep at his desk in the outer room, his face turned sideways over neatly folded arms. The second guard, Coolidge, was snoring on the floor.

"They won't awaken for a while," Amy explained, "and when they do, they'll have no memory of this. You will simply be gone."

Lucius reached down to withdraw Sanders's pistol from its holster, then glanced up to see Amy regarding him with a look of caution.

"Just remember," she warned. "Carter's one of us."

Lucius chambered a round and set the safety and tucked the gun into his waistband. "Understood."

Outside, they walked with measured briskness toward the pedestrian tunnel, keeping to the shadows. At the portal, three domestics were idly standing around a fire burning in an ash can, warming their hands.

"Good evening, gentlemen," said Amy.

They melted to their knees, looks of mild surprise stamped on their faces. Lucius and Amy eased their bodies to the ground.

"That's some trick," said Lucius. "You'll have to teach me sometime."

On the far side of the tunnel, a pair of saddled horses waited. Lucius gave Amy a leg up, then climbed aboard the second horse, taking the reins loosely in his hand.

"One thing I need to ask," he said. "Why me?"

Amy thought a moment. "Each of us has one, Lucius."

"And Carter? Who does he have?"

An inscrutable look came into her eyes, as if her thoughts were carrying her far away. "He is different from the rest. He carries his familiar inside him."

"The woman in the water."

Amy smiled. "You've done your homework, Lucius."

"Things have a way of coming."

"Yes, they do. He loved her more than life but could not save her. She is the heart of him."

"And the dopeys?"

"They are his Many, his viral line. They kill only because they must. It goes hard with them. As he thinks, they think. As he dreams, they dream. They dream of her."

The horses were tamping the dust. It was just past midnight, a moonless sky the only witness to their departure.

"As I of you," said Lucius Greer. "As I of you."

They rode into the darkness.

35

Brothers, brothers.

And away, into the night. Julio Martínez, Tenth of Twelve, his legions discarded, cast to the wind. Julio Martínez, answering the call of Zero.

It is time. The moment of rebuilding has come. You will remake the world again; you will become the true masters of the earth, commanders not only of death but of life. You are the seasons. You are the turning earth. You are the circle within the circle within the circle. You are time itself, my brothers in blood.

In life Martínez had been an attorney, a man of law. He had stood before judges, defended the accused before juries of their peers. Death row cases were his specialty, his professional forté. He had acquired a particular brand of fame. The calls had come from everywhere: Would the great Julio Martínez, Esq., come to the aid of such-and-such? Could he be persuaded to swoop into action? The rock star who had bashed his girlfriend's brains out with a lamp. The state senator with the dead whore's blood on his hands. The suburban mother who had drowned her newborn triplets in the tub. Martínez took them all. They were insane or they were not; they pled or they didn't; they went to the needle, or the tiny cell, or scot-free. The outcome was irrelevant to Julio Martínez, Esq.; it was the drama he loved. To know one was going to die and yet struggle against its inevitability—that was the fascination. Once, as a boy, in the field behind his house, he had come upon a rabbit in a trap, the kind with a spring and teeth. Its iron jaws had clamped onto the animal's hind legs, flaying flesh to bone. The creature's small, dark eyes, like beads of oil, were full of death's wisdom. Life ebbed from it in a series of spasmodic scuffles. The boy Martínez could have watched for hours, and did just that; and when the rabbit failed to perish by nightfall, he carried it to the barn and returned to the house and ate his supper and went to bed in his room of toys and trophies, waiting for morning, when he could watch the rabbit die some more.

It had taken three days. Three glorious days.

Thus, his life and its dark investigations. Martínez had his reasons. He had his rationale. He had his particular method—the rag of spirits, the loyal cord and infinitely pliable duct tape, the dank, unseen compartments of dispatch. He chose low women, those lacking learning or culture, not because he despised them or secretly wanted them but because they were easy to ensnare. They were no match for his beautiful suits and movie-star hair and silken courtroom tongue. They were bodies without name or history or personality, and when the moment of transport approached, they offered no distraction. The timing was all, the orchestrated, simultaneous release. The old choir of sex and death singing.

A certain amount of practice had been required. There had been misfires. There had been, he was forced to admit, a certain amount of accidental comedy. The first one had died well but too soon, the second had kicked up such a ruckus that the whole thing had dissolved into farce, the third had wept so pitiably that he could hardly pay attention. But then: Louise. Louise, with her corny waitress uniform and sensible waitress shoes and unsexily supportive waitress hose. How beautifully she'd left her life! With what exquisite rapture in the taking! She was like a door opening into the great unknowable beyond, a portal into the infinite blackness of unbeing. He had been eradicated, pulverized; the winds of eternity had blown through him, beating him clean. It was everything he'd imagined and then some.

After that, frankly, he couldn't get enough of it.

As for the highway patrolman, the universe was not without its ironies. It gave and took away. To wit: the Jag with a broken taillight, and

Martínez with the woman's bagged body in the trunk; the cop's slow saunter toward the car, his hand resting manfully on the butt of his pistol, and the downward glide of the driver's window; the patrolman's face pressed close, sneering with bored righteousness, his lips saying the customary words—*Sir, could I see . . . ?*—and never finishing. In the harried aftermath, Martínez had managed to dispose of the body in the trunk, his nighttime practices thus to remain forever unknown, unconnected to his fate. But a dead policeman by the side of the highway, everything recorded by his dashboard video camera, well. In the end, the only thing to do, as the saying went, was for the great Julio Martínez, Esq., champion of the unchampionable, defender of the loathsomely defenseless, to pour himself a glass of thirty-year-old single-malt and toss it over his tongue while the windows of the house twirled with the lights of justice and come out with his hands dutifully up.

Which, given the way things had worked out, hadn't turned out to be such an unlucky turn of events, actually.

Martínez couldn't say he cared much for his fellows. With the exception of Carter, who struck him as purely pitiable—the man didn't even seem to know what he was or what he'd done; Martínez hadn't heard so much as a squeak from the man in years—they were nothing more than common criminals, their deeds random and banal. Vehicular homicide. Armed robbery gone bad. Barroom shenanigans with a body on the floor. A century marinating in their own psychological waste had done nothing to improve them. Martínez's existence was not without its irritating aspects. The never quite being alone. The endless hunger always needing to be filled. The ceaseless talk-talk-talk inside his head, not just his brothers but Zero, too. And Ignacio: there was a piece of work. The man was a litany of self-pitying excuses. *I didn't mean to do half those things. It's just the way I was built.* After a hundred years listening to the man's whining, Martínez wouldn't miss him one bit.

There had been something attractively berserk about Babcock, though. You had to hand it to the man for metaphor. Carving out his mother's larynx with a kitchen knife; in another life, he surely would have been a poet. Over the decades, Martínez had mentally sat in that foul kitchen about a million times, and it was true: the woman would *not* shut up. There was a kind of person in this world who needed you to paint a picture, and Babcock's mother was that kind.

And then one day Babcock was simply gone, his signal silenced, like a television station suddenly off the air. The corner of Martínez's mind where Babcock stood, endlessly gouging out the gristly nubbin of his mother's voice box, was empty. All of them knew what had happened;

their collective, blood-borne existence ordained it. One of their brothers had fallen.

God bless and keep you, Giles Babcock. May you find in death the peace that eluded you in life, and what came after.

And so from Twelve, Eleven. A loss, a chink in the armor, but ultimately a matter of lesser concern in the vital period to come. It had been a good century, on the whole, for Julio Martínez. He recalled the early days with poignant fondness. The days of blood and mayhem and the great unleashing of his kind upon the earth. To kill was one thing, one glorious thing; to take was another. A banquet richer still in its satisfactions. From each one Martínez had taken a flavorful bite of soul, drawing them into the fold, expanding his dominion. His Many were not merely *part* of him, an *extension* of him; they *were* him. As he, Julio Martínez, was one of Twelve and the Zero also, concomitant and coextensive, united with one another and with the darkness in which they permanently dwelled.

Brothers, brothers, it is time. Brothers, brothers, the hour is at hand.

For it was inevitable; they had built a race of pure rapaciousness. Their Many, created to protect them, had devoured the earth like locusts, leaving nothing in their wake. Feast had yielded to famine, summer's bounty to winter's scarcity; they would need a home, a zone of protection, of rest. To dream their dreams. To dream of Louise.

My brothers, your new home is waiting. They will bow before you; you will live as kings.

Martínez liked the sound of that.

He discarded them without ceremony. His Many, millions-fold. He called them together from all the hidden places and said to them: *Die.* Dawn was reaching its red-fingered hand over the horizon. They pointed their faces blindly toward it. They showed no hesitation; all that he commanded, so did they. The sun was moving toward them like a blade of light over the earth. *Lie down, my sons and daughters; lie down in the sun and die.*

There followed a certain amount of screaming.

Night by night he made his way east, across the exhausted land. His instincts were acute. The world rippled with sensuousness, caressing him with its sounds and smells. The grass. The wind. The subtlest movements of trees. He lingered, tasting all. He had been away too long. He called to his fellows, their voices threading with darkness as they made their way from every corner to the place of their renewal.

—We are Morrison-Chávez-Baffes-Turrell-Winston-Sosa-Echols-Lambright-Martínez-Reinhardt-Carter. Eleven of Twelve, one brother lost.

And Zero replied in kind:

Oh, my brothers, my pain is as great as your own. But you will be Twelve again. For I have made another, one to watch and keep you in your place of rest.

—Who? they asked, each as one and then together. —Who is the other you have made?

And Zero spoke from out of the darkness:

Our sister.

VI

THE INSURGENT

FORT POWELL, IOWA
POP. 69,172
97 A.V.

Night, you who gather in your lovely lap
The things the shining dawn flung far and wide,
The ewe-lamb you bring back, the straying goat,
The child you lead unto its mother's side.

—SAPPHO, C. 612 B.C.,
Fragment 120

ATTENTION

A MESSAGE FROM THE DIRECTOR

Citizens of the Homeland! There are traitors among us!

The disgraceful methods of the so-called "insurgency" have reached new lows. Dozens of your fellow citizens, including innocent women and children, have been murdered in cold blood by these cowardly conspirators, who act without mercy.

We must defend ourselves!
Stand with your Director!
End the plague of violence!

We call on all citizens to help bring these despicable traitors to justice. The safety of our Homeland is at stake.

Everyone must do his part!

- Be vigilant. The person standing beside you might at this very moment be plotting the deaths of hundreds.
- Report any suspicious activities at once to Human Resources personnel.
- Maintain discipline in your lodging and workplace.
- Stand ready. At any time you may be called upon to assist with defense.
- Anyone offering aid to the insurgency or interfering with the duties of the Homeland Authority will be seen as an **enemy** of the state.

Watch! Listen! Stay on guard!
Together we can restore peace and
security to our beloved Homeland!

Everywhere people were whispering: there had been another bombing in the market.

The November morning broke gray and cold, tasting of the winter to come. Sara awoke to the blare of the horn, followed by a chorus of coughing, throats clearing, bones cracking ambivalently to life. Her eyes and mouth were as dry as paper. The room smelled of unwashed skin and stale breath and delousing powder, a biological vapor of human decay, though Sara barely noticed. Some of the smell, she knew, was herself.

Another pitiless sunrise, she thought. Another morning as a citizen of the Homeland.

She had learned not to linger on her bunk. One minute late to the ration line and you could find yourself dragging through the day without a scrap in your stomach. A bowl of corn mush trumped a few slender minutes of tormented half sleep every time. With her stomach growling, she unwrapped her threadbare blanket and swung her weight around, ducking her head, to plant her sneakered feet on the floorboards. She always slept wearing her sneakers, such as they were— a ragged pair of Reeboks inherited from a bunkmate who had died—because footwear was always being stolen. *Who took my shoes!* a voice would cry out, and the victim would go charging through the lodge, begging and accusing and eventually crumpling to the floor in hopeless tears. *I'll die without them! Somebody help me, please!* It was true: a person would die without shoes. Though she worked at the biodiesel plant, word had gotten out in the flatland that Sara was a nurse. She had seen the blackened nuts of frozen toes, the scabs of worms burrowed in; she'd pressed her ear to the sunken chests and listened to the pneumonic rattles of lungs slowly drowning; she'd felt beneath her fingertips the drum-taut bellies of septic appendicitis, or malignancy, or simple starvation; she'd palmed the foreheads blazing with fever and dressed the weeping wounds that would devour the body with rot. And to each person, Sara said, with the taste of a lie in her teeth: You'll be fine. Not to worry. In another few days you'll be right as rain, I promise. It wasn't medical care she was giving; it was a sort of blessing. You will die, and it will hurt, but you will do it here, among your own kind, and the last touch you feel will be one of kindness, because it will be mine.

Because you didn't want the cols to know you were sick, let alone the redeyes. Nothing was ever said aloud, but people in the flatland had few illusions what the hospital was actually for. Man or woman, old or young, it didn't matter; you passed through those doors and nobody saw you again. Off to the feedlot you went.

The lodges varied in size; Sara's was one of the largest. The bunks were stacked four high, twenty bunk lengths in each row, ten rows: eight hundred souls crammed into a room the approximate dimensions of a feed shed. People were rising, jamming their children's heads into hats, murmuring to themselves, their limbs moving with the heavy docility of livestock as they shambled to the door. Quickly scanning the area to make sure she wouldn't be observed, Sara knelt by her bunk, lifting the mattress with one hand while sliding the other beneath it. She removed the piece of carefully folded paper from its hiding place and secreted it in the pocket of her tunic. Then she drew herself upright.

"Jackie," Sara said quietly, "wake up."

The old woman was curled in a fetal position with the blanket drawn to her chin. Her rheumy eyes stared dully at the wash of gray descending from the high windows of the lodge. Sara had listened to her coughing all night.

"The light," Jackie said. "It looks like winter."

Sara felt her forehead. No trace of fever; if anything, the woman felt cold. It was hard to say how old Jackie was. She'd been born in the flats, but her parents had come from somewhere else. Jackie wasn't one to speak of the past, but Sara knew she had outlived three children and a husband, the last sent to the feedlot for the crime of coming to the aid of a friend who was being sticked by a col.

The room was rapidly emptying out. "Jackie, please." Sara shook her by the shoulder. "I know you're tired, but we've really got to go."

The woman's eyes drew Sara into focus. She trembled with a dry cough.

"I'm sorry, hon," she said, when the spasm had passed. "I don't mean to be uncooperative."

"I just don't want to miss breakfast. You need to eat."

"There you go, looking out for me like you always do. Help an old lady down, will you?"

Sara gave Jackie a shoulder for balance and eased her to the floor. Her body was practically weightless, a form of sticks and air. Another cough hacked through her chest, a sound like pebbles being shaken in a sack. She slowly drew herself erect.

"There now." Jackie took a moment to swallow. Her face was flushed; beads of dampness had risen on her forehead. "All better."

Sara pulled the blanket off her bunk and draped it over the woman's shoulders. "It's going to be a cold one. Stay by me, okay?"

Her lips stretched into a toothless smile. "Where else would I go, hon?"

Sara retained only fleeting images of her capture. A sense of certain death, everything over and done, and then a huge force, merciless in its energy, seizing her bodily. A glimpse of the ground dropping away as the viral hurled her into the air—why hadn't it just killed her?—and then another massive jolt as she was snatched once more, plucked from the air by the second viral, and then the third, and so on, each aerial vault cata-pulting her farther away from the walls and lights of the garrison and into the enveloping blackness, her person passed from airborne hand to airborne hand like a ball in a children's game, all of it beyond the bound-aries of her comprehension, and then the final brain-battering impact as she was slammed into the truck. The awful coming to consciousness, like climbing a ladder from hell into hell. Days without water, without food. The endless bone-banging hours and whispered, unanswerable ques-tions. Where were they going? What was happening to them? Nearly all the captives were women, part of the civilian corps stationed at Roswell, though a handful of soldiers were among them. The cries of the injured and frightened. The smothering darkness.

Sara's mind had not returned to full awareness until their arrival. It was as if time had stretched for the duration of their journey only to snap back into shape when the door opened onto a disorienting splash of daylight. Revealing . . . what? Half of the truck's human cargo had perished—a few dead at the outset and filling the compartment with a stink of gray decay, others from injuries sustained in their capture, the rest from some combination of hunger and thirst and suffocating hope-lessness. Sara was lying on the floor, as they all were, both the living and the dead, inertly limbed and thick-tongued, her back propped against the wall, her eyes clenched against the unaccustomed brightness. An in-version of her physical proportions seemed to have occurred, such that most of her mass had lodged in her head. Over her lifetime, she had seen a lot of people die; lying among them was a first. The boundary separat-ing her from them seemed a membrane as permeable as gauze. Through stinging slits, she watched as a half dozen expressionless men in ragged khaki and heavy, floor-banging boots boarded the compartment and commenced a perfunctory toting away of the deceased. She gathered that the unstructured weight of a dead body was something these men were accustomed to, its purposeless association of parts warranting no more consideration than any other awkward object a person might be forced to carry. Body after body, unceremoniously hauled away. When they came for her, Sara lifted a hand in protest; she might have said something like "Please" or "Wait" or "You can't do this." But these meager efforts were instantly silenced by a hot slap across her cheek, followed, for good measure, by the thrust of a boot that would have caught her midsection had Sara not protectively folded around herself.

"Shut. The fuck. Up."

She did. She shut the fuck up. The man who had struck her was a col Sara would come to know as Sod. Among the citizens of the flatland, all the cols had nicknames. Sod was Sod because he liked raping people. A lot of them did, it was like a game to them, but Sod distinguished himself by the breadth of his appetites. Women, men, children, livestock. Sod would have raped the wind if it had a hole in it.

Sara's turn in the shed would come: brief, brutal, over. In the near term, the pain of his blows had the counterintuitive effect of restoring her senses. Strategies began to form; priorities stepped into line. On balance, staying alive seemed desirable, and the shutting-the-fuck-up seemed the best way to accomplish this. Be quiet, she told herself. Blend in. See what you can see without seeming to. If they want to kill you, they'll do it anyway.

Don't mention the baby.

The clubs came out, poking and prodding as they were marched into the sunshine. They were someplace green. Its lushness mocked her, the cruelest of jokes. The truck had parked in a kind of holding area, a wired compound of stubby concrete buildings with glinting metal roofs; adjacent to this, at a distance of several hundred yards, was a massive, tiered structure, unlike anything Sara had ever seen. It looked like an enormous bathtub. Tall banks of lights lifted from its curving walls, ascending hundreds of feet into the air. While Sara watched, a gleaming silver semitruck, identical to the one they'd just disembarked, drew up to the building's base. Men were jogging alongside, carrying rifles. They wore bulky pads; caged masks were drawn down over their faces. As the truck approached the wall, it seemed to sink into the earth—a ramp, Sara realized, taking it belowground. A gate opened, and it was gone.

"Eyes down. No talking. Two lines, women to the left, men to the right."

Inside one of the huts, they were told to strip and deposit their clothes in a pile. Now they stood naked, twenty-three women in identically reflexive postures of self-protection, one arm held horizontally to shield their breasts, the other extended downward over their genitals. Three of the uniformed men looked on, rocking on their heels, alternating frank leers with laughing faces of disgust. There were gutters in the floor, drains. Slants of light descended from a series of long, barred windows at the roofline. Twenty-three naked women wordlessly staring at the floor, most of them in tears: to speak would be to violate some implied contract to go on living. Whatever was headed their way seemed to be taking its time getting there.

Then, the hose.

The water blasted them like a jet of ice. Water as weapon; water as battering fist. Everyone was yelling, women were tumbling, bodies were sliding on the floor. The hose's operator enjoyed himself spectacularly, whooping like a rider on a galloping horse. He picked off one and then another. He swept them in a line. He zigzagged his pummeling probe from their faces to their breasts and farther down. The water hit you and then it stopped and then it hit you again. There was nowhere to run, nowhere to hide; all you could do was endure.

It stopped.

"Everybody on your feet."

They were led outside again in their shivering nakedness. Water was streaming down their faces, running in rivulets from their hair. Their skin puckered with its evaporation. A single wooden chair had been placed in the middle of the compound. One of the guards stood beside it, languidly sharpening a razor on a leather strop. Four more approached, each bearing a large plastic tub.

"Get dressed."

Clothing was tossed their way—loose pants with drawstring waists, long-sleeved tunics that hung to the hips, all made of scratchy wool with a harsh chemical smell—followed by a random assortment of shoes: sneakers, plastic sandals, boots with the soles split away. Sara found her feet swimming in a pair of leather lace-ups.

"You, step forward."

The man with the razor was pointing at Sara. The other women parted around her. There was something disloyal about this, though Sara hardly blamed them; she might have done the same. Doom weighing in her chest, she approached the chair and sat. She was facing the other women now. Whatever was about to happen, Sara would see it first in their eyes. The man swept her hair into his fist and yanked it taught. A single slice and it was gone. He began to chop indiscriminately at the remains, hewing close to her scalp. There was no pattern to his efforts; he might just as well have been slashing his way through a forest. Sara's hair fell to her feet in golden ribbons.

"Go stand with the others."

She returned to the group. When she touched her head, her fingers came away tacky with blood. She studied its texture with her fingertips. *This is my blood,* Sara thought. *Because it is my blood, it means that I'm alive.* The second woman was in the chair now. Sara thought her name was Caroline. She had met her briefly in the infirmary at the Roswell Garrison; like Sara, she was a nurse. A tall, impressively big-boned girl who radiated health, good cheer, competence. She wept into her hands as the barber hacked away.

One by one they were shorn. So much came down to hair, Sara realized. In their disfigured semibaldness, something private had been stolen, melding them into an indistinguishable collective, like animals in a herd. She was so light-headed with hunger she didn't see how she could continue standing. None of them had had a scrap to eat—no doubt to keep them compliant, so that when food was offered they would feel some gratitude to their captors.

When the cutting was done, they were told to march across the holding area to a second concrete building for something called "processing." They were marshaled into a line before a long table, where one of the guards, radiating the sense of being in charge, sat with a look of irritation on his face. As each was called forward, he reloaded a clipboard.

"Name?"

"Sara Fisher."

"Age?"

"Twenty-one."

He eyed her up and down. "Can you read?"

"I can read. Yes."

"Special skills?"

She hesitated. "I can ride."

"Ride?"

"Horses."

His eyes rolled a little. "Anything useful?"

"I don't know." She tried to think of something safe. "Sew?"

He yawned. His teeth were so bad, they appeared to wiggle in his mouth. He jotted something onto the clipboard and tore off the bottom half of the page. From a bin beneath the table he retrieved a ratty blanket, a metal plate, a battered cup and spoon. He passed these to her, the paper balanced on top. Sara quickly glanced at it: her name, a five-digit string of numbers, "Lodge 216," and, below that, "Biodiesel 3." The handwriting had the blockiness of a child's.

"Next!"

One of the guards took her by the arm and led her down a hallway of sealed doors. A tiny box of a room and another chair, though not like any chair Sara had seen before: a menacing contraption of cracked red leather and steel, its back reclined at a forty-five-degree angle, with straps at the chest, feet, and wrists. Lurking above it, like the legs of a spider descending on silken threads, was an armature of gleaming metal instruments. The guard shoved her toward it.

"Sit down."

He strapped her to the chair and departed. From without the room, the sound muffled by the thick walls, came a burst of ominously high-pitched sound. Was it screaming? Sara thought she might be ill. She would have been, if there had been anything in her stomach to come up. The last of her defenses were collapsing. She would beg. She would plead. She had no strength to resist.

The door opened behind her. A man stepped into her field of vision, dressed in a gray smock. He had a little round belly and clouded glasses perched at the tip of his nose and bushy eyebrows that curled like wings at the tips. Something about his face was kind, almost grandfatherly. Like the guard at the table, he was looking at a clipboard. He raised his eyes and smiled.

"Sara, is it?"

She nodded, tasting bile.

"I'm Dr. Verlyn." He glanced at the straps, frowning as he shook his head. "Those people are idiots. I bet you're famished. Let's see if we can get you out of here."

She experienced a flash of hope that he intended to release her, but as he drew a stool beside the chair, snapping on a pair of rubber gloves, she realized he meant something else. He placed his hand beneath her chin to open her jaw. He peered inside her mouth, then held up two fingers before her face.

"Follow with your eyes, please."

Sara traced his fingers as they made a figure eight and pulled away. He took her pulse, then produced a stethoscope from the pocket of his smock and listened to her heart. He sat up straight and returned his attention to the clipboard, squinting through his glasses.

"Any health problems you're aware of? Parasites, infection, night sweats, difficulty urinating?"

Sara shook her head.

"How about menstruation?" He was checking off boxes. "Any problems there? Excessive bleeding, for example."

"No."

"It says here you're . . ." He paused, flipped through pages. "Twenty-one. Is that correct?"

"Yes."

"Ever been pregnant?"

Something clenched inside her.

"It's a simple question."

She shook her head. "No."

If he detected her lie, he gave no sign. He let the clipboard fall to his lap. "Well, you appear to be in perfect health. Wonderful teeth, if you don't mind my saying so. Nothing to be done there."

Was she supposed to say thank you? Above her face the spider still loomed, gleaming ominously.

"Now then, let's see if we can't finish up quickly and get you on your way."

Suddenly something changed. Sara sensed it in a quick hardening of his features, but not just there; it was as if the air of the room had undergone some subtle alteration. The doctor began vigorously pumping a pedal beneath her chair, producing a whirring sound, then reached above her face to draw down one of the spider's legs. At its tip, spinning in time to his foot strokes, was a buzzing drill bit.

"This will be easier if you don't move."

Some minutes later, Sara found herself standing outside, clutching her meager belongings to her chest. When she'd started to scream, the doctor had given her a leather strap to bite on. On the pale skin of the inside of her forearm, first gouged and then cauterized in place, was a shiny metal tag, engraved with the same string of digits she'd seen on the paper: 94801. That's who you are now, the doctor had explained, removing the strap, now with its embedded impressions of her teeth. He'd stripped off his gloves and stepped to the sink to wash his hands. Whoever you thought you were, you're not that person anymore. You're flatlander number 94801.

The semi was gone, replaced by an open-backed five-ton. Sara saw the words IOWA NATIONAL GUARD imprinted on the driver's door—the first evidence of where she was. A guard motioned for Sara to board; a second guard was standing at the front of the cargo bay, his back braced against the cab, idly spinning his club on its leather strap. Some of the women were already there and a few of the men as well. Everyone was slumped on the benches, their faces carrying the stunned weight of all that had occurred.

She took a place beside one of the men, a young officer she knew as Lieutenant Eustace. He had been the scout who had brought them into Roswell. As she lowered herself to the bench, he angled his shorn head close to Sara's.

"What the hell is this place?" he whispered.

Before Sara could answer, the guard sparked to attention. "You," he barked, gesturing at Eustace with the end of his club. "No talking."

"Who are you people? Why won't you tell us anything?"

"I said, keep quiet."

Sara understood what was about to happen. It was the implied climax of the day's design, the one demonstration of their powerlessness that had yet to be delivered.

"Yeah?" Eustace's face lit with defiance, the last of his energy spitting from his lips. He knew what he was asking for; he didn't care. "Go to hell, all of you."

The guard took a long stride forward and, with a look of absolute boredom, brought the club crashing down on Eustace's knees. Eustace rocked forward, clenching his teeth in barely contained agony. Nobody moved a muscle; everyone was gazing intently at the floor.

"Mother . . . *fucker,*" he gasped.

The guard spun the club around and backhanded the heavy end into Eustace's nose. A wet exoskeletal crunch, like the sound of an insect stamped underfoot; a crimson spray arced into the air, spattering Sara across the face. Eustace's head snapped back, his eyes fluttering in their sockets. He ran his tongue along the inside of his upper lip and spat a shard of a tooth away.

"I said . . . *fuck . . . you.*"

Blow after hammering blow: his face, his head, the bony joints of his hands. By the time Eustace toppled over, his eyes rolled back into his skull, his features crushed into a pulpy mass, blood had rained down on them all.

"Get used to it." The guard paused to wipe his baton on his pant leg and dragged his eyes over the group. "It's pretty much how we do things."

As the truck pulled away, Sara drew Eustace toward her to cradle his ruined face in her lap. The man was barely conscious, his breath gurgling in his throat. Perhaps he would die; it seemed likely. And yet there was a feeling of victory in what he'd done. She bent at the neck and whispered into his ear:

"Thank you."

Thus, in blood, it began.

"One People! One Director! One Homeland!"

How many times had Sara been forced to shout these words? With the morning roll call and the singing of the anthem complete, everyone dispersed to their designated transports. Sara helped Jackie up, then climbed aboard. She saw a new face, one she recognized: Constance Chou, Old Chou's wife. They acknowledged each other with tight nods, but that was all. What had happened at the Colony had come to Sara in bits and pieces over the years. The story was no different from the others she'd heard and differed from the events at Roswell only by degree; in many ways, the greater shock had been that so many other islands of humanity had existed at all. By the time Sara arrived, the Colony's survivors had already dispersed across the flatland. The number Sara heard was fifty-six. How easy it was for fifty-six people to be subsumed into the masses; with their chopped hair and identical tunics, everybody looked the same. Yet every now and then, a familiar face leapt out. She had glimpsed a woman she thought was Penny Darrell, and another who she swore was Belle Ramirez, Rey's wife, though when Sara had called her name, the woman hadn't answered. One morning in the ration line, her bowl had been filled by a man she had seen many times without recognizing as Russell Curtis, her own cousin. He appeared so much older than the man Sara recalled that when their eyes met, it took her a moment to place him. For the better part of a year she had been housed in the same lodge as Karen Molyneau, Jimmy's widow, and her two daughters, Alice and Avery. It was from Karen that Sara took the most information, including the names of the dead. Ian Patal, who had been killed defending the power station. Hollis's sister-in-law, Leigh, and her baby, Dora, who had perished on the trip to the Homeland; Other Sandy, who had died shortly after arrival, Karen wasn't sure how; Gloria and Sanjay Patal. As dark as this news was, Sara still regarded her year with Karen and her girls as a brief respite, a period in which she'd felt connected to the past. But they were always moving people around between the lodges, and one day the three of them were gone, strangers sleeping in the bunks where they had lain their heads for a year. Sara hadn't seen them since.

The ride to the biodiesel plant took them along the river, through a

maze of squalid lodges to the industrial zone at the north edge of the
flatlands. The day gave no promise of improvement; a bitter wind spit
kernels of rain into their faces. The air was ripe with the stenches of the
flatland, pooling animal waste and a compressed and filthy humanity
and, behind it, like a curtain of scent, the dark earthiness of the river.
They passed through a juggernaut of checkpoints, fences opening and
closing, the cols with their clipboards and pens and inexhaustible appetite for paperwork and the structures of authority waving them through.
The far side of the river gave onto open floodplain, denuded and colorless, the crops long picked for winter; to the east, ascending in steps
above the river, rose the Hilltop, where all the redeyes lived, and at its
apex the Capitol Dome, capped with its crown of gold. It was said that
this structure, and those surrounding it, had at one time been a university, which was a kind of school, though with only the Sanctuary for
comparison, Sara had difficulty absorbing this fact. Sara had never been
up the hill, let alone inside the Dome. Some workers were allowed inside,
gardeners and plumbers and kitchen help, and of course the attendants,
who were women selected to serve the Director and his staff of redeyes.
Everybody said the attendants were the lucky ones, that they lived in
luxury with good food and hot water and soft beds to sleep in, but the
information was all secondhand. No attendant had ever returned to the
flatland; once they went in, the Dome became their lives.

"Get a look at that," Jackie murmured.

Sara's thoughts had wandered off, her awareness blunted by the cold.
They were cutting away from the river on the access road; to the north,
beyond the boundaries of the Homeland, Sara could make out the shape
of the cranes spiking through the treetops like a pair of huge, skeletal
birds. The Project, it was called: a decades-long undertaking to erect a
massive steel-and-concrete structure of unknown purpose. Flatlanders
who worked there, nearly all of them men, were searched each day going
to and coming from the site; even to talk about what they did there was
regarded as treason and could get you sent to the feedlot, though rumors
abounded. One theory would hold sway for a time before yielding to
another and then to a third, the first eventually reemerging to start the
cycle anew. Even the men who worked there, when they could be convinced to speak of it at all, did not appear to know what they were constructing. There was talk of mazelike hallways, vast chambers, foot-thick
doors of solid steel. Some claimed it was a monument to the Director,
others that it was a factory. A few claimed it was nothing at all, merely a
distraction concocted by the redeyes to keep the flatlanders occupied. A
fourth hypothesis, one that had gained currency in recent months, was

that the Project was an emergency bunker. Should the Director's mysterious power to keep the virals at bay ever fail, the structure could serve as a refuge for the population. Whatever it was, the work appeared to be approaching completion; fewer and fewer men would board the transports to the site each morning, and they were all older, most having worked there for years.

But the cranes weren't the object of Jackie's attention. As the five-ton drew toward the last guardhouse, Sara saw two words imprinted on the perimeter wall, painted in broad, dripping strokes of white:

SERGIO LIVES!

A pair of flatlanders were dousing long-armed brushes in buckets of soapy water, preparing to scrub it off. A col stood beside them with a rifle cradled over his chest. He glowered as the transport passed, meeting Sara's eye for an icy instant. She looked away.

"Fisher, you see anything that interests you?"

The voice belonged to one of the two cols riding in the back of the truck, a trim man of twenty-five or so, who went by the name Vale.

"No, sir."

For the final five minutes of the ride, she kept her eyes glued to the floor. Sergio, Sara thought. Who was Sergio? The name, rarely spoken in the open, possessed an almost incantatory power: Sergio, leader of the insurgency, bomber of markets and police stations and guardhouses, who, with his unseen fellows, seemed to glide like ghosts through the Homeland, igniting weapons of destruction. Sara understood the words on the fence to be a kind of taunt. *We were here,* they said, *we stood right where you are standing now, we are everywhere among you.* Sergio's methods were marked by an almost incomprehensible cruelty. The insurgents' targets were anywhere the cols might gather, a program of assassination and disruption, but if you were in the wrong place at the wrong time, your presence made no difference. A man or woman would open their coat to reveal the rows of dynamite strapped to their chest, and that would be the end of you. And always, in the final instant, as their thumb found the trigger on the detonator, sending themselves and anyone within the blast radius into oblivion, they would utter these two words: Sergio lives.

The transport pulled up to the plant, and the workers disembarked. A yeasty odor hung in the air. Four more trucks of workers pulled in behind them. Sara and Jackie were assigned to the grinders, as were most of the women. Why this should be so, Sara had never understood—the job was neither more nor less arduous than anything else—but that's how things were done. Corn would be mashed, then combined with fungal enzymes and fermented to make fuel. The smell was so intense that it seemed to be part of Sara's very skin, though she had to admit there were far worse jobs: tending the hogs, or working at the waste treatment plant or slurry pens. They got into line to check in with the foreman, tied their kerchiefs around their faces, then made their way through the cavernous space to their workstations. The corn was stored in large bins with spouts at the bottom; from these openings they would retrieve one bushel at a time and load it into the grinders, where rotating paddles pummeled the kernels into meal. As the moisture in the corn was released it formed a gluey paste, which adhered to the interior walls of the grinder; it was the operator's job to dislodge it, a task requiring great dexterity and quickness, as the paddles did not stop rotating. The difficulty was compounded by the cold, which made even the simplest movements feel sluggish and imprecise.

Sara set to work. The day that loomed ahead would pass in a kind of trance. It was a skill she'd acquired as the years had passed, employing the hypnotic rhythms of work to drain her mind of thought. Not to think: that was the goal. To occupy a purely biological state, her senses absorbing only the most immediate physical data: the whir of the grinder's paddles, the stink of fermenting corn, the nubbin of cold emptiness in her belly where the measly bowl of watery gruel that passed for breakfast had long since been absorbed. For these twelve hours, she was flatlander no. 94801, nothing less or more. The real Sara, the one who thought and felt and remembered—Sara Fisher, First Nurse, citizen of the Colony, daughter of Joe and Kate Fisher and sister of Michael; beloved of Hollis, friend to many, mother of one—was hidden away in a folded slip of paper, tucked like a talisman in her pocket.

She did her best to keep an eye on Jackie. The woman had her worried; a cough like hers was nothing good. In the flatlands a person didn't really have friends, not in the way that Sara had known friendship. There were faces you knew and people you trusted more than others, but that was the extent of it. You didn't talk about yourself, because you weren't really anybody, or your hopes, since you had none. But with Jackie she had allowed her defenses to drop. They had formed a mutual pact, an unstated pledge to watch out for each other.

At noon they were given a fifteen-minute break, just enough time to race to the latrine—a wooden platform suspended above a ditch, with holes to squat over—and gobble another bowl of gruel. There was no place to sit, so you ate standing up or on the ground, using your fingers for a spoon, then got in a second line for water, which was dispensed with a ladle that all the women shared. All the while they were watched by the cols, who stood to the side, twirling their sticks. Their official title was Human Resources Officers, but nobody ever called them that in the flatland. The word was short for "collaborators." Nearly all were men but there were some women, often the cruelest of the lot. One female col, whom they called Whistler for the deep cleft in her upper lip, a congenital deformity that gave her voice a distinctive, reedlike sound, seemed to take special delight in inventing new and subtle ways to inflict discomfort. It was her habit to single out one person, most often a woman, as if she were performing an experiment. Whistler set her sights on you and the next thing you knew you would be pulled out of the latrine line for a pat-down just when it was your turn, or assigned some impossible and pointless job, or switched to a different crew just as your break was coming. The only thing you could do was take it, gritting your teeth through the misery of your aching bladder or empty stomach or exhausted limbs, knowing that soon Whistler's attention would pass to another, though this only made things worse and seemed to be the point of the entire exercise; you found yourself wishing for the suffering to befall somebody else, and thus you became complicit, part of the system, a cog in a wheel of torment that never stopped turning.

She looked for Jackie at the break, but the woman was nowhere to be seen. Sara moved quickly through grinding stations, searching for her friend. The foreman's whistle would blow at any moment, summoning them back to work. She had nearly given up when she turned a corner to find Jackie sitting on the ground, her face damp with sweat, her kerchief balled to her mouth.

"I'm sorry," she managed. "I just couldn't stop coughing."

The cloth was stained with blood. Sara knew what was happening; she'd seen it before, the effects of years of dust in the lungs. One minute a person was fine, the next they were drowning in it.

"We have to get you out of here."

She pulled the woman to her feet just as the whistle blew. One hand wrapped around Jackie's waist, Sara steered her toward the exit. Her goal was to get outside before anyone noticed; what would happen after that, Sara had no idea. Vale was the col in charge. Not the best, but not the worst, either. More than once, Sara had caught him watching her in a way that made it seem like he had something in mind for her, something personal, though he had never acted on it. Perhaps now would be the time. A shuddering nausea passed through her at the thought, yet she knew she was capable of it. She would do what she had to.

They had nearly reached the exit when a figure stepped into their path. "Where do you think you're going?"

Not Vale: Sod. Backlit by the open door, he loomed before them. Sara's stomach dropped.

"She just needs some air. The dust—"

"Is that right, old woman? The dust bothering you?" With the butt of his stick he tapped the woman's chest, igniting a strangled cough. "Get back to work."

"It's all right, Sara," Jackie wheezed, freeing herself from Sara's arm. "I'll be fine."

"Jackie—"

"I mean it." She looked at Sara, her eyes saying, *Don't.* "She's just a busybody, that's all. Thinking she knows what's best for me."

Sod eyes flicked the length of Sara's body. "Yeah, I heard that about you. Think you're some kind of doctor, do you?"

"I never said that."

"Sure you didn't." With his free hand Sod cupped his crotch, rocking his hips forward. "Hey, Doctor, I've got a pain right here. What do you say you get a closer look at it?"

The moment caught and held; Sara thought of Eustace, in the truck. The blood on his face, his shattered hands and teeth. His broken smile of triumph. Standing before Sod, she willed herself to say the words, to utter the curse that would unleash him upon her. It was all so simple, so stark. She could see the scene unfolding in her mind. Just two words, and the flare of anger in Sod's eyes, and then the crash of the stick. These were the terms of her life, a thousand humiliations enacted daily. They had taken everything from her. To accept the worst—no, to embrace it—that was the only resistance.

"Sara, *please.*" Jackie was staring at her. *Not like this. Not for me.*

Sara swallowed. Everyone was looking at her.

"Okay," she said.

She turned and walked away. The space around her had grown strangely quiet. All she could hear was her heart.

"Don't worry, Fisher," Sod called after her with a leering laugh. "I'll know where to find you. It'll be as good as the last time, I promise."

It was later, as Sara lay in her cot, that she permitted herself to consider the full measure of these events. Something had changed within her. She was on the verge, a figure standing at the precipice, waiting to jump. Five long years: it could have been a thousand. The past was disappearing inside her, rinsed away by the wash of time, the bitter cold of her heart, the sameness of days. She had plunged down inside herself for too long. Winter was coming. Winter light.

She had somehow gotten Jackie through the day. Now the old woman slept above her, the straps of her bunk sagging with her restive turning. Jackie's death, when it came, would come badly, in long agonal hours, a strangling from within, before the final stilling. Would her fate be Sara's own? To stumble blindly through the years, a being without purpose or connection, a hollow shell of nothing?

Sara had not returned the makeshift envelope to its hiding place under the mattress. Seized by a sudden loneliness, she withdrew it from beneath the lump of rags that served as her pillow. It had been given to her by the midwife's assistant in the birthing ward—the same woman who had told her that the baby, arriving early in a gush of blood, had not survived. It was a girl, the woman had told her. I'm sorry. Then she'd slipped the envelope into Sara's hand and vanished. Through the haze of grief and pain Sara had ached to hold her daughter, but this hadn't happened; the child had been taken away. She'd never seen the woman again.

Carefully she unfolded the pocket of brittle paper with the tips of her fingers. Inside lay a coiled lock of hair—a baby curl. The room was sunk in darkness, and yet its pale golden color was vivid to her eyes. She brought it to her face, inhaling deeply, trying to capture its scent. Sara could never have another, the damage was too great; Kate was the only one. That was what she'd named her, Kate. How she wished she'd told Hollis. She had wanted to save her news, to choose the perfect moment to give him the present of the two of them conjoined. How foolish she'd been. She thought: I know you're better off, my darling. Wherever you are now, I hope it is a place of light and sky and love. If only I could have held you, just one time, to tell you how much I loved you.

37

This Sergio thing: it had simply gone on too long.

Not that there hadn't been uprisings before. The year 31, wasn't it? And again in 68? Not to mention the hundred little brushfires of defiance put down over the years. And wasn't it true that the problem inevitably boiled down to a single individual, a lone renegade, who simply

failed to get the *point*? That when this man was taken care of (it was always a man), the flames of resistance, deprived of their essential oxygen,
would extinguish of their own accord?

And yet this Sergio: he didn't feel like the others. Standing in the window at the base of the cupola, his gaze directed over the grimy stain of
the flatland and the colorless, winter fields beyond, Director Horace
Guilder took stock. The man's methods were different, for starters, not
merely in quantity but in kind. People blowing themselves up! Strapping
sticks of dynamite to their chests, or pipe bombs crammed with shards
of glass and broken screws, and actually mustering the will to blow
themselves and everyone around them to a bloody mist! It was beyond
madness, a full-blown psychosis that could only mean that this Sergio,
whoever he was, held a deeper psychological sway over his followers than
any who had come before. The flatlanders had safety, they had food to
warm their bellies, they slept in beds at night without fear of the virals.
They were allowed to live their lives, in other words, and this was the
thanks he got? Couldn't they see that everything he'd done, he'd done for
them? That he had built a home for mankind so that it might, against the
prevailing winds of history, continue?

True, there was a certain . . . unfairness to things. An uneven distribu-
tion of resources, one could say, a partitioning of management from
labor, of haves from have-nots, us from them. An unpleasant reliance on
the human capacity for pulling the ladder up behind oneself, and the
time-tested tools—icy showers, endless lines to stand in, the excessive use
of proper nouns, loudspeakers blaring a constant stream of inanities,
etc.—of broad social compliance. "One People! One Homeland! One
Director!" The words made him wince, but a certain amount of stage-
managed demagoguery went with the territory. Nothing really new, in
other words, all of it warranted under the terms of the present age. But
sometimes, such as now, on this icy Iowa morning, the first arctic front
of the season bearing down on them like a runaway train of ass-
hammering cold, Guilder had a hard time maintaining his enthusiasm.

His expansive suite of offices, which also functioned as his living
quarters, had served, at various times in its two-hundred-year history, as
the office of the Iowa territorial governor, the headquarters of the state
historical museum, and a storage room. Its last old-world occupant had
been the provost of Midwest State University, a man named August Frye
(so read the man's stationery), who, from its generous windows, had no
doubt passed many happy hours soaking in the heartwarming sight of
cheerful corn-fed undergraduates flirting like maniacs as they strolled
their way to class upon its well-kept Iowa lawns. On the day Guilder had

assumed residency, he'd been surprised to discover that Provost August Frye had decorated the place with a nautical theme: ships in bottles, maps with serpents, overwrought oil paintings of lighthouses and oceanscapes, an anchor. A strikingly incongruous choice, given that Midwest State (go Bearcats!) was hard aground in about the most land-locked place on earth. After nearly a hundred years, what Guilder wouldn't have given for a smidgen of scenery.

Hence the major problem with immortality, apart from the peculiar diet: everything began to bore you.

At such moments, the only thing that cheered him was taking stock of his accomplishments. Which were not inconsiderable; they had con-structed a city literally from nothing. What excitement he'd felt in the early days. The ceaseless ring of hammers. The trucks returning from their journeys across an unmanned continent, bursting with the aban-doned treasures of the old world. The hundreds of tactical decisions made daily, and the buzzing energy of the staff—men handpicked from among the survivors for their expertise. They had, in short, built a veri-table brain trust from the human leavings of catastrophe. Chemists. En-gineers. City planners. Ag scientists. Even an astronomer (who had come in surprisingly handy) and an art historian, who had advised Guilder (who, to be perfectly honest, couldn't tell Monet's water lilies from dogs playing poker) on the proper preservation and display of a major haul of masterworks from the Art Institute of Chicago, which now decorated the walls of the Dome, including Guilder's office. What fun they'd had! Granted, there was a certain frat-house mentality to the way they'd con-ducted themselves, minus the sexual shenanigans, of course. (The virus pretty much gutted that part of your brain like a trout; most of the staff couldn't even bring themselves to look at a woman without making a face.) But in the main, decorum and professionalism had ruled the day.

Such happy memories. And now: Sergio. Now: Pipe bombs. Now: the bloody mist.

Guilder's train of thought was broken by a rap on the door. He heaved a weary sigh. Another day of forms to fill out, duties to be parceled, edicts to be issued from on high. Taking a seat behind his desk, an ex-panse of eighteenth-century polished mahogany the approximate di-mensions of a ping-pong table, as rightly befit his station as Beloved Director of the Homeland, Guilder braced himself for another morn-ing's ceaseless appetite for his opinions—a thought that gave rise almost instantly to the first inklings of an appetite of a more physical and press-ing nature, a burble of acid-tasting emptiness that ascended from his gut. So soon? Was it that time of the month already? The only thing worse

than the burps were the farts that came after, room-clearing jets of on-
iony gas that even the farter himself could not enjoy.

"Come."

As the door swung open, Guilder drew up his necktie and hastened to
make himself look occupied, shifting documents around the desktop
with manufactured intensity. He selected one arbitrarily—it turned out
to be a report on repairs at the sewage treatment plant, a page literally
about shit—and pretended to study it for a full thirty seconds before lifting his eyes with directorial fatigue toward the dark-suited figure waiting
in the doorway, holding a clipboard chunky with paper.

"Got a second?"

Guilder's chief of staff, whose name was Fred Wilkes, advanced into
the room. Like all residents of the Hilltop, his eyes had the bloodshot
look of a chronic pot smoker's. He also possessed the glossily sleek appearance of a twenty-five-year-old—a far cry from the wiry septuage-
narian of Guilder's first acquaintance. Wilkes had been the first to come
aboard; Guilder had discovered the man hiding out in one of the college's dormitories in the first days after the attack. He was holding—
hugging, really—the body of his late wife, whose hefty proportions had
not been improved by three days of gaseous decomposition in the Iowa
heat. As Wilkes related, the pair had fled the refugee-processing center
on foot when the buses had failed to arrive; they'd made it all of three
sweltering miles before his wife had clutched her chest, rolled her eyes
heavenward, and toppled over, dead of a heart attack. Unable to leave
her behind, Wilkes had scavenged a wheelbarrow and carted her mountainous form to the college, where he'd taken refuge with only her corpse,
and his memories of a lifetime shared, for company. Despite the horren-
dous smell (which Wilkes either didn't notice or much care about), the
two of them made for a genuinely heartrending sight that might have
moved Guilder to tears if he were a certain kind of man, which he might
have once been but was no longer.

"Listen," Guilder had said, kneeling before the grief-sticken man, "I'd
like to make you a proposition."

And so it had begun. It was that very day, that very hour in fact, even
as he'd watched Wilkes take his first disgusted sip, that Guilder had
heard the Voice. As far as he could tell, he was still the only one; none of
the other staffers gave so much as a hint of experiencing Zero's mental
presence. And as for the woman, who knew what was going on inside her
head?

Now, the width of one and a half human lifetimes later, his grand
design coming to fruition and the last of humanity having been gathered

at his feet (the Kerrville thing, like the Sergio thing, being a small but significant irritant, a pea under the mattress of the Plan), here was Wilkes with his omnipresent clipboard and a facial expression, evidently, of not-good news.

"I just thought you should know the gathering party's back. What's, ah, left of it."

With this disconcerting introduction, Wilkes withdrew the top sheet of paper from his clipboard and placed it on Guilder's desk and backed away, as if he were happy to be rid of the thing.

Guilder scanned it quickly. "What the hell, Fred."

"I guess you could say things didn't go exactly as planned."

"*Nobody*? Not one of them? What is *wrong* with these people?"

Wilkes gestured toward the paper. "The flow of oil has been at least temporarily disrupted. That's a plus. It opens a lot of doors."

But Guilder was beyond consolation. First Kearney, now this. There had been a time when scooping up survivors had proved a relatively clear-cut undertaking. The woman appeared; the gates swung open, the wheel of the vault began to turn, the drawbridge descended over the moat; the woman did her stuff, like a lion tamer at the circus; and the next thing you knew, the trucks were galloping back to Iowa, packed with human cargo. The Kentucky caves. That island in Lake Michigan. The abandoned missile silos in North Dakota. More recently, the California raid had been a bona-fide bonanza, fifty-six survivors taken, most of whom had marched like lambs into the truck once the power was cut and the terms were set. (Get in or you're meat.) The usual attrition rate— some died en route, others failed to adapt to their new circumstances— but a solid haul nonetheless.

Since then, it had been one out-of-control bloodbath after another, starting with Roswell.

"Apparently there wasn't much of a negotiation phase. The convoy was pretty heavily armed."

"I don't care if they had a nuclear missile. We knew that going in. These are *Texans*."

"In a manner of speaking, that's true."

"We're about to go on-line here, and this is what you tell me? We need bodies, Fred. Living, breathing bodies. Can't she control these things anymore?"

"We could go in the old-fashioned way. I said so from the start. We'd take some casualties, but if we keep hitting their oil supply, sooner or later their defenses will weaken."

"We *collect* people, Fred. We don't lose them. Have I failed to make myself clear? Can you not do basic math? People are the *point.*"

Wilkes shrugged defensively. "You want to talk to her?"

Guilder rubbed his eyes. He supposed he'd have to make the gesture, but talking to Lila was like playing handball by yourself: the ball came right back no matter how hard you slapped it. One of the most significant aggravations of the job was dealing with the woman's peculiar fantasies, a wall of delusion that Guilder could penetrate only by the roughest sort of insistence. Of all the experts he'd harvested through the years, why hadn't he thought to get a shrink? Keeping her in babies made her calm; the woman's special talent was an indispensable commodity that needed to be managed with care. But in the throes of motherhood she was virtually unreachable, and Guilder worried about further damaging her fragile psyche.

Because that was the thing about Lila. Of everyone who had tasted the blood, only she was endowed with the ability to control the virals.

More than control: in Lila's presence, they became like pets, docile and even affectionate. The feeling was a two-way street; put the woman within two hundred yards of the feedlot, and she turned into a purring cat with a litter of kittens. The effect was nothing Guilder had been able to replicate on his own, though Lord knows he'd tried. Back in the early days, he'd been downright obsessed. Time after time he'd donned the pads and gone into the feedlot, thinking that if he could only find the right mental trick or ingratiating body language or soothing tone of voice they'd fall at his knees the way they did with her, like dogs waiting for their ears to be scratched. But this never happened. They'd tolerate his presence for a whopping three seconds before one of them tossed him in the air—he didn't register as food, more like a man-sized toy—and the next thing Guilder knew he'd be flying around the place until somebody hit the lights to get him out.

He'd long since stopped trying, of course. The sight of Horace Guilder, Director of the Homeland, being batted around like a beach ball wasn't exactly the kind of confidence-inspiring image he wanted to broadcast. Nor could anybody on the medical staff explain to his satisfaction just what it was that made Lila different. Her thymus cycled faster, needing the blood every seven days, and her eyes looked different, displaying none of the retinal stain that marked the senior staffers'. But her sensitivity to light was just as pronounced, and as far as Suresh could tell, the virus in her blood was the same as theirs. In the end, the man had thrown up his hands and attributed her abilities to the less than subtle fact that Lila was a woman—the only woman in the fold, which was how Guilder wanted it.

Maybe that's all there is to it, Suresh had said. *Maybe they just think she's their mother.*

Guilder became aware that Wilkes was looking at him. What had they been talking about? Lila? No, Texas. But Wilkes had told him there was something else.

"Which brings me to, um, the second thing." And that was when Wilkes told Guilder about the bombing in the market.

Fuck! Fuck, fuck, fuck!

"I know, I know," Wilkes said, shaking his head in his Wilkesian way. "Not the best turn of events."

"He's one man. One!"

Guilder's face, his whole body, tingled with righteous anger. Another volleying burp arose. He wanted vengeance. He wanted things to settle the hell down. He wanted this Sergio, whoever he was, with his head on a goddamn *pike.*

"We've got people working on it. HR is asking around, and we've offered double rations to anybody who comes forward with a solid lead. Not everyone down the hill is so enamored."

"And somebody please tell me how he's moving through the flatland like it's a goddamn expressway? Do we not have patrols? Do we not have checkpoints? Can somebody please shed some light on this little detail?"

"We have a theory about that. The evidence points to an organization that's classically cellular. Clusters of just a few individuals operating within a loose operational framework."

"I am perfectly aware what a terrorist cell is, Fred."

His chief of staff made a flustered gesture with his hands. "I'm simply saying that looking for one man may not be the answer. That it's the *idea* of Sergio, not Sergio per se, that we're up against. If you follow me."

Guilder did, and it wasn't a cheering thought. He'd been down this road before, first in Iraq and Afghanistan and then Saudi, after the coup. You lopped off the head but the body didn't die; it simply grew another head. The only useful strategy in these situations was psychological. Killing the body was never enough. You had to kill the spirit.

"How many do we have in custody?"

Thus more paper. Guilder read the full report. According to eyewitnesses, the market bomber had been a female agricultural worker in her thirties. There'd never been any problems with her; by all accounts she was as meek as a lamb, a quality that to a disconcerting extent matched the profiles of other suicide bombers. She had no living family except for a sister; her husband and son had died six years ago, in an outbreak of salmonella. She'd apparently gotten past the checkpoints disguised in a col's uniform (the original wearer's body had been found stuffed into a dumpster, her throat slashed, one arm mysteriously severed at the elbow), though where she'd procured the explosives was unknown. None had been reported missing from the armory or the construction depot, but a full inventory had yet to be completed. Nine of her lodgemates plus her sister's family, including two young children, had been detained for questioning.

"Nobody seems to know anything," Wilkes said with a toss of his hand. He'd taken a seat on the far side of the desk while Guilder read. "Apart from the sister, it's like they barely knew her. We can take it up a notch, but I don't think it's going to produce much in the way of useful intelligence. These people would have caved already."

Guilder placed the file aside, among the many others. The burps, which continued unabated, had painted the walls of his mouth with a foul taste of animal decay, not unlike the stench of the decomposing Mrs. Wilkes. A fact that, if the barely concealed look of olfactory distaste on his chief of staff's smoothly youthful face gave any indication, had not failed to escape the man's attention.

"No need," Guilder said.

Wilkes frowned doubtfully. "You want us to release them? I don't think that's wise. At least let's make them cool their heels a couple more days. Rattle a few chains, see where it takes us."

"You said yourself that if they knew anything, they would have already talked."

Guilder paused, aware that he was about to cross a line. The thirteen flatlanders sitting in the detention center were, after all, people, human beings, probably not guilty of anything. More to the point, they were tangible physical assets in an economy of scarcity. But given the frustrating intractability of the Sergio situation, and the debacle in Texas, and the time-sensitive nature of Guilder's grand designs, which were at long last coming to complex fruition; and in the grip of his own rapidly burgeoning physical need, a titanic biological imperative that, as he regarded Wilkes from across the burnished prairie of his oversized desk, was blossoming inside him like a flower in a time-lapse video, he didn't think for too long. He came to the line, gave it one quick look, and stepped over.

"It seems to me," said Director Horace Guilder, "the time has come to sell this thing."

*　　*　　*

Guilder waited a few minutes after Wilkes was gone to stage his departure. As he had reminded himself many times, a great deal of his authority boiled down to a sense of dignity in his public movements, and it was better for people not to witness him in such an agitated state. He took the ring of keys from his desk and stepped out. Strange, how the hunger had come on so quickly. Usually it crept up on him over a period of days, not minutes. From the base of the cupola, a winding flight of stairs descended to the ground floor, its downward passage flanked by oil portraits of various dukes and generals and barons and princes of the realm, a parade of disapproving, heavy-jawed faces in period costume. (At least he hadn't resorted to having his picture painted—though, come to think of it, why not?) He peered over the rail. Fifty feet below were the tiny figures of the uniformed security detail; members of the leadership, in their dark suits and ties, scuttling briskly to and fro with their officious briefcases and clipboards; even a couple of attendants, flowing diaphanously across the polished stone floor in their nunnish costumes, like a pair of paper boats. It was Wilkes he was looking for, and there he was: by the massive front door with its inlaid carvings of assorted prairie kitsch (a fist gripping wheat, a plow merrily tilling the bountiful Iowa topsoil), his loyal chief of staff had paused to confer with two of the leadership, Ministers Hoppel and Chee. Guilder supposed that Wilkes was already setting the day's orders in motion, bringing them up to speed, but this assumption was belied when Hoppel reared back his head, clapped his hands together, and barked a laugh that ricocheted through the marbled space like a bullet in a submarine. Guilder wondered what the fuck was so funny.

He turned from the rail and made his way to the second, more conventional, and highly unobservable stairway that was his alone to use. By now his insides were roaring. It was all he could do not to take the stairs three at a time, which in his present condition would have probably resulted in some bone-breaking pratfall that would heal within hours but still hurt like hell. Bearing himself like a crystal chalice that might at any moment spill its contents to the floor, Guilder descended one cautious step at a time. The salivation had started, a veritable waterfall he had to suck back between his teeth. Vampire bibs, he thought wryly; now, that would be a moneymaker.

The basement at last, with its heavy, vaultlike door. Guilder withdrew the keys from the pocket of his suit coat. Hands trembling with anticipation, he keyed the door, turned the heavy wheel, and shouldered it aside.

By the time he was halfway down the hall he'd stripped to the waist and was kicking off his shoes. He was riding this thing full-bore now, a surfer skimming down a wave. Door after door sailed past. Guilder could hear the muffled cries of the damned coming from within, a sound that had long since ceased to arouse even a grain of pity within him, if it ever had. He blasted past the warning signs—ETHER PRESENT, NO OPEN FLAME—hit the freezer room at a dead sprint, turned the final corner, and narrowly avoided collision with a lab-coated technician. "Director Guilder!" he gasped. "We didn't know . . . !" But these words were cut short as Guilder, with more violence than was called for, applied the full swinging weight of his left forearm to the side of the man's head, sending him crashing into the wall.

It was blood he wanted, and not just any blood. There was blood and there was *blood.*

He came to the final door, skidding to a halt. With fumbling hands he undid his trousers and tossed them away, then keyed the door and opened it.

"Hello, Lawrence."

38

In the morning, Jackie was gone.

Sara awoke to find the woman's cot empty. Lit with panic, she tore through the lodge, cursing herself for sleeping so deeply. The old woman who bunked in the second row? Had anyone seen her? But no one had, or so they said. At morning roll, Sara detected only the smallest hitch of silence in the space where Jackie's number should have been. Everyone was looking down. Just like that, the waters had closed over her friend. It was as if she'd never existed at all.

She moved through the day in a fog, her mind teetering on the razor-thin edge between desperate hope and outright despair. Probably there was nothing to be done. People disappeared; that was the way of things. And yet Sara could not talk herself out of the idea that if the woman was still in the hospital, if she hadn't been taken to the feedlot yet, there might be a chance. But how could Jackie have been taken right from under Sara's nose like that? Wouldn't she have heard something? Wouldn't the woman have protested? It simply didn't add up.

That was when Sara figured it out. She hadn't heard anything, because there had been nothing to hear. *Not like this. Not for me.* Jackie had left the lodge of her own accord.

She'd done it to protect Sara.

By midafternoon she knew she had to do something. Her guilt was excruciating. She never should have tried to get Jackie out of the plant, never confronted Sod the way she had. She'd all but painted a target on the woman's back. The minutes were ticking away. The virals in the feedlot ate just after dusk; Sara had seen the trucks. Livestock carriers crammed with lowing cows, but also the windowless vans that were used to move prisoners from the detention center. One was always parked at the rear of the hospital, its meaning plain to anyone who cared to consider it.

The cols supervising the grinding teams were Vale and Whistler. Vale she thought she could have worked with, but with Whistler watching, Sara didn't see how. There was only one solution she could think of. She topped off her bushel basket, lifted it from the ground, took three steps toward the grinder, and stopped.

"Oh," Sara cried. She let the basket drop, clutching her stomach. "Oh. Oh."

She melted, moaning, to her knees. For a moment it seemed that amid the noise of the grinders her demonstration had gone unnoticed. She amplified her cries, curling her legs to her chest, hugging her midriff.

"Sara, what is it?" One of the other women—Constance Chou—was crouching over her.

"It hurts! It hurts!"

"Get up or they'll see you!"

Another voice broke through: Vale's. "What's going on here?"

Constance backed away. "I don't know, sir. She just . . . collapsed."

"Fisher? What's wrong with you?"

Sara didn't answer, just kept up with the moaning, rocking at the waist and throwing in a few spastic kicks for good measure. A circle of onlookers had formed around her. "Appendix," she said.

"What did you say?"

She clenched her face with manufactured pain. "I think . . . it's my . . . appendix."

Whistler charged through the crowd, pushing onlookers aside with her baton. "What's her problem?"

Vale was scratching his head. "She says something's wrong with her pendix."

"What are you people looking at?" Whistler barked. "Get back to work." Then, to Vale: "What do you want to do with her?"

"Fisher, can you walk?"

"Please," she gasped. "I need a doctor."

"She says she needs a doctor," Vale reported.

"Yeah, I heard that, Vale." The woman huffed a sigh. "All right, let's get her out of here."

They helped her to a pickup parked behind the plant and laid her in the back. Sara kept up the rocking and moaning. A brief negotiation ensued: should one of them take her or should they call for a driver?

"Fuck it, I'll take her," Whistler said. "Knowing you, you'll dither all day."

The trip to the hospital took ten minutes; Sara used them to formulate a plan. All she'd been thinking about was getting to the hospital, to find Jackie before the van took her away; she hadn't considered the next step. It seemed to her now that she held only two good cards. First, she wasn't really sick; once she experienced a miraculous recovery, it didn't seem likely that they'd ship a perfectly able-bodied woman off to the feedlot. Second, she was a nurse. Sara wasn't sure how she'd put this fact to use— she'd have to improvise—but she might be able to use her medical knowledge to convince the person in charge that Jackie wasn't as ill as she appeared.

Or maybe nothing she did would matter. Maybe once she passed through the hospital doors, she'd never come out. This prospect, as she weighed it, did not appear entirely bad, thus giving her a third card to play: the card of not caring anymore if she lived or died.

Whistler pulled up to the hospital entrance, strode back to the cargo bed, and drew down the tailgate.

"Out with you. Let's go."

"I don't think I can walk."

"Well, you'll have to try, because I'm not carrying you."

Sara sat up. The sun had peeked from behind the clouds, sharpening the scene with its cold brightness. The hospital was a three-story brick building, part of a cluster of low, workaday structures at the southern edge of the flatland. At a distance of twenty yards stood one of three major HR substations. A dozen cols guarded the entrance, which was flanked by concrete barricades.

"Am I talking to myself here?"

She was; Sara was barely listening. She was focused on the car, a small sedan of the type the cols used to move among the lodges. It was headed toward them at high speed, dragging a boiling plume of dust. Sara clambered down from the bed. Simultaneously, she sensed a figure rushing at her from behind. The car was bearing down, its speed unabated. There was something odd about it, and not just the wild velocity of its approach. The windows were blacked out, obscuring the driver; something was written on the hood, the letters scrawled in streaks of white paint.

SERGIO LIVES

As the vehicle sailed toward the barricades, somebody smashed her from behind. In the next instant she was flat on the ground, her body smothered, as the truck exploded with a blast of sound and a wave of superheated pressure she didn't believe could actually exist in the world. The air was sucked from her lungs. Things were falling. Things were sailing through the air and impacting like meteors around her, flaming, heavy things. There was a screeching sound of metal, a rain of tinkling glass. The world was noise and heat and the weight of a body on top of her, and then a sudden silence and a wash of warm breath close to her ear and a voice saying:

"Come with me now. Do exactly as I say."

Sara was on her feet. A woman, no one she knew, was pulling her by the hand against the inertia of her wonderment. Something had happened to her hearing, bathing the scene around her in a milky unreality. The substation was a smoking crater. The pickup was gone; it lay on its side where the entrance to the hospital was, or had been. Something wet was on Sara's hands and face. Blood. She was covered in it. And sticky things, biological things, and a fine, jeweled dust she realized was composed of tiny bits of glass. How amazing, she thought, how very amazing everything was, especially what had happened to Whistler. It was striking, what a body looked like when it wasn't one thing anymore but had been dispersed in recognizably human pieces over a wide area. Who would have guessed that when a body blew apart, as had evidently happened, it actually did that: it blew apart.

She broke away, first her vision and then the rest of her; the woman was running and so was she, running and also being dragged, the energy of her rescuer—for Sara understood that this woman had protected her from the blast—passing into her body through their gripping hands. Behind them the silence had given way to a chorus of screams and shouts, a weirdly musical sound, and the woman skidded to a halt behind a building that somehow still stood (hadn't all the buildings in the world just blown up?) and dropped on the ground. In her hand was a kind of hook, and with this hook she drew aside the manhole cover.

"Get in."

Sara did. She got in. She lowered herself into the hole where a ladder waited. Something smelled bad. Something smelled like shit because it was. As Sara's feet touched the bottom, her sneakers filling with the horrible water, the woman reached over her head and resealed the manhole with a clank, plunging Sara into an absolute darkness. Only then did it occur to her in fullest measure that she had been in an explosion of many deaths and much destruction and that in its immediate aftermath, an interval of probably less than a minute, she had given herself completely to a woman she did not know, and that this woman had whisked her into a kind of nonexistence: that Sara had, in effect, disappeared.

"Wait."

The glow of a small bluish flame igniting: the woman was holding a lighter, touching it to the head of a torch. A blaze leapt forth, illuminating her face. Somewhere in her twenties, with a long neck and small, dark eyes, full of intensity. There was something familiar about her, but Sara couldn't fix her mind on it.

"No more talking. Can you run?"

Sara nodded yes.

"Come on."

The woman began to move at a trot down the sewer pipe, Sara following. This went on for some time. At each of many intersections, the woman decisively chose a direction. Sara had begun to take stock of her injuries. The explosion had not occurred without effect. There was a variety to her pains, some of them quite sharp, others more like a generally dispersed thudding. Yet none was so severe as to prevent her from keeping up with the woman. After more time had passed, Sara realized that the distance they had traveled must have surely placed them beyond the wired boundaries of the Homeland. They were escaping! They were free! A ring of light appeared before them: an exit. Beyond it lay the world— a dangerous world, a lethal world where virals roamed unchecked, but even so it loomed before her like a golden promise, and she stepped into the light.

"Sorry about this."

The woman was behind her. She had reached one hand around Sara's waist, drawing her into stasis; the other hand, holding a cloth, rose to Sara's face. What in the world? But before Sara could utter a single sound of protest, the cloth was covering her mouth and nose, flooding her senses with an awful choking chemical smell, and a million tiny stars went off inside her head; and that was the end of that.

39

Lila Kyle. Her name was Lila Kyle.

Though, of course, she knew that the face in the mirror had other names. The Queen of Crazy. Her Loony Majesty. Her Royally Unhinged Highness. Oh, yes, Lila had heard them all. You'd have to get up pretty early in the morning to pass one over on Lila Kyle. Sticks and stones, she always said (her father said), sticks and stones, but what galled her, really, was the whispering. People were always whispering! As if they were the adults and she the child, as if she were a bomb that might go off at any second. How strange! Strange and not a little disrespectful, because in the first instance, she wasn't crazy, they were one hundred percent wrong about that; and in the second, even if she were, even if, for the sake of argument, she liked to strip naked in the moonlight and howl like a dog (poor Roscoe), what concern of it was theirs? How crazy she was or was not? (Though she had to confess, there were days, certain difficult days when her thoughts would not cooperate, like an armful of autumn leaves she was attempting to shove into a bag.) It wasn't *nice*. It was beyond the *pale*. To speak behind a person's back, to make such vile insinuations—it was outside the bounds of common decency. What had she ever done to deserve such treatment? She kept to herself, she never asked for any-thing, she was quiet as a mouse; she was wholly content to bide her time in her room with her lovely little things, her bottles and combs and brushes and her dressing table, where now she sat—it seemed she had been sitting there for some time—brushing out her hair.

Her hair. As she shifted her attention to the face in the mirror, a wave of warm recognition flowed through her. The sight always seemed to take her by surprise: the rosy, pore-free skin, the dewy glistening of her eyes, the humid plumpness of her cheeks, the delicate proportionality of her features. She looked . . . amazing! And most amazing of all was her hair. How lustrous it was, how abundant to the touch, how rich with its molassesy thickness. Not molasses: chocolate. An excellent dark choco-late from someplace wonderful and special, Switzerland, maybe, or one of those other countries, like the candies her father had always kept in his desk; and if she was good, *very* good, or sometimes for no reason at all, simply because he loved her and wanted her to know it, he would summon her to the sanctified quarters of his masculine-smelling study, where he wrote his important papers and read his inscrutable books and conducted his generally mysterious fatherly business, to bestow upon her the symbol of this love. *Only one now,* he would say to her, the oneness amplifying the specialness because it implied a future in which further visits to the study would occur. The golden box, the lifting lid, the moment of suspense: her little hand hovered over the rich bounty of its contents like a diver poised at the edge of a pool, calculating the perfect angle for her plunge. There were the chocolate ones, and the ones with nuts, and the ones with the cherry syrup (the only ones she didn't like; she'd spit them out into a Kleenex). But best of all were the ones with nothing, the pure chocolate nuggets. That was what she craved. The singular treasure of milky melting sweetness that she was attempting to divine from among its fellows. This one? This one?

"Yolanda!"

Silence.

"Yolanda!"

In a flurry of skirts and veils and windy fabric, the woman came bustling into the room. Really now, Lila thought, what a ridiculous getup *that* was. How many times had Lila instructed her to dress more practically?

"Yolanda, where have you been? I've been calling and calling."

The woman was looking at Lila as if she'd lost her mind. Had they gotten to her, too? "Yolanda, ma'am?"

"Who else would I call?" Lila sighed exorbitantly. The woman could be so dense. Though her English was not the best. "I would like . . . something. If you please. *Por favor.*"

"Yes, ma'am. Of course. Would you like me to read to you?"

"Read? No." Though the thought was suddenly appealing; a little Beatrix Potter might be the very thing to soothe her nerves. Peter Rabbit in his little blue jacket. Squirrel Nutkin and his brother Twinkleberry. The two of them could get into such mischief! Then she remembered.

"Chocolate. Do we have any chocolate?"

The woman still appeared totally out of it. Maybe she'd gotten into the liquor. "Chocolate, ma'am?"

"Leftover Halloween candy, maybe? I'm sure we have some somewhere. Anything will do. Hershey's Kisses. Almond Joy. A Kit Kat. Whatever is fine."

"Um . . ."

"*Sí?* A little choc-o-LAH-tay? Check the cabinet over the sink."

"I'm sorry, I don't know what you're asking for."

Now, this was annoying. The woman was pretending not to know what chocolate was!

"I fail to see what the problem is, Yolanda. I have to say, your attitude has begun to trouble me. A great deal, in fact."

"Please don't be angry. If I knew what it was, I'd be glad to get it for you. Maybe Jenny knows."

"That's my point, you see. That is precisely what I'm saying." Lila sighed heavily. A pity, but there was really nothing left to be done. Better to rip the band-aid off than drag things out.

"I'm afraid, Yolanda, I'm going to have to let you go."

"Go?"

"Go, yes. *No más.* We no longer require your services, I'm afraid."

The woman's eyes seemed practically to pop from her head. "You can't!"

"I'm truly sorry. I wish things had worked out. But under the circumstances, you really leave me with no alternative."

The woman hurled herself at Lila's knees. "Please! I'll do anything!"

"Yolanda, get ahold of yourself."

"I'm begging you," the woman blubbered into her skirt. "You know what they'll do. I'll work harder, I swear!"

Lila had expected her to take it badly, but this undignified display was wholly unexpected. It was positively embarrassing. The urge to offer some consoling touch was strong, but Lila resisted it, lest this draw things out, leaving her hands hovering awkwardly in the air. Maybe she should have waited until David got home. He was always better at this sort of thing.

"We'll provide you with a reference, of course. And two weeks' pay. You really shouldn't take it so hard."

"It's a death sentence!" She hugged Lila's knees as if she were clinging to a life raft. "They'll send me to the basement!"

"I hardly think this qualifies as a death sentence. You're completely overreacting."

But the woman was beyond appeals to reason. Unable to form words through the storm of her uncontrollable sobs, she had given up her pleading, soaking Lila's skirt with mucusy tears. The only thing on Lila's mind was extricating herself from the situation as quickly as possible. She hated things like this, she *hated* them.

"What's going on in here?"

Lila lifted her gaze toward the figure standing in the door, at once breathing a sigh of relief. "David. Thank God. We seem to have a bit of a situation here. Yolanda, well, she's a little bit upset. I've decided to let her go."

"Christ, another one? What's the matter with you?"

Now, wasn't this typical. Wasn't this typical David. "That's fine for you to say, gone all day, leaving me stuck in the house. I'd think you'd back me up."

"Please, don't do this!" Yolanda wailed.

Lila made a get-this-woman-off-me gesture with her hands. "A little help here?"

Which did not prove quite as easy as it might have. As David (not David) bent to extricate the sobbing Yolanda (not Yolanda) from Lila's knees, the woman redoubled her hold and commenced, unbelievably, to scream. What a scene she was making! For goodness sake, you'd think being fired from a housekeeping job really *was* a death sentence from the way she was acting. With a hard yank at the waist, David pulled her free and hoisted her bodily into the air. She kicked and screamed in his arms, flailing like a crazy person. It was only through his superior strength that he managed to contain her. One thing about David: he'd kept himself in shape.

"I'm sorry, Yolanda!" Lila called as he whisked her away. "I'll mail you a check!"

The door slammed behind them. Lila released a breath she realized she'd been holding in her chest. Well, wasn't that something. Wasn't that just about the most uncomfortable business she'd ever had to endure. She felt completely rattled, and not a little guilty besides. Yolanda had been with them for years, and for everything to end so badly. It left a sour taste in Lila's mouth. Though admittedly, Yolanda had never been the best housekeeper, and recently she'd really let things go. Probably some personal difficulties. Lila had never even been to the woman's house, though; she knew nothing of her life. How curious was that? All these years, Yolanda coming and going, and it was as if Lila didn't know the woman at all.

"Well, she's gone. Congratulations."

Lila, who had resumed brushing her hair, examined David coolly through the mirror as he paused in the doorway to straighten his tie.

"And how is this my fault, exactly? You saw her. She was completely out of control."

"That's the third one this year. Good attendants don't grow on trees."

She took another long, luxurious stroke with the brush. "So call the service. It's really not such a big deal, you know."

David said nothing more, evidently content to let the matter drop.

He moved to the divan, drawing up the knees of his suit pants to sit down.

"We have to talk."

"Can't you see I'm busy? Don't they need you back at the hospital or something?"

"I don't work at a hospital. We've been over this a million times."

Had they? Sometimes her thoughts were autumn leaves, sometimes they were bees in a jar, little buzzing things going round and round.

"What happened in Texas, Lila?"

"Texas?"

He sighed grumpily. "The convoy. The Oil Road. I thought my instructions were clear."

"I haven't the foggiest idea what you're talking about. I've never been to Texas in my life." She paused her brushing, meeting David's eyes through the mirror. "Brad always hated Texas. Probably you don't want to hear anything about that, though."

Her words, she saw, had hit their mark. Bringing up Brad was her secret weapon. Though she knew she shouldn't, she took a perverse delight in the expression on David's face whenever she spoke the name—the deflated blankness of a man who knew he could never measure up.

"I don't ask much of you. What I'm beginning to wonder is if you can control these things anymore."

"Yes, well." Buzz, buzz.

"Are you listening to me? We can't have any more disasters like this. Not when we're this close."

"I don't see what you're so upset about. And to be perfectly honest, I don't care for the way you're speaking to me."

"Goddamnit, put that fucking brush *down*!"

But before she could do this, he snatched it from her hand and sent it pinwheeling across the room. He seized her by the hair, yanking her head back, and jammed his face so close to hers it wasn't even a face but a *thing,* a monstrous distorted sluglike thing, bathing her with its rotten bacterial breath.

"I've had it with your bullshit." Spittle splashed her cheeks, her eyes; it launched revoltingly from his mouth into hers. The edges of his teeth were etched with a dark substance, giving them a terrifying vividness. Blood. His teeth were lined in blood. "This *act* of yours. This stupid game."

"Please," she gasped, "you're hurting me!"

"Am I?" He twisted her hair, hard. A thousand pinpoint agonies screamed from her scalp.

"David," she pleaded, tears drowning her vision, "I'm begging you. Think about what you're doing."

The slug face roared in anger: "I'm not David! I'm Horace! My name is Horace Guilder!" Another twisting yank. "Say it!"

"I don't know, I don't know! You're confusing me!"

"Say it! Say my name!"

It was the pain that did it. In a cyclonic rush, her consciousness collapsed upon itself.

"You're Horace! Please, just stop!"

"Again! All of it!"

"Horace Guilder! You're Horace Guilder, Director of the Homeland!"

Guilder released her, stepping away. She was lying backward over her dressing table, shaking with sobs. If only she could go back. *Go back,* she thought, clamping her eyes tight to hide this horror of a man, this Horace Guilder, from her sight. *Lila, go back. Send yourself away again.* She shook with a nausea that rose from a place so deep it had no name, a sickness not of the body but of the soul, the metaphysical core of her fractured self, and then she was on her knees, vomiting, gasping and choking and spewing the vile blood that she herself had drunk that very morning.

"Okay, then," said Guilder, wiping his hands on his suit coat. "Just so that's clear."

Lila said nothing. So powerful was her longing to will herself away, she couldn't have formed words if she'd tried.

"Big days ahead, Lila. I need to know that you're on board. No more of your nonsense. And please, try not to fire any more attendants. These girls don't grow on trees."

With the back of her wrist, she wiped the rancid spittle from her chin. "You said that already."

"I'm sorry?"

"I said, you said that already." Her voice didn't even sound like her own. "About attendants not growing on trees."

"Did I?" He gave a little laugh. "So I did. Funny when you think about it. Something along those lines would sure come in handy, given the exigencies of the food chain and all. I'm sure your pal Lawrence would agree. I tell you, that man can *eat.*" He paused a moment, enjoying this thought, before his eyes hardened on her again. "Now clean yourself up. No offense, Lila, but you've got vomit in your hair."

40

"Sara? Can you hear me?"

A voice was floating toward her. A voice and also a face, one she knew but couldn't place. A face in a dream, which was what she was certain she was having: an unsettling dream in which she was running and all around her were bodies and parts of bodies, and everything on fire.

"She's still completely out of it," the voice said. It seemed to reach her across an impossible distance. A continent. An ocean. It seemed to come from the stars. "How much did you use?"

"Three drops. Well, maybe four."

"*Four*? Were you *trying* to kill her?"

"It was rushed, okay? You told me you wanted her out. So, she's out."

A heavy sigh. "Get me a bucket."

A bucket, thought Sara, what did the voices want with a bucket? What did a bucket have to do with anything? But no sooner had she thought this than a force of cold wetness crashed into her face, blasting her into consciousness. She was choking, drowning, waving her arms in panic, her nose and throat filling with the icy water.

"Easy now, Sara."

She sat upright, too fast; her brain sloshed in its casing, swirling her vision.

"Ooo," she moaned. "Ooo."

"The headache's bad, but it won't last. Just breathe."

She blinked the water from her eyes. Eustace?

It was. His top front teeth were gone, shorn at the root; his right eye was clouded with blindness. With a gnarled hand, he was holding out a metal cup.

"It's good to see you again, Sara. You've already met Nina, here. Say hello, Nina."

Standing behind him was the woman from the pipe. A rifle was slung across her chest, her arms folded casually over it. "Hello, Sara."

"Don't worry," Eustace said. "I know you have a lot of questions, and we'll get to them. Just drink."

Sara took the cup and gulped the water down. It was astonishingly cold and tasted vaguely metallic, as if she were licking a bar of iron.

"I thought you were—"

"Dead?" Eustace grinned, showing his ruined mouth. "In point of fact, everybody here is dead. Nina, remind me, how exactly did you die?"

"I believe it was pneumonia, sir. That or something very heavy fell on me. I can never remember how we did the paperwork."

The explosion, the dash through the pipe; it was all coming back now. Sara drained the cup and took a moment to inspect her surroundings. She appeared to be in some kind of bunker, although there were no windows; she sensed they were someplace underground. The room's only illumination came from a stand of flickering torches.

"Where are we?"

"Someplace the redeyes can't find us." He had a way of looking at her, angling his face to aim his good eye, that somehow added to the penetrating seriousness of his gaze. "Beyond that, I can't tell you. The important thing is you're safe here."

"Are you . . . Sergio?"

Another broken-toothed smile. "I'm flattered you would think so. But no. There is no Sergio. Not in the way you mean."

"But I thought—"

"And you're supposed to. The name is short for 'insurgency.' Nina, if I'm not mistaken, that was your idea, wasn't it?"

"I believe it was."

"People need a name. Something to focus on, a face to attach to the idea. That's our face. Sergio."

She looked at the woman, who was regarding her coolly, then back to Eustace.

"The explosion. That was you, wasn't it?"

Eustace nodded. "Our early reports indicate seventeen cols dead, including your friend Whistler, and two members of the staff who were visiting for an inspection. Not a bad day's work, I'd say. But that's not the real prize."

"It's not?"

"No. The real prize is you, Sara."

Eustace was looking at her intently now. Both of them were. Sara shivered in the cold. A shift had occurred, an inversion of the conversation's energies; he was trying to draw her out. Could they trust her? More to the point, could she trust them?

"This is the part where you ask me why."

Not wanting to concede too much, Sara nodded.

"As of this morning, there is no Sara Fisher. Sara Fisher, flatlander number 94801, was killed in a suicide bombing that took the lives of nineteen loyal security officers of the Beloved Homeland. The only recognizable part of Sara Fisher that remains intact is, conveniently, an arm with your tag on it. This was procured from a female col who, not twenty-four hours ago, was employing it to beat women and children in the dairy barns. We thought that under the circumstances it had better uses, though she seemed not to agree. Put up rather a struggle, Nina, did she not?"

"The woman was a fighter. I'll give her that."

He regarded Sara again. "I see in your expression that our methods come as a shock. They shouldn't."

It was all going by her too fast. "You kill people. Not just the cols. Innocent bystanders."

Eustace nodded evenly. His face was unreadable, almost emotionless. "That's true. Fewer than our glorious director would have you believe, but these things never come without cost."

She was appalled by his casual tone. "That doesn't justify it."

"Oh, I think it does. Let me ask you something. What do you think the redeyes will do after today's attack?"

Sara said nothing.

"All right, I'll tell you. Reprisals. They'll crack down hard. It won't be pretty."

Sara looked at Eustace, then Nina, then Eustace again. "But why would you want that?"

Eustace took a long breath. "I'll put it as simply as I know how. This is a war, Sara. Nothing more or less. And in this war, we're badly outnumbered. We've managed to infiltrate nearly every level of their operation, but the numbers are still on their side. We could never defeat them if we engaged them directly. Our theater of operations is psychological. Rattle the leadership. Draw them out. Every person who's hauled into detention is somebody's father, somebody's wife, somebody's son or daughter. For each one the redeyes send to the feedlot, two more will join us. It may seem brutal. But there it is." He paused, allowing his words to sink in. "Maybe this doesn't make sense to you. Soon enough it will, if my hunch about you is correct. In any event, the upshot of the afternoon's attack is that you no longer exist. And that makes you extremely valuable to us."

"Are you telling me you planned this?"

He shrugged in a manner that suggested the question was more complex than she'd intended. "There's planning and there's planning. A lot of what we do is a matter of timing and luck. But in your case, a great deal of thought went into your extraction. We've been watching you for some time, waiting for the right moment. It was Jackie who put the pieces together and gave the go-ahead. The episode at the biodiesel plant was staged, as was her sudden disappearance from the lodge last night. She knew you would come looking for her at the hospital. Frankly, I found the whole thing a little elaborate, and I had my doubts, but her confidence in you won the day. And I'm pleased to say she was right."

Sara's mind was swimming with disbelief. No, drowning. "Jackie is . . . one of you?"

Eustace nodded. "The woman was with us from the beginning, a senior operative. I can't tell you how many attacks she engineered. Her final mission was to bring you in."

Sara groped for words but found none. She simply couldn't square the woman Eustace was describing with the one she knew. Jackie? A member of the insurgency? For more than a year, the woman had barely been out of Sara's sight. They'd slept three feet from each other, worked side by side, eaten every meal in each other's company. They'd told each other everything. It made no sense; it wasn't possible. Then:

"What do you mean by 'final'?"

Something changed in the air. "I'm sorry," he said. "Jackie's dead."

His words were like a slap. "She can't be!"

"I'm afraid it's true. I know she meant a lot to you."

"They don't move people from the hospital until dark! I've seen the van! We have to get her!"

"Listen to me—"

"There's still time! We have to do something!" She darted her eyes to Nina, still standing impassively with her arms folded over her rifle, then back at Eustace. "Why aren't you doing anything?"

"Because it's too late, Sara." His expression softened. "Jackie was never in the hospital. That's what I'm telling you. Jackie was the driver of the car."

The sensation was of something breaking. That was how it felt. Something broke inside her. A final severing, the last thread binding her to the life she knew cut away. She was floating, floating away.

"She knew how sick she was. At most she would have lasted a few more months before they sent her to the feedlot." Eustace leaned closer. "It was how she wanted it. The crowning moment of a glorious career. She wouldn't have had it any other way."

"She's dead," Sara said, to no one.

"She did what she had to do. Jackie was a hero of the insurgency. And here you are, ready to pick up where she left off."

She couldn't seem to make herself cry. She wondered why this was, and then she knew: the last tears of her life had fallen; there were no more left inside her. How strange, not to be able to cry. To love someone the way she'd loved Jackie and find no mourning in her heart.

"Why me?"

"Because you hate them, Sara. You hate them and you're not afraid of them. I saw it in you that day in the truck. Do you remember?"

Sara nodded.

"There are two kinds of hatred. One gives you strength, the other takes it away. Yours is the first kind. I've always known that about you. Jackie knew it, too."

It was true; she hated them. She hated them for their leering eyes, their easy, laughing cruelty. She hated them for their watery gruel and icy showers; she hated the lies they made her shout; she hated their battering batons and the smiles on their smug faces. She hated them with her bones and blood, each cell of her body; her nerves fired with hatred, her lungs breathed hatred in and out, her heart pumped an elixir of pure hatred through her veins. She was alive because she hated them, and she hated them, most of all, for taking her daughter away.

She became aware that Eustace and Nina were waiting for her to speak. She understood that all they'd done and said had been arranged for this one purpose. Step by careful step, they had led her to the edge of an abyss. Once she stepped off, she'd be herself no more.

"What do you want me to do?"

VII

THE OUTLAW

As flies to wanton boys are we to th' gods;
They kill us for their sport.

—Shakespeare,
King Lear

41

The three of them were rescued the next afternoon by a DS patrol sent to look for them when the tankers failed to arrive in Kerrville. By this time, Peter, Michael, and Lore had left the hardbox and returned to the scene of the attack. The blast had gouged out a wide crater, fifty yards at least; heaps of twisted wreckage lay spread over the adjacent fields. Oily smoke poured forth from still-burning pools of petrol, smearing a sky already inhabited by a cloud of airborne scavengers. Bodies, charred to blackened crusts, mingled with the debris. If any of the grisly remains belonged to their attackers, it was impossible to tell. All that was left of the mysterious gleaming truck were a few sheets of galvanized metal, proving nothing.

Michael was a wreck. His physical injuries—a dislocated shoulder he had rammed back into place against the wall of the hardbox, a sprained ankle, a gash above his right ear that would need stitches—were the least of it. Eleven oilers and ten DS officers: men and women he had lived with, worked with. Michael had been the one in charge, somebody they trusted. Now they were gone.

"Why do you think he did it?" Peter asked. He was speaking of Ceps; during their long night in the hardbox, Michael had told Peter what he'd seen in the side-view mirror. The two of them were sitting on the ground at the edge of the river; Lore had moved upstream. Peter could see her squatting by the water, shoulders shaking with tears she didn't want them to witness.

"I guess he thought there was no other way." Michael squinted upward, watching the circling birds, though he seemed not to be really looking at anything. "You didn't know him like I did. There was a lot to the guy. No way he'd let anybody be taken up. I only wish I'd had the guts to do it myself."

Peter could read the pain and doubt in his friend's face: the disgrace of the survivor. He had known this emotion himself. It wasn't the kind of thing that ever left you. "It wasn't your fault, Michael. If the blame is anyone's, it's mine."

If his words were any comfort, Peter couldn't see it. "Who do you think those people were?" Michael said.

"I wish I knew."

"What the hell, Peter? A truckload of virals? Like they were pets or something? And that woman?"

"I don't get it, either."

"If it was the oil they wanted, they could have just taken it."

"I don't think that's what they were after."

"Yeah, well. Neither do I." A ripple of anger tensed his body. "One thing I do know. If I ever find those people, I'm going to make it hurt."

They spent the night with the search party in a hardbox east of San Antonio and arrived in Kerrville the next morning. Once inside the city, they were separated into different chains of command: Peter to Division Headquarters and Michael and Lore to the Office of the Domestic Authority, which oversaw all ex-murus assets, including the Freeport oil complex. Peter was given time to clean up before his debriefing. It was midday, the barracks mostly empty. He stood in the shower for a long time, watching the greasy soot swirl down at his feet. He knew himself well enough to understand that the full emotional impact of events hadn't quite sunk in. Whether this was a weakness or a strength he could never decide. He knew he was in a lot of trouble, but this concern seemed petty. Most of all, he felt sorry for Michael and Lore.

He dressed in his cleanest fatigues and made his way to Command, a former office complex adjacent to city hall. When he entered the conference room, he was startled to see a face he knew: Gunnar Apgar. But if he'd expected any word of reassurance from the man, it quickly became evident that none was forthcoming. As Peter snapped to attention, the colonel shot him a cold glance, then returned his attention to the papers resting on the long table before him—no doubt the report from the DS patrol.

But it was the second man of the three that gave Peter the most pause. To Apgar's right sat the imposing figure of Abram Fleet, general of the Army. Peter had laid eyes on the man only once in his life; it was tradition that the GA administer the oath of induction for all Expeditionary. There was nothing physically remarkable about the general's appearance—everything about him communicated an almost perfect physical averageness—yet he was who he was, a man whose presence altered a room, seeming to make the molecules of air vibrate at a different frequency. The third person seated at the table Peter didn't recognize, a civilian with a trim gray beard and hair like brushed wheat.

"Have a seat, Lieutenant," the general said. "Let's bring this to order.

You know Colonel Apgar. Mr. Chase is here as a representative of the president's staff. He will serve as her eyes and ears in this"—he hunted for the correct phrase—"unfortunate development."

For over two hours, they pounded Peter with questions. The general did most of the talking, followed by Chase; Apgar was largely silent, occasionally scribbling a note or asking for clarification. The tenor of the whole thing was disquietingly peremptory, as if they were trying to ensnare Peter in a contradiction. The underlying suggestion seemed to be that his story was a cover-up for some man-made catastrophe for which Peter, one of only three survivors, including the convoy's head oiler, bore the blame. Yet as the grilling continued, he began to sense that this suspicion was hollow, a front for some deeper concern. Again and again they returned to the matter of the woman. What was she wearing, what did she say, how did she look? Had there been anything odd about her appearance? To each of these repeated probings, Peter related the order of events as accurately as he could. She was wearing a cloak. She was remarkably beautiful. She said, *You're tired.* She said, *We know where you are. It's just a matter of time.* "We," the general repeated. We who? *I don't know.* You don't know because you don't remember? *No, I'm positive. She didn't say anything else.* Round and round, until even Peter began to doubt his own account. By the time it was over—his questioning came to a close with an abruptness in keeping with its hectoring tone—he felt not just emotionally but physically exhausted.

"A word of warning, Lieutenant," the general concluded. "You are not to discuss what happened on the Oil Road, or the contents of these proceedings, with anybody. That includes the surviving members of the convoy and the search party that brought you in. The determination of this body is that for reasons unknown, one of the tankers exploded, destroying the convoy as well as the San Marcos bridge. Is that clear?"

So, the truth. What had happened on the Oil Road was not the whole story; it was a piece of a larger puzzle the three men were trying to wedge into place. Peter stole a glance at Apgar, whose expression communicated only the manufactured neutrality of someone obeying the orders of his superior.

"Yes, General."

Fleet paused, then continued with a note of caution: "One last matter, Jaxon, and this is also to be treated with the utmost confidence. It seems that your friend Lucius Greer has escaped from detention."

For an instant Peter doubted that he'd heard the general correctly. "Sir?" He darted his eyes toward the others. "How did he—?"

"That's not known at this point. But it seems very likely he had help. The same night Greer went missing, one of the sisters left the orphanage and failed to return. A DS at the western pickets reported seeing two people leaving on horseback just after oh three hundred hours. A man— Greer, obviously—and a teenage girl, wearing the tunic of the Order."

"Are you talking about . . . Amy?"

"So it would seem." Fleet hunched over the table. "Greer is not my first concern. He's an escaped prisoner, and he'll be dealt with. But Amy is a different matter. Though I've always regarded your claims about her with considerable skepticism, she is nevertheless an important military asset." Fleet was looking at Peter with renewed intensity. "We know you visited both of them before departing for the refinery. If you have anything to say, I suggest you say it now."

It took Peter a moment to parse the question's meaning. "You think I know about this?"

"Do you, Lieutenant?"

Peter's mind wrestled with three ideas simultaneously. Amy had broken Lucius out of jail; the two of them had fled the city, their destination unknown; the general suspected him of being an accomplice. Any one of these would have been enough to knock him flat; together, they had the effect of focusing his thoughts on the immediate problem of defending himself. And, rising in the back of his mind, was a new question: what did Amy's disappearance have to do with the woman on the Oil Road? Surely the three men before him were wondering the same thing.

"Absolutely not, General. They didn't tell me anything."

"You're certain? I remind you, this goes into the record as your official statement."

"Yes, I'm certain. I'm as amazed as you are."

"And you have no idea where the two of them might have gone?"

"I wish I did."

Fleet regarded Peter for another moment, his face set. He looked toward Chase, who nodded.

"Very well, Jaxon. I'll take you at your word. Colonel Apgar has relayed your wishes to return to Fort Vorhees as soon as possible. I'm inclined to grant that request. Report to the duty officer at the motor pool, and he'll give you a space on the next transport."

Suddenly this was the last thing Peter wanted. The general's intentions were clear: Peter was being banished to guarantee his silence.

"If it's all right, sir, I'd like to return to the refinery."

"That's not an option, Lieutenant. You have your orders."

A thought occurred to him. "Permission to speak freely, sir."

Fleet sighed heavily. "My understanding is that's what you do, Lieutenant. You might as well get it over with."

"What about Martínez?"

"What about him?"

Apgar quickly met Peter's eye. *Tread carefully.*

"The man in the cave. 'He left us'—those were his words."

"I'm aware of that, Jaxon. I've read the report. What's your point?"

"He wasn't where he was supposed to be, either. Maybe Greer and Amy went searching for him." He looked at each of the three men in turn, then together. "Maybe they know where he is."

A frozen moment followed. Then, from Fleet: "It's an interesting idea, Lieutenant. Is there anything else?"

Just like that, the idea had been put aside. Or maybe not. Either way, Peter sensed that his words had hit the mark.

"No, sir."

The general's eyes darkened with warning. "As I said, you're not to discuss these matters with anyone. I don't think I have to tell you that any indiscretion would not be looked on kindly. You're free to go, Lieutenant."

"I'm sorry, Sister Peg is away for the day."

Sister Peg was never away for the day. The defensive posture of the woman in the doorway made it plain: Peter wasn't getting past her.

"Will you at least tell Caleb I was here?"

"Of course, Lieutenant." Her eyes darted past him in the manner of someone conscious of being observed. "Now, if you will excuse me . . ."

Peter returned to the barracks to pass a restless afternoon on his bunk, gazing at the ceiling. His transport would be leaving the next morning at 0600; he had no doubt that such a swift departure was by design. Men came and went, banging through the room in their heavy boots, yet their presence scarcely registered in his consciousness. Amy and Greer—where could they have gone? And why the two of them together? How could she have broken him out, and how had they made it past the sentries at the portal? He scoured his memory for anything either of them had done or said to indicate they were planning such an escape. The only thing he could come up with was the strange serenity that had radiated from the major—as if the walls that caged him were inconsequential, their substance illusory. How could that be so?

It was a mystery, like everything else about the last thirty days. The whole thing left the impression of figures drifting just beyond the barriers of a heavy fog, there and not there.

As the empty hours wore on, Peter's thoughts were borne back to his evening among the sisters: his time with Caleb, the boy's youthful energy and cleverness; the joy in Amy's face as she turned from the oven to see him standing there; the quiet moment they'd shared as he made his departure, their hands touching in space. The gesture had felt entirely natural, an involuntary reflex without hesitation or resistance; it seemed to have risen from both a deep well inside him and someplace far away, like the forces that propelled the waves he loved to look at, curling onto the beach. Of all the events of the last few days, their moment in the doorway stood most vividly in his recollection, and he closed his eyes, replaying it in his mind. The warmth of her cheek against his chest, and the bright force of her embrace; the way Amy had looked at their joined hands. *Do you remember when I kissed you?* He was still hearing these words in his mind as he fell asleep.

He awoke in darkness; his mouth tasted of dryness and dust. He was surprised he'd slept so long; he was surprised he'd slept at all. He was reaching to lift his canteen from the floor when he noticed a figure sitting on the adjacent bunk.

"Colonel?"

Apgar was facing him, his feet resting on the floor, hands braced on his knees. He took a long breath before speaking. Peter understood that the man's presence was what had awakened him.

"Listen, Jaxon, I didn't feel right about what happened in there today. So what I'm about to tell you is just between us, is that understood?"

Peter nodded.

"The woman you described was seen once before, years ago. I didn't see her myself, but others did. You know about the Massacre of the Field?"

Peter frowned. "You were there?"

"I was just a kid, sixteen. It's not something I talk about. None of us do. I lost my parents and my little sister. My mother and father were killed outright, but I never knew what happened to her. I suppose she was taken up. To this day, I still have nightmares about it. She was four years old."

Apgar had never told Peter anything so personal; he'd never told him anything personal at all. "I'm sorry, Colonel."

The pain of this memory, and the effort that went into telling it: these were plainly written on the man's face. "Well, it was a long time ago.

Condolences noted, but that's not why I'm here, and I'm sticking my neck out telling you any of this. If Fleet found out, he'd have my commission. Or send me to the stockade."

"You have my word, sir."

Apgar paused, then began again: "Twenty-eight souls were lost that day. Of those, sixteen, like my sister, were never accounted for. Everybody knows about the eclipse. What they don't know is that the virals were hiding in the hardboxes, like they knew about it in advance. Just before the attack began, a young DS officer in the tower reported seeing a large truck like the one you described waiting just beyond the tree line. You see where I'm going with this?"

"You're saying it was the same people."

Apgar nodded. "Two men saw the woman. The first was the DS officer I mentioned. The other was a field hand, the foreman of the North Ag complex. His wife and daughters were among those lost that day. His name was Curtis Vorhees."

Another surprise. "*General* Vorhees?"

"I expected you would find this interesting, especially given his friendship with Greer. Vorhees signed on right after the massacre. Half the leadership of the Second Exped came from that day. Nate Crukshank was the other DS in the tower. I'm sure you recognize the name. Did you know he was Vorhees's brother-in-law?"

Crukshank had been the commanding officer at Roswell. The sudden alignment of players felt like pieces snapping together. Peter recalled his days with Greer and Vorhees at the Colorado garrison—the two men's warm, easy friendship, and the stack of charcoal sketches Greer had shown him after the general had been killed. Vorhees had drawn the same image again and again, a woman and two little girls.

"What about the first DS? Who was he?"

"Well, that's a name everybody knows. Tifty Lamont."

This made no sense. "Tifty Lamont was DS?"

"Oh, Tifty was more than that. I owe that man my life many times over, and I'm not alone. After the massacre, he signed on with the Exped too, a scout sniper, maybe the best there ever was. Made captain before he busted out. Vorhees, Crukshank, and Tifty went way back. I don't know the story, but there was one."

Tifty Lamont as Expeditionary, an officer even. From everything Peter had heard about the man, this fact seemed completely incongruous. "So what happened to him?"

"Tifty?"

"The man's an outlaw."

A new look came into Apgar's face. "I don't know, Lieutenant. You'd have to ask him. That is, if you could find him. If, say, you knew somebody who knew somebody."

A silence caught and held. Apgar was looking at him expectantly. Then:

"How many people did you say were in this colony of yours in California?"

"Ninety-two."

"Ninety-two souls, gone without a trace. Pretty puzzling, if you ask me. Doesn't exactly fit the typical MO of a viral attack. Put the sixty-seven at Roswell into the mix and you've got close to two hundred people pretty much vanished into thin air. And now Amy takes off, just when this woman reappears and effectively severs our oil supply. I could see why the brass would be concerned. Even more so when you consider the fact that the only other living soul who's seen this woman is . . . what was the term you used?"

"An outlaw."

"Exactly. Persona non grata. A politically touchy situation, to say the least. On the one hand, you have the military, who want nothing to do with the man. On the other, you have the Civilian Authority, which can't, at least not *officially*. Are you with me here, Lieutenant?"

"I'm not much for politics, sir."

"That makes two of us. Bunch of people covering their asses. Which is why we find ourselves where we are. Just the sort of circumstances that would benefit from a third party. Somebody with a history of, let's say, personal initiative, who can think around the corners. I'm not alone in this opinion, either. Certain confidential discussions have been had in high places. Civilian, not military. Apparently, being your CO makes me an expert on your character. Yours and Donadio's."

Peter frowned. "What does Alicia have to do with this?"

"That I don't know. But I can tell you two things, and the math is up to you. The first is that nobody's heard from Fort Kearney in three months. The second is that Donadio had two sets of orders. I was only privy to the first, which came from Division and were just as I told you. The second came in a sealed pouch from Sanchez's office, eyes only."

"I don't understand. Why wouldn't they want you to know what her orders were?"

"An excellent question. Just who knows what seems to be the crux of the matter. There seems to be a certain interest in questions of confidentiality, and it doesn't only apply to you. So Fleet wants you out of the picture, I'm not telling you anything you don't already know. But just between us, Fleet and Sanchez haven't always seen eye to eye, and the chain of command isn't as clear as you might think. The Declaration leaves a lot of room open to interpretation, and things can get pretty murky. This business of the woman on the Oil Road isn't a matter of, shall we say, general consensus among military and civilian authorities. Nor is Martínez, who, as you succinctly put it, wasn't where he was supposed to be, just when Amy somehow breaks Greer out of the stockade and takes off. All very interesting."

"So you think Martínez is part of this."

Apgar shrugged. "I'm just the messenger. But Fleet has never been what you might call a true believer. As far as he's concerned, Amy is a distraction and the Twelve are a myth. Donadio he can't argue with—she's obviously different—but in his book, that doesn't prove a thing. He tolerated the hunt only because Sanchez made such a fuss it wasn't worth the fight, and what happened in Carlsbad is his opportunity to finally shut it down. There are those who believe different."

Peter took a moment to digest this. "So, Sanchez is going behind Fleet's back."

Apgar frowned ironically. "I wasn't aware I'd said anything of the kind. Talk like that would be above my rank. Be that as it may, I would consider it a personal favor if you could assist me in locating the appropriately resourceful individual to connect a few dots here. Know anybody who fits the bill, Lieutenant?"

The message was clear. "I think I do, Colonel."

"Excellent." Apgar paused before continuing: "Funny thing about that transport. The damnedest coincidence, actually. It seems the paperwork has been misplaced. You know how these things are. Should take about forty-eight hours to sort out, seventy-two at the outside."

"That's good to know, sir."

"I thought you might share that opinion." The colonel slapped his knees. "Well, it seems I'm needed elsewhere. I've been assigned to a presidential task force to deal with this . . . unfortunate development. Don't know how much I can contribute, but I go where I'm told." He rose from the bunk. "Glad you got your rest, Lieutenant. Busy days ahead."

"Thank you, Colonel."

"Don't mention it. And I do mean that literally." He looked at Peter again. "Just be careful with him, Jaxon. Lamont is nobody you want to cross."

They rode through the night and into another. They were east of Luling now. They had no map but didn't need one; Interstate 10 would lead them straight to Houston, into its jungled heart. Greer had been there once before—just the outskirts, but they'd told him enough. The city was an impenetrable swamp, a miasma of tree-tangled muck and sodden ruins, crawling with dopeys. If they didn't get you, the alligators would. They cruised the befouled waters like half-submerged boats, many having grown to gargantuan dimensions, their powerful jaws endlessly searching. Huge clouds of mosquitoes blanketed the air. Your nose, your mouth, your eyes: always they were looking for the body's door, seeking out the soft spots. Houston, what remained, was not a place for humankind; Greer wondered why anyone had ever thought it habitable to begin with.

They would face that soon enough. Now they found themselves in a prairie land of tall grasses and thickets, reclining mile by mile toward the sea. This far to the east, the highway hadn't been cleared. It seemed more suggestion than structure, its surface cracked and subsumed under washes of heavy clay soil. Graveyards of ancient cars frequently blocked the way. Few words had passed between the two of them since their departure: conversation was simply not necessary. Across the days, Greer had sensed a change in Amy, an aura of physical distraction. She was perspiring heavily; at times he caught her wincing, as if in pain. But when he expressed his concern, the girl peremptorily dismissed it. *I'm fine,* she insisted. *It's nothing.* Her tone was almost angry; she was telling him not to press.

As darkness fell, they made their camp in a clearing within sight of a ruined motel. The sky was clear, the temperature falling, calling forth dew from the air. Greer knew they were safe for the night; in Amy's presence he was in a zone of protection. They unrolled their bedrolls and slept.

He awakened later with a start; something was wrong. He rolled to the side and saw that Amy's bedroll was empty.

He did not allow himself to panic. A gibbous moon had risen as they'd slept, slicing the darkness into spaces of light and shadow, a landscape of menacingly elongated forms and pockets of blackness. The horses were obliviously chewing on a stand of weeds. Greer removed the Browning from his pack and moved cautiously into the gloom. He willed his eyes to parse shape from shape. Where had she gone? Should he call out to her? But the silence of the scene and its hidden dangers forbade it.

Then he saw her. She was standing just a few yards from their encampment, facing away. The rhythms of conversation touched his ears. Was she speaking to someone? It seemed so, and yet there was no one.

He approached her from behind. "Amy?"

No reply. She had given up her murmuring; her body was absolutely still.

"Amy, what is it?"

She turned then to face him with a look of mild surprise. "Oh. I see."

"Who were you talking to?"

She gave no answer. She seemed to be only partially present. Was she sleepwalking?

Then: "I suppose we should go back."

"Don't scare me like that."

"I'm sorry, I didn't mean to." She flicked her eyes downward at the gun. "What are you doing with that?"

"I didn't know where you'd gone. I was worried."

"I thought I made myself clear, Major. Put it away now."

She walked past him, headed back to camp.

42

Time interminable; time without end. His existence was a nightmare from which he couldn't awaken. Thoughts floating past like glinting dust motes, darting from wherever he looked. Every day they came. The men with their glowing, blood-red eyes. They unhooked the bloated bags and bore them away on their rattling cart and hung fresh ones on their stands. Always the bags, endlessly needful, constantly filling with their drip-drip-drip of Grey.

They were men who enjoyed their work. They told little jokes, they kept themselves amused. They enjoyed themselves at his expense, like children taunting an animal at the zoo. Here now, they cooed, extending the fragrant dropper toward his mouth, does baby need his bottle? Is baby hungry?

He tried to resist them. He clenched his muscles against the chains, he turned his face away. He mustered every ounce of will to deny them, yet always he succumbed. The hunger soared inside him like a great black bird.

—Say it for Mama. Say, I'm a baby who needs his bottle, I promise to be good. Be a good baby, Grey.

The tip of the dropper wafted enticingly under his nose, the scent of blood like a bomb exploding in his brain, a million neurons firing in an electrical storm of pure desire.

—You'll like this one. An excellent vintage. You like the young ones, don't you, Grey?

Tears squeezed from his eyes. Tears of longing and revulsion. The tears of his too-long life, a century of lying naked in chains. The tears of being Grey.

—Please.

—Say it. I like the young ones.

—I'm begging you. Don't make me.

—The words, Grey. A wave of sour breath close to his ear. Let me . . . hear . . . the . . . words.

—Yes! Yes, I like the young ones! Please! Just a taste! Anything!

And then at last the dropper, its delicious earth-rich squirt on his tongue. He smacked his lips. He rolled the thick muscle of his tongue around the walls of his mouth. He suckled like the baby they said he was, wishing he could make the feeling last, though he never could: an involuntary bob of his throat and it was gone.

—More, more.

—Now, Grey. You know there can't be any more. A dropper a day keeps the doctor away. Just enough to make you keep churning out the viral goodness.

—Just one taste, that's all. I promise I won't tell.

A dark chuckle: And supposing I did? Supposing I gave you just one more dropper? What would you do then?

—I won't, I swear, I just want . . .

—I'll tell you what you want. What you want, my friend, is to rip those chains right out of the floor. Which, I have to say, is pretty much what I'd want in your situation. That's what I'd be thinking about. I'd want to kill the men who put me here. A pause, then the voice coming closer: Is that what you want, Grey? To kill all of us?

He did. He wanted to rip them limb from limb. He wanted their blood to flow like water; he ached to hear their final cries. He wanted this even more than death itself, though just a little. Lila, he thought, Lila, I can feel you, I know that you are near. Lila, I would save you if I could.

—See you tomorrow, Grey.

And on and on. The bags came empty and went away full, the dropper did its work. It was his blood that sustained them, the men with their glowing eyes. They fed on Grey's blood and lived forever, as he lived forever. Grey eternal, in chains.

Sometimes he wondered where the blood they fed him came from. But not very often. It wasn't the kind of thing he wanted to think about.

Occasionally he still heard Zero, though it wasn't like Zero was talking to him anymore. That part of the deal seemed to have expired, long ago. The voice was muffled and far away, as if Grey were eavesdropping on a conversation taking place on the other side of a wall, and all things considered, he counted it a small mercy to be left alone with only his own thoughts for company, no Zero and his talk-talk-talk filling up his head.

Guilder was the only one who took his blood straight from the source. That was what they called Grey, the Source, like he wasn't even a person but a thing, which he supposed he was. Not always but sometimes, when he was feeling especially hungry, or for other reasons Grey couldn't guess at, Guilder would appear at the door in his underclothes, so as not to get blood on his suit. He would unhook the bag from its tube, viscous fluid spurting over him, and place the IV in his mouth, sucking up Grey's blood like a kid taking soda pop from a straw. *Lawrence,* he liked to say, *you're not looking so hot. Are they feeding you enough? I worry about you all alone down here.* Once, long ago, years or even decades, Guilder had brought a mirror with him. It was in what used to be called a lady's compact. Guilder popped the lid and angled it to Grey's face, saying, *Why don't you take a look?* An old man's face gazed back at him, wrinkled as a prune—the face of someone sitting on the fence of death.

He was permanently dying.

Then one day he awoke to find Guilder straddling a chair, looking at him. His tie was undone around his neck, his hair askew; his suit was rumpled and stained. Grey could tell he was late in his cycle. He could smell the rot coming off the man—a dumpstery, corpselike, slightly fruity stink—but Guilder made no move to feed. Grey had the sense that Guilder had been sitting there for some time.

"Let me ask you something, Lawrence."

The question was going to be asked one way or another. "Okay."

"Have you ever . . . now, how do I put this?" Guilder shrugged vaguely. "Have you ever been in love?"

Coming from the man's mouth, the word seemed completely alien. Love was the property of a different age; it was positively prehistoric.

"I don't understand what you're asking."

Guilder's face bunched with a frown. "Really, it seems like a perfectly simple question to me. Choirs of angels singing in their heaven, your feet levitating three inches off the ground. You know. In love."

"I guess not."

"It's a yes or no thing, Lawrence. It's one or the other."

He thought of Lila. Love was what he felt for her, but not the way Guilder meant. "No. I've never been in love."

Guilder was looking past him. "Well I was, once. Her name was Shawna. Though that wasn't her real name, of course. She had skin like butter, Lawrence. I'm totally serious here. That was how it tasted. Something a little Asian about her eyes, you know that look? And her body, well." He rubbed his face and exhaled a melancholy breath. "I don't feel that part anymore. The sex part. The virus pretty much takes care of that. Nelson thought the steroids you were taking might have been the reason the virus was different in you. There might have been some truth to that. But you make your bed, you have to lie in it." He chuckled ironically. "Make your bed. That's funny. That's a laugh."

Grey said nothing. Whatever mood Guilder was in, it seemed to have nothing to do with him.

"I suppose it's not such a bad thing on the whole. I can't honestly say that sex ever did me any favors. But even after all these years, I still think about her. Little things. Things she said. The way the sun looked, falling over her bed. I kind of miss the sun." He paused. "I know she didn't love me. It was all a big act was what it was. I knew that from the start, even if I couldn't admit it to myself. But there you have it."

"Why are you telling me this?"

"Why?" His gaze narrowed on Grey's face. "That should be obvious. You can be pretty obtuse, if you'll pardon my saying so. Because we're *friends,* Lawrence. I know, you probably think I'm the worst thing that ever happened to you. It could certainly appear that way. I'm sure this all might feel a little unfair. But you really left me no choice. Honestly, Lawrence? As odd as it seems, you're the oldest friend I have."

Grey held his tongue. The man was completely delusional. Grey found himself involuntarily flexing against his chains. The greatest happiness of his life, short of dying, would be to pop Guilder's head clean off.

"What about Lila? I don't mean to pry, but I always thought there was something between you two. Which was pretty surprising, given your history."

Something twisted inside him. He didn't want to talk about this, not now, not ever. "Leave me alone."

"Don't be like that. I'm just asking."

"Why don't you go fuck yourself?"

Guilder inched his face a little closer, his voice lowered confidentially. "Tell me something. Do you still hear him, Lawrence? The truth now."

"I don't know who you're talking about."

Guilder shot him a correcting frown. "Please, can we not? Do this? He's real is what I'm asking you. It's not some bullshit in my head." He was peering at Grey intently. "You know what he's asked me to do, don't you?"

There seemed no point denying it. Grey nodded.

"And on the whole, taking everything into consideration, you think it's a good idea? I feel like I need your input here."

"Why does it matter what I think?"

"Don't sell yourself short. You're still his favorite, Lawrence, no doubt about that. Oh sure, I may be the one in charge. I'm the captain of this ship. But I can tell."

"No."

"No what?"

"No, it's not a good idea. It's a terrible idea. It's the worst idea in the world."

Guilder's eyebrows lifted, like a pair of parachutes catching the air.

"Look at you." For the first time in eons, Grey actually laughed. "You think he's your *friend*? You think any of them are your friends? You're their bitch, Guilder. I *know* what they are. I know what Zero is. I was *there*."

He'd obviously struck a nerve. Guilder began clenching and unclenching his fists; Grey wondered, in a lazy way, if the man was about to hit him. The prospect didn't concern him in the least; it would break the monotony. It would be something different, a new kind of pain.

"I have to say, your response is more than a little disappointing, Lawrence. I was hoping I could count on a little support. But I'm not going to stoop to your level. I know you'd like that, but I'll be the bigger man. And just a little FYI: the Project was completed today. A real ribbon cutter. I was saving that as, you know, a surprise, something I thought you'd enjoy hearing about. You could be a part of this if you wanted. But apparently I've misjudged you."

He rose and headed for the door.

"What do you want, Guilder?"

The man turned back, leveling his blood-red eyes.

"What's in it for you? I never could figure that out."

A long silence, then: "Do you know what they are, Grey?"

"Of course I know."

But Guilder shook his head. "No, you don't. If you did, you wouldn't have to ask. So I'll tell you. They're the freest things on earth. Without remorse. Without pity. Without love. Nothing can touch them, hurt them. Imagine what that would be like, Lawrence. The absolute freedom of it. Imagine how wonderful that would be."

Grey made no reply; there was none to be made.

"You ask me what I want, my friend, and I'll give you my answer. I want what they have. I want that little whore out of my head. I want to feel . . . *nothing*."

The vase hit the wall in a satisfying explosion of glass. The car bombing was the last straw. This had to end *now*.

Guilder summoned Wilkes to his office. By the time his chief of staff entered the room, Guilder had managed to calm himself a little.

"Round up ten more per day."

Wilkes seemed taken aback. "Um, anybody in particular?"

"It doesn't matter!" Jesus, sometimes the man could be thick as a plank. "Don't you get it? It *never* mattered. Just pull them out of morning roll."

Wilkes hesitated. "So you're saying it should just be, you know, arbitrary. Not people we suspect of having ties to the insurgency, necessarily."

"Bravo, Fred. That's exactly what I'm saying."

For a second Wilkes just stood there, staring at Guilder with a bewildered look on his face. Not bewildered: disturbed.

"Yes? Am I talking to myself here?"

"If you say so. I can work up a list and send it down the hill to HR."

"I don't care how you do it. Just put it together." Guilder tossed a hand toward the door. "Now get out of here. And send an attendant to clean up this mess."

43

The route to Hollis was more circuitous than Peter had anticipated. The trail had taken them first to a friend of Lore's, who knew someone who knew someone else; always they seemed to be one step away, only to find that the target had moved.

Their last lead directed them to a Quonset hut where an illegal gambling hall operated. It was after midnight when they found themselves walking down a dark, trash-strewn alley in H-town. Curfew had long passed, but from everywhere around them came little bits of noise— barking voices, the crash of glass, the tinkling of a piano.

"Quite a place," Peter said.

"You haven't been here much, have you?" said Michael.

"Not really. Well, never, actually."

A shadowy figure stepped from a doorway into their path. A woman.

"Oye, mi soldadito. ¿Tienes planes esta noche?"

She moved forward from the shadows. Neither young nor old, her body so thin it was nearly boyish, yet the sensual confidence of her voice and the way she stood—shifting from one foot to the other, her pelvis pushing gently against her tiny skirt—combined with the heavy-lidded declivity of her eyes, as they trolled the length of Peter's body, to give her an undeniable sexual force.

"¿Cómo te puedo ayudar, Teniente?"

Peter swallowed; his face felt warm. "We're looking for Cousin's place."

The woman smiled a row of silk-stained teeth. "Everybody's some-body's cousin. I can be your cousin if you want." Her eyes drifted to Lore, then Michael. "And what about you, handsome? I can get a friend. Your girlfriend can come if she wants, too. Maybe she'd like to watch."

Lore gripped Michael by the arm. "He's not interested."

"We're really just looking for someone," Peter said. "Sorry to have troubled you."

She gave a dark laugh. "Oh, it's no trouble. You change your mind, you know where to find me, Teniente."

They moved along. "Nice fellow," Michael said.

Peter glanced back down the alley. The woman, or what he'd assumed was a woman, had faded back into the doorway.

"I'll be damned. Are you sure?"

Michael chuckled ruefully, shaking his head. "You really have to get out more often, hombre."

Ahead they saw the Quonset hut. Blades of light leaked from the edges of the door, where a pair of beefy men stood guard. The three of them paused in the shelter of an overflowing trash bin.

"Better let me do the talking," Lore said.

Peter shook his head. "This was my idea. I should be the one to go."

"In that uniform? Don't be ridiculous. Stay with Michael. And the two of you, try not to get picked up by any trannies."

They watched her march up to the door. "Is this such a good idea?" Peter asked quietly.

Michael held up a hand. "Just wait."

At Lore's approach the two men tensed, moving closer together to bar her entry. A brief conversation ensued, beyond Peter's hearing; then she returned.

"Okay, we're in."

"What did you tell them?"

"That the two of you just got paid. *And* you're drunk. So try to act it."

The hut was crowded and loud, the space partitioned by large, hexagonal tables where cards were being dealt. Clouds of silk smoke choked the air, consorting with the sour-sweet aroma of mash; there was a still nearby. Half-dressed women—at least Peter took them to be women—were seated on stools at the periphery of the room. The youngest couldn't have been a day over sixteen, the oldest nearly fifty, haggish in her clownish makeup. More were moving in and out of a curtain at the back, usually in the arm-draped company of a visibly intoxicated man. As Peter understood it, the whole idea of H-town was to overlook a certain amount of illegal vice but to cordon it off within a specific area. He could see the logic—people were people—but staring it in the face was a different matter. He wondered if Michael was right about him. How had he gotten so prim?

"Not go-to they're playing, is it?" he asked Michael.

"Texas hold 'em, twenty-dollar ante from the looks of it. A bit rich for my blood." His eyes, like Peter's, were patrolling the room for Hollis. "We should try to blend in. How much scrip do you have?"

"Nothing."

"Nothing?"

"I gave it all to Sister Peg."

Michael sighed. "Of course you did. You're consistent, I'll give you that."

"The two of you," Lore said. "What a couple of pussies. Watch and learn, my friends."

She strode up to the closest table and took a chair. From the pocket of her jeans she withdrew a wad of bills, peeled off two, and tossed them into the pot. A third bill produced a shot glass, the contents of which she downed with a toss of her sun-bleached hair. The dealer laid out two cards for each player; then the betting began. For the first four hands Lore seemed to take very little interest in her cards, chatting with the other players, folding quickly with a roll of her eyes. Then, on the fifth, with no discernible change in her demeanor, she began to drive up the bet. The pile on the table grew; Peter guessed there were at least three hundred Austins sitting there for the taking. One by one the others dropped out until just a single player remained, a skinny man with pock-marked cheeks who was wearing a hydro's jumpsuit. The last card was dealt; stone-faced, Lore put down five more bills. The man shook his head and folded his cards.

"Okay, I'm impressed," said Peter, as Lore raked in the pot. They were standing off to the side, close enough to watch without seeming to. "How did she do that?"

"She cheats."

"Really? I don't see how."

"It's pretty simple, actually. The cards are all marked. It's subtle, but you can figure it out. One player at the table is playing for the house so it always comes out ahead. She used the first few hands to figure out who it was and how to read the cards. It also doesn't hurt that she's a woman. In here, no one's taking her seriously. They assume she'll bet when she has good cards, that she'll fold when she doesn't. Three-quarters of the time she's bluffing."

"What happens when they realize what she's doing?"

"They won't, not right away. She'll throw a hand or two."

"And then?"

"Then it's time to leave."

A sudden commotion drew their attention to the rear of the room. A dark-haired woman, her dress torn from her shoulders, arms crossed over her exposed breasts, burst through the curtain, screaming incoherently. A second later a man emerged, his pants bunched comically around his ankles. He seemed to be floating a foot off the floor—suspended, Peter realized, by a man gripping him from behind. As the first man hurtled through the air, Peter recognized him; it was the young corporal from Satch's squad who had driven the transport from Camp Vorhees. The second man, mountainous, the lower half of his face buried in a salt-and-pepper beard, was Hollis.

"Aha," said Michael.

With impressive nonchalance, Hollis hauled the man to his feet by his collar. The woman was shrieking profanities, jabbing a finger at the two of them—*Kill this fucker! I don't have to put up with this shit! Do you hear me? You're fucking dead, you asshole!*—as Hollis half-shoved, half-levitated him toward the exit.

"That's our cue," Peter said.

At a quickstep they made their way for the door, Lore coming up behind them as they exited the hut. The corporal, crying desperate apologies, was simultaneously trying to pull up his pants and scamper away. If Hollis was moved by the man's appeals, he gave no sign. While the two guards looked on, laughing uproariously, Hollis hoisted the corporal by the waistband and propelled him farther down the alley. As he pulled the man upright again, Peter called his name.

"Hollis!"

For a perplexing instant the man seemed not to recognize them. Then he made a small sound of surprise. "Peter. *Hola.*"

The corporal was still squirming in his grip. "Lieutenant, for God's sake do something! This monster's trying to kill me!"

Peter looked at his friend. "Are you?"

The big man shrugged drolly. "I suppose, since he's one of yours, I could let it go this one time."

"Exactly! You could let me go and I'll never come back, I swear it!"

Peter directed his attention to the terrified soldier, whose name, he recalled, was Udall. "Corporal. Where are you supposed to be? Don't bullshit me."

"West Barracks, sir."

"Then get there, soldier."

"Thank you, sir! You won't regret it!"

"I already do. Now get out of my sight."

He scampered away, holding up his pants.

"I wasn't going to really hurt him," Hollis said. "Just put a scare into him."

"What did he do?"

"Tried to kiss her. That's not allowed."

The offense seemed minor. Given all Peter had seen, it didn't seem like an offense at all. "Really?"

"Those are the rules. Pretty much anything goes except for that. It's mostly up to the women." He glanced past Peter. "Michael, it's good to see you. It's been a while. You're looking well."

"Same here. This is Lore."

Hollis smiled in her direction. "Oh, I know who you are. It's nice to finally have a proper introduction, though. How were the cards tonight?"

"Not too bad," Lore replied. "The plant at table three is a real chump. I was just getting started."

The man's expression hardened a discernible notch. "Don't judge me for this, Peter. That's all I'm asking. Things work here in a certain way, that's all."

"You have my word. We all know . . ." He searched for the words. "Well. What you went through."

A moment passed. Hollis cleared his throat. "So, I'm thinking this isn't a social call."

Peter glanced over his shoulder at the two doormen, who were making no effort to conceal their eavesdropping.

"Is there someplace we could talk?"

Hollis met them two hours later at his house, a tarpaper shack on the western edge of H-town. Though the outside was anonymously decrepit, the interior possessed a surprising homeyness, with curtains on the windows and sprigs of dried herbs hanging from the ceiling beams. Hollis lit the stove and put on a pan of water for tea while the others waited at the small table.

"I make it with lemon balm," Hollis remarked as he placed four steaming mugs on the table. "Grow it myself in a little patch out back."

Peter explained what had happened on the Oil Road and the things Apgar had told him. Hollis listened thoughtfully, stroking his beard between sips.

"So can you take us to him?" Peter asked.

"That's not the issue. Tifty's no one you want to mix yourself up with—your CO's right about that. I can vouch for you, but those guys are nobody to fool with. My say-so will only go so far. Military isn't exactly welcome."

"I don't see a lot of options. If my hunch is right, he may be able to tell us where Amy and Greer went. All of this is connected. That's what Apgar was telling me."

"Sounds a bit thin."

"Maybe. But if Apgar's right, the same people might be responsible for what happened at Roswell, too." Peter hated to press, but the next question needed to be asked. "What do you remember?"

A look of sudden pain swept Hollis's face. "Peter, there's no use in this, okay? I didn't see anything. I just grabbed Caleb and ran. Maybe I should have done things differently. Believe me, I've thought about it. But with the baby . . ."

"No one's saying different."

"Then leave it alone. Please. All I know is that once the gates were open, they just poured in."

Peter glanced at Michael. Here was something they hadn't known, a new piece of the puzzle.

"Why were the gates open?"

"I don't think anyone ever figured that out," said Hollis. "Whoever gave the order, they must have died in the attack. And I've never heard anything about some woman. If she was there, I didn't see her. Or these trucks of yours." He took a heavy breath. "The fact is, Sara's gone. If I allowed myself to think different for one second, I'd go crazy. I'm sorry to say it, believe me. I won't pretend I've made my peace with it. But the best thing to do is accept reality. You too, Michael."

"She was my sister."

"And she was going to be my wife." Hollis looked at Michael's shocked face. "You didn't know that, did you?"

"Flyers, Hollis. No, I didn't."

"We were going to tell you when you got to Kerrville. She wanted to wait for you. I'm sorry, Circuit."

No one seemed to know what to say next. As the silence stretched, Peter looked around the room. For the first time he understood what he was seeing. This little shack, with its stove and herbs and snug feeling of home—Hollis had made the house that he and Sara would have had together.

"That's all I've got," said Hollis. "That will have to satisfy you."

"I can't accept it. Look at this place. It's like you're waiting for her to come home."

Hollis's grip visibly tightened on his mug. "Let it go, cuz."

"Maybe you're right. Maybe Sara's dead. But what if she's still out there?"

"Then she was taken up. I'm asking you nicely. If our friendship means anything to you, don't make me think about this."

"I have to. We all loved her, too, Hollis. We were a family, *her* family."

Hollis rose and returned his mug to the sink.

"Just take us to Tifty. That's all I'm asking."

Hollis spoke with his back to them. "He's not what you think. I owe that man."

"For what? A job in a brothel?"

His head was bowed, his hands clutching the edge of the sink, as if he'd taken a blow. "Jesus, Peter. You never change."

"You didn't do anything wrong. You did what you had to. And you got Caleb out."

"Caleb." From Hollis, a heavy sigh. "How is he? I keep meaning to visit."

"You should see for yourself. He owes you his life, and it's a good one."

Hollis turned to face them again. The tide had turned; Peter could see it in the man's eyes. A small flame of hope had been lit.

"What about you, Michael? I know what Peter thinks."

"Those were my friends that got killed. If there's payback, I want it.

And if there's a chance my sister's alive, I'm not going to just do nothing."

"It's a big continent."

"It always was. Never bothered me any."

Hollis looked at Lore. "So what's your opinion?"

The woman startled a little. "What are you asking me for? I'm just along for the ride here."

The big man shrugged. "I don't know, you're pretty good with the cards. Tell me what the odds are."

Lore shifted her gaze to Michael, then back at Hollis. "This isn't a question of odds. Of all the men in the world, that woman chose you. If she's still out there, she's waiting for you. Staying alive any way she can until you find her. That's all that matters."

Everybody waited for what Hollis would next say.

"You're a real ballbuster, you know that?"

Lore grinned. "Famous for it."

Another silence fell. Then:

"Let me pack a few things."

44

The first snow fell on Alicia's third night scouting the fringes of the city, fat flakes spiraling from an inky sky. A clean, wintry cold had settled onto the earth. The air felt hard and pure. It moved through her body like a series of small exclamations, bursts of icy clarity in her lungs. She would have liked to set a fire, but it might be seen. She warmed her hands with her breath, stamped her feet on the frozen earth when she felt sensation receding. There was something suitable about it, this shock of cold; it had the taste of battle.

Soldier was beside her no more. Where Alicia was going, he could not follow. There had always been something celestial about him, she thought, as if he'd been sent to her from a world of spirits. In his deep awareness, he had seen what was happening to her, the dark evolution. The fierce taste uncoiling inside her since the day she had sunk her blade into the buck on the ridge, prying forth the living heart of him. There was an exhilarating power in it, a flowing energy, but it came at a cost. She wondered how much time remained before it overwhelmed her. Before her human surface stripped away and she became one thing only. Alicia Donadio, scout sniper of the Expeditionary, no more.

Go now, she had told him. *You're not safe with me.* Tears floated on the surface of her eyes; she longed to look away from him but couldn't. *You great lovely boy, I will never forget you.*

She had traveled the final miles on foot, tracing the river. Its waters still flowed easily but this wouldn't last; ice had begun to crust at the edges. The landscape was treeless and bare. The image of the city bristled from the horizon as dusk was falling. She had been smelling it for hours. Its vastness startled her. She withdrew the yellowed, hand-drawn map from her pack and took the lay of the land. The dome rising from the hilltop, the bowl-like stadium, the bisecting river with its hydro dam, the massive concrete building with its cranes, the rows of barracks hemmed by wire—all just as Greer had recorded, fifteen years ago. She took out the RDF and adjusted the gain with fingers numb with cold. She swept it back and forth. A wash of static; then the needle nudged a fraction of an inch. The receiver was pointing at the dome.

Somebody was home.

She no longer needed her glasses except in the brightest hours of the day. How had this come to pass? What had happened to her eyes? She examined her face in the surface of the river; the orange light had continued to fade. What did it mean? She looked almost . . . normal. An ordinary human woman. Would that were true, she thought.

She passed the first two days circling the perimeter to gauge its defenses. She took inventories: vehicles, manpower, weaponry. The regular patrols that left from the main gate were easy to avoid; their efforts felt perfunctory, as if they perceived no real threat. At first light trucks would disperse from the barracks to thread through the city, carting workers to the factories and barns and fields, returning as darkness fell. As the days of observation passed, it came to Alicia that she was seeing a kind of prison, a citizenry of slaves and slave masters, yet the structures of containment seemed meager. The fences were thinly manned; many of the guards didn't even appear to be armed. Whatever force held the populace in check, it came from within.

Her focus narrowed to two structures. The first was the large building with the cranes. It possessed the blocky appearance of a fortress. Through her binoculars Alicia could discern a single entrance, a broad portal sealed by heavy metal doors. The cranes sat idle; the building's construction seemed complete, and yet to all appearances it went unused. What purpose did it serve? Was it a refuge from the virals, a shelter of last retreat? That seemed possible, though nothing else about the city communicated a similar sense of threat.

The other was the stadium, situated just beyond the southern perimeter of the city in an adjacent fenced compound. Unlike the bunker, the stadium was the site of daily activity. Vehicles came and went, step vans and some larger trucks, always at dusk or shortly after, disappearing down a deep ramp that led, presumably, to the basement. Their contents were a mystery until the fourth day, when a livestock carrier, full of cattle, descended the ramp.

Something was being fed down there.

And then shortly after noon on the fifth day, Alicia was resting in the culvert where she'd made her camp when she heard the distant wallop of an explosion. She pointed her binoculars to the heart of the city. A plume of black smoke was uncoiling from the base of the hill. At least one building was on fire. She watched while men and vehicles raced to the scene. A pumper truck was brought in to douse the flames. By now she had learned to distinguish the prisoners from their keepers, but on this occasion a third class of individuals appeared. There were three of them. They descended upon the site of the catastrophe in a sleek black vehicle utterly unlike the salvaged junkers Alicia had seen, straightening their neckties and fussing with the creases of their suits as they emerged into the winter sunshine. What strange costumes were these? Their eyes were concealed by heavy dark glasses. Was it just the brightness of the day or something else? Their presence had an instantaneous effect, the way a stone cast ripples across the surface of a pond. Waves of anxious energy radiated from the others on the scene. One of the suited men appeared to be taking notes on a clipboard while the other two shouted orders, gesturing wildly. What was she seeing? A leadership caste, that was apparent; everything about the city implied one's existence. But what was the explosion? Was it an accident or something deliberate? A chink in the armor, perhaps?

Her orders were clear. Scout the city, assess the threat, report back to Kerrville in sixty days. Under no circumstances was she to engage the inhabitants. But nothing said she had to stay outside the wires.

The time had come to take a closer look.

She chose the stadium.

For two more days, she observed the comings and goings of the trucks. The fences were no problem; getting into the basement would be the tricky part. The door, like the portal on the bunker, looked impenetrable. Only when a truck hit the top of the ramp would the door ascend, sealing quickly as the vehicle passed through, all of it perfectly timed.

Dusk of the third day: behind a stand of scrub, Alicia stripped herself of weapons—all but the Browning, snug in its holster, and a single blade sheathed against her spine. She had scouted a spot in the wires where her ascent would be concealed by one of several buildings that appeared unused. A hundred yards of open ground separated these buildings from the ramp. Once the driver of the van rounded the corner, Alicia would have six seconds to cross the distance. Easy, she told herself. Nothing to it.

She took the fence with a single toehold, scuttled against the building's rear wall, and peered around the corner. There it was, right on time, churning toward the stadium: the van. The driver downshifted as he approached the turn.

Go.

When the vehicle hit the top of the ramp, Alicia was just twenty feet behind it. The door, ascending on clattering chains, approached its apex. With a vaulting stride she took to the air, alighting on the van's roof and dropping facedown within half a second of passing beneath the door.

Flyers, was she *good.*

Already she was feeling it, feeling *them.* The too-familiar prickling along her skin and, deep inside her skull, a watery murmuring, like the caress of waves upon a distant shore. The van, at reduced speed, was moving through a tunnel. Ahead she saw a second door. The driver beeped the horn; the door rose to let them through. Another three seconds: the van drew to a halt.

They were in a wide, open space, fifty feet on a side. Peeking over the top of the windshield, Alicia counted eight men. Six were armed with rifles; the other two wore heavy backpacks with tanks and long steel wands. At the far end of the room was a third door, different from the others: a heavy steel contraption with thick crossbars set into the frame.

One of the men sauntered toward the van, holding a clipboard; she pressed herself as flat against the roof as she could.

"How many you got?"

"The usual."

"Are we supposed to do them as a group?"

"Hell if I know. What does the order say?"

A shuffling of paper. "Well, it doesn't," the second man answered. "A group, I suppose."

"Is the betting pool still open?"

"If you want."

"Give me seven seconds."

"Sod has seven. You'll have to pick something else."

"Six, then." The driver's door creaked opened; Alicia heard his feet hit the concrete floor. "I like the cows better. It takes longer."

"You are one sick bastard, you know that?" There was a pause. "You're right, though. It is pretty cool." He directed his voice away from the van. "Okay, everybody, showtime! Let's dim the lights!"

With a thunk the lights extinguished, replaced by a twilight-blue glow emanating from caged bulbs along the ceiling. All the men were backing away from the door at the far end of the room. There could be no doubt what lay on the other side; Alicia sensed it in her bones. A metal gate began to drop from the ceiling, then jolted to a stop. The men with the backpacks had taken up positions on the near side of the gate, wicks of flame dancing at the tips of their wands. The driver strode to the rear of the van and opened it.

"Come on, out with you."

"Please," a man's voice pleaded, "you don't have to do this! You're not like them!"

"It's okay, it's not what you think. Be a good fellow now."

A woman this time: "We haven't done anything! I'm only thirty-eight!"

"Really? I could have sworn you were older." The click of a cocking revolver. "All of you, let's move."

One by one they were hauled from the van, six men and four women, shackled at the wrists and ankles. They were sobbing, pleading for their lives. Some could barely stand. While two men kept their rifles trained, the driver moved among them with a ring of keys, unlocking the chains.

"What are you unshackling them for?" one of the other guards asked.

"Please, don't do this!" the woman cried. "I'm begging you! I have children!"

The driver backhanded the woman, knocking her to the ground. "Did I tell you to shut up?" Then, holding up a pair of shackles to the guard: "You want to clean these things later? I sure don't."

Do not engage the inhabitants, Alicia told herself. *Do not engage the inhabitants. Do not engage the inhabitants.*

"Sod?" the driver called. "Are we ready over there?"

A piggish-looking man stood off to the side at some kind of control panel. He moved a lever, and the gate gave a little twitch. "Hang on a second, it's jammed."

Do not engage, do not engage, do not engage . . .

"There, that's got it."

The hell with it.

Alicia rolled off the roof to find herself standing face-to-face with the driver. "Howdy."

"Son of a . . . bitch?"

She drew her blade and shoved it under his ribs. With a sharp exhalation he staggered backward.

"All of you," Alicia yelled, "hit the floor!"

Alicia unholstered the Browning and moved forward into the room, the weapon cupped in her hands, firing methodically. The guards seemed too stunned to react: one by one she began to pick them off in rusty spurts of blood. The head. The heart. The head again. Behind her, the prisoners had erupted in a torrent of wild screaming. Her mind was focused, clear as glass. The air grew suffused with a sweet intoxication of blood. She popped them off their feet. She lit them up like lightning. Nine bullets in her magazine; she'd finish them off with one to spare.

It was one of the men with the flamethrowers that got her. Though he certainly didn't intend to. At the instant Alicia pulled the trigger, he was trying only to protect himself—an instinctive gesture, to duck his head and turn his back to her.

45

"Papers."

Willing her fingers to stop trembling, Sara held the forged pass out for the guard. Her heart was hammering so hard against her ribs, it was a wonder the woman couldn't hear it. She snatched the pass from Sara's hands and looked it over quickly, darting her eyes to Sara's face before examining it a final time and shoving it back without expression.

"Next!"

Sara pushed through the revolving wire door. A final act: once on the other side, she was on her own. Beyond it lay a fenced chute, like something in a slaughterhouse. A column of day laborers was shuffling through—groundskeepers, kitchen workers, mechanics. More cols stood watch on either side of the chute, holding back snarling dogs on chains, laughing among themselves whenever one of the flatlanders flinched. Bags were searched, everyone was patted down. Drawing her shawl around her head, Sara kept her eyes averted. The real danger was being seen by someone who knew her—flatlander, col, it didn't matter. Not until she was wearing the veil of an attendant would she be safely anonymous.

How Eustace had managed to place her in the Dome, Sara didn't know. *We're everywhere* was all he would say. Once she was inside, her contact would find her. An exchange of code words, ordinary remarks of hidden meaning, would establish their identities. She moved up the hill, trying to make herself invisible by keeping her eyes to the ground, though on second thought, should she? Would it seem more natural to look around? Even the air seemed different here—cleaner, but in a way that seemed laden, humming with danger. At the periphery of her downcast vision she detected a heavy presence of HR personnel, moving in twos and threes. Probably they had ramped up security because of the car bombing, but who knew? Maybe it was always like this.

The Dome was ringed by concrete barricades. She showed her pass at the guardhouse and ascended the wide staircase that led to the entrance, a pair of massive doors set in a bronze frame. At the threshold she drew air into her chest. Here goes, she thought.

The doors were flung open, forcing her to dodge to the side. Two red-eyes brushed past, the collars of their suits turned up against the cold, leather briefcases swinging from their hands. She thought she had escaped their notice when the one on the left halted on the top step and turned to look at her. "Watch where you're going, flatlander."

She was staring at the ground, doing anything to avoid their eyes. Even behind their dark lenses, they had the power to make her insides twist. "Sorry, sir. My mistake."

"Look at me when I'm speaking to you."

It felt like a trap. "I meant no offense," she murmured. "I have a pass." She held it out.

"I said, *look at me.*"

Against all instincts, Sara slowly raised her face. For a fraught moment, the redeye considered her from behind the inscrutable shield of his glasses, making no move to accept the pass. The second one's attentions appeared elsewhere; he was merely indulging his companion with this interruption in their day. There was something distinctly infantile about them, thought Sara. With their soft, unblemished faces and boyishly limber bodies, they were like overgrown children playing dress-up. Everything was a game to them.

"When one of us tells you to do something, you do it."

The other one puffed his cheeks impatiently. "What the hell is with you today? She's nobody. Can we please just go?"

"Not until I'm done here." Then, to Sara: "Have I made myself clear?"

Her blood felt like ice in her veins. It took every ounce of her will not to look away. Those demonic eyes. That curling sneer. "Yes, sir," she stammered. "Completely."

"Tell me. What is it that you do?"

"Do?"

A flicker of a smile, like a cat with a mouse in its paws. "Yes, what do you do. What's your job."

She offered an obsequious shrug. "I just clean, sir." When he made no reply, she added, "I'm going to be an attendant."

The redeye studied her another moment, deciding if this was a satisfactory answer or not. "Well, here's a little word to the wise, flatlander. You go through those doors, you best watch yourself. It doesn't take much."

"I will, sir. Thank you, sir."

"Now get the fuck to work."

Sara waited for the pair to complete their descent before she allowed her body to unclench. *Flyers,* she thought. *For the love of God, get ahold of yourself. You're about to walk into a building full of these things.*

She screwed up her courage and opened the door.

She was instantly overwhelmed by a feeling of expansiveness, her sense of dimension distorted by a vertical vastness of space. She'd never seen anyplace like it: the gleaming marble floor, the tiers of balconies, the massive, curving stairs. The ceiling soared far above. Diminished sunlight descended from the high, curtained windows of the cupola, dimming the interior to a kind of twilight. Everything seemed both loud and quiet at once, the tiniest sounds reverberating before being absorbed by the void. Cols were stationed both around the room's periphery and at regular intervals on the stairs. A line of workers, ten deep, waited at the processing desk in the middle of the room. She assumed her place behind a man with a bag of tools over his shoulder. The desire to glance past him to see what lay ahead was intense but nothing to indulge. The line crept forward as each pass was stamped. She was fifth in line, then third, then second. The man with the tool bag stepped to the side, revealing the figure seated behind the desk.

It was Vale.

Sara's heart jolted with adrenaline. She couldn't move; she couldn't breathe. It would all be over before it had even begun. Her orders were clear: she couldn't be taken alive. Nina had spared nothing in describing exactly what the redeyes would do to her. *It will be like nothing you've ever experienced. You'll beg them to kill you. You can't hesitate.* What could she use? Should she just run and pray they'd shoot her?

"Are you feeling all right, miss?"

Vale was looking at her expectantly, extending a hand to receive her pass.

"What did you say?"

"Are . . . you . . . feeling . . . all right?"

She felt as if she'd been yanked from the edge of a cliff. She fumbled for the correct response. "I'm just a little nervous."

If Vale was surprised to see her, his face did not betray it. Vale was simply a better actor than she was. All those years Sara had known him, and she'd never detected a thing.

"The Dome can be a little overwhelming the first time you see it. You must be the new girl, Dani. Is that correct?"

She nodded. Dani, that was her name now. Not Sara.

"Display your tag, please."

She drew up her sleeve and extended her arm. Eustace, using an insider in the records department, had arranged to have Sara's number assigned to her new, fictitious identity. Vale made a small show of checking it against his paperwork.

"It seems you're to report to Deputy Director Wilkes." He gestured for another col to take his place at the desk. "Come with me."

Sara didn't know the name. But a deputy director—he had to be a member of the senior staff. Vale escorted her down a short hallway to an elevator with reflective metal doors. They stood in silence, both looking forward, as they waited for the car.

"Step inside, please."

Entering behind her, Vale pushed the button for the sixth floor. The car began its upward climb. Still he wasn't looking at her. She wondered if he was going to say anything. Then, as they passed the fourth floor, he reached toward the panel again and flipped a switch. The car abruptly halted.

"We only have a second," Vale said. "You've been assigned to the woman, Lila. This is better than anything we could have hoped for."

"Who's Lila?"

"She's the one who controls the virals. A major target. She's under heavy guard and almost never leaves her rooms."

Sara's mind raced to encode every word he said. "What am I supposed to do?"

"For now, just watch her. Try to win her trust. You and I won't have any more direct contact. Any messages will go through the serving girl who brings you your meals. If the spoon on your tray is upside down, there's a note under your plate. Return any messages the same way, but only do this in an emergency. Got that?"

Sara nodded.

"I always liked you, Sara. I'd like to think I did what I could to protect you. But none of that matters now. If the redeyes figure out who you are, I won't be able to help you." He slid his fingers under his waistband and withdrew a small square of metal foil and pressed it into her hand. "Always keep this hidden on your person. There's a piece of blotter paper inside. It's soaked in the same compound Nina used to knock you out but at a much higher concentration. Put it under your tongue. It won't take more than a couple of seconds. Believe me, it's better than going to the basement."

Sara slid the envelope into the pocket of her trousers. Death was with her now. She hoped she'd have the nerve if the time came.

Vale's hand was on the switch. "Ready?"

With a lurch the car resumed its upward course, then decelerated as they approached their destination. Vale, snapping back into character, placed his hand on her arm, gripping her just above the elbow. The doors slid open to reveal a col, heavyset with dark teeth, glaring at them with his hands on his hips.

"What the hell is going on with this elevator?" Then, locating Sara with his eyes: "What's she doing up here?"

"New attendant. I'm taking her to Wilkes."

The col examined her up and down. His eyebrows wagged suggestively. "Pity. She's a nice one."

Vale led her down a hall lined with heavy wooden doors. Stationed at eye level beside each was a brass plate bearing a name and title, some of which Sara recalled from broadsheets posted in the flatlands: "Aidan Hoppel, Minister of Propaganda," "Clay Anderson, Minister of Public Works," "Daryl Chee, Minister of Material Resource Recovery," "Vikram Suresh, Minister of Public Health." They came to the final door: "Frederick Wilkes, Chief of Staff and Deputy Director of the Homeland."

"Come."

The office's occupant was bent forward over a stack of papers on his desk, scribbling with a fountain pen. A muted winter light filtered through the draped windows behind him. A moment passed; then he looked up.

"Dani, is it?"

Sara nodded.

The redeye shifted his gaze to Vale. "Wait outside, please."

The door clicked shut. Wilkes rocked back in his chair. An air of weariness radiated from him. He pulled a sheet of paper from the pile and looked it over.

"The dairy barns. That was where you worked?"

"Yes, Deputy Director."

"And you have no immediate family."

"No, Deputy Director."

Wilkes returned his attention to the page on his desktop. "Well, it seems this is your lucky day. You're to be Lila's companion. Does the name mean anything to you?"

Sara meekly shook her head.

"Heard rumors, perhaps? We have no illusions that security isn't always what it could be. You can tell me if you have."

With monumental effort, she forced herself to look him in the eye. "No, I haven't heard anything."

Wilkes let a moment pass before continuing. "Well. Suffice it to say that Lila is one of a kind. The job is pretty straightforward. Basically, do whatever she asks. You will find she can be—how do I put this? Unpredictable. Some of the things she asks of you will seem odd. Think you're up to this?"

She returned a crisp nod. "Yes, sir."

"The one thing you must do is get her to eat. This takes some coaxing. She can be extremely stubborn."

"You can count on me, Deputy Director."

He leaned back in his chair again, folding his hands in his lap. "You will find life in the Dome much more comfortable than the flatland. Three square meals a day. Hot water for bathing. Very little will be asked of you other than the duties I've described. If you do a good job, there's no reason you can't enjoy our largesse for years to come. One last matter. How are you with children?"

"Children, sir?"

"Yes. Do you like them? Get on with them? Personally, I find them rather trying."

Sara felt a familiar pang. "Yes, Deputy Director. I like them fine."

She waited for further explanation from Wilkes, but none was evidently forthcoming. He inspected her for another few seconds from across his desk, then picked up the telephone.

"Tell them we're on the way."

*   *   *

Roughly an hour later, Sara found herself garbed in an attendant's robe, standing at the threshold of a room so sumptuously decorated that its volume of detail was difficult to absorb. Heavy drapes were drawn over the windows; the only sources of light were several large silver candelabras positioned around the room. Gradually the scene came into focus. The sheer volume of furniture and bric-a-brac made it seem less like a place where someone lived than a storage room of miscellaneous objects. A voluminous sofa covered in fat, tasseled pillows, as well as a pair of equally overstuffed chairs, stood to one side, facing a low square table of polished wood, its surface piled with books. More pillows of various colors were scattered on the floor, which was dressed by an ornately patterned rug. The walls were covered with oil paintings in heavy gilt frames—landscapes, pictures of horses and dogs, as well as a great many portraits of women and their children in curious costumes, the images possessing a disturbing half reality. One in particular caught Sara's attention: a woman in a blue dress and an orange hat, sitting in a garden beside a little girl. She moved toward it to have a closer look. A small plaque at the bottom of the frame read, "Pierre-Auguste Renoir, *On the Terrace,* 1881."

"Well, there you are. It's about time they sent someone."

Sara pivoted. A woman, arms folded over her chest, was standing in the bedroom doorway. She was both more and less than the image Sara had assembled from the things Vale and Wilkes had said. The person she had envisioned was at the very least a substantial presence, but the figure before her appeared quite frail. She was perhaps as old as sixty. Deep fissures lined her face, cutting borders between its various regions; crescents of drooping skin hung like hammocks beneath her watery eyes. Her lips were so pale they were practically nonexistent, like ghost lips. She was wearing a shimmering robe of some thin, shiny fabric, a thick towel encircling her head like a turban.

"*¿Hablas inglés?*"

Sara stared dumbly, unable to formulate a reply to this incomprehensible question.

"Do . . . you . . . speak . . . English?"

"Yes," Sara stated. "I speak English."

The woman gave a little start. "Oh. So you do. I have to say, that's a surprise. How many times have I asked the service to send somebody who spoke even a little English? I don't even want to tell you." She made a distracted gesture with her hands. "I'm sorry, your name again?"

Never mind that she hadn't told her to begin with. "It's Dani."

"Dani," the woman repeated. "Where are you from, exactly?"

The most general answer seemed the wisest. "I'm from here."

"Of course you're from *here*. I meant *originally*. Your tribe. Your people. Your clan." Another agitated flutter of her hands. "You know. Your *familia*."

With each exchange, Sara felt herself being pulled deeper into the quicksand of the woman's oddness. Yet something about her was almost endearing. She seemed quite helpless, a twittering bird in a cage.

"California, actually."

"Ah. Now we're getting somewhere." A pause; then, with a dawning look: "Oh, *I* see. You're working your way through school. Why didn't you say so?"

"Ma'am?"

"Please," she chirped, "call me Lila. And don't be so modest. It's an admirable thing you're doing. A great show of character. Of course, that doesn't mean I'll be paying you more than the other girls. I made that clear with the service. Fourteen an hour, take it or leave it."

Fourteen what? Sara wondered. "Fourteen is fine."

"And, of course, the Social Security. We'll be paying that, and filing the 1099. David is very particular about these things. He's what you'd call a rule follower. A big ol' stick in the mud. No health insurance, I'm afraid, but I'm sure you get that through your school." She beamed encouragingly. "So, are we good?"

Sara nodded, completely dumbfounded.

"Excellent. I have to say, Dani," the woman, Lila, continued, gliding into the room, "you've come just in the nick of time. Not a moment too soon, in fact." She had taken a box of matches from her robe and was lighting a large candelabra near her dressing table. "Why don't you just put that over there?"

She was referring to the tray Wilkes had given her. On it was a metal flask and cup. Sara placed the tray on the table the woman had indicated, adjacent to an ornately carved wardrobe draped with scarves. Lila had positioned herself in front of a standing mirror and was turning her shoulders this way and that, examining her reflection.

"So what do you think?"

"I'm sorry?"

She placed one hand on her stomach and pressed inward as she filled her chest with air. "This awful diet. I don't think I've ever been so famished in my life. But it really does seem to be doing the trick. What would you say, Dani? Another five pounds? You can be honest."

Standing in profile, the woman was just skin and bones. "You look fine to me," she said gently. "I wouldn't lose any more."

"Really? Because when I look in this mirror what I'm thinking is, who is this blimp? This zeppelin? *Oh God, the humanity.* That's what I'm thinking."

Sara remembered Wilkes's orders. "I think you're supposed to eat, actually."

"So I'm told. Believe me, I've heard *that* before." She placed her hands on her hips, scrunched up her face, and dropped her voice an octave. "Lila, you're too skinny. Lila, you've got to put some meat on those bones. Lila this, Lila that. Blah, blah, blah." Then, her eyes widening with sudden panic: "Oh my goodness, what time is it?"

"I guess it's . . . about noon?"

"Oh my goodness!" The woman began to dart around the room, snatching up various belongings and putting them down again in a manner that seemed arbitrary. "Don't just stand there," she implored, grabbing a pile of books and shoving them into the bookcase.

"What would you like me to do?"

"Just . . . I don't know. *Anything.* Here—" She filled Sara's hands with pillows. "Put these over there. On the whooziwhatzis."

"Um, you mean the sofa?"

"Of course I mean the sofa!"

And just like that, a light seemed to switch on in the woman's face. A wondrous, happy, shining light. She was staring over Sara's shoulder, toward the door.

"Sweetheart!"

She dropped to a crouch as a young child, a girl in a plain smock, blond ringlets bouncing, dashed past Sara into the woman's outstretched arms. "My angel! My sweet, sweet girl!"

The child, who was holding a sheet of colored paper, pointed at the woman's turbaned head. "Did you take a bath, Mummy?"

"Why, yes! You know how Mummy likes her baths. What a clever little girl you are! So, tell me," she continued, "how were your lessons? Did Jenny read to you?"

"We read *Peter Rabbit.*"

"Wonderful!" the woman beamed. "Was it funny? Did you like it? I'm sure I've told you how much I adored him when I was your age." She turned her attention to the paper. "And what do we have here?"

The little girl held it up. "It's a picture."

"Is that me? Is it a picture of the two of us?"

"They're birds. That one is named Martha, the other one is Bill. They're building a nest."

A flicker of disappointment; then she smiled again. "Why, of course they are. Anyone could see that. It's as plain as the nose on your pretty little face."

And on and on. Sara barely ingested any of it. An intense new sensation had come over her, a feeling of biological alarm. Something deep and atavistic, tidal in its weight and movement, accompanied by a focusing of her senses on the back of the little girl's blond head. Those curls. The precise and singular dimensions that the little girl's body occupied in space. Sara already knew without knowing, a fact she also knew, the paradox building a kind of hallway inside her, like images reflected infinitely in two opposing mirrors.

"But how awful of me," the woman, Lila, was saying, her voice at some impossible remove from reality, a transmission from a distant planet. "I've totally forgotten my manners. Eva, I need to introduce you to someone. This is our new friend . . ." She paused, drawing a blank.

"Dani," Sara managed.

"Our wonderful new friend Dani. Eva, say how do you do."

The child turned. Time collapsed as Sara beheld her face. A unique amalgamation of form and features that was the only one in all the universe. There was no doubt in Sara's mind.

The little girl sent her a shining, closed-lip smile. "How do you do, Dani?"

Sara was looking at her daughter.

But in the next second something changed. A shadow fell, a dark presence descending. It jolted Sara back to the world.

"Lila."

Sara turned. He was standing behind her. His face was a man's, ordinary, forgettable, one of thousands like it, but from it radiated an invisible force of menace as incontrovertible as gravity. To behold him was to feel oneself plunging.

He looked Sara contemptuously in the eye, piercing her utterly. "Do you know who I am?"

Sara swallowed. Her throat was as tight as a reed. For the first time, her mind darted to the foil package secreted in the deep folds of her robe; it would not be the last.

"Yes, sir. You're Director Guilder."

His mouth curled downward with distaste. "Put down your veil, for God's sake. Just the sight of you makes me sick."

With trembling fingers, she did so. Now the shadow became a shadow literally, his features mercifully blurred behind the blush of fabric, as if in mist. Guilder strode past her, to where Lila still crouched with Sara's daughter. If his presence meant anything to the little girl, Sara couldn't see it, but Lila was a different story. Every part of her tightened. Clutching the child in front of her like a shield, she rose to her feet.

"David—"

"Just stop it." His eyes flicked disagreeably over her. "You look like hell, you know that?" Then, turning to face Sara once more: "Where is it?"

He was, she understood, speaking of the tray. Sara pointed.

"Bring it here."

Her hands, somehow, managed this.

"Get rid of them," Guilder said to Lila.

"Eva, sweetie, why doesn't Dani take you outside?" She looked quickly at Sara, her eyes beseeching. "It's such a beautiful day. A little fresh air, what do you say?"

"I want *you* to take me," the girl protested. "You *never* go outside."

Lila's voice was like a song she was being made to sing. "I know, sweetheart, but you know how sensitive Mummy is to the sun. And Mummy has to take her medicine now. You know how Mummy gets when she takes her medicine."

Reluctantly, the child complied. Breaking away from Lila, she moved to where Sara was standing beside the door.

With excruciating miraculousness, she took Sara by the hand.

Flesh meeting flesh. The unbearable corporeal smallness of it, its discrete power, its infusion of memory. All of Sara's senses molded around the exquisite sensation of her child's tiny hand in her own. It was the first time their bodies had touched since one was inside the other, though now it was the opposite: Sara was the one inside.

"Run along, you two," Lila croaked. She gave a wave of absolute misery toward the door. "Have fun."

Without a word, Kate—Eva—led Sara from the room. Sara was floating; she weighed a million pounds. Eva, she thought. I have to remember to call her Eva. A short hallway and then a flight of stairs: a pair of doors at the bottom pushed into a small, fenced yard with a teeter-totter and a rusted swing set. The sky looked down with a solemn, snow-filled light.

"Come on," the child said. And broke away.

She climbed aboard a swing. Sara took her place behind her.

"Push me."

Sara drew back the chains, suddenly nervous. How much was safe? This precious and beloved being. This holy, miraculous, human person.

Surely three feet was more than enough. She released the chains, and the girl arced away, vigorously pumping her legs.

"Higher," she commanded.

"Are you sure?"

"Higher, higher!"

Each sensation a piercing. Each a painless engraving in the heart. Sara caught her daughter at the small of her back and thrust her away. Up and out she rose, into the December air. With each arc her hair volleyed backward, suffusing the air behind her with the sweet scent of her person. The girl swung silently; her happiness was bound into a pure occupation of the act itself. A little girl, swinging in winter.

My darling Kate, thought Sara. *My baby, my one.* She pushed, and pushed again; the girl flew away, always returning to her hands. *I knew, I knew, I always knew. You are the ember of life I blew on, a thousand lonely nights. Never could I let you die.*

46

Houston.

The liquefied city, drowned by the sea. The great urban quagmire, none but its skyscrapered heart left standing. Hurricanes, drenching tropical rains, the unchecked slide of a continent's waters seeking final escape to the Gulf: for a hundred years the tides had come and gone, filling the lowlands, carving out grimy bayous and contaminated deltas, erasing all.

They were ten miles from the city's central core. The last days of travel had been a game of hopscotch, seeking out the dry places and segments of passable roadway, hacking their way through thickets of spiny, insect-infested vegetation. In these quarters, nature unveiled its true malevolent purpose: everything here wanted to sting you, swarm you, bite you. The air creaked with its saturated weight and miasma of rot. The trees, gnarled like grasping hands, seemed like something from another age entirely. They seemed positively made up. Who would invent such trees?

Darkness came on with a chemically yellowish dimming. The trip had compacted to a crawl. Even Amy had begun to show her irritation. Her signs of illness had not abated; rather, the opposite. When she thought Greer wasn't looking, he caught her pressing her palms to her stomach, exhaling with slow pain. They quartered that night on the top floor of a house that seemed outrageous in its ruined opulence: dripping chandeliers, rooms the size of auditoriums, all of it spattered with a black, off-gassing mold. A brown line three feet above the marble floor circumscribed the walls where floodwaters had once risen. In the massive bedroom where they took shelter, Greer opened the windows to clear the air of the ammonic stench: below him, in the vine-clotted yard, lay a swimming pool full of goo.

All night long, Greer could hear the dopeys moving in the trees outside. They vaulted from limb to limb, like great apes. He listened to them rustling through the foliage, followed by the sharp animal cries of rats and squirrels and other small creatures meeting their demise. Amy's injunction notwithstanding, he dozed fitfully, pistol in hand. *Just remember. Carter's one of us.* He prayed it was true.

Amy was no better in the morning.

"We should wait," he said.

Even standing seemed to take all the strength she could muster. She made no effort to hide her discomfort, gripping the flat of her belly, her head bowed in pain. He could see the spasms shuddering her abdomen as the cramps moved through her.

"We go," she said, speaking through gritted teeth.

They continued east. The skyscrapers of downtown emerged in their particularity. Some had collapsed, the clay soil having expanded and contracted over the years to pulverize their foundations; others reclined against each other like drunks stumbling home from a bar. Amy and Greer traced a narrow spit of sand between weed-choked bayous. The sun was high and bright. Seaborne wreckage had begun to appear: boats, and parts of boats, splayed on their sides in the shallows as if in a swoon of exhaustion. When they reached the place where the land ended, Greer dismounted, retrieved the binoculars from his saddlebag, and pointed them across the stained waters. Dead ahead, wedged against a skyscraper, lay a vast ship, hard aground. Her stern rose impossibly high in the air, massive propellers visible above the waterline. On it was written the vessel's name, dripping with rust: CHEVRON MARINER.

"That's where we'll find him," said Amy.

There was no dry path across; they would have to find a boat. Luck favored them. After backtracking a quarter mile, they discovered an aluminum rowboat overturned in the weeds. The bottom appeared sound, the rivets tight. Greer dragged it to the lagoon's edge and set it afloat. When it failed to sink, he helped Amy down from her mount.

"What about the horses?" he asked her.

Her face was a mask of barely bottled pain. "We should be back before dark, I think."

He stabilized the craft as Amy boarded, then lowered himself onto the middle bench. A flat board served as a paddle. Seated in the stern, Amy had been reduced to cargo. Her eyes were closed, her hands wrapped her waist, sweat dripping from her brow. She made no sound, though Greer suspected her silence was for his benefit. As the distance narrowed, the ship expanded to mind-boggling dimensions. Its rusted sides loomed hundreds of feet over the lagoon. It was listing to one side; the surrounding water was black with oil. Greer paddled their craft into the lobby of the adjacent building and brought them to rest beside a bank of motionless escalators.

"Lucius, I think I'm going to need your help."

He assisted her from the boat and up the nearest escalator, supporting her by the waist. They found themselves in an atrium with several elevators and walls of smoked glass. ONE ALLEN CENTER a sign read, with a directory of offices beneath. The ascent that lay ahead would be serious; they'd need to climb ten stories at least.

"Can you make it?" Greer asked.

Amy bit her lip and nodded.

They followed the sign for the stairs. Greer lit a torch, gripped her at the waist again, and began to climb. The trapped air of the stairwell was poisonous with mold; every few floors they were forced to step out just to clear their lungs. At the twelfth floor, they stopped.

"I think we're high enough," said Greer.

From the sealed windows of a book-lined office they looked down on the tanker's decking, wedged hard against the building ten feet below. An easy drop. Greer took the desk chair, hoisted it over his head, and flung it through the window.

He turned to look at Amy.

She was studying her hand, holding it before her like a cup. A bright red fluid filled her palm. It was then that Greer noticed the stain on her tunic. More blood was trickling down her legs.

"Amy—"

She met his eye. "You're tired."

It was like being wrapped in an infinite softness. A blanketing, whole-body sleep.

"Oh, damn," he said, already gone, and folded to the floor.

47

Peter and the others entered San Antonio on Highway 90. It was early morning; they had passed the first night in a hardbox in the city's outer ring of suburbs, a sprawl of collapsed and scoured houses. The room lay beneath a police station, with a fortified ramp at the rear. Not a DS hardbox, Hollis explained; one of Tifty's. It was larger than the hardboxes Peter had seen, though no less crude—just a stuffy room with bunks and a garage bay where a fat-tired pickup awaited, cans of fuel in the bed. Crates and metal military lockers were stacked along the walls. What's in these? Michael asked, to which Hollis said, one eyebrow raised, I don't know, Michael. What do you think?

They drove out at first light beneath a heavy sky, Hollis at the wheel beside Peter, Michael and Lore riding in the truck's bed. Much of the city had burned in the days of the epidemic; little remained of the central core save for a handful of the taller buildings, which stood with forlorn austerity against the backdrop of bleached hills, their scorched facades telegraphing the blackened and collapsed interiors where an army of dopeys now dozed the day away. "Just dopeys," people always said, though the truth was the truth: a viral was a viral.

Peter was waiting for Hollis to turn off, to take them north or south, but instead he drove them into the heart of town, leaving the highway for narrow surface streets. The way had been cleared, cars and trucks hauled to the sides of the roadway. As the shadows of the buildings engulfed the truck, Hollis slid the cab's rear window open. "You better weapon up," he cautioned Michael and Lore. "You'll want to watch yourself through here."

"All eyes, hombre," came the man's reply.

Peter gazed at the destruction. It was the cities that always turned his thoughts to what the world had once been. The buildings and houses, the cars and streets: all had once teemed with people who had gone about their lives knowing nothing of the future, that one day history would stop.

They moved through without incident. Vegetation began to crowd the roadway as the gaps between the buildings widened.

"How much longer?" he asked Hollis.

"Don't worry. It's not far."

Ten minutes later they were skirting a fence line. Hollis pulled the vehicle to the gate, removed a key from the glove box of the pickup, and stepped out. Peter was struck by a sense of the past: Hollis might have been Peter's brother, Theo, opening the gate to the power station, all those years ago.

"Where are we?" he asked when Hollis returned to the truck.

"Fort Sam Houston."

"A military base?"

"More like an Army hospital," Hollis explained. "At least it used to be. Not a lot of doctoring goes on here anymore."

They drove on. Peter had the sense of driving through a small village. A tall clock tower stood to one side of a quadrangle that might have once been the center of town. Apart from a few ceremonial cannons, he saw nothing that seemed military—no trucks or tanks, no weapon emplacements, no fortifications of any kind. Hollis brought the pickup to a halt before a long, low building with a flat roof. A sign above the door read, AQUATICS CENTER.

"Aquatics," Lore said, after they'd all disembarked. She squinted doubtfully at the sign, a rifle balanced across her chest in a posture of readiness. "Like . . . swimming?"

Hollis gestured at the rifle. "You should leave that here. Wouldn't want to make a bad impression." He shifted his attention to Peter. "Last chance. There's no way to undo this."

"Yes, I'm sure."

They entered the foyer. All things considered, the building's interior was in good shape: ceilings tight, windows solid, none of the usual trash.

"Feel that?" Michael said.

A basal throbbing, like a gigantic plucked string, was radiating from the floor. Somewhere in the building a generator was operating.

"I kind of expected there to be guards," Peter said to Hollis.

"Sometimes there are, when Tifty wants to put on a show. But basically we don't need them."

Hollis led them to a pair of doors, which he pushed open to reveal a great, tiled space, the ceiling high above and, at the center of the room, a vast, empty swimming pool. He guided them to a second pair of swinging doors and a flight of descending stairs, illuminated by buzzing fluorescents. Peter thought to ask Hollis where Tifty got the gas for his generator, but then answered the question for himself. Tifty got it where he got everything; he stole it. The stairs led to a room crowded with pipes and metal tanks. They were under the pool now. They made their way through the cramped space to yet another door, though different from the others, fashioned of heavy steel. It bore no markings of any kind, nor was there an obvious way to open it; its smooth surface possessed no visible mechanisms. On the wall beside it was a keypad. Hollis quickly punched in a series of digits, and with a deep click the door unlatched, revealing a dark corridor.

"It's okay," Hollis said, angling his head toward the opening, "the lights go on automatically."

As the big man stepped through, a bank of fluorescents flickered to life, their vibrancy intensified by the hospital-white walls of the corridor. Peter's sense of Tifty was radically evolving. What had he imagined? A filthy encampment, populated by huge, apelike men armed to the teeth? Nothing he had seen even remotely conformed to these expectations. To the contrary: the display so far indicated a level of technical sophistication that seemed well beyond Kerrville's. Nor was he alone in this shifting of opinion; Michael, too, was frankly gawking. *Some place,* his face seemed to say.

The corridor ended at an elevator. A camera was poised above it. Whoever was on the other side knew they were coming; they'd been observed since they'd entered the hall.

Hollis tilted his face upward to the lens, then pressed a button on the wall adjacent to a tiny speaker. "It's all right," he said. "They're with me."

A crackle of static, then: "Hollis, what the fuck."

"Everyone's unarmed. They're friends of mine. I'll vouch for them."

"What do they want?"

"We need to see Tifty."

A pause, as if the voice on the other end of the intercom was conferring with somebody else; then: "You can't just bring them here like this. Are you out of your mind?"

"I wouldn't ask if it wasn't important. Just open the door, Dunk."

An empty moment followed. Then the doors slid open.

"It's your ass," the voice said.

They entered; the elevator commenced its downward creep. "Okay, I'll bite," Michael ventured. "What is this place?"

"You're in an old USAMRIID station. It's an annex to the main facility in Maryland, activated during the epidemic."

"What's USAMRIID?" asked Lore.

It was Michael who answered. "It stands for 'United States Army Medical Research Institute of Infectious Diseases.'" He frowned at Hollis. "I don't get it. What's Tifty doing here?"

And then the doors of the elevator opened to the sound of weapons being cocked, and each of them was staring down the barrel of a gun.

*　　*　　*

"All of you, on your knees."

There were six. The youngest appeared to be no more than twenty, the oldest in his forties. Scruffy beards and greasy hair and teeth clotted with grime: this was more like it. One of them, a giant of a man with a great bald head and ridges of soft fat folded at the base of his neck, had bluish tattoos all over his face and the exposed flesh of his arms. This, apparently, was Dunk.

"I told you," Hollis said, kneeling on the floor like the rest of them, hands on top of his head, "they're friends of mine."

"Quiet." His clothing was a hodgepodge of different uniforms, both military and DS. He holstered his revolver and crouched in front of Peter, sizing him up with his intense gray eyes. Viewed up close, the images on his face and arms became clear. Virals. Viral hands, viral faces, viral teeth. Peter had no doubt that beneath his clothes, the man's body was covered with them.

"Expeditionary," Dunk drawled, nodding gravely. "Tifty's going to like this. What's your name, Lieutenant?"

"Jaxon."

"Peter Jaxon?"

"That's right."

Maintaining his crouch, Dunk swiveled on the heels of his boots toward the others. "How about that, gentlemen. It's not every day we get such distinguished visitors." He focused on Peter again. "We don't get visitors at all, actually. Which is a bit of a problem. This isn't what you'd call a tourist destination."

"I need to see Tifty."

"So I hear. Tifty, I'm afraid, is indisposed at the moment. A very private fellow, our Tifty."

"Cut the bullshit," Hollis said. "I told you, I'll vouch for them. Tifty needs to hear what they have to say."

"This is your mess, my friend. I don't think you're exactly in a position to be making demands. And what about you two?" he asked, addressing Lore and Michael. "What do you have to say for yourselves?"

"We're oilers," Michael replied.

"Interesting. Did you bring us any oil?" His gaze narrowed on Lore; a smile, bright with menace, flickered over his face. "Now, you I think I know. Poker, wasn't it? Or dice. Probably you don't remember."

"With a mug like yours, how could I forget?"

Grinning, Dunk rose and rubbed his meaty hands together. "Well, it's been very nice meeting all of you. A real pleasure. Before we kill you, does anyone have anything else to say? Goodbye, maybe?"

"Tell Tifty it's about the field," said Hollis.

Something changed; Peter could sense it at once. The words fell over Dunk's face like a shadow.

"Tell him," Hollis said.

The man appeared stunned into inaction. Then he drew his pistol. "Let's go."

Dunk and his men escorted them down a long corridor. Peter took stock of their surroundings, though there wasn't much to see, just more halls and closed doors. Many of the doors had keypads on the walls beside them like the one beneath the pool. Dunk brought them to a halt before one such door and gave it three hard raps.

"Enter."

The great gangster Tifty Lamont. Once again Peter found his expectations overturned. He was a physically compact man, with glasses perched on the tip of his long, hooked nose. His pale hair flowed over his neck, thin at the top with a crown of pink scalp beneath. Seated behind a large metal desk, he was performing the improbable act of constructing a tower out of wooden sticks.

"Yes, Dunk?" he said, not looking up. "What is it?"

"We've captured three intruders, sir. Hollis brought them in."

"I see." He continued with his patient stacking. "And you did not kill them because . . . ?"

Dunk cleared his throat. "It's about the field, sir. They say they know something."

Tifty's hands halted over the model. After several seconds, he lifted his face, peering at them over his glasses.

"Who says?"

Peter stepped forward. "I do."

Tifty studied him a moment. "And the others? What do they know?"

"They were with me when I saw her."

"Saw who, exactly?"

"The woman."

Tifty said nothing. His face was as rigid as a blind man's. Then: "Everyone out. Except for you . . ." He wagged a finger toward Peter. "What's your name?"

"Peter Jaxon."

"Except for Mr. Jaxon."

"What do you want me to do with the others?" Dunk asked.

"Use your imagination. They look hungry—why don't you give them something to eat?"

"What about Hollis?"

"I'm sorry, did I mishear you? Didn't you say he brought them in?"

"That's the thing. He showed them where we are."

Tifty sighed heavily. "Well, that is a wrinkle. Hollis, what am I going to do with you? There are rules. There's a code. Honor among thieves. How many times do I have to say it?"

"I'm sorry, Tifty. I thought you needed to hear what he had to say."

"Well, sorry doesn't cut it. This is a very awkward position you've put me in." He cast his eyes wearily around the room, as if his next sentence could be found somewhere among its shelves and files. "Very well. Where are you on the roster?"

"Number four."

"Not anymore. You're suspended from the cage until I say otherwise. I know how much you like it. I'm being generous here."

Hollis's face showed nothing. What was the cage? Peter thought.

"Thank you, Tifty," Hollis said.

"Now all of you get the hell out."

The door sealed behind them. Peter waited for Tifty to speak first. The man rose from behind his desk and stepped to a small table with a pitcher of water. He poured himself a glass and drank it down. Just when the silence had begun to strain, he addressed Peter with his back turned.

"What was she wearing?"

"A dark cloak and glasses."

"What else did you see? Was there a truck?"

Peter recounted the events on the Oil Road. Tifty let him talk. When Peter had concluded, the man moved back to his desk.

"Let me show you something."

He opened the top drawer, removed a sheet of paper, and slid it across the desktop. A charcoal drawing, the paper stiffened and slightly discolored, of a woman and two little girls.

"You've seen one of these before, haven't you? I can tell."

Peter nodded. The picture wasn't anything he could easily pull his eyes from. It possessed an overwhelming hauntedness, as if the woman and her children were gazing out of the page from someplace beyond the ordinary parameters of time and space. Like looking at a ghost, three ghosts.

"Yes, in Colorado. Greer showed it to me, after Vorhees was killed. A big stack of them." He lifted his eyes to find Tifty watching him keenly, like a teacher giving a test. "Why do you have a copy?"

"Because I loved them," Tifty replied. "Vor and I had our difficulties, but he always knew how I felt. They were my family, too. That's why he gave this to me."

"They died in the field."

"Dee, yes, and the little one, Siri. Both were killed outright. It was fast, though you know the saying: Make it quick, but not today. The older girl, Nitia, was never found." He frowned. "You're surprised by all this? Not quite what you expected?"

Peter couldn't even begin to answer.

"I'm telling you these things so you understand who and what we are. All these men have lost someone. I give them a home, a place to put their anger. Take Dunk, for instance. He may be imposing now, but when I look at him, do you know what I see? An eleven-year-old kid. He was in the field, too. Father, mother, sister, all gone."

"I don't see what running the trade has to do with that."

"That's because it's only part of what we do. A way of paying the bills, if you like. The Civilian Authority tolerates us because it has to. In a way, it needs us as much as we need it. We're not so very different from your Expeditionary, just the other side of the same coin."

Tifty's logic felt too convenient, a way to justify his crimes; on the other hand, Peter could not deny the meaning of the picture.

"Colonel Apgar said you were an officer. A scout sniper."

Tifty's face lit with a quick smile; there was a story there. "I should have known Gunnar would have something to do with this. What did he tell you?"

"That you made captain before you busted out. He called you the best S2 there ever was."

"Did he? Well, he's being kind, but only a little."

"Why did you resign?"

Tifty shrugged carelessly. "Many reasons. You could say that military life didn't suit me on the whole. Your presence here makes me think it may not suit you particularly well, either. My guess would be you've gone off the reservation, Lieutenant. How many days are you AWOL?"

Peter felt caught. "Just a couple."

"AWOL is AWOL. Believe me, I know all about that. But in answer to your question, I left the Expeditionary because of the woman in the field. More specifically, because I told Command where she came from, and they refused to do anything about it."

Peter was dumbstruck. "You *know* where she comes from?"

"Of course I know. So does Command. Why do you think Gunnar sent you here? Fifteen years ago, I was part of a squad of three sent north to locate the source of a radio signal somewhere in Iowa. Very faint, just little scratches of noise, but enough to catch it with an RDF. We didn't know why, the Exped wasn't in the business of chasing down every random squeak, but it was all very hush-hush, very top-down. Our orders were to scout it out and report back, nothing more. What we found was a city at least two, maybe three times the size of Kerrville. But it had no walls, no lights. By any reckoning, it shouldn't have existed at all. And you know what we saw? Trucks like the one I saw in the field just before the attack. Like the one you saw three days ago."

"So what did Command say?"

"They ordered us never to tell anyone."

"Why would they do that?" Though, of course, they had told Peter exactly the same thing.

"Who knows? But my guess would be the order came from the Civilian Authority, not the military. They were scared. Whoever those people were, they had a weapon we couldn't match."

"The virals."

The man nodded evenly. "Stick your fingers in your ears and hope they never came back. Maybe not wrong, but it wasn't anything I could sit with. That was the day I resigned my commission."

"Did you ever go back?"

"To Iowa? Why would I do that?"

Peter felt a mounting urgency. "Vorhees's daughter could be there. Sara, too. You saw those trucks."

"I'm sorry. Sara. Do I know this person?"

"She's Hollis's wife. Or would have been. She was lost at Roswell."

A look of regret eased across the man's face. "Of course. My mistake. I believe I knew that, though I don't think he ever mentioned her name. Nevertheless, this changes nothing, Lieutenant."

"But they could still be alive."

"I don't think it's likely. A lot of time has passed. Either way, there wasn't anything I could do about it. Not then and not now. You'd need an army. Which the CA more or less guaranteed we didn't have. And in the leadership's defense, these people, whoever they are, never returned. At least until now, if what you're saying is true."

Something was missing, Peter thought, a detail lurking at the edge of his awareness. "Who else was with you?"

"On the scouting party? The officer in charge was Nate Crukshank. The third man was a young lieutenant named Lucius Greer."

The information passed through Peter like a current.

"Take me there. Show me where it is."

"And what would we do when we got there?"

"Find our people. Get them out somehow."

"Are you listening, Lieutenant? These aren't just survivors. They're in league with the virals. More than that—the woman can control them. Both of us have seen it happen."

"I don't care."

"You should. All you'll accomplish is getting yourself killed. Or taken. My guess is, that would be a good deal worse."

"Then just tell me how to find it. I'll go on my own."

Tifty rose from behind his desk, returned to the table in the corner, and poured himself another glass of water. He drank it slowly, sip by sip. As the silence lengthened, Peter got the distinct impression that the man's mind had taken him elsewhere. He wondered if the meeting was over.

"Tell me something, Mr. Jaxon. Do you have children?"

"What does that have to do with anything?"

"Indulge me."

Peter shook his head. "No."

"No family at all?"

"I have a nephew."

"And where is he now?"

The questions were uncomfortably probing. And yet Tifty's tone was so disarming, the answers seemed to spring forth of their own accord. "He's with the sisters. His parents were killed at Roswell."

"Are you close? Do you matter to him?"

"Where are you going with this?"

Tifty ignored the question. He placed his empty glass on the table and returned to his desk.

"I suspect he admires you a great deal. The great Peter Jaxon. Don't be so modest—I know just who you are, and more than the official account. This girl of yours, Amy, and this business with the Twelve. And don't blame Hollis. He's not my source."

"Who then?"

Tifty grinned. "Perhaps another time. Our subject at hand is your nephew. What did you say his name was?"

"I didn't. It's Caleb."

"Are you a father to Caleb, is what I'm asking. Despite your gallivanting around the territories, trying to rid the world of the great viral menace, would you say that's true?"

Suddenly Peter had the sense of having been perfectly maneuvered. It reminded him of playing chess with the boy: one minute he was drifting in the current of the game; the next he was boxed in, the end had come.

"It's a simple question, Lieutenant."

"I don't know."

Tifty regarded him another moment, then said, with a note of finality, "Thank you for your honesty. My advice to you would be to forget about all of this and go home and raise your boy. For his sake, as much as your own, I'm willing to give you a pass and let you and your friends go free, with the warning that speaking of our whereabouts will not, how shall I put this, bring happy things your way."

Checkmate. "That's it? You're not going to do anything?"

"Consider it the greatest favor anybody's ever done you. Go home, Mr. Jaxon. Live your life. You can thank me later."

Peter's mind scrambled for something to say that might convince the man otherwise. He gestured toward the drawing on the desk. "Those girls. You said you loved them."

"I did. I do. That's why I'm not going to help you. Call me sentimental, but I won't have your death on my conscience."

"Your *conscience*?"

"I do have one, yes."

"You surprise me, you know that?" Peter said.

"Really? How do I surprise you?"

"I never thought Tifty Lamont would be a coward."

If Peter had expected to get a rise, he saw none. Tifty rocked back in his chair, placed the tips of his fingers together, and looked at him coolly over the tops of his spectacles. "And you were thinking maybe that if you pissed me off, I'd tell you what you want to know?"

"Something like that, yeah."

"Then you mistake me for somebody who cares what others think. Nice try, Lieutenant."

"You said one of them was never found. I don't see how you can sit here if she could still be alive."

Tifty sighed indulgently. "Perhaps you didn't get the news, but this isn't a what-if world, Mr. Jaxon. Too many what-ifs are just a way to keep yourself up at night, and there's not enough decent sleep to go around. Don't get me wrong, I admire your optimism. Well, maybe not admire—that might be too strong a word. But I do understand it. There was a time when I wasn't so very different. But those days are passed. What I have is this picture. I look at it every day. For now, that's what I have to content myself with."

Peter picked up the drawing again. The woman's shining smile, the lift of her hair on an unseen breeze, the little girls, wide-eyed, hopeful like all children, waiting for their lives to unfold. He had no doubt that this picture was the center of Tifty's life. Looking at it, Peter sensed the presence of a complex debt, allegiances, promises made. This picture: it wasn't just a memorial; it was the man's way of punishing himself. Tifty wished he'd died with them, in the field. How strange, to find himself feeling sorry for Tifty Lamont.

Peter returned the picture to its place on Tifty's desk. "You said the trade was only part of what you do. You never told me what else."

"I didn't, did I?" Tifty removed his glasses and rose. "Fair enough. Come with me."

Tifty manipulated another keypad and the heavy door swung open, revealing a spacious room with large metal cages stacked against the walls. The air was rank with a distinctly animal scent, of blood and raw meat, and the high-noted aroma of alcohol. The light glowed a cool, violety blue—"viral blue," Tifty explained, with a wavelength of four hundred nanometers, at the very edge of the visible spectrum. Just enough, he told Peter, to keep them calm. The builders of the facility had understood their subjects well.

Michael and Lore had joined them. They passed through the room of cages and ascended a short flight of stairs. What awaited them was obvious; it was just a question of how it would be revealed.

"And this," said Tifty, opening a panel to reveal two buttons, one green, one red, "is the observation deck."

They were standing on a long balcony with a series of catwalks jutting over a metal shelf. Tifty pushed the green button. With a clatter of gears and chain, the shelf began to withdraw into the far wall, revealing a surface of hardened glass.

"Go on," Tifty urged. "Look for yourselves."

Peter and the others stepped onto the catwalk. Instantly one of the virals hurled itself upward against the glass, crashing into it with a thump before bouncing off and rolling back to the corner of its cell.

"Fuck . . . *me,*" Lore gasped.

Tifty joined them on the catwalk. "This facility was built with one purpose in mind: studying the virals. More accurately, how to kill them."

The three of them were staring at the containers below. Peter counted nineteen of the creatures in all; the twentieth container was empty. Most appeared to be dopeys, barely reacting to their presence, but the one who had leapt at them was different—a full-blown female drac. She eyed them hungrily as they moved along the catwalks, her body tense and her clawed hands flexing.

"How do you get them?" Michael asked.

"We trap them."

"With what, spinners?"

"Spinners are for amateurs. The gyrations immobilize them, but such devices are no good, really, unless you want to crisp them on-site. To take them alive, we use the same baited traps the builders of this facility used. A tungsten alloy, incredibly strong."

Peter tore his gaze away from the drac. "So what have you learned?"

"Not as much as I'd like. The chest, the roof of the mouth. There's a third soft spot at the base of the skull, though it's very small. They bleed to death if you dismember them, but it's not easy cutting through the skin. Heat and cold don't seem to have much effect. We've tried a variety of poisons, but they're too smart for that. Their sense of smell is incredibly acute, and they won't eat anything we've laced no matter how hungry they get. One thing we do know is that they'll drown. Their bodies are too dense to keep them afloat, and they can't hold their breath very long. The longest any of them lasted was seventy-six seconds."

"What if you starve them?" Michael asked.

"We tried that. It slows them down, and they enter a kind of sleep state."

"And?"

"As far as we can tell, they can stay that way indefinitely. Eventually we stopped trying."

Suddenly Peter understood what he was seeing. The work of the trade was really just a cover. The man's true purpose was right here, in this room.

"Tifty, you are full of shit."

Everybody turned. Tifty crossed his arms over his chest and gave Peter a hard look.

"You have something on your mind, Lieutenant?"

"You always meant to go back to Iowa. You just couldn't figure out how."

Tifty's expression didn't change. His face looked suddenly older, worn down by life. "That's an interesting theory."

"Is it?"

For five seconds the two men stared at each other. No one else said anything. Just when the silence had gone on too long, Michael broke the tension.

"I think she likes you, Peter."

Fifteen feet below, the big drac was looking up at him, her head rolling lazily on her gimballed neck. She uncocked her jaw like someone yawning and drew back her lips to display her glinting teeth. *These are for you.*

Tifty stepped forward. "Our latest addition," he said. "We're all very proud of this one—we've been tracking her for weeks. It's not often we get a full-blown drac anymore. We call her Sheila."

"What are you going to do to her?" Michael asked.

"We haven't decided. More or less the usual, I suppose. A little of this, a little of that. She's too mean for the cage, though."

Peter recalled Hollis's punishment. "What's the cage?"

Tifty's face lit with a smile. "Ah," he said.

Midnight. During the intervening hours, the three of them had been confined to a small, unused room, with one of Tifty's men outside. Peter had finally managed to fall asleep when a buzzer sounded and the door opened.

"Come with me," said Tifty.

"Where are we going?" Lore asked.

"Outside, of course."

Why "of course"? thought Peter. But this seemed to be Tifty's way. The man had a taste for drama. "Where's Hollis?" Peter asked.

"Not to worry, he'll be joining us."

A cloudy, starless night. A truck was waiting for them, parked at the steps. They climbed into the bed while Tifty got into the cab with the driver. They weren't guarded, but unarmed, in the dark, where would they go?

A few minutes passed before the truck drew up to an immense rectangular building, like an airplane hangar. Several other vehicles were present, including a large flatbed. Men milled about in torchlight, conspicuously armed with pistols and rifles, some smoking corn silk. From inside the building came a buzz of voices.

"Now you'll see what we're really all about," said Tifty.

The building's interior was a single cavernous space, lit by torches. A huge American flag, tattered with age, hung from the rafters. At the center was the cage, a domed structure approximately fifty feet in diameter with a hooked chain descending to the floor from its apex. Surrounding it were bleachers packed with men, all talking loudly, urgently waving Austins at a figure moving up and down the rows. At Tifty's entrance a cheer shot up from the crowd, accompanied by a thunder of pounding feet. He did nothing to acknowledge this, escorting the three of them to an empty region on the lower tier of the bleachers, just a few feet from the crisscrossing bars of the cage.

"Five minutes till the betting closes!" a voice rang out. "Five minutes!"

Hollis took a place beside them. "Is this what I think it is?" Peter said.

He nodded tersely. "Pretty much."

"They're actually betting on the outcome?"

"Some are. With dopeys, mostly it's just how many minutes it will take."

"And you've actually done this."

Hollis looked at him strangely. "Why wouldn't I?"

The conversation was cut short as a second, louder cheer erupted. Peter looked up to see a metal crate being toted into the room on a forklift. A figure entered from the other side, walking with a manful swagger: Dunk. He was wearing heavy pads and carrying a pike; a sweeper's mask rode on top of his head, leaving his tattooed face exposed. He raised his right fist and pumped it in the air, summoning a frenzied stamping from the bleachers. The forklift operator dropped the box in the middle of the cage and backed away while a second man hooked the latch to the chain. As he moved clear, Dunk stepped inside. The door was locked behind him.

A hush fell. Tifty, seated beside Peter, got to his feet, holding a megaphone. He cleared his throat and directed his voice over the crowd. "All please rise for the national anthem."

Everyone clambered to their feet, placed their right hands over their hearts, and began to sing:

> *Oh, say can you see, by the dawn's early light,*
> *What so proudly we hailed, at the twilight's last gleaming?*
> *Whose broad stripes and bright stars, through the perilous fight,*
> *O'er the ramparts we watched, were so gallantly streaming?*

Peter, standing too, struggled to recall the words. It was a song from long ago—from the Time Before. Teacher had taught them in the Sanctuary. But the melody had been tricky and the words had made no sense his boyhood self could discern, and he'd never gotten the hang of it. He glanced at Michael, whose eyebrows lifted in shared surprise.

The last screeching note extinguished itself in another detonation of cheers. From the aural chaos emerged a repeated refrain, the beat estab-

lished by thundering feet: *Dunk, Dunk, Dunk, Dunk* . . . Tifty let it run
its course, then raised a hand for silence. He faced the cage again.

"Dunk Withers, do you stand ready?"

"Ready!"

"Then . . . start the clock!"

Pandemonium. Dunk drew his mask down, a horn sounded, the chain
was pulled. For a moment nothing happened; then the dopey popped
free of the crate and skittered up the cage with a quick, insectile movement, like a roach scurrying up a wall. It could have been looking for a
way out or a vantage point for attack; Peter couldn't tell. The crowd had
its opinion. Instantly the cheers turned to boos and catcalls. At the top
of the cage, the dopey grasped one of the bars with its feet and unfurled
its body so that the top of its head was pointed toward the floor, arms
held away from its sides. Dunk stood below it, shouting unhearable
taunts and waving the pike, daring it to drop. *Meat!* the crowd chanted,
clapping in syncopation. *Meat! Meat! Meat!*

The dopey seemed disoriented, almost dazed. Its bland gaze darted
about the room randomly, as if the racket and commotion had short-
circuited its instincts. Its features had a blurry appearance, as if its
human characteristics had been dissolved by strong acid. For five more
seconds it hung there, then ten.

Meat! Meat! Meat! Meat!

"Enough already." Tifty rose to his feet, taking up the megaphone.
"Throw in the meat!"

From without the bars huge, blood-saturated chunks were lobbed
into the cage, landing with smeary splats. This was all it took. The creature released the steel bar and dove for the nearest hunk. The upper section of a cow's leg: the dopey scooped it off the floor and shoved its jaws
into the fatty folds, not so much drinking the fluids it contained as inhaling them. Two seconds and it was drained; the creature flung the desiccated remains away.

It swiveled toward Dunk. Now the man meant something. The dopey
lowered itself to a crouch, balanced on its prehensile toes and massive
splayed hands. The telltale cock of the head, the moment of regard.

It charged.

As the viral leapt toward him, arms extended, claws aiming for his
throat, Dunk dropped to the floor and came up swinging the pike. The
crowd went wild. Peter felt it too, the raw excitement of the contest surging in his veins. Dodging the pike, the dopey scampered back up the wall
of the cage. No dazed retreat this time: its intentions were clear. When
they came, they came from above. Twenty feet up, the dopey pushed it-

self backward off the bars, tucking its body into a headfirst aerial roll, twisting like a corkscrew as it descended in a rush of movement, and alighted on its feet ten feet from Dunk. The same engagement reversed: Dunk lunged; the dopey dropped. The pike speared the empty air above its head. As Dunk fell forward, carried by his own momentum, the dopey shot from its crouch and rammed headlong into his padded midsection, blasting him across the cage.

Dunk wound up propped upright against the bars, obviously shaken. The pike lay on the floor to his left; the mask had been torn away. Peter saw him reaching for the weapon, but the gesture was weak, his hand scrabbling with fogged inaccuracy. His chest was heaving like a bellows, a trickle of blood running from his nose to his upper lip. Why hadn't the dopey taken him yet?

Because it was a trap. The dopey seemed to suspect as much; as it contemplated the fallen warrior, Peter could sense the creature's interior conflict. The drive to kill versus an inchoate tactical suspicion that not all was as it appeared—a vestige, perhaps, of the human capacity for reason. Which would win out? The crowd was chanting Dunk's name, trying to rouse him from his stupor. That or goad the dopey into action. Any death would do. Just by going into the cage, Dunk had already secured the most important victory: to be human. To deny the virals' dominion over himself, over his fellows, over the world. The rest would fall as it fell.

Blood won.

The dopey went airborne. Simultaneously, the wandering hand found and secured the pike. As the creature fell, Dunk lifted the pike to a forty-five-degree angle, aligning it with the center of the dopey's descending chest, bracing the butt against the floor between his knees.

Did the dopey know what was about to happen? Did it experience, in that sliver of time in which the outcome was ordained, an awareness of its race toward death? Was it happy? Was it sad? And then the tip of the pike found its mark, spearing the creature so thoroughly that life breathed out of it in a single, grand, instantaneous exhalation of death.

Dunk shoved the body to the side. Peter had joined the crowd on its feet. His energy was a part of theirs; it flowed in the collective current. His voice rang with the multitude:

Dunk, Dunk, Dunk, Dunk!
Dunk, Dunk, Dunk, Dunk!

Why was this different? Peter wondered, while another part of his brain refused to care, adrift in his unanticipated elation. He had faced the virals on the rampart, in cities and deserts, forests and fields. He had dropped seven hundred feet into a crawling cave. He had given himself to death's likelihood hundreds of times, and yet Dunk's courage was something more, something purer, something redeeming. Peter glanced at his friends. Michael, Hollis, Lore: there was no mistaking it. They felt just as he did.

Only Tifty looked different. He'd gotten on his feet like the rest of them, but his face was emotionless. What was he seeing in his mind's eye? Where had he gone? He had gone to the field. Not even the cage could lighten this burden. Here was Peter's opening. He waited for the cheering to die. In the stands, bets were being counted and paid.

"Let me go in there."

Tifty studied him with one raised eyebrow. "Lieutenant, what are you asking?"

"A wager. My life against your promise to take me to Iowa. Not just tell me where this city is. You have to go with me."

"Peter, this is not a good idea," Hollis warned. "I know what you're feeling. We call it cage fever."

"That's not what this is."

Tifty folded his arms over his chest. "Mr. Jaxon, how dumb do I look? Your reputation precedes you. I don't doubt a dopey is well within your abilities."

"Not a dopey," he said. "Sheila."

Tifty weighed him with his eyes. Behind him, Michael and Lore said nothing. Maybe they understood what he was doing, and maybe they didn't. Maybe they were too dumbstruck by his apparent loss of his faculties to formulate a response. It didn't matter either way.

"All right, Lieutenant, it's your funeral. Not that there'll be anything to bury."

Peter was escorted to a small room at the rear of the arena by Tifty and two of his men. Michael and Hollis were with him; Lore waited in the stands. The room was bare except for a long table displaying armored pads and an array of weapons. Peter suited up. He had initially been concerned that the pads would slow him down too much, but they were surprisingly light and pliable. The mask was a different matter; Peter couldn't see how it would be any help, and it cut down his peripheral vision. He put it aside.

Now for armaments. He was permitted two. No firearms were allowed, only piercing weapons. Blades, crossbows, pikes and swords and axes of various lengths and weights. The cross was tempting, but in such close quarters it would take too long to reload. Peter chose a five-foot pike with a barbed steel tip.

As for the second: he cast his eyes around for something that would serve his purpose. In the corner of the room was a galvanized trash can. He removed the lid and examined it.

"Somebody give me a rag."

A rag was produced. Peter wet it with spit and rubbed the inside of the lid. His reflection began to emerge—not with any distinctiveness, barely more than a blurry shape; but it would have to suffice.

"This is what I want."

Tifty's men burst into laughter. *A trash can lid! Some pathetic little shield against a full-blown drac! Did he intend to commit suicide?*

"Your foolishness is one thing, Lieutenant," said Tifty. "But this. I can't allow it."

Michael looked at him with a quizzical frown. "Like . . . Las Vegas?"

Peter gave him the barest nod, turned to Tifty again. "You said anything in the room."

"That I did."

"Then I'm ready."

He was led into the arena. The crowd erupted in roars and stamping, but the sound was different than it had been with Dunk. Their allegiances had reversed. Peter wasn't one of them; they were excited to watch him die, this arrogant soldier of the Expeditionary who dared to think he could take on a drac. The box was already in position at the center of the ring. As Peter approached, he thought he could see it shaking. He heard, from the bleachers, "All bets now closing!"

"Not too late to back out," Hollis said. "We could make a run for it."

"What kind of odds are they giving me?"

"Ten to one you survive thirty seconds. A hundred to one you make it a minute."

"You get one down?"

"Took you to win in forty-five. I'll be set for life."

"The usual arrangement, okay?" Peter didn't need to elaborate: *If I'm bitten but survive, don't let me. Make it fast.*

"You don't have to worry."

"Michael? Hold him to that."

The man's face was bereft. "Jesus, Peter. You did it *once.* Maybe it was something else that slowed them down. Did you think about that?"

Peter looked at the box in the middle of the ring. It was shuddering like an engine. "Thanks—I'm thinking about it now."

They shook hands. A grave moment, but they had been through similar ones before. Peter stepped inside the cage; one of Tifty's men sealed the door behind him. Hollis and Michael took their places on the bleachers with Lore. Tifty rose with his megaphone.

"Lieutenant Jaxon of the Expeditionary, do you stand ready?"

A chorus of boos. Peter did his best to tune them out. He had been running on pure conviction, but now that the moment was here, his body had begun to doubt his mind. His heart was racing, his palms damp. The pike felt absurdly heavy in his hand. He filled his chest with air. "Ready!"

"Then . . . start the clock!"

In the aftermath, Peter was to learn that the contest had lasted a grand total of twenty-eight seconds. This seemed both long and short; it had happened slowly and all at once, a blur of events that didn't correspond to the ordinary course of time.

What he would remember was this:

The drac's explosion from the box, like water shot from a hose; her majestic airborne leap, a force of undiluted nature, straight to the top of the cage, and then three quick ricochets as she bounded side to side, too fast for Peter's eyes to follow; the picture in his mind's eye of her anticipated release and the arc her body would employ as she fell upon him, and then the moment of its occurrence, exactly as he'd foreseen; the blast of force as their bodies collided, one stationary, one in headlong flight; the drac sending him careening across the cage, and his body—breathless, broken, his own for a moment or two more but no longer—rolling and rolling and rolling.

He was on his stomach. The trash can lid and pike were gone. He rolled onto his back and scrabbled backward on his hands and feet, and then he found what was left of the pike. The pole had snapped two feet from its pointed steel end. He wrapped it with his fist and rose. He would go down swinging; he would die on his feet at least. On a distant planet, crowds were cheering. The viral was moving toward him in a manner he would have described as leisurely, almost sauntering. She cocked her head and opened her jaws to give him a good, long look at her teeth.

Their eyes met.

Really *met*. A bona fide, soul-searching gaze. The moment locked, and in that moment Peter felt his mind plunging into hers: its sensations and memories, thoughts and desires, the person she'd been and the pain of the terrible thing she'd become. Her expression had softened, her posture relaxed a discernible notch. The ferocity of her expression contained something else now: a profound melancholy. A human being was still inside her, like a tiny flame in the dark. *Don't look away,* Peter told himself. *Whatever you do, don't break her gaze.* The pike was in his hand.

He took one step, then another. Still she did not move. He felt a kind of quiet shuddering within himself, not of fear but of longing; this was what she wanted. The crowd had silenced. It was as if the two of them were alone in some immense, still space. An empty church. An abandoned theater. A cave. He drew back the pike, placing his free hand on her shoulder for balance. *Please,* her eyes said.

Then it was over.

The crowd was absolutely still. Peter realized he was shaking. Something irrevocable had happened, beyond knowing. He looked down at the body. He had felt her soul leaving her. It had brushed him like a breeze, only the breeze was inside him, made of words. *Thank you, thank you. I am free.*

Tifty was waiting for him when he exited the cage.

"Her name wasn't Sheila," Peter said. "It was Emily."

Tifty said nothing, wearing an expression of pure bewilderment.

"She was seventeen when she was taken up. Her last memory was of kissing a boy."

"I don't understand."

Hollis, Michael, and Lore were coming down the bleachers. Peter moved toward them, stopped, then turned back to Tifty.

"You want to know how to kill them?"

The man nodded, slack-jawed.

"Look them in the eye."

48

Amy's mind was full of him. Full of Carter and the woman, whose name was Rachel. Rachel Wood.

Amy felt it, felt it all. She felt and saw and knew. The woman's arms around him, pulling him down and down. The taste of pool water, like demon's breath. The soft thunk as they reached the bottom, their bodies entwined like lovers'.

How Carter had loved her. That was what Amy felt most keenly: his love. The man's life had stopped right there, at the bottom of the pool, his mind forever trapped in a loop of sorrow. *Oh please, let me,* thought

Anthony Carter. *I'll die if you want me to, I would die for you if you asked, let me be the one to die instead.* And then the bubbles rising as the woman took the first breath, her lungs filling with the awful water, the deep spasm of death moving through her; and then the letting go.

His was the sadness at the center of the world. The *Chevron Mariner:* that's what this place was. It was the very beating heart of grief.

Blood was dripping from her as she made her way aft across the tilted deck. Amy could feel the change coming, a rumbling in the hills above. It would sweep down upon her like an avalanche. It would obliterate her, fashion her anew. She descended into the bowels of the ship, its maze of halls, its listing passages of pipe. Her feet sloshed through standing water the color of rust. Rainbow shimmers danced upon its surface. She moved by instinct. She homed in. She was the receiver to Carter's beacon, which inexorably drew her down and down and down.

The pump room.

They were hanging everywhere, filling the space with their glow. They clung to every surface. They lay curled upon the floor like children. Here was the reservoir, the lair. The nest of Anthony Carter, his doleful legions suspended in abeyance. *Where are you?* she thought, and as she did her body shook, and in the wake of this convulsive jolt came a massive tightening in her abdomen, as if she'd been clenched by a giant fist. She staggered, fighting to remain upright. Blots of blackness swelled across her vision. It was happening. It was happening now.

I am here.

—Where? Where are you? Please, I think that I am . . . dying.

Come to me, Amy. Come to me come to me come to me . . .

A door stood before her. Had she opened it? She stumbled forward, down the narrow passageway beyond. The floor was slick with oil, the blood of the earth, time's distillate, compressed by a planet. She came to a second portal. T1, it was marked: Tank No. 1. She knew what lay beyond. It had ever been thus. With all her strength she gripped the rusted ring and turned. Space flew open wide around her, as if she'd entered an immense cathedral.

And there he was. Anthony Carter, Twelfth of Twelve. Wizened and small, a wisp of a thing, no larger than the man he'd been and, in his heart, still was. A being of refusal made flesh. He lay on the floor, in the waste of the world; slowly he unfurled himself, rising to meet her. Carter the Sorrowful, the One Who Could Not, locked in the prison that he himself had made.

"Help me," said Amy, a last great shudder moving through her, taking her over, and she fell into his arms.

*　　*　　*

And then she was somewhere else.

She was under a highway overpass. Amy knew this place, or so it felt. Its sights and sounds and smells were laden with a weight of memory. The echoing roar of cars passing overhead; the *click-click-click* of the roadway's joints; the drifting trash and grime and heavy, smoke-choked air. Amy was standing at the edge of the road, holding a cardboard sign: HUNGRY, ANYTHING WILL HELP, GOD BLESS YOU. Traffic streamed by, cars, trucks, no one even looking her way. She was dressed in rags; her hands were black with grime. Her stomach was a stone of cold emptiness. The heedless vehicles flew past. Why would no one stop?

Then, the car. A large SUV, dark and gleaming: it slowed, then stopped, not so much drawing to the curb as alighting, like a great black bird. Its tinted windows fashioned squares of perfect reflection, doubling the world. With a soft mechanical whir, the passenger window drew down.

"Amy, hello."

Wolgast was sitting at the wheel, dressed in a navy suit and dark tie. He was smoothly shaved, his hair swept back from his forehead, shining faintly, as if it were still damp from the shower. "You're right on time." Smiling, he leaned across to open the door. "Why don't you get in?"

Amy placed her sign on the ground and climbed onto the passenger seat. The air inside the car was cool, with a leathery smell.

"It's wonderful to see you," Wolgast said. "Don't forget to buckle up, sweetheart."

Her amazement was such that she could barely form words. "Where are we going?"

"You'll see."

They drove clear of the underpass, into summer sunshine. Around them the shops and houses and cars flowed past, a world of busy humanity. The car bounced agreeably under them on its cushioning springs.

"How far is it?"

Wolgast shrugged vaguely. "Not very. Just up the road a bit." He glanced sidelong. "I have to say, you're looking very well, Amy. So grown up."

"What . . . is this place?"

"Well, Texas." He made a face of distaste. "All of this is Houston, Texas." A memory took hold of his face. "Lila got so sick of hearing about it. 'Brad, it's just a state like any other,' she always said."

"But how are we here?"

"The how, I don't know. I don't think there's an answer to that. As for the why . . ." He glanced at her again. "I'm one of his, you understand."

"Carter's."

Wolgast nodded.

"Are you in the ship, too?"

"The ship? No."

"Where, then?"

He didn't respond right away. "I think it's best if he explains it to you." His eyes shifted quickly to Amy's face again. "You really do look wonderful, Amy. The way I always imagined. I know he'll be happy to see you."

They had moved into a neighborhood of large houses, lush trees, and wide, well-kept lawns. Wolgast pulled into the driveway of a white-brick colonial and stopped the car.

"Here we are. I guess I'll leave you to it, then."

"You're not coming with me?"

"Oh, I'm afraid I'm just the messenger this time. Not even. More like the deliveryman. Just go around back."

"But I don't want to go without you."

"It's all right, sweetheart, he won't bite you." He took her hand and gently squeezed. "Go on now, he's waiting. I'll see you again soon. Everything will be all right, I promise."

Amy exited the car. Locusts were buzzing in the trees, a sound that somehow deepened the stillness. The air was heavy with moisture and smelled of freshly mown grass. Amy turned to glance at Wolgast, but the car had disappeared. This place, she understood, was different in that way; things could simply disappear.

She made her way up the driveway, through a trellised gate wreathed with flowering vines, into the backyard. Carter was sitting at a table on the patio, wearing jeans and a dirty T-shirt and heavy, unlaced boots. He was rubbing his neck and hair with a towel; his mower was parked nearby, exuding a faint aroma of gasoline. At Amy's approach he looked up, smiling.

"Well, there you are." He gestured toward the two glasses of liquid on the table. "I just got done here—come and sit a spell. I thought you might like some tea." The smile broadened to a wide, white grin. "Ain't nothing as good as a glass of tea on a hot June day."

Amy took the chair across from him. He had a small, smooth face and gentle eyes and close-cropped hair, like a cap of dark wool. His cocoa-colored skin was speckled with black spots; flecks of grass were on his shirt and arms. Adjacent to the patio, the pool was a presence of cool, inviting blueness, the water gently lapping at its tiled edges. It was only then that Amy realized it was the same house where she and Greer had spent the night.

"This place," said Amy. She angled her face toward the buzzing trees. Rich sunlight warmed her skin. "It's so beautiful."

"It rightly is, Miss Amy."

"But we're still inside the ship, aren't we?"

"In a manner," Carter replied evenly. "In a manner."

They sat in silence, sipping the cold tea. Beads of moisture dribbled down the sides of the glasses. Things were coming clearer now.

"I think I know why I'm here," said Amy.

"I'm expecting you do."

The air had suddenly chilled; Amy shivered, drawing her arms around herself. Dry leaves, like bits of brown paper, were blowing across the patio; the light had lost its color.

"I been thinking on you, Miss Amy. All the while. Me and Wolgast, we had us a talk. A good talk, like you and me is having now."

Whatever Carter was going to tell her, she suddenly didn't want it. It was the leaves that made her think it: she was afraid.

"He said he's yours. That he belongs to you."

Carter nodded in his mild way. "Man says he owes me, and I reckon that's right, but I set store by him, too. He's the one give me the time to figure it. An ocean of time, Anthony, that's what he said. I took me some there at the start, never said I didn't. Was the hunger made me. But I never could set with it. Wolgast was the one give me the chance to make things right."

"He's the one who sealed you in the ship, isn't he?"

"Yes'm. Asked him to do it when the hunger got too bad. He would have sealed his own self up too, except for you. Go look after your girl, I said. That man, he loves you with his whole heart."

Amy became aware that something was in the pool. A dark shape slowly rising, parsing the surface of the water to take its place among the floating autumn leaves.

"She always there." Carter gave his head a slow, sorrowful shake. "That's the pity of it. Every day I cut the lawn. Every day she rise."

He fell quiet for a moment, his kind face adrift in grief. Then he gathered himself and faced her squarely again. "I know it ain't fair to you, the things you got to face. Wolgast know it, too. But this here's our chance. Never come another."

Her doubt became certainty then, like a seed breaking open inside her. She had felt it for days, weeks, months. The voice of Zero, summoning her. *Amy, go to them. Go to them, our sister in blood. I have known you, felt you. You are the omega to my alpha, the one to watch and keep them.*

"Please," she said, her voice trembling. "Don't ask me to do this."

"The asking ain't mine to do. Telling, neither. This here's just about what *is.*" Carter hitched up in his chair, removed a handkerchief from his back pocket, and held it out to her. "You go on and cry if you want to, Miss Amy. You owed that at least, I reckon. Cried me a river myself."

She did; she wept. In the orphanage she had tasted life. With Caleb, and the sisters, and Peter, and all the others. She had become a part of something, a family. She had made a home in the world. Now it would be gone.

"They'll kill us both."

"I reckon they'll try. I known it from the start." He leaned over the table and took her hand. "Ain't right, I know it, but this here is ours to carry. Our one chance. Ain't never come another."

There was no way to refuse; fate had found her. The light was fading, the leaves were blowing down. In the pool, the woman's body continued on its slow passage, floating and turning in the eternal current.

"Tell me what to do."

VIII

THE CHANGELING

I'm Nobody! Who are you?
Are you—Nobody—too?
Then there's a pair of us!
Don't tell! They'd advertise, you know.

—EMILY DICKINSON

49

The first real snow of winter arrived, as it always seemed to, in the middle of the night. Sara was sleeping on the sofa when she was roused by a tapping sound. For some stretch of time this sound mingled in her mind with a dream she was having, in which she was pregnant and trying to tell Hollis about it. The scene of this dream was a perplexing jumble of overlapping locations (the porch of the house in First Colony where she had grown up; the biodiesel plant, among the roar of the grinders; a ruined theater, wholly imagined, with tattered purple curtains suspended over a stage), and though other characters drifted at the periphery (Jackie, Michael, Karen Molyneau and her daughters), its sense was one of isolation: she and Hollis were alone, and the baby, tapping away inside her—Sara understood this to be a form of code—was asking to be born. Each time she tried to explain this to Hollis, the words came out as different words entirely—not "I'm pregnant" but "It's raining," not "I'm having a baby" but "Today is Tuesday"—causing Hollis to look at her first with confusion, then amusement, and finally outright laughter. "It's not funny," Sara said. Tears of frustration filled her eyes as Hollis laughed in his warm, big-throated way. "It's not funny, it's not funny, it's not funny . . ." and on and on, and in this state the dream dissolved, and then she was awake.

She lay still a moment. The tapping was coming from the window. She pushed the blanket aside and crossed the room, and drew the drapes aside. The grounds of the Dome were kept lit at night, an island of luminescence in a sea of darkness, and through the beams of these lights an icy snow was pouring down, tossed on gusting winds. It seemed more ice than snow, but as she lingered, something changed. The particles slowed and fattened, becoming snowflakes. They descended upon every surface, building a mantle of white. In the other two rooms of the apartment Lila slept, and Sara's daughter, snug in her little bed. How Sara longed to go to her, to lift her child into her arms and carry her back to the couch and hold her as she slept. To touch her hair, her skin, to feel the warm brush of her breath. But this thought was an empty dream, nothing she dared allow herself to imagine was actually possible. Aching with longing, Sara watched the falling snow, welcoming its slow erasure of the world, though down in the flatland, she knew, it meant something else. Frozen fingers, frozen toes, bodies racked with cold. The months of dark and misery. *Well,* Sara thought with a shiver. *The winter. So it begins. At least I'll be inside.*

But when she awoke in the morning, something changed again.

"Dani, look! Snow!"

A glittering light blasted into the room. The little girl, dressed in her nightshirt, had perched on a chair to draw back the drapes and was pressing her nose to the frosted window. Sara rose quickly from the couch and yanked them shut.

"But I want to see!"

From the inner room: "Dani! Where are you? I need you!"

"Just a minute!" Sara looked into the girl's pleading eyes. "I'm sorry, sweetheart. You know the rule."

"But she can stay in bed!"

"Dani!"

Sara heaved a sigh. Lila's mornings were difficult, beset by focusless anxiety and nameless dread. The effect was magnified with each day that passed since her last feeding. Under the blood's restorative spell, she became cheerful and affectionate to both of them, even a little giddy, though her interest in Kate felt more abstract than personal; she seemed not to comprehend fully the child's age, often speaking to her as if she were an infant. On these good days, Lila appeared fully persuaded that she was living in some place called Cherry Creek, married to a man named David—though she also spoke of someone named Brad, the two seeming interchangeable—and that Sara was a housekeeper sent by "the service," whatever that was. But as the effect of the blood waned, over a period of four or five days, she became abrupt and panicky, as if this elaborate fantasy was increasingly difficult to maintain.

"Let me get her in the bath. Then I'll see if I can take you outside to play. Do we have a deal?"

The little girl nodded vigorously.

"Now get dressed."

Sara found Lila sitting up in bed, clutching the folds of her thin nightgown over her chest. If Sara had to guess her age, she would have said the woman looked about fifty; tomorrow it would be more, the lines of her face deepening, her muscles sagging, her hair graying and growing thin. Sometimes the change was so precipitous Sara could actually watch it happening. Then Guilder would bring the blood, Sara would be banished from the room with Kate, and by the time they returned, Lila would be a lush-haired, smooth-skinned twenty-five-year-old once more, the cycle starting over.

"Why didn't you answer me? I was worried."

"I'm sorry, I overslept."

"Where's Eva?"

Sara explained that the girl was getting dressed and excused herself to prepare Lila's bath. Like the woman's dressing table, the bath was a place of totemic importance. In its deep, lion-clawed cocoon, the woman could soak for hours. Sara opened the tap and laid out Lila's soaps and oils and little jars of cream with two fat, freshly laundered towels. Lila liked to bathe by candlelight; Sara took a box of wooden matches from the vanity and lit the candelabra. By the time Lila appeared in the doorway, the air was opaque with steam. Sara, in her heavy attendant's robe, had begun to sweat. Lila closed the door and turned away to remove her dressing gown. Her upper body was thin, though not as thin as it would become, its mass redistributing downward over the days, into her hips and thighs. She turned to face Sara again and regarded the tub with a look of caution.

"Dani, I'm not really feeling myself today. Could you help me in?"

Sara took Lila by the hand as she stepped gingerly over the railing and lowered herself into the steaming water. Once she was immersed, the woman's expression softened, tension departing her face. Sinking down to her chin, she took a long, happy breath, moving her hands like paddles to shift the water to and fro across her body. She leaned back to wet her hair, then shimmied up, bracing her back against the side of the tub. Freed of gravity, the woman's breasts floated over her chest in a pantomime of restored youth.

"I do love the bath," she murmured.

Sara took her place on the stool beside the tub. "Hair first?"

"Mmmmmm." Lila's eyes were closed. "Please."

Sara began. As with everything, there was a certain way Lila liked it done. First the crown of her head, Sara's hands vigorously massaging, then moving downward to smooth the long strands of hair between her fingers. The soap, then a rinse, then the same order of events repeated with the scented oil. Sometimes she had Sara do this more than once.

"It snowed last night," Sara ventured.

"Hmmmm." Lila's face was relaxed, her eyes still closed. "Well, that's Denver for you. If you don't like the weather, just wait a minute, it will change. That's something my father always said."

Lila's father's sayings, duly noted as such, were a prominent feature of their conversations. Sara used a pitcher dipped in bathwater to pour the soap away from Lila's forehead and began to work in the oil.

"So I suppose everything will be closed," Lila continued. "I really wanted to get to the market. We're practically out of everything." Never mind that, as far as Sara was aware, Lila never set foot from the apartment. "You know what I'd like, Dani? A long, lovely lunch. Someplace special. With good linens and china and flowers on the table."

Sara had learned to go along. "That sounds nice."

Lila gave a protracted sigh of memory, sinking deeper into the bath. "I can't tell you how long it's been since I had a long, lovely lunch."

A few minutes passed, Sara working the oil into the woman's scalp. "I think Eva would enjoy some time outside." It felt like a monstrous lie to say this name, but sometimes it was unavoidable.

"Yes, I suppose she would," Lila said noncommittally.

"I was wondering, are there any other children she can play with?"

"Other children?"

"Yes, someone her own age. I thought it would be good for her to have some friends."

Lila frowned uncomfortably. Sara wondered if she'd pressed too far. "Well," she said, with a tone of concession, "there's that neighbor girl, little what's-her-name. With the dark hair. But I hardly ever see her. Most of the families around here keep to themselves. Bunch of sticks-in-the-mud, if you ask me." Then: "But you're a good friend to her, aren't you, Dani?"

A friend. What stinging irony. "I try to be."

"No, it's more than that." Lila smiled drowsily. "There's something different about you, I can tell. I think it's wonderful for Eva, having a friend like you."

"So I can take her outside," Sara said.

"In a minute." Lila closed her eyes again. "I was hoping you could read to me. I do so love to be read to in the bath."

By the time they escaped, it was nearly noon. Sara bundled Eva in a coat and mittens and rubber galoshes and a woolen cap, pulling it down over the little girl's ears. For herself she had only the robe, and nothing for her feet but her ratty sneakers and wool socks, but she hardly cared. Cold feet, so what? They took the stairs to the courtyard and emerged into a world so remade it felt like an entirely new place. The air had a sharp, fresh smell, and the sun was rebounding off the snow with eye-searing intensity. After so many days in the enforced gloom of the apartment, Sara had to pause at the threshold to give her vision a moment to adjust. But Kate had no such difficulty. With a snap of energy she released Sara's hand and bolted from the doorway, propelling herself across the courtyard. By the time Sara had slogged toward her—she might have erred about the sneakers; they were going to be a problem—the child was scooping handfuls of downy snow into her mouth.

"It tastes . . . cold." Her face beamed with happiness. "Try some."

Sara did as instructed. "Yum," she said.

She showed the girl how to build a snowman. Her mind was full of sweet nostalgia; it was as if she were a Little again, playing in the courtyard of the Sanctuary. But this was different; Sara was the mother now. Time had turned its inexorable circle. How wonderful to feel her daughter's infectious happiness, to experience the sense of wonder that passed between them. For the time being, all pain was banished from Sara's mind. They could have been anywhere. The two of them.

Sara thought of Amy, too, the first time in years she had done this. Amy, who had never been a little girl, or so it seemed, but somehow always was; Amy, the Girl from Nowhere, in whose person time was not a circle but a thing stopped and held, a century cupped in the hand. Sara felt a sudden, unexpected sadness for her. She had always wondered why Amy had destroyed the vials of virus that night at the Farmstead, casting them into the flames. Sara had hated them, not just what they represented but the very fact of their existence, but she had also known what they were: a hope of salvation, the one weapon powerful enough to use against the Twelve. (*The Twelve,* she thought; how long had it been since that name had crossed her mind as well?) Sara had never known quite what to think of Amy's decision; now she had her answer. Amy had known that the life those vials had denied her was the only true human reality. In Sara's daughter, this triumphantly alive little person that Sara's body had made, lay the answer to the greatest mystery of all—the mystery of death, and what came after. How obvious it was. Death was nothing, because there was no death. By the simple fact of Kate's existence, Sara was joined to something eternal. To have a child was to receive the gift of true immortality—not time stopped, as it had stopped in Amy, but time continuing and everlasting.

"Let's make snow angels," she said.

Kate had never done this. They lay down side by side, their bodies enveloped in whiteness and the tips of their fingers just touching. Above them the sun and sky looked down in witness. They moved their limbs back and forth and rose to inspect the imprints. Sara explained what angels were: they're us.

"That's funny," said Kate, smiling.

The serving girl, Jenny, would be bringing lunch; their time in the snow was at an end. Sara imagined the rest of the day: Lila lost in fantasy, leaving the two of them alone; wet clothing drying on racks by the fire, Sara and her daughter snuggled on the sofa and the sweet exchange of heat where their bodies touched and the hours of stories she would read—*Peter Rabbit* and *Squirrel Nutkin* and *James and the Giant Peach*—before the two of them drifted together into a sleep of intertwining dreams. Never had she been so happy.

They were walking back to the entrance when Sara glanced up to the window and saw that the drapes were pulled aside. Lila was watching them, her eyes concealed behind dark glasses. How long had she stood there?

"What's she doing?" Kate asked.

Sara summoned a smile to her face. "I think she was just enjoying watching us." But inside she felt a spark of fear.

"Why do I have to call her Mummy?"

Sara stopped in her tracks. "What did you say?"

For a moment the girl was silent. Melted snow was dripping off the branches.

"I'm tired, Dani," Kate said. "Can you pick me up?"

Unbearable joy. The girl's weight was nothing in her arms. It was the missing part of her, come home. Lila was still watching from the window, but Sara didn't care. Kate wrapped her arms and legs tightly around her, and in this manner, Sara carried her daughter out of the snow and back to the apartment.

Sara had received no messages; every day she looked for the inverted spoon, the note tucked under the plate, finding none. Jenny came and went, depositing her trays of bread and cornmeal and soup and wordlessly scurrying away. Having virtually never left the apartment except to take Kate to the courtyard, Sara had glimpsed Vale only once, when Lila had sent her to look for a maintenance worker to unplug the tub's drain. He was walking down the corridor in the company of two other cols, including the jowly one who had met them at the elevator on Sara's first day. Vale had passed right by her. As ever, his disguise—which was really just a way of carrying himself, the confident saunter of his rank—was absolutely seamless. No recognition occurred between them; if Vale knew who she was, he gave no sign.

She wasn't supposed to send a message on her own except for an emergency, but the lack of contact left her anxious. Finally she decided to risk it. There was no loose paper in the apartment, but of course there were the books. One night after Lila had gone to bed, Sara tore a small piece from the back of *Winnie-the-Pooh*. The larger problem was finding something to write with; there were no pens or pencils in the apartment. But in the bottom drawer of Lila's dressing table she found a sewing kit with a cushion of needles. Sara selected the one that looked the sharpest, jabbed it into the tip of her index finger, and squeezed, summoning a bead of blood. Using the needle as a makeshift pen, she scrawled her message onto the paper.

Need meeting. D.

The following day, when Jenny came to collect her lunch tray, Sara was waiting. Rather than allow the girl to simply whisk it away as usual, Sara lifted the tray from the table and held it out to her, making eye contact and then darting her glance downward, lest the point be missed.

"Thank you, Jenny."

Two days later came the reply. Sara secreted the note into the folds of her robe, waiting for a private moment. This didn't happen until later in the day, when Lila napped. She was close to the end of her cycle now, parched and infirm and out of sorts; soon Guilder would be coming with the blood. In the bathroom Sara unfolded the slip of paper, on which was written a time and place and a single sentence of instruction. Sara's heart sank; she hadn't realized she'd have to leave the Dome. She would need to secure Lila's permission under some credible pretext; if she didn't get it, she had no idea what she'd do. With Lila in her impaired state, Sara wondered if the woman would even comprehend the request.

She broached the subject the next day while she was washing Lila's hair. A few hours off, was how she put it. An outing to the market. It would be good to see a few new faces, and while she was there she could look for some special oils or soaps. The request aroused in Lila a palpable anxiety; she'd become more clingy recently, barely letting Sara out of her sight. But in the end she yielded to the gentle force of Sara's argument. *Just don't be too long,* said Lila. *I never know what to do without you, Dani.*

Vale had paved the way; at the front desk, the col handed her the pass with a perfunctory warning that it was only for two hours. Sara stepped into the wind and headed toward the market. Only cols and redeyes were allowed to barter there; currency took the form of small plastic chips in three colors, red, blue, and white. In the pocket of Sara's robe were five of each, part of the compensation that Lila doled out to her every seven days, furthering the fiction that Sara was a paid employee. The snow had been pushed from the sidewalks in what had once been the town's small commercial area, three blocks of brick buildings adjacent to the college. Most of the city went unused and abandoned, fading into soft decay;

nearly all of the redeyes, except for senior staff, lived in a mid-rise apartment complex at the south end of downtown. The market was the heart of the city, with checkpoints at either end. Some of the buildings still bore signs indicating their original function: Iowa State Bank, Fort Powell Army-Navy, Wimpy's Café, Prairie Books and Music. There was even a small movie theater with a marquee; Sara had heard that cols were sometimes permitted to go, to watch the handful of movies that were shown over and over again.

She displayed her pass at the checkpoint. The streets were vacant save for the patrols and a handful of redeyes, strolling in their luxuriously heavy coats and sunglasses. Shielded by her veil, Sara moved in a bubble of anonymity, though this sense of security was, she knew, a dangerous illusion. She walked at a pace that was neither fast nor slow, her head down against the cold gusts that whipped up from the streets and around the corners of the buildings.

She came to the apothecary. Bells tinkled as she stepped inside. The room was warm and fragrant with wood smoke and herbs. Behind the counter, a woman with a scrim of gray hair and a puckered, toothless mouth was bent over a scale, measuring out minute quantities of a pale yellow powder and funneling them into tiny glass vials. She lifted her eyes as Sara entered, then darted them to the col lingering by a display of scented oils. *Be careful. I know who you are. Don't approach until I get rid of him.* Then, speaking in an elevated, helpful voice: "Sir, perhaps you were looking for something special."

The col was sniffing a bar of soap. Mid-thirties, not unhandsome, broadcasting an air of vanity. He returned the soap to its place on the display. "Something for a headache."

"Ah." A smile of assurance; the solution was in hand. "Just a moment."

The old woman selected a jar from the wall of herbals behind her, spooned the dry leaves into a paper package, and handed it to him over the counter. "Dissolve this in warm water. Just a pinch should do it."

He surveyed the package uneasily. "What's in it? You're not trying to poison me, old woman?"

"Nothing more than common dillonweed. I use it myself. If you want me to sample it first, I'd be glad to."

"Forget it."

He paid her with a single blue chip; the woman followed him with her eyes as he departed to a chime of bells.

"Come with me," she said to Sara.

She led her to a storage room in the back with a table and chairs and a door to the alleyway. The woman told Sara to wait and returned to the front of the store. Several minutes passed; then the door opened: Nina, dressed in a flatlander's tunic and dark jacket and a long scarf that wrapped the lower half of her face.

"This is incredibly dumb, Sara. Do you know how dangerous this is?"

Sara stared into the woman's steely eyes. Until this moment, she hadn't realized how angry she was.

"You knew my daughter was alive, didn't you?"

Nina was unwinding the scarf. "Of course we knew. That's what we *do,* Sara: we know things, then we put the information to use. I'd think you'd be happy about it."

"How long?"

"Does that matter?"

"Yes, damnit, it matters."

Nina gave her a hard look. "All right, suppose we've known all along. Supposing we'd told you. What would you have done? Don't bother to answer. You would have gone off half-cocked and done something stupid. You wouldn't have made it ten steps into the Dome without blowing your cover. If it's any consolation, there was a good deal of discussion about this. Jackie thought you should know. But the prevailing opinion was that the success of the operation came first."

"Prevailing opinion. Meaning yours."

"Mine and Eustace's." For a moment, Nina's expression seemed to soften. But only for a moment. "Don't take it so hard. You got what you wanted. Be happy."

"What I want is to get her out of there."

"Which is what we're counting on, Sara. And we'll get her out, in time."

"When?"

"I think that should be obvious. When all of this is over."

"Are you *blackmailing* me?"

Nina shrugged off the accusation. "Don't misunderstand me—it's not something I'm particularly averse to. But in this case, I don't have to." She looked at Sara carefully. "What do you think happens to those girls?"

"What do you mean, 'girls'? My daughter's the only one."

"She is *now.* But she's not the first. There's always another Eva. Giving Lila a child is the only way Guilder can keep her calm. Once they reach a certain age, though, the woman loses interest, or else the child rejects her. Then they get her a new one."

A wave of dizziness filled Sara's head; she had to sit down. "How old?"

"Five or six. It varies. But it always happens, Sara. That's what I'm telling you. The clock is ticking. Maybe not today, or even tomorrow, but soon. Then off to the basement she goes."

Sara forced herself to the next question: "What's in the basement?"

"It's where they make the blood for the redeyes. We don't know all the details. The process starts with human blood, but then something happens to it. They change it somehow. There's a man down there, a kind of viral, or so it's said. They call him the Source. He drinks a distillate of human blood, it changes in his body, something different comes out. You've seen what happens to the woman?"

Sara nodded.

"It happens to all of them, but it's slower in the men. The blood of the Source rejuvenates them. It's what keeps them alive. But once your daughter goes down there, she'll never come out."

A storm of emotions roiled inside Sara. Anger, helplessness, a fierce desire to protect her daughter. It was so intense she thought she might be ill.

"What am I supposed to do?"

"When the time comes, we'll tell you. We'll get her out. You have my word."

Sara understood what Nina was asking. Not asking: telling. They had maneuvered her perfectly. Kate was the hostage, and the ransom would be paid in blood.

"Hate her for it, Sara. Think about what she does. The moment will come for all of us, myself included, just like it came for Jackie. I'll go willingly when I'm asked. And unless this thing comes off, your daughter is on her own. We'll never be able to reach her."

"Where is it?" Sara asked. She didn't have to be clearer than that; her meaning was obvious.

"It's better if you don't know yet. You'll receive a message the usual way. You're the linchpin, and the timing matters."

"What if I can't do it?"

"Then you die anyway. And so does your daughter. It's just a matter of when. I've told you about the how." Her eyes were looking deep into Sara's. There was no compassion anywhere inside them, only an icy clarity. "If this goes according to plan, it will be the end of the redeyes. Guilder, Lila, all of them. Do you understand what I'm saying to you?"

Sara's mind had gone utterly numb. She felt herself nodding, then saying, in a faint voice, "Yes."

"Then do your duty. Do it for your daughter. Kate, is that her name?"

Sara was dumbstruck. "How did you—?"

"Because you told me. Don't you remember? You told me her name the day she was born."

Of course, she thought. So much made sense now. Nina was the woman from the birthing ward who'd given her the lock of Kate's hair.

"You may not believe me, Sara, but I'm trying to right a wrong here."

Sara wanted to laugh. She would have, if such a thing were still possible. "You have a funny way of showing it."

"Maybe so. But those are the times we live in." Another searching pause. "You have this inside you. I know it when I see it."

Did she? The question was meaningless. Somehow she would have to find the strength.

"Do it for your daughter, Sara. Do it for Kate. Otherwise she has no chance."

50

The things they were doing were endurable. Not without pain, and pain's cousin, which was the anticipation of it. But able to be borne. For a long time they asked her nothing. They made no demands of any sort. This was simply the sort of thing they liked to do, and they would go on doing it, taking their dark pleasure, which Alicia did not surrender easily. She silenced her cries, she bore it all stoically, she laughed whenever she could, saying: *Do your damnedest, my friends. I'm the one who must be kept in chains. Do you think this fact, in and of itself, is not a kind of victory?*

The water was the worst of it. Strange, because Alicia had always liked the water. She'd been a fearless swimmer as a child, diving deep into the grotto at the Colony, holding her breath as long as she could, touching the bottom as her ears thudded and watching the bubbles of her exhaled breath ascending from darkness into sunlight far above. Sometimes they funneled the water into her mouth. Sometimes they pulled her down from the chains, strapped her to a board, and dunked her headfirst into an icy tub. Each time she thought, *Here goes,* and counted the seconds until it was over.

Her strength had ebbed discernibly as the days passed. A slight downward adjustment on the whole, but enough. They offered her food, pasty gruel of soy or corn and oversmoked strips of meat hardened to the consistency of leather, their unstated intention being to keep her alive so that they could enjoy themselves for as long as possible, but without the others . . . well. She made a silent vow: when at last she tasted human blood, the unambiguous final act of her transformation, the blood would be theirs. To surrender her membership in the human race was a heavy thing, but there was some consolation in this thought. She would drink the bastards dry.

There was no way to gauge the march of days. Left to herself, she adopted the mental practice of retracing events of her past, moving through her memory as if it were a hallway of pictures: standing the watch at First Colony; her journey with Peter and Amy and the others across the Darklands to Colorado; her strange, arid childhood with the Colonel. She had always called him "sir," never "Daddy" or even "Niles"; from the start he had been her superior officer, not a father or friend. Strange to think of that now. Her memories of her life carried a range of emotions, grief and happiness and exhilaration and loneliness and to some degree love, but the feeling they shared was of belonging. She was her memories, and her memories were her. She hoped she'd get to keep them when all was said and done.

She had begun to wonder if all they had in mind for her was an endless repetition of their painful ministrations when the rhythm of her captivity was disrupted by the arrival of a man who bore the appearance of being in charge. He did not introduce himself, and for at least a minute he didn't say anything at all, just stood before her where she was suspended from the ceiling, examining her with the expression of someone reading a puzzling book. He was dressed in a dark suit and tie and stiff white shirt; he didn't look a day over thirty. His skin was pale and tender, as if it never saw the sun. But it was his eyes that told the real story. Why should she be surprised?

"You're . . . different." Stepping closer, he breathed sharply through his nose, darting it at the air around her like a dog.

"Yeah, I get that a lot."

"I can smell it on you."

"Can't say I've had much of a chance to clean up." She offered her boldest grin. "And you might be . . . ?"

"I'll ask the questions."

"You know, you shouldn't read in the dark like that. It's hell on your eyes."

He reared back and struck her, open-palmed, across the face.

"Wow," Alicia said, waggling her jaw. "Ouch. That kind of stings."

He moved forward again and violently twisted her upraised arm. "Why don't you have a tag?"

"That's a nifty outfit you're wearing. Makes a girl feel a little under-dressed."

Another blow to the face, like the crack of a whip. Alicia blinked her watering eyes and ran her tongue over her teeth, tasting blood. "You know, you guys have been doing that a lot. It's not very welcoming. I don't think I like you very much."

His bloodshot eyes narrowed with rage. Now she was getting some-where. "Tell me about Sergio."

"Can't say that rings a bell."

He struck her again. Little scraps of light twinkled in her vision. She could tell that he was saving the full measure of his strength. He would dole it out one drop at a time, a slow escalation.

"Why don't you cut me down from here and we can have us a real chat? Because this obviously isn't working for you."

Wham went his hand, a fist this time. It was like being hit by a board. Alicia shook it off, spitting blood.

"Tell me."

"Go piss yourself."

A hammering blow to her gut. Her breath froze in her chest as her diaphragm compressed like a vise. The airless seconds passed. The mo-ment her lungs finally expanded, he hit her again.

"Who . . . is . . . Sergio?"

Alicia was having a little trouble focusing. Focusing and breathing and thinking. She braced herself for another blow, but none arrived; she became aware that the man had opened the door. Three figures stepped through. They were carrying a kind of bench, waist-high, with a broad frame at its base.

"I'd like to introduce you to a friend of mine. This is Sod. You've actu-ally already met."

Alicia's vision gradually sharpened. Something was wrong with the man's face. Or, rather, one side of his face, which looked like a slab of inconsistently cooked meat, raw at the center and blackened at the edges. Half the man's hair had burned away, as had most of his nose. His left eye looked melted, vulcanized to a runny jelly.

"Yuck," Alicia managed to reply.

"Sod here was in the holding area when you decided to shoot a tank full of liquid propane. He's not so happy about it."

"All in a day's work. Nice to meet you, Sod. That's quite a name, 'Sod.'"

"Sod is a man of special enthusiasms. You could say the name is well earned. He has a bit of a bone to pick with you." The man in the suit addressed the other two: "Tie her down. On second thought, wait a second."

The blows fell and fell. The face. The body. By the time the man had exhausted himself, Alicia was barely feeling any of it. Pain had become something else—distant, vague. A rattle of chains and a release of pressure on her wrists. She was facing the floor, her waist straddling the bench and her feet bound to its frame, spread wide. Her trousers were yanked from her body.

"A little privacy for our friend here," the first man said, and Alicia heard the door closing, and then the sound, ominous and final, of tumblers turning in the lock.

51

Every night, as Amy and Greer journeyed northward, she dreamed of Wolgast. Sometimes they were on the carousel. Sometimes they were driving in a car, the little towns and the green spring countryside flowing past, mountains looming in the distance, their faces shining with ice. Tonight they were in Oregon, at the camp. They were in the main room of the lodge, sitting across from each other on the floor, their legs folded Indian-style, and on the floor between them was the Monopoly board with its squares of faded color and money in ordered piles and Amy's little hat and Wolgast's little automobile and Wolgast tossing the dice from a cup and moving his piece forward to St. Charles Place, site of one of Amy's six (six!) hotels. The room was warm from the stove, and outside the windows a dry snow was falling through the velvety darkness and the deep winter cold.

"For Pete's sake," he groaned.

He doled out the bills. His exasperation was false; he wanted to lose. He told her she was lucky, making it so with his words. You're lucky, Amy.

Round and round their pieces traveled. More money changed hands. Park Place, Illinois Avenue, Marvin Gardens, the hilariously named "B. & O." Amy's stack of money grew as Wolgast's shrank toward zero. She bought railroads and utilities, she had built her houses and hotels everywhere, a gauntlet of ownership that enabled her to erect more, blanketing the board. Understanding this accelerating mathematics was the key to the game.

"I think I need a loan," Wolgast confessed.

"Try the bank." She was grinning with victory. Once he borrowed money, the end would fall swiftly; he would toss up his arms in surrender. Then they would assume their customary places on the sofa, a blanket drawn up to their chests, and take turns reading to each other. Tonight's book: H. G. Wells, *The Time Machine.*

He spilled the dice onto the board. A three and a four. He moved his car ahead and landed on "Luxury Tax," with its little diamond ring.

"Not again." He rolled his eyes and paid up. "It's so wonderful to be here with you." He lifted his eyes past her, to the window. "It sure is snowing out there. How long has it been snowing?"

"I think it's been snowing a long time."

"I've always loved it. It makes me remember being a kid. It always feels like Christmas when it snows."

The wood in the stove crackled. All through the dense forest the snow fell and fell. Morning would break with a soft white light and silence, though in the place they were, morning would not come.

"Every year my parents took me to see *A Christmas Carol.* Wherever we were living, they'd find a theater and take me. Jacob Marley always scared me something awful. *He wore the chains he forged in life.* It's so sad. But beautiful, too. So many stories are like that." He thought for a moment. "Sometimes I wish I could stay here forever with you. Silly of me, I know. Nothing lasts forever."

"Some things do."

"What kind of things?"

"The things we like to remember. The love we've felt for people."

"The way I love you," said Wolgast.

Amy nodded.

"Because I do, you know," he said. "Did I ever tell you that?"

"You didn't need to say it. I always knew. I knew it from the start."

"No, I should have said it." His tone was regretful. "It's better when it's said."

A silence descended, deep as the forest, deep as the snow that fell upon it.

"Something is different about you, Amy." He was studying her face. "Something's changed."

"I think that it has, yes."

A soft darkness was moving in from the edges. It always happened this way, like lights going down on a stage until all that remained was the two of them.

"Well, whatever it is," he said, and grinned, "I like it." A moment passed, then: "Did you tell Carter how sorry I was?"

"He knows."

Wolgast was gazing past her. "That's something I can never forgive myself for. I knew it just to look at him. He loved that woman with his whole heart." He dropped his eyes to the Monopoly board. "Looks like we're done here. I don't know how you do it. I'll get you next time."

"Would you like to read?"

They took their place on the couch beneath the woolen blanket. Mugs of hot cocoa sat on the table, having arrived, like everything else, of their own accord. Wolgast lifted the book and riffled the pages until he found the right one.

"*The Time Machine,* chapter seven." He cleared his throat and turned his face toward her. "My brave girl. My brave Amy. I really do, you know."

"I love you, too," said Amy, nestling against him.

And in this manner they passed an infinity of hours, the barest blink of an eye, until the darkness, a blanket in its own right, settled down upon them.

52

They followed the eastern supply line north to Texarkana, taking food and fuel and sleeping in the hardboxes. Their vehicle was one of Tifty's, a small cargo truck retrofitted as a portable, which they would soon need: north of Little Rock they'd be sheltering in the open. Fuel was a problem they didn't have, Tifty explained. The truck could carry an extra two hundred gallons in reserve, and on his trip north with Greer and Crukshank, fifteen years ago, they'd scouted sources all the way to the Iowa line—airfields, diesel power plants, large commercial depots with their fields of mushrooming tanks. The truck was equipped with a filtering system they could use to strip out the contaminants, and an oxidizing compound. A slow process, but with luck and good weather, they could reach Iowa by the middle of December.

Their first night in the portable occurred a hundred miles south of the Missouri border. As twilight fell, Tifty retrieved a large plastic jug from the cargo bed, pulled a rag over his face, and poured the contents, a clear liquid, in a line around the vehicle.

"What's in that stuff?" Lore asked. The stink was eye-watering.

"Old family recipe. The dracs hate it—plus, it covers our smell. They won't even know we're in there."

They ate their dinner of beans and hardtack and bedded down on the racks. Soon Hollis was snoring away. Hollis? Peter thought. No, Lore. She slept the way she did everything: however she liked. Peter could understand why Michael was drawn to her—her attraction was powerful—but also why his friend wouldn't come out and say so. Who could withstand being wanted so badly? Even if the quarry wanted to be caught, it put up a struggle. During their days of waiting at the refinery, Peter had wondered, more than once, if Lore was flirting with him. She was, he decided; but it was only a tactic. She was trying to draw herself deeper into Michael's world. Once she got to the heart of it, he'd have no defenses left; Michael would be hers.

Peter shifted on his rack, trying to make himself comfortable; he always had difficulty getting to sleep in a portable. Just when he would begin drifting off, a noise from outside would jar him into wakefulness. One time near Amarillo, the virals had pounded on the walls all night. They'd actually lifted the frame and attempted to turn it over. To keep their spirits up, the men of Peter's squad had passed the hours playing poker and telling jokes, as if nothing of importance were happening. *Hell of a racket out there* was the most anyone would say. *How am I supposed to concentrate on the cards?* Peter would miss that life; he was AWOL nine days, as much of an outlaw as Hollis or Tifty. No matter what Gunnar might offer in Peter's defense, the man's message had been clear: you do this on your own; no one's going to say they knew you.

The next thing he was aware of, Hollis was shaking him awake. They disembarked into the cold. This far north, there could be no doubt of the change of seasons. The sky set low with heavy gray clouds like formations of airborne stone.

"See?" Tifty said, gesturing at the ground around the truck. "No tracks at all."

They drove on. The absence of virals nagged at Peter's mind. Even outside the hardboxes they'd seen no tracks, no scat. A welcome turn of events, but so unlikely as to be disturbing, as if the virals were saving something special for them.

Their progress slowed, the roads becoming vague; frequently Tifty had to stop the truck to recalculate their course, using a compass and maps and sometimes a sextant, a device Peter had never seen before.

Michael showed him how it worked. By measuring the sun's angle to the horizon, and taking into account the time and date, it was possible to compute their location without any other points of reference. The instrument was typically used on ships at sea, Michael explained, where the horizon was unobstructed, but it could work on land, too. How do you know this stuff? Peter asked, but realized as he posed the question what the answer was. Michael had taught himself to use a sextant for that day when he would sail out to find, or not find, the barrier.

The days of travel passed, and still no virals. By now they were openly puzzling over this, though the discussion never advanced beyond noting its oddness. *Strange,* they said. *I suppose we should consider ourselves lucky.* Which they were, but luck had a way of betraying you in the end. Eleven days in, Tifty announced that they were approaching the Missouri-Iowa line. They were dirty and exhausted; tempers were short. For two full days they'd been stymied by a nameless river, backtracking mile after mile, trying to find a bridge still standing. Their fuel supply was getting low. The landscape had changed again, not quite as flat as Texas but close, with gently undulating hills subsumed under waist-high grass. The hour was approaching noon when Hollis, at the wheel, brought the truck to a halt.

Peter, who had been dozing in the back, roused to the sound of the truck's doors opening. He drew upright to find himself alone in the cab. Why were they stopping?

He retrieved his rifle and climbed down. Everything was coated with a fine, pale powder—the grass, the trees. Snow? The air had a tart smell, like something burnt. Not snow. Ashes. Little clouds of whiteness puffed underfoot as Peter advanced to where the others were standing, at the crest of a hill. There he stopped, as his companions had stopped, pinned in place by what they saw.

"For the love of God," Michael said. "What the hell are we looking at?"

53

This woman: who was she?

A spy. An insurgent. That much was obvious; her attempt to free the hostages had all the trademarks, and she had killed six men before making her fatal mistake. But the absence of a tag on her arm didn't add up. That curious odor Guilder had detected; what did it mean? They'd recovered her weapon, a Browning semiautomatic with two bullets remaining in the magazine. Guilder had never seen one like it; it wasn't one of theirs. Either the insurgency had stockpiled a cache of weapons from a source he didn't know about, or the woman came from someplace else entirely.

Guilder didn't like mysteries. He liked them even less than he liked the idea of Sergio.

The woman seemed unbreakable. She hadn't told them so much as her name. Even Sod, that psychopath, a man of notoriously revolting appetites, had failed to extract a scrap of information. The decision to employ the man's services had come about with curious ease. Sending people to the feedlot was one thing; the virals made mercifully short work of it, and the creatures needed to be fed. It wasn't anything nice, but it was over fast. And as for a few blows in detention, or the cautious application of the waterboard, well, sometimes such measures were simply unavoidable. What had the term been, back in the day? Enhanced interrogation.

But sanctioned rape: that was something new. That was a bit of a head-scratcher. It was the kind of thing that happened in small, brutal countries where men with machetes hacked people to bits for no reason other than the fact that they'd been born in the wrong village, or had slightly different ears, or preferred chocolate to vanilla. The thought should have repelled him. It should have been . . . beneath him. This was what Sergio had driven him to. Strange how something could seem completely crazy one day and entirely reasonable the next.

These were the thoughts running through Guilder's mind as he sat at the head of the conference table. If he'd had the option, he would have skipped these weekly meetings, which inevitably devolved into convoluted procedural squabbling, a classic example of too many cooks in the kitchen. Guilder was a firm believer in a clear chain of command and the dispersed authorities of the pyramidal bureaucracy. It tended to create a bloat of busywork at the bottom and an excessive appetite for paperwork and precedent, but it kept everybody in his own corner. Still, the pretense of shared governance needed to be maintained, at least for now.

"Does anybody have anything to say?"

No one seemed to. After an uncomfortable silence, Propaganda Minister Hoppel, who was seated to Guilder's immediate left, next to Suresh, the Minister of Public Health, and directly across from Wilkes, cleared his throat and said, "I think what everybody is worried about, well, not so much worried as concerned, and I think I'm speaking for everyone here—"

"For God's sake, spit it out. And take off your glasses."

"Oh. Right." Hoppel slid the smoke-colored lenses from his face and placed them with nervous delicacy on the conference table. "As I said," he continued, and cleared his throat again. "Is it possible that, maybe, things are getting a little out of hand?"

"You're damn right they are. That's the first intelligent thing anybody has said to me all day."

"What I mean is, the strategies we've employed don't seem to be getting us where we want to be."

Guilder sighed with irritation. "What are you suggesting?"

Hoppel's eyes darted involuntarily at his colleagues. *You better back me up here—I'm not going out on this limb by myself.*

"Perhaps we should de-escalate. For a time."

"De-escalate. We're getting hammered out there."

"Well, that's the thing. There's a lot of talk in the flatland, and it's not going our way. Maybe we should try ratcheting things down a bit. See where that leaves us."

"Have you lost your mind? Have all of you lost your minds?"

"You said yourself that things aren't really working out the way we'd like."

"I didn't say that, you did."

"Be that as it may, a few of us were talking—"

"That's the worst-kept secret in this room."

"Right. So, okay. What we came up with was the idea that maybe we should go in the opposite direction. More of a hearts-and-minds approach. If you follow."

Guilder took a calming breath. "So what you're suggesting, and excuse the paraphrase, is that we should look like pussies."

"Director Guilder, if I may." This was Suresh. "The pattern of a successful insurgency—"

"They're killing people. They're killing *flatlanders*. What about this isn't clear? These people are butchers."

"No one is saying different," Suresh continued with a bland look. "And for a while that worked in our favor. But the roundups haven't produced any usable intelligence. We still don't know where Sergio is or how he moves. No one's come forward. And in the meantime, the reprisals have been an effective recruitment tool for the insurgency."

"Do you know how you sound? I'll tell you how you sound. You sound rehearsed."

Suresh ignored the barb. "Let me show you something."

From a folder on the table he withdrew a sheet of paper, which he slid toward Guilder. One of their own propaganda bulletins, but on the other side was scrawled a different message.

Flatlanders, Rise Up!

The Last Days of the Redeyes Are at Hand!

Join Your Brethren in the Insurgency!

Every Act of Disobedience Strikes a Blow Against the Regime!

And so on, in that vein. Guilder lifted his head to find everyone staring at him, as if he were a bomb that might go off.

"So? What does this prove?"

"HR personnel have found fifty-six of these so far," Suresh replied. "I'll give you an example of the problem this is causing. This morning at roll call, an entire lodge refused to sing the anthem."

"And were they beaten?"

"There were over three hundred of them. And we can only hold half that number in detention. We simply don't have the room."

"So cut their rations in half."

"The flatlanders are on a subsistence diet already. We reduce it any further and they won't be able to work."

It was maddening. Every point Guilder made was instantly parried. He was looking down the barrel of nothing less than an organized insurrection among the senior staff.

"Get out, all of you."

"I think," Suresh pressed with infuriating composure, "that we should come to some consensus on a strategy."

A hot rush of blood shot to Guilder's face. The veins were pounding in his head; he was practically apoplectic. He picked up the paper and waved it in the air.

"Hearts and minds. Do you hear what you're saying? Did you read this?"

"Director Guilder—"

"I have nothing more to say to you. Go."

Papers were gathered, briefcases closed, anxious glances exchanged around the table. Everybody rose and started moving toward the exit. Guilder put his head in his hands. Jesus Christ, this was all he needed. Something had to be done, and it had to be done immediately.

"Wilkes, wait a second."

The man turned, eyebrows raised.

"You stay."

The others departed. His chief of staff lingered by the door.

"Sit."

Wilkes returned to his chair.

"You mind telling me what the hell that was about? I've always trusted you, Fred. Relied on you to keep things running. Don't bullshit me now."

"They're just worried."

"Worried is one thing. I won't tolerate division in the ranks. Not when we're so close. They could get here any day now."

"Everybody understands that. They just don't want . . . well, for things to get out of control. They caught me by surprise, too."

Save your excuses, thought Guilder. "What do you think? Have they gotten out of control?"

"Do you really want to ask me that?" When Guilder said nothing, Wilkes shrugged. "Maybe a little."

Guilder rose, removed his glasses from his jacket pocket, and pulled the drapes aside. This dismal place. This middle of goddamned nowhere. He found himself suddenly nostalgic for the past, the old world of cars and restaurants and stores and dry cleaners and tax returns and traffic jams and waiting in line at the movies. He hadn't felt this depressed in a long time.

"People are going to have to have more babies."

"Sir?"

He spoke with his back to the man. "Babies, Fred." He shook his head at the irony. "Funny, I've never really known much about them. Never really felt the urge. You had a couple, didn't you?"

It was an unwritten rule not to ask about their former lives. Guilder could feel Wilkes's hesitation in his answer. "The missus and I had three. Two boys and a girl. Seven grandkids, too."

"Do you think about them?"

Guilder turned from the window. Wilkes had put on his glasses, too. Was it the light or something else?

"Not anymore." One corner of Wilkes's mouth gave a little twitch. "Are you testing me, Horace?"

"Maybe I am, a little."

"Don't."

The word had more force behind it than Guilder had ever heard from the man. He couldn't decide if this was reassuring or not.

"We're going to have to get everybody on the same page, you know. Can I count on you?"

"Why do you even have to ask that?"

"Humor me, Fred."

A hitch of time; then Wilkes nodded.

The right answer, but Wilkes's hesitancy nagged. Why *was* Guilder asking? It wasn't just the juvenile tenor of the meeting that bothered him; he'd dealt with that before. Somebody was always stepping on somebody else's toes. *Ouch! That hurt! No fair! I'm telling!* Something deeper and more troubling was brewing. It was more than a failure of resolve; it had the feeling of an insurrection in the making. All his instincts told him so, as if he were perched over a widening crevasse, one foot on this side, one on the other.

He closed the drapes and returned to the table. "What's the situation with the feedlot?"

The muscles in Wilkes's face visibly relaxed; they were back on familiar ground. "The blast tore the place up pretty good. It will take at least three more days to repair the gates and lighting."

Too long, thought Guilder. They'd have to do it in the open. Maybe it was better that way; he could kill two birds with one stone. A bit of theater, to get the troops in line. He pushed his notepad across the table to his chief of staff.

"Write this down."

54

"It's just so . . . strange."

Lila had just come off her feeding and was deep within its throes. The blood had been delivered, by Guilder presumably, while Sara and Kate were playing in the courtyard. After two successive days above freezing, the snow had turned into a sticky skin, perfect for snowballs. They'd thrown them at each other for hours.

Now they were playing a game of beans and cups on the floor by the fire. The game was new to Sara; Kate had taught her. Another pleasure, to learn a game from one's own child. Sara tried not to think how fleeting this would be. Any day the message from Nina could come.

"Yes, well," Lila said, as if she and Sara had been having a conversation, "I'm going to have to be going on an errand soon."

Sara paid this little attention. Lila's mind seemed adrift in reverie. An errand to where?

"David says I have to go." Facing the mirror, Lila made the scowly face she always adopted when speaking of David. "Lila, it's for charity. I know you don't like opera, but we absolutely have to go. Lila, this man is the head of a major hospital, all the wives will be there, how will it look if I have to go alone?" She sighed resignedly, her brush pausing on its journey through her lustrous mane of hair. "Maybe just once he'd think about what *I* want to do, the places *I* want to go. Now, *Brad* was thoughtful. Brad was the kind of man who listened." Her eyes met Sara's through the mirror. "Tell me something, Dani. Do you have a boyfriend? Someone special in your life? If you don't mind my asking. My gosh, you're certainly pretty enough. I bet you have dozens of them just beating down your door."

Sara was momentarily disoriented by the question; Lila rarely, if ever, asked Sara anything about herself. "Not really."

Lila considered this. "Well, that's smart. You have lots of time yet. Play the field, don't settle. If you meet the right man, you'll know." The woman resumed her careful brushing. Her voice was suddenly sad. "Remember that, Dani. There's someone waiting out there for you. Once you find him, don't let him out of your sight. I made that mistake, and now look at the fix I'm in."

The remark, like so many, seemed to float in the ether, unable to touch down on any firm surface. Yet over the days of their confinement, Sara had begun to detect a pattern of meaning to these oblique utterances. They were shadows of something real: an actual history of people, places, events. If what Nina said about the woman was true—and Sara believed it to be so—Lila was every inch the monster the redeyes were. How many Evas had been sent to the basement because Lila had . . . what were Nina's words? *Lost interest.* And yet Sara could not deny that there was something pitiable about the woman. She seemed so lost, so frail, so laden with regret. *Sometimes,* Lila had remarked once, apropos of nothing, and with the heaviest of sighs, *I just don't see how things can go on like this.* And, one evening while Sara was rubbing lotion into her feet, *Dani, did you ever think about just running away? Leaving your whole life behind and starting over?* More and more she let Sara and Kate go their own way, as if she were abdicating her role in the little girl's life—as if, at some level, she knew the truth. *I look at the two of you and I think,*

How perfect you are together. That little girl adores you. Dani, you're the piece of the puzzle that was missing.

"So what do you think?"

Sara's attentions had returned to the game. She glanced up from the floor to see Lila looking earnestly at her.

"Dani, it's your turn," said Kate.

"Just a minute, sweetheart." Then, to Lila: "I'm sorry. What do I think about what?"

An effortful smile was plastered to her face. "Coming with me. I think you'd be a great help. Jenny can look after Eva."

"Come where?"

Sara could see it in Lila's eyes: whatever their destination was, the woman absolutely didn't want to go alone. "What does it matter, really? One of David's . . . *things.* They're usually just deadly, to be honest. I really could stand the company." She bent forward from her stool and addressed the child. "What do you say, Eva? How about an evening with Jenny while Mummy goes out?"

The girl refused to meet her eye. "I want to stay with Dani."

"Of course you do, pumpkin. We all love Dani. There's no more special person in the world. But once in a while grown-ups have to go off to be by themselves, to do grown-up things. That's just how it is sometimes."

"Then you go."

"Eva, I don't think you're listening to what I'm saying."

The girl was tugging at the sleeve of Sara's robe. "Tell her."

Lila frowned. "Dani? What's this about?"

"I don't . . . know." She looked at Kate, who had scuttled beside her on the floor, protectively wedging her body against Sara's. Sara put an arm around her. "What is it, honey?"

"Eva," Lila interjected, "what do you want Dani to tell me? Speak up, now."

"I don't like you," the girl murmured into the folds of Sara's robe.

Lila drew back, the color draining from her face. "What did you say?"

"I don't like you! I like *her!*"

Lila's expression was beyond shock. It was a portrait of absolute rejection. Sara suddenly understood viscerally what had happened to the other Evas. *This* was what had happened.

"Well." Lila cleared her throat, her wounded eyes roaming restlessly about the room, seeking some object to attach her attentions to. "I see."

"Lila, she didn't mean it." The girl had resumed her protective huddle against Sara's body, pressing her face into her robe while simultaneously watching Lila warily from the corner of her eye. "Tell her, sweetheart."

"That won't be necessary," Lila said. "She couldn't have made herself more clear." The women rose unsteadily from her stool. Everything was different now; the words had been spoken. "If you will excuse me, I think I'll lie down for a bit. David will be here soon."

She didn't so much walk as stumble toward her bedroom. Her back was bent forward, as if she'd suffered a physical blow.

"Do you still want me to come with you?" Sara asked gently.

Lila halted, clutching the frame for balance. She didn't look at Sara as she gave her answer.

"Of course, Dani. Why wouldn't I?"

They drove to the stadium in darkness. A convoy of ten vehicles, pickups front and rear, each carrying a detail of armed cols in the bed, with eight sleek SUVs in between for the senior staff. Lila and Sara rode in the backseat of the second car. Lila was dressed in a dark cloak with the hood gathered at her neck, oversized dark glasses covering the upper half of her face like a shield. The driver was someone Sara recognized without being able to place, a skeletally thin man with lank brown hair and pale roving eyes that met Sara's through the mirror as they pulled away from the Dome.

"You. What's your name?"

"Dani."

He shot a grin through the mirror. Sara felt a jolt of apprehension. Did he know her? Had his gaze somehow penetrated the obscuring curtain of her veil?

"Well, you're in for a treat tonight, Dani."

Guilder had initially refused to let Sara come, but Lila wouldn't budge. *David, how do you think I feel, being dragged around to all your silly parties with your silly friends? I'm simply not going without her, like it or lump it.* On and on like this until Guilder, with a huff, had relented. Fine, he'd said. Have it your way, Lila. Maybe one of your attendants should see what you really are. The more the fucking merrier.

They were passing the flatland now, following the river, becalmed under a skin of winter ice. Something was happening to Lila. With each minute that passed, the lights of the Dome fading behind them, her personality receded. She was stretching her back like a cat, making little humming sounds at the back of her throat, touching her face and hair.

"Mmmm," Lila purred with an almost sexual pleasure. "Can you feel them?"

Sara had no answer.

"It's . . . *won*derful."

They passed through the gate. Ahead Sara saw the stadium, lit from within, glowing in the winter night. She felt not so much fear as a spreading blackness. The caravan slowed as it ascended the ramp and emerged onto a brilliantly lit field surrounded by bleachers. The vehicles stopped behind a silver cargo truck where a dozen cols were waiting, fidgeting with their batons and stamping their feet in the cold. A tall stake had been tamped into the ground in the middle of the field.

"Mmmm," said Lila.

Doors flew open; everybody disembarked. Standing beside the car, Lila lifted Sara's veil and tenderly touched her cheek. "My Dani. My sweet girl. Isn't it marvelous? My babies, my beautiful babies."

"Lila, what's happening here?"

She rocked her head on her neck with sensuous delight. Her eyes were soft and distant. The Lila Sara knew was nowhere inside them. She moved her face toward Sara's and, astonishingly, kissed her dryly on the lips.

"I'm so glad you're with me," she said.

The driver took Sara by the elbow and led her to the bleachers. Twenty men in dark suits were seated in two rows, chatting energetically among themselves, blowing on their fists. "This is so cool," Sara heard one of them say as she was shown to her place in the fourth row, among a group of cols. "I *never* get to see this."

Down front, Guilder faced the group. He was wearing a black overcoat, a dark tie visible at his throat. He was holding something in his gloved hand: a radio.

"Gentlemen of the senior staff, welcome," he declared with a buoyant grin. His breath puffed before his face, punctuating the words. "A little present for you tonight. A show of gratitude for all your hard work as we near the climax of all our labors."

"Bring 'em on!" one of the redeyes hooted, eliciting cheers and laughter.

"Now, now," Guilder said, waving them to silence. "All of you are well acquainted with the spectacle that is about to unfold. But tonight, we have something very special planned. Minister Hoppel, would you please come forward?"

A redeye in the second row got to his feet and joined Guilder at the front. Tall, with a square-jawed face and brush-cut hair. Grinning with embarrassment, he said, "Gosh, Horace, it's not even my birthday."

"Maybe he's about to demote you!" another voice yelled.

More laughter. Guilder waited for it to die down. "Mr. Hoppel here," he said, placing a fatherly hand on the man's back, "as everyone knows, has been with us from the very beginning. As Minister of Propaganda, he has provided us with a key element in support of our efforts." His expression abruptly hardened. "Which is why, with the greatest regret, I must tell you all that incontrovertible evidence has come to my attention that Minister Hoppel is in league with the insurgency." He darted a hand toward the man's face, stripping off his glasses and tossing them away. Hoppel gave a shriek of pain as he drew his arm up over his eyes. "Guards," said Guilder, "take him."

A pair of cols grabbed Hoppel by the arms; more quickly surrounded him, weapons drawn. A moment of confusion, voices buzzing through the bleachers. *What? What is he saying? Hoppel, could it really be . . . ?*

"Yes, my friends. Minister Hoppel is a traitor. It was he who passed crucial intelligence to the insurgency that led to last week's bombing, in which two of our colleagues were killed."

"Jesus, Horace." The man had gone weak at the knees. His eyes were squeezed tight. He tried to shrug the men's grip off, but he seemed to have lost all strength. "You know me! All of you know me! Suresh, Wilkes, somebody—tell him!"

"I'm sorry, my friend. You've done this to yourself. Take him to the field."

He was dragged away. Beside the silver truck, Hoppel was bound to the stake with heavy rope. One of the cols produced a bucket and poured the contents over him with a crimson splash, soaking his clothing, hair, face. He wriggled helplessly, uttering the most pitiful cries. *Don't do this. Please, I swear, I'm no traitor. You bastards, say something!*

Guilder cupped his mouth. "Is the prisoner secure?"

"Secure!"

He lifted the radio to his mouth. "Hit the lights."

The thunk of tumblers, the screech of the opening door.

Alicia was hanging from the ceiling, her bound wrists stretched above her head, holding aloft her slowly creaking weight. She was tired, so tired. Rivulets of dried blood ran down her naked legs. The man known as Sod, through the days of his dark business, had left no part of her untouched. He had filled her ears and nose with the hot stench of his grunting exhalations. He had scratched her, struck her, bitten her. Bitten, like an animal. Her breasts, the soft skin of her neck, the insides of her thighs, all embedded with the marks of his teeth. Through it all, she had not wept. Cried out, yes. Screamed. But she would not give him the satisfaction of her tears. And now here he was again, lazily swinging the chiming ring of keys around his finger, dragging his one good eye down the length of her body, wearing a greedy, bestial smile on his half-cooked face.

"I thought, since everybody's all off at the stadium for the big show, we might have a little bit of alone time."

What was there to say? There was nothing.

"Now, I'm thinking that the two of us might try something new. The bench feels so . . . impersonal."

He began to undress, a complicated business of leather and buckles. He kicked off his boots, his pants. As he went about his grand unveiling, Alicia could only watch in mute revulsion. She felt like she had about ten different Alicias in her head, each with a single scrap of information lacking any reference to the others. And yet: *alone time*. That was new, she thought. That was a definite wrinkle in the proceedings. Usually there were four of them: one to operate the winch, two to take her down, plus Sod. Where were the others?

Alone time.

"I'm begging you," she croaked, "just don't make it hurt. I'll make it good for you."

"That's very sporting."

"Let me down and I'll show you how good."

He considered this.

"Just tell me what you want and I'll give it to you."

"You're full of shit."

"You can leave the shackles on. I promise I'll cooperate. I'll give you everything you want."

In his face, she saw the idea taking hold. She was naked, beaten. What could a woman in her condition do? The keys were clipped to the belt loop of his trousers, lying on the floor behind him. Alicia forced herself not to look at them.

"There might be something to that," Sod said.

The chains, which ran through a block hung from the ceiling, were operated by a lever affixed to the wall. Pantless, engorged, Sod stepped toward it and unlocked the brake. A rattle overhead; Alicia's feet touched down.

"More slack," she said. "I'll need to move."

A sleepy, sexual grin. "I like your thinking."

The pressure on her wrists released. "A little more."

Her tactic had to be obvious, but the man's anticipation trumped the last of his judgment. Alicia's arms fell to her sides. She now had eight feet of slack to play with.

"No funny stuff, now."

She lowered herself to all fours in invitation. Sod moved behind her, joining her on the floor.

"I'll make it good for you," she said. "I promise."

As he placed his hands on her hips, she drew her right foot to her chest and smashed it into his face. A crack and then a yelp; Alicia shot to her feet and swung around. He was sitting on the floor, holding his nose, dark blood gushing through his fingers.

"You fucking bitch!"

He lurched toward her, going for her throat. The question was who got to whom first. Alicia stepped back, arced one hand from her side, forming a lasso with the chain, and tossed it forward.

The loop dropped over his head. She yanked him toward her, stepping aside and using his momentum to spin him around. Now she had him from behind. With the other hand she formed a second loop of chain and dropped it around his neck. A quick hop and she had her legs around his waist. He was making a gurgling noise, his arms flailing at the air. *Die, you pig,* she thought, *just die,* and with all her strength she rocked her weight backward, tugging the chains like the reins of a horse, sending them pitching toward the ground until with a hard jolt the slack ran out, the block above them caught and held, and Alicia heard the sound she longed for: a satisfying pop of bone.

They were suspended eighteen inches off the floor. Two hundred pounds of dead weight now lay on top of her. She tucked her legs beneath her, arched her back, and pushed. Sod's body folded forward onto its knees, pitching face-first onto the concrete as she unlooped the chains from his neck. She scooped the keys from the floor and undid the shackles and tore them from her wrists.

Then she was kicking him, stomping on his head, smashing his face into the concrete with the hard nub of her heel. Her mind collapsed in a roar of hatred. She seized him by the hair and dragged his lifeless form across the cell and propped him upright to hammer his head against the wall. "How do you like that, you piece of shit? You like that broken neck? You like me killing you?"

Maybe there was somebody outside the cell, and maybe there wasn't. Maybe more men would rush in and chain her to the ceiling and start it all again. But that didn't matter. All that mattered was Sod's head. She would smash it until he was the deadest thing in the history of the world, the deadest man who'd ever been. She was yelling, over and over, "God damn you! God damn you! God damn you!"

Then it was over. Alicia let him go. The body tipped sideways to the floor, leaving a glistening smear of brains on the wall. Alicia slumped to her knees, drinking great gulps of air into her lungs. It was over, but it didn't feel over. There was no over, not anymore.

She needed clothes. She needed a weapon. Strapped to Sod's calf she discovered a heavy-handled knife. The balance was poor, but it would do. She gathered up his trousers and his shirt. Dressing herself in the man's clothing, ripe with his stench, filled her with disgust. Her skin crawled, as if he were touching her. She rolled up the sleeves and the legs of his trousers and cinched the waist. The boots, far too large, would only slow her down; she would have to travel barefoot. She dragged the body away from the door and banged on the metal with the butt of her knife.

"Hey!" she yelled, cupping her mouth to lower the register of her voice. "Hey, I'm locked in here!"

The seconds passed. Maybe no one was out there. What would she do then? She hammered on the door, louder this time, praying someone would come.

Then the tumblers turned. Alicia darted behind the door as the guard stepped into the room.

"What the hell, Sod, you told me I had thirty minutes—"

But these sentiments went unfinished as Alicia, darting behind him, drew one hand over his mouth and used the other to ram the knife into the small of his back, swishing the handle as the tip drove upward.

She eased the body to the floor. Blood was releasing from it in a wide, dark pool. Its rich scent rose to her nostrils. Alicia recalled her vow. *I will drink those bastards dry. I will baptize myself in the blood of my enemy.* The thought had sustained her through the days of torment. But as she looked at the two men, first the guard and then Sod, his pale, naked body like a stain of whiteness on the concrete, she shuddered with disgust.

Not now, she thought, *not yet,* and she slipped into the hallway.

The field sank into darkness. For a moment, all was still. Then, from high overhead, a cool aquatic light pulsed down onto the field, bathing it in an artificial moonglow.

Lila had appeared at the rear of the silver truck. All the redeyes were pocketing their sunglasses. Hoppel had given up his pleas and begun to sob. A van drove onto the field. Two cols disembarked and trotted to the rear of the vehicle and opened the doors.

Eleven people stumbled out, six men and five women, shackled at the wrists and ankles and to each other. They were stumbling, weeping, begging for their lives. Their terror was too great; all their resistance was gone. A cold numbness had taken hold of Sara; she thought she might be ill. One of the women looked like Karen Molyneau, but Sara couldn't be certain. The cols dragged them toward Hoppel and instructed them to get down on their knees.

"This is so awesome," a nearby voice said.

All but one of the cols jogged away, remaining with Lila at the rear of the large truck. Her body was swaying, her head rocking side to side, as if she were floating in an invisible current or dancing to unheard music.

"I thought there were supposed to be ten," the same voice said. One of the redeyes, two rows below.

"Yeah. Ten."

"But there's eleven of them."

Sara counted again. Eleven.

"You better go down there and tell Guilder."

"Are you kidding? Who knows what's on his mind these days?"

"You should check that at the door. He hears you say that, you'll be next."

"The guy has slipped a gear, I'm telling you." A pause. "I always knew there was something off about Hoppel, though."

These words touched Sara like a distant wind. Her attention was now solely focused on the field. Was that Karen? The woman looked older, and too tall. Most of the prisoners had adopted a defensive posture, their bodies folded where they knelt in the crusted snow, hands held over their heads; others, kneeling upright, faces washed by the blue light, had begun to pray. The last col was strapping on armored pads. He wedged a helmet over his head and waved toward the bleachers. Every muscle in Sara's body clenched. She wanted to look away but couldn't. The col moved to the door of the silver truck's cargo compartment, fumbling loudly with keys.

The doors swung open; the col dashed away. For a second, nothing happened. Then the virals emerged, popping from the truck's interior like man-sized insects, landing on all fours in the snow. Their lean figures, striated with muscle, throbbed with glowing vividness. Eight, nine, ten. They moved toward Lila, whose arms were held open at her sides, palms raised. A gesture of invitation, of welcome.

At her feet, they bowed.

She touched them, stroked them. She ran her hands over their smooth heads, cupped their chins like children's to gaze adoringly into their eyes. *My lovelies,* Sara heard her say. *My wonderful beauties.*

"Will you look at that? She fucking loves them."

From the hostages came only a sound of quiet weeping. The end was inevitable; they had no choice but to accept it. Or perhaps it was simply the strangeness of the scene that stunned them into silence.

My sweet pets. Are you hungry? Mama will feed you. Mama will take care of you. That's what Mama will do.

"No, I'm certain there's supposed to be ten."

A new voice this time, coming from the right: "Did you say ten? That's what I heard, too."

"So who's the eleventh?"

One of the redeyes shot to his feet, pointing at the field. "There's one too many!"

All heads swiveled toward the voice, including Guilder's.

"I'm not kidding! There are eleven people out there!"

Go now, my darlings.

The virals broke away from Lila. Simultaneously, one of the hostages shot to his feet, exposing his face. It was Vale. The virals were encircling the group; everyone was screaming. Vale tore the flaps of his jacket aside to reveal rows of metal tubes strapped to his chest. He yanked his arms skyward, his thumb poised on the detonator.

"Sergio lives!"

IX

THE ARRIVAL

And I looked, and behold a pale
Horse; and the name that sat on him
Was Death; and Hell followed with him.

—Revelation 6:8

55

Lila's dressing table detonated with a splintering crash. Guilder hauled her to her feet again and slapped her across the face with the back of his hand, sending her flying back, toward the sofa.

"How could you let this happen?" His face boiled with rage. "Why didn't you call the virals back? Tell me!"

"I don't know, I don't know!"

From the collar of her bathrobe this time: with terrifying effortlessness, Guilder hurled her, face-first, into the bookshelf. A thud of impact, things falling, Lila screaming. Sara was huddled on the floor, her body curled around Kate, the little girl wilted with fear.

"Every last viral! Nine of my men, dead! Do you know how this makes me look?"

"It wasn't my fault! I don't remember! David, please!"

"There is no David!"

Sara clenched her eyes tight. Kate was whimpering softly in her arms. What would happen if Guilder killed Lila? What would become of the two of them then?

"Stop it! David, I'm begging you!"

Lila was lying face-up on the floor, Guilder straddling her, one hand holding her by her collar. The other was balled into a fist, pulled back, ready to strike. Lila's arms lay across her eyes like a shield, though this effort would come to nothing; Guilder's fist would crush her face like a battering ram.

"You . . . disgust me."

He loosened his hold and stepped away, wiping his hands on his shirt. Lila was sobbing uncontrollably. Blood bulged from a cut along her cheekbone. More was in her hair. Guilder flicked his eyes toward Sara, dismissing her with a glance. *You're nothing,* his eyes said. *You're a character in a game of pretend that's gone on far too long.*

Then he stormed from the room.

Sara went to where Lila was whimpering on the floor. She knelt beside her, reaching for her face to examine the cut. In an unexpected burst of energy, Lila shoved Sara's hand away and scampered backward.

"Don't touch it!"

"But you're hurt—"

The woman's eyes were wild with panic. As Sara moved toward her, she waved her hands in front of her face.

"Get away! Don't touch my blood!"

She leapt to her feet and ran to the bedroom, slamming the door behind her.

6:02 A.M.

The vehicles made their way into the flatland in the predawn darkness, gates flying open as they passed. At the head of the line, like the point of an arrow, was the sleek black SUV of the Director, followed by a pair of open trucks, full of uniformed men. Into the maze of lodges they roared, hurling clots of dirty snow from their mudchoked tires, their passage observed by the workers filing from the buildings to assemble for morning roll—weary faces, weary eyes, dully noting the vehicles sailing past. But their glances were brief; they knew better than to look. *Something official; it has nothing to do with me. At least, it better not.*

Guilder watched the flatlanders from the passenger window, full of contempt. How he loathed them. Not just the insurgents, the ones who defied him—all of them. They plodded through their lives like brute animals, never seeing beyond the next square of earth to be plowed. Another day in the dairy barns, the fields, the biodiesel plant. Another day in the kitchen, the laundry, the pigsties.

But today wasn't just another day.

The vehicles halted before Lodge 16. The eastern sky had softened to a yellowish gray, like old plastic.

"This is the one?" Guilder asked Wilkes.

Beside him, the man gave a tight-lipped nod.

The cols disembarked and took up positions. Guilder and Wilkes stepped clear of the car. Before them, in fifteen evenly spaced lines, three hundred flatlanders stood shivering in the cold. Two more trucks pulled in and parked at the head of the square. Their cargo bays were draped by heavy canvas.

"What are those for?" Wilkes asked.

"A little extra . . . persuasion."

Guilder strode up to the senior HR officer and snatched the megaphone from his hand. A howl of feedback; then his voice boomed over the square.

"Who can tell me about Sergio?"

No reply.

"This is your only warning. Who can tell me about Sergio?"

Again, nothing.

Guilder gave his attention to a woman in the first row. Neither young nor old, she had a face so plain it could have been made of paste. She was clutching a filthy scarf around her head with hands covered by fingerless gloves black with soot.

"You. What's your name?"

Eyes cast down, she muttered something into the folds of her scarf.

"I can't hear you. Speak up."

She cleared her throat, stifling a cough. Her voice was a phlegmy rasp. "Priscilla."

"Where do you work?"

"The looms, sir."

"Do you have a family? Children?"

She nodded weakly.

"So? What do you have?"

Her knees were trembling. "A daughter and two sons."

"A husband?"

"Dead, sir. Last winter."

"My condolences. Come forward."

"I sang the hymn yesterday. It was the others, I swear."

"And I believe you, Priscilla. Nevertheless. Gentlemen, can you assist her, please?"

A pair of cols trotted forward and grabbed the woman by her arms. Her body went slack, as if she were on the verge of fainting. They half-carried, half-dragged her to the front, where they shoved her onto her knees. She made no sound; her submission was total.

"Who are your children? Point them out."

"Please." She was weeping pitifully. "Don't make me."

One of the cols lifted his baton over her head. "This man is going to bash your brains out," Guilder said.

She shook her bowed head.

"Very well," Guilder said.

Down went the baton; the woman toppled forward into the mud. From the left came a sharp cry.

"Get her."

A young teenager, with her mother's face. Onto her knees she went. She was crying, trembling; snot was running from her nose. Guilder raised the megaphone.

"Does anybody have anything to say?"

Silence. Guilder drew a pistol from beneath his coat and racked the slide. "Minister Wilkes," he said, holding out the gun, "will you please do the honors?"

"Jesus, Horace." His face was aghast. "What are you trying to prove?"

"Is this going to be a problem?"

"We have *people* for this kind of thing. That wasn't part of the deal."

"What deal? There is no deal. The deal is what I say it is."

Wilkes stiffened. "I won't do it."

"You won't or you can't?"

"What difference does it make?"

Guilder frowned. "Not very much, now that I think about it." And with these words, he stepped behind the girl, pushed the muzzle of the gun to the back of her head, and fired.

"Good Christ!"

"You know what the biggest problem with never growing old is?" Guilder asked his chief of staff. He was wiping down the blood-tinged barrel with a handkerchief. "I've given this a lot of thought."

"Fuck you, Horace."

Guilder pointed the pistol at Wilkes's colorless face, leveling its sights at the spot between his eyes. "You forget that you can die."

And Guilder shot him, too.

A change came over the crowd, their fear turning to something else. Murmurs moved up and down the lines, whispered calculations, the building energy of people who knew they had nothing to lose. Things had moved rather more briskly than Guilder would have liked—he'd hoped to get something useful before the hammer came down—but now the die was cast.

"Open the trucks."

The canvas was pulled away. An eruption of volcanic screaming: no mystery now. Guilder walked briskly to his car, got in, and told the driver to go. They pulled away in a plume of mud and dirty snow as, behind them, the orchestra unleashed its mortal symphony: a melody of shouts and screams, high and wild and full of fear, punctuated by the syncopated rhythm of automatic weapon fire, fading to the final pops as the cols moved through the fallen bodies, silencing the last.

56

Iowa. The ashy bones.

They'd exhausted their fuel near the town of Millersburg, sheltered the night in a roofless church, and set out the next morning on foot. Another seventy miles, said Tifty, perhaps a little more. They'd encountered two more bone fields like the first, the number of dead virals unimaginable. Thousands, millions even. What did it mean? What impulse had led them to lie down on the open earth, waiting for the sun to take them away? Or had they perished first, their corpses reclaimed by the morning light? Even Michael, the man of theories, had no answer.

They walked. Trudged, through snow that now rose in places to their knees. Their rations were scarce; they saw no game. They had been reduced to eating their final stores—strips of dried meat and suet that left a coating of grease on the roofs of their mouths. The earth felt crystallized, the air held in suspension, like bated breath. For hours, no wind at all, and then it came howling. Daylight came and left in the blink of an eye. Heavy parkas with fur-lined hoods, woolen hats pulled down to their brows, gloves with the tips of the fingers cut away in case they needed to use their weapons, though Peter wondered if they could actually manage this. He'd never felt so cold. He hadn't known cold like this existed. How Tifty maintained his bearings in this desolate place, he had no idea.

They passed their eighteenth night in an auto-repair shop that contained, miraculously, a potbellied woodstove of cast iron with a soapstone top. Now, what to burn? As darkness came on, Michael and Hollis returned from the house next door, carrying a pair of wooden chairs and armfuls of books. The *Encyclopaedia Britannica,* 1998. A shame to burn it, it went against the grain, but they needed the heat. Two more trips and they were supplied for the night.

They awoke to brilliant sunlight, the first in days, although the temperature had, if anything, dropped. A hard north wind rattled the branches of the trees. They allowed themselves the luxury of setting one last fire and huddled around it, savoring every bit of heat.

"Like . . . molting."

It was Michael who had spoken. Peter turned toward his friend. "What did you say?"

Michael's eyes were focused on the door of the stove. "How many do you think we've seen?"

"I don't know." Peter shrugged. "A lot."

"And they all died at the same time. So let's suppose what's happening is supposed to happen, that it's part of the viral life cycle. Birds do this, insects, reptiles. When part of the body is worn out, they cast it off and grow a new one."

"But we're talking about whole virals," Lore said.

"That's how it *looks*. But everything we know about them says they function as a group. Each one connected to its pod, each pod connected to its member of the Twelve. Never mind the mumbo jumbo about souls and all the rest. I'm not saying it isn't true, but that's Amy's turf. From my point of view, the virals are a species like any other. When Lacey killed Babcock, all of his virals died. Like bees, remember?"

"I do," said Hollis, nodding along. "Kill the queen and you kill the hive. That's what you said."

"And what we saw on that mountain bore it out. But suppose each one of the viral families is actually a single organism. Each of the Twelve is like a major organ—the heart, the brain. The rest are like the feathers on a bird, or the carapace of an insect. When it wears out, the organism sheds it, in order to grow a new one."

"They don't *feel* like feathers," Lore said acidly.

"Okay, not feathers, but you get the idea. Something peripheral, expendable. I've always wondered what was keeping so many alive. What's left to eat? We know they can go a long time without feeding—Tifty, you proved that—but nothing can survive indefinitely without food. From the standpoint of species longevity, it makes no sense to devour your entire food supply. As predators, they're actually *too* successful. The idea has always bothered me, because everything else about them is so organized."

"I'm not sure I'm following," Tifty said. "Are you saying they're dying out?"

"Obviously something's happening. The fact that it's occurring all at once implies that it's a natural process, built into the system. Here's another analogy. When the human body goes into shock, it draws blood away from the periphery and redirects it to the major organs. It's a defense mechanism. Protect what's important, forget the rest. Now imagine that each of the viral tribes is one animal, and that it's going into shock from starvation. The logical thing would be to radically reduce the numbers and let the food supply come back."

"And then what?" Peter asked.

"Then you start the cycle over."

For a moment, nobody spoke.

"Anyway," Michael continued, "it's just an idea I had. I could be full of shit."

Peter knew different. "So why is it happening here?"

"That," said Michael, "is what worries me."

The time for leaving was at hand; they'd stayed too long as it was. They gathered their gear and zipped up their parkas, bracing themselves for the blast of frigid air that would assail them the second they stepped through the door.

"Six days if the weather holds," said Tifty, hitching up his pack. "Seven at the most."

"Why do I wish it were more?" said Lore.

Grey. Grey.

His eyes popped open.

Can you feel them, Grey?

"Who's there? Guilder, is that you?"

I'm sorry I have been away. You are still my favorite, Grey. Since the very first day we met. Do you remember?

His stomach clenched: the voice of Zero.

"Stop it." His wrists yanked reflexively at the chains. He was lying in his own filth, his body stank, his mouth tasted permanently of blood. "Go away. Leave me alone."

You told me everything about yourself. You didn't even know you were doing it. Did you feel me in your mind even then?

—Get out, he thought. Get out get out get out. Wake up, Grey.

Oh, you're not sleeping. I've always been here. Even as you have lain in chains a hundred years, I have lain with you. Like the story of Job, who lay in the ashes, cursing his fate. God tested him, as I have tested you.

—I don't know you. I don't know what you are.

You don't, Grey? How can you not know? I am the God who abides with you. The one true God of Grey. Can you not feel my love? Can you not feel my wings of love spreading over you, forever and ever?

He had begun to weep.

—Let me die. Please. All I want to do is die.

You love her, don't you, Grey?

He swallowed, tasting the foulness of his mouth. His body was a cave of filth and rottenness.

—Yes.

The woman. Lila. She means everything to you.

—Yes.

Yours is the blood that flows in her veins, as mine flows in yours. Do you see? Do you understand? We are all of a piece, Grey. You lie in chains, but you are not alone. The God of Grey abides with you. The God of all that is, and all that is to come. The God of the next new world. There will be a special place for you in that world, Grey.

—The next new world.

They are coming, Grey.

—Who? Who is coming?

But even as he asked the question, he knew.

Our brothers.

57

And suddenly, she was free. Alicia Donadio, Last of the First, the New Thing and captain of the Expeditionary, was bounding over the wires, into the night, away.

She ran. She ran and kept on running.

She'd killed a few men along the way. Some women, too. Alicia had never killed a human woman before; it seemed not so very different, on the whole. Because in the end, everybody left their life in the same manner. The same surprise upon their faces, their fingers touching the wound with exploratory tenderness, the identical ethereal gaze, aimed into eternity. There was a certain grace to it.

Maybe that's why Alicia liked it as much as she did.

She found her gear where she'd left it hidden in the brush. A pike and cross. The RDF. Her bandoliers of blades. A change of clothes, a blanket, shoes. A hundred rounds of ammo but no gun to fire it. She'd left Sod's knife behind, embedded in the left kidney of a man who had commanded her to stop, as if she might actually do this. Racing from the detention center, she hadn't even known if it would be day or night. Time had been annihilated. The world she found was a changed place. No, that wasn't right. The world was the same; it was she who had changed. She felt apart from everything, spectral, almost bodiless. Above her the winter stars shone hard and pure, like chips of ice. She needed shelter. She needed sleep. She needed to forget.

She took refuge in a shed that at one time might have contained chickens. Half the roof was gone; only the barest form remained: a single wall left standing, the little cages encrusted with fossilized droppings, a floor of hard-packed earth. She wrapped herself in the blanket, her broken body shaking with the cold. *Louise,* she thought, *was it like this?* Her mind tossed with memories, bright flashes of torment that split her thoughts like lightning. When would it stop, when would it stop.

It was still dark when she awoke, her mind climbing slowly to awareness. Something warm was brushing the back of her neck. She rolled and opened her eyes to discover an immense dark form looming above her.

My good boy, she thought, and then she said it: "My good, good boy." Soldier dipped his face to hers, his great nostrils flaring, bathing her face with his breath. He licked her eyes and cheeks with his long tongue. It was a miracle. There was no other word. Someone had come. Someone had come, after all. Alicia had longed for this without knowing it, one soul to comfort her in this comfortless world.

Then, stepping improbably from the gloom, a figure, and a woman's voice, strange and familiar at once:

"Alicia. Hello."

The woman crouched before her, drawing down the hood of her long, wool coat. Her long black tresses tumbled free.

"It's all right," she said softly. "I'm here now."

Amy? But it was not the Amy she knew.

This Amy was a woman.

A strong, beautiful woman with thick, dark hair and eyes like windowpanes lit from behind with golden light. The same face but different, deeper; the impression was one of completeness, a coming into the self. A face, thought Alicia, of wisdom. Her beauty was more than appearance, more than a collection of physical details; it came from the whole.

"I don't . . . understand."

"Shhhh." She took Alicia's hand. Her touch was firm but tender, like a mother's, comforting her child. "Your friend. He showed us where you were. Such a handsome horse. What do you call him?"

Her mind felt heavy, benumbed. "Soldier."

Amy cupped Alicia's chin and lifted it slightly. "You're hurt."

How was this possible? How was anything possible? Beyond the shed Alicia saw a second figure, holding a pair of horses by the reins. A wind-blown swirl of white hair and a great pale beard masked his features. But it was the way he held himself, with a soldier's bearing, that told Alicia who he was; that this man in the snow was Lucius Greer.

"What did they do to you?" Amy whispered. "Tell me."

That was all it took. Her will collapsed, a wave of sorrow came undammed inside her. She did not speak so much as shudder the word: "Everything."

And at long last, a great sob shook her—a howl of purest pain and grief cast skyward to the winter stars—and in Amy's arms, Alicia began to weep.

Guilder. It's time.

Guilder, rise.

But Guilder did not hear these words. Director Horace Guilder was asleep and dreaming—a terrible, oft-repeated dream in which he was in the convalescent center, smothering his father with a pillow. Contrary to history, this did not proceed without a struggle. His father thrashed and flailed, his hands clawing at the air, fighting to break free as he issued muffled cries for mercy. Only when his resistance ceased, and Guilder removed the pillow from his face, did Guilder see his error. It wasn't his father he had killed, but Shawna. Oh, God, no! Then Shawna's eyes popped open; she began to laugh. She laughed so hard that tears came to her eyes. Stop laughing! he yelled. Stop laughing at me! Guilder, she said, you're so funny. You should see the look on your face. You and your crappy bracelet. Your mother was a whore. A whore a whore a whore . . .

Prepare the way, Guilder. Rise to meet them. The moment is at hand.

He jolted awake.

Our moment, Guilder. The birth of the next new world.

The information hit his brain like voltage. He bolted upright in his vast bed, its preposterous acreage of pillows and blankets and sheets, realizing, with faint embarrassment, that he'd fallen asleep with his clothes on. And why, he thought absurdly, did he need, of all things, a canopy bed? A bed so huge it made him feel like a doll? But he shook the question away. They were coming! They were here! He swiveled his feet to the floor and jammed them into the leather lace-ups that he had, apparently, possessed the energy to remove before passing out with exhaustion. Ramming his shirttail into his pants, he dashed to the door and down the hall.

"Suresh!"

The sound of his pounding caromed down the empty hallway.

"Suresh, wake up!"

The door to Suresh's quarters opened to reveal his new chief of staff's sleepy, bronze-colored face. He was wearing a puffy white bathrobe and slippers, blinking like a bear exiting its cave.

"Cripes, Horace, you don't have to yell." He yawned into his fist. "What time is it?"

"Who cares what time it is? They're *here.*"

Suresh startled. "Right now, you mean?"

Rise up and meet them, Guilder. Bring them home.

"Don't just stand there, get dressed."

"Right, okay. I'm on it."

"Move, goddamnit!"

Guilder returned to his apartment and stepped into the bathroom. Should he shave? Wash his face at least? Why was he thinking like this, like a boy on prom night? He ran a damp hand through his hair and brushed his teeth, trying to calm himself. Was this what passed for toothpaste around this place? This awful-tasting gritty goo? For the love of God, why, in ninety-seven years, had they never managed to come up with a decent toothpaste?

He removed a fresh suit from the wardrobe. The blue tie, the red, the green and yellow stripes: he didn't know. He was suddenly so nervous his fingers could barely manage the knot. And hungry. A stone of cold emptiness sat in his gut. A visit with his old friend Grey would have been just the ticket to settle his nerves, but he should have thought of that earlier.

Standing before the mirror, he took a steadying breath. Easy, Guilder, easy. You know what to do. It's just another day at the office. It can't be any worse than a meeting with the Joint Chiefs, can it?

In point of fact, it could. But there was no use in dwelling on the prospect.

By the time he reached the lobby, Suresh was waiting with Guilder's driver. "The trucks are on their way," Suresh said as Guilder drew on his gloves. "You want a full detail to escort you?"

Guilder declined; he would go on his own. Best to keep things simple. The two men shook hands.

"Good luck," said Suresh.

As the car glided down the hill, Guilder's anxiety began to lessen. He was moving into the moment now. At the river they turned north and headed toward the Project. Its dark shape heaved from the earth like a headstone, a square of deeper blackness against the night sky. The portal was open, waiting.

They didn't stop but turned east on the service road. At one time it had been used to move equipment to the site: the quarried blocks of stone, the twirling cement mixers from the concrete plant, the flatbeds with their stacked girders of harvested steel. Now it would carry an altogether different delivery. They passed through the auxiliary gate. Five more minutes and they drew up to where the two semis were waiting in a field of frozen corn stubble.

Guilder told the driver to go. The semis' cabs were empty; their drivers, too, had departed. Guilder pressed his ear to the side of one of the trucks. He heard muffled murmurings inside, interspersed with a female sound of frightened weeping.

The voice in his head was silent. A profound stillness encased him like the anticipatory stillness before a storm. They would be coming from the west. He waited.

Then:

The first one appeared, then another and another, eleven points of glowing phosphorescence spaced at equal intervals on the horizon. The gaps between them narrowed as they neared, like the lights of a giant aircraft approaching.

Come to me, Guilder thought. *Come to me.*

Details began to emerge. Not so much to emerge as to enlarge. One was smaller than the rest—that would be Carter, of course, he thought; the unknowable, anomalous Anthony Carter—but the others took his breath away. In their powerful forms and graceful movements and absolute mastery of themselves they seemed to shrink the space around them, to bend dimensions, to rewrite the course of time. They flowed toward him like a glowing river, bathing him in the light of their majestic horror.

Come to me, he thought. *Come to me. Come to me.*

The moment of their arrival possessed a feeling of absolute completeness. A baptism. The closing covers of a book. A long dive into blue water and the instant of entry, the world wiped away. They stood before him, great and terrible. He drank the majestic, terrifying images of their memories as if dipped into a pool of purest madness. A weeping girl on a dirty mattress. A shopkeeper, hands raised, and the bony press of a gun's muzzle at the vertical crease between his eyebrows. A sensation of utter drunkenness, and a boy on his bicycle glimpsed through a windshield, and the thud of contact followed by a sharp jolt as his little body passed beneath the vehicle's wheels. A delicious feeling of sex, and a woman's eyes expanded to impossible wideness as the cord tightened around her neck. A chorus of terror, depravity, black evil.

I am Morrison-Chávez-Baffes-Turrell-Winston-Sosa-Echols-Lambright-Martínez-Reinhardt-Carter.

Guilder unlatched the cargo door of the first truck. The prisoners tried to run, of course. Guilder had ordered no shackles; he wanted nothing to constrict them. Most made it only a few steps. The few that got farther experienced, perhaps, a fleeting hope of salvation. Their pointless flight was part of the rapture. The moment unfolded in great splashes of blood and abruptly severed screams and living tissue torn asunder, and in the silence that followed Guilder stepped to the rear of the second truck and opened its door in welcome.

"Welcome, my friends. You are home at last. We will see to your every need."

X

THE ASSASSIN

I go, and it is done; the bell invites me.

—SHAKESPEARE,
Macbeth

58

Vale was gone, which could mean only one thing. Sara's turn would come next.

Jenny had disappeared as well. Two days after the bombing in the stadium, a new girl had taken her place. Was she with them? No, Sara would have detected it. A message under the plate, an exchange of reassuring glances. Something. But the girl—pale, nervous, whose name Sara didn't know and was never to learn—came and went in silence.

Lila had taken to her bed. All day long and into the night she tossed and turned. She roused only to bathe but shooed Sara's offers of help away. Her voice was drained; even speaking seemed to require all her energy. "Leave me be," she said.

Sara was alone, cut off. The system was collapsing.

She passed the days with Kate, but this time together felt different, final. The child could sense it too, as children did. What was the source of their powers of perception? Everything was colored by a mood of pointlessness. They played the usual games, not caring who won. Sara read the usual stories, but the child listened only vaguely. Nothing helped. The end of their time was approaching. The days were long and then too short. At night they slept together on the sofa, melded as one. The soft warmth of the girl's body was torment. Sara lay awake for hours listening to her quiet breathing, drinking in her scent. What are you dreaming? she wondered. Are you dreaming of goodbye, as I am? Will we see each other again? Is there such a place? Holding Kate close, she remembered Nina's words. *We'll get her out. Otherwise she has no chance.* My child, thought Sara, I will do what I must to save you. I will go when asked. It's the only thing I have.

On the third morning, Sara took Kate outside. The cold was biting, but she welcomed it. She pushed Kate on the swing for a time, then rode the teeter-totter with her. Kate had said nothing about Lila since the night Guilder had beaten her. Whatever cord had connected them had been severed. When the cold grew too fierce, they headed back inside. Just as they reached the door, Kate stopped.

"Somebody gave this to me," she said, and showed Sara. In her hand was a pink plastic egg.

"Who did?"

"I don't know. She was over there."

Sara followed the girl's gesture across the courtyard. There was no one. Kate shrugged. "She was there a second ago."

For just a few minutes, not more than five, Sara had let Kate wander off by herself.

"She told me to give it to you," Kate said, and held the egg out to her.

The woman had to be Nina, of course. Sara tucked the egg into the pocket of her robe. Her body felt numb. When Jenny had disappeared, she had allowed herself the faint hope that this burden would pass from her. How foolish she'd been.

"Let's keep this a secret—would that be okay?"

"She said the same thing." Then, her face brightening, Kate asked, "Is it a secret message?"

Sara did her best to smile. "That's it exactly."

She didn't open the egg right away; she was afraid to. When they returned to the dark apartment, they found Lila lighting the candelabras with a long match. Her face was drained of color, her hair brittle and askew. She called them over to the sofa and held out a book.

"Would you read to me?"

Little Women: Sara opened the cover to a puff of dust from its yellowed pages.

"I haven't heard this one in ages," Lila sighed.

Sara was made to read for hours. Part of her mind registered the story as interesting, but the rest was in a fog. The language was difficult, and she often lost her place. Kate's attention waned; eventually she fell asleep. It seemed entirely possible that Lila was going to make Sara read the entire book.

"I need to go to the bathroom," Sara said finally. "I'll be right back."

Before Lila could say anything, she stepped briskly to the lavatory and closed the door. She pulled up her robe and sat on the toilet and withdrew the egg from her pocket. Her heart was beating wildly. A flicker of hesitation; then she opened it and unfolded the paper.

The package is in the garden shed at the edge of the courtyard. Look beneath the floorboards to the left of the door. The target is the senior staff meeting in the conference room, tomorrow 1130 hrs. Take the central elevator to the fourth floor, then the first hallway on the right. The last door on the left is the conference room. Tell the guard that Guilder sent for you. Sergio lives.

She had returned the paper to the egg when there came an urgent rapping on the door. "Dani! I need you!"

"Just a second!"

The handle jiggled. Had she locked it?

"I have the key, Dani! Please, open the door!"

Sara lurched off the toilet, sending the egg skittering across the floor. Shit! The key was turning in the lock. She had just enough time to shove the egg into the bottom drawer of the vanity before turning to see Lila standing in the open doorway.

"All done," she said. She heaved a smile onto her face. "What do you need, Lila?"

The woman's face blanched with confusion. "I don't know. I thought you'd gone somewhere. You scared me."

"Well, I did. I went to the bathroom."

"I didn't hear the toilet flush."

"Oh. Sorry." Sara turned and pulled the chain. "That was rude of me."

For a moment Lila said nothing. She seemed completely disconnected from reality.

"Could you do something for me? A favor."

Sara nodded.

"I would like some . . . chocolate."

"Chocolate." What was chocolate? "Where would I get that?"

Lila stared incredulously. "The kitchen, of course."

"Right. I guess that was obvious." Maybe someone in the kitchen would know what Lila was talking about. Sara didn't think it would be a good idea to come back empty-handed. "I'll go right away."

Lila's face relaxed. "Anything would be fine. Even a cup of cocoa." Her eyes unfocused; she gave a little sigh. "I always loved a cup of cocoa on a winter afternoon."

Sara stepped from the apartment. How much had Lila seen? Why hadn't Sara thought to flush the note down the toilet? Had she closed the drawer? She replayed the moment in the mind; yes, she had. There was no reason for Lila to go looking there, though to be safe, Sara would have to retrieve it before the serving girl returned.

The kitchen was located on the far side of the building; she'd have to cross the atrium, which was always full of cols. Still riding a wave of adrenaline, she aimed her eyes at the floor and made her way down the hall.

As she entered the lobby she became aware of a commotion. An attendant was being escorted by two guards, her pitiful cries amplified by the room's expansive acoustics.

"Don't! Please, I'm begging you! I'll do better! Don't take me to the basement!"

The woman was Karen Molyneau.

"Sara! Help me!"

Sara halted in her tracks. How could Karen see her face? And then she realized that she'd made the one fatal error, the one thing she could never forget to do. She'd neglected to pull down her veil.

"Sara, please!"

"Stop."

The command had come from a third man. As he stepped forward, Sara recognized him immediately. The round belly, the fogged glasses riding the tip of his nose, the winglike eyebrows. The third man was Dr. Verlyn.

"You." He was examining her face intently. "What's your name?"

Her mouth had gone dry. "Dani, sir."

"She called you Sara."

"I'm sure she's mistaken." Her eyes flicked reflexively toward the exit. "I'm Dani."

"Sara, why are you doing this?" Karen was wriggling like a fish in a net. "Tell them I'm no insurgent!"

Verlyn's gaze hardened. The corners of his mouth lifted in a smile. "Oh, I remember you. The pretty one. I never forget a face, not one like yours."

Sara bolted for the door. Three strides and she went blasting through it. She tore down the steps, into the sun and wind, shouts rising behind her. "Stop her! Stop that woman!" Where could she run to? But there was no place; cols were racing toward her from all directions, hemming her in like a tightening noose. Sara's hand went to her pocket and found the little envelope of folded foil. Here it was, the end. She stopped on the path; there was no use running anymore—she had only a second or two. The package opened to reveal its lethal contents. She took the blotter between her thumb and index finger and raised it to her mouth. *Goodbye, my child, how I love you, goodbye.*

But it was not to be. As she brought the blotter to her lips, someone rammed her from behind, rocketing her off her feet; the ground fell away and rose again, slowly and then quickly and finally all at once, her skull collided with the pavement, and everything went black.

59

The three of them were lying with their bellies pressed to the upward slope of the culvert, Greer scanning the scene with the binoculars. The late afternoon sun was lighting fires in the clouds.

"You're *sure* this is the place," Amy said.

Alicia nodded. They had lain there for nearly three hours. Their attentions were focused on a wide-mouthed drainage pipe jutting from the base of a low hillside. The snow around the opening was crisscrossed with tire tracks.

The minutes passed. Alicia had begun to doubt herself when Greer raised his hand. "Here we go."

A figure had emerged from the pipe, wearing a dark jacket. Man or woman, Alicia couldn't tell. A scarf covered the lower half of the person's face; a wool cap was pulled down to the tops of the eyes. The figure paused, looking south with a hand to its brow.

"Looks like he's waiting for someone," Greer said.

"How do you know it's a man?" Alicia asked.

"I don't." Greer handed the binoculars to Amy, who pushed a strand of hair aside and pressed the lenses to her eyes. It was amazing to see, Alicia thought; in every aspect, even the smallest gesture, Amy was both the girl she'd always been and someone entirely new. As Greer told the story, Amy had gone into the belly of the ship, the *Chevron Mariner,* as one thing and had come out another. Even Amy couldn't provide an explanation. To Alicia, the oddest thing about it was the fact that it didn't seem odd at all.

"I can't tell either. But whoever's supposed to meet him is running late." Amy drew down the binoculars. Beneath her oversized wool coat, she still wore the shapeless tunic of the Order. Her legs were covered in thick woven leggings, her feet shod in laced boots of crinkled leather. "If we're going to find Sergio, I don't think we're going to get a better chance."

Alicia nodded. "Agreed. Major?"

"No objection here."

The only cover to conceal their approach was a line of brush on the east side of the pipe and a stand of bare trees on the hillside above it. Amy and Alicia left Greer to stand lookout and moved at a crouch along the culvert in opposite directions. Amy would take the right, at ground level; Alicia would drop down from above. Once they were in position, Greer would whistle, diverting the man's attention, and they would make their move.

Everything unfolded according to plan. Alicia scuttled on her belly to the top of the pipe. The crown of the man's capped head was right below her. From this angle, she wouldn't be able to see Amy, but Greer would. She waited for the signal, then:

Where did he go?

Rising to her knees, Alicia rotated in time to receive his full weight slamming into hers. Not *his* weight. Hers. In an airborne embrace they tumbled over the lip, the woman crashing down upon her as Alicia landed on her back in the snow.

"Who the hell are you?" The woman had pinned Alicia's arms with her knees and was holding a knife to her throat, the blade just nicking her skin. Alicia had no doubt that she would use it.

"Steady there. I'm a friend."

"Answer the question."

"Amy? A little help here?"

Amy had moved in from behind. Her approach had been absolutely soundless. Before the woman could react, Amy grabbed her by the collar and flung her sideways; as the woman leapt to her feet and lunged forward with the knife, Amy slapped it away, darted behind her, and locked her in a half nelson, the other arm gripping her around the waist. Alicia's only thought was: *I'll be goddamned.*

"Stop it," Amy said. "We want to talk, that's all."

The woman spoke through gritted teeth. "Go to hell."

"Don't you think I could break your neck if I wanted to?"

"Be my guest. Tell Guilder I said, Fuck you, too."

Amy glanced at Alicia, who had collected the woman's knife and was dusting snow from her pants. Greer was trotting toward them. "Does that name mean anything to you?" Amy asked.

Alicia shook her head.

"Who's Guilder?" she asked the woman.

"What do you mean, who's Guilder?"

"What's your name?" Amy asked. "You might as well tell me."

A moment's hesitation, then: "Nina, okay? It's Nina."

"I'm going to let you go now, Nina," Amy said. "Promise me you'll listen to what we have to say. That's all I'm asking."

"Fuck off."

Amy tightened her grip to make the point. "Do. You. Promise."

Another burst of struggle; then the woman relented. "Okay, okay. I promise."

Amy released her. The woman stumbled forward and spun around. A young face, not much older than twenty, but her eyes told a different tale—hard, almost ferocious.

"Who are you people?"

"That was a nice move," Alicia said to Amy. She twirled the knife around her index finger and passed it to her. "Where'd you learn that?"

"Where do you think? By watching you." She pointed her eyes at Greer. His long beard was clotted with snow, like the muzzle of a dog. "Lucius, could I ask you to stand lookout again? Let us know when the vehicle approaches."

"That's all? Just let you know?"

"It would be good if you could . . . delay them a little. Until we're done talking."

Greer jogged up the ridge. Amy addressed the woman again, making a small but meaningful gesture with the knife. "Take a seat."

Nina glared with defiance. "Why would I do that?"

"Because you'll be more comfortable. This is going to take some time." Amy slid the knife into her belt. *I'm done with this, if you behave.* "We're not at all who you think we are. Now sit."

Reluctantly, Nina lowered herself to the snow. "I'm not going to tell you anything."

"I very much doubt that," said Amy. "I believe you'll tell me everything I need to know, once I explain what's about to happen here."

"I want to play with Dani!"

"Eva, sweetheart—"

The little girl's face was flushed with anger. She snatched one of the leather cups off the floor and hurled it at Lila, missing narrowly.

"You go to bed!" Lila shouted. "You go to bed this instant!"

The girl was immovable. Her face was bright with loathing. "You can't make me!"

"I'm your mother! You do as I say!"

"I want Dani!"

She had filled a hand with dry beans. Before Lila could react, the little girl reared back and launched them with astonishing, hate-fueled force into Lila's face. More beans spattered on the floor behind her, a clattering rain. She leapt to her feet and began to tear through the apartment—yanking books from the shelves, batting things off tables, hurling pillows into the air.

"Stop it this instant!"

The girl picked up a large ceramic vase.

"Eva, no—"

The little girl heaved it over her head and brought it down like somebody slamming the trunk of a car. Not a crack but a detonation: the vase exploded into a million ricocheting shards.

"I hate you!"

Something was happening, something final. Lila knew this, just as she sensed, in a deeper layer of her brain, that all of this had happened before. But the thought went no further; the hard edge of something hit her head. The girl was throwing books.

"Go away!" she screamed. "I hate-you-I-hate-you-I-hate-you!"

But as Lila watched her mouth forming these terrible words, they seemed to be coming from somewhere else. They were coming from inside her head. She lurched forward and grabbed the little girl around the waist and hoisted her off her feet. The girl kicked and screamed, wriggling in Lila's grip. All Lila wanted was—what? To calm the girl down? To get ahold of the situation? To silence the screaming that was tearing through her brain? For every ounce of force Lila applied, the girl replied in kind, shrieking at the top of her lungs, the scene ballooning to grotesque dimensions, a kind of madness, until Lila lost her footing, their combined centers of gravity tilted backward, and they went down hard, crashing into the dressing table.

"Eva!"

The little girl was scooting away from her. She came to a stop against the base of the sofa, glaring furiously. Why wasn't she crying? Was she hurt? What had Lila done? Lila approached her on her hands and knees.

"Eva, I'm sorry, I didn't mean it . . ."

"I hope you die!"

"Don't say that. Please. I'm begging you not to say that."

And with these words tears came at last to the little girl's eyes, though not tears of pain, or humiliation, or even fear. *I will despise you forever. You are not my mother and never were, and you know that as well as I.*

"Please, Eva, I love you. Don't you know how much I love you?"

"Don't say that! I want Dani!" Her tiny lungs expelled an amazing amount of sound. "I hate-you-I-hate-you-I-hate you!"

Lila clamped her hands over her ears, but nothing would block the child's cries.

"Stop it! Please!"

"I-hope-you-die-I-hope-you-die-I-hope-you-die!"

Lila tore into the bathroom and slammed the door. But this accomplished nothing: the screaming seemed to come from everywhere, an obliterating roar. She fell to her knees, sobbing into her hands. What was happening to her? *My Eva, my Eva. What have I done, to make you hate me so?* Her body shook with pain. Her thoughts were swirling, tumbling, shattering; she was a million broken pieces of Lila Kyle spread across the floor.

Because the girl wasn't Eva. No matter how hard Lila wished to make it so, there was no Eva; Eva was gone forever, a ghost of the past. The knowledge poured through her like acid, burning the lies away. *Go back,* Lila thought, *go back.* But she could never go back, not anymore.

Oh, God, the terrible things she'd done! The terrible, awful, unpardonable acts! She wept and shook. She cried, as her father always said, stroking paint on his little boats, a river. She was an abomination. She was a stain of evil on the earth. Everything was revealed to her, everything was of a piece, time stopped and moved again in a reassembled continuum inside her, telling its history of shame.

I hope you die. I hope you die I hope you die I hope you die.

Then something else was happening. Lila found herself sitting on the edge of the tub. She had entered a state beyond volition; she chose nothing, everything was choosing her. She opened the tap. She dipped her hand into its current, watching the water flow through her fingers. So here it was, she thought. The dark solution. It was as if she'd always known; as if, in the deepest recesses of her mind, she'd been performing this final act, over and over, for a hundred years. Of course the tub would be the means. For hours she'd sunk into its warmth; whole decades had passed in its comforting immersion, its delicious erasure of the world, yet always it had whispered to her: *Here I am. Lila, let me be your last deliverance.* The steam swirled upward, clouding the room with its moist breath. A perfect calm encased her. She lit the candles, one by one. She was a doctor; she knew what she was doing. *Soy médico.* She stripped and examined her naked body in the mirror. Its beauty—for it *was* beautiful—filled her with memories: of being young, a child herself, emerging from the bath. *You are my princess,* her father had teased, rubbing her hair to dry it and hugging her in the soft warmth of a freshly laundered towel. *You are the fairest in the land.* The recollections flowed through the water. She was a child, and then a teenager, in her blue taffeta dress with a fat corsage pinned to the shoulder, each picture morphing into the next until finally she beheld a woman, full of maturely youthful strength, standing before the mirror in her mother's wedding gown. The bodice of delicate lace, the descending curtain of shimmering white silk: how her life in all its promise had seemed captured in that image. *Today is the day I will marry Brad.* Her hand fell to her belly; the wedding dress was gone, replaced by a vaporous nightgown. A morning sun was streaming through the windows. She turned and, in profile, cupped the voluptuous curve of her belly. *Eva. That's who you'll be; that is who you are. I will name you Eva.* The steam was rising, the tub nearly full.

Brad, Eva, I am coming. I have been away too long. I am coming to be with you now.

Three blue lines pulsed at the base of each wrist: the cephalic vein, winding upward around the radial border of the forearm; the basilic, commencing in the dorsal venous network before ascending the posterior surface of the ulnar side to join the vena mediana cubiti; the accessory cephalic, arising from the tributory plexus to merge with the cephalic at the back of the elbow. She needed something sharp. Where were the scissors? The ones Dani, and all the others who had come before, employed to trim her hair? She tried one drawer of the vanity and then the next, and when she came to the bottom, there they waited, gleaming with sharpness.

But what was this?

It was an egg. A plastic Easter egg, like the ones she'd hunted in the grass when she was just a girl. How she'd loved the ritual: the wild dash over the field, her little basket swinging in her hand, the dew on her feet and the slow accumulation of treasure, her mind envisioning the great white rabbit whose nocturnal visitation had left behind this bounty. Lila cupped the egg in her palm. She felt the faintest rattling within. Could it be . . . ? Was it possible . . . ? But what else *could* it be?

There was only one answer. Lila Kyle would die with the taste of chocolate on her tongue.

60

Treachery. *Treachery.*

How had the insurgency gotten so close? Could somebody please tell him that? First the redhead, then Vale, and now Lila's attendant, too? That quaking mouse? That anonymous nobody who looked at the floor whenever he entered the room? How deep inside the Dome did the conspiracy reach?

To Guilder's vast irritation, the redhead was still at large. She'd killed eleven people making her escape; how was that even *possible*? They'd never even learned her name. *Call me what you like,* she'd said, *just don't call me early in the morning.* Jokes, from a woman who'd been beaten continuously for days. As for Sod, Guilder, in hindsight, was forced to concede his error. Letting a man like that off his leash had been a one-way ticket to disaster.

Guilder supervised the attendant's interrogation himself. Whatever it was that gave the redhead her strength, this one was made of softer stuff. Three dunks in the tub were all it took to make her talk. The bomb in the shed. The serving girl, Jenny, though nobody had seen her in days. A hideout she didn't know the location of because they'd knocked her out, which made sense; that's what Guilder would have done. A woman named Nina, though the only Nina in the files had died four years ago, and a man named Eustace, whom they had no record of at all. All very interesting, but nothing he could make real use of.

Do you want us to try harder? the guard asked. We could, you know, go a few more rounds. Guilder looked down at the woman, who was still strapped to the board, her hair drenched by the ice-cold water, the last wet gasps shuddering through her. Sara Fisher, No. 94801, resident of Lodge 216, a worker in Biodiesel Plant 3. Verlyn remembered her from the haul they'd brought in from Roswell. So, one of those infernal Texans. Now that the eleven virals had arrived, he'd really have to do something serious about the Texas situation. The woman hardly seemed the type; he had to remind himself that she'd intended to kill him. Though, of course, there was no type; that's what the last violent months had taught him. The insurgency was everyone and no one.

Never mind, he told the guard. Get her hooked up. I think Grey will enjoy what this one has to offer. He always likes the young ones.

He took the stairs from the basement to his office, donned his glasses, and opened the drapes. The sun had just dipped below the horizon, jetting the clouds with ribbons of bright color. The sight was pretty, sort of. Guilder supposed it was the kind of thing he might have enjoyed, a century ago. But a person could only look at so many sunsets in a lifetime and muster an opinion. The problem of living forever, etc., etc., etc.

He missed Wilkes. The man hadn't always been the best company—he'd been far too eager to please—but at least he'd been somebody to talk to. Guilder had trusted him, confided in him. Across the years there wasn't much they hadn't gotten around to saying. Guilder had even told him about Shawna, though he'd masked the story in irony. *A whore, can you believe it? What a jackass I was!* My, but they'd had a good, long laugh at that. The thing was, this was just the sort of unconstructed, vaguely anxious hour when Guilder would have stuck his head from the door, summoning his friend into his office on some pretense—"Fred, get in here!"—but really just to talk.

His friend. He supposed they were. Had been.

Darkness came on. Guilder's gaze traveled down the hill to the Project. It would need a new name now. Hoppel would have been the guy for that; no doubt about it, he'd had a way with words. In his former life he'd been an ad guy with a big Chicago agency, experience he'd put to plentiful use concocting the catchphrases and jingles that kept the troops in rhetorical line, right down to the words of the anthem. *Homeland, our Homeland, we pledge our lives to thee. Our labors do we offer, without recompense or fee. Homeland, our Homeland, a nation rises here. Safety, hope, security, from sea to shining sea.* Corny as hell, and Guilder hadn't been so keen on the word "recompense"—it seemed a little bookish—but the thing scanned nicely and was, by the standards of its genre, not too hard on the ears.

So, what should they call it there? "Bunker" was too martial. "Palace" had the right general ring, but there was nothing palatial about the place. It looked like a big concrete box. Something religious? A shrine? Who would not go willingly into a shrine?

Just how many of the flatlanders would have to go, and at what frequency, remained to be seen; Guilder had yet to receive specific instructions from Zero on this point, the general sense being that things would come out in the wash. The Twelve—or rather, Eleven—might be different from your garden-variety viral, but they were what they were—eating machines, basically. No matter what directives came down from on high, a century of gobbling up everything with a pulse would be a hard habit to shake. But in the main, their diet would consist of a combination of donated human blood and domestic livestock. The right ratios needed to be scrupulously maintained; the human population had to grow. Generation by generation, human and viral, working together—which was, come to think of it, not a bad way to sell the thing. It was positively Hoppelesque. What was the term? Rebranding? That's what Guilder needed. A fresh point of view, a new lexicon, a new vision. A rebranding of the viral experience.

He might have really hit on something with this shrine business. The establishment of something rather like an official religion, with all the mumbo jumbo and ritualistic trappings, might be just the lubricant the gears of human psychology required. State worship was all stick and no carrot; it produced only an arid obedience to authority. But hope was the greatest social organizer of all. Give people hope, and you could make them do just about anything. And not just your average, everyday kind of hope—for food or clothes or the absence of pain or good suburban schools or low down payments with easy financing. What people needed was a hope beyond the visible world, the world of the body and its trials, of life's endless dull parade of *things*. A hope that all was not as it appeared.

And there it was, the name. How simple it was, how elegant. Not a shrine; a templo. The Temple of Life Everlasting. And he, Horace Guilder, would be its priest.

So, not such a worthless day after all. Funny how things could just come like that, he thought with a smile—his first in weeks. Screw Hoppel and his ditties. And while he was at it, screw Wilkes, that ingrate. Guilder had everything in hand.

First the injection, and the wooziness, and Sara, lying on a wheeled gurney, observed the ceiling flowing past.

"Alley . . . *oop.*"

Now she was somewhere else. The room was dim. Hands were lifting her onto a table, tightening straps around her arms and legs and forehead. The metal was chilly beneath her. At some point her robe had been removed and replaced by a cotton gown. Her mind moved with animal heaviness through these facts, noting them without emotion. It was hard to care about anything. Here was Dr. Verlyn, peering down at her through his tiny glasses in his grandfatherly way. His eyebrows struck her as extraordinary. He was holding a silver forceps; a wad of cotton soaked in brown fluid was clinched between the tines. She supposed that since he was a doctor, he was doing something medical to her.

"This may feel a little cold."

It did. Dr. Verlyn was swabbing down her arms and legs; at the same time, somebody else was positioning a plastic tube beneath her nose.

"Catheter."

Now, that was not so nice. That wasn't nice at all. A moan rose from her throat. Other things began to happen, various pokings and intrusions, the alien sensation of foreign objects sliding under her skin—her forearms, the insides of her thighs. There was a beeping sound, and a hiss of gas, and a peculiar odor under her nose, strikingly sweet. Diethyl ether. It was manufactured at the biodiesel plant, though Sara had never seen how this was done. All she remembered were tanks with the word FLAMMABLE stenciled in red on the sides, and their clattering bulk as they were rolled on dollies to a waiting truck.

"Just breathe, please."

What a strange request! How could she not breathe?

"That's it."

She was borne aloft on the softest cloud.

61

Two days had passed since they'd made contact with the insurgency. At first, Nina had failed to believe them, as anyone would. The story was too fantastic, the history too complex. It was Alicia who had finally come up with a way to prove their case. She retrieved the RDF from her pack and led the woman up the ridge and pointed it toward the Dome. Greer was watching the valley below. At this distance, Alicia worried that she wouldn't get a signal. What would they do then to convince the woman? But there it was, fat and clear, a continuous pulsation. Alicia was relieved but also perplexed: if anything, the signal was stronger. Amy was silent a moment, then said, We'll have to hurry now. That sound you're hearing: it means the remaining Twelve are already here. She drew the knife from her belt and passed it to Nina and told Alicia and Greer to disarm as well. We're surrendering to you, said Amy. The rest is up to you.

The truck arrived, carrying two armed men. Alicia and the others met them with arms raised. Their wrists were bound, black hoods drawn over their heads. An interval of time passed, the three of them freezing in the bouncing cargo bed; then they heard the sound of a garage door opening. They were escorted from the truck and told to wait. A few minutes passed; footsteps approached.

"Take them off," a man's voice said.

The hoods were removed, revealing half a dozen men and women standing before them with raised weapons—all but one.

"Eustace?"

"Major Greer." Eustace shifted his broken face toward Alicia. "And Donadio, too." He shook his head. "Why am I surprised?" He turned to the others and gestured for them to lower their guns. "It's all right, everyone."

"You *know* them?" Nina asked.

Eustace looked them over again, noticing Amy. "Now, you I don't think I've seen before."

"Actually," said Amy, "that's not precisely true."

They had arrived on the eve of Eustace's people making their move. Years of painstaking infiltration had reached the moment of culmination. First, the decapitation of the leadership, followed by simultaneous attacks on a range of major targets: HR stations, industrial infrastructure, the power station, the detention center, the apartment complex on the edge of downtown where most of the redeyes lived. Weapons and explosives had been cached throughout the city. Their forces were small, but once the attack was under way, they believed, their numbers would grow. The slumbering giant of seventy thousand flatlanders would awaken and rise. Once that happened, the insurrection would become an avalanche, unstoppable. The city would be theirs.

But something had gone wrong. Their operative in the Dome had been found out. They knew she'd been taken alive, but not where—in all likelihood, the basement.

"I'm afraid there's something I must tell you," Eustace said, and explained who this operative was.

Sara was here. It strained belief. No, it went hurtling past it. And her daughter, too. Sara's. Hollis's. In some deep way, the child belonged to all of them. Their purpose had magnified, but so had the situation's complexity. They would have to get the two of them out.

Amy repeated the story she had told Nina. There could be no doubt that the virals were present somewhere in the city, or what this meant. Here was where they would begin rebuilding their legions. Eustace regarded their tale with skepticism, but then something clicked.

"Guilder will want to protect them," Amy said. "Is there someplace in the city that's unusually fortified? It would have to be large."

Eustace sent a man to retrieve the blueprints of the Project. Three people died to get these, Eustace said, and he unrolled the paper over the table.

"We never knew what this place was for. Lots of stories, but never anything that really added up. The place is a fortress. The redeyes have been building it for years."

Amy examined the blueprints, her eyes making swift calculations. "This is where we'll find them."

"I don't know how you can be so certain."

"Count the chambers."

Eustace bent over the paper. With his index finger, he traced each corridor to its destination. Then he looked up.

Thus their cause was joined to another. The building known as the Project was now the focus. Its design played in their favor: like the cave in New Mexico, the Project's tight quarters could amplify the explosive force of a single bomb detonated at the heart of the structure. But could they get inside? Doubtful—and even if they could, it would be like walking into a lion's den. Their losses would be heavy, and too many men would have to be diverted from other targets.

"So we don't go in to get them," Amy said. "We make them come to us."

"What do you have in mind?"

Amy thought a moment. "Tell me what kind of man Guilder is."

Eustace shrugged. Throughout the proceedings he had taken no umbrage at their presence. It was good, he said, to be among Expeditionaries again.

"He's a monster. Cruel, obsessive, monomaniacal in the extreme. He's absolutely fixated on Sergio."

"What would he do if he captured him?"

"Have the time of his life, probably. But Sergio doesn't exist. It's just a name."

"But what if he did?"

Eustace rubbed a hand over his chin. "Well, the man likes a show. Probably he'd stage a public execution, make a big display."

"Public. Meaning everybody."

"I suppose." Eustace's expression shifted. "Oh. I see."

"Where would he do that?"

"The stadium's the only place large enough. It can hold seventy thousand easily. Which would—"

"Leave the rest of the Homeland undefended. Resources spread thin, major targets exposed."

Eustace was nodding now. "And if he's really interested in making a demonstration of power—"

"Exactly."

Bewildered glances were exchanged around the table. "Somebody, please enlighten me," said Nina.

Amy leaned forward in her chair. "Here's what we do."

It took another twenty-four hours to make ready. Nina returned to the city to contact the leaders of the various cells with new instructions. The insurgency's hideout would be forfeit, of course. They rigged it with trip-wire explosives—barrels of ammonium nitrate fertilizer and diesel fuel connected to sulfur igniters. Nothing would remain but an ashy hole; with luck, Guilder would presume that all inside had been killed, a mass suicide, the insurgency's final blaze of glory.

They prepared the vehicles for departure. Alicia would drive Amy to the pipe, then rendezvous with the rest of Eustace's men to continue to their fallback location. Now all they were waiting on was the weather— they needed snow to cover their tire tracks. It might be tomorrow; it might be a week; it might be never. An hour before sunset on the third day, a tantalizing dust of flurries began to fall. It stopped, then started up again, slowly gathering force, as if the weather had cleared its throat and spoken. *Go now.*

They drove out, a convoy of nine trucks carrying forty-seven men and women. Alicia peeled away and aimed her vehicle north. The snow formed a dense, whirling mass in the truck's headlights. Beside her, Amy, wearing an attendant's robe, was silent. Alicia had warned her what she would be facing; there was no reason to discuss it further, especially now.

Thirty minutes later they arrived at the pipe. Despite her better judgment, Alicia said, "You know what they'll do to you."

Amy nodded. A brief silence; then: "There's a purpose to everything. A shape. Do you believe that?"

"I don't know."

Amy pulled Alicia's hand off the wheel and took it in her own, twining their fingers together. "We're sisters, you know. Blood sisters. I know what's happening to you, Lish."

Amy's words felt like something falling inside her. And yet: of course she would know. How could Amy not know?

"Can you control it?"

Alicia swallowed with difficulty. Over the last two days, the desire had become intense. It was reaching its dark hand inside her, taking her over. Her mind was fogged with it. Soon it would overwhelm her will to resist.

"It's getting . . . harder."

"When the time comes—"

"I'm not going to let it."

All around, the snow was falling. Alicia knew that if she didn't leave soon, she might get stuck. One last thing needed to be said. It took all her courage to form the words.

"Take care of Peter. You can't let him know what happened to me. Promise me that."

"Lish—"

"You can tell him anything else. Make up a story. I don't care. But I need your word."

A deep quiet ensued, encasing the two of them. Alicia had been alone with this knowledge for too long; now it was shared. She searched her emotions. Loss, relief, the feeling of crossing a border into a dark country. She was giving him up.

"In a way, I've always known this would happen. Even before I met you. There was always somebody else."

Amy made no reply. Her silence told Alicia all she needed to know.

"You should go," Alicia said.

Still Amy said nothing. Her face was uncertain. Then:

"There's something I haven't told you, Lish."

Gray day into gray day. The continent's vast inland empire of weather. Would it snow? Would the sun ever come out again? Would the wind blow at their backs or into their frozen faces? They walked and walked, hunched forward against the weight of their packs. There were no signs, no landmarks. The roads and towns were gone, subsumed like sunken ships beneath the waves of snowy prairie. Tifty confessed that he didn't know exactly where they were. Central Iowa, northeast of Des Moines, but anything more specific . . . He made no apologies; the situation was what it was. Why couldn't you have decided to do this in summer? he said.

They were almost out of food. They'd cut their rations in half, but half of nothing would be nothing. As they huddled inside a ruined farmhouse, Lore doled out the meager slices on the blade of her knife. Peter placed his beneath his tongue to make it last, the hardened fat dissolving slowly in the warmth of his mouth.

They went on.

Then, late on the afternoon of the twenty-eighth day, a vision appeared: materializing slowly from a colorless sky, a tall sign, rocking in the wind. They made their way toward it; a cluster of buildings emerged.

What town was this? It didn't matter; the need for shelter trumped every other concern. They passed through the outer commercial ring, with its husks of supermarkets and chain stores, flat roofs long collapsed under the weight of winter snow, and continued into the old town. The usual remnants and rubble, but at the heart they came to two blocks of brick buildings that appeared sound.

"Don't suppose we'll find anything to eat in there," Michael said.

They were standing before a storefront, the front windows of which were amazingly unbroken. Faded lettering on the glass read, FANCY'S CAFÉ.

Hollis said, "Looks like they've been out of business for a while."

They forced the door and entered. A narrow space, with booths of cracked vinyl opposite a counter with stools; except for the dust, which caked every surface, it was remarkably undisturbed. From time to time one found such a place, a museum of the past where the passage of decades had somehow failed to register, more eerie than ruins.

Michael lifted a menu from a stack on the counter and opened it. "What's meatloaf? I get the meat part, but a loaf of it?"

"Jesus, Michael," Lore said. She was shivering, her lips blue. "Don't make it worse."

Hollis and Peter scouted the back. The rear door and windows had been sealed with plywood; a hammer and nails lay on the floor.

"We're not going to get much farther without food," Hollis said gravely.

"You don't have to remind me."

They returned to the front of the café, where the others were bundling themselves in blankets on the floor. Darkness was falling. The room was freezing, but at least they were out of the wind.

"I'm going to look around," Peter said. "Maybe I can figure out where we are."

He slogged his way across the street, then moved down the block, peering in the storefronts. He tried some of the doors, but all were locked. Well, they could come back in the morning and open a few to see what was there.

At the end of the second block he tried a handle without looking—he was just going through the motions now—and was startled when the door swung open. Stepping inside, he holstered his pistol and removed a match from the box in the breast pocket of his parka and struck the tip, cupping the flame against the breeze coming from the open door.

Well, son of a bitch.

Peter knew a supply cache when he saw one. Burlap bags were stacked against the walls of the otherwise bare room. He knelt and opened the nearest bag with a flick of his blade: dried beans. In another he found potatoes, in a third apples. He lit another match and raised it over the floor; there were footprints all around in the dust. Who had left this here? What did it mean?

Their situation was dire, but at least they wouldn't starve. Better to think about what to do next on a full stomach. He sank his teeth into an apple. It was flavorless, hard as a chunk of ice. He polished it off in a frenzy, jammed more into his pockets, and scanned the room for something he could use to carry food back to the others. In the corner he found a bucket full of copper wire. He dumped the wire on the floor, filled the bucket with apples and potatoes, and returned to the street.

He was instantly aware of something odd. The night seemed brighter. The moon? But there was no moon. A prickle of alarm danced over his skin, then he heard the sound. He turned his face away from the wind, listening hard. A distant rumbling. The sound was coming closer, becoming more distinct by the second.

Engines.

He dropped the pail and raced up the block toward the café. A line of vehicles was roaring toward him. He heard voices yelling, then a series of pops. Jets of snow flew up around him.

Somebody was shooting at him.

He tore through the door of the café just as a phalanx of guns opened fire, exploding the windows. *Get down!* he yelled, *Get down!,* but everybody already had. He dove over the counter, landing on top of Lore, who was holding her hands over her head. The blaze of the vehicles' headlights filled the room. Things were splintering, crashing, round after round being pumped into the tiny room.

"Michael! Where are you?"

His voice came from under one of the banquettes: "Who are they? What do they want?"

The question was rhetorical: whoever they were, they wanted to kill them.

"Tifty? Hollis?"

Michael again: "They're with me! Tifty's cut, but he's okay!"

"I've got Lore!"

A pause in the shooting; then they opened fire again.

"Can anybody see anything?"

"Three vehicles straight outside," Hollis called. "More down the street!"

"Maybe we should surrender!" Michael yelled.

"I don't think these are the sort of people you surrender to!"

The room was being pummeled. Peter had only his pistol; he'd left his rifle by the door. They'd never make it to the back, and the doors and windows were boarded up, anyway. The café was a death trap.

"What do you want to do?" Hollis called.

"Can Tifty move on his own?"

"I'm okay!"

Flattened to the floor, Peter swiveled his face to Lore. "What do you have?"

She showed him her knife. "Just this."

He aimed his voice over the counter: "We go on three! Somebody toss us a gun!"

It arrived from Michael's direction, dropping on top of them. Lore took it and racked the slide. The guns outside had fallen silent again. Nobody out there was in any hurry.

"Shooting our way out of here isn't much of a plan," Lore said.

"I'd be happy to hear a better one."

Peter was rising to his knees when Lore stopped him with a hand. "Listen," she whispered.

He heard footsteps crunching snow, followed by a tinkle of glass underfoot. He raised a finger to his lips. How many were there? Two? A hostage, he thought suddenly. It was their only chance. There was no way to communicate with the others; he'd have to go on his own. He pointed to Lore, gesturing toward the far end of the counter, away from the door. He mouthed: *Make a noise.*

Lore slithered along the floor. Peter holstered his pistol and compressed his body to a crouch. When Lore was in position she looked at him, her face set, and nodded.

"Help me," she moaned.

Peter leapt to the top of the bar. As the nearest man turned, Peter drew his pistol and fired at the backlit shape and sailed down upon the second man, sending the two of them crashing to the floor. Peter's pistol clattered away. A moment of mad scrambling, arms and legs tangling; the man had a good thirty pounds on him, but surprise was on Peter's side. A semi was strapped to the man's thigh. Locking a forearm around his adversary's neck, Peter pulled him into a backward embrace, yanked the gun free of its holster, and shoved the muzzle into the curve of his jaw beneath his flowing silver hair.

"Tell them to hold fire!"

From their place on the floor, Peter found himself staring directly at Michael, hidden beneath one of the tables. His eyes grew very wide. "Peter—"

"I mean it," Peter told the man, pressing the barrel deeper. "Yell it, so everyone can hear."

The man had relaxed in his arms. Peter felt him shudder, though not with pain. The man had started to laugh.

"Stand down!" a new voice said—a woman's. "Everybody cease fire!"

The second man wasn't a man after all. She was sitting on the floor with her back braced against one of the booths, her right arm held across her chest to clutch her wounded shoulder.

"Flyers, Peter." Alicia drew her bloodied hand away. Now she was laughing, too. "Lucius, can you believe he fucking shot me?"

62

At the base of the ladder, Amy touched the map to her torch. The paper caught instantly, snatched away in a flash of blue flame. She doused the torch in the trickle of water at her feet, ascended the ladder, and shoved the manhole cover aside.

She was in the alley behind the apothecary shop. She sealed the plate and peeked around the corner of the building; above the heart of the city, the Dome stood imperiously, its hammered surface shining with light. She drew down her veil and walked briskly from the alleyway. Men with dogs were moving along the barricades. She strode up to the guard-house, where two men were blowing on their hands, and displayed her pass.

"This doesn't look right." He showed it to the second man. "Does this look right to you?"

The col glanced at it quickly, then looked at Amy. "Lift your veil."

She did as he asked. "Is there something wrong?"

He studied her face a moment. Then he handed back the pass. "Forget it. It's fine."

Amy threaded past them and headed up the stairs. None of the other men paid her any note; the guards at the gate had verified her presence as warranted. Inside, she marched past the guard at the desk, who barely glanced at her, crossed the lobby to the elevator, and rode it to the sixth floor.

The elevator opened on a circular balcony circumscribing the building's atrium. Four corridors led away, like spokes on a wheel. Amy made her way around the balcony to the third corridor and down its length to the last door, where the guard, a droopy-faced man with a tonsure of gray hair, was sitting on a folding metal chair, flipping through the brittle pages of a hundred-year-old magazine. On the cover was the image of a woman in an orange bikini, her hands pushed upward through her hair.

"The Director asked to see me," Amy told him, drawing up her veil.

His eyes broke from the page, finding Amy's, and that was all it took. She eased him to the floor, propped his back against the wall, and took the key from his belt. His chin was rocked forward onto his chest. She put her lips close to his ear.

"I'm going to go inside now. I want you to count to sixty—can you do that?"

His eyes were closed. He nodded slightly, making a murmur of assent.

"Good. Count to sixty, and when you get there, throw yourself off the balcony."

She unlocked the door and stepped inside. There was something deceptively benign about the room. Two wingback chairs faced an enormous desk, its polished surface gleaming faintly. The floor was covered in thick carpet, muffling everything but the sound of Amy's breathing. One whole wall was books; another displayed a large painting, lit by a tiny spotlight, of three figures sitting at a long counter and a fourth man in a white hat, all seen through a window on a darkened street. Amy paused to read the small plaque at the base of its frame: Edward Hopper, *Nighthawks,* 1942.

To her right was a pair of parlor doors with windows of leaded glass. Amy turned the knob and eased through.

Guilder was lying on top of the blankets in his underwear. A pile of cardboard folders floated in the sea of bedding beside him. Soft, windy snores were issuing from his nose. Where should she stand? She chose the foot of the bed.

"Director Guilder."

He jerked violently awake, darting a hand beneath his pillow. He pushed himself up the headboard, scrambling away from her; with both hands he leveled the pistol at her and cocked the hammer. He was trembling so profoundly Amy thought he might shoot her by accident.

"How did you get in here?"

She sensed his uncertainty. The robe of an attendant, but the face was none he knew. "The guard was very accommodating. Why don't you put that down?"

"Goddamnit, *who are you?*"

She heard voices from the hall, fists pounding on the outer door.

"I am Sergio," she said. "I've come here to surrender."

XI

THE DARKEST NIGHT OF THE YEAR

DECEMBER 21, 97 A.V.

My soul is in the midst of lions;
I lie among ravenous beasts—
men whose teeth are spears and arrows,
whose tongues are sharp swords.

—Psalm 57:4

CAPTURED!

A MESSAGE FROM THE
OFFICE OF THE DIRECTOR

The despicable murderer known as "Sergio" is in custody!

The insurgency has been smashed!

Peace has been restored to our beloved Homeland!

SENTENCE TO BE CARRIED OUT
BY PUBLIC EXECUTION
IN THE STADIUM

ALL WORKERS REPORT TO
HR PERSONNEL AT YOUR LODGES
2130 HRS TOMORROW

Stand together, Citizens of the Homeland!
Rejoice in this glorious day of justice!
Let all traitors know that this will be their fate!

63

Events had followed just as Amy had foreseen. The time and place of her execution were set; only the method had yet to be revealed—the final detail on which their plan depended. Would Guilder simply shoot her? Hang her? But if such a meager display was all he intended, why had he ordered the entire population, all seventy thousand souls in the Homeland, to observe? Amy had baited the hook; would Guilder take it?

Peter passed the next four days lurching between emotional poles—alternating states of worry and astonishment, both overlain with a powerful feeling of déjà vu. Everything possessed a striking familiarity, as if no time had passed since they'd faced Babcock on the mountaintop in Colorado. Here they all were, together once more, their fates drawn together as if by a powerful gravitational force. Peter, Alicia, Michael, Hollis, Greer: they had converged upon this place by different routes, for different reasons. Yet it was Amy, once again, who had led them.

Greer had related the story of her transformation: Houston, Carter, the *Chevron Mariner;* Amy's journey into the bowels of the ship and then her return. The full measure of what had passed between Amy and Carter, Greer couldn't tell them; all he knew was that Carter had directed them here. Beyond that, Amy either wouldn't or couldn't say.

That night at the orphanage, the two of them standing at the door, the tips of their fingers colliding in space: had she known what was happening to her? And had he? Peter had felt in Amy's touch the pressure of something unstated. *I am going away. The girl you know will not be here when next we meet.* Which she had; the girl who Amy was had gone away. In her place was now a woman.

The group clothed their anxieties in unnecessary repetitions of their various preparations. The cleaning of weapons. The examination of blueprints and maps. The going over of checklists and the assorted mental inventories they would carry into war. Hollis and Michael became, in the last days, a kind of closed loop; their purpose had narrowed to Sara and Kate. Alicia dealt with the anxiety the way she dealt with everything—by pretending it wasn't important. The bullet from Peter's pistol had missed the bone and exited cleanly, a lucky thing, but even so. She would be healed in a day or two, but in the meantime the sling on her arm was a constant reminder to Peter of how close he'd come to killing her. When she wasn't barking orders, she retreated into unreachable silence, letting Peter know, without saying so, that she had entered the zone of battle. Greer intimated that something had happened to her in the cell, that she'd been beaten badly, but any attempt to ask her more about this, to offer comfort, was sternly rebuffed. "I'm all right," Alicia said with a peremptory tone that could only mean she wasn't. "Don't worry about me. I can take care of myself." She seemed, in fact, to be actively avoiding him, disappearing for long stretches; if he didn't know better, he would have said she was angry with him. She would return hours later smelling of horse sweat, but when Peter asked her where she'd gone, all she would say was that she'd been scouting the perimeter. He had no reason to doubt this, yet the explanation felt thin, a cover for something unstated.

Tifty, too, had undergone a subtle but significant change. His reunion with Greer had meant more than Peter had expected. They had served in the Expeditionary together, an inarguable bond, but Peter had not anticipated the depth of their friendship. A genuine warmth flowed between them. Peter puzzled over this at first, but the reason was obvious: Greer and Tifty had been here before, with Crukshank, all those years ago. The story of the field, and Dee, and the two little girls: of any man living, Greer best knew the heart of Tifty Lamont.

In this manner the hours, and then the days, moved by. Over everything two questions hovered: Would the plan work? And if it did, could they get to Amy in time?

On the third night, when Peter couldn't stand the waiting for one more second, he left the basement of the police station where everyone was sleeping, ascended the stairs, and stepped outside. The front of the building was protected by a broad overhang that kept the area clear of snow. Alicia was sitting with her back against the wall and her knees pulled to her chest. The sling had come off. In one hand she held a long, gleaming bayonet, serrated near the base; in the other was a sharpening stone. With calm, even strokes she was running the blade of the knife along the stone, first one side and then the other, pausing at the conclusion of each pass to examine her work. She seemed not to notice Peter at first, so intent was her focus; then, sensing his presence, she lifted her eyes toward him. It seemed her moment to speak, but she didn't say anything; her face bore no expression at all, beyond a kind of vague distraction.

"Mind some company?" he asked.

"Sit if you want."

He took a place beside her on the ground. Now he could feel it. The air around her seemed to prickle with barely contained rage. It flowed off her like an electric current.

"That's some knife."

She had resumed her patient sharpening. "Eustace gave it to me."

"You think it's sharp enough?"

"Just keeping my hands busy."

He groped for the next thing to say but couldn't find it. Where have you gone, Lish?

"I should be angry with you," he said. "You could have told me what your orders were."

"And then what would you have done? Follow me?"

"I'm AWOL as it is. A few more days wouldn't have made any difference."

She blew on the tip of the knife. "They weren't your orders, Peter. Don't get me wrong—I'm glad to see you. I'm not even that surprised. In a weird way, it makes sense you'd be here. You're a good officer, and we'll need you. But we all have our jobs to do."

He was taken aback. A good officer? Was that all he was to her? "That doesn't sound like you."

"It doesn't matter how it sounds. That's just how it is. Maybe it's time somebody said it."

He didn't know how to respond. This wasn't the Alicia he knew. Whatever had happened to her in that cell, it had driven her so far inside herself it was as if she wasn't there at all.

"I'm worried about you."

"Well, don't be."

"I mean it, Lish. There's something wrong. You can tell me."

"There's nothing to tell, Peter." She looked him in the eye. "Maybe I'm just . . . waking up. Facing reality. You should, too. This isn't going to be easy."

He felt stung. He searched her face, hunting for any scrap of warmth, finding none. Peter was the first to turn away.

"What do you think's happening to her?" he asked.

He didn't have to be any more specific; Alicia knew whom he was referring to.

"I'm trying not to think about it."

"Why did you let her go?"

"I didn't *let* her do anything, Peter. It wasn't up to me."

A chilly silence fell.

"I could really use a drink," Peter said.

She gave a quiet laugh. "Now, that's new. Those aren't words I believe I've ever heard you say before."

"There's a first time for everything." Then: "Do you remember that night in the bunker in Twentynine Palms when we found the whiskey?"

The bottle had been in a desk drawer. To celebrate the repair of the Humvees and their impending departure from the bunker, they'd passed it around, toasting the great adventure that awaited them on their journey east to Colorado.

Alicia said, "God, we all got so drunk. Michael was the worst. He never could hold his lick."

"No, I think it was Hightop. Remember how he broke open one of the light sticks and smeared that goo all over his face? 'Look at me, look at me, I'm a viral!' That kid was hilarious."

His mistake was instantly evident. Five years later, the boy's death was still a raw wound; in all that time, Peter had never heard Alicia so much as speak his name.

"Sorry. I didn't mean—"

A bright light flashed over the horizon. Lightning? In winter? Moments later they heard the boom, muted but unmistakable.

Eustace appeared at the foot of the steps. "I heard it too. Which direction?"

It had come from the south. It was hard to gauge the distance, but they guessed five miles.

"Well," Eustace said, nodding to himself, "I guess we'll know more in the morning."

Shortly after dawn, a messenger arrived, sent by Nina. The explosives at their hideout had done their work; their ruse had been successful. Minister Suresh, whom Guilder had sent to personally oversee their capture, was rumored to be among the dead. A taste, everyone hoped, of things to come.

But it was the second part of the message that offered the most promise. A semitruck had been parked outside the Project since the prior evening. It was guarded by a large security detachment, twenty men at least. The last piece had fallen into place; the virals were on the move. Guilder had tipped his hand.

Everybody knew the implications of what they were attempting. The plan seemed sound, but the odds were long. Guilder's orders to move the population to the stadium implied that the rest of the city would be only lightly protected, and if everything proceeded according to design, the insurgency would accomplish in one stroke a beheading of virtually every aspect of the regime. But timing would be critical; with so many elements of the resistance acting independently, and lacking the ability to communicate with one another once the siege was under way, it wouldn't take much for things to fall apart. Any variable could throw the operation into chaos.

The greatest variable was Sara. Assuming she was in the basement of the Dome, staging a rescue operation would be strategically cumbersome, and nobody knew where her daughter was. She could be in the Dome, or she could be someplace else entirely. Once they stormed the building and the shooting started, distinguishing between friend and foe would be nearly impossible. The decision they came to was that Hollis and Michael would lead an advance team to the basement. Five minutes would be all they'd have. After that, the building and all its inhabitants would be fair game.

Eustace would head up the operation against the stadium itself. The contents of the explosives package, a form of nitroglycerin, had been stolen from the Project site during construction and subsequently modified to their purpose, making it more potent but also highly unstable. It was of the same type that had been delivered to Sara in the Dome and was now presumed lost. Despite its power, the only way to guarantee the outcome was to deliver it to the eleven virals, as Eustace said, "in person, a bomb with legs." Peter failed to understand this at first; then the meaning came. The legs would be Eustace's.

Their teams would enter the city at four locations, all branched to the main storm pipe. Eustace's team, which included Peter, Alicia, Tifty, Lore, and Greer, would use the confusion at the stadium to infiltrate the crowd; elements of the insurgency under Nina's command would already be in position in the bleachers to seize control when the moment came. Weapons had been concealed in the lavatories and under the stairs to the upper bleachers. Eustace's appearance on the field would be the signal to attack.

At the first touch of darkness, they set out. There was no point in concealing their tracks; one way or the other, they would never be returning. The night was clear, the sky wide and starlit, a vast indifferent presence gazing down. Well, Peter thought, maybe not so indifferent. He certainly hoped that someone up there cared, as Greer had said. It was hard to believe only a few weeks had passed since their conversation in the stockade. They reached the pipe and began to walk. Peter found himself thinking not only of Amy but Sister Lacey, too. Amy was one thing; she was another. The woman had faced Babcock with absolute fearlessness, a pure acceptance of the outcome. Peter hoped he would prove as worthy.

At the base of the manhole closest to the stadium, the group exchanged final words. The other teams, moving to locations throughout the Homeland, would remain concealed belowground until they heard the detonation in the stadium, which would serve as the signal to commence their assaults. Only Hollis and Michael would move sooner. There was no way to predict the moment to act; they would have to follow their instincts.

"Good luck," Peter said. The three men shook hands, then, when this seemed inadequate, embraced. Lore rose on tiptoes to kiss Hollis on his bearded cheek.

"Remember what I said," she told him. "She's waiting for you. You'll find her, I know it."

Hollis and Michael made their way down the tunnel, their images fading, then gone. With handshakes all around and wishes for luck, the other groups departed behind them. Peter and the others waited. The cold was numbing; all of them had wet feet, their shoes soaked by the fetid waters. Eustace was wearing an olive jacket, the deadly cargo concealed beneath. Nobody spoke, but the silence that encased the man ran deeper. In a private moment, Eustace had assured Peter that there was simply no other way. He was glad to do it, in fact. Many people had been sent to their deaths at his orders. It was only right that his turn should come.

It was a little after 1700 hours when, from the top of the ladder, Tifty said, "It's starting. We need to move."

They would exit one at a time at one-minute intervals. The opening lay beneath a pickup truck that a member of Nina's team had left in place on the south side of the stadium. Sooner or later it would be noticed and remarked on—*What's that doing there?*—but so far it had escaped attention. From the manhole each of them would make their way into the lines of people flowing into the stadium. A tricky moment, but only the first of many.

Eustace went first. Greer watched from the top of the ladder. "Okay," he said, "I think he made it."

Lore and Greer followed. Once inside, they would rendezvous at specific points within the structure. Alicia would be the next to last; Tifty would bring up the rear. Peter got into position at the base of the ladder.

Alicia was standing behind him. Like all of them, she was disguised in a flatlander's scratchy tunic and trousers.

"Sorry about your arm," he said, for the hundredth time.

Alicia smiled in her knowing way. It was the first smile he'd seen in days. "Hell, it was probably about time one of us shot the other. We've practically done everything else. I'm just glad your aim is so bad."

"This is a touching scene," Tifty said dryly, "but we really have to *go*."

Peter hesitated; he didn't want those words to be the last thing the two of them ever said to each other.

"I told you you'd get your chance, didn't I?" Alicia hugged him quickly. "You heard the man— get moving. I'll see you when the dust settles."

And yet she did not look at him when she spoke, averting her glance with misted eyes.

The question before him was this: what the hell should he wear?

The era of suits and ties had come to an end for Horace Guilder. That part of his life was over. A suit was the outfit of a government official, not the high priest of the Temple of Life Everlasting.

It was all a little nerve-racking. He'd never been to church much, even as a kid. His mother took him once in a while, but his father never went. But as Guilder recalled it, some kind of robe was standard. Something along the lines of a dress.

"Suresh!"

The man limped into the bedroom. What a sight he was. His face was swollen and pink; his brows and lashes had been scorched away, giving his eyes a startled appearance. He had cuts and bruises all over, puckered and raw-looking. It would all pass in a few days, but in the meantime the man looked like a cross between an Easter ham and the loser of a lop-sided boxing match.

"Get me an attendant's robe."

"What for?"

Guilder waved him toward the door. "Just get it. A big one."

The summoned article was produced. Suresh lingered, evidently hoping for some explanation for Guilder's curious request, or perhaps just looking forward to the sight of Guilder wriggling into the thing.

"Don't you have someplace to be?"

"I thought you wanted me to stay here."

"Jesus, don't be dense. Go see about the car."

Suresh hobbled away. Guilder positioned himself in front of the full-length mirror with the gown held before him. For the love of God, he was going to look like a clown in this thing. But the clock was ticking; HR would be bringing the flatlanders into the stadium any minute. A little delay wasn't necessarily bad—it would ramp up the anticipation—but crowd control would get to be an issue if he dawdled for too long. Best to face the music; over his head went the robe. The image in the mirror wasn't a clown after all, more like the bride at an Amish wedding. The thing was utterly shapeless. He removed a pair of neckties from the rack in his closet, knotted them together, and cinched the waist. A definite improvement, but something was missing. The priests he recalled from his boyhood brushes with religion had always worn some kind of shawl. Guilder went to the window. The drapes were held against the window frame by heavy golden ropes with tassels at the ends. He unhooked them and balanced them over his shoulders, the tassels swaying at his waist, and returned to the mirror. Not bad for somebody who knew absolutely nothing about religion or, for that matter, fashion. What a shock it would be to historians of the future to learn that Horace Guilder, High Priest of the Temple of Life Everlasting, Rebuilder of Civilization, Shepherd of the Dawn of the New Age of Cooperation Between Human and Viral, had sanctified himself with a pair of curtain tiebacks.

He opened the door to find Suresh waiting for him. The man's bald eyes widened.

"Don't say a word."

"I wasn't going to."

"Well, don't."

They rode the elevator to the lobby. The building was strikingly silent; Guilder had sent most of his personal detachment to the stadium. This spread the cols and redeyes thin, but keeping the stadium under control was paramount. The vehicles were waiting, chuffing exhaust into the cold: Guilder's car, the semi with its magnificent cargo, a pair of escort trucks, and a security van. He walked briskly to the van, where two cols were standing at the rear. One thing about a priest's vestment: it didn't offer much warmth on a winter night. He should have brought a coat.

"Open it."

It was hard to believe that the figure seated before him on the bench had been the source of so much trouble. She might have been considered pretty, if Guilder's thoughts ran in that direction. Not that she was dainty—she wasn't. Underneath the swelling and discoloration, she was obviously a solid specimen. Deep-set eyes, strong features, a taut, muscular frame that was nonetheless feminine. But in Guilder's imagination, Sergio had always been a man, and not just any man; the mental portrait he'd concocted was a knockoff of Che Guevara, some banana republic revolutionary with eyes like pinpricks and a scraggly beard. This was Joan of Arc.

"Anything to say for yourself?" Guilder couldn't have cared less; the question was just for fun.

Her wrists and ankles were shackled. Her split and swollen lips gave her voice a thickened quality, as if she had a bad cold. "I'd like to say I'm sorry."

Guilder laughed. Sergio was sorry! "Tell me, what are you sorry for?"

"For what's about to happen to you."

So, defiant to the end. Guilder supposed it came with the territory, but it was nonetheless irritating. He wouldn't have minded banging her around a little more.

"Last chance," the woman said.

"You have an interesting point of view," Guilder replied. He stepped back from the open door. "Seal her up."

For a long time, perched on the edge of the bed, Lila watched her. Slants of light from the window fell across the child's sleeping face, blond curls flowing over the pillow. For days she had been beyond the reach of comfort, alternating between hours of sullen refusal to speak and explosive, toy-throwing tantrums, but in sleep her defenses dissolved and she became a child again: trusting, at peace.

What is your name? Lila thought. *Who are you dreaming of?*

She reached out to touch the little girl's hair but stopped herself. The child wouldn't awaken; that wasn't the reason. It was the unworthiness of Lila's hand. So many Evas over the years. And yet there had only ever been one.

I'm sorry, little girl. You didn't deserve this; none of them did. I am the most selfish woman in the world. What I did, I did for love. I hope you can forgive me.

The child stirred, tightening the covers around herself, and pivoted her face toward Lila's. Her jaw flexed; she made a little moan. Would she awaken? But no. Her palm slid under the curve of her cheek, one dream passed into the next, and the moment slipped away.

Better that way, thought Lila. Better that I should simply fade into darkness. She rose gingerly from the bed. At the door she turned for one last look, bathed in memory: of a time when she had stood at the nursery door with Brad, in the house they had made together with their love, to watch their little girl, this swaddled newborn bundle, this miracle upon the earth, sleeping in her crib. How Lila wished she herself had died, all those years ago. If heaven were a place of dreams, that's the dream she would have passed eternity inside.

Farewell, she thought. Farewell to you, somebody's child.

The scene outside the stadium was one of ordered chaos, a human vastness on the move. Peter slid into the stream. Nobody even looked at him; he was one more anonymous face, one more shorn head and filthy body in rags.

"Keep it moving, keep it moving!"

In four lines they flowed up a ramp and passed through an iron gate into the stadium. To Peter's left, a series of concrete staircases ascended to lettered gates; ahead, a longer flight climbed to the upper decks. The crowd was being divided—two lines to the lower stands, two up the stairs. The field was brilliantly lit; light poured through the gates. Peter tried to catch a glimpse of Lore or Eustace, but they were too far ahead of him. Maybe they'd already broken away. The letters ascended. P, Q, R, then: S.

Peter dropped to one knee, pretending to tie his shoelaces. His successor in line bumped him, grunting in surprise. Whatever you did, you didn't stop.

"Sorry, go ahead."

The line bunched as it flowed around him. Through shuffling legs he glimpsed the nearest guard. He was gazing vaguely in Peter's direction from a distance of ten yards—probably attempting to discern the source of the interruption. *Look away,* thought Peter.

A flick of the col's eyes, and Peter darted into the crawl space underneath the stairs. No shouts rose behind him. Either he had gone unnoticed or the crowd didn't care, locked into their habit of obedience. The entrance to the men's room was ten feet away, at the base of the bleachers. There was no door, only a cement-block wall angled for privacy. Peter peeked around the stairs. An obscuring barrier of shuffling flatlanders marched past. *Now.*

The room was surprisingly large. On the right was a long line of urinals and stalls. He moved briskly to the last and pushed open the door to see a fierce-looking woman with short, dark hair perched on the rim of the toilet, aiming a heavy-handled revolver at his face.

"Sergio lives."

She lowered the gun. "Peter?"

He nodded.

"Nina," she said. "Let's go."

She led him to a tiny room behind the lavatory: a desk and chair, wheeled buckets with mops, and a line of metal lockers. From one of the lockers Nina withdrew a pair of guns of a type Peter had never seen before, something between a rifle and a large pistol, with an extra-long magazine and a second handle jutting from the underside of the barrel.

"Know how to use one of these?" she said.

Peter drew back the bolt to show that he did.

"Short bursts only and fire from the waist. You'll get twelve rounds per second. If you hold the trigger down, the clip will empty fast."

She handed him three extra magazines, then pulled open a drawer-like panel in the wall.

"What's that?" Peter asked.

"The garbage chute."

Peter stood on the chair, wedged himself inside, and dropped down feetfirst. The corridor was tipped like a slide, cushioning his descent, but not enough. He landed hard, his feet skidding out from under him.

"Who the hell are *you*?"

There were two of them, dressed in suits. Redeyes. Lying helplessly on his back, Peter could do nothing. He was clutching the gun over his chest, but shots would be heard. As he scrabbled away, simultaneously attempting to rise to his feet, both men drew pistols from belt holsters.

Then, Tifty. He appeared behind the one on the left and swung the butt of his rifle upward into the man's head. As the second turned, Tifty kicked his feet out from under him, dropped to his knees to straddle his back, yanked him by the hair to angle his head upward, wrapped his neck with his free arm and twisted. A crunching pop, then silence.

"Okay?" Tifty glanced up at Peter. The dead man's head, still locked by Tifty's forearm, sagged at an unnatural angle. Peter looked at the other redeye. Dark blood was seeping from his head onto the floor.

"Yeah," Peter managed.

A rattling from behind them and Nina dropped down. She landed catlike, fluidly raising her weapon to sweep it over the room.

"I see I'm late." She angled the gun to the ceiling. "You're Tifty?"

For a moment the man said nothing. He was staring at her intently.

"You can let go of him, you know," she said. "He's not going to get any more dead."

Tifty broke his gaze away. He released the dead man's head and rose to his feet. He seemed a little shaken; Peter wondered what had thrown the man off.

"We better hide these bodies," Tifty said. "Did Eustace make it in?"

"We'd have heard it if he didn't."

They were in some kind of loading area. A tunnel, wide enough to fit a good-sized truck, led to the left, presumably to the outside; to the right was a smaller hallway. An arrow painted on the wall bore the words VISITORS' LOCKER ROOM.

They dragged the corpses behind a pile of crates and moved down the hall. They were under the field now, on the south side. The hallway ended at a flight of stairs going up. The light was barely enough to see by. Overhead Peter heard the rumble of the crowd.

"We wait here till it starts," Nina said.

In the back of the van, Amy could see nothing. A small window separated the cargo area from the cab, but the driver had left it closed. Her body felt like she'd been dragged from a runaway horse, but her mind was clear and focused on the moment. The van descended the hill and leveled out, the tires spitting up mud and snow into the wheel wells.

"Hey, you back there."

The window had opened. The driver glanced at Amy through the mirror with a smile of wicked delight.

"How's it feel?"

The man in the passenger seat laughed. Amy said nothing.

"You fucking people," the driver said. His eyes narrowed in the mirror. "You know how many of my friends you killed?"

"Is that what you call them?"

"Seriously," he said with a dark laugh, "you should see these things. They are going to rip you apart."

The van was bouncing through deep potholes, jostling the chains. "What's your name?" Amy asked.

The driver frowned; it wasn't the kind of question he expected from a woman on the way to her execution.

"Go on, tell her," the other man said. Then, shifting his weight to angle his face to the opening: "He's Ween."

"Ween?" Amy repeated.

"Yeah, everyone calls him that on account of he's got a short one."

"Ha, ha," the driver said. "Ha, ha, ha, ha."

The conversation seemed over. Then the driver flicked his eyes to the mirror again.

"That thing you told Guilder," he said. Amy could read the uncertainty in his voice. "About what was going to happen. I mean, you were bullshitting, right?"

Amy hooked a foot under the bench and shot her thoughts deep into his eyes. At once the driver stomped on the brake, slamming the second man face-first into the windshield. A crash sent him jerking backward again as the vehicle behind them clipped the van's bumper with a sound of breaking glass and crunching metal.

"What the hell is wrong with you?" The second man was pressing a hand to his face. Blood dripped through his fingers. "You broke my nose, you asshole!"

The convoy had come to a halt. Amy heard a rapping on the driver's window.

"What's going on? Why did you stop?"

The driver replied sluggishly: "I don't know. My foot fell asleep or something."

"Jesus, look at this," the second guard said. He was holding out his bloodied hands for the man at the window to see. "Look what this idiot did."

"Do you need another driver?"

Amy watched the driver's face through the mirror. He gave his head a dislodging shake. "I'm okay. I just . . . I don't know. It was weird. I'm fine."

The man at the window paused. "Well, be careful, all right? We're almost there. Keep it together."

He moved away; the van began to creep forward again.

"You are an unbe*liev*able dick, you know that?"

The driver didn't answer. He darted his eyes to Amy's, their gazes ricocheting in the mirror. A split second, but she saw the fear in them. Then he looked away.

2140 hours. Hollis and Michael were crouched in the alley behind the apothecary. Using binoculars, they'd watched Amy being loaded into the van, followed by the departure of the convoy for the stadium. The assault team that would take the Dome, a dozen men and women armed with firearms and pipe bombs, was still concealed in the storm pipe, fifteen feet below.

"How long do we wait?" Michael said.

The question was rhetorical; Hollis merely shrugged. Though the city had an empty feel, the entrance to the Dome was still defended by a contingent of at least twenty men they could see from the alleyway. The thing they weren't saying was that they had no way of knowing if Sara and Kate were even in the building or how to find them if they were, assuming they could actually get past the guards—a chain of contingencies that in the abstract had seemed surmountable but that now rose before them with stark definition.

"Don't worry about Lore," Hollis said. "That girl can take care of herself, believe me."

"Did I say I was worried?" But of course Michael was. He was worried about all of them.

"I like her," said Hollis. He was still scanning the scene with the binoculars. "She'd be good for you. Better than Lish."

Michael was taken aback. "What are you talking about?"

Hollis pulled the lenses away and looked him in the eye. "Please, Circuit. You've never been a very good liar. You remember when we were kids, the way you two went at it? It couldn't have been more obvious even then."

"It was?"

"To me, anyway. All of it. You, her." He shrugged his broad shoulders and looked through the binoculars again. "Mostly you. Lish I could never read."

Michael tried to assemble a denial, but the attempt collapsed. For as long as he could remember, there had been a place in his mind where Lish stood. He'd done his best to suppress his feelings, since nothing good could come of them, but he'd never quite managed to tamp them down completely. In fact, he'd never managed it at all. "Do you think Peter knows?"

"Lore's the one to worry about. The girl doesn't miss much. But you'd have to ask him. I'd say so, but there's a way of knowing something without knowing it." Hollis tensed. "Hold up."

A vehicle was approaching. They pressed themselves into the doorway. Headlights blazed down the alley. Michael held his breath. Five seconds, then ten; the truck moved away.

"You ever shot anybody?" Hollis asked quietly.

"Just virals."

"Trust me. Once things get going, it's not as hard as you think."

Despite the cold, Michael had begun to perspire. His heart was hammering against his ribs.

"Whatever happens, just get her, all right?" he said. "Get them both."

Hollis nodded.

"I mean it. I'll cover you. Just get through that door."

"We'll both go."

"Not from the looks of things. You need to be the one, Hollis. Understand? Don't stop."

Hollis looked at him.

"Just so that's clear," said Michael.

Like the others, Lore and Greer had successfully faded into the crowd. Where the lines of flatlanders separated, they nudged their way into the stream being directed to the second tier, then the third, and finally the top of the stands. They met beneath the stairs that led to the control rooms.

"Nicely done," Greer whispered.

They retrieved their weapons: a pair of old revolvers, which they would use only as a last resort, and two blades, six inches long with curved steel pommels. The last of the crowd was being ushered into place. Greer marveled at the flatlanders' orderliness, the numb submission with which they allowed themselves to be led. They were slaves but didn't know it—or perhaps they did but had long since accepted the fact. All of them? Maybe not all. The ones who hadn't would be the deciding factor.

"Would you like to pray with me?" he said.

Lore looked at him skeptically. "It's been a while. I'm not sure I'd know how."

They were facing each other on their knees. "Take my hands," Greer said. "Close your eyes."

"That's it?"

"Try not to think. Imagine an empty room. Not even a room. Nothing."

She accepted his hands, her face faintly embarrassed. Her palms were moist with anxious sweat.

"I was kind of thinking you were going to say something, the way the sisters do. Holy this and God bless that."

He shook his head. "Not this time."

Greer watched her close her eyes, then did so himself. The moment of immersion: he felt a spreading warmth. In another moment his mind dispersed into a measureless energy beyond thought. *O my God,* he prayed, *be with us. Be with Amy.*

But something was wrong. Greer felt pain. Terrible pain. Then the pain was gone, subsumed by a darkness. It rolled over his consciousness like a shadow crossing a field. An eclipse of death, terror, black evil.

I am Morrison-Chávez-Baffes-Turrell-Winston-Sosa-Echols-Lambright-Martínez-Reinhardt . . .

He jolted away. The spell was broken; he was back in the world. What had he seen? The Twelve, yes, but what was the other? Whose pain had he felt? Lore, still kneeling, her empty hands outstretched, had experienced it, too: Greer could see it in her shocked face.

"Who's Wolgast?" she said.

Lila's feet seemed barely to touch the ground as she walked down the corridor toward the atrium. There was a feeling of invincibility to her actions; once made, certain decisions could not be undone. The stairs she sought were situated at the end of a long hallway on the opposite side of the building. As she turned the corner she broke into a run, headed for the door as if pursued. The heavyset guard rose from his chair to bar her way.

"Where do you think you're going?"

"Please," she gasped, "I'm starving. Everybody's gone."

"You need to get out of here."

Lila lifted her veil. "Do you know who I am?"

The guard startled. "I'm sorry, ma'am," he stammered. "Of course."

He pulled the key from a cord affixed to his belt and fit it into the lock.

"Thank you," Lila said, making her best show of relief. "You're a godsend."

She descended the stairs. At the bottom she faced the second guard, who was standing before the steel door that led to the blood-processing facility. She hadn't been down here in many years, but she remembered it clearly in all its mercenary horror: the bodies on tables, the vast refrigerators, the bags of blood, the sweet smell of the gas that kept the subjects in everlasting twilight. The guard was watching her with his hand resting on the butt of his pistol. Lila had never fired a gun in her life. She hoped it wasn't hard.

She stepped toward him with a confident gait, lifting her face at the last instant to look him deeply in the eyes.

"You're tired."

Concealed behind the dugout on the north side of the stadium, Alicia dropped the magazine from her semi, examined it to no purpose, blew imaginary dust from the top, and slid it back into the handle, shoving it into place with the base of her palm. She had now removed and reinserted the magazine ten times. The gun was a .45ACP with a crosshatched wooden handle, twelve rounds in each clip. Twelve, thought

Alicia, and noted the irony. Strange, and not unpleasing, how the universe sometimes worked.

A murmur broke through the crowd. Alicia rose on her knees to peer out at the field. Had it begun? A curious object was being towed into the field—a Y-shaped steel armature, twenty feet high, affixed to a broad platform. Chains swung from the booms at the top. The truck halted in the middle of the field; two cols appeared and jogged back to the trailer. They slid blocks under the tires, winched up the nose, unhooked the trailer from the truck, and drove away.

She made her final preparation. The bayonet was tied with rough twine to her thigh. She freed it and slid it into her belt.

Amy, she thought, *Amy, my sister in blood. All I ask is this.*
Let me be the one to kill Martinez.

As the line of vehicles came to a halt outside the main ramp to the stadium, Guilder's nerves were still jangling from the collision with the van. They were lucky it hadn't been worse.

But if he'd thought their safe arrival would bring relief, the sight of the stadium, blazing with light in the winter dark, quickly disabused him of this notion. He exited the car to an immense sound of humanity. Not cheering—these people were much too cowed for that—but a crowd of seventy thousand in one place made a noise of its own, intrinsic to its mass. Seventy thousand pairs of lungs opening and closing; seventy thousand pairs of idle feet bobbing; seventy thousand backsides shifting on cement bleachers, trying to get comfortable. There were voices in the mix as well, and coughing, babies crying, but mostly what Guilder heard was a sort of subterranean rumble, like the aftershock of an earthquake.

"Get her in place," he said.

The guards yanked her from the van. Guilder didn't feel the need to look at her as they dragged her away. He signaled to Suresh to have the semi moved into position. The truck pulled forward and glided up the ramp toward the end zone.

Guilder had given extensive thought to the matter of presentation. Some pageantry was called for. He'd struggled with what to do until he'd come upon an appropriately crowd-whipping analogue: the orchestrated arrival on the field of play of a major sports franchise. Suresh would function as stage manager, coordinating the various visual and auditory elements that would lift the evening's demonstration to the level of spectacle. Together they'd gone through the items on the checklist: sound, lighting, display. They'd done a dry run that afternoon. A few problems had emerged, but nothing that couldn't be dealt with, and Suresh had assured him that everything would come off without a hitch.

They made their way up the ramp; Suresh, limping, did his best to keep up. HR personnel lined both sides of the idling semi; the staff had already been seated in the lower boxes. The noise of the crowd seemed to flow toward Guilder like a wave, immersing him in its energy. The plows had swept the field of snow, leaving behind a muddy landscape; in the center, the platform and armature awaited. A nifty device: it was Suresh who'd come up with the idea. The insurgency had nearly blown him up; who wouldn't be a little mad? As a physician he also seemed to know better than anyone interesting ways to kill people. Suspending her high in the air would give everyone a chance to see her insides unraveling; she'd feel more that way, too, and feel it longer.

While Guilder reviewed his notes, Suresh fitted him with his microphone, running the cable down his back to the transmitter, which he clipped to Guilder's improvised belt of neckties. "Flick this here," Suresh said, drawing his attention to the toggle switch, "and you're on."

Suresh backed away. He drew down his earphones, adjusted his microphone, and began the countdown:

"Sound booth."

(Check.)

"Lights."

(Check.)

"Fire teams."

(Check.)

And so on. Guilder, listening vaguely, shook out his robed arms like a boxer preparing to step into the ring. He had always wondered about this gesture, which seemed like empty showmanship. Now he understood the sense of it.

"Good to go when you are," Suresh said.

So: the moment at last. What a shock the crowd was in for. Guilder slid his glasses onto his face and took a last, long breath.

"All right, everyone," he said. "Let's look alive. It's game time."

He stepped forward, into the light.

64

"Dani, wake up."

The voice was familiar. The voice belonged to someone she knew. It drifted toward her from high above, saying this curious, half-remembered name.

"Dani, you have to open your eyes. I need you to try."

Sara sensed her mind emerging, her body taking shape around her. She felt suddenly cold. Her throat was tight and dry, sweet-tasting. She was supposed to open her eyes—that's what the voice was telling her—but her lids felt like they weighed a thousand pounds apiece.

"I'm going to give you something."

Was the voice Lila's? Sara felt a prick in her arm. Nothing. Then: Oh!

She bolted upright, violently curling forward at the waist, her heart thudding against her rib cage. Air rushed to her lungs, expelled by a dry cough that screeched across the parched lining of her throat.

Lila pressed a cup to her lips, bracing the back of Sara's head with her palm. "Drink."

Sara tasted water, cold water. The images around her began to coalesce. Her heart was still racing like a bird's. Bits of pain, real and remembered, jabbed at her extremities. Her head felt like it was only vaguely related to the rest of her.

"You're all right," said Lila. "Don't worry. I'm a doctor."

Lila was a doctor?

"We need to be quick. I know it won't be easy, but can you stand?"

Sara didn't think she could, but Lila made her try. She swung her legs to the side of the gurney, Lila helping her by the elbow. Below the hem of Sara's gown, white bandages encircled her upper thighs. More bandages dressed her lower arms. All of this had happened without her being aware of it.

"What did they do to me?"

"It's the marrow they take. They start with the hips. That's the pain you feel."

Sara eased her feet to the floor. Only then did it occur to her that Lila's presence was an aberration—that she was freeing her.

"Why do you have a gun, Lila?"

Gone was the frail, uncertain woman Sara had come to know. Her face radiated urgency. "Come."

Sara saw the first body when they stepped into the hall: a man in a lab coat lying face-down on the floor, his arms and legs splayed in the random arrangement of swift death. The top of his skull had been blasted off, its contents splashed over the wall. Two more lay nearby, one shot in the chest, the other through the throat—though the second man wasn't dead. He was sitting upright against the wall, his hands encircling his neck, his chest moving in shallow jerks. It was Dr. Verlyn. Through the hole in his neck, his rapid breathing made a clicking sound. His lips wordlessly working, he looked at Sara with pleading eyes.

Lila was tugging her by the arm. "We need to hurry."

She didn't have to say it again. More bodies—the splashes of blood and startled postures and expressions of surprise in unseeing eyes—flowed past. It was a massacre. Was it possible that Lila had done this? They came to the end of the hall, where the heavy steel door stood open. A col lay beside it, shot in the head.

"Get her out of the building," Lila commanded. "It's the last thing I'll ask of you. Do whatever you have to."

Sara understood that she was speaking of Kate. "Lila, what are you doing?"

"What should have been done long ago." A look of peace had come into her face; her eyes glowed with warmth. "It will all be over soon, Dani."

Sara hesitated. "My name's not Dani."

"I thought perhaps it wasn't. Tell me."

"It's Sara."

Lila nodded slowly, as if agreeing that this was the right name for her to have. She took Sara's hand.

"You will be a good mother to her, Sara," she said, and squeezed. "I know it. Now run."

A hush fell over the crowd as Guilder stepped onto the field, all seventy thousand faces swiveling to look at him. He stood still a moment, drinking in the stillness as his eyes traveled the grandstands. He would make a humble entrance, like a priest's. Time seemed to stretch as he walked to the platform. Who knew it could take so long to cross fifty yards? The silence around him seemed to deepen with every step.

He arrived at the platform. He gazed out upon the crowd, first one side of the field, then the other. His hand slipped to his waist and located the toggle.

"All rise for the singing of the anthem."

Nothing happened. Had he hit the right button? He glanced toward Suresh, who was standing on the sidelines, making a frantic rolling motion with his hand.

"I *said,* please rise."

Begrudgingly, the crowd took to its feet. "Homeland, our Homeland," Guilder began to sing, "we pledge our lives to thee . . ."

Our labors do we offer, without recompense or fee. Homeland, our Homeland, a nation rises here. Safety, hope, security, from sea to shining seu . . .

With a sinking feeling, Guilder realized that almost nobody else was singing. He heard a few isolated voices here and there—HR personnel and, of course, the staff, manfully croaking the words from the fifty-yard line—but this only heightened the impression that the crowd, basically, was on strike.

Homeland, our Homeland, of peace and plenty fair. The light of heaven shines upon your beauty rich and rare. One mind! One soul! Your love is all we see. Let all combine with heart and hand: one Homeland, strong and free!

The song didn't end so much as turn a corner and fall down. Not a good sign at all. The first of several beads of sweat shot from his armpit to slither unimpeded down the length of his torso. Maybe he should have found somebody who could actually sing to warm up the crowd. Still, Guilder had a few things planned to engage the people fully in the evening's transformational festivities. He cleared his throat, glanced toward Suresh once more, received the man's approving nod, and spoke.

"I stand before you today on the eve of a new era—"

"Murderer!"

A buzz of voices shivered through the crowd. The shout had come from behind him, somewhere in the upper decks. Guilder spun around, blindly searching the sea of faces.

"Killer!"

The voice was a woman's. Guilder saw her standing at the railing. She waved a fist madly in the air.

"You butcher!"

"Somebody arrest that woman!" Guilder barked into his microphone, too loudly.

A general catcalling erupted. Objects went sailing through the air, lobbing onto the field. The crowd was throwing the only thing it had. The crowd was throwing its shoes.

"Monster! Assassin! Torturer!"

Guilder was frozen. None of this was what he'd expected at all.

"Demon! Tyrant! Swine!"

"Devil! Satan! Fiend!"

If he didn't do something fast, he'd lose them completely. He gave Suresh the signal; the switch was thrown. To an orchestrated explosion of colored light and smoke, the pickup carrying the woman in its bed bounded onto the field, the semi lumbering behind it. Simultaneously, the fire teams went racing around the edges of the field, igniting barrels of ethanol-soaked wood, making a flickering perimeter of flame. As the pickup halted at the platform, the semi turned in a wide circle and began to back up. The guards dropped the gate of the pickup, yanked the woman from the bed, and flung her to the muddy ground at the base of the platform.

"Get up."

The crowd was in an uproar—booing, whistling, hurling shoes like missiles.

"I said, get up."

Guilder kicked her hard, in the ribs. When she made no cry he kicked her again, then hauled her to her feet and shoved his face so close to hers that the tips of their noses practically touched.

"You have no idea what you're about to face."

"Actually, I do. You could say we're of a very long acquaintance."

He didn't know what to make of this curious claim, but he didn't care. He signaled to the guards to take her away. The woman offered no resistance as they dragged her to the base of the armature and pressed her to her knees. There were streaks of mud on her cheeks, her tunic, in her hair. Under the blazing lights she seemed meager, almost doll-like, and yet Guilder could still discern the defiance in her eyes, an absolute refusal to be cowed. He hoped the virals would take their time, maybe bat her around a bit. The guards unlocked her shackles, then reattached her wrists to the chains that hung from the armature.

They began to winch her up.

With every foot of her ascent, the roars of the crowd intensified. In protest? Anticipation? The pure emotional thrill of watching a person ripped apart? They hated him, Guilder understood that, but they were part of this thing now; their dark energy had joined to the night's transformative power.

The woman came to a rest high in the air, her arms held from her sides, her body swaying.

"Last words?"

She thought a moment. "Goodbye?"

Guilder laughed. "That's the spirit."

"I meant that the other way around."

Guilder had heard enough. He turned toward the rear of the semi. Two cols in heavy pads were posted by the doors. Suresh was watching him intently from the sidelines; Guilder caught his eye and nodded.

Hey, Lila, he thought, you delusional has-been, get a load of *this*.

And suddenly there was silence. A great freezing of all movement as the stadium was dipped in darkness.

A burst of blue.

The time to move had arrived. Greer and Lore burst from their hiding place and charged up the stairs. A single col was standing guard at the door to the control room. Greer got there first.

"What the fuck?" The guard noticed the knives. "Whoa," he said.

Greer gripped him by the ears—conveniently oversized, jutting from the sides of his head like a pair of handles—and rammed his own forehead into the man's skull. Down he went, felled like a tree.

They flew through the door. Again, just one man awaited, a redeye. Wearing chunky earphones with a microphone, he was seated before a panel of lights and switches. A wall of windows looked down on the field, bathed in blue. The earphones were a plus; their entry had gone unnoticed. The tacit understanding between Greer and Lore said that it was now her turn.

The redeye lifted his face. "Hey, you're not supposed to be here."

"True," said Lore, who slipped behind him, placed her left hand on his forehead, and drew her knife across his throat, cutting it like paper.

The doors of the semi swung open.

They emerged in magnificence, like kings. Their movements were stately, deliberate; they showed no haste, only the pure self-possession of their kind. No one could mistake what they were. They towered. They occupied space with a glorious immensity of height and breadth. They had fed on the blood of generations, inflating their persons to colossi. Even Carter, with his modest dimensions, seemed, in the company of his brethren, to partake of their magnificence. At the wondrous sight of them, the crowd made a collective inhalation of breath. Screams would follow, of this fact Guilder had no doubt, but in the moment of the eleven virals' emergence, a deep, anticipatory quiet reigned. The mighty beings stepped forward in rich display. Their backs were erect, their powerful claws articulating like immense devices of pain. They had the aspect of giants. They were legend made flesh, the great bestriders of the earth. The guards raced for the sidelines, to live another day, though Guilder paid this no notice. His mind was full of glory.

My brothers, Guilder thought, *I offer you this token, this foretaste. This tender morsel, this beginning. My brothers, come forward and together we will rule the Earth.*

Nina's team of assassins tore up the stairs. They surfaced at field level in a dugout situated just below the bleachers where the senior staff members were seated. Once Eustace began his run they would spring onto the field, turn to face their enemies, and unleash the contents of their short-barreled automatics.

But now, crouched in the final moments of their concealment, they, like everyone in the crowd, experienced an emotion that was one part terror, one part wonder, one part something else that lacked any point of reference in their lives. Peter was simultaneously attempting to process three competing visual facts. The last of the Twelve were before him, mere yards away; Amy, suspended in chains, was the bait that had drawn them forth; Amy was not Amy but a grown woman. Greer and Alicia had tried to prepare him, but no words could have readied him for this reality.

Where was Eustace?

Then Peter saw him. He was standing at the rail in the end zone—just another flatlander, dragooned into the role of witness. The eleven virals stood before Guilder like a platoon of soldiers awaiting orders. *Goddamnit,* Peter thought, *you're too far apart. Get closer to each other, you bastards.*

Guilder raised his arms.

Lila, alone. The Dome was silent, like a great animal holding its breath. This place, she thought. This tabernacle of pain. How could such a place be allowed to exist on the earth?

The gun was empty; she placed it on the floor and darted back down the hall. Behind each door lay a person on a slab, their life force slowly draining away. There was no time to save them, that was Lila's one regret, but at least she could release them from their torment.

Room by room she traveled, unsealing the doors with the ring of keys she'd taken from the guard. A few words of benediction for each trapped soul within; then she opened the valves on the ether tanks. A cloying sweetness filled the air. Her movements began to feel sluggish; she would have to work quickly. Leaving the doors open behind herself, she made her way down the corridor. The warning signs were posted at regular intervals on the walls of the hallway: ETHER PRESENT. NO OPEN FLAMES.

She came to the final door. She tried one key and then another and another, her fingers heavy and imprecise, the gas already inside her. The serrations bit and held.

Lila's heart shattered at the sight of him. They had chained him to the floor. He lay in naked degradation, suspended eternally at the precipice of death. Monsters! How could she have let this scene of anguish pass? How could she have waited a hundred years to alleviate his pain?

"Lawrence, what have they done to you?"

She hurled herself to her knees beside him. His eyes were open, but his stare seemed to pass through her to another world. She smoothed his wrinkled cheeks, his shriveled brow. She dipped her head to his, their foreheads touching as she stroked his face. "Lawrence," she whispered, over and over, "my Lawrence."

His lips at last formed words: "Save . . . me."

"Of course I will, my darling." The tears were pouring forth, a torrent. The gas was in the hall. From the pocket of her gown, Lila removed the box of matches. "We will save each other."

High above the field, Greer and Lore were also waiting for the eleven virals to move.

"Goddamnit," Greer said, the binoculars pressed to his eyes, "why aren't they doing anything?"

Guilder's hands were still raised. What was happening? He dropped them to his sides and lifted them again, waving with agitation. Still no response.

"Mother*fucker!*"

Lore's hand was poised on the switch. Her voice was frantic. "What should I do? What should I do?"

"I don't know!"

Then Greer saw movement on the field. A figure was racing from the end zone: Eustace.

"Do it! Turn on the lights!"

Even then, it was too late.

Sara, running: she tore across the atrium—was that gunfire outside?—and down the hall to Lila's apartment, rocketing through the door.

"Kate!"

The child was asleep in her bed. As Sara scooped her up, her eyes fluttered open. "Mummy?"

"I'm here. Baby, I'm here."

Now she was sure of it: there was shooting outside. (Though she could not be aware of this, this was the moment when her brother, Michael, rushing up the stairs, took a bullet to his right thigh, a pain he found oddly unimportant, so fueled was he by a rush of pure adrenaline. Hollis hadn't lied: once things got rolling, shooting somebody wasn't hard at all, and he picked off two more guards before his leg folded beneath him, the gun slipped from his hand—the thing was empty anyway—and his vision lit with stars.) Down the hall Sara dashed, carrying her child. *My child, my child.* They would live or they would die, but whichever it was they would do it together; never would they part again.

She hit the atrium at a sprint just as a man came blasting through the front doors. There was blood on his shirt; he was holding a gun. His bearded face was lit with a look of wild determination. Sara stopped in her tracks.

Hollis?

From her position high above the ground, Amy took in the whole of the scene. The crowd of thousands in its wild uproar; Guilder, his arms irrelevantly raised; the emergence of Nina's team from the dugout, and the subsequent unleashing of their firepower upon the rows of suited men, who screamed and dove for cover and sometimes did nothing at all, sitting with uncomprehending composure as their bodies were splashed with rosy arcs of death; Alicia appearing on the field, weapon drawn, ready to charge; Eustace streaming toward them from the end zone, the bomb clutched to his chest, and behind him the col who dropped to one knee, raised his rifle, and took him in its sights; the spurt of blood, and Eustace spinning and tumbling, the bomb squirting away. These events moved around her like planets in their orbits, a whirling cosmos of activity, yet their presence touched her only in passing, brushing her senses like a breeze. She stood at the center, she and her kinsmen, and it was there, on that stage, that all would be decided.

—My brothers, hello. It's been a while.

We are Morrison-Chávez-Baffes-Turrell-Winston-Sosa-Echols-Lambright-Martínez-Reinhardt . . .

—I am Amy, your sister.

That was when she felt him. In the midst of evil, a shining light. Amy sought out Carter with her eyes. He stood slightly apart, his body crouched in the posture of his kind.

It wasn't Carter.

—Father.

Yes, Amy. I am here.

A rush of love swelled her heart. Tears rose to her throat.

—Oh, Daddy, I'm sorry. Look away. Look away.

As the field blazed with light, Amy closed her eyes. It would be like opening a door. That was how she had imagined it. An act not of will but of surrender, to give away this life, this world. Images flashed through her mind, swifter than thought. Her mother kneeling to hug her, the bright force of her embrace, then a view of her back as she walked away; Wolgast, his big hand poised at her spine, standing beside her as she rode the carousel beneath the lights and music; a view of a starlit winter sky, on the night when they had made the snow angels; Caleb watching her with his knowing eyes as she tucked him into bed, asking, "Did anyone love you?"; Peter, standing at the door of the orphanage, their hands meeting in space, saying with touch what could not be said with words. The days flowed through her one by one, and when they had passed, Amy sent her mind outward to those she cherished, saying goodbye.

She opened the door.

At the edge of the field, Peter and the others, having emptied their magazines into the lower tiers, were dropping their clips to reload. They did not yet know that Eustace had been shot, only that the lights had come on as planned, signaling the start of his run; at any moment they expected the explosion to come from behind them.

It didn't.

Peter spun toward the platform. The virals, doused by the lights, had adopted various postures of self-protection. Some were staggering backward with their faces buried in the crooks of their arms. Others had dropped to the ground, curling in on themselves like babes in their cribs. It was an awesome sight, one Peter would remember all the days of his life, yet it paled in comparison to what was occurring above the platform.

Something was happening to Amy. She was convulsing against the chains, wracked by contractions of such violence it seemed she might shatter into pieces. Spasm after spasm, their power intensifying. With a final, bone-breaking jolt she went limp; for a hopeful moment Peter thought it was over.

It wasn't over.

With a deep animal howl, Amy threw back her head. Now Peter understood what he was seeing. Something that should have taken hours was happening in seconds. The facial features melting into fetal vagueness. The spine elongating, fingers and toes stretching into clawed prehensility. Teeth ejected in advance of the picketlike rows, and the skin hardening into its thick, crystalline carapace. The space around her had begun to glow, as if the air itself were lit by the accelerated force of her transformation. With a violent jerk Amy pulled the chains across her chest, snapping them clean from their blocks, and by the time she reached the ground, crouching with liquid grace to absorb the impact of her fall, there were not eleven virals on the field but twelve.

There were Twelve.

She rose. She roared.

Which was when, in the basement of the Dome, Lila Kyle and Lawrence Grey, their fates never to be known, joined hands, counted to three, brushed the match across the striker, and all the lights went out.

65

The explosion in the basement, fueled by the fiery ignition of thirty-two hundred pounds of highly compressed diethyl ether inhalant, produced a release of energy roughly equivalent to the crash of a small passenger jet. With nowhere else to go, its explosive force rocketed upward, seeking any alley of travel to accommodate its rapidly oxygenating expansion—stairwells, hallways, ductwork—before folding back on itself and blasting through the floor. Once it was unleashed into the larger spaces of the building, the rest was up for grabs. Windows blew. Furniture went airborne. Walls were suddenly there no longer. It rose and as it rose it expelled a gyring wake of pure destruction like a tornado in reverse, everything flung up and out from its white-hot heart, until it found the bones of the structure itself, the steel girders and meticulously chiseled limestone blocks that had suspended its roof above the Iowa prairie since the days of the pioneers, and blew them all to pieces.

The Dome began to fall.

Three miles away, the spectators in the stadium experienced the destruction of the Dome as a chain of discrete sensory occurrences: first a flash, then a boom, followed by a deep seismic rattle and a clamping down of blackness as the city's power grid collapsed. Everybody froze, but in the next instant something changed. A new force roused to life inside them. Who could say who started it? Insurgents planted in the stands had already begun their assault on the guards, but now they weren't alone. The crowd rose up in violence, a wild mob. So ferocious was their undammed fury that as they fell upon their captors it was as if their individuality had dissolved into a single animal collective. A swarm. A stampede. A pod. They became their enemy, as all must do; they ceased to be slaves, and so became alive.

On the field, Guilder was . . . dissolving.

He felt this first in the backs of his hands—an abrupt constriction of the skin, as if he were being shrink-wrapped. He held them up to his face. In numb incomprehension—the pain had yet to arrive—he watched as the flesh of his hands puckered and began to split open in long, bloodless seams. The sensation spread, dancing over the surface of his body. His fingertips found his face. It felt like touching a skull. His hair was falling out, his teeth. His back bent inward, drawing him into an old man's stoop. He fell to his knees in the mud. He felt his bones collapsing, crumbling to dust.

"Grey, what did you do?"

A shadow fell.

Guilder lifted his face. The virals filled his darkening vision with a final image of their magnificence. *My brothers,* he thought, *what is happening to me? Help me, my brothers, I am dying.* But he saw no kinship in their eyes.

Betrayer.

Betrayer.

Betrayer betrayer betrayer . . .

Other things were occurring—gunshots, voices yelling, figures running in the dark. But Guilder's consciousness of these events was instantly subsumed into the larger awareness, cold and final, of what was about to happen to him.

Shawna, he thought, *Shawna, all I wanted was a little company. All I wanted was not to die alone.*

And then they were upon him.

The conclusive unfolding of events, which accounted for just thirty-seven seconds in the lives of the participants, occurred in overlapping frames of simultaneous movement collapsing toward the center. Illuminated only by firelight—the barrels at the periphery continued to burn—and the virals' phosphorescent glow, the scene possessed a whiff of hell. The virals, finished with Guilder, his body scattered in desiccated pieces that were more dust than corpse, had assembled in a loose line. They appeared to be regarding Amy with a look of caution. Perhaps they did not know yet what she portended; perhaps they were afraid of her. Peter, his weapon reloaded, was firing in bursts into their massive figures, though without visible effect; the bullets skimmed pointlessly off their armored bodies in bright sparks; they didn't so much as glance in his direction. From the other side of the field, Alicia was moving forward with her pistol raised, just as Nina and Tifty were racing downfield to flank them. The plan was now moot; they had only their instincts. Standing erect on the platform, Amy raised her arms. From each wrist hung a long length of chain. She jerked them into the air and began to rotate them at her wrists, swinging them in wide, accelerating arcs. Spinners, Peter realized. Amy was making spinners, to disorient the virals. Faster and faster the chains whirred in the air above her head, a hypnotic blur of movement. The creatures froze, entranced. With an avian dart, Amy's head tipped to the side; her gaze compacted, calculating the angle of attack. Peter knew what was about to happen.

Amy Harper Bellafonte, fully weaponized. Amy, the Girl from Nowhere, airborne.

As she shot forward, she let the chains fly, snapping them from her body like a pair of whips. Simultaneously she tucked her head to her chest, aligning her posture in midflight so that she would meet the closest among them feetfirst, chest-high, her physical person transformed at the moment of impact into a battering ram with twenty-foot iron wings. She was a fraction of their size, but momentum was on her side; she sailed through the first one, blasting him backward; by the time she landed, the chains had found their targets, wrapping two others around their necks.

With a hard yank she drew the left one toward her, buried her face beneath his jaw, and shook him like a dog with a rag in its mouth.

He howled.

And, with a jet of blood and a bony cracking sound, died.

She unfurled him from the chain with a snap of her wrist, rotating the body away like a top. Her attention turned to the second viral, but the balance had shifted: the element of surprise was gone; the hypnotic effect of the spinners had worn away. The creature launched toward her, their bodies meeting in an uncontrolled collision that sent them both tumbling end over end away from the platform. Amy wrenched the chain free but seemed disoriented; she crouched on her hands and knees in the dirt. A kind of whole-body rippling moved through the remaining virals, their shared consciousness reassembling, achieving focus. One more wink of time and they would fall on her like a pack of animals.

Which they might have, if not for the small one.

Peter's mind had yet to parse them as anything more than a collective; he was forced to do so now. One of the virals was different. In bulk and stature he appeared no larger than a man. In the instant before the others leapt upon Amy, he beat them to the punch; with a compact aerial bound he alighted between her and her attackers, turning to face them, claws raised, his body in a posture of challenge. His chest expanded in a massive intake of breath; his lips pulled back, exposing his teeth.

The blast of sound that followed was completely out of proportion with the size of the body that produced it. It was a howl of purest rage. It was a roar that could have felled a forest, flattened a mountain, knocked a planet off its axis. Peter literally felt himself pushed back by it; his eardrums popped with pain. The small viral had bought Amy only a second, but it was enough. As she rose to her feet, the others shot forward.

Chaos.

Suddenly it was impossible to tell what was happening or where to shoot, the images of battle too quick for human eyes to compute. Peter realized he had expended the last of his rounds, but the gun was useless anyway. He glimpsed Alicia advancing from the far side of the field, still firing her pistol.

Where were Tifty and Nina?

He looked downfield. Nina was racing toward the platform, the bomb clutched to her chest. Tifty was behind her. She waved her free arm over her head, yelling at the top of her lungs: "You bastards! Look over here! Hey!"

The one that took note—did it grasp her intentions? Did it know the meaning of what she held? It did not so much launch as lob itself toward her, dropping in a four-limbed spread like a spider on silk. Tifty saw it first. As he raised his weapon he tried to push Nina aside, but the effort came too late; as with all things falling, the leisureliness of the viral's plunge was an illusion. It crashed into the two of them, Tifty taking the brunt. Peter expected the bomb to go off, but that didn't happen. The viral seized Nina by the arm and flung her away, casting her spiraling over the dirt; then it turned toward Tifty. As Tifty raised his weapon, the creature engulfed him.

A scream. A gunshot.

It wasn't a decision. There were no pros and cons. Peter dropped his gun and made for the bomb where it lay in the dirt, running for all he was worth.

The only two people who saw it all were Lore and Greer. And even then, it was Greer alone, the man of faith, whose prayers had afforded him a deeper comprehension of the scene, who was able to make sense of it.

Viewed from the control room, the battle on the field played out with a flattened quality, rendered more decipherable by distance. At one end lay Eustace, unconscious or dead, and between him and the platform, the body of Tifty Lamont; Nina was gone, hurled into the darkness; Alicia, on the opposite side, was the only one still firing. At the center stood the platform; Amy, having wrenched herself free from the melee, had vaulted to the top of the armature. Her tunic was in shreds, stained with the dark wetness of blood; one clawed hand clutched her side, as if to stanch a wound. Even at this distance, Greer could discern the harsh labor of her breathing. Her transformation was complete, yet one human vestige remained: her hair. Black and wild, it tumbled freely around her face. In another moment her attackers would strike in overwhelming force, yet her posture did not communicate retreat. There was something invincible about her, almost royal.

Then he saw Peter, racing downfield. Where was he going? The semi? No.

Greer blasted from the room and down the stairs. He would part the crowd with his body, his fists, his blade if he had to. *Amy, Amy, I am coming.*

Alicia would not be denied. She had consecrated her existence to this holy fact. She had felt it since the cave: a singular longing drawing her forward, as if she were being pulled down the length of a tunnel. As she moved toward the virals, firing her weapon—her bullets, she knew, would do no actual damage; she only wanted to draw their attention—she was a being of only one thought, one vision, one desire.

Louise, I will avenge you. You have not been forgotten. Louise, you, too, are my sister in blood.

"Show yourself, you son of a bitch!"

Her bullets skimmed and flashed. She dropped her empty magazine, rammed another home, and resumed firing. Through gritted teeth she advanced, murmuring her dark prayer. He would know her, feel her; it could not be otherwise. It was a thing of destiny, that she should be the one to kill him, to wipe him from the face of the earth. He was Julio Martínez, Esq., Tenth of Twelve. He was Sod of the bench and the grunting exhalations. He was all the men in all the years of history who had violated a woman in this manner, and she would drive her blade deep into the dark heart of him and feel him die.

One of the virals swiveled toward her. Of course, Alicia thought; she would have recognized him anywhere. His physique was identical to the others', and yet there was something distinctive about him, an air of haughtiness that only she would be able to detect. He regarded her through soulless eyes lidded with bored languor; he appeared, almost, to smile. Alicia had never seen an expression on a viral's face before; now she did. *I know you,* his bland, arrogant face seemed to say. *Don't I know you? Don't tell me, let me guess. I'm certain I know you from someplace.*

You're damn right you know me, she thought, and drew the bayonet from her belt.

They launched toward each other simultaneously—Alicia with the blade raised above her head, Martínez with his great taloned hands reaching forward like a prow of knives. An unstoppable force meeting an immovable object: their trajectories intersected in a headlong, grappling collision, Martínez's vastly greater mass passing both through and under her, sending her pinwheeling over his head. In her moment of uncontrolled flight, Alicia acknowledged but did not yet feel the lacerations on her arms and face where his claws had torn into her flesh. She hit the dirt and rolled once, twice, three times, each rotation defusing her momentum, and sprang to her feet again. She was winded, stumbling, her head chiming with the impact. Somehow she had maintained her grip on the bayonet; to lose it was to accept defeat, unthinkable.

Martínez, twenty feet away, had dropped to a froglike squat, his hands splayed like paddles on the dirt. The smile had morphed into something else, more playful, full of rich enjoyment. He seemed about to laugh.

Goddamn your laughing face, Alicia thought, raising her bayonet once more.

A shape was falling toward them.

The bomb, the bomb, where was the bomb?

Then Peter saw it, lying just a few yards from Tifty's body. He skidded in the dirt and scooped it to his chest. The plunger was intact, the wires still connected. How would it feel? Like nothing, he thought. It would feel like nothing.

Something blasted him from behind, hard as a wall. For a moment everything left him: breath, thought, gravity. The bomb went spiraling away. The ground unfurling beneath him and a flash of mental blackness; then Peter found himself face-up in the mud.

The viral loomed above him; their faces were mere inches apart. The sight seemed to cross the wires of Peter's senses, as if he were tasting nightfall, or listening to lightning. As the creature tipped its head, Peter did the one, last thing he could think of, believing it would be the final gesture of his life: he cocked his head in concert, willed his mind into absolute focus, and looked the viral dead in the eye.

I am Wolgast.

Then Peter saw: he was holding the bomb.

Help me.

Alicia, sister. Alicia, he is yours.

Martínez never saw it coming. In the fraction of a second before he uncoiled his massive body, Amy landed behind him. With a snap of her wrists she jetted the chains forward to encircle his frame like a pair of lassos, pinning his arms to his sides. The smile melted into a look of surprise.

Now, said Amy.

With a mighty pull she drew Martínez upright, exposing the broad meat of his chest. As Martínez tumbled backward, Alicia landed, straddling his waist, driving his body to the ground. The bayonet was poised above her head, wrapped in her fists. And yet she did not make it fall.

"Say it!" she yelled over the roaring in her ears. "Say her name!"

His eyes sought to focus. *Louise?*

And with these words, and all that she was, Alicia brought it down and drove it home, killing him in the ancient manner.

*   *   *

The final seconds of the battle of the field were, to the crowds in the stands, an incomprehensible blur of movement. Not so to Lucius Greer. Greer understood, as no one else could, what was about to happen. The chains that Amy had employed to restrain Martínez were now pinning her to his corpse. Alicia was struggling to turn him over in order to release her. They were sitting ducks, and yet the remaining virals had yet to fall. Perhaps Martínez's death had caused a break in their communal train of thought; perhaps the shock of seeing one of their own perish beneath a human hand had rendered them immobile; perhaps they merely wished to prolong the moment of victory, and thus extract the fullest measure of satisfaction from their final assault; perhaps it was something else.

It was something else.

As Greer charged across the field, another figure was rushing from his right. A glance was all he needed for his eyes to learn what his mind already knew. It was Peter. He was shouting, waving. But something was different. The virals sensed it, too. They snapped to attention, their noses darting, tasting the air.

"Look over here, you bastards!"

Peter was naked to the waist, his torso slick with blood—warm, fresh, living rivers of blood that coursed down his arms and chest from the long, curving wounds of the blade still clutched in his hand. His intentions were clear: he would draw the virals away from Amy and Alicia, down upon himself. He was the bait; what was the trap?

And Greer heard:

I am Wolgast.

I am Wolgast.

I am Wolgast.

Greer ran.

Alicia saw it, too.

Amy was still pinned to Martínez's body. The chains that tethered her had wound upon themselves; every pull only drew them tighter. Howling in frustration, Alicia saw Peter racing toward the virals; saw their bodies swiveling, heads cocking, eyes blazing with animal attraction, the pleasure of the kill.

Peter, no, she thought. *Not you. After everything, not you.*

She never knew how Amy got loose. One moment she was there and the next she wasn't. The empty shackles would be found just where Amy had left them, attached to chains still hopelessly lashed to Martínez's body; in the ensuing days, as each of them puzzled over the meaning of this fact, opinions would differ. To some it meant one thing, to some it meant another. It was a mystery, as Amy was a mystery; and like any mystery, it said as much about the seer as the seen.

But this came later. In the split second that remained, all Alicia knew was that Amy was gone; she was soaring away. A streak of light, like a shooting star; then she was falling, down upon Peter.

"Amy—"

But that was all she said.

Because Wolgast loved her.

Because Amy was home.

Because he had saved her, and she him.

And Peter Jaxon, lieutenant of the Expeditionary, heard and saw and felt it all; he felt it all at last. In a single meeting of their eyes, Wolgast's whole life had poured into his own. Its comprehensive sorrows. Its bitter losses and aching regrets. Its love for a forgotten girl, and its long sojourn through a hundred years of night. He saw faces, figures, pictures of the past. A baby in its crib, and a woman reaching to lift it into her arms, the two of them bathed in an almost holy light. He saw Amy as she had been, a tiny child, full of strange intensity, alone in the world, and the lights of a carousel and stars in a winter sky and the forms of angels carved in the snow. It was as if these visions had always been a part of him, like a recurring dream only lately remembered, and he felt profoundly grateful to have seen them, to give them witness in the final seconds of his life.

Come to me, he thought. *Come to me.*

He raced headlong. He cast himself into the hands of God. He sensed but did not see Greer streaming toward him, and Wolgast barreling from behind with the bomb clutched to his chest, aiming his body for the heart of the pod. And in the last instant, Peter heard the words:

Amy, run.

And: *Father—*

And: *I love you.*

And as Wolgast dove into their midst, one clawed thumb poised on the plunger; and as Amy likewise swooped down upon Peter to hurl him away, taking the brunt of the destruction in his stead; and as the last of the Twelve in their fury fell upon Wolgast—Wolgast the True, the Father of All, and the One Who Loved—a hole in space opened where he had stood, dark night burst to brightest day, and the heavens rent with thunder.

66

It came to feel as if there were two cities in the minutes that followed: the grandstands, where chaos reigned, and the field below, a zone of aftermath, of sudden calm. A beginning and an ending, standing adjacent but apart. Soon the two would merge, as the crowd, the violence of its uprising exhausted, absorbed the amazing fact of its liberty and began to disperse, going where it liked, including the field; they would find it one by one, drifting down, moving tentatively as their bodies tasted freedom. But in the near term, the combatants on the field were left to themselves, to take a final measure of the living and the lost.

It was Alicia whom Peter awakened to see. She was blackened, bruised, bloodied. Much of her hair had been burned away, tendrils of smoke still rising. Peter, she was saying. She hovered above him, tears streaming down her cheeks. Peter.

He struggled to speak. His tongue moved heavily in his mouth: Amy? Is she—?

Alicia, softly weeping, shook her head.

Somehow Greer had survived. The blast had flung him far away. By all rights he should have been dead, and yet they found him lying on his back, staring at the starlit sky. His clothing was shredded and seared; otherwise he appeared untouched. It was as if the force of the blast had moved not through him but around him, his life protected by an invisible hand. For a long moment he neither spoke nor moved. Then, with an exploratory gesture, he raised a hand to his chest, patting it cautiously; he lifted it to his face, tracing his cheeks and brow and chin.

"I'll be damned," he said.

Eustace, too, would live. At first they believed he was dead; his face was drenched in blood. But the shot had gone wide; the blood was from his left ear, now gone, shorn like a plant plucked from soil and replaced by a puckered hole. Of the detonation itself he had no memory, or none he could fully assemble beyond a chain of isolated sensations: a skull-cracking blast of noise, and a scorching wave of air passing above, then something wet raining down, and a taste of smoke and dust. He would escape the night with only this one additional disfigurement to a face already bearing plentiful scars of war and a permanent ringing in his ears, which would, in fact, never abate, causing him to speak in an overly loud voice that would make people think he was angry even when he wasn't. Over time, once he had returned to Kerrville and risen to the rank of colonel, serving as military liaison to the president's staff, he would come to regard this as less an inconvenience than a remarkably useful enhancement to his authority; he wondered why he hadn't thought of it before.

Only Nina would depart the field unscathed. Hurled away by the viral that had killed Tifty, she'd been thrown clear of the blast zone. She had been moving upfield when the bomb went off, its concussive force blowing her backward off her feet; but in the preceding moment she'd been the only one to witness the death of the Twelve, their bodies consumed and scattered in a ball of light. All else was a blur; of Amy, she had seen nothing.

Nothing at all.

But one of them had fallen.

They found Tifty with his gun still in his hand. He lay in the mud, broken and severed, his eyes rimmed by blood. His right arm was gone, but that was the least of it. As they gathered around him, he labored to speak through his fitful breathing. At last his lips formed words: "Where is she?"

Greer alone seemed to understand what he was asking. He turned toward Nina. "It's you he wants."

Perhaps she understood the nature of the request, perhaps not; none could tell. She lowered herself to the ground beside him. With trembling effort, Tifty lifted his hand and touched her face with the tips of his fingers, the gentlest gesture.

"Nitia," he whispered. "My Nitia."

"I'm Nina."

"No. You're Nitia. My Nitia." He gave a tearful smile. "You look . . . so much like her."

"Like who?"

Life was ebbing from his eyes. "I told her . . ." His breath caught. He had begun to choke on the blood that poured from his mouth. "I told her . . . I would keep you safe." Then the light in his eyes went out and he was gone.

No one spoke. One of their own had slipped away, into darkness.

"I don't understand," Alicia said. She glanced at the others. "Why did he call her that?"

It was Greer who answered: "Because that's her name." Nina looked up from the body. "You didn't know, did you?" he said. "There was no way you could."

She shook her head.

"Tifty was your father."

In due course, there would come a full accounting. A pickup would race onto the field; they would watch three people emerge. No, four. Michael and Hollis and Sara, holding a little girl in her arms.

But for now they stood silently in the presence of their friend, the core of his life laid bare. The great gangster Tifty Lamont, captain of the Expeditionary. They would bury him where he'd fallen, in the field. Because you never leave it, Greer explained; that's what Tifty always said. You might think you can do it, but you can't. Once you'd stood there, it became a part of you forever.

No one ever left the field.

XII

THE KISS

JANUARY 98 A.V.

On the day of victory, no man is tired.

—ARAB PROVERB

67

The weather failed to cooperate. January in Iowa—what had they expected? Bone-numbing day followed bone-numbing day. Food, fuel, water, electricity, the complex enterprise of keeping a city of seventy thousand souls running—the joy of victory had quickly been subsumed by more mundane concerns. For the time being the insurgency had assumed control, though Eustace, by his own admission, had no particular knack for the job. He felt overwhelmed by the volume of detail, and the hastily assembled provisional government, composed of appointed delegates from each of the lodges, did little to lighten his load; it was bloated and disorganized, half the room always squabbling with the other half, leaving Eustace to throw up his hands and make all the decisions anyway. A degree of docility among the population remained, but this wouldn't last. There had been looting in the market before Eustace was able to secure it, and every day there were more stories of reprisals; many of the cols had tried to slip anonymously into the populace, but their faces were known. Without a justice system to try the ones who surrendered, or those who had been captured by the insurgency in advance of the mob, it was hard to know what to do with them. The detention center was bursting at the seams. Eustace had raised the possibility of retrofitting the Project—it was certainly secure enough and had the additional advantage of isolation—but this would take time and did nothing to address the problem of what to do with the prisoners when the population began to move south.

And everybody was freezing. Well, so be it, Peter thought. What was a little cold?

He had formed a close friendship with Eustace. Some of this was their shared bond as officers of the Expeditionary, but not all; they had discovered, as the days passed, that they possessed compatible temperaments. They decided that Peter should lead the advance team that would travel south to prepare Kerrville for the influx of refugees. Initially he'd objected; it didn't seem right to be among the first to leave. But he was the logical choice, and in the end, Alicia sealed the case. Caleb is waiting for you, she reminded him. Go see to your boy.

The exodus itself would have to wait till spring. Assuming Kerrville could send enough vehicles and personnel, Eustace planned to move five thousand people at a time, the composition of each group determined by a lottery. The trip would be arduous—all but the very old and very young would have to walk—but with luck the Homeland would be empty within two years.

"Not everybody will want to go, you know," Eustace said.

The two of them were seated in Eustace's office, in the back room of the apothecary, warming themselves with cups of herbal tea. Most of the buildings in the market had been taken over by the provisional government to serve various functions. The latest project to occupy them was the tallying of a census. With all the redeyes' records having been destroyed in the Dome, they had no idea who was who, or even how many people there were. Seventy thousand was the generally accepted number, but there was no way to know precisely unless they counted.

"Why wouldn't they?"

Eustace shrugged. The left side of his head was still bandaged, giving his face a lopsided appearance, though balanced by his clouded eye. Sara had removed the last of Peter's stitches the prior day; his chest and arms now bore a road map of long, pinkish scars. In private moments, Peter couldn't stop touching them, amazed not only by the fact that he'd inflicted these wounds upon himself but also that, in the heat of the moment, he'd barely felt a thing.

"This is what they know. They've lived their entire lives here. But that's not the whole reason. It's good to right a wrong. I don't know how many will feel that way once we start moving people south, but some will."

"How will they manage?"

"I suppose how people always manage. Elections, the rough business of building a life." He sipped his tea. "It'll be messy. It might not work at all. But at least it will be theirs."

Nina came in from the cold, stamping waffles of snow from her boots. "Jesus, it's freezing out there," she said.

Eustace offered her his cup. "Here, warm yourself up."

She took it in her hands and sipped, then bent to kiss him quickly on the mouth. "Thank you, husband. You really need to shave."

Eustace laughed. "With a face like mine? Who cares?"

That the two of them were a couple was, as Peter had learned, the worst-kept secret of the insurgency. One of the first things Eustace had done was issue an executive order permitting flatlanders to marry. In many instances this was a technicality; people had been paired up for years or even decades. But marriage had never possessed official sanction. The list of couples waiting to be married now ran to the hundreds, and Eustace had two justices of the peace operating night and day out of a storefront down the block. He and Nina had been among the first, as had Hollis and Sara.

"Good news," Nina said. "I just came from the hospital."

"And?"

"Two more babies were born this morning, both healthy. Mothers doing fine."

"Well, how about that." Eustace grinned at Peter. "See what I'm telling you? Even on the darkest night, my friend, life will have its way."

Peter made his way down the hill, hunched against the wind. As a member of the executive staff he was permitted the use of a vehicle, but he preferred to walk. At the hospital he headed for Michael's room. Power had been only partially restored, but the hospital had been one of the first buildings relit. He found Michael awake and sitting up. His right leg, encased in plaster from ankle to hip, was suspended from a sling at a forty-five-degree angle above the bed. It had been touch and go for a while, and Sara had thought he might lose the leg; but Michael was a fighter, and now, three weeks later, he was officially on the mend.

Lore was sitting by the bed, manipulating a pair of knitting needles. Eustace had put her to work as a foreman at the biodiesel plant, but any free moment found her back at the hospital, at Michael's bedside.

"What are you making?" Peter asked her.

"Hell if I can say. It was supposed to be a sweater, but it's coming out more like socks."

"You should really stick to what you know," Michael advised.

"Just you wait till you're out of that cast, my friend. I'll show you what I know. It's nothing you'll forget." She looked at Peter, slyly smiling to make sure he got the joke. "Oh, I'm sorry, Peter. Got a little carried away. I guess I forgot you were there."

He laughed. "It's okay."

She gave one of her needles a wave. "I just want to mention, in case our boy here takes a turn for the worse, I've always thought you had a very nice look to you. Plus, you're a war hero. I'd be interested in anything you had to say, Lieutenant."

"I'll give it some thought."

"Of that I have no doubt." She dropped the yarn to her lap. "As it happens, my shift begins in thirty minutes, so I'll leave you two to talk about me." She rose, bagged her knitting, patted Michael on the arm, then thought better of it and kissed him on the top of his head. "Need anything before I go?"

"I'm fine."

"You're not fine, Michael. You're far from fine. You scared the living hell out of me is what you did."

"I said I was sorry."

"Keep saying it, bub. One day I'll believe you." She kissed him again. "Gentlemen."

When Lore was gone, Peter took her seat. "Sorry about that," Michael said.

"I don't know why you keep apologizing for her, Michael. You're the luckiest guy on planet Earth, as far as I'm concerned." He tipped his head toward the bed. "So how's the leg really?"

"It hurts like hell. Nice of you to finally visit."

"Sorry about that. Eustace is keeping me busy."

"So how many have you found?"

Peter understood that Michael was asking about the other First Colonists. "The number we're hearing is fifty-six. We're still trying to track everyone down. So far we've found Jimmy's daughters, Alice and Avery. Constance Chou, Russ Curtis, Penny Darrell. The Littles are going to take some time to sort out. Everybody's spread all over the place."

"Good news, I guess." Michael stopped, leaving the rest unstated. So many others, gone.

"Hollis told me what you did," Peter said.

Michael shrugged. He looked a little embarrassed, but proud, too. "It seemed like the thing to do at the time."

"You ever want a job in the Exped, you let me know. Assuming they'll have me back. The next time we talk, I might be in the stockade."

"Peter, be serious. They'll probably make you a general for this. That or ask you to run for president."

"Then you don't know the Army like I do." And yet, for just a moment, he thought: what if? "We'll be leaving in a few days, you know."

"So I figured. Don't forget to bundle up. Say hello to Kerrville for me."

"We'll get you in the next trip, I promise."

"I don't know, hombre, the service here is pretty good. The place kind of agrees with me. Who's going with you?"

"Sara and Hollis and Kate, but that's obvious. Greer's staying to help with the evacuation. Eustace is putting a team together."

"What about Lish?"

"I'd ask her if I could find her. I've barely seen her at all. She's been riding out on this horse of hers. She calls him Soldier. What she's doing I have no idea."

"I'm sorry you missed her. She came by this morning."

"Lish was here?"

"Said she wanted to say hello." Michael looked at him. "Why? Is that so strange?"

Peter frowned. "I guess not. How did she seem?"

"How do you think? Like Lish."

"So there wasn't anything different about her."

"Not that I noticed. She wasn't here very long. She said she was going to help Sara with the donations."

As interim director of public health, Sara had discovered that the building that served as the hospital was, as she'd long suspected, a hospital in name only. There was almost no medical equipment, and no blood at all. With so many people injured in the siege, and babies being born and all the rest, she'd had a freezer brought over from the food-processing facility and had instituted a program of blood donation.

"Lish as a nurse," Peter said, and shook his head at the irony. "I'd like to see that."

What became of the redeyes themselves was never fully understood. Those that hadn't been killed in the stadium had essentially ceased to exist. The only conclusion to be drawn, supported by Sara's story about Lila, was that the destruction of the Dome, and the death of the man known as the Source, had caused a chain reaction similar to the one they'd seen in Babcock's descendants on the mountain in Colorado. Those who'd witnessed it described it as a rapid aging, as if a hundred years of borrowed life were surrendered in just a few seconds—flesh shriveling, hair falling out in clumps, faces withering to the skull. The corpses they'd found, still dressed in their suits and ties, were nothing but piles of brown bones. They looked like they'd been dead for decades.

As the day of departure approached, Sara found herself working virtually around the clock. As word had spread in the flatland that actual medical care could now be had, more and more people had come in. The complaints varied from the common cold to malnutrition to the broad bodily failures of old age. A few seemed simply curious about what seeing a doctor would be like. Sara treated the ones she could, comforted those she could not. In the end, the two felt not so very different.

She left the hospital only to sleep, and sometimes eat, or else Hollis would bring meals to her, always with Kate in tow. They had been quartered in an apartment in the complex at the edge of downtown—a curious place, with wide, tinted windows that created a permanent evening light within. It felt a little eerie, knowing that the former occupants had been redeyes, but it was comfortable, with large beds made with soft linens and hot water and a working gas stove, on which Hollis concocted soups and stews of ingredients she didn't want to know about but which were nonetheless delicious. They would eat together in the candlelit dark and then fall into bed, making love with quiet tenderness so as not to wake their daughter.

Tonight Sara decided to take a break; she was dead on her feet, and starving besides, and missed her family keenly. Her family: after all that had happened, how remarkable these two words were. They seemed the most miraculous in the history of human speech. When she had seen Hollis charging through the entrance of the Dome, her heart had instantly known what her eyes could not believe. Of course he had come for her; Hollis had moved heaven and earth, and here he was. How could it have been otherwise?

She made her way up the hill, past the toppled wreckage of the Dome—its charred timbers had smoldered for days—and through the old downtown. To move freely, without fear, still seemed a little unreal to her. Sara thought about stopping into the apothecary, to say hello to Eustace and whoever else was around, but her feet refused this impulse, which quickly passed. With anticipation lightening her step, she ascended the six flights to the apartment.

"Mummy!"

Hollis and Kate were sitting together on the floor, playing beans and cups. Before Sara could uncoil the scarf from her neck, the girl leapt to her feet and flew into her arms, a soft collision; Sara hoisted Kate to her waist to look her in the eye. She had never told Kate to address her by this name, not wanting to confuse her more than necessary, but this had turned out not to matter; the girl had simply done it. Having never had a father before, Kate had taken a little more time to adapt to Hollis's role in her life, but then one day, about a week after the liberation, she had started to call him Daddy.

"Well, there you are," Sara said happily. "How was your day? Did you do fun things with Daddy?"

The little girl reached toward Sara's face, wrapped her nose with her fist, and made a show of snatching it from Sara's face, popping it into her mouth, and pushing her tongue against the inside of her cheek. "I haf yur nose," she said thickly.

"Now, give that back."

Kate, beaming wildly, blond hair bouncing around her face, waggled her head with playful defiance. "Nuh-uh. It's mine."

Thus, the tickling, and laughter from all sides, and the theft of more bodily parts, and the eventual return of Sara's nose to her face. By the time the struggle was over, Hollis had joined in. Cupping the back of Kate's head, he kissed Sara quickly, his beard—warm, familiar, full of his scent—pressing like wool against her cheeks.

"Hungry?"

She smiled. "I could eat."

Hollis dished her out a bowl; he and Kate had already had their dinner. He sat with her at the little table while she dug in. The meat, he confessed, could have been just about anything, but the carrots and potatoes were passable. Sara hardly cared; never had food tasted so good as it had the last few weeks. They talked about her patients, about Peter and Michael and the others, about Kerrville and what awaited there, about the trip south, now just a few days off. Hollis had initially suggested that they wait until spring, when the travel would be less arduous, but Sara would have none of it. *Too much has happened here,* she'd told him. *I don't know where home is, but let's let it be Texas.*

They washed the dishes, set them in the rack, and readied Kate for bed. Even as Sara drew the nightshirt over the little girl's head, she was already half-asleep. They tucked her in and retreated to the living room.

"Do you really have to go back to the hospital?" Hollis asked.

Sara took her coat from the hook and wriggled her arms into the sleeves. "It'll just be a few hours. Don't wait up." Though that was exactly what he'd do; Sara would have done the same. "Come here."

She kissed him, lingering there. "I mean it. Go to bed."

But as she put her hand on the knob, he stopped her.

"How did you know, Sara?"

She almost, but not quite, understood what he was asking. "How did I know what?"

"That it was her. That it was Kate."

It was odd; Sara had never thought to ask herself this question. Nina had confirmed Kate's identity in their clandestine meeting in the back room of the apothecary, but she needn't have; there had never been a trace of doubt in Sara's mind. It was more than the child's physical resemblance that told her so; the knowledge had come from someplace deeper. Sara had looked at Kate and instantly understood that of all the children in the world, this one was hers.

"Call it a mother's instincts. It was like . . . like knowing myself." She shrugged. "I can't explain it any better than that."

"Still, we were lucky."

Sara had never told him about the foil packet; nor would she ever. "I'm not sure if you can even call something like this luck," she said. "All I know is we're here."

It was after midnight by the time she was finishing her rounds. Yawning into her fist, her mind already halfway home, Sara stepped into the last examining room, where a young woman was sitting on the table.

"Jenny?"

"Hi, Dani."

Sara had to laugh—not only at the name, which seemed like something from a distant dream, but the girl's presence itself. It wasn't until she'd seen her that Sara had realized that she'd assumed Jenny was dead.

"What happened to you?"

She shrugged sheepishly. "I'm sorry I left. After what happened in the feedlot, I just panicked. One of the kitchen workers hid me in a flour barrel and got me out on one of the delivery trucks."

Sara smiled to reassure her. "Well, I'm glad to see you. What seems to be the trouble?"

The girl hesitated. "I think I may be pregnant."

Sara examined her. If she was, it was too early to tell. But being pregnant got you a spot in the first evacuation. She filled out the form and handed it to her.

"Take this to the census office and tell them I sent you."

"Really?"

"Really."

The girl stared at the slip of paper in her hand. "Kerrville. I can't believe it. I barely remember it."

Sara had been filling out a duplicate evacuation order on her clipboard. Her pen paused in midair. "What did you say?"

"That I can't believe it?"

"No, the other thing. About remembering."

The girl shrugged. "I was born there. At least I think I was. I was pretty small when they took me."

"Jenny, why didn't you tell anyone?"

"I did. I told the census taker."

Flyers, how had they missed this?

"Well, I'm glad you told *me*. Somebody may be looking for you. What's your last name?"

"I'm not really sure," Jenny said, "but I think that it was Apgar."

68

The day of departure arrived with a hard, bright dawn. The advance team gathered at the stadium: thirty men and women, six trucks, and two refuelers. Eustace and Nina had come to see them off, as well as Lore and Greer.

A small crowd had gathered, family and friends of those who would be departing. Sara and the others had already said goodbye to Michael the night before, at the hospital. Go on, he said, his face red, get out of here. How is a guy supposed to get his rest? But the card Kate had made for him proved his undoing. *I Love Youe Unkle Michel, Get Whell.* Aw, flyers, he said, get over here, and gripped the little girl tightly to his chest, tears rolling from his eyes.

The last supplies were loaded into the trucks; everybody climbed aboard. Peter would ride in the lead pickup, with Hollis; Kate and Sara were riding in one of the large transports at the rear. As Peter fired the ignition, Greer stepped to his window. In Peter's absence, the major had agreed to serve in his stead as Eustace's second-in-command and was now in charge of the evacuation.

"I don't know where she is, Peter. I'm sorry."

Had he been so obvious? Once again, Lish had left him standing at the altar. "I'm just worried about her. Something's not right."

"She went through a lot in that cell. I don't think she's told us even half of it. She'll bounce back—she always does."

There was nothing more to say on the subject. Nor on the other, which in the days since the uprising had hung over them with its unspoken weight of grief. The logical explanation was that Amy had been killed in the explosion, vaporized with the other virals, and yet part of him could not accept this. She felt like a ghost limb, an invisible part of him.

The two men shook hands. "Be careful okay?" Greer said. "You too, Hollis. It's a different world out there, but you never know."

Peter nodded. "All eyes, Major."

Greer allowed himself a rare smile. "I confess I like the sound of that. Who knows? Maybe they'll take me back, after all."

The moment of parting was at hand. Peter ground the truck into gear; with a throb of heavy engines, the line of vehicles drew clear of the gate. In the rearview mirror, Peter watched as the buildings of the Homeland receded from view, fading into the winter whiteness.

"I'm sure she's somewhere, Peter," Hollis said.

Peter wondered whom he meant.

From her hiding place in the culvert, Alicia watched the convoy drive away. For many days she had lived this moment in advance, attempting to prepare herself. How would it feel? Even now she couldn't say. Final, that was all. It felt final. The line of trucks cut a broad arc around the fences of the city and turned south. For a long time Alicia watched it, the image growing smaller, the sound of the engines dimming. She was still watching when it disappeared.

There was one thing left to do.

She'd taken the blood from the hospital, secreting the sloshing plastic pouch beneath her tunic when Sara's back was turned. It had taken all her resolve not to clamp her jaws into it and bathe her face and mouth and tongue in its earthy richness. But when she'd thought of Peter, and Amy, and Michael, and all the others, she had found the strength to wait.

She had buried the pouch in the snow, marking the spot with a stone. Now she dug it free: a block of red ice, dense in her hand. Soldier was watching her from the edge of the culvert. Alicia would have told him to go, but of course he wouldn't; they belonged to each other till the end. She built a fire of crackling scrub, melted snow in a pot, waited till the bubbles rose, and dipped the bag into the steaming water—as if, she thought, she were steeping tea. Gradually the contents softened to a slush. When the blood had thawed completely, Alicia removed the bag and lay in the snow, cradling its warmth against her chest. Within its plastic casing lay a destiny deferred. Since the day the viral had bitten her on the mountain, five years ago, the knowledge of her fate had lain inside her; now she would meet it. She would meet it, and die.

The morning sun was climbing into a cloudless winter sky. The sun. Alicia squinted her eyes against its brightness. *The sun,* she thought. *My enemy, my friend, my last deliverance.* It would sweep her away. It would scatter her ashes to the wind. Be quick now, Alicia said to the sun, but not too quick. I want to feel it coming out of me.

She raised the bag to her lips, pulled the tab, and drank.

*   *   *

By dusk the convoy had traveled sixty miles. The town was named Grinnell. They took shelter in an abandoned store at the edge of town that apparently had once sold shoes; boxes and boxes of them lined the racks. So, a place worth returning to, someday. They ate their rations, bedded down, and slept.

Or tried to. It wasn't the cold—Peter was accustomed to that. He was simply too keyed up. The events in the stadium had been too enormous to process all at once; nearly a month later, he still found himself caught up in their emotions, his mind flashing restlessly with the images.

Peter pulled on his parka and boots and stepped outside. They'd posted a single guard, who was sitting in a metal folding chair they'd brought out from the store; Peter accepted the man's rifle and sent him to bed. The moon was shining, the air like ice in his lungs. He stood in silence, drinking in the night's stark clarity. For days after the uprising, Peter had tried to will himself into some emotion that would correspond to the magnitude of events—happiness or triumph or even just relief— but all he felt was lonely. He remembered Greer's parting words: *It's a different world out there.* It was, Peter knew that; yet it did not seem so. If anything, the world felt even more like itself. Here were the frozen fields, like a vast, becalmed sea; here was the immeasurable, starlit sky; here was the moon with its jaundiced, heavy-lidded gaze, like the answer to a question nobody had posed. Everything was just as it had been, and would go on being, long after all of them were gone, their names and memories and all they were ground like their bones into the dust of time and blown away.

A noise behind him: Sara stepped through the door, toting Kate on her hip. The girl's eyes were open and looking about. Sara moved beside Peter, her boots crunching on the snow.

"Couldn't sleep?" he asked.

She made a face of exasperation. "Believe me, *I* could. It's my fault, I let her nap too long in the truck."

"Hi, Peter," the little girl said.

"Hi, sweetheart. Shouldn't you be in bed? We've got another long day tomorrow, you know."

She pressed her lips together. "Mm-mm."

"See?" Sara said.

"Want me to take her for a while? I can, you know."

"What, out here, you mean?"

Peter shrugged. "A little fresh air should fix her right up. And I could use the company." When Sara didn't answer, Peter said, "Don't worry, I'll keep an eye. What do you say, Kate?"

"You're sure about this?" Sara pressed.

"Sure I'm sure. What else am I going to do? The minute she gets sleepy, I'll bring her inside." He propped his rifle against the building and held out his arms. "Come on now, hand her over. I'm not taking no for an answer."

Sara acquiesced, shifting Kate from her waist to Peter's. The little girl wrapped her legs around him, gripping the lapel of his parka to balance her weight.

Sara stood back a bit to regard the two of them. "I've got to say, this isn't a version of you I've seen before."

He felt himself smile. "Five years. A lot can change."

"Well, it suits you." A sudden yawn seized her. "Seriously, if she gets to be a bother . . ."

"She won't. Now, will you go? Get some sleep."

Sara left them alone. Peter lowered himself into the chair, shifted Kate to his lap, and turned her body toward the winter sky. "So what do you want to talk about?"

"I dunno."

"Not tired at all?"

"Nope."

"How about we count some stars?"

"That's boring." She shifted, making herself comfortable, then commanded: "Tell me a story."

"A story. What kind?"

"A once-upon-a-time story."

He wasn't sure how, having never done this before. Yet as he considered the girl's request, a rush of memories flowed through him: his days as a Little in the Sanctuary, sitting in circle with the other children, their legs folded under them; Teacher, her pale, moonlike face and the stories she told, of talking animals in waistcoats and skirts and kings in their castles and ships crossing the sea in search of treasure; the drowsy sensation of the words passing through him, carrying him away into distant worlds and times, as if he were leaving his own body. They were recollections of another life; they were so distant as to feel historical; yet sitting in the winter cold with Sara's daughter on his lap, they did not seem apart from him. He felt a mantle pass and, with it, a twinge of regret: he'd never told Caleb a story.

"So." He cleared his throat, stalling to assemble his thoughts. But the truth was, he had nothing; every story from his childhood had suddenly fled his mind. He'd simply have to wing it. "Let's see—"

"It needs a girl in it," Kate said, helpfully.

"So it does. I was just getting to that. So, once upon a time there was a little girl—"

"What did she look like?"

"Hmm. Well, she was very pretty. A lot like you, actually."

"Was she a princess?"

"Are you going to let me tell this or not? But now that you mention it, she was. The most beautiful princess who ever lived. But the thing is, she didn't *know* she was a princess. That's the interesting part."

Kate frowned bossily. "Why didn't she know?"

Something clicked then; he felt the contours of a story emerging in his mind.

"That is a very excellent question. What happened was this. When she was very young, not much more than a baby, her parents, the king and queen, took her on a picnic in the royal forest. It was a sunny day, and the little girl, whose name was Princess . . ."

"Elizabeth."

"Princess Elizabeth, saw a butterfly. An *amazing* butterfly. Her parents weren't paying attention, and she followed the butterfly into the woods, trying to catch it. But the thing is, it wasn't a butterfly. It was . . . a fairy queen."

"Really?"

"It's true. Now, the thing about fairies is, they don't trust people. They pretty much keep to themselves, and that's the way they like it. But the fairy queen was different. She'd always wanted a daughter. Fairies don't have children of their own. It made her very sad not to have a little girl to take care of, and when she saw Princess Elizabeth, she was so moved by her beauty that she couldn't help herself. She led the child away, deeper and deeper into the woods. Soon the little girl was lost and began to cry. The fairy queen landed on her nose, and brushed her tears away with her delicate wings, and said, 'Don't be sad. I'll take care of you. You will be my little girl now.' And she took her to the big hollow tree where she lived with all her fairy subjects, and gave her food to eat and a table to sit at and a little bed to sleep in, and before too long Princess Elizabeth had no memory of any other life, except her life among the fairies of the forest."

Kate was nodding along. "What happened then?"

"Well, nothing. Not right away. For a while they were very happy together, the fairy queen especially. How wonderful it felt for her to have a little girl of her own. But as Elizabeth grew, she began to feel that something wasn't right. Do you know what that was?"

"She wasn't a fairy?"

"Exactly. Good for you, for figuring that out. She wasn't a fairy, she was a little girl, and not so little anymore. Why am I so different? she wondered. And the taller she grew, the harder this was for the fairy queen to conceal. Why do my feet stick out from my bed, Elizabeth would ask her, and the fairy queen would say, Because beds are always small, that's just how they are. Why is my table so tiny, Elizabeth asked, and the fairy queen said, I'm sorry, it's not the table's fault, you'll just have to stop growing. Which, of course, she couldn't do. She grew and grew, and soon she barely fit inside the tree anymore. All the other fairies complained. They were afraid she'd eat all their food and there'd be nothing left. They were afraid she'd accidentally squash them. Something had to be done, but the fairy queen refused. With me so far?"

Kate nodded, enthralled.

"Now, the king and queen, Elizabeth's parents, had never stopped looking for her. They'd combed every inch of the forest, and all the lands of the kingdom besides. But the tree was very well hidden. Then one day they heard a rumor about a little girl living in the forest with the fairies. Could that be our daughter? they wondered. And they did the only thing they could think of. They ordered the royal woodsmen to cut down all the trees until they found the one with Elizabeth inside it."

"*All* of them?"

Peter nodded. "Every last one. Which was not a good idea. The woods were home not only to the fairies but to all kinds of animals and birds. But Elizabeth's parents were so desperate, they would have done anything to get their daughter back. So the woodsmen got to work, chopping down the forest, while the king and queen rode out on their horses, calling her name. 'Elizabeth! Elizabeth! Where are you?' And you know what happened?"

"She heard them?"

"Yes, she did. Only the name Elizabeth didn't mean anything to her anymore. She had a fairy name now, and had forgotten everything about her life. But the fairy queen knew what she was hearing, and she felt pretty awful about it. How could I have done this terrible thing? she thought. How could I have taken Elizabeth away? But still she couldn't make herself fly out of the tree to tell Elizabeth's parents where she was. She loved the girl too much, you see, to let her go. 'Be very still,' she said to Elizabeth. 'Don't make a sound.' The woodsmen were coming closer and closer. Trees were falling everywhere. All the fairies were afraid. 'Give her back,' they said to the fairy queen, 'please, give her back before they destroy the entire forest.'"

"Wow," Kate gasped.

"I know. It's a pretty scary story. Should I stop?"

"Uncle Peter, *please.*"

He laughed. "All right, all right. So, the woodsmen came to the tree with Elizabeth and the fairies inside. It was an especially magnificent tree, tall and wide, with a big canopy of leaves. A fairy tree. But as one woodsman reared back with his axe, the king had a change of heart. The tree, you see, was just too beautiful to cut down. I'm sure the creatures of the forest care about this tree as much as I care about my daughter, he said. It wouldn't be right to take it away from them, all because I've lost something I love. Everybody, put your axes down and go home and let me and my wife mourn for our daughter, who we will never see again. It was very sad. Everybody was in tears. Elizabeth's parents, the woodsmen, even the fairy queen, who had heard every word. Because she knew that Elizabeth could never be her real daughter, no matter how hard she wished it. So she took her by the hand and led her out of the tree and said, 'Your Majesties, please forgive me. It was I who took your daughter. I wanted a little girl of my own so much that I couldn't help myself. But I know now that she belongs with you. I'm so very, very sorry.' And you know what the king and queen said?"

"Off with your head?"

Peter stifled a laugh. "Just the opposite. Despite everything that had happened, they were so happy to have their daughter back, and so moved by the fairy queen's remorse, that they decided to reward her. They issued a royal proclamation that the fairies should be left to live in peace, and that all children of the realm should have one special fairy friend. Which is why, to this day, only children can see them."

Kate was silent a moment. "So that's the end?"

"Pretty much, yeah." He felt faintly embarrassed. "I haven't really done this before. How'd I do?"

The girl considered this, then said, with a crisp nod, "I liked it. It was a good story. Tell me another."

"I'm not sure I've got another one in me. Aren't you tired yet?"

"*Please,* Uncle Peter."

The night was clear, the stars shining down. Everything was still, not a trace of movement or sound. Peter thought of Caleb, realizing with a power that startled him how much he missed the boy, how he longed to hold him in his arms. Alicia was right, and Tifty too. But most of all, Amy. *He loves you, you know.* The truth filled him like a breath of winter air. Peter would go home and learn to be a father.

"So, okay . . ."

He talked and talked. He told her every story he knew. By the time he was done, Kate was yawning; her body had gone slack in his arms. He unzipped his coat and swiveled her on his lap, pulling the flaps around her.

"Are you cold, sweetheart?"

Her voice was soft, half gone. "Nuh-uh."

She nestled against him. Just another minute, Peter thought, and closed his eyes. Just another minute, and I'll take her inside. He felt Kate's warm breath on his neck; her chest moved gently against his own, rising and falling, like long waves on a beach. But a minute passed, and then another and another, and by that time Peter wasn't going anywhere, because he was fast asleep.

In the lavatory of the apothecary shop, Lucius Greer was shaving.

The day, and most of the night besides, had disappeared under an avalanche of duties. A meeting of the Council of Lodges, during which Eustace had attempted first to reexplain and then once more justify the lottery procedure for evacuation; the tallying of census data, which had revealed numerous duplicate forms, some made in error, others with deliberate intent by individuals trying to increase their odds of being chosen; a brawl outside the detention center when a group of three cols, half-starved after weeks of hiding in an unused warehouse, had attempted to turn themselves in, only to be intercepted by the small crowd that kept vigil outside the building; nine weddings over which he'd been asked to officiate when one of the JPs had taken ill (all Lucius had to do was read four sentences off a card, yet it surprised him, how weighty it felt to say them aloud); the first official gathering of the evacuation support teams, and the partitioning of their responsibilities in preparation for the first departure; and on and on. A day of one thing and then another and another; Lucius couldn't remember what or even if he'd eaten, he'd barely sat down all day, and yet here he was, past midnight, gazing at his grizzled, hirsute face in the mirror, holding a blade in one hand and a pair of scissors in the other.

He began with the scissors. Snip by snip the wild torrent of his hair and beard fell away, their white leavings gathering on the floor by his feet like drifts of feathered snow. When this was done he warmed a pot of water, soaked a rag and wrung it out, and lay it over his face to soften the bristles that remained. He smeared his cheeks with soap, harsh and chemical-smelling, then went to work with the blade: first his cheeks, then the long arc of his neck, and finally his head, working backward from brow to crown to the base of his skull in short, measured strokes. The first time he had shaved himself in this manner, the night before he'd taken the oath of the Expeditionary, he had cut himself in about twenty places. It was commonly said that you didn't need to look at the uniform to know a fresh recruit; all you had to do was look at his head. But with time and practice, Greer, like all of his fellows, had gotten the knack, and it pleased him to discover that he hadn't lost his touch. He could have done it blindfolded in the dark if he had to, yet there was satisfaction to be had in observing a ritual that after so many years still possessed the power of a baptism. Scrape by scrape his visage was laid bare, and when the task was complete, Greer stepped back to examine his face in the mirror, running his hand over the cool pinkness of his rediscovered flesh and nodding with approval at the image he beheld.

He wiped himself down, cleaned and dried his blade, and put his supplies away. Many days had passed since he had properly slept, and still he was not the least bit tired. He drew on his parka and boots, let himself out the back, and made his way down the alley. It was nearly one A.M., not a soul about, yet from all around Greer sensed a kind of molecular restlessness, a subaural hum of life. He moved past the ruined Dome, down the hill, through the flatland to the stadium. By the time he arrived, the moon was down. He chose not to enter the structure, rather to stand in the absolute quiet and take it in whole, this blot of darkness against the starry sky. He wondered: Would history remember this place? Would the people of the future, whoever they were, give it a name, one worthy of the events that had transpired here, to record it for posterity? A hopeful thought, a bit premature, but one worth having. And Lucius Greer took a silent vow. Should such a future come to pass, should the final battle for earth's dominion be taken in victory, he would be the one to put pen to paper, to give the story words.

He did not know when this battle would be. Amy had not told him that. Only that it would come.

He understood, then, what force had led him here. He was looking for a sign. What form this sign would take, he could not say. It might come now, it might come later, it might not come at all. Such was the burden of his faith. He opened his mind and waited. An interval of time moved by. The night, the stars, the living world; all passed through him, like a blessing.

Then:

Lucius. My friend. Hello.

And on this night of miraculous things, Peter, sitting outside the shoe store, awoke to the feeling that he was, in fact, not awake at all—that one dream had simply opened into the next, like a door behind a door. A dream in which he was sitting with Sara's daughter in his arms at the edge of the snowy fields, all else being the same—the inky sky, the winter cold, the lateness of the hour—except for the fact that they were not alone.

But it was not a dream.

She crouched before him, in the manner of her kind. Her transformation was complete; even her raven mane was gone. Yet as their eyes met and held, the image wavered in his mind; it was not a viral he saw. It was a girl, and then a woman, and then both of these at once. She was Amy, the Girl from Nowhere; she was Amy of Souls, Last of the Twelve; she was only herself. Extending a hand toward him, Amy held her palm upright; Peter replied in kind. A force of pure longing surged in his heart as their fingers touched. It was a kind of kiss.

How long they stayed that way, Peter didn't know. Between them, in the warm cocoon of his coat, Kate slept soundly, oblivious. Time had released its moorings; Peter and Amy drifted together in the current. Soon the child would awaken, or Sara would come, or Hollis, and Amy would be gone. She would lift away in a streak of starry light. Peter would return the sleeping child to her bed, and lie down himself, even attempt to sleep; and in the morning, in the gray winter dawn, they would stretch their bones and load up their gear and continue on their long road south. The moment would pass, like all things, into memory.

But not just yet.

EPILOGUE

THE
GOLDEN HOUR

As easy might I from myself depart
As from my soul, which in thy breast doth lie.
That is my home of love.

—Shakespeare,
Sonnet 109

69

The driver this time was a woman. Amy put down her sign and got into the car.

"How do you do, Amy?" She offered her hand. "I'm Rachel Wood."

They shook. For a moment Amy was rendered speechless, arrested by the woman's beauty: a face of delicate, well-made bones, as if honed with the finest tools; skin that glowed with youthful health; a trim, strong body, her arms articulated with lean muscle. Her hair, pulled away from her face in a taut ponytail, was blond with golden streaks. She was wearing what Amy knew to be tennis clothes, although this knowledge seemed to come from elsewhere, the idea of tennis itself lacking any meaningful reference. Sunglasses with tiny jewels embedded in the arms were perched on top of her head.

"I'm sorry I wasn't here to get you before," Rachel continued. "Anthony thought you'd like a familiar face the first time."

"I'm very glad to meet you," Amy said.

"That's sweet of you to say." She smiled, showing her teeth, which were small and straight and very white. "Buckle up now."

They glided away from the overpass. All was the same as the last time—the same houses and stores and parking lots, the same glowing summer light, the same busy world flowing past. In the deep leather of her seat, Amy felt as if she were floating in a bath. Rachel seemed thoroughly at home at the wheel of the immense vehicle, humming a shapeless tune under her breath as she guided them confidently through traffic. As a large pickup braked ahead of them, blocking the lane, Rachel flicked on her blinker and deftly swerved to pass.

"For goodness sake," she sighed, "some people. Where do they learn to drive?" She looked at Amy hastily and returned her eyes to the road. "You know, you're not quite what I imagined, I have to say."

"No?"

"Oh, not in a bad way," Rachel assured her. "That's not what I meant at all. Honestly, you're just pretty as a picture. I wish I had skin like that."

"So how am I different?"

She hesitated, choosing her words. "I just thought you'd be, you know. Younger."

They continued on. Amy's abrupt arrival in this place had brought about a mild disorientation and, with it, a muting of emotion. But as the minutes passed, she felt her mind opening to her circumstances, the images and her responses to them growing more defined. How remarkable everything was, Amy thought. How very, very remarkable. They were inside the ship, the *Chevron Mariner,* yet she had no physical awareness of this; as before, with Wolgast, every detail of the scene possessed an absolutely firm appearance of reality. Perhaps it was real, in some alternate sense of the word. What, after all, was "real"?

"Right there is where I stopped with him, that first time." Rachel gestured out the window to a block of stores. "Somehow I had it in my head he might like doughnuts. Doughnuts, can you imagine?" Before Amy could assemble a response, she went on: "But listen to me, giving you the grand tour. I'm sure you know all about it. And you must be tired, after such a long trip."

"It's all right," Amy said. "I don't mind."

"Oh, he was such a sight." Rachel shook her head sadly. "That poor man. My heart just went out. I said to myself, Rachel, you have to do something. For once in your little life, get your head out of the sand. But of course I was really thinking about myself, as usual. Which is the thing. I've got enough regrets on that score to last a hundred lifetimes. I didn't deserve him, not one iota."

"I don't think he believes that."

She slowed the car to turn onto a residential street. "It's really marvelous, you know. What you're doing. He's been alone so long."

Soon, they pulled up to the house. "Well, here we are," Rachel announced in a chipper voice. She had put the vehicle in park though she'd left the engine running, just as Wolgast had done. "It was a pleasure to finally meet you, Amy. You'll want to watch your step getting out."

"Why don't you come with me? I know he'd like to see you."

"Oh, no," said Rachel. "It's nice of you to ask, but that's not how this works, I'm afraid. That's against the rules."

"What rules?"

"Just . . . the rules."

Amy waited for more, but there was none; there was nothing to do but climb out of the car. By the open door she turned to look at Rachel, who was waiting with her hands on the wheel. The air was thick and warm beneath the green canopy of the trees; insects were buzzing everywhere with their bright, chaotic music, like the notes of an orchestra tuning up.

"Tell him I'm thinking about him, won't you? Tell him Rachel sends her love."

"I don't understand why you can't come with me."

Rachel directed her gaze over the dashboard, toward the house. It seemed to Amy she was searching for something, her eyes, which had clouded with a sudden grief, pausing at each of its many windows. Tears appeared at the corners of her eyes.

"I can't, you see, because it wouldn't make any sense."

"Why wouldn't it make sense?"

"Because, Amy," she said, "I'm already there."

She found him kneeling in the flowerbeds, working in the dirt. A wheelbarrow was positioned nearby; piles of dark mulch, exuding a heavy earthen smell, were dispersed among the beds. At her approach he rose to his feet, removing his broad-brimmed straw hat and drawing off his gloves.

"Miss Amy, you're right on time now. I was just setting to work on the lawn, but I reckon that'll keep." He waved his hat toward the patio, where glasses of tea awaited. "Come and sit a spell."

They took their places at the table. Amy tipped her face to the crowns of the trees, letting the sunlight warm her. The aromas of grass and flowers filled her senses.

"Thought you'd be more comfortable this way," Carter said. "The two of us can have a time, talking and such. Make the days pass."

"You knew he'd be there, didn't you?"

Carter mopped his brow with a rag. "Didn't send him, if that's what you mean. Wolgast just had his way. No talking him out of it when he set his mind on it."

"But how come the others didn't know who he was? They couldn't have. They would have killed him."

Carter shook his head. "Their kind never could read me, one way or the other. You could say we been out of touch awhile. It's a two-way street, and I ain't sent nothing back their way since the beginning. Shut my mind to all of them." Carter hitched up in his chair and returned the cloth to his back pocket. "You done right, Miss Amy. Wolgast, too. Was a hard and terrible thing, I know that."

She was suddenly thirsty; the tea felt cool and sweet going down and left a bright, lemony taste on her tongue. Carter watched her, waving his hat in a gentle motion to push a breeze over his face.

"And Zero?"

"I expect there's time yet. But he'll be coming for us. This here's personal now. He's surely the worst of 'em. Put 'em all together and you still ain't got one Zero. Bridge we cross when we come to it."

"And until then, here we stay."

Carter nodded in his patient way. "Yes'm. Here we stay."

They sat together in silence, thinking of what would come.

"I've never tended a garden before," Amy said. "Would you teach me?"

"Always lots to be done. Reckon I could use the help. Mower's fussy, though."

"I'm sure I could learn."

"I'm supposing you could, now," he said with a smile. "I reckon that's the case."

Amy remembered her promise. "Rachel told me to send her love."

"Did she, now. I was just thinkin' on her. How she look to you?"

"Beautiful, really. I'd never really had a chance to see her clearly before. But sad, too. She was looking at the house, like there was something she wanted."

Carter seemed surprised. "Why, it's her babies, Miss Amy. I thought you knew."

Amy shook her head.

"Haley and the little one. Woman can't see or touch 'em, where she is. It's her babies she's always dreamin' on. It's the most awful ache to her."

Amy finally understood. Rachel had drowned herself, leaving her children behind. "Will she ever see them again?"

"I expect she will when she ready. It's her own self she has to forgive, for leaving them like she did."

His words seemed to hover in the air, not sounds alone but things of form and substance. The temperature was dropping; the leaves had begun to fall.

"She not the only one, Miss Amy. Some folks can't find a way on they own. For some it's a bad feeling in the mind. Others just can't let go. Them's the ones that love too hard."

In the pool, the body of Rachel Wood had completed its slow ascent to float upon the surface. Amy looked down at the table; she knew what Carter was saying to her. *Every day I cut the lawn,* she thought. *Every day she rise.*

"You got to go to him," said Carter. "Show him the way."

"I just . . ." She felt his eyes on her face. "I don't know how."

He reached over the table and cupped her chin, lifting it upward. "I know you, Miss Amy. It's like you been inside me all my life. You the one was made to set this whole world right. But Wolgast's just a man. It's his time now. You got to give him back."

Tears trembled in her throat. "But what will I do without him?"

"Just like you always done," said Anthony Carter, and smiled into her eyes. "Just like you do now. You *Amy.*"

70

He came to her a final time. Or it was she who came to him. They came to each other, to say a last goodbye.

For Wolgast it began with a sensation of abstract motion. He was in a kind of nowhere, floating through an infinite space, though bit by bit the scene resolved, its spatial and temporal parameters firming, and he became aware that he was, of all things, riding a bicycle. A bicycle! Now, that was strange. Why was he on a bicycle? He hadn't ridden one in years, but he'd loved it as a boy: the feeling of pure freedom and gyroscopic lift, his body's energy flowing through this marvelous mechanism that joined him to the wind. Wolgast was on a bicycle, riding down a dusty country lane, and Amy was beside him, perched on a bicycle of her own. This fact surprised him neither more nor less than anything else about the scene, it all simply *was,* just as Amy was both a little girl and a grown woman, and for a time they rode together without speaking, though the idea of time itself felt strange. What was time? How long had they been riding like this? Some period of hours, perhaps, or even days, and yet the light was always the same—a permanent penumbral twilight that enriched the colors of everything around him with a golden glow: the fields and trees, the dust that rose under his wheels, the small white shapes of houses in the distance. Everything felt very close; everything was far away.

"Where are we going?" Wolgast asked.

Amy smiled. "Oh, it's not much farther."

"What . . . is this place?"

She said nothing more. On they rode. Wolgast's heart was full of warm contentment, as if he were a boy again: a boy riding his bicycle at sunset, waiting for the call that would summon him home.

"Are you tired?" Amy asked.

"Not at all. It feels wonderful."

"Why don't we stop at the crest of the next hill?"

They coasted to a halt. A grassy valley opened below them. In the distance, nestled by trees, was a house: small, white, like the others, with a porch and black shutters. Amy and Wolgast lowered their bicycles to the ground and stood together quietly. There was no wind at all.

"It's quite a view," Wolgast said. Then: "I think I know where I am."

Amy nodded.

"It's strange." He took a deep breath and let it out slowly. "I don't really remember how it happened, but I suppose that's for the best. Is it always like this?"

"I'm not sure. I think sometimes it is."

"I remember thinking I had to be brave."

"You were. The bravest man I ever saw."

He mulled this over. "Well, that's good. I'm glad to hear it. In the end, I guess that's all a person can ask." He sent his gaze over the valley again. "That house. I'm supposed to go there, aren't I?"

"I believe that you are."

He turned to look at her. A second passed; then he broke into a smile of discovery.

"Wait a minute. You're in *love*. I can see it in your face."

"I think I am, yes."

Wolgast shook his head with wonder. "I'll be damned. How about that. My little Amy, all grown up, in love. And does he love you back, this person?"

"I think he does," she said. "I hope he does."

"Well, he'd be a fool not to. You can tell him I said so."

For a moment neither spoke. Amy waited.

"So," he began again. His voice was thick with emotion. "I suppose that means my work here is done. I guess I always knew this day would come. I'm going to miss you, Amy."

"I'll miss you, too."

"That was always the hardest part, missing you. I think that's why I could never bring myself to leave. I always thought, What will Amy do without me? Funny how in the end it was the other way around. I suppose all parents feel that way. But it's different when it's you." The words caught in his throat. "Let's do this quickly, okay?"

She put her arms around him. She was crying too, but not with sadness. Though perhaps a little bit of sadness. "It will be all right, I promise."

"How do you know?"

At the far end of the valley, at the edge of the fields, the door to the house had opened.

"Because that's what heaven is," said Amy. "It's opening the door of a house in twilight and everyone you love is there." She hugged him tightly to her. "It's time for you to go home, Daddy. I've kept you as long as I could, but you have to go now. They're waiting for you."

"Who's waiting, Amy?"

On the porch a woman had appeared, holding a baby in her arms. Amy backed away and touched his tearstained cheek.

She said, "Go see."

71

She awoke to the cold and a vision of stars. Stars by the hundreds, the thousands, the millions. Stars in their slow turning, pinwheeling over her face, and some of them were falling. Alicia watched them fall, counting off the seconds. One one thousand, two one thousand, three one thousand. She tallied the durations of their descents as they plunged across the heavens, and in so doing she came upon the understanding that the world was where she'd left it and she was still alive.

How could she be alive?

She sat upright. Who knew what time it was. The moon had set, dipping the sky in blackness. Nothing had changed; she was just the same.

And yet:

Alicia, come to me.

The sound of her name, whispered on the wind.

Come to me, Alicia. The others are gone, you will be my one. Come to me come to me come to me . . .

She knew whose voice this was.

Alicia climbed from the culvert. Fifty feet away, Soldier was grazing on a frosted stand of weeds. At the sound of her emergence, he lifted his head: Ah, there you are; I was beginning to wonder. His great hooves tossed clumps of white as he ambled toward her with his powerful gait.

—You good boy, she said. She caressed his muzzle, his breath filling her palms with a scent of earth. You splendid, noble boy. How well you know me. I guess we're not done, after all.

Her pack was lying in the culvert. She had no gun, but the bandoliers were there, blades tucked into their sheaths. She pulled the leather straps over her chest and cinched them tight to her frame. She climbed on Soldier's naked back and clicked her tongue, turning him east.

Come to me, Alicia. Come to me come to me come to me . . .

You're damn right I will, she thought. Leaning forward, his great mane filling her hands, she heeled Soldier to a trot, then a canter, and finally a gallop, wild through the snow.

You bastard. Here I come.

DRAMATIS PERSONAE

THE TWELVE

Tim Fanning, a.k.a. "The Zero." Professor of biochemistry, Columbia University. Infected by CV-0 virus on scientific expedition to Bolivia, Feb 21, 20XX.

1. **Giles Babcock (deceased).** Sentenced to death for one count of capital murder, Nye County, Nevada, 2013.
2. **Joseph Morrison.** Sentenced to death for one count of capital murder, Lewis County, Kentucky, 2013.
3. **Victor Chávez.** Sentenced to death for one count of capital murder and two counts of aggravated sexual assault with a minor, Elko County, Nevada, 2012.
4. **John Baffes.** Sentenced to death for one count of capital murder and one count of second-degree murder with depraved indifference, Pasco County, Florida, 2010.
5. **Thaddeus Turrell.** Sentenced to death for the capital murder of a Homeland Security officer, New Orleans Federal Housing District, 2014.
6. **David Winston.** Sentenced to death for one count of capital murder and three counts of aggravated sexual assault, New Castle County, Delaware, 2014.
7. **Rupert Sosa.** Sentenced to death for one count of vehicular homicide with depraved indifference, Lake County, Indiana, 2009.
8. **Martin Echols.** Sentenced to death for one count of capital murder and one count of armed robbery, Cameron Parish, Louisiana, 2012.
9. **Horace Lambright.** Sentenced to death for two counts of capital murder and aggravated sexual assault, Maricopa County, Arizona, 2014.

10. **Julio Martínez.** Sentenced to death for the capital murder of a peace officer, Laramie County, Wyoming, 2011.
11. **William Reinhardt.** Sentenced to death for three counts of capital murder and aggravated sexual assault, Miami-Dade County, Florida, 2012.
12. **Anthony Carter.** Sentenced to death for one count of capital murder, Harris County, Texas, 2013.

YEAR ZERO

Bernard Kittridge, a.k.a. "Last Stand in Denver." A survivor.
April. A survivor.
Timothy. Her stepbrother.
Danny Chayes. A school bus driver.
Lila Kyle. A doctor.
Lawrence Grey. A janitor, Project NOAH.
Horace Guilder. Deputy director, Division of Special Weapons ("The Warehouse").
Major Frances Porcheki. Officer of the Iowa National Guard.
Vera. A Red Cross nurse.
Ignacio. A janitor, Project NOAH.
Nelson. Chief technical officer, Division of Special Weapons.
Shawna. A prostitute.
Rita Chernow. A police detective.

OTHER SURVIVORS

Pastor Don
Wood
Delores
Jamal
Mrs. Bellamy
Joe Robinson
Linda Robinson
Boy Jr.

THE FIELD, 79 A.V.

Curtis Vorhees. Foreman of the North Agricultural Complex, Kerrville, Texas.

Delia "Dee" Vorhees. His wife.

Boz Vorhees. His brother (deceased).

Nitia and Siri Vorhees. Daughters of Curtis and Delia Vorhees.

Nathan Crukshank. Brother of Delia Vorhees; a Domestic Security (DS) officer.

Tifty Lamont. A Domestic Security officer.

OTHER FAMILIES IN THE FIELD

Tyler Vorhees family
Withers family
Dodd family
Apgar family
Cauley family
Francis family
Cuomo family
Martínez family
Wright family
Bodine family

97 A.V.

KERRVILLE, TEXAS

Amy Harper Bellafonte. The Girl from Nowhere.

Lieutenant Peter Jaxon. Officer of the Expeditionary, Army of the Republic of Texas.

Lieutenant Alicia Donadio. Officer of the Expeditionary.

Colonel Gunnar Apgar. Officer of the Expeditionary.

Major Alexander Henneman. Officer of the Expeditionary.

Lieutenant Satch Dodd. Officer of the Expeditionary.

Lucius Greer. A prisoner.

Hollis Wilson. A bouncer.

Dunk Withers. A criminal.

Abram Fleet. General of the Army.

Victoria Sanchez. President of the Republic of Texas.

Sister Peg. A nun, in charge of the orphanage.

Sister Catherine. A nun.

Caleb Jaxon. Nephew of Peter Jaxon, son of Theo Jaxon and Mausami Patal.

FREEPORT, TEXAS

Michael Fisher. Oiler first class (OFC); crew chief at Freeport refinery complex.

Lore DeVeer. An oiler.

Juan "Ceps" Sweeting. An oiler.

Ed Pope. An oiler.

Dan Karlovic. Chief engineer of Freeport refinery complex.

THE HOMELAND

Jackie. A worker.

Eustace. An insurgent.

Nina. An insurgent.

Vale. A human resources officer.

Whistler. A human resources officer.

Sod. A human resources officer.

Dr. Verlyn. A physician.

Dani. An attendant in the Dome.

Jenny. An attendant in the Dome.

Fred Wilkes. Chief of staff.

Vikram Suresh. Minister of public health.

Aidan Hoppel. Minister of propaganda.

ACKNOWLEDGMENTS

Every book needs friends, and this one has many. A big ole tip of the hat to: Ellen Levine at Trident Media Group; Mark Tavani and Libby McGuire at Ballantine Books; Bill Massey at Orion; Gina Centrello, president of the Random House Publishing Group; Claire Roberts at Trident Media; the spectacular production, publicity, marketing and sales teams at Random House, Orion, and my many pubishers around the world; Jennifer ("Jenny") Smith; and the English Department of Rice University. On matters military, I am especially indebted to Adrian Hoppel. Thanks also to Rudy Ramos, sniper-dentist, and Coert Voorhees. Mark and Bill: Pour yourselves a frosty, my brothers; you've earned it. Ellen: No truer friend have I.

To the members of Team Cronin, large and small, I say: Without you, nothing. Thank you for my life.

My gratitude to you all.

ABOUT THE AUTHOR

Justin Cronin is the *New York Times* bestselling author of *The Passage, Mary and O'Neil* (which won the PEN/Hemingway Award and the Stephen Crane Prize), and *The Summer Guest*. Other honors for his writing include a fellowship from the National Endowment for the Arts and a Whiting Writers' Award. A Distinguished Faculty Fellow at Rice University, he divides his time between Houston, Texas, and Cape Cod, Massachusetts.

KU-121-104

Cavan County Library
Withdrawn Stock

INTRODUCING

KATIE MAGUIRE

KATIE MAGUIRE was one of seven sisters born
to a police Inspector in Cork, but the only
sister who decided to follow her father
into An Garda Siochana.

With her bright green eyes and short red
hair, she looks like an Irish pixie, but she is
no soft touch. To the dismay of some of her
male subordinates, she rose quickly through
the ranks, gaining a reputation for catching
Cork's killers, often at great personal cost.

Katie spent seven years in a turbulent
marriage in which she bore, and lost, a son –
an event that continues to haunt her. Despite
facing turmoil at home and prejudice at
work she is one of the most fearless
detectives in Ireland.

THE KATIE MAGUIRE SERIES

White Bones

Broken Angels

Red Light

Taken For Dead

Blood Sisters

Buried

Cavan County Library

Withdrawn Stock

GRAHAM MASTERTON

BURIED

CAVAN COUNTY LIBRARY
ACC No. C/281872
CLASS NO.
INVOICE NO 10278 OM
PRICE € 13.71

First published in the UK in 2016 by Head of Zeus Ltd

Copyright © Graham Masterton, 2016

The moral right of Graham Masterton to be identified as the author
of this work has been asserted in accordance with the
Copyright, Designs and Patents Act of 1988.

All rights reserved. No part of this publication may be
reproduced, stored in a retrieval system, or transmitted in any form or
by any means, electronic, mechanical, photocopying, recording,
or otherwise, without the prior permission of both the copyright
owner and the above publisher of this book.

This is a work of fiction. All characters, organizations, and events
portrayed in this novel are either products of the author's imagination
or are used fictitiously.

9 7 5 3 1 2 4 6 8

A CIP catalogue record for this book is available
from the British Library

ISBN (HB) 9781784081379
ISBN (TPB) 9781784081386
ISBN (E) 9781784081362

Typeset by Ben Cracknell Studios, Norwich.

Printed and bound in Germany by GGP Media
GmbH, Pössneck

Head of Zeus Ltd
Clerkenwell House
45–47 Clerkenwell Green
London EC1R 0HT

WWW.HEADOFZEUS.COM

In memory of my friend Andrzej Kuryłowicz
10 April 1954 – 21 March 2014
You left us on the first day of Spring

'Chan eil saoi air nach laigh leòn'
Irish saying: Even a hero can be hurt

One

'Are you coming inside or not, you useless collop?' Declan demanded.

It was obvious, though, that Christy wasn't going to come any nearer. He stood on the front doorstep, his black and tan fur bedraggled by the rain, and Declan had never seen him look so apprehensive. His eyes were wide, and his nostrils were twitching, and every now and then he tilted his head sideways as if he were trying to peer inside the hallway and in through the living-room door, because he was sure that there was something frightening in there.

Colm called out, 'Declan, for feck's sake, will you stop discussing the weather with that mutt of yours and give me a hand with this fecking fireplace?'

'I'll tell you something, Christy, you're some jibber,' Declan told him. 'If you want to stay out there getting yourself soaked, that's your lookout. But if you die of pneumonia, don't come blaming me for it.'

He left Christy and went into the living room where Colm had knocked the brown-tiled fire surround loose from the wall and was now trying to lever it further away with a crowbar. The air in the tiny room was filled with dust and the floorboards were gritty underfoot so that the soles of his boots made a scrunching sound.

'Never known him act like that before,' said Declan, picking up a shovel and wedging it into the opposite side of the fireplace. 'It's almost like he's scared of something, do you know what I mean? Maybe there's a ghost in here, like.'

1

'That wouldn't fecking surprise me at all,' said Colm, violently wrenching the crowbar from side to side. 'The old feller who used to own this place, they discovered him dead down the bottom of the stairs, that's what that girl from Sherry Fitzgerald's told me. Tripped over his cat, so she reckoned. Broke his neck like a fecking stick of celery and they didn't find him for a month.'

Colm had reckoned that it would take them at least two weeks to renovate the whole house. It was a small two-bedroom property in Millstream Row, Blarney, in a terrace of eleven cottages that had been built sometime in the 1860s to house woollen workers from Mahony's mill.

Although the previous owners had lived in it since 1952, they had decorated it only once during the whole of their years there, with dingy brown floral wallpaper. In 1964 they had built a single-storey lean-to extension in the backyard to accommodate a bath and a twin-tub washing machine, but that had been their only concession to modernization.

Now that the widowed owner had died, the house had been sold to a young professional couple for 123,000 euros as their starter home.

Together, grunting like two prize hogs being prodded to market, Declan and Colm manhandled the fire surround out of the house and into the rain. Christy was still sitting there, soaking wet, and when he stepped back to allow them to shuffle out of the front door he shook himself furiously.

'You're a lunatic, do you know that?' said Declan, after he and Colm had heaved the fire surround, with a deafening crash, into the empty skip that was parked in the narrow road outside. 'Why don't you go in and get yourself dry?'

He bent down and took hold of Christy's collar, but when he tried to drag him into the house Christy stiffened his legs and growled. When Declan pulled harder he scrabbled his claws against the wet pavement and barked, refusing to step over the threshold.

'Sure look at him,' grinned Colm. 'I bet you're right about a ghost. How about it, Christy? Can you see a ghost in there, boy? *Woooooo!*'

'Maybe there's just a smell he doesn't like, dead rat or something,' said Declan. 'Most people don't know it, but your Kerry beagle has an even more sensitive nose than a bloodhound.'

'Yeah, but come on, Dec. How much of him is Kerry beagle and how much is some stray mongrel that gave his mother the lad when her owner wasn't looking?'

'It's all very well you skittin', boy,' Declan retorted. 'This feller can smell if somebody's farted in Limerick, I swear to God. He can smell tripe boiling even before you've lit the gas.'

He yanked at Christy's collar one more time, but Christy snarled and bared his teeth, and Declan gave up. 'Okay, have it your way. You need a bath any road.'

Declan and Colm went back into the house. Now they needed to pull up all the floorboards in the living room because the new owners were going to replace them with hand-scraped Victorian oak.

Colm lit a Johnnie Blue and took three deep drags before pinching it out and tucking the butt behind his ear. Then he picked up his crowbar and used it to jemmy the skirting board away from the wall underneath the window. While he lifted the skirting board over his shoulder and toted it outside to the skip, Declan bent over and gripped the exposed end of the central floorboard, tugging at it again and again until he dislodged the nails out of the joists underneath. He tilted it up and dropped it to one side with a clatter.

Declan was used to finding builder's rubble underneath the floorboards of these old houses, as well as the skeletons of rats and mice. Once he had discovered a black tin box containing thirty-five pounds in Saorstát, the banknotes issued by the Irish Free State, a tarnished harmonica, and a Valentine's card for 'my own dearest Muirgheal'.

In this house, however, it looked as if several bundles of old clothing had been stuffed between the joists – a man's suit, a woman's maroon dress, a girl's yellow pinafore, and a baby's pink nightgown. They were all faded until they were almost colourless and covered thickly in fine grey dust, so it was anybody's guess how long they had been hidden there.

Declan pulled up another floorboard, and then another, the nails screeching in protest, and he was just about to start pulling up a third when he saw that a hand was protruding from the cuff of the man's green coat.

He stared at it for a long time, feeling as if his scalp was shrinking. The hand looked papery and dry, and it was almost completely flat, but he could tell that it was a real human hand all right. Some of the knuckle bones had broken through the desiccated skin and it still had all of its fingernails, even though they had turned amber with age.

He knelt down to examine it more closely, but he didn't have the nerve to touch it. Instead, he reached out and gently squeezed the sleeve from which it was protruding. There was no question about it: there were two stick-like arm bones inside it.

'Lord lantern of Jesus,' he whispered.

He was breathing hard through his nostrils now and his heart was thumping. He let go of the sleeve and cautiously patted the back of the coat, as if he were frisking it. Underneath the fabric he could feel the hard curved bones of a ribcage.

He sat back on his heels. *Holy Mary, Mother of God, if there's a mummified feller inside of this coat, what's inside of the woman's dress? And the children's clothes, too?*

Still kneeling, he shuffled himself sideways to the space between the next two joists where the woman's maroon dress was lying crumpled up, with buttons all down the back. He hesitated for a moment, because it didn't seem right to be touching a woman without her consent, even if she was long dead. Then he reached out and gently pressed against the bodice. Beneath the coarse dyed linen he could again feel ribs, although these ribs were looser, as if they had become detached from the spine.

These weren't bundles of old clothes at all, these were bodies. Years and years ago somebody must have laid them face-down beneath the floor and then nailed the boards down over them. Declan still hadn't pulled up enough boards to be able to see their shoulders or their heads, but it looked to him as if a small family had been hidden there – father, mother, daughter and baby.

He stood up, wiping his hands on his black denim jacket. As he did so, Colm came back from outside, relighting his cigarette.

'Jesus, it's lashing,' he said, his head half hidden in smoke. Then he glanced down at the gap in the floorboards and frowned. 'What the feck's all them old clothes doing down there?'

'They're not just old clothes, boy, they're bodies,' said Declan. 'Man and a woman and their two wains, too, by the looks of it.'

'You're codding,' said Colm, but Declan pointed to the man's dried-out hand. Colm leaned forward and squinted at it short-sightedly, and then he said, 'Feck.'

'I'd say they was probably murdered,' said Declan.

Colm stepped over the gap and crouched down to see if he could make out what the bodies' heads looked like. 'You don't know that for certain,' he said. 'They could have died of the flu or something. People used to die like flies in them days, of all sorts. My old man's youngest sister died of the chickenpox when she was only three years old.'

He stood up straight again and nodded at the bodies. 'Maybe their relatives couldn't afford a funeral.'

'Oh go 'way. Even if you can't afford a funeral you don't bury your nearest and dearest face-downwards underneath the fecking floorboards.'

'I don't know. My Uncle Patrick was buried lying on his left side. That was the way he specified it in his will. Serious. He said that when my Auntie Saoirse was buried next to him he wanted to be looking at her.'

'What, he had X-ray vision did he?' asked Declan. 'He could see through coffins?'

'Don't be soft – he was dead, wasn't he?' said Colm. 'He was just being romantic, do you know what I mean, like?'

'Romantic? Stone-hatchet mad, more like. Anyway, give me a hand to take up the rest of these floorboards.'

Between them, Declan and Colm lifted up all of the floorboards in the living room and carried them outside to the skip. When they had finished they stood and looked in silence at the four bodies lying between the joists. It had stopped raining outside and a silvery sun had appeared behind the clouds, so that the living room was filled with colourless light like an over-exposed photograph.

The man was lying furthest away from the window, with his left arm by his side. His right arm was crooked up, with his forehead resting on it. His hair was thick with dust but it was still brown and curly. The woman had long black hair, very straight, fastened with a simple brown horn slide. The little girl had brown curly hair, too, tied with ribbons into bunches. The baby had a single dark tuft, like a leprechaun.

'Ah, the pity of it,' said Declan.

With a succession of hideous screeches, they prised up the last two floorboards. Underneath they discovered that the space between the joists was crammed with a tangle of thick grey hairs, which at first looked as if it could have been a coat or a shaggy blanket of some kind. Colm took his shovel and prodded at it, and then tried to pick it up. As he lifted it up, however, the blanket tore softly apart and one half of it dropped with a dull thump back into the floor space. Colm immediately dropped the other half, too, because now they could see that what they had uncovered was not a coat or a blanket but the dried-up bodies of two young Glen terriers.

'The family pets, I'll bet you,' said Declan. 'Whoever did this, Jesus, they didn't leave nothing alive, did they? Surprised there's no fecking goldfish down here.'

Because the adults' hair was so thick and so dusty it was not immediately obvious what had happened to them, but Declan and Colm could tell from the baby and the little girl how this family had died. They had all been shot once in the back of the head, including the puppies.

Declan crossed himself. 'You'd best ring the guards,' he told Colm.

Colm nodded and took his mobile phone out of his shirt pocket. Both of them had been deeply sobered by what they had discovered.

6

They could have been sleeping, this dust-covered family, like characters in a fairy tale. Declan was surprised that he wasn't frightened or horrified by them, only saddened. He almost felt as if he had known them, despite the probability that they had been nailed down under the floorboards long before he was born. They didn't smell – not as far as he could tell, anyway – although Christy must have picked up the scent of human decay, even if it was decades old, and that was why he had refused to come inside. Either that, or he was psychic and Colm had been right about a ghost. Or *ghosts*, plural.

Colm had got through to 112. 'That's right,' he was saying. 'Millstream Row, Blarney. You have it, just past the factory. You'll find it easy, there's one of O'Brien's green midi skips directly outside. No, we won't touch nothing. No. Well, if they are, they must be about a hundred and ten years old by now, so I don't reckon they will be. No. Thanks a million.'

Once he had finished his call they went outside. Colm took out his pack of Johnnie Blues and handed one to Declan. They lit up and stood beside the skip, smoking.

'Did the guards tell you how long they'd be?' asked Declan.

'Fifteen minutes at least. The Garda station on The Square isn't manned at the moment.'

'What was that you was saying to them about somebody being a hundred and ten years old?'

'The feller on the switchboard asked me if there was any chance that the person who hid the bodies could still be lurking around, like. You know, in case you and me was in any kind of danger because we'd discovered what he'd done.'

'Holy St Joseph, and they say that criminals are thick.'

'No, fair play to him, I hadn't told him how old the bodies were, like. Well, we don't *know* how old they are, do we? All I told him was, we'd found some people who looked like they'd been shot.'

'Then you're three times thicker than he was. These people must have been shot practically before guns were invented.'

Normally, the two of them would have carried on bantering, but now they lapsed into silence, smoking and stamping their feet to keep warm. Although he was shivering, Christy stayed by the open front door, still looking inside with his head tilted inquisitively, almost as if he was expecting to hear somebody calling out to him.

After a few minutes, a white Garda patrol car came speeding round the curve in front of the woollen mills, its blue lights flashing. It was followed closely by a second patrol car, and then an unmarked blue Focus. There was a chorus of slamming doors.

'You realize we'll be in all the papers,' said Declan, as the uniformed gardaí came towards them.

'So long as they don't print my fecking address,' Colm told him. 'I don't want that Big-Arsed Blathnaid coming after me for child support.'

Detectives Aislin O'Connell and Gerry Barry had been sitting at their stall in Mother Jones Flea Market since it had opened and so far they had made 67 euros from selling two mismatched table lamps, three party dresses and a pink lace-up corset, as well as a stack of old copies of *Ireland's Own*.

It was 3.15 in the afternoon now, but there was still no sign of Denny Quinn, the young suspect they were waiting for. Detective O'Connell had found the time to paint her nails turquoise and Detective Barry had stepped outside five times on to York Street for a smoke, and they were both beginning to think that their informant had either been mistaken or else had been stringing them along. They had been given false tip-offs with increasing frequency lately, almost as if somebody was deliberately trying to waste their time.

A Garda patrol car with two uniformed officers was parked further up the steep slope of York Street, just out of sight in the cul-de-sac of Little William Street, and Detective Barry had been keeping in touch with them via an earpiece and r/t microphone. They had started by regularly keeping in contact with each other, but as the day wore on almost all he heard from them was yawning and complaining that they were busting for a piss.

Detective Barry checked his watch and said, 'I feel like a right gom sitting here. I'll bet money your man never shows.'

He looked almost too young to be a detective, with an upswept quiff of blondish hair like Tintin and a button of a nose. Not that Detective O'Connell looked much older – she was dark-haired, petite but plump, with a pretty, heart-shaped face and lips that could have been the bright red satin bow on a birthday present.

But their appearance was the reason why Detective Superintendent Maguire had picked them for this stake-out. They were supposed to look like typical stallholders at Mother Jones indoor market – youthful and slightly hippy-ish – so that they could watch their target without arousing suspicion that they were gardaí and then approach without him feeling immediately threatened. That was, if he ever put in an appearance.

Detective O'Connell spread out her fingers to admire her nails. 'Maybe the shipment never arrived,' she suggested. 'Or maybe somebody else stroked them.'

'Sure, well, that's always a possibility,' said Detective Barry. 'I know we told the customs to turn a blind eye, but if Billy Duffy knew the fags were coming, and *when*, don't tell me that a whole crowd of other skangers didn't know as well. Maybe Óglaigh na hÉireann got their hands on them before Quilty could pick them up. Or maybe they straight out robbed him.'

'Go away, they'd have to be mental to do that,' said Detective O'Connell. 'Cross Bobby Quilty, Jesus! You might as well say, "Excuse me, boy, would you mind putting a bullet between me eyes?"'

'I don't know. That Brendan Ó Marcaigh, I don't think he's freaked by nothing or nobody. A pit bull went after him once and he got hold of its tail and bashed its brains out on a lamp post.'

'Charming.'

They waited another half-hour. The Flea Market began to fill up with even more customers, wandering in between its yellow-, pink-, green- and blue-painted iron pillars and browsing around the stalls. Detective Barry raised one eyebrow at Detective O'Connell, but he didn't have to say anything because it was clear to both of them that although these new customers were picking up vases and dolls and old Wolfe Tones LPs and making a show of examining them, none of them was actually making a purchase.

Just a few seconds after 4 o'clock a voice in Detective Barry's earpiece said, 'Quinn's arrived. He's just been dropped off outside.'

A few seconds later Denny Quinn entered the Flea Market from the street, carrying two black vinyl rubbish bags, both of them bulging. He was skinny as a rail and pasty-faced, with a spattering of scarlet acne spots across his forehead. Since his last police photograph was taken his gingery hair had been shaved up the sides to give him a cockatoo crest, and he was sporting gold stud earrings in both of his ears as well as several gold chains and a heavy gold identity bracelet. He was wearing a red Cork GAA T-shirt, sagging grey tracksuit bottoms, and white Nike tackies.

'Enter the schwaa,' said Detective Barry.

'At last,' said Detective O'Connell. 'Billy Duffy might have told us what time he was coming. He must have *known*, like. All of these people here do. Eejit.'

'Oh, come on, Billy Duffy can't think and speak simultaneous, you know that.'

Without hesitation, Denny weaved his way between the pillars to the back of the market where there was a vacant alcove with a plywood table and chair. He dropped his black bags on the floor, pushed them under the table with his foot, and then sat down, wiping his nose with the back of his hand.

Almost at once, the six or seven browsing customers began to gravitate towards him. They were all different types: a middle-aged woman with jet-black dyed hair and a tight green satin top; a thirtyish man with a brown beard wearing a grey Marks & Spencer's business suit; an older man with fraying white hair and thick-rimmed glasses and a purple nose; and a girl who couldn't have been much more than school age, with long brunette hair, black eye make-up and tight black leggings. There was also a woman still wearing her blue Dunne's Stores overall, and a thick-set man with a paint-spotted denim jacket and no front teeth who looked like a Polish builder.

The middle-aged woman said something to Denny and then took out her purse and handed him fifty euros in folded notes. He leaned back to stuff the money into his tracksuit pocket before he reached into one of the black bags and lifted out two yellow bricks of two hundred cigarettes. As he passed the cartons across the table, Detective O'Connell had her iPhone held up high in front of her, frowning and prodding at it as if she were texting, although she was actually recording the transaction on video.

The girl with the black eye make-up paid Denny twenty-five euros – one crumpled ten-euro note and the rest in assorted loose change. He gave her one yellow carton which she pushed into a duffel bag and hurried out of the Flea Market with it slung over her shoulder.

Detective Barry leaned close to Detective O'Connell. 'One more sale should do it,' he said, speaking very quietly and looking in the opposite direction as he did so, so that Denny wouldn't guess he was talking about him. 'He might be able to tell the court that one sale was a favour. He might even be able to explain away two. But three – that's a pattern.'

Detective O'Connell said nothing but continued to video the young man as the thirtyish man with the brown beard gave him what looked like at least 200 euros in twenty-euro notes.

'I'm sure I reck that feller,' said Detective Barry. 'I think he works for that estate agents on Marlborough Street, what are they called, Callaghan Screws or something like that? He looks like an estate agent, any road.'

The young man took out four yellow cartons and set them on the table. Detective O'Connell started to stand up, but Detective Barry said, 'Stall it a second, Aislin. Wait till your man actually lays his hand on one.'

The thirtyish man with the brown beard pulled a folded Tesco shopping bag out of his coat pocket and opened it up. As soon as he picked up the first yellow carton, Detective Barry said, 'Right, that's it. Let's go. But real easy, like.' Into his r/t microphone, he said, 'We're hauling him in now, okay?'

The two of them stood up and ambled slowly towards the alcove at the back of the Flea Market, pretending as they went that they were having a conversation. Denny took no notice of them at all as they approached. He had half-turned away from them to serve the elderly man with the wild white hair and thick-rimmed glasses.

Detective Barry reached under his jacket at the back and felt for the handcuffs that were fastened to his belt. 'Okay, then, just as we rehearsed it,' he told Detective O'Connell, nodding his head and smiling as if he were talking about a joke that somebody had told him last night. 'I'll grab him and put the cuffs on him, and you can caution him while we're heading for the door. We need to get him out of here so quick that nobody decks what's happened until we're off and away.'

Detective O'Connell smiled and said, 'I have you, Gerry, don't you worry.'

They had almost reached the alcove now, where Denny was rummaging in one of his black bags for more cartons. The thirtyish estate agent with the brown beard had stepped away and was struggling to push the last of his four cartons into his shopping bag. When he had managed it, however, he looked up and saw Detective Barry, and his face lit up with recognition.

'Well, the dead arose!' He grinned, showing his teeth. 'What are *you* doing here, Detective Barry? Looking for stolen property, is it?'

Instantly, Denny turned around. He saw Detectives Barry and O'Connell making their way between the jumble stalls towards him and he jumped up as if he had been sitting on a powerful spring.

'Tell me, detective, did you ever nick that feller who was robbing those house deposits?' asked the estate agent blithely, still grinning. Detective Barry ignored him and made a dash towards Denny, but Denny pushed the estate agent in the chest so that he stumbled sideways into a display of books and records and second-hand handbags.

'Hey, what the feck?' he exclaimed, but as he regained his balance Detective Barry pushed him, too, to get him out of the way, and this time he fell over backwards on to the floor, knocking a vase and a six-piece tea set off a shelf in a shower of shattered china and purple potpourri.

Denny feinted and weaved between the pillars, trying to obstruct Detective Barry by tipping over antique chairs behind him and kicking over cardboard boxes so that religious figurines and ashtrays and other bric-a-brac scattered all across the floor. There were shouts of '*Hoi!* What do you think you're doing there?' from the stallholders, but none of them seemed to understand what was happening and none of them made any attempt to stop him.

Instead of chasing after Denny, Detective O'Connell made her way directly back to the street door so that she could cut him off. As he neared the entrance, Denny pushed over a coat stand that was heavily laden with second-hand overcoats and hats, which fell across the floor in front of Detective Barry, but then he turned around to find Detective O'Connell standing between him and the street outside, her arms outstretched like a goalkeeper.

By now Detective Barry was climbing over the heap of fallen overcoats. 'Stall the ball right there, boy!' he ordered him, 'You're lifted!'

The young man stopped, both hands raised, although he kept his head down and his back to Detective Barry.

'Turn around,' Detective Barry told him. 'Hold out both of your hands.'

'What for, like?' said the young man. 'I ain't done nothing. Selling a few fags to some friends, that's all.'

'I said turn around and hold out both of your hands.'

Denny started to turn around, but as Detective Barry approached him with his handcuffs raised, he swung back to face Detective O'Connell. With no hesitation at all, he seized her hair with his left hand and swept his right hand diagonally across her face. Detective O'Connell didn't realize what had happened to her at first, but then bright red blood spurted out of her cheek, all the way from the side of her left eye to her chin. She gasped and lifted up her hand, and blood flooded down her wrist and soaked the sleeve of her pale blue blouse. She staggered back and then dropped to her knees.

Detective Barry tried to snatch Denny's arm, but he twisted it away and was bounding through the open door and out on to York Street before Detective Barry could catch him.

Detective Barry crouched down beside Detective O'Connell

and put his arm around her shoulders. She was pressing her hand against her cheek and blood was dripping between her fingers, but she managed to wave her other hand and blurt out, 'Go after him, Gerry, for Christ's sake!'

Two women were hurrying over from the Flea Market cafe to help, so Detective Barry left her where she was and ran outside. He looked left, up York Street, but there was no sign of Denny running up towards Wellington Road, and in any case the hill was so steep that he wouldn't have been able to make it all the way to the top. He must have turned right and run off along MacCurtain Street instead.

Detective Barry went to the corner and again he looked right and left. Between the pedestrians on MacCurtain Street he caught a glimpse of Denny's red GAA T-shirt as he sprinted flat-out past Dan Lowery's Tavern, in the direction of Brian Boru Street. That would lead him to the Brian Boru Bridge across the River Lee, and if he managed to reach the city centre before Detective Barry could catch him he could easily mingle with the Friday afternoon shoppers and get away. Detective Barry started after him, calling up the two gardaí who were waiting in Little William Street as he did so.

'Quinn assaulted Detective O'Connell and gave us the slip,' he told them. 'He's done a legger down MacCurtain Street, heading east.'

He had run only a few more paces before he heard the whooping sound of the patrol car's siren start up. *Got you now, Denny,* he thought. By the time he had reached the blue-painted LeisurePlex building on the corner with Brian Boru Street, however, the siren didn't seem to be coming any closer. He turned his head to see that a mustard-coloured Volvo had turned the corner into York Street and stopped. Since York Street was only one-way, uphill, it was obviously preventing the patrol car from coming down the hill and turning into MacCurtain Street.

He looked ahead and saw that Denny was already crossing the road at St Patrick's Quay towards the Brian Boru Bridge.

'What's the hold-up?' he asked over his radio. 'Denny's crossing the river already. I don't want to lose him in the bus station or the shopping centre.'

'Some gowl's blocking the street and he won't fecking budge. Mulliken's got out to tell him to shift but it looks like he's arguing the toss about it.'

'Jesus. Arrest him. Or push him out of the way. And check if there's any uniforms on Pana who can give me some backup. Come on, *urgent*, like! You saw Denny yourself. Rebel County T-shirt. Grey tracksuit bottoms. Hair sticking up like a fecking red rooster.'

Although the traffic was so busy, and the pedestrian light was red, Detective Barry stepped off the kerb and zig-zagged his way across St Patrick's Quay. A bus and two cars honked their horns at him and one of the drivers shouted out, 'Looking to get yourself killed, you nickey?'

Denny was almost halfway across the bridge now, but he had slowed down so that he was half jogging and half walking and he was clearly out of breath. Detective Barry was in better shape now than he had ever been: he still played Gaelic football for St Finbarr's whenever he could and he regularly worked out at the RB Fitness Centre. Even if the patrol car didn't turn up for another three or four minutes, he reckoned he still had a good chance of catching up with Denny before he reached the bus station and Merchants Quay shopping centre – and holding him, too. *And smashing him on the gonk for cutting Aislin.* He could always plead reasonable force while the suspect was resisting arrest.

Denny had reached the far side of the bridge, but there was so much traffic on Merchants Quay that he was teetering on his Nikes on the edge of the kerb, unable to cross. Detective Barry had to dodge his way past two women with baby buggies and a hugely obese man in a mobility scooter festooned with shopping bags, but he was sure that he had Denny now. Because he had his eyes fixed ahead, though, he hadn't become aware of the silver-grey Land Rover that was burbling slowly across the bridge, keeping pace with him, so that it was holding up all the cars behind it.

For most of the bridge's 200-foot width, cars and pedestrians were separated from each other by steel railings and by the massive cast-iron structure of the bridge itself, which originally used to lift up to allow boats to pass through. The steel railings, however, didn't reach all the way across. As Detective Barry neared the far side, where they came to an end, the Land Rover's engine suddenly roared. With a loud bang from its front suspension, it mounted the pavement, swerved sideways and collided with him, crushing him against the bridge's balustrade.

Detective Barry felt as if a bomb had exploded right behind him and that he had been blown apart. The Land Rover had smashed his legs and snapped his pelvis in half. Even at only 5 mph it had rammed him against the balustrade so hard that his stomach had burst open and his intestines were sliding out between the blue-and-white cast-iron uprights and dangling in loops over the river.

He was so stunned that he felt almost nothing, but as the Land Rover backed away from him and jolted back on to the road he grimly gripped the top of the balustrade to keep himself upright. *I mustn't fall over*, he thought. *If I fall over, I'll die for sure.* He could see the river and the buildings alongside it, and St Patrick's Bridge, and the blue summer sky, and the clouds. He heard the sound of traffic and a woman screaming. *What do I do now?* he thought. But then he heard somebody talking to him and when he managed to turn his head he saw that standing beside him there was a grey-haired man with a reddish face. He smelled strongly of stale Murphy's.

'You just take it easy, boy,' the man was saying, although his voice sounded very muffled. 'You're going to be grand altogether, so long as you don't move. Somebody's called for a white van, okay? Don't move, though.'

Unexpectedly, the sky began to darken. 'Is it night?' whispered Detective Barry. 'I'm killed out, like. I think I need to lie down.'

The reddish-faced man gripped him under his left armpit to help him stay on his feet. 'You're going to be grand altogether so long as you don't move. You're all intertwangled with the railings, like, do you know what I mean? If you move at all you'll just pull yourself apart.'

Detective Barry closed his eyes. He didn't know if he was dead or simply sleeping, but he could still hear voices and traffic so he assumed that he couldn't be dead.

Most of the voices sounded very distant, but then he heard somebody speaking so close to his ear that he could feel their breath.

'My son, my name is Father O'Flynn, from the Holy Trinity Church.'

'Don't let him get away, father,' said Detective Barry, and as he did so blood slid out of both sides of his mouth.

He felt slippery fingertips touching his forehead. He heard Father O'Flynn saying, 'With this anointing, may the Lord in His love and mercy help you with the grace of the Holy Spirit. May the Lord who frees you from sin save you and raise you up.'

He heard sirens. Fantastic. His backup had caught up with him at last.

'Don't let him get away,' he repeated. 'He'll have made it across the road by now. Denny Quinn. Rebel County T-shirt. Don't let him get away.'

Three

Katie was gathering up the papers she needed for her meeting with the County Council Joint Policing Committee when Detective O'Donovan knocked quickly at her half-open door and came straight in. He looked flushed and sweaty and his pink stomach was bulging out of his shirt.

'Garda Brophy just called in,' he told her. 'Gerry Barry's been hit by a car on the Brian Boru Bridge.'

'Oh God,' said Katie, immediately dropping the folder back on to her desk. 'Is it serious?'

'Brophy's still at the scene,' said Detective O'Donovan. 'He says a hit-and-run driver mounted the pavement and smashed him into the railings at the side of the bridge. The paramedics are working on him now but it's not looking hopeful.'

'Right, let's get there now,' said Katie. She crossed her office and took down her pale green linen jacket. 'What about Aislin? Was she hurt at all?'

'She wasn't with him, so far as I know. It seems like Denny Quinn was making a run for it and Gerry was in pursuit of him on foot.'

'Why was he chasing him on foot? We had a car there, backing him up, didn't we?'

'I'm not sure exactly why, like. Brophy said something about them being boxed in, but I don't know the details.'

'What about the vehicle that hit him?'

'A Land Rover. He has a description, although nobody got its number.'

Katie walked briskly along the corridor just as Chief Superintendent Denis MacCostagáin was coming out of his office in his shirtsleeves and braces, looking, as usual, like somebody's miserable uncle.

'Ah, Kathleen, you're on the way to Merchants Quay, then. Michael Pearse has sent out backup already and called Bill Phinner for a technical team. Terrible thing to happen. Terrible. Let's pray to God that young Barry survives.'

'I'll keep you in touch,' said Katie.

Detective O'Donovan had already pressed the button for the lift and was holding the door open. They went down to the ground floor in silence and out to the car park. The morning's heavy showers had passed over and although the streets were still shiny and wet the afternoon was cloudless, with a warm breeze blowing from the south-west. Katie could hear two small children laughing as they ran down the street.

As they sped up Eglinton Street, Katie said, 'A hundred to one it was one of Quilty's thugs. If not Quilty himself. I've said right from the beginning that the only way we're ever going to stop him is if we nail him in person.'

'Sure, I agree with you totally,' said Detective O'Donovan. 'The only trouble with that, like, is getting a conviction. None of his dealers is going to give evidence against him, are they? It's a choice between getting your kneecaps shot off and making six hundred yoyos a week, and I know which of those I'd be going for.'

Clontarf Street, which led to the Brian Boru Bridge, was one-way in the opposite direction, but it had been closed to traffic and Katie and Detective O'Donovan reached Merchants Quay in just three minutes. Five Garda patrol cars were parked at different angles, as well as an ambulance and a Ford Ranger rapid response vehicle from the fire brigade. The pavements were crowded with onlookers and further along the quay, by the bus station, Katie could see an RTÉ television van arriving.

She crossed the road. Detective Barry was lying on a stretcher, with two paramedics kneeling beside him. His face was covered by an oxygen mask and one of the paramedics was holding up an IV drip. Three gardaí and a fire officer were gripping a blue plastic screen between them to shield him from the wind and from public view. The screen made a monotonous flapping sound, but apart from that there was almost complete silence.

'Detective Superintendent Maguire,' said Katie, as one of the paramedics stood up. He was a middle-aged man with flat triangular bags under his eyes, as if his skin were tissue paper, and very pale green irises. 'What are his chances?'

'Somewhere between zero and nil, I'd say,' said the paramedic. 'He's suffered massive crushing injuries to both his legs and pelvis, and his abdomen was split open by the impact. We've done everything we can to replace his intestines and hold him together, but I can't see him surviving this. I'm amazed he's still with us, to be honest with you. The father over there gave him the last rites, so that side of it's been taken care of.'

'He's not conscious at all? If I speak to him, will he hear me?'

The paramedic shook his head. 'We gave him fifteen milligrams of morphine while the firemen were cutting him free from the railings. It'll wear off, of course, and he'll be able to speak to you when it does, but he'll most likely be dead by then.'

Katie looked over towards the blue-and-white balustrade. Three of the uprights had been cut through at stomach height and there was rusty-coloured blood on the surrounding bars. Two firemen were packing away the Holmatro hydraulic cutters which they usually used for extricating dead and injured victims from car crashes.

'We'll be taking him to CUH now,' said the paramedic. 'We've already alerted them that we're bringing him in, and what kind of state he's in, so there'll be surgeons there waiting for him. You never know. We've taken people in before who were knocking on heaven's door and they've come out a couple of weeks later as fit as a butcher's dog.'

Katie bent over Detective Barry. His blonde hair was sticky with blood, but even under the oxygen mask he looked as if he had a smile on his face. She knew that a strong dose of morphine often gives people pleasant dreams, even when they're dying.

'God bless you, Gerry,' she said quietly, and crossed herself.

The paramedics lifted up the stretcher and carried Detective Barry to the ambulance. As they did so, Garda Brophy came over to Katie. He was broad-shouldered and bulky in his yellow hi-viz jacket, with a Neanderthal forehead and an S-shaped nose like a boxer. All the same, he looked grey and strained, and Katie thought he could be very close to tears.

'Quilty's wide to what we're doing, ma'am, no doubt about it,' he told her. 'He definitely has his people hovering around to keep an eye on his dealers. Denny Quinn made a run for it, but as soon as me and Mulliken went after him a car turned into the bottom of York Street and boxed us in.'

'How did Quinn get away? Was somebody keeping sketch for him?'

'It's possible, of course, but Detective O'Connell said that one of the customers in the Flea Market recognized Detective Barry just as they were about to put the cuffs on Quinn and blew the whole thing. She tried to stop Quinn but he slashed her face with a blade of some kind and took flight. That's about all she could manage to tell us. Mulliken's taken her to the Mercy.'

'What about the car that boxed you in?'

'It was a Volvo. We have all its details and Mulliken took the driver's name and address. He may have been working for Quilty or maybe he was just being bold.'

'All right, Brophy, thanks,' said Katie. A white Technical Bureau van was approaching over the bridge, followed by an unmarked green Toyota. Bill Phinner, the chief technical officer, climbed out of the Toyota and came across to join them. He was thin and hollow-cheeked and sharp-nosed, and he always reminded Katie of Dr Van Helsing in Dracula, as if he knew all of the science necessary to catch vampires but found it a constant irritation.

'How's Detective Barry?' he asked, his attention fixed on the gap the firemen had cut in the railings.

'Bad,' said Katie. 'I don't think he's going to live.'

Bill Phinner looked down. The Land Rover's black tyre tracks were clearly visible where it had swerved off the road and mounted the kerb.

'How old is he?'

'Just had his twenty-fifth birthday. One of my brightest.'

'It's always the brightest, isn't it?'

Three technicians in white Tyvek suits were waddling across the road now, carrying cameras and metal cases of sampling equipment.

Katie said, 'There's some bits of orange plastic over there. They may have come from the vehicle that hit him.'

'Well, we'll collect them anyway. If it actually hit the railings, it could well have left some paint on them, too. What type of vehicle was it? Do you know?'

'A Land Rover. Garda Brophy has a full eyewitness description. They didn't get its number, though.'

'Pity. Do you know how many Land Rovers are registered in Ireland? Six thousand three hundred and ninety. And that's if they haven't sold any more since April.'

Detective O'Donovan came over to join them. He had been interviewing eyewitnesses and talking to the firefighter who had been in charge of cutting Detective Barry free.

'No question that it was deliberate, like, do you know what I mean? Five different witnesses say that the Land Rover was driving dead slow across the bridge like it was following him. Then it sped up and went straight for him. The firefighters reckon there was no attempt to brake. Three witnesses said the Land Rover was a silver-grey colour, two said it was goldy. One said there was only two fellers in it, the others were sure there was a third feller sitting in the back.'

'Well, that's a remarkable consensus of opinion, considering,' said Bill Phinner. 'Usually they swear it was a red, green, blue and white Nissan Ford Opel saloon estate car driven by three black Chinese fellers with freckles and red brown hair.'

'They meant to kill him, though,' said Katie. 'That's what worries me. It's only cigarette smuggling, but this takes it to a totally different level altogether.'

Four

Detective Barry had already been taken into the operating theatre when Katie arrived at Cork University Hospital. She had sent Detective Pádraigin Scanlan to the Mercy to talk to Detective O'Connell about exactly what had happened, in case she had noticed some critical details but had forgotten them in her shock at having her face slashed. At the same time, she had sent Detective Sergeant Begley and Detective Dooley to Mother Jones Flea Market to interview any witnesses they could find there, and to confiscate whatever remained of Denny Quinn's bags of contraband cigarettes.

Detective O'Donovan had returned to Anglesea Street to see if the hit-and-run had been caught on CCTV and to help in organizing the search for the Land Rover and for Denny Quinn. Katie had also told him to check on Bobby Quilty's whereabouts at the time, but to be careful not to alert him that he might be under suspicion. Although Detective Barry had been deliberately knocked down while pursuing one of Quilty's dealers, she had no evidence yet that Quilty was responsible, either directly or indirectly, and she didn't want to make him any more wary than he already was.

Katie was prepared to wait at the hospital for as long as it took the surgeons to save Detective Barry's life. He was special to her – one of a crop of five young detectives that she had been working hard to recruit. Some of the older officers called them 'Katie's Kids' and mocked them for their lack of street experience. But they were not only energetic and open-minded, they were highly computer-literate and they had already solved several serious cases of hacking and online fraud, including a complex attempt to divert over two million euros from Permanent TSB.

Katie sat down on a beige-coloured couch in the waiting room, opposite a woman with dyed gingery hair who was continually letting out mewling noises like a cat that wanted to be let in from the garden, and blowing her nose on an increasingly diminishing ball of tissue.

'How are you doing?' Katie asked her. 'Here, look, I have some fresh Kleenex.'

The woman gratefully took the small packet of tissues that Katie offered her. 'It's my daughter, Sháuna,' she said with a sniff. 'She took an overdose this morning and they're doing everything they can to save her. I'm just waiting on news.'

'That's tragic,' said Katie. 'Was she very depressed?'

'She was bullied, that's what it was, and I never even knew the half of it. She was being bullied at school because she's taller than all the rest of the girls, and she was being trollied on the interweb, too, or whatever you call it. She'd been cutting herself and everything, like, and how she managed to hide it from me I just don't understand. I mean, what kind of a mother doesn't know when her own daughter's cutting her arms and thinking of killing herself?'

'Come on, it wasn't your fault,' Katie told her. 'I'm a Garda officer and I've seen this happen again and again. Girls of that age often feel they're worthless and ugly, especially when their so-called friends start to pick on them.'

The woman shook her head and said, 'Holy Mary, Mother of God, if she dies, what will I do then? Her father passed on only two years ago and Sháuna was his bar-of-gold. If she arrives in heaven and she's only fifteen, what's he going to think of me?'

'What's your name, sweetheart?' Katie asked her.

'Brenda. Brenda Molony.'

'Well, give me your address, Brenda, and when Sháuna's recovered I'll send a detective around to call on you and check her computer. We'll be able to identify those bullies and stop them.'

'That's if Sháuna recovers. They said she swallowed a whole bottle of the paracetamol.'

Katie said, 'She'll recover, Brenda. I'll say a prayer to St Benedict for her.'

Brenda's eyes overflowed with tears. 'Ah, you're a good woman, thank you. Here – take your tissues back.'

Katie smiled and shook her head. 'Keep them. I think you need them more than I do.'

Just then, a nurse came into the waiting room and said, softly, 'Mrs Molony? Your daughter's conscious now. Would you like to come up and see her?'

'Good luck,' said Katie, as Brenda followed the nurse out of the room. She couldn't speak, but gave her a complicated wave which expressed her thanks and her despair and her trepidation more than any words could have done. Katie knew exactly how she felt.

She opened her laptop and started to go through the figures she had been intending to present to the County Council Policing Committee. She was concentrating so intently that she didn't notice the young woman with cropped blonde hair who came into the waiting room and sat down very close to her. It was only when she smelled her perfume that she looked up from her computer screen. There was only one person she knew who wore Miracle by Lancôme.

'*Kyna.*' She smiled and put aside her laptop. 'What are you doing here?'

Detective Sergeant Ni Nuallán had lost nearly twelve kilos after she had been shot five months ago, and her face was still gaunt. She had sooty smudges under her eyes and her cheekbones were sharper, but that made her look even more elfin than before. Katie thought she could have been one of the *Aes Sidhe*, the Fairy Folk.

'I've just been for a scan and a check-up with Doctor Kashani,' she said. 'The nurse told me you were here. She said that a detective was seriously hurt, but she didn't know who.'

'Gerry Barry. He was hit by a Land Rover on the Brian Boru Bridge. Crushed against the railings.'

'Mother of God. Was it deliberate?'

'We're almost sure of it. I'm praying that he's going to make it, but the doctors are not holding out a lot of hope. His family's on their way here from Tip.'

'Any notion who did it?'

'I can't say for sure, but it wouldn't surprise me if Bobby Quilty had something to do with it.'

'Quilty. That scummer. He'd run over his own mother if he thought she had a couple of euros in her purse.'

Katie took hold of Kyna's hands. Her wrists were as thin as kindling sticks, so that her large watch and her hospital identity tag were hanging loose. 'So are you okay?' Katie asked her. 'I'm so sorry I couldn't meet you last week. I was up the walls with all those Irish Water lorries getting burned and that Cronin case. It seemed like everybody was setting fire to anything that annoyed them.'

'Oh, I'm grand altogether. Doctor Kashani was worried because my blood sugar was low and I was having difficulty breathing, but he says my stomach's almost completely healed up now and I don't have to worry.'

'You haven't changed your mind, though?' Katie asked her.

'About coming back? No. I've thought about it, like you asked me to, but it wasn't just my body that got shot, Katie.' She tapped her forehead and said, 'It's gone. All my confidence. I'm even scared when I go out for the messages. I was waiting at the checkout in Dunne's the other day and I saw this feen staring at me real narrow-eyed, do you know what I mean, like? I couldn't help thinking, oh Jesus, what if he's a member of a crime gang and recognizes me and shoots me?'

'I could arrange for counselling for you, Kyna. I'm sure you can get over it, in time.'

Kyna shrugged and smiled. 'There's too many other complications, Katie. Losing my confidence is only part of it. There's my feelings for you, too. I'm better off looking for something else to do with my life. I can sing, too, did you know that?'

'No, I didn't. Serious?'

'Oh, yes. I used to sing at The Foggy Dew in Temple Bar. They were always telling me I ought to go professional. I'll sing for you one day. "One Morning in Autumn", just for you.'

'I think you know how much I'll miss you if you *do* decide to quit for good,' said Katie. 'Apart from anything else, I've never known anybody get confessions out of offenders the way you do. They're always so busy fancying you that they'll tell you they robbed a bank just to impress you, even if they didn't.'

She paused, and then she said, 'Will you go back to Dublin?'

Kyna nodded. Katie could understand how she was feeling. She looked haunted. If she was ever going to recover fully, both physically and psychologically, she needed the comfort of her family around her and to forget the grey pavements of Cork City for a while, and the grey waters of the River Lee, and guns, and men who were only too ready to use them.

Kyna lowered her head. Katie, still holding her hands, leaned forward and kissed her parting.

It was then that a surgeon came into the waiting room, still wearing his theatre cap and gown and surgical clogs. He pulled off his cap and approached them with a grave look on his face. His eyes were bulging and sad, like a Boston terrier, and Katie wondered if he had been born with eyes like that or if they had become like that because of all the tragedy he had witnessed. He was dark-skinned and unshaven.

'Detective Superintendent Maguire?' he said, and then he had to stop to clear his throat. Katie started to stand up, but then sat down again. She knew it was bad news and she hadn't eaten all day and didn't want to feel faint.

The surgeon sat down next to her. 'I am Dr Walid. My team and I did everything we possibly could to try and save the life of Detective Barry. Regrettably he died five minutes ago. The trauma he had suffered was too great for him to survive.'

'I see,' said Katie.

There was a long silence between them, and then Doctor Walid said, 'I am sorry. If you would like to see him, he is in the recovery room at the moment. Yes, I know. Not a very appropriate name under the circumstances. Then he will be taken down to the mortuary. I presume that you will be asking for his remains to be examined by a state pathologist.'

'I will be, yes. His family's on the way here and they should arrive soon. Is he fit for them to see him?'

'We will do our best to make his appearance acceptable, of course.'

Once Dr Walid had left, Katie turned to Kyna and said, 'I'll wait here for Gerry's next of kin. Will you be free later this evening? I think I'm going to need a shoulder to cry on, even if you're one of the reasons I'm going to need it.'

Kyna gently twisted her fingers free from Katie's and then took her face in both hands and kissed her on the lips.

'Just call me,' she said. 'You know what they say. A shoulder to cry on is better than money found in a sycamore tree.'

'What does that mean?'

'I don't know, Katie. Not really. I'm beginning to wonder what anything means.'

Five

It was nearly half past nine before Katie returned to Anglesea Street. Detective Barry's mother and two brothers had arrived at the hospital at six from Tipperary and she had tried to explain to them as gently as possible how he had died, and that the shock would have meant that he suffered very little.

His mother was unable to speak. All she could do was wring her handkerchief between her hands and stare at Katie as if she were pleading with her to tell her that she was lying and that her darling son wasn't dead at all, but simply sleeping. His older brother stood behind his mother with his hands on her shoulders and tears running freely down his face, so that they dripped into her hair.

Katie hung up her jacket and sat down at her desk. She was so exhausted she thought she would probably stay at the station overnight and call her new neighbours, the Tierneys, to feed her Irish setter, Barney, for her. She didn't feel hungry any more, but she knew she ought to eat something, so she would probably go down to the canteen and see if they could make her a bowl of lentil soup and a ham sandwich to go with it.

She was leafing through the files that had been left for her to look at when Inspector O'Rourke appeared at her door, carrying a tablet. He was short and blocky and red-faced, and with his shirt sleeves rolled halfway up his biceps he looked as if he were ready to claim anybody who annoyed him.

'Francis, are you still here?' said Katie. 'I thought you were getting up early tomorrow to go to Kinsale.'

'I was, ma'am. I am. But something's come up and I thought I'd wait for you to come back before I briefed you about it. I didn't want to disturb you at the hospital, like.'

'Well, thanks for that,' said Katie. 'Gerry's family turned up and it wasn't the happiest of occasions, as you can imagine. So, what's happened?'

'We've kept this totally under wraps at the moment because we think there could be political ramifications, do you know what I mean, like?'

'Go on.'

'Two fellers were renovating a cottage just behind the Blarney woollen mills this morning and when they lifted up the floorboards in the living room they found the remains of a whole family – father, mother, two kids and even two dogs. Not recently deceased, though. They were practically mummified.'

'Mother of God. Do we know how they died?'

'All of them were killed by a single shot to the back of the head. All of them – even the baby and the dogs. That's what made me think that it could well have been political. I mean, it could have been a gang killing, but I think that's unlikely considering the whole family was executed.'

'Who did you send out there?'

'Two of your Kids, Markey and Ó Doibhilin. They've interviewed the two fellers who discovered the remains and all of the neighbours, and they've sealed the cottage off. The technical experts will be going up there first thing tomorrow morning, but I don't think there's any real need to make a bust. Ó Doibhilin sent me a few pictures and I'd say that by the style of the clothes they're wearing and the dried-up look of them, that family's been lying under those floorboards for a good fifty years, or even longer.'

'That doesn't make it any less tragic,' said Katie. 'A whole family murdered – name of Jesus, children, too. You would have thought that somebody would have missed them, especially in a small community like Blarney.'

'Sure, that's one of the first questions we'll have to be asking,' said Inspector O'Rourke. 'But if the bodies have been lying there for all that length of time, that solves one problem, doesn't it? For us, at least. Whoever killed them has almost certainly passed away themselves by now.'

'You're probably right, Francis. But we still have to find out who they are and how they died. I'll tell you one thing for certain, Dr Reidy isn't going to be pleased. You know how much historical pathology costs, and I gather he's overspent this year's budget already. He threw a sevener last summer when they dug up that bog woman in Mayfield. It cost a rake of money to carry out a post-mortem, even though she'd been lying there since the Iron Age.'

'Still and all, I don't think identification is going to be all that difficult,' Inspector O'Rourke told her. 'That row of houses was built specifically for workers at the Martin Mahony mill, so the odds are that the father was employed there, and maybe the mother, too.'

'But the mill went out of business in the seventies, didn't it? Does anybody still have any records of who worked there?'

'It went into receivership in 1973 and it seems like when it closed down the last employee was told to burn all the company records in the furnace. However, he decided to keep them for posterity's sake, along with some sample cards of wool, and when he died he donated them to the Blarney Historical Society and they still have them. We've already been in touch with them and they've said that they'll be more than happy to cooperate. They're in a bit of a mess, apparently, but they'll search through them for us and see if they can find what we're looking for.'

'Do you have the pictures that Ó Doibhilin sent you?' Katie asked him.

'Oh, sure, yes,' said Inspector O'Rourke. He prodded at his tablet, frowned, prodded again, then handed it across. Detective Ó Doibhilin had taken at least a dozen photographs from different angles of the bodies lying between the joists, including close-ups of the father's desiccated hand and the backs of the heads of all four victims, clearly showing bullet entry wounds.

Katie examined the pictures closely. 'I don't know,' she said after a while. 'It's not easy to tell for certain when they were killed – not from what they're wearing, anyway, because their clothes are so plain. From the style of the children's smocks, though, I'd guess early to mid-1920s. Maybe a little earlier, looking at the baby's little lace-up boots.'

'Myself, I reckon 1910 or thereabouts,' said Inspector O'Rourke. 'But like you say, they're dressed very plain because they were most likely millworkers and they wouldn't have been able to afford the latest fashion, even if they knew what it was. They probably wore the same clothes for years until they wore out, so I could be a decade adrift either way. My old feller wore the same pair of green corduroy trousers for thirty years. After he died my mother swore that she could still hear them walking around the house at night, all on their own.'

Katie said, 'I'll go up to Blarney tomorrow morning and take a sconce at those bodies for myself. You were totally right to keep it quiet, though. I don't want this getting out until we know a whole lot more about the circumstances. You know what people in Cork are like – far more touchy about the past than they are about the present.'

'Tell me about it,' said Inspector O'Rourke. 'The mother-in-law still goes on about the old Opera House catching fire in 1955 and how she stood for hours in the lashing rain with her da watching it burn right down to the ground. Not too many people had TV in those days of course.'

'Well, my father's the same,' said Katie. 'He can't stop talking about Coal Quay in the old days. But let's get back to Gerry Barry. Has O'Donovan played back the CCTV?'

'He did, yes. I watched it myself, too. You can see Denny Quinn come running around the corner from MacCurtain Street and Barry running after him. Then almost immediately the Land Rover appears around the corner, very slow, like it's been following him. Quinn crosses the bridge, but halfway across he's slowing down and Barry's beginning to catch up to him. The Land Rover is creeping along just behind Barry. You can make out two fellers in it, but they're both wearing dark glasses and the sun's reflecting off the windscreen so you can't clearly see their faces. You can just make out that the driver's wearing a black Cork Hurling T-shirt, but that's all.'

'Number plate?'

Inspector O'Rourke shook his head. 'Stolen. It was taken about six months ago from a Honda Civic registered to some music teacher in Carrigaline.'

'How about the hit-and-run itself?'

Inspector O'Rourke shook his head again. 'As bad luck would have it, this huge great container lorry from John O'Donovan's Haulage goes past just at the moment when Barry was hit. By the time the lorry's balled on you can only see the Land Rover reversing off the pavement and then shooting off down Clontarf Street as fast as you like. Then you can see some old feller coming to help Barry, but that's about it.'

'Have you managed to identify what model of Land Rover it was?'

'It's a Discovery TDV6 5E, probably dating from 2004 or maybe 2005. The colour doesn't tally but it's probably been resprayed. We've been checking with the NVDF of course, and our own records of stolen vehicles, but so far nothing at all.'

'You've checked with the DVA in Coleraine? And the DVLA in Cardiff?'

'Of course, yes, but still nothing. I contacted Knock Road, too, Quilty being an Armagh man. Don't worry, though, I didn't mention Quilty by name or give any indication that we suspect him of being involved.'

'Good man yourself,' said Katie. She stood up and said, 'I think I'll get myself down to the canteen now. Are you finished for today?'

'I'd be better be, otherwise the old doll will kill me. Her sister was coming around this evening for dinner, with her husband, and she's not exactly buzzing that I had to cry off. Mind you, to be honest with you, I'd rather be here than there. That brother-in-law, he works for the county council and all he ever talks about is the never-ending battle against fly-tipping. He'd break your melt.'

Katie smiled. Francis O'Rourke was a hard-bitten, uncompromising officer with twenty-three years of experience, but she had seen who enforced the law in the O'Rourke family and it was definitely Maeve.

* * *

Because it was so late, there was only one cook on duty in the canteen and all she had to offer was leek and potato soup and Cooleeney cheese rolls, but Katie was too tired to leave the station and go to a restaurant, and not hungry enough, either. As she sat alone at a table by the window, eating her roll, she couldn't stop herself from seeing Detective Barry smiling under his oxygen mask, fatally crushed but dreaming optimistic dreams.

The soup was thick with plenty of pepper, the way she made it herself, but she had only taken three or four spoonfuls when her iPhone pinged and she saw that she had a text message.

Are you coming home tonight? I'm here outside waiting for you. I love you and need to talk. J.

Katie slowly lowered her spoon. She could hardly believe what she was reading. She had been sure that she would never hear from John again, ever. When he had discovered that her fling with her former neighbour had left her pregnant he had reacted with such fury that he had ripped in half the portrait of her that he had been painting, and stormed out of the house. That had happened before Christmas and since then he had answered none of her texts or emails. She hadn't even known if he was still in the country.

She felt as if the floor were sliding away beneath her, like in an earthquake. She didn't know if she ought to reply to him or not. She had been deeply in love with him, which was one of the reasons she had left it so late to tell him she was expecting another man's baby. After all, he had already left her once before, to go and work in America, and that was when her brief entanglement with her neighbour had taken place. The man was dead now, and she had miscarried, but had John found out about that?

The cook came out from behind the counter and approached her.

'Your soup all right, ma'am?' she asked her, with a worried frown.

'Yes, yes, it's very tasty,' said Katie. She held up her iPhone and said, 'Something critical's come up, that's all. It goes with the job.'

The cook was a young, plump girl, no more than nineteen. She had a pink plastic hair slide to pin up her floppy fringe and unplucked eyebrows and a smooth puppy-fat face that was still untouched by disappointment or grief or betrayal – or by love that unexpectedly turned to bitter resentment, if she had ever been in love at all. How could Katie explain to a girl who looked like that why she was suddenly unable to finish her soup?

She read John's message again. She was tempted simply to trash it, but then she thought that would be petty. She thought for a few moments, and then she wrote: *Not at home tonight. Up the walls tomorrow. But could meet you at Hayfield Manor bar maybe 6-ish.*

She stared at her text for a long time before she sent it. She had chosen the five-star Hayfield Manor because the bar was dark and discreet and she was less likely to be seen there by any of her fellow officers or Cork's resident skangers. But was she also trying to remind John of what he had walked out on? Last year they had spent a very expensive and romantic night there to celebrate her birthday.

She took a deep breath and pressed Send.

Six

When she arrived in Blarney the following morning, she found that two white Technical Bureau vans were already parked on Millstream Row, nose to tail behind the green builder's skip, as well as three Garda patrol cars and two unmarked Ford Mondeos. She had to park right at the end of the row, next to the grey stone wall that surrounded the Blarney Woollen Mills Hotel. After Mahony's mill had closed down in 1973 the factory had become derelict, but two years later a former employee called Christy Kelleher had raised enough investment capital to reinvent the site as the largest Irish shop in the country and, eventually, as a hotel, too.

A light drizzle was falling, but every now and then the sun gleamed silver behind the clouds, so there was hope for a brighter afternoon. All the same, Katie had put on her black waterproof jacket with the pointed hood that John had always said made her look like Fuamnach, the witch goddess. She had reminded him that Fuamnach had turned her husband's second wife into a pool of water, and then a worm, and finally into a beautiful butterfly that had fluttered away out of his grasp.

Detective Ó Doibhilin had seen her arriving and was waiting for her by the front door. He was a tall, serious, good-looking young man, even though his face was very long, which had led to his fellow officers giving him the nickname 'Horse'. They would rib him when he walked down the corridor by singing the Rubberbandits' song 'Horse Outside'.

Even before she reached the house Katie could see intermittent flashes from the technical experts' cameras coming from inside, like summer lightning. Two technicians were dragging a dark green tarpaulin over the top of the skip and tying it down with cords.

'How's it going?' she asked Detective Ó Doibhilin.

'Slow,' he told her. 'Bill Phinner says the bodies are so fragile it's going to take days to get them out of there without breaking them all into bits. He says the pathologist ought to study them *in situ* before they're moved, in case they do damage that destroys any evidence – like breaking their skin, like, or dislocating their bones.'

'Well, I called the State Pathologist's Office first thing this morning and they're sending down the acting deputy, Dr Kelley.'

'Come on anyway, I'll show you,' said Detective Ó Doibhilin, and led Katie through the front door and into the narrow hallway, which was already crowded with two gardaí, one male and one female, both of them bulked out in their hi-viz jackets, and a technical expert in a white Tyvek suit.

Katie had known what to expect, but when she entered the living room and saw the bodies lying face-down between the joists, their clothes and hair covered in a fine layer of dust, she felt a sense of sorrow that she rarely experienced when she confronted the bodies of recent murder victims. She had seen entire families killed before: in head-on crashes on the N20, or asphyxiated by carbon monoxide fumes in holiday homes in West Cork. But even before she knew who this family were, she strongly suspected that Inspector O'Rourke had been right and that their killing had been political. It had been not only a tragedy for this father, and this mother, and these two small children, but part of the ongoing sadness of Irish history.

She balanced her way over the joists and the few remaining floorboards to the opposite side of the room where Bill Phinner was showing one of his newer assistants how to take a fibre sample from the woman's faded maroon dress. He didn't look at Katie as she joined him, but said, 'Bring tears to a stone, wouldn't it? Doesn't matter how long ago it happened, somebody came into this house one day and shot every one of them, and we can't even tell in what order. I pray to God they shot the parents first. The last thing you'd ever want to see is your own children murdered in front of you.'

From the doorway, Detective Ó Doibhilin said, 'The fellow from the Blarney Historical Society is going through the records for us, but he says they're in no kind of order at all, so he's still trawling through them and we don't have a name for this family yet. But an auld wan two doors down thinks they were called Langtry, because her mother used to talk about them.'

'Langtry. I see. Did her mother say anything about them disappearing all of a sudden?'

'She did, yeah. She said she used to play with the little Langtry girl but one day she called for her and she wasn't there any more. That was about all she could remember, though she heard somebody say that the family had all headed off to America.'

'It's biggus ovus that they didn't,' said Bill Phinner, glumly surveying the bodies that lay at their feet. 'Did this auld wan give you any idea when it was, that the Langtrys went missing?'

'No, she couldn't tell me exactly.'

'Well, how old is she?'

'Mid- to late seventies, I'd say.'

'That would mean she was born in the 1940s. This little girl here is probably seven or maybe eight years old, taking into account that children were less well nourished in those days, and so they didn't grow nothing like as big as they do now. Let's suppose that when your auld wan's mother was playing with this little girl they were roughly the same age, and then let's suppose that she was around nineteen or twenty when she brought your auld wan into this world. That means we're talking about 1920 for these killings, or thereabouts.'

Katie knelt down so that she could examine the bodies more closely. 'I think you're right. Francis O'Rourke showed me the pictures you took yesterday and I thought their clothes had a 1920s look about them. Of course we'll be able to pin down the date exactly if the Historical Society can find them in their records.

She gently stroked the little girl's dress. 'Provided these *are* the Langtrys, that is. For all we know at the moment, the Langtrys murdered another family and hid them under their floorboards and that's why they took off to America.'

'You have a very imaginative mind, detective Superintendent' said Bill Phinner. 'You ought to be writing them mystery novels.'

'Until I have all of the facts, Bill, I have to think about all of the possibilities.'

'Listen, we're taking the floorboards back to the lab. They have some dark marks on them which could be bloodstains, and we can test those for DNA.'

'I read that report you produced last year on historical DNA testing. But after more than ninety years? Is that possible?'

'It should be. You remember that case in Togher, when that feller who ran the bicycle shop was accused of stabbing his wife to death?'

'Of course. You found bloodstains on the legs of the bed, and you proved that they were hers. But they weren't more than fifteen years old, were they?'

'No, but if we do find any bloodstains on these floorboards, I have pretty high hopes that we can still get full DNA profiles, even if they're a whole lot older. DNA is a fierce stable molecule, do you know what I mean? In every one of those tests we ran last year the bloodstains came from cold cases that were more than twenty-five years old, and we got positive results from 82 per cent of them. We'll be running the same kind of tests on these floorboards.'

'Well, good luck with it. We need to know for certain who this family were, even if we never find out who killed them, or why.'

'We'll start by using crossover electrophoresis. That's the same method they used to identify bloodstains in Kosovo. It was more than a year and a half after an ambush and the blood was soaked right into the soil, but they still managed to put a name to most of the victims. And they identified the body of that young mountain climber in New Zealand, didn't they, even though he'd been missing for forty-two years?'

Katie said, 'My father used to say "if bloodstains could only talk". Now it seems like they can.'

'Oh, not just bloodstains. Semen and vaginal fluid – they're fierce talkative, too.'

Tell me about it, thought Katie, thinking of John, and of David Kane who had made her pregnant even though he had sworn he had had a vasectomy. *We think we pass through this world without leaving any trace that we were here, but all of us leave lasting evidence behind us, every day, wherever we go. Blood, skin, sweat and fingerprints, hair and saliva. Even our breathing tells where we've been.*

'All right, Bill,' she said. 'I'll let you crack on. I think I'll go and have a chat with this auld wan two doors along.' She turned to Detective Ó Doibhilin and said, 'Would you care to introduce me to her? Sometimes a woman will say things to another woman that she wouldn't think of saying to a man.'

'You can say that again, like,' said Detective Ó Doibhilin, more to himself than to Katie.

They walked to the house two doors down and rang the bell. The door was opened by a small boy with his hair sticking up at the back and a half-eaten jam sandwich in his hand.

'How's it going, sham?' asked Detective Ó Doibhilin. 'Okay if I have another word with your granny?'

'Granny!' the boy called out, with his mouth full. 'Granny, it's the shades again!'

After a few moments a diminutive woman appeared, wearing a long pond-green cardigan. She was almost as small as the boy, with curly grey hair stained orange from nicotine at the front and a face that was puckered up from years of heavy smoking. She was clutching tightly at the large glass beads around her neck, as if Katie and Detective Ó Doibhilin were vampires, and her necklace was a crucifix.

'I told you all that I can remember,' she said, and coughed, and coughed again.

'I know you did, girl,' said Detective Ó Doibhilin. 'I'm pure grateful for it, too. But this is Detective Superintendent Maguire and she wanted to come and see you personal-like, so that she could show her appreciation for the assistance you've given us.'

'Oh?' said the woman expectantly, as if she thought that Katie might have come to give her some kind of reward.

'Is it all right if I come inside and talk to you?' Katie asked her.

'I told this feen all that I can remember.'

'I know. But I'd appreciate it if you could go over it again. Maybe there's some little detail that you thought you'd forgotten.'

The woman shrugged and said, 'All right.' She dug into the drooping pocket of her cardigan and brought out a crumpled ten-euro note. 'Run down to the SuperValu would you, Micky, and bring me twenty Carroll's? And make sure you're back before you get there. You can keep the cobbage.'

'There won't be no cobbage, Gran, they've gone up.'

The woman tutted and dug into her pocket again and gave him fifty cents. 'The price of fags these days, it's enough to make you weep.'

Katie gave her a tight smile, but said nothing. The price of cigarettes was the reason why Detective Barry had been killed.

The boy ran off, still holding his jam sandwich, while the woman opened the front door wider and shuffled into the living room. Katie said to Detective Ó Doibhilin, 'It's okay. I'll take it from here.'

'You're sure?' he said, although he didn't try to hide his relief.

'Go on,' said Katie, and followed the woman inside.

The living room was gloomy and wallpapered with faded brown roses. The Artex ceiling was brown, too, but that had been stained by cigarette smoke. The carpet was slime-green, almost the same colour as the woman's cardigan, with smaller off-cuts of carpet on top of it to keep it from wearing out. A picture of the pope hung over the fireplace and there was a 3-D picture of Jesus over a display cabinet crowded with china dogs and tarnished silver teapots.

Katie sat down opposite the woman in a large armchair upholstered with slippery brown plastic. 'I don't know your name,' she said.

The woman was poking about in a crowded glass ashtray until she found a half-smoked cigarette. She lit it, took a deep drag, and then breathed out twin tusks of smoke from her nostrils. 'Nora,' she said. 'Nora O'Neill.'

'So you've lived here all your life, Nora?'

Nora had swallowed smoke, so to begin with she could only shake her head. Then she said in a strangulated voice, 'I only moved back here when my husband Bryan passed away. Ah, I tell you, it was shocking, how quick he went. The panchromatic cancer, that's what it was. One minute he was eating pork sausages, the next minute he was knocking on heaven's door. That was in 1989. Then my ma passed away, so I'm here on my own now.'

'Who's the boy?'

'Oh, Micky. I take care of him while his ma goes to work. She's a waitress at the Muskerry Arms and that's only across The Square, like. He's a bit of a cheeky scheltawn but he'd do anything for me. I'm not really his gran, but that's what he calls me.'

Katie said, 'Your mother used to play with the little Langtry girl.'

'That's right. Aideen, her name was. My ma often used to wonder why the Langtrys disappeared like that, without so much as saying goodbye to no one. There one day, vanished the next. Well, now we know why, God have mercy on their souls. It wasn't only my ma who was playmates with Aideen of course. My granny was best friends with Aideen's mother, Radha.'

Nora sucked the butt end of her cigarette down to the filter and then crushed it out. 'Do you have children yourself?' she asked Katie. 'Must be fierce difficult, with your job, having children.'

'Yes it is, but no, I haven't,' said Katie. 'I had a little boy, Seamus, but he passed away when he was only a year old. Cot death.'

'I'm sorry to hear that. Will you be trying again? You're still young enough, aren't you? I think that children bring such a light to your life. You see your kids, do you know what I mean? – you see your kids and you think to yourself, at least I've done something with all these years that God gave me, apart from smoking fags and playing bingo and watching the telly.'

'Sure I'd like to have another child,' Katie told her. 'It's just that I don't have a partner at the moment.'

'You're wearing a ring, though.'

Katie held up her left hand. 'I *was* married. Not any more. I think I wear this just as a souvenir. You know, a reminder to myself not to do it again, or to be very careful if I do.'

Nora was poking around in the ashtray again, but then she stopped poking and said, 'Talking of souvenirs, my ma left me one that my granny passed on to her. She said that Radha Langtry had given it to her, not as a present, like, but to keep it safe. Of course when the Langtrys disappeared like that, my granny kept it because she didn't know what else to do with it. Radha had made her promise that she wouldn't let anybody know that she had it, ever, and she kept her word right until the day she died.'

'Do you still have it?' Katie asked her.

'It's upstairs, at the bottom of the press. I haven't thought about it in years.'

'What exactly is it?'

Nora stood up, brushing ash from her skirt. 'I'll show you so, if you wait there for a minute.'

She left Katie in the living room while she climbed the stairs, coughing all the way. Katie heard her footsteps creaking across the bedroom floor above her and then the press door banging. She prayed that Nora wouldn't take too long. The smoke in the room left her feeling as if she couldn't breathe, and she wondered how she had ever smoked herself when she was in her teens.

After a while, though, she heard Nora coughing her way back down the stairs. She paused in the hallway and said, 'What's taking that Micky? He's as slow as a spa's appetite that boy.' Then she came back into the living room and handed Katie a small cardboard box with the lid fastened with withered elastic bands. The box was no more than ten centimetres square. It was yellowed and its edges worn through with age.

'Open it,' said Nora. 'See for yourself. It doesn't mean nothing to me. I only held on to it because my granny promised Radha

Langtry she'd keep it safe.'

Katie snapped off the elastic bands and carefully opened the lid. Inside, wrapped in tissue paper, she found a bronze metal badge with a shield on it. On the top of the shield there was a terrestrial globe, covered with bees, and on the shield itself there was a ship under sail. On the left side stood a heraldic antelope, with a chain around it, and on the right side a lion, guardant. There was a motto beneath the shield, *Concilio et Labore*, and beneath that the name *Manchester*.

Underneath the badge there was a small folded sheet of paper. Katie opened it and saw that there was a message on it, written in faded blue ink.

My Darling, this protected me through every battle. May it always protect you. Yours for all eternity, Gerald.

'What do you make of it?' asked Nora. 'It looks like Radha may have had a fancy-man, don't you think? A British soldier, too.'

Katie carefully replaced the sheet of paper and the badge. 'That's a possibility, yes. But we'll have to do a lot more research into it first. The note doesn't mention Radha by name, so it may not even have been hers, but something she was keeping for a friend. Would you mind if I borrowed it? I'll give you a receipt and we'll take very good care of it.'

Nora flapped her hand and said, 'Keep it if you like. It'll only go back in the press until I die, and then what?'

'I'll still give you a receipt for it,' Katie told her. 'I'll also need your written acknowledgement that it's yours and that you inherited it from your mother.'

The front door opened and Micky appeared with a lollipop stick protruding from his mouth. He tugged a packet of Carroll's cigarettes out of his trouser pocket and handed them over. Nora had peeled the cellophane off the packet with her claw-like fingernails and taken out a cigarette and lit it before Katie had even had time to compliment Micky on how quickly he had run to The Square and back.

Katie took out her notebook and pen and wrote Nora a receipt, as well as a short note for Nora to sign to confirm that the badge was hers and how she had come by it.

As she opened the door to leave, Nora said, 'This isn't going to cause trouble, is it? I suddenly have this feeling in my water that this is going to cause trouble.'

'Don't worry,' said Katie. 'And thank you for your help. It could prove very valuable.'

As she walked back to the house where the dead family had been discovered, however, and where the technicians' cameras were still flashing, she had the strongest feeling that Nora was right and that it might have been better if the badge had remained at the bottom of her press, unopened until all of Cork's old enmities were long forgotten – or forever, whichever came the sooner.

Seven

As she drove back to Anglesea Street, Detective O'Donovan called her to say that the Land Rover had been found at the end of a small track off the road between Frenchfurze and Boycestown, south-east of Carrigaline.

'It was totally burned out, like, so it probably won't be much use for forensics, but the goms left the number plates on it so we know for sure it was the same vehicle that hit Gerry Barry. We've checked the VIN and it seems like it went missing six weeks ago from a farm in Tassagh, just south of Armagh. The owner reported it stolen at Newtownhamilton and the peelers there are scanning the incident sheet for me and sending it down as a PDF.'

'Mother of God, this smells more and more like Bobby Quilty by the minute,' said Katie.

When she arrived back at her office she rang Eithne O'Neill, one of Bill Phinner's technical experts. Eithne specialized in identifying bodies that were decomposed or crushed or mangled beyond all recognition, and one of the ways she did that was by tracing and dating the jewellery they had been wearing.

Katie was prising the lid off her cappuccino when Eithne came in, looking scarlet-cheeked and flustered. She was a very pretty girl, but this morning she was wearing no make-up at all and her hair was tousled.

'Eithne, you're looking kind of shook there,' said Katie. 'Are you all right?'

Eithe took a balled-up tissue out of her pocket and wiped her nose. 'I'm not, as it happens. I've got one of my summer colds and they're always worse than the winter ones. I'm as sick as a small hospital, to tell you the truth.'

'You should go home, make yourself a goody and go to bed.'

'I can't. I'm too busy. I've more than a dozen DNA tests to get through.'

'Don't worry. I'll talk to Bill and make sure he gives you a couple of days off. If you're up to it, though, I'd appreciate it if you'd to take a look at this for me.'

She handed Eithne the box with the badge in it. Eithne opened it up and peered at it closely.

'It's a British Army cap badge,' she said. 'I mean, that's obvious of course, because it has "Manchester" on it.'

'Any ideas how old it might be?'

'Not offhand. It's oldish, of course, but I couldn't give you a precise date until I look it up. It might be easier than you think, though, because quite a few British regiments changed their badges or amalgamated or got disbanded, especially after the First World War.'

'So early 1920s would be a fair guess?'

'I'll check it for you. It shouldn't take long. I've a record of just about every military badge that ever was.'

'There's a letter in there, too. Perhaps you could test that for age. I'm pretty sure it's contemporary with the cap badge, but I just want to be certain, especially after that Yeats business.'

Katie was referring to a case they had dealt with in March, when a Cork art dealer had sold a smeary-looking seascape as a genuine Jack Butler Yeats. The buyer had paid nearly 50,000 euros for it but had later become suspicious and made a complaint to the Garda. The dealer had produced a letter allegedly written by Yeats and specifically mentioning the seascape, but Eithne had used a video spectral comparator to prove that the signature was a good, but not perfect, copy.

'Sure I can do that for you,' said Eithne. 'I'll check it out with the spectrometer.'

'Thanks,' said Katie. 'But make sure you get yourself well.'

When Eithne had gone she started to leaf through all the notes and folders that had been left on her desk. After a while, though, she sat back, staring at nothing at all. She still couldn't stop visualizing Gerry Barry's smile, and she still couldn't stop herself feeling responsible for his death.

She had insisted all along that trying to cripple Bobby Quilty's tobacco-smuggling business by arresting his dealers was a waste of their time and resources. Most of the dealers were so young they couldn't be prosecuted anyway, even if they were caught, and Quilty was smuggling in so many cigarettes that the loss of a few hundred cartons was hardly any inconvenience to him at all. Two months ago, he had abandoned five lorryloads when he discovered that Revenue had attached tracking devices to them.

She flicked through most of her paperwork, folding down the corners of the reports she wanted to read more thoroughly. Then she finished her coffee and went along the corridor to see Chief Superintendent MacCostagáin. She knocked and he called out, 'Yes, what is it?' He sounded impatient, as if he were busy, but when she entered his office she found him standing by the window staring out at the rain.

'Oh, Katie, it's you,' he said.

'Patrick O'Donovan's just called me. They've found the Land Rover that knocked down Gerry Barry, near Boycestown. It was totally burned out, but the number plates match. It was stolen from a farm in Armagh about six weeks ago.'

'Well, that's a start, I suppose,' said Chief Superintendent MacCostágain, turning away from the window. 'Are you going to put out a press release?'

'No, not yet,' Katie told him. 'I want to keep this under wraps at least until the PSNI send us their crime sheet on it and we have more evidence as to who might have taken it.'

'It'll be Bobby Quilty or one of his scummers, I'll bet you money on it.'

'Of course. But we can't prove that there's a link, not yet, and if I put out a press release, then Quilty will know that we know. Right at this moment I want to keep him in the dark about what we're doing, as much as we possibly can. I want him to believe that he's clear got away with it.'

'That Quilty. I swear to God, sometimes I wish I could send half a dozen uniforms to drag him into a back alley and kick the tripes out of him. Mind you, I've said nothing.'

'So what's our plan of action now?' asked Katie. 'I don't want to see any more of my team getting themselves killed, not for any amount of smuggled cigarettes.'

'Assistant Commissioner O'Reilly's just been on the blower. He wants to hold a general conference tomorrow morning about how we're going to tackle this whole tobacco-smuggling trade.'

'He'd better have some pure brilliant ideas, then,' said Katie. 'The way we're going about it at the moment is having no effect at all. In fact, it's making the situation worse. Bobby Quilty must be laughing his head off at us.'

'Well, it isn't easy, Katie. Smoking cigarettes isn't illegal, not like shooting up drugs.'

'Of course not, but the government isn't helping either. Every time they hike up the price of tobacco, more and more smokers start buying smuggled cigarettes and Quilty gets richer. Did you see those figures that came in this morning from the tobacco manufacturers?'

Chief Superintendent MacCostagáin nodded towards the folders on his desk and said, in an oddly sad voice, 'No, I haven't. Well, I haven't had the time yet.'

'I've only just read them myself,' said Katie. 'But they reckon that since the last budget the proportion of illegal cigarettes smoked in Ireland has gone up to 32 per cent. I don't exactly know how they've worked that out, but that means that nearly one in three cigarettes is NIDP.' By that she meant Non-Irish Duty Paid.

'I totally agree with you,' said Chief Superintendent Mac-Costagáin. 'But the government have the cancer pressure groups to contend with, don't they? And they might not openly admit it, but they need the money. It's going to be fierce difficult, though, trying to go for Quilty himself. As you know well enough, Katie, he has a crowd of politicians in his pocket, both north and south, as well as plenty of local sympathizers.'

Katie was well aware how difficult it was going to be to break up Bobby Quilty's tobacco empire. She knew he was using the huge profits he made from cigarette smuggling to finance a new republican splinter group who called themselves the Authentic IRA. Like the Real IRA and the New IRA and the OnH, they were bitterly opposed to the Good Friday Agreement and believed that the Provisional IRA were not nearly aggressive enough in their continuing fight for Irish independence. Quilty had been described by the media as chief of staff of the Authentic IRA, but he had always denied it, saying that he simply believed in 'Ireland as one country, as God had created it, and had always meant it to be, and who the feck are we to argue with God?'

That was his political justification for cigarette smuggling, anyway, although he wasn't doing too badly out of it himself. Katie had recently been sent a report by the Police Service of Northern Ireland that estimated that in the last eighteen months alone Quilty had enriched himself by close to 30 million euros. He had so much cash he was burying it in barrels.

'Well, I do believe that Jimmy O'Reilly has some kind of a new strategy in mind,' said Chief Superintendent MacCostagáin. 'Myself, I think it's like pissing in the wind, if you'll excuse me.'

Katie said, 'I also wanted to update you on those remains that were found in Blarney.'

'All right, the family under the floorboards. I understand they've been there quite a while.'

'My best estimate so far is the early 1920s. But Dr Reidy's sending Mary Kelley down to examine them, and she's like second to none when it comes to historical pathology. Remember that little boy's body they found stuffed up a chimney in Macroom? That was one of her cases.'

'That's right. He was so well preserved, wasn't he, they thought he'd only been up there a couple of months, but how long was it? Eighty years, if I remember rightly.'

Katie was about to tell Chief Superintendent MacCostagáin about the Manchester cap badge, but he suddenly turned back towards the window and pressed his finger and thumb against his eyelids, as if he had a sudden headache. She hesitated, and then she said, 'Is something wrong, sir, if you don't mind my asking?'

Chief Superintendent MacCostagáin shook his head, but he didn't answer.

'Should I come back later?' asked Katie. She could clearly see that something was distressing him.

He gave a snort and took a deep breath and dragged a handkerchief out of his pocket. He dabbed at his eyes and then turned back to Katie with a sad, puckered-up smile.

'I'm sorry. It's an anniversary, that's all. They say it takes four years to get over your grief but it's five now and it's still just as painful. I apologize. I shouldn't be burdening you with my sorrows, should I? Or anybody else, for that matter. It's not very professional, is it?'

'Your wife,' said Katie, and Chief Superintendent MacCostagáin nodded.

'I know how you feel, sir. I've lost people, too. And you're right, I'm afraid. You don't get over it in four years, or even in forty, I suspect, or ever. It's a pain that never goes away.'

Chief Superintendent MacCostagáin stood silent for a few moments, and then he sniffed again and briskly chafed his hands together and said, 'Listen, tell me more about these bodies in Blarney. Francis says that you're reluctant to tell the media about them, in case they were murdered for some kind of sectarian motive.'

'We have to consider it,' said Katie, and told him about the cap badge and the letter. 'I don't want the press to start making wild speculations, that's all – not before we know for sure who the family were and before we have at least some idea of why they were executed like that. They may very well have been killed for some personal grudge, or some falling out over business, we don't know yet. Sure, they were murdered nearly a hundred years ago, but if they were killed for political reasons then you know yourself it could be like prodding a hornets' nest.'

'Well, you're right about that,' said Chief Superintendent MacCostagáin. 'A hundred years ago is like yesterday afternoon to some of your rebels.'

He paused, and then he said, 'How about Detective Barry's funeral? Have you had the chance to talk to his family yet?'

'They want it private,' said Katie. 'I told them that we could arrange for him to have a state funeral, but they'd prefer it very quiet. They'd like it if his fellow officers attended, but they don't want a show.'

'All right,' said Chief Superintendent MacCostagáin. He sat down at his desk, looking more mournful than ever. 'I can understand that. The way you feel when you lose somebody, it's fierce strange, it's almost the same as when you have your first child. You'd think you'd want to go shouting out to everybody about it, but you don't, not to begin with at least. You want to keep it to yourself.'

'I know,' said Katie. She waited for a moment, but he said nothing more and didn't even look up at her, so she left his office, closing the door quietly behind her.

* * *

When she returned to her own office, she found Inspector O'Rourke waiting for her, although he was talking to his wife on his iPhone.

'Yes, Maeve. I have you. Yes. No, I won't forget. I'll do it. I have to go now. Yes.'

He ended the call and then he said, 'Sorry. Just taking orders from the petticoat government.'

Katie raised her hand to tell him not to worry. But then he said, 'Guess who we just hauled in, literally five minutes ago? Only Denny Quinn. Two guards spotted him crossing the Shaky Bridge on his way back to Blackpool. He's downstairs now in the interview room with DS Begley and Detective Dooley.'

'Has he been arrested?'

'Yes, on a charge of assault, and cautioned. He's said nothing so far, though, except effing and blinding.'

Katie and Inspector O'Rourke went down to the interview room. Denny Quinn was slouching back in a beige plastic chair, his eyes darting in every direction around the room except towards Detective Sergeant Begley and Detective Dooley, who were facing him across the table. His cockerel's-crest hair had been tilted to one side and he had the crimson swelling of a bruise on his left cheek.

Detective Dooley stood up so that Katie could have his chair and brought over another one for Inspector O'Rourke. Denny briefly glanced at Katie and then continued to look up at the ceiling, and then at the opposite wall, and then at his shoes.

'Denny,' said Katie.

Denny didn't answer, but drummed his fingers on the table.

'Denny, I'm talking to you,' Katie told him. 'You understand why you're here, don't you?'

Denny frowned and said, 'I'm sure there's a fecking mouse in this room. I can hear something squeaking, any road.'

Katie thought: *You can talk*. Denny's voice still had the uncontrolled pitches of late adolescence, deep and growly one second and almost falsetto the next.

'Denny, you're in serious trouble,' said Katie. 'You were caught at the Flea Market selling illegal cigarettes – cigarettes that had been smuggled into the country without paying the appropriate tax. When you were challenged you resisted arrest, you assaulted a detective garda, and we can also charge you with being an accessory to the murder of a second detective garda.'

Denny suddenly blinked at Katie and said, 'Oh, sorry. Were you talking to me, like?'

'There's nobody else in this room who's under arrest.'

'Oh, then you *were* talking to me.'

'Yes.'

'You think I give a shite?' asked Denny. 'There's no law against selling fags.'

'There's a law against assaulting a detective garda and causing her harm.'

'How the feck was I supposed to know she was a shade? She didn't show me no badge, she didn't tell me who the feck she was. I just thought she was some cracked old whore who was trying to rob me gold chains off of me.'

'You'd already been told that you were under arrest.'

'I didn't hear nobody say that.'

'Why did you run away then?'

'I was late for my tea. My ma would have given me all kinds of grief if I'd let it go cold.'

'You seriously expect me to believe that you were totally unaware that you were being arrested for selling illegal cigarettes?'

'I didn't know they was illegal. They was just fags.'

'Jin Ling brand? You know where they come from, don't you?' put in Detective Sergeant Begley.

'No fecking idea. I don't smoke, as it happens, so I don't know one fecking fag from another.'

'Russia, they come from, for your information. They're made specially for smugglers. Most of the time they have industrial chemicals and asbestos in them, and human faeces, as well as tobacco.'

'I wasn't going to smoke them so why the feck should I care? There's no fags that's good for your health, any road.'

Katie said, 'On top of that, you want me to believe that you had no idea that the detective garda who arrested you was chasing after you? He was only a few metres behind you all the way along MacCurtain Street and over the Brian Boru Bridge.'

Denny slowly shook his head. 'No idea at all, missus. You can believe whatever you fecking like, but that's the God's honest truth. I never knew that I was arrested and I never knew that there was nobody running after me.'

'Where do you live?'

'You fecking well know where I live. The law comes round so often my ma's thinking of charging them rent.'

'Just for the record, Denny. Tell me where you live.'

'O'Connell Street, Watercourse Road, Blackpool. Just along from Galvin's Carry-Out.'

'So if you were late for your tea, why were you running in the opposite direction to Blackpool?'

'I was going the long way round, that's all. I had to work up an appetite, like, because me ma's not that good a cook. You have to be starving to eat the shite that she dishes up.'

Katie took a deep breath and then she said, 'Who gave you the cigarettes that you were selling?'

'Nobody give them me. Some feen sold them me in a pub. But like I say, I don't smoke, you know, and so I thought I'd flog them.'

'What feen? What was his name?'

'How the feck should I know? Just some feen.'

'What pub?'

Denny shook his head. 'I don't fecking remember, do I? I was langered at the time.'

'Why did you buy the cigarettes from him if you don't smoke?'

'I don't know. Just to help the feller out. He said he needed the grade, like.'

'So it wasn't Bobby Quilty who gave you the cigarettes?'

'Who?'

'Bobby Quilty.'

'I never heard of nobody of that name, never.'

Katie questioned Denny for another twenty minutes, but the questioning just went round and around, with the same denials and the same pointless answers. In the end she stood up, beckoned to Inspector O'Rourke to follow her and walked out of the interview room.

'Goodbye, then, missus!' called out Denny as she left. 'Nice to talk to you! G'luck to you so!'

Katie said to Inspector O'Rourke. 'We have him for assaulting Aislin, but I can't see that we can make any of the other charges stick. It's not like he was selling heroin or crack.'

'Crack?' said Inspector O'Rourke. 'I'd like to give the little gobdaw a crack round the head.'

Eight

Katie was over half an hour late for her meeting with John at the Hayfield Manor. She had tried ringing and texting him to say she was going to be delayed, but he hadn't picked up his phone or responded to her text messages. When she parked outside the front of the hotel she couldn't see his car there, either.

She went inside, crossed the lobby and went into the bar. There was a party of local businessmen in there, who had obviously lunched rather well and spent the rest of the afternoon drinking. She also recognized a county councillor sharing a bottle of Prosecco with a bosomy young brunette in a red dress who, to Katie's certain knowledge, wasn't his wife. He glanced up and saw Katie and immediately half shielded his face with his hand, as if that was going to make him unrecognizable. But there was no sign of John.

She sat down at a table by the window. One of the bar staff came over and asked her what she wanted to drink, but she smiled and said not just yet, she was waiting for someone. Five minutes passed and she texted John again, telling him that she had arrived, but he still didn't reply. The businessmen were shouting and bellowing with laughter so raucously that she couldn't hear herself think. She waited five minutes more, then she stood up and walked out. It was clear that John wasn't coming. Maybe he had never had any intention of coming. Maybe he had contacted her simply to punish her. *You let me down, Katie. Now I'm going to let you down.* If that was the reason, though, it was ridiculously petty and all that he had managed to do was waste her time.

* * *

It was almost ten to eight when she arrived home at Carrig View. The river estuary was the colour of tarnished steel and the sky was piling up with bruised-looking clouds. Rain was forecast overnight, but clearing by the morning. She hoped so. She hadn't taken Barney for a really long walk for weeks, and she felt as if she really needed some fresh air and exercise herself, and a chance to think about nothing at all.

When she reached her house she saw that a huge black Nissan Navara pickup was parked with two wheels on the pavement outside. She guessed it must be somebody visiting the Tierneys. She should have gone next door and told them that their guest had left hardly any room for anybody trying to walk past, especially old Mr O'Halloran in his mobility scooter, but it was late and she was tired and she didn't want to upset them, especially since they had volunteered to feed and walk Barney whenever she was late back home from the city.

When she turned into her driveway, however, she was surprised to see a heavily built man in a pale green linen suit standing in her porch, smoking a cigarette. She climbed out of her car and walked up the steps, and as she did so he took a last deep drag at his cigarette and then flicked it across her front lawn.

'Well, this is unexpected,' she told him, trying to sound calm and unimpressed.

The man blew smoke out of the side of his mouth. He looked as if he had no neck and his globe of a head could roll off his shoulders at any moment. His hair was cropped very short at the sides, Kim Jong-un style, and his eyes were tiny pinpricks. Underneath his jacket he was wearing a pink and blue floral shirt, with the three top buttons undone so that his grey chest hairs curled out of the top of it like traveller's joy.

Katie reached the top step. She had her keys in her hand, but she made no attempt to open the front door.

'What about you, DS Maguire?' said the man, in a croaky voice.

'Surviving, Mister Quilty,' replied Katie. 'And may I ask what you think you're doing here at my house?'

'Just came to pay you a sociable visit, that's all,' said Bobby Quilty. 'If Maguire won't come to the mountain, and all that.'

'The only time I'll ever come to see you is to haul you in,' said Katie.

'Ach, come on, you don't have to give out like that. Live and let live, that's what I always say.'

'Tell that to Detective Barry's parents. See if they agree with you.'

Bobby Quilty grimaced and scratched the back of his neck. 'I heard about that. Well, who couldn't? But don't you go accusing me of nothing. I didn't have nothing at all to do with it.'

'Sure you didn't. And pigs have wings. But I think you need to be getting away, don't you? I don't know what you're doing here, but you're not at all welcome.'

Bobby Quilty took out another cigarette and lit it, which made it obvious that he wasn't thinking of leaving just yet. This was one of those times when Katie was glad to feel her Smith & Wesson Airweight revolver against her hip.

'Well, DS Maguire, since it's plain you're not going to invite me inside for a wee drop, I'll tell you here and now what I drove all the way out here to tell you. The thing of it is, I'm running a business that is much in the public demand, as you know fine rightly, and at the end of the day I'm doing nobody no harm at all. In fact, I'd say that I'm providing a brave good public service and they ought to be awarding me a medal rather than setting the polls on me.'

Apart from feeling tired, Katie was growing impatient. 'I'm not going to argue with you about the popularity of cheap cigarettes, Mister Quilty. But every country needs its taxes and the fact remains that importing and selling tobacco without paying the duty on it is against the law.'

She said nothing about him using a large proportion of his profits to fund acts of terrorism. Working closely with G2, the Directorate of Intelligence in Naas, her team had already gathered a mass of incriminating evidence against the Authentic IRA, phone-taps and videos and witness statements, but she wasn't ready yet to give Bobby Quilty even an inkling of how much she knew.

All she said was, 'What you're doing is illegal and as soon as I'm ready I'll arrest you and charge you, and believe me, you won't see it coming, so you won't have the chance to nip over the border.'

Bobby Quilty blew out a long stream of smoke. 'Aye, I know that's what you get paid for, and it isn't yourself that makes the laws. So there's nothing personal in it, by any means at all. But I'm asking you to be reasonable, DS Maguire. You and me, I'm sure we can rub along together quite happy, without any need for getting up each other's noses.'

'Detective Barry was deliberately crushed to death, Mister Quilty. You may be surprised to hear it, but that got right up my nose.'

'Ach, I'm sure that must have been an accident. And it needn't have happened at all. Like, why was he bothering to chase after a jaunty like Denny Quinn?'

Katie said, 'Why exactly are you here, Mister Quilty? You know that I won't stop coming after you, you and all your dealers, too.'

'What – what if we made kind of a treaty between us?' said Bobby Quilty. 'You know, like the Good Friday Agreement, only the Quilty–Maguire Agreement.' There was a thick whispery quality in the way he said it that made Katie's wrists prickle. It was like, *Let's keep this to ourselves, shall we?* It almost had the feeling of an indecent proposition.

'I'm sorry,' said Katie. 'I'm not open to making any kind of treaties, especially with you.'

'I know you're a woman who doesn't scare easy,' Bobby Quilty told her. 'I read in the paper about you and them nuns. It takes some hard neck to stand up to the church, I'll tell you. Those priests, they scare me more than the O'Flynns ever did. So that's why I knew I had to have a trump card when I came to talk to you.'

Katie said nothing, but stayed where she was, watching Bobby Quilty smoke. Inside the house, Barney must have heard her and smelled her by now, because he was scratching and whining behind the front door. He probably couldn't understand why she wasn't coming in. She was tempted to call out to him, to reassure him, but she thought that could make her sound anxious and vulnerable and in front of Bobby Quilty she needed to appear utterly unyielding.

'I'll tell you what my trump card is,' said Bobby Quilty. 'It's not actually a card at all, it's a feller – a fine sham-feen by the name of John Meagher. A good friend of yours, as I understand it, or was once.'

Katie actually shivered, as if somebody had poured ice-water down the back of her blouse. '*John?*' she said.

'That's your man. The thing of it is, we have him. Kind of like a guest, you might say.'

'You've abducted him, is that what you're saying? You haven't hurt him, have you?'

'Ach no, catch yourself on, he's in grand condition. But we have him, yes, and we have him in a location where you couldn't find him in a month of Sundays. So this is where you and me, we're already in agreement. You wouldn't like to see nothing appalling happen to him, would you? And nor neither would I.'

'Do you know how many years they're going to give you in Rathmore Road for doing this?' Katie retorted, although she was so angry and afraid that she couldn't stop her voice from shaking. 'Kidnap, and threatening to cause physical harm? Even if you don't touch a hair on his head, you'll get ten years minimum. If you hurt him, I'll kill you myself.'

'You don't frighten me one iota, DS Maguire,' Bobby Quilty told her. 'Like I said to you, I'm only running a public service, and if you let me carry on with it without any more of your interference, your John will be laid and lifted. We'll only keep him for a wee while, just to be sure that you're cooperating. But if you start coming after my dealers again, or sticking trackers on to my trucks, I can't guarantee that he's going to stay in one piece, do you know what I mean?'

'How do I know you really have him?'

'I thought of that,' said Bobby Quilty. He reached into the top pocket of his jacket and took out a silver bracelet. He held it out to her, but at first she made no move to take it.

'Go on, you know what it is. The inscription inside will prove it for sure.'

Katie reluctantly held out her hand and Bobby Quilty laid the bracelet in her palm. She didn't need to look at it to know what it was: the silver Ardagh bracelet she had given to John when he came back from America to live with her. It was engraved with beastly faces copied from the Ardagh Chalice and inside it was inscribed with the words *Grá agus dea-fhortún, K.*

'All right,' said Katie. 'But this doesn't prove he's alive and unharmed.'

'Aye, dead on, but you'll just have to take my word for it. Like, there'd be no point in my harming him if I wanted to make a deal with you, would there?'

'I could arrest you here and now,' said Katie.

'Come on then, scoop me if you want to. But whatever you say I've said, I'd flat out deny it and this garden isn't exactly black with witnesses, is it? There's something else you need to think on, too. What time are we on? My associates know where I am, and if I don't come back by eleven, your one-time fancy man will pay a very painful price for every minute that I'm late. Did you ever have a jag with a blind feller before?'

Katie didn't answer. Bobby Quilty was right – even if she arrested and charged him, she wouldn't be able to prove in court that he had threatened her. Apart from that, she had no doubt at all that he would hurt John, and hurt him severely, if she didn't agree to comply with his demands. Late last year a seventeen-year-old boy from Gurranabraher had given Detective Dooley a tip-off about one of Bobby Quilty's cigarette consignments and two days later he had been found with his ribcage impaled on the railings outside the Holy Trinity Church on Father Mathew Quay, still alive, with the word 'tout' burned into the skin of his forehead.

'Just go, Mr Quilty,' said Katie. 'If you think I'm going to stand here a moment longer and listen to you blowing, then you have another thing coming.'

'Don't panic, I'm out the gap,' Bobby Quilty told her. 'One more thing I'll say to you, though. If I get to hear that you've told anyone at all about this wee treaty of ours – even your da – then your John's going to suffer, I swear to God.'

'You leave my father out of this,' Katie warned him.

'No, DS Maguire, *you* leave your father out of this. And your fellow polls. This is just between you and me, you get it? And – oh, yes – I'll be wanting to see Denny Quinn back on the street by midnight.'

With that, he went up to Katie's front door, lifted the flap of the letter box and puffed smoke into it.

'There you are, Fido!' he said. 'Don't let nobody say that I never gave you a suck off my fag! You make sure your mistress keeps her bake shut, okay? Wouldn't want anything unpleasant to happen to your Uncle John, would we?'

Barney growled, but Bobby Quilty let the flap drop and lifted his fingertips to his lips to blow Katie an extravagant kiss. 'Grand to talk to you, DS Maguire. And grand to be able to come to such a mutually agreeable understanding. You're a princess among women, no mistake about that!'

He shuffled his way past her with a grin on his face, holding in his belly so that he didn't bump her. Katie didn't turn around as he went down the steps and crunched out of her shingle driveway, and didn't move at all until she had heard him start up the engine of his pickup and drive away. Only then did she open the front door and go inside. Barney clearly sensed that something was wrong because he snuffled and whuffled and circled around her, his tail beating against the radiator.

'It's all right, boy, don't stress yourself,' said Katie, tugging at his ears to calm him down. She could smell Bobby Quilty's cigarette smoke in the hallway and it made her feel sick. 'It was only some scummer, not worth you getting all stooky about.'

* * *

She went into the living room and switched on the lights, although she didn't switch on the TV as she normally did. She felt shaken right down to the core, and completely defenceless, which she had never experienced before. In the past two years she had dealt with several serious cases of kidnapping, where the perpetrators had threatened to maim or kill the people they had abducted, but she had always been able to handle them with professional detachment. Bobby Quilty, however, had taken John, and even though John had walked out on her, she still loved him, and the thought of him being blinded or mutilated or murdered made her tremble.

She looked at the small square clock on top of the bookcase. It was only five past eight, although it felt as if she had been talking to Bobby Quilty for nearly half an hour. She stood in the middle of the living room, gripping John's Ardagh bracelet tightly in her hand, sick with indecision. She knew exactly what procedure she had to follow. She should immediately contact Inspector O'Rourke and the rest of her team and send them out to discover when and where John had been abducted and where he was being held. But that would be critically risky. If Bobby Quilty caught wind that she had broken their 'treaty', she didn't doubt for a moment that he would order John to be mutilated or murdered, just to prove how much of a hold he had over her and that he wasn't a man to be messed with.

She trusted her detectives implicitly but it wasn't beyond the bounds of possibility that Bobby Quilty had one or two officers at the station in his pocket. Even gardaí who had served for five years took home less than 30,000 euros a year and she knew that any number of them had serious debt problems.

Barney stood looking up at her and made that creaking noise in the back of his throat. He needed to be fed and then taken for a walk. But how could she take him for a walk knowing that John was being held hostage and doing nothing to initiate his rescue?

She went to the mirror that hung over the fireplace and stared at herself, as if her mirror image were another, calmer Katie, who could give her an answer. Her dark red hair was looking messy and chopped-about, and her eyes were puffy, as if she had just woken up.

You have to handle this one very, very carefully, she told herself. *You're angry. You're afraid. But don't be rushed into taking some course of action you might regret. Bobby Quilty isn't going to hurt John so long as he thinks you're playing ball, because he knows that if anything happens to John, you'll set the dogs on him.*

For the first time, she held up the Ardagh bracelet and examined it closely. It was slightly bent out of shape, as if it had been forcibly pulled from John's wrist without opening the clasp. She wondered why he had still been wearing it. Did he still love her, in spite of having left her?

She placed the bracelet carefully on the shelf over the fireplace, next to the silver-framed photograph of John which she should have taken down, but hadn't. He standing next to a tractor at the Meagher family farm, stripped to the waist, one eye closed against the sunlight. He was tall, with dark curly hair and a crucifix of hair on his chest. She had always told him that he looked like a Greek god, but like a Greek god he had been jealous and controlling. In the end, that was why their relationship had broken down, because Katie refused to be controlled by any man, even a man she loved.

In spite of that, the Katie that she could see in the mirror was already beginning to work out a way of saving him from Bobby Quilty. It wasn't orthodox, and it was far from accepted procedure. It was probably illegal. But it could be the best way to protect John from coming to any harm and at the same time to bring down Bobby Quilty's cigarette-smuggling empire.

She sat down on the end of the leather couch and picked up the phone. It took the operator at Anglesea Street a few minutes to find Inspector O'Rourke for her, but eventually he picked up, sounding as if he had his mouth full.

'Sorry, ma'am. I was just getting myself a sandwich.'

'That's okay. We all have to eat. How are things going?'

'We're making some progress with the bodies in Blarney. Just after you left, the Blarney Historical Society came back to us. There was definitely a family called Langtry lived in that house, up until February 1921. The father's name was Stephen, so we should be able to trace him through public records.'

'Grand. I think Dr Kelley should be coming down tomorrow afternoon, so maybe we'll be able to make a positive ID within the next few days. I'd still like to keep this under wraps until we do. You haven't had the media sniffing around, have you?'

'Nothing. I reckon they're too busy with this gay marriage vote and this water meter fracas.'

'All right. Listen, the reason I'm ringing you is Denny Quinn. I want you to release him.'

There was a moment's silence and then Inspector O'Rourke said, '*Release* him? Did I hear that right? He's up in the district court tomorrow afternoon. What if he does a runner?'

'Just let him go. We're dropping the charges.'

'What? With all due respect, ma'am, he was flogging illegal fags and he cut Detective O'Connell's cheek wide open. Not forgetting that Gerry Barry was killed when he was trying to arrest him.'

'I know, Francis. But believe me, I have a very good reason for letting him go.'

'Am I allowed to know what it is, this very good reason?'

'Not yet, no. But I'll tell you as soon as I can, and when I *can* tell you I think you'll agree that it was the right thing to do.'

Another silence, longer this time, and before Inspector O'Rourke could answer her Katie said, 'Please don't discuss this with anybody else. If anybody wants to know why we're letting him go, all you have to say is "insufficient evidence". I'll be talking tomorrow to Chief Superintendent MacCostagáin, but it's very important that we keep this as quiet as possible. Let's just say it's a matter of life and death.'

'Okay,' said Inspector O'Rourke, although he still sounded troubled. 'I have you.'

Nine

A broken-down car transporter had caused a three-kilometre tailback on the N25 the following morning and it was raining hard so Katie had to keep her windscreen wipers flapping at full speed just to see the car in front of her. She didn't arrive at the station until 8.35, by which time she was already feeling anxious and irritable.

Detective 'Horse' Ó Doibhilin was waiting for her. He stood smiling expectantly while she took off her dripping-wet witch-goddess jacket, sat down at her desk and had a cursory look through all the folders and messages and letters that were piled up for her attention.

Then, 'Yes, Michael?' she said, as if she had only just realized he was there.

'The fellow from the Blarney Historical Society finally got in touch with me. Douglas Pike.'

'I know, yes. Inspector O'Rourke rang me yesterday evening.'

'He's found copies of the old staff records from Mahony's mill, going right back to nineteen-oh-something. All of their names, how much they got paid and where they all lived. He said that the Langtry family took up residence on Millstream Row in April 1916. They'd moved there from Dripsey. Stephen Langtry had been a machinist at the Dripsey woollen mills but for some reason he gave up his job there and moved to Blarney. Better money, more than likely, that was Douglas Pike's guess. The Langtry family lived in Blarney until the second week of February 1921.'

'But this Historical Society fellow didn't know what happened to them?'

'He had no idea they were all shot dead and buried under the floorboards, no.'

'You didn't tell him that?'

'Oh, no, of course not. But if he had known, he would have told me, for sure. He knows everything about Blarney right down to who drowned whose dog in 1937 for barking and keeping them awake all night, and who won the best barmbrack competition in 1951. He wasn't backward about telling me, either. I thought I was going to be stuck on the blower all afternoon. But—'

Detective Ó Doibhilin held up his notebook. 'I think I have a result. He told me that some of the Langtry family still live in Dripsey, in the Model Village. I've traced two people of that name there, and I've tried ringing them, but neither of them answered, so I'll go out there this morning and see if I can locate them. Tyrone from the Technical Bureau will be coming along with me, to take DNA swabs.'

'Good work, Michael,' said Katie. 'If we can positively confirm who *they* are, then it might help us find out who killed them. Grand. Thank you.'

She turned her attention back to her paperwork, but then she was aware that Detective Ó Doibhilin was still standing there. She looked up again and said, 'Yes, Michael? Was there something else?'

'No, not really, ma'am. It's just that I've never worked on a case like this before – you know, when the crime was committed such a long time ago. It's almost ninety-five years, like.'

'Well, I haven't either,' said Katie. 'Not unless you count that bog woman who was dug up in Mayfield.'

'I was only wondering why we're carrying on this inquiry at all. Like, whoever the offenders were, they must have passed away years ago. And, you know, I would have thought that we'd more than enough on our plates just at the moment.'

Katie said, 'You're right of course, Michael, and believe me, I'm not giving it a very high priority. But justice has to be done, even if it's long overdue, do you know what I mean? You might manage to hide whatever crime it is that you've committed, and nobody might discover what you've done until you're dead and buried, but you still ought to know that one day you could be found out and your name shamed for it.'

'Well, I suppose,' said Detective Ó Doibhilin.

'Look at Sonny O'Neill, for instance. He was the fellow who shot Michael Collins at Béal na Bláth in 1922, but that wasn't known for certain until they opened the files in the 1980s. O'Neill was long gone, but it was still important for us to know that he actually fired the fatal shot, do you know what I mean, whether you think he was a hero or a villain? What happened in the 1920s, it's still resonating, isn't it, even today?'

Detective Ó Doibhilin nodded, and nodded again, and said, 'All right. Yes, I deck that,' and left Katie's office. After he had gone she sat at her desk for a few minutes, thinking about what she had just said to him and hoping it hadn't made her sound too much like her old history mistress, Miss Mulvaney, whose grandfather had been shot dead at Croke Park on Bloody Sunday in 1920, and never let anybody forget it.

She felt frayed and exhausted. She hadn't been able to sleep all night, worrying about John and how she could rescue him from Bobby Quilty. She had also been trying to work out what she was going to say at this morning's operational meeting about cigarette smuggling, and how they were going to change their strategy after the murder of Detective Barry. Up until now – in open and sometimes angry disagreement with Assistant Commissioner Jimmy O'Reilly – Katie had repeatedly argued that they should go after Bobby Quilty in person and not spend valuable time and budget chasing after his small-time dealers and mules. This morning's meeting wasn't going to be easy. Now that John was being held hostage, under threat of his life, she would have to find a way of backtracking without losing authority or credibility or, most of all, face.

* * *

The meeting started fifteen minutes late and everybody in the conference room was growing restless and checking their watches even though there was a large clock on the wall. Superintendent Pearse was having a furious finger-jabbing argument with somebody on his tablet, and Chief Superintendent MacCostagáin was looking deeply disgruntled. In the hoarsely whispered words of Detective Markey, who was sitting close enough for Katie to be able to hear him, he had the face of a bulldog sucking piss from a stinging nettle.

At last, Assistant Commissioner Jimmy O'Reilly walked into the conference room, skull-like and ill-tempered, his thinning silver hair greased back, his eyes as dead as ever. He was still wearing his blue full-dress uniform and Katie remembered that he had attended a formal reception earlier that morning for the new minister for justice and equality, Mary Brennan. Jimmy O'Reilly never enjoyed being reminded that there was somebody up the ladder higher than him, especially when that somebody was a woman.

Behind Jimmy O'Reilly, holding a bulging folder of notes under his arm, came his senior personal assistant, James Elvin. He was a very good-looking young man, with fashionably brushed-up blonde hair and a smart grey suit, and despite Jimmy O'Reilly's permanent scowl James always seemed to be having a secret smirk to himself. Katie had found herself wishing when she first met him that she was ten years younger.

Chief Superintendent MacCostagáin stood up, cleared his throat, and said, 'Before we start, I'd appreciate it if you'd all stand for two minutes in silence to pay our respects to Detective Garda Gerald Barry, who gave his life in the line of duty.'

They all stood. Some crossed themselves and almost all of them closed their eyes or stared down at the floor. Katie kept her eyes open because she knew that if she closed them she would see Detective Barry's smile again and wonder what he had been dreaming as he died.

When they had all sat down, Jimmy O'Reilly rose stiffly to his feet. He was addressing more than sixty detectives and gardaí and technical specialists, but he fixed his eyes on the clock at the very back of the conference room and spoke in a barely audible monotone, as if he were reluctantly reading out a restaurant menu to somebody who had forgotten their glasses.

'Good morning. Tobacco smuggling. Point number one. Strategy. I think we have to accept that it was the way in which we conceptualized our role in dealing with tobacco smuggling that led partly if not almost entirely to the tragic loss of Detective Barry.'

He paused for so long that Katie began to think that he had forgotten what he was going to say next, or that he had even forgotten where he was and that he was supposed to be talking to them. The lengthy silence was punctuated by coughing and shuffling, and one distinctive sneeze.

Eventually, though, he carried on in the same indistinct monotone. 'Point number two. Of course we acknowledge that the smuggling and selling of NIDP tobacco is organized by criminal gangs and our intelligence has clearly shown that some of those criminal gangs are channelling their profits into illegal political activities – such as, for instance, the Authentic IRA. However, the offence of evading duty on tobacco is not of itself a direct threat to public order.'

He paused again, licking his lips with the tip of his tongue, like a lizard that had just swallowed a fly. 'Point number three. Detective Barry is the first and so far the only fatal casualty of tobacco smuggling in Cork, but that is one fatality too many. I, for one, want to see no more lives lost, either gardaí or civilians, not for an offence that is essentially financial. I'm not pretending for a moment that smoking is harmless, or that health care for smokers isn't a serious drain on government resources, but smoking in designated areas is not in itself a crime. I accept that evading duty on tobacco deprives the government of much-needed revenue, but I think we have to ask ourselves how much responsibility the government itself has to bear for bowing to pressure from the cancer lobby and setting the retail price of cigarettes so high, the highest in Europe.

'In my view, An Garda Síochána should be leaving the investigation into tobacco smuggling and the enforcement of duty entirely to

Revenue, except when violence or threats of violence are involved, or when illegal cigarette factories are set up in this country for the purposes of avoiding duty. Furthermore, we should leave the tracing and confiscation of any profits made from contraband tobacco to the Criminal Assets Bureau.'

Again he paused and licked his lips, and then he said, 'I've had detailed consultations with the deputy commissioner and with Chief Superintendent MacCostagáin, and we're broadly in agreement. Since the recent budget cuts, this division has burdened with an increasingly onerous caseload but has fewer officers and less money to cope with that caseload. It's patently clear that our efforts to break up cigarette-smuggling gangs by the piecemeal arrest of their dealers is not proving at all effective. Almost as soon as we arrest one dealer, another one appears on the same spot within minutes, and if we confiscate their stock, the gang simply resupplies them with a whole load more. It's like trying to cut the head off a hydrant.'

'Hydra,' Katie quietly corrected him, though she wasn't sure that he heard her.

Jimmy O'Reilly at last looked down at the faces of his audience, although his emotionless expression showed that he had made up his mind and that he wasn't expecting anyone there to challenge him. 'To sum up, I'm proposing that we curtail our strategy of arresting dealers and in future act only in support of Revenue and the CAB when called upon to do so. Does anybody have any views on that? Detective Superintendent Maguire, you've always been very vociferous when it comes to cigarette smuggling.'

Katie hardly knew what to say, although she was feeling a deep sense of relief. *Thank you, St Raphael,* she thought. St Raphael was the patron saint of lovers and she had said a prayer to him in the darkness of the night, pleading with him to keep John safe.

She hadn't expected for a moment that Jimmy O'Reilly intended to cut back Garda operations against cigarette smugglers. He had given an interview to the *Irish Times* only three weeks ago claiming that his pursuit of tobacco gangs would continue to be 'relentless'. But now she wouldn't have to come up with some fictitious justification for releasing Denny Quinn and suspending her inquiry into Bobby Quilty.

Even though she was relieved, she knew that it would arouse suspicion if she welcomed Jimmy O'Reilly's change of strategy with too much enthusiasm. It was common knowledge in Anglesea Street that there was no love lost between the two of them, either personally or operationally.

'Well, sir, I can't say that I totally go along with what you're suggesting,' she told him. 'In particular, I'm concerned that young people are being tempted by the smugglers to take part in organized crime and that that's going to lead them into much more serious offending as they grow older.'

Jimmy O'Reilly didn't look at her but kept his eyes on the audience, to see what their reaction was. 'Fair play to you, detective Superintendent I can see where you're coming from. But on the whole I think that we can rely on our social services to manage that particular problem – as we mostly do already, to be fair. If the courts won't convict fifteen-year-olds for selling illegal cigarettes, why are we bothering with arresting them and going through all the committal procedure? It needlessly ties up officers who could be going after car thieves and pimps and drug-dealers, and worse.'

Katie lifted both of her hands, as if she couldn't argue with what he was saying. 'All right, then. My team are up the walls at the moment with some very serious inquiries, no question about it, and it would certainly free up some of their time. So, yes, let's break off our surveillance of the dealers for a few weeks and see how things work out.'

'You *agree* with me, then?' Jimmy O'Reilly's lips twisted themselves into something that was almost a smile. 'That's a first. What about Detective Barry? You'll still be pursuing *that* investigation, I imagine?'

'Of course, although it's not going as well as I'd hoped. There's no forensic or CCTV evidence to identify the driver who knocked him down, and no witnesses have come forward yet, although that doesn't surprise me.'

She saw Detective Sergeant Begley shift around in his seat and frown at her. Only yesterday afternoon she had vehemently told him that she would find out who had killed Gerry Barry if it took the rest of her life. But Bobby Quilty or one of his gang were by far the most likely suspects and she wanted to give the impression that she didn't hold out much hope of arresting any of them.

Maybe I'm being more than a little paranoid, she thought. *Maybe there's nobody in this room who's going to contact Bobby Quilty as soon as this conference is over and tell him what I've just said. But how had Bobby Quilty managed to react so quickly to their attempted arrest of Denny Quinn at Mother Jones Flea Market, unless he had known in advance that Denny was under surveillance?*

Katie had little doubt that it would reach his ears somehow, and the less threatened Bobby Quilty felt, the better John's chances of survival.

* * *

She was buttoning up her jacket ready to go out when Detective Ó Doibhilin knocked at her door. He was carrying an old green Governey's shoebox.

'Oh, you're back,' she said. 'How did you get on? I'm in a bit of a rush, I'm afraid. I'm meeting somebody and I'm ten minutes late already.'

'To be honest with you, ma'am, I'm not too sure *what* I got.'

'What do you mean? Did you manage to find any of the Langtry family?'

Detective Ó Doibhilin put down the shoebox on the corner of Katie's desk and took out his notebook. 'I did, yes. Two in fact. The most direct descendant was Dermot Langtry, thirty-nine years old, lives with his wife and three children at O'Mahoney Terrace in the Model Village. He has his own painting and decorating business.'

'All right,' said Katie, trying not to sound impatient. 'So what's his connection to Stephen Langtry?'

'His great-grandfather, Colm Langtry, was Stephen Langtry's

younger brother. That, er, that would make him Stephen Langtry's great-grand-nephew.'

'That's correct. Who was the other one?'

'Dermot Langtry's second cousin, Ronan Fitzgerald. Forty-two years old, married with no children. He's an accountant for Crowley and McCarthy in Macroom. Lives only round the corner in Radharc Na Chroisigin.'

'So, did either of them know anything about the Langtrys' sudden disappearance?'

'Not Ronan Fitzgerald. All he was good for was triangulating our DNA sample. But Dermot Langtry did, yes, and that's why I'm so puggalized.'

'Go on.'

'Well, it seems like the Langtrys took off one day without inform-ing a soul that they were going – the same as that auld wan told us. They didn't tell their family, they didn't tell any of their friends. Stephen Langtry didn't even tell his boss at the mill that he was leaving. The house was cleared, too, all of the furniture gone. After about four months, though, Dermot's great-grandfather received a postcard from Stephen from America. Stephen wrote that the family had settled in New York State and he was working for a company called Glenside Woollen Mills there and that everything was grand.'

'Did he explain why they upped sticks like that, without telling anybody?'

'The postcard's right here in the box, ma'am. There's some letters, too, but I haven't had the time to read them yet. There's five letters and eleven postcards altogether. The last of them is dated Christmas 1923. After that, the Langtrys in Dripsey never heard from Stephen again. They couldn't write back to him and ask him where he was because he never them gave his full address. The letters just say "New York", with the date.'

'But they were definitely sent from America?'

'Take a sconce at them yourself, ma'am,' said Detective Ó Doibhilin. He snapped on a black latex glove, lifted the lid of the shoebox and picked out an envelope. Its address was scrawled in faded purple ink and a cluster of pale green 10 cent stamps were stuck on to it, each with a portrait of President Hayes, as well as two brown 4 cent stamps with a smiling Martha Washington.

Katie could also see a few of the postcards inside the box. Some of them were hand-coloured but most were sepia photographs of tall buildings and streets crowded with men in straw skimmers and women in ankle-length skirts.

'You're right, Michael, this *is* confusing, isn't it? If the Langtrys were shot dead and lying under the floorboards in Blarney, how could they be sending mail from America? These letters and postcards – they certainly *look* genuine, don't they?'

'I'll be taking them down to the lab now to have them tested,' said Detective Ó Doibhilin. 'Unfortunately we don't have any authenticated samples of Stephen Langtry's handwriting to compare them with. Still and all, Tyrone took a DNA sample from Dermot Langtry and he should be able to give us the result of that later today or tomorrow.'

'Good. Dr Kelley will be arriving here about three and she'll be going directly up to Blarney, so we may be able to move the bodies sometime tomorrow. She didn't want them touched until she'd had the chance to examine them *in situ*, in case they fell to pieces. Now, I'm sorry to cut this short, but I really must go.'

As she hurried along the corridor, zipping up her jacket as she went, Detective Ó Doibhilin followed close behind her, carrying the shoebox under his arm.

'I'll tell you the truth, ma'am,' he said, as she pressed the button for the lift. 'You know what I was asking you earlier, why are we are trying to identify this family and find out who killed them even though it happened so long ago? I understand now what you were talking about. Like, I *really* understand. We *do* need to know, don't we? Like, *I* want to know myself. Whoever he is, there's a feller lying in a cemetery somewhere who shot them, the father, the mother, the two little kiddies and their dogs. I want to stand over his grave and tell him that he hasn't got away with it, even if he's dead.'

Ten

John was woken up by a man and a woman arguing with each other. Then he heard a dull thump and a complicated clatter, like furniture being knocked over.

'You're a fecking dirty clart, that's what you are!' the man shouted out in a strong Armagh accent. 'You're a fecking *hoo*-ah! I should clean your clock, so I should! I should kick your fecking teeth right down your fecking throat, you *hoo*-ah!'

The woman screamed something back at him, although John couldn't understand what it was. There was another thump and then she started wailing.

'Stop your gurning or I'll give you something to gurn about!' the man told her, but she carried on mewling and sobbing.

John slowly and painfully sat up. He felt bruised all over and his head was throbbing. His left eye was so swollen that he could barely see out of it and his cheekbone ached.

He looked around the room. It was small and stuffy, with a purple cotton blind pulled down over the window so that he couldn't see out, although he could hear rain pattering sporadically against the glass. It must have been a child's room because the walls were papered with space rockets and flying saucers and planets, and there was a white chest of drawers with stickers of smiling cars and aeroplanes on it. The narrow single bed had a pine headboard covered with more stickers and a stained mattress that smelled of dried urine. The purple carpet was spotted and moth-eaten, and one of the door panels was split as if somebody had once tried to kick it open from outside.

At last the woman stopped crying. John heard the man say something to her which sounded conciliatory, but then she shrilled, 'Away to feck, you frigger!'

He could clearly remember leaving his friend Peter Doody's house in Knocknadeenly, where he had been lodging since he had walked out on Katie before Christmas, and driving down Summerhill into the city. He could remember turning from Western Road into Donovan's Road on his way to the Hayfield Manor Hotel. A young woman had stepped out into the road in front of him with a baby buggy and when she had tried to jump back out of the way the buggy had tipped over. He had stopped and climbed out of his car to make sure that the child hadn't been hurt, but after that everything was a blank.

Very cautiously, he touched the back of his head. His black curly hair was stuck together and he could feel a large lump. He could only assume that he had been hit very hard and knocked unconscious. Not only that, he had a strange, bitter taste in his mouth, as if he been drinking some kind of medicine.

He tried to stand up. He managed to take two staggering steps forwards and then the floor tilted and he had to sit back down on the bed. His head was banging even harder and he felt as if he could hardly breathe.

He was about to try again when he heard a key being turned in the lock and the door opened. Two men crowded into the room. One of them had a huge belly that hung over his belt, a piggy-looking face, and his hair shaved up the sides of his head in what the Northern Irish called a scaldy. The other was scrawny, with tufty grey hair and brown crowded teeth and tattoos of a woman's hands around his neck, as if he were being choked. Both of them were smoking. Behind them, in the next room, John could see the same young woman who had crossed the road in front of him with her baby buggy. She had bleached-blonde hair and enormous breasts that were straining under a tight green T-shirt with a picture of Bono on it, and a dark maroon bruise next to her mouth.

'All right, big lad?' said the huge-bellied man. 'How's it cutting?'

'Who the hell are you?' John demanded. 'What the hell did you do to me? And where am I?'

'Bobby Quilty's the name, and this is my valet, Chisel. My apologies, like, if you've been inconvenienced. But, you know, that's the price you pay for cosying up to the polls.'

'*What?* What in the name of Jesus are you talking about?'

'You and that tasty Detective Superintendent Maguire, that's what I'm talking about.'

'What about her?'

'You and she are a bit of an item, right?'

'What the hell has it got to do with you? Who the hell are you?'

'I told you, big lad. Bobby Quilty. Did your old doll never mention me? Let's just say that I'm one of Cork's most successful entre-pren-hoo-hahs.'

'I still have no idea what you're talking about.'

Bobby Quilty took a deep drag on his cigarette and then blew a long stream of smoke directly into John's face, so that he had to close his eyes and his mouth tightly and turn his head away.

'Calm your knickers, big lad, I'll tell you what I'm talking about. For fecking *months* now, your Detective Superintendent Maguire has been sticking her neb into my entre-pren-hoo-ring something desperate. In fact, she's been doing my fecking head in. So in order to persuade her to leave me in peace, I decided to acquire myself something to negotiate with, like a trump card, like – and that trump card is you. The long and the short of it is, she and me have come to an agreement.'

'What kind of agreement?'

'Catch yourself on, will you, what do you think? If she lets me carry on my business undisturbed, you'll stay sound. But if she keeps on after me, John, and keeps on scooping the people who work for me, well, I can't guarantee that God will preserve you. Not in one piece, any road.'

John said, 'You're out of your mind. You don't seriously think that she's going to leave you alone just because you're holding me hostage?'

'It had crossed my mind,' said Bobby Quilty, taking another drag, but this time blowing it out sharply upwards and sideways.

'Detective Superintendent Maguire and me, we're not even an item any more,' John told him. 'We split up just before Christmas.'

'You were going to meet her last night, though?'

'How the hell did you know that?'

'Ach, that's for me to know and you to find out. But let's just say there's nothing that happens in Cork that Bobby Quilty isn't wise to.'

'So, how long do you intend to keep me here?' John asked him.

Bobby Quilty shrugged. 'I hadn't really given it a whole lot of consideration, to tell you the truth. But I'd say long enough to make sure that your old doll sticks to what she promised.'

'I think you're underestimating her badly,' said John. 'She's far more dedicated to the law than she is to me. She broke up with me because I wanted her to leave the Garda. Whatever you do to me, she'll still come after you. That's what she's like.'

'We'll just have to wait and see, won't we?' grinned Bobby Quilty. 'Well, *I'll* be able to see, but if she chooses not to honour our agreement, it's very possible that *you* won't be able to. But don't worry. I still have my da's old walking stick and a tin of white Dulux.'

Chisel grinned, too, exposing his crowd of mahogany-coloured teeth.

'Just settle yourself down, John,' said Bobby Quilty. 'Sorcia will fetch you some tea later. You're okay with a Bigfoot sausage, are you, from the chippie?'

Eleven

Kyna Ni Nuallán was waiting for Katie in the small alcove just inside the front door of Henchy's Bar, up in St Luke's Cross. She was sitting in the corner with her back to the stained-glass window and even though the alcove was so gloomy she was wearing large black Chanel sunglasses. She had also tied a black silk scarf around her head, pirate-style, and the collar of her black nylon jacket was turned up.

'If I hadn't known who you were, I wouldn't have recognized you,' said Katie, taking off her jacket and sitting down beside her.

'Well, you said to be discreet,' said Kyna. 'Do you want a drink of anything?'

'I could murder a double vodka, but a cup of coffee would be grand.'

Kyna lifted her hand and called out to the bearded young barman, 'Declan, would you do me a favour there and fetch my friend a cup of coffee?'

Katie said, 'You know him? I thought you'd never been in here before.'

'I haven't. But he was coming on to me as soon as I walked in. He said I was the first beour to set foot in the place since Paddy's Day.'

Katie couldn't help smiling. Kyna was very pretty, in a blonde, elfin way. Even her fellow detectives used to come on to her. What they usually failed to realize was that she had no interest in men whatsoever – not sexually, anyway. Katie couldn't stay smiling for long, though. She had asked Kyna to meet her here because she needed to ask for her help. She hadn't been able to think of

82

anybody else who could not only do what she wanted but could be trusted to do it. The trouble was, what she wanted could turn out to be hazardous in the extreme. Kyna had almost sacrificed her life for Katie once already, by stopping the bullet that had been meant for her, and Katie was beginning to wonder if it was too much to ask her to do it again.

It was because of the dangers involved that Katie had arranged to meet her here, at Henchy's. It was less than five minutes north of the city centre, up at the top of Summerhill, but it was not a bar frequented by any of Bobby Quilty's gang, or any other city scobes, or anybody at all who was likely to recognize Katie. Even so, she was wearing a purple beret into which she had tucked most of her dark red hair.

'So what's this about?' asked Kyna. 'I was planning to go back to Dublin tomorrow to see if I can find myself a flat. There's still nearly six months left on my current lease here, but I met a girl from the university last week and she's desperate for somewhere to live so I may be able to sublet to her.'

The barman brought over Katie's cup of coffee with two ginger biscuits in the saucer, so she waited until he was out of earshot.

'It's Bobby Quilty,' she said. 'He's kidnapped John and he says he's going to do him serious harm if I carry on interfering in his tobacco-smuggling business.'

Kyna looked both shocked and baffled. '*John?* You mean *your* John? I thought he was totally out of the picture. Didn't he go back to the States?'

'He might have done. In fact, he probably did. But he's here in Cork now,' said Katie. She took the silver Ardagh bracelet out of her pocket and passed it across the table. 'This was my present to him when he came back last year. Bobby Quilty gave it to me as proof that he really has him.'

'Oh, Jesus,' said Kyna. She handed the bracelet back and squeezed Katie's hand. 'You must be so worried. Have you told anybody at the station?'

Katie shook her head. 'Not yet. They'd want to take immediate action. Or at least, Denis MacCostagáin would. He won't tolerate anybody trying to intimidate individual guards. But Quilty only has to pick up the slightest sniff that we're still after him and God alone knows what he might do to John. I'm sure that Quilty killed Gerry Barry, or one of his henchmen did it on his instructions, and that was over what? A few dozen boxes of Russian cigarettes. I don't think he'd have the slightest compunction about killing John and dumping his body where I'm never going to find him.'

Kyna stared at Katie for a long time without speaking. Eventually, though, she said, 'Do you still love him?'

'John? Love doesn't come into it. He's a human being and Quilty's threatening to mutilate or murder him.'

'But come on, that happens almost daily, doesn't it? Abduction, like, do you know what I mean, and blackmail? I've never known you to pull the plug on any inquiry, *ever*, just because somebody was being held hostage. Completely the opposite, in fact. You've gone after them tooth and claw.'

'Of course,' said Katie. 'But most of the time it's one scummer kidnapping another scummer because he's been horning in on whatever racket he's running. But John isn't a rival tobacco smuggler, or a drug-pusher, or a pimp who's been grooming another pimp's prostitutes. John is totally innocent, Kyna. His only crime was to have a relationship with me.'

Kyna kept hold of Katie's hand for a while, but then let it go. 'You should drink your coffee before it gets cold.'

Katie said, 'It'd be different if I had any idea at all where Quilty's holding him. I could set up a raid, which might be risky but at least we'd have a chance of getting him out of there in one piece.'

'Don't we know anybody who's prepared to grass on Quilty?' asked Kyna. 'What about that Barty McGee? If it wasn't for him, we wouldn't have known half of what Quilty was up to.'

'I don't think Barty's going to be talking to us again, Kyna. Quilty gave him the choice of leaving the country and never coming back or eating his own mebs fried in Kerrygold – or that's what he told Dooley.'

'So what are you going to do?'

'Well, I've had one heaven-sent stroke of luck. Jimmy O'Reilly has decided that after Gerry Barry being killed we should suspend our inquiry into Quilty and instead leave it to Revenue to go after him. He says he doesn't want the lives of any more officers put in jeopardy for such a low-level crime, but I suspect that he's run way over budget this year and this is how he's going to save himself money. Anyway, I said a novena to St Raphael and he must have answered me because at least I didn't have to stand up in front of half the station and come up with some lame excuse why I thought we should lay off Quilty.'

'St Raphael?'

'The patron saint of lovers.'

'So you *do* still love him? John, I mean. You do know that St Raphael is also the patron saint of insanity and nightmares? And short-sightedness, too.'

'Mother of God, you must have been paying attention in catechism.'

Kyna gave her a small, regretful smile. 'No. But I looked him up not long ago to see if he could help me win my ideal partner.'

Katie sipped at her coffee and snapped one of her ginger biscuits in half, though she didn't eat it.

'Officially, you're still on sick leave,' she said. 'You don't have to do what I'm going to ask you, not if you don't want to. It won't be insubordination. And I won't think badly of you, either.'

'I can guess what it is,' said Kyna.

'I'm sure that you can, but believe me, Kyna, if there was any other way, I wouldn't ask. It's no use my pretending that it won't be fierce dangerous, especially if anybody recks you. But you haven't been in Cork all that long, and you haven't been involved in any cases of smuggling or evading tobacco or alcohol duty – nor the Authentic IRA, either.'

'Listen, there's lots of ways I can disguise myself,' Kyna told her. 'I can dye my hair. I've had it all kinds of colours over the years – shamrock green, once! But black looks good on me. And

I can wear clothes that make me look a whole lot younger. Really skinny jeans, loads of bangles and necklaces, and I have a tattoo on my shoulder already, which I can show off.'

'You have a tattoo? What of?'

'A lyre, as a matter of fact. L-y-r-e, not l-i-a-r, although I like the double meaning, too. Sappho the poet used to play the lyre, that's why I had it done.'

'All right,' said Katie. This wasn't the time to go into the implications of that any further. 'If you can do this for me, I'll contact you tomorrow, probably, and tell you where you can find one of Quilty's dealers. They're growing more and more brazen about selling their cigarettes out in the open so it shouldn't be hard to locate one. But, like I say, you don't have to do it. I don't want you getting hurt again.'

'Detective Superintendent Maguire, I'm a police officer. I know what the risks are. I'm not one hundred per cent sure that this is the right way to go about rescuing John, but if this is what you want to do, I'll do it.'

'So how would you handle it? We can't lift Quilty because we don't have any evidence to bring charges against him, and even if we brought him in for questioning his lawyers would have him out again in five minutes flat. In the meantime he'd make sure that something horrible happened to John. He threatened to blind him.'

Kyna took hold of her hand again. 'I've said I'll do it, Katie, and I'll do it.'

Katie reached into her pocket again and took out a pink iPhone in a pink sparkly case. 'Here, take this. It belonged to one of the girls we picked up when we raided that BTB massage parlour on Princes Street. If Quilty asks to check your phone, this one has the numbers of enough pimps and pushers and generally dubious characters to fill Páirc Uí Chaoimh twice over. I've also changed the number marked 'Ma' to my own mobile number, so if he asks you to call your mother just to make sure that you are who you're pretending to be, you'll be able to do it.'

'And who am I pretending to be?'

'Sheelagh Danehy, of Mount Nebo Avenue in Gurra. Late of the support centre for troubled teenage girls at North Pres Secondary School. You went through the copping on course but didn't really cop on, and when they gave you art therapy you got yourself thrown out for emptying your paint water over another girl's head. I'm sure you can improvise the rest.'

'I'll try my best. I was always a goodie two-shoes at school, and of course I never fancied any of the boys. Whenever I walked down the corridor, some of them used to sing out "Kyna, Kyna, with the Untouched Vagina".'

Katie smiled again. 'I'm sure you can act like a slutbag if you try.'

She spent another twenty minutes briefing Kyna on how she could inveigle herself into Bobby Quilty's cigarette-smuggling operation. Soon after she had been appointed a detective garda herself, Katie had been planted undercover into a drug-dealing gang in Togher and she knew how difficult and dangerous it was to repel the sexual advances of some of the men involved.

Expressionless behind her sunglasses, Kyna said, 'I have done it with men, you know. Sometimes because I was langered. Usually out of pity.'

'Don't bother about the cigarette-smuggling itself,' Katie told her. 'I'm not interested in that, nor in Quilty's connections to the A-IRA, or that he was probably responsible for Gerry Barry being killed. Not yet, anyway. All I want to know is where John is.'

'I know,' said Kyna, almost sadly.

Katie didn't embrace Kyna as they parted on the pavement outside, although she would have liked to. It was still raining and there was nobody around, but she didn't want to risk anybody seeing them. As it turned out, there was a white-faced young man watching her from the window of Ladbroke's betting office as she returned to her car. She wondered what he would say if she went in and asked him to give her the odds on John surviving.

Twelve

Katie headed directly to Blarney. Dr Kelley had arranged to meet her at Millstream Row rather than going into the city centre first and then having to come all the way out again. Because she had needed to bring so much specialist equipment with her, she had driven from Dublin with one of her assistants instead of taking the train. That would have taken her nearly three hours, especially in this weather, and she had told Katie that she was anxious to get started as soon as possible.

When she arrived, Katie found that Millstream Row been completely cordoned off and a diversion had been set up around Sunberry Heights for what little traffic there was. A wet and miserable-looking garda unhooked the crime-scene tape for her so that she could park behind the two patrol cars that were already there, as well as two vans and an estate car from the Technical Bureau and a large blue Transit van which was probably Dr Kelley's.

She found Dr Kelley inside the living room, which was lit so brightly with forensic lamps that she had to raise her hand to shield her eyes. Dr Kelley was kneeling on the floor on the opposite side of the room, cutting samples of hair from the head of the mummified man. She was a small, tubby woman, who looked even tubbier in her Tyvek suit. She had a round face with a double chin and round glasses and bushy, mannish eyebrows. In spite of that, Katie thought that if she had plucked her eyebrows and applied a little blusher and lipstick, she could have made herself looked quite sweet and appealing, like a child's doll that had unexpectedly grown to adulthood.

'How's it going?' she asked. Bill Phinner was there, too, standing next to Dr Kelley, and he patted Dr Kelley on the shoulder so that she looked up and saw Katie standing by the door.

'I'll be with you in – *two* seconds,' said Dr Kelley, carefully dropping the hair sample into a clear plastic envelope. Then she stood up and edged her way around the room, tugging off her latex glove and shaking Katie's hand.

'Mary Kelley,' she said, in a brisk, enthusiastic voice. 'I saw you last April, at that forensic symposium at Dublin University. I *so* much wanted to talk to you about the bog woman in Mayfield, but I'd been buttonholed by some *terminally* boring Nigerian biochemist and by the time he'd finished regaling me with his anecdotes about Ebola you'd disappeared.'

'You could have called me any time.'

'Well, time is what I never have. It would be a *blessing*, I can tell you, if so many people in Ireland would stop dying in unusual or unexplained circumstances and give my head some peace once in a while. And now we have this unfortunate family and they passed away before anybody in this room was even born.'

'My guess is the early 1920s,' said Katie. 'The problem is, we have some uncertainty about who they actually are. The records show that in 1921 a family called the Langtrys were living here and that they suddenly vanished without telling anyone they were leaving. A few months later, though, they started sending letters and postcards from America, somewhere in New York State, so maybe they'd just done a moonlight flit. If that was the case, though, who are *these* people, and who shot them, and why?'

Bill Phinner said, 'We should have the results of the DNA tests sometime tomorrow morning, so at least we'll be able to see if they were related to the Langtrys in Dripsey.'

'We'll be moving the bodies, too, first thing tomorrow morning,' said Dr Kelley. 'Once I have them in the morgue I'll be able to carry out comprehensive tests to find out exactly how old they actually are, and how they became desiccated like this, as well as what diseases they might have been suffering from and what their last meal was.'

'Once Mary has retrieved them we'll be testing the bullets, too,' Bill Phinner put in. 'That may give us an idea of what kind of gun was used to kill them – but of course the chances of finding that weapon today are infinitesimal.'

Dr Kelley turned to her assistant, who was a slight young woman who looked as if she were half-Chinese. 'Have you all the photographs you need, Annie? Then we can start on the X-rays.'

Annie went outside to the van and came back after a few minutes carrying a grey handheld MINI Z X-ray machine and the tablet viewing screen that went with it. Katie had seen one of these handheld scanners being demonstrated but had never seen it in use at a real crime scene. It used backscatter technology to detect not only metal and bone but organic material such as drugs and explosives, or even plastic guns that had been made with 3-D printers.

'It's X-ray, all right, but the radiation level is so low we don't have to shield it,' said Dr Kelley. 'I have to tell you, I've been finding it a *boon*, an absolute boon, but it wasn't cheap. Fifty thousand euros, which is why Dr Reidy wouldn't let me take it on the train. He knows me and trains, and what I leave on them. I left a fifteen-hundred-year-old skull on the ten past three from Ballinasloe and it went all the way to Tullamore on its own.'

Katie said, 'What will you do once you've finished the X-rays?'

'We'll be wrapping each of the bodies in polythene and constructing a frame around it to keep it in position so that we do as little damage as possible. Once we have them in the morgue and properly laid out we'll be able to undress them and do full CGI scans and radiocarbon testing.'

'I'll let you crack on, then,' said Katie. 'You have my number, so call me if you need anything at all. You're staying at the Clarion tonight, aren't you? Their restaurant's good, if you like Asian. I'd join you for dinner, but I'm afraid I've a rake of paperwork to catch up on.'

'That's all right,' said Dr Kelley. 'Annie's very good company. I chose the Clarion specially because I knew she'd like the food.'

In reality, Katie had almost finished her paperwork, but she and John had eaten in the Kudos restaurant at the Clarion several times and she knew she wouldn't have the appetite for it, or for any other restaurant.

She stayed for a while to watch Annie carefully scanning the body of the little girl, then she gave a salute to Bill Phinner and walked out of the house into the rain. She was only halfway back to her car, however, when she saw an RTÉ outside broadcast van parked further along the terrace, and then she saw Fionnuala Sweeney from the *Nine o'Clock News* standing by the crime-scene tape, holding up her microphone as if she were carrying the Olympic torch.

'Detective superintendent!' she called out. 'Detective Superintendent Maguire! Can you spare me a minute?'

Katie waved her hand from side to side to indicate that she was too busy and opened the door of her car. Before she could climb in, however, Fionnuala shouted out, '*Langtrys!*'

Katie closed her car door and walked over to the tape. Fionnuala was gingery and white-skinned, but she would have been attractive to men who liked mermaids, especially with the rain sparkling in her hair. Her cameraman was standing close behind her left shoulder and as Katie approached he pinched out his cigarette and tucked it behind his ear.

'I hear that some bodies have been found underneath the floorboards of that house they're doing up.'

'I can't comment at the moment, Fionnuala.'

'I'm given to understand that they're a family called the Langtrys, who disappeared in 1921. Father, mother, two small children and even the family dogs.'

'Who told you that?'

'I'm sorry, detective Superintendent I can't reveal my sources. But it *is* the Langtrys, isn't it, and they've all been shot?'

'Did that Mrs O'Neill tell you that?'

'I'm sorry. Like I say, I can't reveal my sources.'

Katie took a deep breath and looked away. She didn't want to antagonize Fionnuala because she needed RTÉ's support so often in broadcasting appeals for information about robberies or news of missing children, or eyewitness accounts of fatal traffic accidents. On the other hand, she had felt right from the very beginning that the discovery of these bodies needed to be handled with extreme sensitivity. An entire family wouldn't have been shot for no reason at all, especially in 1921, and before she made a media announcement she really wanted to know what that reason had been.

Maybe she was being over-cautious, but she knew from experience that historic grudges could very quickly get out of hand, even if they were nothing more than old family feuds. She had dealt with a case only three weeks ago when a farmer in Curraheen had come close to being killed by his neighbour over a sixty-year-old argument about fifteen and a half metres of scrubby turf.

She turned back to Fionnuala and said, 'All I can tell you now is that several human bodies were discovered during the renovation of one of the houses here on Millstream Row. Currently, they're being examined by the Acting Deputy Pathologist, Dr Mary Kelley, who specializes in historic forensics. That is because our immediate impression was that the bodies had been hidden on the property for some considerable period of time.'

'A family called the Langtrys suddenly disappeared from Millstream Row in 1921. Is it them?'

'We've taken DNA samples, but so far we haven't made a positive identification. We can't yet be sure who they are or when they died or how. As soon as I have more information I will, of course, let you know.'

'It *could* be the Langtrys, though?' Fionnuala persisted.

'As I've just told you, Fionnuala, we can't yet be sure.'

'But they were shot?'

'I can't comment until Dr Kelley has completed her full examination of the bodies.'

'And how long will that take?'

'It will take as long as it takes. That's all I have to say at the moment.'

'Was Radha Langtry having an affair with a British soldier? Do you think that the family might have been shot because of that?'

Katie could have stalked straight to Nora O'Neill's house and taken hold of her by her withered neck and shaken her until she was sick. Instead she said, 'I have absolutely nothing to say about that, Fionnuala. This family have not yet been identified and I am certainly not going to start inventing wild theories about how and why they died until I have all the facts. It's going to be a long and painstaking business, and we may never know the whole truth, but I can promise you that as soon as I know any more, so will you.'

Thirteen

Hours went by, although John could only guess how many because his abductors had pulled off his wristwatch, as well as the Ardagh bracelet that Katie had given him. Eventually he eased himself over on to his side, wincing with pain, and then stood up. He swayed for a moment before taking a single lurching step towards the window. First he held on to the footboard at the end of the bed, and next he reached out for the knobs on the chest of drawers. The top drawer unexpectedly slid open and he almost fell backwards, but there was something inside the drawer that jammed it halfway. He paused, breathing with quick little sniffs, then managed to stagger to the window and hold on to the sill.

When he had first woken up it had already been gloomy outside because of the rain, but now he lifted up the cheap purple blind and saw that it was dark and the street lights were shining. He was in a first-floor room overlooking a small walled yard with green wheelie bins and a bicycle in it. The window handle was stiff, but he managed to wrench it upwards and push the window open, though it had a safety cable fixed to it and would only open about twenty centimetres.

Up on the skyline, only about half a kilometre away, John could make out the spires of St Mary and St Anne's Cathedral. He craned his neck sideways and pressed his head against the glass, even though the lump was still so tender that he gritted his teeth and whispered, 'Ow, *shit*. Ow!' When he did this, he could just see Shandon Bells Tower with its clock faces and pepperpot dome, and its salmon-shaped weathervane. That meant this house was somewhere in Blackpool, on the north-east side of the city centre – maybe on Leitrim Street or Pine Street. If he could get out of here, it wouldn't be difficult for him to find help. He might even be able to walk to Anglesea Street – or hobble there, anyway – and find Katie.

He peered down into the yard. Although the bedroom was on the first floor, there was a lean-to roof directly below the window, probably a toilet or wash-house. Whatever it was, John reckoned that if he could remove the safety cable from the window he would probably be able to clamber down to the yard below. He was badly bruised and his head was pounding with every beat of his heart, but he was still strong and reasonably fit. After he had given up working on his late father's farm he had accompanied Katie to her kick-boxing sessions whenever he could, and after he had walked out on her and moved back to Knocknadeenly he had kept up his running. It was while he was out running last week, under a low grey sky, with only the crows on the telephone wires for company, that he had suddenly realized how much he missed Katie. He knew that he had hurt her. That had been the whole point of his walking out. But standing between the hedgerows on that empty road, panting and sweaty, he saw that he had probably suffered much more pain from his jealousy than she had. She wasn't as tough as most people thought she was, but she knew how to put the past behind her.

He let the blind drop and made his way back to the bed. He sat there for a while, listening. He could hear the muffled sound of a television downstairs, but couldn't hear any voices. With any luck, he could climb out of the window without making too much noise and be out and away before Bobby Quilty and Chisel realized he had gone.

He stood up again, crossed the room, and pressed his ear against the door. He could hear the closing music of *Fair City*, so it must be 8.30. He thought he heard Bobby Quilty barking something and then letting out a harsh, abrasive laugh, but all he could hear after that was the blurting of one TV channel after another as if somebody was using the remote to see if there was anything they wanted to watch.

Okay, he told himself, *if you don't go now, you may never get another chance, especially if Katie doesn't give a damn what happens to you – and who could blame her?*

He crept back towards the window, steadying himself on the end of the bed again and then holding on to the chest of drawers. Looking into the half-open drawer he could see now what had caused it to jam. It was filled with a whole heap of assorted junk – ballpoint pens, Christmas-tree lights, suitcase keys and rolls of Sellotape, as well as a pair of sunglasses with only one lens and a diary for 1996. But what had caused it to stick was a red-handled screwdriver that had tilted upwards and dug its point into the underside of the frame.

John jiggled the drawer and forced it back in. Then he slid his hand in and lifted out the screwdriver. *Exactly what I need to open this window. There is a God. Or at least a patron saint of those whose lives are in danger because they don't have the right tools on them.*

He raised the blind, opened the window as far as it would go and started to unscrew one end of the safety cable. The screws were crossheads and the screwdriver was slightly too large for them, so he had to hold it at an angle. Eventually, though, he managed to loosen both screws to the point where he could twist them out between finger and thumb. With the safety cable hanging loose, he could open the window as far as it would go. It was still raining, but John could smell fresh air, and river, and traffic fumes, and freedom.

He took hold of the window frame and heaved himself up, but as he did so he whinnied in pain and almost bit off the tip of his tongue. When his chest was pressed against the edge of the sill, he realized that Bobby Quilty's men must have broken at least two of his ribs, and he was in agony. He hung there, unable to breathe because the pain was so intense, his mouth filling up with saliva and blood, and for a moment he was tempted to let himself drop back to the floor and give up any attempt to escape.

I can't do it. I can't take it. It hurts too much. But then he thought: *If this is what they've done to you already, John, what do you think they're going to do to you if Katie keeps after them? You heard what Bobby Quilty threatened to do, he threatened to blind you. And that was just for beginners.*

He didn't know how long he stayed there, with his head and shoulders sticking halfway out of the window, blinking at the rain that was spitting into his eyes. At last, however, he summoned up the will to pull himself up even further. The pain in his chest was unbearable, greater than any pain he had ever experienced before, and he could feel his ribs crunching. He began to weep like a small boy and he couldn't help thinking of his mother and the way she used to comfort him when he was little and he had tripped over and scraped his knees on the cinder path. He could almost hear her soft voice cooing at him and smell her perfume as she hugged him better. But his mother was in a home now, with dementia, and he was here, halfway out of this window, and nothing could turn time back.

You're not giving up. Pain is imaginary. Pain is only your body's way of protecting itself, but your body doesn't know what Bobby Quilty is going to do to you, and that will cause you infinitely more pain than the pain you're suffering now.

He tried to lift up his right leg so that he could perch his knee on the windowsill. That would give him the leverage he needed to lift up his left leg, too, and then he would be able to climb or tumble out of the window – tumble, more likely. If he fell, though, he fell. At least he would have escaped.

The first time he tried to lift his leg he simply couldn't summon up sufficient strength for his knee to reach the edge of the sill. He gripped both sides of the frame even tighter and heaved himself a few more inches out of the window.

Oh God, I can't do it. Yes, you can. Oh God, please, I can't do it. Yes, you can. You have to.

He rested for a few seconds, blood pounding in his ears, and then raised his leg again, more slowly. He still couldn't lift it as high as the sill and he had to let it sink back down.

You can. You have to. You have to get out of here.

He tried a third time, whinnying through his nostrils with pain and effort, and at last succeeded in pulling himself up on to the sill, first with his right knee and then, immediately afterwards, with his left.

Holy Mary, Mother of God, please let me survive this. If this was my punishment for abandoning Katie when she needed me, I accept it. But please, Holy Mother, enough is enough.

He clung on to the window frame with both hands, leaning out as far as he could. He had done almost the same thing when he was a young boy, kneeling on his bedroom windowsill at his parents' farmhouse, staring up at the sky at night, trying to see angels – though he had never seen angels. He couldn't see any tonight, either.

This window was too small and he was in too much pain to be able to turn himself around and climb down backwards on to the slates. He would have to climb out head-first and then try to slide and scrabble down the lean-to roof like a body-surfer and hope that when he reached the gutter there wasn't too much of a drop down into the yard below.

Right, he thought, although he was in so much agony that he could hardly think at all. *Count down from five, and then dive, and hope the Lord spares you.*

He bent forward as far as he could, until his fingertips touched the wet lead flashing where the lean-to's slates joined the wall of the house. He was just about to launch himself off the sill when he heard the bedroom door open and almost at once Sorcia's voice screeching out, '*Chisel! For feck's sake, Chisel, your man's only climbing right out the feckin' windie! Chisel!*'

John see-sawed himself out of the window and on to the slates. He might have imagined he was going to surf down the roof on his stomach, but he pitched head over heels on to his back, cracking and splintering the slates as he fell, and then slid down the rest of the way at a forty-five degree angle, still on his back, frantically scrabbling for any kind of a hand-hold. Before he knew it he had reached the gutter. He made a grab for it, but it was rusty and sharp-edged and all he managed to do was rip the skin of his hand and tear the gutter away from its soffit. Together, both he and the length of rusty metal dropped down into the yard.

It wasn't a long drop, no more than two and a half metres, but there was a rabbit hutch directly underneath and a stack of old sash-window frames, with the glass still in them. John fell face-down, smashing one of the windows with his forehead and almost flattening the rabbit hutch, so that the rabbit had to scrabble to the other end. He lay on top of the hutch and the window frames, still conscious but unable to move. He was far too badly bruised and, besides, the wire netting from the hutch had snagged in his sweater. His nostrils were filled with the rancid smell of damp straw and rabbit droppings.

He tried to lift up his head, but when he did so blood dripped down into his eyes and he had to blink furiously before he could see. He felt shattered, smashed to pieces. Every bone in his body felt dislocated from every other bone, and every tendon had been ripped. He didn't care whether he stayed there or not, even though the rain was gradually soaking through his clothes and mucus was dripping from his nose and he was beginning to shiver.

* * *

He heard a door unlocking, and footsteps. He managed to raise his head far enough to see Bobby Quilty and Chisel standing in the yard, the tips of their cigarettes glowing.

'This is pure wick, this is,' said Bobby Quilty. He crouched down close to John and shook his head in exasperation. 'Are you wired to the moon with a faulty plug or something? Look at the fecking state of you.'

John said nothing, but closed his eyes.

'You're not dead, are you?' Bobby Quilty asked him. 'Jesus, you're some quare gaunch, you are. I'm supposed to keep you in one fecking piece. Like that was the fecking agreement. If your old doll could see the condition of you now, she'd scoop me without a second thought. I mean, what in the name of feck did you think you were doing, climbing out the fecking windie?'

'I just hope he hasn't squished De Valera,' said Chisel, shading his eyes so that he could peer into the broken remains of the rabbit hutch.

'As if you give a tinker's shite for that fecking rabbit,' Bobby Quilty retorted. 'When do you ever clean him out? The last time I looked there was so much bobbly shite in that hutch the poor creature was almost crushed to death against the ceiling.'

Chisel had managed to open the hutch door. The rabbit was crouched on its sodden straw, its ears folded back, its pink eyes wide with terror, but it was still alive and it appeared to be unhurt.

'Joseph and Mary, are you going to you help me lift up this looper and get him back upstairs?' Bobby Quilty protested. Chisel reluctantly closed the hutch door again and came round to help.

It wasn't easy, picking John up off the hutch and the window frames, because he had now lost consciousness. Apart from that, the wire netting was hopelessly snarled in his sweater. After two or three minutes of struggling to get it free, Bobby Quilty wrenched all of it away from the front of the hutch and said, 'I can't believe this. This is totally fecking hectic. And what are you doing, Chisel, for feck's sake, wandering around like a fart in a trance? Get ahold of him under the oxters and let's hoick him up.'

'Look at the state of this fecking hutch now,' said Chisel. 'What if De Valera gets out?'

'If he has any luck at all, wee lad, he'll run straight out into the road and get himself flattened by a bus. Better than being flattened by his own shite. Now start lifting, will you?'

'Jesus, he weighs a fecking ton,' Chisel complained as they hoisted John up and shuffled with him over to the open back door.

'Oh, so what do you want to do, leave him out here all night? It's lashing. He'll catch cold, won't he, if we do that, and he'll die of the fecking pneumonics, and then where's our trump card, eh?'

With Chisel holding John under the armpits, and Bobby Quilty holding his legs on either side of him as if he were pushing a wheelbarrow, they carried John into the house and struggled up the stairs with him. Sorcia stood on the landing smoking as they puffed and grunted and swore and eventually managed to wrestle him back into his bedroom and drop him with a crunch of springs on to the mattress. John opened his eyes for a moment but then closed them again. He had regained consciousness but he was in such pain that he could hardly think.

'Don't you say a word,' Bobby Quilty told Sorcia.

'I wouldn't dream of it,' she said. 'I was only going to ask how you're going to stop him from getting away again. Like, what's going to happen when we all go to sleep? If you think that I'm going to stay awake all night watching him, like, you've got yourself another think coming.'

'And if you don't shut your bake, you've got yourself another slap in the kite coming, so you have.'

Sorcia shrugged and blew out smoke, and said, 'Just asking, like. You don't have to go schizo.'

Bobby Quilty turned back to look at John lying on the bed. 'Well,' he said, 'maybe you're not totally away in the head.' He thought for a moment, slowly rubbing his belly as if had eaten something that disagreed with him, and then he said, 'Chisel? Do you still have them nuts and bolts, the ones you used for fixing the trailer?'

'What do you want them for?' asked Chisel.

'I said, do you still have them?'

'Yeah, I'd say so. Somewhere in the bottom of my toolbox, most likely. Why?'

'And you still have your drill here, right?'

'Chalk it down, right. What do you have in mind?'

'Do you know something, Chisel, my life would run a whole lot smoother if you didn't ask so many fecking stupid questions. Go downstairs, will you, and bring up them nuts and bolts, and your drill, too, with a drill bit.'

'What size of a drill bit?'

'A drill bit big enough to make holes for the bolts, you clampit. What else?'

John heard Chisel clomping downstairs. A few more minutes went past during which he could hear Bobby Quilty and Sorcia murmuring to each other. They didn't sound like affectionate murmurs – more like a bitter under-the-breath argument that they didn't want him or Chisel to hear. As Chisel came clomping back upstairs again, Bobby Quilty distinctly said, 'You do that again, you dirty clart, I'll fecking kill you, so I will.'

As Chisel came back into the bedroom John lay still and kept his eyes closed. It was the only way that he could bear the pain and at the same time hide from Bobby Quilty how frightened he was. He had never been frightened like this before, ever, in the whole of his life, even when he had first met Katie and he and his mother had been attacked on their own farm and almost killed. When that had happened he had been surging with adrenaline, but lying here at the mercy of Bobby Quilty he felt helpless. All he could feel was the sickening conviction that Bobby Quilty and Chisel were going to hurt him badly.

Without warning, he felt his left ankle being seized and his shoe tugged off. His sock was pulled off next. Immediately afterwards, his right shoe and sock were taken off, too. While this was happening neither Bobby Quilty nor Chisel said a word, although Sorcia said, 'I can't fecking watch this,' and he heard her clattering erratically downstairs.

Now both legs of John's jeans were dragged halfway up his calves. His ankles were gripped tight and the sole of his bare left foot pressed flat against the bed's footboard. He knew that it was Bobby Quilty who was holding him because he could feel his heavy patterned signet rings pressing into his skin.

There was a *chukk* noise, like a plug being pushed into a wall socket, and then the sudden high-pitched whine of an electric drill. The next thing he knew, John felt a pain in his left foot so intense that he jolted up and down on the mattress and shrieked out loud.

'Jesus!' said Bobby Quilty. 'Shut the feck up, will you, you sound like a woman giving birth to a full-grown pig!'

Almost hysterical, John tried to twist his leg away, but Bobby Quilty's grip was far too strong for him. When he looked down to the end of the bed he saw that Chisel was drilling a bloody hole into the top of his foot. He could feel the bit separating his bones and then biting through the skin of his sole and into the pine footboard.

'*Aaaaahhhhhh!*' he screamed. '*No! Stop it! No! Don't – don't! No-no-no-no-no-gaaaaahhhh!*'

Bobby Quilty and Chisel looked at each other and both of them shrugged. Chisel drilled right through the footboard and then took the drill out. The tip of the bit was still hot from cutting into the wood and John jumped as it touched his flesh.

In a matter of fact way, as if he had been doing this every day of his working life, Chisel took a fifteen-centimetre stainless-steel bolt out of the pocket of his dirty denim waistcoat. He slid a wide penny washer on to the bolt so that John wouldn't be able to tear his foot free from it. Then he inserted it into the hole he had drilled in John's foot and right through the hole in the footboard. John lay back on the mattress, his eyes closed again, shaking, as Chisel took out a nut, spat on it, and twisted it on to the end of the bolt. He tightened the nut by hand, then picked up a spanner from the floor and gave it three or four extra turns so that nobody could loosen it unless they had a spanner, too.

John was rising and falling in and out of consciousness, as if he were struggling to stop himself drowning in the sea at night. The shock of Chisel drilling through his foot was so overwhelming that his brain wanted to drag him down into darkness where he wouldn't feel anything, but the pain kept bringing him up to the surface again. He kept seeing his mother's face again and hearing her voice. *There, there, it's only a scrape, like! Nothing that a poke with sprinkles won't heal!*

But then Bobby Quilty held his right ankle even harder and Chisel started to drill through his right foot, too. There was a brief ripping sound as the drill bit tore through skin and muscle, and then an odd *sqyerkk!* as it glanced off one of his bones. He wanted to pray as the drill bit went through his sole and into the footboard, but his mind couldn't assemble any sensible words. All he could smell was burning wood and flesh, and he was in far too much agony even to scream, let alone pray.

When Chisel had finished drilling through his right foot, he fastened a second bolt through it and tightened that up, too. Now both of John's feet were bolted to the bed.

'There, that's grand altogether,' said Bobby Quilty. 'Now you won't be able to go climbing out the windie again, not unless you take the whole fecking bed along with you.'

'What if he needs a shite?' asked Chisel.

'You've a wee want, Chisel, what do you think? We unscrew the bolts and then he can walk to the jacks on his own. When he's finished dropping the kids off, all we have to do is bolt him back up again.' He mimed the act of twisting the spanner.

'Oh, I have you now, I have you!' said Chisel in admiration. 'I've got to hand it to you, Bobby, that's fierce crabbit, that is. It's exactly like what the Romans did to Jesus when they nailed Him on the cross, except it's more crabbiter than that because the Romans used nails, like, didn't they? So Jesus couldn't come down from the cross to take a shite and then climb back up again. Not that the Romans probably would have let Him, do you know what I mean, like?'

Bobby Quilty said nothing for a moment, but stood over John, breathing in and out through nostrils clogged with catarrh. John opened his eyes and looked up at him, but then closed them again as unconsciousness dragged him down. He couldn't be sure if he was dreaming or not, and that round-faced man with his Kim Jong-un haircut wasn't simply some nursery-rhyme character from his childhood. *The Man in the Moon came down too soon.*

At last Bobby Quilty said, 'Do you know something, Chisel? If I'd been given ten euros for every time you'd ever said anything that made any sense, I'd be flat fecking broke by now.'

Fourteen

The next morning was warm and summery, with huge white clouds that billowed over Cobh like the Spanish Armada under full sail. Katie had slept badly again, so she got out of bed early and took Barney for a walk all the way up to the Rushbrooke Tennis and Croquet Club.

Barney knew this walk well and normally he would trot fifty or sixty metres ahead of her, only waiting at the street corners with his tongue hanging out for her to catch up. Today, he must have sensed that she was anxious, because he stayed very close to her and every now and then turned his head around and looked up at her as if to reassure her that he wasn't going to leave her far behind.

As she reached Grove Garden, her iPhone played 'Buile Mo Chroí' – 'The Beat of My Heart' – which her mother had loved and which had always set her off dancing around the kitchen.

'Good morning, ma'am. It's Detective O'Mara here.'

'Good morning to you, Bryan. How's it going?'

'We've located one of Quilty's fag-peddlers for you. He's sitting in the doorway of that linen shop in the Savoy Centre, the one that closed down, so that you can't see him on the CCTV. I don't know how long he's going to be there, but he has three or four bags of fags with him. He's even got himself a folding chair like he's on his holliers or something.'

'Thank you, Bryan. Just make a note of that, would you, and put it in the case log.'

'You don't want him lifted?'

'No. You know how we're dealing with this now.'

'You don't want me to tip off Revenue or nothing?'

'No. Just leave him be. How old would you say he was?'

'He has a bit of a scobe tash but it wouldn't surprise me if he's hopped off school.'

'Well, there you are. If he's underage that's one good reason not to pick him up. Thanks, Bryan. I'll be into the station by eleven so I'll talk to you after.'

Immediately, she called Kyna. Barney stood patiently beside her while she waited for an answer. She was beginning to think that Kyna wasn't going to pick up when she heard her say, 'Katie – yes, what? Sorry, I've just woken up. What time are we on?'

'Half past eight. Sorry. Did you have a late night?'

'Didn't sleep very well, that's all. I keep having this nightmare.'

'What's it about? Getting shot?'

'I suppose it must be something to do with that. I keep hearing people talking about me in other rooms but when I go to find out what they're saying about me all these doors start slamming – upstairs, downstairs, everywhere.'

'Detective O'Mara just rang me,' said Katie. Although she was concerned about Kyna, because she knew that she was still suffering from post-traumatic stress, she didn't want to start trying to interpret her dreams, not this early in the day. Most of all, she didn't want to hear anything that would put her off sending Kyna to find John for her. Stress could be treated by therapy. Blindness or amputation or death was irreversible.

'One of Quilty's dealers has set up shop in the Savoy Centre. He's probably catering for the early crowd, people on their way into work. O'Mara couldn't say how long he's going to be there, but he says he has a heap of cigarettes.'

'All right. It'll take me a while to squeeze into my leggings and stick up my hair and put my face paint on, but I'll get down there as quick as I can. I'll ring you if he's gone by the time I get there. I'll ring you anyway.'

'Thanks, Kyna. But for the love of God be careful.'

'You know me.'

'Exactly. That's what I'm worried about.'

* * *

Katie had just poured boiling water into her coffee mug when she received a text from Dr Kelley. The four mummified bodies had now been lifted from underneath the floor at Millstream Row and they were being transported to the mortuary at Cork University Hospital. The remains of the two dogs had been sent to VLSI, a specialist veterinary pathologist in Vicar's Road.

Katie tipped her coffee into the sink and went into the bedroom to fetch her purple linen jacket out of the wardrobe. Barney followed her, hopefully expecting another walk, but when she went into the room that had been Seamus's nursery and took her revolver out of the chest of drawers he realized that she was off to work and simply stood in the living-room doorway patiently waiting for her to leave.

'It's all right, Barns,' she told him, tugging at his ears. 'I won't be back too late, with any luck, and I'll bring you something special for your supper.'

When she walked in through the swing doors at the mortuary, Detective 'Horse' Ó Doibhilin was already waiting for her. 'Morning, ma'am,' he greeted her. His voice was oddly watery, and he kept on swallowing, as if his mouth was flooded with saliva. 'They're all here now, the bodies, and Dr Kelley's started work on them already.'

When she saw the man's body lying on the stainless-steel autopsy table, Katie could understand why Horse might be feeling nauseous. All of his clothes had been removed and sent to the Technical Bureau laboratory for testing. Dr Kelley was leaning over him, wearing a lab coat and clear plastic goggles, cutting his breastbone apart with a battery-powered sternal saw. The saw was making a high-pitched screaming sound that set Katie's teeth on edge.

As she made her way across the morgue, Dr Kelley switched off the saw, lowered her surgical mask and gave her a smile. 'Ah, Detective Superintendent! I thought I'd make an early start.

Fascinating, wouldn't you say? I haven't come across a cadaver in this condition for years. Totally *dried out*, like bresaola. It must have been the constant draft under the floorboards and the house being constantly warm.'

The man's skin was so stretched that it looked as if his skeleton had been shrink-wrapped in translucent yellow vinyl, and some of his ribs and finger bones had pierced through it in places. Dr Kelley had combed most of the dust out of his curly brown hair, but his face was grotesque. On the left side it had become flattened, with his eye half-closed, but on the right side his forehead bulged out and his lips were turned down in what looked like a sneer.

'He was shot in the back of the head, about seven centimetres behind his left ear, and slightly upwards,' said Dr Kelley. 'It wasn't a high-velocity bullet. It ricocheted around inside his skull and there isn't an exit wound, so I'll be able to retrieve it once I've opened his cranium. It also appears that he was badly beaten, because his collarbone and several ribs are broken. Of course it isn't possible to say whether this was done before or after he was shot, but logically there wouldn't have been much point in giving him a thrashing once he was dead.'

The bodies of the woman and the two children were lying on trolleys beside the wall, with green sheets draped over them. Katie went over and lifted the sheet that was covering the woman. She had probably been quite pretty when she was alive, but the shot to the back of her head had distorted her face, too. It looked as if she might have been kneeling when she was shot, because the bullet had entered the top of her skull and penetrated her sinus cavity, lodging in the upper side of her hard palate. Her nostrils were tilted upward like a pig's snout and her lips were curled, as if she were singing a very lewd song, or trying to show that she was thoroughly disgusted by what had happened to her.

After she had looked at the girl and the baby boy, Katie was sure that she was going to have bad dreams tonight. Both of their faces had been blown apart by the bullets that had been fired into the back of their heads, so that they looked more like huge dried white chrysanthemums than faces. Only the tiny jawbones among the petals gave away the fact that they were human children.

Dr Kelley came up to Katie and stood beside her as she was staring down at the baby boy.

'Makes you wonder what kind of a person could do that to a defenceless child, doesn't it? Poor mite. He didn't even get to live for a single year.'

Katie lowered the sheet and crossed herself. She couldn't help thinking of her own little Seamus, dead in his cot, although Seamus had simply stopped breathing. 'I almost wish they hadn't been killed such a long time ago,' she told Dr Kelley. 'I would dearly love to find out who did this and make sure they were punished for it.'

'Time stops for nothing at all, I'm afraid, not even us,' said Dr Kelley. 'So you'll excuse me if I get back to my dissection. I have an autopsy scheduled at the Mid-West in Limerick the day after tomorrow and I'd like to get all of these completed.'

'You'll be able to give me some idea of how long they've been dead?' Katie asked her.

'Within a few years either way. Of course I'll be able to tell you if they were born before nuclear testing started in 1945 because of the carbon-fourteen level in their teeth – that's if there is any. I expect the stomach contents will help me a fair bit, too. But their complete desiccation isn't going to help. If anything, I think your best indicators are going to come from their clothing – the style and the fibres and dyes. And any records or photographs that you can find.'

'Well, as you know, we've been given plenty of documentary evidence of who they *might* have been, but it's very contradictory. What you're doing here should at least tell us if these are the Langtrys or not.'

Dr Kelley pulled up her mask and returned to her high-pitched sternum sawing. Katie watched her for a moment and then checked the time. She wondered if Kyna had managed to make contact with Bobby Quilty's cigarette-seller at the Savoy Centre. 'Come on, Michael,' she said to Detective Ó Doibhilin. 'I think we could both use some fresh air, don't you?'

* * *

Before she returned to her office, Katie paid a visit to the Technical Bureau laboratory. There had been a major traffic accident on the N20 to Mallow, so she found that Eithne and Bill Phinner's new assistant were the only ones there. The white cotton blinds were pulled down because the sunlight outside was so bright, and there was a strong smell of hydrochloric acid in the air. Eithne was sitting at her bench under the window, filling an array of test tubes with pale green liquid out of a beaker, while the new assistant was frowning at a tangle of chemical formulae on her computer screen.

Katie went up to Eithne and stood watching her for a moment.

'I thought you were going to call in sick,' she said.

Eithne shook her head and took out a tissue to wipe her nose. 'I'm not too bad today, thanks, ma'am. I've too much to do, any road. I was going to come up and see you after.'

'What are you doing there?' Katie asked her, nodding at the test tubes.

'This is one of the things I was going to come and see you about.'

She reached across and picked up a glass retort that was half-filled with liquid. There were several saturated wool fibres floating in it, like weeds.

'This is a sample from the man's trousers. They were dyed with a water-soluble anionic dye, which was used for almost all garments before 1920. After that, though, there was much wider use of dispersal dyes. That was because more and more manufacturers were using acetates to make clothing and acetates, of course, are hydrophobic.'

'So what does that tell us?'

'In terms of precise dating, not very much. People keep their clothes for years, if not decades, especially if they're less well off. But it does indicate that these trousers were probably made before 1921, and if that's the case, it's likely that your man could either be Stephen Langtry himself or some other fellow who was killed in the Langtrys' house before the Langtrys disappeared. Of course I'm testing the woman's dress and the children's clothing, too. In any case, we're expecting the results of the DNA tests sometime this afternoon, so that should pretty much confirm their identity one way or the other.'

'Did you get anywhere with the cap badge and the letter?' Katie asked her.

Eithne slid off her stool and went across to the opposite side of the laboratory. She came back with the Manchester cap badge that Nora O'Neill had given to Katie, and a clear plastic folder containing the note from *Gerald*.

'I checked this coat-of-arms cap badge against my records. It was worn by soldiers of the Manchester Regiment until 1922, when their commanding officer made an application to the Army Council to change it to a fleur-de-lys.'

'Why did he do that?'

'The troops didn't feel that this badge was very military, especially the ones who came from Manchester. What they didn't like was that the exact same badge was worn by every worker for the City of Manchester Corporation. Like, you know, dustmen and rent collectors and road-menders.'

'So at least we know when it dates from.'

'That's right. And in 1921, C Company of the Manchester Regiment were based at barracks in Ballincollig, only ten kilometres away from Blarney. Even in those days, it would have taken less than fifteen minutes to drive from one to the other. Maybe half an hour by horse and buggy.'

Katie was beginning to feel uneasy again about the political implications of this investigation. She had known ever since she was at school that C Company of the Manchester Regiment was a black name in the history of Cork's struggle for independence in the 1920s. During the war against the British, the IRA had planned to ambush an army patrol as it passed through Dripsey. However, the army had been warned of the intended ambush by a wealthy local woman, Mrs Mary Lindsay, of Leemount House, who had strong loyalist views.

In the late afternoon of Friday, 28 January 1921, seventy men of C Company of the Manchester Regiment outflanked the IRA ambush party and captured eight of them. At the subsequent trial, five were found guilty and sentenced to death.

In retaliation, the IRA abducted Mrs Lindsay and her chauffeur, James Clark, and threatened that if the death sentences were carried out, they would die, too. The authorities ignored their threat and the five IRA men were executed by firing squad and their bodies interred at Cork Gaol. Twelve days later, Mrs Lindsay and her chauffeur were shot, their bodies burned and buried deep in the mountains. The day after, Leemount House was burned down.

Katie's history teacher at school, Mr O'Sullivan, had been passionate about Irish independence. He had even taken the class to see the memorial that had been erected for the IRA men at Godfrey's Cross. She remembered that day clearly, although less for the story of the ambush and more for the fact that it had been raining hard and her mother had made her cheese sandwiches which she had dropped in a puddle.

'What about the letter?' she asked Eithne.

'Genuine, no question at all. I've tested the paper and the ink and it's authentic. And there's indentations in the paper which indicate that the cap badge was wrapped in the letter for a very long time.'

'Okay, Eithne. Thanks for that. All we have to do now is find out who Gerald was. The Manchester Regiment should have records. I'll have Ó Diobhilin get in touch with them.'

Eithne wiped her nose again and then she said, 'If you don't mind my saying so, ma'am, this seems to be bothering you more than a bit, this inquiry.'

'It is, yes,' Katie admitted. 'I'm sure we'll find out what happened to that family eventually, but I'm worried that won't be the end of it. I always have a bad feeling when we start poking around in the past – not because we *shouldn't* poke around in the past, because I think we should. The trouble is, no matter what it is we discover, it's going to upset somebody, even today. I guarantee it. It always does.'

* * *

Walking along the corridor back to her office, she checked her iPhone but there was still no word from Kyna. She told herself not to worry, Kyna was level-headed and highly professional and wouldn't make any careless mistakes that would give her away. In spite of that, though, John's life depended on her. Katie couldn't imagine how she would feel if John were blinded, or maimed, or murdered.

She couldn't imagine how she would deal with her emotions if anything happened to Kyna, either. She felt guilty enough already about asking her to do this, but she hadn't been able to think of any other way of finding out where John was being held. It was far too dangerous to start raiding Bobby Quilty's houses and flats and business premises in the slim hope that they might find John in one of them. They suspected that he owned or rented numerous properties that they didn't know about. After the Dripsey ambush, the British army had set up a huge search in the Inniscarra area for Mrs Lindsay and her chauffeur, but they never discovered where they were because the IRA kept moving them from house to house.

Almost as soon as she had sat down at her desk, Detective Sergeant Begley knocked on her door. He looked flustered. His tight blue shirt had semicircular sweat stains under the armpits and his scarlet braces had slipped off his shoulders and were hanging down behind him like a toddler's reins.

'What's the story, Sean?' Katie asked him, popping open the can of Diet Coke she had brought up with her.

'Look at the state of me,' said Detective Sergeant Begley. 'I saw you out of my window in the car park and I went running down after you but by the time I caught up with you, you'd gone. Jesus and Mary, I'm sweating like a priest in a playground.'

He paused to catch his breath and then he said, 'You saw the *One o'Clock News*, did you?'

'No, I didn't. I was down in the lab to see how what progress Eithne's been making with all the evidence we took from Blarney. That British army cap badge, that definitely dates from the early 1920s, and the love letter that went with it. The dead man's clothing was probably 1920s, too.'

'Listen, it seems like your friend Fionnuala Sweeney from RTÉ News knows just as much about those bodies as we do, if not considerably more. She's sure that they belong to the Langtry family, that's what she said, no question about it, and she even gave out their first names – Stephen, Rahda, and the wains' names, too.'

'Holy Mary, Mother of God,' said Katie. 'It was that Nora O'Neill woman told her all of that, it must have been. It's highly probable that they *are* the Langtry family, though we don't have any idea how Stephen Langtry managed to send postcards from America after he was supposed to be dead, and of course we're still waiting on the DNA results.'

'Oh, there's more,' said Detective Sergeant Begley. 'You're going to love this, I tell you.'

'Go on,' Katie told him.

'According to local legend, Mrs Langtry had been having an affair with a British army officer.'

'Well . . . that's conceivable, considering the cap badge and the letter, and what the letter said. But it's only speculation at the moment. We don't even know for certain that they were hers.'

'Ah, no, but this local legend has it that Stephen Langtry belonged to the IRA and that he actively encouraged his wife to have an affair with a British army officer so that she could tap him for secret information, especially about the movements of army patrols. But the officer found out that she was what you might call a honeytrap, and British soldiers came around one night and shot the whole family.'

Katie sat down, shaking her head in exasperation. 'I don't suppose Fionnuala said who told her this so-called local legend? And if she'd checked to find out if there was any truth in it?'

'No, that's about all she said. After that there was a clip of you looking more than a little fried and saying "no comment", and Mathew McElvey from the press office trotting out his usual excuse that "our investigation is still ongoing and so I can't say anything conclusive". After that they went on to a report about Irish Water warning folks with the lead pipes still in their houses that they could be poisoned.'

'Jesus, I hope that Nora O'Neill has lead pipes in her house. Do you realize what trouble this is going to stir up?'

'I can't say that I do,' said Detective Sergeant Begley. 'But my old grandpa always used to say that there's no treachery worse than the one that you never knew was being done to you.'

Fifteen

It was pay day, so St Patrick's Street was already crowded with shoppers. Kyna had parked her car on the north side of St Patrick's Bridge and walked across the river. Because it was such a warm morning the river smelled even stronger than usual and under the surface she could see a shoal of grey mullet greedily feeding around the effluent pipe. She couldn't help thinking of the song 'The Boys of Fair Hill' – 'the smell on Patrick's Bridge is wicked, how does Father Mathew stick it?'

Kyna was whistled at three times as she made her way past the statue of Father Mathew down to the Savoy Centre. She had gelled up her short blonde hair and she was wearing a low-cut pink T-shirt with TROUBLE printed across her breasts, skintight black jeans and wedge-heeled black patent shoes. She had completed the look with red make-up around her eyes, huge hoop earrings and at least six bangles on each wrist, and she had sprayed herself with too much Obsession.

The Savoy Centre had once been a cinema, but after it had closed in 1975 it had been turned into an indoor shopping mall with stores like Champion Sports and Hickey's Fabrics and a coffee shop. Standing in the entrance was a podgy tousle-haired boy of about nine years old who should have been in school. He kept looking up and down the street as if he were waiting for somebody and Kyna guessed that he was keeping sketch for the law.

She had no difficulty in finding Bobby Quilty's cigarette-dealer. He was sitting in the doorway of a shop called Erin Linens which had sheets of last week's *Echo* stuck all over the windows and a large sign saying *Closing Down Sale*.

Detective O'Mara had told Katie that he was young, and in spite of a wispy black moustache on his upper lip he looked as if he hadn't even taken his Junior Cert yet. He had short black hair with two parallel lines shaved into the side of it, and a milky-white, pimple-spattered face. He was wearing a coral-pink T-shirt from Penney's, a pair of super-skinny blue jeans and Nike runners.

Around his feet were three large black refuse bags, two of them crumpled up and empty, the third half full with red and white cartons of West cigarettes.

Kyna went directly up to him and said, in a high Mayfield whine, 'What's the craic, boy?'

'Twenty-five yo-yos for two hundred,' he told her. 'Buy four and you can have them for eighty.'

'So how much are they paying you?'

The boy blinked at her as if he hadn't understood what she meant. 'I told you, twenty-five yo-yos the box. How many do you want?'

He held up a carton of two hundred cigarettes. On the side Kyna noticed the warning *Rauchen kann tödlich sein*. She knew that West were made in Germany, where they cost 54 euros per carton. They weren't sold in Ireland, but they would have cost 100 euros.

'I didn't say I wanted to buy any,' she told him. 'I want to know how much you get paid for selling them.'

'You what?' the boy retorted. 'What the feck's it got to do with you? Do you want any fecking fags or don't you?'

'I told you, *no*, you gom,' said Kyna, just as aggressively. 'I'm looking to make some grade for myself and I saw you there and thought, that looks like child's play. Better than gobbling manky old scummers in the bus station jacks, I'll tell you.'

The boy glanced left and right. 'I don't know, like. I'm not supposed to talk about nothing to nobody, like, do you know what I mean?'

'Aw, come on,' said Kyna, leaning against the door frame and batting her eyelashes at him. 'Don't tell me they're not looking for gorgeous-looking girls to flog their fags for them. I bet you I could sell twice as many as you any day. Three times more if I was wearing a really short skirt. Four if I didn't wear knickers.'

'Well . . .' said the boy. Kyna could read his mind almost as clearly as if his thoughts were running across his forehead as a text message. Bobby Quilty was always looking for young recruits to sell his smuggled cigarettes on the streets, especially if they weren't already known to the Garda, and Kyna knew from other school-age dealers they had picked up that he would probably drop this boy at least fifty euros for introducing her.

The boy took his mobile phone out of his pocket and tapped in a number. After a few seconds, he said, 'Ger? It's Benny. No, no bother, everything's grand. I reckon another half-hour or so. Listen, there's a beour here who's interested in selling fags. Yeah. That's right, yeah. No. No. She's well fit, like. Yeah. Okay, then. Right. I will.'

Once he had put his phone down, he said to Kyna, 'He's in the Long Valley, sitting at the bar on the left as you walk in. You'll recognize him easy. He'll be wearing a white hat with a black band around it and shades and he has a grey ponytail. His name's Ger.'

'Okay, thanks a million, Benny,' said Kyna. She winked at him and lasciviously licked her lips and said, 'I'll have to think of some way of repaying you, won't I?'

The boy's pimply face flared even redder and he seemed relieved when a young woman came up to them, pushing a buggy with two baby girls in it and a small boy standing precariously on the footrest.

'Give us two boxes, love, would you?' she asked him, opening up her purse. 'No, best make that three.'

Benny rummaged around in his black plastic bag while Kyna walked back to the St Patrick's Street entrance. The boy who was keeping sketch was still there. He was looking bored and assiduously picking his nose.

'Digging for gold?' she asked him.

'Ah, get away to fuck,' said the boy, but all the same he took out his finger and flicked his rolled-up gullier across the pavement.

* * *

Ger was exactly as Benny had described him. When she walked into the Long Valley, the traditional old-style pub at the end of Winthrop Street, she found him perched on one of the barstools like a huge elderly vulture that had dropped directly out of the sky.

He was wearing the white hat that Benny had told her about, although it was grubby and stained. He was also wearing a drooping black jacket with wide shoulders and pockets that were weighed down with loose change and Kyna could only guess what else, as well as raspberry-coloured chinos that were several centimetres too short, so that his bruised white calves were exposed.

Kyna went up to the bar and stood close behind him without saying a word. One of the barmen approached her in his white butcher's apron and said, 'Over eighteen, are you, flower?'

Without turning around, Ger said in a deep, whispery voice, 'You're all right, Séan, she's with me.'

'Oh, no bother at all,' said the barman. 'In that case, what'll it be?'

'Kopparberg Mixed Fruit, if this gentleman's treating me,' said Kyna. She was trying to think what Sheelagh Danehy might consider to be a sophisticated drink to order.

Still without turning around, Ger said, 'How old are you really?'

'Nineteen,' Kyna told him. She doubted that Ger would believe her if she said she was any younger.

* * *

He shifted around on his stool, so that his chinos made a farting noise on the leather. It was difficult to tell what he looked like facially because of his huge dark glasses, but he had a hooked Fagin nose and deeply lined cheeks and a turned-down mouth, as if he wasn't prepared to believe anything anyone told him. His chin was covered in sharp white prickles and his breath smelled of stale beer and garlic and something else rancid.

'What's your name, then?' he asked her.

'Sheelagh. Sheelagh with a "g".'

'A "g" like in "slag", you mean?'

Kyna was hard put to think how the real Sheelagh would have responded to that, but then she decided that the real Sheelagh was probably used to being called names that were a lot worse than 'slag' and would have ignored it.

'My friends call me Sidhe. Or Pixie sometimes.'

'All right, Sidhe. And why are you so interested in selling fags for us?'

'It's only for some spare grade. That's all I want. I lost my job at Coqbull because they said I wasn't being respectful to the customers. Like, you know, it's only a fecking burger bar, what do they expect? Bowing and scraping? I told this one woman that we'd have to charge her for an overnight stay, because if she ate any more we wouldn't be able to get her out the door. I mean, like, scorpy, or what?'

'There's plenty of other work around,' said Ger.

'Oh, for sure, especially for a girl who got herself kicked out of school, with no leaving cert? Like washing-up dishes at O'Brien's, I suppose, or giving the happy-ending massage to stinky old men? I've tried both of them, like, and they was both enough to make a maggot gag.'

Ger took a measured sip of his Murphy's and wiped his mouth with the back of his hand. 'You won't be able to work for us if you don't learn to keep your bake shut. I'll tell you that, girl, for nothing.'

'I'm not stupid,' said Kyna. 'I know you're selling the economy fags. I sold dance biscuits for some feller once and he was so delighted with how quick I sold them and how much profit I made that he wanted me to work for him full-time, and I would have done if he hadn't gone and got himself killed in a car smash.'

'What was his name, this feller?'

'Well, he's dead now, so I don't mind telling you, but I would never have done if he was still alive, not until I was dead myself. So I don't need you telling me to keep my bake shut, thank you very much. His name was Kenny O'Flynn.'

Ger was silent for a moment. Then he patted his left forearm and said, 'Kenny had a tattoo, right here. Can you remember what it was?'

'Of course. It was one of them Celtic knots, like, with *Níl micheart dearmad riamh* written around it.' Kyna thought: *I certainly* should *remember.* She had interrogated Kenny O'Flynn on three separate occasions after he was arrested for dealing D2PM and Bubble in Cork's nightclubs and dance venues, and even outside the gates of the Presentation College on the Western Road.

'So, well, you did know him, then,' said Ger. 'In that case, okay, I reckon we might be able to find you a pitch. All we have to do now is see if the Big Feller takes a fancy to you.'

'Who's the Big Feller?'

'You'll find out soon enough. He's the one who runs the whole business. So take it from me, you want to stay on his good side, like.'

They spent another twenty minutes in the Long Valley, finishing their drinks. Ger seemed to believe that Kyna was who she claimed to be, but all the same he kept asking her questions about her family, and her home life, and where she had said she was living on Mount Nebo Avenue, and why she had got herself into so much trouble at school. Kyna had been trained in interrogation techniques at Templemore and Katie had always been impressed by her ability to persuade suspects to incriminate themselves. But Kayna had to admit that Ger was adept at setting traps in his questions.

'Oh, yes,' he said, 'I used to have a regular scoop with some good old pals of mine who lived on Mount Nebo Avenue. We used to go to that boozer on Gurra Avenue, what's its name?'

'Top of the Hill Bar,' said Kyna. 'I used to go in there when I was only sixteen, hoping they'd serve me a bottle of cider.'

'Top of the Hill Bar, that's right,' said Ger. 'And what was the name of that baldy barman, the one who always looked at you like he wasn't looking at you but whoever it was standing next to you?'

'I don't know,' said Kyna. 'I don't remember no baldy barman.'

Ger lifted one finger. 'You're right there, girl. My mistake. That was Kevin at The Flying Bottle in Knocka. Swivel, they called him, on account of his eyes. Swivel, that was your man.'

Sixteen

Eventually they left the Long Valley and Ger led Kyna across the road to Pembroke Street, beside the main Post Office, where his mustard-coloured Volvo was parked in a disabled bay. There was no blue disabled card displayed behind his windscreen, but the parking attendant who was checking the cars parked along the street simply turned his back when he saw Ger approaching and slowly walked off in the opposite direction.

'Get in,' said Ger, opening up the passenger door. Kyna obediently climbed in and fastened her seat belt. The inside of the Volvo was littered with empty plastic bottles and crumpled copies of the *Irish Racing Post*, and the ashtray was crammed.

'We'll go round and pick up Benny first, then we'll head off to see the Big Feller,' Ger told her. 'I'm presuming you don't have any other engagements, like.'

'I need the grade, don't I?' said Kyna, turning her head away and staring out of the window with a sulky pout. As they drove up Parnell Place, however, she had to turn her head back and half-shield her face with her hand because Detective Dooley was standing on the corner talking to two gardaí and he would have recognized her immediately. How could she explain why she was driving around the city with one of the biggest scumbags in Cork, dressed like a brasser?

They stopped outside the Savoy Centre and the nose-picking lookout went inside to bring Benny out. Benny dropped his black plastic bags into the Volvo's boot and then climbed into the back.

'What's the story, then, Benny?' Ger asked him, shaking out a cigarette and lighting it before he drove off.

'Only two boxes left and they was them Afri Rot fags which nobody wanted.'

'They're so fecking thick, some people! You told them that "rot" is Kraut language for "red"?'

'Well, no, I didn't. I didn't know myself, like. I thought it meant they was humming a bit, like, and that was why they was going so cheap.'

'Jesus, you'd break my melt, you would,' said Ger. 'Didn't I fecking tell you what it meant only this morning when I dropped you off?'

'Yeah, but I thought you were taking the piss, like, do you know what I mean?'

Ger drove up the steep incline of Summerhill and then east beside the high stone walls of the Middle Glanmire Road. Eventually he turned into cul-de-sac of six large brand new houses. Outside the house at the end of the cul-de-sac, three vehicles were parked – a black Nissan Navara pickup, a shiny red Jaguar XF R and an Audi A3.

Ger parked behind the Jaguar, then climbed out and opened the door for Kyna. 'Just remember what I said, girl. You need to keep the the Big Feller smiling, all right, so none of your cheek. And if he wants you to do something for him, no matter what, just fecking do it and no getting uppity.'

Kyna gave Ger a contemptuous Gurra look but said nothing. She and Benny followed him between the cars parked in the driveway and up to the mock-Palladian porch. He rang the door chimes and almost immediately the front door was opened by a tall, gaunt woman with her hair pinned up in a messy brown bun. She was wearing a short summer dress that was splashed all over with huge red poppies.

'Holy Mother of God, Margot,' said Ger. 'You look like you got run over by the 208!'

'Get away, would you?' the woman snapped back. 'I bought this down Opera Lane only yesterday, and if you knew what it cost.'

'Don't tell me. I'm not in the mood for feeling pity for anybody, not today. Besides, it'll probably look massive once you've washed the blood off.'

The woman took them through the house and into the back garden where Bobby Quilty was pacing up and down on the patio, dressed in a jazzy yellow shirt with palm trees and hula girls on it and a pair of flappy khaki cargo trousers. He was giving somebody a dressing-down on his iPhone, barking at them in his strong Armagh accent. He was wearing red flip-flops and Kyna noticed that his toenails were so long that they curled over the ends of his toes. Perhaps his belly was too big for him to bend over and cut them, she thought, although it was obvious from the size of his house and all the cars parked outside that he could have easily afforded a pedicure.

'Don't you be giving me that slabber, wee lad!' he was shouting. 'So far as I'm concerned you nuck that money and I want it back in my hand by Monday morning at the latest. You'll regret it else, so you will, and so will all the family you leave behind you. What do you want it to say on your headstone?'

He wedged his iPhone back into the pocket of his shorts and then looked Kyna up and down and said, ''Bout you, Ger? Who's this? I thought I told you not to fetch any of your slappers back here with you.' He pronounced 'with you' as 'whichew', like a hay-fever sneeze.

'She's all right, Bobby. Her name's Sheelagh. She's looking for a bit of work flogging fags, that's all.'

Bobby Quilty took a pack of cigarettes out of his shirt pocket and lit one with a gold flip-top lighter. He blew out smoke and then he said, 'You know we don't pay good money, sweetheart. You sell two hundred fags for twenty-five euros, you get to keep two euros and fifty cents, that's all. You're a cracking-looking girl, so you are. There's plenty of ways you could be making yourself a shiteload more money than that for a whole lot less effort.'

'I know that, Mister Big Feller,' said Kyna. 'I've tried them. They gave me the gawks, to be honest with you.'

'Call me "Bobby" for feck's sake,' Bobby Quilty told her. His iPhone beeped and he tugged it out and frowned at it, but when he saw who was calling he stuffed it back into his pocket. Then he looked at Kyna more narrowly, with his cigarette dangling between his lips, one eye closed against the smoke, and it was obvious that he liked what he saw.

'Ger, Benny,' he said, 'why don't you go and load up some more fags? A pet day like this, the Peace Park's going to be rammed this dinnertime.'

'Maybe I should go with them, see how it's done,' said Kyna.

'No, no. You come inside with me, girl. I need to give you a briefing before you go out flogging fags. There's a whole lot of ins and outs you have to be familiar with, if you follow me.'

Ger made a strange snorting noise as if he were laughing, and shook his head.

'You all right, there, Ger?' Bobby Quilty asked him. 'I'll see you after, okay?'

'Okay, Bobby,' said Ger, laying his hand across Benny's shoulders and almost pushing him back into the house. Kyna could see them in the hallway talking to Margot and then all three of them disappeared from view.

'Come on, then, sweetheart, come inside, and I'll show you the ropes,' said Bobby Quilty.

'What's to learn?' asked Kyna. 'All you have to do is sit there and sell fags.'

Bobby Quilty grasped her right elbow like a clamp and steered her in through the patio doors. 'Oh no, my darling, there's a whole lot more to it than that. You have to have your regular customers on your phone so that you can tip them the wink when a new shipment of fags has come in, and where and when you'll be selling them. You'll get plenty of casual sales of course, but more than half of your stock will be pre-ordered.'

'But you sell them in shops, too, don't you?' said Kyna. 'Why don't your regular customers just go to the shops?'

'Ach, the polls keep busting the fecking shops, that's the problem. Your shops are an easy target, see, because the polls can fetch in the dogs to sniff out any fags that a shopkeeper might have stashed away in the back or in the ceiling or wherever. Not only that, the shopkeepers are old enough to be hauled up in front of the court. How old did you say you was, sweetheart?'

'Nineteen,' said Kyna. 'Well, nearly nineteen.'

Bobby Quilty propelled her by her elbow along the white-carpeted hallway until they reached the foot of the stairs. There were Jack Vettriano prints hanging all the way up the staircase, couples dancing on a rainy beach, nudes standing in front of mirrors, men in evening wear staring lecherously at women in corsets.

'Away up with you,' said Bobby Quilty and gave a thick, phlegmy cough.

'What do you mean?'

'I mean, away up the stairs with you.'

'What for?'

'Do you want to work for me, or don't you?'

'Chalk it down. I told you.'

'Well, if you want to work for me, you'll do what I tell you, and if I tell you "away up the stairs with you", you'll be away up the stairs.'

Kyna glanced upstairs and then at Bobby Quilty. He jerked his head in an upward direction to emphasize what he had just told her.

She hesitated for a few seconds. She knew that whatever was going to happen upstairs, it wasn't going to be good. She had a choice now. She wasn't on official Garda duty. She was only doing this because Katie had begged her for help, although Katie had made it clear that she wouldn't blame her if she decided that she didn't want to go through with it. But what if she didn't go through with it and John was blinded, or mutilated, or murdered? How could she ever face Katie again?

She took a step up the stairs, and then another. As she climbed, she could still feel the tightness of the stitches where the surgeons had sewn up her stomach after she had been shot. Bobby Quilty watched her, smoking, but it was only when she was halfway up that he began to haul himself up after her.

She reached the landing. The upstairs rooms were furnished in the same soulless modern style as the reception rooms downstairs. They were carpeted in pale grey throughout and every bedroom had white fitted wardrobes with mirrored doors and beds covered with black-and-white diamond-patterned throws. On the walls hung more Jack Vettriano prints and on some of the windowsills stood white earthenware vases of dried chrysanthemums. There was a strong smell of jasmine carpet freshener, which was probably intended to mask the eye-watering reek of Bobby Quilty's cigarette smoke.

Bobby Quilty pointed to what looked like the master bedroom, obviously indicating that Kyna should lead the way inside. Kyna walked in and went across to the window. Through the tall, ivy-covered trees at the end of the garden she could see the dull silvery shine of the River Lee and an orange oil tanker making its way towards the Shell depot.

'Grand view you get from here,' she said.

Bobby Quilty came up and stood close behind her. 'You could make it ten times better. You know that, don't you?'

'Oh, yes?' she said, without turning round. She dreaded to hear what he was going to say next.

'Why don't you pull down your breeks?' he suggested. His smoke was drifting over her shoulder and she could hear the phlegm rattling in his lungs. She started to turn around but he seized her right shoulder, hard, and forced her to remain facing the window. 'You just enjoy the scenery, sweetheart. Pull down your breeks and watch the boats go by.'

'They're too tight,' she said, trying not to sound panicky. 'It took me all the morning just to get them on.'

Bobby Quilty reached around her waist and unfastened her mock-crocodile belt. As he did so, she could feel his belly pressing up against her back.

'What do you think you're doing?' she protested.

'I'm showing you why they call me the Big Feller. I'm also testing you out, just to make sure you're always going to do what I tell you to do, no matter what it is, no questions asked.'

'And what if I tell *you* to take your grubby maulers off me, you fat stinky bastard?'

The instant Kyna said that, Bobby Quilty slapped her around the back of the head so hard that she felt as if her skull had cracked. She staggered forward, her knees giving way, so that she had to grab at the windowsill with both hands to keep herself upright. For a split second, every muscle in her body was tensed up to hit him back. Even though she was still convalescing, she was still fit and she was still highly trained in tae kwon do, and she could have spun around and almost kicked his football-like head clear off his shoulders.

But no, she stayed where she was, her eyes tight shut, her teeth clenched, holding on to the windowsill. *He's not worth it*, she thought, even though her head was ringing. Bobby Quilty was wearing several heavy signet rings and she could already feel where they had bruised her. *Think of John. Most of all, think of Katie.*

'You ever fecking speak to me like that again, sweetheart, and by Joseph and Mary I swear that I'll smack your kite a hundred times harder than that, so I will!' snapped Bobby Quilty. He gripped the back of her neck so hard that she felt as if she were going to black out and for a few seconds she could feel him fumbling around behind her. Then, suddenly, she felt a sharp cold pocket-knife blade pressing against the small of her back and he was sawing roughly through the waistband of her jeans. She heard the stitches tear and then he released his grip on her neck so that he could use both hands to wrench the seat of her jeans apart, and then down. As tight as they were, he managed to pull them nearly down to her knees.

'Keep your bake shut and don't move a muscle!' he told her. His words were indistinct because he still had a cigarette waggling between his lips. 'Don't you even *think* about it, not for a second!'

Kyna was conscious of more fumbling behind her, and more wheezing. Then Bobby Quilty gripped the cheeks of her bottom and spread them wide open, as if he were opening up a book. His fingernails dug into her skin so hard that she couldn't stop herself from sucking in her breath, and then she felt him push his penis in between her thighs, and she sucked in her breath a second time and let out an '*aaaahhhhh*' of sheer discomfort. His penis was stiff and he had been right to boast, it was enormous. But it was very dry, like a wooden rolling pin, and Kyna was dry, too, and he had to force it into her vagina a centimetre at a time. He grunted with every thrust, blowing out ash and cigarette smoke. Kyna kept her teeth gritted and clung on to the windowsill, but he was hurting her now, more and more, and she didn't know how much longer she was going to be able to stand it.

'Jesus, doll, you've a flange like the fecking Sahara Desert!' Bobby Quilty protested.

He tried three or four more thrusts, but all he managed to do was push Kyna's hips repeatedly up against the wall.

'I can't fecking believe this,' he said. He withdrew his penis, took his cigarette out of his mouth, and spat on his fingers so that he could lubricate himself. By the time he managed to jostle himself back into position, however, his erection had begun to subside. He squashed it up against the lips of Kyna's vulva, but it was far too soft now and no matter how hard he squashed he couldn't penetrate her.

'Ach, that's me,' he said and stepped away from her. Kyna turned around to see him bending over so that he could pull up his trousers. 'I never knew any floozy as dry as you, I swear to God. It wouldn't surprise me if you had camels up your cunt.'

Kyna managed to tug up her ripped-apart jeans and buckle her belt. 'I suppose you're going to pay for a new pair,' she said. 'River Island, these are.'

'I'll tell you what I'm going to do with you, you fridge-did bitch,' Bobby Quilty told her. He snatched hold of her wrist, twisting it hard, and when she tried to pull away from him he lifted his other hand as if he were going to slap her again.

'You want another one? You're welcome, so you are.'

With that, he tugged Kyna across the master bedroom and opened the door to the en suite bathroom.

'Fridge-did bitch,' he repeated, as he pushed her inside.

The bathroom was tiled floor to ceiling with mottled grey ceramic tiles with pink flamingos on them and there was a vast jacuzzi and a corner shower with a curved glass door. He pulled her over to the shower and opened it.

'There, get in.'

'What?' said Kyna.

'This is your last chance, sweetheart. Do you want to work for me or not? If you do, then by God you do whatever I tell you. And since you're too fridge-did even to flah, you'll just have to show me in another way, won't you? Now, get in.'

Even though she still had her wedge-heeled shoes on, Kyna stepped into the shower and stood there with her arms crossed defensively over her breasts.

'Kneel down,' said Bobby Quilty. His cigarette had burned down right to the filter now but he gave it a last suck before he lifted the lid of the toilet and flicked it in.

Awkwardly, Kyna knelt down. She couldn't think what he was going to do next. Turn on the shower and soak her in freezing water? But when she looked up at him she saw that he was pulling down his cargo trousers again. He took out his flaccid penis and held it in front of her face. It looked now like a crumpled, grumpy worm.

'Look up,' he said. His voice was strange now – still harsh, but unsteady with excitement. 'Look up, and open your mouth, and keep it open.'

Mother of God, no, thought Kyna. But then Bobby Quilty shivered and started to urinate. He aimed it directly into Kyna's face, stinging her eyes and flooding her mouth with acrid liquid. She spat, and spat again, and shook her head, but he continued to relieve himself all over her. It streamed from her chin and dripped from her earlobes and she could feel it running down warm inside her pink TROUBLE T-shirt.

When he had finished, she stayed where she was, dripping, her eyes closed, trying not to breathe in the alcoholic smell of his urine.

'There, good girl. I think we can say that you've passed the test with flying colours,' said Bobby Quilty as he tucked himself away. 'You stay there, sweetheart, and I'll have Margot come up with some dry clothes for you.'

He walked out of the bathroom, leaving the door open. As soon as he had gone, Kyna clambered to her feet, pulled off her shoes and threw them out of the shower cubicle, followed by her jeans. She was whimpering with disgust as she did so and when she had to drag off her wet T-shirt she retched and would have vomited if she had eaten any breakfast.

Naked, she turned on the shower full, as hot as she could bear it, and soaped herself all over with the shower gel that was hanging from the taps. It smelled of lavender and she knew that she would never be able to smell lavender again without feeling sick.

She was still standing under the shower when Margot came in, carrying a pair of jeans and a top. She stood patiently outside the shower door while Kyna washed her hair again and again. Through the steamy glass she looked like a sympathetic ghost.

Seventeen

At lunchtime, Katie drove to the three-storey building on Lavitt's Quay that housed the Walnut Tree shelter for battered women, which she had helped to set up. It was a run-down nineteenth-century property, which had once been a music shop, and it was still in need of rewiring and some redecorating, but donations had fixed the leaky roof and five of the seven bedsitting rooms were now wallpapered and carpeted.

She was feeling so anxious about John and Kyna that she had almost put off this visit. However, the house manager, Blathnaid O'Keeffe, had called her this morning and told her that they had taken in a new family late yesterday evening and that the mother, Neala Murphy, was very keen to meet her, and thank her.

Katie rang the doorbell outside the dark red-painted facade and Blathnaid opened it so quickly that Katie thought she must have been waiting in the hallway for her.

Inside the house, there was a smell of takeaway pizza and Katie could hear children running about upstairs and laughing. There was always a family atmosphere at Walnut Tree. Katie had insisted from the beginning that it should feel more like a friend's house than a refuge from violence and bullying. There was no lack of crying or arguing, but the women who came here always had a sympathetic counsellor to calm them down and wipe their eyes.

Katie went into the day room, where three young women and their children were watching television. She knew all of them by name. She knew their partners, too, only too well. A fair-haired mother of twin girls was called Moira, and the bruises that still encircled her eyes like yellowish racing-goggles had been inflicted by her boyfriend, Flynn. Fiona was only thirty-six years old but her hair had turned completely white. Her husband, Michael, had burned her with cigarettes all around her genitals and upper thighs and had broken one of her arms so badly that she held it like a pigeon's wing.

Aoife smiled at Katie briefly but didn't speak. As a punishment for cooking meals that he didn't like, her husband, Michael, had kept her locked in a cupboard under the stairs, sometimes for days on end.

'Saw you on the box, Katie,' said Fiona. 'You looked like you was fair odd with that news reporter woman.'

'Oh, you know me,' Katie told her. 'Never happy unless I'm giving somebody a hard time.'

One of Moira's twin girls came up to Katie and held up her a floppy pink bear for her to look at. The girl was only about four years old, with tangled blonde hair and a faded Peppa Pig T-shirt.

'Pink Bear was crying,' she said, very seriously.

'Oh, dear,' said Katie. 'Why was that?'

'She got pushed down the stairs and she bumped her head really, really hard.'

'That's terrible. Who pushed her down the stairs?'

The little girl shook her head so that her hair covered her face. 'She's not allowed to tell.'

'Well, I hope she's feeling better now,' said Katie, touching the little girl gently on the shoulder. She wasn't trained as a child psychiatrist and she knew better than to get involved in conversations like this with children from violent homes.

Blathnaid said, 'Neala's upstairs, Katie. Do you want to come up and have a chat with her?'

'Of course,' said Katie, and followed Blathnaid's large brown-trousered behind up to the second floor.

Neala and her two children had been given one of the newly decorated rooms at the front of the house, overlooking Lavitt's Quay and the river. The ceiling was sloping because it was an attic room, but it was sunny and bright. A boy of about three was kneeling in the window bay playing with two toy cars, while a little girl of about six was lying on one of the beds sucking her thumb.

Neala herself was a taut, nervous-looking young woman with her black wiry hair pulled back in a bunch. Her face was pinched and angular with enormous brown eyes and her wrists were as thin as wooden spoon handles. She was wearing a skimpy purple T-shirt and a voluminous black skirt that looked three sizes too big for her. She started to stand up when Katie came into the room, but Katie said, 'You're all right, Neala, relax.'

'I was hoping you'd come,' said Neala, in a voice that was hoarse from stress and smoking. 'Well, to be honest with you, I was hoping you'd come and I was hoping you wouldn't.'

'You've lovely children,' said Katie. 'What are their names?'

'Peter, and that's Donna.'

Katie smiled at Donna, but Donna stared back at her solemnly, still sucking her thumb.

'I don't know what to call you,' said Neala.

'Call me Katie. This isn't the Garda station and you're certainly not under arrest.'

'That's why I wanted to see you, in a way,' said Neala. She kept glancing around the room as if she were terrified that somebody might be hiding behind the curtains, or under the bed, listening to her.

'Are you all right?' Katie asked her. 'I mean, physically all right?'

'She has some contusions,' put in Blathnaid. 'Doctor Mulroney will be round later to examine her, and the children, too.'

'He's always careful not to leave bruises where anybody can see them,' said Neala, looking at Donna as she did so. She obviously thought that it was pointless not to discuss her husband's violence in front of her children because they had already witnessed it, daily, for themselves.

'Do you want to make a formal complaint against him?' asked Katie. 'If you do, I can send a garda around to take a statement. A female garda.'

Neala shook her head vigorously. 'There's no future in that at all. He was up in front of the court before and all that happened was that he was fined and given a warning and after that he slapped me around worse than ever.'

'You still shouldn't let him get away with it,' said Katie. 'Just because he's your husband, that doesn't make his assault any less serious.'

'I know that. And that's why I wanted to talk to you, to put a stop to it for good and all.'

'Go on,' Katie encouraged her. She could tell from Neala's agitation that she had something very important to tell her, but she was afraid of the consequences if she did.

'That detective garda that was killed on the Brian Boru Bridge – you know, the one who was hit by a car.'

'Detective Barry, yes. We're still looking for the driver.'

Neala glanced around again and then placed her hand over her heart as if she were swearing an oath, or feeling the bruises to remind herself of what her husband had done to her, or both.

'It was Darragh. My Darragh.'

'Your husband was driving the vehicle that hit Detective Barry?'

'That's right. He told me. It was on the news on the telly, like, and he said, "That was me," and he was laughing about it. I was like, "You're codding me, aren't you?" but he was like, "No, serious, that was me driving with Bobby in the front seat. Bobby told me to squish the pig and I did."'

'You're sure he wasn't just boasting, or doing his best to scare you?'

'Darragh doesn't have to say things like that to frighten me. He'd been late back home for his tea that day. We live in Parklands, like, and he only works in a garage in Blackpool, but he said he was late because he'd had to drive all the way down to Boycestown to get rid of the car. He said he'd set light to it. He was pure pleased with himself, believe me.'

Now Katie was convinced that Neala was telling the truth and that her husband, Darragh, hadn't simply been trying to intimidate her. On Katie's instructions, the Garda press office had still not announced that they had found the burned-out Land Rover that had killed Detective Barry. Almost every time they were investigating an unsolved murder some header would come forward to confess to it, especially when it involved a police officer, so she always made sure that several critical details were held back from the media.

'He won't find out that it was me who told you, will he?' said Neala. 'If he ever does, I swear to God he'll do for me. Either *he* will, or that Bobby Quilty. He has the Devil standing in him, that Bobby Quilty. He's totally evil, through and through.'

'Don't worry – it doesn't have to come out that you tipped us off about your Darragh,' Katie told her. 'In any case, we wouldn't be able to get him convicted on your say-so alone. We'd need to find some corroborating evidence first. Otherwise, Darragh could simply deny that he ever said it, or make out that he was joking. There's no law against joking, although sometimes I think that there ought to be.'

'What do you mean, like? What's – what is it? – corrugated evidence?'

'It just means proof that we can show to a judge that your Darragh was actually driving the vehicle at the time that Detective Barry was killed. You know, like fingerprints, or shoe prints, or DNA, or eyewitnesses picking him out and saying it was him. But at least we know now who it is we're trying to identify, and that's going to make our job a whole lot easier, I can tell you.'

'I don't know,' said Neala, worriedly. 'Maybe I shouldn't have told you. I have Donna and little Petey to think about and I'm frightened enough as it is that Darragh's going to find out where we are and come after us.'

'You're safe here, I promise you,' Katie reassured her. 'They never let anybody into the house without checking them first and if there's any trouble they have an alarm connected directly to the Garda station.'

Neala started to gnaw at her thumbnail. All Katie could do was lay her hand on her shoulder and say, 'Please don't worry. Neala. We'll protect you, I promise.'

She waited for a few moments, then she smiled at Donna and went back downstairs to talk to some of the other women in the house. She looked through Blathnaid's notes on the families that Walnut Tree had taken in that week, and then, ten minutes later, she left. When she climbed back into her car, however, she didn't drive off immediately. She sat staring at her sea-green eyes in the rear-view mirror, feeling both angry and frustrated.

If she could have put out an arrest warrant for Darragh Murphy immediately, she would have done. But she knew that she would have to handle any inquiry into Detective Barry's murder with extraordinary caution. She couldn't arrest Murphy on suspicion because he would guess where she had got her information, and she had nothing else to back it up. She would only be putting the lives of Neala and her children in extreme peril – and John's life, too. She couldn't even bring him into the station for an identity line-up. As soon as Bobby Quilty got wind that she was still investigating him, God alone knew what revenge he would take. He would believe that he was justified, too – 'You broke the treaty, DS Maguire, not me.'

Even if she could find enough evidence to put Darragh Murphy behind bars for killing Detective Barry, and Bobby Quilty for inciting him to do it, Neala and John would still be in danger of retribution from other members of Quilty's gang, or his so-called Authentic IRA. In the last week of January, the A-IRA had murdered two suspected members of Oglaigh na hEireann who had attempted to hijack a lorryload of Bobby Quilty's cigarettes. In trademark Quilty fashion, they had both suffered shotgun blasts between the legs before being bound and gagged and thrown off Daly Bridge into the River Lee so that they would float through the city centre at the busiest time of the day.

Katie had seen the bodies for herself and the thought of them still made her stomach clench.

She could fully understand that Neala wanted Darragh to be punished for beating her, and to have him locked up so that he could never threaten her again, but she didn't think that she appreciated what this would mean for her and her children. They would have to spend the rest of their lives in witness protection, under assumed names, even if they left the country and were relocated somewhere in England. Bobby Quilty's most lucrative trade came from the cigarettes that he smuggled from Ringaskiddy into Swansea, or from Dundalk into Liverpool, and he had scores of English cronies who would be only too happy to do him a favour and see that Neala was made to suffer for touting on him.

And John – what would they do to John? She might never see him again – or, if they blinded him, he might never see *her* again, even if she managed to rescue him alive.

She had just started her engine when her iPhone pinged to tell her that she had a text message. It was from Kyna and it read simply, *I'm in. GHMOMS.*

Katie knew what *GHMOMS* meant because Kyna had used it before when she was caught up in a situation that was critical or dangerous or deeply unpleasant. *God Have Mercy On My Soul.*

She was tempted to tell Kyna to pull out if there was too much risk, or if her position was becoming untenable, for whatever reason. But now that she knew for certain that Bobby Quilty was behind Detective Barry's murder it was even more urgent that Kyna should infiltrate his empire even further.

She drove back to Anglesea Street. She had intended to go up to the canteen and have a ham and salad roll, but now she felt too nauseated to eat anything.

Eighteen

Bill Phinner and Eithne came up to her office together. Eithne was carrying a large transparent plastic folder, while Bill was sucking at an unlit pipe.

'Bill!' said Katie, looking up from her paperwork. 'I never knew you smoked a pipe!'

'I don't, as matter of fact,' Bill told her. 'Hardly ever, any road. I can't smoke in the lab, and I can't smoke in the pub, and the missus won't let me smoke indoors at home, and most of the time it's raining and believe you me there's fierce little pleasure in standing down the end of the garden trying to keep your pipe alight when it's lashing down. The only good it does me, it stops me from grinding my teeth. My brother says it makes me look halfway intelligent, too. You can point at things with a pipe and look as if you know what you're talking about.'

'So, what have you got for me?' asked Katie.

Eithne held up the folder. 'Final DNA results on the bodies from Millstream Row. There's no question about it. They're the Langtry family all right.'

'I won't bore you with the minutiae,' said Bill. 'But the charts for all four of the family are here and you'll be able to see for yourself that the segments we've tested are well above the threshold for IBD.'

Katie took the folder and opened it up. She had taken the eight-day refresher course in forensics early last year and she knew that IBD meant Identical By Descent. It was sometimes possible that DNA could be IBC, Identical By Chance, but in the case of the Langtrys she could see from a cursory glance at the charts that the samples had been triangulated with Ronan Fitzgerald and that the matches were undeniable.

'All right, thanks,' she said. 'Of course that leaves me with the question of how Stephen Langtry managed to send letters and postcards from America when he was lying dead under the floorboards in Blarney.'

'A ruse, I'd say, so nobody would find out for a while that they'd been murdered,' said Bill, taking his pipe out of his mouth. 'Their bodies would have stunk for a few weeks but sure most people's houses would have stunk in the 1920s, what with the lack of personal hygiene and the peat fires and the smoking indoors, and the same pot of tripe bubbling on the hob for days on end. And, of course, their killers were haunted that their bodies dried out the way they did, what with the atmospheric conditions under those floorboards being the way they were. I don't suppose they envisaged for a moment that they wouldn't be discovered for another ninety-five years.'

'Well, I think it's pure obvious that somebody else apart from Stephen Langtry sent those letters,' said Katie. 'I'd just be interested to know *who*, and exactly *why*. I mean, there was a war going on and people on both sides were getting killed, but usually it was done quite openly. When Michael Collins was shot they didn't hide his body, did they, and send letters from New York to make out that he was simply fed up with politics and had decided to emigrate?'

'Now that would be a grand idea for a film,' said Bill. 'Especially if they could get that Liam Neeson playing Collins again.'

'I'll have Mathew arrange for a media briefing later this afternoon,' Katie told him. 'I expect Fionnuala Sweeney will be crowing, but it can't be helped. Maybe we'll be able to jog somebody's memory and they'll remember something they were told by their grandparents about the Langtrys.'

'You never know,' said Bill. 'My old grandfather was always rattling on about the time his older brother hid guns on his farm at Inniscarra for Captain Frank Busteed and his boys. From what he said, you'd have believed the Phinners won the war of independence single-handed.'

'Like you say, Bill, you never know. I'll also get Detective Ó Doibhilin to contact US Immigration. It's a ten million to one chance, but their historical records are fantastic and they might be able to tell us if somebody calling himself Stephen Langtry was admitted to the USA in 1921, with or without his wife and children. And the New York State police may be able to discover if a Stephen Langtry ever really worked for Glenside Woollen Mills, especially if Glenside Woollen Mills is still in business.'

'So you think some other family could have gone over to America and pretended to be them?'

'I really have no idea, Bill. I don't think it's very likely, but we have to consider every possibility. The Langtrys might have been murdered a long time ago, but they deserve justice and whoever shot them needs to be named and shamed. Grand work with the DNA, by the way.'

Bill looked towards the window. 'It still looks nice and bright out there. I reckon I'll go and have a smoke to celebrate.'

* * *

The media briefing was called for 4.30 p.m. to give RTÉ and the local radio stations plenty of time to include their reports on their six o'clock news bulletins, and the newspapers time to write it up for their morning editions.

Fionnuala Sweeney was there, of course, sitting right at the front, and so was Dan Keane from the *Examiner* with his usual half-smoked cigarette tucked behind his ear, and Branna MacSuibhne from the *Echo* with her blonde hair sprayed into two rigid buffalo horns. Katie could see a new face there, too: a very thin brunette with enormous brown eyes. She had a tapestry bag slung around her shoulders and a Newstalk badge on her lanyard, although she looked almost too young to be a radio reporter.

At the last moment, Chief Superintendent MacCostagáin came into the conference room to join Katie at the top table, looking even more distracted and out of sorts than usual. Although she had already given him the details of the DNA results, and he didn't often make an appearance at routine news briefings, he shared Katie's concern about the political implications of the Langtry case and he obviously wanted to hear what the media's response was going to be.

Katie stood up and said, 'Good afternoon, ladies and gentlemen. Our Technical Bureau have now completed DNA tests on the four bodies discovered beneath the floorboards at Millstream Row in Blarney, and they have established beyond any reasonable doubt that the four were indeed Stephen and Radha Langtry and their two children, Aideen and Clearie.'

She could see Fionnuala Sweeney nodding her head in self-satisfaction, but she ignored her and looked instead at the young woman from Newstalk.

'Based on this evidence, we'll continue to pursue our investigation into how the family were murdered and who might have been responsible, but I have to emphasize that I am not regarding this case as a high priority. My detectives have many more pressing investigations on their hands, particularly in the areas of drug-trafficking, prostitution, property theft and serious fraud, so the public can rest assured that we're giving our full attention to present-day inquiries.'

Fionnuala Sweeney raised her hand and asked, 'Have you found any evidence yet to confirm or deny that Radha Langtry was having an adulterous affair with a British army officer?'

'I'm aware of that so-called "local legend", Fionnuala, but so far we haven't found any conclusive evidence to back it up.'

'But you do have *some* evidence?'

'No.'

'A British army cap badge wrapped in a love letter?'

'Yes, we have those, but as yet we have no conclusive proof that they actually belonged to Radha Langtry.'

The young woman from Newstalk put up her hand. 'If they *were* hers, though, and she'd been having an affair with a British officer, that could have given the British the motive to shoot them, couldn't it?'

'What's your name?' Katie asked her.

'Muireann. Muireann Bourke.'

'Well, let me say this to you, Muireann, whenever somebody's unlawfully killed, it's part of my job to have theories about who might have done it and why. But I test each of those theories to the very limit and make absolutely sure that I have irrefutable evidence before I start making public pronouncements about them.

'Whatever the "local legend" suggests, it's impossible for me to say for certain if Radha Langtry was having a liaison with a British officer or not, and I certainly have no grounds at all to suggest that the British army was responsible for killing the Langtrys because of it.'

'If you found out that they *were*, though, that would be shattering, wouldn't it? Like, think of the repercussions!'

'Muireann, I can comment only on facts, not wild suppositions, and you should know better than to ask me a question like that.'

Muireann Bourke flushed and looked down at the floor in embarrassment. *She'll learn*, thought Katie. She remembered asking similar questions herself when she was a green young garda and being slapped down for it.

Dan Keane said, 'Even if do discover who murdered the Langtrys, though, what earthly use will that be? What about you, Chief Superintendent MacCostagáin? Don't you sometimes think it's wiser to let sleeping dogs lie?'

'Sleeping dogs, maybe,' said Chief Superintendent Mac-Costagáin. 'In this case, though, the dogs weren't sleeping. They were shot dead, as were the Langtrys.'

'Of course, yes, but it was a very long time ago.'

'There's no statute of limitations on homicide, Dan, even if the offenders have passed away themselves. If you take a life, you will always have to answer to the law, even as you always have to explain yourself to God.'

'Sure, I have you,' said Dan Keane. 'But if we're talking about answering to the law, and to God, can you tell us what progress you've been able to make into finding out who it was that murdered Detective Barry – if any, that is? It's his funeral tomorrow.'

Katie turned her head to give Chief Superintendent Mac-Costagáin a sharp, cautionary look. She was all too familiar with Dan Keane and his interview techniques – 'Keane by Name and Keen by Nature' was the way the *Examiner* described him under his byline. He rarely asked a question unless he already had a good idea what the answer was going to be.

Chief Superintendent MacCostagáin was very guarded when he answered. 'We're still in the process of examining the forensic evidence and collating eyewitness statements,' he said. 'Tomorrow morning we'll be making a fresh appeal for information on all news media, and I understand that Assistant Commissioner O'Reilly has been given approval from Phoenix Park to offer a reward for any information that leads to a conviction. The exact amount hasn't been confirmed yet, but I expect it to be in the region of ten thousand euros.'

'You haven't located the Land Rover that ran down Detective Barry, then?'

'I've no comment to make about that, Dan. Not at this time.'

'But you've located at least *one* abandoned Land Rover?'

'I've no comment to make about that, Dan.'

'Well, fair play to you, Chief Superintendent. I fully understand that your inquiry is still ongoing and that you can't be releasing every doonchy little clue that you come across. But if you'd found the Land Rover that killed Detective Barry, I'd say that was quite a substantial clue, wouldn't you? So would it be safe for me to assume that *this* particular Land Rover has nothing at all to do with his murder and that's why you've announced nothing to the media about it?'

Katie didn't like the way this questioning was going at all, and she knew that Chief Superintendent MaCostagáin wasn't going to be able to get away with answering 'no comment' to every question that Dan Keane put to him.

'Which Land Rover exactly are you talking about, Dan?' she asked him.

'Well, it doesn't really matter, does it, if it has nothing at all to do with your investigation into the killing of Detective Barry?'

Dan Keane's left eyebrow was lifted and he had a calm, superior look on his face because he was confident now that he had Katie cornered.

Katie paused for a moment and then she said, 'A Land Rover was found yesterday on a farm track north of Boycestown. It was totally burned out, with the result that it probably won't yield any meaningful forensic evidence, although our technical experts are still going over it. Apart from that, we're continuing to make inquiries into where it came from and who might have been driving it.'

'You're not denying then that it could be the same Land Rover that killed Detective Barry?'

'I'm not denying it and I'm not confirming it, either.'

'But DS Maguire, it still had its number plates attached. So how could you possibly *not* be certain, when you have CCTV footage of the Land Rover following Detective Barry across the Brian Boru Bridge?'

'Excuse me, Dan, but how you can be so sure that it was still carrying its number plates?' Katie retaliated. Although this briefing wasn't going out on live TV or radio, she was becoming seriously worried now. She was counting on Kyna finding out where John was being held before the evidence against Bobby Quilty became so damning that she had no choice but to arrest him. For John, the consequences of her doing that were likely to be disastrous. She had no doubt at all that only minutes after her detectives turned up at Bobby Quilty's door with a warrant John would be dead, or worse, and that she would never see him, or his body, ever again.

Dan Keane held up his iPhone. 'Just as I was leaving the office on my way here today my picture editor caught up with me and said that two Dutch cyclists came in to see him this morning. It seems like they were on a tour of Cork and Kerry and while they were cycling across country on their way to Kinsale they saw a

Land Rover on fire, and there were two fellows standing watching it. They took a few pictures, but being Dutch they never watched the TV news or read a paper, so they had no idea that they might have witnessed anything significant.'

'Why didn't they report it to the Garda anyway?' said Katie.

'Like I say, they didn't think it was anything of any great importance. Just a Land Rover that had caught fire for some reason and two fellows who were helpless to put it out. They only brought the pictures in to us because they were running low on holiday money and thought we might pay them a few euros for them. And so we did, because one or two of them are pure spectacular. In one of them, there's a great ball of fire going up in the air which must have been the Land Rover's petrol tank exploding.'

'Why didn't *you* bring them in to us?'

'I did. I am. I couldn't have done it any sooner. Here they are now, on my phone. I'll share them with you right away.'

'I must say you certainly picked your moment.'

'DS Maguire, I swear to you on the tomb of St Francis de Sales that I haven't even had the time myself to study them in any detail at all. I can tell you, though, that you can see at least one of the two fellows' faces quite distinctly – so if you knew him, like, you'd be able to tell who he was.'

Katie opened the laptop in front of her and said, 'Go on, then. You have me on your list of contacts, don't you?'

There was a rustle of excitement in the conference room. Fionnuala Sweeney stood up and said, 'You'll be releasing those pictures to all of us, I hope?'

'Not yet, Fionnuala,' Katie told her. 'We need to examine them ourselves first and see if we can identify either or both of the two men in them.'

Katie's laptop pinged and an email from Dan Keane appeared with a Dropbox link to seven photographs. They all showed a Land Rover burning in a narrow country track, with dense black smoke billowing out of it and two men standing some distance away, half hidden by the long grass verge. The second to last picture was the most dramatic, with orange flames rolling up into the sky and one of the men turning his face away from the blast so that he could be clearly seen by the camera.

'Thank you, Dan,' said Katie. 'We'll take a look at these immediately and let you know as soon as we're ready to issue a statement. Meanwhile, I'd appreciate it if you didn't publish them yet.'

'I don't know about that,' said Dan Keane. 'We paid for them, after all. Two hundred and fifty euros. Cash.'

'We appreciate that,' put in Chief Superintendent MacCostagáin. 'However, they amount to material evidence in an ongoing Garda inquiry. If you publish them prematurely and the men in the pictures are alerted to the possibility that we're looking for them and flee our jurisdiction, that could amount to obstruction.'

'I think I'll have to talk to our lawyers about that,' said Dan Keane. 'In the meantime, though, can you now verify that this is the Land Rover that killed Detective Barry? Like, the number plates in those pictures *do* match, don't they?'

'You swore that you hadn't had the time to study them,' said Katie.

'I didn't, no. But I couldn't help myself from giving the number plates a quick lamp. They're BXZ plates, from Armagh.'

'Very well,' said Chief Superintendent MacCostagáin, speaking to all of the assembled journalists. 'You can quote me as confirming that we've located an abandoned Land Rover that appears to be the same vehicle that killed Detective Barry. Further than that, I have no more comments to make at this time.'

Katie said, 'The main purpose of this briefing was to inform you that the bodies found in Blarney have been positively identified as Stephen Langtry and his family. If we manage to come up with any information about who might have killed them and what the motive might have been, we will of course let you know. Thank you for coming.'

Dan Keane said, 'Bobby Quilty, he's from Armagh, isn't he? And Detective Barry was trying to arrest one of his dealers when he was killed.'

Katie closed her laptop and stood up. 'If we could convict people on evidence like that, Dan, three quarters of the population of Cork would be in prison.'

'So they would, DS Maguire, and that would be fierce unjust. But think how peaceful it would be, shopping in Paul Street Tesco on a Saturday afternoon.'

Nineteen

When Kyna came downstairs she found Bobby Quilty sitting on a white simulated-leather sofa in the living room, his legs crossed, one flip-flop hanging loose, jabbing at his iPhone. She stood in the doorway waiting for him to acknowledge her. After all, he was supposed to have humiliated her and shown her in the most degrading way possible that he was the boss.

Her hair was still slicked back wet from the shower and she was wearing a faded pair of Margot's jeans that she had rolled up around her ankles because they were much too long for her, and a loose white sleeveless top, without a bra. Without showing even a flicker of surprise at what Bobby Quilty had done to her, Margot had taken away Kyna's own clothes to wash them.

Bobby Quilty didn't look at her, not directly, but beckoned her to come in and pointed with his iPhone towards the armchair next to him. She sat down and waited until he had finished texting, not saying a word. She had been involved in at least half a dozen undercover investigations before, and the secret was not to act *like* the person whose identity she had assumed but to *be* them. It was never easy. Once, when she was gathering evidence against a Dublin brothel-keeper, she had developed such a crush on her that she had been sorely tempted to warn her that she was about to be arrested and give her time to get away.

"Bout you, then?' said Bobby Quilty with a sniff.

Kyna pulled a non-committal face and said nothing.

'Well, wait till I tell you,' Bobby Quilty continued. 'We've a new shipment of fags just arrived last night and a whole heap of orders from our regular customers. Ger will take you to the lock-up to pick them up and then he'll drive you round so that you can deliver them and collect the cash for them.'

'You don't only sell your fags on the street, then?' asked Kyna.

Bobby Quilty shook out a cigarette and lit it and blew out smoke. 'Ach, no, not at all. Most of our trade comes from shops and bars and office workers. The reason I sell them out on the street is mostly to pick up new business. You know, people who never realized that they could buy two hundred fags for a quarter of the price. Once they know where we'll be flogging them, and when, they always come back for more. Well, wouldn't you? Ten euros for a packet of fags, it's fecking inhuman!'

'You don't trust me to go out selling on my own, though? What, in case I run away with your fags and don't come back?'

'Oh, I think I can trust you. I took a squint at your phone, girl, just to make sure. No, I just want Ger to take you around so that he can show you the ropes, like, and you can meet the regular customers face to face. They'll all take to you, believe me. You're very easy on the eye. You'll be good for business, so you will.'

'Can I have my phone back now?'

'Ach, sure.' Bobby Quilty reached around to the table behind the sofa and then threw Kyna's phone across to her. 'I called a couple of your pals from the massage parlour and they were highly complimentary about you, to say the least. One feller said that he only had to hear your name and it got him all chubbed up.'

Ger appeared in the doorway, with Benny close behind him. He took off his hat to wipe his sweaty forehead and when he came into the room Kyna could smell his body odour. It reminded her of a long-dead cat she had once discovered in the kitchen cupboard of an old woman's house she had been searching in Dolphin's Barn.

''Bout you, then?' asked Bobby Quilty. 'Was the park any use?'

Ger reached into his inside pocket and handed Bobby Quilty a thick bundle of crumpled euro notes. 'We sold thirty-seven boxes altogether. We could have sold more, but the shades was beginning to take too much of an interest.'

'Didn't I tell you not to worry about the polls? We're insured, you know that. I have them totally sorted, so I have. They might sniff around, but they won't scoop you.'

'Well, you might say that, Bobby, but you've never spent two years in the slammer. The shades still give me the fecking palpitations.'

Bobby Quilty was counting out the money that Ger had given him, licking his thumb every now and then.

'Nine hundred and thirty euros,' said Ger. 'One fellow didn't have change but he said not to bother.'

'All right, that's magic,' said Bobby Quilty, once he had finished counting and fastidiously turning all the notes around the same way. 'Now you can load up again and take Sidhe here to do the drop-offs round Blackpool and Shandon – oh, and that newsagent on MacCurtain Street. And on the way back, stop off and see Chisel, would you, and check that our friend hasn't managed to unscrew himself?'

Ger said to Kyna, 'Come on, then, girl. Let's get you to work. You might have a tasty arse but we can't have you sitting on it all day.'

* * *

They drove down to Blackpool. Benny sat in the back with his earphones in and Kyna could hear the faint *tish-tish-tish* of his rap music. Ger said almost nothing except to swear at every cyclist who wavered in front of him and any driver who was slow starting off when the traffic lights went to green. His sweat smelled so strongly now that Kyna put down her window and kept her head turned away from him.

They turned through an archway between the run-down shops and houses along Dublin Street and into a row of tatty lock-up garages. Ger said to Kyna, 'You go stand on the corner, Sidhe, and keep sketch, while me and Benny load up the car. If you see any shades coming, don't shout out or nothing, just walk back over here flapping your hand like you've let off a breezer.'

Kyna shrugged and did as she was told. While she stood under the archway, ostensibly watching out for gardaí, Ger unlocked one of the garages, lifting its door with a harsh metallic squeal like a pig being slaughtered. Even from where she was standing, thirty metres away, Kyna could see that it was stacked right up to its asbestos roof with cartons of cigarettes – the distinctive red-and-white packs of Lucky Strike, West and Marlboro, as well as Goal and NZ Gold and Jin Ling and other brands she didn't recognize.

While Ger and Benny filled up black plastic refuse sacks with cigarettes, Kyna surreptitiously slipped out her iPhone and texted Katie with her thumb. She told her that Bobby Quilty had sent her out on a delivery run, but that he had also asked them to check up on 'our friend', whoever that was, to make sure that he hadn't 'managed to unscrew himself', whatever that meant.

She had only just finished texting when a Garda patrol car came slowly towards her along Dublin Street. She backed into the archway in case the officers recognized her or stopped to ask her why she was loitering there.

The patrol car passed by, though, without even slowing down, and a few seconds later Ger gave her a whistle as if he were calling a dog.

Before they started on their rounds, Ger consulted a torn-off sheet of notepaper with a list of all of their customers pencilled on it. 'Right we are, then. First stop, Ali's Corner Store on Thomas Davis Street, then it's O'Grady's, the bookies and The Scissor Shop, the barber's.'

When they reached Thomas Davis Street, Ger pointed to the corner shop and Kyna climbed out of the car. Benny climbed out, too, opened the boot and handed her two bulging black bags. From the driving seat, Ger whistled to her again, and beckoned to her, and said, 'Smile when you give Ali the fags, okay, and make him think that he could take you into the back of the shop and give you one.'

'*Wha*'? But he's a Paki, isn't he?'

'That's not the fecking point, Sidhe. The point is that this is a cut-throat business, the cigarette trade, and we want him to go on buying from us rather than the Duggans or the O'Flynns. So, you know, give him the eye and wiggle your arse when you take his money. You wouldn't have the time to flah him, any road. We have a dozen more drop-offs yet.'

Kyna kept her mouth closed. She took the bags from Benny and pushed her way between the string bags of onions and sponge mops that cluttered the entrance to the grocery store. Inside, it smelled strongly of fenugreek, and the aisles were so crowded with giant boxes of detergent and tins of okra and cut-price washing-up brushes and racks full of Tayto crisps that she had a struggle to reach the counter.

A bearded Asian in a yellow baseball cap was standing behind the counter, intent on mending a mobile phone.

'Are you Ali?' she asked him. 'Here you are then, boy. Here's the fags you ordered from the Big Feller.'

Ali put down his miniature screwdriver and grinned at her, with his two front incisors missing. 'How about you, then?' he said, in a strong Norrie accent. 'First time the Big Feller's sent a good-looking beour like you to deliver his fags.'

'Well, he only wants to make you happy, Ali, do you know what I mean, like?'

'I don't know if the Big Feller could make me happy, but I think you could. What's your name, girl?'

'Sidhe. S-i-d-h-e like in "fairy", like – not "she" like "her over there who looks like a bit of a goer". And that'll be five hundred yo-yos, please.'

'Sure, but how do I know they're all here, all the fags I ordered? Maybe you can stay for a while and help me to count them, Sidhe, just to make sure. What would happen if I was one box short? Where would I find another box?'

Kyna gave him an exaggerated pout. 'Oh, you're such a bad man, Ali. But not today. I'm up the walls, like, with all my deliveries. One day maybe, when I'm not so pushed.'

'I will look forward to it, my darling.'

Ali opened up his till and counted out five hundred euros. He didn't give them to her, though, until he had come out from behind the counter, put his arm around her waist and escorted her to the door. Even then he held the money just out of reach, until he had kissed her on the lips. The peak of his baseball cap bumped against her forehead.

'Christ on a bicycle!' Benny piped up as she climbed back into the car. 'You only shifted him!'

Ger couldn't help grinning behind his huge dark glasses. 'I'll tell you, there's no way he's going to be ordering his fags from Micky Duggan after that! What was it like?'

Kyna was tempted to spit and wipe her mouth but Ali was still watching from the doorway of his shop and giving her a little finger-wave.

'Suppose a badger sat by mistake in a bowl of curry,' she said. 'Then, after the curry was all stiff and dried up, suppose you kissed that badger's arse. That was what it was like.'

Ger laughed – a thin, cracked laugh – and Kyna knew then that she had won his confidence.

* * *

For the next three and a half hours they drove around Blackpool and Shandon and Gurranabraher, delivering black bags full of cigarette cartons to shops and pubs and offices and private houses. Kyna even took a bag to the manager of an old peoples' home in Sunday's Well, and round to the back door of a dental clinic on Commons Road in Farranree.

At every stop she was greeted with smiles of appreciation and thumbs-up gestures and two of her customers asked her out on a date – a spotty young estate agent with protruding ears and a white-bearded pub landlord who was old enough to be her grandfather. The cash was always handed over with no hesitation at all and by the time she delivered the last three sacks to the Golden Shamrock Bar in Blackpool she estimated that she had taken well over eleven thousand euros.

At last Ger parked outside a terracotta-painted house at the junction of Leitrim Street and Pine Street, opposite O'Keefe's pub.

The house had once been a shop but now its large display windows had grimy, fly-spotted blinds drawn down over them.

'What are we stopping here for?' asked Kyna. 'We don't have any more fags left, do we?'

'You just mind your own beeswax girl and wait here for me,' said Ger. He climbed out of the car, but instead of going to the front door of the house he walked around to a side gate, opened it, and disappeared inside.

'What's here, then, Benny?' Kyna asked, but Benny had put in his earphones and couldn't hear her. After they had waited for a few minutes, though, he suddenly took them out and said, 'I'm fecking parched, me. I've a mouth on me like Gandhi's flip-flop. I'm going to get myself a Coke.'

'Fetch me one while you're at it,' said Kyna.

Benny got out of the car and walked two doors down to Brannagan's Bar. Kyna waited a little while, but when he didn't immediately reappear, she got out, too. She looked up at the terracotta-coloured house, but she couldn't see anybody looking back down at her from the upstairs windows, so she went to the side gate, opened it, and quickly went inside. She found herself in a cramped back yard with wheelie bins and a bicycle in it, as well as a stack of broken window frames filled with shattered glass, and a rabbit hutch that looked as if it had been smashed in half and then crudely repaired with a square of hardboard and a length of frayed electrical flex. The rabbit was sitting on a bed of its own buttons and it stared at Kyna bulgy-eyed, as if it were vainly hoping that she had come to set it free.

The back door of the house had been left ajar and Kyna could see a kitchen sink with dirty plates in it and some chipped cupboard doors. She could hear voices, too: a woman complaining loudly and persistently about something and two slurred male voices, one of which she recognized as Ger.

She went up to the door and pushed it open a little more. The voices sounded as if they were coming from somewhere upstairs, so she carefully stepped inside and went through the kitchen into the hallway beyond. The house was in a desperate state of disrepair. The walls were so damp that the floral paper had been bleached of all its colour, and the pale chocolate stair carpet was threadbare and spotted black with mould. Kyna went to the bottom of the staircase and looked up to the first-floor landing. The voices sounded as if they were coming from a room immediately on the left-hand side, and although the door was almost closed, cigarette smoke was curling around it, so she could be fairly sure that Ger was in there with whoever he was talking to – possibly the person whom Bobby Quilty had referred to as 'Chisel'.

Her heart was beating so hard that it hurt because there was every chance that Ger would suddenly open the door and see her standing there. However, there was no point in her going back. Benny would probably have returned with their Cokes by now and he would see her emerging from the side gate and tell Ger anyway.

She had an excuse ready, to explain why she had followed Ger into the house, but that excuse would only work if she kept on going. She grasped the banister rail, hesitated for a few seconds, and then started to climb the stairs. They creaked loudly, but the woman continued to nag, and Ger continued talking back to her, so they obviously hadn't heard her.

When she reached the landing, she tiptoed over to the right-hand side and opened the first door she came to. It was a bathroom, with curled-up green linoleum on the floor and a bath with dripping taps. The inside of the toilet was stained rusty brown, and its wooden seat had come off and was propped up against the wall beside it.

Kyna opened the next door, which she had to do carefully because the knob was loose and rattled as she turned it. This room smelled strongly as if somebody had been sleeping in it. The ill-fitting orange curtains were still drawn and there was a king-sized mattress on the floor with twisted sheets on it, and pillows that were still dented with the impressions of two heads. A single corduroy-covered armchair was heaped with clothes, men's and women's, including a large pair of stained white underpants.

Just as she closed the door of this room, she heard Ger say, 'How's our friend been keeping, then, Sorcia? Has he been giving you any bother?'

The woman said something Kyna couldn't hear, but then she must have turned around because she heard her say, '—shouting out and moaning and groaning, so I give him five paracetamol and that shut him up. I don't care. I don't like to see nobody suffering like that. I remember when my mam was—'

Kyna paused, still on tiptoe, holding her breath. Ger and the woman must be very close to the door for her to be able to hear them so distinctly. The other man spoke, too, but she couldn't make out what he was saying, only that he had a strong Southside accent.

She went to the door at the end of the landing. On the wall next to it was a faded framed print of Pope Paul VI, holding up two fingers in blessing. She tried the handle, only to find that the door was locked, although the key was still in it. She unlocked it and slowly pushed it open.

It was gloomy inside, like the bedroom, because the blind was drawn. The smell was even worse, though – rancid and sour, but with a sickening sweetness to it, too. Several bluebottles were flying around, while others tapped and buzzed at the window.

Kyna didn't recognize John at first, although she had met him six or seven times and seen dozens of pictures of him and Katie when they were together. He was lying asleep on a single bed, completely naked. His face was startlingly white, and shiny with perspiration, so that he could almost have been a marble effigy of himself, except that his mouth was hanging open and he was snoring.

As she approached him, keeping her hand cupped over her nose and mouth, Kyna saw that both of his feet had been fastened to the wooden board at the end of the bed with metal bolts and that shiny green flies were clustered around the stigmata. He had soiled the mattress and the insides of his thighs were smeared with dark yellow faeces.

She laid her hand on his shoulder and gently shook him. 'John?' she whispered. 'John, can you hear me?'

He stirred and groaned like a door creaking, but he didn't open his eyes. Kyna shook him again, harder this time. 'John? Wake up, John! *John!*'

He made a snuffling sound and then he opened his deep blue eyes and stared at her, unfocused.

'John – we're going to get you out of here. So try and be strong, okay? Katie hasn't forgotten you – she loves you. Do you understand me?'

John frowned at her and said, '*Kyna* . . . is that you?' Then he looked around the room and said, 'Where am I?'

'They're keeping you locked up here, but we'll soon get you out, I promise.'

She could hear Ger coughing, and the woman saying something to him, so she tiptoed out of the bedroom and locked the door. She was halfway back across the landing when the door at the top of the staircase suddenly opened and a skinny man in a black T-shirt appeared, with his belt tied tightly into a knot to stop his jeans from falling down. Right behind him came Ger, and a bosomy young woman in a headscarf. All three of them had been smoking so heavily that they came out in a cloud, like characters in a pantomime.

'What in the name of God are you doing here, Sidhe?' Ger demanded. 'I told you to wait outside, didn't I?'

'I'm bursting for a piss,' said Kyna. 'I couldn't hardly do it down the shore, could I?'

'You could have gone over to the pub, for feck's sake.'

'Oh, give the girl a break, would you?' said the bosomy young woman. 'You're so tight, you are, Ger, wouldn't give a starving nun the skin off your skitter!'

'Any more of that, Sorcia, and there'll be less of it!' Ger snapped at her. But then he said, 'You didn't go in *there*, Sidhe, did you?'

'Where?' asked Kyna.

'In there,' he said, pointing towards the room where John was locked up. 'That door there.'

'Why should I? I just need the toilet.'

Ger gave her a ghastly grin and the smoke from his last cigarette came leaking out from between his teeth. 'That's fierce strange, that is. I thought *you* was the toilet!'

The skinny man laughed, honking like a donkey, but Sorcia came over and opened the bathroom door. 'There, love. It's in there. You'll have to forgive the boggin' state of it. Chisel keeps promising to fix the seat but he keeps fixing himself first and then he's too blootered to know one end of a screwdriver from the other.'

'Holy Jesus, Sorcia, I could see you far enough!' Chisel protested.

Kyna went into the bathroom and closed the door. She turned on the tap in the washbasin to make a splashing noise and then took out her phone and texted Katie to tell her the house number, and exactly where John's bedroom was located, and also that his feet were bolted to the bed. She hadn't seen anybody else in the house apart from Chisel and Sorcia, and she hadn't seen any firearms, but that wasn't to say they didn't have any, or that there wasn't another of Bobby Quilty's gang keeping an eye on the house for him.

Ger knocked on the bathroom door and said, 'Get your skates on, will you, we don't have the whole fecking day!'

'Coming!' Kyna called out, and cranked the cistern handle.

'Is that better?' asked Ger as she emerged. In spite of his earlier irritation, she was sure that he really liked her now and that he would do almost anything for her if she asked. What she would really have liked him to do was lie down on the floor in front of her so that she could stamp very hard on his face.

Twenty

Katie was talking to Mathew McElvey in the press office when her iPhone pinged and she saw that Kyna was texting her.

Mathew was saying, 'I agree with you absolutely, DS Maguire. We have to be very diplomatic in the way we handle this Langtry case. On the one hand, we don't want the Garda to be seen to be stirring up old grievances, but on the other hand, like you said at the briefing, we don't want to be seen to be squandering the taxpayers' money trying to find a murderer who's long dead and buried.

'I still think, though, that there's powerful public interest in knowing who it was that murdered the Langtrys, and why – especially if it turns out that Radha Langtry *was* having an affair with a British officer and it was the Brits who shot them. I had a call only this morning from that Stephen Wright fellow from the *Daily Mail* in London and he was very keen to know if—'

'I'm sorry, Mathew,' said Katie. 'I'll have to interrupt you there. I've an urgent case to deal with. I'll get back to you after, if that's okay.'

'Okay, sure,' said Mathew. 'But I have my fingers crossed about what they're going to be saying on the *Six One News*, I can tell you.'

Katie hurried back up to her office and immediately put in calls to Detective Inspector O'Rourke and Detective Sergeant Begley, as well as Detectives O'Donovan, Dooley and Scanlan. Then she switched on her desktop computer, clicked on to a map of Cork City, and brought up a street view of the terracotta-coloured house where John was being held.

For the first time since Bobby Quilty had visited her at home and told her that he had abducted John, she felt that surge of adrenaline that came from being in control again, although she remained deeply anxious about John. *J's feet bolted to bed*, Kyna had texted her. His *feet*, bolted to the bed? She couldn't even begin to imagine what that must look like, or the pain he must be suffering. Maybe Kyna had just meant that his ankles were fastened with leg-cuffs. Pray that she had.

While she was waiting for Inspector O'Rourke and the other three detectives to reach her office she put in a call to Bill Phinner. Bill had already left, but Tyrone Daley answered. He hadn't yet had time to enhance the pictures of the Land Rover at Boycestown and the two men watching it burn, but when Katie told him it had suddenly become urgent he promised to drop everything else and turn his attention to it.

When he arrived, Inspector O'Rourke was carrying a half-finished polystyrene cup of tea, and Detective O'Donovan had obviously been ready to go home because he was holding a large carrier bag from Saville menswear and an empty sandwich box.

Once all the detectives were gathered in her office Katie announced, 'It's Bobby Quilty.' She stood up and swivelled her computer monitor around so that they could all see the screen. 'Things have moved much faster than I thought they would.'

'Like, what things?' asked Inspector O'Rourke. 'We're supposed to be turning a blind eye to Bobby Quilty, aren't we? And *that* diktat came direct from Our Lord and Master Jimmy O'Reilly himself.'

'We *were* turning a blind eye, Francis, until about five minutes ago. But Jimmy O'Reilly's reasons for turning a blind eye were very different from mine. He was trying to save money by not arresting any more of Quilty's street-peddlers, because the courts have only been letting them off, or throwing their cases out altogether. I was trying to save someone from being mutilated, or even killed.'

'Like, who exactly?'

'You know him,' said Katie. 'His name is John Meagher. My ex, if you want to call him that.'

Very briefly – trying not to sound too emotional – she explained how Bobby Quilty had taken John hostage, threatening to blind him or murder him unless she agreed to back away and leave his cigarette-smuggling business unmolested, and stop trying to prove that he had played any part in Detective Barry's death.

'But I couldn't just sit on my hands and let Quilty get away with it,' said Katie, and she told them how she had asked Kyna to infiltrate Bobby Quilty's gang in order to discover the exact location where John was being held.

'I was pure reluctant to ask her, of course I was. But I couldn't think of anybody else I could trust enough to do it – somebody Bobby Quilty wouldn't recognize.'

Detective Sergeant Begley shook his head in admiration. 'That's one fierce brave girl, Kyna. Holy Mary, Mother of God, she's still convalescing from having herself shot.'

None of them questioned what Katie had done, although she knew Detective Sergeant Begley well enough to read from his expression that he would have acted very differently. Regardless of the risk to his career, he would have arrested Bobby Quilty and subjected him to the kind of 'interview' that would have led to him giving away John's location with no hesitation at all. Katie knew very little about his 'interviews' except that sometimes they involved a broom handle and a woodworking clamp.

'There's more, though,' said Katie. 'I'm fairly sure now that I know the identity of the driver who killed Detective Barry.'

'What, somebody grassed?' asked Detective O'Donovan.

'Not exactly. But a woman was taken into the Walnut Tree shelter this morning, a battered wife, and she told me that her husband had boasted to her that it was him. Not only that, he told her that Bobby Quilty was with him at the time, in the passenger seat, and that Quilty had specifically incited him to do it. Her husband's name is Darragh Murphy. Does that name ring a bell for any of you, by any chance? Darragh Murphy?'

'Oh, it does for me, ma'am, for sure,' said Detective Scanlan, raising her hand if she were in class. 'I must have scooped him four

163

or five times when I was working the clubs – mostly for selling coke, although most of the time it was seventy-five per cent baby laxative. His regular customers called him Diarrhoea Darragh. So far as I know he's still living in Parklands.'

'That's right, Parklands,' said Katie. 'His wife told me about him because he's been beating her so badly and she wanted to see him locked up. Her word alone won't be enough for us to charge him with any realistic chance of conviction, but now we have the photographs the Dutch cyclists took of the two men torching the Land Rover. They're very blurred, but Tyrone's working on them now and with any luck we'll be able to identify one of them as Darragh Murphy.'

'What's the plan, then, ma'am?' asked Detective Dooley.

'I'll talk to Chief Superintendent MacCostagáin and Superintendent Pearse now that I've spoken to you. I'm thinking of setting up three simultaneous raids – very early tomorrow morning, if possible. One to pick up Bobby Quilty, one to pick up Darragh Murphy, and one to rescue John Meagher.'

'Holy St Joseph. That's going to take some organizing,' said Inspector O'Rourke. He looked at his watch and said, 'It's almost five-thirty now. We're going to be fierce pushed for time, even if Jimmy O'Reilly agrees to it, and you know him. He's going to umm and ah about the logistics, and the cost of the overtime, and how sound our evidence is, and what's the price of bodice in the English Market.'

Katie said, 'I know. But we can't drag our feet with this one. The longer we put it off, the greater the risk to Kyna and John. You're right, yes, it won't be at all easy to organize because the coordination has to be faultless, but I'm confident that we can do it. Like, when I say "simultaneous", I mean each of the three raids will have to be synchronized right down to the second. I've no doubt at all that if Bobby Quilty picks up even a *sniff* of what we're doing before we can lift him, he'll have John killed to punish me for breaking our agreement, and Darragh Murphy, too, so that he can't give evidence against him.'

'You really think he'd risk doing that?' asked Inspector O'Rourke.

'You know Bobby Quilty better than I do, Francis. Whatever he's involved in, think of the worst possible outcome you can and then double it. Before we enter any of the three premises I need to be sure first of all that Quilty's at home. I also need to know that his landline's cut and that his mobile phone's jammed: (a) we have to him cornered, and (b) he has to be totally incommunicado.'

At that moment, Katie's phone rang. It was Tyrone, telling her that he had sent eleven enhanced versions of the Dutch cyclists' photos to her computer.

'All the pictures had a lot of noise on them,' he told her. 'I tried a Laplacian filter on them and then unsharp masking. In the end, though, I got some really great edge with that new Fuji doodad that Bill just acquired for us – it's amazing.'

'Can you see the men's faces clearly?' asked Katie.

'You can, yes. One of your subjects is seen only in profile, side-on, like, though I reckon you could easy make a positive ID from that, because he has very distinctive features. Like, his beezer's long enough to take your dog for a walk on it. Your other subject is full-face when he turns away from the petrol tank explosion and now that I've sharpened it up it could almost be a mug-shot. A real sham-feen, I can tell you. The sort that doesn't look as if he would take it kindly if you spilled his drink.'

Katie went over to her desk and clicked up the photographs on her monitor screen. She could see the grassy farm track and the burning Land Rover with thick black smoke rolling out of it, and the two men watching it. The man who had turned to face the camera was wearing a black T-shirt with Cork Hurling in white lettering on it, which matched the T-shirt worn by the driver of the Land Rover seen on CCTV. Both men looked as if they were laughing. Tyrone had succeeded in removing most of the motion blur and graininess and made the pictures remarkably sharp – clear enough to be admissible as evidence in court.

Detective Scanlan came over and stood beside her. 'OMG,

that's Darragh Murphy all right! Grown a bit of a scraggly beard since I last saw him, but that's him in the flesh. And I can tell you who the fellow is with him, the one with the schonk. That's Darragh's best friend Murty – Murty Something, I can't remember his surname. I'm not sure I ever knew it. But he would trail along everywhere behind Darragh, whining through that schonk of his – "where are we going now, Darragh?" "what are we going to do next, Darragh?" "give us a drizzle off your can there, Darragh" – and Darragh would smack him around the head, but he never seemed to mind.'

Katie said, 'All we need now is just one member of the public who saw Darragh behind the wheel that day and that will give us all the evidence we need to charge him.'

'You mean if we can find a member of the public who isn't too terrified to stand up in a court and say so,' said Inspector O'Rourke.

'We can cross that bridge when we come to it,' Katie told him – although, even as she said it, she wished that she hadn't, considering where Detective Barry had been killed.

'I'll go and see Denis MacCostagáin now,' she said. 'I'll meet with you after so that we can discuss exactly how we're going to set up this operation.'

'We'll be calling in some armed backup, I imagine?' said Detective Sergeant Begley.

'Of course,' said Katie. 'At least three of Quilty's scummers have served time in the past for carrying guns and I don't have any reason to think they're not still doing it today. We're going to need three Regional Support Units minimum – one at least at each location. Sean – if Padragain brings up the relevant maps and satellite images, can you give me an estimate of how many personnel we're likely to need? We don't want any of Quilty's people sneaking out the back door simply because we didn't deploy enough officers to surround the entire premises.'

Inspector O'Rourke looked at Katie very acutely and said, 'DS Maguire, I pray this all turns out well for you so.'

Katie touched his arm and mouthed, *thank you.* Then she

picked up her laptop and left her office to go and talk to Chief Superintendent MacCostagáin and Superintendent Pearse.

She took several deep breaths to steady herself as she walked along the corridor. This wasn't going to be easy. Chief Superintendent MacCostagáin had been planning on taking three days off, starting tomorrow, to play golf at Fota, while Superintendent Pearse had been invited to speak at a Freemasons' dinner that evening at the Masonic Lodge on Tuckey Street and had been rehearsing his speech for weeks.

Only God knew how they were going to react when Katie told them that she was proposing to launch a major operation not only to rescue John but to arrest Bobby Quilty and Darragh Murphy at the same time. What was more, she was proposing to do it in the early hours of tomorrow morning, before dawn. The sun would come up at 5.27 a.m., which meant they would have to spend the whole night spent in frenzied preparation.

She desperately wished that she could contact Kyna. She knew where 'Sheelagh Danehy's' mobile phone was because she had assigned one of the technicians in communications to track it for her, although she hadn't said whose phone it really was. In spite of that, she had no way of knowing for certain if Kyna still had the phone in her possession, or even if she did, what kind of a situation she might be in. Even sending her a coded message might put her in jeopardy. Bobby Quilty had kept himself out of prison for thirty years by his paranoid mistrust of anybody who came near him, and by quickly and ruthlessly dealing with anybody he suspected of betraying him.

If Kyna was still with Bobby Quilty when they arrested him, they would have to arrest her, too, just for her own safety, and in any case she would never be able to serve in Cork again. *At least that would solve her emotional problems*, Katie thought, sadly.

* * *

'You're codding me,' said Chief Superintendent MacCostagáin. 'Please tell me you're codding me.'

He had already been snapping shut the buckles of his briefcase when Katie knocked at the door of his office and came in to tell him about her plan for Operation Trident, as she had decided to call it on her way along the corridor.

'I only wish I was,' said Katie. 'But I hope you can understand why I didn't tell you that John had been abducted. You would have felt obliged to set up a search for him, especially after that O'Brien business, but in my opinion that would have been far too risky.'

That 'O'Brien business' was a kidnap case three years before, when Chief Superintendent MacCostagáin had agreed to the kidnapper's demands not to try and find out where he was holding his victim, the wife of a prosperous Cork property developer. The ransom had been paid, but the woman had never been returned and her body had never been found. Chief Superintendent MacCostagáin had been severely reprimanded and nearly lost his job.

'I might have set up a search or I might not,' he said. 'I do trust your instincts, Katie, you know that. But you still should have reported it to me as soon as it happened. What you did, keeping it all to yourself like that, and using Detective Sergeant Ni Nuallán to find him, that was all highly irregular. And if this all goes pear-shaped, it'll be me carrying the can again.'

'I know that right enough, sir. But my primary concern was rescuing John alive and unharmed, and still is. And there's not only that – if I can rescue John, Bobby Quilty won't have any leverage against me any longer. But it's essential that we bring Quilty in before he can get a message to whoever is actually keeping John locked up. And we need to bring in Darragh Murphy, too, for his own protection as much as anything else.'

She didn't add that she wasn't at all confident about the security at Anglesea Street and that she still suspected that a very small minority of officers were taking payment from criminals in exchange for useful tip-offs. Even if they could put Operation Trident into action within the next few hours, she was worried that Quilty would get to hear that she had sufficient evidence to arrest him and that she had discovered where John was being held.

'I'm prepared to stand by my decision, sir, one hundred per cent,' she told Chief Superintendent MacCostagáin. 'Under the circumstances I think it was totally the right call to make. Think on it. If tonight's operations go off as planned, we'll have killed three birds with one stone. We'll have saved John, arrested Bobby Quilty and Darragh Murphy for murder, and put a stop to Quilty's tobacco-smuggling.'

Chief Superintendent MacCostagáin sat down at his desk. 'Very well,' he said, in a tone of voice that meant 'there goes my golfing weekend'. 'Show me the pictures. We'd best call Michael in to look at them, too. He's going to throw a sevener, I can assure you of that.'

*　*　*

As it turned out, Superintendent Pearse wasn't at all upset that he would have to cancel his speech to the Freemasons. He could have delegated Operation Trident to Inspector O'Halloran, especially since Inspector O'Halloran had more than eight years of experience in mounting simultaneous raids on drug-dealing gangs and cross-border car thieves, but he insisted on heading up the arrest of Bobby Quilty himself.

'I won't make any secret of it, Katie,' he told her. 'It's personal. The last time I lifted Bobby Quilty – well, you remember. He walked out of that courthouse sticking two fingers up at me because I couldn't prove a thing. My chief witness against him was found floating in Tivoli Docks with no way of proving that it wasn't suicide and the other two witnesses had vanished off the face of the Earth altogether. That was five years ago and I still don't know what happened to them to this day.'

'Pity to miss your speech, though, Michael,' said Chief Superintendent MacCostagáin dryly.

'Well, that's another reason why I'd like to take over this operation myself. I was dreading it, to be honest with you. It was bad enough when I had to stand up and give a speech at my daughter's wedding. But this was *The Future of Law Enforcement in Cork City and Environs with Special Regard to Immigration and Community Relations.'*

'I'm sure the lodge members will be devastated,' said Chief Superintendent MacCostagáin. 'But you know, Michael, a speech like that doesn't have to go to waste. Next time I can't sleep I'll ring you up and you can read it to me over the phone.'

After that, though, there was no more banter. In spite of their disapproval of the way in which Katie had tracked down John, Chief Superintendent MacCostagáin and Superintendent Pearse both had to acknowledge that this was going to be a rare opportunity to put Bobby Quilty behind bars.

Katie and Superintendent Pearse sat and waited patiently while Chief Superintendent MacCostagáin put in a long phone call to Assistant Commissioner Jimmy O'Reilly, who was in Dublin that day. He explained at length what had happened and what they intended to do, and what the probable costs would be when balanced against the outcome.

Eventually he put down the phone and said, 'We have the go-ahead. He agrees that if we can convict Bobby Quilty for Detective Barry's murder and put a stop to his cigarette-smuggling, too, that will really be a feather in our cap – not just with Phoenix Park but with the government, too. After all, it's no good them putting up the price of fags if it can't be enforced.'

Now they had approval from Assistant Commissioner O'Reilly they had to act quickly. Superintendent Pearse called in the five senior uniformed officers who would be involved in Operation Trident. In less than twenty minutes they had all arrived for a general strategy meeting around the conference table, with Katie chairing it. This was followed by a full briefing of the sixty-three gardaí who would be needed to surround all three target premises – Orange Team, Green Team and White Team. These included eight of Katie's detectives and five armed Regional Support Units, two of which had driven down to give their support from Henry Street Garda station in Limerick. An ambulance would be standing by on Leitrim Street, too, in cased John needed medical treatment.

As she wound up the briefing, Katie said, 'I can't emphasize enough how important the timing of this operation is going to be. We have to enter all three locations at 04.30, on the dot. Speed and surprise are essential. If you have any trouble gaining access, don't stand outside ringing the doorbell, use your door-openers and ferret guns immediately. I would like to think that all three raids will all be over in less than three minutes and that by 05.00 we'll have all of the detainees here, ready for formal charging and questioning.'

'You're not going to let any media in on this?' asked Mathew McElvey. 'It would make for some fantastic TV news footage.'

'Absolutely not, Mathew, sorry. The fewer people know about this in advance, the better. We'll announce it only when Quilty and Murphy are sitting in their cells. You've already been cautioned not to tell your families or your friends why you're on duty tonight. That goes double for anybody you know in the press.'

They returned to Chief Superintendent MacCostagáin's office. His personal assistant had brought in sandwiches and coffee and two bottles of Tanora. Katie stood by the window looking out at the lights of Cork City, sipping coffee. She didn't feel at all hungry.

'Have you decided which team you'll be going with?' asked Chief Superintendent MacCostagáin, sitting behind his desk and taking a bite of a sandwich.

'Orange,' she said. 'I want to arrest Quilty myself. Besides, I've just had an update on the location of Kyna's phone. She's back at Quilty's house on the Middle Glanmire Road, Tivoli Park or whatever it's called. I need to make sure that she's safe and unharmed.'

'So you're not going with the White Team to rescue your John?'

'I can't be in two places at once, sir. I'm not Boyle Roche's bird.'

Chief Superintendent MacCostagáin said nothing for a long moment. Then, 'I know the feeling, Katie. Even though I'm stuck here in the present, I wish I was still in the past.'

Mathew McElvey knocked at the office door and came in. 'For once the Taoiseach has done us a favour!' he announced.

'What kind of a favour?' asked Chief Superintendent Mac-Costagáin. 'I heard that he'd had a mild heart attack.'

'That's right, at a meeting of European finance ministers, as well he might. But it means that the Langtry story was pretty much crowded out of both of tonight's news bulletins.'

'They did mention it, though?' asked Katie. 'I was too tied up at that strategy meeting. I forgot to watch.'

'I have it here,' said Mathew McElvey, holding up his tablet. He switched it on and Katie saw Fionnuala Sweeney standing on Anglesea Street.

'Cork Garda confirmed today that the four bodies found buried under the floorboards in Blarney were in fact those of the Langtry family, who mysteriously disappeared in 1921. Father, mother and two children were all shot in the back of the head. The family dogs were also shot. Gardaí have opened a historical inquiry into who might have been responsible for their murders, but Detective Superintendent Kathleen Maguire emphasized that the case was over ninety years old and was not a high priority.'

'That's a relief,' said Chief Superintendent MacCostagáin. 'No mention of illicit affairs with British officers or other cracked ideas. Tomorrow's going to give us ructions enough without yesterday sneaking up to bite us in the backside.'

Twenty-one

By 4.20 in the morning the three teams taking part in Operation Trident had all been deployed – Orange Team in Tivoli, Green Team in Parklands and White Team on Leitrim Street.

Katie was sitting in a dark blue unmarked Opel with Detective O'Donovan and Detective Scanlan. About two hundred metres further up the Middle Glanmire Road, on the opposite side of the entrance to Tivoli Park, she could see the white Volvo XC70 of the Regional Support Unit with four fully armed gardaí waiting for the signal to move in. Five other uniformed gardaí were already positioned in the woods behind Bobby Quilty's garden to make sure that there was no escape for him that way.

'Hard to work out how many people are in there exactly,' said Detective O'Donovan, leaning over from the back seat. 'Nobody's been seen to leave since we put the house under surveillance, so Detective Sergeant Ni Nuallán's probably still in there, and Quilty's girlfriend, Margot Beeney, but we're not sure if any of his minders are staying overnight.'

'Well, we'll find out soon enough when we get inside,' said Katie. 'Let's hope that whoever's in there, they don't give us any bother.'

Seconds before they entered the house technically trained gardaí would cut the landline and jam all of the occupants' mobile phones. It would have been normal procedure to knock or ring the doorbell first, to give the suspect the opportunity to open the door, but Katie was concerned that Bobby Quilty might have some other means of communication so she had ordered that they break down the door silently to give him no prior warning that they were coming in. They would jam the intruder alarms, too, but if Bobby Quilty had fitted a high-quality alarm system it would almost certainly sense the jam and start ringing. With most alarms, however, there was a polling interval of two minutes and that would give Orange Team more than enough time to force their way inside.

Detective O'Donovan looked up and said, 'Lord, are You listening, Lord? I hope you're not on your cloud asleep at the moment. I think we're going to need a bit of a helping hand here.'

Katie turned round in her seat. 'Just remember, Patrick, your number one concern is finding DS Ni Nuallán and protecting her once you've found her.'

'You can count on me, ma'am,' Detective O'Donovan told her. 'I was just putting in a request for a little divine backup there, that's all.'

Although there was little more than an hour to go before sunrise the sky was still inky black because it was densely clouded over, and the forecast was for low cloud and persistent rain all day. Yesterday had been warm and bright, but Katie found it easy to believe as she waited to arrest Bobby Quilty that summer was over.

She had received no further texts from Kyna, although the latest signal from her iPhone indicated that it was still inside the house. Katie tried to put her to the back of her mind – and John, too. She had prayed to St Leonard to take care of them both, and at the moment that was all she could do.

In her earphone the voice of Inspector O'Rourke blurted, 'Green Team all in position and ready to go in.'

Inspector O'Rourke was on the Parklands housing estate on the far side of Blackpool, outside Darragh Murphy's semi-detached bungalow. As soon as she had received the go-ahead for Operation Trident, Katie had dispatched two plain-clothes gardaí to keep the bungalow under surveillance. They had reported that Darragh Murphy had driven home at 11.17 in the evening, obviously drunk, because his car had struck the low concrete wall around his front garden and then bumped into the garage doors. Once he had managed to climb out and stagger to the front door, it had taken him over three minutes of erratic jabbing to fit the key into the lock.

'White Team ready,' said Detective Sergeant Begley, from Leitrim Street. That house, too, had been watched for most of the previous evening by plain-clothes gardaí. Nobody had been seen entering or leaving, but the officers had heard a man and a woman shouting and arguing until well past midnight.

'There's an alleyway that runs along the back of the houses, past the yard behind Brannagan's Bar,' said Detective Sergeant Begley. 'We have that covered. Unless they land a helicopter on the roof, there's no way anybody's getting out of this place without us catching them.'

'Two minutes and thirty seconds to go, ma'am,' said Detective O' Donovan.

'Right,' said Katie. 'Let's do it.'

As she climbed out of the car five gardaí jogged past her towards Bobby Quilty's house, their all-black combat uniforms rustling, guns clinking and rubber-soled boots pattering on the pavement. All of them were wearing black helmets with protective goggles and black face masks. Two of them were pulling behind them the heavy black case that contained the Holmatro hydraulic door-opener.

One garda ducked his way between the three shiny parked cars in front of the house and headed straight for the side gate, where the telephone junction box was located. Another crouched on the driveway between the cars and took out a mobile phone jammer and a radio signal jammer, both of them not much bigger than a packet of cigarettes, and switched them on.

Detective O'Donovan checked his watch and said, 'Grand stuff. Unless he keeps a carrier-pigeon in his bedroom, that's Quilty totally cut off from the outside world.'

Katie looked up at the bedroom windows of Bobby Quilty's house. The curtains and blinds were drawn in all of them and they were all in darkness, although a single ceiling light was shining on the first-floor landing.

'Do you reckon they're all asleep?' she asked Detective O'Donovan.

'Oh, I'd say so, for sure. They probably only leave that light on in case one of them needs the jakes in the middle of the night. That Bobby Quilty can drink the cape off St Paul.'

Katie was wearing a grade-three protective vest and carrying her Smith & Wesson revolver in a holster on her hip, but all the same she stayed well back in the road. The first few seconds of every forced entry were highly unpredictable. The night was warm, but she shivered. In her experience, the suspects were usually too surprised or drunk or high to retaliate, but occasionally all hell would let loose and there would be wild and indiscriminate gunfire. In only her second week as a detective one of her friends had been killed by a ricochet, and he had been sitting in his patrol car on the opposite side of the road.

'Thirty seconds to go, ma'am. Twenty. Fifteen.'

Now the garda who had jammed the mobile phone signals switched on a software-defined radio to neutralize the burglar alarm. Katie was concerned that this might set off the alarm immediately, but she was relieved when there was total silence. Suddenly, however, an oil tanker on the River Lee below them let out a loud, mournful hoot, like a mother whale that had lost her young.

'Holy Mary!' said Detective Scanlan, close behind Katie. 'That put my heart crossways!'

The two officers operating the Holmatro door-opener carried it quickly and stealthily into the porch and fitted its heavy-duty piston sideways across the door frame. Four armed officers from the Regional Support Unit were lined up next to them, ready to rush into the house as soon as the door fell open.

Detective O'Donovan raised his right hand and said, 'Ten. Five. Zero. Okay – go!'

It took only three strokes of the door-opener's pump handle before there was a sharp crack like a pistol shot and the door frame was forced apart. After that it took no more than a single kick for it to drop with a muffled thump into the hallway. At once the four armed officers jostled into the house, screaming, '*Armed Garda!*

Armed Garda!' Still screaming '*Armed Garda!*' they reached the end of the hallway and began to mount the stairs.

Katie would have preferred them to stay completely silent as they entered the house, but there had recently been legal problems when gardaí had failed to identify themselves when they had raided brothels and crack dens in Cork, and she hadn't wanted to give Bobby Quilty the slightest chance to wangle his way out of being convicted. Neither did she want to give him an excuse to shoot at officers if they burst into his bedroom without warning.

She walked over the fallen front door into the hallway, closely followed by Detectives O'Donovan and Scanlan. As she did so, she looked down at the bronze door knocker and saw that it bore the face of a snarling wolf. A knocker to keep out the *Sluagh*, the spirits of dead sinners, since the doorway faced to the west.

Detective O'Donovan immediately turned left into the living room, beckoning a young woman officer, Garda O'Leary, to follow him. Katie had assigned them both to find Kyna and get her clear of the house as quickly as possible. Detective O'Donovan's mobile phone tracker was showing that 'Sheelagh Danehy' had left her phone downstairs somewhere at the back of the house.

Katie carried on to the end of the hallway. She could hear hoarse shouting coming from the first-floor landing, so she said to Detective Scanlan, 'Come on,' and started to climb the stairs. She was only halfway up, however, when Bobby Quilty appeared at the top, with armed gardaí on either side of him. He had already been handcuffed. He was wearing a sweaty pink T-shirt and a pair of droopy grey boxer shorts, and his bloated face was florid and patchy with rage.

'Ach, it's *you*, DS Maguire! I might have fecking known it! What in the name of *feck* is going on here? A man can't get even snatch a decent night's sleep in his own house without a bunch of polls busting his door down and pulling him out of the scratcher like a bag of dirty washing! You'd better have a fecking good reason for this, I can tell you now, a fecking *amazing* reason, because I'm calling my brief right here and now and he won't be any more delighted than I am to be woken up at half past fecking four in the fecking morning!'

One of the armed gardaí said, 'We've been through all rooms up here, ma'am. There's nobody else here but him.'

'Nobody? Not even Margot Beeney?'

'No, ma'am. We've even checked the presses. He has the place to himself, like.'

Katie carried on climbing the stairs. When she reached the landing she stood in front of Bobby Quilty and stared up at him for a few seconds without saying anything. His huge belly rose and fell as he breathed, and he reeked of stale alcohol and Lynx Fever Body Spray, and some other oily smell that Katie couldn't identify, but which put her in mind of tinned sardine oil. She also noticed for the first time that the wings of his bulbous nose were peppered with blackheads.

She took a deep breath and then she said, 'Robert Boland Quilty, I am arresting you for incitement to murder Detective Gerald Barry. I am also arresting you for the false imprisonment of John Patrick Meagher. You are not obliged to say anything unless you wish to do so, but anything you do say will be taken down in writing and may be given in evidence.'

Bobby frowned at Katie for a moment as if he hadn't caught on, but then his face gradually cracked apart in a grin like a Hallowe'en turnip. 'Is this some kind of a geg, doll?'

'Do you want me to repeat myself? You're under arrest. Now, get yourself dressed and we'll take you into custody.'

'You're having a laugh, aren't you? I told you before that I had nothing at all to do with thon detective getting himself run over. Just because you can't think of anybody else to pin that on. And who in the name of God is John Patrick Meagher? I never heard of anybody of that name in my life. Your head's full of wee sweetie mice, DS Maguire, so it is.'

'Let's talk it over at the station, shall we?' said Katie.

'I want to ring my brief first, so that he can meet us there. I'm not saying a word to you without my brief.'

'You can do that once we've taken you in and formally charged you.'

Bobby Quilty said something back to her. It sounded caustic, but Katie didn't hear it because it was blotted out by an urgent voice in her earphone. It was Inspector O'Rourke, calling her from Parklands.

'DS Maguire? Hallo? We've just found Darragh Murphy.'

'What do you mean "found"? Haven't you lifted him?'

'He's dead, ma'am. He was sitting in front of his telly when somebody shot him in the back of the head.'

'*What?* Serious?'

'Oh, yes. Blew half his head off. I reckon they used a silencer because the surveillance team didn't hear anything.'

'Okay,' Katie told him, trying not to show any reaction in front of Bobby Quilty. 'We've just detained Mister Quilty here so I can be with you in twenty minutes or so. Have you contacted Bill Phinner?'

'Detective Markey's doing that now, ma'am. It's a touch too early to go knocking on doors asking for witnesses, but we'll be starting that as soon as it's reasonable.'

'Don't disturb anything yet, and if the Technical Bureau turn up before I do, tell *them* not to disturb anything either – this is something I need to see for myself. Was there anybody else in the house?'

'No, ma'am. Some women's clothing in the bedroom. Underwear and such. A second toothbrush, too, in the bathroom, but that's all. We'll be searching the premises thoroughly of course, when you give us the say-so, but I thought you needed to know that Darragh Murphy's out of the picture.'

'Yes, thank you, Francis. Just give me a couple of minutes and I'll get back to you so.'

'Problems?' asked Bobby Quilty, with that same hideous grin.

'Nothing that concerns you,' said Katie. Then, 'Get yourself dressed, will you? These officers will go with you. Wouldn't want you jumping out of the window or harming yourself so.'

'None of them are gay, are they?' said Bobby Quilty. 'Wouldn't like a gay garda to see me without my gunks!'

As the armed gardaí escorted him back to his bedroom, Detective O'Donovan came up the stairs with Garda O'Leary behind him. He was holding up a sparkly pink iPhone in his latex-gloved hand. 'We found this in the kitchen waste bin, ma'am. No SIM card in it.'

'There's no sign of "Sheelagh"?' she asked, looking round to make sure that Bobby Quilty was back in his bedroom and out of earshot.

Detective O'Donovan shook his head. 'Nowhere downstairs, no. We took a sconce out in the garden and the fellers in the back are searching through the woods. It might be kind of previous to say so, like, but I get the feeling that she isn't here at all.'

Katie was beginning to feel a cold sinking sensation in her stomach. Her father had always said that when an operation started to go wrong it was like standing on the deck of the *Lusitania* – you know that it's going down under your feet and there's nothing you can do about it. She had planned for Operation Trident to be successfully completed in minutes, but already it seemed to be foundering. If Darragh Murphy was dead, she had lost the only witness who could testify that Bobby Quilty was guilty of incitement to murder. And where was Kyna? If she wasn't here, why hadn't she got in touch? And what about John?

She was about to contact Detective Sergeant Begley at Leitrim Street when he called her.

'We've just this minute finished searching the building, ma'am. Top to bottom. Basement, attic, back yard, everywhere. Not a trace of your John.'

'Nothing at all? How can that be? I was told that his feet were fastened to a bed. *Bolted*, in fact, though I'm not sure what that meant.'

'No beds in the building at all, ma'am, except for some bogging old mattress that the two people who live here use to sleep on. Their names are Charles Rearden, unemployed, and Sorcia MacKenna, part-time hairdresser. Well, that's what she calls herself, any road.'

'And they know nothing about John?'

'They both deny that there's been anybody else in the building since they moved in there five months ago.'

'Who's their landlord?'

'They're squatting, so they say. They found the building empty so they decided to move in. It's actually owned by a property company in Dublin called Watergrass Holdings.'

Katie could have asked him a hundred more questions, but this wasn't the time for it.

'I'll get back to you in a couple of minutes,' she said, and then she turned to Detective O'Donovan. 'Send a car round to Detective Sergeant Ni Nuallán's flat, will you, just to make sure that she isn't at home. I've rung her a few times without getting any answer, but you never know.'

Katie didn't say so, but it was remotely possible that Kyna had become so stressed that she had decided to quit this assignment and go back to Dublin, and that she hadn't had the courage to tell Katie that she couldn't take the pressure any more. After all, she had not only had Bobby Quilty to contend with, she was still recuperating from a serious bullet wound and she was suffering from painful emotional problems.

Katie couldn't believe that Kyna would do that, but even if she had, she could forgive her. What she needed to know more than anything else was that Kyna was safe.

'Padragain, would you contact Detective Sergeant Ni Nuallán's parents and ask them if they've heard from her?' she asked Detective Scanlan. 'Try not to alarm them. Just say that we've lost contact with her – like, maybe her mobile battery's dead or something, or maybe she's staying overnight with a friend – but it's important that we get in touch with her.'

Bobby Quilty reappeared, wearing the same creased green linen suit he had been wearing when he first told Katie that he had abducted John, as well as a lime-green shirt.

'I'll see you at the station, then sweetheart?' He grinned at her, as the armed gardaí escorted him down the stairs. 'I'll be writing out my invoice for having my front door repaired.'

Katie didn't answer. She was aching to ask him where Kyna was – but of course she wasn't supposed to know about the existence of 'Sheelagh Danehy', and until she heard that Kyna was somewhere safe she couldn't risk revealing her real identity. With Darragh Murphy dead it was likely that Bobby Quilty would have to be released from custody within a few hours.

Inspector O'Rourke called her again. He had cordoned off the street in Parklands outside Darragh Murphy's bungalow and had put in a call to the coroner.

'But still no trace of John?'

'Nothing at all, ma'am. I'm sorry.'

Katie took a look around the house and then went back outside. It had started to rain now, a soft drifting rain that had soaked her hair even before she was halfway back to the car. Now that Bobby Quilty had been arrested, all the Garda vehicles had switched on their flashing blue lights. They made the rain sparkle, so that it looked to Katie as if the darkness was swarming with bright blue fireflies.

Twenty-two

At that time of the morning there was scarcely any traffic, so it took them only fifteen minutes to drive north-west across the city to Parklands. Katie left Detective O'Donovan behind at Bobby Quilty's house to supervise an intensive search and, most importantly, to see if there was any evidence, apart from her mobile phone, that Kyna had been there, or where she might be now.

She took Detective Scanlan with her. She knew that Padragain had never attended a homicide scene before, even though she had seen dead bodies in the morgue, and mangled families in traffic accidents, and bloated teenagers hauled grey-faced and dripping from the River Lee. Homicide scenes, though, were something different altogether. They were a silent tableau of the very instant when, for some reason, a person's life had been taken by somebody else. 'Storybooks left open, halfway through,' that's what Katie's father had always called them.

As they made their way through the wet, deserted streets, Detective Scanlan managed to get an answer from the Ó Nuallán number in Dublin.

'Oh, hi there, I'm so sorry to ring you so early, but this is Detective Padragain Scanlan from the Cork Garda. Who am I talking to?'

She covered her phone with her hand and said to Katie, 'Detective Ni Nuallán's sister Bridget.' Then, 'No, no, it's not bad news. Nothing like that. It's just that we need some information about a case that your sister was working on and we haven't been able to contact her. We were wondering if maybe she'd gone back home for a bit of a rest, like. No? Then have you heard from her at all? No? All right. I see. No bother at all. I'm very sorry to have woken you. Yes, I will, of course. Yes. Goodbye.'

Almost immediately Katie had a call from the gardaí that Detective O'Donovan had sent round to Kyna's flat on Wellington Road.

'She's not there, ma'am, no. We talked to her flatmate and she said she hadn't seen her in two days now. She had no idea where she was, no. She didn't usually ask her, like, as a rule, because most of the time Detective Ni Nuallán wasn't at liberty to tell her.'

'Thanks,' said Katie. She sat saying nothing for a while, biting her thumbnail. She was desperately worried now because Kyna's disappearance and Darragh Murphy's shooting led her to one inescapable conclusion: Bobby Quilty had been tipped off about Operation Trident.

Bobby Quilty's nonchalance had made her suspect from the moment she had arrested him that he must have been forewarned – that, and the absence of anybody else in the house. She couldn't believe that he didn't habitually sleep with his mistress and keep at least one bodyguard on the premises to protect him in case of an invasion. He had too many enemies in Cork, and in the North, too – both criminal and political. The Ulster Volunteer Force had twice attempted to ambush his car when he was in Armagh, and his youngest nephew had been shot dead by Red Hand Defenders as he was stepping out of Loughgall Road Spar in Portadown.

By the time they arrived at Darragh Murphy's bungalow the sky was beginning to grow lighter, although the street lamps hadn't yet switched themselves off. The whole street had been cordoned off with blue-and-white tape and there were three Garda patrol cars parked there, as well two vans from the Technical Bureau and an ambulance. In spite of it being so early, and raining, a crowd of about thirty or forty people had gathered on the corner and Katie recognized at least two cars belonging to local reporters parked further up the road.

Inspector O'Rourke was waiting for her in the shelter of the bungalow's porch. He looked tired and bored, shifting from one foot to the other like a hotel commissionaire. The interior of the bungalow was already brightly lit with halogen lamps, although the three technical experts who had arrived to inspect the crime scene were all crowded into the kitchen in their bulky Tyvek suits, along with five gardaí, three in uniform and the other two in plain clothes, all of them waiting for Katie to take a look at Darragh Murphy's body in the exact position where it had been found.

Inspector O'Rourke looked at Detective Scanlan and said, 'Had your breakfast yet, detective? If not, good, because this isn't pretty.'

Katie said, 'Don't worry, Padragain. You can step outside for a breath of fresh air whenever you want to.'

Inspector O'Rourke led them in single file along the hallway. The bungalow was cramped, with threadbare carpets and badly chipped paintwork, and Katie noticed that it had all the telltale signs of a house in which domestic abuse had regularly taken place. One of the living-room door panels was missing and there was a darker rectangle on the wallpaper in the hallway where a picture had once hung. On the windowsill at the end of the hallway stood a single porcelain dog which had probably been one of a matching pair. In spite of the damage, the bungalow was scrupulously clean, which told Katie that Neala had tried her very best to keep Darragh happy, right up until the very last beating.

The living room was papered with a pale green diamond pattern, with darker green velveteen curtains hanging at the windows, although one curtain was sagging where half of its nylon hooks had been pulled down. On a low cabinet in the far corner of the room stood a flat-screen 42-inch television, still switched on to the 5 a.m. *Euronews*, but with the volume muted.

Close behind Katie, Detective Scanlan said, 'Holy St Joseph.'

Darragh Murphy was sitting upright in a large armchair covered with orange stretch nylon. He was wearing light grey trousers with a partially dried damp stain in the crotch, and a grubby yellow polo shirt. On the floor beside his chair there were three cans of

Murphy's. A fourth can had dropped between his grey-stockinged feet and spilled dark beer across the carpet. He had obviously been drinking from it when he was shot.

In the centre of the room stood a three-legged plywood coffee table in the shape of an artist's palette. An untidy copy of yesterday's *Racing Post* lay on top of it, as well as a glass pub ashtray that was heaped with crushed-out cigarette butts, and a fifth can of Murphy's, also with its ring-pull open.

'Looks like he treated his murderer to a swallow before he died,' said Katie.

'It does, too,' said Inspector O'Rourke. 'Some people have no gratitude at all, do they?'

Katie could see that Detective Scanlan was trying not to look at Darragh Murphy's body directly, but that she couldn't stop herself from glancing at it every few seconds, as if she needed to keep checking that what she was looking at was real, not a prop created by the special effects department for some grisly horror film.

Darragh Murphy had been shot directly from behind into the nape of his neck. Katie guessed that his assailant had been kneeling behind his armchair when he fired, although she could only guess what reason he had given for doing so, if he had given any at all. Maybe he had pretended that he had dropped something on the floor and was kneeling down to pick it up. Darragh Murphy must have known his assailant, or at least not felt threatened by him, or he wouldn't have given him a can of stout. Then again, his assailant could have helped himself after he had killed him, as a small reward, or to steady his nerves.

'Padragain, take a close sconce at this entrance wound,' Katie told her. 'You can see by the width of the abrasion collar that the bullet entered just beneath the base of his skull at a slight upward angle. You can also see that the collar has gunpowder stipple marks around it, and that there's this sooty starburst effect directly under the skin. That tells us that it was fired at very close range, even if the muzzle wasn't actually touching him. The starburst was caused by the smoke and the explosive gases dissecting between the skin and the skull.'

'Yes, I have you,' said Detective Scanlan, nodding much more emphatically than she really needed to. She would have seen dozens of photographs of various gunshot wounds during her forensic training, but photographs could never convey the glistening, bloody reality, or the flat, pervasive reek of gunpowder residue. Without a hint of a smile, Bill Phinner had said that it always smelled as if the victim had let off a breezer when they were shot.

Apart from the entrance wound, the back of Darragh Murphy's skull was intact. The rest of his head, though, looked as if a hand grenade had exploded inside it. His eyeless mask of a face was sloping steeply forward, and his jaw had dropped down so that his stubbled chin was resting on the collar of his polo shirt. The sides of his head had been blown wide apart, like the two flaps of a cardboard box, with an ear still attached to each of them. Between them, his brain had been roughly mashed into glutinous beige lumps, and his sinuses and connective tissues had been torn into tangled scarlet strings.

'Typical of high-velocity bullets,' Katie told Detective Scanlan. 'They don't leave much of an entrance wound but they fragment inside the skull so that they leave multiple and very destructive exit wounds. The technical experts will be able to see all the bits and pieces when they X-ray his head. A "lead snowstorm" is what they usually call it.'

'You'd wonder what was inside that brain, wouldn't you?' said Inspector O'Rourke. 'Think of all of the incriminating information he'd have stored up in there. Still, too late to retrieve it now.'

Detective Scanlan pressed her hand over her mouth and made a retching sound and Katie said, 'Go on, Padragain, Get yourself outside. I'll join you in a second when I've talked to Bill Phinner.'

Bill had come out of the kitchen and was waiting for her in the hallway. He gave her a pinched, resigned smile as Detective Scanlan made her way quickly to the front door, retching again before she got there.

'Well, and the top of the morning to you, DS Maguire.'

'What's the story, Bill? Sorry to drag you out so early.'

'Oh, no bother at all. I could see the whole station was buzzing last night, what with all of those off-duty fellows coming in and the armed response lads getting themselves tooled up. I reckoned I'd be needed sometime during the night, so I made sure I turned in early. I slept like a child. Didn't even wake up when the missus came to bed and she usually bounces up and down like she's riding in the 3.15 at Mallow.'

'There's some glaringly obvious things for you to analyse,' said Katie. 'The beer can on the coffee table there, and the cigarette butts. But – I don't know. I have a feeling that none of this fits together.'

'In what way in particular?'

Katie turned towards the kitchen. 'Garda O'Leahy, isn't it?' she asked one of the plain-clothes officers.

'That's right, ma'am.'

'What time did you see Darragh Murphy driving home, did you say? It was after eleven, wasn't it?'

'Eleven-seventeen, though it was eleven-twenty before he managed to get in through the door. He was so wrecked he could barely stand up.'

'So you couldn't have missed seeing him coming home?'

'He crashed into them garage doors and it was like thunder, I'll tell you. Half the street was twitching their curtains to see if a bomb had gone off. You'd have been deaf as a doorpost not to hear that.'

'And you're sure it was him?'

'Well, it was his car all right, and he was wearing that fawny-coloured windcheater that's hanging up there by the door, and that cap. We were watching the house from the other side of the road, like, and the street lighting's not that grand, but there was no lights on in the house before he came home, so who else could it have been?'

'What's on your mind, ma'am?' asked Inspector O'Rourke. He nodded towards the body in the armchair and said, 'You're not thinking that this isn't Darragh Murphy at all? And maybe he's had his head blown off so that we couldn't tell if he was or he wasn't?'

Katie shook her head. 'No, Francis. I don't have any doubt that it's Darragh Murphy. I'm pretty sure, too, that it was Bobby Quilty who arranged to have him taken out. Murphy was the only person who could testify that Quilty incited him to kill Detective Barry, and he was also a loudmouth. If you're suggesting that Quilty had someone else killed in his place and whisked off the real Darragh Murphy away to somewhere safe, that's not Quilty's style at all. What incentive would he have, like, when at any time in the future Murphy could decide to incriminate him? Besides that, Bobby Quilty may sound as if he needs to take his boots off to count to eleven, but he's very far from stupid. He'll be well aware that we'll test Murphy's DNA and it'll only take us a matter of hours to confirm if it *is* him or not.'

'Well, I agree with all of that,' said Inspector O'Rourke. 'I was just wondering why you think there's something askew here.'

Katie said, 'Just look at this scenario. According to our surveillance team, Darragh Murphy came home so langered that he couldn't even fit his key into the front door. What would *you* do if you came home as drunk as that? I doubt you'd hang up your jacket and your cap neatly by the front door, then go and fetch yourself a six-pack of Murphy's out of the fridge and sit down to watch a couple of hours of late-night telly.'

Inspector O'Rourke said, 'You're right. It's been a brave few years since I came home in that condition. Herself wouldn't allow it. But, yes. He'd have been more likely to drop his coat on the floor, stagger into the bedroom and crash out fully dressed on to the bed. That's if he didn't take a detour to the toilet first for a gawk. That's what I always did.'

'It's far too early yet to start jumping to conclusions,' said Katie. 'I think, though, that one of the possibilities we ought to consider is that Darragh Murphy was shot much earlier in the afternoon. Whoever killed him could then have driven off in his car. Somebody returned in the car several hours later. Maybe it was the killer himself, maybe not. If Murphy was already dead, it wouldn't have mattered. But he made as much of a show of it as possible so that if anybody was watching the house he would be guaranteed to attract their attention and lead them into believing it was Murphy coming home. He could have left immediately through the kitchen and of course at that time we didn't have any officers deployed round the back of the house.'

Bill Phinner said, 'Tyrone! Would you test that kitchen door for me? With your gloves on, please. Tell me if it's locked or not.'

Tyrone tried the door handle and the kitchen door opened. 'Not locked, sir.'

'In that case, can everybody make sure that they don't go trampling out into the garden, even if you feel like a smoke. We'll need to be checking the garden for recent footprints.'

Katie said, 'It might be worth calling the dog team out. They could at least confirm if the last person who was sitting in Darragh Murphy's car went out through the back door and which direction they went in. They won't be able to tell us much more than that because your man would probably have been picked up and driven away. If that was the case, though, there must been another vehicle waiting for them somewhere nearby, and if so, one or more of our local residents might have spotted it. There's not much that you can get away with in Parklands without half the estate goggling at you.'

'Fair play to you, ma'am,' said Inspector O'Rourke. 'But once he was home, maybe Murphy sobered up a bit. Like, you know, maybe he *did* sit down with a few cans to watch some telly. Maybe the offender was already in the house waiting for him, or came in through the back door after he had settled down. Maybe he picked the lock, or Murphy had simply forgotten to lock it. After all, there's nothing in here that's worth anybody stroking.'

Katie turned to Bill Phinner. 'If you can give me an accurate time of death, Bill, that would help us no end.'

Bill Phinner looked at Darragh Murphy's burst-open head. The halogen light that had been set up behind his chair shone through the holes where his eyes had been so that it cast a shadowy, ghost-like face on to the carpet.

'We'll be taking his liver temperature now and checking the degree of rigor. Of course we'll be testing his blood-alcohol level, which will give us a much clearer idea if he really was drunk when he came home – if it *was* him, as you say. His temperature will probably give us the best estimate. It's warmish in here so that may give the impression he hasn't been dead as long as he really has been, if you know what I mean.'

Katie checked her watch. 'In that case, I'll leave you to it,' she said. 'I want to go and check on the house where John Meagher was supposed to have been held.'

Bill Phinner beckoned to his technical team and now they all came rustling into the living room, carrying their shiny metal cases of instruments and test tubes and chemicals. They started work right away, taking flash photographs of Darragh Murphy's body from every angle, as well as the living room itself. They carefully packed up the fourth beer can from the coffee table, as well as the brimful ashtray and the *Racing Post*, and sealed them in polythene boxes.

Katie watched them for a while and then walked to the front door. Detective Scanlan was waiting for her, her face drained of colour so that the two spots of blusher on her cheeks looked like a clown's make-up. She was clutching her lavender-coloured waterproof jacket tightly up to her neck

'How are you feeling, Padragain?' Katie asked her.

'A touch better, thanks,' said Detective Scanlan. 'I'm sorry about that. It won't happen again.'

'Oh, don't promise that. I've seen much worse than that, and so will you.'

Bill Phinner had been following closely behind Katie and as she stepped out into the rain he said, 'You're right about the timing, ma'am, in my opinion. Whenever Murphy was shot, it wasn't when we're supposed to think that it was. That scene of crime in there, I was pure suspicious about it the moment I walked in. It looks *staged*, if you understand what I'm talking about.'

Katie stood in the rain with Detective Scanlan beside her. She could tell that Bill Phinner had something more to say to her, but something he was reluctant to tell her.

'Go on,' she said. 'There can't be any question about it, can there? Bobby Quilty knew everything about this operation hours before we'd even finished setting it up.'

Inspector O'Rourke had joined them now. 'Of course he did,' he said, and he sounded angrier than Katie had ever heard him before. 'He's only done it again, Quilty, hasn't he? He's put us into a position where we don't have the evidence to prosecute him and we can't say too much to the media, either, without making ourselves look like an incompetent bunch of culchies, or corrupt, or both, or laying ourselves wide open to a libel action.'

Katie said, 'You and I need to talk about this later, Francis. Meanwhile I urgently need to find out what's happened to John Meagher and Detective Sergeant Ni Nuallán.'

'Don't lose heart, ma'am, that's all I can say,' said Inspector O'Rourke.

Katie looked down the street and she could see Dan Keane from the *Examiner* waiting for her in his long IRA-style trench coat, smoking, as well as Branna MacSuibhne from the *Echo* and Muireann Bourke from Newstalk.

'I want all of our lips sealed tight on this,' she said. 'If it's someone in the station who's been tipping off Quilty, they'll have guessed that we suspect them, but I don't want us to say openly that we have any suspicions of leaked information at all. I would rather say that I personally made a bags of Operation Trident because I didn't double-check the intelligence I was given, something like that. Let's give our mole the confidence to leak more information to Quilty – except that the next time he does it, let's make sure it entraps him. Or *her*, whoever it is.'

'You know something,' said Inspector O'Rourke. 'The mole could just as easy be me. Then what?'

'Then I'll find you out somehow, Francis, I swear it. And by God, you'll suffer for it, believe me.'

Twenty-three

She received two messages on her way to Leitrim Street, even though it was only a ten-minute drive back down towards the city centre.

A dog team had been dispatched to Parklands to see if the killer had left Darragh Murphy's bungalow by the kitchen door, and if he had, which direction he had taken after that. Seconds later, Chief Superintendent MacCostagáin called her to say that he had just received his morning paper.

'It's all over the front page, Katie, about the Langtry family.'

'Well, that doesn't surprise me. It's a very unusual story.'

'Yes, but it has all of this cat's malogian about Langtry's wife having an affair with a British army officer so that she could wheedle information out of him. They've quoted that Professor Pendle and *he* says that it's highly likely that it was the Brits who executed them by way of punishment. Nobody's happy about this, Katie, believe me. I've had Jimmy O'Reilly on to me already.'

'Pendle, Jesus,' said Katie. Sean Pendle was an emeritus professor of Irish history at Cork University and he was notorious for his extreme republican opinions and the way in which he would distort historical facts to suit his agenda. He had published a controversial book, *Fenian Glory*, which many bookstores in Northern Ireland had refused to carry. He was also a relentless publicity seeker, and Katie didn't doubt that by this evening he would be on the television news to give his own explanation of how and why the Langtrys had been shot and buried under the floorboards.

'I'll talk to you about it when I get back to the station,' Katie told him. 'Meanwhile, sir, just to make your morning even brighter,

Operation Trident has turned out to be an utter disaster, beginning to end.'

As briefly as she could, she updated him on the arrest of Bobby Quilty, the murder of Darragh Murphy and the disappearances of Kyna and John. Chief Superintendent MacCostagáin said nothing while she spoke, but she could almost feel his gradually deepening glumness.

'All right, Katie,' he said, when she had finished. 'It looks like we're in for one of those days that we'd rather forget.'

She arrived at the junction of Leitrim Street and Pine Street, where gardaí were already taking down the tapes that had cordoned off Pine Street and were waving traffic through. Detective Sergeant Begley was standing outside the terracotta-painted house where John was supposed to have been held, talking to a sergeant from the Regional Support Unit from Limerick.

'Good morning to you, ma'am,' said Detective Sergeant Begley. 'This is Sergeant Norden from Henry Street.'

'Yes, we've met before,' said Katie. 'You're the one they call "Buzz", aren't you? I really appreciate your backup on this operation, sergeant. Not that any of it has worked out the way we planned.'

'Well, you know what they say about the best-laid plans, ma'am,' said Sergeant Norden. He was a big man and his protective vest bulked him out even more. That was why his colleagues had given him the nickname Buzz, after Buzz Lightyear in *Toy Story*. His head was shaved shiny blue and his eyes bulged and he breathed very laboriously as if he had just finished weightlifting.

'Do you want to talk to the squatters?' asked Detective Sergeant Begley. 'They're upstairs, smoking their heads off and asking us every two minutes when we're going to eff off and give them some peace.'

'There's absolutely no sign that John was being held here?' asked Katie.

'Like I told you, ma'am, there are no beds here except the mouldy old mattress those two scummers use to sleep on. There's three bedrooms altogether. One of them's filled up with old junk so you can hardly open the door. The other one must have been a kid's bedroom at one time, but there's no bed in it now, although there's impressions on the carpet where a bed must have been.'

'All right, let me go upstairs and take a look for myself,' said Katie. 'And, yes, I'll have a word with our friends.'

'Good luck with that,' said Sergeant Norden. 'I was close to lifting the both of them on a charge of pretending to be human.'

They went inside the front door and Detective Sergeant Begley showed Katie the two ground-floor rooms which had once been the shop premises. Both of them were empty, apart from five or six packing cases and a tipped-over chair.

'No indication that there was ever a bed in either of these rooms,' said Detective Sergeant Begley. 'In fact, when you look at the dust on the floor I'd say that nobody's even stepped in here for years.'

He led her upstairs. The first-floor landing was foggy with cigarette smoke and he pointed to the door on the left-hand side and said, 'They're in there, Punch and Judy. I reckon they've been through fifty fags each since we got here.'

'Let me take a look at the rest of the rooms first,' said Katie. 'I don't have any doubt at all that John Meagher was being held somewhere here – probably right up until yesterday evening.'

'Your informant was sound, then?'

'The best, believe me.'

Detective Sergeant Begley opened the doors to the bathroom, and then to the gloomy room where Chisel and Sorcia slept. The sour smell of sweat-stained bedding was so strong that Katie held the back of her hand against her nose, and there were two wrinkled condoms lying on the carpet under the window.

'Holy Mary, Mother of God,' she said, shaking her head. 'Whoever said that romance was dead?'

The next bedroom was stacked with more packing cases, as well as a banjaxed wooden ironing board and a dented paraffin heater. The third bedroom was long and narrow, wallpapered with spaceships and planets. There was a small window at the very end and, as Detective Sergeant Begley had told her, the purple carpet bore four deep impressions from the square legs of a single bed.

Katie went down on one knee and touched the carpet pile. 'There's a damp patch here, did any of you notice?'

'I can't say that we did, ma'am. We had those two squatters hovering around us cribbing and moaning and puffing out smoke like a couple of volcanoes.'

'Well, this would have been where the end of the bed was. My informant said that John's feet were bolted to the bed. I thought that might have meant that he was chained, or fitted with ankle-cuffs, but his feet were really *were* bolted.'

'So there might have been blood on the carpet and that's why it's damp?'

Katie stood up. 'I'll ask Bill Phinner to send a couple of technicians down here. You can scrub a carpet till doomsday but you'll never get the DNA out of it.'

She went to the window and looked out. Then she took her black forensic gloves out of her jacket pocket, snapped them on, and opened the window wide. It was raining even harder now and the rain made a clattering sound as it fell from a broken gutter somewhere below.

'There's a safety cable on here, but somebody's unscrewed it,' she said. 'Recently, too. Look, they've left one of the screws on the windowsill here.'

She stepped back and peered down at the floor to see if she could find the second screw, and as she did so she saw a red-handled screwdriver lying close to the side of the chest of drawers. She left it where it was, because she wanted to have it photographed and then sealed into an evidence bag, but she beckoned Detective Sergeant Begley to take a look at it.

'Here's a couple of questions,' she said. 'Why would those two squatters bother to take off the safety cable? But if they did, why would they just drop the screwdriver on the floor once they'd done it? I can see how messy they are, but that doesn't seem natural.'

'You mean it might have been done in a hurry, like?'

Katie leaned out of the window. She could see that several of the slates were cracked and that four or five of them had been dislodged. The broken guttering was directly underneath them.

'Let's take a sconce outside,' she said. 'I'll talk to those two after.'

They went back downstairs, through the kitchen, and out of the back door into the cluttered yard. The rabbit started snuffling and scratching at the chicken wire at the front of its cage.

'Jesus, you poor creature, the state of you la,' said Katie, bending down to peer into its cage. 'Sean, give Lisa O'Donovan at the ISPCA a call after, would you? If ever there was a case for cruelty to animals, this poor creature is definitely it. This hutch is a wreck. It looks like—'

She stood up straight and shielded her eyes against the rain, frowning up at the broken gutter. When she looked down again she saw the stack of broken window frames next to the hutch, with some of their panes smashed.

'Borrow your flashlight?' she asked Detective Sergeant Begley.

She shone the flashlight on to the shattered glass of the topmost window and lit up a spatter of translucent amber stains.

'That could be blood,' she said. 'I'll have the technicians check that, too. Do you have something we can cover it with?'

'Oh, sure. I've a roll of plastic sheeting in the car. What are you thinking?'

'I don't know for sure. But there's all the indications here that somebody fell out of that bedroom window and dropped down here. Maybe they fell or maybe they were pushed out.'

'So they might have been unconscious, or dead?'

'It's possible. But why didn't they just carry him down the stairs? They must have taken the bed out that way, so why push somebody out of the window, dead or alive?'

Detective Sergeant Begley shook his head. 'Don't ask me. And I doubt you'll get any sense out of those two squatters. I don't think either of them's going to be appearing on *Mastermind* any time soon.'

* * *

'Can we have the window open?' asked Katie as she entered the room where Chisel and Sorcia were sitting. The smoke was filling the air in lazily curling layers.

Chisel was wearing a black short-sleeved shirt and green-striped boxer shorts, while Sorcia was wrapped up in a yellow towelling dressing gown with threads hanging from the hem. They were both puffy-eyed from smoking and lack of sleep.

The garda who had been standing in the corner keeping an eye on them opened up the window and the smoke gradually eddied out into the rain.

'I'm Detective Superintendent Kathleen Maguire,' said Katie. 'I'm in charge of investigating the whereabouts of a man named John Meagher. I have very good reason to believe that he was unlawfully held in this house against his will, and that you two aided and abetted that detention.'

Chisel and Sorcia looked at each other as if they were utterly baffled.

'Come on,' said Katie. 'He was being held in that back bedroom there, on a bed. You disposed of the bed yesterday evening and you cleaned the carpet underneath it. What I want to know is, where was John Meagher taken, and who by?'

'John Meagher?' said Chisel. 'I don't know nothing about no feller of that name. There's been nobody here, like. Only me and Sorsh.'

'So why did you get rid of the bed?'

'Bed? What bed? I don't know nothing about no bed.'

'Don't play stupid,' said Katie. 'There was a bed in that room and even if you didn't dispose of it yourselves, you must know who did.'

'Can't help you,' said Chisel. 'If there *was* a bed, and I'm not saying that there was, maybe it just took off by itself. They have legs, you know, beds.'

He grinned slyly at his own joke and then began to cough so violently that Sorcia had to slap him on the back.

Katie was still waiting for him to recover when Detective O'Mara knocked at the half-open door.

'DS Maguire?' He was holding up an electric drill, with its plug dangling. 'Just found this in the cupboard under the stairs, in a toolbox.'

'What's that?' said Chisel, still coughing. 'I don't know nothing about that.'

'The toolbox has the name Charles Rearden stencilled on it,' said Detective O'Mara. 'That would be you, wouldn't it, Mr Rearden?'

'Yes, well, that's mine all right,' said Chisel. 'Some scummer hobbled that toolbox from me months ago and I've been wondering where the feck it was. If they've put their own stuff into it, that's nothing to do with me whatsoever. Nothing at all. What's that you have there? A drill? I never had any drill like that, not me.'

'There's what looks like dried blood on it and remnants of skin,' said Detective O'Mara. He passed the drill over so that Katie could examine it more closely. He was right. The chuck had prune-coloured blobs of dried blood on it and there were papery shreds of skin twisted around the thread of the drill bit.

'Never saw that before in my life,' said Chisel.

'Seriously, Mr Rearden, do I really look like I was just washed in with the last tide?' Katie asked him. 'I'm arresting both you and Ms MacKenna here on suspicion of falsely imprisoning John Patrick Meagher. You are not obliged to say anything unless you wish to do so, but anything you do say will be taken down in writing and may be given in evidence. Get yourselves dressed and we'll take you into the station.'

'Jesus, Chisel, what a fecking careless browl you are!' Sorcia snapped at him. 'There's no way they could have known, otherwise.'

'I'm afraid you're wrong there, Ms MacKenna,' said Katie. 'There's plenty of evidence that you and your partner here were helping to keep John Meagher imprisoned. I'd just like you to tell me who ordered you to do it.'

'I'm not saying a single word,' said Sorcia.

'You could save yourself a rake of trouble if you did tell me who it was, I can assure you of that. You might even escape prosecution altogether.'

'*Mmmmm-mmmh*,' said Sorcia, shaking her bleached-blonde hair and keeping her lips tightly closed.

'Was it Bobby Quilty, by any chance?'

'Who?'

'Bobby Quilty. Don't try to pretend that you don't know Bobby Quilty. If it was him, you could nod your head. That's all you'd have to do. Then you wouldn't have had to say anything.'

'For feck's sake,' said Chisel. 'You can't ask nobody to tout on Bobby Quilty. You might just as well ask them to jump into the Lee with their pockets full of bricks.'

Sorcia rolled up her eyes in total exasperation. She dug into the pocket of her dressing gown for her packet of cigarettes, momentarily revealing the depths of her cleavage, with a Celtic cross tattooed into it, complete with a rose and thorns.

'Give me a light, you gom,' she told him. 'The condemned woman might as well have one last fag.'

Twenty-four

Not only had the rain been dredging down all morning but now the wind had risen into fierce blustery gusts. Because of that, the traditional football game that would have been played in the yard at Sunday's Well Boys' School for the last day of Rang a Sé was cancelled. Kevin Doherty picked up his son, Tom, just before noon and took him and his little sister, Sibeal, to McDonald's on St Patrick's Street for lunch.

They sat by the window and watched the shoppers struggling along the pavement as if they were drunk, with their umbrellas flapping inside out.

'So, Tom, do you think you could manage a Big Mac?' said Kevin. 'That's your baby school all behind you now. You're almost a man now. You'll be starting at the Mon after the holliers.'

'Miss Cashman was crying,' said Tom seriously. 'She said we were the best Rang a Sé she'd ever taught and she's going to miss us.'

Kevin reached across the table and patted Tom's hand. Tom was a thin, thoughtful boy, with short brown hair that stuck up at the back and very large brown eyes and protruding ears. His grandmother always said that he was going to grow up to be a poet like W. B. Yeats, but in reality he was more interested in wildlife conservation. He had built a hedgehog house in the garden with a sign saying *Gráinneog* over the entrance, although no hedgehogs had yet decided to nest there. His friend Charlie said that was only because hedgehogs had come from England originally and couldn't read Irish.

Kevin could tell that even if Tom wasn't quite tearful himself, like his teacher, the reality had struck him now that he was never going to go back to Sunday's Well BNS, and that he was no longer a senior in Rang a Sé, the sixth form. Next term he would be a new boy in An Chéad Bliain, the first year at North Monastery School. His infant days were over.

Sibeal said, 'I want chicken, but I don't want pissy-bed leaves.'

She was four years old, with blue eyes and long tangly blonde hair. She looked like a miniature version of her mother, Órla, and was just as strong-willed. She was clutching a red-haired rag doll with only one eye and a crazed expression on its face. 'Pissy-bed leaves' – dandelions – was what she called lettuce.

'What's the magic word?' asked Kevin.

Sibeal frowned and then she blurted out, '*Abracadabra!*' and giggled.

Kevin was a little sad, too, that Tom was growing up, but he was feeling mellow and relaxed. He loved taking the children out, especially when he was under less pressure at work. After two months of wrangling he had closed the sale yesterday on that three-storey commercial building on North Main Street that had once housed a branch of Allied Irish Bank, and the lease of a substantial corner property on Tuckey Street was very close to completion.

Although he had wild wavy hair and rather a large nose, he was an attractive man, slim and smart, with the permanent smile of somebody whose career depends on making people feel welcome. He had turned forty in April and while he had been depressed about it at first, he was now feeling mature and confident and in control of his life. He had woken up one morning and suddenly thought: *I'm happy. Jesus, I'm actually happy. This is what it's like, being happy.*

'One week and three days to go and then we'll be off to Gran Canaria,' he said. 'Sunshine, swimming in the sea. We'll be having the time of our lives.'

'I want to take Blossom,' said Sibeal. Blossom was her rocking horse.

'No, sweetheart, you can't take Blossom. She's way too big to fit on the aeroplane. Daddy will buy you a blow-up horsey when we get there.'

Kevin helped Sibeal to cut up her chicken. She sang as she ate, with her mouth full, while Tom swung his skinny legs as he ate his burger and stared out of the window.

After lunch, it wasn't far for them to drive home. The Dohertys lived in a three-storey red-brick terraced house on Military Road, up the hill from St Luke's Cross, where Katie had met with Kyna. When they arrived, Kevin was irritated to see that a battered green van had parked directly outside his front gate, where he usually parked, and it took him several minutes of wrestling with his steering wheel before he managed to manoeuvre his Audi estate in behind it, so close that it was almost touching.

'Some people, you know? They don't think at all that you might need to park outside your own house. I'll bet it's Mrs Doody has the decorators in again. That woman can't let her house be for more than a month without changing the wallpaper.'

'I *like* Mrs Doody,' said Sibeal. 'She gives me Smiley Face Jellies.'

'Well, she shouldn't,' Kevin told her, as he helped her climb out of her child seat. 'Your mother says that too much sugar makes you hyperactive.'

'What's "practiff"?'

As they walked up the brown-and-white tiled path, Kevin was surprised that Órla wasn't waiting for them with the front door open as she usually did when he brought Tom home from school, especially since today was his very last day at Sunday's Well. Sibeal rang the doorbell repeatedly, but Kevin took out his key anyway.

'Órla!' he called out as they went into the hallway. There was no answer, so he called out, 'Órla, are you at home, love?'

The house was silent. Usually Órla had the television on because she liked a constant background noise, even though she barely paid any attention to the programmes. Most likely she had walked down to the Cross to buy sausages from Sheehan's.

'You can change out of your uniform now, Tom,' said Kevin. 'Fetch it downstairs after because Mummy will have it cleaned and we'll take it to the school for another boy who needs it.'

Sibeal said, 'I want a drink.'

'You've only just had a drink at McDonald's.'

'I want another drink.'

'Well, all right, but you can have only water. You've had enough Tanora for one day. You'll be jumping all over the place like a kangaroo and then what will Mummy say? And what's the magic word?'

Kevin was about to usher Sibeal along the hallway to the kitchen when he became aware of an unusual smell. Órla had been making barmbrack when he left, which was one of the reasons she hadn't come with him to collect Tom from school, but this wasn't the warm, fruity aroma of Órla's baking. This was more like musty second-hand clothes in a charity shop, with an undertone of strong, cheapish aftershave.

'Órla?' he said, but quietly this time. The oak-panelled living-room door was only slightly ajar, whereas normally they kept it wide open.

Sibeal looked up at him. 'Do you think Mummy's *hiding*?' she asked him in a conspiratorial whisper.

Kevin didn't answer. He was concentrating too hard on listening. Besides, Órla never played tricks like this: it wasn't in her nature. She would organize proper party games, and face-painting, and singing children's songs like 'The Bog Down in the Valley-O', but she had never been one for practical jokes and pranks. Their marriage had been through some abrasive times because of the constant clash between Órla's seriousness and Kevin's flippancy, and that was one of the reasons why there had been an eight-year gap between their two children. Sibeal, in fact, had been conceived by accident – but a happy accident, as it turned out, because having their little girl had brought Kevin and Órla much closer again.

Kevin reached his hand out towards the living-room door. He was about to push it open when he thought he heard a squeak, and a faint shuffling sound, and he hesitated.

'*Do-you-think-Mummy's-in-there?*' whispered Sibeal.

Kevin pressed his fingertip to his lips to shush her. It was *his* house: he didn't know why he didn't just push the door open and march straight in to see if Órla really was playing hide-and-seek. For some reason that he couldn't fully understand, however, he sensed that something was badly wrong. Either Órla was in there, acting completely out of character, or else there was nobody in there at all – in which case, why did he feel so apprehensive?

Not just apprehensive – actually *frightened*. But why? Órla was probably standing at the counter in Sheehan's even now, buying sausages, and she'd be back in five minutes. Yet why was the door almost closed like that? And what was that smell?

He touched the door cautiously, but as soon as he did so a man's voice called out in a strong Antrim accent, 'Kevin! Why'n't you come on in here, big lad? What are you footering for outside of the door there for? You're not jibbing it, are you?'

Sibeal looked up at Kevin in alarm.

'It's all right, sweetheart,' said Kevin, although he felt as if his heart had stopped. He pushed the door so that it swung wide open, but he didn't immediately step inside.

Órla was standing on the oval rug in the middle of the living room. She was wearing her long brown apron and her hands were still white with flour. Her fine reddish hair looked frayed where she had tied it back in a scarf and her face was even whiter than usual, ivory white, which showed up the tawny freckles across the bridge of her nose, and her pale pink lips.

Two men were standing close to her, on one either side. The man on her right was bald-headed, with the lumpy face of a former boxer, and an S-shaped nose. He was barrel-chested, but his legs were short and his droopy black jacket made him look even shorter, almost like an amputee.

The man on her left was skinnier and taller, with a messy mop of grey hair and a long, indented face. His eyes were glittery and near-together and he had a downward-pointing nose as sharp as a stalactite. He was wearing a cheap bronze nylon windcheater and tight black spindly jeans. He could have been taken for a giant bird of prey rather than a man.

Both men were holding automatic pistols, the short man in his left hand, the tall man in his right. Kevin reached down and gently pushed Sibeal so that she was standing behind him.

'Come along in, Kevin,' said the short man, beckoning him with his gun. 'There's nothing for you to be nervous about. We're only paying you a social call that's long overdue, that's all.'

'Who are you?' asked Kevin. 'Órla, have they hurt you at all? No – Sibeal – stay behind me, sweetheart.'

Órla looked at Kevin with a desperate expression on her face, her floury fists gripped tightly, but said nothing.

'If you've hurt her—' said Kevin, turning to the short man.

'Ach, away on,' the short man replied. 'We've hardly come here to hurt you. This is all going to be painless, I can assure you.'

'Who are you?' Kevin repeated. 'What do you want? I've some cash upstairs if that's what you're looking for, but otherwise there's not much of any value.'

'Oh, I wouldn't agree with that at all, big lad. What you have here is the most valuable commodity that Ireland ever has to offer. Settling old scores.'

'What in the name of Jesus are you talking about? What do you want?'

The tall man spoke in a slow, mournful voice, almost as if he were giving a sermon. He, too, had a distinct Antrim accent, but it sounded more precise and more educated than his companion's. 'I thought you Catholics were very conscientious when it came to admitting your transgressions. For the Lord loveth judgement, and forsaketh not His saints, but the seed of the wicked shall be cut off.'

'What? What are you talking about?'

'Exactly what I said Kevin – cutting off the seed of the wicked. The sins of the fathers shall be visited upon the children, and rightly so. If there's one thing we never do in Ireland, it's forget those who trespass against us. No sinners should ever go unpunished, but if by some rare chance they do, then their descendants should be punished for what they did, no matter how many generations it takes.'

'I still don't follow you. What sinners?'

'All of the sinners. Every one of those bloody-handed IRA murderers, and you can go back as far as you like. How many anti-Treaty men were never captured during the civil war and held to account? Hundreds! You could argue that they're long dead now, but that's no reason why their heirs and descendants shouldn't be justly punished for all their atrocities.'

'Am I hearing you right? You think people should be locked up for what their fathers and their grandfathers did a hundred years ago – even if they never knew about it?'

'I wasn't talking about prison, Kevin. I was talking about justice. An eye for an eye and a bullet for a bullet. Listen, today's weak-kneed politicians may have gone soft on murderers, granting them amnesty and letting them out of the Maze and sending comfort letters to those on the run. But the fact remains that they are murderers still – bloody-handed murderers! They will never be forgiven by the Lord our God – and no matter how many years go by they will never be forgiven by those grieving families whose parents they killed, or whose grandparents, or whose great-grandparents, *ad infinitum*, and so on and so forth. Why should a murderer's children be allowed to live a happy life when the people they murdered were robbed of all the years that were left to them and never had the chance to see their own children grow up?'

Kevin laid his hand on Sibeal's shoulder and said, 'Wait there, sweetheart. Just stay where you are. No, *please*, magic word, darling, stay where you are.'

He walked into the living room and approached Órla until he was standing directly in front of her, so close that he could have reached out and touched her. He heard a cough and a sniff behind him and he turned round to see a third man sitting in the window seat overlooking the garden – a young man with a khaki woolly hat pulled down right to his eyebrows, wearing a denim jacket and jeans. He looked only about eighteen years old and he had angry red spots on his cheeks and a wispy black moustache. He, too, was holding a gun – an AK-47 semi-automatic rifle which he was holding at a slope across his knees.

Kevin had to try hard to keep his voice steady. Without taking his eyes off Órla, he said, 'Maybe I'm very stupid, but if you haven't come here to rob us, I'd very much like you to explain to me exactly what you're doing here and why you're threatening my wife and my family like this. What's all this talk about settling scores and punishing people? All I want you to do is get out of our house and leave us in peace and I swear on my children's lives that I won't breathe a word of this to anyone.'

'Could you believe it – that never entered my mind, do you know that? – your breathing a *word* to anyone!' said the short man in mock surprise. 'Like, if you're not breathing, like, you *can't* breathe a word, can you, big lad?'

Kevin stared at him, hardly able to believe what he had said, but the short man didn't even look up. He was too concerned with ejecting the magazine from his automatic, frowning at it, and then clicking it back into place.

'You've come here to *kill* me?' said Kevin. 'What have I ever done to anybody? What? You're just going to shoot me, in front of my wife and my children? I don't even know who you are!'

'No, you're right there, you don't know who we are,' said the tall man. 'But the whole point of this is, we know who *you* are. Have you not been listening to the news and reading your paper in the past few days?'

Kevin was beginning to hyperventilate. Almost silently, Órla had begun to cry now and tears were running freely down her cheeks. She kept opening and closing her mouth as if she wanted to tell him something important but was too distressed to get the words out. In the hallway, Sibeal had started to whimper, too, clutching her rag doll as tightly as she could.

'If you've been paying attention to the news, Kevin, you'll be aware that the guards discovered some bodies under the floorboards of a cottage in Blarney. A whole family – father, mother, two children and even the family dogs.'

'I heard about that of course,' said Kevin. 'But they'd been dead for nearly ninety years, hadn't they? I think that's what they said on the news. So what does that have to do with me?'

'It has everything to do with you, Kevin. The Langtrys, that family was called, and it was members of your family who shot them.'

'You're *cracked*!' Kevin protested. 'My family never had anything to do with anything like that!'

'Maybe they never told you about it, but they did. The Langtrys came from Dripsey originally, to work at the woollen mills in Blarney. Everybody was told that they had simply done a moonlight flit. But now we know for sure that they were shot by your great-grandfather, Martin Doherty, and your great-uncle, Killian Doherty, amongst several others.'

'Are you out of your *mind*? My great-grandfather was a grocer! Doherty's Grocer's, in Coachford. He was never anything to do with shooting anybody. I don't know what my great-uncle did for a living, but I think it was something to do with shipping.'

The tall man shrugged, 'There were plenty of men in those days who were shopkeepers by day and soldiers by night. Your great-grandfather was one of them. Didn't you know that after the Dripsey ambush in 1921 he was hauled in by the British army and interrogated for nearly a month before they had to let him go?'

Kevin said, 'No, I didn't. All I know about him was that he was a grocer and my grandfather was a grocer, too. In the end, my grandfather sold the shop and ran a pub for a while, the Mills Inn at Ballyvourney.'

The tall man came around and stood closer to Kevin. He had a large brown wart on his chin instead of a dimple. Now that he was standing so near to him, Kevin could tell that he was the one who made the living room smell like a charity shop.

'You can say what you like,' the tall man told him. 'My family had it on the best possible intelligence that Martin Doherty and

Killian Doherty had been sent to do for the Langtrys. We never once believed for a moment that it was the Brits who did it. It was Captain Frank Busteed of the IRA at Kilcullen who ordered it.'

Kevin didn't know what to say. He felt as if he had opened the living-room door and stepped into a world of total madness. He was terrified and he was sure that these men were intent on killing him, but he couldn't even begin to understand why.

The tall man said, 'The only reason that the Brits let your great-grandfather go was because a letter arrived from the Langtry family in America to say that they had taken it upon themselves to emigrate and that they were all alive and well. Under the circumstances, the Brits could hardly charge him with murder, could they? Our family, though, we were never totally convinced that they had actually emigrated – but what else could we do? The Langtrys sent more letters from America, and there was no sign of them anywhere around Blarney, and no graves found – no bodies burned or buried in bogs. We had to assume that they really *were* in New York. No emails in those days. No phones, even.'

He paused and then he said, 'You can understand why we've been so devastated that their bodies had been found, can't you? After all this time, we've found out at last that our suspicions had been right all along and that they *had* been murdered by the IRA.'

'I still don't see how you can blame *me* for what happened,' said Kevin. 'Not in a million years.' He lifted his chin and flared his nostrils, trying to look defiant.

'Are you having a laugh? Of course we can blame you! Your family murdered one of our families – *all* of them, even the bairns. Even the fecking *dogs*, man! It's time you lot paid for it.'

'You're not a Langtry, though, are you?'

'No, of course not. The Crothers, we are. Our family used to keep Leemount House for Mrs Mary Lindsay, back in those days. My great-great-grandfather Payton kept the gardens. My great-great-great-grandmother Aideen did the cooking and their youngest daughter, Radha, helped her and did the house-cleaning.

'I still don't—' Kevin began, but the tall man interrupted him and now his voice was shaking with indignation.

'It was Radha who married Stephen Langtry and ended up buried under those floorboards. She was the flower of the family, that's what they used to call her. I should have brought you a photograph of her so that you could see for yourself what kind of a beauty she was. The loveliest young woman that you could ever imagine. But your great-grandfather – *your* great-grandfather, whose blood is flowing in your veins even now – he forced his way into Radha's house, that beautiful young woman, and he shot her with no hesitation whatsoever.'

To emphasize his outrage, the tall man lifted his own automatic and pressed the muzzle against his forehead. '*Shot* her,' he repeated. 'Killed her.'

Kevin raised both hands, as if to show the tall man that he was sorry for Radha and her family being murdered, but he could think of no way of making up for it, even if his great-grandfather had been responsible for it. If Radha hadn't been shot she would have been dead by now, anyway, no matter how beautiful she was.

None of them spoke for almost half a minute. The rain spattered against the living-room windows and Órla continued her painful, muted sobbing, although Sibeal had stopped whimpering now and stood silent, swallowing and swallowing as if she were close to being sick.

It was then that they heard Tom bounding down the stairs, calling out, 'Dad! I can't find my blue top! Do you know where my blue top is? I didn't put it in the wash!'

Kevin froze for a second. Then he strode to the living-room door and just as Tom came jumping to the bottom of the stairs he shouted, '*Tom! Get out of the house now, quick as you can! Run to Mrs Doody's next door and tell her call for the guards! Go!*'

Tom hesitated, blinking in bewilderment. He was wearing only his black tracksuit bottoms and a white vest, and he was carrying his grey school uniform bunched up close to his chest.

'*Go!*' Kevin told him, and this time he was almost shrieking.

The short man came out of the living-room door behind Kevin and roughly pulled at his sleeve. 'What the feck you playing at, big lad?'

'*Tom! Go and call the guards!*'

Tom dropped his school uniform on to the doormat and reached for the front door latch. As he tugged it down, however, the short man levelled his pistol at him, left-handed, still gripping Kevin's shirt sleeve with his right. The distance between the muzzle of the gun and the back of Tom's head was less than three metres.

In films, guns are fired in slow motion, so Kevin would have had time to twist his sleeve free from the short man's grip, dive towards Tom and rugby-tackle him to the floor, while the bullet would have slammed harmlessly through the door panel.

Instead, Kevin heard a sharp crack and at the same time a splash of bright red blood appeared on the door panel in front of Tom's face. Tom hesitated for a split second, still holding the door latch, but then he dropped sideways on to the staircase. He slid lifelessly down to the bottom, his arms and legs jumbled, his face turning towards Kevin as he did so. His eyes were open, but above his eyebrows his forehead been blown away and the top of his head was filled with bright red lumps like roughly mashed tomatoes.

Sibeal may have screamed. Kevin didn't seem able to hear anything. Even though the pistol was fitted with a silencer the shot had still been loud. He couldn't even hear himself let out a rising groan of grief. He dropped heavily on to his knees beside Tom, and collected him up in his arms, and held him close. He was warm, he was still warm, and when Kevin hugged him tight he let out a breath.

The tall man came out of the doorway to see Kevin hunched over Tom's body, his head nodding up and down in anguish like a religious penitent. He looked with obvious distaste at the blood that was already smothering Kevin's hands and drenching the front of his shirt, and at the fan-shaped spray of blood on the front-door panel.

212

'Man, dear, would you believe the fecking state of this place? It's going to be a right pain in the arse cleaning all this up.' There was no more emotion in his voice than an interior designer who disapproved of his client's choice of colour.

'The kid was going for the peelers,' the short man explained. 'What else could I do?'

'I don't care *where* the feck he was going, you didn't have to make such a fecking pig's dinner out of it. Oh well, it's not like we'll be trying to keep *this* family hidden for the next ninety years.'

Kevin raised his head. His eyes were almost blinded with tears and his mouth was dragged down in anguish.

'Come on, then, you can kill me, if that's what you came here to do. But don't hurt my wife, don't hurt my daughter. You've taken my son, you evil bastards, isn't that enough?'

The tall man looked back down at him, heavy-lidded. 'I think you've missed the point, big lad. An eye for an eye, that's what I said. A bullet for a bullet. A father and a mother, a boy and a girl. And I saw you have a couple of cats in the kitchen. You have to pay in full.

'Ker-*ching*,' he added, making the noise of a cash register.

Kevin looked down at Tom's staring eyes and the bloody chaos where the top of his head had been. 'This is not real,' he whispered to himself. 'This is a nightmare. None of this is real.'

'I expect our Radha said that, too, or something very like it,' said the tall man, while the short man gripped Kevin's arm and started to pull him up on to his feet.

Twenty-five

Katie drove home before she interviewed Bobby Quilty. She needed a shower and a change of clothes and something to eat, even if she didn't manage to get any sleep.

As soon as she had returned to Anglesea Street she had initiated a nationwide search for Kyna and John by ordering bulletins to be sent out to all six police regions in the Republic, and the same information to all eleven districts of the Police Service of Northern Ireland. After that she had gone to Chief Superintendent MacCostagáin's office to give him an outline briefing on the disaster that had been Operation Trident. She hadn't tried to make excuses for what had happened. She had told him, though, that Bobby Quilty must have been warned of the raids in advance.

'You think it might be coming from inside?' Chief Superintendent MacCostagáin had asked her. 'Is it somebody here at the station?'

Katie could only shrug. 'I don't know yet, sir. I really have no idea. But I *will* find out, you can count on that.'

That morning there had already been several discussions on both TV and radio about the Langtrys. Professor Pendle had repeated his assertion that the British army had shot them, and Oraltih Mac Aindríu of Sinn Fein had said that it was high time the British came clean about some of the atrocities they had committed in the 1920s. So far, however, there had been no response from London. Katie had given a short and non-committal statement to Mathew McElvey in the press office to keep the media at bay until later, but she was anxious not to compromise her arrest of Bobby Quilty in any way.

She had been passing the station's front desk when a call came in for her from Bobby Quilty's solicitors in South Mall. She had flapped her hand and mouthed '*no – not in!*' to the telephone operator and the girl had told them that she was still tied up in a strategy meeting and she would ring them back later. She knew Bobby Quilty's solicitors only too well: Fairley and O'Counihan, especially Terence O'Counihan – a tall, handsome bully with swept-back hair who represented some of the wealthiest businessmen in Cork, and some of the most unsavoury, too.

She arrived at her front door back in Cobh almost at the same time as Jenny Tierney, her neighbour. Jenny had been taking Barney for a walk, in spite of the rain. Jenny was a small, bustling woman who never stopped talking. All bundled up in her pink plastic scarf and yellow vinyl raincoat and bright red rushers she looked as if somebody had brought a rather untidy Russian *matrioshka* doll to life.

'Oh, thanks a million, Jenny, you're a saint,' said Katie, as she took Barney's lead. Barney snuffled up to her and then shook himself violently so that the rain flew off him. 'Barns! You've *soaked* me now, you silly mutt!'

'Were you working all last night, Kathleen, were you?' Jenny asked her as she unlocked her front door. 'Did you get any sleep? I couldn't do without my sleep myself. Sure and I'd be dozing off in the middle of the day if I didn't get my full eight hours, and it doesn't help with himself snoring like Dooley's timber yard.'

Katie switched off her security alarm. 'Did you enjoy your walk, Barns?' she asked him. 'Where did you go?'

'He used to be pure reluctant to go out in the wet now, didn't he?' said Jenny. 'Last week, though, I took him down to the end of Whitepoint Drive for a bit of a change, like – down by the water, you know where I mean, and there's a lady golden Labrador he's taken a fancy to who lives down there, so now he doesn't object to going out at all, even if it's lashing. I have only to say, "Come on, Barney, let's go and see Oona," and if he could clip on his lead himself, he'd be doing it like a shot, I can tell you.'

'Barns!' said Katie. 'You didn't tell me you were in love!'

'Oh, I'd say he's head over paws, but that Oona's awful flirty with him, too. You should see the pair of them together! They'll be voting for dogs to marry next, I shouldn't be surprised, now they've legalized the gays! I expect you're tired, girl, but why don't you come next door to mine for a bit of a sit-down? A cup of tea will crown you.'

'That's very kind, Jenny,' said Katie. 'Right now, though, I have a heap of things on my mind. I don't think I'd be very good company.'

'Well, if you change your mind, like. I have some Guinness gingerbread my sister just sent me and if I don't share it out I'll be finishing it off all by myself, like.'

Jenny kept on talking until Katie had taken off her coat and hung it up and smiled and said thank you again and slowly but firmly closed the door. Then she had gone through to the living room and sat down on the couch to take off her shoes. She felt exhausted. Her head ached and her ankles were swollen and she would have given anything to go to bed and close her eyes and sleep for the rest of the day. All she could think of, though, was Kyna and John. She knew that Bobby Quilty had spirited them away, but she couldn't even begin to imagine what he had done with them – where he might be hiding them, or if he had hurt them, or even if they were still alive. She felt a deep nauseous guilt in the pit of her stomach about both of them, especially Kyna. She should never have sent her to try and infiltrate Bobby Quilty's gang, she should have known that it would end in tragedy. It made no difference that Kyna had agreed to do it: her life was worth a hundred of Bobby Quilty's.

And John – there he was, with his ink-blue eyes and his black curly hair, smiling down at her from his photograph frame on the fireplace. She could almost feel the wind on the day that picture had been taken, on the beach at Dingle Bay, with only the sound of the sea coming in and the thumping of horses' hooves on the sand as five riders galloped by.

She suddenly realized that she was crying.

Barney had been in the kitchen lapping up his water but now he trotted into the living room and stared at her, licking his lips.

'Don't you worry, Barns, I'm grand altogether,' she told him, wiping her eyes with the back of her hand. 'Just tired and emotional, that's all. It's what I get paid for. And what about you? I would have thought you'd had enough of water outside, visiting your fancy-woman in the rain, like.'

She went into the bedroom, unfastened her holster and laid her gun on top of her dressing table. It was her new Smith & Wesson .38 Airweight, which she had only recently changed for her previous revolver. She preferred this because it weighed only 425 grams, lighter than her previous weapon and less than half the weight of the SIG Sauer P226 automatics issued to most of the Regional Response Units. It also had a concealed hammer which guarded against accidental snagging in her clothes. She hadn't yet fired it on duty, and maybe she never would, but she had practised with it every week since she had been issued with it. It had a hard kick to it because it was so light, but she had learned how to handle that, and the grip really suited somebody with small hands like hers.

She undressed and went into the bathroom for a shower. She was surprised to see in the mirror over the basin that she didn't look as tired or as anxious as she felt. In fact, she looked unnaturally calm and composed, and the neat new cut that her hairdresser, Denis, had given her, which tapered into the nape her of her neck, was completely unruffled.

After her shower she wrapped herself in her thick white towelling dressing gown and lay on her back on her bed, crossing her arms over her breasts like a medieval saint on a tomb. She closed her eyes, but after a few seconds she had to open them again. She knew that she wouldn't be able to sleep, so she would have to take two or three caffeine pills if she wanted to be fresh and focused when she faced Bobby Quilty.

She almost felt like asking God why He had created men like Bobby Quilty. Maybe it was just to test the faith and moral courage of people like her.

'All You had to do was *ask* me if I believe in You,' said Katie to the ceiling. Barney heard her talking and let out a gruffing noise, as if he agreed with her.

She was about to get up and get dressed when her iPhone played '*Buile Mo Chroí*'. It was Inspector O'Rourke, sounding as croaky and tired as she was.

'What about you, ma'am? I've just had a call from a retired CID inspector from the PSNI.'

'Oh, yes? What did he want?'

'One of his former colleagues in the Crime Operations Department in Belfast told him about the bulletin you put out regarding DS Ni Nuallán and John Meagher.'

'Okay. And?'

'And if they're still alive he says he has a reasonable suspicion that he knows where they are. Or even if they're not.'

Katie sat up. 'Serious?' she said. 'He must still have some contacts.'

'I think that's the gist of it, ma'am. Any road, he said he'd like to talk to you personal, if he could. I think he remembers you from that time you went up to Belfast to help them to break up that child abuse ring.'

'What's his name?'

'Harte. Alan Harte. He said he's living in Cherryvalley now, in East Belfast.'

'Cherryvalley? He must have been given a golden handshake and a half. I'm not sure I remember him, though.'

'Well, let me give you his number and you can talk to him for yourself.'

'I'll get back to you after, Francis, as soon as I have. Stall it for a second, would you, and let me find a pen?'

Katie jotted down Alan Harte's number and as soon as Inspector O'Rourke had rung off she called him. The phone rang and rang for a long time and she began to think that there was nobody home. Just as she was about to put the phone down, however, it was picked up and a man with a clogged-up voice said, 'Alan

Harte,' then cleared his throat and repeated, softly but much more distinctly, 'Alan Harte.'

'Oh, hallo to you there, Alan. This is Detective Superintendent Kathleen Maguire, from Cork Garda headquarters. I was told you'd been trying to get in touch with me.'

'Well, well, DS Maguire! Thanks a million for calling me back! I don't know if you remember me at all. I met you when you came up to Belfast two years ago and you helped us to scoop those toerags in the Khan–Norris gang.'

Katie said, 'I should have called you on Skype and then I would have been able to see what you look like.' She didn't tell him that she was wearing only her dressing gown, so the Skype conversation would have had to have been one-sided. 'Not to worry. Detective Inspector O'Rourke tells me you might have some information on those two people we're looking for.'

'That's right. One of my old colleagues from Lisnasharragh called me as soon as he saw your message. He's always promised to let me know if a certain name comes up, and there it was, that certain name, big and fat and unmissable.' He quoted from Katie's bulletin: '*These two have been missing since a Garda operation at 0430 hours to detain Robert Boland Quilty on suspicion of keeping them unlawfully imprisoned.*'

'So, you and Bobby Quilty have history, do you?' asked Katie.

'Oh, aye, we have history all right. Why do you think I had to quit the force? We tried to pull a sting on Quilty when he was smuggling drugs in through Larne. To this day I still don't know who he paid off or who he threatened, but nearly seventy-five thousand pounds' worth of heroin was found hidden in my garage roof at home and I could offer no explanation at all as to how it got there. I resigned on grounds of ill health – in inverted commas, if you know what I mean – and it was all hushed up. But of course it was Bobby Quilty who set me up and I swear to God that I will get him one day and fasten his family jewels to the floor with a nail-gun, so I will, if you'll excuse me for saying so.'

'Well, maybe this is your big chance,' Katie told him. 'If we can locate John Meagher and Detective Sergeant Ni Nuallán, and they're still alive, they should be able to give us all the evidence against Bobby Quilty that we could need.'

'Even if they're dead they should be able to,' said Alan.

'I'm trying not to think about that possibility yet,' said Katie.

'No, I can understand that. But I think we have to be realistic about this. Both you and I know what Bobby Quilty is capable of.'

'All right, Alan. Let's concentrate on John Meagher and DS Ni Nuallán. Where do you think we might find them?'

'This is not one hundred per cent, DS Maguire, but it's very much more than just a wild guess.'

'Oh, come on, Alan, call me Katie. You're a civilian now and I'm not in the mood for formalities. I don't mind you knowing that both John Meagher and Kyna Ni Nuallán are personally very close to me.'

'Right you are, then, Katie it is. And like I was telling you, this is more than just a wild guess. Bobby Quilty always used to envy Chunk O'Connell because of the way O'Connell's farmhouse straddles the border, and it was said that all Chunk ever had to do to avoid arrest was cross from one side of his yard the other. About five years ago, Bobby Quilty bought a very similar property in South Armagh. When I say "bought", it was almost a compulsory purchase. He persuaded the owners that it might be better for their general health if they sold up for a derisory sum of money and moved away.'

'Where is it, exactly, this property?' asked Katie.

'It's just off the Shean Road at Forkhill. You can see it clearly enough when you're driving past, even though it's set well back. You won't find it in any official records that it belongs to Bobby Quilty. It belongs to some trust that belongs to proxy that belongs to some holding company. I didn't discover myself that Quilty owned it until two or three weeks before I was forced to resign. But he has the same kind of arrangement as Chunk O'Connell: if the police come to lift him, he simply walks out of the sitting room into the kitchen and they can't touch him. He can stand a foot in front of them eating sausages and there's nothing legally that they can do about it because he's in another country.'

'And you think John Meagher and Kyna Ni Nuallán might be there?'

'Let's just say that when I first joined the CID there's one or two people in South Armagh that I did favours for. Right from the beginning I always considered that it was good policing to turn a blind eye to what the Lesser Bastards were up to, because the Lesser Bastards could help me catch the Bigger Bastards. What would you rather have? A dozen convictions for stealing second-hand cars, or a single conviction for conspiring to plant a three-kilo bomb in the middle of a crowded shopping centre?'

'Yes, I follow you,' said Katie, a little impatiently.

'Anyway, Katie,' Alan went on, 'one of my Lesser Bastards works part-time in the bar now at the Welcome Inn in Forkhill. Every night when he cycles home he passes Bobby Quilty's place and if ever he sees anything unusual going on there, no matter what it is, he sends me a text about it. In return I keep my mouth shut about some of the stunts he got up to with his two brothers after the Good Friday Agreement. They were all three members of the Provos' Second Battalion. This feller never killed anybody himself, but he smuggled the explosives for a bomb that did.'

'So you're telling me that he saw something unusual last night?'

'Aye, he did. I won't read you his text verbatim because you wouldn't be able to make a scrap of sense of it, but he said that just before midnight last night he saw a black or maybe a dark blue van turning into Bobby Quilty's house and parking outside. Two fellers got out of the front and opened the back doors. They lifted out a stretcher with a man lying on it, but then a girl jumped out and started running towards the road.

'One of the two fellers went running after her and caught up with her pretty quick because it looked like her wrists were tied together, which meant she couldn't run so well. He pulled her back to the house and then another three fellers came out of the house and helped to carry the stretcher inside.'

'Did your informant say what the girl looked like?'

'He said she had short blonde hair, that's all. Well, *shoe blind air* is what he actually texted, but I think we can safely assume that's what he meant.'

Katie said, 'I didn't mention it in my bulletin, but I was told that John Meagher had been physically bolted to a bed. If he'd actually had bolts fixed through his ankles or his feet, it would make sense, wouldn't it, for him to have been carried on a stretcher?'

'And Detective Sergeant Ni Nuallán is a blonde?'

'It does all seem to fit together,' said Katie. 'If they were just arriving at Bobby Quilty's house at midnight, that means they would have left Cork around eight, and that makes sense time-wise.'

She didn't say anything to Alan, but by 8 p.m. the preparations for Operation Trident had been fully under way. If Bobby Quilty had been tipped off about Trident immediately after their tactical briefing, he would have had plenty of time to arrange for the bed to removed from the house on Leitrim Street and for John and Kyna to be stowed into in a van and driven north on the M8 to Dublin, and then on to Dundalk presumably, and the border.

'I can't pretend that this is going to be a doddle, by any means,' said Alan. 'The Public Prosecution Service and the top brass at Knock Street are ultra-wary these days of having anything at all to do with Bobby Quilty. Chief Superintendent Shields said herself that it's worse than trying to prosecute a wasps' nest. No witnesses can ever be cajoled into speaking out against him, not even for money and the promise of a lifetime's protection, and you wouldn't believe the number of times he's sued the police service for harassment or wrongful arrest. Successfully, too. The last time he was awarded 15,000 euros.'

Katie knew that Alan was right. In spite of all the incriminating information that the police forces and intelligence services on both sides of the border had gathered against him, neither An Garda Siochána nor the Police Service of Northern Ireland had been able to bring a prosecution against Bobby Quilty that would stand up for five minutes in court.

Not only that, she doubted if Chief Superintendent Mac-Costágain or Chief Superintendent Shields would grant her authority for a raid on Bobby Quilty's house at Forkhill, even though cooperation between An Garda Siochána and the PSNI was mostly excellent these days and they frequently exchanged officers.

How could she justify going after Bobby Quilty yet again? She could imagine the conversation with Chief Superintendent MacCostagáin.

'I strongly believe that Bobby Quilty is holding Detective Sergeant Ni Nuallán and John Meagher imprisoned in his house in South Armagh.'

'Oh, yes, and what evidence do you have for this strong belief?'

'I was told by an ex-detective inspector of the PSNI.'

'*Ex*-detective inspector?'

'He resigned after he was suspected of drug-dealing, but he claims that Bobby Quilty framed him.'

'And where did he get *his* information from?'

'A former Provo who works in a local pub. While he was still in the service, the ex-detective inspector let this fellow off several charges of handling explosives. In exchange for that, the fellow keeps a sneaky eye on Bobby Quilty for him so that one day he can get his revenge.'

'And that's your evidence?'

She knew what this would look like, especially to Acting Commissioner Jimmy O'Reilly, and to several of the more misogynistic senior officers at Anglesea Street. They would think that she felt so humiliated by the fiasco of Operation Trident that she had worked herself up into a hormonal tantrum and now she was trying to bring down Bobby Quilty in any way she could, no matter how flimsy her evidence might be. 'Policing by PMT,' Jimmy O'Reilly had once called it when she had lost her temper with a particularly sarcastic Cork pimp.

But supposing she was given the go-ahead to set up a raid? What if it turned out the same as Operation Trident? What if

Bobby Quilty was again tipped off in advance and when they broke into his house there was no sign that Kyna and John had ever been there? For Katie, that could well lead to serious disciplinary proceedings – probation, suspension, or even demotion. Jimmy O'Reilly wouldn't take kindly to the Garda being made to look like fumbling culchies, especially in front of the PSNI.

She was desperately worried about Kyna and John, but she had to be rational. If she failed to rescue them at the first attempt and was taken off the case, or suspended, or worse, then she would have very little hope of rescuing them at all.

'I know what's running through your mind, Katie,' said Alan. 'I talked to my old pal at Lisnasharragh before I phoned you and he was of the same opinion. With a cute hoor like Quilty you can't just go barging in with all guns blazing without knowing in advance how it's all going to work out. My informant saw the fellow on the stretcher and the girl with the blonde hair, but let's be serious, we don't know for sure if they're the two people we're looking for, and even if they *are* the two people we're looking for, how do we know they're still there now, or if they're likely to be still there if we burst in looking for them?'

'So what are you suggesting? Further surveillance?'

'You have it exactly. I'll go down there myself and have a scout around. I'll see what pictures I can get and if there's any forensic evidence there to be picked up. And – well, you know, it's surprising what you can hear when you keep your ears open.'

'You mean you're going to hack their mobile phones and tap their landlines?'

'Away on with you, Katie! As if I'd do any such thing!'

'Of course not – not as a civilian, and not without a warrant. Who knows what you might overhear?'

'Katie, I'll get back to you as soon as I can,' said Alan. 'I would have trod careful in any case, but now I know that these two mean so much to you personally yourself, I'll tread extremely light indeed, I promise you. A couple of years ago one of our sergeants got on the wrong side of Bobby Quilty and his Authentic IRA and you don't want to know what they did to him, except that it involved his own baton tightly wrapped in razor wire.'

'You're right, I don't want to hear what they did to him,' said Katie. 'It's bad enough trying not to think what they might be doing to Kyna and John.'

Twenty-six

'I'm sorry that I never thought to bring a priest along with us,' said the tall man. 'Very remiss of me, not to think that you Taigs wouldn't be expecting the last rites and all.'

'Let me cover him up at least,' said Kevin. He hauled himself to his feet, gripping the banisters with one bloodied hand to help himself up. His teeth were chattering as if he were freezing cold.

The tall man went over to the coat rack and lifted down Kevin's own long grey raincoat. Kevin took it and gently draped it over Tom's body. From the living room, he could hear both Órla and Sibeal weeping. Their sobs were so anguished that they barely sounded human – more like lonely seals crying on an ice floe after their cubs had been culled.

'Please,' said Kevin. 'You can do anything you like to me, but please don't hurt my wife and my baby girl. I'm begging you. If you have any human mercy at all, please don't hurt them.'

The tall man looked away, as if he were thinking about something else altogether – like, did I remember to book my car in for its NCT?

Kevin waited, swaying slightly with shock. After a few moments the tall man seemed to have collected his thoughts because he said, 'All right, then, let's get you in here all together. Come on now, big lad.'

'I beg you,' said Kevin. His throat was so dry that he could hardly speak.

'What? Like Stephen Langtry begged for Radha, more than likely, and his kids, too? Come on, come in here and let's get this over and done with.'

The short man pressed his hand against Kevin's shoulder and pushed him into the living room. Órla and Sibeal were standing next to the fireplace, clutching each other, their eyes swollen and their faces dripping with tears. The younger man had propped his AK-47 up against the window while he rolled up the large red Ashanti-patterned rug in the middle of the floor. Once he had done that, he left the room and Kevin heard him open the front door. He came back shortly afterwards, carrying a large roll of translucent polythene sheeting almost two metres long.

'You can't do this,' said Kevin. 'This is just barbaric.'

'Ach, there's been a surfeit of barbarity in Ireland down the years,' said the tall man, without looking at him. 'But there's a way to end it, so there is, and that's to punish every act of barbarity with an act of equal barbarity. I know fine rightly that you're innocent yourself, Kevin, and so are you wife and your bairn, but the Langtrys were just as innocent and somebody has to be punished for their murder, and if not you, then who?'

The young man had unrolled the wrinkled polythene sheeting and spread it all across the polished oak floorboards. Kevin had sanded and polished those floorboards himself, soon after they had first moved in.

Kevin knew that he wasn't dreaming, although everything that was happening felt utterly unreal. It was more like being very drunk than dreaming. It felt like those times when he had been quite aware that he was drunk, and hadn't wanted to be drunk, but hadn't been able to speak properly or walk without stumbling down the stairs.

Now that the sheeting had been unrolled across the floor, the tall man touched Kevin very lightly on the back of his head and said, 'Kneel, will you, Kevin.'

Kevin knelt down, his arms by his sides. He couldn't stop himself from crying now even though he wanted to be brave in front of Órla and Sibeal. He didn't want to look at them. He didn't want to witness the distress in their faces, but he couldn't help it. These might be the last few seconds in which he would ever see them.

The short man came up and stood right behind him. He was expecting to be shot in the head at any moment and wondered what it was going to feel like. Did you feel anything at all? Or could you feel your brain exploding, the way Tom's had exploded? Were you aware of everything that you had ever thought or learned or experienced bursting apart like a supernova? How much would it hurt?

He was still waiting for the shot when the tall man went across to the fireplace, took Órla's arm and led her over to the middle of the room, next to Kevin. Órla tried to twist her arm away from him, but he was gripping her sleeve too tightly.

'Kneel,' he told her. When she hesitated, he repeated in the same unemphatic monotone, 'Kneel.'

Órla knelt. She was close enough for Kevin to be able to reach out and touch her, but when he lifted his hand towards her the tall man pursed his lips and shook his head.

'*Mummy!*' sobbed Sibeal.

'Don't you worry, wee girl,' said the tall man. He went over and put his arm around her shoulders and gently steered her over to stand next to Órla.

'Now, you kneel, too, darling, just like you do in church when you're saying your prayers to the Holy Mother. "Hail Mary, full of grace, why do you make that self-satisfied face?"'

Sibeal knelt, awkwardly, but at the same time Kevin started to get to his feet again.

'You lay one finger on her! You touch one hair of her head and I'll find you in hell! I'll find you in hell, you bastard, and I'll make sure that you suffer for all eternity!'

The short man grasped both of Kevin's shoulders and forced him back down into a kneeling position, jarring his left kneecap painfully against the floor. The tall man said, 'I may very well end up in hell, Kevin, but you won't be able to find me. You – you'll be in paradise with your family, big lad, strolling happily from cloud to cloud and you'll have forgotten all about me. Or even if you haven't, you'll have forgiven me. That's what you Taigs do, isn't it? Forgive?'

'Don't you dare hurt her!' Kevin warned him.

'Ach, she won't feel a thing,' said the tall man. With that, he lifted his automatic, cocked it, and pointed it directly between Sibeal's eyes.

Kevin didn't have time to speak before he pulled the trigger and shot Sibeal in the centre of her forehead. Blood sprayed over the glass of the china cabinet directly behind her and up the wall, spattering a small framed picture of St Felicity. Sibeal pitched backwards on to the floor, but still kneeling, as if her knees were hinged. Her blue eyes were still open and, like St Felicity, she was staring up at the ceiling, except that there was a powder-black entry wound between her eyebrows. A large triangular segment had been blown from the back of her skull so that her brains were now tangled with her hair.

Órla screamed and tried to stand up. The short man made a grab for her and as she turned herself around to fight him off the tall man shot her in the right eye, at point-blank range. The fragmentation bullet didn't penetrate all the way through her skull, but her head was violently distorted off to the left so that her face now sloped in a surrealistic parody of herself. She dropped sideways on to the floor close to Kevin's knees and blood ran out of her eye socket and across the bridge of her freckled nose. She was wearing the thin silver bracelet that Kevin had given her on her thirtieth birthday, because that was all he had been able to afford.

Kevin closed his eyes tight. He thought, *Kill me, go on, you're going to do it anyway, and there's nothing left for me to live for now*, but he didn't speak.

The tall man was standing very close in front of him. Kevin couldn't smell him with all that gunpowder stench in the air, but he could sense that he was there.

'Strange thing, revenge, isn't it?' the tall man asked him. 'The sweetest morsel in the mouth that was ever cooked in hell. That's what Sir Walter Scott called it.'

Kevin still said nothing. He could hear the rain sprinkling against the windows and in the distance he could faintly hear the rumbling of a plane taking off from Cork airport. *So this is how my life ends*, he thought. *This is where my destiny was always leading me.*

He pictured the first time he had seen Órla, standing behind the counter at Ryan's, the baker's, with the sun making her look so pale and ethereal, like the ghost of a beautiful girl, rather than a real girl.

'Are you getting?' she had asked him.

He opened his eyes. The tall man was staring at him with an expression that he had never seen on anybody's face before, ever. It was closer to helplessness than anything else, as if he had no choice but to do this because Irish history wouldn't have it any other way.

'I am now,' he said – but of course the tall man didn't understand that this was in reply to the very first question that Órla had put to him and had nothing to do with the bloody tragedy in this living room.

The tall man slowly circled around him, his shoes making a rustling sound on the polythene sheeting. He stood behind him for what seemed to Kevin like an hour, but was less than a minute. Then he raised his automatic until the silencer was only a centimetre away from the back of Kevin's head.

'This is for Radha,' he said. He fired, and Kevin's face blew open from the inside out.

* * *

The tall man and the short man wrapped up each of the four bodies tightly in polythene sheeting, sealing them with silver gaffer tape. While they were doing that, the younger man used a crowbar to prise up six floorboards in the middle of the living-room floor.

Between them, they lowered the bodies into the spaces between the joists and then they carefully nailed the floorboards back down. They replaced the rug and positioned two of the armchairs on top of it.

This took them nearly two hours and then they had to spend a further twenty minutes to clean up Tom's blood from the hallway. Fragments of the bullet that had gone through his head had scarred the upper right-hand door panel, but the younger man had the idea of covering these up by pinning over it a list of reminders that Órla had written to herself and stuck to her fridge.

'Let's put it this way, you're not going to walk in here and immediately think, "Ah, she's stuck her to-do list on the front door to hide some bullet holes", now are you?'

They took a last look around. The Doherty house was silent, as silent as the Langtrys' house must have been when their murderers had finished nailing down their bodies and cleaning up the blood. Then they closed the front door behind them, climbed into their van and drove off.

It was still raining, even more heavily now, and the rain drifted across the city as if God were trailing shrouds across the streets.

Twenty-seven

It was past 2.30 p.m. before Katie arrived back at Anglesea Street. A lorryload of live pigs had broken down in Jack's Hole and the traffic had tailed back all the way to the Euro Business Park. Apart from that, it was raining so hard now that she had to set her windscreen wipers to flap at full speed, and visibility was down to less than thirty metres.

As she came out of the lift she almost collided with Detective Ó Doibhilin.

'Oh, there you are, ma'am,' he greeted her. 'I was just coming back from your office because you weren't there, but here you are now yourself.'

'What's the story, Michael?' Katie asked him. She walked briskly down the corridor to her office and Detective Ó Doibhilin came trotting after her. He was waving a green plastic folder as he did so.

'I heard back from a fellow called Bracewaite, who's like an unofficial historian for the Manchester Regiment. All of their regimental records are kept in the Tameside Local Studies and Archive Centre in Ashton-under-Lyne in Manchester.'

'Did he know who this "Gerald" might have been?'

'He's one hundred per cent sure of it. Lieutenant Gerald Seabrook, whose family came from a place near Manchester called Hale Barns. He'd seen service in France during the First World War and in 1919 they posted him to Ballincollig.'

Katie took off her waterproof jacket and hung it up. 'What we really need to know is, is there any record of his having had a relationship with Radha Langtry?'

She sat down and Detective Ó Doibhilin popped open the plastic folder and handed it to her. 'There's no specific record of that, like, but there's a copy of a letter that was sent just before Christmas in 1920 from the regiment's headquarters in Manchester to Lieutenant Seabrook's commanding officer here in Ireland. I'd say that there's at least an implication in it that Lieutenant Seabrook was doing a line with Radha Langtry.'

Katie took out the typewritten letter and quickly read it. It had been sent by Major D. R. Kettering from Ladysmith Barracks, Ashton-under-Lyne, to Lieutenant Colonel F. H. Dorling, commander of the 1st Battalion of the Manchester Regiment in Ballincollig. It was dated 17 December 1920.

> *Sir,*
> *I have received an appeal from Mrs J. Seabrook,*
> *the wife of Lt. G. K. Seabrook, urgently requesting*
> *information about his wellbeing and whereabouts.*
> *It appears that she has had no word from him*
> *whatsoever for more than three months, neither has*
> *she received the usual monthly payment from him to*
> *meet her household expenses and the care of their two*
> *young children.*
>
> *She is particularly distressed since Christmas is*
> *almost upon us.*
>
> *I would be grateful if you could have this matter*
> *raised with Lt. Seabrook and inform me of the*
> *position regarding his contact with his wife and*
> *financial contributions to his family.*

'Is this all?' asked Katie, holding up the letter. 'Did this Major Kettering get a reply?'

'I'm afraid that's all, ma'am – all that's in the archive, any road. There's no further word about why Lieutenant Seabrook hadn't been in touch with his missus. But there *is* a record of what happened to him.'

'Oh, yes? And what was that?'

'He went missing in March 1921. They thought at the time that he'd deserted, because four private soldiers failed to show up for duty at the same time. Here they are – Privates Pincher, Mason, Caen and Roughley. A whole rake of British soldiers went AWOL, according to this Bracewaite fellow, because they'd just come back from fighting the Germans in France and suddenly they found themselves up against the IRA. The stress and the totally different circumstances they were fighting under was too much for some of them. That was in the days before post-traumatic stress disorder was thought of, you know. They'd only just invented shell-shock.'

'But he hadn't deserted, this Lieutenant Seabrook?'

'No, ma'am, he hadn't at all, and neither had any of those four privates. If they *had*, like, we wouldn't be able to check up on it. There's a file called "arrests and illegal absences" in the regimental archives, but it's sealed for a hundred years and nobody's allowed to take a sconce at it until 2040 at the earliest. No, in 1923 the Brits and the IRA were doing some further political bargaining, like, and as a concession to the Brits the IRA told them that Lieutenant Seabrook and the four privates had been abducted and shot and their bodies buried underneath a hedge in Muskerry.'

'So it wasn't only Radha and the rest of the Langtry family who were shot. It was "Gerald" as well?'

'That's what it looks like. At first, all five of the soldiers' bodies were squashed into a single coffin and buried in Bandon, but after some more negotiations in 1924 they were dug up, like, and sent to the regimental headquarters in Ashton-under-Lyne. They were separated and all of them were buried with the full military honours in Hurst Cemetery, which is where they still are.'

Katie leafed through the letters and papers that had been emailed to Detective Ó Doibhilin from England. There was even a photograph of Lieutenant Gerald Seabrook, MC. He was standing in a summery garden somewhere, in his uniform, his eyes half closed because of the brightness of the sun. He didn't look to Katie as if he were particularly tall, maybe five foot seven or eight inches, and his shiny dark hair was parted in the middle, but he was handsome in a cheeky Tom Cruise way and he had an engaging smile.

'Strange to think that he's been dead now for over ninety years, isn't it?' said Katie. 'Taken away, shot and buried under a hedge. And look at him, still grinning away like he doesn't have a care.'

She felt that the motive for the Langtrys' murders was gradually becoming more distinct, as if she were cleaning successive layers of dirty varnish from a very old painting. The information that Detective Ó Doibhilin had gleaned from the Manchester Regiment archives hadn't really helped much, but at least it had confirmed who 'Gerald' had probably been. He could have been shot by the IRA for no other reason than he was a British army officer, but Katie thought it increasingly likely that they had killed him out of revenge for the Dripsey ambush, and that they could have shot the Langtrys for the same reason.

All she had at the moment was 'what-ifs', but the 'what-ifs' made sense and it was worth following them up to see if they helped to make the picture any clearer. Stephen Langtry had been a member of the IRA. What if he had told Radha about the imminent ambush? He might have done it for her own safety, or so that she could caution her employer, Mrs Lindsay, to stay away from Godfrey's Cross that day. If anything happened to Mrs Lindsay, Radha would have been out of a job, and secure jobs like that in those days weren't easy to come by – or, indeed, any jobs at all.

But what if Radha had been having an affair with Gerald Seabrook and she had told *him*, too, in case he were killed? What if the British army's informant hadn't been Mrs Lindsay at all, as the IRA had first thought and the history books still suggested – or at least, not the only informant?

Whether it was Mrs Lindsay or Radha or both of them who had warned the British about the ambush, Katie could understand why the IRA might have been set on revenge once it had gone so calamitously wrong. Most of their men had escaped because they knew the countryside so well, but one had been mortally wounded and eight had been captured, and of those eight, five had been sentenced to death and executed.

In retaliation, the IRA had abducted and shot Mrs Lindsay and her chauffeur. But if they had subsequently discovered that Radha was the source of the leak, it was more than likely that they would have made a point of going after Gerald Seabrook, and the Langtrys, too. That was only another 'what-if', of course, and Katie knew that she might never find the evidence to back it up. But unless the Langtrys had been murdered because they were having some kind of bitter personal feud with another family, it seemed like the most logical explanation.

After all, she thought, the killings had been a classic example of an IRA punishment: you were taken, you were shot, you were buried, and nobody ever saw you again or knew exactly what had happened to you. It was infinitely more traumatic than being murdered in the open, in front of witnesses, especially for your family and friends. You had simply been 'disappeared'. They didn't even have a grave on which they could lay flowers.

'This fellow Bracewaite said he's happy to do some more snuffling around for me,' said Detective Ó Doibhilin. 'He said he might be able to trace the Seabrook family, especially if they're still living around the Hale Barns area. From what he told me, you have to be fierce *flathúl* to live around there – it's all big five-bedroom houses and swimming pools, do you know what I mean, like? – so families don't tend to move so often.'

'That's grand, Michael, keep banging away at it,' said Katie. She looked at the clock on her desk. 'Now I have to go and have a word with our friend Bobby Quilty. After that, I'll be holding a general debriefing about Operation Trident.'

'You don't want to know what they're saying in the canteen about Operation Trident,' said Detective Ó Doibhilin.

'Yes, I do,' said Katie.

'Serious?'

'Tell me. I won't get odd with you, I promise.'

'Well, they're saying, "Two wrongs don't make a right. Three prongs weren't worth a shite."'

'I'll ignore that,' said Katie. 'Just warn them that if I overhear anybody saying that myself, I'll be sending them out in the rain to lick my car clean.'

Twenty-eight

Katie took Detective Sergeant Begley and Detective O'Donovan down with her to the interview room. When she walked in Bobby Quilty was deep in murmured conversation with his lawyer, Terence O'Counihan, their heads almost touching, and even though he flicked his eyes towards the door he didn't stop murmuring and showed no other sign that he had seen her come in.

'Mr Begley, Mr O'Counihan,' said Katie, drawing out a chair. Terence O'Counihan turned around as if he were surprised to see her, and stood up. He was so tall that Katie had to tilt her head back to look him in the eye and he made her feel like a child rather than a grown woman. He was wearing an expensive grey shark-skin suit, double-breasted, and a blue silk tie with a repetitive pattern of herons on it. He was very handsome, in a smooth, well-moisturized way, with black hair that was greying at the temples and immaculate eyebrows. Whenever he was amused, or quizzical, one eyebrow would rise like a raven lifting itself off a rooftop. His nose was very straight, his eyes were slightly hooded. His tan had come from somewhere very much more exotic than Santa Ponsa.

'Well, well, Detective Superintendent Maguire. We must stop meeting like this.'

'We would, Mr O'Counihan, if you were more selective in your choice of clients.'

'Ouch!' Terence O'Counihan grinned. 'You still float like a butterfly, sting like a bee! However,' he said, lifting his wrist to look down with those hooded eyes at his gold Patek Philippe watch, 'time is flying by, Detective Superintendent *tempus fugit.*

238

I must insist either that you release Mr Quilty on station bail or immediately bring him up in front of the District Court on the charges for which you arrested him.'

'I need to ask him a few questions first,' said Katie.

'My client has nothing to say.'

'He does realize the seriousness of the charges against him? Incitement to murder and false imprisonment?'

'He does, of course. But he vehemently denies both. Whatever it is you're accusing him of saying, he didn't say it, and whoever you're accusing him of imprisoning, he doesn't know them and in any event he wasn't there.'

'We have forensic evidence that John Meagher was held in a property on Leitrim Street belonging to Mr Quilty.'

'He knows nothing at all about that and he has no comment to make.'

Katie found it hard to look at Bobby Quilty, but he didn't take his eyes off her. He sat there with his chubby fingers squashed together like sausages, and a porky, self-satisfied twinkle in his eyes. Now and then he gave a catarrhal snort in his left nostril, and swallowed. He didn't yet know that she had discovered where he was holding Kyna and John, and of course she wasn't going to tell him, because he would either have them moved at once to some other safe house or kill them – she had absolutely no doubt that he was capable of it. She was so angry and afraid that she had to stop and take a steadying breath now and again, in case she burst out and told him how vicious and loathsome she thought he was, and how deeply he disgusted her. Detective Dooley always referred to him as 'Bobby the Hutt', after Jabba the Hutt in *Star Wars*.

'Very well,' she said. 'If Mr Quilty doesn't wish to answer any questions, that's his right in law. However – as you know full well yourself, Mr O'Counihan – if he fails to tell me now anything that he later relies on by way of his defence, the judge will be very much less than amused.'

'I'd say the key to these accusations is evidence, wouldn't you?' Terence O'Counihan replied in a warm, smooth voice. 'May I ask who's going to be standing up in the witness box to confess that my client incited them to murder your unfortunate detective? And may I ask who's going to testify that they were party in any way to the false imprisonment of Mr – what was his name?'

'John Meagher,' said Katie. Her mouth was dry, as if she were reading his name from a gravestone.

'Of course, John Meagher,' said Terence O'Counihan. He spread his hands wide and said, 'But Mr Meagher's whereabouts are still unknown, or so I gather, and apart from some forensics which you claim to have recovered, and which we have not yet had the opportunity to examine ourselves and contest, what evidence do you have to prove that he was falsely imprisoned at all? My client is being in no way uncooperative or obstructive by declining to answer your questions. The plain fact is that there is no case for him to answer.'

'Well, we'll see what the district judge has to say about that,' said Katie. 'Meanwhile, I'm extending Mr Quilty's detention here until we've arranged a time for his appearance in court.'

'I must object to that,' said Terence O'Counihan.

'Your objection is noted, Mr O'Counihan.'

Katie was turning to leave when Bobby Quilty let out a sharp whistle between his front teeth, as if he were calling a dog, and beckoned Terence O'Counihan towards him. Terence O'Counihan leaned over while Bobby Quilty muttered something in his ear. Then he stood up straight again and said, 'My client would like a private word with you, Detective Superintendent if that's possible.'

'What does he mean by that – "a private word"?'

'He's asking if there's somewhere in the building where you and he can go to talk confidentially, without anyone overhearing and without any microphones or other recording equipment. That kind of private.'

'Why would he want to do that?' asked Katie, still not looking at Bobby Quilty directly.

'He says it's a personal matter. But it does have some bearing on the charges against him.'

If any other offender had asked to speak to her in confidence, on a 'personal' matter, Katie would have refused outright. But Kyna and John were in Bobby Quilty's house in Forkhill, in South Armagh, and God alone knew what condition they were in and how they were being treated. She had felt a sickness in her stomach ever since she had talked to Alan Harte, and she kept tasting bile in her mouth, and this morning's coffee.

'All right,' she said. 'If it helps us to clear this matter up.'

'You're welcome to talk in my car, in the car park,' said Terence O'Counihan. 'That would be private.'

'No,' Katie told him. 'For all I know you have a recording device inside it.'

'Or a bomb, even,' put in Detective Sergeant Begley, but nobody laughed.

Katie said, 'We can go upstairs to the fourth floor and out on to the balcony. An officer will be able to keep an eye on us then from inside, but nobody will be able to hear what we're saying.'

'Fair play to you, Detective Superintendent' said Terence O'Counihan. 'Floats like a butterfly, stings like a bee. Sharp as a knife, I should have added.'

* * *

Katie and Bobby Quilty went up to the top floor of the station, accompanied only by a single garda, although he was big and muscular and they could barely all fit into the lift together.

'Ach, this is fierce intimate,' said Bobby Quilty, holding in his belly with both hands. 'But look at the bake on you, Detective Superintendent! You look like a wee bag of weasels the day!'

Katie said nothing, but gave a quick, sour smile.

They went out on to the balcony that overlooked Anglesea Street, although they stayed away from the railing because of the rain. The garda remained inside, his arms folded, watching them bored and stony-faced through the window.

Bobby Quilty took a pack of cigarettes out of his shirt pocket stuck one between his lips.

'There's no smoking in the station,' said Katie.

'Not until now, anyway,' said Bobby Quilty, lighting up his cigarette and blowing smoke out into the rain. The garda took a step towards the door, but Katie raised her hand to indicate that he should stay where he was.

'Well?' said Katie. 'What was this private and personal matter you wanted to talk to me about?'

'Ach, sure, you know yourself that you'll never make those charges stick,' said Bobby Quilty. 'Do you think that I came up the Lagan in a bubble? I respect you, Detective Superintendent Maguire, don't make any mistake about that. But I'm a survivor, and I know how to protect my interests, and you need to give me the credit for that.'

'I give you credit for nothing, Mr Quilty, except for being a dangerous scumbag. You were responsible for Detective Barry being killed, and I have every reason to suspect that it was you who ordered Darragh Murphy to be disposed of so that he couldn't give evidence against you. You told me yourself that you were holding John Meagher, so I don't think I need much more proof of that.'

Bobby Quilty blew more smoke and shook his head in amusement. 'Catch yourself on, will you? As if you'll ever get me to admit that to a judge. No – what I'm trying to say to you now, doll, is what I was trying to explain to you before, but it seems like it fell on deaf ears the last time. You and me, we both have to find a way to rub along together without constantly getting up each other's noses.'

'The thought of getting up *your* nose gives me the gawks, if you must know, Mr Quilty.'

Bobby Quilty laughed and gave another cackling sniff. 'I love you, Detective Superintendent Maguire, do you know that? If you weren't a fecking poll I'd ask you to marry me. I know you have to enforce the law, that's what you get paid for, but at the same time I have to scrape a wee living myself. So if you won't agree to a treaty, I have to have some kind of insurance policy so that you won't keep coming after me and disrupting my business. Like I said to you before, I'm only flogging a few fags at economy prices and there's no desperate harm in that.'

'You're still holding John Meagher, is that what you're telling me?'

'Oh, you catch on quick, no question about that. Yes, Mr Meagher is still a guest of mine and that's how he's going to stay until I'm convinced that you're going to live and let live.'

'How is he? Is he still well?'

'As fit as a butcher's dog. In fact, I'd say he's treating his stay with us as something of a holiday.'

'Don't take me for a fool, Mr Quilty. There was blood on the carpet in that house on Leitrim Street.'

'I wouldn't know about that, Detective Superintendent. Your man is still living and breathing and eating cheesy beanos for breakfast – what more do you want than that? And I would never take you for a fool. I've heard that you have to pass all kinds of fierce hard exams to be a guard. Why, some of the guards I've met, they can count from twenty to one, backwards, and walk forwards at the same time.'

'I don't need to remind you what a serious offence it is, false imprisonment. Not to mention trying to influence a senior police officer by means of menaces.'

'I know that fine rightly, of course. But you haven't left me any alternative, have you? Which is why I wanted to talk to you now, in private. I wanted to let you know that in the light of what you did last night, busting into my house like that, I've doubled my insurance policy and Detective Sergeant Ni Nuallán is now a guest of mine, too.'

'Is she safe?' asked Katie. There was no point in acting surprised. 'She's not hurt in any way?'

Bobby Quilty flicked his cigarette butt over the side of the balcony. 'I think her pride is a wee bit dented, but that's all. She played her part amazing, though, I'll give her that. For a while there she had me believing that she really was some slapper from

Gurra. I even sent her out on a fag run and the boys said she was beezer at it.'

'Who tipped you off?' said Katie.

'Nobody tipped me off, doll,' said Bobby Quilty. He tapped the side of his nose and said, 'I can smell peelers a mile off. It's a kind of a *blue* smell, you know, like rotten fish. You can't mistake it.'

'So you're telling me that you have both John Meagher and Kyna Ni Nuallán as hostages?'

'Hostages! That's the exact fecking word I was looking for and couldn't think of it for the life of me. That's it, Detective Superintendent! Hostages!'

'And in return?'

'In return for them being given bed and board and not beaten on a regular basis, you'll be dropping all of the charges against me and on top of that you'll be recompenserating me for my busted front door.'

Katie stared at him for a long time. Behind him, from the south-west, the grey sky was gradually growing brighter, almost silvery.

'What if I say no?' she said.

'Well, I thought you might be asking me that,' said Bobby Quilty. 'That was the whole reason I wanted us to talk in private, with nobody earwigging. If you say no—'

He didn't finish his sentence. Instead, he drew his finger across his throat and opened his eyes wide, and nodded, and nodded again, to make it clear that he meant it.

Twenty-nine

After Bobby Quilty had been escorted back to the interview room Katie went back upstairs to see Chief Superintendent MacCostagáin.

'Katie!' he said. 'What's the craic? What time are you having your post-mortem on Operation Trident? And you're holding a media briefing directly afterwards, is that right?'

'Yes, sir,' she told him. 'But I wanted to tell you that I've decided to drop the charges against Bobby Quilty. It was probably a misjudgement on my part to arrest him in the first place.'

Chief Superintendent MacCostagáin looked down at the papers on his desk and then looked up at Katie again, and his expression was even more miserable than usual.

'This won't be doing our public image a great deal of good, will it? God knows we've been fighting hard enough to prove to the people of Cork that we're competent and efficient, and that we're making serious progress against organized crime. This is going to set us back badly.'

'It might do, yes, temporarily,' said Katie. 'But I'm totally confident that I can build up enough evidence against Bobby Quilty to bring him in again, sooner rather than later, and on charges that will get us a conviction.'

Chief Superintendent MacCostagáin stood up and went across to the window. 'This is strictly between you and me, Katie, but I know you're a realist. One of the main problems here is that you're a woman, and as you're perfectly well aware, there's still a hard core in the force who resent your promotion, even now.

They'll take advantage of every opportunity they can get to see you demoted or removed altogether, and of course that won't go down well with Commissioner O'Sullivan. She's been busting a gut to make sure that women gardaí are given equal advancement, but of all people I don't have to tell *you* that in reality that still means that women officers have to perform twice as well as men. This Bobby Quilty business isn't going to help her cause at all. In fact, to be frank with you, it's an expletive deleted disaster.'

'Yes, sir,' said Katie. 'I'm not making any excuses. But I think it would do our reputation even more damage if we tried to take Bobby Quilty to court on the evidence we have at the moment, or rather the lack of it. He'll make a great big media show out of it and it'll make it harder for us to go after him the next time because he'll accuse us of harassment.'

'And?' asked Chief Superintendent MacCostagáin, turning away from the window. All his years of experience had given him a very sensitive ear and Katie could tell that he had picked up something in her voice – an unspoken 'and' which might have betrayed that she had a much more pressing reason for dropping the charges against Bobby Quilty than the possibility of negative headlines in the *Examiner*.

'And – nothing,' she said. 'Even if the blood that we found on the bedroom carpet in Leitrim Street turns out to be John's, we have no way of proving that Bobby Quilty knew he was there, and even if we did, we have no way of proving that he was responsible for kidnapping him. There's no chance that those two squatters will give evidence against him, even if they really *are* squatters, not unless they want to risk having their heads blown off like Darragh Murphy.'

'So what's your plan?' asked Chief Superintendent Mac-Costagáin.

'I've been working closely already with G2, of course, and we've a heap of circumstantial evidence against Bobby Quilty and all of his associates – phone-taps, emails, surveillance photographs. On top of that, though, I'm hoping to get some more background information from the PSNI. Nobody can spend twenty years running the cross-border rackets that he's been running without leaving *some* incriminating evidence behind them.'

'All right, Katie,' said Chief Superintendent MacCostagáin, in his usual sad voice. 'Good luck with the media so.'

* * *

The atmosphere in the conference room was subdued. There was a strong smell of stale cigarettes and damp clothing, and Katie kept the post-mortem on Operation Trident short and direct.

'I want to thank everybody who took part in Operation Trident. You all carried out your assignments in a highly professional manner, and I particularly wish to compliment the restraint and efficiency of the Regional Support Units. I accept complete responsibility for the outcome, which was obviously not what I had been expecting. I can only plead that I misinterpreted the intelligence that I was given.'

She was quite aware that she was doing herself no favours by accepting the blame for the disaster of Operation Trident. However, if there was anybody in the assembled audience who might be passing information on to Bobby Quilty, she wanted to give them no hint that she was even more determined than ever to see him arrested, charged, and locked up for the rest of his life in Portlaoise maximum security prison.

'I will, of course, be making a full report to the assistant commissioner,' she said. 'Meanwhile, I want you to know that I intend to drop the charges against Bobby Quilty at this time. If you happen to come into contact with him during the course of your duties, I expect you to treat him with the same respect that you give to any other citizen of Cork.'

There was a loud derisory raspberry from someone at the back of the room and a few of the gardaí shook their heads in exasperation, but nobody else had anything else to contribute.

As everybody shuffled out of the conference room, Inspector O'Rourke came up to Katie and said, 'You didn't have to take all the blame, you know, ma'am. You could have come up with some almost nearly true story about Quilty getting wind of it somehow.'

'I would have, if things had been different,' said Katie, snapping shut the clasps on her briefcase.

'Different – like, how?'

'I'm sorry, Francis, you don't have the whole picture yet and I'm not in a position to give it to you. When I can, though, you'll understand at once. Let's just say that if I get myself demoted because of this, it won't kill me. On the other hand, if I'd given out even the slightest suggestion that I suspected anybody here in the station of being a tout for Bobby Quilty—'

Inspector O'Rourke looked at her narrowly for a few moments, expecting her to finish her sentence. When she didn't, but simply raised her eyebrows, he understood what she was telling him, even if he could guess only roughly what it was.

She hated this secrecy, especially since she really felt the need for somebody to confide in, and to support her. Just as she was walking out of the door of the conference room, however, her iPhone pinged with a message. A visitor had arrived for her and was waiting for her downstairs. He didn't have an appointment, but he had said that she would know who he was and why he was here. His name was Alan Harte.

When she arrived at the front desk, a short ginger-haired man was just pushing his way out through the front doors and she thought for a moment that it was him, grown tired of waiting for her. Then she looked across to the opposite side of the reception area and there he was, his face in shadow, wearing a long grey raincoat with shoulders that were still sparkling with raindrops.

'Alan?' she said, and he stepped out of the shadow.

'Katie,' he said, in the same soft Belfast brogue that she had heard on the phone, and held out his hand.

He was tallish, just under six foot she would have guessed, and he looked as if he had once been very slim but had filled out with middle age. His hair was steel-grey, cut short and sharp. His eyes were grey, too – Irish-sky grey. He had a broad face, with strong cheekbones and a square chin. Katie would have guessed some Scottish ancestry. He was carrying a black overnight case.

'You could have let me know you were coming,' said Katie.

'I'm sorry. I didn't know myself until this morning.'

'Come up to my office,' she said – then, as soon as she had pressed the button for the lift, 'What about Kyna and John? Have you seen them?'

Alan nodded. 'I have, yes. That's the main reason I'm here. I could have called you or texted you, but you never know who might be hacking your phone and I didn't want to risk it. I drove down to Forkhill at first light this morning, even though it wasn't very light. I parked my car about a half a mile away from the house and walked through the fields so that I could sneak my way into the paddock at the back. It was lashing down so there was nobody outside in the yard, and I doubt they expected anybody else to be out there, either.'

The lift arrived and Katie and Alan stepped in. Close up to him, Katie caught a smell like a combination of black pepper and cinnamon. Maybe it was some aftershave that he was wearing, or maybe just his shower gel.

'How did they look?' said Katie. 'The last time you saw John they were carrying him on a stretcher, weren't they?'

'They were in a large downstairs room at the back. Your friend John was lying propped up with a cushion on a couch and your detective sergeant – what was her name, Kyna? – she was sitting beside him in armchair. So far as I could make out, she was feeding him out of a bowl with a spoon. I don't know what that says about his physical condition. The room was gloomy enough so it wasn't easy to see them too distinctly. They were alive, anyway. I was going to take some pictures but then some wee man came into the room and pulled the curtains across.'

'And you're sure they didn't see you?'

'Not a chance. I was hiding myself beside this tool shed, and like I say it was lashing. I stayed there about ten minutes longer, trying to see if I could pick up a phone signal, although I had no luck with that. Nobody came out, though, so they obviously didn't know I was there.'

'And you're sure it was them? Kyna and John?'

'No question at all. It was fair gloomy in that room, like I say, but I recognized them straightaway from the pictures on your bulletin. They looked tired and kind of nervous, but if they were being fed I'd say that was something to be optimistic about. If you were intending to kill a pig you'd feed it up, but a human being? You wouldn't bother, would you? Why waste good food?'

Katie gave him a quick sideways look. 'That's not very encouraging.'

'I know, I'm sorry. I didn't mean it like that. Too many years being a copper, that's my trouble. I think it's made me impervious to other people's feelings. I'm not even sure I have too many of my own any more.'

'I've dropped the charges against Bobby Quilty,' said Katie, as they entered her office and she switched on the lights. 'I should never have arrested him in the first place. I suppose I was hoping that St Francis would conjure up some miraculous piece of evidence before I had to let him go.'

'So what happened?' asked Alan.

Katie sat down at her desk, but Alan remained standing. She told him as briefly as possible how Operation Trident had gone so disastrously wrong, and how Bobby Quilty had been one step ahead of her and made a mockery of each of the three simultaneous raids. Alan nodded when she told him about Darragh Murphy being shot, and nodded again when she described what they had found at the house on Leitrim Street – or rather, what they had failed to find.

'Tip-off,' he said. 'You have a tout there, no question about it.'

'Oh, no doubt at all,' said Katie. 'The problem is, I have no idea at all who it could be. To begin with, only a handful of people knew that I'd asked Kyna to work undercover for Bobby Quilty, but on the night we had to warn the Regional Support Unit that she might be inside his house, in case it came to a firefight and they shot her by mistake.'

'Believe me, Bobby Quilty was doing the same in Armagh,' said Alan. 'What makes him so hard to scoop is that he has contacts in all walks of life – politicians, business executives, prostitutes, criminals. He knows everybody from Bamba's Crown to Cranfield Point, I can tell you. He knows bank managers, so that he can easily find out if any police officers are having a struggle financially. He knows hotel keepers, who tell him if they're having affairs with any woman that they shouldn't be. He knows club owners and drug-dealers, so he's always aware if they've ended up addicted to the crack that they're supposed to be confiscating. At the very least he always has three or four poor peelers who are going to be passing him inside information, either in exchange for cash, or for keeping his mouth shut, or for not posting pornographic photographs of them on Twitter for their wives to see. He'll have at least one tout here in Anglesea Street, possibly more than one. As you say, though, Katie, the problem is finding out who. It could be anybody at all, from the highest to the lowest.'

'Well, I have some ideas how I can winkle them out,' said Katie. 'In the meantime, though, what do you suggest we do about Kyna and John?'

'I'd recommend absolutely nothing at the moment. Bobby Quilty's going to be confident now that so long as he holds them hostage, you'll be leaving him well enough alone. He's not so stupid that he'll kill the geese that guarantee him the golden eggs. We had a similar situation in Belfast in 1988. The Provos kidnapped the owner of Sheen's department store and said that they would only return him in exchange for two of their own men who had been caught by the RUC the previous week. The poor store owner suffered a heart attack and died, so the Provos no longer had anything to bargain with. That lesson won't have been lost on Bobby Quilty.'

'So, what else are you doing here?' Katie asked him. 'You didn't come all this way just to tell me about Kyna and John, did you?'

'To be honest with you, Katie, I thought I could maybe help you to do for Bobby Quilty once and for all. I'll admit it's personal, but the man's a general menace. If you could let me look through all of the intelligence that you have on him and I can see first-hand for myself what kind of a set-up he's running here in Cork, there's a fair chance I might spot something that you've overlooked without realizing it, do you know what I mean? If I can help you to build up a strong case against him that will stand up in court, and see the bastard sent down, it'll be like five Christmases rolled into one, I'm telling you.'

'You understand that I couldn't allow you to do that officially? I mean, the Garda and the PSNI swap officers all the time, but you're not an officer any more, and all of the intelligence on Bobby Quilty is highly confidential. If I let you look at it, you'll see how we acquired it, and the names of our informants, and that's all confidential, too, of course.'

'I get that, Katie. And I'm not even a former officer. I'm an *ex*-officer. But this is a fierce unusual problem we're up against here and it's going to take some fierce unorthodox measures to solve it.'

'I don't know, Alan,' said Katie. 'I'll have to give this some very serious thought. I can't see Chief Superintendent MacCostagáin agreeing to it. He's a stickler for protocol, and it's not like you retired from the service in a blaze of glory, if you'll forgive me saying so.'

'I understand that, of course. But I was hoping you might take me on as a kind of unofficial adviser. Let's face it, Katie, what are the options? The second you tell anyone here that Kyna and John are being held hostage, and that you want to raid Bobby Quilty's house to rescue them, Quilty will get to hear of it and the best you can hope for is that you find their bodies. It would be exactly the same if I tried to persuade Chief Superintendent Shields in Armagh to do the same.'

'I know,' said Katie. She was about to answer him, but she knew he was right.

Alan stood there watching her for a while, saying nothing. She opened the file on her desk in front of her, which was a lengthy report on the tightening of border controls between the Republic and the United Kingdom because of the number of illegal migrants who were using Ireland as a back door into England. She read the first two paragraphs and then closed it.

'Where are you staying?' she asked.

'Jury's probably, on the Western Road. I brought my toothbrush with me and a change of gunks.'

'Look – I have a media briefing in ten minutes,' Katie told him. 'It shouldn't take long. I'll take you to the canteen if you like and you can have a coffee while you're waiting. We can talk some more afterwards.'

'Aye, grand, that's fine by me. I've all the time in world, so I have.'

* * *

The usual crowd of reporters and freelance journalists had arrived for the media briefing – although Dan Keane from the *Examiner* was in hospital for X-rays on his lungs and Roisin Magorian was standing in for him, a quiet, thin, sharp-looking woman in a dark green linen suit. Her lips were almost always tightly pursed, which had led Detective Sergeant Begley to christen her 'the Pencil Sharpener'.

Fionnuala Sweeney was there, too, as well as Branna Mac-Suibhne from the *Echo* and Muireann Bourke from Newstalk.

Superintendent Pearse joined Katie to give her moral support and explain the logistics of Operation Trident.

'Everything went exactly as planned,' he said, by way of conclusion. 'No firearms were discharged, no gardaí were injured, and there was no risk to the public at any time. It was a textbook operation from beginning to end.'

'Well, one firearm was discharged, wasn't it?' asked Roisin Magorian, holding up her pencil. 'The firearm that killed Darragh Murphy.'

'I'm sorry, but that was done several hours before Operation Trident was actioned,' said Superintendent Pearse. 'And not by us.'

'You say it was a textbook operation, but the man you wanted for killing Detective Barry was murdered before you could arrest him. Not only that, there was no hostage in the house on Leitrim Street where you suspected there was one, and even though you arrested Bobby Quilty you later dropped both of the charges against him and released him. What kind of a textbook operation was that?'

Katie said, 'Our failure to get a satisfactory result from Operation Trident was entirely down to me. I was given intelligence which I interpreted to the best of my ability, but the intelligence turned out to be misleading, to say the least. That's not to say we shouldn't have acted on it, or that there was any mishandling of the operation whatsoever. If the information had in fact been correct and we had failed to act on it, we would have been guilty of gross dereliction of our duty and it could have resulted in injury or even death.'

She paused, and looked at theTV camera, and added, 'I'm not infallible. None of us are. But I would rather be guilty of making an error of judgement than guilty of causing the death of an innocent person by failing to respond to what seemed like genuine information.'

'I spoke to Mr Quilty before I came here,' said Roisin Magorian. 'If you'll forgive me for quoting him more or less verbatim, he says that the Cork Garda have a certain part of their anatomy hanging out of the window while their grannie throws snowballs at it.'

'Mr Quilty is entitled to express his opinion in whatever language he chooses, provided it isn't obscene or slanderous.'

'However, he says that he isn't a vindictive man and that he's satisfied that his future relations with the Garda are going to be cordial. *Warm*, even. Would you agree with that?'

'An Garda Siochána will treat Mr Quilty in the same way that we treat every other citizen of Cork, no matter who they are.'

'No special treatment, then, in case he sues you for wrongful arrest?'

'No comment,' said Katie. 'In fact, that's a question that doesn't deserve an answer.'

'There's no need to get stooky about it, Detective Superintendent' said Roisin Magorian. 'I was only asking. You can't deny that the Garda have given preferential treatment to certain people in the past, naming no names.'

'Can I ask what progress you're making with the murder of Darragh Murphy?' put in Branna MacSuibhne.

'Nothing dramatic so far,' said Inspector O'Rourke. 'Several Parklands residents saw a yellowy Volvo estate waiting at the end of the alley that runs behind the houses in Darragh Murphy's street. It was there for at least twenty minutes with its motor running, which is one of the reasons it caught their attention. One witness said she saw a skinny feen in a grey hoodie walking out of the alley and climbing into the Volvo and then it immediately drove off.'

He looked down at his notes and then he said, 'She told our officer, "Your man was walking very quick, like he thought the Devil was close behind him but didn't want to turn around to look, and once he'd jumped into it, the car took off with its tyres screaming like all the bats of hell."'

'Could this have been the same Volvo estate you were looking for after the murder of Detective Barry?' asked Branna.

'I won't deny that's a possibility,' said Inspector O'Rourke. 'However, none of the witnesses at Parklands made a note of the vehicle's index marks. We still have a name and address for the owner of the Volvo that may have been involved in the incident in which Detective Barry was fatally injured, but we haven't yet been able to trace him. Charles Daly, of Rathpeacon. The address was real enough, but there's nobody living there who matches the name in which the vehicle was registered. We're still making inquiries of course.'

'You wanted to talk to Darragh Murphy in regard to the death of Detective Barry,' said Muireann Bourke. 'Now that he's dead, does that mean that the case is closed? Or do you have other suspects?'

'The case is still very much open,' said Katie. 'As yet we have no conclusive proof that Darragh Murphy was responsible for fatally injuring Detective Barry, or that other parties weren't involved. That's all I have to say for now.'

After the media conference had ended, Katie was about to go back to the canteen when Roisin Magorian caught up with her.

'What's the story, Roisin? Anything more I can help you with?'

Roisin reached into her bulging green leather tote bag and took out a springbound notebook. 'This is nothing to do with Operation Trident, Detective Superintendent. This is another story I've been working on altogether.'

'Go on.'

Roisin Magorian had a pair of half-glasses hanging around her neck and she perched them on to the end of her nose. 'I have a friend who has a friend who's an accountant for the Diamond Club casino. He told me in confidence that some very influential people in Cork have desperate gambling debts, some of them running into six figures.'

'That doesn't surprise me one bit,' said Katie. 'You remember that case we had only last year, don't you – that manager at AIB? He'd lost a fortune at the roulette table – a fortune! – and so he lent himself nearly a quarter of a million euros from his customers' accounts so that he could save himself from having his legs broken. Well, when I say "lent", he was never going to be able to pay it all back.'

'This is much more serious, in its way,' said Roisin Magorian. 'There are several politicians who have run up enormous gambling debts and they've borrowed money to keep their creditors off their backs. At least three county councillors and a TD, too. Not just politicians, either. A senior manager in Revenue and a buyer of pharmaceuticals for the HSE. *And* – a senior officer in the Cork Garda. Which is why I'm asking you about it.'

'Do you know who it is?' asked Katie.

'No. Your man from the Diamond Club wouldn't name any names because it would be more than his job's worth. In fact, he said it might be even more risky than that. Most of the money has been lent by sources with powerful vested interests, like developers looking for planning permission, or drug companies that want their product bought by the health service at an inflated price. Or, in some cases, by criminals – criminals who wouldn't be too happy if it got out who they'd been lending money to.'

'Do you have any evidence for this at all, apart from what this fellow from the Diamond Club told you?'

'Some. But I'm gathering more day by day. I just wanted to ask you if you had any inkling that it was true, and if you know that at least one of your senior officers is up to his ears in gambling debt.'

'You're taking a chance, aren't you? It might be a "she", not a "he". It might be me, for all you know.'

'No, I may not know his name yet, but it's a "he".'

Katie could see that Inspector O'Rourke was waiting to talk to her. 'I'm sorry, Roisin,' she said. 'You know more about this than I do. Even if I do find out, I'm not at all sure that I'll be telling you.'

'Well, we'll see,' said Roisin Magorian. 'You might be inclined to, in return for some information from me. I may not know who your gambling Garda officer is, but I'm pretty sure who it was that lent him the money.'

Katie waited for her to continue, but Roisin Magorian did nothing more than tuck her notebook back into her tote bag. 'Good luck to you, DS Maguire,' she told her, and turned to go.

Katie was tempted to call her back, but she knew that she wouldn't tell her any more. She went to join Inspector O'Rourke and make her way back to the canteen where Alan was waiting for her.

'How do you reckon that went?' asked Inspector O'Rourke.

'Not quite as bad as I'd expected. But let's wait until we see the *Six One News* and tomorrow morning's papers.'

* * *

Alan looked up from the copy of the *Echo* he had been reading and said, 'How did it go?'

'As well as could be expected,' said Katie, pulling out a chair and sitting opposite him. 'In other words, somewhere between desperate and disastrous.'

'Have you had any word from upstairs yet?'

'Nothing so far, but I'm sure I will. Jimmy O'Reilly isn't going to let me get away with making a hames of an expensive operation like that. It's all budget with him. That man, I'll tell you. He wouldn't spend Christmas.'

She wondered why she was talking to Alan like this. After all, she hardly knew him. She hadn't even checked if he really had been a detective inspector with the PSNI. But she felt exhausted with worry and badly in need of an ally. Apart from that, he was the only other person who knew where John and Kyna were, and what danger they were in, and everything he had said had rung true so far.

'You look tired, if you don't mind my saying so,' Alan told her.

Katie scruffed her hand through her hair. 'I'm fair beat out, if you must know.'

'Then why don't we leave this till tomorrow? If you don't want me seen around here too often, we could always meet for breakfast.'

'No, I won't be able to sleep until we've talked through how we're going to handle this. I probably won't be able to sleep anyway. I keep getting this picture in my head of John lying on a couch and Kyna feeding him, the way you described it. I mean, like, Mother of God, John was a very fit man.'

'We have to take it careful, Katie. If we try to rush this, it's going to end up like your Operation Trident, only worse. We have to nail Bobby Quilty before we do anything else, and nail him securely.'

'Don't worry, I'll make sure you get copies of all the intelligence we have on him,' said Katie. She was becoming aware that other gardaí in the canteen had noticed her talking to Alan and were obviously wondering who he was and why they were having what must have looked like such an intimate conversation. Katie's personal life was even more riveting to her fellow officers at Anglesea Street than their four-times-a-week dose of *Fair City*.

'How did you get here?' she asked Alan. 'Did you drive?'

'Came on the train,' he told her. 'I didn't fancy driving for four and a half hours in weather like this, and besides there's five kilometres of resurfacing works on the E201 at Two-Mile Borris.'

258

Katie couldn't help thinking to herself: *Even if he never was a detective inspector, he certainly sounds like one.*

'Listen,' she said. 'Instead of going to Jury's, why don't you come back to Cobh with me? I've a spare room and it'll cost you nothing. I have to take my dog for his walk and get myself something to eat. That's if you don't mind reheated lasagne. It's home-made, not Tesco's best.'

'Katie, I didn't come here to impose on you. I can see that you have quite enough on your plate already, so you have.'

'No, it wouldn't be an imposition. I'd be glad of the company right now, to be honest with you. There's not a lot of consolation in talking to yourself, like.'

* * *

They drove to Katie's house on Carrig View in Cobh and it rained harder and harder all the way there. When they climbed out of her car and hurried to the front porch, Katie noticed the living-room curtain in the Tierney's house next door twitching back and Jenny Tierney peering out to see who it was. Oh, there'd be some chinwagging now all right. *C'mere till I tell you, that Detective Maguire brought a feller home with her last night and he didn't leave until the morning so.*

Barney greeted Alan with his usual suspicious snuffling, but when he realized that Katie was quite comfortable with him he relaxed and went into the kitchen to make some loud lapping noises in his water bowl.

'Sorry about the sniffing,' said Katie.

'Oh, don't worry. They say that dogs can sniff if a man has prostate cancer, so I'm relieved that he's given me the all-clear.'

'Would you care for a drop of coffee?' asked Katie, walking into the living room. Her table lamps were on timers but it had grown so dark so early that she switched them on herself.

'No, no thanks. I've been drinking coffee all day. If I have any more caffeine I'll be gibbering like a baboon.'

'A beer, then?'

'All right, twist my arm. It's a little early for me, but the sun's gone down. It's not visible, any road.'

Katie switched on the television. The *Six One News* would be on in five minutes and she wanted to hear Fionnuala Sweeney's report on Operation Trident. She went into the kitchen and came back with a bottle of Murphy's and a glass for Alan, then she poured herself a vodka and topped it up with lemonade.

'So tell me about yourself,' she said, sitting down on the couch next to him and tucking her feet up.

Alan shrugged. 'There's not much to tell. If I'd followed my heart maybe there would have been. I always wanted to be a musician and have my own folk band, The Cuchulains I was going to call them, do you know? But my older brother went off to England to work in insurance, and my younger brother got himself a managerial job with Green Isle Foods, and my sister married this Belgian fellow she met on holiday, a bit of a looper but pleasant enough, and went off to live in Belgian land.'

'What happened to The Cuchulains?'

'Oh, they never came to nothing, sadly. The problem was that our da was a chief inspector in the RUC. There've been Hartes in the Northern Ireland police service since my great-grandfather was a county inspector for the Royal Irish Constabulary in 1912, and my da was dead set on the family name being carried down through the generations.'

Katie shook her head and smiled. 'You don't have to tell me. You were the only one left and you didn't want to let him down. That was exactly what happened to me. Seven Maguire sisters and the only one to join the Garda was muggins.'

'Still, Katie, fair play to you, you've done yourself proud. And your father proud, too. My da's dead and buried now, but he was mortified when I had to leave the service. Mortified!'

'Are you married?' Katie asked him, nodding towards the gold ring on his wedding finger.

'Separated. Coming up for eight years now. Somehow we never got around to divorcing, and somehow I never got around to taking off this ring. I suppose if nothing else it's a great contraceptive.'

They watched the *Six One News*. A major fire had gutted a whiskey distillery in Midleton, with seven workers injured and three still missing. There had also been a critical vote in the Dáil on further cuts to the health service, so the report on Operation Trident had been dropped altogether.

'There you are, Katie,' said Alan. 'There is a God.'

Katie finished her drink and stood up. 'I'm not so sure about that. I still have to take Barney for his evening patrol and it's flogging outside.'

'Hey, I'll come with you, so I will. There's no point in just the one of us getting skited.'

As soon as Barney heard her take his lead down from the hook in the hall he came running out of the kitchen.

'Look at him,' said Katie. 'He thinks I'm going to take him all the way down to Whitepoint Drive to see his girlfriend, Oona. Sorry, Barns, not on a night like this. We're going as far as the ferry and back again, and that's it, and if you don't do your business by then you'll just have to bottle it up till the morning.'

Alan laughed, and Katie turned to him, and suddenly realized for the first time in days that she had something to smile about, no matter how briefly.

Thirty

'Oh, Jesus!' John cried out. He sounded desperate, as if he had been trying to keep silent for the past half-hour but couldn't contain his agony any longer. 'Oh Jesus – oh holy Jesus, my feet!'

Kyna opened her eyes. The clock outside in the hallway had only just struck half past seven and the overhead light was still on, but she had been awkwardly curled up in her armchair trying to sleep. She was exhausted, and there was nothing else to do in this large, dull, brown-wallpapered room – no television, no radio, no books, not even a newspaper, and the only picture on the walls was an autumn landscape of County Fermanagh that was almost as brown as the wallpaper.

When John started moaning, however, Kyna lifted herself out of her armchair and went across to the couch to kneel down beside him. She said, 'Ssh, I'm here, John,' and gently laid her hand on his forehead. He felt chilled and sweaty, and he was trembling uncontrollably from head to foot.

'They'll have to call a doctor for you,' she told him. 'You can't go on like this. You'll get blood poisoning, if you haven't already. Let me look at your feet.'

John shook his head. 'No, no, please don't touch them. Please. It's like they're on fire. It's like they're on fire and my legs are starting to burn, too.'

'John, you have to let me take a look. I might be able to clean them up for you. If you leave them wrapped up like that they're only going to get worse. You could die from septicaemia.'

John was wearing only the dirty blue shirt and boxer shorts

that he had been wearing when he had first been snatched on his way to the Hayfield Manor. His legs were bare, but both of his feet were swaddled in thick white towels – the left towel very much larger than the right, more like a bath towel, so it looked disproportionately huge. Both towels, though, were stained with brown and yellow blotches, and they smelled strongly of dried blood and pus.

Even before she started to unwind them, Kyna was disturbed to see that John's calves were swollen and red, almost up to his knees.

'I'll be as gentle as I can,' she said. John nodded, gripping the edge of the cushion with one hand and pushing the knuckle joint of his other hand into his mouth and biting it.

She lifted up his left leg and carefully began to unwind the towel. John sucked in his breath and bit harder on his hand. Although she hated to hurt him, she knew she couldn't let his feet continue to fester like this.

With every layer she unwound, the brown and yellow stains became wider and wetter and the smell became stronger. She retched, although she tried to suppress it because she didn't want to John to become any more distressed than he was already. All she had eaten since this morning was a ham and tomato sandwich that Ger had bought at a petrol station on the way here, so she had nothing to bring up except saliva.

When she finally dragged off the last corner of the bath towel, she could see how badly John's feet had become infected. His whole foot was swollen and purple and his toes were black. The hole that Chisel had drilled through his foot was now clogged with glistening greenish-beige pus.

She stared at it helplessly. She couldn't bandage up his foot again, not with the same sodden towel, but she had nothing to clean it with. She always had make-up wipes in her bag, but Ger had taken that away from her, and in any case they wouldn't have been enough to clean out John's suppurating wounds. All she had now was the clothes in which she had first met Bobby Quilty, which Margot had washed for her: her pink TROUBLE

T-shirt, sports bra and skinny black jeans. Ger had even taken her shoes.

She turned to John. He was biting his knuckle so hard that blood was sliding down his wrist and his eyes were crammed with tears. He was in so much pain that he couldn't even look at her.

She laid her hand gently on his forehead again and then she said, 'That's it, John. They have to call a doctor for you. You need to be in hospital.'

John took his hand out of his mouth and said, 'Please, Kyna, for the love of God. I can't take this take any more. I don't care if they kill me. Just make it stop.'

Kyna stood up and went to the living-room door. She banged on it with both fists and shouted out, 'Open the door! Open the door! We need a doctor! You have to send for a doctor!'

She stopped, and listened, but all she could hear was the muffled sound of a television in another room.

'*Open this fecking door, you bastards!*' she screamed, and beat at the door panels even harder. '*We need a doctor! This man is dying in here! Open this fecking door!*'

She waited again. This time she could hear the television suddenly become louder as a door was opened, and then footsteps coming along the corridor outside. The key was turned and the door pushed inwards, so that she had to step back two or three paces. Ger was standing there, beaky-nosed, smoking, barefoot, in a crumpled striped shirt with no collar and his usual raspberry chinos. He was still wearing his huge dark glasses, and even indoors he was wearing his stained white hat.

'What the feck is this all this fecking commotion for, girl?' he demanded. 'Jesus, you're making as much noise as ten pigs stuck in a gate!'

'It's John,' said Kyna. 'He needs a doctor, urgently. Look at his foot. I mean, *look* at it, will you, he's going to die of the blood poisoning if we don't get him treated.'

Ger wrinkled up his nose and looked at John over Kyna's shoulder. 'Mother of God, I don't have to look at his fecking foot, I can smell it from here. Worse than a knacker's flange. I don't know how you can stand it. Except you don't have the choice, do you?'

'You need to call for an ambulance,' said Kyna.

'Oh, is that right? So I call for an ambulance and then what happens? The paramedics will want to know what happened to your man's feet and who he is and what he's after doing here, won't they? And I don't suppose you'll be keeping your bake shut either, will you, Sidhe, or whatever your fecking name is?'

Kyna tried to snatch at Ger's sleeve and pull him into the room so that he could see close up how badly infected John's feet were. He wrenched his sleeve free from her and said, 'Away to feck, would you? There's feck all I can do about it. If I call for an ambulance, the next person who'll be needing a fecking ambulance will be myself, don't you have any doubts about that. And you, too, more than likely.'

'At least fetch me a bowl of hot water and something I can bandage his feet with. And maybe you have some disinfectant – iodine, anything will do. And some Nurofen, if you have it, or aspirin. Anything. He's in terrible pain.'

'You have some nerve, you know,' Ger told her. 'Making out you're some skanger and all the time you're an undercover guard. My sense of smell fair let me down then, I should have smelled bacon the minute you walked into the pub. Mind you, it's come back since. The stink in here is pure mank. I'm not codding, I'd feel sorry for you if you weren't a shade.'

Kyna was close to tears. 'Have you no heart in you at all, for God's sake? Look at the state of him. All I'm asking you for is some hot water and some disinfectant, and a few bits of old torn-up sheet or something to bandage his feet with. If he dies, you'll be done for manslaughter at the very least.'

'If he *dies*, darling, nobody will ever find him, or know what became of him, and the same will go for you, too. The Big Feller doesn't like to leave evidence behind him or people to open their yaps and say what he did.'

'*Please*,' Kyna begged him.

After thinking and smoking for a few moments, Ger nodded and said, 'Okay. I'll see what I can do. But, you know,' and as he said this he looked Kyna up and down, 'maybe there's something that you can do for me in return, do you know what I mean, like?'

Kyna said, 'Please, whatever you want. Just fetch me something to clean his feet.'

'That's a promise, like?'

Kyna closed her eyes and nodded. She couldn't imagine that Ger could do anything worse to her than Bobby Quilty.

When Ger had gone, she knelt down beside John again and held his hand. John was still trembling, but he managed to glance at her quickly two or three times and say, 'Katie – does Katie know about this?'

'I'm sure she does. Maybe she doesn't know exactly where we are, but she'll find us. You know she will.'

'Do *you* know where we are?'

'Not exactly. But we must have been driving for at least three hours, and judging by their accents I'd say we're north of the border somewhere. Probably South Armagh, because that's where Bobby Quilty comes from originally.'

'Holy Mary, Mother of God, my feet hurt. Even if they won't call for a doctor at least they must have some painkillers.'

'I've asked him. Whether he brings some or not, I couldn't tell you.'

'I walked out on her,' said John.

'Katie? Yes, I know.'

'Did she tell you why? She was expecting another man's baby and I was jealous. Seems petty, doesn't it, when you look at me now? Hurting so much that I can hardly think and expecting her to come and rescue me.'

'She lost the baby.'

'I know. I heard. I know one of the radiographers at CUH.' He paused and clenched his teeth, his face a mask of a suffering. After a while, though, he relaxed a little and said, 'Comes in waves.

266

One second I feel better, the next I feel like I'm being cremated alive, feet first.'

He clenched his teeth again and groaned in the back of his throat. Then he breathed out and said, 'She didn't – she didn't get rid of the baby because of me, did she?'

Kyna said, 'No. She was going to keep it. We even talked about names. Brendan, she was thinking of, if it was a boy, or Cliona if it was a girl. She liked the idea of naming a little girl after a fairy.'

'I was worried it was my fault.'

'Then you don't know Katie very well, do you? Katie takes total responsibility for everything she does, no matter how bad it is. No – she had a serious scuffle with some scummer while she was trying to make an arrest and got herself kicked. She hasn't got over it, even now.'

John turned his head and looked at Kyna through eyes that were slitted with pain. 'You almost sound as if you know her better than me.'

Kyna squeezed his hand and tried to smile, and said, 'I love her.'

They heard the key in the door again and Kyna stood up. Ger came into the room, followed by one of the men who had helped carry John into the house on a stretcher – an unshaven, narrow-faced man in a dark grey turtleneck sweater, his hair brushed forward in a widow's peak.

Ger was carrying a grubby white flannelette sheet over his arm. He rolled it up and threw it over to Kyna. 'There, that's the best I can do you in the way of bandages.'

'This is filthy,' said Kyna. 'This is only going to make the infection even worse.'

'Well, in case of that, I fetched you some disinfectant,' said Ger. He turned around to the man with the widow's peak, who handed him a blue plastic bottle of Domestos bleach, with the top already taken off. He walked over to the couch where John was lying and held up the bottle as if it were the Olympic torch.

'What are you *doing*?' asked Kyna. John looked up at him in pain and bewilderment.

267

'First aid, that's what they call it, isn't it?' said Ger, and poured undiluted bleach all over John's exposed left foot.

The only scream that Kyna had ever heard that was higher and more agonized than the scream John let out then was when a young woman had thrown herself in front of a train at Heuston station in Dublin. He arched his back and dug his fingers into the seat cushions and kicked his left leg again and again as if he were trying to kick it off. He was incoherent with pain.

Kyna dropped to her knees and twisted the sheet that Ger had given her around John's foot. She tried frantically to dab the bleach out of the blackened, pus-clogged cavity that Chisel's drill hole had now become, but every time she touched it John's whole body went into a spasm and he started to pant as if he had been running to the point of exhaustion. At last he clutched at her arm and said, 'Stop, stop, Kyna, leave it, leave it, don't touch it any more!'

'Oh, Kyna, is it?' said Ger. 'So that's your real name? You're not Sidhe then, after all?'

'Fetch some hot water!' Kyna told him, standing up. 'You could have killed him with shock, doing a stupid thing like that, you gowl!'

'What did you fecking call me?' Ger demanded. He brandished the Domestos bottle in front of Kyna's face and said, 'How would you like a splash of this straight in your eyes, Miss Undercover Shade?'

'Just stop acting the maggot, will you, and fetch me some hot water,' Kyna screamed at him, 'If you don't, I'll go fetch it myself and damn you!'

Ger swung back the bottle. Before he had the chance to throw any bleach at her, however, Kyna spun around and kicked him in the face, her right heel hitting his left cheekbone so hard that his neck jerked sideways. His sunglasses snapped and his dirty white hat flew off. He staggered backwards in a complicated dance, dropping the bottle of bleach so that it emptied down one leg of his chinos. He nearly fell over but the man with the widow's peak made a grab for his upper arm and he managed to regain his balance.

Without his hat, Kyna saw that Ger was almost bald, except for a few stray clumps of wild grey hair. Without his dark glasses, she saw that he was blind in one eye. His right eye was totally white and bulging in its socket, like a hard-boiled quail's egg.

He bent down and picked up his hat, jamming it back on to his head at a rakish angle, as if he had done it for comic effect. The man with the widow's peak found his dark glasses on the floor and handed them to him, but the right lens was missing and Ger slung them across the room in a fury.

He advanced on Kyna, holding up both fists. Kyna stayed where she was, tense but calm, her knees slightly bent and both hands lifted, and it was obvious that she wasn't afraid of him at all – not in a fair fight, anyway.

Ger's chin was tilted upwards and his one good eye was wide open, staring at Kyna without blinking.

'Ger – don't try it, Ger,' Kyna warned him. 'It's not worth it. You won't prove anything except that you're older and slower and blinder and that I can give you a fierce bad beating if I want to.'

Ger thought for a moment. He opened and closed his mouth as if he were about to say something, but then thought better of it. He slowly lowered his fists, stepped back and said, 'No, maybe you're right, girl. Maybe you're right. I wouldn't stand a chance in hell against all that martial arts jiggery-pokery of yours, now, would I? That take-one-door or whatever the feck you call it.'

'*Now* can I have some hot water?' said Kyna.

'Sure, yes. Absolutely. Of course you can. Grady, there's a plastic bowl under the sink in the kitchen. Fill that up with hot water, will you, boy, and bring it back here, quick as you like.'

The man with the widow's peak left the living room. Kyna knelt down beside John again and took hold of his hand. 'John?' she said. 'How are you feeling?'

John's eyelids were fluttering and he was licking his lips as if he were thirsty, but he was only barely conscious and he didn't answer. Very carefully, she unwound the towel that was still wrapped around his right foot, and when she lifted it away she could see that his right foot was even more seriously infected than the left one. It was charcoal-black from his toes to his ankle and glistening with thin liquid pus, as if it had been varnished.

Ger was standing close behind her. He whistled and said, 'Jesus Christ on a fecking wagon wheel! That feller's going to be needing some replacement plates of meat, if you ask me.'

The man with the widow's peak came back with another, younger man, who was carrying a blue plastic washbasin half filled with steaming water. The younger man set it down beside Kyna and grinned at her as he did so. He had fair curly hair thick with dandruff and raging red spots and he was wearing a red baseball cap backwards. He smelled strongly of skunk.

'Thank you,' said Kyna.

'Oh, you're very welcome,' he told her. As he stood up, however, he seized her left arm, gripping it very tight, and at the same time the man with the widow's peak took hold of her right arm.

'You – *bastards*! Let – *go* of me! *Let go!*' she shrilled at them, trying to wrench herself free, but the two of them were far too strong for her and they hauled her up on to her feet. She bent her knees so that they would have to drop down to the floor, but she weighed less than fifty kilos and they easily held her up between them, even with her feet in the air. They turned her around to face Ger and she could see by the look on his face that he hadn't forgiven her for kicking him and breaking his dark glasses, not one bit. His left cheekbone was crimson and swollen now, and his one good eye was beginning to close up.

'Do you know what happened to the last old doll who tried to hit me?' he said, and gave her a grin. 'I have to say *tried*, because you're the only old doll who's ever succeeded. But even though she only tried, she got herself beat up so bad that her own mother couldn't recognize her when we dropped her off home, and I'm not shitting you, I promise.'

Kyna lowered her feet to the floor and took a deep breath. 'Let me tell you this, Ger. I was shot in the stomach less than six months ago. I'm still recovering. Look here, if you don't believe me.'

Even though the man with the widow's peak was holding her arm, she was able to lift up her TROUBLE T-shirt to show him the swastika-shaped scar next to her navel. Ger stared at it and then said, 'All right, doll, I believe you. What the feck does that have to do with the grass and the goose on the side of a mountain?'

'If you beat me, I'll start to bleed again internally and you won't be able to stop it and I'll die. You probably won't give a damn yourself, but Bobby Quilty will. Why do you think he's gone to all of the trouble to keep me and John here as hostages? In fact, if you kill me, he'll probably kill *you*, and if he doesn't they'll find my body whatever you say and you'll be done for murder.'

Ger couldn't stop himself from grinning. 'Fair play to you, girl, I think that's the best fecking excuse for not getting beat up that I ever heard anybody come out with.'

'You can call it an excuse but you know it's true,' Kyna told him. She was trying to sound brave, but her heart was beating so hard against her ribcage that it hurt, and she had wet herself a little.

Ger came up very close to her so that she was almost suffocated by the smell of stale tobacco and alcohol. She had always dreamed that she would die in some loving woman's arms, with the sun going down and filling the bedroom with its last tangerine light – not beaten to death in a shabby living room by a one-eyed criminal with poisonous breath.

'No beating, then,' said Ger. But then he grasped both of her shoulders and tilted his head back. For a split second she wondered if he were going to give her some kind of mock-benediction, but then he butted her hard in the face with his forehead. Her nasal bone snapped and blood gushed out of her nostrils, and her knees gave way from under her. The two men let her collapse on to the floor, concussed, both of her eyes rolled up like Ger's one blind eye.

John was still unconscious, too. Ger looked over at him and then down at Kyna, and said, 'There. Let that be a fecking lesson to the both of them. Don't try messing with Ger Daley because that's what you'll get. Grady – find my glimmers for me, would you, boy, and the lens that dropped out of them? See if you can't stick them back together for me.'

He left the room. Grady and the spotty young man scouted around the floor for his sunglasses and the missing lens, giggling to each other like children, and once they had found them they left the room, too, and locked the door behind them.

More than twenty minutes passed before Kyna became aware of her surroundings again. She was seeing double and her head was banging so hard that she could barely think. She was struggling to breathe, too, and when she put her hand up to her face she found that the blood had dried hard around her mouth and chin like a Hannibal Lecter mask. With extreme caution she touched the bridge of her nose, and sucked in her breath when she felt the broken bone crunch inside it.

'Mother of God,' she whispered to herself, and awkwardly sat up. John was still lying on the couch with his eyes closed, his face an asbestos grey, although she could hear him softly snoring.

She wanted to sob, but she bit her lower lip hard to stop herself because it would have hurt too much. She had never felt so hopeless and abandoned in the whole of her life.

Thirty-one

The rain began to ease off as they took Barney for his walk up to the Carrigaloe Rushbrooke pier. On the way back the wind was blowing dry and cool and the ferry terminal lights glittered on the river. Katie began to feel calmer and more composed than she had for days.

In the back of her mind she was still fretting about Kyna and John, but she knew that Alan was right. So long as they remained alive, Bobby Quilty had a guarantee that the Garda would turn a blind eye to his cigarette-smuggling business and that they wouldn't try to implicate him in the murder of Detective Barry or the shooting of Darragh Murphy.

When they reached Katie's house she saw the next-door curtain twitching again, and Jenny Tierney peering out, and she gave her a little finger-wave.

'Nosey neighbour,' she told Alan, as she opened the door. 'She's sound out, pure helpful, I'll give her that. She feeds Barney and takes him for walks when I'm late back from work. But she does like to keep herself abreast of everything that's going on, like.'

They went inside. Katie had left the oven on low while they were out and there was a herby smell of lasagne in the hallway.

'I'm starved,' said Alan, following her into the kitchen. 'I've eaten nothing at all since breakfast and that was only toast.'

'Would you like another beer?' she asked him. 'Then I can show you where you'll be sleeping.'

She refilled his glass with Murphy's and poured herself another vodka, and then she took him into the spare room, which had once been the nursery. She had redecorated it less than three months ago, so it no longer looked like the room in which her little Seamus had died in his cot. There was a new double bed and the walls had been painted cream, with four framed samplers hanging on them.

Alan read one of the samplers and said, 'Here, I like this, *Three things there are that can never come back . . . the arrow shot forth on its destined track . . . the appointed hour that could not wait . . . and the warning word that was spoken too late.* How true is that.'

In spite of herself, in spite of the room looking so different now, Katie couldn't help thinking of the morning she had walked in and found Seamus lying chilly and wet-lipped and as white as wax, with his small blue teddy bear lying close to him, smiling.

Alan frowned at her. 'Have I said something I shouldn't?'

'No, not at all,' she told him. She opened the fitted wardrobe and said, 'Here, look, there's a dressing gown here you can use.'

It was John's black silk Japanese dressing gown with a picture of a flying crane on the back, a *tsuru*. She had bought it for him because cranes always mate for life and the Japanese regard them as a symbol of fidelity. Alan said, 'Thanks,' and laid it on the bed. It was rather James Bond-ish, and Katie could see that he was tempted to make a comment, maybe even a joke, but he resisted the temptation.

* * *

They ate lasagne and salad at the kitchen table and talked more about Bobby Quilty and how they could incriminate him. Even if they couldn't find anybody who was brave enough to stand up and testify against him in open court, Alan thought that he might be able to bribe one of his gang to pass him enough material evidence to sustain a charge against him.

'I doubt if we'll ever be able to get him for incitement to murder, but false imprisonment . . . I think we might have a reasonable chance there. He's holding Kyna and John in his own house, after all.'

'So long as we can prove that it's his house.'

'Well, yes, there's that. But I know some solicitors in Belfast who may be able to help us untangle who the deeds really belong to. Wellings and McCormack, on Victoria Street. They used to be some of my Lesser Bastards and I have quite a lot of background on them, so I'm pretty sure they'll oblige.'

After they had eaten they went into the living room for a nightcap and talked about their families and their different lives in law enforcement. Barney came and sat close to Katie and put his head in her lap so that she could stroke his ears for him. Katie found Alan very easy company, much easier than her late husband, Paul, had been. As economic times in Ireland had grown harder, Paul had frequently been involved in less than legitimate dealings in the building trade and he had never felt he could tell her the whole truth about what he was up to. Alan was easier than John, too. John had always been so jealous – not just of other men who found Katie attractive and came on to her, but of her career. She had made it clear to him that An Garda Síochána was her vocation and she couldn't give it up to follow him to America, or anywhere, and that had made him deeply resentful.

'Have I misunderstood something here?' John had shouted at her once, in the middle of an argument. 'You belong to me, don't you? Or don't you?'

'Apart from Jesus, there's only one other person I belong to,' Katie had retorted. 'That's myself.'

What made Alan so relaxing to talk to was that he had served as a police inspector, so she didn't have to explain to him the stresses of the job, nor the antagonism she had faced from so many of her male colleagues when she was promoted over their heads. Alan understood police procedure and what they could do in the name of the law and what they couldn't. He also knew what corners were cut, and what rules were bent, and what evidence was fabricated, and how, and why. After talking to him for nearly four hours, and asking him scores of questions, Katie felt confident that if anybody could help her to put Bobby

Quilty out of business, and rescue Kyna and John, then Alan could.

Maybe he was telling the truth about why he had been forced to resign from the PSNI and Bobby Quilty had set him up. On the other hand, maybe he *had* been involved in the drug-dealing. She had no way of knowing for certain, but whatever he had done in the past, she needed him now.

Just after midnight, Alan went to take a shower while Katie watched television with the sound turned down. He came into the living room, his grey hair still wet and sticking up, wrapped in John's dressing gown.

'I'll say goodnight, then,' he told her. 'And thanks a million for putting me up.'

Katie stood up and he came over and gave her a kiss on the cheek. He no longer smelled of black pepper and cinnamon but her own peach shower gel.

'We'll save your John and your Kyna,' he added, and gave her a reassuring smile. 'Sleep well and I'll see you in the morning. I'll make you my famous Ulster egg-in-a-cup if you fancy that for breakfast. Do you have breadcrumbs?'

* * *

It took her a long time to fall off to sleep. The wind had risen even more and she could hear her rotary clothes line rattling in the yard outside. She couldn't stop herself from thinking about John, and what Kyna had meant about his feet being bolted to the bed, and about Kyna, too, because she still hadn't fully recovered from her gunshot wound. It had badly torn her small intestine and she had needed more than seventy centimetres cut out of it.

Three things there are that can never come back, she thought, but the words on that sampler didn't make her feel any less responsible for what had happened. John and Kyna were being held because of her, and she couldn't turn back the clock.

When she slept, she dreamed that she was in her father's house in Monkstown, across the river. It was a large, green-painted

Victorian house with a garden that had long since become tangled and choked with weeds. Inside the house it was gloomy and cold and empty, and there was no sign of her father anywhere. The fire had died in the grate and was nothing but a heap of ashes.

She had opened the front door and was about to leave when she heard whispering upstairs, like someone saying a novena. She went to the bottom of the staircase and looked up. The first-floor landing was in darkness and she was filled with dread at what she might find if she went up there. But the whispering went on and on and she knew that she couldn't go until she found out who was praying.

'Da?' she called out. 'Da, is that you?'

There was no answer, only the whispering, so reluctantly she began to climb the stairs. For every step she went up, it seemed as if two more appeared ahead of her in its place, so it felt as if it took her hours to reach the landing. The doors to all of the bedrooms were closed, except for one, and she thought she glimpsed somebody in white moving around inside. The whispering had stopped and now she could hear only rattling, faint but persistent.

'*Da?*' she said, although she wasn't sure that she had said it out loud.

She seemed to glide across the landing and through the open bedroom door. The bedroom was dimly lit with a silvery luminescence, as if everything in it were radioactive. Beside the window stood a nun, dressed in white, her face hidden by her cowl. She was praying, and it was her rosary beads that were making the rattling sound.

In the middle of the room were two single beds, side by side, and on each bed a body was lying, covered with a white sheet. Katie didn't have to go over and lift up the sheets to know who they were. Her chest tightened in panic and she tried to turn round and leave the room. Every time she turned round, however, she found that she was still facing the same way and that she couldn't find the door.

She circled round and round, but the door was always behind her and the two bodies were always there in front of her. The nun came sliding towards her, her rosary still rattling, and Katie knew that she was going to take away the sheets and show her who was lying underneath. She didn't want to see them. She didn't want proof that they were dead.

'*Three things there are that can never come back,*' the nun whispered and reached out to tug the first sheet away.

Katie screamed, and turned around again, and this time the open door appeared in front of her. Before she could reach it, however, the nun caught her around the ankles and wound her scapular around them, over and over, so that she was powerless to move her legs.

'*Let me go!*' she screamed. '*Let me go!*' – so loudly that she woke herself up.

She wasn't in her father's house at all. She was in her own bed, hot and tearful, and all twisted up in her duvet. Her pillow had dropped on to the floor and her patchwork bedcover had slipped halfway off. The rattling of rosary beads was her clothes line, rattling in the wind.

She heard a tentative knocking at her bedroom door.

Alan said, 'Katie? Katie, what's wrong? Are you all right in there?'

'I'm fine,' she called back. 'I had a bad dream, that's all. You can come in, if you like.'

She reached over and switched on the bedside lamp. Alan came in, wearing John's dressing gown, tightly belted at the waist.

'Boys a dear! The way you were screaming there, that must have been one bad dream and a half. I thought some intruder had broken into the house and you were being murdered – serious.'

Katie dried her tears on the duvet cover and then picked up her pillow and straightened the bedcover. 'I had a dream about John and Kyna. Both of them were dead.'

Alan sat down on the side of the bed and took hold of her hand between both of his. 'I can understand you feeling guilty, Katie – but them being taken like that, it's Bobby Quilty's doing, not yours.'

'But he wouldn't have taken them, would he, if it hadn't been for me?'

'Oh, so you're blaming yourself for being some kind of a jinx, are you?'

'Why shouldn't I? It's true.'

Alan shook his head. 'From what you've told me, you and John only got together in the first place because you saved him from having his throat cut. And whatever you say, Kyna's a cop, and cops know the risks of what they've chosen to do. If anything, Katie, it's you who're keeping them alive right now.'

Katie said nothing. Alan lifted one hand and brushed her damp red hair away from her forehead.

'Come on,' he said. 'It was a nightmare, that's all. I've had worse ones myself, especially during the Troubles. One night I dreamed that the Provos had planted a bomb in my car and my legs were blown off. Can I fetch you anything? Maybe a drop of tea?'

'No thanks, Alan. I'm grand altogether. I just need some sleep.'

He stood up and said, 'Okay, then. But if you have any more dreams like that, just scream before you wake up and I'll chase them away for you, so I will.'

He was halfway to the door when Katie said, 'Stay.'

He stopped, but he didn't turn around. Katie pulled back the duvet and said, 'Stay. Alan. Please. I really need somebody to hug me.'

Now Alan turned. It was difficult to read the expression on his face. It was questioning, but interested, his eyebrows slightly lifted, and there was a sparkle in his eyes, too.

'Do you think it's a good idea?' he asked her.

'I don't need to apply to the District Court for a warrant, do I?' said Katie. 'I just want you to hold me and help me get to sleep.'

She had no idea what this might lead to. Nothing at all, probably. But she simply didn't want to switch off the light and lie there alone for the rest of the night, afraid to go to sleep.

Alan hesitated a split second longer and she was almost tempted to tell him to forget it. But then he came back, and she shifted herself over to give him more room, and he climbed into bed with her. They lay there, face to face, looking into each other's eyes.

'This wasn't what I expected, when I got on the train this morning,' said Alan.

'Me neither,' said Katie. She touched his cheek, where silver prickles of stubble were beginning to grow. There was something about him that made her feel secure and protected. He hadn't spent all evening challenging her or teasing her, like so many men did. He hadn't even flirted with her. He was handsome, too, but in a mature, confident way, as if he didn't need to keep checking himself in the nearest reflective surface to make sure that he still looked the berries.

'I have to tell you that I find you very attractive, Katie,' he told her. 'A fellow could put to sea in those green eyes of yours, and sail away, and never come back.'

'I thought you were a peeler, not a poet,' she teased him.

Alan jostled himself into a more comfortable position and then put his arms around her.

'I'm sorry, I'm a bit sweaty,' she said.

'Jesus.' He smiled. 'Have I had that effect on you already?'

They stared at each other, so close that the tips of their noses were almost touching, and then he kissed her forehead, and her eyelids, and her cheeks, and then her lips. She kissed him back – little friendly pecks at first, with her eyes only half closed, but then deeper, and longer.

As she did so, she felt his penis rising under the thin silk of John's dressing gown. That was when she stopped kissing him and touched his lips with her fingertip and said, 'Now I must get some sleep. It's going to be a long difficult day tomorrow and I don't want to look beat out.'

She gave him one more kiss and then turned herself over, with her back to him, although she reached around and took hold of his wrist and placed his hand against her stomach, so that he was holding her very close. His erection was pressing hard against her bottom, but he made no move to lift her nightdress, and somehow she felt that there was an understanding between them. She took his stiffness as a compliment, that he was doing nothing to hide the fact that she aroused him, but was prepared to wait until she was ready. She was highly stressed, and exhausted, and she had asked him for comfort, and that was what he was giving her, comfort.

She fell asleep after only a few minutes, but she had no more nightmares. She was woken just after five by the hooting of a ship in the estuary and for a moment she thought that John was lying next to her. When she turned her head and saw that it was Alan, however, she felt a sense of both grief and relief. His eyes were closed, but she could see that his pupils were darting from side to side under his eyelids in REM sleep, so he must have been dreaming. Maybe he was dreaming of her, she thought. She snuggled herself in closer to him and took his left hand and cupped it over her breast.

Thirty-two

Celia rang the doorbell three times but nobody answered. The last time, she pressed it and kept it pressed for more than fifteen seconds. Still no answer.

She stood on tiptoe so that she could peer into the living-room windows, but there was no sign of Órla Doherty or either of the children.

That was very queer, because the children were on their summer holidays now, and it was only 8 a.m., which was very early for Órla to take them out anywhere. Even if she *had* taken them out, she would have been sure to have told Celia last week what her plans were. After Celia had finished cleaning the house they always sat down together for a cup of tea and an intimate chat.

What was even queerer, both of the Dohertys' cars were still parked in front of the house – Kevin's Audi estate and Órla's pale blue Ford Focus. Kevin always took his car to work, and if Órla had gone anywhere with the children she must have walked, unless a friend had picked them up.

Still, Celia had her own key so if the Dohertys were out she could at least make a start with the hoovering. Over five years she had been cleaning for them now, so she was almost part of the family.

She let herself in. The house was silent and Celia was immediately struck by the smell. It was only faint, but it was acrid, like the smell of spent fireworks, and the house had never smelled like that before. Maybe Kevin had been setting off some indoor fireworks to celebrate the beginning of the holidays.

She opened the cupboard under the stairs and reached inside for her floral housecoat. As she was lifting out the vacuum cleaner, though, she stopped and listened, and sniffed again, and looked around her. She wasn't used to the house being so quiet because Órla always had the television on, regardless of whether it was *Shortland Street* or *The Doctors* or the RTÉ news. She had the strangest feeling, too, that something wasn't quite right.

It was then that she saw the list pinned to the back of the front door. She went up to it and stared at it. It was Órla's list of things to do – dry-cleaning to collect and birthday cards to buy and bills to be paid. But it was usually stuck on to the fridge, this list. It had *always* been stuck on the fridge. Why had she suddenly decided to pin it up here in the hallway?

She went into the living room. There was something strange in there, too. Two of the armchairs were side by side, on top of the rug, at an awkward angle so that people sitting in them would have been facing away from each other. Órla was always meticulous in the way she arranged the furniture, and she never placed the armchairs on top of the Ashanti rug.

Celia could see herself in the mirror over the fireplace, biting her thumbnail and thinking. She could carry on with her cleaning and leave when she had finished, but where had the Dohertys disappeared to? Órla hadn't even left her a note to say when they might be back.

She went back into the hallway and took down the list. It was then that she saw the jagged splintering in the door panel, and even though she had no idea what might have caused it she knew at once that the Dohertys must be in some kind of trouble. Maybe they had argued and their argument had turned into a fight. She knew from what Órla had told her over tea and biscuits that the Dohertys' marriage hadn't always been the smoothest. Maybe she had left and taken the children with her and Kevin had simply gone off to work.

But why had neither of them taken their cars?

Celia went next door and knocked at Mrs Doody's. It took a long time for Mrs Doody to answer and for a while Celia was worried that she might have disappeared, too. At length, however, she opened the door, cradling a black-and-white miniature schnauzer in her arms. The instant it saw Celia, the schnauzer started barking.

'Corky, will you whisht awhile!' Mrs Doody snapped at him. She had her hair pinned up in a tight grey bun and was wearing a splashy summer dress with huge yellow chrysanthemums all over it. She had an oddly tiny head and a pinched, shrivelled-up face, with black-rimmed spectacles that looked enormous by comparison.

'Sorry to be bothering you, Mrs Doody,' said Celia. 'But have you seen any sign of Kevin and Órla today by any chance?'

Mrs Doody thought about it and then shook her head. 'No, girl, not today. Órla I haven't seen since yesterday morning. She came around to borrow some brown sugar for her barmbrack. Yesterday afternoon I saw Kevin out the window bringing the kids home, but that was all. They were very quiet last night, I have to tell you, and I haven't heard a squeak from them today. Usually I can hear their telly, like, and the kids running up and down the stairs.'

'They're not at home this morning, but look, their cars are still there. And the house . . . I don't know, come and see it for yourself. There's something desperate quare gone on there, I'm sure of it.'

'Let me find my slippers and I'll be with you.'

She disappeared for a few moments and then returned, still carrying her miniature schnauzer, which barked at Celia when it saw her again.

'*Whisht*, Corky, will you? Oh, they tell you when you buy them that they're affectionate, these little fellows, and they are, but they don't tell you that they've more bark than Gougane Barra forest.'

The two of them went next door to the Dohertys' house. Both Mrs Doody and Corky started to sniff suspiciously as soon as they stepped into the hallway. Corky barked once and then started to make an extraordinary squeaking noise in the back of his throat. He wriggled and twisted in Mrs Doody's arms so that she had to drop him on to the floor. He trotted without hesitation into the living room.

'Well, you're right, this is desperate quare,' said Mrs Doody. 'I can't think what that smell puts me in mind of, but it's not the way this house usually smells, and that's for sure. Órla's always squirting that flowery room spray around.'

Celia showed her the splintered door panel. She lifted her huge glasses a little so that she could focus better and then she said, 'Now, then. A bullet's done that, no mistake about it.'

'A bullet? Serious?'

'My uncle used to run Hickey's Bar in Bandon and in the back room there was panelling which the Brits had shot at during the war. The marks you could see on the wall there were the identical spit of these, I'll tell you.'

'Mother of God,' said Celia. 'I know that Kevin and Órla have their fights all right, but I can't see them *shooting* each other. You didn't hear a gun going off, did you?'

'No, I didn't,' said Mrs Doody. 'By the looks of it, though, by the *smell* of it, I'd say that nothing good's happened here.' She reached up to touch the splintered front door, and then she turned around and snapped out, '*Corky!* For the love of all that's holy, will you hold your whisht!'

Corky had started barking again, a high-pitched monotonous yapping, and they could hear him scratching at the floor, too.

'What's that little pesht up to now? *Corky!*'

They went into the living room and saw that Corky had managed to scrabble the red patterned rug to one side and was clawing furiously at the floorboards. Mrs Doody picked him up and tried to stop him barking by holding his jaws together, but he struggled and kicked and jumped down out of her arms again.

Celia went down on one knee and ran the palm of her hand over the floorboards. 'Look here,' she said. 'There's marks here like somebody's pulled the floor up – see, there's holes where the nails were taken out and they've been knocked back in different places.'

There was nothing that either of them could do to stop Corky from barking and scratching, and every now and then he pressed his snout against the cracks in between the floorboards and gave a deep, quivering sniff.

'There's something under there,' said Mrs Doody. 'He can smell it, like. He's not exactly a bloodhound, but he can always tell when I fetch home tripe in my shopping bag.'

'Oh, God,' said Celia. 'You don't think—? Did you see that programme they had on the telly a couple of days back, about that family in Blarney that was found buried under the floorboards? Father and mother and children, too. And dogs.'

'I saw that, yes. There was a piece about it in the *Echo*, too. But that occurred back in the 1920s. Jesus, that was before even *I* was born!'

'I know. But where are the Dohertys?'

'Like you say, they could have had an argument,' said Mrs Doody, although she sounded more than a little apprehensive. 'What's under here, though – it's more likely to be a pigeon that's got itself stuck, don't you think? Or a cat maybe, or a rat.'

Celia hesitated, but then she crouched forward and sniffed at the floorboards herself. Immediately she sat up straight, cupping her hand over her face.

'I can smell something all right. Something *sweet*, like. Sweet but bad, do you know what I mean? Like when you buy a chicken and it's off.'

'Do you have Órla's mobile phone number?' Mrs Doody asked her. 'Why don't you try ringing her? Maybe she and Kevin had a fight, but it's the first day of the holliers, isn't it? Maybe she's just taken the kids out shopping for some summer clothes.'

Celia went out to the hallway to find her purse and came back with her mobile phone. She pressed Órla's number and waited.

After a short while they heard a ringtone. It was muffled, but there was no question where it was coming from – underneath the floorboards. Even Corky stopped barking and listened.

'Call the guards,' said Mrs Doody. Then she stepped back so that she was no longer standing in the centre of the living room, where the rug had been, and crossed herself.

Thirty-three

When she opened her eyes again and reached across the bed, Alan had gone.

She lay there for a while, looking towards the window. The wind that had been blowing most of the night had died down now and it appeared to be quite bright outside, even though it wasn't sunny. She couldn't hear rain, anyway, and that was a blessing.

She thought about Alan. She wasn't sorry that she had invited him into her bed, especially since he had given her all the emotional comfort she had needed, and at the same time had been so restrained. They weren't yet lovers – maybe they never would be, but they were as close now as two acquaintances could be.

She lifted her head from the pillow to check the time. It was nearly ten past eight – later than she had slept in for months – and she felt all the better for it. She wasn't due in to Anglesea Street until lunchtime, when she was supposed to be having a meeting with Assistant Commissioner O'Reilly and Chief Superintendent MacCostagáin about their future strategy for dealing with Bobby Quilty and other cigarette-smugglers.

She hadn't yet thought how she was going to explain to them why her investigations into the killings of Detective Barry and Darragh Murphy were making such slow progress. She would probably tell them that after the fiasco of Operation Trident she was insisting that every piece of evidence against Bobby Quilty was triple-checked – fingerprints, DNA matches, witness reports, phone-taps, everything.

She closed her eyes again for a few seconds, but then she heard the bedroom door click and she opened them again. Alan came in, still wearing John's black silk dressing gown. He was carrying two mugs, one with a picture of Pope John Paul on it, the other with the badge of An Garda Siochána.

'Ah grand, you're awake!' He smiled. 'I made us some coffee. I guessed that you like yours black, no sugar.'

'You don't know me that well, then,' said Katie, sitting up. 'One level spoonful of demerara. You'll find it in the brown glass jar next to the microwave.'

'Your wish is my command, o Detective Superintendent. You outrank me, after all.'

He set down one mug on the bedside table and went back to the kitchen. He returned, stirring her coffee, and sat down on the side of the bed.

'You've given yourself the pope mug,' said Katie.

'You don't have one with the archbishop of Armagh on it, that's why. But I don't think God will strike me down for drinking out of a Catholic vessel. Careful, it's very hot still.'

'I wasn't going to drink it straightaway,' Katie told him. 'I didn't want to have coffee breath when you kissed me.'

Alan looked at her very steadily. This was the moment when he could have said no, this will get far too complicated. But Katie was telling him that she needed him, for the time being at least, or somebody like him. Somebody she could come home to at the end of each increasingly disastrous day. Somebody who would understand what stress she was suffering and support her, and hold her close in the middle of the night.

He leaned forward and kissed her. Then he kissed her again and she kissed him back. She shifted herself further across the bed to make more room for him and turned down the duvet cover. Then she crossed her arms and pulled off her white short-sleeved nightdress. She was large-breasted for a small woman and her breasts swung a little when she lifted it over her head.

Alan stood up and unfastened the tie-belt, letting his dressing gown slide to the floor. He was broad-shouldered and muscular for a man in his early fifties, although his stomach was slightly rounded. The hair on his chest was as grey as the hair on his head and formed a V-shaped pattern, like grey cirrus clouds. His pubic hair was grey, too, and wiry.

He eased himself into the bed next to her. His penis was already stiff and his testicles were wrinkled tight. Katie took hold of the shaft and pressed the ball of her sharp-nailed thumb up against the opening. He was very big, and very hard, and she squeezed him tighter and tighter until his purple glans turned a dark plum colour.

He cleared his throat. 'Have you condoms?' he asked her.

'I'm on the pill,' she told him.

'Better to be safe, you know. Don't want to be sending another one to school.'

Katie had been taking the pill ever since she had accidentally become pregnant to her former neighbour, who had sworn on his life that he had had a vasectomy. She hadn't thought she was likely to have another sexual encounter quite so soon, but she was terrified that she might have another unplanned pregnancy, and she would never consider an abortion. Her mother had died after giving birth to the last of her sisters. She had been warned that there were complications and she should terminate the pregnancy early, but she had refused. *Only God gives life, and only God can take it away.*

Alan kissed her again, on her lips, and then her neck, and took hold of her breast and caressed it, tugging gently at her nipple and rolling it between his fingers until it stiffened. She felt his glans becoming slippery, so she learned back on the pillow and opened her thighs. With a faint, moist click, like the quietest of kisses, the lips of her smooth waxed vulva opened up to reveal how wet she was.

'Oh, Katie, you're such a beautiful, beautiful woman,' Alan breathed. He ran his fingers lightly down her side, all the way to her hip, which made her shiver. Then he slid his finger between her lips and stroked her clitoris so gently that she could barely feel it.

She kept her grip on his penis and guided it between her legs. He was arousing her with his finger-play and it was almost making her delirious, but she wanted him inside her, as deep as he could go.

He entered her and she let out a moan of pleasure that was almost a laugh. He felt enormous, as if he were far too big for her, and she opened her legs as wide as she could so that he could bury himself inside her, right up to that grey wiry hair, and his testicles bobbed against her. The tip of his glans touched the neck of her womb and she jumped, and laughed again.

He felt so different from John. Most of the time John had been sensual and slow, almost dreamy, although he had sometimes been forceful, when he was drunk or he hadn't made love to her for several weeks. Alan was strong and blunt and deliberate and heavy, pushing himself into her again and again, harder and harder each time, as if he were trying to drive her into the mattress. His skin had the smooth dry texture of unpolished marble, so that Katie almost felt as if she were being penetrated by a life-size statue of a man. He made her feel physically helpless, but at work she was always in charge and in a way she found it exciting to be dominated like this.

He was panting now, as if he had been running a half-marathon. Without warning he levered his penis out of her and ejaculated all over her stomach. She was close to reaching a climax herself and she smeared his warm semen around and around, and over her breasts, so that her nipples were stiff and slippery.

Alan lifted himself off her and lay close beside her, quickly and lightly flicking her clitoris with his finger. It was as hard now as a little bird's beak. She felt that tight, dark, shrinking sensation between her legs, tighter and tighter. Then she was shaking and jerking and gasping and she could see stars.

They lay side by side for over twenty minutes, while Katie felt him drying on her stomach. She looked at him closely and he smiled back at her, but she realized that she was searching for some telltale clue in his expression – like a detective rather than a lover. At the moment he had climaxed all over her she had found it erotic, but now she wondered why he had done it. Surely a man's strongest sexual urge was to climax as deeply as he could inside the woman he was making love to – especially since this was their very first time.

Had he wanted to degrade her in some way, maybe without fully realizing it himself? She was a serving detective Superintendent after all, while he was an ex-detective inspector who had been forced to resign under a cloud of suspicion. As he had said, '*You outrank me.*'

Or maybe there was another reason. Maybe he hadn't believed her when she had assured him that she was on the pill. She was only in her late thirties, after all, still young enough to have a baby, and when they were talking the previous evening she had described how she had lost little Seamus and how much she still missed him.

'Your coffee's probably gone cold by now,' Alan told her.

'Ah well, you can make me some fresh, can't you? And what about that Ulster egg-in-a-cup? I need to take a shower.'

'Katie,' said Alan.

She touched his lips with the tip of her finger. 'You don't have to say anything, Alan. Let's just wait and see where this goes. *Three things there are that can never come back*, and that was a fourth.'

* * *

Katie showered and dressed in her light grey suit. By the time she had blown her hair dry and put on her make-up, Alan had showered and dressed, too, in a tattersall country shirt and dark brown chinos.

Katie sat at the kitchen table with her laptop while Alan brewed some fresh coffee and boiled four eggs for their breakfast.

He had shelled the eggs and was mashing them up with butter, salt, pepper and breadcrumbs when Katie's iPhone rang. It was Detective Sergeant Begley.

'What's the craic, Sean?'

'You're not going to believe this, ma'am, but it's Blarney all over again.'

'Blarney? What do you mean?'

291

'There's a family of four's been discovered murdered in a house on Military Road. The father, the mother, and two kids, a boy and a girl. Shot dead, by the look of it, all four of them, and nailed down underneath the floorboards.'

'Holy Mother of God. How long do you think they've been there?'

'Oh, these aren't historic bodies, like. The technical experts have only just taken up the floor and they haven't touched them yet. They're all wrapped up in plastic sheeting. The woman who lives next door saw them yesterday afternoon at about three o'clock, so they must have been killed sometime after that.'

'All right, Sean. I'll be with you directly.'

'The reason I said it's Blarney all over again, ma'am, there's a note with them.'

'Do you have it there with you? Read it to me.'

'It says, "This is to show you that we never forget our own. It was the IRA killed the Langtrys and these are the blood relations of those murderers. The score is settled now at long last. *Quis separabit?*"'

'UDA,' said Katie. 'I can't believe it, after all these years. That's all it says?'

'That's all. And it's been printed on a computer and there's no signature or nothing.'

'*Quis separabit?* That's signature enough, isn't it?'

Quis separabit? – Who Will Separate Us? – that was the motto of the Ulster Defence Association, the Protestant paramilitaries that had fought against the Provisional IRA during the Troubles. They were known to have killed at least 260 people, but they were supposed to have ceased their armed campaign in November 2007. It was common knowledge, though, that some of them still harboured grudges – not only against the Provisional IRA but against others in their own organization.

Alan was standing by the table with a mug of mashed-up eggs in each hand. 'Don't tell me – you have to go.'

'I'm sorry,' said Katie. 'They've found a family murdered, just like the Langtrys were murdered. Shot and buried under the floorboards.'

'Jesus Christ.'

'Well, I don't think He had anything to do with it. More like the UDA.'

'I heard you. You want your breakfast?'

Katie shook her head. 'I haven't much appetite now. Sorry. Maybe you can make them for me some other time.'

'All right. But I'll come into the city with you and start poking around to see what I can find out about Bobby Quilty. That's unless you want me to stay here and take Barney for his walk.'

'No, Jenny will do that for me. I think I've given her enough gossip by way of compensation.'

Alan scraped the eggs into the waste-disposal unit, rinsed out the mugs and put them into the dishwasher. Katie could tell that he wanted to say something to her, but he stayed silent. As she had told him, what had happened that morning could never come back.

Thirty-four

She dropped Alan off at the corner of Merchant's Quay and St Patrick's Street. He leaned across the car to give her a kiss, but two uniformed gardaí were strolling towards them and she placed her hand on his shoulder to keep him away.

'I think we've caused enough of a stir already.' She smiled. 'But call me later and don't get yourself into any trouble. You know yourself what Quilty's people are like.'

'I will, and I won't,' he promised, as he climbed out of the car. Once the gardaí had passed them by, however, he turned around and blew her a kiss.

Katie drove across St Patrick's Bridge and up Summerhill to Military Road. She wasn't at all sure what she felt about Alan. She found him comforting and reassuring and very masculine, but at the same time she wasn't entirely convinced that he was everything that he seemed to be. She wondered if he regarded her as more of a conquest than a companion. Or maybe she was just being hypersensitive, and feeling guilty about John.

Military Road was crowded with vehicles when she arrived. Two vans from the Technical Bureau, four patrol cars, two ambulances and six or seven other cars. She was relieved to see that RTÉ's outside broadcast van hadn't arrived yet.

Detective Sergeant Begley met her at the Dohertys' front gate, along with Detective Dooley. When she went inside the house she saw that Detective Scanlan was in the kitchen, talking to Celia, the Dohertys' cleaner, and Mrs Doody from next door. Clearly she wasn't finding it easy because Mrs Doody was still holding

294

Corky and for all the *whishts awhile, will you*, he wouldn't stop barking.

Katie went into the living room. Bill Phinner was in there, as well as Eithne O'Neill and Tyrone Daley and two other technical experts, all wearing white Tyvek suits and masks. Seven of the oak floorboards in the centre of the room had been prised up and stacked against the wall by the fireplace. In the space under the floor, Katie could see the four bodies, all tightly wrapped up in vinyl sheeting and bound around with silver gaffer tape. The vinyl was transparent enough for her to be able to make out their pale faces and the colour of their clothes, and also the rusty bloodstains around their heads. Not only that, but she could smell the distinctive faecal odour of recent death.

'What's the story, Bill?' she asked him.

'Two adults, a man and a woman, and two children, a boy and a girl. Without taking that plastic off it looks pretty clear they've all been shot in the head. There's bullet fragments in the front-door panel, so that would confirm that a gun was involved.'

'Do we know their names?'

'We won't be able to tell for sure if they're all from the same family until they've been formally identified, but we're assuming for the moment that they are. The Dohertys – Kevin and his wife Órla, Tom and Sibeal. Kevin's an estate agent for Thomas Mahoney's down on South Mall.'

Detective Sergeant Begley said, 'Their cleaning woman found them. Well, actually it was that dog from next door that sniffed them out.'

'Clever dog,' said Katie. 'He should come and work for our canine support unit.'

'I don't think they could stand the noise,' said Detective Sergeant Begley. 'He's been yapping ever since I got here. He's worse than her I married, I'll tell you.'

'We've taken all the pictures we need, ma'am,' said Bill. 'It was washed off, but we've also found blood spatter on the wall here with the infra-red, and some in the hallway, too, by the stairs.

We'll be lifting the bodies out now, but we'll be keeping them parcelled up like this until we get them to the mortuary. You'll be calling the pathologist.'

'Of course, yes. The woman next door – did she not see anybody unusual visiting the house? Didn't she hear anything?'

'She said that the Dohertys were very quiet last night, that's all. She can usually hear their telly. But of course she didn't imagine there was anything wrong. Nothing like this, any road.'

'Come and take a sconce at the door,' said Bill. 'I'd say that it was hit by fragments from a soft-nosed bullet, but only fragments, which could mean that it had passed through something else first – like a human skull, for instance. The blood spatter we found by the stairs would verify that. According to the cleaning woman, there was a shopping list pinned over the door to hide the damage.'

'How often does the cleaner come?'

'Once a week.'

'So if it hadn't been for our doggy friend, the Dohertys may not have been found for days?'

Katie took a close look at the splinters in the front door and then went back into the kitchen to introduce herself to Celia and Mrs Doody. Celia was red-eyed and tearful, and twisting a handkerchief in her hands.

'They were such a lovely family. I'll tell you, Kevin and Órla, they had their arguments sometimes, but they were lovely people. Why would anybody want to do such a terrible thing to them?'

'They had arguments?' asked Katie. 'What about?'

'Oh, nothing serious, like. Maybe they couldn't agree on what colour they were going to paint the bedroom. Or Kevin was getting on her nerves because he was never ready in time for Mass. Or he kept giving Tom those orangey sweeties even though they made the little fellow go stone-hatchet mad.'

'So, Órla used to confide in you?'

'Well, yes, we always had a bit of a chat when I was done

with my cleaning. Only about women's stuff, you know, and family gossip.'

'Thank you, Celia. We'll probably want to talk to you again later. You too, Mrs Doody. In the meantime, I think you can go. We have the sad business of taking out the bodies and I don't think you'll want to witness that.'

Katie went back into the living room. 'Do you have that note?' she asked Detective Dooley.

He handed her a plastic evidence envelope. She read and re-read the message that had been left with the bodies, and as she did so an idea began to form in her mind.

'If the offenders really were UDA, they must have come down from the North especially to do this.'

'They could have been local, though, ma'am, and only signed it *Quis separabit?* to put us off the scent, like.'

'Well, you could be right,' said Katie. 'It just seems a bit too clever for that, that's all. If they were trying to make out that they were UDA, or UFF, but they weren't, I wonder if they wouldn't have simply signed it that way, UDA, or UFF. Like, if I was a murderer and I was trying to make out the Garda had done it, I'd sign it "Garda", not "To Achieve the Highest Level of Personal Protection, Community Commitment and State Security".'

'I'm glad you can remember all that, because that's more than I can,' said Detective Sergeant Begley. 'Mind you, I can't even remember what I had for breakfast.'

It's all right for you, thought Katie. *At least you had some.*

'We'll start knocking on doors along the road, then,' said Detective Sergeant Begley. 'If the old doll next door didn't see or hear nothing, though, I doubt if anybody else did. They keep themselves to themselves around here.'

Katie looked down at the vinyl-wrapped bodies and crossed herself. She just hoped they hadn't suffered. As she turned to leave the room, Tyrone said, 'Oh! By the way, ma'am. We should have had the DNA results back by now on those bloodstains we found in that bedroom on Leitrim Street. I'll call you later so, as soon as I get back to the lab.'

Katie close her eyes for a moment. *John*, she thought. *I haven't abandoned you, don't worry.*

'Thanks a million, Tyrone,' she told him, and stepped outside.

* * *

She had very little to say to the media waiting in the road – only to tell them that four bodies had been found in the house and that they had almost certainly been murdered. She declined to confirm that they were the Doherty family and she didn't mention that they had probably been shot. Neither did she say that a note had been found with the bodies.

'Was this some kind of domestic tragedy?' asked Fionnuala Sweeney from RTÉ. 'I mean, like, the father killing the family and then himself? Or are you looking for somebody else?'

'It wasn't domestic, no. We're looking for a person or persons who might have visited the house sometime yesterday afternoon after three o'clock or later in the evening. If anybody in the locality saw anything suspicious or unusual, or has any other information, obviously we'd be very grateful to hear from them.'

'Who found the bodies?' asked Roisin Magorian from the *Examiner*. 'And can you tell us where exactly in the house they were located?'

'I can't answer that for you just yet, Roisin. I'll be asking the press office to get in touch with you as soon as I can give you more information.'

'Any further thoughts on the other matter we talked about?'

'No, Roisin. Not yet. But I haven't forgotten what you told me.'

Thirty-five

Driving back down to Anglesea Street she kept thinking: *Quis separabit?* The killers hadn't been able to resist taking the credit for what they done and they had made it clear that their revenge had been not only personal but political.

The more Katie thought about the wording of that note and the way it was signed, the clearer her next plan of action took shape in her mind. It wasn't an orthodox plan by any means, but hadn't Alan said that they were faced with a fierce unusual problem – a problem that called for some fierce unorthodox measures?

She was fully aware that she might be placing her entire career in jeopardy, but on the other hand it could be the making of her. Noirin O'Sullivan hadn't been promoted to Garda commissioner by being cautious or indecisive.

The first person she met as she walked along the corridor to her office was Chief Superintendent Denis MacCostagáin, looking even glummer and more preoccupied than usual.

'Ah, Katie. You've been up to Military Road, then? Any ideas?'

'It's a little early to say yet, sir. But believe it or not, there was a note left with the bodies claiming that they were killed in revenge for the Langtry family. It said that the Dohertys were blood relations to the members of the IRA who shot the Langtrys, and that "we never forget". It was signed with the motto of the UDA. *Quis separabit?*'

'Jesus, it's unbelievable. After all these years? Were there any witnesses at all?'

Katie shook her head. 'Not that we've found so far. But I'll be putting óut a media statement later. Look, I'll have to postpone our meeting with Jimmy O'Reilly. Maybe we can rearrange it for tomorrow morning.'

'Well, that suits me,' said Chief Superintendent MacCostagáin. 'I'm up the walls right now, to tell you the truth. It's like I'm personally taking the bang for all these attacks on elderly folks out in the rural community that we've been having lately. For God's sake, it's not my fault we've had to close so many local Garda stations! Then there's these ridiculous water meter protests, and on top of that, how are we going to cope with all these migrants? Bobby Quilty and his cut-price Lucky Strikes are about the last thing on my mind. Do you want to fix up another time with Jimmy or shall I?'

'Don't bother, sir,' said Katie. 'There's a couple of other things I want to talk to him about, so I'll do it myself.'

'Thanks a million. I'll talk to you later so.'

Katie continued to walk along the corridor towards Assistant Commissioner Jimmy O'Reilly's office. As she approached it she saw that the door was already a few centimetres ajar and she could hear voices – quite loud, too, as if they were arguing. She was about to knock when she caught what they were saying and hesitated, and listened.

'You'll be the ruin of me, you know that.' That was definitely Jimmy O'Reilly talking.

'But *Jesus*, Jimmy, you know full well what they'll do to me if I don't—' The rest of that sentence was unclear, but it was a young man's voice. Katie thought that she recognized him, but she couldn't be absolutely sure.

A long pause, and then Jimmy O'Reilly said, 'You know it can't go on like this. You'll have to find a way to stop yourself.'

The young man was almost whining now. 'I *can't*, Jimmy! That's the whole trouble! It's not like giving up the fags or coming off coke. At least with coke it's a physical thing, do you know what I mean, like? You can just stop snorting it. But this is . . .' The voice became indistinct. 'This is like it's inside my brain. No, it's more than that. It's *me*. It's what I live for. Without it, do you know, I might as well be fecking dead and buried.'

Another long pause. Katie was ready to knock when Jimmy O'Reilly walked across the room and she saw his reflection appear in the glass-fronted bookcase that stood against the left-hand wall of his office, quite close to the window. It was a very dark reflection, like a reflection in a pond, because the shelves inside the bookcase were lined with leather-bound volumes of Clarus Press case law. Nonetheless, there was no mistaking him – the curved new-moon shine on the top of his head, and his glasses.

She lifted her hand yet again, but then she saw the young man's reflection appear in the bookcase, too. He crossed the room and stood close beside Jimmy O'Reilly, and from his brushed-up hair and his height she realized now who it was – James Elvin, his senior personal assistant.

'So, come on, tell me,' snapped Jimmy O'Reilly. 'How much?'

'Only three thousand this time. Well, three thousand seven hundred. Three thousand seven hundred and thirty-two.'

Very long silence this time. Katie could see Jimmy O'Reilly turn his back on James Elvin and stare out of the window.

'All right, then,' at long last. 'I'll have it for you by tomorrow morning.'

'No chance of tonight? I can't go back there till I pony up. Can't even put my foot through the door.'

'It wouldn't do you any harm at all to take a night off. It might do you some good.'

'Oh, please, Jimmy. Please!'

'I don't know. I'll see what I can do.'

'Oh, thank you, Jimmy. Thanks a million million. You're my gold-plated angel.'

'Angel? You think? More like your gold-plated handpump.'

It was then that Katie saw Jimmy O'Reilly turn back from the window so that he and James Elvin were facing each other. To her disbelief, they put their arms around each other and embraced. At first it seemed like nothing more than a manly hug, but they remained holding each other closely for almost twenty seconds. Katie couldn't see from their reflections if they were actually kissing, but neither of them spoke. Even after they had eventually parted, they said nothing further, and both of them walked back across the room, so that their reflections disappeared from Katie's sight.

Only two or three times in her career had Katie come across critical evidence by accident. Once she had been investigating the embezzlement of public funds from City Hall and a taxi driver had handed in to the Garda station a briefcase that had been left in the back of his cab. It had contained all the duplicate accounts books of the official against whom she had been trying unsuccessfully to gather evidence for months.

Another time she had been drinking with her husband, Paul, in the Old Oak in Oliver Plunkett Street when a man sitting close behind her had boasted to his companion that he was responsible for beating up a car dealer from Togher who had almost died and would have to spend the rest of his life in a wheelchair.

She could hardly believe what she had just seen and heard in Jimmy O'Reilly's office. If she had arrived a split second earlier she would have heard nothing at all, knocked and walked in. *Perhaps God has been watching me today*, she thought, *and forgiven me for putting John and Kyna in such jeopardy. Or at least granted me the means I've been looking for to set them free.*

She tiptoed hurriedly back about twenty metres down the corridor, then bustled back to Jimmy O'Reilly's door, rapping sharply on it with the gold Claddagh ring on her right ring finger.

'Who is it?' called out Jimmy O'Reilly.

Katie stepped into his office and he said, 'Oh, it's you, Katie,' with all the enthusiasm of a man who has just seen the prospect of hours of tedious deskwork walk in through the door.

James Elvin was gathering up papers on Jimmy O'Reilly's desk and sliding them into a green manila folder. He looked up and grinned boyishly at Katie, as if he were flirting with her, and said, 'DS Maguire! What's the craic with those murders up at St Luke's?'

'We'll know more when Dr Kelley has had the chance to examine the bodies,' Katie told him in a dismissive tone of voice. Then she turned to Jimmy O'Reilly and said, 'I'm sorry, sir, I'll have to call off our meeting about Bobby Quilty. Perhaps we can reschedule it for tomorrow sometime.'

'That's fine by me,' said Jimmy O'Reilly. 'James, what's my diary like for tomorrow?'

'You're in Limerick at eleven o'clock tomorrow morning, sir,' said James. 'Garda Sergeant Mulligan's funeral. Then you have a meeting at two-thirty in the afternoon with Kieran Fitzgerald from the Garda Ombudsman. Then at six-thirty there's that reception for the Cope Foundation.'

'Oh, yes, the slow people.' Jimmy O'Reilly pursed his lips and made a thoughtful sucking sound. 'Sorry, Katie. Looks like we'll have to make it the day after tomorrow. You'll have your hands full anyway, won't you? And I don't think that Bobby Quilty's duty-dodging is exactly a priority, do you?'

'No, sir, you're right,' said Katie. 'We're tight enough as it is for time and money. And that's another thing I need to discuss with you, apart from Operation Trident – my budget.'

Jimmy O'Reilly glanced across at James Elvin and Katie saw the younger man frown, as if to say, *Come on, Jimmy, beat on, will you, the clock's ticking and I need my cash.*

Jimmy O'Reilly squinted at his watch. 'Katie,' he said, 'I'd love to go over your budget with you. Unfortunately some unexpected business has just come up and I have to shoot out to deal with it. Besides, it's going to take us a fair bit of time for you to tell me how much you need, isn't it, and what you can justify?'

'Again, yes, sir, you're absolutely right,' said Katie. All she wanted to do now was to let him go. She wanted to give him no hint at all that she knew the real reason for him needing to leave so urgently – or at least that she had a very strong suspicion.

She even managed to give James Elvin a smile as she left Assistant Commissioner Jimmy O'Reilly's office. Not only did he smile back at her, she could have sworn that he winked.

You just wait, you cheeky young steamer, she thought, still smiling at him. *I'll be giving you something to make you both your eyes blink.*

* * *

As soon as she got back to her own office she closed the door behind her and called Detective O'Mara.

'Bryan – listen to me! Assistant Commissioner O'Reilly is about to leave the station. I want you to follow him for me and see where he goes. That's all. You can take pictures of any address he visits, but be very careful and don't let him see you.'

'Assistant Commissioner O'Reilly? Am I allowed to know the reason for this, ma'am?'

'Let's just say it's security.'

'Security?'

'All right – security and health and safety. And time-and-motion study. And anything else you can think of. Just do it, Bryan, and let me know as soon as you're back.'

'Yes, ma'am.'

Next she called Alan. It took him a long time to answer and when he did it sounded as if he was walking along the pavement by a busy road.

'Alan? How's it going with Bobby Quilty?'

'Fair to middling, I'd say, but I've made some progress. I was just about to ring you and tell you. I kicked off by looking for one of Quilty's fag-sellers and I found one just inside the gate to the Bishop Lucey Park. Skinny wee rat, so he was, only about fourteen years old. He was doing a roaring trade with the lunchtime crowd from that takeaway coffee bar.'

'Can you speak up a bit?' Katie asked him. 'You sound like you're down the bottom of a well.'

'I don't exactly want to be shouting this out in the middle of the street!' said Alan. 'Here – hold on, there's an office doorway I can go into. That's better. So, anyway, I found this skinny kid and I bought two hundred fags off him myself so that I could get chatting with him. I wanted to make sure he was one of Quilty's minions. I don't think he meant to tell me anything much, Quilty had probably warned him not to. But I made out that Bobby and me were best pals from way back, and the next thing I knew the kid was even boasting to me how much money he'd made that morning, and how he'd have to go back to Bobby to get some more stock.'

'So of course you went with him?'

'Well, no, because the last thing I wanted to do was bump into Bobby. Bobby never forgets a face and he never forgets a grudge. But I followed the kid at a distance, all the way to this parking lot on Keeffe Street.'

'I know it, yes. Demolition site, more like.'

'There was a black Nissan Navara parked there, with some hard-looking fellow keeping guard on it. He filled up the kid's bag with cartons of Marlboros and the kid went off again.'

'A black Nissan Navara? That's Bobby Quilty's car all right. Did you make a note of its index number?'

'I did, yes. But it wasn't really necessary. I hung around for about half an hour and then Bobby himself came out of the building opposite with two other thugs and some blowsy-looking woman. Quilty had a few words with the fellow who'd been keeping guard and then they all went back in again.'

'Quilty doesn't own or rent any property on Keeffe Street, so far as I know. But with him you can never be sure. He probably owns half of Cork by now, under different names.'

'I managed to take a couple of pictures, so I'll show you when I see you.'

'Where are you now, Alan?'

'Only a couple of minutes away from you now. Copley Street. I thought I'd drop into that pub opposite and treat myself to a cold one.'

'The Market Tavern. All right. But try not to treat yourself to too many cold ones. I've found out something today purely by chance and I may need you do to a bit more following for me later. Let me know when you get there and I'll come across and tell you all about it.'

'Katie—'

'What?'

'Nothing. It can wait. I'll see you after, okay!'

* * *

Katie put down the phone, although she stood looking at it for a few seconds afterwards, as if she expected it to ring again and God to tell her what to do next. From out of the blue, He had given her some highly compromising information about Assistant Commissioner Jimmy O'Reilly. Could He not reassure her that what she was intending to do with that information wouldn't turn out to be madness – or, worse than that, pointless and ineffective? She didn't think her career could stand another Operation Trident.

She realized that she might have misunderstood completely what Jimmy O'Reilly and James Elvin had been arguing about, and that she might have misinterpreted the shadowy reflections in the bookcase. Yet what she had seen and heard made sense of what Roisin Magorian had suggested to her. More than that, it had given her a key to unlock one of the most difficult and dangerous investigations that she had ever had to deal with.

She went into her toilet to brush her hair and fix her make-up. Her eyes were puffy and she hoped she didn't look as slutty as she felt. At home she always kept two teaspoons in the freezer to pat around her eyes if they were swollen.

No, come on, Green Eyes, she told herself. You're going to win this. And you're not a slut. Everybody needs comfort sometimes, especially when they have the world on their shoulders, like you do, and the lives of two people they really care for depend on them being confident, and brave.

When she came out, Tyrone was waiting for her. He was staring out of the window at the bright, grey day like a young man in a dream.

'Tyrone!' said Katie, and he gave a little start and turned round.

'Sorry, ma'am. I was miles away there. It's that family this morning, the Dohertys. I can't get them out of my mind, like, do you know what I mean?'

'Yes. It's terrible. It's worse than terrible. Mother of God, it's hard enough when one person in a family dies or gets killed. A whole family gets murdered together, I don't know, it's like some kind of Greek tragedy.'

'Well, yeah,' said Tyrone, although she suspected that he didn't know exactly what a Greek tragedy was.

He held up a printout. 'I have the DNA results from Leitrim Street. The stain on the carpet was blood and it also contains traces of flunitrazepam. The DNA matches the hairs you gave us from John Meagher's comb. So he was there, all right. I suppose the question you're asking yourself is where is he now?'

Katie nodded and said, 'Thanks, Tyrone. Much appreciated. I don't think I tell you technical experts often enough how much we rely on you. If it weren't for you, do you know, we'd be still be crawling around the floor with magnifying glasses, like Sherlock Holmes.'

Tyrone's cheeks went pink. 'It's our job, ma'am. But Bill Phinner told me that John Meagher was a friend of yours, like, and so this meant a lot to you, this test.'

'Yes,' said Katie. 'A very close friend. Well – let's hope that he still is.'

After Tyrone had left Katie called Detective Sergeant Begley. 'Sean, that couple of so-called squatters at Leitrim Street. The fellow that called himself Chisel and that mouthy moth of his. Will you bring them in for questioning, the both of them? Take Scanlan with you. Not tonight – very early tomorrow morning will do it. Tyrone's just confirmed that the blood on the bedroom carpet was John Meagher's.'

'I doubt you'll get them to say anything, to be honest with you.'

'I doubt it, too, Sean. In fact, I'm sure of it. But the DNA test is positive evidence that John Meagher was there and I can't just ignore it.'

'Leave it with me, ma'am. I'll have somebody around there fonya-haun and we'll bring them in for breakfast.'

Katie was absolutely sure that neither Chisel nor his girlfriend would answer any questions, which is why she was willing to take the risk of bringing them in. Now that the technicians had come up with a positive DNA result she had to show Chief Superintendent MacCostagáin, and the media, too, that she was taking steps to find out who had abducted John and where he was now. It was the first investigation about which she had pretended to know less than she actually did, rather than more.

Thirty-six

Alan was waiting for her in the Market Tavern across the street. The tavern's walls were bare yellow brick decorated with brewery mirrors and GAA scarves, and the furniture was rustic-style pine. The bar was often packed out, mostly with a young crowd of students, but this was the middle of the afternoon and it was almost empty except for a young couple having a whispered but intense argument in one corner and Alan sitting under a picture of Muhammad Ali knocking out Joe Frazier, with a bottle of Satz in front of him, reading the *Echo*.

He folded up his paper, stood up and kissed her on each cheek. 'What about you?' he said. 'You look like you lost a cent and found a hundred euros.'

'You could say that I'm the victim of a happy accident,' she told him, sitting down. 'Oh – I'll just have an orange juice, thanks.'

She quickly told him what she had seen and overheard outside Jimmy O'Reilly's office. He listened without interrupting her, but then he said, 'Were you ever aware before that this Jimmy O'Reilly might be gay?'

Katie shook her head. 'He was married before, but his wife left him for some store manager from Dunne's, I think. I never really thought about it. I always assumed it was because he was such a misery-guts.'

'Well, he might well be dancing at both ends of the ballroom, you never know. It certainly sounds like this young man is cadging money off him for some reason. Blackmail would seem the most likely. Maybe he's found out that Jimmy O'Reilly is

309

the father he never knew, or that he's been fiddling the Southern Region's performance records. But there could be any number of reasons.'

'Of course,' said Katie, 'and I'm not counting eggs before they're laid. I have O'Mara following him right now to see where he goes to get the money. It may be the bank, in which case I'll have to think again. But Roisin Magorian definitely gave me the impression that he was being funded by somebody shady and that maybe that somebody shady was demanding more from him than compound interest.'

'I never had you for such a theorist.' Alan smiled.

'I'm not, Alan. Not as a rule. But I'm looking for any way at all to rescue John and Kyna, and so long as there's still a mole in the station I daren't do anything official. I don't want to set up a raid on Quilty's house only to find they've been spirited away, the two of them, or that they're dead already.'

Alan nodded. He traced a pattern on the tabletop with his finger for a moment, like a butterfly, around and around. Then he said, 'I'm going to ask you a favour. I'm thinking of taking a look at that premises on Keeffe Street.'

'What do you mean by "taking a look"? You mean "breaking in and snooping around"?'

'I mean paying a visit after dark without the owner's knowledge or permission, yes. I'm personally interested in anything that might connect Quilty to drug-trafficking, or to his financing of the Authentic IRA, but of course if I can find anything else incriminating – anything relating to John and Kyna – I'll let you know at once.'

'And if you're caught at it?'

'That's the reason I'm asking you a favour. If I'm caught at it, and arrested, you can make sure that it's filed and quietly forgotten.'

'What if it's Bobby Quilty or one of his scumbags who catches you?'

'Katie – I won't be caught. I'll go in there, I'll search the place, I'll leave. That's all. It shouldn't take me longer than a half-hour or so. Nobody will ever know that I've been there. But if I can find evidence that will help us to bring down Bobby Quilty for good and all—'

'No, Alan,' said Katie. 'I can't let you do it. It's way, way too dangerous. Not just for you, but for John and Kyna, too. Don't think that plenty of people haven't seen us together, you and me. If Quilty catches you there, or finds afterwards out that you've been poking around there, he's going to blame me for it.'

Alan puffed out his cheeks and made a soft popping noise in resignation. 'Very well. This is your manor, after all, which is why I needed to ask your permission in the first place.'

'It's not that I don't want you to do it,' said Katie, reaching across the table and taking hold of his hand. 'But at the moment it's still too risky. Let's take it one step at a time. Softly softly, catchee whatever.'

'Not a bother,' said Alan, taking his hand away. 'I understand exactly where you're coming from.' He turned sideways in his chair and crossed his legs and looked towards the bar, making no secret of the fact that he was put out.

'Alan—' Katie began, but then she thought: *Don't say it, don't go there. You may be wrong and you need Alan right now. If you tell him what you really think – that he's far more interested in clearing his own name than he is in saving John and Kyna – you could well be utterly unjust and he may refuse to work with you any more.*

'Apart from that,' she said, trying to sound conciliatory, 'I want you to follow James Elvin when he leaves the station tonight. See where he heads off to. If I understood their conversation correctly, he's going to go somewhere and gamble. He might even come in here. They have Texas Hold 'Em nights every Wednesday. My guess, though, is The Bank at Clarke's Bridge, or the Diamond Club on Father Mathew Street.'

'Okay, I'll do that,' said Alan. 'What time does this James Elvin usually finish?'

'Five-thirty, give or take, unless Jimmy O'Reilly wants him to stay on for anything special. If you wait in reception you'll be able to see him leave the station and follow him from there.'

'Does he have a car? Supposing he drives off? What then?'

'I don't think that's likely, because it's a pig to park near either of those gaming clubs and they're only a five-minute walk away.'

'Okay. Grand. I'll keep in touch with you and let you know if and when he goes into any gaming clubs. I'll tell you what I'll do, though. I'll stay here in the city tonight.'

'You left your bag at my house. What will you do for a change of clothes? And your razor and toothbrush?'

'Marks and Spencer's. I'll manage.'

'Is it something I said? We don't have to sleep together if you don't want to. You're welcome to use the spare bedroom.'

'No, no, Katie. It's nothing like that. I just think you may be right. Let's take one step at a time. Softly, softly and all that.'

'I've upset you.'

'No, you haven't. We're grown-ups, aren't we? Not only that, we're police officers. At least you are.'

There was a long uncomfortable silence between them.

'Would you be wanting any more drinks there?' the barman called over.

'No, we're grand, thanks,' said Alan. 'I'm on duty tonight, any road.'

* * *

She had only been back at her desk for five minutes before Detective O'Mara knocked at her door.

'He didn't see me,' he said, a little out of breath. 'I don't think he saw *nobody*, to tell you the God's honest truth, the way he was pushing people off the pavements.'

'So where did he go?'

'I was hard put to keep up with him, I can tell you. And he was wearing this maroony jacket which I never saw him wear before, and a grey hat pulled down over his eyes. If I hadn't have known it was him I wouldn't have known it was him.'

'So . . . where did he go?'

'Over the Trinity Bridge and then up Morrison's Quay.'

'Don't tell me. He went up to Keeffe Street.'

Detective O'Mara looked decidedly peeved, as if to say why the feck did you send me chasing out after Jimmy O'Reilly on a humid afternoon like this when you already knew where was going?

'That's right,' he said. 'Keeffe Street. Like there's a tatty old office building on the left-hand side opposite the car park and he went inside. I didn't follow him in, but I saw him at one of the upstairs windows for a moment, with his hat still on. He came out again – ooh, no more than ten minutes later – and then he came straight back here.'

'Was he carrying anything? A bag, or a briefcase?'

'A plastic shopping bag in his jacket pocket when he was on his way there, but he was carrying it on the way back like it had something in it, though I couldn't see what it was.'

'Thanks, Bryan. That was really good work.'

Detective O'Mara hesitated for a moment, then he said, 'Aren't you going to tell me what this is all about? Assistant Commissioner O'Reilly walks to Keeffe Street dressed up like some busker and comes back again carrying a bag full of something.'

Katie smiled at him. 'I'll tell you as soon as I can, Bryan. But it's like you've come running into the room with another piece of the jigsaw that I've been missing. Only two or three more pieces to go and it'll be finished.'

'Okay, ma'am, if you say so.'

* * *

It was nearly 6 p.m. before Alan rang her.

'I nearly missed him. I had to go to the jakes and when I came out he was just going out through the front door. But I'm after him now. He's on foot all right. He stopped by the car park and I thought he was going to go in, but he was only chatting to somebody there. Now he's on the move again.'

'Thanks, Alan. Ring me as soon as he gets to wherever he's going.'

'No problem.'

She closed the folder on the desk in front of her and stood up. It would be a good idea if she went to the canteen for a coffee and a sandwich because she had a feeling she would be working late tonight. She had nearly made it to the door when her phone warbled again.

'DS Maguire? It's Dr Kelley.'

'Oh – Dr Kelley. How are you? How's it going?'

'Slow. We've removed the plastic sheeting from all four victims now. I just wanted to tell you that one of Kevin Doherty's brothers has come in to identify them. It's the whole Doherty family all right – Kevin and his wife Órla, née Cronin, and their two children Thomas and Sibeal. All four of them died from massive gunshot trauma to the head.'

'Dear God in heaven,' said Katie.

'I have two technical experts working with me now. We won't have any clear results for several days, I shouldn't think, but they're trying to recreate the crime scene from the angle of the bullet wounds and the blood spatter on their clothes. It looks as if they were very close to each other when they were shot and that they were probably kneeling. That's all I can really tell you at the moment, except that they were all shot with .38 calibre hollow-cavity bullets.'

'That fits in with the damage on the front door,' said Katie.

'Exactly. And as soon as the technicians can check the striations on the bullets, what's left of them, we'll know for sure how many weapons were involved.'

'I'll try to come by tomorrow morning and take a look for myself,' Katie told her. 'Meanwhile, thanks a million.'

She went to the canteen and bought herself a latte and a chicken salad sandwich. She had taken only two bites before Alan rang her again.

'Katie? You were dead on. The Diamond Club on Father Mathew Street, only two doors up from the Gospel Hall. I tried to follow him inside but there was a doorman who wouldn't let me in unless I became a member. Well – when I say "doorman", I mean muscle-bound Neanderthal in a dinner jacket. He was more than willing to sign me up on the spot, but I thought I'd better ring you first. Your wee man James might have seen us together at the station, so I didn't want to go inside there and have him recognize me, in case it messed up whatever it is you're up to.'

'That's fantastic, Alan, thank you. He probably wouldn't know who you were, but it's better to be safe. Listen – do you think you can just keep an eye on the place for me, maybe for half an hour or so, just to check if he leaves? I'm going to go in after him myself.'

'You're codding me, aren't you? He's going to know you the moment you walk in through the door.'

'Trust me, he won't.'

'Okay, then, if you say so. There's a bus shelter right opposite Father Mathew Street. I'll sit there and read my paper and look as if I'm waiting for a bus.'

'Alan,' said Katie. She was conscious that she was treating him like one of her own team of detectives and she didn't want him to feel that she was demeaning him. 'Thanks a million for this. I mean it. It's just that I can't trust anybody else but you. Not at the moment.'

'Katie, don't bother yourself. Anything that helps us nail the Big Feller.'

Katie called for a taxi and then finished her coffee in a series of gulps even though it was still too hot. She left the rest of her sandwich. She had intended to eat it only as a precaution in case she felt hungry later.

Normally she would have asked a garda to drive her, but she didn't want anybody in the station to know where she was going – not that it would have given them any indication of what her plans were. God or Fate had given her a precious lead in saving John and Kyna, and she wasn't going to compromise it in any way.

A red taxi from Sun Cabs was waiting for her outside as she left the station. She could have walked to St Patrick's Street in less than the ten minutes it took drive there, but the early evening was still humid and she didn't want to end up flustered and hot.

The taxi dropped her off outside the Brown Thomas department store. Inside it was all bright lights and the smell of perfume. She went up the escalator to the first floor, to women's designer fashions. A thin middle-aged sales assistant came gliding out to meet her with a beatific smile and her hands clasped together and said, 'Madam? Is there anything in particular you're looking for?'

The sales assistant looked so saintly that Katie almost felt she could have said 'redemption'. Instead, she frowned at the rails of designer dresses all around her and said, 'Something that's eye-catching, do you know what I mean? And sexy, and a little too young for me.'

'Eye-catching?' said the sales assistant. 'I see. Did you have any preference as to style or colour?

'Red, I think. Red would be perfect. And short. And maybe off-the-shoulder. Something that shouts out at you. Something that says "Look at me, I'm out for a bit of fun."'

The sales assistant blinked at her, but Katie said, 'Don't worry about it. It's only for a laugh. We're having a bit of a hen party, that's all.'

'I see. Well, why don't you come and take a look at some of the Carven dresses? Some of them are very eye-catching. And, ah, *fun.*'

It took Katie less than five minutes to choose a scarlet taffeta mini-dress. It was very short and swirly, and cut on a diagonal so that the left shoulder was bare.

'It certainly shouts out, doesn't it?' said the sales assistant when Katie came out of the changing room and did a twirl in front of the mirror. 'Not too young for you, though. In fact, I'd say it makes you look even younger.'

The dress was priced at 390 euros, but Katie intended to bring it back for a refund the next day, when she had finished with it. Once she had paid the sales assistant, she went back down to the shoe department on the ground floor and bought herself a pair of red Kurt Geiger stilettos to match. They were tagged at 120 euros, but she thought she might keep them afterwards because they would go with her own red velvet dress. She could always put them down to expenses: 'specialist footwear for undercover operation'.

She checked her watch. She had taken twenty-five minutes already and she didn't want to keep Alan waiting at that bus stop for too much longer. She bought a blonde urchin-style wig for 45 euros and then carried all of her bags into the ladies' toilet, locked herself into a cubicle, and changed. In the next cubicle she could hear a woman quietly crying and normally she would have asked her what was wrong, but she had no time.

She had entered the store a businesslike woman with dark red hair and a pale grey suit. By the time she emerged on to St Patrick's Street, she was an exhibitionist blonde in a provocative scarlet dress who looked ready to party. She hadn't yet changed her shoes, though. It would be quicker to walk to South Mall where Alan was waiting for her, rather than take a taxi, and she wasn't going to try to teeter there on six-inch stilettos. On her way down Winthrop Street several young men turned round to look at her and she was given two or three appreciative whistles. One even called out, 'Hey, darling! Fancy coming to the Voodoo Rooms with me, do you?'

Oh, yes, she thought. *I can imagine what your friends would say if you brought a detective superintendent into one of Cork's ravingest night clubs.*

As she turned into South Mall, Katie could see Alan sitting in the glass bus shelter He was holding up his folded copy of the *Echo* with a pen in his hand, as if he were trying to do the crossword, but she could see that he had his eye on Father Mathew Street across the road.

She put on her gold-framed, pink-lensed sunglasses and sat down right next to him. He glanced at up at her, but then went back to his crossword.

'What's the craic, sweetheart?' she asked him, in a throaty voice.

He looked up and stared at her, and then he said, 'Jesus! Katie! I thought I was being accosted there! I was just about to tell you that I couldn't afford you!'

He couldn't stop staring at her, shaking his head. 'Well, you're a fine beour now, no question about it! If you hadn't opened your mouth I could have sat here beside you for the rest of the evening and I wouldn't have recognized you.'

'That's the point,' said Katie. 'I'm going to go into that Diamond Club now and see what I can pick up about young James Elvin. This must be the first undercover job I've done in seven years.'

'So, what can I do?'

'There's nothing much more you can do, Alan, not until tomorrow. Then we'll see how this all starts to come together. *If* it comes together. I have my fingers crossed that certain people will act to type, but as you know yourself, they don't always do that.'

'Oh, I know that fine rightly, I can tell you. I'll go and book myself a room at Jury's, then. Do you want me to take all those messages for you?'

'You can still stay the night at home with me, Alan. We don't have to – you know.'

Alan shoved his newspaper into his jacket pocket and bent over to pick up Katie's Brown Thomas shopping bags. 'No, I think it's better if I don't. Not that I don't think you're stunning, not at all. You know I do. And not that I don't want to. But sometimes I think two people can meet and be attracted to each other, strongly attracted, but they're not right for each other. All they'll ever do is end up hurting each other for no real reason at all.'

Katie was taking off her flat work shoes. She dropped them into one of the shopping bags and said, 'Is that what happened with you and your wife – what was her name?'

'Alison, yes. More or less. We nearly tore each other to shreds. I wouldn't want to go through anything like that again, Katie.'

'Is that what you think? That we'd tear each other to shreds?'

'No, not really. I'm just being wary, that's all. Once bitten.'

Katie said nothing. She hadn't been expecting to have a long-term relationship with Alan, but she thought it might have turned out to be more than just a one-night stand. It was clear, though, that he was afraid of committing himself. Perhaps that accounted for his last-second withdrawal when they had made love.

She had a suspicion, though, that there was more to it than that. Maybe he wouldn't fully feel like a real man again until he had harpooned his Moby-Dick. Bobby Quilty had destroyed him and he needed to destroy Bobby Quilty in return, more than anything else.

'I'll ring you after, anyway,' she told him. 'Maybe I'll drop into Jury's, if it's not too late, and we can have a drink in the bar.'

They stood up and he kissed her. She touched his prickly cheek with her fingertips and looked into his eyes to see if she could read what he was really thinking, but they seemed clouded, like one of those grey misty days over the estuary when she could never be sure which was the land and which was the sea.

* * *

Katie crossed the road. Father Mathew Street was narrow and dark and damp-smelling, with high buildings on either side. The Diamond Club was a few doors short of halfway down it, with a purple neon diamond sign over the entrance, flickering intermittently. Inside the front door there was a small purple-carpeted foyer, with a reception desk and a potted palm, where the dinner-jacketed Neanderthal was waiting with his hands cupped over his genitals. He smelled strongly of Aramis aftershave.

'Your boss in?' Katie asked him.

'Might be. Who wants to know?'

'I'm looking for a job, like, that's all.'

'A job is it? What as?'

'Blackjack dealer. I used to work at the Gold Rush on MacCurtain Street, but I don't know, I was fair fried there after a while.'

The doorman looked up and down the street and then said, 'Okay,' and picked up the phone on his desk. 'Mister Kerrigan? I have a girl down here says she's a blackjack dealer looking for a job. Yeah. No. Yeah. Well, put it like this, you wouldn't kick her out of bed for eating Taytos. Okay, then. Yeah.'

He put down the phone and said, 'You can go on up. Mister Kerrigan's tied up with a bit of business at the moment, like, but he shouldn't keep you longer than ten or fifteen minutes, so he says. He says that you can have a drink on the house while you're waiting.'

'What, and some Taytos to go with it?'

'He didn't say nothing about that. Just a drink.'

Katie decided that it wasn't worth trying to explain that she had only been joking. She climbed the narrow staircase at the back of the reception area. At the top there was a small landing and a doorway covered with a curtain of purple and green glass beads. She rattled her way through them and found herself in a long, low, purple-carpeted room with purple Tiffany lamps hanging from the ceiling. All down the right-hand side there were card tables with purple baize tops, and gilt-painted chairs, and in the centre there were two blackjack tables, with a roulette table at the very far end.

On the left-hand side there was a bar with a short fat barman in a white dinner jacket standing behind it. He was throwing dry-roasted peanuts up in the air and trying to catch them in his mouth, ducking his head from side to side like a performing seal.

It was early yet, so the club was almost empty. Four men were playing poker, while another six or seven were gathered around the roulette table, along with three bored-looking girls in low-cut purple dresses. The female dealer had piled-up black hair, Amy Winehouse style, and was wearing a tight purple satin blouse. Standing between two of the girls, his face in profile, was James Elvin. He had loosened his tie and his forehead was shiny with sweat. One or two of the other men looked around when Katie walked into the club, but James Elvin's attention remained fixed on the roulette layout.

The ball clattered to a stop and the dealer announced, 'Red, twelve.'

James Elvin said nothing, but raised his fist to his mouth and bit at his knuckles. One of the other men let out a little whoop.

Kaie went up to the bar. As she did so, the barman missed the last peanut he had been trying to catch and it bounced across the bar.

'*Shite*,' he said, then, 'Sorry about that, girl. How's it going there?' He had a cast in his eye so that it was difficult for Katie to tell if he was looking at her directly or not. On his upper lip he had a thin black moustache of the type that Katie's husband, Paul, used to call a 'thirsty eyebrow'. His elasticated purple bow tie was so greasy it was almost black.

'What can I be getting for you?'

'Vodka tonic, if you don't mind, boy,' said Katie, in a high Mayfield whine. She knew that, like several other casinos in Cork, the Diamond Club didn't have a liquor licence, but the barman took a large bottle of Smirnoff from the neon-lit shelf behind him and poured out a large glass for her, topping it up with Tesco tonic water and a tired slice of lime.

'This your first time?' he asked her, as she climbed up on to a barstool, crossed her legs and tugged up the hem of her dress. 'Haven't seen you in here before, have I?'

'I thought I'd try it out, like,' she told him, perching her sunglasses on top of her wig. 'I was fair bored out of my mind at The Bank and the Gold Rush, do you know what I mean? Same old faces every night.'

'Well, you have your regulars here, of course,' said the barman. 'But there's a lively crowd in later most nights, and at weekends.'

Katie looked around. 'Yes, I like it. It has what-do-you-call-it, you know? Atmosphere.'

'Just as well, right, or we couldn't fecking breathe, could we?' said the barman.

God spare me, thought Katie, *a comedian*. 'What's your name?' she asked him.

'Bertie, that's my real name. Bertie. But everybody calls me Tache. On account of my 'tache, like.'

'Good to know you, Bertie. My name's Nessa.'

'Good to know you, too, Nessa. What do you do, then, Nessa, or are you a woman of leisure?'

'I wish. I'm working at the Clarion at the moment. Receptionist, like. Well, I have to make ends meet, do you know what I mean?

My husband and I split up about six months ago and he's not exactly forthcoming with the maintenance.'

'Sorry to hear that, Nessa,' said Tache. 'Suppose you're looking to supplement your income, then, playing the tables?'

'That – and looking for some rich and handsome feller to take care of me for the rest of my life.'

Tache swivelled his eyes around the club and then shook his head. 'Nobody of that description in yet, girl. You'll have to wait for the late, late crowd. There's a car dealer comes in around eleven most nights, Paddy McGuigan. You might take a fancy to him.'

I doubt it, thought Katie. *When I was a detective sergeant, I arrested Paddy McGuigan for cutting and shutting insurance write-offs.*

She nodded in the direction of the roulette table. 'That fair-haired feen there, between them two girls. He's a good-looking feller.'

Tache let out a raspberry-blurt of amusement. Then he beckoned Katie to lean closer to the bar so that he could speak to her confidentially.

'There's two reasons why he wouldn't suit you, pet. One is, he *always* loses, big-time. He comes in every night, but when he leaves he's hundreds of yoyos down – thousands, sometimes. I'll say this for him, though, he's always back next day with all the grade he needs to settle up. I can't tell you where he gets it from, but he doesn't get it from playing roulette, I know that much.'

'Well, he must have money, then,' said Katie. 'I don't mind a loser so long as he's a rich loser.'

'Yeah, but the second reason he wouldn't suit you is because he's gay as Bogley.'

'You're codding me, aren't you? Him? He doesn't look it.'

'Oh, take my word for it,' said Tache. 'He's a corned-beef inspector, him, no question about it. Comes in here with some twinks some nights and they can't keep their hands off of each other. I've even caught him shifting some feller in the jacks.'

'What a waste.'

'You're not the first girl who's said that and you probably won't be the last. I'm surprised Mr Kerrigan tolerates him sometimes, especially after he's had a few drinks, like, and starts acting like a right batty boy. I don't know what he does for a living but he has friends in high places, I'd say, and that's why Mr Kerrigan never complains to him, not ever.'

'Oh, well,' said Katie. 'The Lord works in mysterious ways.'

'How's your drink?' Tache asked her. 'Like a top-up, would you?'

'No, you're all right,' Katie told him, although a second drink probably wouldn't have affected her. Apart from the tonic being flat, she could tell that the vodka was watered down.

'Now that auld feller right opposite your man, he's minted,' Tache was saying, although Katie was watching James Elvin so intently that she was hardly listening to him. The roulette ball had clattered again and the dealer had called the winning number, and again he was gnawing at his knuckles.

'. . . not only that, he's always on a winning streak. Talk about rubbing fat into a fat pig's arse. I asked him once why he comes here every night, because he doesn't need the money. He said he tries to stay away from the club but his feet always bring him here. Like he has club feet. Do you get it? Like he has—'

'Sorry?' said Katie.

Tache was about to start telling her again when a door opened next to the roulette table and cigarette smoke billowed out. Two men appeared, both of them smoking, but they put their cigarettes into their mouths to shake hands.

One of the men was tall and skinny, with a high shock of wavy red hair that was turning white at the sides. He was wearing a cream suit with wide padded shoulders which must have been at least fifteen years old. She assumed that this was Fintan Kerrigan, who owned the Diamond Club – or managed it, anyway. The other man, in his familiar pale green linen jacket, was Bobby Quilty.

Katie stayed on her barstool, but lowered her pink-lensed sunglasses.

'How about some peanuts?' Tache suggested. 'I have the dry-roasted or the chilli-flavoured.'

'No, you're all right,' she told him. She could see Bobby Quilty having a last few words with Fintan Kerrigan. When they had finished Bobby Quilty raised one hand in salute and walked away, past the roulette table. He stopped, though, when he reached James Elvin. He said something, and James Elvin said something back, and Katie wished desperately that she could lip-read.

Before he walked on, though, Bobby Quilty put his arm around James Elvin's shoulders and gave him a squeeze, like a proud father with his bar-of-gold, or a GAA football manager with his favourite player.

He crossed over to the bar and said loudly, 'What about you, Tache? How's your belly off for wrinkles?'

'Oh, I'm grand altogether, thanks, Big Feller,' said Tache. 'Do you fancy a scoop before you go?'

Bobby Quilty was standing next to Katie now, so close that she could smell him. Cigarette smoke was still curling out of his nostrils as if he were a dragon.

'Well, now, here's an improvement on your usual floozies,' he said, grinning at her, and more smoke leaked out from between his teeth.

Katie said nothing, but Tache said, 'Bobby, this is Nessa. She's bored of The Bank so she's dropped in here to give us a try-out. It's dead right now of course, but I told her we're always buzzing later on.'

'Fierce pity I can't stay,' said Bobby Quilty, angling his head to one side and making no attempt to hide the fact that he was trying to look up Katie's dress. 'Otherwise I'd say you're pulled.'

Still Katie didn't speak. Bobby Quilty continued to stare at her as if he was beginning to suspect that he might have met her before, but couldn't put his finger on where exactly, or when.

'Cat got your tongue, Nessa?' he asked her. 'It's not every day I pay a woman a compliment like that.'

Katie felt her chest tighten. She had her gun in her purse, along with her make-up bag, but she still felt threatened. It was Bobby

Quilty's sheer physical grossness that was so intimidating, as well as his obvious belief that he could say and do whatever he liked to anybody. She was reminded of what she had read in school about the Roman emperor Caligula, who had told his dinner guests that he could have any of them killed at a moment's notice for no reason except that he felt like it.

'So, what do you want me to say?' she replied, exaggerating the Mayfield whine that she had adopted when she first started talking to Tache.

He narrowed his eyes. 'Are you *sure* we don't know each other?' he asked her.

'I think I'd remember you, boy,' said Katie. 'You're not exactly Mister Missable, are you?'

Long pause, then, 'Take off them shades,' said Bobby Quilty.

'Oh, I will, yeah.'

'Take them off. Let's take a look at you proper-like.'

He reached out as if he were going to take them off himself, but Katie was quicker. She seized his wrist and gripped it very tight, digging the ball of her thumb deep into his tendons.

There was a moment of high tension between them. Bobby Quilty tried to force his hand nearer to her face but she wouldn't let him. He didn't speak, but she could almost hear him thinking: *How come this floozy's so quick to react, and so fecking strong?*

He half lifted his left hand and for a split second Katie was afraid that he was going to try to slap her. Just then, however, the bead curtain rattled and a grey-haired man in a brown jacket came through.

'Boss?' he said. 'I have the car outside, but I'm blocking up the street and the guards have just told me to move it.'

'All right, coming,' said Bobby Quilty. He stopped pushing and Katie released her grip on his wrist. He continued to stare at her, though, as if he could penetrate her sunglasses with X-ray vision to see what she looked like without them.

'I'm sure I fecking know you,' he said.

'Maybe you do and maybe you don't,' said Katie.

Bobby Quilty stared at her a moment longer and then went stamping off, crashing his way through the bead curtain to follow his driver downstairs.

'Good luck to you so, Big Feller!' called Tache. Then he turned to Katie and said, 'What in the name of Jesus was all *that* about? I hope you don't have that effect on *all* the fellers who come in here!'

It was then that Fintan Kerrigan came over to the bar and said, 'You're the young lady who's looking for a job, right?'

Tache looked baffled, but Katie slipped off her barstool and said, 'Thanks for the drink, Tache, and for all the gossip,' and followed Fintan Kerrigan into his office.

Thirty-seven

Her interview for the job of blackjack dealer lasted less than five minutes, as she had known it would, because whatever Fintan Kerrigan was going to offer her as a salary, she was going to tell him it wasn't enough.

'You'll have all your tips, too, though,' said Fintan Kerrigan, lighting up another cigarette and leaning back in his black leather chair. 'Good-looking girl like you, Nessa, you should make at least double what I'll be paying you. On a good night, a whole heap more.'

'Supposing it's a real quiet night, like tonight? Then what?'

'It's early yet. The place will be black later on.'

'That's what Tache said. But I don't know. And you say that I'll have to wear purple? I've never been keen on purple.'

'All my girls wear purple, It's the Diamond Club colour.'

'I'll have to think about it,' said Katie. 'Purple, you know. It doesn't suit me at all. Reminds me of funerals, like, do you know what I mean?'

Fintan Kerrigan sat back with the smoke fiddling upwards from his cigarette. After a while he said, 'You don't really want this job, do you?'

'What do you mean?'

'It's that Denny from The Bank, isn'it? He sent you here to find out how much I'm paying my dealers these days.'

'No, he didn't.'

'Oh yes he fecking did. What kind of a gom do you think I am? Go on, away with you. And I'll have ten euros off of you for the drink.'

Katie stood up, opened her purse, and tossed two five-euro notes on to his desk. 'Desperate the price of water these days, isn't it?' she said.

* * *

She met Alan afterwards in the bar of Jury's hotel. She thought that he was looking jaded, but she didn't feel tired at all. Maybe it was the stimulating effect of the dress she was wearing, and her new stilettos, and her swept-forward blonde wig. In the past three hours she had received more compliments and appreciative looks than she had in the past three months. Maybe blondes really did have more fun, especially if they wore very short red dresses.

'I'm not at all surprised that Bobby Quilty didn't recognize you,' Alan told her, pouring a Satz into his glass. 'I can hardly recognize you myself, for God's sake.'

'I'm fierce glad that he didn't,' said Katie. 'That could have wrecked everything. I might be adding two and two together and making five and a half, but I think I have more than enough evidence now that either James Elvin or Jimmy O'Reilly himself has been tipping off Bobby Quilty. It could be the both of them.'

'It looks that way, I agree with you,' said Alan. 'But even if they have, what do you plan to do about it? If you blow the whistle on them now, they'll just deny it. And don't tell me that Quilty has been lending O'Reilly cash that you can trace. If you hadn't seen and overheard O'Reilly and Elvin the way you did, you never would have guessed what was going on, would you? And like you said yourself, it's still possible that you might have misinterpreted what they were talking about and what they looked like they were doing.'

'I know,' said Katie. 'But I'm sure I didn't, and I'm sure that I can prove it. Jimmy O'Reilly's days are numbered, you mark my words. Not only that, I think I can nail Bobby Quilty at the same time.'

'So what do you have in mind?' Alan asked her. 'I know how worried you are about John and Kyna, but you're not rushing things here, are you? If you're going to pull in Bobby Quilty, your evidence has to be watertight, one hundred and ninety per cent, or else his lawyers will make mincemeat out of you – and I'm speaking from bitter experience.'

'You told me yourself that Bobby Quilty knows almost everybody in the North. I assume that includes almost all of the IRA and all of the the loyalist paramilitaries, too.'

'Of course he does. As you rightly know yourself, he was a Provo until they laid down their guns – or laid them down officially, anyway. Then he got himself involved with the Real IRA but he fell out with them about who was in charge of what, particularly the finances. That's when he suddenly discovered that he could carry on the cause but make a heap of money for himself while he was doing it. Hence the Authentic IRA.'

Alan took a sip of his lager and then he said, 'Believe me, Katie, I wouldn't say he knows *almost* all of the paramilitaries. He knows every single man jack of them, full stop. Not only the men who carry the guns but the sons and the daughters of the men who carry the guns, and the grannies and grandpas of the men who carry the guns, and the names of their goldfish. On both sides, too – republican and Orange and all shades in between. If by any remote chance he doesn't personally know somebody, then one of his minions will.'

'That's what I've been counting on,' said Katie. 'If he knows that many loyalists, he'll probably know who it was who shot the Doherty family.'

'Oh, for sure, he's bound to. The killers boasted about who they were on the end of their note, didn't they, with that *Quis separabit?*, even if they didn't actually put their names to it. Take it from me, they'll be boasting about it even louder on the Falls Road or Sandy Row, or wherever it is they come from. Quilty will soon get to hear who did it, if he doesn't know already. Not that he would ever tell *you*, or the PSNI. Not that he would give a damn, either.'

'What if I fixed it so that he *did* give a damn?'

'Sorry? I don't follow you. How could you make a heartless shitehawk like Bobby Quilty care about anything at all that doesn't affect him in the slightest?'

Katie said, 'You're right, you couldn't. Not normally, anyway. But supposing the Dohertys' murders *did* affect him – and I mean personally? Supposing the Dohertys were actually related to him, cousins of his, only two or three generations removed? What's the Big Feller going to look like if he allows some loyalist gang to shoot four of his close relations in cold blood and get away with it unpunished?'

'No question about it,' said Alan. 'He'd track them down and blow their brains out. The slight snag is, they *weren't* related to him, were they?' He paused, and then he said, 'They weren't, were they?'

'It won't make any difference if they were or they weren't,' said Katie. 'Not so long as Bobby Quilty *believes* that they were.'

'And how are you going to make him believe that? You can't tell the media that they were, can you? Apart from that, the Doherty family could easily check with the General Register Office and prove that you were telling a porky. That wouldn't do your reputation a whole lot of good, would it?'

'Just remember that most of Ireland's public records were destroyed when they burned the Four Courts in 1922, so it wouldn't be all that difficult to be a little creative when it came to the Doherty family tree. Besides, I'm not thinking of telling the media. I'm thinking of telling Assistant Commissioner Jimmy O'Reilly. Nobody else. Just him.'

'Jesus. And I thought my Alison was devious,' said Alan. 'But what if O'Reilly *isn't* your tout?'

'Then I'll just have to make sure that Quilty finds out some other way.'

'And then what?'

'He'll go after the killers himself if he behaves true to type, which is what I'm counting on. He'll make sure that he gives them one of his pontificating lectures before he has them executed. He doesn't only want to be the big cheese, he wants the whole of Ireland to *know* that he's the big cheese.'

'Am I understanding you right here, Katie? You're going to feed false information to Bobby Quilty in the expectation that he's going to lead you to the shooters who murdered the Dohertys?'

'You have it exactly. You should have been a cop, do you know that?'

Alan ignored Katie's light-hearted sarcasm. He was open-mouthed with disbelief. 'He'll *kill* them. He'll kill them and you'll be responsible. You won't just be destroying your career, Katie. You could end up in the slammer.'

'I'm not going to let him kill them. *We're* not going to let him kill them, you and me. We can track him and stop him before it's too late. If we do that, we'll know who shot the Dohertys, and have them arrested, and also have Quilty arrested for aiding and abetting attempted murder.'

'For the love of God,' said Alan. 'What if Jimmy O'Reilly or James Elvin aren't your touts at all? What if they are but they smell a rat and they don't tell Quilty that he's related to the Dohertys? What if they don't tell him anyway? What if they tell him but he doesn't give a shite?'

'In that case, I'll just have to carry on my investigation into the Dohertys' murder in the usual humdrum way. But it's going to be well-nigh impossible to find out who did it, especially if they came from the North. I'll need the full cooperation of the PSNI, if they'll give it to me, but I don't think they'll be too devastated that some Catholics got shot in Cork. And I *still* won't be able to touch Bobby Quilty.'

'There are so many "what-ifs", Katie, that's what worries me,' said Alan. 'What if Quilty doesn't go after the Dohertys' killers in person? What if he simply gets in touch with one of his minions in Belfast and tells them do the dirty deed for him? What if the Dohertys' killers are shot and buried under the floorboards like the Langtrys and the Dohertys and nobody finds them for another ninety years?'

'Alan, I have to do *something*. I can't just plod on with nothing but forensic evidence and witness reports and hope that I might get lucky. I've already got lucky, overhearing Jimmy O'Reilly and James Elvin together. Like, what were the odds against that? I have to try and take advantage of it, even if it doesn't work out. If anything happens to John and Kyna and I didn't at least *try*—'

Alan reached across the table and laid his hand on her arm. 'All right, Katie. I'm with you. I think it's a mad idea altogether – totally insane – and it could be very dangerous. I'm prepared to give it a go with you, though, just to watch your back for you if nothing else, and see you stay safe. So, when do you plan on telling O'Reilly that the Quiltys and the Dohertys are related?'

'I'm going to the mortuary tomorrow morning to talk to Dr Kelley – she's the pathologist. I'll tell him when I go back to the station after that. He's in Limerick anyway for a garda's funeral until two o'clock at least.'

'I must say I'm beginning to regret staying here tonight and not coming home with you,' said Alan. She thought he looked dejected as well as tired, and older than when she had first seen him standing in the reception area at Anglesea Street in his sparkling wet raincoat.

She could almost hear her grandmother Aileen, who always used to say, 'It's *life*, that's what it is. It grinds you down like a millstone, life – day after day, week after week, year after year – until one day you're ground down to dust. Then the wind blows you away, *piff!* and that's you gone for good!'

'Here,' said Alan, passing Katie the Brown Thomas shopping bags which were resting against the chair beside him. 'You'd better have your real identity back.'

Thirty-eight

On her way home that evening Katie stopped off at her father's house in Monkstown to see how he was recovering from his recent bunion operation. As she arrived outside she was surprised to see her sister Moirin's green Hyundai blocking the driveway, so that she had to park in the street.

When she rang the bell, it was her younger sister Siobhán who answered. Siobhán was taller than Katie, and plumper, with masses of curly red hair. This evening she was wearing a pink short-sleeved blouse and jeans, and her hair was tied back, and Katie hadn't seen her look so pretty in a long time.

'*Katie!*' she squealed and gave her a hug and wouldn't let go. After a while Katie had to gasp for breath and say, 'I love you, too, Siobhán, really I do, but you're spifflicating me here and I'd like to get inside and see Da.'

'I have a kitten now,' said Siobhán, taking hold of Katie's hand as they walked through the hallway into the living room. 'The Finnegans next door had five kittens – well, six, but one of them died. They gave me one for free.'

Katie could tell that her father's cleaner, Bláithín, had been today because the house smelled of lavender furniture polish and there was a vase of fresh orange-tipped gladioli on the windowsill. Her father was sitting in the kitchen while her sister Moirin was noisily washing saucepans in the sink.

'Don't get up, Da,' Katie told her father. She was pleased to see that there was a tinge of colour in his cheeks and he had filled out a little since the last time she had seen him. He was even showing the first signs of a small pot-belly underneath his pale grey cardigan. She put that down to Bláithín feeding him. Bláithín cooked for the Roaring Donkey pub, not far from Katie's, and she brought him back any unsold meat pies or bread-and-butter puddings.

'How's your bunion?' she asked him, and he heaved up his right leg to show her his hugely bandaged foot.

'I don't *have* a bunion any more, thanks to Dr Murphy. I'll be able to wear slippers of the same size as soon I'm all healed up. Lately, I've always had to buy two pairs, so that I could walk around with an eight on one foot and a ten on the other.'

'Did I tell you that I've got a kltten?' said Siobhán.

'Yes, darling, you did,' said Katie. 'What's the kitten's name?'

'Zebby the Giraffe.'

'That's a pure strange name for a kitten. What colour is it?'

'It's a she. She has grey and black and white stripes, and a pink nose. And a pink bottom hole, too.'

'*Siobhán*,' Moirin admonished her.

Siobhán had turned thirty now but while she was staying with Katie she had been attacked and hit violently on the head with a hammer by her lover's jealous wife. She had suffered irreversible brain damage and now had a mental age of six or seven. Moirin and her husband, Kevin, had been taking care of her ever since.

'Hi, Moirin, what's the story?' said Katie.

Moirin dried up the last copper saucepan and hung it up, so that all the other copper saucepans jingled and clanked against each other. She took off her apron and said, 'You've missed supper, Kathleen. It was chicken pot roast.'

'I didn't come for supper, Moirin. I just came by to see how Da was.'

'That's just as well, then. There wouldn't have been enough for all of us.'

'Where's Kevin?' asked Katie. 'Has he got over that terrible rash yet? What was causing it, red peppers?'

'He's better for now, but don't you worry, he'll be allergic to something else soon. Gluten, or ivy, or beef hand pies. Kevin's never happy unless he's itching and scratching. He's in Waterford at the moment, at some estate agents' conference. Three days of peace. Well, apart from Siobhán.'

'I know a joke,' said Siobhán.

'That's good,' said Katie. 'Why don't you tell us?'

'Mother of God,' said Moirin. 'It's enough to make me wish I still smoked.'

'Go on, Siobhán,' Katie smiled at her. 'Tell us your joke.'

Siobhán stood up like a child standing up to give a recital at school. 'There was this old feller and he was standing by a puddle outside a pub. He had a stick with a bit of string tied to the end of it and he was jiggling the stick up and down, like this.'

'All right,' said Katie. 'Then what?'

'Another man said, "What are you doing?" and he said, "Fishing." So your man felt sorry for him and took him into the pub and bought him a drink. And when they were having the drink your man said, "How many have you caught today?" And the old feller said, "You're number eight."'

Katie laughed and said, 'That's a good joke, Siobhán. Who told you that?'

'A man I met in the Garden of Time. Moirin takes me there a lot. There's fountains.'

Moirin pursed her lips in disapproval. 'Between you and me, I think he was after a whole lot more than making her laugh. Nothing more tempting than somebody with the body of a woman and the mind of a child.'

'It didn't make me laugh,' said Siobhán. 'I don't understand it.'

'Then why in the name of God do you keep repeating it to everybody you meet?' Moirin snapped at her.

'Because it makes *them* laugh.'

Now that Moirin had finished clearing up they went into the living room. Katie poured a whiskey for her father and a vodka and Coke for herself and sat down on the couch next to him. Moirin busied herself with her crochet – a baby's bobble-hat that she was making for a friend – while Siobhán sat on the floor and played with two dolls from *Frozen*, Elsa and Anna, making them talk to each other in squeaky voices.

Katie's father took hold of her hand and said, 'What's wrong, darling? You didn't drop by just to ask about my bunion, now, did you?'

'You make me sound as if I don't care about you.'

'I know you care about me, Katie. You're the first person here when I need anything. But something's bothering you, isn't it? Something serious.'

Katie leaned towards him a little and very quietly told him all about John and Kyna and how Bobby Quilty was holding them in his house in South Armagh – and how she was planning to rescue them.

'What frightens me is, that everything depends on this one snatch of conversation that I overheard outside Jimmy O'Reilly's door and what I saw reflected in his bookcase. They might not have been hugging each other at all – maybe they were close together but from my angle it looked like they were.'

'But Jimmy went to see Quilty after, didn't he, and came back with a bagful of money?'

'I don't know for sure that it was money.'

'Well, I doubt if it was drisheen. Come on, Katie, darling, sometimes you have to trust your own instincts and in this case I think your instincts are sound.'

'Dear God, I hope so. It could all so easily go wrong and I dread to think what Quilty would do to John and Kyna if it does. The bags I made of Operation Trident doesn't fill me with a whole lot of confidence.'

'You know full well yourself that Operation Trident would have gone like clockwork if somebody hadn't tipped off Quilty beforehand. It was decisive, it was bold. You put it all together in only a few hours. It was good police work, Katie, don't you have any doubt about it.'

'Thanks for the compliment, Da, but police work gets judged on results and in this case the result was total disaster. I really don't know if I ought to be taking even more of a risk by trying to lift Bobby Quilty and whoever murdered the Dohertys *and* expose Jimmy O'Reilly, all at the same time. I'm worried that it's going to turn out to be Operation Trident the Sequel.'

Katie's father glanced across at Moirin, who still appeared to be concentrating on her crochet, although she had her head slightly inclined towards them, as if she were trying to catch what they were saying. Siobhán was singing 'Let It Go' in a penetrating off-key falsetto, so it was clearly hard for Moirin to hear them. Katie knew that her father trusted Moirin, like he trusted all of his seven daughters, but she would only have to say a careless word within earshot of the wrong person and Katie's plan could be seriously jeopardized.

'You're right about Jimmy O'Reilly,' he said, not even looking at her, and speaking with his lips nearly closed, like a ventriloquist. 'He was only a sergeant, of course, when I knew him, but there were always rumours about him. You never saw him with a girl, and he was a scouter in his spare time. Sorry to be offensive, but some of the fellows in the station used to call him "Jimmy O'Piley".'

'Just because he was a scouter, that didn't mean that he was gay – or if he was, that he was sexually active,' said Katie. 'Scouting Ireland have the strictest child protection policy you could imagine. Like, all scouters have to be screened by the Garda Central Vetting Unit, don't they? They're not even allowed to put on a pair of shorts until they can produce two references.'

'Jimmy O'Reilly slipped through the net somehow,' Katie's father told her, still in that ventriloquist's mutter. 'There was an incident at the Fota summer camp one year. I'm not sure exactly what he was accused of, but he was forced to give up scouting and he was posted to Limerick. The whole thing was hushed up because he was a garda sergeant, but it was common knowledge around the station.'

'He was married, though, wasn't he?' asked Katie.

'Yes, to a woman who worked in the Dooradoyle library. Beibhinn, her name was. She was a fair few years older than

Jimmy and I think she'd given up hope of ever getting wed. I remember one of the girls saying that she would rather have taken holy orders than marry the most miserable gay in Ireland.'

Katie said, 'So we're fairly sure that Jimmy O'Reilly is gay. But that still doesn't prove that I'm right about him feeding information to Bobby Quilty.'

Katie's father turned to her and looked her steadily in the eye. 'Katie, if you're wrong, you're wrong, and you'll soon find out if Bobby Quilty *doesn't* go after whoever it was who murdered the Doherty family. In which case you'll have to come up with a plan B. My only advice to you is to play this very, very close to your chest. This PSNI fellow who's helping you out, what's his name?'

'Alan – ex-Detective Inspector Alan Harte.'

'Are you sure you can trust him? From what you've said, it seems like he's pursuing some vendetta of his own against Quilty. If that's all that matters to him, maybe he won't be so worried about John and DS Ni Nuallán. So if I was you, I'd be doggy wide with him. After all, if he was slung out of the police service, for whatever reason—'

He paused for a moment and then he said, 'You like him, don't you?'

Katie flapped her hand at him. 'Who'd have a former garda inspector for a father? Mother of God, Da, you can read me like a Book of Evidence. Yes, I like him. But, yes, you're right, I'm not completely sure of him.'

'I have some old RUC contacts who might know him, or who might be able to find out more.'

'I don't know, Da. If he thinks that I've been checking up on him behind his back—'

'*Let it go!*' sang Siobhán, higher and higher, almost screaming. '*I am one with the wind and the sky! You'll never see me cry!*'

Moirin said, 'I don't suppose you can take care of her for a day or two, can you, Katie? This song's breaking my melt!'

'I'd love to,' said Katie. 'Let me wrap up this investigation I'm working on right now and then I'll give you a ring. Maybe I'll take her down to Kerry and stay at Parknasilla. Sometimes you get seals coming right up on to the shore for a sunbathe, close by the hotel. You'd like that, Siobhán, wouldn't you?'

'*Let it go!*' sang Siobhán, oblivious, holding up Elsa and Anna so that they danced in the air. '*The cold never bothered me anyway!*'

Thirty-nine

'I'm starved!' said Chisel. He was lying on his back on the couch with a copy of the *Racing Post* spread over his middle and his big toes sticking out of the holes in his sock, with toenails that needed cutting. 'I could eat the decorations off of a hearse, I tell you!'

'Does that mean you want me to cook you something?' asked Sorcia from the armchair in front of the television. She was sitting with her feet up on a vinyl-covered pouffe, her yellow towelling dressing gown gaping open. An unlit cigarette waggled between her lips as she spoke.

'Of course not,' Chisel retorted. 'It means I want you to dance round the room in the nip whistling "The Broad Black Brimmer" out of your ganny. What do you think?'

'I couldn't do that any road, not while I'm in me flowers. Apart from that, I don't feel like cooking and we don't have anything in to cook unless you count a tin of tuna and a beetroot that looks like my grandmother's arse.'

'Jesus, you're fecking lazy, you are, Sorsh. If there was work in the bed, you'd sleep on the floor. You can ring for a takeaway, can't you? What's the time? The Golden Wok'll still be open.'

'It's either that or Murphy's chipper.'

'Nah, I don't fancy fish. Jesus, I've been smelling you all day.'

Sorcia switched the television to mute and reached down to the floor for her mobile phone. 'I'll say this for you, Chiz. You're the most fecking romantic man I ever met in the whole of my life.'

'I'll have the chow mein and the chicken spring rolls and them chilli spare ribs. And don't go forgetting the eggy rice like you did the last time.'

Sorcia rang the Golden Wok while Chisel went into the kitchenette and took two more cans of Murphy's out of the fridge. He popped the tops on both and handed one to Sorcia before he lay down on the couch again and lit himself another cigarette.

'What's this shite you're watching?' he asked her.

'I don't know. Some fillum about some feller whose brother's a bit on the slow side, like.'

'Why don't you turn the sound back on?'

'Because I don't understand what the feck they're talking about, that's why.'

'That's because you've a wee want yourself, Sorsh.'

'Oh go away and eff yourself.'

'That's more than you ever do for me, you dirty clart.'

Sorcia was just about to snap back at him when they heard the front door downstairs being opened. Opened – pause – and then closed.

'Who's that?' said Chisel, sitting up.

'How should I know?' asked Sorcia. 'You didn't leave the door unlocked, did you?'

'I never go out the front, do I? I always go out the back.'

'That doesn't mean you didn't leave it unlocked. I know you. You'd forget your scunders if they wasn't stuck to your arse.'

Now they heard heavy footsteps drumming up the stairs – at least two people, maybe three. Chisel stood up and said, 'Christ, I hope it's not the guards again. I left my gun on top of the toilet.'

'Typical,' said Sorcia, sitting up straight and wrapping her dressing gown around herself more tightly.

'Who's that?' Chisel called out in a strangled voice. 'This is like private property, like! You're trespassing!'

The living-room door opened and Bobby Quilty came in. Unusually for him, he was wearing a wide-shouldered black suit, and a white shirt with one tail untucked, and a mottled red tie.

He reeked of David Beckham aftershave.

'I know it's private property, Chisel,' he said, with a grin. 'That's because it's *my* private property. You can't trespass on your own private property, now, can you?'

'Oh, it's you, Bobby! What about you, big man? I wasn't expecting to see you the day.'

Bobby Quilty nodded at Sorcia and said, 'All right, Sorsh? Gave you a quare gunk, did I?'

Sorcia pulled her dressing gown even tighter across her breasts. 'You could have given a body a moment's notice, Bobby. I'd have dressed up for you.'

'Don't bother yourself, doll. You'd scare rats out of a stone ditch no matter what you wore.'

Normally, Sorcia would have lashed back at him, but she clearly sensed that this unexpected visit wasn't simply social because she carefully placed her can of Murphy's on the floor and stood up, smoking in quick, nervous puffs and blowing the smoke out sideways.

Chisel was trying to see who Bobby Quilty had brought with him. The two men were waiting on the landing, both shaven-headed, one wearing a black T-shirt with a demonic face on it, the other in a loose-fitting denim shirt that looked two sizes too big for him. Neither of them came into the living room and neither of them spoke. Although it was dark out on the landing, and their faces were in shadow, Chisel was sure that he had never seen either of them before.

'Who's that you've fetched along with you, Bobby?' he asked, tilting his head to one side, trying to see them more clearly behind Bobby Quilty's bulk.

'Business associates,' said Bobby Quilty. 'That's because you and me, Chiz, we have a little business to be sorting out.'

'What sort of business would that be, then? I thought we were all squared up, you and me.'

Bobby Quilty stepped forward and rested one hand on Chisel's bony shoulder. Chisel glanced down at it uneasily, as if a fat predatory bird had just perched there.

'I asked you to do something, didn't I, when we took away that John Meagher fellow? I asked you to clean up the place, didn't I, so that the polls couldn't tell that we'd been keeping him here?'

'We did, Bobby. We scrubbed the whole place thorough, I swear to God. We scrubbed the whole place thorough, didn't we, Sorsh?'

Sorcia puffed at her cigarette and nodded. She was beginning to look seriously frightened now.

'The problem is, Chiz, you didn't scrub hard enough. See, there was a bloodstain left on the bedroom carpet.'

'I know that, Bobby. I saw it, and we scrubbed it. That bloodstain, we even scrubbed it with the bleach. You never would have known it was a bloodstain by the time we finished with it.'

Bobby Quilty pulled a face. 'Maybe *you* wouldn't have known that it looked like a bloodstain, but the polls knew. They took a sample and they checked the DNA and now they have all the evidence they need that John Meagher *was* here, no matter how much you swore that he wasn't.'

'I couldn't help that, Bobby! Me and Sorsh, we did everything we could to make sure that the place was spotless. I don't even know what D and A look like, otherwise we would have scrubbed them off, too.'

'It's DNA and it doesn't fecking look like anything, you tube! It's micro-fecking-scopic! You should have lifted up the whole fecking carpet and taken it down to the dump!'

'I didn't realize that, Bobby. Honest to God, cross my heart, if I'd have known that there was anything microscopic there at all, I would have taken the carpet down along with the bed. I would have thrown away the whole fecking bedroom if I could have.'

'Do you know something, Chiz? You astound me sometimes,' said Bobby Quilty. 'If you didn't exist, I think they'd have to invent you, just to prove how fecking stupid it's possible for one man to be.'

'Away on, big man,' said Chisel, with a sheepish smile. He was beginning to think that Bobby Quilty had come around simply to give him a telling-off and that was all. But Bobby Quilty kept his hand resting on Chisel's shoulder and abruptly his expression turned very grave, as if he had been keeping the bad news until last.

'The reason that this is a problem, Chiz, is that the polls will be knocking on your door here tomorrow morning bright and early and they'll be pulling you in for questioning.'

'I won't tell them anything, Bobby! You know that! I won't say a word! Jesus, I've never been a tout and never will be!'

'Yes, Chiz, I know that. But they have this DNA, see, and whatever you say they can prove to a court that John Meagher was here, and they can call on witnesses to prove that you and Sorsh were here at the very same time that he was.'

'What witnesses? Who can prove that we were here? All we have to do is say that we weren't!'

'So if you weren't here, where the feck were you? And what are you going to say when they put the delivery lads from half the takeaways in Blackpool on to the stand and ask them who it was who answered the door when they came around here with two meat feast pizzas or a chicken kebab?'

'We don't have to say nothing at all, Bobby. That's the law. The polls can't make you discriminate yourself.'

'But what if they say to you that you and Sorsh are both guilty of keeping John Meagher here against his will, and even if you say nothing you're still going down for it, the both of you. And then what if they say to you, "Chisel, wee man, if you *confess* that you kept him here, if you admit it, and if you tell us who asked you to do it, then you won't face any charges at all, and you can both skip off free?" What if they say *that* to you, Chiz? Do you think you'll be able to keep your bake shut, even then?'

'Of course, Bobby. What do you think? You wouldn't squeal, would you, Sorsh? And neither would I. You can count on us, big man, I can tell you that.'

'You've spent some time up on Rathmore Road, haven't you, Chiz? Like it up there, did you? Food was *cordon bleu*, was it? And how about your cell-mates? All decent spuds, were they? None of them wanted to stick it up the old chocolate speedway? And how about you, Sorsh? How do you think you'll enjoy the women's wing in Limerick? There's some desperate rugmunchers in there, from what I'm told.'

Chisel tried to lift Bobby Quilty's hand off his shoulder, but Bobby Quilty gripped him even tighter, so that he winced.

'What more can I say to you, Bobby?' Chisel appealed to him. 'If the polls are coming in the morning, maybe you could find us somewhere to hide out for a while – you know, until this all blows over.'

'This is *never* going to blow over, Chiz. Wherever you go, the polls are going to find you, especially with that mankin' tattoo round your throat.'

Sorcia crushed out her cigarette in an ashtray that was already heaped with crushed-out cigarettes. 'So what are you going to do, Bobby?' she demanded, with a catch in her throat. 'Chuck us in the river, or what?'

'Ach, come on, you two have been brave good when times were good, and you've been brave good, too, when times were bad. The bogging state of that river, I wouldn't do a thing like that to you. I'll make it quick and easy, you won't feel a thing.'

'You're going to kill us?'

'Sorsh, doll, I didn't come round here for a cup of tea. If I had my druthers, I'd give you both tickets for the Maldives, or Lanzarote at least, but money's tighter than a duck's arse these days. I can't risk you being questioned by the polls and that's all there is to it. I have to think of my business, and all the people who depend on me.'

'Do you know what you are, Bobby Quilty?' said Sorcia. 'You're the Devil himself, that's who you are. The Devil Incarnate. I know you're going to hell when you die because that's where you came from. You'll be going off home, that's all.'

With that, she took two steps forward and spat in his face. A lump of tobacco-stained phlegm slid down his cheek and dripped on to his shirt collar.

He wiped his cheek with the back of his hand, then wiped his hand on his sleeve. He made no move to retaliate, but kept his eyes riveted on Sorcia as if he could kill her just by staring at her.

'Bryan, Feilim,' he said, over his shoulder. 'Come here, would you, lads, and take hold of these two for me? Go easy, though. They're good and loyal friends of mine, aren't you, Chiz?'

'Bobby, you don't have to do this, you truly don't,' said Chisel. 'Me and Sorsh could be down to Ringaskiddy and off on the first ferry before it even gets light. We'd be off and away and you'd never see us again ever so long as you live.'

'And what do you think running away is going to prove? Running away is the same as admitting you're guilty. And you don't think the polls have discovered the electrified telephone yet? They only have to call the British cops and tell them to watch out for a feller with a pair of hands tattooed around his neck and a fag-smoking floozy and you'll be back here and banged up before you can say that shite is thicker than water, and that you two are thicker than shite.'

'Bobby, I'm pleading with you now. Don't do this. I thought that you and me were like brothers.'

'I did have a brother once,' said Bobby Quilty. 'In fact, if you must know, I was twins. My brother was stillborn, and my mam never forgave me, ever, not until the day she died herself, as if I'd strangled him in the womb to make sure that I always got the best of everything.'

'Bobby—'

'Shut your teeth, Chiz,' Sorcia snapped at him. 'You're sounding like you sit down to pee. You know that the Big Feller's come here to do us, no matter what you say, so why don't we just get it over with?'

She turned to Bobby Quilty and said, 'Come on, then, wee man. Do what you came here for. Or would you rather we went outside and stepped under a bus, so it wouldn't look like you who'd done us?'

'You have a quare ticket on you, Sorsh, I'll say that,' said Bobby Quilty, shaking his head. 'Come on, lads, let's take them through to the bedroom.'

The two shaven-headed men came into the living room. In the light, they looked surprisingly young and not nearly as hard as they had first appeared when they were standing on the landing in the shadows. The man in the black demonic T-shirt was missing his upper front teeth and wore gold hoop earrings, while the man in the denim shirt had a livid harelip scar.

'Where in the name of Jesus did you find these two scobes?' said Sorcia. 'Did the circus leave them behind?'

'The bedroom,' Bobby Quilty repeated, still staring at Sorcia as if he could happily kill her there and then.

'Don't you fecking touch me,' said Sorcia as the man in the black demonic T-shirt came towards her. 'I'll go there under my own steam, thanks very much.'

She pushed her way past Bobby Quilty and across the landing to the open bedroom door. The man in the denim shirt approached Chisel, but Chisel waved him away and followed Sorcia. His mouth was puckered tight and he had tears in his eyes. He looked up appealingly at Bobby Quilty as he passed him, but Bobby Quilty simply patted him on the back and said, 'You'll be grand, Chiz, don't you worry. It comes to all of us, you know, sooner or later. Think of my brother. He never even got to see the sun for one day.'

The five of them crowded into the untidy bedroom and stood around the mattress with its stained, twisted sheets. The only light in the room came from a pink china lamp on the floor beside the mattress, with no shade on it.

'Okay, let's have you taking your clothes off,' said Bobby Quilty.

'What?' said Sorcia.

'I want you in the nip , the both of you.'

'Oh, I see, you want me scundered, as well as dead. Forget it, wee man. There's no fecking way.'

'*Feilim!*' said Bobby Quilty, and the man in the denim shirt bounded across the mattress in his boots. Sorcia was clutching her dressing gown around her as tightly as she could, but he grasped the lapels in both hands and wrenched it wide open. Then he roughly turned her around, pulling the collar down at the back and dragging her arms out of the sleeves. Within a few seconds she was standing there naked and pale and freckled. Her rounded stomach was decorated with a multicoloured tattoo of a parrot, its wings spread wide, rising from her pubic hair as if it were launching itself out of its nest and its tail was the string of her tampon. Her legs were bruised and marbled with blue varicose veins.

She made no attempt to cover herself, but stood there defiantly with her hands resting on her hips, as if to say, *You can do what you like to me, you Devil, but I refuse to be ashamed.*

Without being prompted, Chisel crossed his arms and lifted off his sweat-stained orange polo shirt and then unbuckled his belt and stepped out of his faded blue jeans. He left his holey socks on, but he was wearing no underpants. Apart from the tattoos around his neck of the two hands throttling him, the rest of his body was covered with snakes, and lions, and naked women, and on his sunken breastbone the face of Jesus, with His crown of thorns, but looking more like Bob Geldof than Jesus..

'Lie down on the bed,' said Bobby Quilty.

'Bobby,' said Chisel. 'I'm begging you, man. Look at me here, bollock-naked, and Sorcia, too, no threat you at all. If we can do this on your say-so, do you really think we'd squeal to the polls about you?'

'Lie down,' Bobby Quilty told him.

Awkwardly, Chisel and Sorcia lay down next to each other, their arms by their sides, but their eyes darting around them – from Bobby Quilty to the man in the black demonic T-shirt, to the man in denim. Chisel tried to hold Sorcia's hand, but she snatched it away.

'Now, turn back to back,' said Bobby Quilty.

'What? What do you mean?'

'I mean, lie with your backs to each other, and real close, so that your heads are touching.'

They did as they were told, although as he turned over Chisel suddenly let out a high, girlish laugh. He was beginning to think that this was all an elaborate joke, just to frighten them. He couldn't see any weapons. He knew for a fact that Bobby Quilty never carried a gun in case he was stopped and searched by the guards, and neither of the two men appeared to be armed, unless the man in the denim shirt had a gun tucked into his belt.

'That's it, Chiz, good man yourself,' said Bobby Quilty. 'Heads together. That's cracker.'

He went to the bedroom door, opened it wider and stepped out on to the landing. There was silence for a while, except for Sorcia occasionally coughing and the man in the black demonic T-shirt monotonously sniffing. That, and the muffled sound of the traffic outside.

Chisel was tempted to call out to Bobby and ask him how much longer they were going to have to lie here, as naked as the day they were born, with the backs of their heads pressed uncomfortably hard together and Sorcia's sweaty buttocks sticking to his.

He had already taken a breath when he heard footsteps coming up the stairs, light and businesslike and quick. He heard Bobby Quilty saying something like, 'Ready for you, Sandy.'

Sandy? he thought. *Who for feck's sake is Sandy?*

The bedroom door was flung wide open now, so hard that it banged against the wall. A thin man dressed in a black sweater and grey trousers stalked in, like the long-legged scissorman, his head completely covered in a black balaclava. He dropped to his knees beside the mattress and before either Chisel or Sorcia could react he gripped Chisel's tufty hair by the roots. Chisel said, '*Ow!*' but without any hesitation, the man pressed the muzzle of a silenced automatic hard against Chisel's forehead and fired.

Chisel's head swelled up and blood and brains squirted out of his ear. Sorcia's head ballooned, too, and her face exploded all over the pillow.

The man in the black demonic T-shirt retched and covered his mouth with his hand and said, '*Jesus Christ!*' The man in the denim shirt stared at the bloody hollows that had once been Sorcia's face, his hand held up to his forehead as if he were stunned. Her jawbone was hanging wide open so that she looked as stunned as him. One of her brown eyes was hanging off the edge of the pillow on the end of its stringy pink optic nerve, peering anxiously down at the floor.

Bobby Quilty came back into the bedroom and looked down at the two naked bodies lying on the mattress, with their mangled heads. There was no emotion in his face, but his tongue was roaming around inside his mouth as if he were trying to dislodge shreds of his lunch that might still be stuck between his teeth.

'Grand job, Sandy,' he said at last. 'Nothing like a suicide pact to sort out a feller's problems, especially mine.'

Sandy quickly unscrewed the silencer and dropped it into his pocket. Then he lifted Chisel's right hand and bent his fingers one by one around the butt of the automatic, leaving his trigger-finger until last. Finally, he angled Chisel's arm and bent back his wrist so that it would appear that he had shot himself in the forehead, killing Sorcia at the same time.

'Nice piece, that SIG Sauer,' he said. 'Fierce pity to leave it.'

'Don't you worry,' Bobby Quilty told him. 'With what I'm paying you for this, you'll be able to buy yourself another five like it. Now, away with you.'

Sandy got up and left, and after Bobby Quilty had taken a quick look around he and his two 'business associates' left, too. They clattered down the stairs, but as they were letting themselves out of the front door a noisy moped pulled into the kerb outside. A young man climbed off it and started to unbuckle a large red food-delivery bag on the back.

'What you got there, wee man?' Bobby Quilty asked him.

'Takeaway order from the Golden Wok, for Chisel.'

Bobby Quilty stuck out his lower lip and shook his head. 'Nobody called Chisel living here. Not any more, any road.'

Forty

By the time Katie arrived at the mortuary Dr Kelley was already at work. She was closing the gaping Y-shaped incision she had made into Órla Doherty's chest, using quick, tiny sutures that were almost as neat as a dressmaker's stitches.

'Good morning to you, DS Maguire,' she said, looking up from her suturing and standing back. She was a tall, willowy woman in her mid-forties, with a long, exotic face. Her eyes were very dark, even without make-up, and her eyebrows were finely arched. Even in her long white lab coat, Katie thought that she looked like a figure from an ancient Egyptian frieze.

'A pure tragedy, this one,' she added. 'I thought I'd grown impervious over the years, do you know? But to see the little ones murdered like this, for some historical grudge—'

Katie nodded. The bodies of the other members of the Doherty family were lying side by side against the far wall, all three of them draped in dark green sheets. They were lit up by the shafts of sunshine that fell from the clerestory windows high above them, as if they were lying in a chapel.

'Any other injuries, apart from the gunshot trauma to the head?'

'A few fresh bruises on the father's and mother's arms, as if they were manhandled. Your technical experts took pictures and they thought it might be possible to make a match from one of the bruises on the father's left biceps because his assailant was wearing two rings.'

Katie went up to the side of the stainless-steel autopsy table. She knocked accidentally against the analogue scale that was used to weigh dissected organs, such as livers and brains, and its metal pot dolefully clanked like a funeral bell.

Órla's eyes were closed and the way in which her face had been distorted by the fragmentation bullet made her look as if she were dreaming some surrealistic dream.

'You would have to check her medical records to find out whether she knew it, but she was showing early signs of systolic heart failure,' said Dr Kelley. 'If it had been left untreated, she may have had only a few years left before she suffered a serious or even fatal heart attack.'

'She doesn't have to worry about that now,' said Katie sadly. Like Dr Kelley, she had seen scores of dead bodies, including children, but there was something about this whole family lying here that was particularly poignant. If they had really been killed in retaliation for the Langtrys, it made her feel sorry for Ireland, too. Could there still be people in this country with such long memories and such a lack of forgiveness?

'Once I've closed Mrs Doherty here, I'll be finished,' said Dr Kelley. 'I'll send you my full report as soon as I've written it up, but the long and the short of it is that all four of them were killed by a single devastating gunshot wound to the head. The boy was hit in the back of the head and not at point-blank range like the others, so it's possible that he may have been trying to escape when he was shot. Your technical experts had some theories about that, and about the sequence in which they were killed.'

'I'll be talking to them later,' said Katie. 'Meanwhile, thanks for all the work you've done on this. Let's pray that we don't get any more like it.'

* * *

As Katie was climbing into her car to drive to Anglesea Street her iPhone pinged. It was a text from Alan, saying: *BQ's pickup @ Keeffe St. CU 18er.*

She texted him back, telling him that she would arrive at the station in less than fifteen minutes.

Almost immediately, before she could start the engine, Detective Sergeant Begley called her.

'I'm at Leitrim Street, ma'am, but we're getting no response at all. We've been shouting and hammering fit to wake the dead, but not a squeak. We called around at five-thirty, but they didn't answer and we thought that maybe they were wrecked, the way they smoke and drink, those two, and we just couldn't stir them out of their scratcher. But we came back twenty minutes ago to try again and we're still getting nothing. I didn't want to go barging in without a warrant, though, especially after all the trouble we had with Operation Trident.'

'No, good man yourself, Sean. You're wise to hold off. The courts have been taking a very dim view lately of raids without warrants – and apart from that, I don't want to be ruffling Bobby Quilty's feathers again, not so soon, anyway. Post a uniform there to keep an eye on the place, will you, just in case the two of them make an appearance, and find yourself a District Court judge for a warrant. I'm on my way back to the station from Wilton so I'll see you after.'

As she drove east along the South Link Road, Katie began to feel increasingly apprehensive. She wasn't particularly worried that Chisel and Sorcia couldn't be roused. It wouldn't surprise her if Bobby Quilty had kicked them out of the house on Leitrim Street, or maybe Detective Sergeant Begley was right and they were too hung over to be woken up. But it was time now to put her plan into action and she was losing confidence that it was going to work out. There was so much that could go wrong, right from the very start, or simply not happen at all. What if she had completely misjudged Assistant Commissioner O'Reilly and James Elvin? Even if she hadn't, what if Bobby Quilty didn't react the way she expected him to? It was like one of those elaborate games in which a ball rolls down a slide and drops on to a hammer which activates a catapult which knocks over a row of dominoes.

She turned into the Garda station car park. The trouble was, she still couldn't think of any other way to try to rescue

John and Kyna that wouldn't risk them being moved to another location where they couldn't be found, or even killed. Bobby Quilty had to be put out of action quickly and effectively, and if possible, legally – although she had decided that she would worry about the legality of what she was planning if and when it had worked.

She was pleased and relieved to see Alan waiting for her in the reception area. He was wearing a light fawn Gentleman's Quarters jacket which was obviously new and he looked as though he had slept well last night. Before she went over to him, though, she approached the garda sergeant at the front desk and said, 'Has Assistant Commissioner O'Reilly come back yet?'

'About ten minutes ago, ma'am.'

'Thanks,' said Katie, and walked across to where Alan was sitting.

'You're looking worried,' he said. He stood up and half raised his arms as if he wanted to hold her close, and kiss her, and reassure her that everything was going to be all right – but of course he couldn't, not in front of the desk sergeant and all the other gardaí and visitors who were coming and going.

'Let's go up to my office,' she said. 'I have the tracker ready for you, and the briefcase.'

'Good. I walked past Keeffe Street on my way here and Quilty's pickup is parked exactly where it was before, with the same shamfeen guarding it.'

'I'll give you fifteen minutes and then I'll go and see Jimmy O'Reilly. That should light the blue touch-paper.'

'You're still sure you want to go ahead with it?'

'I don't have any choice, Alan. If it doesn't work, it doesn't work. But I have to try.'

They went up to Katie's office in the lift. She smelled that black pepper and cinnamon fragrance on him again, but they still didn't touch or exchange any kind of intimate look. There was CCTV in the lift and more cameras along the corridors.

Once they had reached her office Katie went straight over to her desk, unlocked her top drawer and took out a black GPS tracker, about the size and shape of a small mobile phone.

'Here,' she said. 'MicroMagnetic Four, one of the newest available. I "borrowed" it yesterday from my drugs team. You can stick it under a wheel arch or anywhere you like. I've already set up the mapping panel for it on my laptop and a mapping app on my phone. The second Quilty moves off we'll be able to see where he's headed, and it'll show his position every five seconds after that.'

She handed it to Alan, as well as a cheap brown briefcase packed with thirty or forty sheets of A4 paper. 'Don't worry if you lose any of the documents. They're only last year's council minutes on flood defences.'

'Okay,' he said. 'Give me fifteen minutes or so, that should be easy enough. In any case I'll text you as soon as it's done.'

There was no CCTV inside her office and Katie was tempted to give him a kiss. Even if his true motive was revenge, he was being brave and he was helping her. Instead, though, she touched her fingers to her lips and smiled at him and said, 'Be careful, that's all.'

'Careful? Do you know what they called me in the service? "The Underwriter." Before we went out on a shout I always insisted that we ran through every conceivable risk. I might have been mocked for it, but it saved some lives, I can tell you.'

'Just make sure you take care of your own life,' said Katie.

Alan touched his fingers to his lips in the same way that she had, and left.

* * *

It was a bright, warm afternoon, with a gusty breeze blowing so that the grey surface of the River Lee's south channel was ruffled. It took Alan less than five minutes to walk along Copley Street, cross the river on to Morrison's Quay, and walk up towards Keeffe Street. He walked quickly because he was keeping his fingers crossed that Bobby Quilty hadn't finished his business for the day and driven off home.

When he reached Keeffe Street, though, he saw that the black Nissan Navara pickup was still parked on the demolition site, and that the hard-looking guard was still leaning against it, with his arms folded, looking almost terminally bored.

Alan entered the demolition site, walking slowly between the double line of parked cars. He stopped when he was less than twenty metres away from Bobby Quilty's pickup and took out his mobile phone, as if he were answering a call. Loudly, he said, 'Yes, yes! Of course, Bill! No, man, I have it with me! Hold on, I'll find it for you!'

With deliberate awkwardness, he wedged the mobile phone between his ear and his upraised shoulder, lifted the briefcase and opened it. He took out the sheets of paper and started to shuffle through them.

'I have it here somewhere, Bill! Yes, just hold on a moment, would you?'

Bobby Quilty's guard showed no interest in him, but yawned ostentatiously.

Alan shuffled through more papers, and just as another gust of wind rose up, he dropped them all. They flew everywhere, flapping and dancing across the demolition site. Some of them caught against the wheels of Bobby Quilty's pickup and some of them disappeared underneath it altogether. Some of them wrapped themselves around the guard's ankles and he irritably kicked them off.

'Sorry! Sorry! My fault! Sorry!' said Alan, bending down repeatedly like a penitent monk and making futile attempts to snatch at the papers as they skipped away. The guard started picking them up, too, particularly those that were trapped up against the pickup's wheels.

Alan circled round to the opposite side of the pickup and went down on his hands and knees so that he could reach for some of the papers that had blown underneath it. At the same time, he took the magnetic tracker out of his pocket and clamped it in a small rectangular space next to the exhaust pipe. Even if the underside of the vehicle was inspected with a mirror, it would be very difficult to detect it.

Eventually, he and the guard had gathered up all of the papers except for three of them that were tumbling away towards Fitton Street.

'Thanks a million,' said Alan, as the guard handed him two handfuls of crumpled-up papers. 'I'm like a pig in reverse, me. Always dropping stuff. Dropped a scalding hot cup of coffee right on me foot only yesterday. Thanks.'

'You'd best be getting after them,' said the guard, pointing towards the papers that were blowing out of sight.

'Yes, thanks! Thanks again!' said Alan, and went off at a jog, stuffing the papers back into the briefcase as he went. Before he turned the corner, he glanced back and saw that the guard was leaning against the pickup again, with his arms folded exactly as before, oblivious to what had really happened.

Alan took out his mobile phone and texted Katie: *Stuck!*

* * *

Assistant Commissioner O'Reilly was on the phone when Katie knocked at his door, but he called out '*Come!*' and when she stepped into his office he indicated that she should sit down opposite his desk.

'Oh yes, it was pure moving,' he was saying. 'A fitting tribute to a very fine officer. Yes. So I'll see you next week when I come up to Phoenix Park. That's right, Thursday. All right, Diarmuid. Good luck to you so.'

He hung up the phone and then looked at Katie inquiringly, with his hands steepled and his head cocked slightly to one side.

'Can I help you at all, Katie?'

'Not really, sir, but there's something you need to be aware of – just in case there are any repercussions, you know, like Operation Trident.'

'Yes, well, I have some news for *you* on Operation Trident. It seems as if Bobby Quilty is prepared to withdraw his complaints about his home being broken into, and his unjustified arrest, so long as we compensate him financially for the damage caused to his property. He has also asked that we issue a media statement to the effect that we were acting on misleading information and that he is not under suspicion for any offence or misdemeanour.'

'Holy Mary, what else does he want? A civic reception and a year's free subscription to *Ireland's Own?*'

'There's no need for cynicism, Katie. I understand that you feel defensive about Operation Trident, but if Bobby Quilty is prepared to overlook it then so am I – and so, too, is the deputy commissioner in charge of operations.'

'You've discussed it with her?'

'Of course. I have to say that she's prepared to be much more lenient than I would have been if I had been in her position, but then it's all girls together these days, isn't it, from Frances Fitzgerald downwards. So long as you've learned a lesson from this, and we don't have any more debacles like Operation Trident.'

He pronounced 'debacles' with a long 'a' like 'di-*bahh*-kulls'.

'I can't guarantee it,' said Katie. 'In this job, you can never tell what misleading information you're going to be fed, can you?'

'All I can say is, Katie, don't let anything like it ever happen again. Now, what was this something that I need to be aware of?'

'It's the Doherty family, sir.'

'Oh, yes. What about them? Very sad case, that.'

'It said in the message that was found with their bodies that they were shot in revenge for the Langtrys back in 1921. Because of that, we checked up on their genealogy. You know, just to see if they really *were* related to any known IRA soldiers at the time. Apart from anything else, we were hoping that it might solve the question of who shot them, and why.'

'So did it?' asked Jimmy O'Reilly. He started to open and close his desk drawers as if he were looking for something, or wanted to show Katie that he wasn't really very interested.

'No, it didn't, unfortunately. But the big surprise was that the Dohertys were direct descendants of Niall Quilty, who was one of Captain Frank Busteed's men – you know, the IRA contingent who set up the ambush at Dripsey.'

Jimmy O'Reilly stopped opening and shutting drawers and looked up. 'Niall *Quilty*, did you say? You're not telling me that he was related in any way to *Bobby* Quilty?'

Katie held up a torn-off sheet from her notebook. 'I have it all here, sir. According to the Quilty family tree, Niall Quilty was a cousin of Bobby Quilty's grandfather. One of his daughters married a Doherty and *their* youngest son was Kevin Doherty's grandfather, so the family connection to Bobby Quilty is very close. Essentially, the Dohertys were Bobby Quilty's cousins, only three generations removed.'

'Oh, I see. That *is* a surprise. So how's your investigation into the Doherty murders coming along? Do you have any idea yet who might be responsible?'

'Apart from that message, and the suggestion that the killers might have been UDA or UFF, nothing at all so far. Dr Kelley has only just completed her autopsy and the technicians are working on the ballistics, but there was scarcely any forensic evidence and no eyewitnesses.'

'So how do you rate your chances of catching them?'

'At the moment, zero to nought per cent,' said Katie. 'But it's very early days yet. I'll be in touch with the PSNI and they may be able to give us a lead.'

'Fat chance of that, if they really were UDA.'

Katie nearly said, *There's no need for cynicism*, but she kept her mouth shut. Jimmy O'Reilly stood up, walked over to the window, and then came back and sat down again. Katie could tell that he was deeply agitated by what she had just told him. He drummed his fingers on his desk as if he were trying to make up his mind about what to do next, and Katie could easily guess why. *Should I tell Bobby Quilty that the Dohertys were related to him, or should I say nothing at all? What if I don't tell him but it comes out later?* At least, that's what she imagined he was thinking. She could be wrong.

After a long silence, Jimmy O'Reilly said, 'What do you have there? The family tree, is it?'

'That's right. Of course, most of the family records before 1922 were lost in the Four Courts fire, but we found the connection between the Quiltys and the Dohertys in the parish register in Inniscarra.'

'Can you make me a copy of that?'

'Have this one,' said Katie and handed him the sheet of note-paper. 'I thought you ought to know about it, that's all, in case Bobby Quilty was accused of something else that he hadn't done.'

'It's not a joke, Katie,' said Jimmy O'Reilly. 'We know perfectly well what Bobby Quilty gets up to, but it all comes down to man-power and budget. Let Revenue deal with him. He's much more their problem than ours.'

Katie stood up and said, 'I'll let you get on, then, sir. Thank you for the update on Operation Trident. I appreciate it.'

Jimmy O'Reilly was frowning at the family tree that she had given him. 'Hmm,' was all he said, and raised his hand to acknowledge that she was going.

Forty-one

Half an hour later, when she was sorting through all the paperwork that had piled up on her desk, she heard a *click* from her laptop and saw that Bobby Quilty's pickup was leaving the car park on Keeffe Street. She kept her eye on the little blue vehicle symbol as it flashed up every five seconds on the MicroMagnetic mapping plan. She watched it crossing over the Michael Collins Bridge and then turning north up Ship Street and she wondered if it would continue heading north. It stopped at the end of Ship Street, but then it turned eastwards on the Lower Glanmire Road, towards Tivoli, in the direction of Bobby Quilty's house.

Alan had only had coffee for breakfast so he had gone across to the Market Tavern for a drink and a beefburger. He, too, was following Bobby Quilty's progress with his mobile phone app, and he texted Katie: *The Big Fellers on the move. Going home by the looks of it.*

Katie thought: *Maybe Jimmy O'Reilly hasn't been in touch with Bobby Quilty yet. Or maybe he* has *been in touch with him, but Bobby Quilty isn't interested in historical vendettas. Or maybe he* is *interested, and he's raging about it, but he's going to arrange for somebody else to do the dirty deed for him. On the other hand, maybe I'm dead wrong about Jimmy O'Reilly and he would never pass confidential information to anybody, especially a scummer like Bobby Quilty, no matter what personal pressure he was under.*

She almost felt guilty for suspecting him. So what if he was homosexual and James Elvin was blackmailing him for money?

That didn't necessarily mean that he would breach Garda security, just to protect his own reputation. He had a very impressive record of service, even if he was old-school and intolerant of women being promoted any higher than tea-makers and crossing-patrol officers.

Bobby Quilty's pickup turned into Tivoli Park and stopped. There was nothing that Katie could do now except wait and see if he suddenly drove off somewhere else. Alan texted her: *Dont panic. He may not have heard yet. Or hes making some calls to find out who did it.*

Glad UR so confident! Katie texted back.

There was a pause, then Alan replied: *It wont be over till the fat man gets scooped.*

Katie went back to her paperwork. She was having to deal with complaints from victims of crime in rural areas that detectives were either late in responding to robberies and assaults or not turning up at all. In some villages the closure of Garda barracks was leading to crime waves, with hundreds of thousands of euros of farm machinery being stolen and elderly people assaulted and robbed in their own homes.

'I never answer the front door now after dark,' one complainant had written. 'I never know who it might be – a neighbour come for a chat, a priest come to pray, or a knacker come to rob me.'

Katie jotted down some notes. She was trying to think of ways in which she could improve response times without incurring extra costs, and it wasn't easy. If Bobby Quilty had been guilty of nothing more than cigarette-smuggling, she would have been inclined to agree with Jimmy O'Reilly that present budget restrictions made it uneconomical to go after him. As Detective Dooley had said just yesterday, 'It's only money, after all, and the nation's health, and when did we ever care about either of those before now? What about the Godfather fry-up at Tony's Bistro? Eight sausages and six rashers and four slices of black pudding! I know it's in aid of charity, but how healthy is that?'

As Katie worked, she continually flicked her eyes across to the mapping plan on her laptop, but Bobby Quilty's pickup remained stationary outside his house.

She had almost finished her report on response times when Detective Sergeant Begley rang her. She could tell immediately from the sound of his voice that something was badly wrong.

'Sean! Did you get the warrant all right?'

'Oh, sure, I got the warrant,' he told her. 'Judge Coughlan was kind of uppity about it at first, but when I told her that we were looking to build a case against Bobby Quilty she issued it straight off. I got the feeling that she's allergic to the Big Feller.'

'I know that. She had to let him off twice last year on charges of extortion because we couldn't find any witnesses with enough nerve to give evidence against him. So, what have you found? Anything? Have the lovebirds flown the nest?'

'No, they're still here, the both of them.'

'And? Are you bringing them in?'

'They're both dead, ma'am. Shot in the head. Looks like a suicide pact, but if Bobby Quilty's involved, you never can tell, can you?'

'*Dead?* Mother of God! Where did you find them?'

'In bed, lying with their backs to each other, but head to head. Chisel blew his brains out and hers, too, with just the one bullet. It's a pig's dinner, I can tell you. Here – hold on – I'll go back into the bedroom so that you can see for yourself.'

After a moment's hesitation a view of the bedroom at Leitrim Street appeared on Katie's desktop computer, tilting sideways as Detective Sergeant Begley approached the mattress and slowly scanned the two naked bodies lying back to back. Then he held his camera close to Chisel's hand, so that she could see the gun that he was holding.

'How long do you think they've been dead?' asked Katie.

'They're both in full rigor, so they were probably lying here dead when we first came around this morning. We've called the technicians, so they should be able to give us a more accurate time once they've taken their temperature and all that.'

'Any sign of a suicide note?'

'No, nothing. Mind you, I doubt if either of those two could read or write.'

'No witnesses? Nobody heard anything, or saw anything?'

'Nobody that we've talked to so far. This is a fierce noisy junction between Leitrim Street and Pine Street, especially first thing in the morning, so that's hardly surprising.'

'All the same, Sean, that's a SIG Sauer 2022. Nice gun, but not the quietest weapon in the world.'

Detective Sergeant Begley slowly walked around the mattress, giving Katie a panoramic view of the two white bodies, and then a close-up of Sorcia's devastated face. When Katie saw the beef-red sinus cavities and the flapped-down letterbox jaw she was glad that she hadn't eaten anything since she had come back from CUH.

She glanced again at the mapping plan. Bobby Quilty's pickup still hadn't moved.

'All right, Sean,' she said. 'I'll come straight up there. You have Detective Scanlan with you, don't you?'

'Scanlan and two uniforms. They've already called Super-intendent Pearse for backup.'

'Is Scanlan okay?'

'Scanlan? She's grand altogether. To tell you the truth, I think her stomach's stronger than mine. I was craw sick when I first walked into that bedroom and found those two squatters lying there with their heads blown off. Jesus, they smelled bad enough when they were alive.'

'I'll bring Dooley with me,' said Katie. 'He has a cast-iron stomach, too.'

Katie rang Alan and told him what had happened and where she was going.

'Rather you than me,' he told her. He paused, and hiccupped. 'I've only just finished an eight-ounce beefburger and I think I wolfed it down too quick.'

'Keep a watch on Quilty for me, won't you, and ring me or text me as soon as you see any sign of movement.'

'Don't you worry, Katie,' he said, and hiccupped again. 'He'll only have to budge an inch and I'll know about it.'

'Hold your breath and count to a hundred,' Katie told him. 'I'll ring you later so.'

* * *

She stood by the door and watched while three of Bill Phinner's technical experts examined the bodies and the bedroom. One of them was taking photographs of Chisel and Sorcia, while the other two were down on their hands and knees with SPEX Forensics HandScopes. Centimetre by centimetre they were systematically shining infra-red and ultra-violet light on to the carpet and the skirting boards and walls, searching for shoe prints and any other kind of indentations, as well as hairs and fibres and fluids.

Bill Phinner stood close beside Katie, with his brow furrowed, and he kept making little sucking noises, as if this was the very last place he wanted to be. Katie had sprayed perfume on to her handkerchief and was holding it over her nose and mouth. The bedroom smelled overwhelmingly of stale cigarette smoke and excrement and dead fish, and with their pallid skin and all their tattoos Chisel and Sorcia reminded her of the common goby that her father used to catch in the River Lee estuary. He never ate them, because they were the bottom of the food chain. *Rather like Chisel and Sorcia*, thought Katie, even though she knew that was less than Christian.

'So what time did they die, do you think?' she asked Bill. 'They were in rigor already when Detective Sergeant Begley broke in, so he reckoned that they must have been dead before he came round at half past five this morning.'

'From their rigor and their body temperatures, I'd say at least eighteen hours ago. We've taken some blood samples so we can narrow it down more exactly than that, but a fairly good estimate is ten or eleven last night.'

Detective Sergeant Begley came into the room behind Katie.

'That bedside lamp was lit when we first entered the room, so I think it's fair to assume that it was night-time.'

Katie took her handkerchief away from her face, but tried not to breathe in too deeply. 'Let's face it, we see a fair number of double suicides don't we? But they're mostly old couples, when one or both of them is terminally ill, and in practically every case they take an overdose.'

'Oh, we've had one or two exceptions,' Bill Phinner put in. 'You remember that poor old couple who jumped in front of a train at Kent station last year, hand in hand?'

'Of course. And those two who drove their car into Lough Mahon and just sat in it while it sank? But double suicides like that are very rare, like. And whenever guns are involved, it's almost always the man who shoots the woman and then shoots himself. I've never seen a double suicide like this, with only one shot. How did he know that she wasn't going to sit up at the very last moment and he'd only end up killing himself and not her?'

Detective Scanlan appeared behind Detective Sergeant Begley. Katie thought she was looking a little pale, and there were dark circles under her eyes. 'Do you want to come and take a sconce at the living room, ma'am? I think it poses more questions than it answers, do you know what I mean?'

'Yes, I'll come now,' said Katie. 'I think I need a breather, anyway.'

'Don't entirely blame you,' said Bill Phinner. 'There's some whiff in here, isn't there? Would you believe that before I decided to take up forensics I was going to go and work for Topps in Ballincollig making lollipops and Life Savers? It might not have been so meaningful, the work, but by God it would have smelled sweeter.'

Katie went across to the living room where Detective Dooley was taking notes and another of Bill Phinner's technical experts was taking photographs.

'So what are the questions?' asked Katie, although she could see for herself that the TV was still on, even though the sound was muted, and there were open cans of Murphy's on the floor, as well as packets of cigarettes, two over-full ashtrays and a copy of the *Racing Post*. She was reminded of the scene of Darragh Murphy's murder – an ordinary evening that had been suddenly and violently interrupted.

'It strikes me as fierce quare that they should have been sitting here drinking and smoking and watching the telly but then they decide to get up and go into the bedroom and take off all of their clothes and kill themselves. Those two cans of stout are still nearly full, like they had only just been opened.'

'That's right,' said Detective Dooley. 'If it really was a suicide pact, you'd have thought they would have sat here and finished their drinks. A last toast to life, do you know what I mean? And if they didn't finish their drinks because they had a blazing argument, they wouldn't have gone to bed and laid down that way back to back and shot themselves together. One of them would have shot the other, or vice versa, and then himself, or herself, as the case may be.'

'I spoke to the woman who lives in the flat next door,' said Detective Scanlan. 'She said they were always at each other's throats and some of the rows they had were, like, epic. Always effing and blinding. The language they used would have a made a knacker blush, that's what she said. But she didn't hear them argue last night, or this morning.'

'And she didn't hear any gunshot, either,' added Detective Dooley. 'If she could hear them swearing at each other, surely she could have heard a SIG Sauer blowing their heads off – that would have been more than 140 decibels. On the other hand, they were always slamming doors and throwing furniture at each other, so she might not have realized that it was a gunshot and not a chair.'

'So your thinking is . . .?' Katie asked them, looking around. The smell of cigarettes was so strong in here that it made her eyes water. It permeated everything, the curtains, the carpet, the furniture. The ceiling was stained brown with nicotine, the way that pub ceilings used to be.

'Well, like you're always telling us, ma'am, don't jump to any premature conclusions,' said Detective Scanlan. 'In this case, though, both Dooley and I believe that they were murdered by a third party – or *parties*, most likely. And they were taken by surprise, like, because we found a Browning Hi-Power automatic on top of the toilet cistern, which was probably Chisel's. It's an old one, with gaffer tape around the butt, but it was loaded and made ready. So he would have been able to defend himself against an intruder if he had been given enough warning.'

'The downstairs doors were both locked, front and back,' said Detective Dooley. 'They hadn't been forced, either. If it *wasn't* suicide, which we don't believe it was, then there's four possibilities. The first is that one of the doors was originally unlocked, so that the intruders could just walk in. The second is that Chisel or Sorcia opened the door for them because they knew them. The third is that they opened the door for them even though they *didn't* know them but they were immediately forced to let them in. The fourth is that the intruders had a key.'

'I think you're right,' said Katie. 'And since this building is owned by Bobby Quilty, even though it's only through a holding company, I think your fourth possibility is by far the most likely.'

'Wouldn't Bobby Quilty have done more to cover his tracks?' asked Detective Dooley. 'I mean, leaving the telly on like that, and these half-empty cans of stout. That's pure amateur.'

Katie shrugged. 'Maybe Bobby Quilty wasn't involved in person, although the way these two were murdered, that has all the hallmarks of a Bobby Quilty punishment – like Darragh Murphy's. Well – maybe not punishment so much as insurance, to make sure they couldn't give evidence against him and to frighten off anybody else who might be thinking of informing on him.'

She thought for a moment and then she said, 'I believe it *was* him, and I have the feeling that he *was* here, but I don't think he gave a tinker's damn about the details, like the telly and everything. All he needed was an alibi in case we lift him on suspicion – "It was suicide, your honour, I didn't have nothing to do with it." Nobody else is going to be brave enough to say different.'

Bill Phinner came into the living room, still frowning – always sour and serious, with a permanent air of professional disappointment about him.

'I heard what you said, ma'am, and you're absolutely correct. It wasn't suicide, either double or single. The male victim is holding the gun, but the HandScope showed that he has no gunpowder residue on his fingers whatsoever, so he didn't fire it himself. Firing that particular weapon can sometimes leave redness on the web between finger and thumb, and there's no sign of that either.

'On top of that, there's a semicircular impression in the skin around the entry wound in the male victim's forehead. It doesn't match the muzzle of the gun, but it's consistent in diameter with the muzzle of a silencer being pressed hard against his forehead. My armaments expert in there is probably showing off, but he thinks it could have been a Griffin Revolution or a Gemtech Tundra, which is a lightweight silencer that's ideal for a SIG Sauer 2022. Personally, I doubt if we'll be able to identify the make of silencer conclusively. Whichever one of those it was, though, it was fitted to the gun when it was fired, and they're eighteen centimetres in length, which would have made the weapon far too long for the male victim to hold it against his own head at that particular angle.'

'So it was murder,' said Katie.

'No question,' said Bill Phinner. 'I'd go further than that myself, even as a man of science, and say that it was an execution.'

He had only just uttered the word 'execution' when Katie's iPhone pinged. 'Excuse me,' she said. It was a text message from Alan.

BQ on the move. On N8 headed east.

Katie said, 'Okay, everybody. I have to go now. A summons from on high. Bill, thank you, as usual. Sean, Michael, Padragain, I'll leave you to finish up here. See you after at the station.'

With that, she hurried down the stairs and out on to Leitrim Street. Two more patrol cars had just arrived and five gardaí had cordoned off the entire pavement in front of the building. She ducked under the blue-and-white tape and crossed over to her car.

If Bobby Quilty was heading east on the N8 it could be that he was simply driving to Fota to play a round of golf. He was a member, after all. But if he turned left at the second roundabout he would be joining the M8, which could take him north to Belfast.

She turned on the engine, but before she drove off she texted Alan: *On my way. 5 mins.*

Forty-two

She was turning into MacCurtain Street when Alan texted her again: *BQs taken M8. Going N.*

She drummed her fingers on the steering wheel as she waited at the lights at the end of the Brian Boru Bridge, where Detective Barry had been crushed. If Bobby Quilty was on his way north, then maybe her plan was going to work out – at least partially. The driver in front of her was slow to move off when the lights turned green and she repeatedly blew her horn at him. He turned around and glared at her as if she had interrupted him saying a novena to St Monica, the patron saint of patience.

Alan was waiting for her outside the Market Tavern. She lifted her laptop off the passenger seat and when he had climbed in and fastened his seat belt she handed it to him.

'There . . . It's already logged in to the mapping plan.'

Alan showed her the app on his phone. 'He's just passed Rathcormac. He'll be going through Fermoy in a couple of minutes. He's really giving it the tittie, if you'll excuse the expression.'

Katie watched as the tiny car symbol flashed up on the screen every five seconds. It looked on the app as if Bobby Quilty was gradually creeping his way north, but in reality he must be driving at over 130 kph, at least 10 kph over the speed limit. Against all of her professional instincts she found herself praying that he would slow down – the last thing she wanted was for him to be pulled over for speeding.

As she drove eastwards alongside the river she put in a call to Detective Inspector O'Rourke. When he answered he sounded as if he had his mouth full.

'What's the story, ma'am?'

'I'm sorry to do this to you at such short notice, Francis, but I've had a bit of a family crisis and I'll be needing to take the rest of the day off, and probably tomorrow as well. Have you heard from DS Begley about that pair found dead at Leitrim Street?'

'I have, yes. Don't worry about it. Do you want me to make a statement to the media about it? I can liaise with Superintendent Pearse if you do.'

'All you need to tell the media at the moment is that we suspect the deaths were murder and that we're investigating further,' Katie told him. 'And of course make the usual appeal for witnesses. How's it going with that water meter protest?'

'They've called it off, thank God. For now, anyway. I never had to deal with such a bunch of raving headbangers in the whole of my career, I'll tell you. The way they talk, you'd think that water meters were invented by Satan.'

'Thanks, Francis. If anything urgent comes up you can contact me at any time. I'll send you a text as soon as I know when I'll be back.'

Alan was keeping his eye on the mapping plan. 'He's passing Fermoy now. He's still heading north on the M8. Just going over the Blackwater River. Still speeding.'

Then he turned to Katie and said, 'You're a consummate liar, you know that, don't you? "Family crisis" – I almost believed you myself when you said that!'

'Well, it's true in a way. John is practically family, and so is Kyna. Take a look in the glovebox.'

'What?'

'Take a look in the glovebox. See what's in there. But be careful.'

Alan opened the glovebox. He put in his hand and took out two black woollen balaclavas, and then a Garda-issue SIG Sauer automatic.

'You're really going to do this, aren't you?' he said.

'What did you think? That I was going to chase Bobby Quilty all the way up to Belfast and then do nothing but phone the police?'

'No. Of course not. But you're taking one hell of a risk here. You're an awful scary lady, did anyone ever tell you that? I think I'm more afeard of you than I am of Bobby Quilty.'

'You've used one of these SIG Sauers before, have you?'

'Oh yes. I did all my firearms training with a two-twenty Carry.'

'We'll have to make it snappy, Alan. Really, really snappy. No hesitation at all. There won't be any time for procedure or warrants or calling for backup.'

'I'm with you all the way. You know that, don't you? And I've done a fair few things myself that were off the menu, so to speak. But this – *fewfff* . . .'

'Where he is now?' asked Katie. They were approaching Fermoy themselves now, although she was keeping to the speed limit. There was no need to have Bobby Quilty's pickup in sight when they were tracking him on the mapping plan.

'Oh—' said Alan. 'He's just passed the turn-off to Mitchelstown. He'll have crossed the Cork county border into Limerick in a couple of minutes.'

Katie had guessed for herself how far Bobby Quilty had progressed but she had wanted to change the subject. She had enough doubts about what she was doing without Alan asking her if she wasn't being too reckless.

Ever since they had left Cork City she had seen heavy grey clouds following them in her rear-view mirror, trailing veils of rain, and by the time they crossed over the Blackwater themselves the clouds were on top of them, like a huge grey blanket being dragged over their heads, and large clear droplets were starting to patter on the windscreen. As they reached Limerick it began to lash down, so that Katie had to turn on the windscreen wipers at full speed and the road ahead of them vanished in a fog of spray.

Alan said, 'Weren't you even tempted to go to America with John? I mean, for the love of God, think of the weather, if nothing else.'

Katie shrugged. 'I still wake up in the night thinking that I made a terrible mistake. I could be living in San Francisco right now, happily married, working for Pinkerton's. I might even have a child. Who knows?'

'What was it that decided you? Not only your sense of duty, surely. I have a sense of duty – that's part of what makes you decide to be a police officer in the first place. But I make plenty of selfish decisions, too.'

'You decided you weren't going to sleep with me again. Was that a selfish decision?'

'No. Yes. In a way. Let's just say that it was self-preservation.'

'Meaning what, exactly?'

'Meaning that I find you incredibly attractive, and sexy, and strong, and self-willed, and that I would probably find myself falling in love with you even if I haven't already. And like I said before, having a relationship with you would probably rip us to bits. Well, it would probably rip *me* to bits, anyhow.'

Katie said nothing for nearly half a minute, while the windscreen wipers furiously flapped from side to side and the tiny car symbol on the mapping plan continued to click every five seconds.

At last she said, 'Don't you trust me?'

'Of course I trust you. But I'm not sure that I could handle you. What we're doing now, I don't know how you had the nerve to think about it, let alone actually carry it out. From what you've told me, you fought tooth and nail to get yourself promoted to Superintendent but now you're putting your entire career at risk, not to mention your life. And all for a man you never really loved.'

'I didn't say that I didn't love him.'

'You didn't have to, Katie. If you'd ever really loved him, you'd be in San Francisco right now, sunning yourself, with your new child on your knee, instead of raking through the pissing rain in Limerick chasing after some fat revolting shitehawk like Bobby Quilty.'

Katie was about to answer, but then she didn't. Maybe Alan was right. She had adored John. She could still close her eyes and think of the way that he used to make love to her, strong and slow and rhythmical, so that sometimes it was like being in a boat on a gently swelling tide, rather than a bed. She could still picture him standing naked by the bedroom window in the morning looking out, but then she could also remember that his eyes seemed to be focused far away instead of on the yard outside, and that she had always felt that she was gradually losing him. Once a man has left Ireland, he never finds it easy to return, not for good. But John was in danger now, appalling danger, and she couldn't imagine how devastated she would be if she lost him.

'Crossing into County Tipperary,' said Alan.

* * *

The rain slowed Bobby Quilty's pickup down to 90 kph, but on Katie's laptop it still kept on clicking its way relentlessly northwards. After two hours Katie and Alan reached Kildare, where Katie pulled on to the hard shoulder at the side of the road and they changed places so that Alan could drive for a while. The rain was still hammering down, so they scurried from one side of the car the other as quickly as they could, like two characters in a silent comedy.

'Jesus,' said Alan, as he fastened his seat belt. 'You hardly need a car in this weather. You'd be better off with a fecking speedboat!'

Katie said, 'I'm going to close my eyes for a while. Wake me up if Quilty does anything strange.'

'It has occurred to you that it may not be Quilty himself in his pickup, only a couple of his minions?'

'It's him all right,' Katie told him.

'What makes you so sure?'

'Because he's driving to Belfast to show the whole of the country that he's not to be messed with, either him or his family. And the only way he can do that is by doing it in person. He thinks somebody's challenged him and he's not going to let them get away with it.'

'But what if it's not him? What if Jimmy O'Reilly hasn't even told him and he's just sent one of his little scummers on some errand or other?'

'Then I'll have egg on my lap, won't I?'

'Face.'

'What?'

'It's "egg on my face". Not "lap".'

'If that's not Bobby Quilty in that pickup, then I'll probably have both.'

She didn't think she would be able to sleep, but the monotonous flapping of the windscreen wipers and the continual clicking of the laptop soon began to make her feel drowsy. She dreamed that she was in a car, driving through the rain, and then she dreamed that she was sitting in the kitchen at home, talking to her mother.

She was surprised and pleased that her mother was still alive. She looked very much like Katie, with her coppery red hair tied back in a loose, untidy pleat, and intense green eyes. She was wearing a cream-coloured smock with a broderie anglaise collar, which she had been wearing the day before she was taken to hospital to give birth to Moirin, and died.

'I think you're making a terrible mistake,' said her mother, without looking up from her embroidery.

'Why? I love him.'

'You think you love him, but you've never been in love so you don't know what love is. Not real love. Not the way your da and I love each other. Not only that, he's a desperate chancer. You know he is. It won't do you any favours in the Garda, being married to a man like that.'

'Ma, I don't care what you think. Me and Paul are going to get married and that's an end to it. *Paul!* Come on, we're leaving!'

Alan said, 'Who's Paul?'

Katie jolted and opened her eyes. Her shoulder was stiff from leaning sideways against the passenger door and her mouth felt dry. It was still raining and the windscreen wipers were still furiously throwing themselves from side to side.

'Did I say "Paul"?' she said. 'I was dreaming. I was having an argument with my mother about my first husband. Well, my only husband. He's dead now.'

She peered out of the window and asked, 'How long have I been asleep? I didn't think I would actually sleep! Where are we?'

'You've been out for half an hour at least. We've just passed Rathcoole. We'll be going around the Dublin ring road in a few minutes, God help us. Let's hope the traffic's not too sticky.'

'Where's the—?' Katie began, but Alan lifted up her laptop from where he had tucked it down the side of his seat.

'I've been keeping track on the Big Feller on my mobile,' he said. 'He's still heading north.'

Katie opened her laptop and saw that Bobby Quilty's pickup had now bypassed Dublin city centre on the M50 ring road and was passing through Swords. From here, it would take them about another hour to reach the border with the North and then a further fifty minutes to get to Belfast. She reached behind her to the back seat, where she had left her large maroon leather tote bag, and took out two bottles of Celtic Pure water. She opened one and passed it to Alan.

'Thanks. A cold Satz would have hit the spot, but this'll do.'

The late rush-hour traffic around the M50 was slow, a carnival of red brake lights, but it kept moving and as soon as they had bypassed Dublin Alan was able to speed up. The rain was gradually easing off, too, and as they drove over the twisting River Boyne between County Meath and County Louth the clouds began to break up, so that the sun held up a few last silvery swords of light before it sank behind the distant trees.

At last they reached the southern suburbs of Belfast. Alan stayed in the driving seat because he knew the city so well, while Katie kept the mapping plan open on her lap and gave him directions.

'He's turning off the main road, left, on to the A55,' she told him.

'That's the Monagh bypass, which goes off to the west,' said Alan. 'He won't find many loyalists in that direction.'

Bobby Quilty's pickup had slowed down now and they were less than two kilometres behind it.

'He's heading along Springfield Road.'

'I think I know where he's going,' said Alan. 'His cousin Maxy

O'Mara lives just up here in Dunboyne Park. Maxy was always Bobby's fixer. He'd get guns for him if he needed guns, or a car with a number plate that nobody could trace, or rent him a lock-up where he could store his smuggled fags if he'd shipped in too many. Jesus, Maxy O'Mara. We scooped Maxy more times than I can remember, but we were never able to get him up in front of a court.'

'Not even a Diplock Court?'

Alan shook his head. 'He wasn't strictly a terrorist, that was the trouble. And we could never get enough admissible evidence against him. You remember that poem, "The other day, upon the stair, I met a man who wasn't there"? That's what we used to call Maxy O'Mara when I was in the COD – "the Man Who Wasn't There". No matter where a witness testified that Maxy had been, he could produce two more who would say that he hadn't been there at all.'

Katie watched Bobby Quilty's pickup as it turned off the Springfield Road into Highcairn Drive. It travelled a few metres and then it turned left into a short cul-de-sac called Dunboyne Park, just as Alan had predicted. There it stopped.

Alan pulled into the forecourt of the Mount Alverno petrol station, about a kilometre and a half short of Highcairn Drive. 'Okay then,' he said. 'Now what do we do?'

'We'll have to wait, that's all,' said Katie. 'He might just have stopped for a comfort break. In fact, I'd say that's a certainty, knowing him. But it all depends on what he does next.'

'On balance, I think it's unlikely that he'll try to do anything tonight,' said Alan. 'He might have found out by now who it was who shot the Dohertys. If they were loyalists, though, like they made out they were, then even *he's* going to be cautious about going into a staunchly loyalist area at this time of night. That's if there isn't an interface around it and it's locked for the night.'

'Quite honestly, I could use a comfort break myself,' said Katie. 'Keep an eye on him, would you? I won't be long.'

When she came back from the petrol station toilet, Alan was standing beside the car with her laptop open on the roof.

'Any movement?' she asked him.

'No. He hasn't budged an inch. I reckon I'm right and he's going to stay there till the morning. Listen – we don't want to be sitting in the car all night, do we? What do you say we go back to my place? It's only twenty minutes away and we can take it in turns to keep a watch on him. I can knock us up something to eat, too.'

Katie thought for a moment. It was a very high risk. If Bobby Quilty did decide to go after the Dohertys' murderers tonight, and they lived in one of the nearest loyalist enclaves like Ainsworth Avenue or the Highfield Estate, it would take him only a few minutes to get there and by the time she and Alan arrived it might be too late. On the other hand, the murderers might live further away, and in any case she guessed that Bobby Quilty would want to spend some time relishing his revenge and making sure that his victims knew exactly what a fatal mistake they had made by killing anybody related to the Quilty family.

'I don't know,' she said. 'I'm beginning to think I was out of my mind, doing this.'

'Well, me too,' said Alan. 'But like you said, if it doesn't work, it doesn't work, and we'll have to think of some other way of rescuing John and Kyna.'

He laid his hand on her shoulder and said, 'Listen, if it would make you feel happier to stay close by and keep a watch on Quilty all night, I don't mind doing it. I've done plenty of stake-outs before, albeit when I was a few years younger. The garage sells sandwiches and drinks, and there's a toilet. What more do we need?'

Katie couldn't help smiling even though she felt so tense and confused. 'No . . .' she said. 'Let's go back to your place. So long as we're ready to scramble the second that Quilty makes a move. I have the feeling that you're right and that he won't try anything until tomorrow.'

'You're sure about that? I mean, you're in charge.'

She looked at him and for the first time she could see in his expression that he accepted that she outranked him, even if he was no longer in the service, and that he was prepared to do whatever she told him. She couldn't stop herself from wondering what he would be like if they went to bed now, if he would make love to her any differently than he had the first time.

'Yes, I'm sure,' she said. 'But before we do, let's just cruise past Dunboyne Park and take a look.'

Alan started the engine and they drove further along Springfield Road until they reached Highcairn Drive. On the left-hand side of the road there was a low brick wall and a hedge. On the right-hand side, there was a patch of rough grass, with a spiked steel fence behind it, and beyond the fence two terraces of houses. On the end wall of each terrace were paintings of masked men with guns, and loyalist badges, and the letters UFF, for the Ulster Freedom Fighters.

Katie had visited Belfast many times before, but mostly to the city centre, for meetings with the Crime Operations Department, and she had forgotten how blatant the hostility still was between republicans and loyalists. UFF could almost have stood for Us? Forgive and Forget?

Dunboyne Park was two neat rows of red-brick houses with neatly tended front gardens. About two thirds of the way down Katie could see Bobby Quilty's Nissan Navara, with one of his men leaning against it, smoking. Even as Katie and Alan drove slowly past the entrance to the cul-de-sac she saw the man leave the side of the pickup and disappear into one of the houses.

'All right,' she said. 'Let's hope they're all inside, sitting down to a pasty supper and tapping their feet to the Wolfe Tones' greatest hits.'

'I wish I'd met you years ago,' said Alan.

They turned around and then Alan drove them into the city centre. They crossed over the River Lagan, with the street lights sparkling in the water, and out to King's Road, in the Cherryvalley area, which was lined with large detached 1930s houses – the prosperous Protestant part of the city. They turned into a small mews with modern blocks of flats at the end of it.

'Home,' said Alan.

Katie's attention had been fixed on her laptop, making sure that Bobby Quilty's pickup was still parked outside Maxy O'Mara's house. 'Oh,' she said. 'We're here. That was quick.'

Alan led her in through the communal entrance and upstairs to his third-floor flat. He opened the door and switched on the lights and said, 'Sorry about the mess. I keep meaning to tidy up, but somehow I never get around to it.'

The flat was very small, but very modern, with polished wooden floors and a kitchen with pine cupboards and black faux-marble work surfaces. The living room was bare except for a purple couch, a glass-topped coffee table and a bookcase. The only mess that Katie could see was a heap of crumpled shirts at one end of the couch and a stack of scribble-filled notebooks on the coffee table, along with a half-empty coffee mug and an oat bar wrapper.

'I expect when I said I lived in Cherryvalley you imagined somewhere very grand,' said Alan, picking up the shirts and carrying them through to the bedroom. Katie could see that there was a double bed, unmade, with a pale yellow bedspread, and a fitted wardrobe, but hardly enough space between the bed and the walls to walk around sideways.

He came out of the bedroom and said, 'When I was married, of course, we had a three-bedroomed house and a garden and all. But can you imagine what this place cost me? €129,000! For a flat no bigger than a bus shelter!'

Katie sat down. She was beginning to feel very tired now.

'What can I get you?' he asked her. 'Tea? Coffee? Wine? Beer?'

'Tea would be good. I don't drink on duty.'

When she said that, they both looked at the mapping plan on the laptop. Bobby Quilty's pickup was still in Dunboyne Park. What he was saying, or doing, or planning to do, Katie couldn't even guess.

* * *

She had a shower and dressed again in her black trousers and grey blouse. She always carried clean underwear in her tote bag because she never knew when she would unexpectedly have to stay out overnight.

While she was putting on her make-up in the bathroom mirror she thought that there was nothing more poignant than a single toothbrush, standing in a tumbler.

'What can I fix you to eat?' Alan asked her when she came out of the bathroom. 'I have pizza in the freezer. Or I can beat up some eggs and make you a cheese omelette. I'm renowned throughout Ulster for my cheese omelettes.'

'Pizza would be grand,' said Katie. 'That's what I always have when I'm too tired to cook.'

'Okay,' he said. 'Pizza it is. We can catch some shut-eye then, but we'll have to take it in turns.'

'Well, that solves *that* moral dilemma,' said Katie.

Alan took hold of her shoulders and gave her a kiss. 'More like *im*moral dilemma.' He smiled. Then he pointed at the blue car icon on the mapping plan and said, 'Quilty, you bastard, if you move so much as one inch before I've had something to eat I'll clean your clock when I see you, so I will. Your own father won't know you – not that he ever did.'

* * *

Alan slept first, fully dressed except for his shoes, while Katie kept herself awake by watching television with the volume turned right down and her laptop open on the coffee table right beside her.

After a while she stood up to stretch her legs and look through the books in Alan's bookcase. Most of them were dog-eared paperback thrillers, Clive Cussler and James Patterson, but there were two or three hardbacks on Irish history and even *Hunger Strike* by Danny Morrison. *Hunger Strike* was an anthology by various writers about the dirty protests and hunger strikes by republican prisoners in the Maze prison in the 1970s, which struck Katie as an unusual book for a former PSNI officer to have on his shelves. Perhaps he had wanted to see the Troubles from both points of view.

There was also a photograph of a dark-haired woman in an oval silver frame. She was quite pretty, but wistful. Katie looked at the back of the frame, but there was nothing written there, so there was no indication of who she was. Alan had said that he and his wife, Alison, had nearly torn each other to shreds, so was it likely to be her?

Alan had set his alarm for 3 a.m., and when it buzzed she heard him stir himself and groan. After a few moments he came shuffling into the living room, blinking and scratching the back of his neck.

'Your turn,' he said. 'But I pray to God you don't have anything like the nightmares I've just been having.'

'No, I think I'd rather keep my eyes open,' said Katie. 'It's going to be daylight before we know it and if I go to sleep now I'll be wrecked when I wake up.'

'In that case I'll make us some coffee.'

When he came back with two mugs of espresso, Katie said, 'I see you have Danny Morrison's book on the hunger strikes.'

'I bought it when it first came out. I thought, "know your enemy".'

'You don't think of them as your enemy now, do you?'

'It's still hard not to. Our next-door neighbour, Tommy, was a prison warder and he was shot one day when he went out shopping with his five-year-old daughter.'

'So, what do you think? Are we forgetting or are we just pretending to forget?'

'If you're right about Bobby Quilty, then we're not even pretending. Do you know how many interfaces we have in Belfast?'

'Fifty? Sixty? I know it's quite a few.'

'Ninety-nine, even today. What kind of people in a so-called civilized city need concrete walls and locked gates and barbed wire to keep them apart?'

Katie was on the verge of asking Alan about the woman in the photograph when there was an insect-like click from the mapping plan on her laptop. It was 5.11 a.m. and although the sky was cloudy and overcast it was growing light outside. Bobby Quilty's pickup was moving to the end of Dunboyne Park and turning round. It came out on to Highcairn Drive and then turned into Springfield Road, heading east towards the city centre.

'That's it,' said Alan, reaching under the couch to retrieve his shoes. 'He's on his way!'

Katie slipped on her shoes, too, and then stood up to clip on her holster and tug on her short black jacket. She picked up her laptop and the two of them left the flat and hurried down the stairs.

They ran across to Katie's car and climbed in. As soon as she had fastened her seat belt Katie opened her laptop and said, 'He's just turned right on to Cupar Way. Any idea where he might be headed?'

'Sandy Row, somewhere like that. Hardcore loyalist territory, anyway.'

Mother of God, thought Katie. *Bobby Quilty's actually fallen for it.* She didn't know whether to be elated or terrified.

Forty-three

Bobby Quilty's pickup turned right on Blythe Street and then into Felt Street in the Blackstaff ward. It went a third of the way along Felt Street and stopped.

'He's in Felt Street,' said Katie. She waited for two more five-second clicks and then said, 'He hasn't moved. That looks like his final destination.'

'Felt Street is totally loyalist,' said Alan. 'There's more Union flags hung up there than washing.'

'How long is it going to take us to get there?'

'Ten minutes, if I put my foot down.'

'Okay then, put your foot down. He's still hasn't moved.'

They crossed over the Lagan again. Because it was so early there was hardly any traffic in the city centre apart from a street-sweeper and two or three buses with pasty-faced shift-workers staring listlessly out of their windows. It took them less than eight minutes to reach Felt Street, a long red-brick terrace, and as soon as they turned the corner they saw Bobby Quilty's pickup.

Alan pulled in behind a white builder's van and parked. Katie opened the glovebox and handed him one of the black balaclava helmets and the SIG Sauer automatic.

He checked the gun's magazine and then said, 'Okay. So what's the plan of action?'

'There is no plan of action, except that once we see Quilty, we have to neutralize him before he has a chance to use his phone.'

'"Neutralize" meaning—?'

'Make him drop his phone and any weapon that he might have

on him, although in my experience he's not usually armed. It's his minions who carry the firearms.'

'And if he refuses?'

'Alan, I haven't given you that gun for the fun of it.'

'Whatever you say. Let's do it, then, shall we? But for the love of God, Katie, be careful, will you? I've already attended one too many funerals.'

She held out her hand and he squeezed it tight. 'Okay,' she said. 'Showtime.'

They pulled on their black balaclavas. Alan looked at Katie and said, 'Holy cow! I thought I was afeard of you before. You should see yourself now. Hallowe'en Part Two!'

They climbed out of the car and walked side by side along Felt Street. There were Union flags hanging outside almost every house and even from the lamp posts. There was no wind, though, none at all, and they hung down limply under a sky as grey as human ashes.

One of Bobby Quilty's men was standing outside the house where his pickup was parked. He had a shaven head and a tight white T-shirt which emphasized his body-builder's muscles. Katie took out her revolver, but the man had his back to them as they quickly and quietly approached, so he didn't see them until they had almost reached the metal garden gate.

'Hey – what the *feck*—?' he began, but Katie pointed her gun directly at his face and said, 'Shut your bake. Not a sound. Get inside.'

'What?'

'I said get inside. *Go*. But *no* – don't put your hands up. Just walk in normal.'

The maroon-painted front door was already half open and the overhead light in the hallway was on. The shaven-headed man pushed the door open wider and stepped inside. Katie followed him, with Alan close behind. Alan had cocked his automatic and was holding it up in both hands.

The hallway was narrow with a floral carpet and gilt-framed prints of flowers on the walls. On the right-hand side there was a steep staircase, and down at the end of the hallway two open doors, the left-hand door leading to the living room and the right-hand door leading to the kitchen. Katie was about to ask the shaven-headed man where the Big Feller was when she heard Bobby Quilty's distinctive voice coming from the living room. She could also smell cigarette smoke.

'—but *now* look at the three of you, wee men!' Bobby Quilty was saying. 'Not so fecking scary now, are you?'

Katie prodded the shaven-headed man in the back with the muzzle of her revolver. 'Go on. In you go.'

The shaven-headed man glanced over his shoulder at her and it was obvious that for all of his muscular bulk he was frightened – probably more of Bobby Quilty than of her. He had a single gold earring and although his T-shirt was very white he smelled of stale sweat.

'Are you dee-efff, man?' said Alan. 'Get yourself in there before the lady makes a hole in you.'

'Who's that?' called Bobby Quilty. 'Murtagh, is that you? Who's that out there with you? Is that the kids back already?'

The shaven-headed man went reluctantly in through the living-room door. Katie went in after him and then shoved him hard between the shoulder blades with the heel of her left hand. He staggered forward two or three steps and that allowed her to step smartly to one side of him and point her revolver directly at Bobby Quilty. Alan came in close behind her, although he still kept his gun raised, James Bond-style, ready to point it at anybody who looked like a threat.

'What in the name of God—?' said Bobby Quilty. He was standing in front of the brown-tiled fireplace with the back of his cannonball head reflected in the mirror behind him. He was wearing a baggy cream jacket and drooping blue jeans, and a shirt with camels and pyramids and desert sunsets all over it. There was a cigarette stuck to his lower lip, and as he spoke the long ash on the end of it dropped on to the carpet.

A mock-onyx coffee table had been picked up and was now perched on top of the living-room couch, because the space had been needed for the three men who were sitting back to back in the middle of the floor. The first man was bald and beefy-shouldered, with a broken nose. The second was thin, with a wild mess of grey hair and hollow cheeks. The third was spotty and young, with a straggly black moustache. The older man was wearing green-and-white-striped flannelette pyjamas, but the other two had on nothing but underpants – large white Y-fronts for the man with the broken nose, and pink boxer shorts for the spotty boy.

Katie could see that all three men had their hands fastened behind them with nylon wrist restraints, the same kind of PlastiCuffs that the Garda used. In between them, behind their backs, there was a battered black briefcase, standing on its end.

Another of Bobby Quilty's men was sitting in an armchair by the window, with his legs crossed, also smoking. His hair was bright orange and it had been cut short so that it stuck up like a scrubbing brush. His face was rat-like, with icy blue eyes and protruding front teeth.

Bobby Quilty was holding up his mobile phone. Katie said, 'Drop it, Bobby. Drop the phone.'

'Or you'll do *what*, whoever you are, wee doll? Shoot me?'

'I said drop the phone.'

Bobby Quilty looked down at the phone as if he were surprised to see it. 'Ach, there might be a bit of a problem with that.'

'I'll give you till three. Drop it.'

'Just hold your horses and listen,' said Bobby Quilty. 'The problem is that we've paid these three fellers a visit this morning to settle a score. These are the Crothers – Sam Crothers, he's the baldy one, Stephen Crothers, the one who looks like a bomb went off in a scouring-pad factory, and young Kenny MacClery, who's a nephew.'

'I don't care who they are,' Katie repeated. 'Drop the phone.'

Bobby Quilty raised his left hand like the pope giving a bene-diction. 'I asked you to hold your horses and hear me out. These three fellers have done my family a desperate injustice and because of that they have to be punished for it. An eye for an eye and all that. That case you see in between them happens to contain 450 grams of C4, as well as more than a hundred three-inch nails. The detonator that can set off that C4 is activated by guess what, wee doll?'

He held up his mobile phone and grinned at her. 'If I drop it, then ba-*doom*! These three fellers, as well as the rest of us here in this room – well, we'll all end up as pasty filling.'

'In that case, lay the phone gently down on the floor and step away from it.'

'Or what? You'll shoot me? And what do you think will happen if you shoot me? I might press the key that sets off the bomb, out of spite. Or maybe I'll just drop my phone on the floor. Whichever it is, ba-*doom*!'

Katie guessed that the chances of Bobby Quilty's phone setting off an explosion if he simply dropped it on to the floor were infinitesimal, if not zero. All the same, she didn't know exactly what kind of connection had been set up between his phone and the detonator in the bomb – if it really was a bomb.

'Lay the phone down on the floor, gently,' said Katie.

'Why?' Bobby Quilty retorted. 'What the feck has any of this got to do with you, any road? Who are you? Don't tell me the Sandy Row Women's Wombles are back in business.'

For nearly half a minute, nobody moved and nobody spoke, and with every second that passed the tension in the room racked up higher. Bobby Quilty continued to stare at Katie with contempt, while his three handcuffed victims in the middle of the room looked up at her in desperation. The man with the orange hair sat in the same casual position, with his legs crossed, but now his pose was rigid and although a ribbon of smoke was still rising from his cigarette he made no attempt to smoke it. The shaven-headed man in the white T-shirt moved, but only to take two cautious steps backwards – as if that would make any difference if it was a bomb and it really did explode.

Katie couldn't see Alan because he was standing too close behind her, but she could hear him breathing hard and quick. In fact, he sounded almost like a pole-vaulter hyping himself up for his run towards the bar.

'Meara will be back very soon, with the girls,' said Stephen Crothers in a voice that was little more than a croak. 'You can't harm them. They're innocents. Whatever you do to us, you have to spare Meara and the girls.'

'Oh, like you spared the Doherty children?' said Bobby Quilty.

'That was different. That was a long-standing debt that had to be paid. We thought the account would be settled for good after that.'

'Well, you thought wrong, didn't you, wee man?' Bobby Quilty retorted. 'Those were relatives of mine that you did for, very close relatives, and nobody lays a finger on any member of my family without suffering for it. You – look at the three of you, you miserable friggers. Thought you'd make history, did you? Well, you will, I swear to God, but it won't be in the way you thought you would. There'll six coffins all right, so there will, but they won't know which bit to put in which. They might just as well bury you in soup kettles after what's going to happen to you.'

'Nothing's going to happen to them,' said Katie. 'You're going to put down that phone and I'm going to call the police.'

Bobby Quilty suddenly frowned. He took the cigarette off his lip and looked at Katie with his eyes narrowed.

'It's you, isn't it?' he said. 'It's only fecking you.'

'What are you talking about?'

'It's *you*. Detective Superintendent Maguire. I thought I recognized that Corky whine on you. I'm right, amptnah? What in the name of Jesus do you think you're playing at?'

'Holy shite,' said the orange-haired man in the armchair. 'You're having a laugh, aren't you? She's that peeler you was talking about?'

Katie dragged off her balaclava and stuffed it into her pocket. 'Well done, Mr Quilty. I was going to tell you who I was in just a moment, anyway, before I arrest you for making a threat to kill and possession of explosives with intent to endanger life.'

'This is Belfast, wee doll, in case you hadn't noticed,' said Bobby Quilty. 'This isn't Cork.'

'That makes no difference. I still have the power to arrest you here and I'm sure the PSNI will be delighted to assist me in taking you in and bringing charges against you.'

'I don't fecking believe this,' said Bobby Quilty. 'You've set me up here, haven't you? You've only gone and fecking set me up. And who's that knobhead with you?'

Alan pulled off his balaclava, too. 'Reck me, do you, Bobby? It's been a long time.'

Bobby Quilty slapped his hand against his forehead. 'I don't fecking believe this! This is like some kind of fecking bad dream! Detective Inspector Alan Harte, as was! Harte the Fart, that's what we used to call you! All wind and no action!'

'Alan,' said Katie. 'Call for backup, would you? And tell them we'll need bomb disposal, too.'

'Hey, now then, that's enough of that,' said Bobby Quilty, and now his tone was deadly serious. 'You and I have an understanding, Detective Superintendent Maguire, don't we? If I was you, I'd turn around and walk out of here and say no more about what you've seen here, ever, because if you don't, you know what the consequences will be, don't you?'

He held up his phone again. 'I have only to call my pal Ger and even if I don't say a single word he'll know why I've called him and he'll know exactly what to do.'

'You're not getting away with this any longer, Bobby,' said Katie. 'Alan, make that call, will you, please?'

'I wouldn't do that, Detective Inspector Harte the Fart,' Bobby Quilty warned him. 'I don't know if Detective Superintendent Maguire here has, like, *apprised* you of the arrangement that she and me have between us. But you push just one button on that phone of yours and I'll be pushing one on mine – the one button that tells my pal Ger to do for two good friends of hers.'

Katie said, 'It's okay, Alan. Stall it for a moment.'

'It's beyond me why you've showed up here today, Detective

Superintendent Maguire,' said Bobby Quilty. Still holding up his phone, he took a packet of cigarettes out of his shirt pocket, placed one between his lips and then lit it, all left-handed. 'I thought our arrangement was working very well on both sides.'

'That was because I could never find anyone who was brave enough to give evidence against you,' said Katie. 'But now I believe I have.'

'What, these three friggers here? They're *murderers*, wee doll. They were the ones who shot the Doherty family. They shot the father and the mother and the poor wee children, too. I know that for a fact, because I know the scumbag who sold them their guns and not only that, they've been bragging about it all around Blackstaff. Who's going to believe what *they* have to say, even if they have the guts to say it?'

'Oh, you'd be surprised,' Katie told him. 'A court will believe them, if their story rings true. And I think they'll have the guts to say it if it means a substantial reduction in their sentences for shooting the Dohertys.'

There was another long, tense, uncomfortable silence. Then Bobby Quilty said, 'Why don't you call it a day, Detective Superintendent Maguire? Forget you ever came here, wee doll. That way, your two dear friends will stay safe and we can carry on like nothing ever happened.'

'And if I do that, what will you do? Blow these people up? Them and their children?'

'Retribution, that's all it is. Justice. What they did to us, we're going to do the same to them.'

'The Langtrys and the Dohertys were shot and buried beneath the floorboards. They weren't blown up.'

Bobby Quilty blew out a long stream of smoke. 'There was kind of a snag there. I wanted to do that, so I did, bury them under the floorboards. It would have been historically appropriate, do you know what I mean? But I was told when I got here that all the houses along this street have concrete floors, and we couldn't have spent three days hammering away with pneumatic drills, now could we? – and then mixing up the concrete to pour over them.'

The man with the orange hair suddenly spoke up. He had a thin, rusty voice, as if were making a complaint rather than a comment.

'I'll tell you this, too, Mrs Peeler. If you *really* want to make a point in this city, a bomb's always the best way of doing it. A shooting, they'll forget that after a few weeks. Shootings are ten a penny. But if you blow up half the street, they'll remember that for a brave lot longer.'

Katie ignored him and turned back to Bobby Quilty. 'But what's the point that you're trying to make here, Bobby?'

'I'm making the point that nobody murders members of my family and gets away with it, that's all – no matter what their excuse is.'

'The Dohertys were no relations of yours.'

'They were, too. I have the family tree to prove it.'

'And where did you get that from?'

Bobby Quilty squinted against the smoke from his cigarette. 'A reliable source. A very reliable source.'

'Bobby – I invented that family tree myself, for the specific purpose of getting you here and identifying the men who shot the Dohertys for me.'

'Away on!' said Bobby Quilty. Then, 'You're not serious.'

'I was never more serious in the whole of my life. Now lay the phone down carefully on the floor and step away from it. Robert Boland Quilty, I am arresting you under the Non-Fatal Offences Against the Person Act 1997, for making a threat to kill or cause serious harm to another person without lawful excuse. You are not obliged to say anything unless you wish to do so, but anything you do say will be taken down in writing and may be given in evidence.'

If the atmosphere in the living room had been tense before, it was now so charged that Katie almost expected the front windows to crack from the pressure. The orange-haired man uncrossed his legs and slowly stood up, as if his knees were as rusty as his voice. The three handcuffed men in the middle of the floor kept turning their heads around in bewilderment and panic, looking first at

Katie and then at Bobby Quilty and then at the orange-haired man.

Bobby Quilty said, 'You disappoint me, Detective Superintendent Maguire. You fecking disappoint me. I thought you were a woman of your word, but all the time what were you doing? Deviously plotting, that's what you were doing. But now you're going to find out that I'm the kind of man who keeps his promises.'

'I'm telling you this for the very last time, Bobby,' said Katie. 'Put down the phone.'

Bobby Quilty changed the phone over to his left hand and defiantly raised it even higher, angling it so that Katie could see the screen. Then he held up his right index finger and said, 'This is where you learn a lesson, Detective Superintendent Maguire. This is where you learn not to mess with Bobby Quilty. Execution by telephone. But you'll never find out what happened to your friends or where their bodies might be buried, and you'll never be able to prove a thing against me because I didn't do it and I wasn't there, and you're a witness to that yourself.'

Katie kept her revolver pointed at Bobby Quilty's chest but she knew that she wasn't going to shoot him. He was no immediate threat to *her* life, because he wasn't armed, and it would be almost impossible for her to prove that he was a threat to John and Kyna's lives, either. He was threatening these three members of the Crothers family, and their children, too, when they came home, and that was a serious offence in itself, but whether it justified shooting him and possibly killing him was another matter altogether.

For the first time since she had thought of this plan for stopping Bobby Quilty, she hesitated. It could come down to a choice between saving John and Kyna and saving three alleged murderers. She had been prepared to risk her career setting up Bobby Quilty like this, but she wasn't prepared to kill him and go to jail for it.

She could walk out now and call the PSNI, but Bobby Quilty would only have to get the first hint of a police raid and he would almost certainly give the word for John and Kyna to be done for.

'I tell you what, Bobby,' she said. 'I'll give you a choice. I'll walk out of here if you do, too, and take your briefcase with you. You've led me to the men who shot the Dohertys, as I was hoping you would, and now I can deal with them myself. They won't go unpunished, I can promise you that.'

Bobby Quilty drew deeply on his cigarette, and when he spoke, smoke came leaking out of his mouth and his brown-rimmed nostrils. 'How do I know that you weren't codding me when you said that the Dohertys were no relations of mine?'

'You'll just have take my word for it, that's all.'

'I had the information from a very reliable source, wee doll, and that very reliable source never mentioned you.'

'He wouldn't have done. He's not an enthusiast when it comes to female police officers.'

Bobby Quilty's eyes narrowed when she said that, but he didn't respond. For all he knew, she was only guessing that his 'very reliable source' was a garda officer and she was trying to trick him into saying who it was.

'So what do you say?' said Katie. 'Deal or no deal?'

'I'll tell you what I think,' said Bobby Quilty. 'I think you're trying to pull a fast one here, Detective Superintendent Maguire. If I walk out of here and let these friggers live, then the word's going to go around that any scummer can do for Bobby Quilty's relations and he won't have the balls to hit back. That's what this is all about, isn't it? You want me to look windy. You'll get all of the credit for solving the Doherty murders and I'll end up looking like a sooner.'

'Holy Mother of God, Bobby, how many times do I have to tell you? You're not related to the Dohertys. I made it up.'

'I don't fecking believe you. I've seen the family tree for myself. There was a Quilty served with the IRA at Kilcullen and he married a Doherty.'

'There wasn't, and he didn't. I invented it.'

Bobby Quilty shook his head in disbelief and turned to the orange-haired man. 'What's your opinion, Sandy? I definitely think we're being taken for eejits here, don't you?'

As soon as Bobby Quilty looked the other way, though, Alan seized Katie's left arm and swung her violently round behind him, as if they were dance partners and some furious flamenco had just started up. He caught her completely by surprise and she hit her shoulder hard against the door frame, dropping her revolver, which bounced into the hallway. For a split second she thought: *My God, he's been fooling me – he's on Bobby Quilty's side.*

Dropping down on to her knees to pick up her revolver, however, she heard an ear-splitting bang, and then another, and another. She twisted round to witness what looked like a waxwork tableau in which time had stood still and nobody was moving. Through a gauzy curtain of gun-smoke, she saw Alan holding his automatic in both hands, pointing it directly at Bobby Quilty. She saw Bobby Quilty himself, his mouth open in surprise and his cigarette hanging from his lower lip. The sunset pattern on his shirt was so colourful that it was impossible to tell if he had been shot, but his shoulders were hunched forward and his arms were outspread like a man preparing to jump off a wall. He had dropped his mobile phone and it was bouncing across the floor.

The man with the orange hair had hauled up the left side of his mustard-coloured tank top and was tugging a large pistol out of his belt. The shaven-headed man was reaching out towards Alan, his mouth distorted in a silent shout. In the middle of the room, the three handcuffed men had ducked down, hunching their shoulders and squeezing their eyes tight shut, since Alan had fired only a few inches over their heads.

'*Alan!*' Katie shouted, although she could hardly hear herself because the shots had half-deafened her. The orange-haired man had taken his pistol right out now and was cocking it and aiming it at Alan.

Katie picked up her revolver and scrambled out into the hallway on her hands and knees. She heard another shot, a deeper *boom!* this time, then the sharper crack of Alan's SIG Sauer. She stood up, went back to the open door and leaned cautiously sideways, holding her gun up high, so that she could see inside the room.

The orange-haired man was sitting back in his chair with his arms and legs spreadeagled, and there was a blood on his tank top. The shaven-headed man with the white T-shirt had jumped on to Alan's back and grabbed his right wrist and was trying to wrestle his gun away from him.

'*Get us the fuck out of here!*' Sam Crothers screamed, throwing himself from side to side in an attempt to free himself from his nylon handcuffs. Kenny MacClery was trying to bump himself across the room on his bottom. Stephen Crothers's teeth were gritted in pain and concentration as he, too, tried to wrench his hands out of his cuffs.

Katie was about to step into the room and point her gun directly at the shaven-headed man in the white T-shirt so that he would let Alan go, but then she saw Bobby Quilty. He had collapsed sideways into the fireplace and there was a wide triangular bloodstain on his jacket and blood running out of his nose. His eyes were bulging and his chest was heaving, but he was managing to inch his way out of the hearth and across the carpet, reaching out in front of him with his bloodied right hand.

A second too late, Katie realized that he was trying to reach his mobile phone, which had fallen close to Sam Crothers's bare foot. He jabbed at the phone with his index finger, missing it twice, but then he hauled himself a few inches nearer.

'*Alan!*' Katie screamed at him and tried to get into the room. But Alan and the shaven-headed man were struggling around and around, blocking the doorway, and as she tried to force her way past them they toppled against her, grunting and panting, and pushed her back into the hall.

Even when she thought about it later, she didn't remember hearing the explosion. But the whole house shook as if it had been hit by an earthquake and a blizzard of debris was blasted out of the living-room door – bricks, tiles, bits of furniture, curtains, as well as a shower of glittering nails and large pieces of human bodies. Alan and the shaven-headed man were both lifted up bodily and blown across the hallway into the kitchen where they landed with a double thump, splattering blood up the sides of the green kitchen cabinets.

Katie was knocked over backwards, almost as far as the front door. She made a grab for the coat-stand to try and stop herself from falling over, but the coat-stand fell over, too, and she was buried for a moment in donkey jackets and children's duffel coats. The explosion had split the wallpaper in the hallway and made all the pictures drop off, but it hadn't been powerful enough to bring down the wall itself.

As Katie struggled to her feet, a thick grey cloud of smoke and dust rolled out of the living room, so that she was almost blinded as well as deafened. She stood still for a moment, leaning with one hand against the wall to steady herself, then holstered her revolver and dragged her balaclava out of her pocket so that she could press it over her nose and mouth.

Shaking with shock, she stepped carefully over the broken bricks and lumps of plaster until she reached the kitchen. She didn't have to go inside to see that both Alan and the shaven-headed man were dead. They were lying face to face, both of them soaked in blood, and staring at each other with their eyes wide open, like two boxers challenging each other before a match.

She didn't want to look inside the living room but she knew she had to. Right inside the doorway a headless torso was lying against the wall. Its heart and deflated lungs were still inside it and lacerated strings of bloody beige intestine still connected it to the pelvis and legs, which were sitting in the middle of the room. She couldn't see its head, but she could tell from the white underpants that it was Sam Crothers.

The whole of the front of the living room had been blown out, so that she could see the street outside. Half the ceiling had collapsed and the front garden was heaped with bricks and broken window frames and jagged pieces of plasterboard. Lying on his back on the pavement, still sitting in his chair, was the orange-haired man. His face had been blasted off so that he looked as if he was wearing a piece of raw pig's liver as a mask.

Bobby Quilty's pickup was parked right outside. Its windows were shattered and its doors dented and peppered with holes.

Katie was feeling swimmy and there were tiny stars prickling in front of her eyes. The metallic stench of blood and faeces and exploded C4 made her retch. *Stay steady*, she told herself. *This is your job and it was you who brought this about.*

Like Sam Crothers, Stephen Crothers and Kenny MacClery had been sitting with their backs to the briefcase and they taken the full force of the C4 and the nails that were packed inside it. Apart from their hips and legs, there was hardly anything left of either of them but plaited piles of intestines and a jumble of ribs and stringy rags of red flesh.

Bobby Quilty's body, in contrast, was almost unscathed. He had been lying on his side when he had detonated the bomb and the Crothers had shielded him from the worst of the blast and its devastating hail of nails. His eyes were closed and although his his chin was bearded with blood, and the front of his jacket was blood-soaked, too, he could have been contentedly sleeping.

Katie looked down at him and thought: *You always knew, didn't you, that your life would end like this? And you were never going to die alone, were you? You had to have the satisfaction of taking some other scumbags with you – especially since you believed that I was lying to you, and that they had murdered your relatives.*

Now, however, Katie forced herself to switch into professional mode. She could hear people shouting in the street outside and a woman screaming. The police and the fire brigade would be here in a matter of minutes and she needed to be out of here and gone before anybody started asking who she was and what she was doing. She had been shaken to the core, but she had to think about John and Kyna. How long would it be before Bobby Quilty's minions heard that he was dead and made their own decisions about what to do with them? Without Bobby Quilty holding them as hostages to keep the Garda off his back they would be nothing but a useless liability.

She bent down and lifted Bobby Quilty's hand so that she could pick up his mobile phone. It was like a pig's trotter and his fingers were sticky and still warm. She dropped the phone into her pocket and then she searched around for Alan's SIG Sauer automatic. She couldn't see it among the wreckage in the living room, so she had to go back into the kitchen. She didn't want to look at Alan lying there dead, but she couldn't stop herself. His expression had changed and he appeared to be sad now, rather than angry. She knew that it was only the primary flaccidity that occurs immediately after death, before rigor mortis begins to set in, but ever since their night together she had thought of Alan as being sad about something.

She found his gun halfway underneath the gas cooker, with only the butt visible. Once she had retrieved it she de-cocked it and tucked it into her belt. She had been anxious not to leave without it because she had logged it out of the armoury at Anglesea Street and it could easily be traced through its code number.

'*Is there anybody in there?*' she heard a man shouting. '*Hallo? Is there anybody in there?*'

She heard somebody else call out but she couldn't hear what they said. They were probably warning the first person to stay well clear until the bomb squad had determined that there wasn't a second device intended to catch first responders.

Next to the kitchen there was a small utility room, with a washing machine and a clothes horse. There was also a door leading out to the back yard. As quickly and as quietly as she could, Katie let herself out and closed the door behind her. The yard was cluttered with an old enamel bathtub and a bicycle with no wheels and some broken fencing, and she had to climb over two worn-out car tyres, but there was a gate that gave access to the next street. When she opened it she was relieved to see that the street was deserted, so there wouldn't be any witnesses to say they had seen a red-haired woman in black hurrying away from the house after the explosion.

She walked quickly up to the main road and back into Felt Street, where her car was parked. She dropped the SIG Sauer and her balaclava back into the glovebox, as well as Bobby Quilty's mobile phone. Then she started up the engine, did a quick three-point turn, and drove away. As she turned the corner into Blythe Road a police patrol car came speeding past her with its lights flashing and siren scribbling. It was followed almost immediately by another, and then by a fire tender.

Her hand was still shaking as she set her satnav for Forkhill. In current conditions, it told her, the drive would take her slightly less than an hour. She prayed that, apart from using his mobile phone to set off the briefcase bomb, Bobby Quilty hadn't put in a call to the men who were holding John and Kyna.

As she turned on to the main M1 she glanced in her rear-view mirror and could see clouds of dirty smoke still rising over the rooftops from Felt Street. It gave her a strange feeling, driving away from a crime scene like this, instead of towards it. It went completely against her training and her experience, and her natural instincts.

But her plan had worked out so far, even though it had turned out to be more tragic than she could ever have imagined. She had to see it through to the very end, for John's sake, and Kyna's sake, and as a tribute to Alan.

She was passing Loughbrickland when it began to rain again, not lashing down, but a soft, persistent mizzle. She stayed dry-eyed. The time for crying would be later.

Forty-four

She made slow progress south because of the weather, and a broken-down car transporter at Newry reduced traffic to a single lane, but it was still only ten minutes past eight when Katie arrived in Forkhill.

She passed the Welcome Inn, where Alan's Lesser Bastard worked – the young man who had seen John and Kyna taken into Bobby Quilty's house. It was too early for it to be open and the only person on the village street was a woman in a hooded raincoat walking past McCreesh General Store and Funeral Director, with a miserable-looking mongrel on a string.

Alan had told her exactly where Bobby Quilty's house was, only two and a half kilometres further south, right by the border. She drove past it to see how many cars were parked outside, if any. Behind the trees she could make out only one: a mustard-coloured Volvo. She would have bet 100 euros that it was the same mustard-coloured Volvo that had obstructed the gardaí who had been trying to give Detective Barry backup as he chased the cigarette-seller along MacCurtain Street, and the same 'yellowy' Volvo that had been seen in Parklands after Darragh Murphy had been shot.

Bobby Quilty had said that he would call 'my pal Ger' to have John and Kyna dealt with. Katie had guessed that he meant Ger Carmody, who she knew to be one of his closest henchmen, who kept an eye on his affairs in Cork when he was away in the North.

On the opposite side of the road, a few metres further south, there was a narrow farm track with overgrown hedges on both sides. Katie drove down it until she was out of sight of Bobby Quilty's house. She parked her car close to the verge, in case a tractor needed to get past, although it looked as if the track was no longer in use.

Alan had said that when he had visited the house to check up on John and Kyna he had sneaked round the back, so Katie decided to do the same. She crossed the road and walked about 150 metres past the low stone wall in front of the house until she came to its perimeter fence. She looked around. All she could see were the low hills on either side of the road, and fields. The next house was more than a third of a kilometre away. It was still drizzling and there was nobody else in sight. At that moment, she could almost have believed that she was the only person left in the world.

She climbed over the wall and followed the three-bar wooden fence to the rear of the property, keeping her head down. There were enough bushes around the driveway to hide her from anybody who might be looking out of a downstairs window, and although there was a single upstairs window facing in her direction, it had a blind drawn down over it.

She climbed over the fence into the garden. As soon as she dropped down on to the other side, she froze. The back door of the house opened and a man appeared, wearing a white hat and sunglasses and a sagging black jacket. Ger Carmody – that grubby white hat was his trademark. He sucked at the butt-end of a cigarette and then flicked it out into the garden. Katie crouched low, hoping he wouldn't see her in the long feathery grass. He blew out smoke, then he went back inside and closed the door behind him.

Katie waited for a few moments and then made her way towards the house. There was the shed that Alan had used for cover, and there was the large living-room window through which he had seen John and Kyna. The living room was dark inside, so all she could see was the reflection of the garden, and the hills in the distance.

Please God don't tell me Bobby Quilty managed to make that call and they've been shot, or taken away somewhere else.

She wasn't quite sure what she should do next. Maybe she should risk it and try to enter the house. With any luck, Ger Carmody had left the back door unlocked, or she could kick it open. But what if he hadn't, or she couldn't? Should she go to the front door and knock, and demand entry as a Garda officer? Supposing John and Kyna weren't there any longer, and there was no trace that they had been?

She hunkered down beside the shed. She was feeling shivery now, although the morning wasn't cold, just damp. The shock of the bomb on Felt Street was beginning to get through to her and she knew that what she really needed was a hot drink, and quiet, and a good long sleep.

Now that Bobby Quilty was dead, maybe she should give up trying to rescue John and Kyna single-handed and call for the police, although that could still be a highly dangerous option. There was only one car outside, but she didn't know how many more of Bobby Quilty's men might be inside the house. Apart from that, Ger Carmody had a record of extreme violence and if he were found guilty of unlawful imprisonment he would face going to jail for the rest of his life, so if police cars arrived outside he might feel he had nothing to lose. Bobby Quilty had been prepared to go out in a blast of glory, so it was possible that his Ger Carmody might do the same, and take John and Kyna with him.

Alan had been right, she thought. Her plan had been fraught with too many 'what-ifs', and that was what had killed him. She had to make a conscious effort not to think of him lying on that kitchen floor, looking so sad.

She was still trying to make up her mind what to do when she saw a shadowy movement inside the living room. Somebody was walking towards the window – a woman, by the look of it. When she came close, she saw that it was Kyna. She had a fawn blanket wrapped around her shoulders and her hair was all messed up. It was her face, though, that shocked Katie. Both of her eyes were purple and almost closed up, and her nose was swollen.

There was no sign of John, but Alan had said that his informant had seen him carried into the house on a stretcher, so maybe he was still unable to walk.

Katie made her mind up immediately. She drew her revolver out its holster and ran with her knees bent towards the window. As soon as Kyna saw her she dropped the blanket from her shoulders and flapped her hands wildly, as if to tell her to *Come, and come quickly.* She looked startled and relieved, but she was a Garda officer, too, and Katie knew that she wouldn't panic. She mouthed something that Katie couldn't hear, but she raised one finger, as if to tell her that there was only one man guarding the house. Katie lifted her hand to show her that she understood, then she went to the back door and tried the handle. Ger Carmody had left it unlocked. Bobby Quilty clearly hadn't rung him, and he couldn't have heard yet that he was dead.

Katie opened the door and stepped inside. She found herself in a gloomy kitchen with a pine table in the middle of it. The table was crowded with empty pizza boxes and KFC buckets and dirty paper plates and beer cans and coffee mugs and two ashtrays heaped with so many cigarette butts that they looked like maggots. The terracotta-tiled floor was so sticky that Katie's shoes made a crackling sound as she walked across to the hallway.

The door to the hallway was already half open, but she stopped and listened before she opened it any further. She could hear a television, though she couldn't make out what station it was tuned to.

She waited a little longer, but as she reached out to open the door wider she heard footsteps approaching up the corridor outside. Hurried, squeaky footsteps, as if somebody in crêpe-soled shoes had an urgent message to deliver.

She heard a door being unlocked and even though her ears were still singing from the explosion she could clearly hear voices. She heard Kyna saying, 'What in the name of Jesus do you want now, you bastard?' Kyna sounded very clotted, as if she had a cold.

'Mother of God, that's some bang off your man,' said a deep, harsh voice with a strong Cork accent. She guessed that was Ger.

'He's desperate sick, that's why,' Kyna retorted. 'He's nearly dying and you haven't the human heart to send for a doctor.'

'Well, we don't have to bother about it now. Things have changed. It turns out now that you and your manky friend here are surplus to requirements.'

'What are you talking about?'

'It's over, sweetheart. The Big Feller's bought the farm.'

'You *what*?'

'It's just been on the news, on the telly. There was a bomb set off in Belfast and seven fellers were done for, including the Big Feller.'

'You're not serious.'

'It was on the news on the telly only a couple of minutes ago. How more serious do you want to be than that?'

'I can't believe it. So what happens now?'

'So, like I say, you're surplus to requirements. I'm out the gap, like, but I don't need you and your stinky pal here.'

'You can't—' Kyna began, but Ger must have closed the living-room door then because Katie couldn't hear the rest of what she was saying. Not that she needed to. It was chillingly clear what he intended to do.

She pulled open the kitchen door. The living-room door was next to it, on the right-hand side, and she kicked that open. She stepped into the room with her revolver raised high up in front of her.

Kyna was standing by the window, her shoulders still wrapped in her blanket. Ger had crossed the room to the couch where John was lying and he was jiggling a large Colt automatic in his hand as if he were weighing it. John's legs were draped in a sheet that was stained brown and amber with blood and pus, with several bluebottles crawling over it, and he looked appalling. His face was dead white except for the dark circles around his eyes. His jaw was hanging slack and his arms were crossed over his chest, like an effigy on a medieval tomb. His eyes were open but he was staring at the ceiling, and he didn't acknowledge Katie's appearance with even a flicker. Underneath that stained sheet, his infected feet were rotting and the stench in the living room was thick and sickly.

'Put the gun down, Ger!' Katie shouted at him, and she wished that she hadn't sounded so shrill.

Ger jerked with surprise. 'Christ on a bicycle, it's you! And I thought the only bang I was getting in here was off of this feller's feet.'

'I said, put the gun down, or so help me I'll drop you.'

Ger pointed his Colt at the crown of John's head. 'Oh, no. I think I have the advantage here, sweetheart. If you don't put your little peashooter down, I'm going to blow your friend's head halfway to Dundalk.'

'You were going to do that anyway,' said Katie. 'So put the gun down or, believe me, I'll kill you where you stand.'

Ger said, 'You won't, because you don't want to see your friend here die, too. Which he will, if you shoot me, and you know it.'

Kyna dropped her blanket to the floor and said, 'Listen, Ger. You want to get out of here, don't you? I'll tell you what I'll do. I'll come with you as a hostage until you're well clear of here. Then you won't get killed, and John here won't get killed, and by the grace of God I won't get killed, either.'

Katie said, 'If you agree to that, Ger, I'll put down my gun.'

'Even if you do that, darling, you'll still be chasing after me, won't you, and you'll have these two as witnesses against me?'

'Ger – if I *do* manage to find you and bring you up in front of a court, you'll be better off facing a charge of false imprisonment than two charges of cold-blooded murder.'

Ger continued to point his automatic at John's head, but there was no doubt that he was undecided.

'You can say what you like,' he told her, 'there's no way I'm going back to that fecking Portlaoise prison again. I'd rather die than go back to that fecking hell-hole.'

'If you walk out of here peacefully today, without hurting any of us, then I'll testify on your behalf,' said Katie. 'That's if I ever catch you, which I probably won't. If you have any sense, you'll get out of the country and never come back.'

Almost half a minute passed. Katie's hand was trembling from holding up her gun for so long and she could actually taste the rank smell of John's decaying feet.

At last, Ger shook his head and said, 'Nah . . . no chance. I know you, DS Maguire. You look like butter wouldn't melt in your mouth but you have some fierce sharp teeth in that same mouth, too. No matter where I go, you'll make sure you lift me. Jimmy Malone – he was in Gran Canaria, wasn't he, and you still had him extramadited, and what had *he* done?'

'Jimmy Malone set fire to a house with six children in it.'

'Wasn't his fault they died. He didn't know they was home.'

'Come on, Ger, let's all be reasonable,' said Kyna, coming closer to him, with both hands outspread. 'We can't spend all day discussing this. The rest of the boys are going to be back soon, aren't they, and how much do you trust *them*? You're going to let them witness you shooting us? They'll rat you out as soon as look at you. Much better if they come back and all of us are gone.'

She looked across at Katie and said, 'There's four more of them altogether. They went shopping to Newry early this morning because they'd run out of fags and bacon and booze. You know – the three staples of a civilized life.'

Katie didn't take her eyes off Ger. He was talking tough and she found it almost impossible to read his expression behind those dark glasses. All the same, she was beginning to deduce from his indecision and his body language that he was actually frightened of her – or what she represented, at least. When he looked at her he saw Portlaoise high-security prison and that made him doubly unpredictable. From her experience, he was much more likely to pull the trigger if he was frightened, and if he killed John his adrenaline would start pumping and he would find it easy, if not exhilarating, to kill both Kyna and herself.

She went over to the bookcase and laid her gun down on it.

'There,' she said, although her heart was beating so fast that she was breathless. 'All you have to do now is walk out of here. Kyna's offered to go with you, to make sure that you get clear away. I promise you we won't try to stop you or come after you, and I won't put out any bulletins about you for at least twenty-four hours. You have my word on that, Ger.'

Ger lifted his automatic away from the top of John's head, obviously trying to make up his mind. The instant he did so, however, Kyna spun around on one foot and kicked the gun out of his hand.

He said, '*Shite!*' and staggered backwards, but she went after him and kicked and punched him again and again, so fast that to Katie it was nothing but a blur of arms and legs. She kicked him hard in the crotch, and when he doubled forward she kicked him under his chin so that his jaw cracked and his hat flew off. He tumbled backwards into the space between the end of the couch and the wall, and she used the arm of the couch as a vaulting horse so that she could stamp on his ribs, right over his heart.

Katie circled around her and scooped up Ger's automatic from the floor, then went back to the bookcase and collected her own revolver. Meanwhile, Kyna was kicking Ger repeatedly in the side of his head. Finally she stood on his face, using her full weight, so that his dark glasses and his nose-bone both crunched.

'Kyna! Jesus and Mary! I think that'll do it,' Katie told her.

'The *bastard*!' said Kyna in her clogged-up voice. 'The total, absolute *bastard*! I was begging him to call for a white van for John, but he wouldn't. Instead, he headbutted me and broke my nose.'

Katie looked down at Ger, with his dark glasses smashed on the bridge of his nose and blood running in streams down both sides of his face.

'He won't be doing a whole lot to stop us getting out of here now,' she said. She knelt down next to John and took hold of his ice-cold hands. He stared back at her but he didn't seem to know who she was.

'John, it's Katie. Do you understand me? It's Katie. I've come to take you away from here.'

John continued to stare at her, and he whispered something, but at first she couldn't make out what he was saying.

'It's okay, John. Everything's going to be grand now. We'll take you to the hospital to have your feet patched up and then you'll be fine.'

'Barney,' whispered John. 'Time for Barney's walk.'

Katie's eyes filled up with tears. She squeezed his hands and said, 'Yes. Yes, it is. And soon you'll be able to take him out your-self. Let's just get you up off that couch and out of here. Kyna?

Do you think you could give me a hand here? He won't be able to walk by himself.'

Kyna was crouching next to Ger, who still hadn't stirred. She was pressing her fingertips up against his neck, feeling for his pulse.

'I think he's dead,' she said.

'Serious?'

'I can't feel a pulse and he isn't breathing. I think I've broken his neck.'

'Mother of God, that's all we need.'

'He deserved it. The same as Bobby Quilty. He just told me that Bobby Quilty was dead, blown up by a bomb or something like that. That's why he came in to kill us. We weren't useful any more. Surplus to requirements, that's what he said.'

'I know,' said Katie. 'I heard him telling you about Quilty. It's true. I was there myself when the bomb went off.'

'*What?* You were actually there?'

'I nearly got blown up myself. There were six others killed, too. Listen, I'll tell you all about it after. Are you certain he's dead?'

Kyna leaned over Ger's face to make a final check that he wasn't breathing. After a few seconds she said, 'He's gone, yes. I'll bet you he's in hell already.' She stood up and then she said, 'You're here by yourself? Like, this isn't official? There's no other officers outside?'

'This is a highly unofficial one-woman raid. And we need to get out of here fast, especially if those scummers are coming back from doing their messages in Newry.'

Kyna looked around the living room. 'We can't leave the place like this. There's enough fingerprints and blood and DNA to identify us ten times over. What's going to happen when the cops come in and find Ger's body like this, with my footprints on his face? Or are you going to file an official report and admit to everything?'

'If I do that, I might as well hand in my resignation at the same time. This is not only unofficial, it's probably illegal as well. Well, it *is* illegal. You've just killed a man.'

'Self-defence. I wish I'd been there to kill Bobby Quilty, too.'

Katie saw that there was an old Zibro paraffin heater standing in the corner, probably placed there to mollify the drafts that came through the north-east-facing window in the middle of winter. She went across to it, opened up the front panel, and saw from the dial on the tank that it was over half full.

'You're joking, aren't you?' said Kyna.

'Why not? Bobby Quilty's dead, so he won't have anything to complain about.'

'Holy Saint Joseph.'

Katie lifted the fuel tank out of the paraffin heater and unscrewed the lid. The smell of the paraffin reminded her of her childhood, when her father had kept a paraffin heater on the upstairs landing to keep the bedrooms warm. She knew that what she was doing was madness, but her whole plan to rescue John and Kyna had been madness, right from the beginning, and it was better to see it through to its insane conclusion than to start trying to wrap it up by the book. She had seen too many operations falter and fail because officers had been unwilling to break the rules at a critical moment.

She walked from one end of the living room to the other, sloshing paraffin on to the carpet and the curtains. When she reached the couch, she put down the paraffin tank and gently lifted the stained sheet from John's feet. He whimpered and clutched at her arm, and she could see why. Both of his feet were ink-black and bubbling with pus, and the darkness had spread almost up to his knees.

'Here – help me lift him up,' she told Kyna.

'*I can't*,' whispered John. '*Just leave me here.*'

'You have to,' said Katie. 'We're going to burn the place down.'

'*Well, let me burn with it. I can't.*'

'John, we're going to do it anyway.'

Katie and Kyna put their arms around him, and between them they heaved him up to a standing position. He was panting and shuddering, and he kept closing his eyes tight shut because of the pain, but with Kyna supporting him he managed to stay upright.

As quickly as she could, Katie splashed paraffin on to the couch and the bloodstained sheet. Then she knelt down and rummaged in the sagging pockets of Ger's black jacket, her lips pursed tight with disgust, until she found his plastic cigarette-lighter. After that, she turned the tank upside down and emptied the last of the paraffin all over him. It wouldn't burn his body sufficiently to hide who he was, but it might obliterate any evidence of who had killed him.

'Right,' she said, with her eyes watering from the paraffin fumes. 'Let's get out of here.'

They both wrapped John's arms around their shoulders and half-carried, half-dragged him to the living-room door. Katie worked out in the gym whenever she could, but she was impressed with how strong Kyna was. She could almost have humped John out of the house by herself.

When they had managed to heave John into the hallway, Katie went back into the living room. She flicked Ger's lighter and set fire to the bottom of the curtains. Then she lit the hem of the bloodied sheet on the couch. When she lit the carpet, the flames scurried across the floor and set fire to the curtains at the other end. Finally, coughing from the fumes, she stood over Ger himself.

Although he had been so criminal and vicious, Katie still felt deeply disturbed about burning his body like this. This wasn't the way that people were supposed to end their lives – broken and alone and incinerated like so much rubbish. She also had an irrational feeling that, once he had burst into flames, he might jump up screaming.

'Come on,' Kyna urged her from the doorway. 'We need to go now. Poor John's going to drop at any minute.'

Katie bent down and lit the cuff of Ger's jacket. At once, he was enveloped in blue and green flames. His sparse grey hair shrivelled and the plastic frame of his sunglasses melted and dripped down the sides of his face, as if he were weeping black tears.

The heat in the living room suddenly began to intensify and the hot air made the fire burn even more fiercely. Flames were leaping up the curtains like angry dogs to lick at the ceiling, while the polyester covering of the couch was ablaze and its foam filling was already pouring out dense brown billows of noxious smoke.

Katie went back out into the hallway and lifted John's left arm around her shoulders. He looked as if he were close to losing consciousness, because his head kept dropping forward, but together she and Kyna carried him along the hallway to the front door. They passed the room where Ger had been watching television and seen the news that Bobby Quilty had died. The television was still on, but now it was showing a weather forecast. Persistent rain across Northern Ireland for the rest of the day, and tomorrow.

Kyna opened the front door and they carried John outside, his bare black feet trailing across the shingle.

Blinking against the drizzle, Katie said, 'My car's just across the road there, off to the right.'

She twisted her head around so that she could look behind her. Smoke was rising from the back of the house, thicker and thicker, and then she saw flames in the hallway.

They were only a third of the way up the driveway, however, when a dark blue van appeared from the direction of Forkhill and turned into it.

'Oh God,' said Kyna. 'The boys are back from Newry.'

Katie stopped, breathing hard from the effort of carrying John. She had her right arm around his waist and she was gripping his left hand tightly, so without letting go of him she wasn't able to pull out her gun. Kyna might have been able to keep him upright on her own, but she was panting, too. The only alternative would be to lie him down on the wet shingle driveway.

The dark blue van stopped about thirty metres ahead of them. Katie could see three men staring at them through the windscreen, with the wipers squeaking monotonously as they cleared away the drizzle.

Now the wipers stopped and three men climbed out. Two of them were the men who had held Kyna's arms while Ger head-butted her – the man with the widow's peak and the fair-haired spotty youth. The third was tall, with a chestnut-brown beard.

Katie could see a fourth man in the back of the van, but he stayed where he was.

'Hey! Where do you think you're heading off to?' shouted the thin man with the widow's peak. 'Look at it, Jesus, the whole fecking house is on fire! Where's Ger?'

Katie didn't turn around again to look at the house, but she could smell the smoke now because the drizzly wind was blowing from the south-west, and she could hear crackling and popping and the chiming of breaking windows. The three men started to walk slowly towards them, but she could see that none of them was very confident. She could imagine why they were so uncertain. There was no sign of Ger to tell them what to do, and even though the house was on fire they didn't know whether they ought to call the fire brigade. The fire brigade would call the police and that would mean they would be found out for keeping John and Kyna unlawfully imprisoned – not to mention any other illegal activities they might have been involved in, like tobacco-smuggling or drug-running or storing weapons for the Authentic IRA.

Katie was about to tell Kyna to try and support John for a few seconds while she took out her gun. She had only managed to say, 'Kyna, can you—' when there was a shattering bang from behind her and she felt a shock wave pushing the three of them from behind, like a gust of strong wind. The next thing she knew they were being showered with fragments of brick and tile and sparkling glass.

She looked around, and as she did so there was another explosion, even louder than the first, and half of the roof of the house appeared to jump into the air and then collapse completely into the floor below. A cloud of grey smoke rolled up into the rain, and then there was a third explosion, and a fourth, and then a sound like a hundred firecrackers. Part of the facade of the house fell forward, leaving a single chimney stack, and then that, too, teetered and fell sideways with a rattle of bricks.

What was left of the house was still burning and even some of the trees around the garage were ablaze. A huge ivy-covered oak had been uprooted by the blast and fallen on top of Ger's mustard-coloured Volvo, crushing the roof and shattering the windows.

'God Almighty!' shouted Kyna, because both of them were deafened now. 'Bobby Quilty's arms dump!'

The three men who had been approaching them were already running back to their van. They climbed into it and slammed the doors, and then the van swerved backwards, skidded on the wet road, and sped off, heading north.

There was a series of ten or eleven sharp bangs which Katie recognized as hand grenades. More debris flew up into the air and clattered on to the driveway all around them.

'Let's go!' Katie shouted. 'This time, I think God was on our side!'

Forty-five

Katie had only just returned home and given Barney a pat and a cuddle when Detective Inspector O'Rourke rang her.

'How's your family problem, ma'am?' he asked her.

'All sorted, thank you, Francis. I'll be back at my desk at the crack of dawn tomorrow.'

'That's grand. I've been trying not to bother you, but one or two things have cropped up. You've heard about Bobby Quilty, I suppose?'

'Yes. What a turn-up for the books that was. I'd say it was an act of God.'

'Well, whatever, there must have been be a rake of people on both sides of the border who breathed a sigh of relief when they heard that he'd been topped.'

'I certainly did,' said Katie. 'Any information yet on who did it?'

'That's a bit of a mystery at the moment. Of course, they're still examining the house where it happened, but Detective Inspector Humphreys called me from Knock Road and said that it looked like Quilty had intended to murder the people who lived there, for some inexplicable reason. He had them all tied up and he was going to blow them up with a briefcase full of plastic explosive and nails.'

'So, what went wrong? Or should I say right?'

'They don't know yet, not for sure. They can't work out how the bomb was triggered, although it was probably set off by a signal from a mobile phone. I can give you all the details when you come in tomorrow.'

'Do they know who these people were – the ones that Quilty wanted to kill?'

'A family called the Crothers. They had very strong loyalist connections, apparently, but that's hardly surprising. They lived in the Blackstaff ward, and that's more Orange than a case of Tanora.'

'Do they have any idea *why* he wanted to kill them?'

'Not at the moment. But there was one quare thing. Quilty was *shot*, as well as blown up, although they don't know yet who shot him. One of the seven people killed in the blast was an ex-PSNI police inspector, but he didn't appear to be armed. We'll obviously find out more when their technical experts have completed the forensics and they've finished collecting witness statements, but you know what they're like in Belfast. Very tight-lipped.'

'Thanks, Francis. I'm back home now, so you can ring me at any time.'

She put her iPhone down on the coffee table, while Barney looked at her expectantly, wagging his tail. The hopeful expression in his eyes said: *Walk, walk! Please say the word 'walk'!*

She tugged at Barney's ears, but before she could think about taking him for a walk she needed to know that John and Kyna were being treated, especially John. She rang CUH and spoke to a staff nurse in the Acute Medical Unit.

'John Meagher's extremely unwell, I'm sorry to tell you. His feet and his lower legs are badly infected. He's also seriously dehydrated. Doctor O'Connell has instigated several tests and we should be receiving the results tomorrow afternoon. We'll keep in touch with you, of course.'

Next she rang Kyna. She was at CUH, too, being treated for a skin infection.

'They've booked me in next week to have my nose reconstructed. Don't worry. In two or three weeks I'll be as beautiful as ever.'

'How are you feeling?' Katie asked her.

'You mean how am I feeling about Ger? Very mixed. I loathed him and I wanted to pay him back for hurting me like that, and most of all for not allowing John to be treated. But I honestly didn't mean to kill him. I would have preferred to see him sent to Portlaoise again. Then he would have suffered for the rest of his life and I wouldn't be feeling so guilty.'

'Anyway, take good care of yourself,' said Katie. 'Are you staying in the hospital or are they sending you home?'

'I'm just waiting for some pills and then they're going to discharge me.'

'You could come and stay with me for a while. I could use the company.'

There was a very long pause. Katie could hear hospital noises in the background, and a woman calling, *'Nurse!'* Then Kyna said, 'Thanks, Katie, but no . . . I think we've got each other into enough trouble already.'

'Somehow I don't really care any more.'

'Well, you should. This city would be a much worse place to live in if it wasn't for you.'

'I'll see you tomorrow so,' said Katie. 'Maybe you can meet me for lunch. How about Elbow Lane?'

'I don't know. The more I see you the more I want to stay here in Cork and I'm not so sure that we're very good for each other. Maybe in another life . . . if we were florists, or dress designers. Something girly and harmless. Besides, I don't really want to go out looking like this.'

'You look like you've walked into a door, that's all.'

'Every battered woman uses that excuse. No, Katie, let's leave it for a while. I can't thank you enough for what you did to rescue us – the risk you took. I think you're amazing. But I need to meditate for a while, and get myself back together again, body and spirit.'

'Okay,' said Katie, a little sadly. 'But call me when you're ready, won't you?'

'I promise.'

Katie switched off her iPhone and looked at Barney. He could sense that something was wrong because he cocked his head to one side and made that mewling noise in the back of his throat.

'Come on, Barns,' she told him, standing up. 'Let's go outside and get ourselves soaking wet.'

* * *

She was reading through the files that had been left on her desk when there was a complicated rapping at her office door. She looked up as Assistant Commissioner Jimmy O'Reilly came in.

'Katie,' he said. 'Francis O'Rourke told me that you'd been having some family problems.'

'They're all resolved now, thank you, sir.'

Jimmy O'Reilly stood watching her for a moment, then he cleared his throat and said, 'Fierce dramatic news about Bobby Quilty, wasn't it?'

'Yes, sir.'

'Not that much is going to change, I shouldn't think. Somebody else will take over the cigarette-smuggling, no doubt, and all the other rackets the Big Feller was running.'

'There's a couple of likely contenders,' said Katie. 'Matty Fegan, for one. I'm keeping a close eye on him. Fatty Matty Fegan.'

'It looks as if Bobby Quilty did us one favour, though,' said Jimmy O'Reilly. 'He caught the fellows who shot the Dohertys – even if he did set himself up as judge, jury and executioner, and execute himself in the process. I doubt if we would have found those Crothers in a million years.'

'I just wonder why he went after them,' said Katie.

'Come here to me? He went after them because they'd murdered his relations. To Bobby Quilty, that was a personal challenge. He couldn't let them go unpunished. Come on, Katie, you knew Bobby Quilty as well as any of us. To him, that would be unthinkable.'

'But how did he know it was them?'

'Because he had contacts everywhere in Belfast, didn't he? He knew everyone – republican, loyalist, and everybody in between. The PSNI are doing a thorough test on the Crothers' bodies, of course, and what remains of their house, but I was talking on the phone to Detective Chief Inspector MacReady about it yesterday afternoon and he was convinced that the Crothers shot the Dohertys. According to some of his informers, they were boasting about it in their local pub.'

'What I actually meant was, how did Bobby Quilty find out that he was related to the Dohertys?'

Jimmy O'Reilly frowned. 'How should I know? Perhaps he'd *always* known. Perhaps he looked up his family tree. You can do it online these days, can't you? Look Up Your Granny dot.com, or some such.'

Katie was tapping her pen on her desk like a metronome. She knew what she was going to say next, but she also knew that she would have to phrase it very carefully.

'I made a mistake,' she said.

'I don't understand. What kind of mistake?'

'I made a mistake when I was checking up on the Dohertys' genealogy.'

'And?' said Jimmy O'Reilly. It was obvious that he was beginning to sense that Katie was playing him along and he was growing irritated. 'What exactly are you trying to tell me?'

'Bobby Quilty wasn't related to the Dohertys. There *was* a Niall Quilty who served with Captain Frank Busteed, that's true – but he was shot by the British when he was only seventeen and he never got married and he never had a daughter. I mixed him up with somebody else.'

Jimmy O'Reilly stared at Katie as if she were a doctor who had just told him she had failed to diagnose the lump on his neck and he had less than six weeks to live.

'You mixed him up with somebody else?'

'Yes . . . silly mistake. I was working very late and I was tired. But the only person I told about Bobby Quilty being related to the Dohertys was you.'

'You gave me that family tree,' said Jimmy O'Reilly.

'Yes, I did, but it was erroneous. So I know how *you* came to believe that Bobby Quilty and the Dohertys were related. What I can't understand is how Bobby Quilty came to believe it, too.'

'I have no idea. It must have been a coincidence.'

'A coincidence?'

Jimmy O'Reilly suddenly grew angry. 'I've just told you – I have no idea! Maybe he had some other grievance against the Crothers! What are you trying to say here, Katie? Come on, spit it out! Are you accusing me of passing confidential information to Bobby Quilty?'

'Yes.'

'Give me one reason why I should have done. Go on!'

Katie stood up. 'I can give you several thousand reasons why, Assistant Commissioner, and all of them are euros. You were constantly borrowing money from Bobby Quilty to settle your boyfriend's gambling debts. Bobby Quilty had you in his pocket and so did James Elvin. In fact, James Elvin still does. He would only have to tell the media why you've been going easy on Bobby Quilty's cigarette-smuggling and you'd be finished.'

Jimmy O'Reilly looked at her with his eyes narrowed, then he walked over to the window. He watched the rain trickling down it for a while and then he said, 'What do you expect me to do now?'

'Nothing,' said Katie. 'I'm not the commissioner and I'm not the Garda Ombudsman. Well – there's one thing you *could* do, and that's to refuse to give James Elvin any more money. He might go to the media, but that's a risk you'll just have to take.'

Still watching the raindrops, Jimmy O'Reilly said, 'You're a witch, do you know that, Katie? Right from the beginning I said you were a witch, but nobody would listen. They were all too keen at Phoenix Park to be politically correct and show that the Garda were moving with the times.'

He turned around and said, 'You've *done* something, haven't you? You've pulled some fecking evil trick. I don't know what you've done or how you've done it, but I swear to God that I'll find out one day and I'll see you burned at the stake, like the witch that you are.'

Without saying anything else, he walked out of her office, leaving the door open behind him.

Katie sat down again. She was trembling slightly, but that was mostly from tiredness and the delayed shock from what she had been through the day before. She had dreamed about Ger last night, with his glutinous black plastic tears and the flames dancing out of his face. She had dreamed about Alan, too, and in her dream about Alan he had lifted his head from the kitchen floor in Felt Street and said, 'You don't love me, do you? So why did you make me love *you*?'

As soon as he had uttered those words, he vomited a huge gout of bright red blood and it splashed all over the floor.

* * *

It was almost lunchtime when Detective Ó Doibhilin came in to see her. She had heard nothing more from Assistant Commissioner O'Reilly, and when she had walked along to Chief Superintendent MacCostagáin's office to talk about a new gang of Romanian pimps who had opened up an internet page called Magic Massage, she had looked down into the car park and saw that his car had gone.

Detective Ó Doibhilin was holding up a plastic folder. 'Do you have a moment, ma'am? I've heard this morning from that Bracewaite fellow in Manchester – you know, the historian who was trying to see if he could find out more about Lieutenant Seabrook and Radha Langtry.'

'What's he come up with?' asked Katie.

'A letter. It's only the one letter, but I think it's shattering, do you know what I mean, like?'

He came over to her desk, set the folder down in front of her, and opened it. Inside, there were the scanned copies of two sheets of notepaper. They were handwritten, in a strong, well-formed hand, the kind of copperplate script that was taught in schools in late Victorian times.

It was headed 'Ballincollig Barracks, February 23rd'.

My dearest Jane,
I understand how much pain I have caused you by
my infidelity, and I beg your forgiveness. I can plead
only that the horrors of the Front and the unnatural
stress of fighting against the Fenians led me to seek
solace in another's arms; and for this I have no excuse
whatsoever, except to admit my own weakness.

Now, however, a tragedy has occurred and you are
the sole person to whom I can express my grief – a
grief which is compounded by the way in which I have
betrayed you. I have to tell someone about the terrible
events of the past three weeks or I will surely go mad.
I cannot confide in Lt. Col. Evans for that would
inevitably lead to my being cashiered.

The young woman with whom I was involved
was Mrs Radha Langtry, whose husband Stephen
was a member of the Irish Republican Army. She had
learned from her husband that an ambush of our
regular Friday patrol from Macroom to Cork had
been planned, at a place called Godfrey's Cross. He
had informed her because she daily went to work
that way, to Leemount House, the home of Mrs Mary
Lindsay, and he cautioned her to take another route.

Radha did not want me to be harmed, and that
is why she told me, but of course I had no choice
but to warn Lt. Col. Evans of the intended ambush.
However, she also warned her employer Mrs Lindsay,
because Mrs Lindsay was due to drive through
Godfrey's Cross that day to take her car to the
barracks here in Ballincollig for military inspection. (It
is a new regulation because of the number of cars that
have been commandeered recently by the IRA.)

Mrs Lindsay told the local priest, Father Ned
Shinnick, about the ambush, and he warned the IRA
command that their intended attack was no longer a

secret. Unfortunately he was known to have nationalist sympathies and they refused to believe him.

The consequence of this was disastrous. You may have seen in the newspapers that the IRA party were surprised and outflanked and eight of them were captured. They are being held in Victoria Barracks in Cork, court-martialled, and found guilty, and may very well be shot.

Because she is such a staunch nationalist, the IRA blamed Mrs Lindsay for this catastrophy [sic] and have abducted both her and her chauffeur. I have to assume that under great duress Mrs Lindsay informed her captors that it was Radha who had warned her about the ambush.

I attempted to contact Radha, but without success. Eventually I was informed by the local priest in Blarney, Father Thomas, that the Langtry family had decided on the spur of the moment to emigrate to America. I found this difficult to believe, since Radha had never mentioned that she and her husband had any such intention.

The priest saw that I was greatly distressed and took some pity on me. He told me in the utmost confidence that the Langtrys had not, in fact, emigrated, but that the local IRA commander had ordered that they be punished for informing the British about the ambush. Their friends and relatives would believe that they had gone to America because letters would be regularly sent home here to Ireland by IRA sympathisers in New York.

I tried to persuade Father Thomas to tell me what the Langtrys' punishment might have been, but he refused to say any more. Although of course I am not a Roman Catholic he granted me absolution but of what possible use was that?

I am trying to cling to the belief that the Langtrys may have been forced to move to another part of Ireland, but in my heart of hearts, my dearest Jane, I know they have not. I know that they have been shot, and their bodies buried somewhere in the mountains, or in a peat bog, and that they will never be discovered. What has become of their two children I cannot guess.

You will hate me for this, Jane, but I always loved you and I love you still, in spite of my treachery. I am riven with grief, and I have been weeping so bitterly that I have to pretend to my men that I have an eye infection.

You will probably burn this letter and forget that you ever knew me, but I had to share my agony with somebody, and also tell how it really came about that the IRA ambush was foiled.

If I had not had a relationship with Radha, our own soldiers would have been killed; but since I did, eight Irishmen will almost certainly be executed, and Radha is surely dead, too. How can there be a God, if these were the only alternatives which He gave me?

I am crying now, my dearest dearest, as I write this to you. I am so sorry for what I have done, and the pain is unbearable. Give my fondest love to Kitty and James.

Yours, Gerald.

Katie read the letter again and then sat back. 'Mother of God. Where did this historian of yours find this? I mean, like, it sheds entirely new light on the Dripsey ambush. It looks like poor Mrs Lindsay and her chauffeur, they weren't to blame at all.'

'He found it in the files in the family solicitors' office,' said Detective Ó Doibhilin. 'He says there's some other correspondence from the time that shows that all of the Seabrook family were aware of it, but didn't want to shame Gerald's name, especially since he was killed only a few weeks later. They preferred Jane Seabrook to be the grieving widow of a military hero, rather than the abandoned wife of a love rat who got himself tangled up with the IRA.'

'I'll have to talk to Chief Superintendent MacCostagáin about this,' said Katie. 'Maybe this is something that needs to be filed and forgotten. As if enough innocent people haven't lost their lives because Lieutenant Seabrook "sought solace in another's arms".'

'I'll leave it with you, then,' said Detective Ó Doibhilin.

'Thanks, Michael. You've done some incredible work on this. I'll make sure you get a commendation for it.'

Detective Ó Doibhilin left her office and she picked up the letter and read it yet again. *Love,* she thought, *what disasters it can lead to.* If Lieutenant Seabrook hadn't fallen in love with Radha, the Doherty family would still be alive – and if she hadn't loved both John and Kyna, Bobby Quilty wouldn't have taken them hostage, with all of the fatalities that had followed, especially Alan's.

Her phone warbled. It was Detective O'Donovan.

'Patrick! What's the story?'

'We've just had a message from the PSNI. There was a serious house fire yesterday up at a village called Forkhill, near Newry. Not only a fire, a series of major explosions. They reckon the house contained an arms dump for an IRA splinter group, although they're not naming any names yet, except for one.'

'Go on. Was it somebody we know?'

'Only Ger Carmody, burnt to a cinder. They believe it was, anyway, because his car was outside and they found what was left of his hat.'

'Ger Carmody? What was he doing up in South Armagh?'

'Search me. But what a day, ma'am, wouldn't you say? What a result! Bobby Quilty and Ger Carmody both going off to meet their Maker within hours of each other. You didn't say a prayer to St Bonaventura by any chance?'

'Why St Bonaventura?'

'He's the patron saint of bowel disorders. If you'll excuse my language, my auld feller used to say that he takes care of all the shits.'

The following morning she drove to Cork University Hospital before she went into the station. It had rained heavily during the night but now the clouds had cleared and it was sunny and humid.

She had pressed the button for the lift when her iPhone played 'Buile Mo Chroí'.

A distant voice said, 'Is that Detective Superintendent Maguire?'

'It is, yes. Who is this?'

'Inspector Wallace from the Crime Operations Unit in Belfast.'

'Oh, yes, inspector? How can I help?'

'I'm a friend of Alan Harte. I was the one who passed him your bulletin about your two missing persons. Have you heard about Alan?'

'What about him?'

'He's dead, I'm sorry to say. You obviously know about that bomb in Belfast, the one that killed Bobby Quilty and six other individuals. Well, Alan was one of those six individuals.'

'Oh, God. That's tragic.'

'I know. I'm sorry to give you such bad news. He told me that he was in contact with you. After I told him about the bulletin and he realized you were after Bobby Quilty – well, he was itching to talk to you. He couldn't wait.'

'Yes, he came down to Cork to see me,' said Katie. 'We exchanged information about Quilty, but that was about all we could do. Quilty was never an easy man to corner, as you know.'

'We're still going over the house where it happened, and we will be for several days yet,' said Inspector Wallace. 'One of the things that has us really puzzled, though, is that Bobby Quilty was shot and fatally wounded before the bomb went off. We thought at first that Alan might have shot him, but there's no sign at all of the gun he might have used. One of the other individuals had a weapon, but it wasn't the same calibre as the gun that killed Quilty, and it had only been fired once, while Quilty was shot three times.'

'Maybe somebody else came into the house and shot him but left before the bomb went off.'

'Well, it's possible. But I'd like to know who had more of a motive for shooting Bobby Quilty than Alan.'

'Yes – he told me about Quilty setting him up with all those drugs,' said Katie.

There was a long pause, and then Inspector Wallace said, 'Drugs? What drugs?'

Katie was confused. 'Alan told me that Quilty planted heroin in his house so that he would be suspected of drug-dealing, and that's why he had to resign from the PSNI.'

'I don't know why he should have told you that,' said Inspector Wallace. 'Maybe he didn't want to tell you the real reason.'

'You mean it wasn't true? He resigned because of something else?'

'He resigned because he simply couldn't handle the job any more. He was right on the verge of having a breakdown. He couldn't think of anything else but killing Bobby Quilty. He probably didn't tell you because you would have thought that he was obsessed and unstable and you wouldn't have cooperated with him.'

'So why was he so determined to kill Quilty?' asked Katie.

'He was building a good case against Quilty for drug-smuggling. Quilty knew that he had some sound evidence, and even a couple of witnesses, and was getting quite close to arresting him. So Quilty sent him a message that if he didn't lay off, his family would all be shot, one by one, starting with his wife.'

'I thought that he and his wife were divorced.'

'Are you joking? They were totally inseparable, those two. He would have run stark-naked down the Falls Road if she had asked him to. But Alan called Quilty's bluff and went on gathering evidence against him, and one day Alison was coming out of Wyse Byse and a fellow walked up to her and shot her in the head.'

Katie didn't know what to say. All of a sudden, everything about Alan and his behaviour made sense. And now she knew who the woman was in the framed picture on Alan's bookshelf.

'Detective Superintendent Maguire?' said Inspector Wallace.

'Oh, sorry. What? That – that just took me by surprise.'

'I wondered if you wanted to attend Alan's funeral. I don't have a date yet, of course, but I can let you know when I do.'

'Yes, please do. And thank you for calling me.'

Another pause, and then he said, 'I haven't upset you, have I?'

* * *

She took the lift up to the Acute Medical Unit. At the nurses' station she was met by Staff Nurse Abara, a small, dark, quietly spoken woman with huge brown eyes. Katie had met her several times before and had always thought that she would have taken holy orders if she hadn't trained as a nurse.

Nurse Abara led her along the corridor to the room where John was being treated.

'He is sleeping now,' she said. 'We have given him a massive dose of antibiotics and in the meantime we are considering the various options for treatment.'

She opened the door and they went inside. John was lying on his back, with his eyes closed. He was wearing an oxygen mask and was attached to two intravenous drips. Underneath the mask his face was so pale that he looked as if he were wearing white foundation. There was a hump under the lower half of his blanket where a cage protected his feet and calves.

Katie approached the bed and stood and watched him breathing. He was so deeply asleep that she could tell he wasn't going to wake up.

'So, what *are* the options?' she asked.

'Dr O'Connell can tell you all about them in greater detail when he comes in later. But John's feet and his legs up to his knees are gangrenous and he will require some very radical treatment. One option is debridement, where all the gangrenous flesh is surgically cut away. There is also maggot therapy, which can be very successful in cases of gangrene.'

'Yes, I've heard of that. I didn't know you did it here.'

'Yes, we breed tiny bacteria-free maggots in the laboratory. We bandage them firmly to the gangrenous flesh and they eat it. The wonderful thing about maggots is that they don't touch the healthy flesh, and they also give off substances that kill bacteria and promote healing.'

'Is there another option?' Katie asked her.

'Well, yes, there is, of course, and I'm afraid that Dr O'Connell is already thinking that he won't have any choice.'

Katie reached out towards John's curly black hair, but didn't touch him. She wondered if he were dreaming, and what about. *Once you leave Ireland, you can never go back. Not for good. Everything you loved here will destroy you, in the end. Your memories, your friends – not to mention the music, and the rain.*

'You're talking about amputation,' said Katie.

Staff Nurse Abara nodded. 'Below the knee, hopefully.'

'Both legs?'

'Yes.'

'And then what? Prosthetic legs?'

'They're marvellous these days. Even if we do have to amputate, which we probably will, he'll still be capable of leading a very full life.'

Katie took a deep breath. 'Does he know this?'

'Dr O'Connell has briefly discussed it with him, yes.'

'And what did he say?'

'He said that he was lucky that he survived, and that he owes his life to you, although he didn't explain how, or why.'

'Is that all?'

'No. He also said that he wasn't afraid of the future, even if he did have to lose his legs. You saved him and he knows now that you're always going to take care of him.'

* * *

Katie didn't wait to talk to Dr O'Connell. She walked quickly back along the corridor and went down in the lift. She was shaking again, even worse than after the bomb. She kept her face turned away from the mirror so that she wouldn't have to look at herself, as if she had been disfigured in a serious accident.

Below the knee, hopefully. He knows now that you're always going to take care of him.

As she crossed the reception area the revolving door flashed with reflected sunlight and Kyna came in, in a loose white sweater and jeans, with a plaster across the bridge of her nose.

Katie didn't say a word but went up to her and put her arms around her and held her tight. Several people stared at the two of them as they passed by, but Katie couldn't see them because she was blinded with tears.

CAVAN COUNTY LIBRARY